Star Trek®
The Captain's Table

For orders other than by individual consumers, Pocket Books grants a discount on the purchase of **10 or more** copies of single titles for special markets or premium use. For further details, please write to the Vice President of Special Markets, Pocket Books, 1230 Avenue of the Americas, 9th Floor, New York, NY 10020-1586.

For information on how individual consumers can place orders, please write to Mail Order Department, Simon & Schuster Inc., 100 Front Street, Riverside, NJ 08075.

Star Trek®

The Captain's Table

War Dragons

James T. Kirk
and Hikaru Sulu
as recorded by L. A. Graf

Fire Ship

Kathryn Janeway
as recorded by
Diane Carey

Dujonian's Hoard

Jean-Luc Picard
as recorded by
Michael Jan Friedman

Once Burned

Mackenzie Calhoun
as recorded by
Peter David

The Mist

Benjamin Sisko
as recorded by
Dean Wesley Smith and
Kristine Kathryn Rusch

Where Sea Meets Sky

Christopher Pike
as recorded by
Jerry Oltion

The Captain's Table Concept by
John J. Ordover and Dean Wesley Smith

POCKET BOOKS
New York London Toronto Sydney Singapore

This book is a work of fiction. Names, characters, places and incidents are products of the authors' imagination or are used fictitiously. Any resemblance to actual events or locales or persons, living or dead, is entirely coincidental.

POCKET BOOKS, a division of Simon & Schuster Inc.
1230 Avenue of the Americas, New York, NY 10020

This book is published by Pocket Books, a division of Simon & Schuster Inc., under exclusive license from Paramount Pictures.

ISBN: 0-671-04052-9

First Pocket Books trade paperback printing March 2000

10 9 8 7 6 5 4 3 2 1

Printed in the U.S.A.

These titles were previously published individually by Pocket Books.

Contents

War Dragons

James T. Kirk

and Hikaru Sulu

as recorded by
L. A. Graf

One

KIRK

TRANSPARENT ALUMINUM SPUN A DELICATE MEMBRANE BETWEEN THE SPINDLY green of transplanted Martian foliage and the blue-black Martian sky. As he watched one of the shipyard's many crew transports crawl patiently starward along a sparkling length of duranium filament, it occurred to James Kirk that man-made atmospheres were always the most fragile. Mars's chilly surface, although no longer the frigid wasteland of just a few centuries before, still clung to the planet only through the heroic efforts of her tenants. Outside the tame habitat of interlinked domes and tunnels, carefully tended flora transplanted from Earth's highest mountains and harshest tundras braved Mars' seasonal extremes, while the excess carbon dioxide from captured comets and a few million adventurous humans preserved just enough water on the surface to reward the plants with the occasional rain shower. The end result was a certain defiant beauty—spidery junipers and upright bracken reaching toward the teal spark of a homeworld their ancestors had left generations ago.

Not unlike humanity. Granted, humans pampered themselves with heaters, oxygen cogenerators, and pressurized suits and homes. But they still survived where nothing larger than a dust mote had survived before them, and Kirk liked the view they'd created.

Utopia Planitia's shipyards stretched from the skirt of the colony's main dome to beyond the horizon, arcing magically upward in the guise of shuttle-bees and crew elevators. The twinkling strings of force and fiber bound the orbiting ships only temporarily. Some nearly finished, others bare skeletons of the great leviathans they would become, they'd all turn outward soon enough. Darkened engine rooms would thunder with the pulse of great dilithium hearts, and the blood and muscle organs in the chests of her eager crew would leap up in answer, until that combined symphony of animal and mineral, creature and machine finally ignited her sleeping warp core. It was a song that kept an officer's heart beating long after no other passion could. *Old captains never die . . .*

Kirk stepped off the moving walkway in the northernmost Agridome, the one dedicated to the sparse rock gardens and dark succulents of a Terran gulf environment whose name Kirk no longer remembered. It wasn't crowded the way so many of the lux-enhanced Agridomes always were. Everyone wanted to watch the crews ship out while surrounded by bright Colombian parrots or Hawaiian orchids, as though they'd never really dared to leave Earth at all. But here the lack of tall plant life offered an unobstructed view through the sides and top of the dome, and the foliage reflected the reddish moonslight in silver washes, as though leaves and stems were spun from raw pewter. Kirk remembered coming here as a freshly minted ensign the night before he rode a crowded elevator up to his first assignment on board the *U.S.S. Farragut.* He'd stayed here until dawn, trying to count the multitude of stars he could see in the single patch of sky surrounding the ship that was to be his home, his life, his family for the next five years. That was more than forty years ago, but it felt like only yesterday. He could still hear the reverent hush of the leaves against his trousers as he picked a path through the foliage, and he still remembered the cool surface of the rock that served as his perch at the foot of the dome's widest panel. Best seat in the house.

He found the man he was looking for seated in exactly the same spot, shoulders square, head high, hands folded neatly in his lap. Beyond him and a thousand miles above, the brilliant glow of a refurbished starship dwarfed the dimmer signatures drifting around her.

Kirk smiled, and paused what he hoped was a respectful distance away. "Quite a view, isn't it?"

The younger captain rose, turning with an alert smoothness born of courtesy rather than surprise. That was something Kirk would always associate with Hikaru Sulu—the politeness which came to him apparently as naturally as breathing, with no taint of impatience or condescension. That, and an endless capacity for brilliance.

Sulu mirrored Kirk's smile, looking only a little embarrassed as he stole one last look at the magnificent ship hanging over his shoulder. "All the way into forever." He kept one hand cradled close to his waist, and extended the other as he stepped away from his now vacated stone seat. "Captain."

His grip was firm and even, as befitted a man of his position. Kirk returned the warm handshake in kind. "Captain."

"I didn't realize you were in-system," Sulu told him. "If I'd known, I would have stopped by to give my regards." It might have just been politeness, but Kirk could tell from his former helmsman's voice that the sentiment was sincere.

"Just passing through on my way to finalize the Khitomer negotiations," Kirk assured him. "I heard at the commodore's office that you were laid over to take on your new executive officer." A movement from the vicinity of Sulu's cupped hand caught Kirk's attention, and he found himself suddenly eye-to-eye with the small, spotted lizard that had clambered up onto Sulu's thumb for a better view. "He's shorter than I remember."

Sulu glanced fondly down at his stubby-tailed companion, tickling it under the curve of its bemused little smile until it blinked. "Actually, we're not scheduled to rendezvous for another two hours. This is just one of the friendly locals." Or as local as any living thing on Mars. It's anteriorly bilateral eyes and five-toed little feet hinted at a Terran origin, but it was the nearly identical gold-and-brown speckled relatives Kirk could now see lounging among the thick-leafed shrubs that gave its ancestry away. The Martian Parks Service didn't like mixing one planet's flora with another planet's fauna. Therefore, Terran landscaping equaled Terran lizards.

Each chubby little eublepharid had staked out its own rock or branch or hummock, blunt little noses lifted skyward, hindfeet splayed out behind them as though they were laconically bodysurfing on their own bliss. Kirk envied their abandon.

"Anything on your agenda for those next two hours?" he asked Sulu.

The younger captain shrugged one shoulder, startling his small passenger to abort its scrabble partway up his wrist. It paused there, as though forgetting where it meant to go, and Kirk noticed that unlike its lounging neighbors, this lizard's tail looked recently broken. Its curiosity and boldness must have gotten it in trouble recently. "I've got nothing in particular to do," Sulu admitted. "Just some long overdue relaxation while I have the chance." Kirk wondered if he'd been watching the meditating lizards instead of his own starship after all. "Did you have something in mind?"

"Some*place.*" Kirk caught the politely questioning cock of Sulu's head, and smiled. "The perfect spot for overdue relaxation, as a matter of fact."

"Sounds good." Sulu glanced down as the lizard squirmed determinedly under the cuff of his uniform jacket. Before he could stop it, all that was left was a sausage-shaped bulge and an exposed nubbin where its brown-banded tail should have been. "Are they friendly toward nonhumanoids?"

"I've never known that to be a problem before," Kirk assured him. "And I'm sure that in the lizard world, that little guy was the captain of his very own rock somewhere. He'll be welcome in the Captain's Table."

He led a willing Sulu back out of the Agridomes and down the stately, curving avenues that led eventually to the spaceport proper. The door to the bar was where Kirk remembered it, looking as always like the entrance to a supply cabinet rather than to the cozy tavern he knew lay within. Plain, nearly flush with the Martian stone of this ill-lit subterranean passageway, it was set apart from the other, more ostentatious establishments on either side by nothing except a neatly painted sign just to the right of a hand-operated doorknob: The Captain's Table.

Sulu cocked his head with a thoughtful wrinkling of his brow, and Kirk knew he was trying to remember why he'd never noticed the little entrance before. "This must be new," the younger captain decided at last. He still held his arm balanced across his midsection in deference to the small passenger up his sleeve.

Kirk hid his smile by stepping forward to take hold of the door. "I found it the first year I commanded the *Enterprise,* but some captains claim it had been around for dozens of years before that."

Sulu gave a little grunt of surprise, then moved back to let the door swing wide. "Sounds like the Federation's best kept secret."

A gentle swell of warmth, and sound, and scent rolled over them like a familiar blanket. "More like the galaxy's most exclusive club." And, just like a dozen times before, Kirk found himself inside without specifically remembering stepping through the doorway.

The Captain's Table had never been a large establishment, and that didn't appear to have changed over the years. A brief, narrow entry hall spilled them abruptly into the bar's jumble of tables and chairs, and Kirk found himself veering sideways to avoid tripping over the tall alien seated directly in his path. Slitted eyes shifted almost imperceptibly within an almost featureless skull; one long, taloned finger dipped into a fluted glass half-full of viscous red liquid. It was a dance they'd performed the first time Kirk came into the Captain's Table, thirty years ago, not to mention every other time he'd stumbled onto the place on Argelius, Rukbat, or Vega. He stopped himself from laughing, not sure the lizardine patron would appreciate his humor, and instead nodded a terse apology before turning to join Sulu in the search for a table.

"Jimmee!"

It seemed everyone was here tonight.

Kirk spun around just in time to catch Prrghh at the height of her leap. It wasn't one of her more spectacular jumps—Kirk would never forget watching her pounce from the second-floor bannister to land on her feet amid a particularly rousing discussion—but she still contacted him almost chest-high and entwined legs and arms around his torso in lithe, feline abandon. Kirk felt himself blush with pleasure when she stroked her own sleekly furred cheek against his. Acutely aware of all the other eyes in the bar, he resisted an impulse to wind his hands in her long primrose mane.

"James!" The bartender's roar collided with the low ceiling and ricocheted all over the room. "How in hell are you? Long time gone, boy-o!"

At least seven years, Kirk admitted to himself. But not a damned thing about the place had changed. Not so much as a dust mote.

"Don't be silly, Cap!" Prrghh squirmed around in Kirk's arms to look back over her shoulder, a position that would certainly have dislocated the spine of any anthropoid species. "Jimmy is always here!"

"Everyone is always here," a gruff voice behind them snarled. "Especially tonight." The female Klingon pushed past Kirk as though she had somewhere to go, then stopped abruptly and crouched to thrust her nose into Prrghh's pretty face. "If you're staying, sit down. If not, get out of the way and take your *mris* with you."

Prrghh's hiss was dry, but rich with hatred. Kirk turned them away from the Klingon, already knowing where things could lead once Prrghh's ruff had gotten up. "Why don't we find a seat, then?" he suggested smoothly. The Klingon grunted, but made no move to follow.

Kirk swung Prrghh to the floor as though he were twenty years younger or she twenty kilograms lighter. He let her fold her hand inside his, though, basketing his fingers with lightly extended claws. Her palm felt soft and familiar despite the years that had passed since it had last been fitted into his. Beside him, he noticed Sulu's failed efforts to hide a knowing grin by pretending to check on the lizard now peering curiously from beneath his cuff. Kirk wondered briefly what sorts of tales Sulu might tell out of school, considering his former commander's reputation. This time the heat in Kirk's cheeks had a little bit more to do with embarrassment.

It might have been a Saturday night, the place was so packed with bodies and voices and laughing. But, then, Kirk's memory said that it *always* looked like Saturday night, no matter what the day or time. Never too crowded to find a seat, thank God, but always just threatening to burst at the seams and overflow into the rest of the world. Kirk snagged Sulu by the hem of his jacket when the captain started toward the bar along the long end of the crowded room.

"A seat," Sulu said by way of explanation, lifting a lizard-filled hand to indicate his objective. Kirk glanced where the captain pointed and shook his head. The empty seats in question surrounded a grossly fat Caxtonian freighter pilot who appeared to have congealed around a tankard of milky brown fluid.

"He's Caxtonian," Kirk said. "By this time of night—"

Prrghh wrinkled her delicate nose. "He stinks fiercely!" Her long, supple tail snaked up between the men to twitch their attention toward the foot of the stairs. "This other human is looking at you."

The captain Prrghh pointed out looked human enough, at least. Salt-and-pepper beard, with hair a matching color that hung just a little longer than the current civilian standard. Kirk liked the well-worn look of his leather jacket, with its rainbow shoulder patch and anomalously fleece-trimmed collar. He was lean and wiry, with an earnest smile and tired but friendly eyes. Two other seats at his table were already filled by a rapier-thin dandy with black hair pulled back into a neat queue, and a broad bear of a man with a wild white beard and a curl of pipe smoke covering most of his head. When their leather-jacketed comrade waved again, Kirk acknowledged his gesture by slipping between a knot of standing patrons to blaze a path to the table.

"Gentlemen. Welcome to the Captain's Table." The salt-and-pepper haired human took Kirk's hand in a firm, somewhat eager shake. "Humans?" he asked, with just the slightest bit of hopefulness in his tone.

Kirk glanced at the freighter designation stenciled beneath the ship name on the leather jacket's patch, and recognized the wearer for a fellow captain. Of course. "The genuine article." He stole a chair from an adjacent table and offered it to Prrghh as Sulu conscientiously offered the freighter captain his left hand for shaking to avoid disturbing the reptilian passenger sprawled happily across his right palm.

The freighter captain pumped Sulu's hand without seeming to notice either the deviation from convention or the little passenger. "I'm sure pleased to see you," he grinned. "We were feeling a bit outnumbered tonight." He tipped a cordial nod to Prrghh as she slipped into her seat. "No offense, Captain. I just sometimes get real tired of aliens."

Her ears pricked up and green eyes narrowed on the other captain's lean face. Kirk recognized the expression—she liked a challenge. "Perhaps you have not met the right aliens."

The freighter captain lifted an eyebrow, and Kirk suspected he enjoyed his share of challenges, too. "Perhaps not," he admitted with a smile. "Maybe you can educate me."

"A surprisingly trusting lot, all points considered." The black-haired dandy tipped the tankard in his hand and squinted down its throat to verify it was empty. He hadn't interrupted his story for Kirk and Sulu's arrival, and didn't interrupt it now as he waved the tankard over his head to catch a server's attention. "They brought us neatly upside, lashed our hulls together, and came aboard with every thought of liberating our hold of its treasures. Alas, our only cargo was a crew of well-armed men and the good old Union Jack. By the time we'd taken our due, that was one Jolly Roger which never flew again."

"A clever story." The white-haired captain bit down on his meerschaum pipe and nodded wisely. "You're a cunning man, Captain, using that pirate crew's own expectations against them."

"The best judge of a pirate is one of his own," the Englishman admitted. His tankard still waggled above one shoulder. "My duties may seal me now to the queen, but I'm loathe to believe that any man who never ran with pirates can ever be their match."

Kirk straightened in his seat, stung by the remark. "Oh, I don't know about that."

The table's patrons turned to him almost as a unit, and he found himself momentarily startled by the frank challenge in their stares.

"Do you mean to disavow my own experience?" There was steel in the dark-haired Englishman's voice despite his friendly countenance.

The white-haired bear lifted one big hand in an obvious gesture of placation. "Easy, my friend. He sounds like a man with experience of his own."

"Some." Kirk settled back as a wiry serving boy scampered up to their table with a tray full of drinks. He gave the others first pick from the offerings, knowing what he wanted would still be there when they were done. "Pirates were never my primary business, but I've run across my share." He wrapped his hands around the mug of warm rum the boy placed in front of him, well familiar with the price every captain had to pay for the first round of drinks after his arrival. "Let me tell you about a time when I rescued the victims of some pirates, only to find out they weren't exactly what I'd expected. . . ."

I told myself it wasn't resentment. I didn't have the right to resent him. He hadn't killed my helmsman; he'd never placed my ship and crew in danger; he hadn't forced my chief medical officer to retire. He hadn't even murdered my best friend. He had never been anything but responsible, conscientious, and reliable. In these last few weeks, he'd stepped into a position made vacant by my own actions—not because he wanted it or because he hoped to prove anything to anybody, just because it was necessary. He was that kind of officer; service without complaint. Duty called, and he answered.

Still, I hadn't quite figured out how to separate him from everything that had come before. So while he stood there in the gym doorway, waiting for my answer with his damned impenetrable patience, my first instinct was to tell him to go to hell. Instead, I asked in the mildest tone I could muster, "Mr. Spock, can't this wait until later?"

I must not have sounded as patient as I'd hoped. He lifted one eyebrow a few micrometers, and peered at me with the same keen interest he probably applied to alien mathematics problems. Subtle emotions often had that effect on him, I'd noticed. It was as though he couldn't decide what informational value to assign such a random variable, and it annoyed him to settle for an imperfect interpretation.

Except, of course, that annoyance was a human emotion.

"Regulations stipulate that a starship's captain and executive officer shall meet once every seven days to coordinate duties and exchange pertinent crew and mission information." He didn't fidget. He just folded his hands around the data pad at his waist and settled in as though there was no place else he needed to be. "Our last such meeting was eleven days ago."

I turned back to my interrupted workout, leaving him to recognize the implied dismissal. "Then a few more hours won't make any difference." I aimed a high sweep-kick at the sparring drone, and earned a flash of approving lights for smashing into the upper-right-quadrant target.

Spock was silent for what seemed a long time, watching me with his usual cool fascination, no doubt, as I did my best to sweat out my personal demons at the expense of a supposedly indestructible robot.

In the end, they both managed to outlast me. I stopped before I started to stumble, but not before I was forced to suck in air by the lungful, or before I raised dark welts on the edges of both hands. I still secretly believed that if I could push myself just a little further, a little longer, I'd finally beat out the last of my uncertainty and guilt. But I'd entertained this secret belief for at least three weeks and hadn't yet found the magic distance. And now I refused to fall down in front of my new executive officer while I still struggled to find it.

He gave me what was probably a carefully calculated amount of time to catch my breath, then said to my still-turned back, "May I remind the captain that when he is not eating, sleeping, or engaging in some necessary physical activity, he is on duty. As senior science officer, my duty shift is concurrent with the captain's. As acting executive officer, my second duty shift coincides with when the captain is off-duty. Logic therefore suggests that rather than disrupt the necessary human sleep function, the most efficient time period during which to conduct our required conferencing would be during the one-hour fifteen-minute interval between the termination of my secondary duty shift and the beginning of your regular tour." He paused as though giving my slower human mind a moment to process his argument, then added blandly, "Which is now."

I swiped a hand over my eyes to flick away the worst of the sweat, and heaved an extra-deep breath to even out my panting. "Is this your way of telling me you're working a few too many hours, Mr. Spock?"

Both eyebrows were nearly to his hairline; I could almost feel the lightning flicker of his thoughts behind those dark Vulcan eyes. "No, Captain."

He was as deadly serious as if I'd asked him to contemplate the course of Klingon politics over the next hundred years. "My current schedule allows ample time for research, personal hygiene, and the intake of food. Since Vulcans are not limited by the same stringent sleep requirements as humans, I find the hours between my shifts more than sufficient for meditation and physical renewal."

I tried not to sigh out loud. My entire Starfleet career would be a success if I could teach even one Vulcan to have a sense of humor. "What would you like to discuss, Mr. Spock?" I asked wearily.

Where anyone else—anyone human—would have promptly flipped up the pad to consult its readout, Spock announced, apparently from memory, "According to the first officer's log, there are currently eight hundred fifty-four individual crew evaluations which are late or incomplete."

I paused in the action of scooping up my towel to frown at him. "There are only four hundred and thirty crew on board the *Enterprise*."

Spock acknowledged my point with a microscopic tilt of his head. "Four hundred twenty-four evaluations are still outstanding from the quarter ending stardate ten thirteen point four. The other four hundred thirty were due at the end of the most recent quarter, which ended on stardate twelve ninety-eight point nine."

And Gary—perpetually behind when it came to such mundane administrative duties—died before he had the chance to turn in even one from the most recent batch. I tried to disguise a fresh swell of frustration by scrubbing at my face and scalp with the towel, and began to dictate, for the record: "Since last quarter, Lt. Lee Kelso was killed in the line of duty. Dr. Elizabeth Dehner—killed in the line of duty. Lt. Commander Gary Mitchell—" I hid a bitter scowl by turning and banning the sparring drone back to its storage locker. "Killed." The word still tasted like cold gunmetal in my mouth. "I've ordered the lateral transfer of Lt. Hikaru Sulu and Ensign David Bailey from astrosciences to cover the vacant bridge positions, and have accepted Lt. Commander Spock's application for temporary assignment as ship's first officer." Snatching up my tunic and boots with a brusqueness that surprised even me, I came to a stop just shy of touching Spock, knowing full well how discomforting such proximity tended to be for Vulcans. "On a brighter note, Chief Medical Officer Mark Piper has retired to a safe, well-paying civilian position at Johns Hopkins University on Earth, and his replacement, Leonard McCoy, seems to be adapting nicely." That last was half a lie, since I hadn't actually spoken to my old friend McCoy since the day he first came aboard. I hadn't managed to say much even then, thanks to the doctor's colorful tirade against the ship's transporter. I hadn't remembered him being quite so technophobic, and found myself wondering if this was going to be a problem. "Why don't you put all that in Gary's files and call them done?"

Spock said nothing as I pushed past him on my way to the showers, merely stepping neatly to one side to avoid any unseemly physical contact. These were the kinds of little skills he must practice daily, I realized. Memorized patterns of behavior, movement, and response based on the thousands—perhaps millions—of social interactions he'd endured with a species whose conduct must seem positively arcane to him. I doubted he even understood much of the social data he mentally collected about his crewmates—he simply noted which interactions produced what results, and adjusted his model accordingly. If there was a difference between that and how a soulless machine would make use of the same information, at that particular moment I couldn't see what it was.

He followed me into the showers at what was no doubt a carefully calculated distance. Why did his patient silences always make me feel so guilty about whatever random bitterness popped into my head? Probably just another side effect of his conversational style. I made a note to read up on Vulcan social customs, naively believing that I might find some understanding of Spock in their workings.

"The completion of Commander Mitchell's reports should pose no undue difficulty. I calculate that, by committing only forty-two point three percent of my on-duty time, I can deliver the reports to you within sixty-eight hours."

I hoped he didn't expect me to vet them quite so quickly. Eating and sleeping aside, I still had too much shoring up to do with the ship's new crew assignments to catch up on nearly 900 reports over the next three days.

"I must confess, however . . ."

Reluctance? I paused with the water crashing over my head to stare at him.

He all but rushed on before I could say a word. "I find the guidelines as laid out by Starfleet . . . baffling."

That admission of near-weakness surprised me more than almost anything else he could have said. I turned off the water and leaned out to study him. "How so?"

If he was human, I almost think he might have blushed. Not in embarrassment, but from the stone-faced frustration young children sometimes display when confronted with an impenetrable question they secretly suspect is a joke at their expense. I wondered if Vulcan children ever teased each other, or if the Vulcan Science Academy practiced hazing.

"The precise goal of such record keeping in the format specified is unclear," he said, quite formally, yet somehow without actually meeting my eyes. "There are no statistical data to be compiled, no discrete procedures to be followed. The desired end result is entirely inadequately conveyed."

I felt a strange warmth when I realized what he was saying. Sympathy, almost. "The desired end result is insight," I told him. He looked at me, and I smiled gently, explaining, "It's the first officer's job to be liaison to the crew. As captain, I depend on your observations—your instincts and feelings about the crew's state of mind."

Any emotion I might have imagined in his features evaporated with the infinitesimal straightening of his shoulders. "I am Vulcan. I have no instincts or feelings, only logic."

But the crew is human, I wanted to tell him, *just bubbling over with emotion.* Who in God's name had ever thought a Vulcan could serve as a human crew's XO?

The chirrup of my communicator saved us from pursuing a discussion neither of us was sure how to follow. I ducked out of the shower, careless of the water I dripped as I scooped up the communicator and flipped back the grid. "Kirk here. Go ahead."

The communications officer's honey-rich voice seemed strangely out of place in the conflicting Vulcan-human landscape of our interrupted conversation. "Sir, sensors have detected a disabled ship two point two kilometers to our starboard. There're some shipboard functions, but they don't respond to our hails."

A real problem. Not overdue reports, Vulcan emotional illiteracy, or misplaced captain's angst. A way to avoid feelings of helplessness by directing all my energy toward something I could change. "Plot a course to intercept, and scan the ship for survivors. I'm on my way to the bridge." I was already shaking my tunic free from the rest of my clothing by the time I snapped the communicator shut and tossed it to the bench. "I'm afraid you're on your own with those reports, Mr. Spock." As we left for the bridge, I flashed him a grin over the collar of my shirt, one that was probably as reassuring as it was strictly sincere. "Just do the best you can."

The bridge felt alien and strangely quiet when the turbolift deposited us on its margins. I missed Gary's laughter. It had been omnipresent—sometimes irritatingly so—and I found myself missing the sudden guilty hush that meant Gary had been sharing some particularly bawdy story with the rest of the crew. I missed his liar's smile, and his all-too-innocent, "Captain on the bridge" to announce my arrival.

Instead, the smoothly deep voice of my new helmsman made the call, and nobody abruptly ceased what they were doing or ducked their heads to hide a sudden onset of blushing. Decorum reigned, and I felt like I'd stumbled onto some other captain's vessel.

Still, I made that first step beyond the turbolift's doors without any outward sign of hesitation, briskly taking the steps down to my chair as Spock rounded behind me to head for his own station at the science console. "Mr. Sulu, report."

The helmsman—*my* helmsman, I reminded myself firmly—half turned in his seat, one hand still hovering possessively over his controls. "Sensors detect life on the vessel, but still no response to our hails. Their power exchange is in bad shape—the distress call might be on automatic."

Meaning the crew either couldn't use ship's systems to respond, or were too badly injured to make the attempt. I drummed my fingers on the arm of my command chair, thinking. On the viewscreen, the flat, elongated vessel drifted lazily clockwise, passing into a long silhouette, presenting us her nose, wafting lengthwise again. Her engines had been burned down to nubs, and the characteristic shatter of disruptor fire carved jagged stripes down her sides. It looked like at least half the ship was in vacuum, and the other half looked too dark to be getting anywhere near normal power. If there was anything or anyone still alive on board, they wouldn't stay that way forever.

"Spock, do we have any idea what kind of ship that is?"

He was silent for a moment. I gave him that—I'd figured out early on that he didn't like giving answers until he'd looked at all the data.

"Sixty-three percent of the identifiable ship's components strongly resemble an Orion Suga-class transport," Spock said at last, still scanning the computer's library screens. "Eleven point six percent are from an Orion-manufactured slaving facility. Four point two percent still bear the registration codes for a Klingon unmanned science probe. The remaining twenty-two point two percent resemble nothing currently on record."

I rubbed thoughtfully at my chin. "Could they be Orions?" I asked after adding up those bits and pieces. "Or maybe Orion allies?"

"Starfleet has reported no recent Orion pirating activity in this sector." While it wasn't exactly an answer to my question, it still led me a few steps closer to something that was. Spock swivelled in his chair to lift an eyebrow at the screen. "To my knowledge, the Orions have no allies."

Which told you everything you needed to know about the Orions. Still . . . "Just because we don't know about any allies doesn't mean there are none." I resisted an urge to toss Spock a puckish grin he wouldn't appreciate. "After all, even the Devil had friends."

He tipped his head in grave acknowledgment of my point, and I felt for one startled moment as though he were teasing me. *He's a Vulcan, not Gary Mitchell. Vulcans don't tease.* I turned forward again to hide my chagrin, and tapped my chair intercom with the side of my hand. "Bridge to transporter room."

"Transporter room. Scott here."

It worried me sometimes that my chief engineer spent so much time with the transporter. I tried to reassure myself that it was a fascinating piece of equipment, with all manner of systems to explore. But sometimes I just couldn't shake the suspicion that there was more to Scott's constant tending than mere affection. Probably not something I should mention around Dr. McCoy. "Scotty, can you get a fix on the life-forms inside that alien vessel?"

"Fifteen to twenty of them," he reported, managing to sound pleased with himself and a little frustrated all at the same time. "Maybe as many as twenty-four—the numbers are hopping all over the place."

"See if you can isolate them with a wide-angle beam." I muted the channel and glanced aside at Spock. "What sort of environment does that ship hold?"

He opened his mouth, took a small breath as though to say something, then seemed to change his mind at the last minute. Without having to reconsult his equipment, he informed me, "Slightly higher in oxygen and nitrogen than Earth normal, and at a slightly greater atmospheric pressure. Fluctuations in their gravitational equipment average at just a little less than one Earth gravity." Then he continued on without pausing, saying what I suspected had been the first thing to cross his mind. "May I infer from your questions that you intend to bring any survivors on board?"

"Indeed you may." I sent an automated request to security for a small reception committee, and a similar request to sickbay for an emergency medical team. "I've never ignored another ship's distress signal, and I don't intend to start now."

Spock stood smoothly as I jumped up from my chair, his own quiet way of announcing that he was following me down to the transporter room. "And if the captain who initiated this distress call is an Orion ally, as you speculate?"

I looked up at the viewscreen, quickly refreshing my image of its crumpled superstructure and ruptured sides. "Then they still need rescuing." We certainly couldn't tow them anywhere—I doubted their ship would stand up to the grasp of the tractor beam, much less to having its tumble forcibly stilled and its whole mass accelerated along a single vector. Besides, towing wouldn't take care of their wounded. I wouldn't put any captain in the position of being helplessly dragged along while his crew died around him. Not if I could help it.

"Don't worry, Mr. Spock," I continued as I circled my command chair and took the stairs to the second level in a single step. "We can isolate our guests in rec hall three until arrangements are made to drop them off with whatever allies they're willing to claim." The turbolift doors whisked aside for me, and I slipped inside with one hand on the sensor to hold them open as Spock caught up. "No one's going to get free run of the ship just because we're giving them a ride."

He stepped in neatly beside me, pivoting to face the front of the 'lift with a precision that seemed to be just a part of his movement, not something he planned. "Worry is a human emotion," he stated, as though correcting me on some particularly salient fact.

I stepped back from the doors and let them flash closed on us, taking up my own place on the opposite side of the turbolift. "Of course it is," I said, rather flatly. I kept my eyes trained on the deck indicator to avoid having to look at him. "How could I have forgotten?"

TWO

SULU

The resounding crash of furniture interrupted Captain Kirk's story. Hikaru Sulu swung around to see what kind of trouble might be brewing in the shadowy depths of the Captain's Table. All he saw was the female Klingon heading for the bar with an empty tankard swinging in one large fist. Apparently, kicking over her chair with a booted foot was her method of politely disengaging herself from a conversation when she wanted more blood wine. There was something a little odd about the Klingon, something that nagged at the edge of Sulu's usually reliable memory, but he couldn't pin down exactly what it was. Did the Imperial medals of honor on her chest look just a bit outdated, or were they slightly futuristic? He felt as he often did back in the old days, when he and Chekov would spend their shore leaves in cheap spaceport flight simulator games that hadn't been reprogrammed or updated in years. Nothing looked quite right, and yet none of it seemed quite serious enough to worry about either.

"Relax," Kirk said softly, when Sulu turned back to their table and his unfinished drink. "That's what you came here to do, remember? And this is the one place in the galaxy where you don't have to feel responsible for everything that happens."

Sulu gave him a quizzical look. "Because I'm not the only captain in the room, you mean?"

"Because there is no one in the room who is *not* a captain." The felinoid alien on Sulu's other side wrapped a slender hand around his biceps, flexing her pearly claws at his involuntary look of surprise. Sulu was grateful that Kirk had caught him only a few steps out of the station commander's office, so that he still wore the tough red synthetic wool of his Starfleet jacket. "Yes, silly. Even me. Captains come in many shapes and sexes." She aimed a wicked look across the table at the freighter captain in his worn leather jacket. "And *species,*" she added meaningfully.

The human's salt-and-pepper beard split with a rueful wince. "Very true, *Captain.*"

"About all we have in common are the headaches," said the massive, white-maned man next to him. He took his meerschaum pipe from his mouth and made an old-fashioned gesture of respect toward the felinoid. "Or whatever part of your anatomy responds to having too few hours in the day to solve too many problems."

"Spine," she said and curled herself into a cat-smooth stretch that would have put her into traction if she were a human. "Ahh! That last run to Andor was a killer. The only good thing about it was—" She paused and glanced across the table at the English dandy, then lowered her voice to a hiss, "the Orion pirates left us alone, *this* time."

The freighter captain watched her with appreciative eyes. "Pirates are the one thing I've never had to deal with, knock on wood." He wrapped his knuckles on the table, startling the stub-tailed lizard into a short skittle from where it had been basking in the light from their table's lamp. The passing bartender promptly dropped another bottle of Martian Red Ice Ale onto the space the lizard had vacated. Since his own mug was still full, the bearded human offered it to the felinoid, who accepted with a flirtatious flick of her long eyelashes. "As bad as it must be to hunt them, I bet it's even worse to be the one they're hunting."

"Not if you keep your hull clean and your sails mended," said the Englishman. With his thigh-high boots and cutlass, he could have walked straight from the pages of a swashbuckling Rafael Sabatini adventure novel. Whatever costume party he was attending later that night, he'd probably win a prize for best historical accuracy. Even his boots were a perfect reconstruction from the days when shoemakers hadn't bothered to make different shoes for right and left feet. "Trust me, there's not a pirate in the world who ever bothered to scrape all the barnacles off his belly."

"Very true," agreed the man with the meerschaum pipe, with a look of grudging respect. "If you have a good steady wind behind you, you can loft your canvas and leave them wallowing like garbage scows."

The felinoid captain shook her caramel-colored mane of hair. "I theenk thees pirates are not sso eezee to run from, or to fyght," she said definitively. "I haf heard thiss story, how thees Nykusss mersenries almost start a war wiss the Klingons." She wrinkled her nose in the direction of the loud female Klingon who was just returning to her own table with a fresh drink. "Who can blame them?"

"That was later," Kirk told her. "The Anjiri and the Nykkus were on the run when I met them. But a few years after that, when they came after *us*—that was when things really got interesting." He gave Sulu a sidelong look, his hazel eyes gleaming with laughter. "Of course, you really should hear that part of the story from the man who got attacked by them on his first cruise with a brand-new ship—"

Sulu winced at the reminder of his initial botched mission on the *Excelsior,* but he couldn't help smiling as well. As soon as he recognized the story Captain Kirk was spinning he should have guessed that he wasn't going to escape without telling his part of it. And considering who he was waiting for here at Utopia Planitia, recounting that particular encounter with pirates did seem like an appropriate way to pass the time. Sulu glanced around at the circle of waiting faces and took a fortifying sip of Red Ice ale.

"It all started back on Deep Space Three," he said. He tickled the lizard under its chin until it wiggled up onto his hand, feeling strangely reassured by its cool presence against his skin. "Of course, we didn't know then that Captain Kirk's story was just the beginning of ours. Or that ours was the finish of his, I guess. All we knew was that we had a delivery to make, and a brand-new starship crew to make it with. . . ."

This really should be more nerve-wracking, I thought, watching the coordinated array of industrial-sized transporter beams play over the sleek, gull-winged shape of an FL-70 Falcon. After all, this unusual procedure—beaming a fleet of small reconnaissance ships directly into a starship's shuttle bay—wasn't just being tested for the first time, it was being tested on a newly designed and newly commissioned starship. *My* starship, the *U.S.S. Excelsior.* I know you'll say I'm prejudiced, but I had come to be extremely fond of the *Excelsior* in the short time since I'd been promoted to be her captain. She was a big muscular ship, built for maximum self-sufficiency and self-defense rather than speed and sleekness. The result was a work-horse, not anywhere as pretty to look at as the *Enterprise,* but the working model for a future line of long-range Starfleet cruisers.

Right now, however, the *Excelsior* was the only one of her kind and thus the only starship in the fleet whose main shuttle bay was big enough to carry all twelve Falcons. With the current level of diplomatic tension that existed between the Klingons and the Federation, that meant she was the only way those reconnaissance ships could get transferred to the Neutral Zone without making the Empire suspect they were being invaded. So, despite the fact that her shuttle bay doors were precisely one meter too small for the Falcons to fly through, this critical assignment had fallen to me, my ship, and my newly trained crew. You can see why I should have been shaking in my boots.

But as I watched the first FL-70 begin to glitter and fade out of existence, all I felt was the sweet relief of finally being done with testing and shakedown cruises and getting down to actual work. We'd spent months putting the *Excelsior* and her crew through every torturous test and trial that Starfleet's Corps of Astronomical Engineers could devise. In theory, our goal was to locate and correct any mechanical or computer flaws before we actually took the big ship out on her first mission, but I'd come to suspect that there was another, more subtle reason for shakedown cruises. By the time they were done, your entire crew was so hardened to crisis—and impatient for action—that any potential for nervous human error had been entirely burned away.

It took a surprisingly long time for the first Falcon to vanish from Deep Space Three's huge docking hanger. Its edges sparkled with transport effect long moments before the center did, and it vanished the same way, with a gleaming curve of cockpit windows lingering to the end like the Cheshire Cat's smile. The power drain created by the transport generators made the hangar lights dim, and the catwalk on which I was standing shook with subsonic vibrations as inertial dampeners cut in to compensate for the sudden shift in mass from the old-fashioned revolving station to the *Excelsior.* There was a lengthy pause after the Falcon was gone, then the slim communicator on my wrist chirped a request for attention.

"Sulu here."

"First Falcon's in the nest, sir," said Tim Henry gruffly. My chief engineer didn't have Montgomery Scott's rolling brogue or his tendency to prophesy disaster any time the ship's systems were stressed, but Henry had his own idiosyncracies. He spent all his off-duty hours building molecular model cities out of nano-machinery, creating what his xeno-biologist wife Sandi affectionately called "quantum flea circuses." This quirk was more than outweighed, however, by his superb trouble-shooting intuition. While all the engineers around him were scratching their heads and reaching for their computer models to determine which of the *Excelsior*'s many newly designed systems could be causing a ship malfunction, Henry already had panels off and was testing circuits. Ninety percent of the time, his first guess turned out to be the right one. If there was one thing my years on the *Enterprise* had taught me, it was that you could forgive a lot of eccentricity in a good engineer.

"Any problems with inertial compensation?" I craned my head to glance over the transporter tech's shoulder at the monitor which showed the *Excelsior,* docked high on the station's outer ring. It was an irrational thing to do, of course, since I couldn't possibly tell from the outside if the transport of this enormous and unwieldy piece of cargo had damaged my starship's delicate link to Deep Space Three. But the unlikely vision of my ugly metal behemoth floating like a swan against the background swirl of stars always made me smile.

"Barely a flicker on the readouts, sir," Henry reported. "If anything, we started to compensate for the mass a few milliseconds too soon. I'm going to synchronize our inertial dampeners with the transporter power surge next time. Clear for number two."

"Acknowledged." I nodded at the station's transporter chief and she punched in the coordinates of the second FL-70. This time I watched the power gauges instead of the glittering sweep of the beam, and whistled at the energy consumption they recorded. If we had been anywhere near an inhabited planet, that much diversion of sunlight might have caused a noticeable climate change. However, the massive red giant that Deep Space Three orbited had long ago engulfed and charred any planets it once had. The space station was free to drain off as much radiant energy as it needed.

"We've got the highest capacity cargo transporters in the sector, Captain." The station commander had seen the direction of my gaze and interpreted my whistle correctly. Wendell Barstow was an older man, brisk and businesslike as befitted someone who oversaw both Starfleet and mercantile operations on his watch. "And we've handled bigger packages than those FL-70s of yours. Don't worry, we'll get them all into your shuttle bay without burning out any power circuits."

"But will the Neutral Zone outpost we're heading for have the transporter capacity to get them out again?" asked a grim voice from beside me. "If not, the *Excelsior*'s shuttle bay doors aren't going to fit anymore."

I glanced over at my executive officer, a little surprised that this long-awaited call to action hadn't ignited the same cheerfulness in him that it had in me. "Our orders are to deliver the Falcons to Elaphe Vulpina Nine," I said. "Last time I checked, that was the Neutral Zone outpost set up specifically to guard the Vulcans' main transporter research station. Don't worry, Mr. Chekov, those patrol ships won't have to blast their way out of the *Excelsior*'s belly."

"Assuming the Klingons haven't recently blasted Elaphe Vulpina," Chekov reminded me. "You know we've been on the brink of war with them ever since we butted heads on the Genesis planet. If they decided to attack—"

"A dozen little reconnaissance ships built for stealth and speed won't be any help to us. They can stay right inside our cargo bay while we stop any Klingon incursion." I eyed my second-in-command with more attention than I'd paid to him since the day he'd first reported to his new post on the *Excelsior.* He looked older than in the days when we'd manned the helm of the *Enterprise,* of course, but then so did I. Less muscle and more bone showing in our faces, less rashness and more wisdom in our eyes. But the lines carved between his dark eyebrows seemed sharper than usual today, and his eyes met mine reluctantly. I frowned, and took a few steps away from the station commander and his transporter chief, trusting that the rumble of the big inertial compensators would cover our lowered voices.

"Pavel, what's the matter? I told you when you came aboard, if there's some part of a mission you don't like, it's your job as my executive officer to say so." That was another thing I'd learned from serving with Captain Kirk and Commander Spock back on the *Enterprise.* "Are you worried the Klingons will find out we're delivering a fleet of military ships to the border and attack us?"

Chekov shook his head, but remained silent. I held my tongue as the second Falcon slowly began to vanish. Ten years of serving together, and nearly twenty years of friendship, let me know when to push this man and when to let him be. At length, he made a face. I don't think it was the stale smell of Deep Space Three's regenerated air that inspired it.

"I think this all just reminds me a little too much of the *Kobayashi Maru,*" my executive officer admitted. "Why did Starfleet Command have to make our very first mission one that involves the Klingons and the Neutral Zone?"

"Our mission parameters don't have us coming within fifty kilometers of the Neutral Zone itself," I reminded him. "Unless they happen to be patrolling near Elaphe Vulpina, the Klingons should never even know we were there."

"Right." I couldn't tell from his clipped-off voice if Chekov was being sardonic or just serious. He watched in silence as the second Falcon disappeared. This time, it was the sensor-deflecting nose array that lingered until last. "Just promise me you won't answer any mysterious distress calls from the other side of the Klingon border."

"Don't worry," I said dryly. "I got that out of my system back at the academy." My wrist communicator chirped again, and I tapped the channel open. "Sulu here."

I was expecting Tim Henry's confirmation that the second small patrol ship had arrived intact, but what I got instead was the younger voice of Nino Orsini, my chief security officer. "Captain, we just got a call from the ship's resupply team. They've gotten delayed down on level eight because of a little alien trouble."

I frowned. "What kind of alien trouble?"

"A confrontation with some—er—revenue agents from the local dilithium supplier. The station quartermaster insists their tax claim on Deep Space Three's dilithium stock isn't valid, but they're refusing to let our supply team take it without paying a tariff. Should I take a detail from the *Excelsior* down to deal with it or call in station security?"

I glanced over at Chekov and got an answering nod without even needing to ask the question. "Neither, Lieutenant. Commander Chekov is going to straighten out the situation."

"Aye, sir. And by the way, Chief Henry says to tell you that the second Falcon came in just fine with the modified inertial dampening procedure."

"Acknowledged. Sulu out."

By the time I'd lifted my thumb off the communicator controls, Chekov had already vanished into the nearest turbolift. I sighed, and turned back to the glitter of transporter beams scything through the station's cargo hold. The third Falcon was beginning to vanish, leaving nine more to go. If the truth be told I was already bored, but being a starship captain meant more than just making all the hard decisions in times of crisis. It also meant being present at all of your ship's momentous occasions, from major events like the signing of peace treaties to small ones like the arrival of new crew members and the first-ever transport of ships into shuttle bays.

It also meant delegating authority, something I was still trying to accustom myself to. I knew better than to try dealing with every problem and crisis in person, but part of my brain was still down in that turbolift with Chekov, trying to foresee and solve the problems he'd encounter on deck eight. Was that the right way to delegate, or was I supposed to just hand the problem over to a competent member of my crew and then forget about it? It was something I still wasn't clear on, and in this case it was no use asking myself what my mentor, Captain Kirk, would have done. Delegating authority was the one thing he was notoriously bad at.

"Problem, Captain Sulu?"

"A minor one." I joined Wendell Barstow back at the transporter desk in time to see the third Falcon dissolve into glitter. "How long has your local dilithium supplier been trying to levy a tariff on Starfleet requisitions?"

"What?" The station commander looked as blank as if I'd told him that the Klingons had just signed a peace treaty with the Federation. "Who says they are?"

"My resupply team. They've been asked to pay a surcharge to top off the *Excelsior*'s stocks."

Barstow snorted at that and pressed his wrist communicator on. "Barstow to Operations Room. How many non-Starfleet ships do we have in port now, Rebovich?"

"Four, sir," said the voice of his second-in-command. "An Andorian luxury liner, an Earth courier, a Tellerite merchant ship, and an Orion private yacht."

"Thanks. Barstow out." The station commander gave me a tolerant look. "Sounds to me like your resupply team is getting itself caught in a classic Orion swindle. You did say this was the *Excelsior*'s first full-fledged mission, didn't you, Captain Sulu? You should have warned your greenhorns never to pay a toll to the trolls."

I felt my cheeks tighten with embarrassment, and it wasn't just at the stationmaster's blunt frontier slang. It was hard enough to be a brand-new captain without the additional burden of shepherding a brand-new crew through all the pitfalls that unscrupulous aliens could throw at them. "I'll warn my XO not to fall for it," I managed to say calmly enough, but I tapped my communicator channel open with more force than it needed. Fortunately, Starfleet built its equipment to sustain worse things than a captain's irritability.

"Sulu to Chekov."

"Chekov here." From the slowing pitch of the turbolift whistle in the background, I could tell he had almost arrived at his destination. It made his disgruntled tone understandable. "Change of orders, Captain?"

"No, just a change of context. Commander Barstow thinks our 'dilithium revenue agents' are probably Orion swindlers. I thought you'd want to be prepared—"

"To rescue the supply team from their clutches," Chekov finished for me, the irritation in his voice replaced by a veteran space-traveler's amusement. "Understood. Chekov out."

I released the communicator button and stood watching a fourth Falcon fade into glimmers beneath the scouring of the station's immense transporter beams. It looked like pure magic, as any sufficiently advanced technology does, but I knew that billions of complex computer functions were being carried out during each second of that transfer, accompanied by an input of solar power so vast that magnetically confined power conduits were required to supply it. And the net result of all this technological wizardry? Twelve little two-man reconnaissance ships were moved a distance they could easily have coasted to on the strength of their own warp exhaust, if the engineers who designed the *Excelsior*'s shuttle bay doors had only foreseen the need to admit them.

My communicator chirped again, but this time it didn't wait for me to announce myself. "Captain, you and the station commander need to hear this," said my security chief's voice. Before I could respond, the crackle of a poor-quality or very distant subspace transmission burst from the speaker on my wrist.

"Ships converge Deep Space Three attack wait explosion capture ships converge Deep Space Three attack wait explosion capture ships converge—"

Orsini's voice replaced the ominous babble. "We picked it up on a routine scan of subspace frequencies, sir," he said before I could ask. "About a minute ago."

"Klingons?" I demanded. Deep Space Three was the major restocking point for the entire length of the Klingon Neutral Zone, although it wasn't anywhere near the boundary itself. If it was under attack by the Klingon Empire, a major incursion was in progress and Chekov's gloom regarding our mission had been well-justified.

"No, Captain. The transmission signature isn't Klingon, and the language was barely decipherable." That was my chief communications officer, Janice Rand. Her composed voice, the result of long years of deep space experience, contrasted noticeably with Orsini's youthful urgency. "Our universal translator found a comparable alien language sampled twenty years ago in a sector near here, but the translation you just heard only has a forty-five percent confidence interval. We're not even sure that we caught the entire text of the message."

"Can you pinpoint the source?"

"No, sir. It was broadcast in a part of the subspace spectrum no one uses much because of interference from black holes. That's the crackling noise that you heard."

"So it could be coming from anywhere." I watched the last glittering fade of the fourth Falcon and frowned. "Have our sensors picked up unusual ship movements anywhere near the station?"

"Several vessels are in the vicinity, sir, but their flight paths don't seem to be coordinated." Science Officer Christina Schulman sounded as if she was frowning, but then she almost always did when she was trying to interpret long-range sensor data. I had never seen anyone coax more information from sensor arrays and be less satisfied with it. "Some of the ion trails do show an unusual enhancement in the heavier transperiodic isotopes, which means their warp drives are getting pretty old. Other than that, we don't have much information."

"Which means they aren't broadcasting their identification profiles the way most merchant ships do." I swung around to face the station commander, who'd been listening in thoughtful silence beside me. "Commander Barstow, I suggest we stop the transport and place the station on red alert—"

"Based on a single badly translated transmission?" The older man gave me the same tolerant look that had greeted my resupply crew's encounter with Orion swindlers. "Captain Sulu, do you have any idea how many times a week we get hit with this kind of thing out here on the frontier? Garbled messages with just enough words to make the universal translator think it knows the language—and by the time you track it down, you find out it was just a subspace echo that got bounced through a singularity from one side of the quadrant to the other. Or maybe the Klingons along the Neutral Zone amusing themselves by trying to destroy our crew's morale. We can't raise our shields every single time it happens—it would disrupt all our cargo loading operations."

I frowned out at the silver crescent of docking rim I could see through the cargo bay windows. All of those ships, including my own, lay vulnerable to attack unless the station raised its shields to protect them. I might be succumbing to new-captain jitters, but something about the brutal simplicity of those intercepted attack orders told me they weren't idle Klingon chatter. And Captain Kirk always said to trust your instincts.

I shot out a hand and caught the transporter chief's hand away from her controls before she could begin the transport of another Falcon. "I can't force you to shield your own station, Commander Barstow," I said quietly. "But I *can* order this loading operation to be halted so that I can raise the shields on my own ship."

"But if we power down the beam generators now it'll take two hours of recalibration before we can start up again," the transporter chief protested. "We have other ships waiting to be loaded—"

"I'll take full responsibility for the delay." I could see Barstow's exasperation deepen to annoyance. "You can put a reprimand in my file if this turns out to be a false alarm, but for now I'm taking it seriously. I want my ship shielded in case of attack."

"Shut down the transporters," Barstow told his transporter chief reluctantly. She swept a hand across her controls, and I felt the vibration of the immense plasma cables that fed the beam generators fade to a shiver and then vanish. A moment later, the deep-throated growl of the inertial dampeners faded too. Inside the shroud of silence that had fallen over the station's main cargo bay, the chirp of my communicator seemed as loud as the whoop of a distress siren. I thumbed it on, expecting the *Excelsior.*

"Sulu here."

"It's Chekov." His tense whisper probably wouldn't have been audible a moment before. "Captain, our resupply team's not being swindled, they're being held hostage in the quartermaster's office. They must have been forced to call in a false report to explain their delay in returning to the ship."

I lowered my voice to avoid giving his position away in case anyone was listening. "How many Orions are there?"

"None," Chekov said grimly. "I only got a glimpse of the aliens guarding the door, but they don't look like Orions or anything else I've ever seen. And they don't look friendly. I think they're trying to break into the dilithium storage area."

I glanced over at Barstow. "Attack wait explosion," I reminded him and saw his face tighten with dismay. He pressed his own communicator and began calling for security. "Chekov, do what you can to keep those aliens out of there until station security arrives," I told my second-in-command. "They may be trying to sabotage Deep Space Three."

"Understood. Chekov out."

I slapped the communicator to another channel. "Sulu to *Excelsior.*"

"Henry here." My crew had obviously taken the intercepted threat as seriously as I had, since they'd summoned the next-in-command back from the shuttle bay to the bridge. "Orders, Captain?"

"Put the ship on red alert. Disengage from the station and back away far enough to raise shields." The interference from a starship's powerful electromagnetic defenses had been known to play havoc with space station circuits, especially if the station hadn't raised its own external shields. "Warn all Starfleet vessels in port that we have a hostage situation in progress, potential sabotage on Deep Space Three, and an attack force of unknown proportions on the way." I glanced at Barstow and found him heading for the turbolift without waiting to consult with me. I didn't hold his departure against him—now that he knew the threat was real, the safety of Deep Space Three had to be his top priority, just as the safety of the *Excelsior*'s crew and her cargo was mine. "Beam me back aboard before you raise shields."

"Too late, sir." The sweeping glare of phasers across the cargo bay windows had already told me that. "We just came under attack."

"Then get those shields up, *now!*" To my relief, I could see docking clamps opening all along the silver rim of Deep Space Three, as one Starfleet vessel after another disengaged and prepared for battle. The *Excelsior* was already several meters from the station and moving fast for all her workhorse bulk. As I watched, a sudden shiver of phosphorescence ran across her starboard side as her rising shields brushed past Deep Space Three's own defensive screens.

Phaser bursts exploded again across the cargo windows, too bright this time to be anything but a direct hit off the screens in front of them. I thought it was a stray shot until it happened again, a few seconds later. I frowned and glanced over at Deep Space Three's transporter chief, but she was so busy recalibrating her instruments that I wasn't sure she even knew an attack was in progress. I tapped her shoulder and got a startled upward look.

"Is there a weapons array near here?"

"Not really. The nearest one is on the lower docking ring."

"What about life-support? Shield generators?"

She shook her head again, looking puzzled. "Cargo transporters are never placed near any critical station systems. The interference from our power circuits would mean constant retuning. Why?"

I squinted up at another burst of light. "Because whoever these attackers are, they seem to be concentrating their fire on us."

"On *us?*" She craned her head upward. "But the screens over the cargo bay were never designed to withstand heavy fire—"

"I think they know that." I frowned, watching the swoop and flash of surprisingly small and mismatched fighters behind the phaser explosions. This was starting to look more like a pirate raid and less like a military attack. "They're staying tucked between the station wheels, where the weapons arrays can't reach them. And any return fire from the starships out there will just add to the damage they're doing."

The transporter chief looked back down at her panel, winced, then swept her hand across it, taking all her systems back to zero again. "We'd better get out before that hull breaches. At least the Falcons won't mind being exposed to vacuum—"

"No, but they will mind being exposed to phaser fire." I wasn't going to let my very first mission be wrecked by a bunch of alien buccaneers who'd picked Deep Space Three to loot that week. If I couldn't be aboard the *Excelsior,* overseeing this fight, then I could at least be a participant in it. "Get up to Operations," I told the transporter chief, giving her a little push to separate her from her station. "If the station shields fall, tell your security chief to try activating the shields on the other seven Falcons by remote command."

"The other *seven* Falcons?" she repeated, and blinked at me in confusion. "But we only transported four over to the *Excelsior.*"

"I know." I took a step away from the transporter desk and felt the weight of the last five months—the constant decisions, the endless complications, and the unrelenting responsibility—slide unexpectedly off my shoulders. I started to understand why Captain Kirk always insisted on leading all those landing parties himself. "The eighth one will already have its shields raised. From the inside."

Three

KIRK

In my case, defending the *Enterprise* from imminent attack wasn't my primary concern. After all, we'd found no evidence of unidentified ships loitering about, and sensors verified that any detectable engine residue belonged only to the damaged vessel in front of us. If you'd asked me at the moment Spock and I arrived in the transporter room, I would have said our biggest challenge would be figuring out our visitors' dietary needs.

I would have been wrong, of course. But I was still young; I had a lot to learn.

So with all the other dire considerations that could have been racing through my head as Engineer Scott activated the transporter, what actually struck me first about them was that they should have been bigger.

Not that I had any expectations—we still hadn't been able to establish voice contact with them, much less visual. The only thing we knew for certain from our sensor readings was that they *weren't* Orions; whether or not they were sympathizers toward that dyspeptic race still remained to be seen. Still, the flashes of transporter cohesion that came just ahead of total solidity suggested terror, speed, and ferocity far beyond anything the Orions had ever achieved.

So when the transporter's whine finally drifted to silence and left behind a half dozen armored creatures not much taller than my shoulder, I felt a little twinge of surprise.

I heard Spock later call them therapods, but at the time the only word that came to my mind was "reptile." Pebble-skinned, a uniform sand gray in color, they had the lidless, jewel-toned eyes of a gecko and the fierce, conical teeth of a crocodile. They were thick limbed, with broad, brutish heads; their crouching, forward-leaning posture would have made them look ready to attack even if they'd been the most gentle, open-minded people in the world, which I had a feeling they were not. The armor was mechanical—no biological elements at all, as far as I could see—but fitted them so tightly that it might have been chitinous plates or thickened skin. When one of them lowered its muzzle to make direct eye contact with me, I swallowed my first surge of alarm and decided I'd interpret the gesture as one of leadership rather than aggression.

Realizing how easily the rod-shaped universal translator could be mistaken for a weapon, I kept my hand scrupulously relaxed at my side as I took a single step toward the transporter pad. "I'm Captain James T. Kirk of—"

They exploded into the room as a single unit, like shrapnel from an old-fashioned bomb. I'd brought an escort of security personnel—I was altruistic, not stupid—and the shriek of phaser fire filled the tiny room as lashing tails and brilliant claws struck out in every direction. I had less than an eye-blink to glimpse two men go down under a powerful double-footed kick from one attacker, then one of the armor-plated monsters slammed me full in the chest and we hit the deck so hard my vision grayed.

It missed gutting me by a few inches—I heard the heavy claws on its feet screech against the decking. Instinctively, I heaved as much strength into my counterblow as I could muster, aiming for the fetid stink of its breath so close to my own face. The translator in my hand impacted with bone and armor, smashing snapping teeth aside but clearly doing nothing to discourage my attacker from another try. Dread clenched at my belly as its big lizard face swung back toward me—

Then the referred jolt of a phaser blast made my hands go numb and knocked the glint of consciousness from the creature's eyes.

I thought I had managed to muscle it aside myself, valiantly ignoring the adrenaline shakes that were making my stomach feel like liquid. But, as it rolled to flop prostrate on the decking, I saw Spock straighten from where he'd bent to haul it off me. I also saw the phaser still in his hand.

"Thank you, Mr. Spock." No sense spoiling the moment by pointing out the legendary Vulcan reputation for nonviolence.

He glanced at the phaser as though unimpressed with how it looked in his hand. "Merely being prudent, Captain."

Because arranging for a new commander officer would prove an annoyance this far away from a Federation starbase? Or because he'd had just enough exposure to the executive officer position to know he didn't want the captaincy? There are some questions better left unasked.

Turning, I made a quick survey of the damage around the transporter room. Spock was one of the few people in front of the console still standing—apparently, our visitors hadn't marked him as a threat when it came to picking targets. Which showed what both of us knew, I guess, since I probably would have discounted a Vulcan, too. But the attackers themselves lay in huddles all over the room, twitching as though in feverish sleep. I was surprised but pleased by how little human blood had been spilled in the brief skirmish. You could say a lot of things about Starfleet security squads, but that they were tough as nails should be top on anybody's list.

"Call sickbay," I told Scott. He and his transporter tech were still safely ensconced behind the control console, wisely staying out of the way. "Get that medical team down here."

"Presumptive, Nykkus sometimes are." The voice was feather-light, and drifted up to us from the dented device still clutched in my right hand. "Incendiary, Nykkus most times are."

The alien still crouched near the back of the transporter pad blinked at me from beneath the arms he'd crossed over his head. He'd been completely screened from view by the armored creatures now spread out on my floor, who I now realized were probably protecting him. His own armor was lighter, more like a tense skin of protective clothing, and he was slim and more delicately boned. What struck me most, though, was how humanoid his face and eyes appeared when compared to his guards'—like the features of a human compared to those of a gorilla. He stood with a fluid grace that was neither threatening nor submissive and splayed one long-fingered hand against his chest. "Vissith am I." One finger curled out to point down at my side while the little nubbin that was all he had for a tail twitched nervously. "From this elongation, a voice I sense. This alteration, what I eject tells you?"

I glanced down at the translator, then back up at him. "Yes. This is a translation device." Which I very likely addled by bashing it against one of Vissith's guards. It spun out a musical braid of hissing and clicks which I hoped made for better syntax in his language than it did in mine. "Can you understand what I'm saying to you?"

Vissith's head cocked almost over onto his shoulder. His whole body seemed to fidget, fingers moving, knees flexing arrhythmically. "Yes," he said at last. But even the voice given him by the translator sounded uncertain. "Although very bad your decoration of words is."

I couldn't help but smile. "The translation should improve as we talk longer." I was almost hypnotized by his constant movement, and had to make myself blink and look back up at his jewel-tone eyes. "I'm Captain James T. Kirk, of the Federation starship *Enterprise*. We mean you no harm."

He bobbed a short staccato, toes clicking. "Our existence you broken have." Fingers fluttered to dust hissing words over his fallen guards. "My domestic Nykkus killed you have."

"Your Nykkus aren't harmed, only . . ." I glanced at their crumpled forms, trying to decide on the best way to explain "sleeping." Which word should I have used for Vissith's guards—domestic or Nykkus? I chose the one I didn't recognize, hoping it would translate more directly back into the alien's language. "Your Nykkus will wake up again in a few minutes." And, God willing, we'd have everything sorted out with Vissith by then. I wasn't really looking forward to defending myself with a handheld translator again.

The transporter room doors whisked open, and Vissith jumped as though someone had stung him. I responded only a little less strongly—I'd almost forgotten the emergency medical team. I certainly hadn't expected my new chief surgeon to come along with them. Piper'd had a tendency to delegate such duties to his younger medtechs. Snapping an appraising look at the downed aliens and my one injured security officer, McCoy raised both eyebrows at me the way he used to when he was a dorm monitor at Starfleet Academy and I was the cadet he'd caught at an inappropriate party. I waved him to get his team to work without ever really pulling my attention away from Vissith.

"My ship is not the one which attacked you," I tried to explain, turning back to our guest. "But our sensors detect no other vessels in the vicinity—"

"Pirates. Cargos loosened, our pod set adrift."

I resisted an urge to slap the translator against the palm of my hand. Vissith's abrupt interruptions made it hard to follow the flow of our discussion, but the translator's bizarre word choices weren't helping, either. "Any pirates are long gone. We detected your automatic distress beacon and only came to offer assistance."

"Fix our hovel."

The request—the *order*—caught me by surprise. I shook my head slowly, biting back an impulse to point out that someone who'd been minutes away from sucking vacuum was really in no position to be demanding anything. "I'm afraid we can't do that," I explained. Quite reasonably, I thought. "Your ship has sustained serious damage." *And I have no intention of sending a repair crew to poke around a scrap heap so hot that sensors still don't have a definitive fix on the number of life-forms on board.* "But if you're willing, we'll give your crew shelter and medical care, and take you back to your own people."

His rocking and weaving never slowed, but it took him a long time before he spoke again. "Packages within our belly, these as well you bring."

Spock beat me to that explanation. "Our sensors detect no mass left within your cargo bays, and very little atmosphere beyond where your crew has taken shelter."

I wasn't sure how much of that would make it through a garbled translation, so added, "What your crew has with them is all you have." Then I gave Vissith a moment to absorb the concept, not to mention for the translator to finish skreeling out its own interpretation. "There's nothing left we can steal from you," I said gently. "And if we meant to harm you, we could have done so already. If you'll trust us, and step down from there, we can use our transporter to bring over the rest of your crew and set you up in guest quarters."

For the first time since he'd climbed to his feet, Vissith stood stone still. "Interrogative."

Even the translator had no suggestion as to what he'd meant to say. "I don't understand."

That admission at least seemed to turn into something on its way out the other end of the translator. I listened to what seemed an incongruously long string of hissing, then an equally long silence. "Suspicious your suggestion is." He seemed to be speaking very slowly, carefully. I was more sure than ever that the translator wasn't working any better in his direction than in mine. "Vacuum and vacancy your only improvements will be."

Ah, we got nothing from helping them. Yet from where I stood, we humans actually had a lot to gain—friendship with a new race, expanded knowledge about the galaxy we all lived in, maybe even some information that could help us ferret out any acts of piracy in this sector. Still, I wasn't sure how to explain all that to Vissith, especially through a communications device I wasn't confident could accurately translate our names. "We call it kindness." Could the translator convey the meaning of a smile? "It's a human custom."

Perhaps the slow blinking of alien eyes meant something equally as subtle and untranslatable as a smile. "This gesture to me has no meaning. My people this word do have not."

No meaning in a smile? Or no such word as "kindness." Either way, I should have known right then that something was wrong.

We learned that they were called the Anjiri. There were seventeen of them on board their disintegrating ship, plus another twenty-three of the burly, battle-scarred pit bulls that Vissith referred to as Nykkus. I'd tried to get McCoy to do thorough scans of both, to see if they were related species or no more similar than humans are to Vulcans. Looks can be deceiving. But he was busy inventing appropriate medical treatment for the four Nykkus injured when their ship was first attacked, and his efforts weren't helped by Vissith's continued insistence that he was wasting his time. "Nykkus people are not," he offered, as though that should have been obvious to any casual observer. "Into the dark outside pressure doors toss them you should. This often do we. Injuries unseemly are. To the cold with them."

So when the Nykkus balked at following the Anjiri into the rec hall we'd prepared to house them, I wasn't entirely surprised. How could they be sure there were no airlock doors inside? I let McCoy lead the Nykkus down the corridor to the gymnasium; it wasn't until the last Nykkus rounded the corner out of sight that Vissith and the rest of the Anjiri finally deigned to cross the threshold to the rec hall without them. So much for happy race relations.

"Nykkus people are not," Vissith had said again, seeming to dismiss the whole incident with no more concern than he'd dismissed the Nykkus's injuries earlier. "Nykkus dance fitless ever, flee the face with seeing now."

Which, of course, was the second half of my ever deepening problem. Instead of improving as it sampled more of the Anjiri's language, the translator's syntax and word choice seemed to be getting steadily worse. "It's not working," I complained to Spock. Not unless I planned to believe that the Nykkus "pilled for fees and reasons" or that their Anjiri masters had "baked the halls in the candles of their brains."

"The device is fully operational." Spock didn't even disassemble it—he'd already done that twice on my insistence; this time he simply watched it burble through yet another self-diagnostic, then handed it back to me with no more breach of his Vulcan composure than a testily arched eyebrow. "The Hayden-Elgin model translator has the lowest malfunction rate of any current translation device."

McCoy snorted without looking up from the readings his tricorder compiled. "Fat lot of good that does us." It was the first thing the doctor had said since rejoining us in the rec hall. "We might as well go back to smoke signals and tom-toms."

Spock didn't sigh, but I somehow got the impression he wanted to. He was hitting it off with McCoy about as well as I'd expected. "Doctor, I fail to see the relevance—"

"Bones," I reached past Spock to catch McCoy's elbow, "did you have problems with your translator, too?"

The doctor glanced up, his face an elegant display of disgust. "Who can tell?" he grumbled. "I don't think the Nykkus said two words the whole time I was with them. Not a chatty lot. What they did say made no more sense than a dog barking at the moon."

"Captain . . ." Spock turned quite pointedly to me, his hands gripped patiently behind his back. "Such subjective anecdotes do not constitute a scientific observation—"

I cut him off, already knowing what I planned to do. "I want a communications officer."

He snipped short whatever he'd been about to say, took two mental steps backward, and plowed forward again on a new track. "Translator repairs fall more directly into engineering's purview."

"I don't want repairs." I thrust the translator at Spock until he deigned to bring one hand around and take it. "I want a *new* translator—a living one. I want somebody who'll take into account more than just what comes out of the Anjiri's mouths." When he raised an eyebrow, I qualified, "We've got trained linguists in communications. I say we use them."

And what the captain says, goes.

The young lieutenant who answered my summons fifteen minutes later was in her late-twenties, slim and brown, with the kind of dark mocha eyes that seem to look through you as much as *at* you, and a smile so white it made me blink. I had a feeling she raised attentiveness to a whole new standard. So petite that she could have walked under my outstretched arm, she still managed to exude an ease and confidence that would make me remember her as taller for several months afterward. To this day, I have no memories of ever looking down at her, only of facing her squarely eye-to-eye.

"Lieutenant Uhura." I summoned her with a wave of my hand, then stepped aside to widen our circle when she approached. She joined us with the politeness appropriate to a junior officer, but with no sign of shyness or fear. Her long golden earrings jangled musically as she listened to my quick summation of events with a series of attentive nods. The whole while, her deft hands neatly dismantled the Hayden-Elgin translator so she could examine the pieces, wipe them off, then fit them back together again.

"Well, Mr. Spock is right," she said when I was finished. "There's nothing wrong with the device." She aimed a stunning smile up at Spock, as if either offering him apology or support. "But the inherent problem with all field-style translators is that they're almost entirely dependent on audio and electromagnetic input. There's *some* visual data collection, but the units don't allow for enough storage and processing to really make good use of it." Her eyes danced over the Anjiri, who gathered with their bevy of Federation-supplied security guards around the food service equipment. Her expression reminded me of the way Scotty looked at really tricky technical problems. "Let me talk to them for a few minutes and see what I can do."

Of course, as in all alien dealings, it took more than just a few minutes. Uhura stood in a knot of suspicious Anjiri, tricorder in one hand and translator in the other, for more than an hour—long enough for McCoy to apparently run out of disgruntled comments and head back for sickbay to escape the boredom, long enough for Spock to decide it would be most logical to fill our waiting time by examining two of the overdue crew reports he was finding the most impenetrable, and long enough for me to wish I had insisted on following Uhura when she first strode over to exchange introductions with the Anjiri. I hate waiting. More specifically, I hate doing nothing. Even when there's not a damned thing I can do, I'd still rather be inventing some kind of work for myself than standing around waiting for a junior officer's report.

Still, I'd like to believe that I honestly noticed the moment when Lieutenant Uhura's interactions with the Anjiri moved from linguistic Q&A into actual conversation. Silencing Spock with an upraised hand, I walked away from him without taking my eyes off Uhura and without bothering to notice if he'd even stopped talking.

When neither Uhura nor Vissith interrupted their chatter for my approach, I stopped a few feet away and summoned, "Lieutenant?"

"Captain!" Her eyes shone bright with an unmistakably professional pride. I like an officer who's possessive about her discipline. "I believe we've made some progress."

I could have guessed that from the tangle of wires and patch clips littering the table beside her. The translator, partially gutted again, lay nestled against the bottom of her tricorder, held in place by a wrap of wire and an umbilicus of data cables and conduits. On the tricorder's tiny screen, a little lizard-like simulacrum danced and flowed in rhythm with Uhura's words. I almost recognized some of the movements from Vissith's eternal fidgeting, but they looked awkward and primitive when projected in two lifeless dimensions.

"There's a detailed physical component to the Anjiri language." Uhura stole a look at Vissith, as if knowing—expecting—him to overhear, and eager for his verification. "The position of the body—and various body parts—in space can change the very definition of a word. If anything, the translator's efforts to combine those apparent variations in meaning was only making matters worse."

Rather than meeting Uhura's eager gaze, Vissith's own eyes remained fixed on the dancing lizard on her tricorder screen. "What about now?" I asked. "How do you know what physical movements to attach to whatever word the translator puts out?"

"The tricorder has better visual pickup, and a lot more processing power." She played with one of the wire connections, but I couldn't see that it accomplished anything. "I'm letting it mate the audio portion from the universal translator to its own visual input to create a single English output, then just reverse the process to take the English back into visual and audio Anjiri components." Then a quick smile back at Vissith. "How am I doing?"

His eerie, lidless eyes remained locked on the small screen. "Strange, it is, dealing in conversation with myself in a small black box." The simulacrum did look passingly like him; as near as I could tell, the hissing Anjiri voice it produced was his, as well.

"It's better than struggling with no real communication at all." I studied the little mini-Vissith as it danced out a translation of my words. While Vissith himself said nothing I could hear in response, the translator/tricorder arrangement said, "Yes" in the voice it had given him. I couldn't help but wonder if something in his bobbing and weaving was the equivalent of a human nod. "My apologies for any difficulties we experienced before," I went on. "You and your people are welcome on my ship. Do you understand what's happened? Why you're here?"

"Your podmate much has clarified for us."

I assumed he was refering to Uhura, but nothing in his body language made that clear.

"Returned to our homes, we will be. Honored guests of the captain, until that time we will be."

"Very honored guests," I said. "Our doctor has seen to your Nykkus—"

Vissith brushed off my unfinished sentence so thoroughly that he nearly turned his back on me. "Nykkus people are not. Nykkus live, Nykkus die. Little the concern is to us."

So that much, at least, had translated accurately. I made a mental note to remember this point—how much any race tolerates its siblings tells you a lot about it. And about how it will tolerate you.

"If you'll tell us where you'd like to be delivered, I can have my helmsman set a course."

"Pilots of our own we have." His hands cut short, definitive circles in the air to either side. "Courses of our own we will set. To your bridge you may escort us once we have eaten, have slept."

I blinked at him, caught off guard. "I'm afraid it doesn't work that way. This is my ship." *You lost yours to pirates.* "Tell my crew where you would like to go, and we'll be more than glad to take you there."

"Where we wish to go, our own business is. The path to our own homeworld, the right to know you have not. Our own courses we shall plot, or we shall go not."

Is reason a human concept? It was something I'd have to debate with Spock—later, after we'd managed to off-load our passengers somewhere we could all agree upon. "This is a very advanced vessel. Your crew isn't trained—"

"Anjiri pilots quite cunning are," Vissith insisted with an almost human stubbornness. "Anjiri pilots anything can fly." He turned to Uhura, as though convincing her mattered more than convincing me. "Anything. Our own courses we shall plot or we shall go not."

"Captain . . ." Spock edged about as close as Vulcan comfort would allow. I could almost feel the electric charge building around him, like a capacitor right on the verge of letting go. Because he was a Vulcan, he burst into words, not action. "Captain, I do not advise—"

"All right, Vissith, you can do the course plotting yourselves." I know what you're thinking, but I really don't make it a habit to ignore the advice of my first officers. Usually. The words, the agreement seemed to jump out of me of their own accord. I'd learned a long time ago to trust whatever little corner of my brain tossed out such gems, and I wasn't about to stop listening to it now. "But only if you allow my crew to remain on the bridge in case you need assistance."

Vissith stared hard at the flashing tricorder screen, then flicked his bright eyes up at me. "Watch our piloting they may not. The path to our homeworld, the right to know they have not."

"No one will watch you as you pilot. I only want to make sure my ship can be taken care of if problems should arise." I don't know whether I managed to read something on Vissith's immobile face, or if it was intuition kicking in again. "In case your pirates return," I added smoothly.

This time, Vissith's long silence didn't produce even a flutter from the translator. He had to rattle a whole string of alien sounds before Uhura's device offered up, "Agreed. For you we shall send when our eating finished is." He whisked his hand lightly down Uhura's face, so quickly she didn't have a chance to flinch. "This podmate on the use of your food creation devices instruct us will."

I waited for Uhura to show her acceptance with a curt nod in my direction, then echoed that nod toward Vissith. "Lieutenant Uhura will know how to contact me when you're ready."

I left them all clustered around the food dispenser, their backs turned to me and their hands weaving intricate patterns of talking in the air.

Spock actually managed to keep quiet until we were almost to the turbolift. Then, when he spoke, it was with the cutting precision I'd eventually learn to recognize as the sign of a Vulcan snit. "Captain, Starfleet regulations expressly prohibit granting bridge access to non-Federation personnel."

"Starfleet's regulatory board isn't here." I punched the controls to summon the 'lift. "Besides, I've got no intention of either hauling the Anjiri around indefinitely *or* of handing them over to Starfleet as though we'd collected them as prisoners of war."

He stopped neatly at my side and folded his hands behind his back. "My personal experience is that this practice is unsafe. If we do not know where they intend to take the *Enterprise,* we cannot be properly prepared for whatever we find there."

"Oh, I intend to know where they're taking us, Mr. Spock."

He peered at me with one eyebrow lifted. "I heard you give your promise to Vissith." The coldness in his voice surprised me. "Did you do so intending not to keep it?"

I shrugged. "I promised no one would spy on them while they plotted their course. I never promised to erase the navigation computer's buffer. Or to let them *go* wherever they wanted without my approval." I punched at the call button again, eternally impatient. "We can download the course information from the main computer as soon as they're finished, then I'll decide whether or not we actually follow whatever course they plot. We're not going anywhere without knowing what's ahead of us." The turbolift whooshed open for us, and I graciously waved Spock ahead of me, meeting his skeptical frown with a smile. "A captain never has to lie, Mr. Spock, as long as he's careful about the promises he makes."

Four

SULU

"AND WHOSE REPTILE MIGHT THIS BE?"

Sulu glanced across the bar in surprise. He'd become so engrossed in Captain Kirk's story of his first days serving with Mr. Spock that he hadn't even noticed that the little tailless lizard who'd been sleeping quietly on his hand was gone. Across the bar, a white-bearded old sailor in a gaudy waistcoat and a magnificently oversized hat was holding a fuzzy-looking animal of indeterminate species up off the ground. His pet was scrabbling frantically with all its paws, although since they encountered nothing but air, it wasn't making much headway in its struggle to reach the brownish-gold squiggle crossing the floor.

"Uh—I guess it's mine." Sulu pushed his chair back and went to scoop up the adventurous little lizard. It promptly squirmed out of his grip, but only to leap across to the folded lapel of his uniform. From there it swarmed up the jacket latch to his shoulder where it pulsed the white skin of its throat and made nearly inaudible hissing noises at the leashed bundle of fur below it.

"Sorry about that," Sulu said to the other captain. "I didn't realize it had wandered away."

"You ought to've been paying closer attention, lad," the old man said reprovingly. "You don't want to go losing a crewmate in a place like this. No telling what kind of ship the poor thing would end up on."

Sulu lifted an eyebrow, watching an Elasian female captain draped in dilithium jewelry try to fend off a gnomish-looking alien with enormous wrinkled ears. "I see what you mean." He lifted a hand to keep the little lizard in place as he retreated back across the bar to their table. By the time he got there, he found the chairs had been rearranged—the felinoid captain had relocated herself to the lap of the leather-jacketed freighter captain, and her seat had been taken by a human female with a mane of fire-red hair and a dancing smile. For all her youth and merriment, however, the look this new captain threw across the table at the English dandy was sharp as a sword-thrust.

"I heard you mention pirates over here," she said. "And I came to hear the rest of the tale, if you don't mind the extra company."

"Not at all," Kirk assured her gallantly, but the old man with the meerschaum pipe snorted. The swashbuckling Englishman just looked amused.

"Being a pirate yourself, I suppose you have a natural interest in them, Anne," he commented.

"Not all of us choose to be as we are, Peter, which you should know better than most." The redhead reached out to snag his unfinished mug of beer with a rope-calloused hand. "There are those who are forced into the corsair life by sad and evil circumstance."

"And those who take to it like ducklings to water," muttered the white-bearded man through a cloud of pipe smoke.

"And there are those who use it as a shield, to cover even more ambitious and dangerous crimes," Sulu said, before the clash could flare into anything serious. "I suspected that might be the case with the pirates who attacked Deep Space Three, but I couldn't have been more wrong about what those other crimes might be."

The Englishman, his amusement still half turned on the bold redhead, helped himself to Sulu's drink in turn. "The crime of piracy isn't crime enough where you come from?" he asked.

"More than enough," Sulu told him. Even the memories of that long-ago day still made his stomach churn. "But by the time we found out what else they had in mind, it was more than just a simple crime—it was personal. . . ."

"Sulu to *Excelsior.*"

It was the second time I'd made the request, and I was starting to wonder if the FL-70s communicator was functional. I could see the massive shadow of my starship through the occasional breaks in the phaser glare outside Deep Space Three's cargo bay, and she didn't look incapacitated, or even damaged enough to account for my crew's lack of response. "Sulu to *Excelsior.* Come in."

Despite everything, it felt good to be at the helm of a ship again, even if it was just a little Raptor-class reconnaissance vessel with an overpowered warp engine and a bizarre sensor-deflecting design that made it look as if it had crushed its needlenose into a brick wall. It felt even better to hear the airtight thunk of the Falcon's gull-winged door close behind me and listen to the hum of her shields coming online as the phaser explosions outside the cargo bay grew fire-bright through Deep Space Three's fading defensive screens.

I ran a quick systems check while I waited for my crew to respond. I only had a single phaser unit, added almost as an afterthought to the FL-70's reconnaissance systems, but my sensor readouts were almost the equal of a starship's in terms of their sensitivity and swift response. The entire story of the battle outside the space station flickered across my display panel now in symbols and running captions that told me the status of all the participants. I could see the undocked Starfleet vessels shielded and arrayed in protective formation around the defenseless Andorian liner and Earth courier, a thousand meters out from Deep Space Three. The Tellerite merchant vessel was moving to join that sanctuary, but the Orion yacht was still locked onto the lower docking ring.

None of the attackers' fire hit it, though—they were concentrating their phaser strikes on the centrally located cargo bay with only a few blasts flickering back toward the Starfleet force. The sensor readouts showed only occasional bursts of return fire, whenever one of the pirate ships swooped above the station's circumference on a strafing run. Someone out there must have ordered a limited response to the attack, to keep Deep Space Three from falling victim to our own friendly fire. Not that it was helping much—my Falcon's sensors were also precise enough to show me exactly how little protection remained above my head.

"Sulu to *Excelsior*." This time I used my wrist communicator instead of the ship's larger transmitter, but I still got back the same anomalous silence. Interference from the double set of shields I was trying to transmit through must be jamming my communications signal. I turned my attention to the tentative ship identifications that the Falcon's highly tuned sensors had made based on our attackers' ion trails. One seemed to be a Rochester-class cruiser, a short-range battleship that Starfleet had mothballed twenty years ago. Another looked like a Romulan patrol-ship retrofitted with an Orion warp drive, and the third was a lightly armed Vulcan scientific probe, probably hijacked from whatever mission it had been carrying out. The fourth ship was the most powerfully armed, but seemed cobbled together from so many different recycled ship parts that the Falcon's data banks couldn't begin to guess at its original identity.

The FL-70 shook with the impact of the first phaser blast to break through the station's failing shields. Another blast followed, and another and another, until a sudden crystalline condensation of clouds around my cockpit windows told me the cargo bay had breached to outer space. I brought the impulse engines online with a sweep of my hand. I didn't need them to send the Falcon rising toward the roof of the cargo bay—the decompressing rush of air lifted us along with it toward the shattered hull of Deep Space Three. I used the impulse engines merely to control our upward lurch, intending to keep the Falcon hovering in the phaser-burned rift so no pirates could get through. But as our own upward velocity slowed, the gleaming shadows of seven other airborne ships ghosted past us, drawn toward the stars by the relentless suck of vacuum. I cursed and hit my communicator again.

"Sulu to *Excelsior!*"

"Captain!" There was a surprising tinge of relief in Janice Rand's usually calm voice. "When we lost contact with you and Commander Chekov, we thought—"

"Get me Henry," I said and heard the click of an opened channel, then the familiar background sounds of a bridge on full alert. It wasn't exactly soothing, but the lack of anything that sounded like damage reports did reassure me a little.

"Orders, sir?" said the gruff voice of my chief engineer.

"Tell everyone to stop firing—the FL-70s got torn loose by the decompression blast." Long years of piloting experience let my eyes and hands maneuver my craft through the shattered cargo bay roof while my mind was working out other problems. I tried to scan the Falcon's crowded sensor displays, but the information was scrolling by too fast for me to catch it with a glance. "What are the attackers doing now?"

"They've stopped firing, but they haven't come out from between the docking rims." That was Orsini reporting from the *Excelsior*'s weapons panel. "They seem to be just waiting there."

"And I'll bet I know what for." Two of the unmanned FL-70s had gotten snagged by the maze of broken steel and duranium at the top of the cargo bay, but the rest had drifted through and were now spinning aimlessly in the station's microgravity. I sent my own dish-nosed craft surging out beyond them, hoping the unexpected movement would delay the thieves from scooping up their loot. "Break ranks and get the *Excelsior* in position to slap a tractor beam on the loose Falcons. The pirates are after them, not the civilian vessels."

"Aye, sir." I might not have been able to read all the information on the Falcon's sensor display, but I knew the largest symbol on it had to represent my oversized starship. She began moving toward the shattered cargo bay, but I never saw a quiver in the position of the four small red-circled icons that were our attackers. I took another looping orbit around the Falcons, but the pirates had apparently retreated back around the curve of the station—the only place they showed up was on my display screen. I wasn't going to leave the Falcons unguarded for long enough to go and spot them, but I wished I knew why they weren't moving. If I was in command of such a small and ragtag fleet of pirate ships, the sight of something like the *Excelsior* coming after me would have frozen my blood faster than deep space. Unless they had another surprise in store for us—

Ships converge Deep Space Three attack wait explosion capture . . .

"Sulu to Deep Space Three." I was getting more used to the controls of the little reconnaissance ship, and managed to actually read some of my sensor display on my third loop around the drifting FL-70s. Its scan of the station showed severe damage only around the main cargo bay, but my hail was answered as breathlessly as if a total warp core meltdown were imminent.

"Rebovich here—we're in the middle of a firefight with the intruders—Commander Barstow's been wounded and we don't know the status of the hostages. Orders, Captain Sulu?"

"Secure your dilithium supply room and your warp core," I commanded. "Lock down every door and bulkhead in their vicinity and scan them both for possible sabotage."

I heard the instructions tapped into the computer, then another indrawn breath. This time it sounded startled instead of panicky. "Someone with a top-level Starfleet security clearance already gave that order to our computers, sir. About fifteen minutes ago."

Thank you, Chekov. "Then contain the attackers in whatever sector of the station they're in—"

"That's what we did, sir!" Rebovich was starting to sound frantic again. "They massacred the security team that was locked in with them, then they deliberately weakened a section of the main plasma conduit. If we don't let the seals down and send a repair team in soon, we'll lose that whole side of the docking rim!"

"And the hostages will die along with their captors in the resulting plasma explosion," I said grimly. Despite the ragtag appearance of our attackers, their tactics for sabotaging Deep Space Three were ruthlessly elegant. When their initial attempt to blow up the spare dilithium stocks had been foiled by Chekov's intervention, they'd promptly engineered a wordless blackmail threat that would either get them free or get the station blown up anyway. And that set all my military instincts clamoring. Were these actually Klingons, disguising a border incursion as a pirate raid to avoid diplomatic repercussions? Or was this the first careful probing by a new race of hostile aliens, looking for weaknesses in our defenses? Either way, I was beginning to see why Rebovich sounded so frazzled.

I glanced at my sensor screens again, seeing no movement from the four mismatched ships of the attacking force. The first gleam of the *Excelsior*'s primary hull had just appeared over the curve of the upper docking rim. If they had any sensors of their own, the attackers must know we were only seconds away from securing the floating Falcons in a tractor beam too strong for them to break, yet they still didn't make a move toward the loose flotilla of patrol ships. That surprising inactivity, combined with the tactical brilliance of the landing party on Deep Space Three, let me guess that the ones who'd planned this attack were among the hostage takers rather than the outside forces.

I frowned and glanced back down at my display screens, this time looking for the small symbol that represented the private Orion yacht. It was still firmly attached to the lower docking ring. "Deep Space Three, how far away are the intruders from docking port one-seven-one?"

"About thirty meters, sir. They appeared to be heading in that direction when we locked the bulkheads down on them."

"Then evacuate all personnel from that sector of the ring and open the bulkheads to let the intruders through to their ship," I said. I didn't like giving the saboteurs even a slim chance of escaping with their hostages, but I suspected that nothing less than a clear path back to their ship would entice them to abandon their current position. "As soon as sensors show them moving, slam the bulkheads down behind them and beam in an engineering team to repair the damaged conduit."

"Aye, *sir.*" Rebovich sounded so inordinately relieved that I knew the safety margin on the conduit must be falling fast. The silence that followed her acknowledgment seemed far too long, but that was only the time-dilation caused by my own tension. Even the *Excelsior* seemed to be moving with excruciating slowness, and the diamond glitter of her tractor beam seemed to crawl rather than shoot out to capture the four loose Falcons.

"Intruders are moving, sir," Rebovich said, but she sounded more agitated than ever. "Our sensors still show one life-form near the damaged plasma conduit. Should we beam it in?"

It could be an alien suicide guard, I knew. It could also be my executive officer, although my instincts said that if he had shadowed the hostage takers this far, he would have followed them all the way to their ship, looking for a chance to rescue his fellow crew members. "Can you do a bioscan?"

"It's a Vulcan, sir. And—and almost dead, according to our sensors."

"Then beam him out," I ordered. "And evacuate the entire lower docking ring while you try to get that plasma conduit stabilized." My sensor displays were showing an alarming instability in the station's normally steady plasma discharge. I swung my Falcon away from its tractor-held siblings, heading for docking port 171. On my display screen, I could see the pirate fleet moving at last, converging to form a tight knot around the still-docked Orion yacht. I felt my stomach clench in dismay, and it wasn't at the military precision of that maneuver. No ship escort needed to fly that close to protect an unarmed vessel. This formation was specifically designed to put the central vessel at risk if any of its escort were fired on. And that meant the hostages had been taken aboard.

"*Excelsior* to Captain Sulu." I could tell from my chief engineer's voice, harsher than usual with restrained anger, that my bridge crew had come to the same deduction I had. "Request permission to release the tractor beam and pursue the attacking force."

"Permission denied," I said between clamped teeth. "Tow those FL-70s away from the station, at maximum impulse speed. *Now!*" The Orion vessel was disengaging from its docking clamp with such reckless haste that it had nearly slammed one of its clinging escort ships into the station's hull. I sent my own Falcon plunging around to the right, taking advantage of that momentary wedge of opening to aim and fire—

The warning flashed across my sensor displays only a second before the plasma flare punched through the hull of Deep Space Three. I felt the Falcon lifted and hurled helplessly into the backwash of that superheated blast. All I had time to do was throw full power to my shields and hear the howl of the collision warning systems before the little ship sprang violently backward and slammed me into oblivion.

"This," said my chief medical officer crisply, "is the reason why captains should not go running around trying to do *everything* themselves. Haven't I told you before that you should practice delegating a little more of your authority?"

I jerked my head away from the keening hum of the tissue regenerator, not because it hurt but because I knew the cut on my chin barely needed its attention. "All I did was hit my face on the sensor display panel when the collision avoidance rockets engaged—"

"People with glass chins should refrain from piloting ships with uncalibrated inertial dampeners." She might be younger and more detail-oriented than Leonard McCoy, but I had found Judith Klass to be every bit as opinionated as the doctor on the *Enterprise.* Perhaps it was a trait they hammered into them at Starfleet Medical Academy.

"I don't have a glass chin." I rolled off the sickbay bunk with a wince to avoid her skeptical look. I really couldn't complain about the FL-70's automatic collision avoidance system, since it was the reason I was sitting here instead of being splattered across the hull of Deep Space Three. But before we delivered those reconnaissance ships to the Neutral Zone, I was going to make damned sure their inertial dampeners were calibrated. "Call the bridge and tell them I want a senior officers conference in five minutes, main briefing room."

Klass's pale eyes glittered at me from out of her strong-boned face. "I called them as soon as I saw you were almost awake," she said, and caught my chin in her determined fingers again, running the tissue regenerator across the throbbing cut on my chin before I could protest. "They're waiting in the medical briefing room next door."

I couldn't decide what was more annoying—the fact that Klass thought she knew what I was going to want while I was still unconscious, or the fact that she had been right. I settled for saying, "Thank you, Doctor," in as neutral a tone as I could manage before I headed for the door. The amused look I got as she followed me suggested I hadn't entirely managed to disguise my irritation.

It took me a minute, coming into the small and unfamiliar conference room, to place exactly what was wrong. Engineer Tim Henry looked a little grim and Security Chief Nino Orsini was tapping a more urgent rhythm on his data pad than he usually did, but Communications Officer Janice Rand and Science Officer Christina Schulman both seemed as calm and professional as ever. Scott Walroth, my young navigator, kept glancing at my more experienced pilot, Heather Keith, for reassurance, but since this was his first tour of duty on a starship, he had a tendency to do that anyway. It wasn't until I sat down and saw the empty place at my right where by custom my executive officer would have been that I realized it was the reverberations of Chekov's absence that I was feeling in the room.

"Gentlemen," I said. "By my watch, I've been unconscious for over twenty minutes. I assume our attackers are either captured or gone. Which is it?"

"Gone," Orsini said glumly. "Deep Space Three needed the transporters on every Starfleet vessel to evacuate their lower docking ring. By the time we were done, the attack ships had vanished off our sensors and the plasma explosion had erased all traces of their ion trail."

"How many of the *Excelsior*'s crew are missing?"

"Five of the six people on the dilithium resupply team. And Commander Chekov, too, I'm afraid," my young security chief added reluctantly. As a former security chief himself, Chekov had mentored Orsini throughout the shakedown cruise. "We couldn't ping a signal from his wrist communicator, either on the station or among the evacuees."

It was exactly the bad news I had expected, but hearing it spoken out loud still sent a stab of dismay through me. You don't lose a friend of twenty years easily. "And none of the pirate ships were caught in the blast?"

"None, sir." That was Schulman's quiet voice. "The brunt of the explosion came straight toward you. If it hadn't been for the Falcon's collision avoidance rockets, you would have slammed right into the station."

I deliberately avoided meeting Doctor Klass's pointed look. "What's the status of the station now?"

Tim Henry cleared his throat. "Between the cargo bay hull breach and the plasma burst, sir, they're operating at about thirty-percent efficiency over there. The other Starfleet vessels in port have sent down some engineers to help get their main power circuits up and running, and a new plasma generator is on the way from Deep Space Two."

"Casualties?"

"None." My chief engineer slanted me a regretful look. "Unless you count the two Falcons we lost when the plasma flare hit the cargo bay—"

I felt the newly healed skin on my chin tug with my half smile. "A couple of Neutral Zone outposts might cry over those losses, Chief, but I think they're acceptable. How about the station cargo transporters? Any chance of Deep Space Three getting them up and running in the next hour or so?"

Henry couldn't restrain a snort. "About as much chance as they have of sucking all their plasma back in from outer space. Why, Captain?"

I gave him a quizzical look. "Because I'd like to take the rest of those Falcons with us when we leave. It'll slow us by two warp factors to fly with them in formation."

That seemingly simple statement sent a discreet ripple of surprise and confusion through my bridge officers. I watched them think it over for a moment, waiting patiently until one asked the obvious question. There are few pleasures quite as satisfying to a captain as being able to surprise a crew as competent as this one.

It was Nino Orsini who cleared his throat at last and asked, "We're leaving in an hour, sir? Why the hurry?"

"Because we've got pirates to catch," I said. I'd expected that to cause a stunned silence, and it did. I'd also expected the silence to dissolve into a barrage of startled questions, but Tim Henry gave me a single sharp-eyed glance before it could.

"Nano-machined subspace transponder?" he demanded.

I let my smile widen. It was nice to have a chief engineer who kept up with more than just the latest developments in warp drive technology. "Actually, a hundred thousand of them, Chief. The FL-70s are equipped to fire projectile bursts of nano-transponders, enough to blanket an area where you suspect a cloaked vessel to be. They can't penetrate shields, of course, but that Orion yacht didn't have its shields up yet. And I got a nice clear shot at them right before the plasma flare hit me."

Janice Rand was already on her feet and pulling Orsini with her. "Nino, you find the specifications on that transponder frequency, and I'll start scanning for their signal—with your permission, of course, Captain," she added belatedly.

"Granted, with pleasure," I told her. "Walroth, Keith—get up to the bridge and prepare a course as soon as we know the heading. Schulman and

Henry, see if you can work out a system we can use to piggyback those five remaining Falcons onto the *Excelsior.* If not, assign them pilots and send out two of our best-armed shuttles to escort them after us. We're not going to slow down for them."

"Aye, sir!" said six voices in unison. A moment later, the medical briefing room was empty except for Doctor Klass and me. She arched one thin eyebrow in amusement.

"Did my lecture about delegating authority sink in, or are you still feeling the aftereffects of the concussion I healed you of fifteen minutes ago?"

I frowned at her. "I had a concussion?"

"Severe, with accompanying brain swelling," she affirmed. "Why else do you think I put off fixing that scratch in your chin for twenty minutes after we beamed you aboard? Do you have a headache now?"

"No."

"Any dizziness or nausea?"

"None." You couldn't really fault Klass for her annoying air of superiority. She was actually an even better doctor than she thought she was.

Her strong-boned face took on the mildly inquisitive look that was her equivalent of a puzzled frown. "So why are you still sitting here?"

"Because I want to know what happened to the sixth member of the dilithium resupply team," I said. "Deep Space Three reported that he was nearly dead when they beamed him out. Is he still there? Did they transfer him back to our sickbay? Or did he die before anything could be done?"

Klass startled me with another amused look. "Indeed not, Captain. Vulcans are capable of sustaining life over a much wider range of physical endurance than humans, as I'm sure you know. And in any case, a great deal of Cadet Tuvok's problems were caused by himself."

"What do you mean?"

In answer, she stood up and gestured me back toward sickbay. "I think I'll let him explain."

The young Vulcan wore the colors of a science officer on his opened uniform and fading bruises on the skin of his neck and chest, despite the time he'd obviously already spent under tissue regenerators. I sat on the stool Klass pointed me to beside him, to spare him the effort he was making to sit up.

"Mr. Tuvok, at ease. I'd like to ask you a few questions." I glanced over at Klass and saw that she had already programmed her medical tricorder to record his answers. "You feel well enough to answer?"

"Of course, sir." The security guard glanced across at Klass. "Did the doctor explain that I was in *us'tar-ja?"*

"The Vulcan healing trance?" I shook my head. "Were you that badly injured?"

"Actually, no." Tuvok rubbed his fingers across the fading bruises on his chest, looking slightly guilty. "I was engaging in what you humans call 'playing possum.' My assumption was that the aliens who captured us would not wish to take a corpse along as a hostage."

"And you gambled they wouldn't phaser you to make sure you were really dead?"

The Vulcan's face never changed expression. "That is correct, Captain. But although our captors were quite needlessly violent, I had observed that they preferred their hands and tails to their sidearms. In fact, some of them seemed almost uncomfortable with the equipment they used, as if it were new to them."

"Hands and tails?" I repeated. "What kind of aliens were they, Cadet?"

"I did not recognize their species, Captain, although I have memorized the appearance and names of the two hundred and fifty known races of this quadrant. But they were clearly of saurian descent—their skins were lightly scaled and they used their tails both as cantilevers and as strong lashing devices." Tuvok paused, looking thoughtful. "They worked as a coordinated unit throughout the sabotage attempt, but I did not get the sense that they were a trained military force."

"A covert terrorist operation? Or a spying mission to prepare for a later invasion?"

Tuvok shook his head. "I cannot be sure, sir. But I am sure of one thing—this was not a chance encounter. The leader of that attack came to Deep Space Three specifically to obtain the FL-70 reconnaissance ships."

I nodded. It confirmed my own guess, although it didn't make me any happier to know we were facing a determined enemy rather than a random pirate raid. "And now that they've failed to get them? Did you get any sense for what they might do next?"

"Yes, sir. That was why I risked entering the healing trance, in the hope of getting the information to you." The Vulcan science cadet sat up despite Klass's glare and his own wince of pain. "Our universal translator did not work well with the language they spoke, and they did not speak much. But toward the end, the leader made it clear through his questions and threats that he wanted the FL-70s so he could take over the Federation outpost at Elaphe Vulpina. He kept asking us if we had any security clearance codes or weapons that would allow him to access it."

I glanced across at Klass's grave face. "And did he get an answer, Cadet?"

"Not from the *Excelsior*'s crew, sir." Even through his Vulcan reserve, I heard the quiet pride in his voice. "But I do not believe the station quartermaster will be able to hold out forever under that kind of torture. The aliens will soon have a Starfleet key to Elaphe Vulpina's defenses."

"Which makes it even more imperative to catch them before they get there. The last thing we want is a firefight that will attract the attention of the Klingon Empire." I pushed him back down on the medical bed. "Relax, Mr. Tuvok. You did the right thing by staying behind."

That got me a surprised lift of his eyebrows. "I never doubted it, sir," said the young Vulcan, and I was reminded again that guilt was not an emotion his race indulged in. "I only regret that the other members of my party did not have the ability to do as I did."

"So do I, Cadet." I stood and winced as my own sore spots complained at the sudden movement. I didn't want to think about how much worse Chekov and the other hostages were probably feeling at this moment, but some morbid part of my brain wouldn't let that thought go once it had kindled there. "So do I."

Five

KIRK

I KNOW HOW TO KEEP A PROMISE—I DIDN'T SPY ON THE ANJIRI. I REALLY didn't. From the central seat of my command chair, I couldn't see much of the helm controls even when a human sat there. The Anjiri, though, had surrounded themselves with their battle-scarred Nykkus so thoroughly that they barely had their own view of the main screen. Even if I'd wanted to peer over their shoulders, I'd have had to practically crawl on top of their heads to do so.

So I made an effort to conceal my impatience by pacing the circumference of the bridge, pretending to micromanage all the other stations while I waited. And waited.

"Captain, please. Can't you make them let us help?"

Sulu shushed Bailey into silence, but I stopped to clap the younger man on the shoulder with as much reassurance as I could muster. "Everybody's got to learn for themselves, Mr. Bailey. Even aliens."

"It's just . . ." His brow furrowed so seriously, you might have thought he was contemplating some great quantum mechanical argument. "Sir—" Another scowled frown from Sulu, and he dropped his voice to a whisper. "They don't have the faintest idea what they're doing! Look at them! I can't believe they even managed to get out of their home star system."

I'd been wondering myself if they actually knew how to get themselves back. Glancing over my shoulder, I watched Uhura carefully explain something to the Anjiri currently in Bailey's seat while he leaned nearly into her lap to watch the translation simulacrum on her tricorder screen. "They probably had a preprogrammed navigation module on their last ship. The kind where you pick a course from a menu, the ship remembers where you started, and all you have to do is reverse your course to get home."

"If that's true, sir," Sulu interjected, "they couldn't possibly have programmed the module themselves."

Bailey gave a defeatist little laugh. "Considering what happened to their last ship, I don't know if we should count on that." I wasn't sure if he meant to blame them for having taken their ship into dangerous space, or for not being good enough pilots to then extricate themselves from an unwanted fight.

My navigator's comment notwithstanding, I didn't think the Anjiri could fairly be blamed for wrecking their own ship. There'd been plenty of battle damage evident, and it wasn't like this whole sector wasn't a prime candidate for an incursion of opportunistic feeders. Still, the Anjiri's total lack of understanding of even the most basic navigation and course-plotting skills was almost surreal.

For three hours—while Sulu and Bailey waited like the true Academy gentlemen they were—the Anjiri had alternated at the helm, a kind of interstellar musical chairs. Occasionally, one of them would hiss viciously at a Nykkus, apparently for stepping in front of the forward screen and blocking their view. I wondered if they could actually tell where in space they were from that display, or whether they'd notice if I had Spock project a view from several weeks ago. For hours they'd touched, sniffed, moved, and activated controls on the helm, making more individual movements for the sake of a fairly straightforward course than Sulu would have made to chart a covert path through the Neutral Zone.

"I think a lot of what they're doing is exploring." I hesitated a moment over how much to reveal. "They've been generating a lot of error messages." At least a dozen for every successful course calculation—and that included making unsupported requests such as access to our library files or attempting to order beverages from the dining hall.

"Let's hope they don't explore too much." Sulu looked apologetic for having brought the subject up. "I don't think that letting strangers know too much about what we're flying is good for business."

But at least we knew exactly how much they were learning. Deciding that wasn't for public consumption just yet, I said only, "Hang in there, gentlemen. You'll have your stations back soon enough," and headed for my own abandoned command chair.

I didn't see the subdued indicator on my command display until I was almost seated, but I glanced up to verify that no one else was looking anyway. While the Anjiri were still hissing and jittering over their arcane course inventions, Uhura stayed intently by their sides, recording every word that passed between them, and Sulu and Bailey continued their extended fret over the nefarious use of their consoles. I thumbed the switch next to my display, and sat back to watch it scroll.

The tiny screen filled with the same convoluted and mostly meaningless data that had been filtered over to me since the Anjiri first began their flight. As promised, we'd been letting them plot their course (such as it was) without interrupting; Uhura had even been on hand to explain anything about the stations they found confusing, and she'd more than once ferried questions back to Bailey and Sulu, then translated their answers for our guests. Meanwhile, the navigation computer stored every keystroke the Anjiri made in a virtual buffer zone until they either accepted it as a final course or input alternative data to overwrite it. I'd assigned Spock the task of creating a shunting program to snapshot the data before it vanished from the buffer, which meant I only examined the data after the Anjiri themselves had declared they were done with it. Whether I looked at the data ten hours after they left the ship or ten minutes after they deleted it struck me as having no real ethical difference, so I had Spock forward the buffer dump to my command console as soon as he'd had a chance to make sense of it.

All of this Spock performed at his science station without sending so much as a glance in my direction. I might have given him credit for some otherwise unexpected theatrical skill, except that he hadn't spoken to me—with the exception of a few well-placed "Yes, Captains" and an equally few "No, Captains"—since our conversation outside the rec hall. I resisted assuming this meant he was irked with me. After all, Vulcan's didn't get irked, they merely withheld comment until they had further data. He was no doubt distracted, thinking about how to phrase his official report on why I had insisted on such an illogical course of action.

So when I first noticed his neat, block-style handwriting on the information drifting by on my screen, I had a perverse moment where I felt like a schoolboy, passing notes during class. Then I saw what he'd written, and my focus galvanized on what was in front of me.

We are within five parsecs of the highlighted station. Orions respond hostilely to approaches of closer than two parsecs. If you choose to allow this course, preemptive radio contact might be in order.

I keyed back to the top of the data, scrolled down through it again twice as fast as before. The station Spock had highlighted in the stats was what the Orions preferred to call a waystation. In reality, it was a place for their pirate skiffs to stop and disgorge ill-gotten gains when being chased by Federation craft, so they could then claim never to have had the goods on board to begin with. The probable cause which might have let us search a fleeing pirate vessel didn't extend to searching an Orion civilian facility. Thus did many Orion pirates escape through legal loopholes and avoid extradition and indictment by our government. It bothered me that the

Orions felt it necessary to erect such a station on the border of what had so far been a fairly quiet sector.

I ran across Spock's note again: *Preemptive radio contact might be in order.*

Indeed it might. If I didn't allow the ship to take the heading the Anjiri had chosen, they were sure to notice eventually, and at least figure out that they'd been tricked in some fashion, even if they couldn't precisely figure out why. At the same time, if I initiated contact with the Orions before their self-imposed two parsec boundary, I was also giving away that I'd been using my own legal loophole to keep track of the Anjiri's doings. I let instinct guide me again, and decided, without giving myself a chance for second thoughts, that we'd never find out precisely what the Anjiri were up to if we didn't find out who they knew. Let the Orions save me from grappling with the dilemma about whether or not to call. I sent Spock the signal to let the course run.

He raised one eyebrow until it nearly disappeared into his hairline, but did as he was told.

"Captain." The advantage of not letting your command crew in on absolutely everything is that they then sound convincingly surprised when they pipe up with such announcements. "We're being hailed on an Orion broadband channel."

I did my best to look surprised in an appropriately commanding fashion. "Put it on screen, Ensign."

An Orion's big, bulldog face solidified out of the stars like a chancre on perfect skin. He wore the dreadlocks of a lower-class citizen, but the wealth of earrings and nose rings dangling from his pushed-in face announced his importance on the station. "I am Akpakken, supreme commander of this station. Identify yourselves and prepare to be destroyed!"

A bold threat, considering most of these floating pawn brokerages didn't have the weaponry to fend off a good case of the chills much less a Federation starship. Still, my mission description didn't include punching holes in overinflated Orion egos, no matter how great the temptation. "I'm Captain James T. Kirk of the *U.S.S. Enterprise,*" I answered with somewhat less bravado. "We're here on a peaceful transport mission. We don't want any trouble."

"Then turn your rodent warren around and flee back to your own space, hairless maggots."

No one ever accused Orions of having the most elevated social skills.

"We have friends of yours on board, Akpakken." I didn't look down at the Anjiri and Nykkus at the front of my bridge. I was waiting for Akpakken to do that first, so I could judge the recognition in his eyes. "Perhaps you'd like to speak with them before you send us packing."

He blew a fierce snort that threatened to fog both our viewscreens. "We are Orions," he announced with phlegmatic pride. "We have no friends."

I offered a little shrug. "Be that as it may, the Anjiri are the ones who brought us here." This time, I angled a quick glance toward Vissith, making sure he was listening via the little figure on Uhura's translation device. All other activity around the helm console had frozen. "They claimed this was their home."

The translation simulacrum in the tricorder danced madly. *I hope it's saying I no longer believe a word you've ever said to us,* I thought at the back of the Anjiri's narrow skull. It's one thing to have someone distrust you so much they won't even let you pilot your own ship, another thing entirely to have them fly you right into the mouth of a compromising situation that could actually lead to fighting.

"We know of no Anjiri," Akpakken insisted. "They lie to you, pink monkey-weasel."

It's a secret vice of mine, but I have always loved listening to what our translators do to Orion speech.

"Now go away!"

Akpakken lifted one meaty fist to slam closed the comm channel, but Vissith leapt in front of the viewscreen before the Orion could complete the movement. "Halt!"

I was surprised first by the speed and agility of Vissith's unexpected movement. I was surprised even more when Akpakken hesitated, squinting down at the lithe saurian with a certain suspicious greed.

I hardly recognized the Anjiri's voice when Vissith first burst into speaking. Not in their language—not in anything that made Uhura's translator activate its display, not in anything the communication channel's translator could turn into understandable English. When Uhura glanced anxiously back toward me, I motioned her to my chair, then leaned forward to whisper, "What are they saying? Why aren't the translators working?"

Uhura shook her head slowly, eyes darting between the two aliens instead of down toward her device. "They keep switching languages, too quickly for the translator to keep up. I think it's some sort of trader argot." She fell silent and listened for a while longer. "I can only recognize a few of the languages myself, but I think Vissith is . . . negotiating with him. He's promising Akpakken something."

I drummed my fingers on the arm of my chair. "As long as it isn't my ship, I don't care what they negotiate for." In truth, I had never liked blind negotiations.

Abruptly, Akpakken declared with traditional Orion directness, "All right—leave them."

Knowing the quality of Orion translators, I couldn't help wondering if what Akpakken thought they'd just discussed bore any resemblance to what Vissith thought they'd been discussing. "We have forty passengers," I began. "Are you prepared—"

He cut me off without even an excusing gesture. "I am prepared. I was mistaken—the Anjiri are our allies. You may approach Pleck Station and leave them." This time his hand completed the termination command. "Akpakken out."

"Food service records indicate an increase of twenty-four point three percent in what is otherwise a consistent average consumption of point seven four liters per twenty-four hours on all other days."

I'd mastered the art of nodding sagely during graduate seminars at the Academy. A necessary component of the practice, of course, was accurately judging when you really had to listen and when you didn't. My elbows propped on a rec hall dining table, hands wrapped around a cup of rapidly cooling coffee, I'd quickly ascertained that the important part of this scenario was the work Scott and his engineering team performed on the hall's exposed machinery. They'd come to make sure the Anjiri hadn't tampered with anything during their stay; I'd come to watch over them while picking through my dinner. Spock had been a last-minute addition after he followed me into the turbolift outside my quarters with a new list of reasons why we had to discuss personnel records before the end of the watch.

Which was why he'd been regaling me with duty schedules and overdue physicals all throughout my roast chicken and potatoes.

I watched the engineers bolt a panel back into place next to an environmental outlet. "Scotty says the only thing he's found missing so far is a programming chip from one of the battle simulation games." I turned to Spock, shaking my head. "All the other useful devices they could have tried to take, and they steal a computer game."

The disparity apparently didn't strike him as fascinating. "Perhaps they did not recognize which among the surrounding equipment was valuable. They might not have known that it was only a simulation game they stole." He tipped his pad meaningfully toward me. "I believe we were discussing Ensign Maudie's caffeine ingestion during his weekend duty tours."

I turned my back to the engineers, facing my first officer full on. "Mr. Spock, I don't care how much coffee Ensign Maudie drinks the morning after he's been out having a good time with his friends."

Spock settled back into his seat, one eyebrow lifting testily as he slowly crossed his arms. "Is there relevant data regarding Ensign Maudie's social activities which I should consider in preparing my report?"

I scrubbed at my eyes to hide my frustration. "Mr. Spock . . ." I really didn't want to snap at him. He was like a child sometimes, honestly trying to do his best even though he didn't fully understand what was expected of him. Dropping my hands to the table, I looked at him as earnestly as I could. "When Starfleet suggests the first officer compile reports on the behavior and performance of a starship's crew, they don't mean surveys on how many hours of sleep the crew is getting or how much caffeine they've ingested."

"However, both are directly relevant to a crew's performance levels. Ingestion of large quantities of caffeine can cause humans to experience light-headedness, trembling, frequent urination—"

"As captain," I cut him off, "my responsibility is to the ship itself, our mission, how we do our job out here. The first officer's responsibility, then, is to the crew—but the details of how they're assigned, who needs disciplinary action, where we need additional staff, not what they choose as their breakfast beverage." My own coffee was too cold now to drink. I set it aside with a sigh. "We're supposed to have a synergistic relationship, Mr. Spock. I decide what needs doing, you help me understand how the crew can best get that done."

The way he stiffened in his seat might almost have been prickly if he'd been human. "I believe I have been timely in providing the captain with assignment rosters and leave requests."

"You have. Your thoroughness and attention to detail is . . . remarkable. Commendable. But . . ." Does it make sense to worry about hurting a Vulcan's feelings? Does a lack of emotional fragility on their part mean I'm no longer obligated to be polite? "This is a primarily human crew, Mr. Spock. That means our feelings will have an impact on the performance of our duties, even when that's not appropriate. Humans will get frightened, or decide they can't work with someone else they don't like, or lose their confidence, or fall in love. I need those feelings to be taken seriously, and tended to, if this crew is going to function at its best." I paused for what felt like a very long time, considering how best to phrase this. "I need a first officer who can understand those details."

He nodded, once, precisely. "Although I am Vulcan, Captain, I have served in the company of humans for many years. Human frailty and prejudice are concepts with which I am well acquainted." The prejudice remark stung. But I didn't try to protest—it would only make things worse, and I didn't really have the right. "In addition, I have had ample opportunity to observe unfettered emotion and its effects on human behavior." A pause, so long I couldn't interpret it in any way but as embarrassment. "My mother was human."

I felt a bizarre impulse to say, "I'm sorry," the way you might if someone just told you a beloved relative had died. It wasn't that I felt there was anything strange or wrong about what he'd said, although it was certainly unexpected, only that he seemed so ashamed for having said it. Like admitting some distant member of your family was a dog. "I hadn't realized."

"It is a personal matter," he continued, once it became apparent I wasn't going to say anything more. "It is not a subject for public discussion."

"I understand." And I did, sort of. I understood that he didn't want his half-human status becoming general knowledge among the crew. I didn't entirely understand why.

"Merely because Vulcans have chosen not to let emotional states dictate our behavior does not mean we are incapable of understanding them. Indeed, I am well-versed in human hormonal urges, whether or not I happen to share them." Now he folded his hands on the table and leaned forward as though he were the one lecturing to me. "What you fail to grasp, Captain, is that emotion is not quantifiable. One must rely entirely upon subjective reports from the human in question regarding what that human is feeling, and why. There is no protocol by which to double-blind data collection and verify that such subjective observations are accurate. Nor are the results of emotion reproducible. An event which invokes strong emotion in one human may have no affect on another human of similar construction and experience. A human who responds emotionally to a particular event may be unmoved by a similar event at a later date." He took on that air of effortless pedantry that was apparently coded in the Vulcan genes. "Surak taught us generations ago that emotion is little more than arbitrary responses to arbitrary events. It is not valuable as data, and is therefore ignored."

"But that's where you're wrong, Spock!" I made myself straighten again when he recoiled slightly from my lean across the table. "Whether or not emotions make sense, they are part of the human equation, part of what makes humans behave and function in the ways they do. By refusing to acknowledge human emotions as real when you deal with the crew, you're willfully ignoring a variable, then wondering why your sums don't add up. What matters is that *humans* believe in what they feel. *Humans* will always have that variable in motion, whether or not you choose to allow for it."

I gave him a long time to think about that, watching the path of his thoughts in his dark eyes. After what seemed a small eternity, he said with care, "Your argument is unexpectedly logical." As if he didn't want to get caught saying anything rash. "I must take it under consideration."

I didn't grin at him, but I wanted to. "Mr. Spock, I believe there's hope for you yet."

Just then, the intercom's urgent whistle split the rec hall's quiet. Sulu's voice quickly followed. "Bridge to Captain Kirk."

Exchanging a glance with Spock, I pushed away from the table and jogged to the nearest wall intercom. "Kirk here. Go ahead."

"Captain, we're being approached by four Orion heavy merchant vessels." The official designation of what we all knew were pirating ships. "They've already fired a few—well, I guess they're warning salvos, sir, but they're too far out of range for the shots to even register on our shields."

"Any luck hailing them?" I asked. Spock had moved to my side by now, eavesdropping in the way good first officers always should.

"Not so far, sir, no."

"Patch me through to communications and hit them with a wide-beam transmission. I want to talk to them." I waited for Uhura's go ahead, then declared into the comm, "Commander Akpakken, this is Captain Kirk of the *Enterprise.* You are within the vicinity of my vessel. Cease fire! I repeat, cease fire! If you fire your weapons, and even a single shot comes in contact with my ship, I'll have no choice but to take retaliatory action. Do you understand?"

Addressing Akpakken by name had been something of a calculated guess, but it paid off in spades when his rattling roar came back at me. "Spineless monkey-rodents! To throw your filth into our warrens, then tuck your tailless rear-parts between your monkey legs and flee!"

I raised my eyebrows at Spock, and he merely shook his head. "Commander, perhaps you'd like to tell me what exactly we did to earn your wrath?"

"The pirates!" Akpakken bellowed. "Slimy Anjiri pirates! You fling them into our laps through your deceit, telling us they are victims, without danger. And within hours of your retreat, they have stolen the premiere yacht of our quadrant and escaped with four thousand kilos of precious metals!"

Six

SULU

THERE WAS A UNIQUE FEEL TO THE *Excelsior* WHEN SHE WAS TRAVELING AT maximum warp, a repeated subliminal shiver that no amount of fiddling with the inertial dampeners or calibrating the warp drive ever seemed to erase. I didn't mind it myself, although Doctor Klass claimed it drove her crazy and was always requesting Tim Henry to get rid of it. Twenty-five years of piloting experience told me it was only an internal resonance between the hull and the warp engines, but I still often thought of that shiver as my starship's living pulse and a reflection of her crew's eagerness to be out working among the stars. Since we'd left Deep Space Three, that shiver had felt stronger and more persistent than before. I wasn't sentimental enough to anthropomorphize my ship, so I didn't assume that reflected the urgency of our mission to rescue our lost crewmates. All it meant was that we were pushing the envelope of our sustained warp capability.

It had taken us longer than I'd expected to set out after the pirate convoy. Commander Barstow had been injured badly enough in the initial firefight with the aliens that he had to be sent in stasis back to Earth for reconstructive surgery. That meant a quick round of approving new security clearances and promoting people to acting positions of command, a process that had to be carried out by the nearest available starship captain. I had known that by taking command of the *Excelsior* I would become a de facto Starfleet dignitary, but I'd expected that to be a minor responsibility, limited to entertaining ambassadors or making a glittering display of brass at Federation ceremonies. That might be true in the inner systems, but out here on the frontier, a starship captain was the embodiment of Starfleet authority for deep space stations and border outposts like these. Transmissions from headquarters were fine for everyday matters, but when you had a crisis and a crew badly in need of a morale boost, a starship captain was needed to personally fasten those rank pins to the new commander's lapel.

By the time we finally departed Deep Space Three, with our small armada of FL-70s and shuttle escorts trailing behind us, the low-powered signal from the pirate yacht had been entirely overwhelmed by the subspace bubbling of black holes and cosmic strings. The FL-70s' nano-transponders, each no larger than a human blood cell, were designed to be followed from the moment they were launched, not detected long after the quarry had escaped. I ordered a course to be set toward Elaphe Vulpina, then sat gritting my teeth while my communications and science staff searched for the fragile transponder signal along the way. It was a gamble that Starfleet Headquarters had agreed was worth the delay, but if a certain Vulcan junior science officer had misunderstood or misheard the alien pirates' intentions, there was a good chance we might never pick up their trail again. It was a tribute to my hardworking bridge officers that we managed to catch the transponder's call only two hours later, at the feathery edge of its range. My sigh of relief turned to a startled curse when the tracking data were analyzed a moment later—and showed the pirate convoy moving in a completely different direction than we were.

"Plot the transponder's position relative to Deep Space Three and Elaphe Vulpina and put it on the viewscreen," I commanded, as soon as our own course had been altered to match theirs. I watched the outside starscape ripple and dim behind a computer-generated overlay of glowing symbols. "Is this the heading they've been on since they left the station?"

"I don't think so, sir." My science officer frowned down at her panel rather than the viewscreen, although both of them now showed the same view. "If we extrapolate their current velocity and direction backward—" A glowing yellow line shot out from the moving flash of blue that was our quarry to the solid green of Deep Space Three. "You can see that they should have gotten a lot further away from the station than they did. In fact, we should never have been able to pick up their signal at all—it should have gone out of range while we were still sorting out security clearances."

"Maybe they stopped for a while," Orsini suggested. "After all, they don't know we're following them."

"Maybe, but I think it's more likely Cadet Tuvok was right about their original destination." Schulman ran a stylus across her panel and another glowing line, this one red and distinctly dog-legged, snapped into existence on the viewscreen. "If we assume the pirates started out toward Elaphe Vulpina at their current velocity, then turned onto a new heading about an hour into the flight, they would have ended exactly where they are."

I regarded the pattern before us with thoughtful eyes. "Extrapolate their current heading ten parsecs, Ensign Walroth, and tell me what star systems it passes through."

"None, sir." The navigator punched the request into his panel again, more emphatically this time, but even from my command chair I could see that his screen still came up blank. "The pirates are heading straight into one of the empty sectors in this part of the quadrant. There are no inhabited star systems within a month's travel in that direction."

That information made a troubled silence lap across the bridge, while one of my officers after another gave the viewscreen a baffled glance. "Could it be a red herring?" Orsini asked at last. I glanced at him and saw Chekov's wariness looking out of the younger man's eyes. "Maybe the pirates consolidated their forces after the battle and didn't need the Orion yacht anymore."

"Schulman, do long-range sensors detect anything yet at the site of the transponder signal?"

"No, sir. We're still too far away." She glanced over at me intelligently. "But Elaphe Vulpina's sensors should be able to detect the rest of the convoy by now, if it's still headed their way."

I looked back at my communications officer. "Rand, send a message to Elaphe Vulpina on a secure channel. Warn them to scan for ships and prepare for a sabotage attempt or an outright attack if they see anything approaching from that heading." Satisfied that we had given the border outpost all the forewarning we could, I sat back and scrubbed a hand across my face, trying to guess what my enemy's change in plans might mean.

"The sector of space they're headed for now, Walroth—is it part of the Federation or the Klingon Empire?"

"It's mostly Neutral Zone, sir." Ensign Walroth gave his navigation panel a puzzled look, then glanced over at Keith as if her display might show something different. "Captain, it looks as if the pirates have begun to decelerate."

"For another course adjustment?" I demanded.

"No, sir. They seem to be stopping right in the middle of nowhere."

I frowned and rose to my feet, leaning over the young man's shoulders to scan his glowing star charts. He was right—the faint pulse of light that was our transponder source had begun to decrease speed, at a rate that would put it at rest deep within interstellar space. That might have made sense as an evasive maneuver, but the pirates shouldn't have known they were being followed. I swung toward my science officer.

"Are we getting close enough for them to detect us?"

"No, sir," said Schulman promptly. "Our long-range sensors still can't pick up any ships at the source of the transponder signal. I can't imagine that the pirates have better instruments than we do."

"Neither can I." I returned to my chair, still frowning. "What the hell are they up to out there?"

Heather Keith glanced over her shoulder at me, an unusual enough occurrence when we were moving at top warp speed that it caught my attention immediately. "Captain, I spent a lot of time patrolling this part of the Neutral Zone with the *Venture,*" she said. "It's not well-known, but there's a traffic pattern the Klingons tend to follow around here, a route through the Neutral Zone that connects the Klingon homeworld with their colonies in the Treghar1 cluster."

I lifted my eyebrows. I could see why the Klingons wouldn't make much noise about that, since the Neutral Zone was technically supposed to be entered only on journeys to or from the colonies the Organians had permitted us to establish there. But given the multi-variate curvature of that border zone, there were times when it could put a substantial detour in an otherwise straight journey between one part of the Federation and another. Apparently, it posed the same problem for the Klingon side of the border.

"Transfer the coordinates of that route to the science desk, Lieutenant," I said. "Schulman, how does it correlate with the position of our transponder signal?"

"That's about where they'll be stopping when they complete deceleration," she agreed. "I'm starting to get some reliable telemetry from the long-range sensors as we get closer and I'm fairly sure—"

I waited a moment. It wasn't like my science officer to start a sentence and not finish it, especially when it was something she was "fairly sure" about. Christina Schulman had once admitted to being only "fairly sure" about Plottel's Universal Field Equation and "pretty certain" of Einstein's Theory of General Relativity.

"Lieutenant?" I probed after another minute.

"I think I may have spoken too soon, Captain." She was running one analysis after another on her long-range sensor panel, her troubled look deepening as she did so. "Initial readings suggested there were two ships at the transponder's location, but now I'm picking up four—no, five. And now they're all gone again—"

"Signal interference?" asked Tim Henry from the engineering station in back of the bridge.

"I think you're right, Chief. The number of ships keeps shifting moment by moment." Schulman looked frustrated. "But I've done three system checks and there's nothing wrong with our side of the link."

Nino Orsini swung around from his weapons panel. "It could be phaser afterglow from a ship battle. At this range, sensors couldn't separate real ships from the reflected images bouncing off their shields with each blast."

"That would make sense of the sensor data," Schulman admitted.

"Although it doesn't make sense to *me.* Why would you stop to attack a ship while you were fleeing from Deep Space Three?"

"They're not fleeing if they don't know they're being followed," I reminded her. "And for all we know, that other ship attacked them first. The Klingons can be touchy about finding unauthorized ships in the Neutral Zone." I swung back to Walroth and Keith. "Estimated time of arrival at the battle site, gentlemen?"

"We should be within firing range in another thirty minutes, sir," said my navigator.

"Twenty-five, if we push the deceleration curve." Heather Keith didn't look back at me this time, but she must have heard my quick intake of breath. She added reassuringly, "I know we didn't do it often on the shakedown, sir, but trust me. The *Excelsior* can take it."

"Very well, Lieutenant. Make it twenty-five minutes." I forced myself to take a long, slow breath after I spoke, startled by the surge of adrenaline that had spiked into my blood. What difference did it make, I asked myself, if we met the pirates in twenty-five minutes or the original two hours that I had thought it would take to catch up to them? The sooner the better, as far as the safety of the hostages was concerned.

But that logic didn't quell the churning uneasiness I felt. Neither did a circuit of the *Excelsior*'s bridge, although it did make my officers look more confident to have their various data screens inspected and approved by the captain. The only one who seemed to notice my restlessness was the chief engineer. He gave me a commiserating glance and rubbed at his own stomach.

"Butterflies," he said gruffly. "Always get 'em before a ship's first real engagement."

I nodded and clapped a hand on his broad shoulder as if it were I and not he who was the veteran of two other prototype ship launches. "We'll do fine," I said, and moved on to the security station. It was there, glancing back across the *Excelsior*'s bridge at the star-streaked viewscreen, that I caught a glimpse of my own empty captain's chair and realized what was really wrong. I'd been through a hundred mock combats and another hundred simulated emergencies with this crew, but in every single one of those situations I'd always had the inner confidence of knowing that my second-in-command could take over if something went wrong. It wasn't the fact that this was the *Excelsior*'s first real crisis that bothered me. It was the fact that Chekov wasn't here to support me through it.

That thought startled me so much that I had to grit my teeth to keep from cursing. Was I really so unready for command, after all the years I'd prepared and longed for it, that the absence of a single one of my thousand competent crew members could disrupt my confidence like this? Granted, he was the only one who'd trained with me under Captain Kirk, who had absorbed that living legend's strategies and maneuvers more thoroughly than I had. And of course, we had the complete mutual trust that came from saving each other's lives more times than we could count. After escaping volcanic eruptions, serving undercover on an Orion pirate ship, and helping each other survive a hundred other critical situations, was it any wonder that I'd come to think of Pavel Chekov as my other self, the man I might have been if I'd been born in cold, grim Russia and not vibrant San Francisco?

I'd asked for him as my executive officer as soon as I'd been given command of the *Excelsior,* knowing he was long overdue for reassignment. Chekov had seemed a little reluctant to accept, perhaps remembering his previous stint as executive officer on the unfortunate science research vessel *Reliant.* But once we'd begun the shakedown cruise, our ability to mesh our talents and working styles had blossomed back into existence as easily as if it had been only yesterday that we'd manned the helm of the original *Enterprise* together. He'd seconded my hardest decisions, volunteered opinions I knew I could trust, and helped me weather all the ups and downs of getting a new crew adjusted to an even newer starship. I had just never realized before how much I'd come to depend on him throughout that process.

"We're nearing Klingon space lanes, Captain." It was the way Scott Walroth had to twist around to glance at me that reminded me I was still frozen beside the security console, staring at the funneling rush of stars that marked our passage without actually seeing them. "We'll be within firing range in twelve minutes."

"Thank you, Ensign." I cast a guilty look down at Orsini, hoping my long silence hadn't unnerved my young security chief. Fortunately, he was still scrambling to update his battle plans for the new ETA, and seemed to think my pause had been for his benefit rather than my own.

"I'm almost done recalibrating, sir," he said. "If you can just wait another minute—"

I did so, leaning over his display panel to scrutinize the battle plans as they coalesced. "Why are you assuming we'll have to fight six opposing ships, Lieutenant? Even counting the Orion yacht—"

"The pirates should only have five," Orsini finished. "But if the vessel they're engaged with is Klingon—"

"They might object to being rescued by Starfleet?"

The security chief shrugged. "Or they might assume we're using the pirates as a cover for an invasion, the same way we suspected them at Deep Space Three. Commander Chekov always says you can't go wrong if you expect the worst."

Despite my tension, I felt a smile tug at the corners of my mouth. I might not have Chekov here to depend on, but I did have a crew that he had shaped and molded as much as I had. "Very prudent, Lieutenant," I said. "Why don't you and Lieutenant Commander Rand work out a message we can send to the Klingons assuring—"

"Captain!" Christina Schulman spun around at her station, her urgent gaze sweeping the bridge until she found me. "The transponder signal is moving again."

I strode back to my console at the center of the bridge. "Walroth, can you verify that?"

The navigator hurriedly requested a different set of star charts from his console. "I'm sorry, sir, I was trying to coordinate with Orsini's battle plans—"

"Never mind that now, Ensign. Just tell me if that transponder heading has changed since the attack on that unknown ship."

"Nine-nineteen mark one. No, sir, it's the same." The young man gave me an almost apologetic look. "The pirates are back up to speed and still heading for nowhere."

"Schulman, do sensors indicate any ships still present at the battle site?"

"No, sir." Her reply came so fast that I knew my science officer had asked herself that question long before I did. "My long-range sensors showed several ships leaving the area together, but I lost resolution before I could get an accurate count."

It was beginning to look as if the caution Chekov had hammered into my security chief had been justified after all. "Could you tell if they were all traveling on the same heading?"

My science officer shook her head. "No. We decelerated below warp five and lost sensor contact before I could determine that."

"Should we resume our previous speed, sir?" My pilot had her hands already poised above the controls, waiting for the order. I was opening my mouth to grant that permission when Janice Rand swung around and interrupted with the confidence of a veteran officer who knows how important her information might be.

"Captain, I'm receiving an automatic distress signal from an emergency life-pod. It appears to be coming from the vicinity of the battle site."

The *Excelsior*'s viewscreen still showed the usual rush of flying stars around us, but a glance at Heather Keith's display screens told me we were decelerating below warp three now. "Did any emergency message or ship identification come in with the distress signal?" I asked Rand.

"None, sir. It's just a simple subspace alarm, the kind most life-pods emit automatically as soon as they're launched." My communications officer glanced over at me, her eyes reflecting the staccato flash of light that marked the incoming alarm on her display panel. "Based on its specific range of frequencies, I'd say the ship it evacuated from was Klingon."

"Just promise me that you won't answer any mysterious distress calls from the other side of the Klingon border . . ."

"What do long-range scanners show at the battle site now, Lieutenant Schulman?"

"They've detected several escape pods at the coordinates of the distress call, sir, but no sign of a wrecked ship. I can't detect any life-signs in that vicinity."

"Would you expect to, at this distance?" Heather Keith asked.

"If there are enough survivors in those pods I would." Schulman threw another aggravated look at her long-range sensors, whose output was never good enough to satisfy her. "But our biodetectors aren't sensitive enough to pick up one or two stray individuals at this distance, especially through the afterglow of that battle."

I frowned, seeing from Lieutenant Keith's piloting screens that I had less than five minutes to decide whether to stop and investigate. "Security, science—rapid analysis of the situation."

"It's a trap," Orsini said at once. "A distress call where no one is actually in distress—any ship can jettison an escape pod and manufacture that."

"Agreed," said Schulman. "But this can only be a trap if someone's waiting there to catch us. According to my sensors, there are no other ships in the vicinity."

"There could be Klingon ships waiting under cloak," said my security chief.

"There could," she agreed. "But Ockham's Razor says that the simplest explanation is most likely to be correct. And those escape pods are drifting in the exact area where our pirate convoy stopped to engage a ship in battle twenty minutes ago."

I glanced at Lieutenant Keith's display again, eyeing the diminishing distance between us and the flashing icon that marked the distress signal. "Ensign, update on the transponder signal?"

"Still maintaining speed and direction on heading nine-nineteen, sir," Walroth said. "Assuming we accelerate back to maximum warp speed now, we'll intercept them in approximately forty-five minutes."

And if we stopped to investigate these escape pods, we would end up a full two hours behind them again. I curved my hands around the arms of my captain's console, feeling uncertainty twist in my stomach. It was so easy to make the right decision in simulated battles, when you were positive there *was* a right decision to be made. But this was the real world, and none of the decisions I could make seemed remotely close to being right. If I stopped to check the distress signal, I might possibly endanger the *Excelsior,* and I would certainly add another hour or so to the time the hostages had to spend in jeopardy. If I didn't stop, I would certainly be breaking Starfleet regulations and possibly condemning battle survivors to death. Depending on what the pirates had decided to do with their hostages after their change in plans, some of those survivors might even be members of my crew.

"Maintain deceleration, Lieutenant Keith," I told my pilot. "Ensign Walroth, plot a course that will put us within maximum transporter range of the source of that distress signal. Schulman, I want a continuous sensor scan of this entire region. If a vessel appears from any heading, put the ship on red alert."

"Aye, Captain," said three voices in unison. The slowing streaks of stars on the *Excelsior*'s viewscreen announced our arrival at the battle site. A moment later, my pilot glanced up from her stabilized display. "We've arrived at the alarm coordinates, Captain."

I frowned up at the unhelpful viewscreen, which showed nothing but deep space and distant stars. "Can we locate and magnify the pod?"

Schulman shook her head, but it was more in bafflement than negation. "Sensors seem to be having a little trouble with it, sir. What we're looking at there is the precise location of the distress signal's generator. It just doesn't seem to coincide with any significant mass in the area."

I glanced back at Rand. The somber look in her blue eyes told me the answer to my question, but for the sake of the ship's records I had to ask it anyway. "Commander Rand, could that alarm continue to generate a distress call if the life-pod itself was destroyed?"

"Most of our distress signal generators are self-contained and self-powered devices, sir," she replied. "I would assume the Klingons use similar methods."

"So would I." I fought with a brief, treacherous desire to send the *Excelsior* leaping back into immediate pursuit of the pirate ship. But now that we were here, it would be stupid not to take a little time to learn about our enemies. And about their victims. "Lieutenant Schulman, I want you to scan this entire area for wreckage. Chief Henry, beam whatever we can find to a secured cargo bay and see if you can use it to identify the vessel that was attacked. Rand, alert Doctor Klass to be prepared to identify organic remains, if any happen to be found." I glanced at my watch and made a quick calculation in my head. "You have twenty minutes from my mark to reconstruct the crime, gentlemen—the same amount of time the pirates had to commit it. Mark."

The cargo bay was full of bodies. Rows of bodies, large and small, all of them stiff, all of them exhaling the glittery smoke of space-cold flesh put back in contact with air and humidity far too late to do them any good. All of them Klingon.

"I think it must have been a colony ship." My medical officer waited for a response to that statement, but I found myself unable to speak in the presence of so much senseless slaughter. After a moment, Klass cleared her throat and went on. "Chief Henry has only found a few shards of exploded life-pod, but he says the alloy is typical of unarmed Klingon vessels. We found seventy-six adults and eighteen children in the twenty minutes you allowed us to scan and beam them aboard. We might have found more if we'd stayed to sweep the whole area."

"Twenty minutes was all we could spare," I said curtly. Actually, it had been more than we could spare—we had lost the fragile signal of the nano-transponders just before we reengaged our warp drive, and only found it again by following the pirates' last known heading. It was the second time that gamble had paid off, but we were once again two hours behind in the chase. "What killed them? Not phasers."

"No, Captain, or we wouldn't have bodies," Klass said with patient logic. "Most of the adults and all of the children appear to have been ejected directly from stasis tubes into space. They died from vacuum exposure, and there is no medical evidence to indicate they even regained enough consciousness to take a breath during their last moments."

My throat muscles lost a little of their convulsive stiffness. "And the rest?"

Klass's thin lips tightened. "Judging by the explosive decompression of the capillaries in their lungs, some were thrust into vacuum alive. Others seem to have been killed by blunt force trauma before being ejected from the ship. The tricorder picked up traces of non-Klingon DNA in most of the wounds, indicating the wounds were inflicted by hand. Or by tail," she added dryly.

I nodded, remembering Tuvok's description of the way his captors had fought. "Can that incorporated DNA be matched to any of the known alien races in your medical records?"

"Absolutely none," my chief medical officer admitted. "But the aliens in question are sauroid in morphology, not quite two meters in height, strongly muscled and heavily clawed, and quite possibly passive rather than active endotherms."

I blinked at her. My specialty in biology had been plants, but I'd had the requisite course in zoology and knew the terms she was using. "You think the pirates who did this are literally cold-blooded? Wouldn't that be unheard of in a sentient race?"

"It would be unheard of for them to be *ectotherms,*" Klass corrected me, in the professorial voice all doctors seemed able to assume at will. "But there are several sentient races known to have internal heat generation and warm blood without having the ability to regulate their blood temperature.

Studies have shown that this lack of control predisposes them to mood swings, violent outbursts and racial paranoia. Even from the little we know of them so far, I suspect the pirates may be of similar temperament. The presence of ceremonial scarification—"

"Hold it," I said, frowning at her. "How did you infer a social phenomena like scarification from a few genetic samples?"

"I didn't," said my infuriatingly logical doctor. "I inferred it from the abundance of geometrically placed scars on the face, arms, and chest of the body—"

"*Body?* What body?"

"The single non-Klingon body we recovered in our scan of the battle site." Klass allowed herself a very small smile, one that was more a quizzical upward curve of the lips than any real indication of amusement. "You wouldn't expect Klingons to surrender their ship without inflicting *some* casualties—"

"Show it to me," I interrupted her without ceremony. An austere raised eyebrow reminded me that if DNA analysis and Klass's perfect memory couldn't give our enemies an identity, a quick inspection by a brand-new captain wasn't likely to, either. I didn't bother responding to that look, since I wasn't sure myself what I was going to accomplish. Perhaps I merely needed to see one of my enemies face to face, to have a concrete image of what I was facing in this battle.

"This way." Klass led me through the rows of frozen, fog-shrouded bodies to a form so blocky and solid that it looked as if it had been hewn from ice rather than turned to it. I frowned down at the face, seeing a toothy snout and deep eye-sockets whose unlidded eyes were now ice-punctured and colorless. A strong nasal ridge continued across the forehead with its scarred, lumpy scales, then rose into a cranial crest, vacuum-burned but impressively frilled further down the strong back. The body was covered in scales, ranging in color from mahogany to dark steel-gray. Over them, armor plating like thickened plates of chiton clung to the body, still emitting a warmth I could see in the cold drift of fog off the chilled flesh. That thermal augmenting unit probably kept the passively warm-blooded sauroid inhabitant more active than he could be on his own, but it wasn't doing its owner any good now.

"A single individual of a theropod species, origin unknown, age unknown," Klass reported. "Death resulted from attack with a Klingon *bat'leth.* Ejection into vacuum followed after a period of several minutes."

"Toward the end of the battle, in other words," I said grimly. "He was thrown out into space by his own people."

My chief medical officer lifted an eyebrow at me again, this time inquisitively. "On what evidence do you base that conclusion, Captain?"

"On the evidence of having heard them talk about doing it," I retorted. "Back when I was the helmsman on the *Enterprise* and we rescued a bunch of these guys from what they claimed was a pirate attack."

"Ironic," Klass said calmly, without a flicker of surprise crossing her strong face. "Why was the data on their species never entered into Starfleet medical records?"

I shook my head, still feeling the misty sense of déjà vu that had led to my recognition of this scarred alien. "I'm not sure. It happened a long time ago, and it was never actually an official mission. All I know is that Captain Kirk followed them back to their homeworld and made some kind of deal with the authorities there. And we never heard from them again."

"Until now," she said.

"Yes." I studied the dead face again with its strong projecting muzzle, triangular teeth, and fierce net of ceremonial scars. It seemed as if I should remember the name of such an unusual alien race, yet no word stirred in my memory. If all of Starfleet's computer records were equally blank—

"Put the Klingons' bodies into vacuum storage until we can deliver them to an appropriate location," I told my chief medical officer. "But I want this body kept in stasis until it can be examined."

"By another medical doctor?" Although her tone was polite, there was a spark in Klass's pale eyes that made me realize she had another similarity to Leonard McCoy: a keen sense of professional pride.

"No, Doctor. By the man who's most likely to know why these aliens are here and what they're trying to accomplish." I took a step back from the sauroid's mist-blanketed body, hoping I was doing this for the right reasons and not because I wanted the strong presence of my former captain to support me now that my first officer was gone. "Let's just hope the *Enterprise* isn't on the other side of the galaxy right now."

Seven

KIRK

"WHO SPREADS VILE LIES ABOUT THE GORN?"

Kirk wasn't sure what startled him most—the outraged roar of a familiar alien species, or the equally familiar cadence of its slow words. He twisted around in his chair just in time to come face-to-muzzle with a double row of sharp teeth and a blast of warm, meat-smelling Gorn-breath.

He gripped the edge of the table and leaned back slightly, wincing at the stench. "No one said anything about the Gorn."

The dandy across the table from him ruined the assertion by asking in a voice much louder than necessary, "Captain, isn't this one of the incompetent reptiles about which you've been regaling us?" He returned Kirk's glare with a saber-thin grin that left the starship commander momentarily unsure which fellow captain he would end up hitting.

"No!"

The Gorn lurched upright with a steamy hiss. Whatever thick, stinking fluid had been in the bucket in its hand splattered its feet and the floor around it. "What stringy human dares call the Gorn incompetent?"

Kirk noticed with some annoyance that not all the fingers that rose up to point at him came from his table.

"We weren't talking about the Gorn," he began, in what was meant to be his most soothing and reasonable voice.

He interrupted himself to duck out from under the Gorn's sluggish roundhouse swing.

I remember this, he thought as his chair overturned and he hit the floor rolling. Slow, deliberate, but persistent and strong as hell. Kirk watched the

Gorn's second swing impact with the table, sending glasses, patrons, and wood flying off in all directions. It occurred to him that a drunk Gorn was probably the scariest thing he'd seen in the last few years.

"My lizard!" Sulu jumped to his feet, away from the alcohol-soaked mess. A few meters ahead of him, a squiggling flash of gold-and-brown whisked under the boards of the staircase and out of sight.

If the Gorn noticed either the fleeing lizard or the other Starfleet captain, it gave no indication. Swaying mightily, it turned in a laborious circle to snap pearly teeth at Kirk. "Hold still, leaping mammal! I will be merciful!"

"I've heard that before." Kirk bounced into a squat, ready to dive in any direction. No matter how slow moving, this was still the creature who, while sober, had once heaved a rock the size of a shuttlecraft at him. Kirk had no intention of taking this Gorn captain lightly. "Captain, let's discuss this like civilized creatures—"

The Gorn's languorous swipe would have passed over him by a good half meter if not for the dangling bucket. Ducking, Kirk scrabbled sideways to avoid being drenched.

"You've had too much to drink—"

No bucket this time, just a talon-filled swipe wide enough to let Kirk jump to his feet and out of range.

"And I think you've misunderstood—"

The sauroid's roar rattled like a snake's angry tail. "You claim now that I don't even understand your speaking?"

"You've gotta admit," the human freighter captain leaned his elbows back against the long bar, looking almost as puckish as the dandy, "the translation devices seem to be working a lot better this time around—the stuff he says almost makes sense!"

Of course there were no translation devices—there never were here, and never needed to be. Which is why Kirk felt perfectly justified in raising his voice loudly enough for everyone present to hear. "This is a Gorn, not an Anjiri *or* a Nykkus!" He swept a chair between himself and the staggering Gorn, more for the appearance of distance than because he thought it would protect him. "They look completely different, and don't function even remotely the same. This is *not* the race we had dealings with!"

"Lies!" the Gorn raged, stretching up to its full, towering height. "The Gorn have had dealings with the humans for decades—one long history of conflict!"

It crushed the chair with one foot. Kirk took refuge behind another table as its patrons fled.

"So," the dandy asked mildly, "exactly how many different reptile people have you managed to irritate in your career, Captain?"

Obviously one more than was good for him. Dodging swiftly to his right, Kirk let the Gorn get halfway into a slow-motion spin to confront him, then dashed just as quickly leftward to place himself behind the alien's broad back. He might have felt guilty about kicking anyone else between the shoulder blades, but he'd done enough hand-to-hand grappling with this mighty species to know that any kick he delivered was likely to feel more like a friendly thump on the back. Much as he expected, the Gorn barely stumbled under the blow. It wouldn't have fallen at all if it hadn't tripped over Sulu.

The whole bar seemed to shake as the Gorn hit the floor. Sulu threw himself valiantly toward the struggling lizard he'd finally relocated, barely managing to avoid being crushed by the toppling behemoth. Even so, the little tailless reptile seemed to squirt from the middle of the imbroglio like a watermelon seed, beelining for the cracks in the stone fireplace. Kirk performed what felt like a particularly blundering tap dance around the fleeing gecko and his former helmsman, and ended up pouncing on the Gorn's chest more to cover his own stumbling than because he'd actually intended to pin the alien.

As long as he was there, though, he planted his knees on the Gorn's shoulders and caught the end of its muzzle in both hands to protect his face from being bitten off. "Now, listen to me." Its hot breath whistled past his fingers, stinking eloquently of something pale and fermented. "Yes, we've been talking about a reptilian race that we clashed with a number of years ago. No, that race was *not* the Gorn, although the Gorn have been our worthy opponents in the past." That seemed to mollify the Gorn captain a little. He gave a little burp and stopped trying to shake off Kirk's hands. "The Gorn have always been honorable," Kirk continued. "The race we're talking about was very different."

The Gorn captain's voice hissed against Kirk's palms, but his grip on its muzzle blocked whatever words it made against the back of its own teeth.

Lifting his hands away, Kirk asked civilly, "What was that?"

"What became of these other people who were not Gorn?"

A request was always better than a blow. Rocking back on his heels, Kirk took his weight off the Gorn's chest and rose neatly to his feet. "That's what I've been trying to tell you." He offered the Gorn a hand, but was still a bit surprised when the big creature reached up to take it. "Why don't you join us over here—" Although he had to lean back into his pull to heave the other captain upright, they both managed to make it without falling down. Sulu still stood, looking disconsolately around for his gecko, but the others had already regrouped at the bar and resupplied themselves with fresh beverages. "I'll buy you a drink," Kirk offered the Gorn, "and you can let me explain what happened. . . ."

• • •

"Captain Kirk, I'm detecting another heading shift in the *Nevekke's* ion trail."

Before I could order our own course change to compensate, Lieutenant Sulu quickly scanned his own helm readings, then leaned over to examine Bailey's navigations console. "No . . ." Even in correcting the younger man, his voice was calm and nonjudgmental. "The yacht moves back to its original course twelve kilometers later." He glanced over his shoulder at me. "I think they're flailing. They either don't know how to use the *Nevekke*'s controls, and are changing course without meaning to, or this is their idea of evasive maneuvers."

I had a feeling I knew which it was, but didn't want to take anything for granted. "Keep on them."

Sulu nodded curtly, swiveling back to his controls with only a brief pause to murmur some words of encouragement to Bailey. I fidgeted in my command chair, too mad at myself now to even pace the bridge.

I hadn't taken the Anjiri lightly—hadn't been impressed with their technological savvy, perhaps, but also hadn't assumed they were harmless because of that. Their original ship had been such a mishmash of different technologies that I'd simply taken for granted that they were a poor race, the kind that couldn't afford the high-quality technology that made spaceflight safe. That they were living off other races' leavings. In a sense, I was right. In this case, though, the "leavings" weren't whatever obsolete technology their trading partners were willing to part with, but whatever the Anjiri themselves could find lying around. Or whatever they could steal. Technological scavengers, opportunistic feeders off of more advanced races who probably should have known better.

"You are indulging in an exercise of fruitless emotional narcissism, are you not?" When I angled a dark look at Spock, he added, "I meant no disrespect. You are human, I understand. It is your lot."

Before he was promoted to first officer, he stayed at his science console instead of hovering at my right shoulder. "I'm reassessing how I handled the Anjiri," I sighed. It was strangely gratifying to have him standing there, as though his presence gave me the right to vent. "I was so damned eager to get them off the ship, I didn't even care where we off-loaded them."

He seemed to consider that for a moment. "As I recall, you exerted no undue pressure on Commander Akpakken to accept the Anjiri."

"I should have warned him," I grumbled.

"Illogical." Spock folded his hands behind his back, warming up for full lecture mode. "Contrary to human conviction, data obtained after the fact cannot be applied retroactively. We had no reason to believe Akpakken would be incapable of taking the necessary precautions to protect his station from the Anjiri."

In fact, the Anjiri didn't even attempt a sophisticated hijacking once they got on board the station—they took the Orion yacht in a straightforward smash and grab, without bothering to string the Orions along, much less come up with a believable excuse to get access to their hangar bay. After blasting their way off the station—the Orions were threatening to bill the Federation for repairs to their hangar bay doors—they then made no attempt to mask their drive signature or damp their ion emissions. Not exactly the actions of your top-flight pirate crew.

"At least Akpakken had the sense to map their course for the first few parsecs." I sighed again, but this time without the conviction of a true sulk. "Saved us a lot of time."

"And presents us with interesting data on Orion sensor and navigational techniques," Spock added. "Given the Orions' skill in predicting the location of Federation patrol ships, Akpakken's information should prove quite useful in avoiding future pirating activity in this sector."

I managed a wry smile. "I'm glad we could at least provide you with interesting study material, Mr. Spock." He didn't seem to get the joke.

The chirrup from the helm's long-range sensors caught my attention, and I knew what it meant even before Sulu announced, "Picking up a small craft dead ahead."

"Put it on screen. Full magnification." I hadn't expected a lengthy chase—there hasn't been a yacht built with any hope of outrunning a starship. I watched the *Nevekke* ripple into view against a hazy ribbon of gas and debris and cocked a look toward Spock. "Asteroid belt?"

He was already back at his station, bent over his sensor display. "Planetary remnants, including residual ring structures." He gave the viewscreen a pensive frown. "The outermost of fifteen planets around a class K star."

At the helm, Sulu was suddenly a whirlwind of activity. "They're accelerating!"

On the screen, the Orion yacht's small warp engines brightened, squeezing a rippling puff of exhaust leakage out of the belly of the ship. They were pushing the little ship way too hard, and I had a feeling why.

"Close with them!" I shouted, half vaulting from my chair. "I want a tractor beam on them before they make that field. All hands, yellow alert!" That last was peremptory—if we ended up dodging and weaving through that debris field in a ship the size of the *Enterprise,* I wanted the crew ready for anything.

I felt the *Enterprise* gather herself for the leap forward, like a racehorse plunging in the gate, but I knew with sick certainty that we'd never catch *Nevekke* before she made the debris field. Still, I almost snapped at Bailey to take a stab at them with our tractor beam, even though they were woefully out of range. Instead, I cursed at *Nevekke*'s vapor trail when she didn't so much as fire her retrojets before diving into that sea of gas and distraction.

"Mr. Sulu," I ordered grudgingly, "cut speed. One half impulse." We weren't *Nevekke.* We wouldn't win this battle with speed, any more than they'd made any headway with cunning.

Spock jerked his head up from his console. "Captain . . . ?"

"We promised the Orions we'd bring back their yacht, Mr. Spock." I fumed as discreetly as possible, clenching my fist against my thigh. "We can't do that unless we follow them in."

Ahead of me, I saw Bailey start, and even Sulu's voice carried a certain note of skeptical acceptance when he acknowledged, "Aye, aye, sir. One-half impulse."

Instead of leaping into action, the warp engines pulsing at my ship's heart growled down to a frustrated rumble. The asteroid belt no longer rushed up on us like the edge of a cliff, and we lost visual with the yacht a lot faster than I would have liked. All that was left was the ripple of her warp exhaust where she'd ducked into a cloud of tumbling rock.

"Look at their speed!" Bailey shook his head at that visual remnant of the Anjiri's escape. "They're going to ionize themselves on a planetoid."

We should be so lucky. "Let's try not to follow their example," I cautioned. "Be conservative, Mr. Sulu, but keep that ship in range."

Sulu gave only a terse nod in acknowledgment—he was already fixated on his controls as the forward screens began to glow with vaporizing dust and microimpacts. Our treacherous waltz had begun.

Proximity alarms exploded into life all around me.

"Kill those sirens." I waved irritably at Giotto at the security console. He hurried to comply, and I hunkered down in my chair to glare at the blurring starscape before me.

You have to understand astronomical distances—there wasn't a one of those rocks closer than several kilometers away. If the *Enterprise* had been a human on foot, traversing this debris field would have been like navigating around a set of football goalposts without slamming into one. But the *Enterprise* wasn't a human—she was a huge, massive, warp-powered vessel that has more inertia than some small moons and enough of her own gravitational field to perturb the orbit of every piece of space debris she passed. "Several kilometers" in a Constitution-class starship starts to seem a lot more like tiptoeing across a trampoline covered with hand grenades.

Screen magnification adjusted itself downward, then downward again as we crept deeper and deeper into the morass. I couldn't see a damned thing to justify our caution. Most of the planetoids and asteroids we brushed past weren't even close enough to get a meaningful visual, and once magnification reached zero the stars beyond the nose of the ship looked hardly different than what I usually saw there, just a little more cloudy and yellow.

Spock's deep voice interrupted my glowering. "Captain . . ."

I spared him a glance, then realized that whatever he'd picked up on his sensors had seized his full attention. I doubted he'd have noticed me looking at him if I bounced a hand phaser off his head. I thought about Sulu, equally engrossed in the business of keeping us out of any unfriendly gravity wells, and stood to join Spock at his station so that whatever he had to say wouldn't distract my helmsman. "What is it?"

He still didn't look up from his readouts, but his response was more alert than I'd expected. "I'm detecting signs of primitive industrialization on one of the planetoids currently within sensor range."

I don't know why I glanced at the viewscreen. I didn't really expect to see anything—there wasn't even a discernable star this far out, and no other full-sized planets in sight. "Intelligent life? Here?"

Spock lifted his shoulder in a minimalist Vulcan shrug. "Not indigenous, certainly. The planetoid in question does not appear to support even a noxious atmosphere, or show any indication of tectonic activity. Logic suggests that these are colonists, perhaps shipwreck survivors."

"The Anjiri?"

"Possibly." But his voice gave no indication how likely he thought that possibility to be. "Readings reveal the same eclectic collection of technologies and metals."

"A good place to hide, if you've got ships agile enough to access it." Which an Orion yacht wasn't, really. "What about reinforcements? Any sign of other ships in the vicinity?"

He bent back to his sensors for a moment. "I assume you are only interested in ships which are capable of lifting off to engage us in combat?"

What the hell kind of question was that? "Do you detect some other kind?"

"The inhabited planetoid is . . ." He hesitated, just enough to make the hair on the back of my neck start to rise, "encrusted with a great variety of vessels. I read no engine activity, yet their life-support systems appear to be powered and fully operational." He turned a cool look toward me without straightening from his station. "The Anjiri appear to be using them as living quarters."

And what could make for nicer living quarters than a well-appointed Orion yacht?

"We can't let them land that yacht." Taking the steps to my command chair in a single stride, I swung into the seat as I demanded, "Mr. Sulu, where are we relative to the *Nevekke?*"

The helmsmen stole a series of short but directed glances at his readings. "Ninety-three kilometers," he shook his head apologetically, "and pulling away. I'm sorry, sir. We're losing too much velocity on the turns."

Damn. "Don't blame yourself for the laws of physics, Mr. Sulu." I slapped open a channel on my chair console. "Bridge to Engineering."

"Engine room. Scott here."

"I've got a civilian yacht at a hundred klicks dead ahead that I need to stop. Can you route extra power to the tractor beam so it'll hold across that distance?"

Scott sounded wary of my request, as always. "Aye, I can route half your shield output through the tractor beam array. I can't promise your civilian ship'll hold up to the stress, though."

"Let me worry about that. You get me that power." I closed our connection before he could protest further. "Mr. Sulu, where's our quarry?"

"A hundred twelve klicks, still pulling away."

"Mr. Bailey, activate tractor beam. Let's see if we can slow our friends down a little."

I heard Spock stir slightly to my right. "Captain," he interrupted, "if we should attach our tractor beam to an asteroid rather than the *Nevekke*—"

We'd be a living example of that old joke: What's the last thing to go through a starship commander's mind when his ship hits a moon? Answer: His warp drive.

"Mr. Bailey will endeavor to be careful."

The jolt of deceleration hit the ship so powerfully, I came out of my command chair and went down on one knee. "*Careful,* Mr. Bailey!" I reminded the navigator.

He shook his head frantically, hands flying across his panel. "That wasn't me!" he protested with youthful indignation. "I mean, that wasn't us! The engine room hasn't even given me the go-ahead yet."

So when the second tremor rocked the ship, I swung an urgent glare at Spock. It was wasted—he'd already buried his attention in his station, and didn't need me to prompt him for a report. "Captain, we've been caught by someone else's tractor beam."

I leaned hard over the railing between us. "*What?*" In the background, somewhere decks away, I could hear the ship's core systems straining as the *Enterprise* tried to plow forward despite the drag.

"Two tractor beams," Spock continued, as calmly as though we were discussing dyes in a petri dish, "at a one hundred twenty degree angle from each other."

I twisted to shout at Sulu, "Helm, full stop!"

Sulu went to work without replying. Nothing betrayed our drop in speed, but the third jolt which rocked the ship didn't jar us so violently, thanks to our reduced momentum.

Spock's announcement was only what I expected. "Captain, we're suspended in a triangulated tractor beam. The beam generators appear to be situated on three separate planetoids around the main industrialized homeworld."

Maybe the Anjiri weren't so ignorant of how to use their stolen technology after all.

"Any of them within phaser range?" I asked. I prowled back to the command chair, but couldn't make myself sit down.

"Negative. The power of each individual beam is unprecedented, allowing them to be situated a great distance from our position." Spock actually looked impressed. "I will speculate that this is how the Anjiri make use of the reaction piles from their various captured ships."

What a nice little lesson in recycling. I chewed my lip, absently bouncing a fist off the edge of my chair back as I pondered our options. "Uhura, open hailing frequencies. Broad band."

"Sir, I—" She hesitated, and I turned to face her. "We're being hailed," she told me, looking a little startled. "The channel's low frequency and the coding very primitive, but . . ." Her eyes glazed with listening for a moment longer. When they cleared again, she said, "It sounds like they're speaking Anjiri."

Of course they were. I rounded my seat, glaring at the still obstructed view. "Put them on screen."

The already dusty and fragmented stars fragmented further, shattering into a pale, unremitting buzz. I waited for a face to appear, but instead heard only the growling hiss of a voice that might have been Vissith's, yet was somehow clearly not Vissith's. The tortured translator-syntax was unmistakably Anjiri.

"Your ship to our revered coordinates shall proceed. Into our company yourselves you shall present. All of this within one specified unit of time you shall accomplish, or torn into prenatal bits you shall be."

Eight

SULU

CAPTAIN'S LOG
U.S.S. Excelsior
Stardate 8730.1

We are in pursuit of the alien pirates who attacked Deep Space Three and took six members of our crew hostage, then slaughtered ninety-four innocent Klingon colonists. Their heading and velocity have put them deep within an uninhabited portion of the Neutral Zone and their ultimate destination remains unclear. So far, we have received no answer to our requests for either a conference with Captain Kirk or the records of his previous encounter with these aliens. What we have received are strict orders from Starfleet not to cross the Klingon side of the border. We are therefore proceeding at maximum warp to intercept the pirates.

I RELEASED THE RECORDING BUTTON ON MY CONSOLE ARM WITH A QUIET, guilty sigh. In these days of visual computer records, a captain's log was a personal journal, intended to document its maker's mental and emotional state in case his or her command decisions were later brought into question. I could remember Captain Kirk back on the bridge of the *Enterprise,* pouring out his frustrations and venting his fears into his log entries. So far, all I felt able to record in front of my crew were brief and banal statements of fact: Where we were, what we planned to do, what our orders were. I suspected that later examination of this journal would merely conclude that its captain lacked the inner confidence he needed to carry out his duties.

"Captain Sulu, long-range sensors are picking up some telemetry on the transponder source," said Lieutenant Schulman. The aggravation in her voice added the unspoken words, *"at last."* "It looks like six ships, traveling together in tight formation. We're not close enough to separate out their ion trails and identify them yet, but from the size of the sensor reflections, I'd say one is much larger than the others."

"The Klingon colony transport," I guessed and saw my science officer nod agreement. "Time to intercept, Ensign Walroth?"

"Nine-point-three minutes, sir." The words might have a Vulcan precision, but the suppressed excitement in the young man's voice betrayed an all-too-human sense of anticipation.

"And our current distance from the border?"

"Fifty million kilometers and closing," said my pilot without looking away from her display. "We're going to be kissing Klingon space by the time we catch up to them, sir. We can't let them run any further."

I swung around and caught my security chief in the process of doing the same thing, so that our glances caught and held. "Battle strategy, sir?" Orsini demanded.

"Overshoot before engagement," I said. "If we come at them from the direction of the Klingon border, their best hope of evasive action is to break back toward our side."

"Assuming they're not running for that border as a sanctuary," Henry put in from his engineering station.

Heather Keith snorted. "After killing almost a hundred Klingons, I doubt they'll find a warm welcome in the Empire, Chief."

"Unless they captured that colony ship to use as a Trojan horse," I said. "We'll concentrate our fire on it first and see if that draws the other ships in to protect it."

"If it doesn't?"

I paused, trying to decide how best to balance the safety of our missing crew with our urgent need not to let their captors cross the Klingon border. In the part of their missive coded for my eyes only, Starfleet Command had made it very clear that any incursion into the Empire's space right now was likely to set off a round of attacks and reprisals that would at the very least rouse the Organians' wrath. At the very worst, it might catapult us into full-scale interplanetary war with the Klingons before those superior beings even had time to intervene. Balanced against that, the six lives that had drawn us here were clearly of lesser importance—and yet every fiber of my body rebelled against subjecting them to the kind of crushing attack the *Excelsior* was capable of.

Janice Rand interrupted before my internal conflict could betray me into a jumble of contradictory battle orders, or even worse, no battle orders at all. "Captain, we're getting another message from Starfleet, security code alpha."

That meant all of my bridge officers had the clearances needed to hear it. "Put it on the main viewscreen, Commander."

The glittering rush of stars going past us at maximum warp speeds vanished, replaced by the calm face and piercing dark eyes of Rear Admiral Hajime Shoji. "Captain Sulu," he said with the politeness he was legendary for, even at the times of greatest crisis. "I apologize for the delay in responding to your earlier request for information, but it was necessary to consult with Captain Kirk before we made a decision." The slightly ironic emphasis the rear admiral put on the word "consult" suggested that it was a tactful euphemism for "cross-examine." Given that no official medical records seemed to have been filed from the *Enterprise*'s previous encounter with these aliens, I could see why Starfleet Command might have been a little vexed.

"Were you able to discover the identity of the aliens?" I asked, since the rear admiral seemed to be waiting for some response.

"Indeed," he replied, as imperturbably as a Vulcan ambassador. "And I'm pleased to be able to tell you that upon hearing of your encounter with them, Captain Kirk volunteered to assist you in any way he can. He has just finished a mission in an adjacent sector and should be arriving within two standard hours."

That news, which would probably have made me bristle with offended pride a day ago and sigh in relief two hours ago, now felt like nothing more than extraneous information. "We're five minutes away from contact with the alien convoy, Admiral." I tried to sound as imperturbable as he did, but I wasn't sure I succeeded. "Is there *any* information you can give us that might be of some help?"

Shoji inclined his head in a gesture as ambiguous as it was gracious. "Starfleet Command is forwarding you all the information we can—"

"Captain!" It was a tribute to Rand's poise and confidence that she felt no more compunction about interrupting a rear admiral than a fellow bridge officer. "We're being hailed on a Klingon emergency channel—but the message says it's from our resupply team!"

"Match and verify voice patterns," I ordered my communications officer. "Orsini, raise shields and prepare for attack in case this is a trap. Schulman, locate the source of that transmission and cross-check it with the flight path of the alien convoy. Admiral, if you'll excuse me—"

The appreciative glint in those dark eyes told me the order in which I'd issued my commands hadn't been lost on my sector commander. "By all means, Captain Sulu. Shoji out."

I swung around without waiting to see the uninformative stars that replaced him on the viewscreen. "Schulman, let me know as soon as you've received and scanned the information Starfleet sends us. Where are the alien ships now?"

"Two are continuing on their original heading toward the Neutral Zone, Captain," she reported. "Three others have split off on a heading which is roughly parallel to the Klingon border, and the largest one—the former Klingon colony transport—seems to have come to a complete stop, then turned around to go back to where it came from."

I glanced at Rand. "Status of the emergency hail?"

"Voice patterns are matched and verified, sir. It's Ensign McClain from Ship Services Division. He says the rest of the resupply team is there with him."

"Put him on the main screen," I commanded and swung around to face it. This time, the transition from star-streaks to a human face was much less smooth, fragmented around the edges in a way that meant the transmitter was calibrated for a different type of rastering system and had been transformed to fit our screen. Inside that fractal halo, a young and swollen face squinted back at me through a splatter of deepening bruises.

"Ensign McClain, what is your status?"

"Alive and abandoned, Captain." McClain's voice held the kind of toneless exhaustion I'd heard before in survivors of torture, the same tone Chekov's voice had held when the Klingons had used an agonizer on him so many years ago. "The damned snakes who took us killed the station quartermaster trying to get a Starfleet security override code he didn't even know. When they started in on us, Commander Chekov managed to cut some kind of deal with them. They kept him and threw all the rest of us out in a Klingon life-pod."

I wasn't sure whether the tightness I felt in my throat was pride that my first officer had been able to save his crew, or dismay about his own fate. "What kind of deal did Chekov cut?"

"I don't know, sir. The universal translators could barely make sense of the snakes when they talked. All I know is that as soon as he cut it, the aliens changed course away from Elaphe Vulpina and stopped slapping us around. They didn't get around to actually throwing us out until later, after they'd attacked that Klingon ship and had the life-pods to spare."

Something about that sequence of events didn't feel right to me, but now wasn't the time to dissect it in detail. "All right, Ensign. We've got the coordinates of your signal fixed and will be within transporter distance in just a few minutes." I could see the flashing beacon of his emergency signal on Heather Keith's piloting boards, and years of piloting experience told me exactly what its position meant in terms of travel time. "Does anyone in your party need to be beamed directly to sickbay?"

"It looks like Neely has a pretty bad concussion, sir, and Vanderpool thinks her wrist might be broken. The rest of us are just banged up."

"Good. Notify us if anything in your situation changes, Ensign. *Excelsior* out."

Before I had even touched the button that closed the channel, his battered face vanished from the screen, replaced by a dim vision of stars and a glowing overlay of ship movements. "Captain, our long-range sensors show that the convoy ships have all come to a stop just outside normal sensor range," my science officer said urgently. "They seem to be massing for some kind of surprise attack."

"Red alert," I ordered, then scanned that sensor-constructed array, wishing I had the kind of running captions the FL-70s used to identify each vessel. The large image now somewhere behind us was certainly the Klingon colony transport, lightly armed but a significant threat if she made any kind of suicide run. Off to the side, where their parallel course had taken them, the three smaller images probably represented the smallest ships of the pirate convoy: the former Orion yacht, the captured Vulcan science probe, and the retrofitted Romulan patrolship. Of the three, only the patrolship was much of an offensive threat. Still out in front of us, close to the Klingon border, the final two images must be the Rochester-class cruiser and the unknown alien battleship. With their heavier armor and powerful phaser banks, they were the most threatening part of the little fleet.

"Walroth," I said without turning away from the screen. "How long will it take those ships to reach the coordinates of our resupply team's life-pod?"

He punched the request into his board and visibly stiffened at the answer. "Under one minute for most of them, sir. The Klingon transport would take longer."

"And our current ETA for the life-pod?"

Lieutenant Keith answered before he could. "One minute and forty-three seconds, sir. Even at maximum deceleration, we're not going to beat them to it."

"Then take us to the outside edge of transporter range. I don't want that pod getting caught in the cross fire if a battle starts." I vaulted out of my chair and crossed to the weapons desk. "Orsini, those ships are probably going to wait for us to drop our shields and start beaming our crewmen aboard before they attack. As soon as we stop, I want you to cut power to our shields—"

"*Cut* power, sir?" he repeated, looking puzzled.

"Yes, Lieutenant. We want to look unshielded and defenseless just long enough to lure them toward *us.* When they're all within firing range, raise shields and counterattack."

My security officer slanted me an inquiring glance. "Won't that still put the life-pod on the edge of a battle, sir?"

"Yes." I was beginning to regret having left our two strongest shuttlecraft to escort the remaining FL-70s to Elaphe Vulpina. One could easily have defended the life-pod from attack while the other tractored it out of danger. Instead, I was forced to rely on split-second timing and luck, that most fickle of allies in outer space.

"Sulu to main transporter room," I said into my console's communicator panel, and waited for the response of Transporter Chief Renyck. "Lock on to the five life-forms in that Klingon life-pod and prepare to beam them out on my command. If the pod gets hit by a stray phaser shot, we're going to lower shields and beam the crew aboard. If we've disabled the strongest attack ships by then, we can probably endure a few minutes of unshielded phaser fire—"

"Nearing life-pod coordinates, Captain," Walroth interrupted. Hearing Commander Rand cut off a rear admiral seemed to have given him a little more confidence in his own ability to issue reports. "We've established a stationary position at a distance of approximately twenty-five thousand kilometers."

"Shields down," I told my security chief, and heard the almost subliminal whisper of the power generators fade. "Schulman, can we get an image of that life-pod now?"

"I'll put it on-screen," she said, and a magnified image of a tiny Klingon life-pod floated through the glowing diagram of alien ambush still covering the screen. The flimsy hull of plastic and raw duranium barely reflected the deep space star-glow, and not a sign of light leaked from its single porthole. It didn't look like it could survive too much more exposure to vacuum, much less a glancing phaser blast. Doubts about my strategy started to creep into the confidence with which I'd begun this encounter.

At the communications station, Rand cleared her throat. "Sir, I'm getting another message from Ensign McClain. He says they can see the *Excelsior* from their porthole, and want to know why we're not beaming them aboard."

I scowled, knowing there was no way I could send a secure message back on that Klingon frequency. "Tell him we're dropping shields and will be beaming them over soon. With any luck, overhearing that exchange will kick our friends out there into motion."

But five long minutes crawled by and the glowing symbols on the viewscreen made no attempt to converge on my unprotected ship. More doubts began to cloud my conviction that I knew what the pirates were up to. Could they be waiting out there for some other reason? Perhaps this close to the edge of the Neutral Zone, they were hoping the life-pod's distress call would draw in some Klingon border guards and precipitate a military confrontation they could then take advantage of. But that strategy implied Pavel Chekov had made the destruction of the *Excelsior* part of his deal with the "snakes," and I knew that was the last thing my executive officer would ever do.

"Captain, we've received the information packet from Starfleet on the *Enterprise*'s previous encounter with these aliens," my science officer said, in what was obviously an attempt to fill the silence. "I've scanned over it, and there doesn't seem to be very much there. It mentions the same kind of translation problems we've noticed in their speech, and it refers to them as interstellar pirates, but there's not even a consensus about what they're called. Sometimes they're referred to as the Anjiri and other times as the Nykkus."

I scrubbed a hand across my cheeks and chin, amazed I didn't feel beads of sweat popping out as the impasse lengthened. "That's because there were actually two species working together in the group we rescued back then, Lieutenant," I said absently. "I remember thinking at the time that they looked like congener species—"

Neither of whom had evinced very much respect for the life of the other. I felt my frown deepen as I recalled the cavalier way both those sauroid species seemed unable to value others' lives. Now that I had time to think, I also remembered what had bothered me about Ensign McClain's story. It wasn't the fact that Chekov had cut a deal to save his crewmen from torture—that part rang utterly true. But why had the Anjiri and Nykkus, whose regard for each other's lives was minimal to say the least, needed to wait until they had a *spare* life-pod available for the hostages to be freed in? Surely the Vulcan science probe had life-pods large enough to carry five humans, and if they didn't the Orion yacht certainly would have. Just as surely, neither the Anjiri nor the Nykkus would have worried about saving all those life-pods for each other. So why did they wait for several hours after Chekov convinced them to turn away from Elaphe Vulpina before they released the hostages in a Klingon pod several sizes larger than it needed to be?

I didn't like any of the reasons I could think of.

"Lieutenant Orsini, I want a thorough security scan of that life-pod," I said crisply. "Life-forms, systems integrity, possible explosive devices—"

"You think the *life-pod* is the Trojan horse?" demanded Tim Henry.

"I think there's some good reason we're being watched and not attacked," I said somberly. "And if there aren't any Klingons on the way, I suspect they've planted a surprise for us along with the crew. They seem to be awfully fond of trying to sabotage their victims before they come in for the kill. If they're really smart, they didn't even let the hostages realize anything was wrong."

"We're out of range of my weapons sensors, sir," Orsini said. "If we could get a few thousand kilometers closer—"

I eyed the hovering threat that ringed us on the viewscreen, and shook my head. "That might be exactly the move they're waiting for, Lieutenant. Schulman, what can you get on the long-range instruments?"

"Life-forms all read human, sir, and there are only five of them," my science officer said promptly. "But I am picking up an unusual power drain from the pod's impulse engines. Their fuel cells seem to be functioning normally, but all the power is getting siphoned off before it reaches the cabin."

"That's why it looks so dark?"

"Yes, sir."

"Captain!" At the helm, Heather Keith stared up at the viewscreen. "One of those ships out there is moving!"

I sat up straighter, noticing the slight divergence of one of the three smaller glows from the others. "Projected course," I said sharply, and heard the tap of orders input to both Schulman and Walroth's stations. Instants later, twin white lines appeared on the viewscreen, lancing out from that moving ship directly toward the drifting Klingon life-pod.

"Pirate ship will enter firing range in twenty seconds," said my security chief. "Orders, Captain?"

I paused, feeling nearly overwhelmed by mounting doubts and indecision. "Hold your fire," I said, just before the twenty-second deadline passed. "Prepare to raise shields and counterattack if she changes course to come at us. If she doesn't, scan for weapons activity or subspace transmissions. I want to know if they're planning to attack the life-pod or rendezvous—"

"Captain." The tangible calm of Rand's voice made me realize how much tension was vibrating in all the others, including my own. "I'm picking up a transmission from the approaching ship to the rest of the convoy, on the same subspace frequency they used before they attacked Deep Space Three. But this time our universal translator can barely make sense of it—" She broke off and keyed a tab on her communications console. The familiar deep growl that emerged made the hair on my forearms rise in apprehension.

"Wait explode escort wait explode escort . . ."

"It must be another sabotage attempt," I said, but the confirmation of my suspicions about the Klingon life-pod didn't make me feel any better about losing the innocent crewmen who were stranded there. "Do we have scan results on the approaching ship yet?"

"Fifteen life-forms aboard, of a type unrecognizable to the sensors," Schulman said. "I assume they're either Nykkus or Anjiri. Power flows from impulse engines—"

"Phaser banks are charging, sir," Orsini broke in on her unceremoniously. "They'll be within firing range of the life-pod in thirty seconds."

I tapped the button that made my communication console reestablish its most recent connection. "Transporter room, get those hostages out of there!"

"Aye, Captain," said my transporter chief's competent voice. "Transporter beam is locked and engaged. We have partial recovery—"

Rand swung around from the communications station, and for the first time that I could remember since our voyage began, her voice actually sounded strained. "Captain, I'm receiving a transmission from the Klingon life-pod. It sounds like Ensign McClain—"

I clamped my jaw shut on the urge to say something time-consuming and useless like *What?* or *That's impossible!* "Main screen," I said between my teeth. I didn't wait to hear what Ensign McClain had to say—one glance at his bruised and frantic face, and I smacked a hand back on my communicator controls.

"Transporter room, abort transport!"

"Captain Sulu!" McClain's voice was no longer toneless, but the note of terror I heard in it wasn't much better. "You beamed over five snakes instead of us! They were in stasis tubes programmed to snag the transporter beam—"

I pressed the reconnect button again, this time even harder than before, as if that could somehow get me through to my endangered transporter chief. "Renyck, abort transport! Can you hear me?"

"It's too late," Schulman said. "The ship's logs show that transport was completed ten seconds ago."

That made Renyck's lack of response ominous rather than frustrating. I swung around toward Orsini. "Get security—"

"Captain, the pirate ship is firing at the life-pod!" He had his hands poised over his weapons array, his face lifted to watch the brilliant flare of phasers across the viewscreen. "Orders?"

I gritted my teeth again, this time on an impulse to curse this entire chain of insanely impossible events. "Hold your fire until we have those hostages out! Helm, take us on an intercept course between the pirate ship and the pod. Try to draw their attack back toward us." The glowing sensor-pattern of ambush disappeared into a stomach-churning swoop of stars and a quiver of phaser beams as Keith launched us into the middle of that strafing run. I could feel the ship shake as one blast caught us amidship, and a few seconds later a damage alarm began to sound at the engineering desk. "Rand, contact the auxiliary transporter room and get those hostages beamed out of there, *fast.* We'll be unshielded and open to attack until we get them."

They may have responded to my orders with shouted "aye-ayes" or they may have carried them out in silence for all I knew. With the external crisis taken care of, my attention immediately snapped back to the crisis on my own ship. "Security alert, all decks. We have hostile intruders on deck five, repeat—"

"Not deck five, sir," Schulman said grimly. "There was another transport forty-five seconds after the first, but this one was intraship." Transport at such close range was always dangerous, but given the *Excelsior*'s brand-new and carefully calibrated transporter pads, I knew we couldn't depend on finding our intruders splattered across a bulkhead. "Four life-forms were transported that time. One of them must have stayed behind to make sure the transporter chief didn't send them back to where they came from—"

"Where *did* they go?" I demanded. On the viewscreen, radiance scythed and lanced its way across the nearby sky, laying down a lattice of destruction for our helm to dodge through. But the *Excelsior*'s workhorse bulk wasn't exactly built for evasiveness. I saw Lieutenant Keith wince as the ship shuddered with impact again, more strongly this time.

Schulman glanced over her shoulder, a surprising clench of anxiety on her normally composed face. "According to my records, sir, the second transport was to the ship's main shuttle bay."

"Where the FL-70s are." I knew I was the one who said that, although I barely recognized that grating voice as my own. I could hear the ominous silence that followed and wondered if my officers felt as betrayed as I did by the fact that all the shakedown cruises in the world could not prepare us to meet this crisis. "Orsini, beam down to the shuttle bay and secure those Falcons. If the pirates capture even one of them, they'll be able to gut the whole ship." He vanished a step away from his security console as Schulman punched the emergency order into the computer. Without a word, Scott Walroth left navigations and took his place at the weapons panel. "Henry, can you throw a stronger version of the phaser dampening field across that shuttle bay?"

"No, sir. It's too broad to span without internal amplifiers."

"Then beam some in there," I said sharply. "If the Falcons can't fire their phasers, it'll take a suicide run to damage us from the inside." A phaser blast glanced off our bridge carapace, making the ablative armor scream in a protest I hadn't heard since the last explosive decompression I'd survived. I remembered that we still weren't shielded. "Walroth, target phasers on that ship! Rand, did we manage to get the hostages out of the life-pod yet?"

"Yes, sir."

"Then I want full power returned to shields—"

"No, sir!" Henry's words were as gruff as ever, but the unusually deep pitch of his voice caught my entire attention. "Our shields were designed to ward off phaser fire from *outside.* If any of those FL-70s fire at them from the inside while they're in place, they'll set up a runaway internal resonance through the entire node-generating network. It'll blow the ship apart within minutes."

I grimaced, feeling the shudder of another glancing phaser blast. This one slanted past one of our warp nacelles, then caught the drifting Klingon life-pod in a brilliant embrace. The little pod promptly blew itself to bits in an explosive decompression whose shrapnel slammed against the *Excelsior*'s unguarded hull. I winced and hit my communicator panel.

"Orsini!" I was probably yelling louder than I needed to, but by then I didn't care. "Are those Falcons secured yet?"

"Sir . . ." His strained voice barely emerged from the noise of what sounded like a hundred cascading waterfalls. I didn't need to hear any more of my security chief's response than that. I recognized the sound of several impulse engines throbbing in a confined space, and felt my gut twist in painful dismay.

"Captain Sulu." Walroth turned from the weapons desk, his smooth face suddenly looking older than its years. He knew what that sound meant, just as did the rest of the bridge crew. We weren't going to be able to put up our shields to defend ourselves, and we weren't going to be able to stop the Falcons from blasting their way through the *Excelsior*'s undersized shuttle bay doors. "The other members of the pirate fleet are all converging on us now. Orders?"

I took a deep breath, bitter with the smell of smoke from overloaded circuits and the knowledge of my own failure. "Return fire, Ensign. Take out as many of them as you can." In the time I had left before my brand-new ship was reduced to a ruined hulk, the least I could do was make these unknown aliens pay a steep price for what they had done. "Keith and Henry, prepare for imminent hull breaches in sectors six, seven, and eight. Schulman, track each of those Falcons. The minute they're out of the cargo bay, I want our shields back in place." That was assuming the shields still worked by then, and that the pirates weren't smart enough to remain inside and blast the *Excelsior* into oblivion.

I turned toward Rand last, barely able to make my throat muscles spit out the last set of commands I had to issue. "Order all nonessential crew to begin evacuation procedures. Alert essential crew that total ship destruction is possible within the next few minutes. And send Starfleet—" I had to pause to swallow something that tasted like bile. "Send Starfleet an emergency distress call along with a complete copy of our ship's log."

I paused, wishing I were done there, but the most unpleasant task still remained. Bad enough that I had made a wreck of my very first mission and turned my ship into a blackened and possibly lifeless hulk. Even worse, though, was the fact that I had to send the news of that disaster back to the one man who probably could have avoided it, if he'd been the captain here. But I had no choice—for the safety of my crew and for the Federation, I had to let go of my last shreds of personal pride. "And Rand, I want you to send the same message directly to Captain Kirk on the *Enterprise*."

After that, I sat back in my captain's chair, scowling out at the glowing viewscreen and preparing to direct the last few evasive maneuvers and phaser blasts we could get in before the hammering I could already feel in the *Excelsior*'s gut spread out to destroy all her essential systems. For the sake of my crew, I had to pray that the *Enterprise* was close enough by now to come to our rescue. For myself, however, James Tiberius Kirk was the last man in the galaxy I wanted to see.

Nine

KIRK

"Cosa pensa!" LIEUTENANT COMMANDER GIOTTO CROWDED BETWEEN THE pilot and copilot's seats, staring out the shuttle's front window like a kid staring into an adult establishment he'd never be allowed to enter. "This place looks as bad as the hull of my grandpap's fishing boat."

I eased back on the throttle for what felt like the hundredth time since leaving the *Enterprise,* irrationally afraid of bumping into something. "Your grandfather should have cleaned his ship more often."

Giotto's snort was as crass as it was eloquent. "Yeah—so should the Anjiri."

I couldn't argue with him there. If the asteroid ahead of us had been an ocean liner, the barnacling on her hull would have kept her from leaving port at all. Except these barnacles were the size of shuttles, the size of houses, the size of ships. Passenger transports had been sunk into the rock's upper layers right alongside ore carriers; private skiffs were welded nose-to-nose with garbage scows. The original dimensions of the planetoid were impossible to determine. Individual life-pods distorted its silhouette like warts on a frog, and what could only be disconnected cargo trunks formed an uneven seam around its middle like a poorly stitched-up scar. I found myself counting the number of individual ship designs represented in this coagulated flotsam, but quit when I reached the mid-twenties.

"Are any of those Federation ships?" Uhura asked.

I'd brought her along for the same reason I'd left Sulu back on board the *Enterprise*—I wanted the best I had in the places where I could use them most. Given the universal translator's problems with the Anjiri language, I was hoping Uhura and her improved equipment would let us avoid any fatal misunderstandings once we were in front of whoever had levied this summons. Meanwhile, if this little trip to the Anjiri principal's office didn't go well, I wanted a pilot at the helm who could thread the *Enterprise* between these rocks and back to open space at record speeds. Sulu was my best bet for that, which left only me to pilot the shuttle.

I split my attention between the shuttle's controls and the couple of likely Federation candidates in the junkyard now filling our view. "I don't think so," I answered Uhura at last. Then, because it seemed more honest than any flat statement about the Anjiri's architecture, "At least, I don't see any Federation ships among what's there."

"We're not exactly deep in Federation space here." Giotto all but braced his elbows on the control console to maintain his view out the window between us. His dark eyes scanned along behind mine. "With all the troubles we've been having with your translators, Lieutenant, I'm almost sure these Anjiri have never run across us before."

I was more than just almost sure—I would have bet my command on it. Their twisted mistranslations and inappropriately self-important behavior would have fueled too many good stories for a captain to keep quiet about them, and their own lack of knowledge about our equipment and ways was too thorough to be feigned. As if that weren't enough, these asteroid-bound Anjiri had repeatedly insisted we come to them in a ship—no mention of beaming. No mention, even, of *not* beaming. No indication at all that they even realized such a thing was possible. I was hoping we could keep it that way, at least for a little while. Even though their tractor beam generators were out of our phaser range, the coordinates they'd given us for this rendezvous were well within the range of our transporter. As long as the Anjiri didn't know that, it increased my chances of snatching my people out of there when *I* decided we were ready to leave, and not just when the Anjiri decided they were ready to let us go.

As if alerted by my musings about them, the female Anjiri who'd radioed us before—or at least the same translated voice—announced grimly, "Near to our landing specifications you are. Speed reduce you shall, docking undergo."

I looked up, past Giotto's shoulder, and focused on a set of rusty bay doors just as the docking lights circling it blinked into life one at a time. "And there she blows . . ."

The sleeve that housed the doors was half sunken in the asteroid's surface, not even attached to a recognizable ship anymore. I could glimpse metal plating along the outer edges, but couldn't tell if it continued on to become part of some buried transport or had been cut free of the bigger structure for mounting here. All I knew for sure was that the doors began their slow sideways rumble much later than I would have liked. I down-throttled again, waiting for the gap between the doors to widen enough to admit us.

It felt like an optical illusion—movement so gradual as to seem like no movement at all, then a sudden increase in the distance, then no movement again for an achingly long time. I think I noticed the chains about the same time my heart started racing with the realization that we were moving too fast and the doors were moving far too slow.

"Oh . . ." Giotto's exclamation sounded more like a soft moan, "Oh, I don't like this, sir."

I couldn't see exactly how the chains were being taken up inside the doors' mechanism, but the stop-start nature of the movement hinted at living creatures, not machines, struggling to haul the huge bay open. The gigantic bolts on the exterior of the doors might have been welded in place, or even simply screwed forcibly into the metal, although both options assumed the incongruity of a Nykkus inside an environmental suit. I couldn't believe the Anjiri had risked themselves for such a task. The chains on either side passed through what might have been natural holes in the rock, terminating somewhere out of sight in what could only have been a hundred Nykkus engaged in the galaxy's largest tug-o'-war. "Not comfortable with technology" didn't even begin to describe this.

"Captain, this is bad," Giotto insisted, in case I hadn't heard him the first time.

"Observation noted, Mr. Giotto." Again easing back on the throttle, again feeling strangely as though nothing I did at the controls was having enough effect on the shuttle's velocity. "Now you and your team go strap in. That's an order."

He proved the worth of his training by ducking back beyond my range of sight with nothing more than a crisp, "Aye, sir." Then I heard him in the passenger compartment, ordering his security squad into their seats with no trace of resentment in his voice. He was a good officer, never misjudging when to speak his own mind and when to just obey.

I wish I could claim my own judgment was as good. About all I can say in my defense is that I'd had the same minimalist pilot training as every other Starfleet commander—just enough to think I can pilot my own shuttles into danger, but not enough to reliably get them out of it again.

Uhura stirred uneasily in the copilot's seat beside me. "Captain . . ."

She had *not* had pilot training, which was why I'd inactivated the console in front of her. This, however, didn't mean she couldn't tell a bad approach when it was happening right in front of her.

"Captain . . . !"

"Lieutenant—" I gritted my teeth and killed the shuttle's engines completely. "Please, don't sideseat drive . . ."

It was already too late, of course. I'd brought us in too close to bleed off any more momentum before impact, and the view through the doors had grown just wide enough to reveal that the entire bay was much shallower than I'd expected. Not a bay at all, as it turned out, just a pair of stolen doors mounted over an uneven hole. If I made it through the narrow gap they called an entrance, I didn't see how I was going to keep us from crumpling *Galileo*'s nose against the back wall.

Inspiration is nine-tenths desperation. I didn't so much plan to flip us ninety degrees starboard as I suddenly found us that way while trying to squeeze past the slow doors. Our drive nacelles scraped metal so long and hard that the whole ship rumbled. My own stomach crawling up my throat, I heard Uhura gasp, and saw her hands shoot down to grab the edges of her seat. I hoped Giotto had succeeded in getting his people strapped down in back. Snapping us upright as swiftly as I dared, I let the rough bottom of the bay drag on us until I could almost feel the friction heat eating its way through our hull. When the nose bumped the rear wall, though, our momentum was down to only a few meters per second. It sounded more like a love tap than the shaking we'd just been through.

I did a quick check of the boards to make sure no breach alarms were flashing, then tried to disguise my own pounding heart by showing Uhura a charming smile. "Any landing you can walk away from . . ."

The shaky expression on her face was probably meant to be a smile, too, although she looked neither amused nor reassured.

"I don't think we need to mention the details of this to Mr. Spock," I continued, prompting her with a small nod. I waited for her halting echo of the gesture, then reached across in front of her to open our channel to the ship. "*Galileo* to *Enterprise.* We're in."

"*Enterprise,* Spock here." As though somebody else might have answered and I wouldn't have known who it was. "Landing noted, Captain. I shall place Mr. Scott on standby for shuttle chassis repairs when you return." I knew he couldn't see the color that flushed into my cheeks, but it annoyed me that Uhura would. "Might I suggest a lower velocity approach on our own shuttle bay?"

The lieutenant bent over her pile of translation gear, a stifled giggle bringing the warmth back into her face.

"Thank you, Mr. Spock. I'll keep that in mind." Then, in the hopes of avoiding further embarrassment, I directed him toward business. "Do you have a lock on our transponders?"

Spock proved willing as always to follow my lead. "Affirmative. Sensors indicate no evidence the Anjiri are capable of generating an energy shield which might interfere with either reception or transportation."

"Good." But I tried not to worry about how deep we could go beneath this planetoid's heavy metal cladding before it amounted to the same thing. "One word of warning from any one of us, and you pull us all out."

"We shall be standing by."

"I'm counting on it. Kirk out."

I couldn't hear those big slow doors bang shut on the vacuum, but the whole stone bay shuddered with their impact. Unbelting, I joined Giotto and his team in the rear, peering out the shuttle's side windows while the security squad checked their weapons and pulled themselves together. Nobody waited for us in the bay, and the pinging and moaning of slowly building outside pressure made me wonder how long it would take before anyone could safely stand in that cramped chamber. We weren't entirely alone, though; the walls all around us were filled with cloudy windows. And every one of those windows was crowded with row upon row of staring Nykkus.

I waited for one of the inside doors to slide open, and even then made no move to open our own hatch until I glimpsed a few rounded Anjiri heads protruding above the emerging Nykkus. If they'd sent a group of Nykkus all alone, I wouldn't have trusted the atmosphere was something any of us could survive—after all, Anjiri threw Nykkus out airlocks when they became inconvenient. Who knew what they did with meddling starship captains? I was trusting they wouldn't sacrifice members of their own elite class for the sake of a crude trap.

Poising my hand above the door controls, I waved for Giotto and the security team's attention. "Stay here, and keep the hatch closed. I don't want to find out we've been welded into the scenery when I get back."

Giotto nodded brusquely. "Anybody tries that, they go through us." He took one polite step backward to leave Uhura a place at my side. "We'll be here, sir," he promised. "Just don't keep us waiting."

I didn't intend to.

The air in the bay felt thin, and it carried just enough chill to sting my nose and make my breath feather steam in front of my face. The Anjiri and Nykkus, I noticed, either didn't breathe or didn't steam when they did so. I'd assumed when we first met them that their quick metabolisms meant they couldn't be true ectotherms. Now I wondered, and wondered as well how they kept moving when the temperature was so low. Perhaps their armor had built-in thermal-circuits to keep them warm.

Three of the Anjiri stepped forward as a unit. They didn't even need to elbow the Nykkus aside—the guards simply parted for them as though knowing all along what was expected. "My image, you will follow." The voice offered by Uhura's translator was male, and I couldn't tell which of the three Anjiri had spoken. "The Egg Bringers to you will speak."

They all turned away just as abruptly, striding back for the door.

Glancing aside at Uhura, I found her frowning over her translator, playing with the readings and giving no sign she realized our hosts were walking away. I caught her elbow and hurried her along beside me. I didn't want to find out what would happen if we ended up left in the bay all alone.

Once we'd been ushered into the only slightly warmer hallway, I leaned down to ask her quietly, "Egg Bringers?"

Still frowning, she tapped through several screens of data. I don't know how she kept from stumbling along the rough-hewn floor. "The concept's confusing—the translator is offering other possible meanings. 'Mentor/teacher,' 'wise one,' 'life bearer,' 'mate.' " She glanced up from her readouts, looking almost embarrassed to suggest, "Sir, I think they mean females."

The dark, winding interior of this cold rock's tunnels didn't look significantly different than the surface. Stone-carved walls gave way to scarred stretches of steel, various hatches and doors and even partial ship's hallways jerry-rigged one into the next like a huge three-dimensional crazy quilt. I felt surrounded, smothered, weighed down by this metal-and-mineral termite mound. I didn't want to be part of this—I didn't want my ship to end up as part of this. With a start, I realized that my biggest fear all along was that the Anjiri had only brought me here as a diversion, that their real goal was the *Enterprise*. How to explain to Starfleet that your first command was dismantled and turned into part of some floating alien apartment complex? How to reconcile that horrible prospect within yourself?

I shook the idea off. It wasn't going to happen. Even before I left the ship, Spock had already figured out how to overload at least two of the Anjiri tractor beam generators using our own defensive screens and a fatal feedback cascade. I didn't like thinking about Anjiri and Nykkus civilians caught in the explosions that kind of tactic would cause, but I liked thinking about the *Enterprise* in pieces and my crew exposed to vacuum even less. Spock had his orders. If I couldn't work things out with the Anjiri, he was to make sure the ship and crew got free, no matter what the cost.

I don't like to lose.

Uhura drifted ahead of me, unconsciously placing herself as close as possible to the sibilant voices of the Anjiri who led us. She reminded me a little of a Vulcan just then, so intent on her tricorder and its cascade of linguistic codes that it didn't seem to occur to her that Anjiri might not appreciate tailgating any more than starship captains appreciated piloting advice. I realized our escort was slowing as the tunnel widened into an anomalously bright and smooth-sided room, and I had just reached out to pull Uhura back to my side when the trio of Anjiri spun on her, snapping at the air.

"What weapon?" they rattled, flashing their claws at the device. They'd dissolved into a single stalking cacophony, but still only one voice spiraled out from Uhura's small speaker. "What weapon this is?"

My communications officer looked up, her face registering startled hurt at their suggestion. "Why, it's not a weapon." She turned the tricorder carefully, so as not to tear loose any of its eccentric connections. "It's a translation device. See the figure?" As it metamorphosed into an Anjiri simulacrum, her words seemed friendly and warm. "It turns my words into language you can understand, and turns your words into my language."

Alarm spiked through me as the Anjiri rushed to cluster around her. But the Nykkus fell back, almost as though unwilling to listen in on their masters' translated thoughts, and I imagined I recognized the childlike tilt of utter fascination in the Anjiri's hairless heads. When Uhura shuffled around to stand shoulder-to-shoulder with two of them, lifting the translator so they could see, I couldn't help but smile.

I think that's when I realized what a treasure I had standing before me. In an outfit like Starfleet, competence is easy to come by; brilliance is only slightly harder. More valuable than either, though, is the ability to transcend species and transfix creatures you have never even met before. In a communications officer, that skill becomes priceless. It's what elevates a comm officer's job beyond mere talking and makes him or her a vital member of the crew. I knew she belonged on a starship's bridge, and felt an instant of shame that I hadn't seen fit to place her there sooner.

Then a hoarse, breathy rumble swept over us with almost physical force. I jerked around, expecting the frigid rush of escaping air through a breached hull, or, at the very least, a weakened seal on one of the many stolen airlocks we'd passed for the last hundred meters. Instead, I was met with a wave of confused movement as the Nykkus on all sides dropped as though pole-axed, and the Anjiri around Uhura shrieked before flinging themselves prostrate to the floor. When I saw what had swept into the alcove behind me, I had an irrational moment when I considered the wisdom of joining them.

What could only have been the threatened females ducked through the doorway one right after the other, bursting upright as though furious with the restrictive hallways they escaped. They were startlingly similar to the Anjiri males, and because of that, somehow more frightening. Bigger and sleeker, their heads sculpted into the suggestion of an elegant crest and their eyes swirling with colors I can't even begin to describe, there was a heat to them, a presence or a smell. I was suddenly acutely aware of how much taller than me they all stood, how much more quickly their rangy muscles could move. With no defining sexual characteristic but their size, they seemed strangely more male than the males; any possibility of external variation in their structure was hidden by the close-fitting armor wrapped around their gracile frames. It was some sort of environmental suit, I decided. Something that kept them warmer, primed, eternally faster than I had any hope of being. My instincts wanted to give way before them, offer them apologies for things I'd never done. So instead, I got angry. The fact that their impact on me was clearly something as natural to them as breathing didn't make me feel any better about it. It just made me rail against my own apparent frailties, and promise to prove that I was better than that.

"Such clucking cease you will." A strange chill laced the females' translated words. They swept in so close against each other that they might have been one big creature. Behind them, inching along the floor like the train of a living gown, Vissith and his Anjiri crew couldn't have looked more obsequious if they'd had hair to pull and clothes to rend. What had to have been the group of Nykkus we'd originally rescued with them slithered silently along in their wake. I realized with an unexpected jolt of discomfort just how indistinguishable the individual Nykkus were, and wondered if that was why the Anjiri viewed them as such interchangeable cogs.

"Robbers of our vessel these things be?" The largest of the females hissed the question back toward Vissith, her bright eyes glittering for all that she never truly deigned to look at him. The rest of them glared unblinkingly at me. They all bobbed and danced as though carrying on some inner conversation. I got the impression all of their gestures impacted the one speaker's meaning, but decided this wouldn't be the best time to initiate that conversation with Uhura. "Stealers of the ship which to your weakling fangs we granted?"

I'm a loyal mammal—if I'd had hackles, I'd have raised them. "We didn't 'take' anything," I objected. I tried hard to keep my voice civil, but guessed from the sharp glance Uhura cast my way that I wasn't entirely successful. The consummate professional, though, she kept her translation device aimed at the cluster of females, even though only half of them watched what it had to say. "We found your people stranded on a ship so badly damaged that I was under the impression we *rescued* them." I scowled down at Vissith, taking what satisfaction I could in the way he nearly wormed himself through the stone flooring. "We *offered*—very generously, I believed—to return them home."

The females rounded on Vissith like a pack of lions. One of them planted a taloned foot in the middle of his back, and I thought for a moment they would shred him. "And to *here* you bring them did?" The voice from Uhura's translator sounded so calm, so untroubled. I found myself wishing the Anjiri had tails, so I would have some way to gauge the subtlety of their moods beyond just what I imagined I could read in their expressionless faces. I didn't like having to wait until they struck at something. "To these dens and nurseries lead them you did?"

"No!" His translated voice equally dispassionate, Vissith's body language, at least, was clear even to me. Splayed hands crept up to cover his head, and he turned one eye toward the floor as though he could barely stand to watch the females circling. "Fooled them did we! Clever we were, so as to prideful make you—to a place of fine ships take us did we make them. A ship new, clean did we abscond!"

The threatening foot shifted, and a bright rake of purple-gray blood blossomed on the male's exposed back. "Tiny what you have brought home is."

"Inside you must yet see," Vissith insisted. If he felt any pain, he didn't display enough in either his speaking or his movement to change the timbre of the translation. "Inside this ship very fine is."

"Yet these creatures a huge ship behind you do trail." They all looked at me then, and I made myself meet their combined gaze with equal fierceness. "Careless."

Vissith squirmed beneath the shelter of his own hands. "Many fine things from that ship did we salvage." He made no coordinated movement that I could recognize, but some communication obviously passed through the males groveling behind him. It ran aground among the silent Nykkus. A knot of them slithered forward without ever really standing, and produced double handfuls of all-too-familiar trinkets. It was like magic—I don't know where on their bodies they could have been hiding it all. Perhaps inside the seams of their body armor. Perhaps inside alien orifices I didn't want to know any more about. Either way, it was an astonishing volume of trinkets, things Scott hadn't even reported yet as missing. Knobs and buttons, probably from the transporter room, computer chips, decorative trim, and a few pieces of McCoy's medical equipment. There were even two communicators and a phaser jumbled into the mix. I didn't know whether to be horrified or amused.

I didn't make a move to interfere when the females spread themselves to each pick up their own piece of the loot. "They took useless things," I announced, trying to keep an eye on everything as they began to pass them around. "Games and trinkets. And the ship they brought here was stolen. It belongs to someone else."

Three of them shrugged, then squatted to examine the phaser. "To us belongs it now."

"None of this belongs to you." I wanted to know where in hell the Nykkus had picked up that weapon. Its presence in the pile bothered me more than everything else combined. "You can't simply take things."

The biggest of the females tipped her head toward me. "Interrogative."

I dared a glance at Uhura. She looked at me, then back down at her translation equipment. "I think she means, 'Why not?' "

I felt like someone had elbowed me in the stomach. How do you explain human morality to an alien?

"Where we come from," I said, rather slowly, "we have respect for the other peoples we live with. We feel that stealing things from others is disrespectful."

It took a long moment for the translator to make something of that. At least half the females lost interest in the jittering simulacrum before the audible sounds of my speech had finished translating. "Needed things are," the larger female informed me as she turned a communicator over in her hand and watched the golden lid drop open. "Needed is needed. Our eggs quickly mature do, we more room soon require. What other should do we? Our children to crowd and die we must allow?"

I didn't have an answer for that.

"Can't you make your own living spaces?" Uhura finally spoke up. She looked impossibly tiny and fragile, wedged in among those powerfully muscled bodies. "You have plenty of room here. You could tunnel—"

When two of the females slashed their hands through the air near her, I was terrified they meant to strike at her. But Uhura calmly held her ground, so I gritted my teeth and refrained from leaping to her rescue. "Tunnel? No. When ships there are all about for our use lying? Tunneling for rodents is."

That was the second time I'd been called a rodent in a single day. "These ships aren't just lying about," I tried to explain. "They belong to someone—maybe someone a lot bigger and more powerful than yourselves." I reached out to scoop the communicator out of her hands. She hissed at me, but didn't resist. "When you go around taking things that don't belong to you, you run the risk that the actual owners are going to come take their ships and equipment back."

The dorsal ridge only hinted at on the Anjiri males lifted into a stubby crest of anger on the females. "A threat from yourselves this is?"

Even as she asked it, the stinging tingle of an ultra-close transporter beam chased itself all through my hands. I could almost smell the ionization of the air molecules as the communicator in my grip shimmered and evaporated into nothing.

No one said anything for an elongated moment. Then I heard myself announce, as if I'd known all along what I'd intended to say, "Yes, that's a threat."

The second communicator sparkled away in the wake of the first, with the phaser not far behind. The females rattled with alarm, dropping whatever else they held and leaping together in a protective circle

"Trickery! Foolery!" Their leader tore through the Nykkus closest to her like a whirlwind through paper. I knew the guards were dead even before their bodies spun to the floor, but I hadn't a hope of interfering with that terrifying speed. I thought for sure Vissith and his companion males were next, but instead the females only crouched menacingly atop them, howling. "Items of false death, these be! Items to destroy themselves made these be!" One of them I couldn't see clearly struck a male who was already on the ground. "Cold-born! Foolish!"

"No! No!" I'd never heard the Anjiri make such shrill noises before. Vissith writhed and twitched in submission as he pleaded with them. "Their pod this trickery reaps!" he squealed. "Things to dissolve and remake elsewhere they have! Stole my pod from our ship in this way they did! Seen it we have. Felt it also we have."

Sparkles rang into thin air from random places on the floor, but I couldn't tell what had dematerialized.

"He's telling you the truth." I recaptured the females' attention, at least half in the hopes of preventing any further bloodshed. "We can take back every item you stole from us by making it vanish here and reappear on board our vessel. We could take anything else we wanted the same way."

They'd pulled into an elongated formation, the largest female still boldly facing me while her sisters arrayed themselves by descending size behind her. "Disrupt our breathing bubbles would you?" Only one of them was speaking now. "Vanquish air and heat from our hatchlings would you?"

"I *could.*" I paused for effect, letting the transporter's whine underscore my silence. "But I won't." That announcement seemed to upset them even more than the prospect of my potentially beaming away sections of their hull. The rearmost females lowered themselves halfway to the floor, mouths agape. Ah, culture shock. "My people are peaceful. We have no intention of harming you or your hatchlings. All we ask in return is that you give us the same courtesy. Don't abscond with our starships. Don't steal our devices."

The females fell very still. "Conjunction of query."

This time I didn't have to look toward Uhura for the translation. " 'Or'?" my communications officer suggested. "As in, 'Or else you'll do what?' "

I didn't want to make threats. Peaceful people didn't make threats to their less sophisticated neighbors, especially threats they honestly had no intention of keeping. Once you've promised something dire, you'd better be prepared to deliver the first time they decide to test your resolve, otherwise it's as good as making no threats at all. And that didn't get us anywhere.

"You should be more concerned about what races less peaceful than mine could do," I said at last. "There are many powerful peoples out there who wouldn't hesitate to destroy your colonies and expose your hatchlings to vacuum." I was thinking about the Klingons when I said it, but even the Orions had been known to unleash some nasty vendettas on trading partners gone astray. "You could never defend yourselves against them, and even my people wouldn't be able to help you."

"Always dangers have there been." She threw a snarl toward the males, but they couldn't have cowered more deeply if their lives depended on it. Which they probably did. "Cold-born males by these dangers culled should be. Fool-born males to steal and never fight commanded have been. Things of use to their homes and pods they must bring. Far from pleasantness of society until hours of breeding to keep them we prefer."

"Instead of stealing," Uhura said gently, "have you considered establishing trade friendships with other peoples?"

A short snap of sound, which the translator converted to the familiar, "This word no meaning for us has."

I found myself wondering if the word they lacked was "trade" or "friendship." It didn't really matter. "I can't tell you how to conduct yourselves with other races, I can only give you my advice. And my advice—my *strong* suggestion—is that you direct your scavenging expeditions away from my people's region of space." That would at least steer them clear of most of the galaxy's major powers, and send them instead to contend with the master merchanters who tended to array themselves behind the Orions the way flies gathered on rotting meat. If anyone could usher them into the world of interstellar capitalism, it would be that cabal. And if they couldn't survive that . . . Well, then they wouldn't survive the Romulans or Klingons or Rigelians, either, and Darwin was right after all.

I like to believe it was serious thinking the females did when they drew back into a tight knot and fluttered and shushed at each other. At least what their leader proclaimed at the end of their strange conference was a point both well considered and true. "Useless scavenging be if goods return home do not."

I nodded. "My point exactly."

"Cold-brained males elsewhere to scavenge shall be sent." They flashed a unified look of some fierce emotion straight at me. "From our dancing, lidded eyes of yours away shall you turn. To ourselves leave us you shall."

"You have my word." And I had the last of my equipment. I kept half-an-eye on what could only have been the chip from the simulator game as it shimmered in to nonexistence from where it had ended up beneath a female's talons. Males and females both were already skittering away from that last transportation site when I flipped open my own communicator and startled them with the chirp. "Kirk to *Enterprise.* Mr. Spock, lock on to me and Lieutenant Uhura and beam us directly to the *Galileo* on my mark." And to hell with the Orion pleasure yacht. We'd made unexpected progress in our negotiations with the Anjiri; I wasn't about to compromise that by dickering over a ship we could just as easily claim had been destroyed in the pursuit.

"Transporter locked on," Spock answered briskly. "Captain, your coordinates prompt me to ask if you noticed that I successfully located—"

"I know what you did, Mr. Spock." Which didn't mean the Anjiri needed a full explanation right at this moment. "Now energize, please."

The song of imminent dissolution was louder now, strong enough to make the polished walls sing. A few of the bolder females kept their intent eyes on us as the transporter began to catch hold and fade us into transparency. Most of them, though, averted their eyes, or took positions on the floor next to their kowtowing males. I had a brief glimpse of what it must feel like to be a young god.

"Bright and fierce your heat is." The large female even came a step closer, and I felt a strange, undeserved pride in her bravery. "Eggs of many great fire may bear you."

At the time, I thought it just some untranslatable Anjiri good luck wish that had no English meaning. As it turned out, I was both right and very wrong.

"They thought I was *what?"*

"It is the only logical explanation, Captain." I tried to remember that Spock couldn't possibly be enjoying himself as he sprang this on me. The emotions were certainly just too complex for a Vulcan—enjoyment itself, vindictiveness over my perhaps not so open-minded treatment of him these last few weeks, and of course the undeniable necessity of empathy with my own very human sense of pride. But as he folded his hands atop the briefing room table and turned that studiously considering frown in my direction, the only thing I could think was that he'd determined ahead of time what reaction his observation would elicit, and he was now tickled green to see things playing out as planned. "Judging from your and Lieutenant Uhura's observations, females hold the dominant positions in Anjiri society. You allude to a strong biological basis for this situation, similar to that among primate species on Earth. However, even on Earth, female-dominated aggressive hierarchies are not unheard of. In the Terran species *Crocuta crocuta,* for example—"

McCoy's delighted chuckle cut off whatever long explanation was sure to have followed. "They thought you were a girl, Jim."

What in hell did everyone find so funny about this?

Spock seemed to be thinking something similar, although I still found it hard to believe he hadn't expected as much. He turned an imperiously arched eyebrow on McCoy, for all that he ostensibly addressed only me. "In acknowledging your position of power, it was the only conclusion they could draw. Indeed, Captain, you should be flattered."

I tried not to look too sour as I played with the cream at the bottom of my coffee cup. "I'll remember to thank them if we ever cross paths again."

"Do you think that's likely?" Scott asked. He seemed a little surprised when we all turned to look at him. "That they'll break their word, I mean. It's sure to get them into all manner of trouble."

"I don't think they'll bother us." Uhura had conducted herself throughout the briefing with the same quiet dignity she'd displayed when surrounded by volatile Anjiri breeders. She was proving an excellent addition to my command crew. "Their main concern was for the safety of their children and their homes. No matter how their intraspecies behavior might seem to us, they weren't outwardly hostile—they weren't doing any of this because they wanted to pick a fight, and they never once put us in any real danger, even though they could have."

"Either that," McCoy pointed out, "or they're just smart enough not to pick a fight they can't win."

"Whichever the case," I said, "we've got to give them a chance to keep their word. It's hard to find your sea legs in a great big galaxy—it's not our place to tell them which way to go." I swept together my own notes as a signal that this debriefing was over. "Let's keep our reports minimal on this encounter. I'll recommend to Starfleet that we send an occasional scout to check this border for the first year or so. After that—" I shrugged. "They're on their own."

McCoy downed the last of his coffee as he stood. "Aren't we all?"

In a very big sense, yes. And sometimes that was the point.

Other times, the point was to learn how to step beyond our independence and forge a bond with the species that Fate had arrayed all around us. I tried to catch Spock's gaze as he stepped past me on his way to the door. "Mr. Spock, a moment please."

He paused, ubiquitous data pad in hand, but didn't retake his seat.

I waited for the door to close behind McCoy and the others before saying, "Good work retrieving those items." I tried on a smile more for my benefit than his. "It might have proved embarrassing to explain how they all disappeared on my watch."

He acknowledged that with a minuscule tilt of his head. "As property of the ship, they fell into the realm of the first officer's responsibilities, did they not?"

I smiled, forced once again to give him credit for a sense of humor that I suspected he'd had in him all along. "Yes, Mr. Spock, they did." Settling back in my seat, I punched up an order for a large pot of coffee and two cups. I didn't think Spock would use his, but it seemed the proper gesture, given the hours we'd be putting in together over the next five years. "Take a seat, Mr. Spock. First officers don't have to stand during their weekly meetings with their commanding officers. Now—isn't there the matter of some eight hundred crew evaluations we need to get through before tomorrow?"

Ten

SULU

"A MOST SATISFYING TALE." THE RED-HAIRED PIRATE CAPTAIN THUMPED HER mug of Martian ale on the bar to emphasize her approval of Captain Kirk's story. They had repaired to the long polished counter while a twitchy young boy and the unruffled bartender replaced the smashed remains of their previous table. The arrangement would have suited Sulu fine, except that his skittish little lizard had disappeared at some point during the fracas. He'd have worried that the massive Gorn had stepped on it, but the entire fight had happened in such drunken slow-motion that even a gecko could have kept out of its way. "Oh, what I wouldn't give to be one of these fierce lizard-women, who can tether their men with just a flash of their claws!"

"I wish you were one, too," Sulu said, eyeing the potted Andorian palm whose delicate fronds draped one end of the bar. He saw a gauzy spider perched on one inner leaf, but no sign of the gold-and-brown reptile that had ridden into the bar in his sleeve. "Then maybe you could get my little lizard-friend to come out from wherever he's hiding."

That brought the Gorn's heavily scaled muzzle up from his bucket of Gondwana Pale Ale. "I am not hiding," he said with ominous slowness. "Any skittering mammal who says otherwise insults my honor!"

"No, no!" The last thing Sulu wanted was to start another barroom brawl with their new drinking companion. It wouldn't be as easy to replace the mahogany bar as it was to replace the table, and for all its sturdiness, he wasn't confident it could stand up any better under a direct impact from the Gorn. He leaned forward, trying to phrase his response in the same slow syllables the big sauroid used. "I said 'little' lizard-friend, Captain. No one could *ever* think that referred to you."

The murmur of agreement that rippled down the bar seemed to soothe the alien captain's vanity. "In that case, I no longer say you skitter," he said magnanimously. "Even though you do."

"Thank you," Sulu said wryly. The Gorn grunted and dipped his muzzle back into his drink, throat muscles bulging and compressing like a snake's with each swallow. Across the broad expanse of glittering greenish scales that was his massive neck, Sulu saw a tiny patch of gold-dusted brown stir and then settle back happily among the warm folds of skin. He thought about reaching out to pluck the little gecko from his new perch, but decided that had too high a probability of being interpreted as another attack on the Gorn. Instead, he finished the last of his own ale and glanced at the time display built into his wrist communicator. It seemed as if far too much had occurred in the brief span of time the chronometer said had passed since they'd entered the Captain's Table. Sulu consulted with his own internal clock and reluctantly decided against a second drink.

"If you'll excuse me, gentlemen . . ."

Kirk lifted an eyebrow at him. "What's your hurry? I thought you had two hours before your new executive officer was due in port."

"That's true, but—" Sulu wasn't sure quite how to phrase his suspicions that inside these comfortable walls, time wasn't running quite at the pace it should. It seemed ungracious to accuse Captain Kirk of bringing him to a place where you couldn't trust the clocks. "I still need to get some dinner."

"Eat here." The large sauroid head lifted from its bowl to bare an immense jawful of teeth. Sulu hoped that was a smile. "Finish story."

"Yes." The felinoid captain squirmed out of the freighter captain's lap and over the polished top of the bar, coming back with a menu and a large bowl of Elyrian spice-almonds, which she pushed toward him. "You cannot leave us in suspense."

"Indeed." The elderly captain still chewed all his words around the stem of his meerschaum pipe. "The Captain's tale may be well-finished, but yours was left at a most sorrowful pass. What became of your gallant new ship and her crew?"

"And why did those wayward Anjiri and Nykkus males commit those atrocities on *Excelsior* more than twenty years after Captain Kirk had negotiated his truce with them?" The English captain might look like a debonair Elizabethan dandy, but he had the keen instincts of a seahawk. "Did the females of their species send them out to attack and pillage for some new purpose of their own? Or were they cannons loosed upon the deck by some twist of fate?"

"Precisely what we wondered at the time," Kirk agreed. "But that part of the story is Captain Sulu's to tell."

Sulu paused, strongly tempted to stay and enjoy the strong feeling of camaraderie he'd found among this strange assortment of captains. While he debated, the quiet bartender came back to his station and made his choice for him by pouring out another Martian Red Ice Ale. Caught between its mellow honeyed scent and the spicy aroma of the almonds, Sulu sighed and opened the menu.

"Pot-stickers and the satay chicken," he told the bartender, then passed the menu on to Kirk. "You're sure we'll have enough time to eat?"

"Steak sandwich, extra fried onions. Don't worry, Captain. We'll be done before the sun sinks over the yardarm."

That promise brought nods of agreement from the redheaded pirate, the elderly captain, and the Englishman, but made both the Gorn and the felinoid look puzzled. "What iss thiss planet called Yardarm?" the felinoid asked the freighter captain. "And why must we be done before local sunset there?"

He scrubbed a hand through his salt-and-pepper beard to hide a smile. "Uhh, I think that's just another way to say 'happy hour.' So, Captain, what happened after the pirates boarded your ship?"

"They didn't board it," Sulu admitted. "I wish they had, we might have had a chance against them then. But all they did was blast the Falcons free and rake our warp nacelles and impulse engines with enough phaser fire to keep us from following them. Then they vanished, leaving us unarmed and defenseless—right on the edge of Klingon space."

"Bridge to Captain Sulu."

I reached out and caught hold of the nearest bulkhead, to keep myself from drifting into some critical piece of equipment while I tapped my wrist communicator on. The entire secondary hull had lost gravity in the pirate attack, and the large room that housed our gravity generators had become a floating minefield of debris, spare parts and old coffee cups. After working in this chaos for two hours, my chief engineer's temper had become understandably short. Even the captain who'd stopped in momentarily to check his progress wasn't immune to being snapped at if he bumped into the wrong thing at the wrong time.

"Sulu here."

"Sir, we're being hailed by the *Enterprise.* Captain Kirk would like to speak to you personally."

I winced, but my dismay was muted now by exhaustion and a resurrected sense of pride. Despite all the damage that the Anjiri and Nykkus pirates had inflicted on my ship—the shuttle bay breached to space where the Falcons had blasted their way out, the warp nacelles blackened by phaser fire, the shields still offline, and the computer networks out in over half the ship—not a single member of the *Excelsior*'s huge crew had been lost. Our months of training might not have prepared us to avoid the pirate's attack, but they had paid off in smooth emergency evacuations and flawless disaster response both during and after it. On deck after deck, my resilient crew had begun repairing equipment and reconnecting circuits within minutes of our opponents' departure. It might not have renewed my faith in my own decisions, but it reassured me that one way or another, the *Excelsior* would survive my tenure as her captain.

"Put the call through to me here, Marquez." From the dazzled tone in which the other captain's name had been spoken, I'd known the voice emanating from my wrist communicator wasn't Janice Rand's. Like my other command officers, Rand was roving through the ship, troubleshooting, coordinating and approving the crew's repair efforts. Only Tim Henry had been excused from that morale-boosting duty—his engineering intuition was needed to put the severed control circuits of the secondary hull's gravity generator back together.

"Sulu." The crisp voice from my communicator brought back wistful memories of the days when all I had to do was carry out orders to the best of my ability, without worrying about whether or not they were the right ones. "We're fifteen minutes away. Is there any chance the Anjiri are using you as bait in another trap?"

My first instinct was to protest that my ship's long-range sensors were down and I had no idea what the pirates might or might not be up to. But the *Enterprise* had long-range sensors every bit as good as ours. If they were within minutes of a rendezvous, Captain Kirk wasn't asking me for raw data—he was asking for a fellow captain's analysis.

"Possibly," I said after a pause. "The Falcon reconnaissance ships they stole from us are designed to deflect long-range sensors and might not appear on your screens. However, they're only very lightly armed and shouldn't be able to damage the *Enterprise* as long as its shields stay up."

"Then we'll launch our big cargo shuttle and run both it and the *Enterprise* into the area fully shielded," the captain said with his usual decisiveness. "The *Jocelyn Bell* should be large enough to bring over all the repair equipment as well as the extra team of engineers you requested."

I cleared my throat. "Sir, you won't be able to use our main shuttle bay—it was breached to vacuum in the attack. And I'm afraid the *Jocelyn Bell* won't fit into our auxiliary bay."

"How do you know that, Mr.—I mean, Captain Sulu?"

"Because I flew her prototype back at White Sands, a few years ago." There were people who said I'd spent too many years as a Starfleet pilot before I'd applied to a command post, but I'd never regretted the experience. "You'd have to dock her at the emergency airlock on the primary hull, which would still leave you exposed to a pirate attack."

"We could fly into your main shuttle bay, then drop our shields and let you beam us in from there," Kirk suggested. "Your transporters are still working, aren't they?"

I glanced over at Tim Henry, surrounded by the glowing ends of so many severed optical cables that he would have looked like a haloed saint if it hadn't been for the irritated frown on his face. "Are the main transporters back on line, Chief?"

"Yes, but Klass says the dais is off-limits until she's done collecting DNA samples," he said absently. "They'll have to use the auxiliary transporters in the secondary hull."

"DNA samples?" my former captain repeated, sounding as if the overheard words were disturbing. "What for? You're not worried that Chekov was one of the infiltrators who beamed aboard to steal the Falcons, are you, Sulu?"

"No." My mouth had framed that answer before my mind could even decide if the question was a valid one. I forced myself to spend a moment thinking about it, and decided that it was impossible. If Chekov had been one of the infiltrators who'd stolen the reconnaissance ships, he'd have turned his phasers on the others before he'd let them destroy the *Excelsior.* "My chief medical officer has been studying the dead Nykkus we've got and she's noticed some discrepancies with the report Starfleet sent us. Can you bring Doctor McCoy and Mr. Spock over so we can examine the bodies and compare notes?"

"We'll be there in ten minutes," was all the captain said in reply. "Kirk out."

I really didn't remember much about our initial encounter with the Nykkus and Anjiri. It had been my very first mission as chief helmsman for the *Enterprise,* and so mostly what I remembered was my intense concentration on every technical detail of the voyage. The only distinct visual memory I had of the aliens we'd rescued and then chased after was of the several hours they'd spent canoodling with the ship's navigational systems, while navigator David Bailey and I watched from the back of the bridge and fretted. I remembered the Anjiri officers looking as slender and elegant as the house geckos who used to live among my boyhood plant collection back in San Francisco. Their Nykkus security guards and subordinates had seemed much more burly and brutish, with a stronger predatory tilt to their sauroid torsos and a twitchy animal nervousness in their eyes and tails. I vaguely remembered that they spoke, although not often, so they were sentient but you could hardly call them sophisticated. Certainly not the kinds of minds who could have planned and carried out the shrewd infiltration of the *Excelsior.*

I hadn't thought much about finding a Nykkus body in the wreck of the Klingon colony ship—I assumed he'd just died in the course of guarding some Anjiri superior. But when the suicide guard we'd found floating in the airless space of the breached shuttle bay had turned out to be Nykkus, too, I started to wonder exactly who our attackers were. A visit to sickbay to interview the former hostages had yielded a description of the pirates that seemed to fit the Nykkus far more closely than the Anjiri. And Doctor Klass's examination of the two dead Nykkus bodies had, as I had reported to Captain Kirk, raised some additional questions.

Questions that now lay on the autopsy table between us, shrouded by a gentle shimmer of stasis.

"Notice the hypermorphosis of the cranial crest," Klass said, without looking up from the screen of her medical tricorder. She didn't need to glance at the body she was discussing, since she'd spent the last hour dissecting and analyzing every part of it, but I couldn't look away. This limp gray body, with its lacing of thick ritual scars and the dark vacuum bruises under the swollen and lightly scaled skin of its throat and face, seemed to stare back at me as aggressively in death as in life.

"So he's got a big bump on the top of his head." That was Leonard McCoy, of course. His years sat lightly on him—the eyebrows he lifted at my chief medical officer were still brown and the sardonic note in his voice was as tart as ever. "Without any real knowledge of physical variation within the Nykkus as a species, we can hardly conclude—"

"Doctor." That Vulcan voice was just as measured as Klass's but significantly deeper in pitch. Spock said nothing more, nor did he stir out of the watchful pose I remembered from years of serving together—hands behind his back, chin tucked into his chest, one eyebrow slightly elevated. Still, McCoy scowled and settled back into silence with grudging respect. It was as if, after all their years of sparring with each other, these two best of enemies had distilled their arguments down to single words loaded with meaning only they understood.

Klass cleared her throat and continued. "Note also the significant increase in bone thickness, tooth differentiation, and secondary sexual characteristics such as the dorsal frill. These physical features suggest elevated levels of hormones linked with sexual differentiation and sexual dimorphism. This hypothesis was confirmed by the discovery of significant concentrations of cortico-steroids in the blood—"

"Measured after being freeze-dried in outer space?" McCoy demanded, as if he couldn't keep himself quiet any longer. "I hardly think you could make a valid case for comparison there."

Klass glanced up from her tricorder, exchanging steely looks with her fellow physician. "I cannot make *any* case for comparison, Doctor, since blood samples were never taken from the Nykkus specimens encountered by the *Enterprise* twenty years ago. All I would postulate is that these hormone levels seem unusually high for an adult, even in a fast-growing, passively endothermic sauroid species like the Nykkus."

For all his years of decorated service, McCoy didn't seem to take that amiss. I had noticed before that there was very little attention paid to rank in Starfleet Medical Academy, or among ship's doctors. "Hmpphh," he said. "Have you looked at chromosomal abnormalities?"

"Indeed," said Klass. "The DNA I collected from the two specimens and from the transporter pad all showed similar, and thus presumably normal, chromosomal patterns. I did note a great deal of complex coding in the regions which appear to control sexual development. If similar samples had been taken on our previous encounter with the Nykkus, we'd know whether that was an inherent feature of their genetic heritage—"

"Or a recent mutation, or even a result of genetic engineering," McCoy said testily. "But until you've tried to get blood samples from a batch of grouchy reptiles who can barely communicate through a universal translator, young woman, I suggest you refrain from pointing any fingers!"

Klass lifted an eyebrow at him with steely hauteur. I intervened before she could make matters even worse. "I don't think Doctor Klass meant to criticize you, Doctor McCoy. She's just trying to say that we don't have enough data to know exactly what's causing this physical change in Nykkus."

"It's not just a physical change," said the trim, hazel-eyed man at the end of the autopsy table. Captain Kirk had been eyeing the dead alien even more intently than I had, but his words showed that he hadn't missed any of that medical exchange. "The Nykkus we met twenty years ago could never have planned the kind of attack that sabotaged Deep Space Three and disabled the *Excelsior.* Hell, I'm not even sure the *Anjiri* we met back then could have carried off something like that. At least," he amended thoughtfully, "not the males. Are we sure these *are* males?"

It might have seemed a strange question to ask in front of a naked corpse, but like many sauroid species, the Nykkus did not have or need external reproductive organs. Their passively warmed bodies probably put less stress on genetic haploid cells than our hot mammalian blood did, allowing their reproductive systems to be kept in safe internal storage until needed. Spock lifted an eyebrow in thoughtful consideration of the question, but Klass was moving her chin in a precise and tiny motion of negation.

"Chromosome analysis of all the DNA I collected turned up the single shortened variant that we universally assign to the male of the species, Captain. Unless the females dispatched the males here while they remained on board the ship, I believe we are dealing with a single-sex expedition, just as you were twenty years ago."

"Then something's changed their whole mentality and level of intelligence." Kirk paced from this autopsy table to the next one. This Nykkus body was far more damaged around the eyes and muzzle, since he'd still been alive when he'd encountered the absolute chill and emptiness of space. "Although not their willingness to sacrifice themselves, it seems. Your transporter chief said this guard beamed himself into empty space after he forced her to transfer the Nykkus who stole the Falcons?"

"That's what she told me," I said. "But I had one of the other transporter technicians check the coordinates he had her beam him to. If the shuttle bay had breached to vacuum five minutes later, he'd have been right next to one of the Falcons and able to climb aboard."

"So he just mistimed his getaway." Kirk frowned down at the rictus of asphyxiation that distorted this alien's vacuum-bruised face into a more savage expression than life could have given it. "I see why you thought we should compare notes, Captain. These may be Nykkus, but they're not the kind of Nykkus I encountered twenty years ago." He leaned closer to the damaged face with its lidless eyes frozen milk-white. "Spock, do you remember the Nykkus we transported having these elaborate scars?"

"No, Captain," his science officer said. "The scars I recall seeing on those Nykkus looked like random relicts of battle, nothing more."

It was my turn to lift an eyebrow across at McCoy, who rolled in his eyes in wry response. Only a Vulcan scientist as brilliant and retentive as Spock could recall minor physical details of beings he had seen for only a few hours, twenty years before. "What do you think these scars represent?" I asked him.

"Tribal identification," McCoy said before Spock could answer. "Rite of passage ceremonies. Military hazing."

"All of which," said Klass clinically, "are dysfunctions associated with excess levels of masculine hormones during and after adolescence."

Kirk made a face. "You don't have to talk about it like it's a disease—"

"But indeed, Captain, it can be," Spock replied. "In many species, unusually high levels of normal reproductive hormones can result in unacceptable levels of antisocial behavior among both males and females."

McCoy snorted. "Don't beat around the bush, Spock. Are you saying that we're dealing with nothing more than a case of testosterone poisoning here?"

Klass gave McCoy another cold look, but the Vulcan science officer didn't even lift an eyebrow. After so many years, I supposed he was resigned to McCoy's insistence on rephrasing all his insights in more casual and less precise language. "That might indeed be one part of the change that has occurred in the Nykkus," Spock agreed. "Although I do not believe it satisfactorily accounts for their increased intelligence and remarkable military strategy."

"But the excess levels of reproductive hormones are not in themselves the cause of this problem," Klass said. "They are merely a symptom of whatever disease or mutation or genetic engineering the Nykkus have been subjected to."

McCoy opened his mouth as if he planned to continue that cause-and-effect debate, but I cleared my throat and intervened. "This—er—hormone poisoning might explain how the Nykkus were able to do what they did these past two days, but it doesn't explain *what* they're trying to accomplish by it."

Captain Kirk threw me a frankly approving look, and I found to my surprise that it felt as good now as it did back when I was a young helmsman making suggestions on battle strategy. "You're right, Sulu. Whatever their medical problems are, we can't solve them if we can't find them, and to find them we have to figure out what they're trying to do."

"That's obvious," said McCoy. "The reports I read said they attacked Deep Space Three to steal those new Falcon reconnaissance ships, right? And when that didn't work, they lured in the *Excelsior* with the hostages they held and went after the Falcons again."

"Yes, but now that they have the Falcons, we don't know what they plan to do with them," I said.

Kirk steepled his fingers, looking down at the fallen face of our enemy. "We're on the edge of Klingon space," he said. "And the Nykkus just brutally attacked a Klingon civilian ship, something that's bound to lead to reprisals once it's discovered. If these were Orions, I'd say they were trying to stir up a war between the Federation and the Empire for their own purposes."

Klass gave him an inquiring look. "Does the fact that these are not Orions preclude them from having the same motive?"

"I suspected the pirates might be Klingons in disguise when they first attacked Deep Space Three," I admitted. "If we hadn't stopped to answer that Klingon distress call, we might never have realized the Nykkus were the ones attacking us."

"And the Klingons would sure as hell assume we were the ones who attacked *them,*" McCoy agreed. "Starfleet Command's already chewing their nails to the quick about *that* situation."

"But from what we know of the Anjiri, they seem determined to stay as isolated as possible from galactic politics," Captain Kirk reminded us. "They're subsistence spacefarers with only a small asteroid for a homeworld, unable to manufacture their own ships or homes or weapons. A little raiding to augment their aging technology was all the dominant females were willing to sanction their males to do. They knew any attacks more ambitious than that would have brought down the wrath of a superior race upon their heads."

"Do you think these hypermasculine Nykkus would subscribe to that same caution, Captain?" Spock inquired.

"Perhaps not—but I don't think they're just out to raise a little manly hell, Spock. Or to steal whatever kind of technology they come across, the way their Anjiri cousins were twenty years ago. If that were the case, they'd pick easier targets than Starfleet and the Klingon Empire." Kirk was pacing around the stasis table now, his stride as restless and energetic as ever. "No, they've got some more specific plan in mind and the FL-70s are crucial to accomplishing it. What advantage can those four little ships give them?"

It might have been a rhetorical question, but I answered it anyway. "They're lightly armed, but they have the best sensor-evading technology in Starfleet right now. It's not as good as a Klingon cloaking device, since you can still see them once they're in visual range, but until then they can fly virtually undetected through space. And they're almost impossible to target with weapons sensors."

McCoy shook his head, looking puzzled. "But if the Nykkus need stealth for whatever they're planning to do, doesn't that imply an attack against a superior enemy after all?"

Captain Kirk and I exchanged thoughtful glances. "Quite possibly," he said. "Or a terrorist attack against their own species. If they've already been outcast for their—er—antisocial and hypermasculine tendencies—"

"But that wouldn't explain why they captured that Klingon colony ship," I pointed. "Unless it's going to be used as a decoy . . ."

The silence that followed my remark was a profound one, with both Klass and Spock slitting their eyes in the most thoughtful look they could manage and even Kirk looking arrested and enlightened. Only McCoy was left to stare around at the rest of us in puzzled expectation. "Well?" he asked after a moment. "What does that mean?"

"It *could* mean the Nykkus do plan to attack their own homeworld, and will use the Klingon ship to lull the suspicions of their siblings," Spock said. "Or—"

"It could mean that the Nykkus plan to attack a Klingon outpost," Klass finished.

I had already tabbed on my wrist communicator. "Sulu to Keith," I told the computer. After a brief pause, I heard a background wail of duranium welders, so loud that I could barely hear the sound of my pilot's voice shouting for them to be silenced. Someone had heard her, though—the wail dropped to an idle whine.

"Keith here, Captain. What do you need?"

"Information," I said. "When you used to patrol this area with the *Venture,* where were the closest Klingon border outposts?"

She paused, but like any good pilot she didn't need to think about it long. "There're no nearby border patrol stations, Captain, but there is some kind of research station out at Kreth. It's in a system we call Alpha Gaudianus, an uninhabited red sun with only a few gas planets."

"Thank you, Lieutenant." I thumbed the communicator off and turned back toward Kirk. "Does that sound like a potential target for the Nykkus to attack?"

He nodded, looking grim. "But we can't discount that they may also be heading back to their homeworld, armed with weapons that are far superior to anything the Anjiri ever dreamed of."

"So what do we do?" demanded Doctor McCoy. "Flip a coin to see which way we go?"

The lines engraved between Kirk's eyes deepened. "If there's even the slightest chance the Nykkus are heading for Kreth, we have to stop them. We can't afford to take even the risk that their attack might incite the Klingons to war."

I'd expected McCoy to be the one who objected to that cautious strategy, but to my surprise it was Spock who did so. "The borders of the Federation may be endangered by a Klingon incursion, Captain, but the future of our united races is not cast in doubt. However, if these Nykkus outcasts are allowed to raze their homeworld with weapons that we gave them—"

"Sulu didn't *give* them those Falcons," the captain said in exasperation. "And we don't know that they want to use them for anything more nefarious than a palace coup."

"Their treatment of Deep Space Three and the colony would argue otherwise," Klass pointed out. "I agree with Mr. Spock. The Nykkus and Anjiri's homeworld at least deserves to be warned about this threat."

"That's easier to say than do," Kirk said regretfully. "Even if we send a subspace signal to the coordinates of their homeworld, we have no idea what frequencies they use or if they even use subspace communicators at all."

"So we actually know the coordinates of their homeworld?" I asked in surprise.

A corner of Captain Kirk's mouth jerked up wryly. "*We* know it, even if Starfleet officially doesn't. The record of our voyage to the Anjiri homeworld was erased from the official ship's log with Starfleet's permission, but it's still preserved in my captain's logs. Why?"

An idea was starting to glimmer in my head, one I found both seductive and frightening. It would give me a chance to solve the current dilemma, but at the same time it would take me away from my ship. Was that separation what I really wanted? Was I running away from my problems, or was I trying to surmount them? I was unsure enough of my own motives to rephrase my original proposal.

"If the Anjiri females are dominant, and can only be overcome by stealth, a warning may be all they need. You could send Mr. Spock and the *Jocelyn Bell* to the coordinates of the Anjiri homeworld, Captain, while you take the *Enterprise* out to Kreth."

"A good idea, except for one thing, Captain Sulu." Kirk gave me a speculative look. "Why should I lose a first officer when there's a perfectly good Starfleet captain sitting around twiddling his thumbs while his ship gets put back together?"

I frowned. "But with the *Excelsior* this close to Klingon space—"

"The *Enterprise* can easily tow her to a safer distance before we leave for Kreth," Spock said. "And upon your return from the Anjiri homeworld, Captain Sulu, you can use the *Excelsior*'s own tractor beam to attach her to the *Jocelyn Bell,* and finish towing your ship to safety that way."

I took a deep breath. "How far away are the Anjiri from here?"

Kirk grinned at me, as if he knew that asking that question was as good as saying yes. Which perhaps it was. "Several hours, at top warp speeds. Spock will program the coordinates into the *Jocelyn Bell*'s navigational computer before we leave. And I'll let you pick your shuttle crew from your own ship, Captain Sulu. Once we enter Klingon space, I'm going to need every crewman I've got to keep the *Enterprise* in one piece."

"I'd like to take one of your officers, sir, if you don't mind," I said. "If I remember correctly, Commander Uhura was the only one who really seemed to understand what came out of our universal translators when the Anjiri talked to us. If we post Janice Rand temporarily to the *Enterprise* to take her place—"

"That's acceptable." Kirk cast a grim glance at the dead Nykkus lying on the autopsy tables. "Somehow, I suspect that even if I manage to catch up to the Nykkus between here and Kreth, they're not going to do much talking to us. Any other questions, gentlemen?"

"Yeah." That was McCoy, predictably enough. "Am I the only one who's noticed that we've got two of everyone in this meeting except first officers? What are we going to do to rescue poor Chekov?"

I exchanged glances again with Kirk, reading the grim reality in his face that I already felt in my heart. "We'll do what we can, Bones," the captain said. "But that may not be much."

"And Chekov would understand that," I said quietly. After twenty years of friendship, I knew in my bones what my first officer would have said if he'd been there. "He'd be the first to tell you that his life isn't worth saving if it means putting the Klingons at war with the Federation."

"No," Kirk said somberly. "No more than any of ours would be."

Eleven

KIRK

SHE WAS A BIG, AWKWARD, FRONT-HEAVY GIRL, WITH A FRAGILE REAR END and inertial dampeners that were shot all to hell. As willing as her captain might be, I knew if we just slapped a tractor beam on her and started to pull, we'd stress her structural frame badly enough to compromise seals and welds all across her secondary hull. Looking at the damage wrought on her shuttle bays after the FL-70s' exit, I was frankly afraid we'd snap her in half. So I sent over my chief engineer and the best team of tube-crawlers he had, and we waited nearly three hours for the combined *Enterprise-Excelsior* tech force to wake up the red-lined impulse engines enough to break the huge ship's inertia.

The *Enterprise* took over as soon as the *Excelsior* was drifting free. Even so, we accelerated her along as smooth a vector as we could manage, and I kept wishing Hikaru Sulu was the one piloting the *Enterprise* as we did it. They say it's hard sometimes for young officers to "grow up" out from under their charismatic commanders. I'm here to tell you that it's also hard to be the commander who lets them go, especially when you know that kind of talent doesn't come along every day. Even without Sulu at the helm, we managed to safely tow *Excelsior* a good ten parsecs into Federation space; it took another ten to ease her to a full stop and send word back to Starfleet that she'd be sitting here for a while.

The *Excelsior*'s crew breathed a collective sigh of relief when we finally released her. I wasn't celebrating just yet. McCoy once told me I'd be a captain until the day I died—if not longer—because something inside of me just wouldn't let it go. I suspect that something is the niggling certainties, the agitating instincts that tell you where to go and what to do, even when you have no clear idea what you're reacting to. Good commanders learn to trust those silent impulses; I'd given myself over to them years ago. Apprehension with no direct target had started burning in my belly about halfway through our oh-so-careful tow, and by now it had almost eaten me through. There was something about this mission already not going as planned, something still an unreachable distance away, something I wouldn't know about until it was too late. I didn't say anything to Sulu. He had his own problems, his own ship to worry about, his own peace to make with whatever urges and instincts his captaincy woke in him. It was bad enough that my instincts already insisted we wouldn't be bringing his first officer back; I didn't need to complicate his mission with worries about the safety of my ship and crew as well.

Still, we left Sulu and his shuttle crew still gearing up for their trip to the Anjiri homeworld. "No time to waste," I'd insisted. In reality, if I'd had to hover around doing nothing even one moment longer, I was going to explode. At least on the way to Kreth, I could be doing nothing at maximum warp.

When Spock's call found me in my quarters late that night, more than ten hours after we'd left the *Excelsior* picking up her pieces on the friendly side of the Neutral Zone, I had raised doing nothing to a fine art. I'd undressed at bedtime, and had centered my head on the pillow the way you're supposed to when trying to guarantee you get enough sleep to be a fit commander for your loyal crew. Then I'd stared at the ceiling and thought about the Anjiri we'd met twenty years ago, worried about Chekov, and faced head-on every horrible thing I could think of that might result from the Nykkus reaching Kreth ahead of us.

The chirrup of the bridge channel, then, didn't exactly wake me. Stretching one arm toward my bedside comm, I hit the switch with the side of my hand without actually bothering to roll over. "Kirk here."

"Captain—" Spock's deep voice sounded as awake and unbothered as always. "We have come within sensor range of the first FL-70."

I bolted upright, scowling down at the dark comm panel as though Spock himself were sitting there. "The first?" The lights in my cabin bloomed to half brightness when I stood, and I had to shade my eyes with my fingers to keep from being blinded as I made my way toward the viewscreen on my desk. "What about the others?"

Spock's face appeared on the small screen, looking as neat and alert as when I'd left him on the bridge three hours ago. "Unknown. We only became aware of this craft's presence because sensors detected leakage from damage to its engines and weapons array. Its shields are not active and life support appears to be nonfunctional."

"Do we have a visual?"

An inset view from the ship's main screen took over the bottom half of my display. The little Falcon floated in a cloud of luminous particles; I could see the faint, corkscrew trail of its drift over the last hundred kilometers or so. Phaser burns streaked its flanks, and a good portion of its blunt, shovel-nose was simply missing. I tried to tell if there were lights on in the cockpit, but couldn't see past an opaque glaze of fog on the windows. "Looks like she's been in a fight."

"A ninety-nine point nine nine percent probability," Spock agreed. His own image was turned in profile, apparently examining the ship as it appeared on the bridge's main screen. "Damage to the aft quarter is consistent with that sustained by ships retreating from a more heavily armed opponent."

I scrubbed at my eyes, getting used to the light, and considered the options. "Maybe the Klingons found them." The FL-70s might have been minimally armed, but they were still more powerful than a lot of small ships. And I found it hard to believe that any battle this deep into the Neutral Zone hadn't attracted a whole swarm of Klingon cruisers eager to share in the glory.

Spock was quiet for a time, turning to consult his sensors until all I could see was the back of his dark head. I stood to dig a clean pair of trousers and a tunic out of my closet, so was halfway across the cabin pulling the tunic over my head when he finally said, "Klingon attack is unlikely. Weapons residue suggests phaser cannons of Federation design."

So much for easy answers. "Well, who else out here—" I pulled the tunic's collar down past my eyes, and so saw the Falcon and its mist-whitened windows as though for the first time. Fog. Condensation.

Breathing.

"Spock, somebody's alive in there." He'd reported that the life-support systems were inoperable, not that the ship itself was in vacuum.

My first officer's answer was so studied, so carefully precise, that I knew he'd made this same deduction minutes ahead of me. He must have been hoping to present all the truly relevant information before inconvenient human emotions came into play. "May I remind the captain that the *Excelsior* was enticed to drop her screens, and thus nearly destroyed, using much the same ploy."

I thrust my arms through the sleeves of my tunic and hastily shook out my pants. "It's human, isn't it?" I knew the answer without having to demand it of him. "Spock, it's Chekov."

"It is not possible to obtain a positive identification using only ship's sensors."

"Who else could it be?" I insisted. I'd left my boots by the door, so swept my jacket off a chair back and started buckling up. "The Federation phaser fire—it's from the other Falcons. Chekov got his hands on one somehow and used it to escape." And got this far before the systems finally failed. "He must know what the Nykkus are planning."

"Provided the human life-form inside is Commander Chekov and not some other human hostage of whom we are unaware." He met my gaze across the channel with frank coolness. "And provided the Nykkus have maintained Commander Chekov in a fashion which leaves him still capable of communicating."

In other words, not dead, but maybe even worse than dead. The thought made my stomach turn sour. "Point taken." I paused in latching my last shoulder clasp to drag one hand across my face. "All right," I said, sliding back into my desk chair. "The last time, the Nykkus used *Excelsior*'s own transporter beam to bring soldiers aboard straight from stasis. Any chance they're counting on the same tactic here?"

I pulled up a general schematic of the FL-70s while Spock spent what felt like hour-long moments verifying his own sensor scans. "I detect no anomalous power usage," he reported at last.

"And the Falcon itself is barely big enough for two people, much less a cargo of stasis pods." I looked up from my private research. "What about outside attack once our screens are down? Is there any way we can be sure those other Falcons aren't hanging around?"

"Assuming they are all still fully functional?" Spock gave the micrometer headshake that I sometimes suspected less-experienced observers couldn't see. "No. Not until they come within visual range. However, the window of opportunity afforded by a single transporter operation would not be sufficient to put us in any appreciable danger from such small craft."

Unless, of course, the Nykkus had managed to add a few more ships to their arsenal. Like a nice cloaked Bird of Prey.

I caught sight of the small ship's clouded main window again, and my heart clenched like a frustrated fist. It's easy to maintain your professional objectivity as long as you don't remember that the officer who's suffocating inside his damaged shuttle while you debate is someone you know.

"Send a double security squad to the main transporter room." I sounded marvelously decisive, as though I was already sure this was exactly the right thing to do. "And keep an eye on our internal sensors—if anyone beams in *anywhere* except that main dais, I want to know about it." But I keyed off the screen before turning to retrieve my boots, unwilling to watch the little death-trap's tumble any longer. "Do I have time to get to the transporter room?"

I couldn't see him turn toward his sensors, but I recognized the slight delay. "Carbon dioxide within the Falcon will not reach fatal concentrations for approximately fifteen minutes."

Oh, good—we'd be saving a man's life with barely ten minutes to spare.

"Have McCoy meet me at the transporter." I palmed off the lights, then turned my back on the darkness. "I'll call you when we're ready."

There are times when I feel like the transporter is really just some malicious genie. We let it out of its bottle, point it at something we can't really see, and it snakes out like a giant hand to bring back whatever we've wished for, uncaring of the consequences or details. That genielike literalness had brought a nest of vipers aboard the *Excelsior* and nearly caused her destruction. I didn't begrudge my security team's caution, then, when the transporter dais began its wailing song and a dozen phaser rifles leapt to a dozen shoulders. Whoever first said, "Better safe than sorry" must have been a Starfleet security chief. Or, if not, they must all have it tattooed on their hearts during their training.

But when the first cloud of randomized matter coalesced near the floor of the transporter pad, the bundle it formed looked fearfully still and small. By the time colors had solidified and the last molecule of doubt was erased, I knew there was no Nykkus ambush waiting to blow my ship apart. Just a Starfleet officer curled into a motionless huddle, the sour stench of sweat and stale air hanging over him in the bubble of atmosphere we'd brought along for the ride.

I let McCoy move in first, before the incoming carrier wave had fully faded, and took the extra second to wave the security team at ease. The moment of post-transport stasis broke before I turned back; I heard Chekov take a hoarse lungful of oxygenated air, and caught a glimpse of purple-gray Nykkus blood sprayed so liberally across his front and arms that I didn't want to imagine what had happened to put it there. Then McCoy knelt in front of Chekov, blocking my view, and I heard the doctor's gentle voice murmur, "Easy does it—you're safe now."

I don't think Chekov hit him. McCoy reared back when his patient exploded into movement, nearly overbalancing himself down the transporter steps, but I caught him by the shoulder of his jacket before he could fall. He looked startled, not injured, and he still had the good sense to fling an arm out to stop me when I would have vaulted the rest of the way onto the dais. Chekov, in the meantime, had ended up with his back to the alcove wall, crouched on one knee with both hands thrust out in front of him. He shook so hard, I expected him to shatter. What must have been an energy weapon burn traced a thin line up one cheek, and it looked like his nose had been broken. Still, I found myself strangely reassured that he wasn't anywhere near as battered as the survivors we'd left back on the *Excelsior.* I think I noticed all of this, including the stark panic in his eyes, a good second or two before I noticed the gun. "Chekov . . ."

It was an impossibly old Romulan pulse cannon, almost as long as his arm. I'm not sure he even realized he had it. It was corroded and damaged, like everything the Nykkus owned, and just as spattered with gore as its holder. I had a sudden, clear insight into how he'd managed to wrench himself free from his captors, but it was smashed aside by the clamor of booted feet thundering up the dais stairs behind me.

I twisted a stern glare over my shoulder. "Freeze!"

The rumble of their halt was almost more frightening than their advance. The whole security squad was so close I could have roundhoused them, a staggered arc around the floor and steps of the transporter. Their commander, tight on my right shoulder, didn't even twitch when I informed her evenly, "Lieutenant Benni, take your team and fall back."

Benni's eyes remained fixed and passionless, like a hunting dog unwilling to be called off her mark. "Sir—"

I saved her the dilemma by reaching out calmly and closing my hand over the front of her phaser. "We're dealing with a fellow Starfleet officer," I told her, pushing her arm gently but firmly to her side. "No one's is going to be shooting anyone. Now fall back."

If she'd hesitated an instant longer, I might have tipped over into anger. But she was new, a veteran only of one so far woefully pedestrian tour. She didn't understand yet how I did things, and she didn't understand the fragile tightrope command sometimes walked between controlling a crew and losing your temper with them—much like being a parent. I gave her an extra instant, and Benni saved herself from a reprimand by stepping her squad back so carefully they might have been moving through a minefield. Phasers dropped dutifully to their sides, but I noticed not one team member put them away.

When I turned my attention back toward Chekov, he met my gaze with a feverish intensity I wasn't sure how to interpret. "You're on the *Enterprise.*" I came a step further up onto the dais. "We picked up the engine discharge from the Falcon you hijacked, and we pulled you aboard."

He nodded, as though my announcement only confirmed what he already suspected. "What about the *Excelsior?*"

I made the mistake of trying to placate him. "The *Excelsior*'s fine—"

"She's *not* fine!" He let the old Romulan cannon drop, but didn't let go of the grip. "I saw what they did to her!" One hand strayed to clutch at a patch of wetness high on his right thigh, and I realized that the black of his trousers had hidden a fairly substantial flow of blood. It pooled now into a dark stain beneath his knee. "I saw what I helped them do to her," he insisted, less forcefully than before. "She's *not* fine . . ."

I wished McCoy had been able to sedate him, and wondered how long we had before he passed out on his own. "All right, she's not fine." I mounted the last step and came forward to squat right in front of him. "But she's not destroyed."

He didn't believe me. I could tell by the bone-deep sorrow that flashed into his eyes, and by the way he brought one shaking hand up to cover his eyes, and by the way he asked, very, very quietly, "Where's Sulu?"

Even knowing I was telling the truth, I felt a liar's rabbit-punch of guilt. "He's not here." So often, it's how things are perceived that really matters.

He nodded again, resigned this time, and sank wearily back against the wall. The ancient gun finally clattered from his grasp, and he drew his knees as a brace for his elbows as he buried his face in his hands. Edging closer, I leaned in to slip a finger through the cannon's trigger guard and slide it back across the transporter pad.

"You should have left me out there." He said it so softly, I almost didn't hear him over the clatter of security guards dashing forward to take custody of the gun. He didn't even sound bitter.

I stared at him, acutely aware of McCoy rushing up from behind me but not wanting to leave the remark just lying there. "You know I couldn't do that."

"But you should have." He brought his hands away from his face with a sigh, lacing them atop his updrawn knees. It was such a strangely casual gesture, it worried me more than everything else that had gone before. "You should have just left me to die."

"Captain, I have the *Jocelyn Bell* online."

I glanced aside at Chekov, trying to gauge his reaction to Rand's announcement. Waiting quietly, his hands folded on the table, he proved as impenetrable as he'd been since I spirited him out of sickbay. His silence made the empty briefing room feel huge.

Punching the button to answer Rand, I leaned over the pickup to order, "Put them through, Commander." Then I moved to a seat just far enough to one side that I could watch both Chekov and the small comm screen without having to give away my thoughts to either.

I'd had this idea while pretending not to loiter in sickbay, supervising from afar while Scotty towed the Falcon's remnants into our own shuttle bay and trying hard not to interfere while McCoy did whatever a doctor could with Chekov's physical injuries. For maybe an instant, I'd even entertained the thought of speaking privately with Sulu before I let this call go through. Had everything on the *Excelsior* gone well over the last few months? Had Chekov given Sulu any reason to suspect he had unfinished business from his last starship assignment? One look at our silent guest now, though, and I knew I'd done the right thing by letting this contact go through cold. My former navigator was many things, but inattentive was never one of them. He'd have sensed immediately that there'd been words between Sulu and me, and the last thing I needed was to give him more reason to suspect me of trying to fool him.

Distance stole some of the detail from Sulu's face, but none of the animation. I was suddenly fiercely glad I hadn't polluted this—no one could have feigned the pure relief that flooded the captain's face when he first caught sight of his pale and weary first officer. "Pavel! Oh, God, I'm glad they found you. Are you all right?"

"Yes." A lie, but not mine to expose. Sulu could see enough of the truth without my interference. Chekov had been patched up but not fixed. With broken bones mended and the wound in his leg mostly healed, the bruises under his eyes still stood out so starkly that he looked like he hadn't slept in a year. "What about the *Excelsior?*" he asked his captain. "What about the crew?"

"Henry's going to be a while getting everything glued back together, but we didn't suffer any casualties. Even the resupply team made it home all right." Sulu met his first officer's eyes with touching sincerity. "You did good by getting them out of there," he said, stressing each word as though pressing it into his friend's palm. "I'm just glad you got yourself out in one piece, too."

Chekov cast such a faint glance in my direction, it barely registered as a look at all. "Blame that on Captain Kirk."

"Is the captain with you?"

I responded more to Chekov's shift away from the comm than to Sulu's question. But once Sulu's exec had averted his eyes, I pulled the screen slightly aside to put myself in the captain's view. "Yes, Captain."

"I take it we're now sure the Nykkus are headed for the Kreth research station and not for home. Do you want us to turn around?"

I'd already thought about that and decided on my answer. "No. If we're going to have to fight the Nykkus, I want all the information we can get. Check in at their homeworld and see what you can find out."

He gave me a brisk nod of understanding. "Aye-aye, sir." Then, his expression relaxing again as he turned to his XO, "Commander Chekov, take care of yourself."

What hopes I had for Chekov's recovery lay entirely in the warmth that passed briefly through his eyes when he answered, "You, too, Captain."

We sat in silence for what seemed a long time after Sulu closed the channel. I let the screen go black, then settled back in my chair to let Chekov sort through whatever must have been churning behind his studiously controlled expression. "Are you satisfied now that I'm not lying to you?"

He nodded mutely. That was all.

I remembered only once before when he'd been so uncharacteristically stoic. We sat near a row of windows during a grim San Francisco winter, waiting our turns at a Starfleet Command inquest I'd strenuously insisted should never take place. But it was what Starfleet did when starships were destroyed—they questioned the survivors and everyone involved in rescuing them until even the most gruesome details became rote and polished smooth from too much handling. I'd watched Chekov then, as gray and quiet as the weather outside, and wanted to make sure, incongruously, that everything was all right. But I hadn't said anything. I'd respected his silence, and the silence of the more than two hundred *Reliant* crewmen whose deaths had brought us to that place. And now we were here, and I couldn't believe the silence had done any of us any good.

"Does Sulu know?" It wasn't what I thought I'd say.

But it broke the ice-jam. He shook his head, still not raising his eyes toward mine. "I didn't even know." He pushed himself to his feet, and limped away from me down the long length of table. It would take a lot more than twenty minutes with a tissue regenerator to put that leg to rights, but that was more than could be said for the Nykkus whose body we'd scraped out of the Falcon once we got it on board. It had gotten in only the one good blow before losing to the Romulan pulse cannon. "I got so good at . . . not thinking about any of it. And it isn't as if I ever run into old crewmates . . ."

Of course not—everyone he had served with on the *Reliant* was dead. But I couldn't have said that out loud. I didn't need to. I could tell by the way he paused to lean heavily against a chair back that not a moment went by when he wasn't painfully aware of that reality.

"I thought if I kept busy with another assignment, another crew, it wouldn't be a problem," he went on, very deliberately. I could almost see him picking through his turmoil to choose the proper words. "I thought it wouldn't be the same."

Yet apparently it had been. "What did you promise the Nykkus to free the resupply team?"

"The aliens—the Nykkus?" He glanced at me to verify the word, then looked away again once I nodded. "The Nykkus weren't well-armed when they left Deep Space Three. They wanted the Falcons to use as Trojan horses against Elaphe Vulpina—they somehow believed that the research facility there was working on technology to replicate matter using the transporter."

Information no doubt pried from the crew of the Vulcan science ship Sulu had reported among the pirate force. Information which also hadn't trickled down below the rank of admiral, as far as I knew. Chekov couldn't possibly know how prescient the Nykkus were in choosing their target. "Something had gone wrong on their homeworld; there weren't very many of them. They intended to replicate themselves into an army." He turned to face me, one hand still braced on the chair, the other clenched at his side. "I couldn't let them torture my crew." It was the most passion I'd heard in his voice since leaving the transporter room. "I couldn't just stand by and watch another research facility be destroyed. It's supposed to be my job to protect them from that." Pain, raw and earnest, made his eyes almost glow. "I convinced them that Federation replication equipment had governors to prevent its use with living organisms. But that Klingon transporter duplicators didn't have the same restraints."

The logical leap caught me temporarily off guard. "But you knew the Klingons weren't doing replicator research," I guessed. I realized only after I said it how much of the reality I gave away.

If my slip meant anything to him, he didn't show it. A ghost of his old smile threatened. "No one's doing it," he pointed out. "It only mattered that they believed someone was. The Nykkus had a handful of out-of-date warships and an old pleasure yacht. I traded them the coordinates to Kreth in exchange for the resupply team's release. I know how Klingons arm their stations. By the time the *Excelsior* was close enough to be in any danger, the Klingons would already have destroyed the Nykkus fleet."

And you along with them. But maybe that had been part of the plan. Maybe that had seemed easier than facing the loss of another starship and another crew. I kept my mouth shut and let him finish.

"I didn't mean to help them bait an ambush. If I had known what they were planning—"

Another damned platitude escaped me before I could stop it. "No one's blaming you."

And the steel doors slammed down in his eyes, so bitter and dark that I despaired of ever breaching them again. "Of course not," he spat, so choked with self-loathing it made me wince. "The first time—with the *Reliant*—all I did was turn my ship over to a madman and do *nothing* while he massacred my captain and crew. And Starfleet declared it nobody's fault, so everyone forgave me. Well, this time I gave the enemy everything they need to start a war between us and the Klingons." He slammed his empty chair against the table and turned his back on me for the final time. "I don't need anyone else to blame me anymore. I know whose fault this is."

Twelve

SULU

For a long time after Chekov's signal cut off, I sat quiet at the helm of the *Jocelyn Bell,* trying to decide what it was that had bothered me about that call from my first officer. Was it the briefness of the contact, or was it the far-too-normal sound of his voice in those few sentences we had exchanged? I remembered the bruises and broken bones, the troubled looks and numbed voices of the hostages we had beamed out from the Klingon escape pod. My frown deepened. Chekov's face had worn the same bruises, but not the same traumatized expression. Had his age and past experience allowed him to survive being tortured by the Nykkus? Or did that carefully correct demeanor of his hide an experience so much worse that it couldn't be expressed at all?

"Something about that didn't sound right." Uhura glanced over at me from the communications station of the cargo shuttle. Her coffee-colored eyes were as warm and thoughtful as ever, but the years had subtly chiseled her good looks, adding distinction to their beauty. "Was Chekov giving you some kind of coded message?"

"Not that I could tell." I kept one eye on my helm control while I talked, although our course hadn't varied since we'd left the *Excelsior* a few hours ago. Piloting the *Jocelyn Bell* myself wasn't just an attempt to keep my mind and hands occupied during this long, tense trip. It freed up another of the cargo shuttle's limited seats for a xenobiology specialist to accompany my science officer, my borrowed communications chief, and my handful of security guards. The fact that it also kept my mind and hands occupied was a fringe benefit. "Why?"

"Because Janice Rand is filling in for me back on the *Enterprise,*" Uhura said. "If Chekov wanted to make sure the *Excelsior* and her crew had survived, all he had to do was ask her."

"I'm not sure why he needed to ask anyone." Lieutenant Sandi Henry was never shy about sharing her concerns and opinions, which was one of the reasons I'd brought her along as our xenobiology specialist. The other reason was that it gave her something else to worry about besides the amount of overwork her chief engineer husband was currently subjecting himself to. "Surely Captain Kirk told him the *Excelsior* was all right. Why wouldn't Commander Chekov believe him?"

"Maybe for security reasons," Nino Orsini said loyally from where he sat in the back of the shuttle with his squad of eight security guards. "Commanding officers can't always tell the truth in front of everybody. Not if there are important Starfleet secrets at stake."

Uhura shook her head, making the beaten gold sunbursts and silver moons that dangled from her ears chime. "That can be true sometimes, Lieutenant—but I'm not sure what secrets the Anjiri and Nykkus could have that would matter to Starfleet or to the Federation. You never saw their homeworld, did you?"

"No," I said, knowing the question was directed at me instead of my security chief. I wasn't the only one on board the shuttle who had served on the *Enterprise,* but I was certainly the only one old enough to remember that particular mission. "I was back on the ship, preparing to make a quick getaway in case the Anjiri stormed out at us. Why?"

"Because if you had, you wouldn't have been worried about them storming out at us." Amusement danced in her voice the same way the shuttle instrument lights danced over her jewelry. "They had the most ragtag technology I've ever seen, even worse than on Omega Four. I can remember thinking it was a miracle the Anjiri were there at all, considering they lived in unshielded shipwrecks on a hollow planetoid. They must have inherited their first spaceships from an earlier civilization, or maybe were given them by the Orions in payment for some term of service. By the time we ran across them, everything they had was secondhand, stolen or rescued from scrap."

"Including their weapons?" asked Orsini.

Uhura shook her head and her earrings chimed again. "I really didn't see those. I was too busy trying to translate the Anjiri's language by watching their body language."

"I don't remember them having much in the way of handheld weapons," I told my security chief. "But they had a real kicker of a tractor beam. They used it to drag in small ships and space debris from parsecs away."

"Like Charybdis in her cave, pulling in all those Greek and Roman ships," Schulman said whimsically.

Orsini gave her an uncertain look. "Uh—right. That's probably how they got that little Vulcan science vessel. Don't the Vulcans have a scientific prospecting treaty with the Orions in this sector, Cadet?"

"Indeed," said a deep, collected voice from the row behind him. I glanced back at Tuvok and thought that for all his youth and inexperience, he looked much calmer than I would have felt about returning to the stronghold of my torturers. There were advantages to the rigid training in emotional control that his culture practiced. "I reviewed our tapes of the space battle as you suggested, Lieutenant, and deciphered the Vulcan ship's identification number from them. The Vulcan Science Academy reported it missing only two weeks previous to our encounter with it as a pirate vessel."

"And its last reported location, Cadet?" I asked, frowning.

"The Orion system Greshik Tyrr, sir. Approximately two parsecs from the coordinates Captain Kirk gave us for the Anjiri-Nykkus home system."

I glanced at the helm display and saw that we had ten parsecs remaining in our voyage. "Can you calibrate our long-range sensors to scan for the fringes of that tractor beam, Lieutenant Schulman? It might be good to let the Anjiri bring us in as unpowered flotsam rather than drop out of warp at their doorstep."

"I'll try, sir." Far from being frustrated with her task of scraping data out of the cargo shuttle's less sensitive sensors, my chief science officer seemed positively energized by the challenge. I was beginning to suspect that her ongoing battle with the *Excelsior*'s long-range sensors had less to do with the quality of our equipment and more to do with Christina Schulman's delight in getting a system to perform above and beyond its specifications. "I should be able to give you at least a parsec of warning."

"Good enough." I checked our heading once again to make sure it hadn't wavered, then swung back toward Uhura and Henry. "All right, tell me everything you know about the Anjiri and the Nykkus."

Uhura inclined her head at the xenobiologist first. "I looked over Doctor Klass's autopsy and the DNA reports on the two dead Nykkus, as well as the limited information from the previous contact mission," Lieutenant Henry said promptly. "I agree with the doctor's conclusion that some sexual hypertrophy exists in the specimens we recovered, but nothing in their DNA patterns looked genetically engineered to me. And given the extreme improbability of random genetic mutations producing beneficial results, I would also hesitate to attribute the change to any kind of teratogenesis."

"What *would* you attribute it to?" asked Schulman, glancing over curiously from her sensor panel. "Environmental toxicity?"

"That would be possible if the Anjiri and Nykkus lived in a natural environment," the other scientist agreed. "Pollutants that mimic natural reproductive hormones have been known to cause serious disruptions in sexual development, particularly among herptile species. However, I would be very surprised if a ship or manufactured planetoid, with all the filtration systems that are needed to recycle the air and water, could create the same kind of chemical poisoning."

"Even in an old, cobbled-together environment like the Anjiri's?" I asked.

Henry nodded. "The extent of filter breakdown you'd need to cause hormonal poisoning would cause other effects, like heavy metal toxicity and pernicious anemia. The Nykkus we found didn't have any of those problems."

"So what's the bottom line, Lieutenant?"

"The bottom line," said Sandi Henry, "is that we simply cannot make generalizations about the range of genetic variability in an alien species from a few minimal encounters. For heavens sake, look at the Klingons—judging on appearance alone, you can't even tell some of them are the same species."

Uhura gave her a quizzical look. "So what you're saying is that these 'new' Nykkus who attacked the *Excelsior* may be genetic variants that have existed all along in the home population?"

"Or whose genetic code existed all along in the gene pool, at least," Henry agreed. "Perhaps as a recessive trait, like the gene for dark color that only showed up occasionally in white English moths until the Industrial Revolution. Traits like that are essentially in storage, waiting for conditions to change—"

"And favor them," Schulman finished, nodding. "At which point the recessive gene becomes selected and begins to be expressed more frequently."

"Exactly."

The shuttle was silent for a moment. I suspected that most people aboard were wondering, as I was, how the conditions at the Anjiri homeworld could have changed to favor the devious, savage intelligence we'd experienced from their sibling species of Nykkus. Had the same change occurred to the Anjiri as well? If so, perhaps a state of war now existed between the former allies, and any incoming ship would be regarded as a threat.

"Three parsecs to the Anjiri homeworld." My pilot's instinct had told me that even before I glanced at the helm display to confirm it. "No sign of a tractor beam yet, Schulman?"

"No, sir. No sign of any sensor sweeps, either. Either the Anjiri are tractoring in any random debris they hit, or they're just not out fishing today."

"Keep looking," I ordered. "They may pulse their sweeps to avoid detection." I glanced across at Uhura. "No hails from that direction either?"

She glanced across her boards and shook her head. "Not from any direction, Captain."

"All right, then, Commander. It's your turn to tell us what you know about the Anjiri and the Nykkus."

"About the Nykkus, not much," she admitted. "The Anjiri did most of the talking back when we encountered them. Although the Nykkus clearly understood the Anjiri's commands and could think for themselves, they weren't very verbal."

"Neither were the Anjiri, were they?"

She shook her head, suns and moons jangling at her ears. "Most of their language was nuanced through their body postures. They only had a few basic sounds—hisses, snarls, intakes of breath—so they made each combination mean different things according to how they stood and moved as they said it."

"And the Nykkus didn't make any of those sounds?"

"They made all of them, but their posture was always so defensive and submissive that with the additional body language added to it, the universal translator just kept repeating 'sorry, sorry, sorry' for everything they said." Uhura picked up the communications tricorder she had brought with her and toggled its display on. "I did a preliminary linguistic analysis of the original signal the *Excelsior* picked up and translated just before the attack on Deep Space Three. It codes out as essentially the same language as the Anjiri and Nykkus spoke twenty years ago, but with an emphasis on deeper growling vocalizations rather than higher-pitched hisses. A different accent, perhaps, or maybe a new kind of military slang. Either way, I have to agree with Lieutenant Henry. We could just be seeing a segment of Nykkus society that we were never exposed to before."

I nodded, glancing back at my helm display. "One and a half parsecs from Anjiri homeworld. Still no sign of a tractor beam or any sensor sweeps, Schulman?"

"No, sir." She gave me a worried look. "Actually, Captain, I'm not picking up much sign of activity from the homeworld at all. I should be getting some ionic emissions from their power plants by now, or some signal leakage from their communications circuits."

"Perhaps they've relocated their floating planetoid to another solar system," Orsini suggested. "It sounds like the whole thing could have been towed with a few good ships."

"Perhaps." I watched the distance between us and the Anjiri homeworld dwindle, eaten away by the *Jocelyn Bell*'s powerful warp engines. At half a parsec, I could finally make out the sullen twinkle of the Anjiri's home star by its unmoving position in the center of the helm display. At twelve billion kilometers, we streaked through the unseen halo of space-dark ice that was the system's cometary belt and the twinkle kindled to a dim charcoal glow. At two billion, the ember brightened to a flare, and at half a billion it became a furious boil of bloody fire at the center of a crowded gas-giant system. I swept a hand across the warp controls and brought the *Jocelyn Bell* sweeping out into normal space, at a deceleration rate fast enough to make the safety warnings on our inertial dampeners strobe as redly as the Anjiri sun. Uhura winced and braced herself against her communications panel as the shuttle continued its weapons-evading slam to the position I had selected for our stop, just outside the heavy metal gates of the Anjiri's manufactured worldlet.

"Sulu," said my old *Enterprise* crewmate between her teeth. "This is exactly how fast Captain Kirk brought us in the last time I was here. Please tell me I was right in thinking for twenty years that we wouldn't have crashed into the Anjiri's docking bay if you had been our shuttle pilot."

"We're not going to crash into the Anjiri docking bay." I watched the exponential downward curve that was keeping our inertial dampeners stretched to their limit. Nonpilots never realized just how much tolerance was built into Starfleet's systems, but I had spent a few lost years of my life determining the width of that safety margin to a hair. We would end that deceleration a safe kilometer away from the Anjiri's fortress, arriving too relativistically fast to aim at and stopping too close to fire at. "Don't worry, the sensors are picking up the planetoid and it's still in the same position—"

"Yes." Uhura's somber voice told me that wasn't necessarily a good thing. I spared a look up from my controls as the dampeners stopped flashing their warnings, and saw the dark shadow of the Anjiri's little planet, wearing its haphazardly welded encrustation of spacewrecks and flotsam. That looked familiar enough, but as soon as my eyes adjusted to the dim reflection of red star-shine, I saw what Uhura had already seen. The great metal gates of the Anjiri docking bay were blasted through as savagely as the *Excelsior*'s own shuttle bay. And not a trace of light leaked from within.

"Schulman," I snapped while the *Jocelyn Bell* swooped to a graceful but completely unnecessary stop inside the asteroid's safe firing range. "Sensor readings on life-support and life-signs inside there."

"Negative, sir, at least for the sectors I can read from here." My science officer frowned at her sensors, for once looking justifiably frustrated. "The problem is, these systems just don't have the power to sweep through more than a few hundred meters of that metal cladding. There could be lots more areas intact deeper inside, or on the other side, and we'd never know."

"Well, we're damn well going to find out." I saw Uhura's lifted arch of eyebrow and realized how grim I must have sounded. But I hadn't come all this way, leaving behind a wounded starship and a damaged first officer, just to turn and leave at the first hint of an obstacle. Even if not a single Anjiri or Nykkus remained alive in there, we needed to know what had happened to them to understand the rampage on which their survivors had embarked. "Schulman, keep scanning. I'm going to loop around this rock and give you a chance to scan as much of the first hundred meters as we can."

"And then what, Captain?" Lieutenant Henry's clear blue eyes couldn't mask her doubt the way her well-trained voice could. "We don't have a transporter aboard, and even if we use the environmental suits, we may be breaching all the rest of their atmosphere just by going in."

"I know that." I sent the *Jocelyn Bell* into a slow spiral around the augmented Anjiri planetoid, watching its welded carapace slide past. Most of the flotsam I saw was unrecognizable, but here and there a space-blackened nacelle or carelessly welded weapons turret caught my pilot's eye. The blackest, most buried ones were ships I'd only seen in books or museums, while the ones that still gave off an occasional glint of steel gray or duranium silver beneath our scanning lights were spaceships that had flown in my boyhood. None of them had what I was looking for.

"What are your sensors reading, Lieutenant?"

"Atmosphere, I think, sir. But it seems to be pretty deep inside—no, wait, it's starting to hold a lot closer to the surface." We'd passed a barren projection of the planetoid's original iron-nickel core a moment ago, and seemed to be orbiting now around a different sector of this manufactured world. The welded wrecks were fresher here, and carefully arranged to allow views of the sullen red sun through scattered portholes.

"This side looks better than the other one." Despite her curious gaze and comment, Uhura's hands never stopped moving across her communications panel. She was scanning all possible frequencies, not just the normal subspace channels, in search of a distress call. I doubted the secretive Anjiri and Nykkus would ever resort to begging the outside galaxy for help, but I didn't try to dissuade her. Even a slim chance was better than not looking at all. "I wonder why."

"Maybe it's how the other half lives," Sandi Henry suggested. "The Anjiri half. From the reports filed after the *Enterprise* encountered them, there seemed to be a wide social gap between the two species."

"Despite their obvious relationship," Uhura agreed.

"Captain, I'm reading life-signs inside," Schulman said abruptly. "Bearing five-fifteen mark nine."

"Affirmative." I sent the cargo shuttle slanting over to the new heading without taking my eyes off the barnacled mass of welded ships passing beneath our lights. The pack rat Anjiri had apparently used anything they'd found to expand their limited space habitat. I recognized an early Vulcan unmanned probe, an antique Orion colony supply ship, an M-class Starfleet courier—

"Captain?" Schulman gave me a puzzled glance as the *Jocelyn Bell* swerved from its heading into a back-looping spiral. "The life-signs are still seven hundred meters away."

"Is there atmosphere in the section right below us, Lieutenant?" I asked, bringing the shuttle to a slow idle over the familiar Starfleet insignia. On one side, I could see a crudely welded patch over the dusky star of a photon torpedo hit. Since the Nykkus had never used torpedoes against us, I presumed that meant this was a wreck from some early space battle with the Romulans or Orions, found and salvaged by the sauroid space-gleaners.

"Yes, sir, there is." Schulman's startled look had melted into comprehension. "Oxygen levels and pressures are a little low, but well within human tolerance."

"No worse than paying a visit to the cloud-cities on Ardana." I made a tighter looping spiral around the wreck. The port side of the courier ship was preserved intact, welded into the planetoid's metal husk in a way that seemed to deliberately leave her emergency docking port clear and accessible. I wondered if the Anjiri had used it as an airlock themselves. "Orsini, have someone pack along a few oxygen bottles from the emergency lockers in case anyone gets sick."

"Yes, *sir,*" my security chief said enthusiastically. Uhura glanced over her shoulder at the away team he was already forming from his squad, then back at me. Her lifted eyebrow would have done Spock proud.

"You're actually planning to *dock* here?"

"Why not?" I had the *Jocelyn Bell*'s own emergency docking port already centered over the courier's airlock, her guide-lasers locked onto target and her impulse engines adjusted for a slow descent. Without an order being given, Schulman began downloading data from her sensor station to a tricorder and Henry fastened her xenobiology equipment belt around her waist. "Starfleet emergency docking ports have been made to the same specifications for the past ninety years, Commander, for situations just like this."

"I don't think this was *exactly* what Starfleet had in mind." But Uhura scooped up her own communications tricorder as soon as she heard the solid thud of the magnetic docking plates latching onto each other. I cut the *Jocelyn Bell*'s impulse engines and engaged the cargo shuttle's autothrusters to keep her from pulling away as the Anjiri homeworld rotated beneath her. Fortunately, this little planetoid had an unusually strong gravitational pull that would help keep us mated. It must have been a chunk of pure iron-nickel core blasted free when its primordial planet was destroyed in a cosmic collision. And the outer layers of duranium and metal cladding slathered onto it by the Anjiri had only added to its density.

"We've got the old docking port plugged into ship power and online, Captain," called Nino Orsini's voice from the back of the cargo shuttle. I couldn't see him behind the advance group of guards, but suspected he'd be the first one through that airlock when I gave the order to enter it. "We're ready to go when you are."

"Proceed at your discretion, Lieutenant." I spun my pilot's chair around and moved to join Uhura, Schulman, and Henry in the center of Orsini's carefully arrayed security guards. For all its age, the M-class courier's emergency port made no more noise irising open than our own shuttle's had. The only sign that we had opened a gateway to the Anjiri homeworld was the gust of air sucked out of the ship and a drop in air pressure so sudden it made my ears pop. As a former test pilot, I was used to ignoring that, although I saw Henry and Uhura both wince and rub at their ears.

"I don't remember the air being this thin before." Uhura watched the first party of security guards climb down into the open airlock and disappear. "Or this cold."

The temperature change that followed our exchange of atmospheres with the planetoid was striking, especially in an artificial habitat created by a sauroid species. "Maybe the life-support systems are failing and causing environmental problems after all," I said. "Schulman, did the life-signs you picked up show any indication of medical distress?"

"Not that I could see, sir. There was one that seemed much weaker than the others, but it could have just been coming from deeper in the planetoid. The metal alloy this world is made of is highly recalcitrant to sensor scans." Schulman grimaced at the tricorder she'd brought with her. "The bioscan on this thing probably won't work for more than a hundred meters in any direction."

All of the advance guard had now vanished through the airlock, leaving a tense silence behind them. I pushed past our own escort and risked a glance down through the short tunnel made by the magnetically mated portals. All I saw was darkness, lit by an occasional distant gleam from a security guard's hand lamp. A strong smell, tart as corroded metal but at the same time more musky, rose up to prickle at my nose. I frowned and toggled on my wrist communicator. "Sulu to Orsini."

"Orsini here." My security chief sounded a little breathless from the change in oxygen levels, but otherwise untroubled. "The advance team has secured the courier hull and adjacent tunnel passages, sir. It should be safe for the rest of you to enter. It's a drop of about twelve feet, but the gravity change will soften it."

"Tell your men not to explore more than a hundred meters away from the airlock until we're all through," I ordered, then tapped off my wrist communicator and swung myself down into the airlock first. I felt the Anjiri homeworld's lighter gravity make my stomach lurch when I dropped below the courier's hull, but I still hit the metal floor below with enough of a thud to make my teeth clack together. I stepped back, shaking my head at Orsini's idea of a soft landing. When the next guard to drop through the airlock also grunted with pain on arrival, I told him to help the rest of the party down, then went in search of my security chief.

There didn't seem to be much else left of the M-class courier beyond its docking port and upside-down bottom deck. A jerry-rigged Romulan bulkhead had been used to close the area off, in case of accidental portal opening I supposed. The glow of a handheld light inside its opened door panel shed enough light to let me recognize Orsini's aquiline features.

"Any sign of recent Anjiri or Nykkus activity in this sector, Lieutenant?"

Orsini shook his head, looking puzzled. "Not really, sir. Certainly no evidence of a recent attack or any kind of space battle. All we found was a lot of toys scattered around down one of the tunnel passages."

"Toys?" My voice must have been loud enough to catch Uhura's attention even as she dropped through the airlock—I recognized the soft jangle of earrings that accompanied the sound of approaching footsteps. "What makes you think that's what they were, Lieutenant?"

He held out what looked like a limp bundle of fiber cable. On closer inspection, I could see that it was knotted at each end to form a series of oil-darkened handholds. One of the knots still wore the embedded glitter of an ash-dark scale. "If that's not for playing tug-of-war, sir, I don't know what it is," Orsini said apologetically. "We found a lot of other ropes like this strung along a high tunnel wall and across a section of roof. There seemed to be a lot of claw marks in the metal around them."

"A jungle gym?" Uhura asked.

"That's what it looked like to me, sir."

"Or maybe a military training ground," I reminded them. "That military strategy the Nykkus have been using on us didn't come from nowhere." I glanced back to see the rest of the landing team gathered on the courier's lower deck. "Schulman, what direction were those life-signs from here?"

"Seven-nineteen mark nine, sir." She came to join us, scanning her tricorder around the spokes of metal-walled tunnels radiating out from this docking port. "That tunnel seems to lead in the right direction, sir."

I nodded at Orsini, and he called his guards together with a single snapped command, then led us down the passageway the science officer had selected. Its welded walls must have been torn from several generations of wrecked spacecraft—engraved Orion filagree gave way to the simple gleam of Vulcan steel, then to the rusting crunch of ancient Klingon armor. After a while, the crazy-quilt passage gave way to the dull purple-black of the planetoid's own native metal. It seemed to suck the light from our massed handlamps into itself, leaving me with an uneasy sense of being surrounded by echoing space instead of solid walls.

"Anything showing on the bioscan, Schulman?"

"No, sir. My calculations show we're still approximately four hundred meters from where I first picked up the life-signs."

I frowned. The strange smell that had reminded me of corroded metal and a carnivore's breath was growing stronger the deeper we penetrated into this passage. "Orsini, pull back your advance guard," I said after a moment. Maybe I was being overcautious, but a captain doesn't have to explain his orders. My security chief not only didn't question them, he pulled his rear guards in as well to make a solid protective diamond around us. He'd apparently mistaken my unease for the kind of battle intuition I'd always envied in Captain Kirk.

"What is it, Captain?" Uhura asked.

"I'm not sure, but I think—"

"Life-signs," Lieutenant Schulman interrupted, her voice crackling with frustration. "Only forty meters away and moving toward us fast, *damn* this tricorder—"

"Phasers set on stun," I snapped and heard the adjustments click around me. "Heavy stun," I added after a moment when I felt the passage shake with the approaching thunder of footsteps and roaring voices.

"Twenty-five meters," said Schulman.

The din rose to a clamor. At a sign from Orsini, the front line of security guards dropped to one knee to give the rear line a clear line of fire. I crouched behind them, seeing Uhura and Henry join me, while Schulman still stared down at her tricorder. Before I could snap out an order, the xenobiologist tugged Schulman down with us, out of the line of fire. "Fifteen meters," the science officer said without even seeming to notice. "Ten . . . five . . ."

A massive glitter of purple-black hurtled around the curve of the passage ahead of us, and for a moment it looked as if we were being attacked by the metal planetoid itself. Then the solid onrush broke for an instant into the chaotic surge and eddy of a charge arrested in mid-stride, and the thundering roar dropped into startled silence. Ten meters away, the knot of attacking Nykkus had crashed to a stop and now stood staring at us like a stymied pack of natural predators, interlacing restlessly through each other without taking another step toward us.

"Hold your fire," I said softly. "Wait and see what they decide to do."

They were undeniably Nykkus rather than Anjiri, this hunting pack in front of us. They had the same savagely muscular shoulders, the same strong sauroid skulls, the same gleaming teeth. But the flaring rills on their skull-crests brushed the top of the two-meter tunnels they stood hunched in, and their jeweled reptile eyes blazed in the darkness like fire-opals lit from behind. They lacked the ritual scarring on their scales that had distorted the two Nykkus bodies we had found. In its place they wore a glittering network of copper and silver droplets that they'd either pierced through their overlapping scales or somehow soldered to them, in intricate patterns that followed the curves of their environmental armor and their own strong muscles. The brightness of that metallic bodywork was reflected and intensified by the rich luster of the scales beneath.

The Nykkus and Anjiri we'd met twenty years ago aboard the *Enterprise* had been sand-gray and dust-brown, Captain Kirk had said. The Nykkus who'd attacked Deep Space Three and the *Excelsior* had been significantly deeper and richer in color, their scales grading from polished mahogany to wet steel. But the Nykkus before us made the previous ones look like pale imitations of themselves. Their scales had the intense shine of dark gemstones—the charcoal gleam of smoke quartz, the dried-blood glitter of garnet, the gray-black glint of polished hematite. The colors seemed to shift and melt as they gradually stilled into silence, cooling from their original overcast of angry purple-black to a more watchful midnight-blue. I suspected it was a side-effect of their scales settling back into place as they cooled and lost the purple-gray flush of blood vessels in the exposed skin below.

Their restless shifting had settled at last into a wedge formation that almost echoed ours, the tallest and darkest Nykkus at its point and the others arrayed behind in order of descending size. A deep rumbling snarl broke the silence, but before any of our nervous security guards could take it for a threat, Uhura's specially adapted translator had already transformed it into a rush of words. I was so startled that I rose from my crouch and stared across at our attackers. The universal translator was always sensitive to gender, and armed with Uhura's Anjiri-Nykkus database, it had turned that snarled demand into a strong but undeniably *female* voice.

Twenty years ago, James T. Kirk had found the females of the Anjiri species to be more powerful, assertive, and intelligent than the males. Now we were facing their Nykkus equivalents—even stronger, even more aggressive, and perhaps even more intelligent than the military strategists who'd blown up Deep Space Three and left the *Excelsior* in ruins.

God help us all.

Thirteen

KIRK

KLINGON RESEARCH. THE ULTIMATE OXYMORON.

Racist of me, I know, but I've always found the concept of Klingon scientists a little hard to wrap my brain around. What did Klingon science look like? Steel-jawed geologists extracting information from rocks using agonizers and *d'k tahg?* Armor-clad physicists smashing atoms with *bat'leths?* After all my years in the service, the only thing I knew for sure was that the Klingons defended their research outposts as ruthlessly as their military bases.

Kreth was apparently no exception. From parsecs away, we could see the flash and glow of weapons discharge like lightning against a black storm sky.

"So much for avoiding a war," Benni muttered from her weapons console.

She had a lot to learn if she thought I gave up that easily.

"Sensors detect massive damage to most station sections." Spock, already well familiar with my tenacity, had bent to his sensors the moment the Alpha Gaudianus system, which was Kreth's home, came within range. "Quantum interference in the region is anomalously high, but I believe there are only three ships engaged in the attack."

I heard Chekov stir to the left of my command chair. "The Falcons." McCoy had released him from sickbay with no caveats more than an hour ago, but he still looked tired and a little lost with no position to go to, no job to do. He must have seen the movement when I glanced at him, because he turned to face me before continuing, "The Nykkus will use the FL-70s' stealth capabilities to get in close and pick the station apart without risking their weaker ships. They've got their soldiers—the ones they plan to duplicate—packed into the other ships like livestock. They won't put them in danger."

"Not yet at least." Once they were on the station and faced with hand-to-hand combat against the Klingons, I had a feeling they'd have to be a little more free with their resources. "Spock, any sign of damage to those Falcons?"

He hadn't yet lifted his face from the sensors. "Negative."

Which meant the damned things could keep nickel-and-diming the station for days. Clenching one fist in frustration, I told myself it wasn't reasonable to resent Starfleet for building a reconnaissance craft that was everything they claimed it would be. "Mr. Benni," I called to my weapons officer, "shields up. Helm, warp three."

"Captain—" Spock took a single step away from his station, a sure sign that I'd startled him with the order. I will admit to occasionally feeling a sting of pride that I can still startle my Vulcan first officer after so many years.

"Those Falcons are Federation property, Mr. Spock. They're also the only thing in sensor range, which means Kreth's record of this attack is going to look one hell of a lot like a Federation invasion."

He gave that reasoning the considering nod it deserved. "Bringing a Constitution-class starship into the fray will not go far toward convincing them otherwise."

"It will if we can clear out those Falcons," I insisted. "And if we make sure there are Klingon eyewitnesses left to tell the tale."

The Nykkus themselves certainly weren't going to stick around to greet the Klingon cavalry. From everything Chekov had said, they were unsophisticated but not stupid. Smarter, even, than their Anjiri counterparts from two decades before, who for all their flailing managed to do quite well with other races' stolen technology. It wouldn't take the Nykkus long to figure out that there were no prototype replicators on Kreth. Once they realized they'd been duped, they'd abandon the station, leaving only the misleading battle records to explain what had happened. And, unless I missed my bet, they'd be back at Elaphe Vulpina about the time the first salvo was being fired in the Federation/Klingon war.

When the first rough judder rattled my teeth, I put it down to the quantum wreckage ringing any battle whose main projectiles were photons and gamma rays. Then the ship rocked as though we'd skipped her belly across an open moon, and I gripped the arms of my command chair in alarm. "Spock . . . ?"

He ran down the list with stoic precision. "Debris from at least two

Birds of Prey . . ." The traditional guard dogs of Klingon posts. "Also remnants of a Veth-class Klingon colony transport . . ." The Nykkus's Trojan horse. "A vast amount of subspace fracture as well."

"Subspace fracture?" That hadn't been what I'd bargained for when I first called for this heroic swoop to the Klingons' rescue. I swivelled my chair to frown at Spock. "From what? Some sort of natural phenomenon?" At the time, I was thinking a nearby singularity, or perhaps the fading wavefront from a long-ago supernova.

My science officer merely lifted both eyebrows in a thoughtful Vulcan shrug. "Insufficient data at this time. However, it is not consistent—"

It was no subspace fracture that slammed us broadside. The whole ship seemed to buck like a startled horse, and I shouted, "Shields *up,* Lieutenant!" toward the weapons panel even as I dragged myself back into the command chair. Chekov, on his knees now, wisely took hold of the bridge railing but made no move to stand.

"Shields are up, sir!" Benni's hands were already flying across her controls, her face contorted in what I knew was anger at that situation, not me. "Whatever hit us—"

It came to her call, kicking us so hard I could almost feel the strutwork break.

"God . . . !" she breathed. Her face had the stunned look of someone facing a power greater than she'd ever conceived. "That's off the scale."

I motioned sharply at Chekov. "If you're staying, Commander, take a seat." Because I had a feeling things were only going to get worse, and it was no time to ride out a battle on your knees.

He gave me a brusque nod, then scrambled under the railing toward the empty auxiliary engineering station. I don't know if he picked that seat because it was the first his eyes happened upon, or because it was immediately behind the weapons console. Whatever the reason, he was poised between the two when the third impact slammed us, and barely made it past the weapons alcove before being all but thrown into his chair.

A breach alarm for somewhere in the lower decks shrilled so loudly I couldn't hear which department sent out the call for a medical team. "Spock, where the hell is that coming from?"

He stared now at the light show on the viewscreen, as though that could tell him something more than his sensors. "As the Falcons are outfitted with only a single phaser array, I must infer that we are being fired upon by the station."

What does Klingon science look like? Weapons research.

I mouthed a fistful of profanities as I swung toward Janice Rand. "Commander, get that station on the comm!"

"Trying, sir." She already had one hand to her earpiece, that familiar glazed look in her eyes as she played across the bandwidths. "There's no response."

Of course not—if I were a Klingon, the word "surrender" wouldn't even exist in my dictionary. And in the height of battle, what else could an enemy commander possibly want to discuss?

"Then punch through to them," I snarled. "Tell them what we're here for and get that gun turned away from us!" I turned to find Benni's eyes already fixed on me, awaiting her orders. "Lieutenant, let's prove our good intentions. Lock on to those Falcons."

She was working before I'd even finished the command. I heard the telltale beep of the weapons system searching for its target, but never the staccato chirrup signaling an imminent phaser strike. "I can't get a fix," she finally complained after what felt like a dangerous eternity. "The readings have them all over the place."

"Then go to visual," I told her. "Get a manual lock."

This time, the target-lock sang out triumphantly. A blue-white burst of phaser fire stitched the vacuum behind a Falcon, between two Falcons, seeming to pass through the body of both without even generating a defensive flicker in their screens. Even inertial dampeners couldn't completely negate the stomach-wrenching shift in vector as the *Enterprise* slewed toward port and shouldered downward. A bouquet of gas-shrouded fires bloomed along the damaged curve of Kreth's silhouette as our own phasers tore aside its outer plating.

"Dammit . . . !"

The helmsman, Plavi, shook his head in apology but didn't glance away from his boards. "I'm keeping her as steady as I can without getting us hulled."

No one was blaming him. The rending pulse of whatever the Klingons were firing distorted the space in front of us like a column of heavy water. It sheared aside as if changing its predatory mind, and I realized we'd dropped into another laborious half-roll only when my ribs collided roughly with the arm of my chair. If the Klingons didn't kill us, we were going to tear our own ship apart trying to avoid it. The only thing the Klingons weren't hitting with their damned cannon was the Falcons.

"Spock—" God, I hated to do this. But if the Klingons destroyed the *Enterprise,* the Falcons would keep at Kreth until she fell, and there'd be no way to keep that from looking like a Federation attack when the Empire came to pick up the pieces. "Can you get me a fix on the station's weapons array?"

Spock, wisely, didn't bother to point out that firing on the station ourselves wasn't exactly stacking the deck in our favor. "Two four seven mark three eight three one mark one seven five."

What's that old saying about making an omelet by breaking some eggs? "Weapons, lock on phasers, half power—"

"Wait!"

Chekov's shout brought my heart up into my throat. But I bit off the command I would rather not have been giving and swung my chair around to find him already out of his seat, sliding into the back of the weapon's alcove. "Targeting's off by forty degrees." He pointed at the readings as though I could see what was displayed there. "The Falcons—it must be part of their detection avoidance mechanism—"

"We're on visual—" Benni argued sharply.

Chekov scowled at her with senior security officer's disdain for the uppity young. "Then they're throwing chromatic echoes," he said, reaching over her shoulder for the targeting controls, "or projecting false visuals off their shields, but they aren't where we're seeing them!"

Benni glanced an irate question in my direction. I felt only a moment of guilt about betraying a current officer in favor of the instincts of a previous one. "Give it your best shot, Mr. Chekov." Because if it didn't work, we'd be opening fire on the Klingons. I would grasp at any straw that might avoid that.

Even standing, he seemed oddly relaxed at the controls. As if by touching the station where he'd spent so much of his youth, he temporarily rediscovered the unquestioned self-assurance that came with that territory. A spiral of phaser fire circled the closest Falcon like a bracelet of fire. I started to bite down on an oath when no single shot hit home, then the Falcon kicked back suddenly on a ball of exploding gas, and went tumbling.

My heart felt like it would explode with relief. "Keep on them!"

Unlike the Falcons, we made an all-too-easy target. Another great fist of force smashed us almost head-on, and I saw Chekov's next shot swirl so wild not even a forty degree deviation in tracking would help put it close to its target. "Dammit, can't they see—?"

I don't remember how that angry shout would have finished. When I caught sight of the wounded Falcon bearing down on the Klingon weapons array, all I could think was that they were idiots if they thought they stood a chance by putting themselves in such close quarters. Then I remembered the Nykkus we'd seen on board the *Excelsior,* who had trustingly beamed himself into vacuum because that was his part in someone else's greater plan.

And I realized what this crippled Falcon had been ordered to do.

"Mr. Chekov, stop that ship!"

He didn't take the time to acknowledge, only opened fire. He couldn't possibly have been faster—I don't even think he'd been waiting for the order. I saw what I thought was the flash of shields repelling a phaser blast across the Falcon's aft, but its nose carved into the station at too close to the same instant for me to be sure. Or maybe the Klingons unleashed their big weapon in one last defiant attempt to take the little ship down. All I know is that the energy pulse that swelled out from the ruptured station when the Falcon ignited was tremendous. The wave of supercharged subspace slammed the *Enterprise* full in the face, throwing her almost ninety degrees straight upward. It sounded like the whole world exploded, then reality tore itself out from under me, and everything went black.

Whatever stimulant Starfleet arms their medics with tends to tear through your nervous system like a phaser bolt, yanking you into wakefulness just before it exits out the top of your head.

At least, that's how it always felt to me. For all I know, it had more to do with being knocked unconscious than with how Starfleet chose to wake me up. I must have been lifted into a sitting position. All I remember is rolling onto my hands and knees with my skull throbbing like a pulsar. Blood stung my eyes, and something skin-warm and slick moved just under my hairline. I didn't need to touch my hand to my scalp to know it was more blood.

Smoke blurred the air on the bridge into a gray pall. Lighting had dimmed to emergency levels, and the ghostly chatter of distant voices over the intercoms filled the background with requests for medical help, damage teams, and rescue. Helm and navigation were mostly dark, with a lower section of the helm console blown completely open. My helmsman, Plavi, was nowhere to be seen, and Navigator Chambers did her best to attend both positions, although I didn't know what good she could possibly be doing. Just keeping herself busy, maybe. A badly burned corpse, half-obscured by the singed duty jacket draped across its face, lay neatly arranged on the deck between the weapons and auxiliary engineering stations. When Chekov slid, sans jacket, out of the maintenance hatch beneath the weapons console, I realized the corpse was Benni.

I caught the arm of my chair to crawl upright and check the starboard half of the bridge. My attendant medtech made the mistake of trying to pull me back down to the deck. "Go take care of someone else," I told him. When he didn't let me go, I shrugged him off with captainly force and turned to look for Spock.

My first officer—my friend—worked at his own station as calmly as if we weren't up to our asses in dead machinery and dead crew. I've never been sure if the too-hot stench of burned circuitry and burned flesh simply didn't faze a Vulcan's discipline, or if some peculiarity of biology rendered them unable to smell it. Either way, I envied him.

Dragging myself to the front of my command chair, I summoned the closest thing to a command crew I had left. "Spock, Chekov . . ."

I could tell as soon as they started toward me that both officers had escaped any serious damage. Spock had a tear across one shoulder of his jacket, but the tinge of emerald that marked Vulcan blood was so faint that I doubted he'd bled much even before the medics reached us. Chekov, meanwhile, rounded the railing with most of his attention focused on the blackened circuit boards in his hands. He shuffled through them like a gambler displeased with a poker hand, and didn't seem to notice the fresh bruise running up the length of his cheekbone.

For just an instant, I wondered if I should send him below. Wasn't this the mistake I'd made last time? Letting him stay as though the only way to deal with losing your starship was to keep working as though nothing unusual had happened? I'll admit, I didn't know what else I could do. Especially now, with casualties so high, I couldn't afford to turn down any experienced officer's help. The fact that the message sent by banishing him from the bridge would have been intolerable was only incidental.

I eased myself into my seat as they joined me. "Report." God, what had I done to my shoulder? My whole arm ached like mad.

Spock folded his arms behind his back in that gesture that always made him look like a student about to deliver an oral presentation. But his voice now was low and serious. "We have sustained seven fatalities shipwide, including Lieutenant Benni. Ensign Plavi and thirty others are listed by sickbay as having serious injuries, and there are hundreds others still being treated at their stations."

Better than I had feared, but worse than any captain ever hopes for. I used my sleeve to wipe blood away from my eyes while I let him go on.

"Hull breaches in sectors four and five of the secondary hull," Spock continued. "Life-support systems are down all over the ship, and gravity is unavailable below deck twelve. Warp engines are off-line, impulse engines are marginal. Commander Rand is confident she can reinstate communications within the hour, but we are at seven percent shield strength and without long-range sensors."

I realized then that part of the background comm noise had been Rand reestablishing vital ship channels. "So we can't defend ourselves." I turned toward Chekov. "Can we fight?"

He looked up from his damaged boards for the first time, shaking his head. "Most of the torpedoes in storage survived undamaged, but launch bays one and two both took crippling hits. Automated targeting systems are off-line. Phasers are functional at one-quarter power, but only for microbursts." A little gesture with the boards, as though showing me something there. "We can't put up a sustained barrage."

Settling gingerly into my command chair, I aimed a silent curse at the shattered station still drifting near the bottom of the viewscreen. It took me a moment to realize that the screen's snowy resolution wasn't damage to its systems, but just the physical debris and waste plasma from our combat. "So they got in one last good shot." I couldn't even see the Klingon weapons array from here. "Dammit."

"I do not believe our damage was caused by the Klingons." Spock frowned up at the station as well, his head cocked ever so slightly. "At least, not directly. Based on my analysis before we lost power, I infer the Klingons here on Kreth were experimenting with focused multiphasic resonance waves." He seemed to feel that peering at me intently would help me better understand the more lofty concepts of his profession. "This would explain how their weapon was able to inflict such great damage even through our shields, as well as why destruction of the weapon would create such a powerful subspace pulse."

Chekov, on the other hand, believed in placing lofty concepts in perspective. "Like trying to disable a hydrogen bomb by blowing it up."

So it was the destruction of the weapon that crippled us, not the weapon itself. I felt weirdly sorry for the Klingons. However much that exploding resonance wave rocked us, it must have been immeasurably worse for them. "I suppose it's too much to ask that the Nykkus ships were caught in the pulse."

"Except for the Falcons," Chekov said, "they were all out of range. They came in after the resonance wave had passed, and the *Rochester* battleship towed the Falcons in to dock."

"And left us alone . . ." That detail ate at me. I tried to find the Nykkus ships through the sullen subspace glare—the Vulcan science probe, the Orion yacht, the overgunned mutt that had torn up Deep Space Three. But they were all out of sight beyond the edge of the viewscreen. If it weren't so damned unimportant, I might have asked Chambers to realign the pickups to provide a more satisfying view. "The way they used that damaged Falcon to take out the Klingon array . . ." I caught myself thinking out loud, and made an effort to carefully arrange what I was trying to say. "They'd counted on the Falcons being impossible to hit," I explained, including both men in my brainstorming. "Counted on them to clear out the Klingon weaponry before moving in their more valuable personnel carriers. But once we proved we could shoot them, they couldn't take their time anymore. So they sacrificed one damaged ship to clear the way for the rest of their fleet." Which proved they were not only clever, but ruthless as well. Always a chilling realization. Made worse by the fact that they obviously had someone calling the shots who thought fast enough to take advantage of downturns during combat.

"They cannot have known the result of their actions would also disable the *Enterprise,*" Spock pointed out.

"No," I agreed. "But they could recognize that it had happened." I had to wipe my eyes clear again, and my head responded by banging my pulse against my ears. "So why not attack us? Why just leave us sitting here?" It occurred to me for the first time that I could conceivably pass out from loss of blood. The thought made me angry at my own human weakness.

Before I could take advantage of our silence to summon the medtech back over, Chekov said with sudden conviction, "We're the red herring." And a whole host of certainties poured through me.

Klingons were not known for broadcasting distress calls, but that didn't mean no one would come to find out what had happened here. If nothing else, patrol ships somewhere between here and the Federation border would pick up on the pulse sent out by the dying resonance gun, and one of them somewhere would know what that had to mean. They'd come expecting a tragic laboratory accident, perhaps, but they'd find the *Enterprise.* Would the two seconds they spent blasting us to atomic dust give the Nykkus time to sneak out under the confusion of the local space distortions? Who knew? We certainly wouldn't be around to find out.

"This is where we could really use those Klingon eyewitnesses," I sighed.

Spock turned to head back toward his sensors. "We have seven."

I spun so sharply in my chair that my head felt like it would explode. "What?"

"Short-range sensors are functioning at reduced range." He brought up a display on the viewscreen as though to prove his claim. "We have located a small concentration of Klingon life signals in one of the intact areas of the station."

Of which there were not many. I looked at Kreth's blackened hulk and the aurora of quantum fury suspended around it. "Let me guess—we can't beam them out because of the local subspace damage."

Spock lifted a thoughtful eyebrow. "I suspect that would present additional considerations during transporter operations," he admitted. "However, our primary obstacle is the station's own defensive screens."

"Shields?" This time I actually came up out of my seat and leaned across the railing between us. "Spock, you're kidding—that thing still has operational *shields?"* I was unexpectedly envious of the fruits of Klingon research.

"I can only infer the Klingons employed some form of multiple node shield generator network, in which part of that network remained operational even after the resonance wave."

That part must have been shielded like all hell. I forced my thoughts back to the problem at hand. "All right, so we can't pull them out. Maybe we can lead them out." I turned, still holding on to the rail, and asked

Chekov, "Can you get past whatever general security measures they'd have in their labs and corridors?"

He looked only a little surprised by the question. Chekov hadn't worked full-time in security for more than eight years, but he had always been meticulous about detail and, as near as I could tell, remembered every damned thing Starfleet had ever put into his head. He'd all but majored in Klingon weaponry at the Security Academy, which made him the closest thing to an expert I had on board.

"With the right equipment," he said at last, very slowly, "yes, sir, I think I can."

From a Starfleet officer, that promise had always been good enough for miracles. I gave Spock a nod toward his console. "Tell Mr. Scott to start working on those 'additional considerations during transporter operations.' I need a one hundred percent reliable transporter for local conditions in under an hour." Then one last look at the battered research station before motioning Chekov toward the lift. "We've got Klingons to rescue."

The inside of a stripped-down FL-70 is cramped, hot, and a little too close to vacuum for my tastes. We'd torn out the weaponer's seat—along with the weapons, the engines, both wings, and just about anything else with more than ten grams of mass—to make room for a portable airlock and both environmental suits, not to mention reduce the Falcon itself to as close to a pressurized tin can as possible in under forty minutes. As it was, Chekov and I ended up wearing the torso shells and carrying our helmets, but it still made for a damned uncomfortable way to drift into the dragon's lair.

Of course, the plan was to arrive without being noticed by the dragon. Thus the removal of anything that might possibly be detected as an energy source, and our faith in the Falcon's naturally sensor-deflecting design. In the shuttle bay, long minutes before two dozen flight technicians joined forces to heave our unpowered vault into space, I suffered a moment of doubt about whether it might actually be safer to risk the half-repaired transporter and beam over. McCoy would probably say I had some unexpressed need to flaunt my own perceived immortality. But, then, he said that every time duty placed me in physical jeopardy, and it hadn't yet altered how often the situation arose. Doctors don't really know everything. Still, it was the physical limitations of the Kreth station that finally decided what form our little rescue mission would take, bulky environmental suits and all.

Spock had used one of the detached wings to spread a surprisingly concise version of the station's schematics in front of me while Chekov helped the engineers finish welding gas canisters to the Falcon's ruined nose.

"Docking facilities here, here, and here were destroyed in the combat." Spock pointed to the most convenient airlock sites, all on our side of the station. "This sector of the facility housed the resonance wave cannon—"

"So is no longer there," I finished for him. I sat down on the edge of the wing, not liking where this was going.

"The Nykkus have control of the only landing bay," he went on, "as well as all of the external docking airlocks."

I studied the clean lines of the printout, trying to reconstruct it in three dimensions with all the little alterations Spock's report implied. The end result was a very sorry picture. "That doesn't leave us a lot of places to access the station." At that point, I'd still been hoping to mate with an airlock and get on board the easy way.

Spock turned the schematic to show me the details of the section blown open by the resonance cannon's destruction. "You should be able to wedge the Falcon between decks here." He indicated a wide open gap that used to be someone's sleeping quarters. "Portions of these decks are necessarily breached to vacuum, which will guarantee you meet no Nykkus resistance while securing the Falcon."

"We'll have to go aboard in environmental suits . . ."

I glanced back at Chekov, who'd approached so quietly during our discussion, I hadn't even realized he stood on the other side of the wing until then. Behind him, what maintenance personnel Scotty would spare us busily collected their gear before heading off to tend to the ship at large. Chekov stared at the station map with his lips pressed tight, reading something in its layout that I wasn't able to see.

"Is there a problem, Commander?" I asked when he didn't say anything further.

His eyes flicked up to mine, his train of thought apparently disrupted by my question. "No . . ." Then, more firmly, as though whatever he'd been thinking was trivial and he was now convinced of the answer. "No, sir. I'm just concerned about doing the delicate bypass work in full suit."

He wasn't the only one.

"Trust me, we'll get into atmosphere as soon as we find some." I rapped my knuckles against the station proper. "Where are the Klingons in all this?"

Spock circled an area surprisingly deep in the structure, the lines of its decks and bulkheads highlighted in bright green. "They have not moved since we first detected them." He didn't have to say that this could mean anything—from the Klingons all being massively injured, to them being in stasis, to the readings being just plain wrong. I chose to believe it simply meant they were prudent, and had chosen not to roam about. I couldn't afford to have any of the other options be true. "The Nykkus are here." A much bigger area, in red, radiated outward from the airlocks the Nykkus had claimed. I noted the main operations center right in the middle of it all. "To avoid interference from the station's shields, you will need to bring the Klingons at least this far outside the shields' operative range. I would recommend the highlighted path as the most efficient route of travel."

Not to mention the one that kept us nicely away from where the Nykkus had established their foothold.

I gave us two hours to accomplish our objective. "If you detect Klingon cruisers approaching," I ordered Spock as I climbed inside the gutted ship, "or the Nykkus start pulling their ships away from the station, get the *Enterprise* out of here." In either situation, Chekov and I would have failed. The only question remaining would be whether or not the *Enterprise* could get back across the border in time to warn the Federation about the impending war.

Fourteen

SULU

"NOT-NYKKUS YOU ARE."

The dark-scaled female heading up the wedge formation blocking our tunnel passageway may have repeated her words, or my dazed brain might just have finally realized what she'd said before. The emphasis put on the connected words "not-Nykkus" made me wonder if it was a derogatory term for all beings who were not their own magnificently scaled selves.

I glanced over at Uhura, and she rose from her crouch, stepping forward with a calmness few communications officers could have summoned under the circumstances. She stood between two of the kneeling security guards, careful to go no further than that, then lifted her tricorder and held it out so the Nykkus females could see its translating display. A dozen fire-opal eyes swung from me to her, hot as predators watching prey, but still not a member of that female hunting pack stirred out of their careful wedge. They were waiting, with what might have even been termed politeness, for a spoken response.

"I am a human, and an officer of Starfleet." I spoke slowly, to give Uhura's jittering figures a chance to be seen on the tricorder display. "I cannot speak your language well, but the drawings you see on this machine might help you understand me better."

"Nykkus speech in machine this stored is," said the lead female, her powerful torso tilting forward then swaying side-to-side to nuance each of her rumbled words. "Nykkus you before met have. Where?"

I tried not to let her see how much she startled me with that swift deduction. Instead I glanced at Uhura, wordlessly giving her permission to answer that question.

"Nykkus and Anjiri we have met in this place, many years ago," said the communications officer. "Anjiri speech we have studied and kept in our machines since then."

That response, watched with all its visual nuances by a dozen intent eyes, seemed to send a jostling tide of surprise and disappointment through the pack. "Anjiri speech Nykkus speech now is." The bobbing head and lashed tail of a slightly smaller female in the second row of the wedge showed that she was the one speaking now. "Anjiri withers and gone soon is."

"Nykkus only soon remain," echoed another female. The translator ran their words together, but I suspected that was because their deep rumbling voices overlapped almost as closely as their own scales. The physical movements of their powerful torsos, lashing tails and rising heads was what really distinguished one speaker from the next in this species, and even that seemed to ripple across this coordinated hunting pack like a wave across a kelp forest. "Nykkus walk—"

"Nykkus wait," said a third.

"Nykkus return," finished the leader. It sounded like a war chant, or perhaps a sort of prayer. "Your docking hear we, Nykkus are you think we. Attack we not, if we otherwise knew."

This time the look I exchanged with Uhura was one of pure astonishment. The last thing I'd expected, when this pack of fiery-eyed predators had lunged around the corner, was an explanation and an apology for their thundering approach. I tried to remind myself that these creatures might be even more devious than their spacefaring brothers, but something about their steady gazes and interwoven voices didn't seem to allow that possibility.

"We have come to find out why *some* Nykkus have attacked our ships and space stations in the past few days," I said, putting as much emphasis as I could on the word "some" to avoid giving offense. My vehemence expressed itself by making one of the stick Nykkus figures on Uhura's display screen leap high into the air, something that seemed to amuse the females watching it. At least, I assumed that the hisses, slitted eyes and in unison swaying represented amusement.

"Rebellion *some* Nykkus made have," the lead female replied at last, her opalescent eyes still narrowed to brilliant slits. Her voice seemed to echo the emphasis I'd put on the word "some," although perhaps with a more mocking tone. "Atrocities *some* Nykkus committed have. On homeworld ours, on Egg Bringers. Meeting would wish we, dominance would do we, blood would spill we from *some* Nykkus."

I frowned, trying to follow the sense of her words. "Were they slaves of the Anjiri, these Nykkus who rebelled?" A slave uprising would explain the decimated homeworld, especially if some environmental or genetic change had altered the willingness of the Nykkus to remain subordinate to their Anjiri cousins.

"Nykkus slaves *never* were!" The leader flattened her powerful torso so that her frilled crest-rill had room to rise and express her indignation. Behind her, her sisters snarled and hissed their own rills erect in swift support. "Cold-born Nykkus leaders required, Anjiri cold-born no better would be. Cold Anjiri may have us made, but Nykkus slaves never were." Her eyes narrowed again, as if a new thought had occurred to her. "Lies *always* told are, tricks *always* played are, by Nykkus too warm born yet not hot enough. This truth you have obtained not yet?"

I opened my mouth, then closed it again and thought over her statement. I might not understand all of its subtleties, but I couldn't differ with the gist of it.

"This truth we have begun obtaining," I agreed. "These Nykkus who play tricks and tell lies—did they play a trick and leave you here when they abandoned this place?"

That question brought a chorus of deep hoots from the entire group. I waited impatiently for the translator to give me the meaning of those sounds, and only understood them to be laughter when Uhura turned to give me a wry smile of her own. She had her fingers flexed on the controls of the translator so that her words remained in English.

"I'm glad you're amusing them, Captain. But remember that for all their politeness, these Nykkus females could be even more unpredictable and quick-tempered than the Anjiri females Captain Kirk and I met twenty years ago."

"I haven't forgotten." I listened to the roar of hooted laughter continue. "What did I say that was so funny?"

"I'm not entirely sure," Uhura admitted. "But when they were referring to the Nykkus who were 'warm-born yet not hot enough,' something in the way the translator handled that made me wonder if it wasn't another way of saying 'male.' "

"Male?"

Uhura began to answer me, but the soft echoes of the last Nykkus hoots were already dying. She turned back and released the translator's input control, holding the display screen up again just in time to catch the female leader's definitive snarl.

"Of Nykkus ignorant you must be, to think warm-born could us disdain or defy!" She paused, tilting her head to regard me with her swirling, fire-bright eyes. "If tormented by warm-born you now are, with the wisest speak you must. Come!"

• • •

It wasn't until the Nykkus had led us several hundred meters along the twisting length of one passageway and down the descending spiral of another that I noticed they weren't carrying lights. The glow of our hand-held lamps didn't seem to bother them, but clearly they didn't need them to see, even in the thick darkness cast by the purple-black metal into which these tunnels had been carved. The realization made me clutch my lamp in sweaty fingers, abruptly aware of how much of a disadvantage we could be put at even if all the Nykkus did was take our illumination and leave us. I glanced over my shoulder at Schulman.

"You've recorded the route we've taken since we left the ship, Lieutenant?"

"Of course, sir." Her response was absentminded rather than indignant, even though I was questioning her on one of the most basic rules of landing party safety. Clearly, her mind was elsewhere. "Lieutenant Orsini is keeping track, too."

"Yes, sir." My security chief spoke softly, although with Uhura's augmented translator again turned off, none of our Nykkus escorts should have been able to understand him anyway. Still, after all that we had endured from this surprising alien race, I couldn't entirely blame Orsini for his caution. "I've linked my tricorder's recording loop to my communicator, so the rear guard we left aboard the *Jocelyn Bell* will know exactly how to get to us if they need to."

"Good." Most security guards would have simply assumed the signal from our communicators could provide enough information to track us down in an emergency, but in a three-dimensional maze like this planetoid, precious time was lost finding the correct route to the final location. Reporting the entire path was the kind of extra precaution Chekov would have taken, if he'd been securing this mission. Just as questioning the science officer about her distraction was the kind of extra initiative Captain Kirk would display if he'd been leading it. I slowed down a step so I could fall into stride beside her.

"What are these strange readings you're getting from your tricorder, Lieutenant?"

Her frowning gaze lifted from her display for a startled moment. "How did you know, sir?"

"By the expression on your face," I said wryly. "What's the matter?"

The corners of her mouth kicked downward. "I don't know if it's interference from all this metal ground-matrix or the way I tried to reprogram the bioscan after it did such a bad job picking up those approaching Nykkus. I thought I had fine-tuned it, and it did start picking up more life-signs ahead of us awhile ago, but none of the readings look right. One seems to be the weak one I caught before, and it's still weak, which suggests an organic rather than instrumental cause—"

"In other words, a person who's sick or injured?"

"Yes, sir. It's the other ones that really bother me, though. I'm getting at least a dozen life-signs that just don't make sense to me at all. There's a definite pulse and associated brain activity with each of them, but absolutely no respiration or thermal signature."

"Eggs," said Uhura from several steps ahead of us.

Schulman looked thoughtful. "I suppose that could explain the readings—"

She broke off as we passed through a metal-carved arch and unexpectedly found ourselves in a huge, echoing space. After a moment, I recognized it as the inverted belly of a cargo ship, welded onto the planetoid and lit with the anomalous flicker of firelight instead of the usual ship's fluorogens. The red-gold dance of flames was bright enough to drown out our hand-lamps and warm enough to banish the metallic chill of the tunnels we had traveled through. It was also wide enough to encompass a ring of what looked like large fire-charred stones in its halo of warmth.

"Eggs," Uhura repeated, as we joined her in gazing at the blackened lumps. Each was almost a meter long, smoothly rounded on one end but sharply pointed on the other, and each sat in a hollow scooped out of the native metal of the planet. Other hollows pocked the metal floor around us in concentric circles around that fire, and further out in the darkness, I thought I could see the charred pits where other fires had once burned. "This must be their nesting grounds—the place where they incubate their young."

"Lieutenant?" I asked Schulman, who'd discreetly managed to point her tricorder at the nearest lump. Our Nykkus escorts had paused with us, making respectful gestures with tails and lowered frills toward their incubating cousins. "Are these your mysterious life-signs?"

"Aye, sir. All except for the single weak one." My science officer stooped to press her hand against the purple-black metal of the floor and looked surprised. "Whatever this alloy is, it's holding a lot of the fire's warmth. In fact, it's hot enough all the way out here that I wonder—" She scanned her tricorder across the ring of eggs again, and her surprised look darkened into a frown. "Henry, can this be right? It says the ambient temperature inside those eggs is sixty degrees centigrade."

"What?" The xenobiologist came over to frown at the tricorder readings. "That's not incompatible with life—but it's highly unusual. Most of the sauroid species I've encountered incubate their eggs between thirty and forty degrees."

I glanced around the ring of eggs again, seeing their fire-blackened shells in a new light. If they'd been kept so close to the fire's heat that even the crystal matrix of the eggshells had been charred—a ghost of boyhood memory rose to tickle at my consciousness. I'd never been allowed to keep all the reptiles and insects I would have liked to propagate my exotic plant collection, but that hadn't stopped me from reading everything I could about them, in the hope that my parents would someday relent. They hadn't, and a few years later I'd transferred my enthusiasm to flying lessons instead of reptile husbandry, but I still remembered some vague rules about incubation. I glanced out at the shadowy marks of all those other empty egg-hollows, arrayed in concentric arcs farther away from the leap of flames, and my suspicions deepened.

"Henry, what effect would an overheated incubation generally have on a sauroid species?" I asked softly.

The xenobiologist threw me a glinting but unsurprised look, as if I'd caught the trend of her own thoughts. "It depends, Captain. The eggs of some species have very little temperature dependence, other than the basic threshold required for survival. Others sauroids can link sex, size, and even life-span to the temperature at which the egg was gestated." She paused, glancing back at our escort of female Nykkus. Their tails had begun to rasp impatiently across the floor and their fierce eyes refracted the firelight into blood-opal glimmers. "In temperature-dependent species, excess heat could cause malformed limbs, fused spinal disks, and infertility in extreme cases. In less severe cases, you might get more rapid development both in and out of the egg, aberrant color patterns, and inappropriate—or exaggerated—sexual behaviors."

The lead Nykkus female roared out a warning, then leaped into a powerful surge of motion again. Orsini hurriedly motioned for us to follow her, then spread his security guards around us in a protective cordon. I suspected the large, echoing space had made him fear an attack from behind or from the flank, and given the way these gem-dark Nykkus blended in with the native shadows of their homeworld, I wasn't sure I blamed him.

The resounding crash and thunder of Nykkus footsteps led us across what seemed like half a kilometer of nesting ground, until the glow of the fire looked as dim and sullen behind us as the red cinder of the Anjiri sun did in front, glittering through some salvaged porthole. The sides of the inverted cargo ship swept in like metal wings, and the space between its deck and the raw metal floor dwindled until the Nykkus had to slow to a walk and go single file, flattening their rills against their skulls for protection. I was the first to follow them, with Orsini treading right at my heels. As the space narrowed even further, the smell of corroded metal that permeated the Anjiri homeworld finally faded, but only because it was overlain with such a strong smell of musk and fetor that I could no longer smell anything else.

The dull red eye of the Anjiri sun seemed to wink at us, and the dark female Nykkus slowed to a stop, dropping to her knees with all her sisters in a single, coordinated motion. I followed suit, but it wasn't until a moment later that I realized the sun's temporary darkness had been caused by the jerky lift of a dark hand from a cluttered dais, heaped with thermal blankets and pillows. The pile looked so utterly still and crumpled in the dim sunlight, I hadn't realized there was a body buried in it. And the sound that followed that painful gesture was barely recognizable as a voice—hoarse coughing like distant gusts of wind, interspersed with long whistling noises that must be painful breaths.

"Comes . . . is . . ."

The universal translator had again given us a female voice for this speaker, but it had parsed the words out with long pauses between them, as if there were missing pieces it couldn't translate. I glanced over my shoulder at Uhura, who had lifted her augmented translator up over Orsini's shoulder. The slanting red sunlight threw exotic shadows across her sculpted face, but lit her coffee-dark eyes with sympathy.

"What's going on, Commander?"

"I'm not sure, sir, but I think she's too sick to do anything but whisper. The translator will need a little time to recalibrate for her."

Unfortunately, I wasn't sure we were going to be given that time. The female Nykkus leader had twisted around to stare at us with sun-flamed eyes and an aggressively out-thrust jaw.

"Egg Bringer answer you must." Her snarl sounded like a whipcrack after the ghost-whisper of the sick female's voice. "Respect, obedience you show!"

"I wish I could," I said, hoping both she and the senior female could see the translating dance of stick figures on Uhura's screen that nuanced my words. "But our speaking machine can't hear all of the Egg Bringer's words."

"Perhaps if you could repeat what she says for a while, our machine could understand her better," Uhura suggested politely.

The tall female Nykkus tipped her head, as though listening to something we couldn't hear, then lashed her tail in swift acknowledgment, pushed herself to her feet, and launched herself toward us. I struck Orsini's hand away from his phaser, hoping to God I had guessed right about this. The massive hematite-dark body came to a halt only centimeters away, so close I could smell her own reptile musk and feel the exuded heat of her thermal armor.

"Close to Egg Bringer this machine take," she ordered. "Her own speaking to your ears must go."

I reached back to take the translation device away from Uhura, but she had already slipped past me on the Nykkus's other side and was approaching the bundle of blankets with her usual calm fearlessness. I went to push after her and bumped into a scaled, breathing wall of Nykkus instead. I scowled up at the female leader.

"Allow me through to answer the Egg Bringer!"

"Reason?" she demanded. "Not hottest of your egg pod you are."

I scowled, but before I could try to argue about something I wasn't even sure I understood, an audible hiss from the invalid interrupted. The lead Nykkus female's head snapped around and then, with a hot exhaled breath that sounded remarkably like a human sigh, she stepped back and let me through.

I joined Uhura at the edge of the blankets, crouching down as she had so the female lying there wouldn't have to lift her head too far to look at us. It was clear, now that I could actually see her painfully thin, shriveled body slumped across the stack of pillows, that this Egg Bringer wasn't just sick—she was old and probably dying. The hand she lifted to point at Uhura was twisted by some kind of degenerative bone disease into what looked like a single massive claw, while a dowager's hump of softened bone lowered her sauroid head deep onto her sunken chest. Even her lower jaw looked deformed by her illness, slid sidelong and drooping. Only in the gemstone glow of her eyes did she seem to resemble her Nykkus companions, but her far slimmer build and complete lack of tail told me the resemblance ended there. This was not an older Nykkus—it was one of the more aristocratic Anjiri species, the first we had seen in all our current dealings with these formerly allied races.

"Memory of you have we." Now that we were closer, the augmented translator seemed to be working a little better, although without the ability to nuance her words through movement, I suspected the Anjiri invalid had difficulty articulating even in her own language. "Trinkets by wanderers stolen, to air turned by you were. Promises kept."

I opened my mouth to ask what she meant, but Uhura's gentle tug on my sleeve stopped me. "She thinks you're Captain Kirk," the communications officer said softly, her fingers flexed on the translator's control panel so no figures danced her words through to the old Anjiri. "Tell her we know she kept her promise, and that we kept ours, too."

"Promises were kept on both sides," I said, as soon as Uhura released the controls again. "We left your area of space alone, and you did ours. Until now."

Her bright eyes followed the stick figure's interpretative dance across Uhura's display screen with enough understanding that a breathless snarl bubbled out of her deformed jaw when the final words were spoken. "Until now, Nykkus with Anjiri worked, promises together kept we." The bitterness of the words sizzled even through the imperfect translation. "Until fire touched. Nykkus warriors perfect were, Anjiri blood on their hands not, no eggs they destroy. Cry the day when fire Nykkus eggs did touch! Promises broken all, Anjiri warm-born by they killed all. From then ever, eggs all fire-touched, eggs all Nykkus were. Gone, gone, this world's future all. With warm-born Nykkus gone, returning never."

The ancient Anjiri's coughing of words stopped, seemingly exhausted by that final spate of fury. I spared a glance back at our Nykkus escort, but they didn't seem to be offended by the old Anjiri's rant against their own species. I remembered their apology when they first met us: "Nykkus are you think we. Attack we not, if we otherwise knew."

"What happened to cause such a tragedy between the Nyykus and Anjiri?" I asked, although I was starting to get a glimmer of the answer. The crumpled figure on the dais jerked a hand up again, this time pointing the fused claw past us at the largest of the Nykkus.

"Of birthing tell," she ordered, in her hoarse snarl. The dominant Nykkus ducked her powerful head in respectful submission, then turned her opalescent eyes toward us and the translating device.

"Hatched in fire, hot-born Nykkus, first in millennia are we," she said simply. There was no pride in her voice, just a simple realization of anomaly. "Nykkus eggs always warriors hatch, Egg Bearers and young guard they. Cold-born obedient warriors hatch, no eggs lay, no eggs destroy. Nykkus eggs far from fire kept, pale their shells remain. Anjiri eggs closer and darker are, heat in brains and loins burn they."

I frowned, beginning to see the pattern. With temperature the deciding factor in intelligence among these sibling species, it was clearly to the Anjiri's advantage to keep their stronger and fiercer cousins as cold as possible while they incubated, so that the Nykkus hatched out slow-witted and docile. But if fertility was also predetermined by the effects of temperature on the egg, as the young female Nykkus seemed to imply, why hadn't her species died out centuries ago?

I didn't have time to ask—the dark female had drawn another exasperated human-sounding breath and was continuing her story. "Mistaken, one pod of eggs long ago was. Anjiri eggs thought to be, close to fire set were they. Put to be Egg Bringers well would be, hot-born danger make not we. Warm-born Nykkus instead hatched, heart-hot but brain-shadowed always are they. Skulls crushed at once, well would be, but cold-born caretakers this truth obtain do not. Warm-born live, warm-born fast grow, warm-born rebellion against Anjiri make."

"They made smarter Nykkus males by mistake," Uhura said, lifting her fingers from the translator during the next, longer pause. "And then paid the price for all those years of repression."

"Yes," I said.

The dominant Nykkus female threw us a fiery opal gaze, as if she'd guessed what we were saying without the need of a translation. I reminded myself that if the females of her species were as superior in intelligence to their males as the Anjiri females had been to theirs, I was quite probably dealing with a being much smarter than I was.

"Lies *always* told are, tricks *always* played are, by Nykkus too warm-born yet not hot enough," she repeated fiercely. "This truth in times past all obtained, to make no warm-born Nykkus agreed *all.* Lost to time, this knowledge was—in blood and murdered pods regained was it. No Anjiri warm-born alive left they, all Anjiri eggs destroyed did they! Nykkus eggs only to be hatched were, an army of glorious renown to make."

I frowned. "But how could they—"

"Captain." I recognized the urgent voice from my wrist translator, so nearly noiseless that even Uhura's translator didn't detect it as that of my xenobiologist. "I've done preliminary DNA scans on the Nykkus and Anjiri, and you need to know the results. These aren't sibling species, sir, these are co-sexes of the same species. The females can lay fertile eggs for both variants, probably because they have two different kinds of ovaries."

I glanced over at Uhura, startled, and saw her pitying look swing back to the last female Anjiri. "The warm-born Nykkus forced the Egg Bringers to bear too many eggs, so they could raise more of themselves, didn't they?" she asked.

The Anjiri female didn't answer, but her Nykkus sister—or daughter—tilted her torso far forward and opened her jaw to bare her scimitar teeth, a position that made the translator's voice roar with anger. "Egg Bringers birth-killed, bone-rotted with swift bringing did they, stupid warm-born. No more Anjiri Egg Bringers made they, stupid warm-born. Nykkus Egg Bringers to make and use thought they, *stupid* warm-born!" Her teeth glinted, reddish-purple sunlight dripping across them like blood. "One pod only in the fire burned and hatched. Even wet from eggs, *dominance* did we, blood from warm-born Nykkus spilled.

"Crush our skulls ordered they, but cold-born caretakers knowledge obtained had and wiser were. Taken far were we, taken far to ancient burrows. By cold-born alone raised were we, come the time to return and dominance do." Her gape became what looked distinctly like a grimace. "But the warm-born Nykkus in theft of ships spent, too late to do dominance came we. One bone-rotted Egg Bringer alive left they. Into space all warm-born young took they, only one pod in fire put to burn left they, more Nykkuss Egg Bringers. Here wait we, here with sisters yet unborn, to dance dominance when the wanderers return do."

"But *will* they return?" I asked grimly. The question wasn't meant for the Nykkus or Anjiri around me, but Uhura's translator made it snarl and dance across the display screen nonetheless. The crumpled Anjiri female lifted her deformed snout from the thermal blankets and fixed me with a steady glare. Her coughing voice was fainter still, as if her last reserves of strength were fading, but the translator gave its human equivalent a steely note.

"Warm-born Nykkus your ships among the star battled have?"

"Yes," I admitted.

"Warm-born tricks and lies and cunning traps witnessed have you?" she persisted.

"Yes." This time the admission nearly got snapped between my teeth on its way out.

"The warm-born to this refuge return do, here to stay they forever, would have done you?"

"If possible, yes."

The sway of her head, so precariously slung on the calcium-exhausted bones of her spine, might have been either a nod or a shake or some other more alien gesture, but the triumphant gleam in her eyes was unmistakable. "This dilemma of warm-born, foreseen long have I. Broken promises vengeance upon their breakers bring, as long ago foretold you. But if complete vengeance is, disaster upon our race brings also. No more eggs can make I, warm or cold, Nykkus or Anjiri. Without warm-born to quicken them, no eggs these hot-born daughters make. Gone, all this world's future, gone with warm-born Nykkus." Her eyes flared with a last spike of determination, and her fused claw lifted to point directly at me. "Unless the hot-born to dominance among the stars bring you."

My immediate reaction was to step back in surprise, to frown at her, to ask her what she meant. But something hard and inexorable rose up inside and stopped me before I could do any of those things. It wasn't newfound strength or newly acquired wisdom. It was the relic of my defeat at the hands of the Nykkus, something I could thank them for all the rest of my life—a deep conviction that the easy, unthinking, natural response to a situation could sometimes be utterly the wrong one.

This time, that conviction held me silent and impassive as I thought over what the ancient Anjiri was suggesting. "Are you sure," I asked her at last, "that these young hot-born of yours can dominate the older Nykkus?"

Her misshapen face gaped with the ferocity of her hoarse snarl. "When wet with egg-blood, dominance did they on Nykkus many hatchings older," snapped the translator. "Close enough to warm-born see and touch, these daughters bring must you. No further battles, tricks, or lies upon your stars must Nykkus do. Home to quicken eggs and serve will come they, and glad at their bidding be."

I glanced at Uhura, not so much for consensus as to check the depth of concern in her eyes. It might be risky to take intelligent female Nykkus out into the galaxy, but their behavior had been honorable even before they'd known who we were, and their Anjiri sisters had certainly kept their end of the previous bargain they'd made with Starfleet. I thought we could count on these gem-dark female warriors to do likewise, provided we could get them close enough to get their rogue males back under control. We had to at least give them the chance to save their race—we had no other alternative. Members of the Federation are taught from childhood to avoid the needless loss of any species, and to abhor the extinction of any sentient alien race.

"We will take your daughters to the stars, to do dominance on the warm-born there." I didn't look back at my officers for consensus or support before I made that promise. It was a command decision, made because there wasn't any other choice. "But by now, your warm-born will have made enemies of other powerful starfaring empires besides our own, and we may not come in time to save them from vengeance wreaked by others."

"Swiftly go, and what can be saved, save you." The crippled Anjiri made a final gesture of benediction toward the powerful female Nykkus, then closed her fire-bright eyes and slumped torpidly down into her blankets. "For one more turning of sun alive will stay I, hope of future generations homeward brought to see. If not, then in fires of my birth will burn at last these weary bones, and to hell the souls of Nykkus with them take."

Fifteen

KIRK

THE SECURE PANEL BLOCKING THE MOUTH OF THE MAINTENANCE TUNNEL leapt aside so unexpectedly, I steeled myself for an out-gush of poison gas, or the concussion of a plasma grenade. Instead, we were met with only a gentle exhalation of cool air changing places with warm, and Chekov leaned inside to squint up into yet another long column of darkness. "Don't Klingons believe in emergency lights?"

A question which had grown near and dear to my heart during the last half hour. We'd stumbled across atmosphere barely a hundred meters into the station, but a positive pressure hadn't come with the other amenities I'd hoped for. Our helmet lights provided enough illumination to install the portable airlock and fill its narrow confines with gas. They could not, however, show us any way to coax open the bulkhead door which led into the pressurized station. That required an extra ten minutes of suit time while we ate most of our airlocked oxygen by cutting through the massive door with a phaser torch.

"I don't like not being able to secure this door again," Chekov had complained when we finally crawled through to the pitch black hallway on the other side. "If anything happens to our lock, we're going to evacuate the rest of the station."

With us inside. Not an unreasonable fear. Also, I suspected, not the reason he peeled out of his environmental suit soaked with sweat.

"What's your suit temperature?" I'd asked, tossing my own helmet into the web sling I'd bolted to the corridor wall. I'd managed to just reach the lower end of uncomfortable during our short trek, nowhere near hot enough to plaster my hair to my forehead much less drench my jacket.

Chekov glanced almost peremptorily at the reading on the inside collar of his breastplate, then stuffed it into the storage sling alongside mine. "Twenty degrees Centigrade."

What my mother used to call "room temperature." Perfectly normal. Unlike almost everything else about this mission.

By the time we'd reached this maintenance passage, a good kilometer further along, I'd started to wonder about the nature of equipment failures. Here we were, picking apart a space station's defenses one security door at a time, then sealing them behind us so that a casual glance would look like nothing at all had happened. Deceiving through appearances. Lying by the expediency of what others believed of what they'd see. And I thought about how easily humans could accomplish the same trick, by locking all their doors behind them, by allowing the appearance of functionality to substitute for the real thing whenever no one took the time for more than a casual glance.

The cool dry air of the station had dried Chekov's hair, but there was nothing to be done about his heavy uniform. I stood a little behind him as he verified there were no other security measures on the maintenance tunnel's hatch, and I wanted to ask him if he'd been in an environmental suit since losing the *Reliant.* If he'd known when he agreed to come with me that the first ten minutes of our trip would be the longest of his life. If he'd considered what might have happened if we'd been forced to stay in suits for thirty minutes—or an hour.

Instead, I rolled up the map in my hands and said, "Sixteen Klingon security points in less than thirty minutes. I'm impressed."

He tossed a look back at me that seemed both surprised and slightly pleased. "It only looks impressive because no one's home." He scooted away from the opening and pushed the cover plate completely aside before stuffing his tools back into their case. "Unlocking a few security doors is one thing. Doing it without anyone noticing is something else."

I went first up the open-runged ladder, my hand lamp wedged into my grip alongside the ladder's holds. The climb was the worst. Twelve steps up, the only thing I could see below me was the flicker of Chekov's light as he brought up the rear; ahead, my lamp cut a pitifully small swath out of the darkness. We could have dangled four hundred miles above the abyss and it wouldn't have been more black. We had phasers we couldn't reach, communicators that did us no good whatsoever now that we were deep inside the Klingons' shield, and a satchel filled with security-technician paraphernalia that was only worth its weight against pass boxes and sector doors. If someone closed in behind us or swooped down from above, about the only good either of us could do would be to warn the other. Not exactly my idea of an equitable division of risk.

I felt better once we reached a side passage. It was decadently wide by human standards, built to accommodate Klingon shoulders. I couldn't have hit my head on the ceiling without standing almost upright. All fours still made for the best mode of transport; I clenched the wrist cord on the lamp in my teeth and let it dangle as I pushed the map ahead of me one arm's-length at a time. The cone of light swung and jiggled, but it managed to catch enough details off the conduit-crowded walls and ribbed flooring to give me some vague idea where we were. Impressionistic map interpretation. Pausing, I settled back on my heels to stretch my spine, and to give my eyes a break from the headache-inducing wobble of light against dark. "We need to start looking for an exit hatch," I called back to Chekov. "If the Klingons haven't moved, we should be practically on top of them by now."

The floor in front of me shattered with enough force to pitch the map into the air and slap the light out of my teeth. A flurry of self-indictments raced across my mind—I should have sent Chekov first to search out booby traps; I should have led with a tricorder, not a phaser, to verify each centimeter of the structure's integrity; I should have known that Klingons would never let themselves be rescued without a fight.

The *bat'leth* twisted savagely into the metal, ripping it like paper. The floor beneath me tore downward in a single ragged sheet, and I had time for only one abortive grab at an overhead conduit before pitching down into blinding brightness.

Instinct made me roll the instant my shoulders slammed into a hard surface. In theory, this would be the deck, and being in motion would render me harder to hit while I tried to explain what I was doing here. In reality, the table now forced to catch my weight, in addition to a Klingon's armored mass, collapsed with a splintered crash. My attempt at evasion gained me only a metal-clad boot in the chest, and I ended up sprawled face-up beneath a *bat'leth* with someone's heel grinding into my throat.

A harsh female's voice commanded, *"Mev!"* just as my own eyes flashed to a movement in the hole above me and I saw Chekov lean through with his phaser armed.

"Hold your fire!"

Klingon and human both obeyed with laudable speed. The Klingon froze in midswing, his *bat'leth* swept back over one shoulder in what I'm sure would have ended up as a clean decapitation. Chekov more prudently shrank back from the opening, leaving only the washed-out glow from the lantern he'd discarded in the passageway behind him.

"What unexpected guests." This time I recognized the flat burr of an intercom in the still distinctly female voice. "Vardok, release him."

I've never understood how Klingons manage to balance their enthusiasm for battle with unquestioning obedience to sometimes less than blood-happy commanders. Vardok, though, proved himself a warrior with mettle. Taking two long strides away from me, he let his *bat'leth* fall across his front, the way a ballplayer might stand while awaiting his turn at bat. I noticed he was missing most of the flesh along one side of his face, and three of the fingers on one hand had been torn away. I'd never seen anyone, excluding Vulcans, sustain such hideous injuries in stoic silence. I didn't know whether to be respectful of the Klingon's inner strength, or just very, very afraid.

I opted for keeping one eye on him while doing what I'd come for. Heart pounding, I rolled carefully to my knees and took stock of the surroundings before trying to stand. At first glance, it looked like a sickbay. Then I realized there were no beds, no diagnostic tables, not even the shelf after shelf of hyposprays that I'd grown used to seeing in McCoy's domain. The six other Klingons detected by Spock's sensors all clustered behind a long stretch of transparent aluminum. They wore jumpsuits of a trim, pocket-filled design, with silver and hematite piping that I suspected denoted rank, or position, or perhaps what areas of the station they were allowed to access. I wondered if they were part of some closed environment experiment, or if they'd fled here seeking safety when the Nykkus attack began.

Then I remembered that even Klingon scientists probably never fled.

"Captain—" The speaker turned out to be a female young enough to be Vardok's daughter. Her angular face showed only the disdainful pride I'd learned to identify as the Klingon default expression, but near her hip she clutched a small data pad so tightly that she'd cracked the screen. Perhaps Klingon scientists weren't quite as fierce as their military counterparts after all. "Please," she said, sounding strangely like she meant to be both fierce and courteous, "do us the honor of bringing your soldier down to join us."

I stepped clear of the hole Vardok had torn in the ceiling, keeping my hands carefully away from my sides. "Chekov, come on down. This is what we came here for."

He slid through the hole without answering, catching the edge in both hands and lowering himself toward the ground. All in all, a neater landing than my own. As he moved to stand beside me, the female behind the transparent wall remarked to the other five crowded in with her, "What more proof do you need that Federation ships do not necessarily mean Federation attackers?" But she said it just a bit too loudly, as though meaning it for my ears as much as theirs. "Even Starfleet is not foolish enough to send only two human warriors to deal with us."

I took her assertion as a promising sign. "We're not here to fight. I'm Captain James T. Kirk—"

It was Vardok, his voice slurred and bloody, who rumbled, "We know who you are."

I've never been sure how to react to having my reputation proceed me. I turned partway toward Vardok, including him in the discussion. "Your attackers are pirates who hijacked Federation ships. We came to try to stop the attack, but our ship was caught in the subspace pulse when your resonance cannon was destroyed."

A little murmur of what might have been recognition passed through the Klingons behind the barrier. Vardok had returned to stoicism, not even meeting my gaze when I looked at him.

"So your ship is crippled," the female said. Implying they understood at least a little of what their cannon could do, and perhaps even what it had done to their own station. "Surely you did not come here to apologize for being defeated in combat."

"I came here to appeal to your honor." I felt Vardok's eyes on the back of my head, and reminded myself to tread carefully. The Klingons behind the partition might seem to be calling the shots, but Vardok was still the one out here with the sword. "Even if the Nykkus haven't found you yet, they will soon. You'll be killed, the Nykkus will leave, and your government will arrive to find a research outpost that was apparently destroyed by the Federation." I gave them a moment to follow that thought a few months, or years, into the future. "There is no honor in declaring war against the wrong enemy."

The female nodded slowly. "You have a keen understanding of Klingon honor, James T. Kirk." She seemed to notice the data pad in her hand for the first time, and slipped it out of sight into one jumpsuit pocket. "So you would have us stand witness for what truly happened here. How did you plan to use your crippled ship to ensure that?"

"We have a transporter. Right now, you're underneath one of the station's remaining defensive screens. If you would follow us—"

She pounded one fist against the transparent aluminum wall, so hard I would have expected the material to crack. But it didn't even rattle. It just made a deep, dull thumping, like stones against a starship's hull. I understood what she was telling me even before she said it. "We can follow you nowhere. The automatic security systems sealed these rooms when the attack began. It cannot be opened from inside, or from where you stand." She spread her arms in the almost universal gesture of helplessness. It looked particularly ill-fitting on a Klingon.

That stirring in my gut that had kept me awake nights since leaving the *Excelsior* kicked in with renewed vigor. I didn't like the precedent set by having the fundamental elements of a plan go awry. "If we can't move you out from under the shield, then we have to bring the shield down." I extended a helpless gesture of my own. "Where's the generator?"

Hesitating only momentarily, she motioned me to approach the divider.

Inside, probably the last working computer terminal on the station cast a pale glow across her face as she sat to wake up its system. It must have been shielded inside this isolated clean room, along with at least some small computer dedicated to keeping it alive. The other Klingons clustered in a ring barely big enough to let me see what she was doing.

"The generator is here." The kind of layout starships often keep on hand for new personnel popped up on her screen, and she pointed with authority at the general operations center. Smack in the middle of Nykkus country. She split the screen to display an innocuous square housing, its front marked by nothing except the Klingon "Do Not Enter" that Chekov and I had gotten so skilled at ignoring lately. "You need to use a maintenance command code to open the housing." She glanced over her shoulder at an older male Klingon in a dull gray robe. He spoke to her briefly, and she typed the run of figures onto the screen. "Lork says this code will serve that purpose. The generator itself is inside."

I studied the numbers, but the code was really the least of my worries. "There are Nykkus all over that part of the station. We can't very well just walk in and turn it off."

She swivelled away from her computer to look at me, then beyond me. "This warrior with you—he understands how our weapons work?"

I didn't have to glance back at Chekov to know where she was looking. "Yes. He knows them well."

"Then we will show you the place on Kreth where research was done on directional explosive devices." I knew the kind she meant—the kind you planted ahead of your own troops that projected its force so specifically, you could be sure it would only wipe out things in one direction. "You should be able to find everything you need to build a very useful bomb," she assured me with great sincerity. "Blast your Nykkus out into space. You will have us alive to speak on your behalf to our people, and we will have our revenge for the dead." A truly Klingon smile bared her teeth, and I wasn't sure I liked how they gleamed. "An elegant solution to both our problems, don't you think?"

The fact that any explosion which destroyed the operations center would probably also suck most of the air out of the rest of the station didn't seem to concern them. Why should it? They were in an airtight room, and had nothing better to do with their time. They could be beamed out once the explosion was over. Vardok, meanwhile, would be honored to join his fallen comrades at the gates of Sto'vo'kor. At least, so they assured me. Vardok himself had surprisingly little to say on the matter.

Unlike Vardok, we had suits, which made me feel only marginally better about it. I hailed the *Enterprise.* "Pick up any Klingon life-signs not grouped tight with the others," I told Spock. "Beam him in first." But it was a messy, interference cluttered communication, and I wasn't entirely sure he understood what I'd asked him to do.

"Still no word from Sulu," I announced once I'd closed the channel and turned back toward the inside of the lab. It didn't seem prudent to mention that, with as spotty as our own communication with the *Enterprise* was, it probably wasn't reasonable to expect to hear from the other captain until he was right on our doorstep. "Are we ready to go?"

Chekov sat in front of the workbench with his hands folded on top of it, his chin resting on his hands, and his dark eyes boring into the exotic contraption he'd just put together one piece at a time. "I'm thinking it through." It was a bit unnerving to watch—I could almost see him reexamining the parts in his mind, stepping through each of their functions until the final point where detonation destroyed them all. About the time I was thinking of urging him to hurry, he sat back with a sign and reached for the small, studded cylinder that he'd already told me was the detonator/timing device for the bomb. I remembered finding it eerie to be saving such an innocuous yet deadly piece for last. "It's not as focused as I would like," Chekov admitted as he quickly examined the detonator under his light, "but it should work."

So we stood a little farther behind it, or we would do what armies sometimes did and completely retreat from anywhere near the device before setting it to explode. If it could do even half the damage Chekov predicted for the little device, it would work more than just well enough.

I stayed in the laboratory doorway as he primed the last piece for insertion. It was dark in here, just like everywhere else. I'd let Chekov take both lanterns so as not to ruin my night vision as I crouched outside to guard the hall. Now he sat in the midst of their combined glow with half the contents of his equipment kit spread out on the workbench, a confusion of Klingon tools, devices, and parts discarded nearby. In that moment, while he put the finishing touches on the one item that meant the success or failure of everything we'd come here to do, he seemed so comfortably settled and sure of his work, so far removed from the guilt-wracked officer I'd beamed aboard a few hours ago, that I had to ask, "What's the difference?"

He tossed me a silent question out of the corner of his eyes, but didn't stop working.

"Between this and command," I added. I stepped inside the doorway, as though for privacy, even though there wasn't anyone within this whole section of the station who might possibly hear. "At this moment, you're responsible for the ship, those Klingons, for both our lives . . ."

He gave a little nod of understanding, finally catching up to my thought processes. "No, sir," he said, clicking the detonator firmly into place, "*you're* responsible. I'm just one of the tools you use to get the job done." A single white light blinked alive on top of the device. "I wasn't very good at taking care of my own tools."

I watched the care with which he collected his kit together, checking each piece for damage, wiping each one clean on the sleeve of his jacket. I found it hard to believe he'd been any less conscientious with his people. "You had some pretty heavy extenuating circumstances."

"That doesn't bring them back." He slipped the last piece into its slot in the satchel, and closed the case. "I thought at first that I should somehow make up for being the only one left . . . by not running away from my duty, by taking the new assignment and being better . . ." But then he shook his head, as if even he realized how little sense thoughts like that made when you had to speak them aloud. "Now . . ." He slid the bomb into one hand and stood. "I'm ashamed at how good I am at this." He looked not at the bomb, or at his tools, but just at me, presenting himself with all these pieces as his evidence. "At being someone else's tool, and not the craftsman."

I wished—not for the first time since bringing him aboard—that we had the leisure to do more than just stumble across these things in the midst of crisis. Instead, all I could say was, "You have nothing to be ashamed of. You'd make a fine addition to any crew."

An unexpected flush dashed up his cheeks. "We should get going." He reached back for the lanterns, tossing mine toward me with a neat underhand. "It's a long walk back to our suits."

Not as long as the walk out from them. The already opened security doors helped, I'm sure, but it was adrenaline that pushed me at a near-trot the whole way. Just before we rounded the last corner leading to the storage sling where we'd left our suits, I mentally cautioned myself not to get too comfortable with this apparently abandoned station. We'd traveled the same routes too many times now, grown too used to the idea that the routes Spock had marked for us were somehow magically more safe than others. Once we were suited up again and making our clumsy way through the corridors closest to the Nykkus base of operations, we couldn't afford to be so cavalier.

In that regard, then, the Nykkus clustered around our ruined suits were not a complete surprise. Nor was their speed in dashing in to surround us, nor was their fierceness in tackling Chekov and slamming me against the wall. In retrospect, the only thing that I could never have expected, even after reading the *Excelsior* crew's reports, was how hideously a Nykkus tail could hurt when it smashed into you at full, whistling speed.

I crashed back into consciousness while half-choking on pain.

"Captain . . . easy . . ."

It was like zero-G, with no concept of up and down, only brighter and smelling pungently of reptile musk and Klingon blood. I couldn't see clearly, couldn't seem to remember how to breathe. I tried to push myself away from whatever crowded against my cheek and shoulder, but just the thought of shifting my elbow ripped such pain through my chest that I shouted profanities and curled in on myself.

"Sit up!" Hands gripped the front of my jacket, heaving me upright through pain's sticky surface tension. As soon as I was vertical—even before I realized it was a wall that patiently took my weight—the crushing heaviness lifted off my rib cage. I took a careful, pain-clouded breath as Chekov instructed me, "Captain, take this."

It's amazing what being able to breathe does for one's perspective. Taking the wadded-up jacket he thrust into my arms, I hugged it against myself like a lifesaving float. More stress removed from my protesting rib cage, and a return to vision as my blood pressure came down. Much more practical first aid than anything I'd ever been forced to study. They must teach them this stuff at the Security Academy.

We'd made it to central operations a bit more straightforwardly than I might have preferred. A big, open room with dark metal walls and only the ghost of emergency lighting ringing the ceiling and every empty panel. Stations cluttered the space in what seemed a thoroughly nonergonomic manner, but perhaps it was just an expression of Klingon aesthetics. There were no chairs.

Nykkus milled in groups of two, three, seven, walking over what was left of dead Klingons with as little reaction as when they walked over their own filth. Moving, upright, their dark, metallic scales flashing, they were more intimidating than they'd seemed on a cold morgue slab. Infinitely more intimidating than a mere two decades ago. Four of them entertained themselves by chuffing and barking into our confiscated translators, but they were too far away for us to hear what they were saying. Probably the Nykkus equivalent of "the quick brown fox." Two others sat together in a corner, one studiously carving fresh whorls into the other's cheeks. The largest group of them, though, busied themselves with our phasers, targeting objects all throughout the room. They'd apparently discovered the heat generation settings. Every time they fired on something and sent it bursting into flame, they went into a frenzy of excitement, racing in and out among each other, leaping into the air. They reminded me of a bunch of nine-year-old boys shattering glass bottles with an air rifle.

It was the angular lump of gray metal on the far side of the room, agonizingly distant from my hurting self, that made my stomach twist in frustration. "The shield generator."

"I know." Chekov, on his knees in front of me, twisted a grim look over his shoulder. "I don't think they've even tried to get it open."

Of course not. The housing could have been a seat, or one of a dozen other strange structural irregularities that jutted out from walls and floors around the place. It occurred to me that I had no idea what all those other boxes might contain. I found myself wishing we had the time to examine them all.

But we had time for very little, really. Regaining my sense of command, I focused on Chekov for the first time since he'd pulled me upright. "Are you all right?" The sleeve of his blue tunic was wet with blood from the elbow down, as though one of the Nykkus had gripped him a bit enthusiastically, but his eyes looked remarkably bright and clear from pain.

"Better than you." He stretched his arm out—to flex his hand and prove nothing was broken, I thought. But then he closed his fingers firmly around my wrist and squeezed. I felt the smooth regularity of metal pressed against my skin, and realized with a start what it was: my wrist communicator. I glanced down and saw Chekov's own communicator on his wrist, its little status display informing me that it was turned on and a channel to the ship already open. Apparently, the Nykkus were better at recognizing weapons.

"The Nykkus found our environmental suits and destroyed them," Chekov explained. His eyes never left mine, but I knew the words were for the sake of whoever else might be listening. "You have at least a few broken ribs, and probably a concussion—you've been unconscious for nearly twenty minutes. We have fourteen minutes left of the window you afforded Mr. Spock for this mission."

And we were either close to completing that mission or farther from it than ever before. "Whether or not Mr. Spock sticks around past that will have to be up to him." We might as well supply him with some useful information in the meantime. "We're obviously in the main operations center. Why are we still alive? What are they waiting for?"

"The Raask has to visit each of their cargo ships in order to check with the crews." He added with a certain amount of satisfaction, "I don't think their communications equipment is working very well."

I frowned, still on his first bit of information. "What's the Raask?"

A commotion at the other end of the room sucked the attention of all the other Nykkus like a fireball sucks oxygen. They dropped their toys, jumped away from their wrestling and dancing, and clattered for the source of their fascination with high, grating squeals and breathy hisses. In front of me, Chekov shuffled quickly back as though anxious to make room between the two of us. The glare he threw toward the approaching band was pure hatred.

"The Raask," he said grimly, "is them."

They stood out from the rest of the Nykkus the way a mastiff stands out from a herd of deer. Seven of them, their bodies a mass of ritual scarring, their dorsal crests erect, their muzzles crowded with at least one extra row of teeth. They were obviously older than the less scarred, less finished males around them, their dominance dripping off them like hot wax. All of them carried Klingon disruptors, and three had what looked like raw Klingon skull plates fastened to their body armor. Their tails were plated with scales so sharp, I knew they must augment their natural shape with filing. If I'd been hit with one of those tails, there'd have been little left between my collarbones and pelvis for Chekov to worry about taking home. Every detail of their hot, closely knit unit was so intensely beautiful, so terrifying that I momentarily despaired of ever standing up to them.

They spread into a flying wedge as they drew close to us. Chekov stood, drawing their attention, and they swept into a prowling circle around him, tails rattling against the floor in a private rhythm that seemed to pass back and forth between them.

"Hurtful things from this creche fine are. Objects beauteous . . ." They each wore a Starfleet translator—stolen, no doubt, from the *Excelsior*'s resupply team. Their voices—one voice—slithered out of all the units at once, granting them a strange sibilance that wasn't at all inappropriate.

One of them, taller and more heavily boned than the others, halted its prowling to roll our newly made bomb out of the pouch it wore around its waist. "The Raask this thing as one with the others knows. Design and housing, prettily the same are." It leaned close to breathe the question into Chekov's face. "What this creates?"

Chekov tipped his chin a bit defiantly upward, and told them, "It's a bomb."

The Raask blurred into movement. I rocked up onto my knees in alarm, choking back an uprush of pain and praying I didn't see one of those sharpened tails lash out in a spray of blood and human entrails. "Scaleless!" The large, dark Nykkus—the leader?—pummeled its siblings aside and bent low over where Chekov had ended up sprawled on the floor. "Toothless-born! Think mammals not their faces the Raask can know? Think this mammal tricks and lies no payment to the Raask bear must?"

I tried to see past the swarm of their bodies, but even after struggling upright, I had to content myself with watching for signs of blood on Nykkus teeth and tails.

"Know this mammal well the Raask do. Lies and slinking dance this mammal do." It sank into a squat, the bomb cradled like a baby on its taloned hand. "Star-bright vast expansion not," it declared, almost sweetly. "This mammal always lie do. The Raask this so knows does. Thing hurtful the Raask believe this does do. Object beauteous to mammal for all lying pay. See?"

It rolled the bomb from hand to hand, metal-polished talons clicking against its duranium surface. When one arching thumb claw pried at the detonator tab, I couldn't keep my mouth shut any longer. "Stop!"

Half the Raask whirled on me, crouching in suspicion. Their leader simply ceased all movement, its gemlike eyes staring into space with what I could only take to be annoyance at my interruption. "What mammal dancing so this is?" it asked at last.

I heard Chekov's voice call frantically from within their cluster, "Captain, don't—!"

He had caught their attention again with horrifying efficiency. I lurched a few unsteady steps forward, still hugging the balled-up jacket against me and hoping it would prove enough support to save us both. "I mean it!" Shouting made my head spin in sick circles. "If you kill him, I won't tell you a damned thing, and you'll all die."

One of the Raask slammed its tail against the floor, making the younger Nykkus around their edges skitter back and sink low. "Dancing so this mammal also touted." The words came from all of them, any of them. "This mammal lies make did."

"But I'm not lying." I shuffled a few steps close, still trying to get a good look at Chekov where they kept him pinned to the floor. "And neither is he. He's trying to trick you. He's counting on you not believing him so that you'll experiment with that device and blow yourselves up."

A ripple of coordinated movement passed among them. "Mammal's death also this dance make would."

Yes, but I don't think he cares about that right now. "Why do you think I'm stopping you? I don't want to die." I staggered to a stop next to one of the dead control consoles, only to discover that nothing feels like useful support when your ribs are too battered to let you lean. "You think I'm lying? This mammal—" I jabbed a finger toward Chekov, who was in the middle of their bundle. "You believe he hates you? You believe he would do anything to destroy you, even destroy himself?"

For the first time, very little movement wove through their pod. I wondered if they were thinking, or if there were gestures in their language so subtle the human eye couldn't even see what they were.

"If you think I'm lying," I said, "then hand that device to him and see what he does with it."

Tails rattling, teeth clacking in obvious threat, the Raask drew apart like a door irising. Chekov stood slowly, relieving at least a little of my breathlessness, and looked at me with incomprehension clouding his expression. He wasn't hurt, though. For all their speed and ferocity, they apparently knew how to temper their outbursts so as to preserve a victim for torture. What interesting evidence of civilization.

The lead Raask balanced the bomb on the palm of its broad hand, and thrust the device toward Chekov. My officer stared at the bizarre gift while I thought as fiercely as I could, *Do what you said you're good at—be the tool!*

Let me be the captain, and just do what I expect of you without questioning it.

As though my thoughts arced across the distance and into his brain, Chekov gave a decisive little nod, took the bomb from the Raask, and pulled out the switch. Squawking a brief Klingon warning, the bomb began its countdown.

If they'd learned nothing else in capturing Kreth station, the Nykkus had learned the difference between a handgun and a weapon of mass destruction. They fell on Chekov like football players all going for the same ball. One of them came up with the gleaming metal device in both hands, and dashed toward me while commanding shrilly, "Undo! *Undo!*"

I jerked my chin toward where the other members of the Raask might very well have killed Chekov already. "Let him go." They might not be able to read the Klingon numbers marching across the face of the bomb in their hands, but I could. I knew exactly how much time we had.

I made them place Chekov next to me and back two large steps away before finally taking the heavy device. I pushed the timer back inside the body, and the countdown stopped. The Raask insisted on examining the quiescent, but not defused, bomb.

"Why this mammal's entrails safeguard you do?" one of them asked, tossing the bomb to one of its companions now that it was no longer interesting. "Why its bones protect you do?"

I looked at Chekov, who still bore the slightly stunned expression of a man who'd avoided unwanted death by far too close a margin. I took that as a good sign. "Because he still has uses. I'm not done with him yet." I stood as straight as possible, hoping that made me appear honest. "I can show you how to find the replicator equipment you came here for."

"No objects of duplication smelled have we!" But there was a certain hopeful lust in the lead Raask's eyes when it dashed foward. It never shifted its eager attention from me, but still slashed a hate-filled glare at Chekov. "Lies this mammal do!"

"He's not the one telling you this—I am." Clinging to my wad of jacket like a lifeline, I pushed away from the station I'd been using for support. Chekov caught my arm, and I leaned on him as heavily as I dared as I limped toward the generator housing. "This station belongs to our enemies. You can build a hundred armies in their space and I wouldn't care. You'll just keep them busy." It was smaller than the upright consoles, just the right size to sit on when you didn't think you could stand a moment longer. "They know how dangerous their replication technology could be in the wrong hands. So they've hidden it under a masking field. That's why your sensors don't work well around this station, why you're having trouble communicating with your ships." I thumped one foot against the innocuous housing. "The controls are in here."

I motioned Chekov to slide aside the access door, but the Raask was faster. Snatching him away from me, their leader flattened its hand across the commander's middle in a gesture whose threat was more than merely obvious. "Like this mammal you falsehoods do, like this mammal also you die do."

I attempted a thin smile. "I was already clear on that."

Thank God for Starfleet training and the sense to pay attention to everything. I hesitated only long enough to recall the Klingon figures Lork had donated to our cause, then keyed open the housing with an authority I didn't entirely believe myself. The inside surprised me with an intricate network of displays and colored lights. I'd almost forgotten how working Klingon equipment looked. I found the master circuit near the rightmost edge of the generator's system board; prying it out was harder. Sweat stung my eyes, and I felt more than just a little dizzy by the time I succeeded in wedging a finger under the flange and popping it upward. Almost immediately, the lights on the face of the generator died. I imagined I could feel the mighty shielding fall.

Straightening, I clenched the master circuit in my fist as tightly as I could. And I smiled. All triumphant traitors should face their captors with a smile.

The lead Raask dashed forward to thrust its big muzzle into the open housing. It's throat rippled with a purr of delight. "Field of masking gone now is. What now we do?"

"Now we see if Mr. Spock decided to stick around."

Even these new and improved Nykkus were faster physically than mentally. By the time the transporter's whine grew into a wail around us, it was already too late for them to stop us. Too late to do more than swipe harmless talons through our fading silhouettes, too late to seek another sheltered part of the station.

Too late, even, to snatch back the shield master circuit that I still held safely clenched in my hand.

Sixteen

SULU

"Still no contact with the *Enterprise?*"

I'd made the request enough times in the last few minutes that Uhura didn't even bother to glance up from the controls of her communications console on the *Jocelyn Bell* when she answered. "No, Captain. I've even tried tight-beaming a signal directly to her presumed location at Kreth, but there's no reply."

I swung my frown to the console on the left and my chief science officer. "The *Enterprise* still hasn't appeared on our long-range sensors? We're within ten minutes of arrival."

Christina Schulman shook her head. "The integrity of subspace itself seems to be badly damaged around that Klingon research station, Captain. It's almost as if some kind of phase demodulation of space has occurred there. I don't think you're going to get sensor or communications contact until we're within visual range."

"Warm-born there known still to be?"

I glanced over my shoulder at the two-meters-plus of Nykkus leaning forward to peer at the *Jocelyn Bell*'s small viewscreen. I could remember thinking on the journey out to the Anjiri homeworld that this wide-bellied cargo shuttle was almost too big for comfort. The once roomy command console in front of the two long rows of passenger seats now seemed small when the rear cargo area held a restless coil of Nykkus, conversationally snarling and snapping and jostling each other with powerful shoulders as they vied for places behind the viewscreen. My nervous security chief hadn't taken his eyes off them since we'd boarded, but there'd been no attempt to break the agreement we'd made back in the sullen red light of their own sun. Unlike their male counterparts, the hot-born female Nykkus seemed to understand the wisdom of not making enemies when you didn't need to.

"We won't know that until we get there," I told her. The Nykkus made the snapping sound with her jaws that seemed to be their equivalent of a nod without even glancing at the jittering stick figure on the augmented universal translator. The Nykkus were growing more and more comfortable with just the sound of our translated voices as this trip progressed, at a rate I might have found disturbing if I didn't have more important things to worry about. Like whether Captain Kirk and the *Enterprise* had fallen victim to the warm-born Nykkus the way the *Excelsior* had, or if the Klingons had simply annihilated all of them together in a fit of imperious wrath at the infringement of their territory.

"This vessel cannot faster go?" The female's fire-opal gaze slanted past my shoulder at the *Jocelyn Bell*'s display of warp output and velocity. It was such a reasonable thing for someone to do while asking that question that it took me a minute to realize this particular young sauroid had never been trained in space-flight procedures.

"No," I said flatly.

She snapped her scimitar teeth together again, equably enough, and gave up her place to another of her sisters. This one used her time to simply stare at the viewscreen for several long moments. Then, just as I began the *Jocelyn Bell*'s smooth deceleration curve, she stabbed a single onyx-colored claw at the display's polysilicon surface. "This star our destination is," she said, not making it a question.

"Yes," I said, wondering how she'd calculated that. We decelerated out of warp and promptly entered a region of normal space lit with a pale, ghostly glow, as if a shred of nebula or planet-forming plasma had streaked through and left it subtly energized. I ran a quick systems check of all my piloting controls, but saw no interference on the boards. "Schulman?"

"I think we're seeing the effects of that subspace dephasing I picked up earlier on sensors, sir." My science officer was hunched over her sensors now, running one analysis after another. "I don't think it's natural, sir. Some kind of subspace explosion or cosmic string eruption—"

"Or space-battle?" I asked grimly, seeing the darkened silhouette of a Klingon station slide into view without any indication of lights or power glowing within. There was still no sign of the *Enterprise,* but at this range the station could be blocking her from us.

"Possibly, sir. But if so, the weapons used don't match the output of anything in Starfleet's data banks."

"This world builds, who?" asked the Nykkus, peering at the station on the viewscreen so intently that her powerful head hung nearly level with my own. "You?"

"No. It belongs to our enemies, a race of warriors called Klingons." I began to cut back the *Jocelyn Bell*'s impulse engines as we drew closer to Kreth. From behind me, I could hear Lieutenant Orsini whistle in soft astonishment at the black stabs of phaser burns and lesions of hull breaches that marred the station's sides. "Why?"

"Built too simple it is," said the charcoal-colored female, crinkling her muzzle in distaste. "Windows too few, floors too few. And to space, too many holes is."

Before I could explain that hull breaches hadn't been included in the original Klingon blueprint, the architectural critic was shouldered aside by the largest and most dominant of the pod. I was starting to be able to tell the Nykkus apart by the different undertones of garnet, sapphire, and amethyst that gleamed like a raku pottery glaze across their dark scales. The leader of the group was almost completely black, with only a splash of twilight color at her throat. I wondered if that meant her egg had received the most charring and heat.

"Weapons of distant murder at this place have they." She pointed to the phaser scars showing on the viewscreen, confirming my suspicions that she was not only the biggest but also the brightest of her pod. "If warm-born now this place control, dominance afar must we first do, with our own distant weapons use. Weapons powerful enough we have?"

I gave her a startled look. These hot-born sauroids with their gleaming hematite scales and opalescent eyes had seemed utterly adapted for their simple life back in the tunnels of the Anjiri homeworld. I'd wondered how they would react to the cultural shock of Starfleet technology, but I'd never suspected they would absorb and encompass it in a few short hours. They'd given such close scrutiny to every move we made since boarding the *Jocelyn Bell* that by now I had the uneasy feeling they could have flown the ship themselves if they wanted to. That swift Nykkus adaptability helped me understand how their rogue male counterparts had cut such a swathe of destruction through two overwhelmingly superior space-powers. It also made me wonder what would have happened if this complex sauroid species had decided long ago to control their disruptive Nykkus males by incubating warrior eggs too hot rather than too cold.

Uhura swung around before I could answer the hot-born female's question. "Captain, I'm getting a reply from the *Enterprise!*"

"Sulu." That was Kirk's grim face, unmistakable even through the drizzle of interference on the viewscreen. "Security protocol delta."

I nodded as the communications officer made the necessary encryption modifications to her console. "Protocol engaged, Captain," I said and saw his own confirming nod. "What is your situation?"

"We've got the leaders of the Nykkus pirates in our brig, but we're not going anywhere with them soon," Kirk said. He looked tired. We'd all had a very, very long day. "The Klingon station sent a distress call out when the Nykkus first attacked it. About an hour ago, our old friend Captain Koloth showed up with a couple of Klingon warships."

"Is he holding the Federation responsible for the attack on the research station?"

"No, thanks to a few surviving Klingon eyewitnesses." Kirk threw a wry glance over his shoulder, and I finally realized that the familiar figure manning the *Enterprise*'s security station was my own executive officer. Chekov's dark gaze lifted to meet Kirk's—and mine—for a rueful moment, then dropped to his panel again. "But Koloth is demanding that we give the Nykkus ringleaders over to him for the execution of Klingon justice."

"Which usually boils down to plain old execution," added Doctor McCoy sardonically, from his usual place beside Kirk's command chair.

I glanced back at the knot of hot-born Nykkus in the cargo shuttle, guessing from the way their scales had lifted and flushed with purple blood that they'd had no problem following this conversation. A strong tang of musk now pervaded the shuttle's atmosphere. "Is Koloth threatening to attack if you don't surrender the Nykkus to him?"

"No, but if we don't he's threatened to take his revenge against the shipload of younger Nykkus he captured when he took control of the station." Kirk's face turned grim again. "That's why I need to know what you found out at the Anjiri homeworld, Captain. Are these Nykkus pirates criminals in their own society? Can we turn them over to the Klingons with a clear conscience?"

The image of a crippled and dying Anjiri female rose in my mind and I opened my mouth to say "yes." But my new inner reluctance to accept easy solutions at their face value stirred again, forcing me to stop and turn toward the silent Nykkus at my back. She opened her mouth wide, in the snarling gape that seemed to be an expression of both anger and resolution among her species.

"Criminals are they, criminal to us before all others!" she declared. "But to us must these criminals return, or else forever our race dies. Warm-born males by mistake were made, and their tricks and lies on Anjiri first they played. Now only hot-born females we remain. Warm-born Nykkus need we, both race of Nykkus and Anjiri to re-create." Even their translated syntax was getting better.

Kirk's eyebrows shot upward. "Sulu? Is that true?"

"Yes, Captain. The Anjiri and Nykkus are members of the same species, their sexes and personalities decided by the temperature at which their eggs are incubated. Thanks to those megalomaniac pirates out there, the Nykkus males on their ships and these few females are the only ones left. We need to save as many as we can, to give their race a chance to survive."

The dominant female had listened to my succinct report in silence, but her fire-opal eyes glowed with determination by the time I was done. "Survive must we and dominance must do we," she told the viewscreen. "But even if not so, first victims of the warm-born are we. Belongs justice first to us, before to any other."

Captain Kirk stared at her from the viewscreen so intently that I wondered if he already saw the potential danger—and opportunity—in these intelligent sauroids as clearly as I did. "You want to punish the pirate ringleaders yourselves?"

"Punish, avenge, and dominance do!" The bubbling snarls that echoed her own roar showed the sentiment was shared by her sisters. "This right on our world have we. This right among the stars have we also?"

"Considering Klingon concepts of justice, you just might," Kirk said thoughtfully. "Commander Rand, hail Captain Koloth and patch a three-way contact through to the *Jocelyn Bell.*"

While we waited for the channel to open, our shuttle finally rounded the shattered corner of the Klingon research station, and the equally burned and blasted silhouette of the *U.S.S. Enterprise* floated into view with two sleek Klingon warships hanging ominously above her. I took a deep breath, feeling suddenly and quite illogically better about my entire engagement with the Nykkus. If they could do this to Captain Kirk, there was no shame in their having done it first to me.

A dark face with slashed eyebrows above glittering black eyes appeared on half the shuttle's viewscreen. From the way Kirk's frown jagged deeper into his forehead, I could tell that Koloth's scornful look was aimed at him. "Please don't tell me you're going to dither at me some more about justice, Captain," he said. "Just transport those reptile criminals over to my custody, and I might be able to forget that you're currently invading Klingon territory."

Kirk's scowl deepened. "The criminals you're referring to have been claimed by a third party in this dispute, Captain Koloth. It seems the Nykkus themselves have a claim to settle against these pirates."

"And how many fleets of starships do the Nykkus have, that I have to worry about their claims?" Koloth asked coldly.

"None," Kirk said between his teeth. "So far. But they are an emerging and warlike race who own a highly strategic piece of Orion real estate, close to the Klingon border."

I saw the considering look that entered Koloth's dark eyes at that information, despite the fact that he must have known Kirk had deliberately thrown it out to make him pause. I added my own quiet persuasion. "Captain Koloth, isn't there a Klingon proverb that says, 'Choose your enemies more wisely than your friends. Your friends do not come back to kill you later.' "

"Indeed, there is." The Klingon captain turned his gaze slightly in the viewscreen and his slanted eyebrows went up. I suspected the fierce wall of Nykkus arrayed shoulder to shoulder behind my back, teeth bared and frills defiantly erect, also had a salutary impression on him. "Well, what crimes do these Nykkus have to complain of, and what justice do they intend to exact for them?"

Kirk opened his mouth to reply, but a roaring Nykkus voice drowned out whatever he meant to say. "Murder of our species, would commit they!" spat the dominant Nykkus female. "Of justice final givers are we, dominance dance upon their bones until remains defiant none!"

"That sounds interesting," Koloth admitted. "Would you mind an audience?"

Kirk scowled into the viewscreen at him. "You don't have the right to interfere—"

The Klingon's mouth curled into a cruel smile. "Oh, indeed, I do, Captain. My two *undamaged* warships give me that right." This time, it was the mocking emphasis in his voice that made Kirk's face darken. "Your Nykkus friends will dance their dominance right here, on my ship and in front of me, so that I can see that it satisfies the demands of Klingon honor. Otherwise, I will simply blow them and you to bits."

"Where dominance is done care not we," declared the lead female, before I could interfere. "Fire's daughters are we, the Vorsk, first to hatch in centuries. Dominance on the most-scarred, the Raask, will do we, matters not the place or time."

"That sounds like agreement to me." Koloth was still smiling. "In precisely three minutes, Captain Kirk, I will drop my shields and beam over the—er—reptile ladies. You can beam over the gentlemen you're holding at the same time, along with any witnesses you care to bring. A truce of encounter will hold until justice is delivered to my satisfaction. After that, you can—as you humans say—go on your merry way. Provided that the merry way you go takes you straight out of Klingon territory. Agreed?"

"Agreed," the captain said grudgingly. "Kirk out."

Koloth's cynical face vanished from the viewscreen, leaving only my former captain to look at me with foreboding in his eyes. "Sulu, how many of these female Nykkus were you able to rescue?"

"A full pod of twelve, here have we," said the Nykkus leader before I could answer. "Why ask you?"

Kirk snorted. "Because we have at least seven of the Nykkus ringleaders in custody, the ones marked with all the scars, plus another twenty younger ones who supported their attack. And they all seem to be just as big and strong as you are."

"Strength in more than tail and teeth have we," said the dark female, her teeth parting then meeting again with a startling rasp instead of the usual click. "Sufficient to this meeting be we."

"I hope so," Kirk said grimly. "Because if you're not, Koloth will be doing dominance on all of us."

We materialized in yet another cargo hold, this time one dank and chill to suit Klingon cargo, but well-lit and cordoned off by a watchful line of Klingons armed with *bat'leths* and stern looks. I arrived with Kirk, Spock, and Chekov as the designated Starfleet witnesses in this distinctly odd court of justice. The Nykkus females had already been transported over by the Klingons, punctual to the minute on their promise. We arrived only a moment later, but Koloth was already scowling. The expression pulled his pencil-slim beard into a sour curve across his face.

"Gentlemen," he said reproachfully. At first I thought he was addressing us, but a moment later his voice surged into a peal of annoyance. "*Gentlemen.* Where are the reptile gentlemen these ladies are so eager to punish? You gave your word of honor to bring them over, Captain Kirk."

"And I'll keep it," Kirk said. His voice had taken on the tone of no-nonsense curtness that irritable Klingons so often brought out in him. "In stages." He saw Koloth's face darken and added, "Even a trial doesn't put everyone in the dock at the same time."

"They do on Qo'nos."

Kirk ignored that petulant protest, turning instead to the impatient line of female Nykkus. They were unarmed and unarmored, except for the links of thermal plating that kept their temperature up. Their gold and silver scale-piercings glittered in the light. "Which of the criminals do you wish to confront first?"

"Dominance on the Raask, the first-to-hatch, would do we," said the largest. In the actinic Klingon lights, her opalescent eyes had turned an eerie, opaque white, and a tense flush of purple shone through her lifted black scales. "Now, while strong we are."

Kirk lifted his wrist communicator and toggled it on. "Scotty, beam over the main set of prisoners," he ordered.

There was almost no pause—Montgomery Scott must have been waiting for that order with the Raask already targeted and caught in the transporter's clutches. Forms with familiar sauroid tails began to coalesce in the middle of the open area framed by Klingon guards, forms as broad-shouldered as the female Nykkus who waited for them, but neither as tall nor as dark. Nor as quick.

I wasn't sure what I had expected from this clash of warring sexes. A negotiation, or even an exchange of threats and counterthreats seemed unlikely, given the participants' nonverbal natures. Perhaps I thought the mobile Nykkus bodies would establish heirarchy through gestures and posturing, or that some invisible interplay of pheromones and female musk would bring the rogue males under control.

I couldn't have been more wrong.

The female Nykkus slammed into motion as soon as the glitter of the transporter had faded, as if the smell and sound of their snarling male counterparts had ignited something explosive inside them. Almost thirty meters separated them from the Raask, but they covered the distance in enormous, leaping steps, hurtling into the knot of males while the Raask was still swinging around to see where the thunder of footsteps was coming from.

The scarred Nykkus met that charge with fierce aggression, powerful tails lashing and jaws snapping fiercely for a hold on gem-dark skin, but in even in the chaotic roil of battle, it was clear who the superior warriors really were. With swift and silent precision, the female Nykkus split into pairs and harried five of the scarred males into separate areas of the cargo bay so they couldn't back themselves defensively together. The two largest females took on the remaining males as a pair, leaping in and striking, then flashing away again before marginally slower male reflexes could catch them.

Purple-gray blood ran across the clean metal deck, and roars of anger turned slowly to snarls and groans of pain. And still the male Nykkus battled, stubbornly refusing to yield to their dominant sisters. There was a single instant, more felt than actually seen, when it seemed to me as if all the females of that jeweled fighting group somehow paused in the midst of battle to confer with one another. Before I could even be sure if it had happened, a chorus of final unbelieving shrieks ripped out of the males. A moment later, they all lay dead, their throats bitten across so fast and lethally that no human eye had even seen the killing blow.

Their panting, amethyst-flushed killers stepped back from that carnage, grimacing a little at their various bites and bruises. The largest turned toward us, her opaque white eyes brilliant as a sodium flare against her hematite skin.

"The next domination ready to do are we."

I glanced over at my fellow witnesses to Nykkus justice. Koloth looked as surprised and delighted as if he'd found a secret treasure, while Chekov's pale face wore the half-stunned, half-pained look of a torture victim unexpectedly released but not yet healed. Spock's face remained impassive, of course, but Captain Kirk scowled at the ruthless sauroid killers in what looked like deep anger and dismay.

"Is this how you will preserve your race? By killing all those who are not yourself?" he demanded fiercely.

The lead Nykkus female shook herself, head to tail, in a powerful gesture that still managed to seem surprised at its own power. "To murder planned not we," she said, but she sounded resigned rather than repentant about that. She watched the Klingon guards drag the dead bodies from the combat ground. "If dominance had accepted the Raask, alive would they now be. But to live wished not they anymore."

"I think I agree with her, Captain," I said quietly. "I don't think those particular Nykkus could ever have agreed to stay quietly at home after what they'd done."

"And I don't think we could have trusted them to stay there." Chekov finished my thought in the way we'd fallen into doing during the *Excelsior*'s shakedown cruise. I glanced at his still-pale face and hoped that whatever demons seemed to have been plaguing him had begun to settle now.

"It should also be remembered, Captain, that these Nykkus pirates had the blood of ninety-eight Klingon colonists on their hands. They were not innocent victims." His first officer's words finally eased the troubled look from Kirk's grim face. Despite his own Vulcan imperturbability, Spock had known better than the rest of us what was causing his commander's anger.

"Death honors them with its swiftness." Koloth gave us a look of glittering amusement that didn't quite match his solemn Klingon proverb. "Now please don't be a spoilsport," he added, sounding more like his usual self. "That was a superb clash of warriors. Bring over the others and let us see more!"

Kirk frowned, but lifted his wrist communicator nonetheless. "Scotty, send over the second party."

This time, there were more sparkling transporter beams than usual—Scotty must have had both the main and auxiliary transporters locked in to work together. I watched twenty slighter and less scarred Nykkus forms materialize in the middle of the cargo hold. From the outset, these males seemed less aggressive, perhaps because they were younger, or perhaps because they smelled the blood of their slain leaders under their feet with their first indrawn breaths. The change didn't seem to affect the females—they lunged at this overwhelming group of twenty with the same explosive ferocity as they'd used on their seven older siblings. There was a moment filled with snapping jaws, lashing tails, painful snarls, and more than a few startled yelps as the Nykkus seemed to realize just who was attacking them. For another moment, a few small pockets of resistance roiled within the mass, as one male Nykkus or another tried to break and run. But by the time I'd finished taking my third tense breath, the snarls subsided into a chorus of plaintive hissing, and the young Nykkus males had lowered themselves in crouching submission to the bloodstained victors.

"Now that wasn't anywhere near as much fun," complained Koloth. "In fact, it reminded me entirely too much of a bad Klingon marriage."

Kirk snorted. "You can spare yourself any further sight of it by releasing the rest of the Nykkus into our custody."

The Klingon captain frowned, but with seven blood-soaked bodies heaped along his deck, he couldn't very well claim that his demands for justice hadn't been served. "Release the rest of the little lizards from that Orion yacht we captured, and bring them up here, Tulrik," he ordered one of his lieutenants, sulkily. "And don't forget, Kirk—I expect you to be gone within the hour."

"We will be," the captain said, although after Koloth had turned away, he added under his breath, "Although we may have to row to manage it. Spock, get back to the ship and tell Scotty to prepare for departure. Chekov, I want a security team ready to meet the Nykkus when we beam them back aboard, and quarters arranged for them on a secured deck of the ship." He glanced out at the mass of subdued young sauroid males, looking wry. "Not that I think they'll be causing much trouble, but it never hurts to be safe. We'll beam over with them as soon as the younger ones are here."

"Aye, sir," the two men said in unison. I waited until the transporter beam they'd called for had swept the last gleaming motes of them away before I let my concern and indignation show.

"You're demoting Chekov back to security chief?" The way he'd given my executive officer those orders told me that, even if Chekov himself hadn't felt able to. "Why? Because he helped the Nykkus when they held him hostage?"

"Of course not." Kirk put a hand out to catch my shoulder, looking for once almost as old as I knew he was. "Sulu, you know what happened when Chekov was first officer on the *Reliant.* That's a lot for anybody to stand up under, and he might have found his way through it if you'd managed to get a year or two of routine missions on the *Excelsior* before this happened . . . but you didn't. And this Nykkus disaster has got him doubting everything except the one thing he knows he can still do. Take orders, and carry them out."

My frown deepened. "But, Captain, he's first officer material—"

"I know that, and you know that," Kirk agreed. "But right now, Chekov doesn't know that. Give him a few more years, and maybe he'll remember it again. Until then, let him take his old position on the *Enterprise.* He'll be the better for it."

No doubt he would, but would I? For a minute, clinging uncertainty and self-doubt still insisted that I needed Chekov on the *Excelsior,* that having him there with me would be the easiest way to handle my own new and stressful position. But that inner voice that now mistrusted every easy, obvious answer rose up and informed me that was exactly the reason Chekov shouldn't be there. Maybe, in a few years when I knew for sure that I *didn't* need him, it would be time for us to serve together again.

"Whenever he wants it," I said at last, "there'll be an executive office on the *Excelsior* waiting for him."

"I'll let him know that." Kirk gave me an approving thump on the back, then turned to survey the Nykkus again. A flood of half-grown, snarling males had just been herded into the room. They headed instinctively for the little groups of females and sub-adult males that had coalesced out of the general submission, clustering around them in obedient formations that soon looked as tightly bonded and efficient as trained military teams. The transition wasn't lost on Koloth—I could see him looking across at the Nykkus with speculation gleaming in his dark, shrewd eyes. Apparently, Captain Kirk saw it, too.

"After all this, I hope we didn't just give the Klingons a new ally in this sector," he commented dryly.

I looked across at the dark army of Nykkus and shook my head with determination. "Not if we play our cards right. We'll just have given them a new reason to respect the Federation's allies."

"Spoken like a true captain." Kirk reached out and wrung my hand in his own sturdy grip. I smiled and returned the handshake just as strongly. "Congratulations, Captain Sulu. It's nice to have you in the club. Oh and by the way," he paused with his wrist communicator not yet toggled on, "there's a nice little place on Utopia Planitia that I should probably show you someday. Remind me, next time we both happen to be in port."

"I will," I promised.

Seventeen

THE CAPTAIN'S TABLE

"And did you?"

Sulu glanced up from his empty mug of Martian Red Ice Ale, wondering who'd asked that question. The English sea captain was draining his own mug, and the old man with the meerschaum pipe was busy trying to get it to light for about the fiftieth time that night. The felinoid and the human freighter had slipped away, arm in arm, to some more private part of the bar during the last part of the storytelling session, and the Gorn was lying facedown in his beer bucket. The voice had been too low to be the red-haired pirate's, which meant that it either belonged to the barman or to Captain Kirk himself. Both of them were smiling at him, so he gave up trying to track down the source of the question and simply answered it.

"No," he admitted. "It's been so many years, I'd forgotten all about that promise until I told the rest of the story. Captain Kirk was the one who remembered it, and came to find me." He returned his mentor's smile. "You're right, sir. It was a good way to pass the time."

"I thought you'd like it," Kirk said, pushing his own glass away and buttoning up the flap of his uniform jacket. He slid off his bar stool, then gave the Gorn captain's massive green shoulder a comradely thump. "I hope you enjoyed the story, Captain."

The Gorn lifted an enormous ale-stained snout from his bucket. "What story?" he rumbled. "I forgot to listen." Then he fell back onto the bar and began to snore again.

"Well, now that you know about the place, Captain Sulu, you can come back and find it on your own anytime," the barman said, twisting a rag through a long, triangular glass. "We're open whenever you're passing through."

"I'll remember that." Sulu reached in his pocket for a handful of coins to throw onto the bar, but the red-haired pirate reached out and caught his hand before he could drop them. She had perched herself cross-legged on the bar across from him for the last part of his story, so she wouldn't miss a single exciting detail of the triumph of female Nykkus over their rogue males.

"You can't leave now," she protested. "You haven't finished your story!"

Sulu threw Kirk a rueful look. "That's true, I haven't, but that's because the epilogue hasn't actually happened yet. If you can wait until after I pick up my new first officer tonight—"

"No, I meant about the lizard-women! Did the evil Klingons add them to their archipelago? Or were they invited to join your federation of good nations?"

"That's a whole other story," Kirk informed her. "You'll just have to wait until the next time we drop in to hear it."

"Or ask some other captains to tell you." Sulu couldn't be sure, since the Captain's Table bar was so crowded and wide, but he thought he'd seen a pod of familiar faces enter the room from the other side, dressed in the same Starfleet red Kirk and he wore. The glitter of their dark scales reminded him of his short-tailed stowaway, but he glanced around in vain. The slump of the sleeping Gorn's neck showed no brown and gold gecko anywhere in sight. "Has anyone seen the little lizard I came in with tonight?"

The barman shook his head, looking concerned. "I hope the little furry animal didn't eat him."

"No." The white-maned sea captain pointed with the stem of his pipe. "I saw him squiggle off toward those dark-skinned girls, over there."

Kirk evidently had a better view of the group than Sulu did. He lifted his eyebrows in amusement. "Your gecko knows superior officers when he sees them, Mr. Sulu. You'll have to get another pet tonight."

"Actually, sir, I think I've had enough exposure to reptiles for a while." Sulu stepped away from the bar, then paused to give their companions a respectful nod. "It was a pleasure meeting all of you. Fair skies."

"And fairer stars," said the Englishman seriously. "Travel safe among them."

Sulu smiled and followed Kirk out into the midnight-blue Martian night. The two small moons weren't up yet, and the desert-clean atmosphere made the stars burn like diamonds sprinkled on dark velvet. He glanced up, wondering just how many of them he'd visited so far in his life, and just how many more he'd get to see before he died.

"It was good to work with you on the *Excelsior*'s first mission, sir," he said, as they matched strides down the avenue that led back through the spaceport. "I don't remember if I ever thanked you for everything you did back then."

Kirk shook his head, smiling. "Maybe not, but it doesn't matter. You'll pay back the favor to some other young captain who rises out of your ranks someday. That's the way Starfleet works." His smile widened. "And in any case, I got a superb security officer out of the whole mess. If I weren't retiring soon, I'd try to keep him awhile longer."

Sulu laughed, knowing from the way Kirk had let his voice drift ahead of them that the words weren't meant for him, but for the dark-haired man waiting at the spaceport's gate. "And he'd probably let you, Captain, but I wouldn't. I've got a hundred free flight simulator games coming to me, after the bet we made about whether you really were going to retire after the Khitomer treaty signing. And with the *Excelsior*'s schedule of deep-space missions for the next five years, the only way I'm ever going to get my payoff is if he comes along as my first officer."

"Very funny," said Chekov. "You're late."

Sulu glanced at his watch, suddenly worried that all that time in the Captain's Table had really been the hours that it seemed. The time displayed there assured him otherwise. "By ten minutes, Pavel! Don't tell me you never found a nice little Russian bar on shore leave and forgot exactly what time you were due back at the ship, because I remember—"

"That was different, there were two diplomats and an alien tax collector involved—"

A hand fell on both their shoulders, warm and friendly. "It's good to see you two working out so well," said Captain Kirk. "Enjoy your mission on the *Excelsior,* Mr. Chekov. And Captain Sulu—let me know how everything goes next time we happen to be in the Captain's Table together."

He left them with a final clap on the shoulders, his strides fading away into the night. Chekov looked curious.

"The Captain's Table?" the Russian asked. "I've never heard of that bar here on Mars. Is it new?"

"New to me, but I think a lot of people have already found it." Sulu paused, remembering what Kirk had said about passing the favor on to a captain who would someday rise out of his ranks. He smiled at his new second-in-command. "Maybe I'll get the chance to take you there someday. I don't suppose you want to bet on whether—"

"No," said Chekov firmly. Sulu laughed, and swung around to walk beside him, heading back toward the spaceport, toward the *Excelsior,* and toward the stars.

Star Trek

The Next Generation®

—THE CAPTAIN'S TABLE—

Dujonian's Hoard

Jean-Luc Picard

as recorded by

Michael Jan Friedman

For Jason, Roni, Jesse, and Dana,
who love to go a-wanderin'

Madigoor

Captain Jean-Luc Picard looked around at the thickening fog and decided he would never reach his destination.

In the pea soup that surrounded him, every building looked like every other. Floating street illuminators were few and far between. And as Madigooran cities were known to have their deadlier sides, he wasn't at all comfortable not knowing where he was going.

Turning to his friend and colleague Captain Neil Gleason of the *Zhukov,* Picard shrugged. "Maybe we ought to turn back," he suggested. "Return to the conference center."

"Nonsense," said Gleason, his face covered with a thin sheen of moisture, his blue eyes resolute beneath his shock of thick red hair. "We can't turn back. We're almost there."

Picard cleared his throat. "Forgive me for sounding dubious, Neil, but you said the very same thing ten minutes ago, and—unless I'm mistaken—ten minutes before that."

Gleason stopped and clapped his colleague on the shoulder. "Come on, Jean-Luc. I've never attended a more useless excuse for a conference in my life. Trade routes, transitional governments, border disputes . . . it's enough to make me wish I'd become an engineer."

Picard had to agree.

A year earlier, the Federation had signed its treaty with the Cardassian Union, with each side ceding certain planets to the other. After that, matters along the border had gotten complicated rather quickly.

For one thing, the Maquis had entered the mix, using guerrilla tactics to make it known they weren't going to accept Cardassian rule—treaty or no treaty. Like it or not, that compelled Starfleet Command to formulate a whole new line of policy.

Hence, the strategic conference on Madigoor IV, which Picard and Gleason had been asked to attend. But in its first day, the conference had dealt little with practical matters—such as where and how the Maquis might strike next—and more with a host of attendant political considerations.

"We owe ourselves a little relaxation," Gleason insisted with a smile. "A little diversion, if you will. And there's no place in the galaxy as diverting as the Captain's Table."

"Yes," Picard responded. "You told me. A pub to end all pubs."

"An understatement, I assure you."

The captain ignored the remark. "At which point, if you'll recall, I said my pub-crawling days were well behind me."

"That's right," Gleason agreed. "And I told you *this* pub would make you change your mind."

Truth be told, Picard had had another reason for trying to decline his friend's offer. He'd had a lot on his mind lately—an *awful* lot—and he still needed to sort it out.

However, there had been no arguing with the man. So Picard had accompanied him—a decision he was rapidly beginning to regret.

Looking around again, all he could make out were vague shapes. Fortunately, none of them were moving, so there was no immediate danger. But the fog was getting denser by the moment.

"I'm sure you're right," he told his companion reasonably. "I'm sure this Captain's Table is a perfectly wonderful establishment. But if we can't find the place . . ."

"Oh, we'll find it all right," Gleason assured him. He frowned and peered into the fog. "It's this way," he decided, though he sounded even less sure of himself than when they'd left the conference facility. "Yes, this way for certain, Jean-Luc."

And he started off again. With a sigh, Picard followed.

But after another ten minutes, they still hadn't gotten where they were going. A little exasperated by that point, the captain took Gleason by the sleeve of his civilian garb.

"Listen," he said, "this is absurd, Neil. At this rate, we'll be wandering these streets all night."

Gleason scratched his head and did some more looking around. "I just don't get it," he replied at last. "Last time, it seemed so close to the conference center. And now . . ."

"That was a year ago," Picard reminded him. "Maybe it's closed down in the interim. Or moved."

Gleason didn't say anything, but his look admitted the possibility his friend was right.

"At any rate," said Picard, "this is looking more and more like a wild-goose chase. And as someone who has actually chased a wild goose in his youth, I can personally attest to the fruitlessness of such an endeavor."

Clearly, Gleason wasn't as sure of himself as before, but he still didn't seem willing to admit defeat. "Look," he sighed, "maybe if we just go on a little farther . . ."

Having reached the end of his patience, Picard held his hand up. *"You* go on if you like. I'm going to call it a day."

Of course, he was so lost at that point, finding the conference center would be no mean feat. But at least he knew the place still existed. That was, unless the Madigoorans had hidden it as well as they'd hidden Gleason's pub—which seemed fairly unlikely.

Gleason squinted into the fog. "It's here somewhere," he insisted. "I could've sworn it was . . . " Suddenly, his face lit up. "Right there!" he announced triumphantly. And he pointed.

Picard followed the man's gesture. Through the concealing, befuddling fog, he could make out a whimsical sign handpainted in bright colors. In flowing Madigooran characters, it read *G'kl'gol Ivno'ewi.*

Gleason translated. "The Captain's Table." He held his arms out like a performer seeking applause. "You see? I told you I'd find it."

"So you did," Picard conceded.

Funny, he thought, how that sign had seemed to loom up out of nowhere. Looking at it now, he didn't know how he could have missed it.

"Come on," Gleason told him, tugging at his arm.

They crossed what appeared to be a square and reached the door beneath the sign. It was big, made of dark wood and rounded on top, with a brass handle in the shape of a mythical, horned beast. All in all, a curious entrance—even for Madigoor, which had its share of antique architecture.

Without a moment's hesitation, Gleason took hold of the handle and pulled the door open, allowing a flood of noise to issue forth from inside. Then he turned to his colleague with a grin on his face.

"After you, Jean-Luc."

Picard took Gleason up on his offer. Tugging down on the front of his shirt, he went inside.

His friend followed and allowed the door to close behind them. "Well?" Gleason asked over the sounds of music and clattering glasses and conversation. "What do you think of it?"

Picard shook his head. After hearing his colleague's description of the place, it was hardly the sort of ambiance he had expected. The place wasn't a pub at all, was it?

Rather, it was reminiscent of a French country inn, from the elegant but faded wallpaper to the violin melody coming from somewhere to the ancient hearth blazing in the far wall. There was even an old French nation-flag, hanging from the smoky, dark rafters.

Also a stair, off to the side and just past the bar, that led upstairs to another floor. No doubt, the captain mused, there were rooms to let up there, for those who had drunk a bit more than their fill.

Tables stood everywhere, a veritable sea of them, each illuminated by an oil lamp in the center and liberally stocked with half-empty wine bottles. And there was hardly a vacant seat to be had, except in the farthest reaches of the place. Nearly every table was surrounded with guests, some sitting and some standing.

Picard couldn't help but remark—if only to himself—on the assortment of species in evidence there. He had run into almost every kind of being in known space at some point in his career, and he was hard-pressed to think of one absent from the proceedings. In fact, there were a fair number of patrons whose like he'd never even heard of.

As he continued to examine the place, something caught his eye. A display case, actually, with—unless his eyes were failing him—something remarkable inside it.

Something *quite* remarkable.

"Jean-Luc?" said Gleason.

"Just a moment," the captain replied.

He wound his way through the closely packed crowd, drawn by his curiosity. Moments later, as he stopped in front of the display case, his initial conclusion was confirmed.

There was a bottle inside the case. And inside the bottle was a model of a Promellian battle cruiser—much like the one he had built as a boy, which stood now in his ready room on the *Enterprise.*

Picard had never seen another such model in all his travels. It was hard enough to believe another child somewhere in the universe had been so fond of Promellian ship design. But the chances of that child being inclined to build something in a bottle . . .

He shook his head. It staggered the mind.

Yet here it was, an exact replica of his boyhood trophy. The captain turned to comment on the coincidence. "Look at this, Neil. I—"

But Gleason was gone.

Picard looked about, imagining his fellow captain had merely strayed in another direction. Toward the bar, perhaps. But the longer he looked, the more certain he was that Gleason was nowhere to be found.

Now, that's strange, Picard thought. Gleason was so eager to show me this place. Why would he bring me in and then abandon me?

The captain didn't wish to jump to any unfounded conclusions. However, it occurred to him he knew almost nothing about this establishment. The hair prickled on the back of his neck.

If Gleason *had* somehow fallen victim to foul play . . . perhaps someone he'd met here on a previous occasion and offended . . .

Picard stopped himself. You're overreacting, he thought. A massive conspiracy aside, the place was too crowded for Gleason to have been shanghaied without witnesses. And not every bar was a playground for kidnappers and cutthroats, despite his experiences to the contrary.

He'd simply give his friend a chance to turn up, which he would no doubt do in the fullness of time. And in the meantime, Picard would take a closer look at the bottled ship.

As he did this, Picard found himself marveling at the model—at both the care that had gone into its construction and the choices that had been made. For instance, the method used to put the metal hull joints together.

They weren't glued, as one might have expected. They were fused—just the way *he* had done it. In fact, if he hadn't known better, he would have suspected the thing had been taken from his ready room and placed here only a few hours ago.

An unlikely event, the captain conceded. A ridiculously unlikely event. Still, the resemblance was—

Suddenly, he saw something out of the corner of his eye. Something shiny. And it was flying in his direction.

Whirling, he snatched at it—and found himself holding a foil by its leather-wrapped pommel. For a moment, he stared at it, for it was clearly an antique—six hundred years old if it was a day. Then he looked up to see how it had come hurtling his way.

There was a man standing not twenty paces away, carving the air between them with a twin to the foil. He was human, about Picard's height, with a roguish mustache and the fine, worn clothes of a swashbuckler. No doubt, one of those who fancied period styles.

The man smiled. "En garde, mon ami."

The captain held a hand up for peace. "Excuse me," he said with the utmost diplomacy, "but I think you've mistaken me for someone else. I didn't come here to duel with you."

"Ah," said the man with the mustache, "but I believe you have."

"Jean!" came a deep, commanding voice.

Picard whirled. Unless he was mistaken, the summons had come from the direction of the bar. Sure enough, the bartender seemed to be looking in the captain's direction.

He was a tall, heavyset human-looking fellow with long, silver hair and a starched white apron. His gaze looked sharp enough to cut glass. Not unlike his tone of voice, it carried something of a warning.

"Are you speaking to me?" Picard asked, wondering how it was the man knew his name.

"I'll have no bloodshed here," the bartender insisted. "Not like the last time, Jean."

The *last* time? the captain wondered. There hadn't been any last time. Not for him, at least.

"You needn't worry," the swashbuckler said. He inclined his head to the bartender even as he pointed his blade at Picard. "There will be no dire injuries tonight. Only a few welts in the name of fun."

Abruptly, Picard realized the swashbuckler was called Jean, as well. And with narrowed eyes and rippling jaw muscles, the man was advancing on him, his point extended.

The assembled patrons pushed a couple of tables aside and scurried out of the way. They seemed eager for a little entertainment, and the swashbuckler seemed only too happy to give it to them.

Under most circumstances, the captain would have declined. After all, he stood a chance of getting hurt, and in a strange milieu at that—and he still didn't know what had become of his friend Gleason.

However, the challenge, delivered so recklessly, had stirred in him an emotion he thought he'd suppressed long ago—the bravado of a young cadet. Besides, the swordsman had said he intended no serious violence. And if it were welts he was eager for, as he had announced . . . Picard smiled. He would do his humble best to oblige the man.

"Well?" asked the other Jean, stopping a couple of strides from the captain. "Will you fight me?" He tilted his head slyly. "In the name of good fellowship if for no other reason?"

Picard chuckled. "In the name of good fellowship . . . why not? The game is one touch. Agreed?"

His adversary grinned broadly. "Let us make it first blood."

The captain frowned. He was somewhat less comfortable with that approach, but he agreed to it.

"First blood, then," he said.

They raised their swords and advanced on one another. Before Picard knew it, he was engaged in a storm of clashing blades.

The captain's opponent was clearly an expert with the foil, flicking it about with deadly accuracy. But Picard was no novice, either. He had studied in some of the most famous fencing dens on Earth, under some of the most exacting masters. Before long, he proved himself equal to any assault his adversary cared to mount.

Then, after about thirty seconds or so, the fellow's attacks began to speed up. It became clear to the captain that his opponent had been testing him to that point, gauging his skills. And now, having educated himself on that count, mustached Jean was beginning to fence in earnest.

Still, Picard kept up with every cut and thrust. He foiled every attempt to bind his blade. And all the while, he looked for an opening, an opportunity to beat his opponent with minimal risk to himself.

But then, was that not what fencing was all about? Anyone could become a swordsman on the physical plane. But the mind game, the contest of wills and wits . . . that was another matter entirely.

Picard barely noticed the cheering of the crowd. He was too intent on keeping up with the play, too focused on seeking a weakness he could capitalize on before his opponent discovered one in him.

Their blades whipped back and forth as if they had a life of their own. It was lunge and parry, counter and retreat, over and over again. Each exchange was a thing of beauty—even to Picard himself, though he had little time to appreciate it.

And then he spotted his opening. The other Jean, a little fatigued perhaps, had lowered his blade a couple of inches. Picard pretended to launch an assault on the fellow's shoulder.

Seeing it, the other Jean reacted, bringing his weapon up to fend Picard off. But the captain's true target wasn't Jean's shoulder at all. In midlunge, he dropped his blade and came in under his opponent's armpit.

Not hard enough to hurt him, of course, but hard enough to pierce his white, ruffled shirt and break the skin beneath it. After all, the game *was* first blood.

"Alas!" Picard bellowed suddenly, commiserating with his adversary as fencing tradition demanded.

The other Jean took a step back and raised his sword arm. Clearly, the fabric of his shirt had been pierced. And there was a bloodred mark just to the side of the hole.

Eyeing Picard with a mixture of disappointment and admiration, the fellow hesitated for a moment. Then he brought his blade up to his forehead and swept it down smartly in a fencer's salute.

"You've won," the other Jean conceded.

"So it appears," Picard replied, returning the salute with one of his own. "But it was well fought."

His opponent nodded. "I thought so, too."

A hearty cheer went up from all assembled, shaking the very walls of the place. And before it died, someone had thrust a glass of wine into the captain's hand. From the background, he could hear the stirring strains of ancient France's national anthem.

As the patrons of the Captain's Table clinked their glasses and put their own words to the music, Picard wondered at their careless enthusiasm. What kind of place *was* this? he asked himself.

He had a thought. A very disillusioning thought, at that.

Could this be his old nemesis Q at work again, showing off his vaunted omnipotence for some purpose the captain couldn't begin to fathom? He searched for Q in the crowd, but couldn't find him.

Suddenly, the captain felt an arm close around him like a vice. He looked up into dancing eyes and a dense, white beard and for a moment—just a fraction of a second—imagined he was face-to-face with Santa Claus. When the stranger laughed, filling the room with his mirth, it didn't do anything to dispel the illusion.

"Why, you're more solid than you look," the big fellow guffawed. He thrust a meaty paw at Picard. "Name's Robinson, lad. Just Robinson. It's a pleasure to make your acquaintance."

The captain took the man's hand and found his own enveloped. "Jean-Luc Picard. The pleasure is mine."

"There's a lad," Robinson rumbled. He pulled the captain in the direction of a table in the corner. "Come and say hello to my friends. They want to meet the man who bested the best sword-fighter in the place."

The best? Picard considered the inn in a new light. Did that mean there were *others?*

A moment later, he was deposited in a chair. Looking around, he found himself in the company of Robinson and his friends. The big man introduced them one by one.

The tall, slender being with the green skin and the white tuft atop his head was Flenarrh. The muscular Klingon female was named Hompaq. Bo'tex was the overweight, oily-looking Caxtonian nursing his oversized mug of ale—and exuding an unfortunately typical Caxtonian odor. And Dravvin was the heavy-lidded Rythrian with the loose flaps of skin for ears.

"And this is Jean-Luc Picard," Robinson announced. "Master swordsman and captain extraordinaire."

Taken aback, Picard turned to the man. "How did you know I was a captain?" he asked.

Robinson laughed and slapped Picard on the back, knocking him forward a step. "Didn't anyone bother to tell you, lad? We're *all* captains here, of one vessel or another."

Picard looked around the table. "I didn't know that," he said. And of course, he hadn't.

"That was some duel," Bo'tex remarked, changing the subject a bit. "Best I've seen in this place in quite a few years."

"Admirable," agreed Flenarrh, placing his hands together as if praying. It gave him an insectlike look.

"Here," said Hompaq, pouring a glass of dark liquid into an empty glass. "There is only one drink fit for a warrior."

Picard recalled his tactical officer's dietary preferences. He couldn't help wincing as the glass was placed before him.

"Prune juice?" he ventured.

Hompaq's eyes narrowed. "Of course not. It's bloodwine—and you'll find no better on Qo'Nos herself!"

"Not everyone *likes* bloodwine," Dravvin noted, his voice as dry and inflectionless as the other Rythrians of Picard's acquaintance.

"He will like it," the Klingon insisted. She thrust her chin in Picard's direction. "Drink!"

He drank—though perhaps not as much or as quickly as Hompaq would have preferred. To be sure, bloodwine was a powerful beverage. The captain didn't want to be caught at a disadvantage here—especially when his comrade was still missing.

"Excuse me," he said, "but has anyone seen a fellow named Gleason? He's human, a bit taller and broader than I am, with bright red hair turning gray at the temples."

His companions looked at one another. Their expressions didn't give Picard much hope.

"I don't think so," Bo'tex replied, speaking for all of them.

"Worry not," Robinson assured Picard with the utmost confidence. "People have a way of appearing and disappearing in this place. Your friend'll surface before long." He sat back in his chair, as if preparing himself for a good meal. "What's important now is the storytelling contest."

Picard looked at him. "Contest?"

Robinson nodded. "Indeed. We have one every night, y'see." He eyed the others with unmitigated glee. "This evening, we're out to see who can tell the most captivating tale of romance and adventure."

"Yes," Bo'tex confirmed. "We were just about to begin when you and Lafitte started flashing steel."

Picard looked at him. "Lafitte?" he echoed. And now that he thought about it, the bartender had called the man . . .

"So?" Hompaq rumbled, interrupting Picard's thoughts. She leaned across the table toward Bo'tex, accentuating an already ample Klingon cleavage. "You have a story for us, fat one?"

The Caxtonian's complexion darkened. "I'm afraid I'm not much of a storyteller," he demurred. "The . . . er, exigencies of command haven't left me much time to perfect that art."

"Rubbish and nonsense," Robinson boomed, dismissing the idea with a wave of his hand. "You always use that excuse. But captains make the best storytellers of anyone, and Caxtonian captains are no exception."

"If that's so," Bo'tex countered in a defensive voice, "why don't you get the ball rolling for us, Robinson? Or is it possible you haven't *had* any romantic experiences?"

Robinson shot the Caxtonian a look of reproach. "As it happens, Captain

Bo'tex, I've had not *one* but *three* great loves in my life. All of them transcendent beauties, and educated women to boot." He cast his eyes down and sighed. "One died young, bless her soul. The second died in middle age, just as I was about to propose marriage to her."

"And the third?" the Rythrian inquired.

Robinson's features took on a decidedly harder line. "She died not at all," he said.

But he didn't go on to say how that could be, or what effect it had on him. And since no one else pressed the man for an explanation, Picard thought it best to keep silent as well.

Robinson turned his gaze on Bo'tex again, obviously not done with him. "And what of you, sir? Is it possible any female could stand the unwholesome smell of you?"

Bo'tex smiled a greasy smile. "I'm not smelly at all—at least, not to other Caxtonians. In fact," he went on, waxing poetic, "my full-bodied scent is actually a pheromone bouquet unequaled on my homeworld. I've often got to fight females off with a stick."

Dravvin closed his eyes. "Somehow, I'm having difficulty conjuring that image in my mind."

"You're not the only one," said Flenarrh.

Hompaq spoke up. "I once had a lover," she growled.

"Oh?" said the Rythrian. "What happened to him?"

The Klingon grinned fondly, showing her fanglike incisors. "I had to gut him, the mangy targ. But he'll always live in my heart."

Dravvin rolled his eyes. "Delightful."

Hompaq eyed the Rythrian with undisguised ferocity. "You mock me?" she rasped, challenging him.

Dravvin was unflustered. "Me?" he said dryly. "Mock you?"

It wasn't exactly an answer. However, it served the purpose of keeping the Klingon in her chair while she pondered it.

Suddenly, a half-empty mug of ale slammed down on the table, causing it to shudder. Picard turned to see its owner—a short, stocky alien with mottled, gray skin and tiny, red eyes. The fellow leaned in among them, between Bo'tex and Robinson.

"Kuukervol," Flenarrh sighed.

"That's right," said the newcomer, who seemed more than a little drunk—though not so much so he hadn't caught the gist of their conversation. "Kuukervol, indeed. And I've got a story that'll make the heartiest of you quiver and the weakest of you weep for mercy—a tale of blood and thunder and love so powerful you can only dream about it."

The assembled captains exchanged glances. Picard noted a certain amount of skepticism in their expressions.

"He was on his way to Rimbona IV . . ." Hompaq growled.

". . . minding his own business," Bo'tex continued, "when he ran into a Traynor Disturbance. Level one, perhaps a little more."

"Enough to rattle my sensor relays!" Kuukervol protested.

"And necessitate repairs," Dravvin amplified.

"There he was," said Hompaq. "Blind on his port side, vulnerable to enemy attack and the vagaries of space . . ."

". . . except he *had* no enemies," Bo'tex noted, "and he'd already stumbled on the only real vagary in the sector. Nonetheless . . ."

". . . I hurried desperately to make repairs," Kuukervol pointed out, "when who should show up but . . ."

". . . a Phrenalian passenger transport," Dravvin added. "And lo and behold, it was headed for Rimbona IV just as he was."

"Of course," Hompaq said, "it wasn't going to stop for him."

"It was full!" Kuukervol declared. "Full to bursting!"

"So it was," Dravvin conceded. "Which is why it could rescue neither our friend nor his crew. However, its commander promised he would alert the Rimbonan authorities to Captain Kuukervol's plight."

"Which he did," said Robinson.

"And they would have arrived just in the nick of time," Bo'tex gibed eagerly, "had they seen any reason to effect a timely rescue—or indeed, effect a rescue at all."

"Unfortunately," Dravvin went on, "there was no discernible danger to ship or crew."

"No *discernible* danger," Kuukervol emphasized. "But the *un*discernible lurked all around us!"

"Under which circumstances," said Flenarrh, "Captain Kuukervol and his courageous crew had no choice but to take matters in their own hands—and repair their sensor relays on their own."

"At which point," Hompaq chuckled, "they went on to Rimbona . . ."

". . . warier than ever . . ." Kuukervol said.

". . . and," Dravvin finished, "arrived without further incident."

The newcomer's mouth shaped words to which he gave no voice, as if he hadn't spoken his fill yet. Then he gave up and, wallowing in frustration, took his half-full mug and wandered away.

The Rythrian looked pleased. "I think we've taken the wind out of his sails. And good riddance."

Robinson made a clucking sound with his tongue and turned to Picard. "The poor, benighted sot tells the same story every night. Except for a few middling changes, of course, so it'll fit with the evening's theme."

Flenarrh smiled benignly. "If we've heard him tell it once, we've heard it a hundred times."

"Come to think of it," said Bo'tex, "we never did get to hear the juicy part. I wonder . . . would it have been the Phrenalian commander who served as Kuukervol's love interest? Or perhaps he would have singled out some member of his command staff?"

"The possibilities boggle the mind," Dravvin observed ironically.

"Minds being boggled," said a voice from over Picard's shoulder. "Sounds like my kind of place."

Picard turned and saw another fellow coming over to join them—one dressed in a navy blue pullover with a white symbol on the upper right quadrant. He had dark hair with hints of gray and a goatee to match. Also, something of an antic sparkle in his greenish brown eyes.

"Ah," said Robinson. "The Captain of the *Kalliope.*"

The newcomer smiled. "Good to see you again, Captain Robinson. What's it been? A year or more?"

"Time has little meaning in a place like the Captain's Table," Robinson replied. "How's your wife? And the little ones?"

"Not so little anymore," said the Captain of the *Kalliope.* "The big one's trimming the sails now and his brother's taking the tiller." He glanced at Picard. "I wondered if you would drop in here someday."

Picard looked at him. The fellow seemed awfully familiar, somehow. Picard tried to place him, but couldn't.

"Have we met before?" he asked the Captain of the *Kalliope.*

The man shrugged. "In a manner of speaking. Let's just say your fame has preceded you." He raised a mug of dark beer until it glinted in the light. "To Jean-Luc Picard, Starfleet's finest."

The others raised their glasses. "To Jean-Luc Picard."

Picard found himself blushing. "I'm flattered."

"Don't be," said the Captain of the *Kalliope.* "These guys will drink to anything. I learned that a long time ago."

The others laughed. "How true," Hompaq growled. "Though I am not, strictly speaking, a guy."

Bo'tex snuck a sly look at her bodice. "It appears you're right," the Caxtonian told her.

Her eyes narrowing, Hompaq clapped Bo'tex on the back, sending him flying forward across the table. "How clever of you to notice," she said.

As Bo'tex tried to regain his dignity, the Captain of the *Kalliope* sat and winked at Picard. "Some group, eh?"

The fellow reminded Picard of someone. It took him a moment to realize who it was. Riker was a little taller and more sturdily built, but otherwise the two had a lot in common.

Picard nodded. "Some group."

"Now, then . . . where were we?" Robinson asked.

"A tale of romance and adventure," Flenarrh reminded him. "And we still haven't got a volunteer."

"Don't look at me," said the Captain of the *Kalliope.* "You know I can't tell a tale to save my life."

Flenarrh looked around the table—until he came to Picard, and his eyes narrowed. "What about you, Captain? You look like a fellow just steeped in romance and adventure."

Robinson considered Picard. "Is that true, Captain? Have you a tale or two with which to regale us?"

Picard frowned as he weighed his response. "In fact," he said, "I do. But it's one I would rather keep to myself."

His companions weren't at all happy with that. Dravvin harrumphed and Hompaq grumbled, both clear signs of displeasure.

Robinson leaned closer to Picard. "Come, now," he said. "We're all friends here. All *captains,* as it were. If you can't share your tale with us, who the devil can you share it with?"

Picard looked around the table. Normally, he was a man who kept his feelings to himself. Nonetheless, he felt remarkably at ease in this place, among these people. He drummed his fingers.

"All right," he said at last. "Perhaps I'll tell it after all."

Robinson smiled. "Now, there's a lad."

"A warrior," said Hompaq.

Indeed, thought Picard. And he began weaving his yarn.

The Tale

MY STORY BEGINS A COUPLE OF MONTHS AGO. I AND MY SHIP, THE FIFTH Federation vessel to bear the name *Enterprise,* were performing a routine planetary survey when we received a communication from Starfleet Command.

It was an eyes-only communication—which meant I needed to receive it in private. Leaving my first officer in charge of the bridge, I repaired to my ready room.

As it turned out, the communication was from Admiral Gorton—a very likeable fellow with whom I shared an interest in equestrian sports and French wines. I asked him what I could do for him.

Gorton frowned, making the lines in his weathered face seem deeper than usual. "Normally," he pointed out, "Starfleet doesn't ask its captains to search for missing persons. In this instance, however, I'm afraid I've got to make an exception."

I leaned back in my chair. "Very well, then. I take it there is something unusual about this missing person?"

"There is indeed. His name is Brant, Richard Brant. Ring a bell?"

I thought for a moment. "Wasn't there a Richard Brant aboard the *LaSalle?* Its first officer, as I recall?"

"Your memory is as good as ever," Gorton confirmed. "For reasons of his own, Brant resigned from Starfleet almost a year ago. His intention was to charter expeditions to exotic destinations."

"And?" I prodded gently.

"He dropped out of sight about a couple of months ago, as far as we can tell. At first, we suspected he had been abducted by the Maquis, since his expeditions took him into the vicinity of the Badlands."

"The Maquis haven't engaged much in kidnapping," I noted.

"True," said Gorton. "That doesn't seem to be the way they normally operate. Still, we couldn't rule it out as a possibility. Then, less than a week ago, Command received word that the Maquis had nothing to do with Brant's disappearance."

"You have a lead on him, then?" I asked.

Gorton nodded. "We've learned that Brant was seized by mercenaries in the Caliabris sector."

I was puzzled. "Mercenaries? What would they want with him?"

"Jean-Luc," said the admiral, "have you ever heard of something called the Hoard of Dujonian?"

I nodded. After all, I had been a student of archaeology since my days at Starfleet Academy.

"The Hoard," I said, "was part of a treasure unearthed on Cardassia Prime some two hundred years ago, when the Cardassians excavated a series of large Hebitian tombs."

For those of you unfamiliar with the Hebitians, they were the cultural ancestors of the Cardassians—a peaceful and spiritual people who are said to have loved justice and learning.

It seems that wasn't all they loved. Their burial chambers were magnificent vaults, filled from wall to wall with priceless, jeweled baubles.

But it wasn't merely the *quality* of their gems that made some of the Hebitian artifacts so priceless.

"One variety of jewel unearthed with the treasure was called glor'ya," I continued. "It was found to have properties similar to dilithium, but vastly superior. Cardassian scientists saw in it unlimited potential, certainly with regard to propulsion capabilities—but also when it came to weapons design."

"Exactly right," said Gorton. "Then you must also know the rest of it—how, according to legend, a twenty-second-century Cardassian named Dujonian managed to steal all the Hebitians' glor'ya-encrusted artifacts and hide them somewhere off-planet."

"Nor was he ever heard from again," I mused, "so the truth of the matter could never be proven, nor Dujonian himself taken to task for his actions."

However, I was unaware of any link between Brant and the Hoard. I said so.

Gorton frowned. "Our source tells me these mercenaries believe Brant can lead them to Dujonian's treasure trove."

I grunted softly. "Why would they believe this?"

The admiral shook his head. "We don't know. Maybe they unearthed a clue to the Hoard's location and it led them to the Caliabris sector."

I saw the connection. After all, the *LaSalle* had done considerable work in that part of space. "In that case, Brant's knowledge of the sector would have been invaluable to them."

"Exactly," said Gorton. "Or maybe the mercenaries simply got wind of something—a clue that told them Brant had located the Hoard. In any case, the man was abducted."

"And you want him found," I concluded, "and rescued—before these mercenaries can find the Hoard and make use of the glor'ya in it."

"Or even worse," said Gorton, "sell it to the Cardassians."

"Who would employ it," I responded, "to make their warships even more dangerous than they are already."

The admiral nodded. "That's our concern. Of course," he went on, "there are several agents we could have assigned this task, but you're the only one with any real archaeological background. You'll need it to verify if you actually encounter the Hoard."

"I understand," I told him.

Gorton regarded me. "At this point, I'm sorry to say, I don't have much else in the way of hard information. I can only point you to the source I mentioned—the one who reported Brant's abduction in the first place."

He suggested I go undercover to make the contact, so as not to compromise our informant. I agreed that I would do that.

"Good," he said. "I'm transmitting all pertinent information on him. Needless to say, you'll have to use discretion in sharing what I've told you with your officers."

"Needless to say," I echoed.

The admiral smiled grimly. "Good luck, Jean-Luc. And godspeed."

"Thank you," I told him.

Then he ended the communication. His image vanished from my monitor, to be replaced with the starred symbol of Starfleet.

I pondered the task Gorton had set for me, leery of entering a situation I knew so little about. All sorts of questions came to mind, none of which was the least bit trivial.

What if Brant's kidnapping were not what it seemed? What if, far from being their victim, he had joined these so-called mercenaries of his own volition? Indeed, what if Brant's disappearance had nothing at all to do with Dujonian's long-lost treasure?

With luck, I would have some of the answers before long. Without luck, I would be operating at a considerable disadvantage.

Abruptly, a beeping sound told me there was someone at the door to my ready room. "Come," I said, inviting him or her in.

As the door slid aside, I saw that it was William Riker, my executive officer. He looked curious.

"Something interesting?" he asked, a boyish smile on his face.

"I should say so," I replied. And I described my assignment in as much detail as possible.

After all, I trusted the man implicitly. Given the option, there was nothing I would have considered keeping from him.

Before I had finished briefing him, the boyish smile vanished. After all, Riker was rather businesslike when it came to my welfare, and had been from the time we first met. It's the mother hen in him.

"You're not going alone?" he asked. It wasn't really a question. At least, not in *his* mind.

"I hadn't really thought about it," I answered.

"I'd go with you," he said, "except one of us should stay on the *Enterprise.* Just in case."

"Agreed," I told him. It was common sense.

Riker frowned. "You'll need someone tough and adaptable. Someone who's gone undercover before."

There was one obvious choice. I spoke the man's name.

My first officer nodded. "He's the one."

"All right," I said at last. "I'll ask him to come along. But that's it, just the two of us. I don't want to be too conspicuous, Number One."

My first officer sighed good-naturedly. "I'd prefer more, sir. You know that. But Lieutenant Worf is worth several ordinary officers."

I found myself hard-pressed to disagree.

As it was still very early in the morning, I found Worf in the ship's gymnasium, teaching his Mok'bara class. As Hompaq can attest, Mok'bara is a ritual Klingon martial-arts form designed to enhance one's agility in hand-to-hand combat.

Though there were no other Klingons on the ship besides Worf, the class had become a popular one. On that particular day, I saw my Betazoid ship's counselor and my human chief medical officer among those striving to achieve perfection under my Klingon lieutenant's watchful eye.

When I entered the room, Worf hesitated, his expression one of concern. But with a gesture, I assured him there was no urgency to my visit. I would stand there and watch while he completed the morning's exercises.

Nor did I mind in the least. Mok'bara was as elegant a discipline as any I had encountered, and I had encountered my share.

That said, I had no desire to take part in it myself. When it came to exercise, my tastes at the time ran more toward horsemanship and fencing. They still do, as you have seen, in part, for yourselves.

When the ritual exercises were over, one of Worf's students—a young woman—asked him about a particular maneuver. Apparently, it was a method of dealing with an attack from behind.

With a patience he seldom displayed in other circumstances, the

Klingon showed the woman how to turn her attacker's wrist and grip it just so. Then he came around behind her and let her attempt the move on him.

It worked like magic. The woman performed the maneuver as Worf had indicated, turning, twisting and throwing her hip out—and the Klingon went spinning to the mat.

Of course, I had to wonder how much of the Klingon's fall was involuntary and how much of it an attempt at encouraging his disciple. Still, it was an impressive display.

The woman thanked Worf and withdrew, enlightened by his lesson. I must say, I was enlightened a bit as well. Even if I was not a practitioner of Mok'bara, I was intelligent enough to pay attention when there was something valuable to be learned.

Worf's class didn't last much longer after that. As his students filed out, muscle-sore but exhilarated, I approached him.

"You do not come down here often," he noted.

"That's true," I said. Lately, I had gotten in the habit of taking my exercise in the holodecks. "And as you seem to have guessed, this isn't just a casual visit. I have need of you, Mr. Worf."

My tactical officer looked at me, his very posture an assurance that he would do whatever I asked of him. Klingons place a premium on loyalty, as Hompaq will confirm—and Worf was no exception.

"When do we leave?" he asked.

I hadn't yet told him we would be working undercover. I hadn't even said we'd be disembarking from the *Enterprise.* He just seemed to know.

"As soon as I can make arrangements," I replied. "It all depends on when we can find a ship headed for the Caliabris sector."

His brow furrowed. "Why the Caliabris sector?"

"Allow me to explain," I said.

In the next few minutes, I briefed him on our mission, and he absorbed the data dutifully. But the particulars mattered less to him than the fact that there *was* a mission.

"I will be ready," he told me.

And of course, when the time came, he was.

With the help of Starfleet Command, Worf and I obtained passage on a Thriidian freighter bound for the Caliabris sector.

As far as the Thriidians were concerned, my companion and I were just two of the many characters who spent their lives drifting from one end of known space to the other, taking work where they could get it. The fact that Worf was a Klingon drew a few extra stares, but I had anticipated that and accepted the risk before we set out.

Certainly, there were those in the galaxy who harbored a burning hatred for Worf's people. However, we didn't run into any of them on the freighter. In the end, we reached our destination on time and without incident.

Soon we found ourselves in orbit around Milassos IV, a backwater planet on the fringe of the Caliabris sector. Our informant, an Ethnasian named Torlith, was there to meet us at our prearranged beam-down site—a clearing in the fragrant, blue-green forest that surrounded that world's largest city.

Ethnasians were broad, slow, and ruddy-skinned, with black eyes and a collection of equally black spines projecting from their lumpy skulls. Torlith was even broader and slower than most of his species, but his wits were quick—and to Starfleet Command, whom he served as an invaluable conduit of information, his wits were all that mattered.

"Captain Picard?" said Torlith, his eyes gleaming darkly in the light of three full moons, the shadowy foliage an eerie backdrop behind him.

"I'm Picard," I confirmed. I indicated my security chief with a tilt of my head. "And this is Lieutenant Worf."

The Ethnasian regarded the Klingon and nodded. Then he turned back to me. "You know," he said, "as long as I've worked with Starfleet, I've never met a starship captain."

"Well," I replied, not much interested in his assessment, "you've met one now. Shall we go?"

Torlith chuckled at my eagerness. "Of course. I've got a hovercar parked less than a kilometer away. And I've booked some lodgings for you, as I was instructed. If they're not to your liking—"

"They'll be fine," I assured him. "But if it's all the same to you, I'd prefer to go straight to the tavern."

The Ethnasian dismissed the notion with a wave of his pudgy hand. "The one I spoke of won't be there until later. A couple of hours, at least."

"That's all right," I told him. "I want to get the feel of the place before she arrives."

Torlith may not have thought that was necessary, but he acquiesced quickly enough. "The tavern it is," he said, and led Worf and myself in the direction of his hovercar.

The Ethnasian was true to his word. His vehicle was less than a kilometer's walk from our beam-down site, concealed from the casual observer by a thicket of leafy branches.

Looking around, however, I saw no freshly cut stumps, no sign of phaser burns on the surrounding flora. By that sign, I decided Torlith had used this place for his business dealings before—and I didn't imagine all of them had been on behalf of Starfleet.

His hovercar was efficient, if noisy. It took us out of the forest and into the city—if one could call it a city. More accurately, it was a maze of haphazardly erected edifices, altogether without reason or focus. None of the buildings was remarkable in any way, either by virtue of its size, its shape, or its appearance.

My first officer would no doubt have called the place "a dive." However, it was the logical and seemingly unavoidable starting point of our search for Richard Brant—and, if the legends were true, for a good deal more.

Landing his vehicle in an open lot designated for such a use, the Ethnasian led us through the city's winding streets. They started out deserted but became increasingly more populated as we went on.

Most of the faces we encountered were those of the native Milassoi, a towering but pale and ultimately fragile-looking species who wore dark robes and hoods. However, there were at least half a dozen other space-faring races present as well, humans sprinkled among them.

Finally, we came to the tavern in question. Torlith led us inside, making his way through the crowd until he found an empty table in the back. Then he sat and gestured for Worf and myself to do the same.

It was nothing like the Captain's Table. The place was dark, rough-hewn, almost cavelike in its appearance, with vials full of Veridian glow-beetles providing the only real illumination.

On the other hand, none of its patrons seemed daunted by the lack of artifice. In fact, they seemed to like it just fine.

A moment after we sat down, a serving maid approached us and asked for our preferences in libations. It took only a couple of minutes for her to bring the order to the bar and return with our drinks.

As I sampled my synthehol, I took quick stock of those around us. The crowd was what one might find in a great many other "watering holes" I had encountered—noisy and full of furtive glances, but basically harmless.

"I see no particular danger," Worf confirmed.

"Nor do I," I returned. "Still, the evening is young."

Suddenly, Torlith grabbed my arm. "It's her," he said. And he jerked his spiny head in the direction of the bar.

I peered at the crowd, but didn't see whom he was talking about. "Where is she?" I asked.

The Ethnasian jerked his head again. "Keep looking. She's on the other side of that Moqausite."

A moment later, the Moqausite moved—and I saw her. At first, it was only her back I spotted, with her red hair cascading down it. Then she turned around and I got a glimpse of her face.

Her eyes were a languid blue, her lips full and expressive, and she had a spray of girlish freckles across the bridge of her chiseled nose. It was the visage of a poetess, perhaps, or a dreamer. She didn't at all look the part of a veteran transport captain.

"That's our woman?" I asked our informant, unable to quite keep the incredulity out of my voice. "Are you certain?"

"Absolutely," said Torlith.

Worf scowled. "You said she would not arrive until later."

"She doesn't," said the Ethnasian, "usually."

I watched her move among the other denizens of the tavern, all of whom were male. She was slender and graceful, yet sturdy in a way. After a while, she joined a longhaired Orion and a wiry-looking human—a man with a scar across the bridge of his nose.

Part of her crew? I wondered. They didn't seem to show any particular deference to her.

"What's her name?" I asked.

"They call her Red Abby," Torlith told us. "If she's got another name, she doesn't use it."

Worf leaned closer to the Ethnasian. "And she was your source with regard to Brant's kidnapping?"

Torlith nodded. "Of course, she didn't say how she knew, but she seemed pretty certain of it. She's put out a call for experienced hands—so she can follow in what she says are Brant's footsteps."

Interesting, I thought, continuing my observation of the woman's interactions at the bar. Interesting indeed.

"And where do these footsteps lead?" the Klingon demanded.

"How should I know?" Torlith replied in an attempt at humor. "Red Abby's the one who's shipping out, not me."

It was fairly obvious the woman was seeking the same treasure as Brant's abductors. I said as much. "Why else go after him?"

"As you say," our informant agreed, "it seems pretty obvious. In any case, you've got a golden opportunity on your hands."

"What's that?" Worf asked.

"Just say you've heard she's looking for a crew. If you're lucky, Red Abby will sign you up and take you right to Brant—and maybe the Hoard of Dujonian, to boot."

My companion eyed Torlith. "If we're lucky," he echoed.

The Ethnasian nodded again. "Yes."

"And why are you not offering to sign up yourself?" Worf inquired. "Are you not eager to make yourself rich?"

Torlith laughed. "Because, if you must know, Klingon, I don't believe in the Hoard. I think it's a one-eyed sailor's tale, made of wind and weather and not much else."

"Of course," I interjected, "none of that really matters—at least with regard to our mission. The important thing is that we find Brant and extricate him from his captivity."

"If he *is* a captive," Worf reminded me.

"Yes," I said. "If."

"Of course," Torlith agreed. "Brant's your objective." His black eyes slid slyly in my direction. "But be honest, Picard. In the back of your mind, where you're more man than officer, aren't you hoping Red Abby's got a line on the Hoard after all? And maybe, just maybe, you'll have a chance to lay your eyes on all that treasure?"

I was honest, as he'd asked. "I don't deny it. But my mission remains the same, treasure or no treasure." I glanced at Worf. "Let's get going. We've a new captain to meet."

My officer grunted at the irony and got to his feet. I did the same. Together, we made our way to the bar. We hadn't gotten more than halfway before Red Abby noticed our approach.

Her companions noticed it, too. The Orion made no move, but the human's hand drifted to his belt, beneath which he probably had a weapon.

"What can I do for you gentlemen?" the woman asked us.

Her voice, like her appearance, was smooth and even a little seductive. But her tone was that of a businesswoman.

"We've heard you're looking for some experienced hands," I told her. "My name's Hill. My friend here is called Mitoc." They were names I'd made up during the hovercar ride, mine inspired by a fictional detective I had come to admire. "We'd like to sign on."

Red Abby eyed me. "Even though you don't know where we're headed? Or what the dangers may be?"

I shrugged as if such matters didn't faze me. "It won't be the first time," I said. "Or the last."

Red Abby turned to Worf. "You say you're experienced? Then tell me where you've served."

My lieutenant thrust his bearded chin out. "I have served on several Klingon trading vessels," he answered. "Unfortunately, you would not know them. I also worked the *Coridanni* and the *Jerrok Mor.*"

The woman nodded judiciously, then turned her gaze on me. "And you?" she demanded. "Where have *you* served?"

"On the *Jerrok Mor,* as well," I said. "Also the *Nada Chun,* the *Ferret,* and the *Erron'vol.*"

"As what?" she asked.

"You name it," I told her. "Helmsman, navigator, engineer."

"A jack-of-all-trades," she concluded.

"Something like that."

"The rest of that saying is 'master-of-none.' "

I chuckled a little. "That part wouldn't apply, then. I'm good at what I do. *All* of it."

She regarded me a moment longer, then turned back to Worf. "And you, Mitoc? What are *you* good at?"

"I can also perform several different functions," he said. "However, my specialty is tactics and armaments."

Red Abby raised an eyebrow. "Really. Then you know how many pre-fire chambers are in a Type II phaser?"

"Four," Worf answered without hesitation.

She grunted. "I'll take your word for it. Personally, I don't know anything about phasers and I couldn't care less—as long as the damned things work when I need them to."

"Then we're hired?" I asked.

Red Abby considered me. "As soon as my officers check your references. As it happens, I know Captain Goody rather well. I'll want to ask him about your tour on the *Ferret* personally."

"I'd expect no less," I assured her.

Of course, both Worf and myself had been careful as to which ships we mentioned. The *Erron'vol* had been destroyed in a spatial anomaly the week before, about the same time the *Ferret* was caught smuggling weapons to the Maquis—so neither of their captains would be available to refute our stories.

In the same vein, the captains of the *Coridani,* the *Jerrok Mor,* and the *Nada Chun* were all retired Starfleet personnel. Starfleet Command had told them enough to make them useful to us, but not so much as to leave our mission open to discovery.

In short, Red Abby would find our references impeccable. That is, if she even bothered to check, which I suspected she would not.

"One more thing," she told us.

"And that is?" I asked.

The woman seemed to look inside me with her soft, blue eyes. "Have you got any enemies I should know about, Hill? Anyone at all?"

I pretended to think for a moment. Then I shrugged. "None that come to mind," I said.

"And you?" she asked Worf.

He curled his lip. "None who still live," he told her, giving her an answer worthy of a Klingon.

Red Abby nodded, then turned to me again. "See me tomorrow night, same place. If everything checks the way it should, you'll ship out with me the following morning."

"The sooner, the better," I said.

Unexpectedly, she smiled at that. It was a stern smile, without any humor in it. "Always," she replied. Then, having dismissed us, she resumed her discussion with the Orion and the man with the scar.

Exchanging glances with Worf, I headed back to our table, where our contact had been waiting for us. His eyes crinkling at the corners, he asked, "So? Are you gainfully employed?"

"I suspect we are," I replied.

Madigoor

"AND WERE YOU?" ASKED THE CAPTAIN OF THE *Kalliope,* LEANING FORWARD in his seat at the Captain's Table. "Employed, I mean?"

Picard nodded. "We were. And as I would find out later, I had been right about Red Abby checking our references. She hadn't bothered."

Dravvin's eyes narrowed with interest. "And you took off the morning after you signed on, as this Red Abby said you would?"

"Yes," said Picard. "We beamed up to her ship, the *Daring,* along with a number of other recruits."

"What kind of ship was she?" asked Bo'tex.

"An old Ammonite vessel," Picard replied, "sleek and black, with a few worn spots on her hull showing her age. Nonetheless, she was in good working order for a ship of that age. Red Abby had added some improvements to her as well, particularly in the areas of propulsion and armaments."

"To her credit," Hompaq remarked.

"In any case," Picard continued, "neither we nor any of the other newcomers to the Daring were apprised of our destination. As I understood it, only three people on board had that kind of knowledge."

"Presumably," said Robinson, "the ones Red Abby felt she could trust."

Picard nodded. "One was her first officer, the Orion we had met. He called himself Astellanax. The second was the human with the scar, who went by the name Sturgis and served as her navigator. The third was a half-Romulan, half-Bolian named Thadoc, who helmed the vessel."

Flenarrh rubbed his hands together thoughtfully. "A half-Romulan, half-Bolian, you say?" He smiled. "I don't believe I've ever seen a joining of those particular species."

"What did he look like?" Hompaq asked.

Picard recalled Thadoc's features. "Like a hairless Romulan with blue skin and a subtle ridge running down the center of his face. But his demeanor was strictly Romulan."

"Relentless," Robinson observed.

"Relentlessly *efficient,*" Picard noted. "Red Abby couldn't have asked for a more capable officer."

"And the other two?" asked Flenarrh. "What were they like?"

Picard shrugged. "Sturgis didn't say much, so it was difficult to tell—though I had a feeling he would as soon have cut my throat as looked at me. Astellanax, on the other hand, was as talkative as most Orions, and what he talked about most was the *Daring.*"

"The ship?" asked Hompaq.

"Yes. He said he had never served on a vessel so quick and responsive." Picard looked around the table. "Of course, he had never been on the bridge of a Galaxy-class starship."

Hompaq regarded him. "But you must have had *some* idea of where you were going. You could see the stars, could you not?"

"Not well," Picard told her. "Once we left Milassos Four, we assumed a pace of warp six or better. But Lieutenant Worf and I could glean enough to determine our general heading."

Robinson's eyes seemed to twinkle. "And that was?"

"A portion of the Caliabris sector sandwiched between the Cardassian Union and the Romulan Empire, though claimed by neither. I knew little about it," Picard conceded, "as the Federation had not charted its worlds. But I had a feeling I was going to find out."

"What about the rest of Red Abby's crew?" asked Bo'tex. "Were there any Caxtonians aboard?"

Picard shook his head. "Most of the crew was either human, Andorian, or Tellarite, though there were more than a few Ferengi and Yridians present as well . . . and a Pandrilite named Corbis, with whom Lieutenant Worf had—shall we say—a small difference of opinion."

"Do I detect a note of sarcasm?" asked Dravvin.

"Judge for yourself," Picard said.

The Tale

HAVING BEEN AMONG THE LAST TO SIGN ON WITH RED ABBY, WORF AND I were given the graveyard shift. That meant we had some time on our hands. Several hours' worth, in fact.

If we spent it apart from the rest of the crew, Red Abby would surely hear of it—and begin to wonder what we were up to. So rather than arouse her suspicions—or anyone else's, for that matter—we opted for a public venue in which to while away the hours. Since the ship boasted no lounge or recreation areas, the only choice left to us was the mess hall.

It was a severe place, as gray and dimly lit as any of the corridors, and devoid of observation ports. That and its location on the ship led me to believe it hadn't always been a mess hall, but a storage area of some kind.

The place stood in stark contrast to the lounge on the *Enterprise.* Still, the trio of replicators behind a rounded, gray rail seemed to be in working order, and the chairs, though flimsy-looking, appeared to be reasonably comfortable.

There were several other crewmen already occupying the mess hall, seated at one table or another. Obviously, they were graveyard-shifters as well, and they'd had the same idea we had as to how to pass the time.

Approaching the replicators, Worf and I each took a tray from a stack in a recessed compartment. I ordered a ham-and-egg sandwich, an old favorite from my boyhood on Earth, then found a seat at an empty table and waited for Worf to join me.

Unfortunately, Worf's replicator wasn't working as well as he had hoped. As we would learn later, it simply wasn't programmed for a great variety of Klingon dishes. After making several attempts, the lieutenant rumbled deep in his throat and reached for the replicator I'd used.

The result was the same. Refusing to believe he couldn't have his heart's desire—a plate of rokeg blood pie, as it turned out—Worf reached for the third replicator. However, by then, a Pandrilite had come up behind him for a second helping and was reaching for the same set of controls.

As you may have guessed by now, this Pandrilite was Corbis, of whom I spoke. If I told you the fellow was big, it would be an understatement. He stood a head and a half above my security officer, and Worf was not puny by any means.

In any event, in reaching for the replicator, my lieutenant inadvertently upset Corbis's tray. Before the Pandrilite could react, his plate slid into his chest and deposited the greasy remains of a stew.

With a curse, he righted his tray and the plate slid back. But by then it was too late.

Corbis looked down at his tunic, where the stew had left a dark, oily stain. Then he looked at Worf.

"What are you, blind?" he rumbled with a voice like thunder. "Who's going to clean this tunic?"

The Klingon shrugged. "That is your problem. You would not have soiled yourself if you had not been so eager to grab for more food."

"I soiled *myself?"* the Pandrilite echoed, towering over Worf. "It was *you* who pushed my tray over."

"I pushed *nothing,"* the Klingon insisted, his lips pulling back to show his teeth.

"You're a liar," Corbis grated, leaning forward so his eyes were only inches from Worf's. "You shoved my tray and you'll clean my tunic—or you'll take your next meal through a tube."

I had overheard everything, of course. At first, I let it go, thinking the incident would blow over. But when I heard the Pandrilite's threat, I knew I had been overly optimistic.

Getting up from my seat, I hurried over to intervene. In the process, I saw a couple of Corbis's friends rush over, as well. One was an Oord, judging by the tusks protruding from either side of his mouth. The other was a rather husky Thelurian, his facial markings an angry green.

It was a disaster in the making. However, I intended to head it off. After all, I had negotiated treaties between entire species. Surely, I thought, I could make peace between Worf and a Pandrilite.

I was mistaken, of course. It wasn't the first time, and, sadly, it would not be the last.

Worf, I must say, was showing admirable restraint. At least, by Klingon standards. His eyes narrowing, he said, "I would advise you not to make threats you cannot carry out."

"Oh, I can carry them out all right," Corbis replied—and flung the remnants of his meal in the direction of Worf's face.

The lieutenant must have been expecting it, because he ducked. Instead of hitting him, the Pandrilite's tray went hurtling across the room and struck a bulkhead, then clattered to the floor.

Arriving just in time—or so I thought—I interposed myself between Worf and Corbis. "Gentlemen," I said, "this is a simple misunderstanding. I'm sure if we cool down for a moment, we can settle everything."

The Pandrilite looked at me for a moment, as if trying to decipher my existence. Then he drove his fist into my face, sending me hurtling like his tray—except not quite as far.

As I regained my senses, I saw Worf had not taken kindly to the battering of his commanding officer. Hauling off, he drove a blow of his own into the center of Corbis's face, snapping the man's head back and sending him staggering over the replicator rail.

Unfortunately, the Pandrilite's friends had entered the fray by that time. Spinning Worf around, the Oord head-butted him between the eyes. Dazed, the Klingon was an easy target. The Thelurian took advantage of it by planting his fist in Worf's midsection, doubling him over.

By then, I was on my feet again. As the other diners roared encouragement at us, I charged the Thelurian and shoved him into a bulkhead as hard as I could. Then I turned toward the Oord—just in time to see him lunge savagely for my throat.

Sidestepping his rush, I chopped at his neck as he went by. It had some effect, but not nearly as much as I'd hoped. Then again, Oord are known for their ability to endure punishment, and I'd probably missed the nerve bundle I was aiming for anyway.

Suddenly, I was grabbed from behind and dragged over the serving rail. Rather than resist, I flipped backward and caught my attacker by surprise, sending him crashing into the wall behind him.

Twisting to free myself, I saw it was Corbis. Before he could react, I struck him once in the belly and a second time in the jaw. The crowd bellowed its approval.

But Corbis was a Pandrilite. Even my best blow couldn't have incapacitated him, especially in the cramped quarters of the serving area.

He tried to respond with a pile driver of his own, but I vaulted over the rail again and he connected with nothing but air. Unluckily for me, he followed me over the rail.

Corbis swung his fist at me and I ducked. He swung again and I ducked a second time.

I thought to sweep his legs out from under him when something—or rather, someone—hit me from the side. We rolled a couple of meters together before we could even begin to disengage.

I was about to lash out at my attacker when I was realized it was Worf. Apparently, one of his opponents had sent him flying in my direction.

"Are you all right?" I asked.

"Yes," he said. "You?"

"I've been worse," I told him.

And that was all the time we had for conversation because our enemies had come together and were headed straight for us. What was worse, we had precious little room to maneuver, thanks to the tables wedged behind us.

There was no shortage of chairs either. But that wasn't a problem. Far from it, in fact. With one mind, Worf and I reached back and grabbed the nearest chairs to hand. And as our adversaries closed with us, we swung at them for all we were worth.

There was a great clatter and cry, in the course of which I believed I had connected with my target. Nonetheless, something barreled into me, sending me hurtling end over end across the table in back of me. In fact, over *several* tables in back of me.

As I struggled to my feet, reluctant to let Worf carry on the battle all alone, I caught sight of a leather boot. Looking up, I saw that it belonged to the captain. Red Abby was glaring down at me.

"That's enough!" she snapped, her voice like a whip.

Suddenly, everything stopped. Looking back toward the replicators, I saw that Worf and the Oord were locked in midstruggle. Slowly, their anger wilting under Red Abby's scrutiny, they let each other go.

A moment later, Corbis and the Thelurian got up from the floor. They looked bruised. The Thelurian was bleeding from a broken nose.

I got to my feet. I was bleeding, as well, I realized, from a cut across my cheek. I looked at Red Abby, then the rest of the diners, whose enthusiasm for the brawl had cooled considerably.

Red Abby turned to me. "I don't like fighting on my ship," she said. She eyed Worf and then the Pandrilite and finally his friends. "I don't care who was right and who was wrong. If there's a repeat of this, I'll jettison the lot of you into space. Do I make myself clear?"

"Eminently," I said.

After all, there was a mission at stake. I was willing to swallow my pride, to do whatever was necessary to see it to a successful conclusion.

For Worf, it was a little harder. But he managed to appear humble nonetheless. "It will not happen again," he vowed.

Red Abby extracted the same kind of promise from Corbis and his friends, though the lot of them had to be seething inside. Then she turned and left the mess hall.

In her wake, things returned to normal. Tables and chairs were righted and the crew sat down to eat. The only exceptions were the Pandrilite and his allies. They chose to leave instead—but not before Corbis shot us the dirtiest of looks.

As Worf and I took up positions on the replicator line, our meals having been casualties of the altercation, I leaned in to whisper a warning to my officer. After all, the Pandrilite and his comrades didn't seem eager to forgive and forget.

"We'll have to keep an eye on Corbis," I told him.

Worf nodded. "I agree."

However, Corbis would soon be the least of our worries.

Madigoor

DRAVVIN SHUDDERED. "NASTY, THOSE PANDRILITES."

"They can be," Picard replied. He thought of Vigo, who had served under him on the *Stargazer.* "On the other hand, I had a Pandrilite weapons officer who was gentler than you could ever imagine."

Robinson grunted. "Not when it came to the enemy, I trust."

"No," Picard conceded. "Not then."

"I knew a couple of Pandrilites once," said Bo'tex. "Twin sisters. Lovely creatures, too. They had an intriguing little stage show on a station called Mephil Trantos . . ."

Hompaq held her hand up. "Spare me, Caxtonian."

Bo'tex fell silent. However, he looked as if he would have dearly loved to say more.

"Captain Hompaq is quite right," said Robinson. "This table is no place for the tawdry and the tasteless. At least, not tonight it's not. Until the sun comes up—or suns, as the case may be—we're dealing exclusively in remarks of delicacy and refinement."

The Caxtonian looked contrite. But he also looked as if he would speak of his Pandrilites if only someone would let him.

"I've never actually seen a Pandrilite," said the Captain of the *Kalliope.* "Are as they as big as people say they are?"

"Probably," Dravvin replied.

"They're not only tall, you see," said Flenarrh, "but also extremely muscular. However, the most impressive thing about them is their diet."

Picard recalled Vigo's favorite dish. "That officer of mine used to like something called *sturrd.*"

Flenarrh nodded. "I've seen it. It looks like a pile of fine sand mixed with shards of broken glass."

The Captain of the *Kalliope* made a face. "Sounds appetizing."

Dravvin cast a sidelong glance at Hompaq. "Appetizing is in the eye of the beholder," he noted. "Even Pandrilites like their food *cooked.*"

Taking the bait, Hompaq curled her lip at him. "Klingons prefer to cook their *enemies.*"

Picard knew it was a joke. So did the others, he imagined. Still, Dravvin looked too disgusted to come up with a reply.

"Now, then," said Robinson, "let's not get too far afield. Our friend Picard was regaling us with a tale, remember?"

"That's right," said Bo'tex, leaning forward with curiosity.

"Tell me," Flenarrh asked the captain, "what did you mean when you said Corbis would soon be the least of your worries?"

Picard smiled sympathetically. "That would be getting ahead of myself."

The Tale

As Worf and I were newcomers to the *Daring,* I had expected Red Abby to relegate us to scut work—running diagnostics in engineering, perhaps, or safety-checking the ship's half dozen life-pods. Apparently, that was not to be the case.

When the duty list was posted, we found that we had been assigned to the *Daring*'s bridge. Exchanging looks, Worf and I said nothing. We merely made certain not to be late.

When we arrived on the bridge, a place marked by gray-and-black metal bulkheads and pale green lighting globes, we saw Astellanax occupying the rounded captain's chair. Red Abby herself was absent, no doubt getting some rest.

The Orion turned to me. "You, the jack-of-all-trades. You'll be manning the helm." He glanced at Worf. "And I'll need you at tactical. Any questions, either one of you?"

We shook our heads from side to side. "No questions at all," I said, for the sake of clarity.

Astellanax nodded. "Then get to it."

I felt strange assuming any other post but the center seat. After all, it had been more than twenty years since I served as anything but the captain of a spacegoing ship.

Nonetheless, I did as I was bidden.

As I approached the helm, Thadoc unfolded himself from behind his console. "She's all yours," he told me. Then he added, in a decidedly more sober tone: "Treat her right."

"I have every intention of doing so," I assured him, and sat down in the helmsman's place.

Sturgis, who was sitting at navigation and showed no sign of leaving, cast a wary eye at me as I joined him. I mumbled something. He mumbled back. It was the extent of our camaraderie.

Worf's position was behind mine, so I couldn't watch as he acclimated himself to the ship's weapons control console. It was just as well. I had my hands full getting to know the *Daring*'s helm.

Still, I took note of two officers whom I had not yet met. One was the operations officer, a blond man with a boyish smile and a long, ornate earring—though it wasn't of the Bajoran variety. I would learn later that the fellow's name was Dunwoody.

The other officer, a dark-haired woman, was at the bridge's engineering station. Her name was Sheel—a Trill, as I would also learn, though not the joined kind.

We soared through subspace at warp six, the stars streaking by us, all periodic system checks coming up negative. In short, the *Daring* was in admirable working order.

It wasn't until near the end of our tour, when the captain and her morning-shift personnel came out onto the bridge, that we hit our first snag. What's more, it had nothing to do with the workings of the ship.

Our first hint of it was when Sturgis scowled at his navigation monitor, where long-range sensor scans were reflected. "Captain," he said, "sensors show something dead ahead."

"Something?" Red Abby echoed.

The man's scowl deepened. "Ships," he said. "Five of 'em."

The captain came over and peered at Sturgis's board. "Let's see them," she said, her voice cool and even.

A moment later, the image on the viewscreen changed. It showed five specks. And though I couldn't see them very well, their precise positioning confirmed they were spacegoing vessels.

"Increase magnification," Red Abby ordered.

The image changed again. We were no longer looking at a collection of specks. They were ships, as Sturgis had indicated, though no two were of the same design.

Pirates, I thought. It was the inescapable conclusion.

Worf and I traded looks. This was precisely the sort of obstacle we had hoped to avoid. After all, we were only pawns on this chessboard, subject to the whims of our captain and her newfound adversaries. And with their superior numbers, those adversaries had us at a distinct disadvantage.

Red Abby cursed beneath her breath. "Battle stations. Raise shields. Power up the phasers."

Our communications officer turned in his seat. "They're hailing us," he told the captain.

Red Abby glanced at him. "On screen."

A moment later, the image of a swarthy, heavily bearded human appeared on the viewer. His thick, unruly hair, shot through with strands of silver, was bound at the nape of his neck in a tight braid.

I recognized him. His name was Marrero Jaiya, a key figure in the Maquis rebellion. I'd clashed with him on two separate occasions, more to his chagrin than my own.

Apparently, he'd abandoned his post among the Maquis since our last encounter. Otherwise, he wouldn't be pirating in this sector—or holding up our vessel at the point of his phasers.

Turning to Worf, I saw his Klingon brow furrow at the sight of Jaiya. When he shot a glance at me, there was a warning in his eyes—one I had no trouble at all understanding.

If the pirate recognized either one of us, our cover was blown. We had to make sure that didn't happen. And as there was a good chance we were both on screen, we had to slink *off*-screen before disaster struck.

"What do you want of us?" Red Abby demanded of Jaiya.

Little by little, Worf and I made our way toward the periphery of the bridge. Nor did the former Maquis seem to notice.

"You've got a big, beautiful vessel there," he told our captain. "We could find a thousand uses for a vessel like that. Maybe a million."

"No doubt you could," Red Abby replied tautly. "I hope you get your hands on one someday."

"Actually," Jaiya said offhandedly, "we were thinking we might get our hands on one *today.* That is, if you were inclined to be . . . how can I put it? Generous as well as realistic."

Red Abby shook her head. "I'm not very generous. Any of my men will tell you that. But when it comes to realism, I'm a past master."

Worf and I kept moving, inch by careful inch. And still no reaction from the pirate. Finally, we removed ourselves to a position from which we didn't think we could be spotted.

"I see," Jaiya said. "Then you'll stand down your weapons and drop your shields, so we can inspect our new vessel."

"I'll do nothing of the kind," Red Abby replied evenly.

"But you're outnumbered," he pointed out. "And outgunned."

"And I've got a big, beautiful vessel, remember? One you wouldn't covet unless you appreciated its tactical capabilities—which are more than enough to send your people to their respective makers."

The pirate looked at her for a moment. "You know, I'd heard you could be stubborn on occasion."

"You heard right," Red Abby assured him.

"Even when the odds are five-to-one?"

"All that means," she said, "is I've got five times as many targets to choose from."

"I see," Jaiya responded. "Then, as they say, the ball is in my court. Do I wish to mar that beautiful vessel by blowing big, ugly holes in her hull—and perhaps take a few lives into the bargain? Or do I grant you safe passage for the time being?"

"That's the choice," Red Abby agreed. "But as you consider it, consider something else as well. If the situation becomes a violent one, your vessel will be the one I'll go after first."

The pirate's eyes narrowed slightly. "A threat?"

Our captain smiled grimly. "A piece of information I thought you should have. Certainly, if our positions were reversed, *I'd* want to have it."

"I'll take that into account," said Jaiya. And without another word, his image vanished from the screen, to be replaced by the forbidding spectacle of the five mismatched fighters.

Astellanax looked at Red Abby, the muscles rippling in his temples. "What do you think they'll do?" he asked.

She shook her head. The bravado she'd displayed for the pirate seemed to melt away before my eyes, revealing the worried creature underneath.

"I don't know," Red Abby answered at last.

She was being honest, of course.

As you all know—as *any* captain knows—it's impossible to determine an adversary's intent without reading his or her mind. One can guess, perhaps even point that adversary toward a particular logical progression. But one can never say for sure.

For what seemed like an eternity, the pirates hung there in space, neither attacking nor retreating. Sheel muttered something under her breath. Dunwoody drummed his fingers on his console.

And still the pirates didn't make a move.

Then, all of a sudden, Jaiya's ship peeled off. The other vessels followed him, one after another. And in seconds, they were gone.

Sturgis turned to Red Abby. "You did it, Captain."

She nodded. "He believed me when I said I wasn't going to give up without a fight. The only thing he was going to win was a cloud of space debris, and it would have cost him a few ships to obtain it."

I glanced at Worf as we yielded our posts to Thadoc and the morning shift. The lieutenant was smiling. But then, he was a Klingon, and they appreciated bravado almost as much as a good battle.

"Resume course," Red Abby said. "Steady as she goes, Mr. Thadoc."

"Aye, Captain," the helmsman replied, working his controls.

I regarded Red Abby. Until that point, I had thought of her mainly as a means to an end, and not a particularly pleasant means at that. But after seeing her stand up to Jaiya and his pirates, I was forced to look at her in a new light.

I was also very much relieved. Had the pirates boarded the *Daring* as they had threatened to, Jaiya would almost certainly have recognized Worf and myself. And he wouldn't have hesitated for a moment to make the most of such valuable captives.

Worf and I entered the lift at the rear of the bridge and let its doors close behind us. As I programmed the mechanism for the deck where our quarters were located, my lieutenant turned to me and smiled. It was the same smile I had seen on his face a few moments earlier.

"She has the heart of a warrior," he said.

"Red Abby?" I responded, though I knew whom he meant.

"Yes," he said, his grin widening. "Red Abby."

I found myself forced to agree.

Worf and I went straight from the lift to our sleeping quarters. After all, we were rather weary by that time, not having slept since our departure from Milassos IV.

As captain of the *Enterprise,* I enjoyed an entire suite of private quarters. Not so on the *Daring.* Worf and I shared a single cabin with the same black metal bulkheads and green lighting globes that we had seen on the *Daring*'s bridge. The place held six bunk beds and a replicator.

As it would turn out, the beds were never in use at the same time. At least half of our roommates were always on duty or about the ship at any given moment—so though our accommodations were rather cramped, they never became crowded enough to seem intolerable.

That first morning, Worf and I had the place all to ourselves. We shared a bunk bed, I above and he below. I slept well, but not long—five hours at most. And yet, my lieutenant was already awake when I opened my eyes.

We didn't discuss our mission, on the off chance we were being watched via some shipwide surveillance system. I didn't believe that was the case, but there was no reason to take chances.

Instead, we talked about breakfast. We didn't wish to draw any more attention to ourselves by getting involved in another brawl, but the thought of eating in our quarters was unappealing. In the end, we decided to revisit the mess hall.

Luck was with us. Corbis wasn't present, nor were his comrades, the Oord and the Thelurian. And though there were some other tough-looking crewmen seated here and there, they didn't make the slightest move to cross us. Perhaps word of our prowess had gotten around.

Or, more likely, word of the captain's wrath.

However, as we took our places in the replicator line, a voice cracked like a whip. "Hill," it snapped. "Mitoc."

It was Red Abby.

I looked up at the intercom grid. "Here, Captain."

"I want to see you," she said. "Both of you. In my quarters. Now."

Her tone spoke clearly of her impatience. Exchanging glances with my lieutenant, I wondered what had irked the woman.

"We're on our way," I assured her. Then Worf and I left the mess hall and took a lift to the appropriate deck.

The Klingon scowled as we emerged from the lift compartment. "I do not like this," he said under his breath. "Why would Red Abby have summoned us and no one else?"

"There's only one way to find out," I told him.

True enough.

Following the corridor, we came to the captain's quarters. A moment later, the door whispered open and we went inside.

The place was made of the same gray and black metals we had seen on the bridge and in our own quarters—except here, there were no green globes to provide illumination. Instead, Red Abby had fitted the floor and ceiling with plain, white lighting strips.

The furnishings were simple as well, constructed of a hard, gray material with which I was not familiar. There was a bed, a desk, and a couple of chairs, nothing more.

Red Abby herself was standing in the center of the room—but she wasn't alone. First Officer Astellanax was with her. So were Sturgis and Thadoc.

As the door closed behind us, I focused my attention on the captain. "Here we are," I said.

She nodded. "I can see that."

Suddenly, all three of her officers pulled their phasers from their belts. In accordance with what had obviously been a prearranged command, they trained them on us.

Apparently, Worf's instincts had been accurate. Unfortunately, I had waited too long to heed them.

I eyed Red Abby. "What's all this about?"

"Who are you really?" she asked me. She glanced at my lieutenant. "And who's your friend?"

"What do you mean?" I inquired.

Red Abby frowned. "When I was speaking with those pirates, I noticed you two moving away from me . . . as if you didn't want to be recognized. That's not the behavior of men who have no enemies."

The situation could have been much worse, I thought. It seemed I had a chance of salvaging it if I worked quickly.

"All right," I said reasonably. "You've got us. But it's no big deal. We were Maquis operatives for a while—until we had a run-in with some of our comrades in the movement."

"A run-in," she echoed.

"That's right. It was purely a philosophical rift—no treachery involved on either part. Still, the Maquis know we could give them away. They'd sleep better at night if they could do away with us."

Red Abby weighed my "confession." Then, without warning, she pulled out her phaser, took a step forward, and pressed its barrel to my forehead.

For a moment, I thought she would activate it. At that range, almost any setting would be a kill setting. I could see Worf out of the corner of my eye, restraining himself as best he could.

Then Red Abby lowered her weapon. A moment later, she signaled for her officers to do the same.

"Get out of my quarters," she told us. "And if I find out either of you has lied to me again—about this or anything else—I'll kill you just as quickly as the Maquis would."

I assured her she wouldn't have occasion to do that. And taking Worf by the sleeve, I escorted him out of the captain's quarters.

It had been a close call for us. Nor would it be the only one we would have to endure.

Madigoor

Bo'tex chuckled. "And what would you have done if this Red Abby of yours had sniffed out the truth?"

Picard shrugged. "At that point, I suppose, there wouldn't be much I *could* do—except, perhaps, accept my fate."

"And what would that have been?" asked Dravvin.

"Yes," said Flenarrh, "what indeed? Would Red Abby have shot you in the brain, as she threatened?"

Hompaq looked at him disdainfully. "You heard Worf's assessment of her. The woman had the heart of a warrior. How could she have done otherwise?"

Robinson eyed Picard with a sly grin. "Well, Captain? Care to resolve the matter for us? Would she have shot you or not?"

Picard smiled back at him. "You asked for a proper story, did you not? As I recall, that requires me to reveal everything in good time—and nothing before that time."

Robinson laughed. "Touché, my friend. By all means, proceed, and rest assured we'll vex you no more."

Picard accepted the promise in the spirit it was offered—a rather ironic one, he thought—and moved on.

"For a time," he related, "the *Daring* proceeded through the void without obstacle or incident. However, Red Abby continued to keep the details of our destination to herself."

"No doubt, a frustrating situation," Bo'tex commented.

"As you say," said Picard. "However, Worf and I trusted we would soon have the information we required. All we would have to do is play our parts and the pieces would fall into place."

Robinson harrumphed. "The best-laid plans of mice and men."

Dravvin looked at him. "I beg your pardon?"

"They oft go astray," Robinson explained, completing the saying.

"How right you are," Picard told his fellow human.

"And what made them go astray on the *Daring?*" asked the Captain of the *Kalliope.*

Picard smiled a tight smile. "A Galor-class warship."

"Galor-class?" Hompaq repeated. Her eyes narrowed beneath her brow ridge. "You ran into the Cardassians?"

Picard grunted. "Much to our chagrin."

The Tale

The day after Red Abby's reprimand, I took charge of the helm again—despite whatever suspicions our captain may still have harbored about me. Perhaps she just wanted me where she could see me.

In any case, the first task I set myself was to conduct a long-range sensor sweep. Mind you, I never thought it would turn up a Cardassian warship. I only wanted to see if Jaiya and his pirates were still on our trail.

Imagine my surprise when I saw something bigger and a lot more dangerous than Jaiya. The vessel was at a considerable distance, but it was clearly keeping pace with us.

"Cardassians," I announced. "One ship. Galor-class."

Sturgis switched to long-range sensor capability and studied his monitor. "Hill's right," he confirmed.

Red Abby straightened in the captain's chair. "On screen."

Sturgis ran his fingers over his controls. A moment later, the viewscreen filled with the sight of the warship. It looked like some great, tawny predator savoring the prospect of a kill.

And the kill it was savoring, no doubt, was *us.*

Red Abby bit her lip, none too happy with the spectacle. "Hail them," she said at last.

At the tactical station, Worf complied with the order. The seconds ticked off slowly.

"No response," he told the captain.

"Keep trying," Red Abby insisted.

I didn't like the odds. The *Daring* was an able ship, but not a fighter.

On the best of days, she was no match for a Galor-class warship. If the Cardassians decided to attack . . .

And then, it was no longer a matter of *if.*

"Captain," Worf called out suddenly. "The Cardassians are accelerating to warp eight."

For a moment, I imagined he was speaking to me. Then I remembered where I was and what station I held there.

"Full power to the shields," said Red Abby.

Sturgis muttered a curse at navigation. "They're powering up their weapons batteries," he reported.

Our captain eyed the enemy vessel as it loomed larger and larger on our viewscreen. "Ready phasers," she said.

"Ready," Worf replied.

"Target and fire," Red Abby barked.

The Klingon did as she said. Our phasers lashed out furiously at the Cardassian vessel, but her shields appeared to be a match for us. I glanced at Sturgis's monitors.

So did the captain.

"Not much effect," the navigator told her.

Worf made a sound of disgust. "They're returning fire!"

The viewscreen confirmed his warning. We held on to our consoles as the Cardassian's weapon batteries raked us with a blinding barrage.

The *Daring* shuddered and bucked with the impact, but not so badly that anyone was hurt. Recovering quickly, I glanced again at Sturgis's monitors to see how severely we had been damaged.

"Shields down forty percent," he reported.

Red Abby turned to me, the glare of the viewscreen glinting in her eyes.

"Evasive maneuvers, Mr. Hill. And for all our sakes, I hope you're as good as you claim."

I hoped the same thing. After all, it had been a long time since I'd done any tactical piloting, and I wasn't nearly as intimate with this ship as I would have liked.

As I directed the *Daring* into a sudden, gut-wrenching turn, sending a couple of my comrades tumbling out of their seats, the Cardassians unleashed another energy barrage. This time, they missed.

It seemed I had gotten us one step ahead of them. It was a step I was reluctant to relinquish.

With that in mind, I whipped the *Daring* about in the opposite direction. The move elicited cries and curses from my shipmates, but this time they hung on. Again, the Cardassians attempted to skewer us on their beams. Again, they fell short.

However, I couldn't elude them forever. It was only a matter of time before I made a fatal mistake—or they anticipated our next move and made us pay for it. With this in mind, I gambled everything on a single maneuver.

It was one that had originated in the skies over Earth's European continent some four hundred years earlier, in a conflict called World War One. The idea was to loop over and back behind one's pursuer, instantly transforming oneself from hunted to hunter.

In the *Enterprise,* the move would have been a difficult one. And the *Daring* was by no means as quick or maneuverable as the *Enterprise.* Still, I felt compelled to try it.

"Hang on!" I bellowed.

Suddenly, I brought our nose up and accelerated, straining our ship's inertial dampers to their limit. I was thrown back in my chair with enough force to rattle my teeth.

The deckplates screamed as if with a human voice, but I showed them no mercy. In for a penny, I thought, in for a pound. I pulled us up and back into the tightest arc the *Daring* could handle.

On the viewscreen, a shower of stars plummeted past me. For a moment, I lost all sense of up and down. My stomach flip-flopped and I experienced a brief but awful moment of vertigo. As I mentioned earlier, this was definitely *not* the *Enterprise.*

Through it all, I kept my eye on my controls. When the Cardassians tried to shake us with a course change, I compensated. Jaw clenched, fighting inertia, I reached out and activated the starboard thrusters.

We were on their tail. At least, all my instruments indicated as much. But I wouldn't be satisfied until I saw the back of the Cardassian loom up on the screen in front of me.

Another few seconds, I told myself. Just hold on. Another few seconds and we would know if our effort had paid off.

Abruptly, I saw what I was so desperately looking for. The Cardassian warship fell into view, filling our screen with its nearness, its nacelles spilling streams of photons on either side of us.

We were so close to the enemy, we could almost see the seams in her hull. For the first time in our encounter, we had the upper hand. Immediately, I leveled us off.

Nor was our captain slow to recognize her advantage. "Fire!" cried Red Abby, her eyes alight.

Our phasers stabbed at the Cardassians. And this time, at considerably closer quarters, they had more of an effect. The enemy's shields began to buckle under our barrage.

"Keep firing!" Red Abby snarled.

The Cardassians fled, executing some evasive maneuvers of their own.

But I maneuvered right along with them, keeping them in our sights so Worf could worry their hindquarters.

The *Daring*'s weapons batteries were hardly up to Starfleet standards, but the lieutenant didn't seem perturbed in the least. His aim was unerring, his timing impeccable. In a matter of seconds, he had knocked out one of the warship's shield generators—and was going after the other one.

Then the tide turned.

The Cardassians' shields jumped to full strength again, no doubt drawing on energies from less crucial systems. Once again, our beams spattered harmlessly before they could do any damage.

I engaged the port thrusters, knowing what was coming next. But, despite my best efforts, I was too late.

The Cardassians' weapons banks erupted at us with renewed fury. The *Daring* shivered and jerked sideways under the force of the attack. A console exploded, sending out a shower of sparks. Smoke filled the bridge.

I felt a hand clutch my shoulder. "Get us out of here," Red Abby demanded of me.

Then the Cardassians struck again. I was flung out of my seat. The next thing I knew, I was dragging myself off the deck, a ringing in my ears and the taste of blood in my mouth.

My comrades had been tossed about, as well. One by one, they began to stir, to show signs of consciousness. All except Sheel, whose head lay at a fatally awkward angle at the base of a blackened console.

Red Abby, who was only a few feet away from Sheel, crawled over and checked the woman's neck for a pulse. Apparently, there wasn't any. The captain cursed and looked to Worf.

By then, he had regained his post.

"Report," she rasped, her blue eyes glittering as they reflected a sudden burst of sparks.

"Shields are down," the lieutenant told her, blinking away the smoke that wafted around him. "Weapons are disabled. And the engines are offline—impulse as well as warp drive."

"What about life supports?" asked Red Abby.

Worf consulted his monitors. "They still function," he concluded. Then he added, "For now."

I looked at the viewscreen. The Cardassian warship wasn't firing on us any longer. But then, it didn't have to.

We were dead in the water.

Madigoor

"BUT WHY DID THEY ATTACK YOU IN THE FIRST PLACE?" ASKED HOMPAQ.

"I wondered that myself," said Dravvin.

"Did they suspect you of aiding the Maquis?" asked Bo'tex.

Flenarrh grunted. "Perhaps they were asserting a right to territory beyond the borders established by treaty."

Robinson nodded. "Perhaps."

"Unfortunately," said Picard, "I was destined to wait some time before I received an answer. At the moment, my comrades and I were more concerned with the Cardassians' intentions than their motivations. And since they weren't making a move to destroy us . . ."

The Captain of the *Kalliope* shook his head. "They had decided to board you," he concluded.

Picard smiled. "That was our guess as well."

The Tale

Red Abby took in everyone present with a single glance.

Her hair was wild and fiery amid the spark-shot smoke, her eyes slitted with desperation. She had to know there was little chance of winning this encounter, but she was still determined to try.

"We can't let them take the bridge or engineering," she told us adamantly. "Any other section, but not those. Then we'll still have a shot at getting out of this."

"I'll head for engineering," Astellanax volunteered. "They'll need someone to give orders down there."

"I'll go with you," said Sturgis.

The captain nodded. "Take Hill and Dunwoody too. The rest of us will try to hold things together up here."

Brushing aside a loose strand of hair, she looked up at the intercom grid. "All personnel, listen up. We've taken a beating and we're expecting a visit from the Cardassians. For now, find yourself a place you can defend and keep your head down."

Assad, a broad, dark-haired man, chose that moment to speak up. "Captain," he said, "the Cardassians can beam us *off* the *Daring* as easily as they can beam themselves *on*."

It was true, of course. But I knew the Cardassians. The one thing they would *not* do is bring an armed enemy onto their vessel.

Judging by the look Red Abby shot at Assad, she knew the Cardassians, too. "Next time I need someone to state the obvious, I'll know whom to call on." She turned to Astellanax. "Get a *move* on."

As the first officer started for the turbolift, I cast a glance at Worf—a warning not to do anything I would consider foolhardy in my absence. After all, I needed him more than ever if we were to complete our mission. But I knew my admonition would carry limited weight with him.

The Klingon held only one thing higher than his sense of duty, and that was his warrior's code of honor. If the situation became such that he could survive only through cowardice, he would simply choose not to survive.

With this grim thought in mind, I followed Dunwoody into the lift. Then Astellanax slammed his fist into the appropriate stud on the control strip and the turbo-compartment took us down to the engineering level.

"I've fought the Cardassians before," the Orion told us, though he declined to say where. "They're merciless. We've got to be merciless as well."

I agreed with the sentiment—up to a point. Still, I wasn't going to take part in a bloodbath if I could help it. I set my phaser on stun.

A moment later, the lift doors opened. Astellanax stuck his head out cautiously, scanning the corridor in one direction and then the other. Satisfied it was safe—at least for the time being—he gestured for the rest of us to come after him.

We proceeded in the direction of engineering. As the newcomer in the group, I brought up the rear.

It gave me a chance to watch the others in action. Astellanax and Sturgis looked ahead and behind at every step. They seemed to know all too well what they were doing.

Dunwoody, on the other hand, was something of a novice at this sort of thing. I made a mental note to stay clear of him if and when we ran into the Cardassians.

Moving cautiously, we took a couple of minutes to cover fifty meters of winding corridor. As we approached an intersection, we heard what sounded like the scrape of footfalls up ahead. A second later, it was followed by the rasping of furtive voices.

Those of our crewmates? Or the enemy? We all wondered the same thing.

His back to the wall, Astellanax began inching toward the intersection. Sturgis came next. Dunwoody and I followed. None of us dared even to breathe, lest we give away our presence there.

Abruptly, the Orion—whose hearing was more acute than anyone else's in our party—stopped and turned to look at us. "Those aren't Cardassians," he said. "They're human."

Accelerating his progress, he peeked around the corner and confirmed his observation for himself. Breathing a sigh of relief, he went out into the intersection and signaled with his phaser.

When I followed, I saw a woman, an Yridian, and a Ferengi at the far end of the corridor. I recognized the Ferengi as someone I'd seen in the mess hall, just before our conflict with Corbis.

Our comrades looked surprised to see us. But for some reason, they didn't seem relieved. Suddenly, I realized why that might be. The insight sent chills up and down my spine.

I searched their faces more closely. The five of them seemed tense, fearful, as if they perceived a danger more urgent and immediate than the general threat of invasion.

Almost as if they had already *encountered* the enemy . . . as if he were close enough to shoot them in the back if they didn't obey his commands.

"Commander Astellanax," called the Yridian. "I'm glad to see you."

"And we, you," the first officer replied. "Didn't you hear the captain when she told you to take cover?"

"Yes," the woman said. "We did. In fact, the three of us were on our way to a cargo bay to do just that."

Her voice trembled ever so slightly. Perhaps I wouldn't have heard it if my suspicions hadn't been aroused already, or if I hadn't been human, too. But I *did* hear it—and I could delay no longer.

Without a word to any of my fellow bridge officers, I moved past them. And not only them, but the crewmen we'd encountered. To forestall the questions I knew would follow, I held up my left hand. Then I planted myself against the wall, took a breath, and waited.

I expected the Cardassians to burst out of concealment at any moment, eager to spring their trap. They didn't disappoint me.

Aiming carefully, I took out the first one with a beam to the center of his chest. As he went sprawling, a second one appeared and took hasty aim. Fortunately, he managed only to sear the bulkhead above my head. And he never got off a second shot because I shot first.

But there were other Cardassians behind them. They poured out into the corridor like locusts—nearly a dozen of them—firing their lethal beams at anything that moved. And since we had orders to reach engineering, we stood our ground and fired back.

The corridor became a lurid, screaming vision of hell, lances of seething energy crisscrossing madly in midair. My back pressed against the wall, I fired this way and that, trying to make out my nearest adversaries between flashes of fire.

Then, just as I was spearing one Cardassian with my phaser beam, I saw two more coming at me. Both of them had me in their sights and there was no time to beat them to the punch. So I did the only thing I could think of—I threw myself at them.

Not at their weapons, of course, because that would have spelled disaster. Rather, I launched myself at their ankles, hoping to knock them off their feet in the manner of an ancient Terran bowling ball.

I was fortunate. They missed me and went down in a heap of tangled limbs. But my phaser was kicked out of my hand in the process, leaving me a lot more vulnerable than I had planned.

As the first Cardassian tried to get to his feet, I planted my hands on the deck and lashed out with my foot, knocking him unconscious with a blow to the head. Then I hurled myself onto the other Cardassian.

He turned out to be a more formidable opponent than I had expected. First, he snapped my head back with a teeth-rattling blow to the jaw. Then, reaching for my throat with both his hands, he squeezed my windpipe until he had cut off my air supply.

I tried to wrench his hands away, but it was no use. He was too strong. As I felt myself blacking out, I struck him in the face.

A second time.

And then again.

The third blow was the charm. It loosened his grip on me, enabling me to suck in a desperately needed draft of air.

Turning the tables on the Cardassian, I hit him in the throat with the heel of my hand. And as he gasped for air, his eyes popping as if they wished to escape their sockets, I knocked him senseless.

That accomplished, I cast about for my fallen phaser—and found it less than a meter away. I was just about to close my fingers on it when a boot came down on my hand rather painfully.

Suppressing a yelp, I looked up and saw a Cardassian soldier aiming his weapon at me. This time, it seemed there would be no escape. But no sooner had I thought that than a bright red beam punched my enemy in the chest, sending him hurtling into a bulkhead.

I sought out the source of the beam and saw it was Dunwoody who'd rescued me. But there was no time to thank him for it. Grabbing my phaser, I looked around for a target.

Only a couple of Cardassians were still standing. And as I watched, Astellanax and Sturgis made short work of them. The skirmish over, an eerie silence filled the corridor.

Of the dozen or so Cardassians who had attacked us, none moved. But we had taken casualties, as well. The Ferengi was staring at the ceiling, his eyes no doubt fixed on some celestial treasury. The woman was dead, too, her chest a smoking ruin.

I regretted what had happened to them. Nonetheless, the rest of us still stood, and our goal hadn't changed.

"Come on," said Astellanax. He glanced at the Yridian. "Pick up a weapon and let's go."

"Go where?" asked the Yridian.

"Engineering," the first officer told him.

Without further explanation, Astellanax took the point again, advancing to the intersection of the two corridors and looking about. When he saw the way was clear, he went on.

As before, we were right behind him.

Madigoor

"STIRRING," SAID DRAVVIN.

"I daresay," Robinson added.

Hompaq didn't speak. She just growled deep in her throat.

The Captain of the *Kalliope* looked at her. "You disagree?"

The Klingon eyed him. "A warrior does not set his phaser on stun. A warrior sends his enemies to their deaths."

Picard returned her gaze evenly. "Perhaps. But I do not fancy myself a warrior, Hompaq. Nor would it have furthered my mission to destroy every Cardassian I laid my eyes on."

"Nonetheless," said Flenarrh, "you were fighting for your life. A stunned enemy is one who can rise again and prove your undoing."

"True," Picard conceded. "But I was willing to take that chance."

"And this Dunwoody," said Bo'tex. "It turned out you were wrong about him. He saved your life."

Picard smiled. "He did indeed. But again, I find I'm getting ahead of myself. As I was saying . . ."

The Tale

WE NEGOTIATED THE CORRIDORS OF THE *Daring,* PHASERS AT THE READY, on the alert for the enemy. But, initially at least, all we encountered were a couple more strays.

One was a tall, slender Bajoran named Murrif, who looked uncomfortable holding a phaser—even more so than Dunwoody. The other was an Oord, though not the one who had stood by Corbis in the mess hall.

"Have you seen any Cardassians?" asked the Oord.

Astellanax nodded. "We got the best of the encounter. But there are bound to be more of them around."

"What about the captain?" asked Murrif.

"She's defending the bridge," said the first officer. "Or anyway, she's supposed to be. Our job's to get to engineering."

"And get there we will," Sturgis added.

There were nods all around. As wary as ever, we resumed our journey. After a while, the Yridian came up beside me.

"I didn't want to fool you," he told me.

"No?" I replied.

"It turned my stomach," he went on. "But the Cardassians said they would kill us if we didn't cooperate."

I glanced at him. "And now two of you are dead anyway."

"*I'm* alive," he pointed out.

I frowned. But all I said was, "Yes. You're alive."

As I turned away from him, I heard a curious sound—as if someone were pushing metal over metal. It seemed to be coming from the stretch of corridor directly behind us.

I whirled. At the same time, a half-dozen Cardassians dropped from the ceiling, where they had slid away a series of access plates. Even before they landed, they began firing their weapons at us.

"Back here!" I shouted to my comrades, pushing the Yridian in one direction as I threw myself in the other.

A couple of directed-energy beams sliced past us. Someone screamed, though I didn't see who it was.

Then Astellanax and the others fired back, and the battle was joined in earnest. The air around me shivered and seethed with barrage after deadly barrage. One even came close enough to blind me for a moment.

As my eyes cleared, I leaned as far into the curvature of the bulkhead as I could and picked out a target. Doing my best to ignore the chaos all about me, I took aim and fired.

My beam hit the Cardassian square in the center of his chest. It knocked him off his feet and sent him skidding backward down the corridor. But no sooner had he fallen than another came forward to take his place.

Then that one fell, too, spun about by a blow to his shoulder. A third took a shot to his midsection and rolled over, clutching himself. The tide of battle seemed to be turning in our favor.

Unlike the prior combat, this one never devolved into a hand-to-hand struggle. We simply fired and fired some more, and kept firing until none of the Cardassians were left standing.

In the strange, dense silence that followed, I surveyed the corridor. Two of my comrades had been hit by enemy fire. One was the Oord, who had sustained only an injury to his shoulder.

The other was the Yridian. In his case, the damage was a bit more serious. Moving to his side, I closed his gaping, dead eyes with a sweep of my hand. Then I glanced at Astellanax.

The first officer didn't say anything. He just walked over to the nearest Cardassian, who happened to be still breathing, and picked him up by the front of his uniform.

"I want to know one thing," he said evenly. "Why didn't you just materialize behind us? Why did you have to try to take us from above?"

The Cardassian looked at him. For a moment, I thought he would give Astellanax an answer. Then he spat in the Orion's face.

Astellanax let him slump to the floor and wiped the spittle from his cheek. Then he took aim at the Cardassian and killed him.

"Obviously," said the first officer, "the enemy is having trouble beaming men aboard the *Daring*. My guess is the captain has found a way to resurrect our shields."

"It's possible," Sturgis remarked.

"Or," I said, "we managed to disable the warship's transporters when we fired on her."

Astellanax looked at me. "I'd like to think so."

Then he made his way down the winding corridor again, this time with a bit more haste.

Madigoor

DRAVVIN HELD UP HIS HAND. "A QUESTION, IF I MAY."

Picard nodded. "Go ahead."

"You didn't seem very happy with the Yridian. I take it you didn't approve of his decision to survive at the expense of others?"

"That's true," Picard replied. "I *didn't* approve. Mind you, I think one should do whatever one can to keep body and soul together, but I stop short of endangering the lives of others."

"I agree," said Robinson. "If you've got coin, buy what you like. But don't reach into someone else's pocket."

The Captain of the *Kalliope* stroked his beard thoughtfully. "Then, in the Yridian's place, you would have refused to cooperate? Even at the expense of your life?"

Picard shrugged. "I might have given the appearance of cooperation—so as to make myself useful at a later time. But I would not have cooperated with the Cardassians in fact."

Bo'tex laughed a hearty laugh. "You wouldn't make a very good Caxtonian, Captain Picard."

"Nor a very good Yridian, apparently," said Hompaq.

"Would he make a good Klingon?" Flenarrh asked.

Hompaq grunted. "A Klingon would not have allowed himself to be captured in the first place."

Picard couldn't help but chuckle at that.

"In any case," he continued, "we pressed on. And, as luck would have it, we reached the engine room without further violence."

The Tale

THE PROBLEM, AT THAT POINT, WAS GETTING INSIDE THE PLACE. AFTER ALL, the doors to the engine room were closed, and the last thing we wanted to do was blast our way in.

Under normal circumstances, we could have contacted the engineering staff via ship's intercom. However, the Cardassians were no doubt monitoring for such messages.

Fortunately, Astellanax carried a portable communications device that could interface with the workstations in the engine room. Pulling it out, he tapped out a message and waited.

A message came back. Those in the engine room wanted to know how they could be sure of the first officer's identity. They suspected the Cardassians had captured Astellanax and were using his device to try to gain entry.

The Orion frowned and tapped out another message. It wasn't a sentence, as it turned out. It was some sort of code—one that someone in the engine room was capable of recognizing.

A moment later, the doors slid apart, revealing a by-now-familiar gray and black decor. The engine room contained a surprising number of working consoles, all of which reflected the pale green glare of the bulkhead globes.

However, there was no one at the consoles that we could see—no one to greet us or ask us in.

Astellanax seemed undaunted by the fact. He started for the entrance—until I grabbed him by the arm.

"Wait a minute," I whispered. "What if this is a trap like the other one? What if the enemy is waiting for us inside?"

Murrif seemed less than impressed with the possibility. "If it's a trap," he said, "they don't seem very eager for us to enter it. The engineers made us give them the password, didn't they?"

"It could be they're just playing their parts," I pointed out.

"It could be," Astellanax echoed thoughtfully. "But our people weren't under any pressure to respond to my signal. It's not as if the Cardassians would've known I was sending it."

I bit my lip, wishing there were a way to allay my fears. "I don't suppose there's a countercode?" I asked.

The first officer looked at me with just a hint of a smile. "Next time," he said.

"I've got an idea," said Dunwoody. "I'll go in and check things out. If there's a problem, you'll know it."

"What if they threaten your life?" asked Murrif.

Dunwoody eyed him. "They'll have to make good on their threat. I'd die before I'd let them use me the way they used the others."

Sturgis glanced expectantly at the first officer. "Sounds like a plan to me," he said.

Astellanax considered the offer—as well as the man who had made it. "All right," he said at last. "Go ahead, Mr. Dunwoody. And good luck."

With that wish on his side and little else, Dunwoody made his way down the corridor and walked through the open doors into engineering. He turned to someone we couldn't see, waved, then turned back to us.

"It's all right," he called. "There's no one here but—"

Before the fellow could get the next word out, a couple of Cardassians materialized behind him. Sensing that something was amiss, he whirled and fired his phaser at them.

One Cardassian went sprawling, propelled by the force of Dunwoody's beam. But the other invader was already taking aim at him.

"Watch out!" I cried, and fired.

It wasn't the cleanest shot I had ever made, but it had the desired effect. The Cardassian spun about, his weapon falling from his hand.

Cursing, knowing how close he had come to death, Dunwoody leveled his phaser at the Cardassian—but his hand was trembling so badly, his beam missed by several inches. It was only with his second shot that the man hammered his adversary senseless.

Suddenly, the Oord bellowed a warning. Turning, I saw a group of Cardassians materializing in the corridor behind us.

"Quick!" Astellanax cried. "Into the engine room!"

But there were Cardassians materializing there as well. I saw Dunwoody retreat from my view, presumably to join a clutch of engineers already holed up behind their consoles.

I hesitated just long enough to consider our options. The Orion's advice still seemed to make sense. Engineering remained a key to control of the ship—and it was easier to defend than an open corridor.

Firing at the Cardassians behind me to keep them at bay, I made for the open doors of the engine room. So did Astellanax, Sturgis, and Murrif, and with equal haste.

Only the Oord stayed behind. Battered shoulder and all, he stood his ground, giving the rest of us time to escape.

It was a suicide stand—the Oord had to have known that. But he stood there anyway, firing his phaser with deadly accuracy into the oncoming ranks of the enemy. As we charged into engineering, I heard a sound that could only have been the Oord's body hitting the deck.

At that point, I was too much in the thick of the conflict to mourn my comrade. The engine room was full of Cardassians—perhaps twenty in all, none of them eager to give up their foothold. They sent a barrage at us that should have dropped us all in our tracks.

As it happened, it only dropped one of us. An energy beam hit Murrif square in the face, breaking his neck with its force—and his momentum slid him into an unmanned console.

I knew from watching Dunwoody that at least some of the engine room's defenders were to my left. As I returned the Cardassians' fire, I retreated in that direction. Then I picked a spot between two workstations and dove full length, hoping to make it to cover before our adversaries' volley could tear me apart.

Directed energy beams crisscrossed in the air around me, scalding it with their passage. But none of them hit me. I landed, rolled, and felt myself grabbed by several pairs of hands.

I looked up into the faces that went with them. To my relief, one of them was Dunwoody's.

"Glad you could join us," he quipped, though the sheen of sweat on his face belied the casual tone of his remark.

"Not half as glad as I am," I replied.

I glanced about. Astellanax and Sturgis had made it as well, joining the handful of engineers and assorted crewmen holed up there already. We exchanged the grateful looks of men who had risked their lives together and emerged from the experience unscathed.

The Cardassians chose that moment to send a barrage into the workstation I was hiding behind. There was a wretched whining sound and a geyser of sparks, but my comrades and I remained unharmed.

Hefting my phaser, I peered across the engine room at the enemy. What I saw was not encouraging.

The Cardassians were continuing to beam reinforcements into the place. If the captain had discovered a way to befuddle the enemy's transporters for a time, that time was now past.

It made me wonder if the Cardassians had taken the bridge. It made me wonder if they were assuming control of the *Daring* even as we risked our lives to save her. It made me wonder what had become of Worf, though my lieutenant had proven himself a difficult man to stop.

And it made me wonder if they had killed Red Abby.

It cut me to think so. Despite her avarice, the woman had shown herself to be a brave and able commander—one of the few I had met outside Starfleet. She had won my respect.

And perhaps something more, though I was reluctant to admit it at the time—even to myself.

At any rate, I had no way of knowing Red Abby's fate—or Worf's, for that matter. All I could do was fire away at the Cardassians in their increasing numbers, hope we could hold them for a while, and watch faithfully for a window of opportunity.

It came, all right. But not for *us.*

Up until then, the workstations in front of us had been our salvation, protecting us from the increasingly fierce attacks of the enemy. In a single moment, they became our greatest danger.

One by one, they began to blow up. With a sinking heart, I realized the Cardassians had taken the bridge after all. And they had found a way to overload the circuitry in the workstations.

The result? Chaos.

Half of us bolted like rabbits driven from their warren—only to be cut down by the invader's relentless barrage. I and some of the others stayed where we were, continuing to fight from cover as long as we could.

Unfortunately, there was no pattern to the explosion of the engineers' workstations—or at least, none I could discern. No doubt, the Cardassians meant it to be that way. I remember wondering whether the console in front of me would be the next to blow up.

Then I didn't have to wonder anymore.

Madigoor

"IT EXPLODED?" ASKED ROBINSON.

Picard grunted. "Right in front of me."

"But it didn't kill you," Bo'tex observed.

"Obviously," said Dravvin.

"I was lucky," Picard told them. "All I suffered was a few burns. However, the force of the explosion was enough to knock me out."

"Then what?" asked the Captain of the *Kalliope,* obviously caught up in the particulars of the tale.

"I regained consciousness perhaps half an hour later," Picard replied. "I found myself in the *Daring*'s small, gray transporter room with a Cardassian energy rifle in my face. But it was only one of a dozen carried by a contingent of stony-faced guards."

"You were alone?" asked Flenarrh.

Picard shook his head. "There were some forty of us being held there."

"Forty survivors," Robinson mused.

"Precisely," said Picard.

"What about Worf?" Hompaq demanded.

"To my immense relief," Picard told her, "Worf was among that number—though the Cardassians had opened a dangerous-looking gash in his temple. Looking around, I saw Astellanax, Sturgis, and Thadoc as well. Also Corbis, and his friends the Oord and the Thelurian. And Dunwoody, though he was holding a limp and painful-looking arm."

"And Red Abby?" asked Robinson.

Picard nodded. "Our captain was there, too, though I didn't notice her at first. She was kneeling, tending to one of the wounded. Though she had been bruised and battered as badly as any of us, she managed somehow to maintain an air of defiance."

Bo'tex smiled. "I see where this is going."

"So can I," said Dravvin.

"This woman inspired you," Bo'tex speculated. "She gave you hope in the midst of despair."

"And when the Cardassians let their guards down," said Dravvin, "you attacked them and freed yourselves."

Picard chuckled grimly. "Had you been there, you would have known an uprising was an impossibility."

"Indeed," said Flenarrh. "Charging your captors would no doubt have cost you dearly."

"I believe so," Picard agreed. "And even then, we would not have gained anything. We would still have had to escape our cargo bay."

Flenarrh leaned forward. "And with the *Daring*'s transporters under the Cardassians' control, they could have beamed in all the reinforcements they required."

"Aye," said Robinson. "Or beamed out you and your comrades, one at a time. The Cardassians held all the cards."

"Still," Hompaq snarled, "if it had been me in that cargo bay, I would have gone for a Cardassian throat." She glared at Picard. "And if I had died, at least it would have been a warrior's death. Only a coward allows himself to be herded like a pack animal."

Picard, of course, knew a few things about Klingon ethics. He had, after all, been the Arbiter of Succession—the man who picked Gowron as the leader of the Klingon High Council.

"Only a fool wastes his life on a useless gesture," he told Hompaq pointedly. "I had a mission, remember—a duty to Starfleet. In order to fulfill that duty, I had to survive my captivity."

Hompaq bared her teeth, less than thrilled with Picard's tone. For a moment, he thought she might pull a concealed weapon—or at the least throw herself across the table at him. In the end, however, she made a sound of disgust and stayed in her seat.

Not that the Klingon was fearful of facing him. Quite the contrary. Rather, it seemed to Picard, she had a healthy respect for the establishment in which they were seated.

For the Captain's Table.

"As I was saying," Picard continued, "we may have thought about an uprising, but we didn't attempt one. We simply waited, exchanging grim glances, until the Cardassians received an order via the ship's intercom."

The Tale

I UNDERSTOOD ENOUGH CARDASSIAN TO MAKE SENSE OF THE ORDER. Apparently, my fellow prisoners and I would shortly be beamed to the enemy's warship. It was better than being destroyed out of hand, I thought.

A moment later, my comrades began to disappear, two and three at a time. Corbis and his friends were among the first to go. Worf, Thadoc, and Sturgis came soon after. I myself was among the last.

We materialized in a place not unlike the one we had left. Of course, the bulkheads around us were of a decidedly darker hue, and the recessed lighting gave off a smoldering, orange glow, but it was clear we were in a cargo bay.

A *Cardassian* cargo bay. It was a chilling thought, to say the least.

Once all of the prisoners were assembled, a stocky Cardassian officer entered the bay with something like a tricorder in his hand. Glancing at it, he scanned our ranks until his eyes fell on our captain, who endured his scrutiny with a scowl.

The Cardassian pointed at her. "You," he said in a tongue she could understand. "Come with me."

Astellanax and some of the others looked ready to intervene. Obviously, they didn't like the idea of leaving their captain alone in the hands of the Cardassians. For that matter, neither did I.

Abruptly, the issue became an academic one. The officer pointed to Astellanax as well. "You will come, too," he said.

Then he eyed the rest of us and glanced again at his handheld device. After a moment's consideration, the Cardassian picked out Worf, Sturgis,

Thadoc, and myself, and informed us that we would be accompanying him.

We didn't know on what basis we had been selected—though I might have ventured a guess—but we didn't argue with the decision. When the officer left the cargo bay, we left with him, flanked by a pair of armed guards.

The Cardassians escorted us down a corridor to their version of a turbo-lift. The door irised open and we went inside. Then the officer punched in a destination code.

Unfortunately, I couldn't see it from where I was standing. A few moments later, the lift stopped and the door irised open again, allowing us to enter a dimly lit corridor.

I looked right and then left. To my right, the corridor wound out of sight. To my left, it ended in a rather ornate egress.

Only then did I realize where we were headed.

Remember, the Federation had been at war with the Cardassians years earlier. In the course of that war we had taken some of the enemy's ships. Though I hadn't personally toured one of those vessels, I had seen the schematics disseminated by Starfleet.

That's how I knew we were headed for the bridge. But for the life of me, I couldn't see what purpose our presence there was meant to serve.

The six of us were herded in the direction of two ornate doors. Just before we reached them, they parted for us. As I had predicted, the warship's bridge was beyond them, as dark and smoldering with orange light as the rest of the vessel.

Like the other Cardassian bridges I had seen, this one had five stations—two forward, two aft, and a massive-looking captain's chair. Graphics in gold and electric blue gleamed at us from tactical screens situated on every bulkhead.

My attention was drawn to the viewscreen, which was considerably smaller than that of a Starfleet vessel and oval in shape. It gave us a view of the *Daring* as she hung in space, her port nacelle and parts of her hull charred beyond recognition.

I glanced at Abby. She seemed transfixed by the sight. You all know what she was feeling, I imagine. Certainly, I did. She was, after all, the captain of that crippled vessel.

The gul in charge of the warship turned and took note of our arrival. He was a tall, almost gangly specimen, with the self-assurance bordering on arrogance that I had come to associate with Cardassian leadership.

"I see everyone has arrived," he said. He turned to Abby. "As you will note, your bridge officers are all present—at least, insofar as our sensor data could identify them. In general, we took pains not to kill any more of your people than we absolutely had to."

"That was generous of you," Abby replied, no doubt meaning to inject a note of sarcasm.

But her voice was hollow, drained of energy. Of course, a stun blast would have had that effect on even the strongest victim.

The Cardassian smiled. "I am accustomed to being addressed by my name and title. From now on, you will call me Gul Ecor whenever you speak to me. Is that clear, human?"

Abby frowned. "It's clear."

"It's clear, *what?"* asked the gul.

The woman's eyes blazed with hate, despite her fatigue. "It's clear," she said, "Gul Ecor."

The Cardassian nodded, then glanced at the viewscreen. "Unfortunately," he remarked, "I can't treat your ship as I have your crew. It would serve as a marker with regard to our encounter here, and that might cause me problems in the future."

He gestured to his weapons officer, whose fingers flew over his controls. A moment later, the Cardassian looked up.

"Ready, Gul Ecor."

Ecor paused a moment, as if to build up the drama. Then he made a gesture of dismissal. "Fire."

Suddenly, a pair of disruptor beams shot across the viewscreen, stabbing the *Daring* in her aft quarters. The ship buckled and blackened under the barrage. Then there was a blinding burst of white light—the kind that might be created by an exploding warp core.

As it subsided, we could see that the *Daring* was gone.

I turned to Red Abby. Her eyes had become ice chips and her features had gone as hard as stone. But to her credit, she didn't look away from the *Daring*'s demise. She stared at the Cardassian viewscreen without flinching, as if trying to etch the moment in her memory.

I empathized with the woman. I had never seen a ship under my command so completely destroyed, though I had seen one wrecked so badly I was forced to abandon her.

But that is a tale for another time.

"Unfortunate," said Gul Ecor. He gazed at Abby with hooded eyes.

"Isn't it . . . Captain Brant?"

Brant? I thought.

That was the name of the man Worf and I were searching for. Clearly, Ecor had some inkling as to Red Abby's objectives. That wasn't good news for her—or for myself and Worf either.

However, the Cardassian had made a mistake. Brant wasn't Red Abby's name. I looked at her, then at Ecor, then at her again. I waited for Red Abby to point out the gul's error.

But she didn't. She just stood there, looking more wary than defiant all of a sudden. And by that sign, I realized the Cardassian hadn't made a mistake after all.

My mind raced. If Red Abby's name *was* Brant, our expedition was not what I had been led to believe. Far from it, in fact.

Back on Milassos IV, I had concluded Red Abby was a shallow fortune hunter—a money-hungry adventurer who had gotten a whiff of Dujonian's Hoard. At the time, it was the only possibility that made sense.

Now, I saw the matter in a new light. If Red Abby was related to Brant, perhaps even his wife . . . she was no mere fortune hunter after all. She was a brave and determined woman risking her life for someone she loved.

The Hoard might still have played a part in it, I conceded. But more and more, it looked like the icing rather than the cake.

Not that it would matter to Gul Ecor why Abby had set out after Brant. It would only matter that she *had*—and that she might lead him to the glor'ya lost to Cardassia hundreds of years ago.

Finally, Red Abby spoke again. "How do you know who I am?" she demanded of the gul.

Ecor shrugged. "We have our sources in this sector. They told us who you were and what you were after."

Astellanax's eyes narrowed considerably. "So you've been tracking us since we left Milassos Four?"

The Cardassian nodded. "We remained patient for a long while, waiting for the proper moment to overtake you." He smiled a thin smile. "That moment came rather precipitously, I'm afraid. But once you conducted a long-range sensor sweep and discovered our presence, we could no longer be content to pursue you from afar."

There was a gleam of more than triumph in Ecor's eye. But then, he had a lot to be pleased about. He was on the verge of advancing his career by leaps and bounds.

For a Cardassian, the Hoard of Dujonian was the prize to end all prizes, its recovery the accomplishment to eclipse all accomplishments. Indeed, what could have brought more prestige, more glory to Ecor and his superiors, than the retrieval of the Hebitians' legendary glor'ya?

Clearly, Ecor would go to any length to get what he wanted. Almost certainly, he would resort to torture. In fact, the gul was probably savoring the prospect of it even as we confronted one another.

I knew from personal experience how masterful the Cardassians could be at that grisly art. I knew how easily they could destroy their victim's mind as well as his body.

Or, in this case, *her* body.

I gazed at Red Abby and feared what might happen to her. Not because she was weak, but because she was strong . . . because, if I was any judge of character at all, she would sacrifice herself rather than reveal the whereabouts of Richard Brant.

And then, just in case there was any doubt as to Ecor's intentions, he smiled at Red Abby. "I'm glad to have had this chance to meet you. You and I have much to talk about," he told her.

She met his gaze. But again, she fell silent.

For a moment, the gul seemed inclined to say more. Then he gestured and the Cardassians behind us prodded us with the barrels of their weapons. It appeared the show was over.

Madigoor

"HAH," SAID ROBINSON, GRINNING BROADLY IN HIS BEARD. "SO RED ABBY wasn't at all what she seemed to be."

"Not at all," Picard confirmed.

"People seldom are," the Captain of the *Kalliope* observed.

"Not so," Bo'tex countered. "I am *exactly* what I seem to be."

"More's the pity," Dravvin said under his breath, eliciting a belly laugh from Hompaq.

Bo'tex looked at the Rythrian. "Excuse me?"

Dravvin dismissed the remark with a wave of his hand. "Nothing. Really." Then he turned to Picard. "I've had a couple of run-ins with the Cardassians myself. The second time, I nearly lost my life to them."

"And you'll regale us with that story in due time," said Robinson. "But right now, it's our friend Picard who's spinning the yarn."

The Rythrian regarded Robinson for a moment. Then he inclined his head slightly, causing his ears to flap.

"Of course," Dravvin said flatly. He turned to Picard. "My apologies. Spin away, Captain."

Picard leaned back in his chair and resumed his tale. "As I was saying, the show was over . . ."

The Tale

We were herded back down the corridor under the careful eyes of our captors and returned to our cargo bay. The rest of Red Abby's crew awaited us there. Or rather, the portion that had survived.

At that point, our guards left, closed the doors behind them, and activated the forcefield. It didn't appear we would be going anywhere.

"What happened?" one of the crewmen wanted to know.

"Where did they take you?" asked Assad.

"They destroyed the *Daring,"* Red Abby replied evenly.

The news of their ship's demise made the crewmen's eyes grow round with dread. After all, without a vessel in which to escape, what kind of future could they expect? A life of hard labor in some Cardassian prison camp, ended only by death?

"They wanted us to watch," Red Abby went on. "Me, in particular."

"What for?" someone wondered.

The captain shrugged. "Out of spite, I think, as much as anything else. They *are* Cardassians, remember."

Corbis glared at Red Abby. "I can see them showing *you*—you're the captain." He jerked his head to indicate me and Worf. "But why *him?* And this other one?"

"Because they were working the bridge," Astellanax explained. "At least, that's what our friend the gul told us." He frowned. "They identified us by the sensor readings they took of our bridge."

Corbis turned to me. If looks could have killed, I would have been stricken dead on the spot.

"It's your fault we're here," he snarled.

"My fault? And how do you come to that conclusion?" I asked.

The Pandrilite pointed a meaty blue finger at me. "You were at the helm when the Cardassians showed up, weren't you?" He glared at Worf. "And unless I'm mistaken, the Klingon was at tactical."

My lieutenant raised his chin. "What of it?"

I stepped in front of Worf, coming between him and Corbis. "We did our best," I said. "I can't help it if we were overmatched."

The Pandrilite grunted. "Couldn't you?" He looked around at the others. "I've never seen this Hill character before—and I've been on a lot of voyages to a lot of different places. How do we know he wasn't in the Cardies' pay? How do we know he didn't hand the ship to them on a platter?"

There was a rumble of assent—mostly from the Oord and the Thelurian. But a few others had been swayed by the Pandrilite's speech as well.

"You're insane," I said, refusing to yield an inch. "I was the one who discovered the Cardassians."

"Did you?" Corbis sneered. "Or did you just make it look that way—so you could go on spying for them?"

"I'm not a spy," I told him. "Not any more than you are."

The Pandrilite smiled a nasty smile. "And all we've got to go on is your word, eh? Well, I'll tell you what I think, human. I think it's *you* we've got to thank for where we are." He cast a glance at Worf. "You and your cowardly cur of a Klingon."

That settled it.

It was no small thing to question a Klingon's loyalty. But to question his courage? The accused had little choice but to take the remark as a challenge—and that is precisely the way Worf took it.

I tried to restrain him, but it was no use. Barreling past me, the lieutenant bared his teeth and went for Corbis.

What's more, the Pandrilite was ready for him. When Worf smashed him in the face, he staggered but didn't fall. The Klingon tried to connect with a second punch, but his adversary warded it off—then struck back with a hammerlike blow of his own.

I tried to get between Worf and Corbis, but the Thelurian leaped on me from behind and dragged me down. Digging my elbow into his midsection as hard as I could, I freed myself of his company and got to my feet.

However, my freedom was short-lived. Corbis's other friend, the Oord, bowled me over. By the time I stopped rolling, he was on me again, trapping me beneath his bulk.

I struck the Oord once and then again, but it didn't seem to faze him. If anything, it made him hold on to me that much tighter.

By then, much of the crew was cheering, though I wasn't sure whom they were cheering for. Perhaps they weren't sure, either.

Worf, meanwhile, was standing toe to toe with the Pandrilite, trading one devastating blow after the other. Both fighters were bloodied, but neither seemed likely to yield until he was knocked unconscious—or worse.

"That's enough!" cried Red Abby, her voice cutting through the emotion-laden atmosphere in the cargo bay.

She kicked the Oord in the side with the toe of her boot, doubling him up. With a hard shot to his jaw, I got him to roll off me.

Next, Red Abby tried to separate Corbis and Worf. After all, she was still their captain, still the one to whom they had given their allegiance. It was her job to maintain order.

She might as well have tried to stop a matter-antimatter explosion. The Pandrilite dealt her a backhanded smash to the shoulder, spinning her around so hard she reeled into the bulkhead.

It occurred to me that I might have stopped Worf, at least, with a direct order. However, our comrades didn't know I was his commanding officer and I sincerely wished to keep it that way.

Gritting my teeth, I resigned myself to the physical approach. Needless to say, I had little faith in it at the moment.

But before I could throw myself into the fray again, the door to the cargo bay opened—and a handful of armed Cardassians stepped inside. A hush fell over the prisoners.

Worf and Corbis didn't seem to notice. They kept pummeling each other, making the cargo bay resound with the crack of their blows. That is, until Gul Ecor walked in and gestured to his men.

I cried out a warning, but it was too late. The Cardassians hit my lieutenant and the Pandrilite with a couple of seething, white energy beams, sending them flying off their feet.

For a moment, I feared the beams might have been lethal. Then I saw Worf and Corbis stir, if only feebly, and I knew the Cardassians' weapons had been set merely to stun.

I went over to Worf and knelt beside him. He looked up at me, disgusted with the way the combat had ended, but remarkably lucid for a man who had taken the kind of punishment he had.

"Well," said Ecor, "it seems I've stumbled on a disagreement. I *do* hate to see a lack of harmony amongst my prisoners."

I wondered why he was there. Clearly, not just to break up the fight. He could have sent an underling to do that.

Ecor turned to Red Abby. "I just discovered something interesting," he told her. "At least, I found it so. As it turns out, we have quite a celebrity in our midst."

Red Abby and her men looked at each other. No one had the faintest idea what the Cardassian was talking about.

Suddenly, Ecor turned to me. "Isn't that so . . . Captain Jean-Luc Picard of the Federation *Starship Enterprise?*"

There was silence in the hold for a moment. Shocked silence—and *I* was perhaps more shocked than anyone. I felt all eyes upon me, reinterpreting my presence there, and Worf's as well.

Corbis cursed colorfully beneath his breath. "A damned spy, after all," he rumbled menacingly.

Red Abby's eyes narrowed. "I should have known."

"Well," the gul replied amiably, "you know now."

Briefly, I considered denying my identity—telling Ecor I didn't know what he was talking about. However, this was no wild guess he had made. He obviously knew whereof he spoke.

As I riffled through my options, seeking a way out of my narrowing straits, I realized how the Cardassians had made the identification. I didn't have to wait long before Ecor confirmed it for me.

"In case you were wondering," the gul explained, "every Cardassian warship carries a record of recent encounters with the Federation in its computer. When one of my bridge officers decided you looked familiar, he accessed those records—and came up with a positive match."

It was just as I had suspected. "How enterprising of him," I told Ecor. "No pun intended."

The gul chuckled, obviously savoring his confrontation with me. After all, I had had my share of run-ins with the Cardassians. It would have been a coup for Ecor to bring me back to Cardassia Prime with him.

But he still had a greater coup in mind—the same one Red Abby had set her sights on. For the time being, at least, a trip to Cardassia was hardly at the top of our agenda.

Ecor pressed his palms together. "I must admit," he said, "I believed this was a private expedition at first. A grab for treasure. I see now it was a Starfleet effort all along."

His conclusion couldn't have been further from the truth. However, I wasn't about to mention that. The less he knew, I thought, the better.

"Now, then," the gul declared, turning to Red Abby, "I would very much like to know the coordinates of the Hoard of Dujonian."

The woman remained silent. She didn't deny that she had what Ecor wanted. She just wasn't going to give it to him.

After all, Richard Brant's life hung in the balance. Whatever Red Abby's relationship to him might have been, she obviously didn't want to place the fellow in jeopardy.

Though the Cardassian continued to smile, his eyes took on a decidedly harder cast. "Come now, Captain Brant. I can save you a lot of pain if you divulge the information on your own. That is, without my having to . . . extract it from you."

Red Abby had to be scared out of her wits, but somehow she managed not to show it. "I have nothing to say," she replied, her voice remarkably unwavering under the circumstances.

The muscles rippled in Ecor's jaw. Clearly, he wasn't pleased with her response. As a result, he turned to *me* again.

"What about you, Captain Picard? Will you prove a bit wiser than your colleague and share the coordinates with me?"

"I don't know them," I answered truthfully. "Though if I did," I went on just as truthfully, "I don't know that I'd be inclined to share them."

Out of the corner of my eye, I saw Red Abby glance at me. She seemed surprised. And perhaps, I think, a bit more impressed with me—though it hadn't been my intention to impress her.

Having found a couple of strong links in the chain, Gul Ecor eyed the rest of the crew. He had to have known that Worf, a Klingon, wouldn't crack under his threats. But to his mind, no doubt, there were a great many others who might have.

The Cardassian scanned them, making the same kind of threats he had made to Red Abby and myself. Thadoc seemed unmoved. Astellanax muttered a curse and received a rifle butt in the ribs for it. But in the end, Gul Ecor found his weak link.

It was Sturgis, the navigator. "All right," he said, his complexion pale and waxy with fear. "I'll tell."

Red Abby glared at him and shook her head. "Don't do it," she said.

Sturgis looked at her apologetically. "I can't help it, Captain." He tried to smile and failed badly. "The prospect of torture has never held much appeal for me."

"And what *is* your destination?" Ecor asked him.

Sturgis hesitated for a moment, knowing there would be no turning back once he revealed the information—no returning to Red Abby's fold. He took the plunge anyway.

"Strange as it may seem," he told the gul, "the *Daring* was on its way to Hel's Gate."

At first, I thought I had misheard the man. Then I saw the astonished expressions on everyone's faces—except those of Red Abby and her officers, of course—and I realized I'd heard correctly after all.

No one was more astonished than Gul Ecor. "Hel's Gate?" he echoed. "But how can that be?"

It was a good question—one to which we all wanted to know the answer. Hel's Gate, after all, was a celestial anomaly of great turbulence, which was rumored to emit deadly radiation in powerful waves. No one in his right mind would have made such a place his destination.

And yet, Red Abby had done just that. Or so it appeared.

"To tell you the truth," Sturgis replied, "I don't *know* what the captain had in mind. She never told me that much. But it was the Gate we were heading for, as plain as the nose on my face."

The gul leaned into the man's face. "You're certain of this?"

Sturgis nodded. "Certain."

"No other possibility?"

"None," the navigator confirmed.

Ecor studied him a second longer. Then he gestured to one of his men. "Put him in a cell. And equip it for torture."

Sturgis's eyes opened wide. "What are you saying?" he piped, stricken with fear. "I *told* you what you wanted to know!"

The gul watched as two of his men grabbed the navigator by his arms. "Quite possibly," he told Sturgis, "you *have* been honest with me. If that's so, I'll know it."

"But by then—" the navigator protested.

"By then," Ecor interrupted, "it won't do you any good, I grant you. But it will benefit *me* immensely."

"No!" Sturgis shrieked, struggling against his captors to no avail. "No, dammit, no!"

But his cries fell on deaf ears. The gul pretended not to notice as his men dragged the human away. I exchanged glances with Worf, but we were hardly in a position to help the poor wretch.

"I told you the truth!" Sturgis wailed. "The truth!"

And then he was gone, though the echoes of his screams still remained. Finally, even those were gone.

The irony of Sturgis's plight had not been lost on me. The fellow had betrayed his captain and his crewmates to escape the torture chamber—yet he was to be tortured nonetheless.

A grisly prospect, I reflected. I did not envy him.

Ecor turned to Red Abby then. And to me.

"For the moment," he said, "you've been spared. After all, I can torture you only once—and our discussions will prove more fruitful after I've spent some time with your friend."

The gul's mouth twisted with anticipation. It was the first clear-cut sign of his sadism.

"You see, my friends, getting answers is largely a result of knowing which questions to ask. And before long, I expect, I will have a great many questions for you."

I didn't doubt it for a second. Ecor didn't appear to be the sort who gave up easily.

As I watched, he left the cargo bay, his guards trailing in his wake. Then they were gone and we were left alone to contemplate our fate.

Madigoor

"SO YOUR COVER WAS BLOWN," FLENARRH OBSERVED.

Picard nodded. "Thoroughly. I was revealed as a Starfleet captain—in the midst of those who had reason to hate and fear Starfleet. It was not a positive development, as you can imagine."

"But . . . were you *truly* headed for Hel's Gate?" Dravvin asked. He sounded more than a little skeptical.

"Yes," said Bo'tex. "Was that really what Red Abby had in mind? Or was it simply what she had told Sturgis?"

"A good question," Picard responded. "In fact, I found myself mulling the same one, as I sat there in the Cardassians' cargo bay. Why on Earth would anyone purposely chart a course for something like Hel's Gate? It seemed foolish, to say the least—perhaps even suicidal."

Robinson eyed him. "And yet?"

Picard shrugged. "I decided to put the question to the only person who would know for certain—Red Abby herself."

"Wasn't she wary of you?" asked Hompaq.

"Naturally," Picard said. "However, I pointed out that we were in the same boat, so to speak. Whatever we had been in the past, we were at that moment fellow prisoners."

"And she accepted the argument?" asked Dravvin.

"Apparently," Picard answered.

The Tale

"Is it true?" I asked.

Red Abby looked at me. "About Hel's Gate, you mean?" She nodded. "It's true all right."

I frowned. "But how *could* it be?"

She chuckled grimly. "I asked the same question. Hel's Gate is a maelstrom, I said. Why the devil would anyone want to go near the place?"

"And?" I prodded.

"And it's a maelstrom all right." Her eyes took on a faraway look. "But it's also a dimensional wormhole of some kind. And beyond it, on the other side, is Dujonian's Hoard."

"You've seen it?" I asked.

Red Abby shook her head. "No." She smiled bravely at me. "I mean not yet. But I will. Bet the farm on it."

I had to admire her courage if not her grasp of the trouble we were in. But she still hadn't satisfied my curiosity.

"If you've never been there yourself . . ." I began.

Red Abby spoke softly, so no one else would hear her. "My brother's been there."

"Your brother," I echoed just as softly. "You mean Richard."

She nodded, a lock of red hair falling across her forehead. "The one in trouble. And the one you're supposed to rescue, I imagine. Or is it strictly the Hoard you're interested in?"

I considered how much I ought to tell her. The part about Richard Brant had become obvious. There didn't seem to be any harm in confirming it.

"Your brother is part of it," I replied. "At least, to me he is. He was Starfleet, after all."

Red Abby smiled a grim smile. "But the Hoard is the bigger part. You don't want it falling into the hands of the Cardassians."

She had hit the nail on the head, of course. I shrugged noncommittally. "I suppose one could read that into it."

The woman laughed. It was a good laugh, an open laugh, not the kind I had heard from her before. "Always so circumspect, you Starfleet types."

"Are we?" I asked.

"Why not come out and say it? You're here to save my brother from a pack of mercenaries. But unlike me, you're not doing it out of any real concern for him. You've got your own agenda. There's no shame in that."

"It's not that simple," I told her.

She grunted. "No, it never is."

Certainly, the woman could be exasperating. "What I mean," I continued, "is that there is no lack of concern for your brother—either on my part or on Starfleet's. But I would be lying if I said it's our *only* concern."

Red Abby leaned back against the bulkhead. "Honesty," she said. "I'm impressed. Especially in light of all the lies you told me."

"Regrettable," I told her. "But necessary."

She looked at her hands, as if she'd suddenly found something fascinating about them. "Not bad, actually. I really thought you were some kind of adventurer. When I learned you were a Starfleet officer . . . a captain, no less . . . as I say, not bad."

"People don't fool you very often," I observed.

Red Abby turned to me. "No," she agreed, "they don't, now that you mention it. You either, I'd guess."

"Not often," I conceded. "Though you did."

"Me?" she said. "How?"

"I thought you were motivated strictly by greed," I explained. "Now it seems you're out to save your brother from his abductors."

"I didn't make any claims one way or the other," she reminded me.

"That's true," I said. "But you fooled me nonetheless."

For a moment, we looked at each other—not as captain and crewman or as adversaries, but as two people might look at each other. And I found a great deal to like in Abby Brant.

Then she looked away. "What are our chances of getting help from that Starfleet of yours?"

I frowned. "Almost nil. My associate and I were out here very much on our own. Due to the delicate nature of our mission, you understand."

"I do," said Red Abby. "I guess his name's not Mitoc, then?"

I shook my head. "It's Worf."

She grunted softly. "You might as well have called him Worf. I wouldn't have known the difference."

"At the time," I said, "I had no way of knowing that."

Silence again. But this time, she didn't look at me. In fact, she seemed to be making a point of *not* looking at me.

"Have I said something to offend you?" I asked.

Finally, Red Abby looked up. "No," she told me. "You haven't offended me. But you *have* managed to—"

Just then, I heard the cargo bay's door iris open. A handful of Cardassian guards came in, their weapons at the ready. Finally, Gul Ecor entered and stood among them.

"Unfortunately," Ecor announced, "our friend Sturgis didn't survive his interrogation. It seems he wasn't as durable as he looked."

I could hear Abby curse under her breath. What's more, I understood her anger and her pain. In the end, Sturgis had fallen victim to his fear, it's true. But prior to that, he had been a loyal and efficient crewman—a man she had trusted and perhaps even liked.

I, of course, had another reason for mourning the man. As you'll recall, he and I had fought side by side against the Cardassians. For all I knew, Sturgis had saved my life.

"However," the gul went on, either ignorant of Abby's muttered curse or unimpressed by it, "the fellow swore with his dying breath that he hadn't lied to me—and that Hel's Gate was indeed the *Daring*'s destination."

He turned to Red Abby. "That presents me with a problem, Captain Brant. I know where you were headed—but not what you planned on doing when you got there, or how it was going to help you find the Hoard."

"And?" she said.

"And I don't intend to expose my ship and crew to a phenomenon like Hel's Gate until I have a better understanding of the situation."

"You won't get it from me," she told him.

Ecor smiled tautly. "I beg to differ with you." He gestured to his fellow Cardassians. "She's next."

As the soldiers reached for Red Abby, I determined I wouldn't stand by and allow them to take her. The fact that I had little or no chance of stopping them didn't enter into the equation. I simply couldn't let her be seized without a fight.

Apparently, Lieutenant Worf was of the same mind. But then, as I've noted, he is a Klingon.

Since there was a Cardassian standing behind me, I drove my elbow into his ribs. As he doubled over, I shoved him as hard as I could into the bulkhead behind him.

Worf attacked the nearest guard as well, with much the same results.

His man lay on the deck, bloodied and gasping for air, before he or anyone else could prevent it.

But that was as far as either of us got. I felt something strike me in the side with the force of a sledgehammer—a directed energy beam, no doubt, fortuitously set on stun. As I lay on the deck, half-numb, I saw my lieutenant had suffered the same fate.

Gul Ecor came to stand over me. "Be patient, Captain Picard. If Captain Brant doesn't prove cooperative, you'll get your turn." He laughed. "In fact, you'll get your turn no matter what. I'm sure there's a good deal I can learn from the commanding officer of a starship."

As I mentioned earlier, I had already suffered at the hands of a Cardassian torture master. I had no desire to suffer that way again.

Still, as Abby was led away, I found I was more concerned for her than I was for myself.

Madigoor

"OUR HERO'S PROSPECTS ARE NOT GOOD," THE CAPTAIN OF THE *Kalliope* said slyly. "Nor, for that matter, are his friend Red Abby's."

"As is often the case," Dravvin noted, "in a tale of high adventure."

"Indeed," Flenarrh added, "why else would anyone listen to such a tale—except to see how the hero escapes his bad prospects?"

"Sometimes he *doesn't* escape," the Captain of the *Kalliope* said.

"True," Hompaq agreed. "Sometimes he has the good sense to perish. In fact, that is the hallmark of a good adventure story—a brave death in the face of terrible odds."

"I suppose that's good *sometimes,*" Bo'tex allowed.

Hompaq glanced pointedly at Picard and made a derisive sound deep in her throat. "Not sometimes, fat one. *All* the time. An honorable death is not an enemy, to be feared and avoided. It is a prize to be coveted, the ultimate reward for courage and devotion."

Flenarrh chuckled, enjoying the Klingon's remark. "I do believe our friend is baiting you, Captain Picard."

"Baiting him *again,*" Dravvin noted.

Picard could see that Hompaq's annoyance with him wasn't going to go away. At least, not without some effort.

He smiled, the picture of tolerance. "As well she should," he replied. "After all, Hompaq makes a valid point—a particularly Klingon point. And like any Klingon, she's willing to stand up for it."

Hompaq's eyes narrowed. "Then you agree with me?"

Picard shook his head. "Not completely, no. I'm not quite so eager to embrace death as you are. But I respect your opinion nonetheless."

Hompaq considered him for what seemed like a long time. "Perhaps I spoke too soon," she conceded at last. "It seems you have an appreciation for the Klingon soul after all."

"A great appreciation," Picard assured her.

"That still doesn't tell us how you escaped your predicament," Bo'tex reminded him.

"Allow me to correct that deficiency," Picard said. "As you'll recall, Red Abby had just been taken away for interrogation. And I was recovering from the stun beam a Cardassian had inflicted on me . . ."

The Tale

As soon as the Cardassians left us alone, Astellanax knelt by my side. "Are you all right?" he asked.

I nodded. The numbness in my arm and my side was already beginning to wear off, leaving a dull ache in its place.

"I'll live," I told him. I glanced at the door, which had closed in the Cardassians' wake. "But I'm not so sure about your captain. She'll die before she gives Ecor what he wants."

The first officer nodded. "Agreed."

"We can't just let them kill her," protested Thadoc, who was standing behind Astellanax. "We must do something."

"This is a Cardassian warship," Dunwoody reminded him, "full of trained soldiers. It won't be easy."

"No," said another voice. "It won't."

I turned and saw it belonged to Corbis. He looked around the cargo bay at his fellow prisoners, captivating them by virtue of his size.

"I don't know about the rest of you," he went on, "but I signed on to find treasure—not to risk my skin for a captain I hardly know."

"She is not just our captain," Thadoc countered. "She is one of us."

"And if I don't do something to help her," said Astellanax, "what right have I got to expect help when they take *me* away?"

"Well said," I declared, getting to my feet—no easy task, I might add, but one I deemed necessary. "However, Mr. Dunwoody has a point. As I told Red Abby herself, there is no easy way out of here."

"Oh, no?" asked a broad, dark-haired Tellarite named Gob. His tiny eyes squinted at me expectantly.

Corbis grunted, picking up on the Tellarite's meaning. "Not even when we've got a high-and-mighty Starfleet captain among us?" He turned to Worf. "And his Klingon lapdog?"

I eyed my lieutenant, counseling patience with my glance. Somehow, he found the wherewithal to embrace it.

"Not even then," I told the Pandrilite reasonably. "Certainly, I have a working knowledge of Cardassian vessels and the technologies that drive them. But before I can use that knowledge to advantage, we've got to get out of this cargo bay."

"Then, let's do it," Astellanax said. He looked around. "There's got to be a way out of here. It's just a matter of finding it."

I frowned. The Orion was long on enthusiasm but short on suggestions. And as it happened, I'd been racking my brain for a way out since the Cardassians threw us in there.

Assad pointed to a narrow, raised section of ceiling running from one bulkhead to another. If you've ever seen the schematics for a Cardassian vessel, you know it contained power-distribution circuitry.

"If we could get up there," he said, "maybe we could short out the ship's energy grid." He looked around at his fellow prisoners. "It's worth a try, isn't it?"

Worf scowled. "Even if there was a way for us to reach it, we would be risking an explosion that would rip this bay apart."

Astellanax started to suggest it might not be so bad a risk after all. I emphasize the word "started," because at that moment we heard the shrill complaint of a half-dozen klaxons.

Clearly, something had gone wrong on the warship. Something *serious,* I told myself, with a certainty that depended on instinct more than logic.

I looked at Worf, wondering what it could be. An accident in the engine room? Or perhaps the approach of an enemy?

Either way, it represented a danger to us—one we were helpless to do anything about. If something was amiss, the Cardassians would likely worry about themselves first and about us not at all.

Then something else happened. We felt a jolt, right through the deck-plates. The lights went out at the same time, leaving us nothing to see by except the ghostly glow of blue-green emergency strips.

Corbis moved to the doors and pounded on them with the flat of his big, blue hand. "Let us out!" he cried.

I knew he'd get no satisfactory response. As it happened, he got no response at all.

But that was good—the best outcome we could have hoped for, in fact. It meant our guards had abandoned us to attend to an emergency elsewhere on the ship—and with the power that maintained the force field down, the only thing that stood between ourselves and our freedom was the doors themselves.

Standing beside the Pandrilite, I tried to dig my fingers into the tiny crevice between the rhodinium surfaces.

"What are you doing?" asked Thadoc.

"Trying to pry the doors open," I explained. "And if it's all the same to you, I could use some help."

Even before I spoke, Worf had come over to join me. As he and Thadoc dug their fingers into the opening, Corbis lent his efforts, as well.

"Heave!" I cried.

We heaved. The doors parted ever so slightly.

"Heave!" I cried again.

This time, with a little better grip, we made more progress. A space the width of two of my fingers opened between the doors.

"Heave!" I cried a third time.

We put our shoulders and our backs into it, tugging as hard as we could. I felt some unseen restraint give way and the doors slid back into their wall-pockets, clearing the way for our escape.

The corridor outside our cell was dark as well, only the lighting strips providing illumination. With a cheer, the other prisoners pushed us into it, unmindful of what we might find there. Fortunately, there wasn't a single Cardassian in sight—but that didn't mean it would stay that way.

Even if all other systems were down, internal sensors from other parts of the ship might pick up the movements of so many beings. It would only be a moment or two before the Cardassians realized what had happened, and less than a minute before they responded.

Two things were clear to me. First, we had to go on the offensive. Second, if we didn't recover Red Abby immediately, we might never get another chance to do so.

And there was only one place they would keep her.

"This way," I shouted over the tumult of voices, and started down the corridor toward the nearest lift.

"Where are you going?" asked Astellanax.

"The gul's quarters," I told him.

"Why there?" asked Thadoc.

"Because," I said, "that's where we'll find your captain, assuming she's still alive."

"Wait a minute!" someone bellowed.

The Oord—Corbis's friend from the melee in the mess hall—stepped forward with a belligerence characteristic of his species. He made an exaggerated gesture of dismissal with his arms.

"I don't give a *damn* about the captain," he rumbled. "I want to know where the escape craft are."

More than a dozen voices went up in support of the Oord's demand. With the casualties we had sustained on the *Daring* and the loss of Sturgis, that represented almost half our number.

But there was no time to argue. "Very well," I said, pointing past them. "They're over there. Two decks down."

The Oord looked at me with narrowed eyes, no doubt wondering if I had any reason to lie to him. Then he took off in the direction I'd indicated, with the green-splotched Thelurian and several others on his heels.

To my surprise, Corbis wasn't one of them. The Pandrilite watched his friends go for a second, then turned to me. He seemed ready to follow where I led—at least for the moment.

Suddenly, the deck rocked beneath our feet, forcing us to grab the bulkheads for support. I was no longer willing to accept the accident theory. More and more, it was becoming clear to me that the ship was under attack—though I couldn't divine by whom and for what reason.

"The captain!" Astellanax cried, even before we'd recovered.

Thrusting myself away from the bulkhead, I made my way toward the lift. Ideally, I'd have proceeded with the kind of caution we had employed on the *Daring,* but there simply wasn't time for that.

So when we came around a corner and met our first squad of Cardassians, we were almost nose to nose with them before either party knew it.

As we were unarmed, the close quarters worked to our advantage. I drove an uppercut into the jaw of one Cardassian while Worf decked a second with an open backhand. Corbis lifted a third soldier and sent him flying into his comrades, just as Thadoc used a Romulan lightning jab to crush the windpipe of a fourth man.

The fighting was savage and unrestrained, but mercifully quick. And when the proverbial dust cleared, our side had emerged victorious. In fact, we hadn't lost a single combatant. Knowing how lucky we'd been, we grabbed whatever arms we could and surged down the corridor.

Reaching the lift, we jammed in and Worf programmed it for the main deck. I half-expected the compartment to halt in midtransit, interdicted by a command from the bridge. But it did nothing of the kind.

While we were in the lift, the ship lurched twice. The second time was the worst one yet. All the more reason to move quickly, I mused.

When the doors opened, I took a quick look around in the darkened corridor. Seeing no evidence of an ambush, I tightened my grasp on my Cardassian pistol and led the way to Gul Ecor's suite.

Our goal was almost in view, I told myself. There was a chance we would make it—an outcome on which I wouldn't have wagered a strip of latinum just a few minutes earlier.

We came to the end of the corridor, turned right and then right again. And there before us, not more than fifty meters away, was the entrance to the gul's quarters. Unguarded, no less.

It seemed too easy. And it was.

Someone cried out and we whirled. A moment later, the Cardassians' energy beams exploded in the darkness. All but one of them missed.

In the eerie half-light of the emergency strips, Astellanax glanced just once at the blackened, oozing mess that had been his stomach. His eyes grew round and wide. Raising his weapon, he fired off a blast. Then he toppled forward, dead before he hit the ground.

The rest of us fired as well, sobered by the Orion's destruction. I regret to say he was not the only casualty we suffered in that encounter. One of the humans among us cried out and crumpled, followed by a Bajoran and a squat, light-haired Tellarite.

Still, we created equal havoc in the ranks of the Cardassians. Before long, we had forced them to retreat to the joining of corridors behind them.

"The gul's quarters!" I rasped, ducking another flash of deadly energy. "Move if you value your lives!"

I didn't dare check to see who had responded to my command. I was too busy laying down cover fire for them, with Lieutenant Worf on one side of me and Corbis on the other.

"Picard!" a voice said, crackling in the darkness. "Quickly!"

It was a woman who had called me—and not just any woman. The summons had come from the throat of Red Abby.

"Dammit, Picard, get in here!" she cried.

As if to emphasize the urgency of her summons, a whole new flood of Cardassians filled the corridor, stepping over the bodies of their fallen comrades. Worf and Corbis and I retreated as one, continuing to provide cover for the other prisoners.

Then we ducked into the gul's quarters, and the door irised closed in our wake. It cut off any possibility of our being hit by enemy fire—temporarily, at least.

In the muted blue-green glow of the emergency lighting, I turned to Red Abby. She was hefting a Cardassian energy rifle, scanning the ranks of those who had retreated into the room with me.

Abruptly, she turned to me. "Astellanax?" she asked, her brow creased deeply with concern.

I shook my head. "He didn't make it."

Madigoor

FLENARRH SIGHED AND SHOOK HIS HEAD. "I WAS HOPING," HE SAID, "THAT Astellanax would survive this adventure."

The Captain of the *Kalliope* nodded. "I was beginning to like him."

"So was I," Picard replied. "He was loyal, dependable—all the things a first officer should be."

"He was a warrior," Hompaq said. "He died as one."

Picard decided Hompaq's epitaph was as good as any he could have come up with. Satisfied, he went on with his story.

The Tale

RED ABBY WAS SADDENED BY THE ORION'S DEATH—THAT MUCH WAS CLEAR. But she didn't let it incapacitate her.

"What about the others?" she inquired.

"Some chose to leave in a shuttle while they could. Those you see elected to stay and effect a rescue."

Red Abby spared them a glance. There was gratitude in it, spoken without words but sincere nonetheless.

Then she grabbed my arm. "We don't have much time," she said, and pulled me in the direction of the next room.

Through the open archway, I could see a shadowy pair of legs lying on the gray, carpeted floor. Unless I was mistaken, they belonged to Gul Ecor. Yet, the last I had seen of the gul, he was accompanied by a contingent of guards.

I turned to Red Abby. "What happened?"

"The lights," she said, "couldn't have gone out at a better time."

She didn't seem inclined to provide more of an explanation than that. But then, she didn't have to. I had an imagination.

As I entered the room, I saw that Ecor wasn't the only one lying there. Two of his guards were sprawled on the floor as well. I didn't need a medical officer to tell me all three Cardassians were dead.

Red Abby led me across the room to the gul's workstation, which stood in the starlight cast by an oval-shaped observation port. The workstation would give me access to the warship's entire command network—assuming, of course, that the system was still operational.

Some of the others entered behind us and moved the corpses over to a bulkhead. Perhaps *pitched* them would be more accurate.

Again, the deck bucked beneath us. Reminded that time was of the essence, I sat down at the chair in front of the workstation, propped my energy rifle against the bulkhead beside me, and got to work. A minute or so later, I found the entry point I was looking for.

It gave me access to not only the ship's command logs, but its sensor logs as well. I took a moment to scan them, to assemble the pieces of the puzzle. What I learned caused me to exclaim in surprise.

"What is it?" asked Red Abby.

I looked at her. "We've been attacked all right—and not just by anyone. It seems our adversary is a Romulan warbird—C Class."

Dunwoody cursed. Worf scowled at the mention of the Romulans, for whom he had no great love. After all, they had killed his parents in the now-infamous Khitomer Massacre.

I turned back to the monitor. "The Romulan commander, an individual who identifies himself as Tacanus, claims the Cardassians were trespassing in Romulan space."

"A likely story," Red Abby commented.

"They're after the Hoard of Dujonian," Worf observed.

"Like everyone else," Assad noted.

"What do we do now?" asked Dunwoody.

Red Abby bit her lip. "This tub is no match for even a C Class warbird. It's a wonder it's held out this long."

Our ship shuddered, as if for emphasis. Not that any was required, mind you. We were acutely aware of our disadvantage.

"If the Romulans win," I said, "it won't help to try to escape in a shuttlecraft. They'll hunt us down like Gosalian hacklehawks descending on a field mouse."

"Agreed," said Red Abby. "Somehow, we've got to stand up to the Romulans and beat them." She looked around. "Any ideas?"

No one seemed to have one, at first. Then it hit me, like a phaser beam on a heavy stun setting.

"If Worf's right about the Romulans coveting the Hoard," I said, "they won't be content to just destroy the Cardassians. They'll want to interrogate them as the Cardassians interrogated us."

Corbis eyed me. "So?"

"What he's saying," Thadoc informed the Pandrilite, "is the Romulans will have to send boarding teams to take prisoners—or at least, beam some Cardassians onto their vessel."

"And they can't do either of those things," said Dunwoody, "unless they drop their shields for a moment."

I nodded. "Precisely. And that's when they'll be vulnerable."

Understanding dawned in Red Abby's eyes. "Very clever. But we'll need to get to a transporter room."

"We will indeed," I replied thoughtfully, weathering yet another quaking of the deckplates.

And yet, as far as we knew, there were still Cardassians laying in wait for us outside the gul's suite. Clearly, we would have to get past them in order to reach our objective.

Once again, my knowledge of Cardassian ship design stood us in good stead. I pulled my chair halfway across the room until it stood directly beneath an oval-shaped vent in the ceiling.

"What is he doing?" Corbis wondered.

"Your guess is as good as mine," said Gob.

Stepping up onto the chair, I pried the vent cover loose and stuck my head into the opening. A rather ample passageway was revealed to me—much larger than the vent itself had suggested.

"Of course," said Thadoc, a note of admiration in his voice.

"A ventilation shaft," Red Abby noted, for those who still hadn't figured it out. "Where does it go, Picard?"

"Not very far," I told her. "The ventilation nexus for this section of the ship is only about fifty meters away. But it should be enough to get us past the Cardassians watching our door."

Dunwoody grunted. "They pulled the same trick on us back on the *Daring*. Crawling through the ventilation shafts, I mean."

I glanced at him, remembering all too vividly the vicious nature of that firefight. "That's correct," I said. "And I see no reason why we should not return the favor."

"Nor do I," said Red Abby.

"Then, follow me," I told her, and hoisted myself up into the shaft.

She followed. So did the others, including Lieutenant Worf. I led them along the length of the shaft, bypassing several vents until I came to the one I was looking for.

Peering through its slats, I checked to see if there were any Cardassians in the immediate vicinity. The corridor seemed empty in the glow of the emergency strips, though a bulkhead panel at the far end had exploded and was sparking savagely.

Satisfied that we wouldn't be dropping into a trap, I removed the vent cover and lowered myself to the floor. Phaser in hand, I looked around. There was still no sign of trouble.

I gestured for the others to descend, as well. They did this with the utmost dispatch, ghostly figures in a taut, blue twilight. Then I led the way down the corridor, Worf and Red Abby right behind me.

My comrades and I negotiated passageway after twisting passageway, enduring one vicious jolt after another as the warship absorbed the Romulans' attacks. After a while, we came to a corridor filled with smoking, sparking chaos, and a slew of Cardassian corpses.

We made our way through it slowly, carefully, unable to see more than a few inches in front of our faces. The smoke seared our throats and invaded our lungs, until we were coughing as much as breathing.

The skin on the back of my neck prickled. I felt as if, at any moment, I would be cut in half by a Cardassian disruptor beam.

Fortunately, it didn't happen. We came to the end of the corridor without either firing or being fired upon. As I wiped my watering eyes and proceeded through the thinning smoke, I saw what looked a great deal like the transparent doors of a Cardassian transporter facility.

It was a dozen meters ahead, perhaps less. What's more, it appeared to be unguarded—but as we had seen before with regard to the Cardassians, appearances could be lethally misleading.

As it happened, I was still in the lead at that point. With the utmost caution, I advanced on the transporter facility. When I got close enough, its door began to iris open.

Madigoor

Picard paused to take a sip of his wine. He was approaching the bottom of the glass.

"And?" said Bo'tex. "What did you find?"

"What do you think?" asked Hompaq. "The place was as empty as a poor man's feast hall."

"Empty?" said the Captain of the *Kalliope.* He stroked his beard. "Why would you say that?"

"Because they are Cardassians," the Klingon spat. "If they had the brains to safeguard a transporter facility, they would never have lost Dujonian's Hoard in the first place."

Robinson chuckled. "A good point."

"Perhaps it is, at that," said Flenarrh.

Dravvin turned to Picard. "And *was* it empty?"

Picard set his glass down. "Not exactly," he replied.

The Tale

THE PLACE WAS GUARDED BY A SINGLE CARDASSIAN—ONE WHO HAD OBVIously been surprised by the opening of the door. As I spotted him, he was still drawing his disruptor pistol.

Leveling it, he fired at me. I fired as well.

Luck was on my side. I dispatched the fellow with my first shot.

Of course, we didn't yet know he was alone. We had to approach the facility carefully, looking and listening for evidence of other Cardassians. Finally, satisfied the place was secure, we swarmed inside.

Like every other place on that vessel, it was cast in a blue-green glow. Immediately, I located the room's control console and commandeered it. Presetting as many controls as possible, I obtained a lock on the Romulan ship and waited for its commander to do as I had predicted.

By then, the doors had closed behind us, fortifying us against unwanted interruptions. Corbis came up beside me.

"What now?" he asked.

"Now we exercise patience," I replied.

"Patience?" he said, as if it were a curse.

I nodded. "That's right."

As it turned out, we needed quite a bit of it. The minutes dragged by, unmindful of our anxiety. We looked at one another, searching for answers our comrades couldn't provide.

As captains of your own vessels, you know uncertainty is a terrible thing. It can gnaw at you until your very sanity gives way. We began to get a taste of that in the Cardassian transporter room.

After a while, we wondered if we had guessed wrong about the Romulans' plans. Perhaps they had already obtained the information they needed. Perhaps, in destroying our Cardassian captors, they were merely eliminating a competitor for the Hoard.

I had already begun to consider alternative schemes, none of which was particularly satisfactory, when the sensors showed me what I had been hoping so desperately to see. The Romulans had dropped their deflector shields. Almost at the same time, they began to conduct transporter activity on one of their middle decks.

Encouraged, I activated the Cardassian transporter system and darted across the room. The Cardassian version of a transporter pad wasn't very impressive looking, but it was very nearly as efficient as the Federation model. Taking my place on it alongside Abby, Thadoc, Corbis, and three other men, I drew my phaser and waited.

In a heartbeat, we found ourselves on the Romulan bridge.

The commander of the warbird was sitting in a central chair with a rounded back. He was surrounded by seven or eight officers tending to various duties, their faces caught in the glow of bright green status screens on the bulkheads around them. Before they could register our presence or react to it, the place came alive with a host of diamond-blue energy beams.

Every one of the Romulans fell instantly—with one exception, and Thadoc took that one out with a blow to the back of the neck. Worf and the rest of our comrades materialized in the next second or two, but to their chagrin there was nothing for them to do. A bizarre stillness reigned as the magnitude of our victory sank in.

Through sheer audacity, we had taken over the bridge of a Romulan warbird—and as far as we knew, no one on the vessel except us had any inkling of it. Of course, that would change soon enough.

Advancing to the Romulan commander's seat, I moved his unconscious form aside. Then I turned to Thadoc.

"We need a security lockout," I said. "Can you give us one?"

I was only guessing that he'd had some experience serving on Romulan vessels. Being only half-Romulan, he might not have. It didn't occur to me that, even if he did have the expertise, he might not be willing to apply it on my behalf.

After all, we were no longer fighting for our lives in some corridor. We were on a bridge again, even if it wasn't that of the *Daring*. The situation cried out for a captain—and Thadoc turned to the one he had in mind for the position.

In other words, Red Abby.

It was no time for politics. Taking the woman by the arm, I pulled her off to the side, where we could speak one-on-one.

"Listen," I said, "I don't care who sits in the center seat once we have secured this vessel. But for now, I need the cooperation of everyone—you included."

She frowned, clearly reluctant to comply. But after a moment, she turned to Thadoc.

"Do whatever he says," she commanded.

Without a word, Thadoc opened the Romulan commander's control panel and gave me the lockout I had requested. "From this point on," he announced, "no one will be able to enter the bridge without our permission."

"Sounds good to me," Dunwoody remarked.

Thadoc turned to me. "What next?"

I didn't need much time to think about it. "Conduct an emergency override, deactivating all transporter facilities. Then check to see how many Romulans have already been sent to the Cardassian ship."

Again, Thadoc complied. After a second or so, he looked up. "Transporters are all locked down. As for how many have left the warbird . . ." He shook his head. "All boarding parties are still here."

"No one left?" I asked. "Are you sure?"

His expression told me he was *very* sure.

I frowned. "Some astute Romulan officer must have noticed our transport and called a halt to the boarding operation."

"Let's make sure the situation doesn't change," said Red Abby. She turned to Thadoc. "Raise the shields."

He nodded. "Done."

Red Abby looked at me, the epitome of cooperation. "What now?" she asked.

"Now," I told her, "I give them their walking papers. Mr. Thadoc, would you activate the ship's intercom?"

It took only a moment for him to do as I had requested. Choosing my words judiciously, I addressed the warbird's crew, trusting the system's translation protocols to make my announcement understandable to them.

"Attention," I said. "We have secured control of your vessel."

A chorus of cheers went up from the throats of Red Abby's men. Or most of them, anyway. Red Abby herself remained silent. If she harbored any resentment toward me, she didn't show it.

Not that I would have stepped aside in any case. I was clearly better prepared for this stage of the operation than she was.

"At this time," I continued, "we recommend you leave the ship by any means available to you."

Thadoc glanced at me, his brows raised in surprise.

"They are Romulans," he whispered, too softly to be heard over the intercom system. "That recommendation will *not* sit well with them."

"I'm aware of that," I whispered back. "But they are also painfully vulnerable under the circumstances. And though I have no desire to take advantage of their vulnerability, they have no way of knowing that."

In fact, the Romulans had no idea who I was or what I was capable of. What's more, I had no intention of enlightening them.

"It's all right," Red Abby told Thadoc. "Picard's got the ball." She looked at me. "Let's see if he can run with it."

If it was a vote of confidence, it was hardly a resounding one. Nonetheless, I went on.

"I will allow you to make use of all shuttles and life-pods," I told the crew. "If you decline to do so, I will cut off your life support and you will die slowly for a lost cause. The choice is yours."

At that point, I terminated the communication. Worf was standing in a corner from which he could keep an eye on the Romulans lying about the bridge. He nodded approvingly.

"Do you think they'll respond to your generosity?" Assad asked.

"I suspect they will," I told him. "But one never knows. There are Romulans and there are Romulans."

A moment later, an indicator lit up on the commander's board. Someone was boarding one of the life-pods.

"I've got at least one taker," I noted.

In the next several seconds, I saw five more indicators. Three of them were life-pods, the others shuttles. Obviously, at least part of the crew had decided to take me up on my offer.

"It's working," Worf observed.

"So it is," Thadoc said. He looked at me. "But what do you propose to do if there are stragglers? Romulans who would rather die than renege on their oaths and abandon their ship?"

It was a fair question.

"I have a plan for them," I assured him. I jerked my head to indicate the Romulans we had knocked unconscious. "Just as I have a plan for our sleepy friends here."

"What about the Cardassians?" Corbis asked.

Another fair question. To be sure, something had to be done about them.

I turned to Thadoc again. "The Cardassians must be caught in some kind of tractor beam. See if you can release them."

As he got to work, I looked at the viewscreen. The Cardassian warship hung there in space, battered and blackened, its hull glowing a savage red in the places where it had taken the most damage.

After a few moments, the vessel began to drift away from us. With all it had gone through, its crew had no control over its movements.

"There," I said. "That should take care of the Cardassians."

The warship would hang in space like a broken toy until such time as its fellow Cardassians saw fit to look for it. It might take quite some time, of course. However, we were showing our captors more kindness than they had shown us.

Meanwhile, the Romulan evacuation was proceeding apace, shuttles and life-pods issuing from the warbird in several different places. But it seemed Thadoc had been right to ask about stragglers. Some of the escape vehicles were being ignored, even in what should have been the most populous sections of the ship.

Red Abby seemed to have noticed as well. "If you've really got a plan," she told me, "this would be a good time to implement it."

I checked the sensor readout on the commander's control panel. Three of the shuttles had left their bays, but two were still close to the ship. I turned to Thadoc and indicated the Romulans lying among us.

"Obtain a transporter lock on them," I said, "and beam them onto one of those shuttles. Then find another half-dozen Romulans and do the same, again and again—until we're alone on this vessel."

The helmsman regarded me for a full second, no doubt trying to find a flaw in my scheme. Apparently, he was unsuccessful, because he eventually bent to his task.

As he worked the warbird's transporter controls, the Romulan bridge crew began to shimmer. Almost instantly, it was gone. And in the next few minutes, the same thing took place all over the ship.

Thadoc seemed to be enjoying his work. But in time it ended, as all good things will.

Red Abby looked around and nodded. "Well," she observed, "I suppose that's one way to get rid of unwanted guests."

I found myself smiling—not so much at the quip itself as at the tone she had used. It was the first time I had heard the woman even come close to making a joke.

"So it is," I agreed.

Thadoc looked at Red Abby. "We should get out of here. There may be additional warbirds in the vicinity."

She looked at me. I nodded, telling her the captain's chair was hers again. I would keep my end of the bargain.

"You've got the helm," she told Thadoc. "Chart us a course for Hel's Gate."

Madigoor

"A BOLD MOVE," SAID HOMPAQ, "THIS TRANSPORT ONTO THE ENEMY'S SHIP—even if it *was* just a pack of Romulans."

Flenarrh looked at her from beneath his white tuft. "I wouldn't take the Romulans lightly if I were—"

The Klingon snarled at him.

"—me," he finished lamely.

"I'm impressed, too," said the Captain of the *Kalliope.* "I don't think I ever would have thought of that tactic myself."

Robinson chuckled. "Don't be so hard on yourself, lad. Where you come from, they don't *have* transporters."

The Captain of the *Kalliope* grunted good-naturedly. "That's true. Still, it was a clever maneuver."

Dravvin stroked his chin. "From what you've said, Picard, there couldn't have been more than thirteen or fourteen of you left to man the warbird—and to effect repairs where it was damaged in the battle."

"That's correct," said Picard.

"It doesn't seem any of you would have gotten much rest," the Rythrian noted.

"Not much at all," Picard agreed, "though it was sorely needed after all we had been through."

"I can't operate without rest," Bo'tex remarked. "No Caxtonian can. If we don't get our beauty sleep, we're liable to run our ship into the nearest asteroid belt."

"I'm sure you're exaggerating," said Robinson.

"Not one iota," Bo'tex insisted. "Ever hear of Captain In'dro?"

Robinson shook his head. "I don't believe so, no."

"He and his crew were models of Caxtonian efficiency. Then they were kept up one night by engine noise. The next day, they fell asleep on their bridge and got caught in a subspace anomaly." Bo'tex paused for dramatic effect. "They were never heard from again."

"Enlightening," Dravvin said dryly. "But tell me this, Captain Bo'tex . . . if In'dro and his crew were never heard from again, how do you know exactly what happened to them?"

The Caxtonian stared at him for a moment. "I . . . er, that is . . ."

The Rythrian grunted. "As I thought."

The Captain of the *Kalliope* turned to Picard. "While our colleague Bo'tex is trying to answer Captain Dravvin's question, you may want to go on with your story."

Picard nodded. "Indeed. As I was saying, rest was certainly on all our minds. And repairs were needed as well. But before she addressed those concerns, Red Abby had something to say to us. To *all* of us."

The Tale

As you may have gathered, this wasn't a woman who liked to stand on ceremony. She spoke plainly and from the heart.

"When a captain picks her crew," she said, "there's no science to it. All she can do is listen to her instincts and hope they're right more often than they're wrong."

Red Abby paused. "Astellanax was one of the best choices my instincts ever made. He was smart and diligent and faithful, and that's pretty much what you want from a first officer. I'm grateful for all he did for me, not just on this voyage but also on those that preceded it."

Her gaze seemed to soften as she scanned the remnants of her crew, her disordered red hair catching light from the Romulan monitors. She was taking some care in selecting her words.

"I want to thank everyone on this bridge as well," she said. "Without you, I'd still be holed up in that gul's quarters, waiting for the Romulans to come and drag me out. As long as I live, I'll never forget your loyalty or your courage. And with luck, I'll still be able to reward you for what you've done . . . with Dujonian's treasure."

I was touched by Red Abby's words. Judging by the looks on their faces, I'd say my comrades were as well. At that moment, inspired by her gratitude, they would gladly have followed her into hell.

Or, at the least, through Hel's Gate.

Corbis, perhaps, was the lone exception to the rule. He stood in the corner, scowling. But if he was less than electrified by his captain's speech, he kept it to himself.

"Now, then," Red Abby went on in a more businesslike tone, "we'll need to assess damage and make repairs. If we run into another hostile ship, Romulan or otherwise—and at this point, it wouldn't surprise me in the least—I don't want to get caught with our pants down."

"Nor do I," I replied. "On the other hand, we need some sleep. We've barely shut our eyes in the last two days."

"I agree," said Red Abby.

She set up a schedule of duty assignments. Thadoc and I would eventually take turns at the helm—though until I familiarized myself with the Romulan control panel, we would have to work together.

Worf and Dunwoody would switch off at tactical. The remainder of the crew would try to effect repairs as best they could, with at least two teams roaming the warbird at any given time.

Whoever wasn't on duty would find a place to sleep. Whoever *was* on duty would find something useful to do. There were no exceptions—not even Red Abby herself, apparently. To make that clear, she volunteered to begin the first shift by leading a repair squad.

I was pleasantly surprised by the woman's egalitarianism. After all, I had seen her reluctance to cede me the captain's chair even temporarily.

Then again, as I noted earlier, we were no longer on the *Daring*. We were ensconced aboard a Romulan vessel, with which Red Abby had little familiarity. It made sense for her to help however she could.

"If there's the least sign of trouble," she told Thadoc pointedly, "contact me immediately."

"I will," he assured her.

Then Red Abby departed with the repair teams, leaving Thadoc, myself, and Worf on the bridge alone. While my lieutenant busied himself running diagnostic routines at tactical, Thadoc taught me what he knew about the Romulan helm console.

As it turned out, it wasn't so different from the Klingon version, which I had come to know in my dealings with the Empire. Nor did the similarity come as a surprise to me.

As you may know, the Klingons and the Romulans were allies for a while, in the middle of the twenty-third century. During this period, they pooled their expertise in a great many areas of military technology, ship design being only one of them.

"It's quite simple, really," Thadoc told me.

I nodded. "Of course, I won't feel comfortable until I've performed some maneuvers myself."

He shrugged. "There's no time like the present. Perform some maneuvers now, if you like."

I took Thadoc up on his offer. Without diverging substantially from our course, I put the warbird through one rigor after another, testing the precision of her steering system and the responsiveness of her engines.

I was pleased with the results. While the Romulan helm *looked* like its Klingon counterpart, there was no comparison between the two systems in terms of performance. The Romulans had clearly outdistanced their former allies over the last hundred years.

"She turns on a dime," I said.

Thadoc looked at me quizzically.

"An old expression," I explained. "It means she handles well."

He grunted softly. "That, she does."

His eyes lost their focus for a moment. It seemed to me Thadoc was lost in some long-ago memory.

"You served on a warbird," I noted, guessing that that was what he was thinking about.

"I did," he confirmed. "For six years."

"As helmsman?" I asked.

"Eventually," Thadoc told me.

"But you left."

He nodded. "I did indeed."

"Didn't you like it anymore?" I asked.

Thadoc looked at me. "I was good at what I did, make no mistake. Still, I was not held in wide esteem. Perhaps it was the Bolian blood in me, I don't know. A few years ago, shortly after the Klingon Civil War, our warbird ran into a Federation vessel in unaligned space."

I thought for a moment. "The *Potemkin?"*

He seemed impressed with my knowledge of the incident. "Yes. In any case, we lost the encounter. My commander needed a scapegoat so he wouldn't have to take the blame himself."

I understood. "And he made you that scapegoat."

"I was accused of incompetence," said Thadoc, "and a failure to heed my commander's orders. All I could do was exercise my right of statement and deny the charges. In the end, it did me no good whatsoever."

"You were sentenced to death?" I asked.

He shook his hairless, blue head. "My commander knew I had done nothing wrong, and he was not entirely without conscience. He saw to it I was sent to a penal colony instead."

"Charitable of him," I commented.

"En route there," said Thadoc, "our transport vessel ran into a subspace anomaly. There was considerable damage to the ship—hull breaches and the like. Casualties ran heavy. As luck would have it, most of the survivors were prisoners like myself."

He stopped himself. After a moment, he frowned.

"No," he decided. "They were prisoners—but not like myself. The others were violent, desperate men, guilty of the crimes for which they were to be punished. I alone was innocent."

I asked him what happened then. Thadoc told me, dredging up memory after vivid memory.

"The prisoners took over the ship, but it was useless to them. The engines had been damaged irreparably by the anomaly. We couldn't go anywhere. Worse, we discovered a buildup of energies in the artificial singularity that powered the warp drive. You're the captain of a starship; I don't need to tell you what kind of threat that represented."

"You were in danger of being destroyed," I said.

"Precisely," he confirmed. "Fortunately, the buildup was a slow one. We sent out a distress call and hoped for the best. Days went by, with no response. We wondered if our communication equipment had been damaged as well, in some way we couldn't detect."

"Entirely possible," I remarked.

"Time passed painfully," said Thadoc, "with no improvement and none in sight. Tempers flared. There were arguments—and bloodshed, even among the prisoners. Every day, it seemed, someone was found dead in some corridor. The last of the guards was killed just for spite. And all the while, the singularity grew more and more unstable."

Hellish, I thought. But I didn't want to interrupt.

"There were several attempts on my life," he noted, "though I kept mostly to myself and offended no one. The first few times, I was able to ward off my assailants. In time, however, I was forced to kill them to keep them from killing me.

"Then the energies in our power source, which had been building slowly to that point, began to accelerate. If we were lucky, we realized, we had a few hours left. With no possibility of survival and no fear of punishment, my shipmates tore at each other like fiends, their hatreds fueled by the pettiest of slights.

"Except for me. I alone fought to defend myself, though I had no more reason to hope than they did. I sequestered myself on the bridge, which no one else seemed to care about any longer, and endured the sounds of the others slaughtering one another.

"It was fortunate that I was there," said Thadoc, "and not somewhere else, or I might have missed the communication that lit up the tactical console. Apparently, someone had received our distress call and responded. What's more, they were nearly in transporter range."

He looked at me. "It was the *Daring.*"

I nodded. No wonder the helmsman was so loyal. Red Abby had taken him off a doomed ship. She had saved his life, and perhaps his sanity as well.

"At great risk to herself and her vessel," he told me, "the captain transported me off, along with the others who still lived. There were shockingly few of them left.

"Once our injuries were treated, we were invited to tell Red Abby our stories. Mine was the only one she believed. She put off the others at the nearest port of call, giving them a chance to make of themselves what they could. I, on the other hand, was invited to join her crew.

"Unable to return to Romulus, faced with the possibility of having to sign on with someone less scrupulous, I took Red Abby up on her offer. Nor," said Thadoc, "have I ever had reason to regret it."

I smiled. "Not even now? With our numbers depleted and Hel's Gate looming on the horizon?"

He didn't hesitate to answer. "Not even now."

Madigoor

PICARD WAS ABOUT TO SAY MORE . . . WHEN SOMETHING LONG AND GREEN skittered across the table.

Suddenly, the intruder stopped and looked around with almost comical intensity. It was some kind of lizard, it seemed—a gecko, unless the captain was mistaken—and contrary to his earlier assessment, it wasn't entirely green after all. In fact, it wore a sprinkling of bright yellow spots.

Bo'tex pushed his chair back, his face twisted with loathing. "What *is* that?" he demanded.

"It's a gecko," said the Captain of the *Kalliope.*

Picard nodded. "That's what I thought."

"As I recall," said Robinson, "the little fellows are found in the tropics. And don't worry, Captain Bo'tex. As fearsome as they look, their diet is restricted to insects."

The Caxtonian scowled. "Very funny."

"Where did the thing come from?" asked Dravvin.

"Where indeed?" said Flenarrh. "In all the time I've been patronizing this place, I've never seen anything like it."

"Could it be someone's pet?" asked the Captain of the *Kalliope.*

"I don't know how else it could've gotten in here," Bo'tex replied.

"That's true," said Robinson. "Unless it's a captain in its own right, and we simply haven't recognized the fact."

Hompaq chuckled. "Too bad it doesn't have a little more meat on its bones. It looks like it would make a tasty snack."

Bo'tex grimaced. "You want to *eat* it?"

The Klingon grinned. "I'd eat *you,* my plump friend, if I wasn't loathe to catch your stench."

The Caxtonian harrumphed. "I told you, dammit, it's *not* a stench—it's a mating scent. On my homeworld, other males envy me. They'd kill for a bouquet like mine."

"That may be true on your homeworld," said Hompaq. "Here, people are willing to kill to get *away* from you."

Bo'tex thrust out his chest. "If my smell is so offensive, why do you put up with me?"

The Klingon bared her teeth. "I have a cold," she told him.

By then, the gecko seemed to have made itself at home. It looked at Picard and blinked.

"It wants to hear the rest of your story," Robinson quipped.

Picard looked at him. "Far be it for me to disappoint a lizard," he said—and went on with his tale.

The Tale

I WAS STILL TESTING THE OPERATIONAL PARAMETERS OF THE ROMULAN HELM when I received a summons from Red Abby.

I looked up from my console. "Picard here."

"I'm in the commander's quarters," the woman told me. "I need you to take a look at something."

Returning the helm to Thadoc, I left the bridge and took a lift to the deck in question—a residental one, apparently. Then I made my way down the corridor to the commander's suite.

The doors opened at my approach, revealing a large room with tan and gray walls, in keeping with the ambiance that characterized the rest of the vessel. There was a triangular mirror set into one wall. On the wall facing, a winged predator clutched two globes, one green and one blue—a symbol of the Romulan Empire, which claimed the planets Romulus and Remus as homeworlds.

I didn't see Red Abby right away. It was only after I had looked around for a moment that I found her hunkered unceremoniously between a long Romulan divan and an opening in the wall. A bulkhead panel was lying on the deck beside her, along with the Romulan equivalent of a tricorder.

"You asked to see me?" I said.

She turned away from the cavity in the wall long enough to glance at me. "I'm glad you're here. Come take a look at this."

I knelt beside Red Abby, craned my neck, and glanced into the opening. There was something inside—a dark mechanism about the size of my fist lodged in a tangled nest of colored circuitry.

It bore a string of raised characters—distinctively Klingon characters, I noted—which was, I supposed, why the woman had summoned me to see it instead of Thadoc.

"Do you know what it is?" Red Abby asked.

I nodded. "Those characters form a Klingon phrase: Wa' DevwI' tu'lu. Translation: There is one leader."

I thought she might comment on the saying's applicability to our own situation. She refrained, however.

"That's nice," she said. "What does it mean?"

"It's a threat," I explained, "meant to intimidate potential mutineers. After all, one may often be tempted to destroy one's commanding officer—especially if one is a Klingon. However, the temptation diminishes dramatically when such an act ensures one's own destruction."

Red Abby's eyes narrowed. "One's . . . own destruction? Are you telling me this is a self-destruct mechanism?"

I confirmed that it was. "It's designed to initiate a sequence of events that will blow up a vessel from within. It became quite popular among Klingon captains several years ago—until a couple of ships exploded and the High Council was forced to outlaw it."

Picking up her tricorder, I took some readings. They allayed my concerns—at least for the time being.

My companion shook her head. "But what's it doing *here,* in a Romulan warbird?"

I could only speculate, of course. "Perhaps the commander of this vessel had reason to distrust his subordinates. Perhaps he was about to give them reason. Perhaps he was simply paranoid. In any case, he must have obtained the device on the black market and installed it himself, then announced its existence to his staff."

"So they would think twice about taking him down," Red Abby noted.

"That's my guess," I said. "On the other hand, he might not have mentioned it at all. His only motive might have been revenge."

"Sour grapes," she observed. "If I can't have command of this vessel, no one can."

"Exactly," I told her.

Red Abby leaned back against the divan. "Good thing the device isn't active."

"Actually," I pointed out, "it *is* active."

She eyed me. "It *is?"*

"Without question," I said.

"Then why do you look so damned calm?" she asked.

"There's no need to panic," I told her, putting the tricorder on the floor beside me. "The device is not set to go off for several hours."

"Good," said Red Abby. "Then I can panic later."

I shrugged. "If you like."

"I don't get it," she said. "We stunned that Romulan commander before he could move a muscle. Unless . . . someone else came in here and activated the mechanism. But that—"

"Doesn't make sense in light of my speculations?" I suggested.

Red Abby frowned. "Unless I'm missing something."

"It's rather simple," I told her. "Unlike the self-destruct mechanisms one finds on Starfleet vessels, this one is not *armed* by a sequence of commands—it's *dis*armed."

My companion looked at me, surprised. "So . . . this thing is set to go off all the time?"

"Exactly," I said. "Every twenty-six hours, the commander of this vessel was required to reset the mechanism—because if he failed to do so, his ship would be reduced to atoms."

Red Abby's nostrils flared. "That's very interesting. But as you may have noticed, the commander of this ship is no longer aboard. So we either have to disarm the mechanism permanently, figure out the reset code, or get the hell off the ship before she blows."

It was an accurate description of our options. "I vote for disarming the mechanism," I told her.

"That's fine," she said. "I take it you've done this before?"

"I have not," I confessed, turning my attention to the device again. "But faint heart and all that."

"Faint heart?" Red Abby echoed.

"Never won fair lady," I said, finishing the thought. I glanced at her. "Surely, you've heard the expression before?"

"Not until now," she told me.

"Well, then," I replied amicably, "this would appear to be a first for both of us."

"A first?" Red Abby seemed wary of me suddenly.

"Yes, I said, smiling. "For you, the first time you've heard the saying about faint hearts. And for me, the first time I've disarmed a Klingon self-destruct device."

She seemed to drop her defenses again. "Right."

I considered the mechanism. "You know," I said, "I hate to leave this sort of thing unattended."

"But?" Red Abby prompted.

"But I could use some tools. You'll find them in whatever storage compartment you got the tricorder from."

"Any particular kind?" she asked.

"Whatever looks useful," I said.

"Consider it done," Red Abby muttered.

As I analyzed the connections between the self-destruct mechanism and the surrounding circuitry, she left the room. A couple of minutes later, she returned with an armful of Romulan tools.

"One of everything," Red Abby stated, laying the implements down in front of me.

I inspected them and chose what looked like a charge inverter. It was long and narrow, with a handle at one end and a tiny bulb at the other, much like the Federation version.

"You're sure that's the right thing?" she asked.

"I will be," I said, "once I scan it with your tricorder."

I proceeded to do just that. As luck would have it, I had chosen well. The tool was precisely what I needed.

"We're in good shape?" Red Abby inquired.

"For the moment," I told her.

By then, I had worked out exactly what I would have to do. As far as I could tell, the self-destruct mechanism interfaced with the circuitry in three separate places. I would need to deactivate all three interfaces without creating an energy imbalance in the circuitry—because that would trigger a self-destruct command as well.

It wasn't a complex job, but it was an exceedingly delicate one. It would require several minutes to complete, perhaps more.

"Let me know if you need anything else," Red Abby said.

I nodded. "I will."

Then I set to work.

Disabling the first connection took the most time and attention, largely because of my lack of familiarity with the Romulan charge inverter. Despite its appearance, the implement was significantly slower and less precise than its Starfleet counterpart.

Once I got past that hurdle, however, I felt comfortable enough to engage my companion in conversation. Nor, to be honest, was it merely a way of easing the tension. I was driven to know more about the woman who called herself Red Abby—and this was my first opportunity to speak with her in private.

"Were you especially close?" I asked her—rather abruptly, I'm afraid. "You and your brother, I mean?"

Red Abby looked at me, as if trying to decide whether to answer such a personal question. In the end, she decided in my favor.

"He was my brother," she said. "My only sibling. How could it have been any other way?"

I too had possessed but a single sibling—my brother, Robert, back on Earth. He had perished in a fire. I took his death rather badly. But for most of our lives together, we had failed to see eye to eye.

I said as much.

Red Abby shook her head. "It was never that way with Richard and myself."

"No?" I said.

"Not in the least. Growing up, we were always very much alike—rebellious and undisciplined, determined to blaze our own paths instead of following those of others." She paused. "Somehow, my brother managed to ignore those qualities in himself and wound up in Starfleet Academy."

"Where he did rather well," I noted.

The second interface was deactivated. Without pause, I went on to the third one—trying not to notice how alluring the smell of Red Abby's hair was. Like lilacs, I thought.

"Yes," she said. "Richard did *very* well."

Her tone of voice told me she meant to say more. "But?" I prodded gently, hoping to hear the rest.

"But he didn't have an easy time of it."

"I'm sorry to hear that," I said.

"The regimentation, the lip service he had to pay to his so-called superiors . . ." She shrugged. "He hated all that. But he managed to accept it because he wanted to explore the galaxy and Starfleet seemed like the best way to do that."

"He must have derived some satisfaction from the job," I suggested. "A person doesn't often rise to the rank of executive officer without a certain degree of commitment."

Red Abby nodded. "It satisfied him, all right—even more than Richard expected, I think. But only for a while. Then it got to him, little by little, just as I told him it would."

"He felt stifled?" I asked.

I glanced at her, suddenly aware of how close she was to me. Aware of her every feature. Her fiery red hair, flowing over one slender shoulder. Her eyes, with the mystical blue of a summer sky in them.

Her mouth, full and inviting.

"Claustrophobic," said Red Abby. "Restrained by one rule or another. But even then, he didn't give it up. Someone always seemed to be counting on him for something, depending on his skills and experience—and Richard never in his life let anyone down."

She lapsed into silence for a moment. Perhaps, I thought, she was renewing her resolve not to let *him* down.

"In any case," Red Abby went on, "his tour eventually ended and he took the opportunity to resign his commission. He'd had enough. He wanted to try something different. Something without so many rules."

The last of the three interfaces gave way, rendering the self-destruct mechanism harmless. Breathing a sigh of relief, I took hold of the device and withdrew it from the bulkhead cavity. Then I showed it to Abby.

"That's it?" she asked.

"That's it," I told her.

Red Abby nodded. "Good work."

Neither of us got up, however. That was fine with me. I still yearned to know more about her.

"And you've never had the urge to try Starfleet yourself?" I asked. "Never wondered what it was like?"

Red Abby laughed and leaned back against the Romulan divan again. "I know myself too well."

I gazed at her. "What does that mean?"

"I've grown even less patient than Richard, less tolerant of sprawling bureaucracies and red tape." Her tone grew more serious. "Frankly, Picard, there's only one thing in Starfleet I've ever coveted, and that's only a very recent development."

Her remark made my curiosity boil. "If I may ask," I said, "what *is* that one thing?"

She didn't answer right away. Then, unexpectedly, she swung her legs beneath her and leaned forward, and kept leaning until her face was right beside mine. I could feel the warmth of her breath in my ear as she answered with remarkable frankness.

"You."

Madigoor

PICARD PAUSED IN HIS TALE. BUT HIS COMPANIONS AT THE CAPTAIN'S TABLE wouldn't hear of it.

"Go on," Flenarrh spurred him.

"By all means," said Bo'tex, leaning forward in his chair. "We're just getting to the good part."

Picard looked at him. "The good part?"

The Caxtonian shrugged. "Yes, well . . . you know."

Picard looked at Bo'tex askance. "I believe you're reading something into my remarks that wasn't there. I've merely related what Red Abby told me, as faithfully as I can. I've described a conversation."

Flenarrh laughed suggestively. "But there was more than conversation, was there not?"

Picard hesitated.

"Well?" said Hompaq. "Flenarrh asked you a question."

Even the gecko seemed to want to know what had transpired.

Suddenly, a Bajoran youth seemed to appear out of nowhere. He was carrying a tray full of drinks with practiced ease.

"Refills," he said.

Picard didn't recall ordering one. Still, he was glad to see it arrive, as it brought him a respite from the other captains' questions.

Dravvin frowned. "What timing," he said dryly.

"The worst," Bo'tex grumbled.

The Bajoran looked at them. "Should I come back later?"

The captains exchanged glances around the table.

"Er . . . perhaps not," said Robinson. "One never knows when one will suffer an awful thirst."

"That's true," Flenarrh confirmed.

"All right, then," said the youth. "Who had the bloodwine?"

"Here," Hompaq told him.

"And the Ferrin's Dark?"

"That would be me," said the Captain of the *Kalliope.*

"Romulan ale?"

"Mine," said Bo'tex.

The Bajoran picked up a long, thin glass and scrutinized it in the light. "Um . . . some kind of green stuff?"

Robinson grinned in his beard. "You can set that one down here, lad."

And so it went.

Before long, the youth's tray was empty of its cargo. Only then did he seem to catch sight of the gecko sitting on the table.

"Uh . . . where did *that* come from?" he asked.

"Beats me," said the Captain of the *Kalliope.*

"In case you were wondering," Robinson declared cheerfully, "it's a gecko."

"Tropical," said Dravvin.

"Eats insects," Hompaq noted.

"But, then," said Bo'tex, jerking a thumb at the Klingon, "so does *she.*"

The Bajoran frowned. "Do you, uh . . . want me to get rid of it?"

Flenarrh shook his head. "Don't do so on my account. I've gotten accustomed to the little fellow."

"Me, too," said the Captain of the *Kalliope.*

The lad considered the lizard for a moment. "Then, I guess I'll just leave it here."

"I guess you will," said Dravvin.

The Bajoran started off through the crowd. But before he could get very far, Hompaq reached out and pinched the youth's buttocks.

Wincing with pain, he looked back over his shoulder at her—at which point she leered at him. The Bajoran scurried off as if the devil himself were after him—and perhaps she was.

The Klingon made a clucking sound with her tongue. "Too bad he's built so sparsely—even worse than the lizard there. I bet I'd enjoy making a warrior out of him."

Dravvin chuckled. "If you attempted it, you'd have to notify the poor lad's next of kin."

Everyone at the table took a sip of his or her drink—except Hompaq, who downed half of it at a single gulp. Then they turned to Picard.

"I hope," Flenarrh said, "you didn't think we had forgotten about you."

Hompaq laughed. "He's not off the point of the bat'leth yet."

"So," said Bo'tex, "*was* there more than conversation? Between you and Red Abby, that is?"

Picard regarded him. "Let us assume, for the moment, that there was—except it was you on whom Red Abby had bestowed her admiration. Would you recount it for us now, detail for detail?"

"Damned right I would," Hompaq interjected. She pounded her powerful fist on the table, making it and the beverages on it shudder with the impact. "What's a conquest without a hearty song to commemorate it?"

Ignoring her, Picard fixed Flenarrh with his gaze. "Would you?" he asked his fellow captain.

Flennarh thought about it for a moment. Then he smiled. "Perhaps not. I see your point, my friend."

Hompaq heaved a sound of disgust. She folded her arms across her ample chest and leaned back in her chair. "I should have stayed in the Empire," she rumbled sourly.

"Then we're to hear nothing of your dalliance?" Dravvin asked.

"I didn't say there *was* a dalliance," Picard reminded him.

The Rythrian sighed. "But surely, *something* followed."

Picard reflected on the comment, but declined to respond to it directly. Instead, he took a circuitous route.

"What ultimately came to pass," he said, "was this: An alarm sounded through the warbird, summoning us to the bridge."

"Another instance of poor timing," Bo'tex noted.

Picard ignored him. "Red Abby and I took a lift and arrived on the bridge in a matter of moments—only to find ourselves face-to-face with a viewscreen full of strange vessels."

The Tale

THEY WERE PIRATES, LIKE THE ONES WE HAD ENCOUNTERED BEFORE. At least, the diversity of ships in their fleet seemed to indicate as much.

But this time, there were twice as many of them.

"Jaiya again?" I wondered out loud.

"No," said Abby appraisingly. "This isn't Jaiya's bunch. Unless I'm sorely mistaken, this one's a damned sight more aggressive."

I nodded. "Lovely."

We were seriously outnumbered. If it came to a battle, we would find ourselves at a marked disadvantage.

Abby turned to me. "Stand off to the side. You don't want anyone to see you." She glanced at Worf. "You, too."

As it happened, Assad was on the bridge at the moment. Without waiting to be ordered, he took over at tactical. Thadoc simply remained where he was, at the helm.

As Worf and I moved to the periphery of the Romulan bridge, I considered the irony inherent in our situation. Not so long ago, my lieutenant and I had had to conceal our desire to remain anonymous. Now, Abby was more concerned with our anonymity than we were.

But then, she didn't want to lose us. And if we were recognized by the pirates, she might well have done so. After all, as I noted before, a pair of Starfleet birds-in-the-hand were worth a great deal on the open market—perhaps even more than some fabled bird-in-the-bush.

Satisfied that we were out of sight, Abby turned to Assad. "Hail them," she said, referring to the pirates.

Assad complied. Less than a second later, the wrinkled, ratlike face of an Yridian filled the screen.

Abby seemed to know him. "Captain Dacrophus," she said, not bothering to conceal the antipathy in her voice.

The pirate captain seemed genuinely surprised at the sight of her. But then, when one hailed a Romulan vessel, one expected to find oneself conversing with a Romulan.

"It's good to see you," he said at last.

Abby frowned at Dacrophus. "I'd say that, too, if I were too stunned to think of anything else."

The Yridian shrugged. "Frankly, when I found the remains of your worthy ship, I thought you and your crew had been murdered. I'm glad to see my fears were groundless—especially since I'd rather deal with someone I know than some stranger." He paused to inspect our bridge. "Funny," he said. "You don't *look* Romulan."

"But I'm in charge of this warbird nonetheless," Abby told him. "What the hell do you and your people want from me now?"

Dacrophus smiled. "I know. It must appear that we're hounding your every step. But then, we have been—ever since we discovered what you were after." His smile deepened. "That is, the Hoard of Dujonian. As you can imagine, we'd like to unearth that treasure ourselves."

Abby muttered a curse. "Even if we assume I know where it is, why would I tell anyone—you especially?"

"Because if you don't," the Yridian warned her good-naturedly, "we'll blow you out of existence."

A compelling argument, I mused.

Dacrophus rubbed his hands together. "On the other hand," he said, "we pirates are not as greedy as people seem to think. If you're willing to be reasonable, we'd be perfectly happy with only half Dujonian's treasure. That way, no one has to go home empty-handed."

Abby frowned again. Dacrophus had cleverly given her an option she could live with—assuming, of course, she could trust him to honor it.

"All right," she said finally. "You can tag along if you like. But don't give me any reason to doubt your sincerity."

The Yridian chuckled. "I would never be so foolish," he told her. On that note, he cut off the communication, leaving us nothing to contemplate but a view of his fleet.

I moved to Abby's side. "I'm not sure that was wise," I said, in a low voice so no one else could hear it.

"Everything's under control," she assured me.

"I hope you're right."

Abby glanced at me sharply. "I *said* it's under control."

Something else occurred to me. "Tell me," I said, "how is it our friend the pirate seems to know you so well?"

"You sound suspicious," she replied.

"Merely curious," I told her.

Abby turned away from me and sighed. "All right. I suppose you have a right to know."

Know? I thought. What *else* had she concealed from me?

Abby's eyes seemed to glaze over as she stared at the Romulan viewscreen. "I was a pirate myself, once upon a time."

"You?" I asked, caught by surprise—though in retrospect, I probably should not have been.

"Me," she said. "Mind you, it wasn't for very long. I doubt anyone except Dacrophus remembers. But it was long enough to offend some of my fellow pirates. The most important ones, apparently."

"And that's why you're not with them anymore?" I asked.

"That's why," she confirmed. "Actually, they did me a favor kicking me out when they did."

"Why is that?" I asked.

"Had I stayed any longer, I would've known too much. They would've been forced to kill me."

"Thoughtful of them," I agreed a bit sarcastically.

It reminded me of the story I'd made up about myself and the Maquis, when I was still masquerading as Hill. I said so.

Abby nodded. "Now that you mention it, you're right."

She was silent for a moment.

"The funny thing," she went on abruptly, "is sometimes I can't help wishing I were still with them."

For a moment, I thought she was joking. Then I realized she was telling me the truth.

Abby shook her head. "There was a sense of camaraderie about them, a feeling of belongingness. And they weren't just privateers. Once in a while, they did something for someone who needed it."

I must have seemed skeptical, because her expression became more insistent. "At least," she said, "some of them did."

"If you say so," I remarked.

"In any case," Abby went on, "what's done is done. As you can see, my pirating days are behind me."

I couldn't resist. "Yes," I said, glancing pointedly at the viewscreen. "*Directly* behind you."

She didn't dignify the remark with a response. Under the circumstances, I couldn't blame her.

"Steady as she goes," she told Thadoc.

The helmsman nodded. "Aye, Captain."

For the next two days, we sped toward our legendary destination. And all the while, Dacrophus's pirate fleet remained close on our heels, a pack of jackals trailing a lioness in hopes of sharing her spoils.

On the other hand, we encountered no additional obstacles. That gave us ample time to effect repairs to our ship, though it turned out mercifully few were needed. It also gave us a chance to study the warbird's operating systems—an exercise that would soon prove useful.

For on the third day after our defeat of the Romulans, we came in sight of the phenomenon known as Hel's Gate.

Madigoor

"HEL'S GATE," FLENARRH REPEATED, SAVORING THE NOTION LIKE THE BOUQUET of a fine wine.

The Captain of the *Kalliope* chuckled. "With a fleet of treasure-hungry pirates on your tail."

"And Brant's kidnappers somewhere up ahead," Bo'tex noted.

"No danger of being bored, at least," remarked Robinson.

Flenarrh leaned forward. "What was it like?" he asked, his eyes alight. "The Gate, I mean?"

Everyone waited to hear his answer—even the gecko, it seemed.

"Was it everything you expected?" Dravvin inquired.

Picard took a moment to answer. "Everything I expected," he said at last, "and more."

The Tale

Hel's Gate lived up to its reputation in every way. It was a dramatic, even spectacular phenomenon—and at the same time, a decidedly dangerous one.

The thing's core was a pure, blinding white, difficult to look at even with our screen's light dampers in operation. But the fields that played around it, changing size and shape before my eyes, were quite the opposite. So beautiful were they, so varied in the iridescent hues they presented, it was difficult not to be mesmerized by them.

As I watched, enthralled, a dark red light appeared in the core and discharged itself into space. It happened again a few seconds later, and yet again a few seconds after that, as if the phenomenon were shooting gouts of blood from a severed artery.

A grisly image, I'll admit. Nonetheless, it was the one that sprang readily to mind.

"There it is," said Abby, unable to keep a note of awe and amazement out of her voice.

I turned to her. "You sound surprised."

She shrugged. "Maybe I am. I don't know."

Then I realized how it had been with Abby. She had been so intent on getting her brother back, so focused on putting together a ship and an adequate crew for that purpose, she hadn't had time to fully consider what she was getting herself into.

And now that she was able to see it with her own eyes, now that it blazed before her with a wild and hideous intensity, it had taken on a reality for which she was unprepared.

But Abby was nothing if not resilient. She turned to Thadoc.

"Any sign of the mercenaries' ships?" she asked.

She was unconcerned about giving away any secrets. After all, there were only four of us on the bridge at the moment—myself, Worf, Thadoc, and Abby herself—and we were all aware of her search for her brother.

The helmsman consulted his monitors. "No, no sign."

To be sure, there were no mercenary vessels represented on the viewscreen either. But then, with the light display coming out of Hel's Gate, it would have been easy for a ship or two to conceal themselves.

"But they *were* here," Worf pointed out from the tactical station.

Abby looked back over her shoulder at him. "How do you know?"

My lieutenant frowned. "I've picked up traces of at least three ion trails and possibly more. The traces are faint but unmistakable. And they all lead into the phenomenon."

"Into it," Abby echoed pensively.

But not necessarily through it, I thought. What's more, I suspect I was not the only one completing her comment that way.

"Even if there *is* a dimensional entry in there," I said, regarding the savage brilliance of the thing's core, "I don't see how anyone could have lived to reach it."

"A point well taken," Thadoc grunted.

I had a sudden flash of insight. "That is," I noted, turning to Abby, "unless you've got something up your sleeve."

She returned my scrutiny without giving away a single emotion. "In fact," she admitted, "I *do*." She eyed the screen. "The approach typically taken by those who enter Hel's Gate is that they try to negotiate the phenomenon under full power."

"A mistake," I deduced.

"A big mistake," Abby explained, "since Hel's Gate tends to reflect energy back at its source. The key, according to my brother, is to enter the phenomenon under absolute minimum power."

"Without active propulsion," I noted.

Abby nodded. "Exactly. You just coast through it on momentum, at the lowest possible speed."

"Sounds nerve-wracking," I observed.

"And difficult," she agreed, "in that you've got to figure out what the lowest speed might be. But it's the only way through."

Indeed, I couldn't think of any other. I considered the phenomenon anew, weighing what Abby had told me.

"Let's try it, then," I said.

Of course, Abby would have done so with or without my encouragement. In any case, she had Thadoc plot a course and a speed.

"What about the pirates?" Worf asked.

Abby looked at him, a smile finally pulling at the corners of her mouth. "They'll have to figure it out on their own."

The Klingon didn't object to the strategy—and neither did I. After all, I had no great desire to remain in the company of Captain Dacrophus and his cronies. And if it took something like Hel's Gate to pry them away from us, so be it.

"Full impulse ahead," Abby ordered.

"Full impulse," Thadoc confirmed, and moved us forward.

"Captain Dacrophus is hailing us," Worf reported.

Abby hesitated a moment. "On screen," she said, obviously no longer concerned about concealing my identity.

A moment later, the Yridian's visage filled the viewscreen. "What are you doing?" he demanded.

"What does it look like?" Abby answered evenly and unflinchingly. "I'm entering the Gate."

Dacrophus's eyes narrowed. "Then I'm following. But don't try any tricks, my friend. You'll regret them."

Abby nodded. "No doubt." She cast a glance at Worf. "You may terminate the communication, Lieutenant."

The Klingon complied. The Yridian disappeared, replaced by the violent splendor of the phenomenon.

We proceeded for about thirty seconds on impulse power, Hel's Gate looming before us. Then, hoping for the best, we minimized energy usage on board, cut power to our engines, and entered the phenomenon on momentum alone.

"There," said Abby, leaning back in her captain's chair. "Now we'll see who regrets what."

Over the years I had served in space, I had developed a great respect for those oddities the universe had thrown in my path. And yet, there I was, arrogant enough to believe we could defy something as fierce and powerful as Hel's Gate and live to tell about it.

I felt like a particularly small and foolhardy minnow offering myself up to the leviathan of legend. And the closer we came to the heart of the phenomenon, the more apt the analogy seemed.

Running only on emergency power, we couldn't have provided Hel's Gate with much energy with which to batter us. Yet, batter us it did. The warbird lurched this way and that like a creature in torment, threatening to tear itself apart with its gyrations.

"I thought we would be safe if we cut power," Worf barked.

"There must have been some energy already trapped inside," I responded, grabbing the back of the captain's chair for support. "Perhaps from previous attempts to run the Gate."

"Thadoc," Abby cried out, hanging on to her captain's seat as best she could. "Report!"

"Shields down to seventy percent," the helmsman shouted back, fighting a jolt. "No—make that sixty percent. And falling."

The captain turned to Worf. "Can we reduce power any further?"

My officer shook his shaggy head as an unnerving shudder ran through the ship. "Not without losing helm and life support."

He'd barely finished when the captain's seat seemed to fly out of my grasp. I had time to recognize that as an illusion, to realize it was I who was flying away, head over heels, before I came up against something hard with bone-rattling force.

Tasting blood, I fought to remain in control of my senses. Raising my head, I looked around—and saw the bridge littered with bodies. No—not corpses, I told myself, unless corpses were capable of groans and curses. My comrades were still alive.

But no one was at his or her post. And most alarming of all, with Thadoc stretched out limply against a bulkhead, there was no one piloting the Romulan vessel. In a place like Hel's Gate, such a deficit could have proven devastating—the difference between survival and being torn into a hundred bloody fragments.

In Thadoc's absence, the helm was my post. My responsibility. Girding myself, I grabbed the bulkhead behind me and staggered to my feet. The deck jerked beneath me and I almost went sprawling again. But somehow, I stood my ground, and even took a few steps toward the piloting controls.

Another impact. Another few steps. Impact, steps. By then, I was close enough to hurl myself at the console.

My fingers closed on it just as the warbird whipped me backward again. But this time, I managed to hang on, my muscles screaming with the effort. With an immense application of will, I hauled myself into the helmsman's seat.

My monitors showed me we were still on course, more or less. Making whatever adjustments I could without applying thrusters and adding to our miseries, I rode out the next upheaval and the one after that.

By then, Worf had wrestled himself back into place behind the tactical station. He called to me in his deep, booming voice.

"Are you all right, Captain?"

"Well enough!" I replied, despite the numbness in my side and the ringing in my ears.

Mercifully—or so I thought—the tremors began to subside a little. One by one, Abby and Thadoc dragged themselves off the deck and came to stand beside me. Unfortunately, Thadoc was cradling one of his wrists. Judging by his wretched expression, he had broken it—perhaps in more places than one.

On the viewscreen, the nature of the phenomenon changed. After all, we were no longer attempting to peer into Hel's Gate, speculating on what it could possibly represent. Now, for better or worse, we were fully and irrevocably *inside* it.

What had earlier seemed like an flawless center of brilliance now showed us its true colors—more specifically, striations of midnight blue and neon green and rich umber, running lengthwise along the inside of a colorless cylinder. And it all seemed to tremble with uncertainty, as if it might take on another appearance at any second.

Despite a bruise on the side of her face, Abby smiled. It was a welcome sight, to say the least.

"We're in," she said, collapsing in the Romulan commander's chair.

"So we are," I added.

Our vessel had lost momentum, of course, in the process of entering the Gate. But as I checked my instruments, I realized we were no longer doing so. Clearly, this was a frictionless vacuum, though it was nothing like any vacuum I had ever seen.

Abby turned to Worf. "Status?"

The Klingon checked his monitors. "Shields down to fifteen percent," he reported. "Some of our internal sensor nodes are off-line, but otherwise the ship is functional."

The captain nodded. "Excellent."

"How much longer before we emerge on the other side?" I asked.

Abby shrugged. "My brother didn't say."

As it turned out, our stay in the cylinder lasted only another thirty seconds or so. Then we saw a bright light at its end, similar to the one we had seen at its beginning, and we began to experience turbulence again.

Considerable turbulence.

"Brace yourselves!" I shouted.

It didn't help.

As badly as we'd been tossed about on the way in, we were treated even worse on the way out. Clutching my console for dear life, I was wrenched this way and that, feeling like little more than a rag doll.

Finally, the deck bucked and dipped and spun me loose, sending me crashing into the base of someone else's console. Nor can I say what took place immediately after that, as I wasn't conscious to witness it.

Madigoor

"BUT YOU GOT THROUGH," SAID FLENARRH, "DIDN'T YOU?"

"Of course he did," Bo'tex laughed derisively. "What kind of story would it be if he hadn't?"

"A rather pointless one," Dravvin agreed. "And I don't think our guest would tell a pointless story." He regarded Picard with a glint of irony in his eyes. "Would you, Captain?"

Picard smiled. "Not if I could help it, no."

The gecko tilted its head.

So did Robinson. "Then you *did* make it to the other side."

Picard nodded. "I did indeed."

"And what did you find there?" asked Flenarrh.

Picard recalled the moment of his awakening on the far side of the Gate. "I found another part of space," he replied. "Or perhaps another universe altogether. I can't tell you for certain. All I can say is that the constellations I saw were unfamiliar."

"And the Hoard?" Flenarrh prodded.

Dravvin rolled his protuberant eyes. "For the sake of Canarra, he'll get to it. Be patient, will you?"

Picard couldn't help but chuckle at Flenarrh's eagerness. "Indeed, at the moment when I woke from my battering, I wasn't thinking of the Hoard. I was thinking of Dacrophus and his pirates, who were rather conspicuous by their absence. We and our warbird were coasting through the void all alone."

"They hadn't followed you in?" Bo'tex asked.

"Or had they followed and been torn apart?" Robinson inquired.

Picard shook his head. "To this day, I don't know."

"But they were gone," the Captain of the *Kalliope* established.

"They were," Picard agreed.

"And good riddance," Bo'tex chimed in. "Lazy lungwarts. Why don't they go out and get themselves real jobs?"

"Mind you," said Picard, "I was not pleased at the prospect of the pirates having lost their lives. To my knowledge, they hadn't committed any serious crimes—and even if they had, I'm not certain anyone deserves to perish that way. In any case, they were no longer a problem for us."

"Again," Bo'tex exclaimed, "I say good riddance."

Picard smiled tolerantly.

The Tale

As I suspected, Thadoc's wrist had been broken. Dunwoody, who had had some medical training, confirmed that conclusion.

However, Thadoc insisted that he remain on the bridge—if not as helmsman, then at least as navigator. Abby agreed, and I was the first to applaud her decision. Though it fell to me to become full-time helmsman, Thadoc's expertise with a warbird was still far superior to my own.

There were other injuries as well, but none too severe. In effect, we were bloodied but unbowed.

Remarkably, when I ran a diagnostic check of our propulsion system, I found the engines hadn't been damaged in the least. I was pleased to report this—almost as pleased as Abby was to hear it.

"Tactical systems are also functional," Worf announced. "Shields at seventy-five percent and improving. They should be back to full strength in a matter of minutes."

"What about weapons?" Abby asked.

The Klingon paused. "One of our aft control centers is off-line. However, I can route commands through a backup center."

"Do so," Abby told him.

Worf arched an eyebrow.

"Please," she added.

The internal sensor network had suffered the greatest disruption, but that was of no immediate concern to us. All in all, we had been lucky.

"You see?" Abby asked me, looking satisfied with herself. "I told you I had everything under control."

I grunted sarcastically. "If you can call nearly costing us our lives being under control."

"*Nearly* doesn't count," she declared.

There was no winning that argument. I could see that with the utmost clarity. "If you say so," I replied.

Our viewscreen showed us a great many stars, but one was burning a lot more brightly than the others. Abby pointed to it.

"That's our destination," she said.

Thadoc worked his controls with his one good hand. "Long-range sensors indicate seventeen planets. Two of them are inhabitable."

Clearly, I thought, if we were to find the Hoard, it would be on one of those two worlds. Apparently, Abby saw it that way as well.

"Chart a course," she told Thadoc.

He did as he was asked. Moments later, I had the warbird clipping along at warp four, the solar system in question dead ahead.

But even at warp four, it would be several hours before we got there. Abby and Thadoc opted to get some rest in that time, leaving Worf and me on the bridge by ourselves.

"You are injured," the Klingon observed.

I glanced back over my shoulder at him. "You can tell that from all the way back there?"

Worf nodded. "You are bleeding. From a head wound."

My hand went to the back of my head. I found a sore spot. When I inspected my fingertips, there was blood on them, but not a lot. Idly, I wondered if it was a new wound or an old one that had reopened.

"A scratch," I concluded.

My lieutenant grunted with something like humor. "A Klingon would no doubt say so. Most humans would not."

I turned back to my console and smiled. "I hope you don't think I'm like most humans, Mr. Worf. After all the years we've served together, I should hope you know me better than that."

His response wasn't long in coming. "I do, sir."

A moment later, the lift doors opened and my old friend Corbis stepped out onto the bridge. He wasn't alone, either. The Tellarite known as Gob was at his side.

"Is something wrong?" I asked Corbis.

He eyed me with some of the hostility he had harbored toward me earlier. "That's between me and the captain, Starfleet."

It didn't seem he was speaking of any danger to the ship, so I refrained from forcing the issue. "Suit yourself," I told him.

"Where is she?" asked the Tellarite.

I glanced at him. "You mean the captain?"

"Yes," he said, "the captain."

"She's sleeping, as far as I know." I returned my attention to my instruments. "I'd advise you not to wake her. She'll need her wits when we get where we're going."

Gob snorted. "That's what we want to talk to her about—where we're going." I imagined his tiny eyes narrowing as he scrutinized me. "Has she located the Hoard of Dujonian?"

Again, I glanced over my shoulder at him. "I thought you wanted to discuss that with the captain."

"We do," said Corbis.

"*You* do," the Tellarite told him. "I just want an answer. I don't particularly care who gives it to me."

"The captain thinks she knows where the Hoard is," I responded. "But as I'm sure she told you from the beginning, there are no guarantees."

"We've gone through hell," Gob grumbled. "And we've lost a lot of men. I'd hate to think it was all for nothing."

I nodded. "So would I."

And that was the end of it. Corbis and his newfound companion left without another word.

But as soon as they were gone, Worf spoke up. "I will be watching Corbis even more closely than before, sir. And Gob as well. They will pose a problem for us before this is over."

Unfortunately, I found myself agreeing with him.

Madigoor

"I *TOLD* YOU PANDRILITES WERE NASTY," DRAVVIN REMINDED THEM.

Robinson nodded. "So you did."

"Tellarites are no picnic, either," said Flenarrh. He looked around to make sure there was no one of that species in earshot. "No one's quicker to anger, not even the Klingons."

Hompaq cleared her throat. "Present company excepted, of course."

Flenarrh inclined his tufted head. "Of course. By no means did I mean to imply your fuse was anything but short."

The Klingon eyed him, suspecting that she was being toyed with. But she found no evidence of it in Flenarrh's face, so she flashed her long, sharp teeth and let the matter pass.

"What happened then?" asked the Captain of the *Kalliope.* He indicated the gecko with a tilt of his head. "My friend and I want to know."

"Nothing," said Picard. "At least, not right away. In fact, my whole shift went by without anything remarkable happening."

The Tale

At the end of it, I turned to see Abby and Thadoc walk out onto the bridge. They appeared refreshed by their respective naps, and the helmsman looked a bit more comfortable with his arm in a sling.

I glanced at Abby. "You're in a good mood."

"A little sleep can work wonders," she said.

But I knew it wasn't sleep alone that had caused her spirits to rise. It was the prospect of finding her brother.

Abby cast a look at the viewscreen. "How are we doing?"

"As you can see," I told her, "we're approximately halfway to our destination. In fact—"

Worf interrupted me. "Three ships off the port bow, sir."

I turned my attention to my monitors. As the Klingon had indicated, our sensors had detected three small vessels on an intercept course. Not surprisingly, I had never seen their fluted design before.

"Shall I hail them?" asked Worf.

I looked to Abby, who was standing by the captain's seat. "I think it's a good idea," I told her.

True, I was unfamiliar with this milieu and its politics, and we might well have been trespassing in someone's territory. But if we had ruffled any feathers, it was all the more important to establish communications so we could smooth them.

And in all honesty, the explorer in me yearned to see what kind of beings we had encountered.

She considered it for a moment, then nodded to Worf. Dutifully, he carried out the order. A moment later, our viewscreen showed us the grim-looking individual in charge of the alien formation.

His skull was oblong and hairless and his skin was bone white, providing a striking contrast with the faceted, ruby red ovals of his eyes. Jagged, brown horns protruded from either temple, echoed by smaller versions at the sides of his long, narrow chin.

"Greetings," said Abby. "I'm—"

She never finished her sentence. The alien didn't give her an opportunity to do so.

"You have entered Abinarri space," he advised her in a gravely voice, "in blatant violation of seventy-seven separate Abinarri statutes."

"I assure you," said Abby, "it wasn't our intention to break any laws. We'll be gone before you—"

Again, the alien interrupted her. "Do not attempt to flee. Our tractor rays will take hold of your vessel momentarily."

She shot the Abinarri a disparaging look. "The *hell* they will. Terminate communication, Mr. Worf."

The image on the viewscreen changed. Once more, we found ourselves gazing at the alien formation.

Abby turned to me. "Get us out of here, Picard—and I mean now."

I did the last thing the Abinarri would have expected. I shot right through the center of their formation. By the time they wheeled in response, we were making good on our escape.

"Maximum warp," said Abby.

"Maximum warp," I confirmed.

As we accelerated, I could feel a subtle pull on my face and body. After all, inertial dampers are not as high a priority in warbirds as they are in Federation vessels.

But then, Romulans are by all measures stronger and more durable than most Federation races. It would have come as no surprise if their tolerance for G-forces was higher, as well.

In any case, after a few moments I expected to have given the Abinarri the slip. As I discovered, I was quite wrong. Not only had they not been left behind, they were actually *gaining* on us.

Thadoc deposited himself behind the navigation console. "Quick little vessels, aren't they?"

"Yes, they are," I replied.

I could have made the warbird go faster, as well, but I didn't think I could maintain such a rate of speed for long. Could the Abinarri maintain it? At the time, I had no idea.

"Rear view," said Abby.

Worf manipulated his controls. Abruptly, the image on the viewscreen changed, showing us the Abinarri vessels in hot pursuit.

"They are powering up their weapons banks," the Klingon reported.

"Let's do the same," said Abby, staring at the viewscreen.

Worf worked for a moment. "It is done," he announced.

Abby tapped a stud on the armrest of the commander's chair. "This is Captain Brant. We're about to go into battle again. If I were you, I'd find someplace cozy and brace myself."

It occurred to me that Corbis and Gob would be displeased. Of course, this was hardly my greatest concern at the moment.

"Target and fire!" Abby barked.

Worf unleashed a barrage of disruptor beams, striking the lead ship in the Abinarri formation. According to my monitors, the aliens' deflectors were all but obliterated.

Thadoc glanced over his shoulder at Worf. "Good shooting."

The Klingon didn't respond to the compliment. He was too busy targeting the lead ship again.

"Fire!" Abby told him.

Worf looked at me, knowing his next volley would destroy the Abinarri if he wished it. I didn't want that.

"Target their propulsion systems," I said.

"Aye, sir," he responded.

Abby shot me a dirty look but didn't say anything. It was an awkward command situation, especially in the middle of a battle. Still, we were both resolved to make the best of it.

"Fire!" Abby cried again.

Worf fired.

This time, our disruptors tore into the alien's hindquarters, disabling their warp drive or whatever equivalent means of propulsion they employed. Instantly, the craft dropped out of warp.

That left only two Abinarri on our tail, though they were getting closer with each passing second. If they hadn't fired yet, it was no doubt because we were outside the range of their weapons.

A moment later, that no longer seemed to be a problem for them. Our viewscreen lit up with a greenish burst of light. It jolted us.

Another burst, another jolt.

"Damage?" asked Abby.

"Nothing serious," said Thadoc, his features cast in the orange glow of his Romulan controls. "Shields are down only fifteen percent."

Apparently, the Abinarri's bark was worse than their bite. Not that I was complaining, mind you.

"Fire at will!" Abby commanded.

Having already received my approval, Worf did as he was told. A second Abinarri vessel saw its shields shredded by our disruptor beams. Then the Klingon disabled it as he had disabled its sister ship.

This one, too, dropped below the speed of light. That left only a single adversary with which we had to concern ourselves.

But the Abinarri hadn't had their fill of us yet.

Even closer than before, they fired again—and at short range, their beams packed more of a wallop. I felt the impact through the deckplates—once, twice, and a third time.

"Shields down thirty-six percent," Thadoc noted.

When Worf returned fire, our greater proximity to the Abinarri worked in our favor as well. His first barrage ripped through their shields and breached their hull. The next one destroyed not only their propulsion system, but also half their weapons banks.

Like the other Abinarri, the vessel dropped back as if it had reached the end of its tether—while the warbird continued to knife through the void at maximum warp. The alien was millions of kilometers behind us before we could draw another breath.

Abby nodded approvingly. "Well done," she said, watching the stars fall away in our wake.

Worf inclined his head—his way of saying thank you.

Abby looked at me. "You too, Picard."

"What did *I* do?" I asked her.

"You had the sense to dart right through their formation," she observed. "If you hadn't, they might have caught us in a cross fire. Then our encounter might have had a different ending."

I shrugged. "Perhaps."

After all, I wasn't looking for accolades. My only objective was to bring my mission to a satisfactory conclusion. At least, that was what I kept telling myself as I used my controls to return to warp four.

There was, of course, the matter of myself and Abby Brant. Not Red Abby the captain, not the tough-as-nails transport commander, but the woman with whom I had forged something of a bond.

A bond of mutual respect, one might say. Of camaraderie—and maybe a bit more than that.

Such were my thoughts. No doubt, they ended up commanding more of my attention than they should have.

"Picard," said Thadoc.

I looked at him. "Yes?"

"If you like," he told me, "I could take over the helm for a while. It's time for the change of shifts, and one hand should be enough as long as there's no trouble."

I nodded. "Of course."

Standing, I turned the helm over to him. At the same time, the lift doors opened and Dunwoody emerged onto the bridge—at which point Worf moved aside and let the other fellow man the tactical station.

But the Klingon didn't leave the bridge. Instead, he moved to one of the aft stations.

I looked at him. "What are you doing?" I asked.

He looked back. "Going over the data I obtained."

"The data . . . ?" Red Abby repeated. Obviously, the woman had no idea what Worf was talking about.

But then, I was only beginning to understand myself.

"While the Abinarri ships were unshielded," I ventured, "Mr. Worf must have taken the liberty of establishing a datalink with their computer."

"A subspace datalink," the Klingon explained. "Though it was in existence for only a few seconds in each case, I was able to upload a significant amount of information."

If I had ever underestimated my tactical officer, I promised myself never to do so again.

Abby too looked at the Klingon with new respect. "Of course. In case we happen to run into the Abinarri a second time."

"Either the Abinarri," I granted her, "or any of the other species described in their database. One never knows what sort of knowledge will prove useful in uncharted waters."

"Very impressive," said Abby.

Worf shrugged. "It seemed like a good idea at the time."

Then he turned his attention to the data coming up on his screen. His brow beetled in response.

"Captain," he said, "take a look at this."

I followed his gesture to a list of Abinarri statutes—which their commander had cited as reasons for detaining us. It turned out there were rather a lot of them. Thousands, in fact.

"Quite the busy little legislators," I said, "aren't they?"

My companion grunted. "And it seems they impose their laws on a great many other species."

The data on the monitor screen bore that out. The Abinarri had subjected no less than thirty other species to their peculiar brand of justice, and they were currently attempting to add two more.

I frowned. It was one thing to follow one's own cultural imperatives. To force others to follow them was another matter entirely.

"I don't understand," said Thadoc, who had apparently overheard our conversation. "How can they lord it over so many other worlds when their vessels are so unimpressive?"

"Unimpressive to us, perhaps," Abby pointed out. "In comparison to all the other civilizations here, they probably boast the height of technology."

Dunwoody smiled. "For our sake, let's hope so."

Silently, I added my hope to his own. Then I turned back to the monitor, eager to learn all I could about the tyrannical Abinarri.

Madigoor

"AND WHAT DID YOU LEARN?" ASKED THE CAPTAIN OF THE *KALLIOPE*.

"Yes," said Flenarrh, "what?"

"A great deal," Picard said. "It seems the Abinarri were originally a rather wild and iconoclastic people."

"A nation of hermits," Dravvin observed.

"More or less," Picard confirmed. "Time and again, their primitive attempts at civilization were brought down by anarchy and lawlessness."

"Not unlike my own people," Hompaq grumbled.

"Actually," said Picard, "the ancient Abinarri make early Klingons look polite and reserved."

Hompaq's eyes narrowed. "You lie."

"I do not," Picard assured her. "They were utterly savage, capable of the most heinous acts one can imagine. It was not unusual for an early Abinarri to kill his mate or his children over a shortage of food. Cannibalism not only ran rampant, it was the preferred diet in some places."

"Lovely," said Robinson.

Picard glanced at him. "Indeed. It was only after long years of chaos and unrestrained brutality that a strange, new caste emerged among the Abinarri. The data we had didn't tell us how or why, but it did say these people were known as the Lawmakers."

"Apt," said Bo'tex.

Dravvin rolled his eyes. "If rather obvious."

Picard continued. "The Lawmakers decided that their people were incorrigible. Unless an elaborate system of laws was instituted, the Abinarri would simply destroy one another."

"And how were these laws to be enforced?" asked Flenarrh.

"At the point of a spear," Picard told him. "At least, at first. But after a while, the laws simply became the laws, and people obeyed them. Again, our information was incomplete on this point. But two things were clear to us: Chaos gave way to order, and civilization thrived."

"By all accounts," Bo'tex remarked, "a good thing."

The gecko blinked. No doubt, he thought so, too.

"In any case," Picard said, "the Abinarri came to understand the world around them as never before. They produced superior scientists and philosophers, painters and musicians . . ."

"And writers?" the Captain of the *Kalliope* suggested.

"Those as well," said Picard. "But the Lawmakers—who had eliminated the earliest obstacles to civilization and were therefore still venerated—were needed less and less as time went on."

Robinson grunted. "No doubt, a difficult pill to swallow."

"So difficult," Picard noted, "that the Lawmakers refused to recognize the fact. Instead, in the grand tradition of self-perpetuating institutions, they went on creating law after superfluous law. Before long, they had rendered the Abinarri system of justice nearly impossible to understand—and even more impossible to apply."

The Captain of the *Kalliope* frowned. "I can only imagine what this did to personal freedoms."

"As you suggest," said Picard, "it trampled them. It ground them down, spit them out, and made people forget they ever existed. Finally, the time came when there were no Abinarri behaviors left to be prescribed, no Abinarri freedoms left to curtail or regulate."

"And?" Flenarrh asked, apparently sensing there was more.

"And," said Picard, "that was the day the Lawmakers looked up and gazed greedily at the heavens."

Robinson sighed. "It's an old story, I'm afraid. When you're finished oppressing your own people, you set your sights on oppressing others. On my world, we called it colonization."

"A good analogy," Picard mused.

Dravvin eyed him. "I take it the Abinarri had begun to explore space by that time?"

"Yes," said Picard, "though they had yet to make contact with other self-aware species. Under sudden pressure from the Lawmakers, their stellar expansion program was drastically accelerated. All Abinarri resources and technologies came to be focused on the noble effort to find sentient beings on distant worlds."

Robinson chuckled mirthlessly in his great, white beard. "So they could impart the beneficial Rule of Law to the infidel."

Picard nodded. "And that is what they did. They found any number of civilizations, conquered them, and imposed their statutes on them. Where Abinarri statutes didn't seem to apply, the Lawmakers were only too happy to make up new ones."

"How interesting," said Flenarrh.

"Yes," Dravvin replied sardonically. "Especially for all those species the Abinarri were generous enough to subjugate. Those people must have found the situation *extremely* interesting."

Picard looked at the Rythrian. It was only natural that he should make such a comment. His people had labored under an off-world tyrant for nearly a decade in the early part of the twenty-fourth century.

"At any rate," said Picard, "that is the way matters had proceeded in that universe for well over two hundred years. The Abinarri had taken control of world after world, star system after star system, all for the purpose of spreading their gospel of Law. And no one had had the wherewithal to stand against them."

"Until you came along," said Bo'tex.

Picard shook his head. "We only succeeded in winning a skirmish. The Abinarri barely felt our passage."

Suddenly, Hompaq made their table shudder with a thunderous blow. Everyone looked at her.

"I have heard enough about these Abinarri," she said. "If they are inferior warriors, as your account suggests, they are beneath my notice." She leaned forward, her lips pulling back ferociously from her teeth. "Tell me instead about the Hoard of Dujonian."

Picard smiled. "Rest assured, Captain Hompaq, the Hoard was still very much on our minds—and even more so on the minds of our crew."

"But did you *find* it?" the Caxtonian asked.

"A fair question," Dravvin judged.

"You'll learn that soon enough," Picard told him. "After all, we're coming to the most important part of the story."

The Tale

WORF AND I COULD HAVE CONTINUED TO STUDY THE ABINARRI ALL DAY. However, our rest period was over before we knew it. I replaced Thadoc at the helm and Worf took back the tactical station from Dunwoody.

As I got myself settled, I found the stars sailing by me as they did when I was on the bridge of the *Enterprise.* I found myself thinking about my Starfleet crew, wondering how things were going for them.

I had no doubt they were doing fine without me. My executive officer was more than capable of running a starship on his own, and the rest of my staff was seasoned as well.

Still, I dwelled on each one of them. I couldn't help it. I was, after all, their captain.

One of them in particular kept turning up in my thoughts. His name was Data and he was my second officer. He was also an android—that is, an artificial being created in the mold of a man—who was discovered by Starfleet on a world called Omicron Theta in the year 2338.

Data was the superior of any human in almost every way one could name. For one thing, he was eminently more durable than any man or woman. For another, he could survive indefinitely without food or air.

Data could exercise superhuman strength and incredible quickness when the need arose. His mind could race at computer-like speeds. But since the day I met him, he had aspired to only one thing—the single aspect of the human condition denied to him.

In short, he wished to experience emotions. *Human* emotions.

For a long time, it seemed such an experience was beyond Data's reach. Then it came to light that his creator, Dr. Noonien Soong, had manufactured a positronic chip that would grant the android his fondest wish.

By inserting the chip into his brain, the android could know love, rage, happiness, jealousy—the gamut of human feelings. However, as great opportunities often do, this one came with a terribly steep price.

As you can imagine, a human overcome by emotion might injure his or her companion. But an android overcome in such a way would almost certainly kill that companion. And so it would be with Data.

All too aware of this danger, he chose not to insert the emotion chip—his legacy and only route to real happiness. Instead, he placed it in a safe place in his quarters on the *Enterprise-D.*

Perhaps one day, Data would incorporate the chip into his positronic matrix and discover what it was like to be a human being—the joys and the sorrows, the delights and the disappointments, the pride and the pain. But for the time being, he took his responsibilities to others more seriously than his hopes and dreams.

It was a brave decision. I believed that at the time Data made it, and I believed it still as I sat there on the bridge of the warbird with Abby Brant at my side.

I hoped that, under similar circumstances, I would have the courage and the wisdom to make the right choice—as it seemed to me Data had.

Putting the android aside for the moment, I checked my Romulan instrument panel. I found we were on the brink of the system we had made our destination. Its outermost planets were almost in our grasp.

Abby had noticed, too. "Slow to warp factor one," she told me.

"Aye," I replied, and did as she said.

She then asked Thadoc to set a course for the sixth planet from the sun. It was one of the two spheres we had noticed earlier that appeared capable of supporting life.

At warp one, which was equivalent to the speed of light, it would take us another couple of hours to reach the sixth planet. Still, it was prudent not to go in any faster.

One never knew what sorts of complex gravitic relationships one might find in an uncharted solar system, especially one with seventeen planets whirling around it. And as comfortable as I now felt at the helm of the warbird, it was still an alien vessel, with eccentricities that might manifest themselves at the most inopportune times.

As it happened, the time passed quickly—for me, at least. The deeper we delved into the system, the more I was able to learn about the various bodies that comprised it.

For instance, the smallest worlds were either the closest to their sun or the farthest away from it—a common configuration. However, what was far from common was the size of the planets in the middle distance.

In most cases, the largest world in a system is no more than thirty times the size of its smallest sister planet. As captains of spacegoing vessels, you are no doubt aware of this.

In this system, two worlds—both of them gas giants—drastically exceeded the traditional proportion. The ninth planet from the sun was almost two hundred times the mass of the first planet—and the tenth planet was an incredible seven times as massive as the ninth.

I couldn't help speculating. After all, when gas giants of that size collide, as the proximity of these two suggested they might someday, the greater one has a chance to grow heavy enough to begin fusion.

If that happened, it would be reborn—not as a planet, but as a star, blazing within the formerly ordered bounds of an existing solar system. The term for it was super-Jovian planet ignition. Its result? Cataclysmic, in the case of systems with populated worlds.

First, the clash of the two gas giants would create new gravitic relationships. Other planets would be realigned, perhaps crash into each other or be drawn into their new sun. And those events, of course, would give rise to still further changes.

Second, whatever life may have existed on planets proximate to the new sun would be destroyed. Either they would be baked to death or perish from an excess of ultraviolet radiation.

This gave me yet another reason to glance over my shoulder at Worf every so often, it being his job to conduct long-range scans of the solar system. I wished to know if there were sentient life-forms on the planets we had made our destinations—and to estimate their chances of survival in the event of a super-Jovian planet ignition.

Not because I thought we would be able to help them. That would be an impossibility, since the ignition would take place eons hence if at all. I simply had a need to know.

It was the same impulse that had compelled me to explore space in the first place. I longed to know things about distant places. No doubt, you have all felt the same way at one time or another.

It is, after all, why we are what we are.

Finally, Worf looked up from his console—but not to report on the planet to which we were headed. "I have located a vessel," he said.

Abby looked at him. "A vessel?"

The Klingon nodded his shaggy head. "It is of Orion manufacture."

I could see the excitement in Abby's face. And the urgency. More than likely, this was the vessel of the mercenaries who had abducted her brother.

"Where is it?" she asked.

"In orbit," he replied, checking his instruments again. "Around the fourth planet from the sun."

She didn't hesitate. "Set a new course, Mr. Thadoc."

"Aye, Captain," came the reply.

Abby turned to me. "Take her in, Picard. Full impulse."

"Full impulse," I acknowledged.

We found ourselves approaching the fourth planet in the system. It was small, mountainous, and mostly barren, with but a single small ocean. Still, it was what we in Starfleet would have called a Class M world—one that possessed an oxygen-nitrogen atmosphere not unlike Earth's and was generally suitable for human habitation.

Soon, Worf was able to tell us something new. "Sensors show humanoid life-forms aboard the vessel. Twenty-two of them in all. However . . ." He looked up—first at me, and then at Abby. "None of them resemble any species known to the Federation."

Abby frowned, no doubt wondering what to make of the information. Unfortunately, I was unable to help her.

Up to that point, we believed Richard Brant had been kidnapped by mercenaries from our universe. Nor could we rule that out, given the presence here of an Orion spacecraft.

Now it seemed possible that Brant's abductors had been denizens of *this* universe—either working on their own or in concert with the mercenaries we suspected earlier. The plot was thickening.

Abruptly, Worf spoke up again. "Captain Brant, I am receiving a message for you. Eyes only."

Abby's eyes narrowed. "For *me?* From the *ship?*"

The Klingon shook his head from side to side. "From the fourth planet. Do you wish to view it in private?"

She considered her options for a moment. "No," she said at last, "I'll take it at the captain's chair."

"Acknowledged," Worf replied. He did what he had to in order to send the message along.

Abby took the captain's seat and turned to one of the monitors in her armrests. For a moment or two, her expression remained wary and uncertain. Then it began to change.

Abby's mouth quirked at one corner. Then, slowly and subtly, a smile began to spread across her face. It was a beautiful smile, too—all the more so for its rarity.

"What is it?" I asked from my position at the helm.

She didn't answer my question.

"Captain?" said Thadoc.

Finally, Abby looked up. "We're beaming down," she said evenly.

"*Who* is?" asked her helmsman.

She thought about it—but only for a moment. "I am," she replied. Abby turned to me, still beaming. "Picard, too."

"I *am?*" I said.

I wished I knew what she had in mind. But then, I hadn't seen her monitor or the message on it.

"Come on," Abby taunted me. "Where's your sense of adventure, Picard?"

Obviously, she knew how to get to me.

"All right," I responded, getting to my feet. "I'll beam down with you—if only to satisfy my curiosity."

Abby turned to Thadoc. "Take the helm," she said, "and establish a synchronous orbit. We may be gone a few hours. And don't worry about the Orion. It won't give us any trouble."

"Aye," Thadoc replied. If he was the least bit skeptical, he managed not to show it.

Worf was another story. He was scowling as only a Klingon could scowl, not at all thrilled with the idea of exposing me to the unknown.

"I will go as well," he resolved.

"That won't be necessary," Abby responded. She was looking at me as she said it, requesting a favor with her eyes.

I decided to trust her. "Remain here, Lieutenant. I'll contact you if I need you."

Worf made a sound of disgust. "As you wish, sir."

Madigoor

"But what was it Abby saw on her monitor?" Bo'tex wanted to know. "And who was it from?"

Flenarrh grunted. "*Now* who's the impatient one?"

The Caxtonian looked at him indignantly. "I'm just asking, is all."

"Just as I said," Flenarrh countered, "you're being impatient."

"It never hurts to ask a question," Robinson conceded, pacifying Bo'tex before he could emit an odor the others would come to regret. "However, I sense our friend Picard was about to *answer* your question—and perhaps a number of others in the bargain."

The gecko turned to Picard as if it knew what was going on.

The captain smiled. "True enough," he said.

The Tale

ABBY AND I EXITED THE ROMULANS' BRIDGE AND REPAIRED TO THEIR TRANSPORTER room. Once there, we took our places on a hexagonal transporter grid, under the Romulan symbol of the birdlike predator with the globes in its claws. Assad did us the favor of beaming us down.

We materialized in a sunny, ochre-colored valley beneath a vast, blue-green sky. But we weren't alone. Not by a long shot.

There were several white, domelike enclosures scattered about. Among them stood a wide variety of humanoids, none of whom looked the least bit familiar to me. What's more, every one of them was armed—and at least half had leveled their weapons at us.

"I hope you know what you're doing," I told Abby, eyeing our hosts.

"So do I," she said.

Abby didn't make a move to go anywhere, so neither did I. The two of us just stood there, waiting for something to happen. I dearly wished I knew what it was.

Suddenly, someone else emerged from one of the domes. He was wearing a worn, brown coat made of some leatherlike material. And though he appeared somewhat scruffier than his Starfleet file image, it didn't take me long to determine his identity.

It was Richard Brant.

Abby, it seemed, had recognized him a moment before I did. She was making her way to him through the alien crowd, ignoring the weapons trained on her as if they presented no danger at all . . . looking to her brother with mingled joy and relief.

Richard was pushing his way toward her, as well, just as eager to embrace his sister as she was to embrace him. And a moment later, both of them got their wish.

"Richard," she said, hugging him as hard as she could.

"Abby," he replied. He rested his head against hers.

Though I'd missed it before, I began to see the resemblance between them. The eyes, the nose, the light sprinkling of freckles . . . there was no doubt in my mind they were brother and sister.

"I was afraid you were dead," Abby told him.

"But I'm not," Brant chuckled. "As you can see, I'm very much alive." He held her away from him so he could look at her. "You look pretty hearty yourself for a women who's gone through Hel's Gate."

"It wasn't as bad as you made it out to be," she said.

He laughed. "Only you would say that."

Abby turned to me. "Picard, I want you to meet my brother. Richard, this is Jean-Luc Picard. He's—"

"The captain of the *Enterprise,*" Brant finished. "I recognize the name." He extended his hand. "Good to meet you, Captain."

He seemed untroubled by my presence there. But then, he must have suspected that Starfleet would take an interest in his disappearance.

"Likewise," I said, grasping the fellow's hand. "I'm glad to see you're in one piece, Mr. Brant. For a while there, we weren't so certain that would be the case."

"For a while there," Brant echoed, "neither was I."

I had some questions for him. I said so.

"About my friends here?" he asked.

With a sweep of his arm, Brant indicated the aliens assembled around us. Of course, they had put away their weapons by then, though a few of them still eyed me warily.

I shrugged. "If that's where you would like to start."

Brant dug his hands into the pockets of his coat. "Several months ago," he said, "I was on a one-man science vessel running medical supplies to the Badlands when I found myself pursued by a Federation starship. As I recall, it was the *Trieste* . . ."

"Hold on a second," I said. "You were smuggling for the Maquis?"

"Just medical supplies." Despite his admission, he seemed very much at ease with himself. "Does that shock you?"

"Yes," I said, "it does. On the other hand, you wouldn't be the first officer of my acquaintance to be drawn into the Maquis web."

Brant smiled tightly. "I wasn't drawn into anything, Captain. I was simply trying to make a living—and the exotic expedition business wasn't as lucrative as I had hoped."

"You could have returned to Starfleet," I pointed out.

He shook his head. "Trust me, it was no longer an option."

I remembered what Abby had told me on that count. "Go on."

"The *Trieste* was about to overtake me," he said. "I was in the vicinity of Hel's Gate and I couldn't think of any other way to elude pursuit, so I ducked inside the phenomenon. As I had hoped, the *Trieste* embraced the better part of valor and decided not to follow."

Abby looked at her brother askance. "You went into the Gate with your engines active?"

"I did," he told her. "But before the Gate could really work me over, my engines went off-line—warp as well as impulse. That saved me. It forced me to coast on momentum."

"And that was how you learned to make it through," I deduced.

Brant nodded. "When I emerged, my ship was damaged—but not as badly as it could have been. Unfortunately, I didn't know where the hell I was. None of the stars around me looked the least bit familiar."

"Tell me about it," said Abby.

Her brother continued. "With no other course of action open to me, I began to effect repairs. At some point, my ship turned up on someone's sensors. That someone came by to have a look at me."

I looked about. "One of *these* people?"

"She *was,*" Brant explained soberly. "She's dead now, but that's another story. The important thing is she brought me to a planet very much like this one and introduced me to her comrades."

"Comrades . . . in what?" I wondered.

Brant glanced at them with an air of pride. "These people are rebels," he told me. "Not unlike the Maquis, though the analogy may not appeal to you. And that planet—like this one—was their base of operations, where they fought the good fight against an oppressive interstellar regime."

"An oppressive regime," I echoed, making a connection in my mind. "It wouldn't, by any chance, refer to itself as the Abinarri?"

His eyes hardened. "You've met them, then."

"We've sampled their hospitality," I replied.

"And taken down three of their ships," Abby added.

Brant seemed impressed. "I'm glad to hear it. In any case, they told me about their cause—and before I knew it, I was hooked. Their rebellion stirred something in me in a way I can't explain."

Still, he searched for words to describe it. Not for my sake, I'm certain, but for his sister's.

"It seemed to me," he said, "that this was what I'd been looking for all my life—something so right, so pure and untainted, I could put my entire being into it and never look back."

Abby didn't say anything. She just nodded.

"But," I said, "at some point you came *back* to our universe. What were you doing there if your fight was here?"

"Good question," said Brant. "One I would have expected from a Starfleet captain, in uniform or out."

"It's my duty to inquire," I told him stiffly.

"So it is," Brant agreed. "And believe me, Captain, I've got nothing to hide in that regard. I was just doing some recruiting on my old turf. That is, trying to gather people to our banner."

"People?" I asked.

"Yes," he said. "Adventurous sorts who might be attracted to a good cause, even if it was in unfamiliar territory." He scowled. "Unfortunately, it seems my efforts backfired."

"In what way?" asked Abby.

Her brother looked at her. "The mercenaries? The ones who kidnapped me, hoping I'd lead them to the Hoard of Dujonian?"

"Yes?" she said.

"That's how they got wind of me," Brant explained. "Through someone I tried to recruit for the rebellion. The next time I saw that person, it was a trap. The mercenaries showed up in their Orion ship and spirited me off—forced me to show them the way through Hel's Gate."

"But they didn't know what they were getting into," I ventured.

"That's correct," said Brant. "My comrades didn't take long to realize a ship had come through the gate—or that I was on it. In short order, they got me back and gave the mercenaries what they deserved."

I absorbed all the man had said—which was quite a lot. Then I asked the Question of Questions.

"And what about the Hoard?"

Brant looked at me uneasily. "Ah yes. The Hoard."

I pressed on. "Did you unearth it somewhere in this universe, as the mercenaries seemed to believe? Or was it, say, an enticement you dangled as part of your recruitment drive?"

Abby regarded him. "Is it here, Richard?"

Her brother smiled. "It is indeed. Just a couple of star systems from where old Dujonian left it two hundred years ago." He turned to me. "You'd like to see it, I suppose?"

I confess I felt a thrill of anticipation. "I would," I told him.

Abby's brother pulled a small device from its place beneath his tunic. Then he spoke into it.

"This is Brant. I need you to transport our visitors and myself into the vault."

There was a pause. "As you wish," came the response.

Brant eyed his sister, then me. "Brace yourself," he told us.

A moment later, I found myself in another place entirely—a large but low-ceilinged cavern full of stalagmites and stalactites, illuminated by blue lamps set up on tripods. Abby and her brother were there, as well, and by the ghostly light of the lamps, we laid eyes on the splendor of Dujonian's Hoard.

It stretched luxuriously into the farthest recesses of the cave, an alien terrain of glor'ya-bearing goblets and armbands, necklaces and serving platters, statuettes and tiaras.

It was breathtaking, to say the least—and not only for the regal brilliance with which its every artifact flashed and glimmered, exhibiting the deep, rich colors of the spectrum.

To me, it was also a window into the minds and sensibilities of the ancient Hebitians, of whom not even their Cardassian ancestors had accurate records. On that count, it was priceless beyond any mercantile measure.

"Incredible," said Abby, the light reflected in the Hoard reflected a second time in her eyes.

She approached the mounds and valleys of casually strewn treasure with an almost religious awe. Then, kneeling in the midst of it, she picked up a long, glor'ya-encrusted necklace and let it spill like a river from one hand to the other.

"I never thought . . ." she began.

"What?" asked her brother, kneeling beside her. "That you would ever see it? Or that it would be so beautiful?"

Abby shrugged. "Both, I suppose."

I too knelt to inspect the stolen treasure. Picking up a goblet, I turned it in my hand, watching its glor'ya catch the light one by one. But before I was done, I noticed that two of the stones were missing.

"A pity," I said out loud.

Brant looked at me. "You mean the missing gems."

I nodded. "Yes."

"If you look closely," he said, "you'll find that's the case with the majority of these artifacts. But I assure you, it's not out of carelessness."

"Out of what, then?" I asked.

Brant picked up a tiara and ran his fingers over the glor'ya embedded in it. "My rebel friends discovered the Hoard a good many years ago, or so they tell me. Like the Cardassians, they understood these gems were useful as well as beautiful."

I began to see what he was saying. "They used the glor'ya to power their ships."

He nodded. "Of course, they could have used the gems all at once, and made their vessels juggernauts of destruction—just as the Cardassians might have. But they realized that their fight would be a long one, so they opted to use the glor'ya sparingly."

"Which is why most of them are still here," Abby concluded.

"Where they will stay," Brant said pointedly, putting the tiara down again. "At least, until we see the need to establish a new headquarters for ourselves. Without these little jewels, there would be no rebellion—so we've learned to guard them jealously."

He stood and gestured to indicate the limits of the cavern. "This place is several meters below a rather nondescript stretch of ground, and there's no way in or out of it except by transporter."

"So your enemies won't find it," Abby noted.

"Enemies," her brother replied with a smile, "and friends alike." He took out his communications device again. "This is Brant," he said. "We're ready to leave now."

"Wait," I told him.

He looked at me. "Stand by," he ordered his transporter operator.

"I'd like to take a gem with me," I told Brant. "Just one. So Federation scientists can replicate it and study it."

He considered the request for several seconds. "All right," he replied grudgingly. "Just one."

I took a closer look at the goblet in my hand. It was quite beautiful. Had it not already been deprived of some of its beauty, my task would have been a great deal more unpleasant.

Finding the glor'ya that seemed the loosest, I grasped it between thumb and forefinger and gradually worked it back and forth. Finally, it came out of its setting.

Showing it to Brant, I deposited it in a pocket of my jacket. Then I put the goblet down and got to my feet.

Abby rose as well, shaking her head at what we were leaving behind. Then she looked at her brother.

He spoke into his device. "Transport," he said.

I took a last look at the lost majesty of Dujonian's Hoard. Then I found myself back on the planet's surface, standing among Brant's fellow rebels as before.

He looked at his sister. "Disappointed?"

"About the Hoard?" asked Abby. She shook her head.

"Are you sure?" her brother asked.

"I'm sure," she replied honestly. "Oh, I'll admit it was exciting to think we might take home a legendary treasure. But to tell you the truth, Richard, it never mattered that much to me. I was much more interested in finding my brother."

Brant blushed and glanced at me. "I'm afraid Abby's always been this way, Captain. I may have been born first, but my sister has never stopped looking out for me."

I nodded. "As it should be," I said, wishing I had looked after my older brother a little better.

"And you need not worry about whom I recruited," Brant said knowingly.

I smiled. "My concern was that obvious?"

"It was written all over your face," the man told me. "I only approached a couple of my Starfleet colleagues about joining the rebellion, and neither of them was tempted to join me. In fact, my efforts didn't meet with much success in general."

"Much?" one of his comrades echoed.

The fellow was tall and thin, with orange scales in place of skin and distinctive, black markings under his eyes. He seemed to take exception to Brant's choice of adjectives.

Abby's brother heaved a sigh. "All right, Ch'wowtan. Make that *none.*" He took on a rueful expression. "Apparently, there aren't nearly as many adventurous souls out there as I'd imagined."

Madigoor

"I RESENT THAT," SAID DRAVVIN.

Hompaq bared her teeth. "I wish the p'tak were sitting at this table. I'd give him an adventure he would never forget."

"If he managed to survive it," Bo'tex suggested.

The Klingon grunted her assent.

"Obviously," said Picard, "Brant's luck would have been better if he had done his recruiting here."

"Absolutely right," Bo'tex agreed.

"But, of course, he *couldn't* have done his recruiting here," Flenarrh was quick to point out.

Picard smiled. "Ah, yes. Captains only."

"Indeed," Robinson commented slyly. "Keeps out the riffraff."

"Enough of that," said the Captain of the *Kalliope.* "Where were we? Or should I say, where was our friend Captain Picard?"

Dravvin harrumphed. "As I recall, Mr. Brant had told him there were no adventurous souls to be found."

"Damn his nostrils," Bo'tex spat.

"And no Hoard to be taken home," Flenarrh added wistfully.

"Damn his ears and his eyes as well," the Caxtonian hissed.

Robinson regarded them. "Listen to the two of you. It's not as if the Hoard would have been yours, in any case."

"True," said Flenarrh. "But I can dream, can't I?"

Hompaq made a sound of disgust. "We have discussed the treasure at length, have we not? Now, for the sake of Kahless, let us move on."

"A spendid idea," Dravvin said, in effect seconding the motion.

Bo'tex harrumphed. "Spoilsports."

"Indeed," said Flenarrh.

Making a point of ignoring them, Robinson stroked his ample, white beard. "As I recall, the erstwhile Mr. Brant was complaining about his inability to attract recruits."

"That's right," said Picard, glad the man had set them back on track. "However, our conversation took a different turn after that."

"In what way?" asked the Captain of the *Kalliope.*

Picard turned to him. "Once again, an alarm went off."

The Tale

By that, I mean a high-pitched whooping that came from a dozen speakers around the rebel camp, stopping everyone in his or her tracks. At the same time, there was a beeping sound in our immediate vicinity.

Responding to it, Brant pulled out his communications device. His features were taut with urgency as he flipped the thing open again and spoke into it.

"What is it?" he asked.

The voice on the other end was deep and gruff. "A fleet of Abinarri ships, not more than a few minutes away."

Brant cursed. "How did they find us?"

"Does it matter?" asked the voice on the other end.

"I suppose not," Brant answered. He looked at Abby, then me. "Looks like they know this is our headquarters."

"Could our appearance have led them here?" Abby wondered.

Her brother shook his head. "Not likely—unless they had a pretty good idea of our whereabouts to begin with."

"The question," said the tall fellow with the orange scales, "is what we're to do now. All of our vessels except the mercenary are off tormenting the Abinarri elsewhere."

Brant frowned. "And the mercenary can't stand up to a fleet all by herself." He bit his lip. "She can't outrun it, either. And even if she could, we couldn't all board her in time."

"Planetary defense systems?" I suggested.

"Good idea," Brant told me. "That is, if you're planning on staying in one place for a while. We can't afford to do that." He tilted his head to indicate the sky. "For this very reason."

The muscles fluttered in Abby's temples. "There's another possibility," she pointed out.

Her brother's eyes lit up with newfound hope. "Of course," he breathed. "The warbird!"

It was true—the Romulan vessel would make a difference in the battle. She was a powerful ship, as fit as she had ever been, and in the last few days Abby's men had begun to get the hang of her.

Abby looked at me with fire in her eyes. "I need your help, Picard. With Thadoc hurt, you're the only one capable of taking the helm."

I couldn't argue with the accuracy of her declaration. However, I wasn't a rebel like Richard Brant. I wasn't a treasure hunter. I was a Starfleet officer, who had vowed to serve one master and one master only—and that master was the Federation.

But I knew who the Abinarri were now. I understood how they operated and what they could do to a subject society. And though I hadn't seen their tyranny with my own eyes, I didn't have to.

Because I wasn't just a Starfleet officer. In the final analysis, I was also a man.

Abby's features went taut. "Don't think for a minute you're getting out of this," she told me.

"I wouldn't dream of it," I said, unable to keep my mouth from pulling up at the corners. "You've got yourself a helmsman."

Tapping my communicator, which I still wore under my tunic, I called up to the warbird. "Mr. Worf?"

"Aye, sir?" came the reply.

"Two to beam up."

A couple of seconds later, I found myself on the Romulan bridge again, Abby alongside me. Without a word, she swung into the center seat.

In our absence, Corbis, Gob, and a couple of others had come up to the bridge. All four of them were standing by the aft stations, staring suspiciously at Abby and myself.

I was not thrilled about their presence there. But for the time being, there were more important matters on the agenda.

Worf looked at me. I could tell from his expression that he had already detected the Abinarri on his sensor grid.

I joined him at tactical for a moment. "Brant's down there," I said sotto voce. "He's joined a group of interplanetary rebels. Those ships you see are bent on destroying them."

The Klingon wanted to know only one more thing. "Will we be fighting on the side of the underdog?"

I nodded. "We will indeed."

Worf smiled a grim smile. "I was hoping you would say that."

Just then, Corbis spoke up. "What's going on?" he demanded.

"We're engaging an enemy," Abby told him.

"Who is it?" asked Gob.

She whirled in her seat, her eyes spitting fire. "I told you—it's an enemy. That's all you have to know."

"That's what *you* think," Corbis snarled. He pointed a long, thick finger at Abby. "I'm done fighting, done putting my life on the line. I want to see that treasure I've been waiting for!"

"Get off my bridge," Abby told him sternly.

The Pandrilite advanced on her. "Like hell I will."

She stood up and faced him. "I told you to leave the bridge, Mr. Corbis. If I were you—"

Before she could complete her warning, the Pandrilite belted her across the face. Unprepared for that kind of force, Abby flipped backward over her center seat and landed on the floor.

Then, before anyone could get to her, Corbis drew his weapon and put it to her head. I exchanged glances with Worf and Thadoc, but there was little any of us could do at the moment.

"Don't you see?" Corbis snarled at his comrades. "There's something going on here they don't want us to know about!" He turned to me, his eyes red-rimmed with fury. "Isn't that right, Starfleet scum?"

I swallowed. "You don't know what you're doing, Corbis. We've got to act quickly or we'll be destroyed."

It was no more than the truth. The Abinarri would likely take us for an enemy whether we entered the fray or not. We had to undertake evasive maneuvers or we would be ripped open.

Corbis's eyes narrowed dangerously. "We'll act quickly all right. We'll get the hell out of here." He glared at Thadoc, who had risen halfway out of his seat. "And we'll do it now, won't we—or I'll vaporize your precious little captain!"

"Don't listen to him," Abby said, wiping blood from her mouth. "Let him kill me. Just don't abandon those people down there."

The Pandrilite made a sound deep in his throat. "So there are people down there. Is that what this is about?"

Abby didn't say anything. No doubt, she regretted having opened her mouth at all.

"Is that why you came through Hel's Gate, dragging the rest of us along?" asked Corbis. "Is that why you risked the life of everyone aboard this ship? What happened to the Hoard, Captain? What happened to riches beyond our wildest dreams?"

"Yes," said Gob, his grotesque nostrils flaring wildly as he took a step toward Abby. "What *about* those promises you made us?"

"I made no promises," Abby told him. "I—"

Corbis silenced her with a jab from the barrel of his weapon. "Shut up," he said. "I've had my fill of your lies."

"I've got an idea," said Gob, grinning greedily. "We'll take the warbird and make a run for it. Then, when we're on the other side of the Gate, we can sell her to the highest bidder."

"That's what you think," I countered. "Once the Romulans find out you have their ship, you won't live long enough to find a buyer. They'll reduce you to atoms first."

"He's right," Abby groaned, despite the weapon held to her head. "Your only chance is to stay here and—"

The Pandrilite jabbed her again in the temple. "I thought I told you to keep your mouth shut."

It was all I could do to keep from charging at him.

Madigoor

"You see?" said Dravvin.

Flennarh nodded. "You called it, all right. You *said* Pandrilites were trouble, and here's the proof of it."

The gecko looked appropriately astonished.

"Enough of that," Bo'tex declared. "I want to hear how Picard here got out of his spot."

"So do I," said the Captain of the *Kalliope.*

"What did you do?" asked the Caxtonian.

"Weren't you listening?" Hompaq snarled. "He said there was nothing he *could* do."

"Actually," Robinson explained, "that's a figure of speech. At the time, it *seems* there's nothing one can do. But inevitably, one finds some way to prove oneself wrong."

"And *do* something," Dravvin interpreted.

"Exactly," said Robinson.

"True," Picard noted. "At least, *most* of the time. In this case, however, there was literally nothing we could do. Nothing at all, if we valued Red Abby's life."

Robinson looked at him. "Nothing? *Literally?"*

"Nothing," Picard confirmed.

"Then how was she saved?" Flenarrh asked.

"Perhaps she wasn't," Hompaq pointed out. "Perhaps she died at the hands of the Pandrilite."

Dravvin snorted. "That would suit you, wouldn't it?"

"It would indeed," said the Klingon.

"It's not a matter of what would *suit* us," Robinson reminded them. "It's a matter of what *was.* Either Red Abby died on that warbird or she didn't—there's no middle ground."

Everyone at the table looked to Picard—the gecko included.

"As I was saying," he continued, "I restrained myself from making a run at Corbis. As for the possibility of the Romulans taking their ship back, Gob seemed thoroughly unimpressed."

The Tale

THE TELLARITE LIFTED HIS CHIN AT ME AND SNORTED. "THE ROMULANS," he said, his beady eyes gleaming, "are a risk we'll be glad to assume. At least we'll know who we're fighting—and why."

Corbis pointed to Thadoc with his free hand. "Get us out of here *now,* half-breed—or your captain's a dead woman!"

But before Thadoc could respond, the bridge jerked savagely beneath us. Corbis lost his footing like everyone else and grabbed a bulkhead for support. Seeing my chance and knowing I might never get another one, I threw myself across the space between us.

The Pandrilite fired at me. Somehow, his bloodred beam missed and vaporized a section of bulkhead instead. I grabbed for his phaser, and my momentum slammed us into a console. Then the deck jerked again and we went down in a tangle of arms and legs.

As we hit the floor, I tried to roll on top of him, but he snapped my head back with a blow to the jaw. Gritting my teeth, I got hold of Corbis's wrist and slammed his weapon-hand against the metal surface beneath us.

Once. Twice. And again.

The third time proved to be the charm. Crying out, Corbis relinquished the weapon, bellowing as it fell from his battered hand.

Quickly, I kicked it away. It skittered across the floor. Of course, by that time, the Pandrilite's weapon wasn't the only one I had to worry about. There were phasers discharging all around me, their beams crisscrossing wildly in the close quarters of the bridge.

As I tried to gather myself, I felt a cluster of powerful fingers close on my throat from behind. I tried to claw them loose, but Corbis was too strong for me. I could feel my windpipe closing, my air supply shutting down.

Little by little, I felt myself lifted into the air. Before I knew it, my feet were dangling inches above the deck.

I kicked backward while I still could, felt my heel hit the Pandrilite in the shin. It made him drop me to the deck, but it didn't loosen his grip one iota. If anything, it tightened it.

I could feel the blood pounding ferociously in my temples, see the darkness closing in at the edges of my vision. My hands and feet were beginning to lose all sense of feeling.

Then I remembered something I had learned not so long ago. Something I had seen a young woman do in the gym on the *Enterprise-D,* under the tutelage of her Klingon instructor.

I could only hope it worked as well for me as it had for her.

Groping for one of Corbis's wrists, I found it and took hold of it as Worf had demonstrated. Then I turned it and twisted as well as I could, considering I could already feel my eyes popping out of my skull.

The Pandrilite cried out and went spinning over my hip, just as if he had been propelled by a phaser blast. I made a mental note to thank Worf if and when I had a chance to speak with him again.

Taking the deepest breath I could, I put some oxygen back in my bloodstream. Then I advanced on Corbis, hoping to capitalize on the surprise I had dealt him.

Unfortunately, it was he who dealt the surprise. As he came up, he had a phaser pistol in his hand—either the one he had lost earlier or someone else's. The Pandrilite's eyes were feral with hatred as he raised the weapon and pointed it at me.

But before he could press the trigger, a bright red beam knocked him off his feet and slammed him into a bulkhead. I heard a crack and saw Corbis slump to the deck, his neck bent at an impossible angle.

Impossible, that is, for someone still alive.

Turning, I saw where the beam had come from. Abby was on her knees behind me, a phaser pistol locked in both her hands. When she realized Corbis was no longer a threat, she lowered it.

I looked around in the unnatural quiet. Gob was lying on the other side of the bridge, the side of his face blackened beyond recognition. Corbis's two other companions were dead as well.

Thadoc stood up from behind his helm console, which featured a smoking hole the size of a phaser beam. He seemed whole, though—or at least, no worse off than before.

Worf hadn't been quite so lucky. His tunic was charred and ripped open in the vicinity of his rib cage—and blood had begun to soak into what was left of the material.

"Are you all right?" I asked him.

He nodded. "Fine."

That didn't tell me anything. He would have said he was fine if he was writhing in agony on his deathbed.

Suddenly, the warbird lurched under the heaviest barrage yet. A plasma conduit broke, unleashing a stream of white-hot vapor. The viewscreen sputtered and went dead for a second; when it came back on, it was plagued by wave after wave of static.

Through them, I could make out more than a dozen triangular ships. They were coming at us from different directions, waiting until they got closer before they opened fire again.

And why not? We had yet to protect ourselves or get a shot off. It must have seemed to them that we were dead in the water—which would be true enough if we didn't act soon.

I flung myself into the helmsman's seat. At the same time, Worf took charge of the tactical panel. Cradling his wrist again, Thadoc deposited himself beside me at navigation.

"Report!" cried Abby.

"Damage to decks seven and eight," Thadoc grated. "One dead. Dunwoody's team is making repairs."

"All weapon arrays are still functional," Worf growled. "Shields down forty-two percent."

"The helm's responsive," I noted. That was the good news. "But the warp coils seem to have taken a beating. We could be limited to impulse power at any moment."

Abby frowned, her cheek bruised where Corbis struck her. "We'll worry about that if and when it happens. Evasive maneuvers, Picard. Let's see what you can do with *these* Abinarri."

If she had hoped to inspire me with a challenge, it was unnecessary. My desire to keep us alive was inspiration enough.

"Hang on," I said grimly. As I noted before, Romulan vessels weren't known for the effectiveness of their inertial dampers.

I engaged the impulse engines and executed a turn that took us out of the Abinarri's midst. However, they were on us again in a matter of moments, stinging us repeatedly with their energy weapons like a swarm of bees on an intrusive bear.

"Fire at will!" cried Abby.

It wasn't necessary. Worf was already attending to it.

On the viewscreen, two of the Abinarri vessels glowed with the force of our disruptor barrage. A second later, another Abinarri was dealt a glancing blow. But if they were damaged, it didn't stop them from harrying us.

The enemy seemed to prefer working at close quarters. That didn't surprise me in the least. As I'd noted in our last encounter, their weapons were significantly more effective that way.

But beyond any practical considerations, I got the feeling that was simply the way these people liked to hunt. Very likely, it was the way their ancestors had done it—by surrounding their prey and bringing it down through sheer weight of numbers.

I was determined that *this* prey wouldn't go down so easily. Working furiously at my controls, I negotiated the maze of enemy vessels and emerged from it a second time.

But a second time, the pack caught up with me.

Worf did his best to hammer at the Abinarri, managing to score several more hits. One ship even exploded in a paroxysm of blue fury. But as before, the Klingon's efforts didn't seem to faze the survivors.

"Shake them!" cried Abby.

"I'm trying!" I bellowed back.

I looked for the mercenary vessel, hoping it could offer us some relief. But my monitor told me our ally had troubles of her own. Like us, she was besieged on all sides.

On the other hand, the mercenary's attackers were fewer in number. They must have understood that she was the weaker of us and focused their efforts on the warbird.

Suddenly, one of the aft stations sparked savagely and began to flame. Someone grabbed an extinguisher and began to put the fire out, but the station next to it ignited as well. Smoke began to fill the bridge, searing our throats and making our eyes sting.

"Shields at twenty-eight percent!" Worf reported over the din. "Starboard phaser banks partially disabled!"

On the viewscreen, a half-dozen Abinarri slid toward us. One by one, their weapons spat red fire at us. I was able to dodge some of the blasts, but not all of them.

The bridge was wrenched this way and that, sending us sprawling over our control panels. I thrust myself back and regained my chair, only to be flung to the deck by another energy assault.

A console exploded, sending pieces of hot metal spinning across the bridge. As black smoke twisted up from the thing, I saw one of our men slump against Abby. It was Assad.

He was dead, his throat a gaping wound.

With a stricken look, Abby lowered him to the deck. Then she took in the carnage all around her.

"Mr. Worf?" she said, her voice thick with emotion.

"Shields at thirteen percent," he told her, reading the information off his monitors. "The starboard phaser array is down."

Thadoc chimed in with more grim news. "Damage to decks four and five as well now."

I took us through a twisting turn, eluding one volley after another. It worked better than the other maneuvers I had attempted, buying us some time. But not enough, I told myself.

At this rate, we wouldn't last another ten minutes. Nor, I thought, would the mercenary vessel. The Abinarri were simply too good at this game, and we didn't have the resources to change the rules.

Then it came to me—perhaps we had the resources after all. Perhaps we had just what we needed.

Madigoor

"AND WHAT WAS THAT?" ASKED BO'TEX, UNABLE TO CONTAIN HIMSELF.

Robinson laid a hand on Picard's shoulder. "Don't get our friend the Caxtonian too excited," he advised. "He's capable of smells you wouldn't wish on your worst enemy."

"I'll keep my pheromones to myself," Bo'tex promised. "I only want to know what came next."

"Obviously," Dravvin concluded, "our friend came up with a scheme. He's all but said so."

"Yes," said Bo'tex, "but *what* scheme? Did he transport a tiny bit of antimatter onto each of the enemy's ships? Did he use his tractor beams to send one Abinarri crashing into the other?"

Picard shook his head. "We did neither of those things. For one thing, we were on a Romulan vessel, and they don't carry antimatter."

"That's right," said Flenarrh. "As Picard told us, they get their power from an artificial singularity."

"What's more," Picard noted, "transporting antimatter is a ticklish business. A *very* ticklish business. I've yet to see the containment field that would allow antimatter to pass through the pattern buffer."

"But what about using your tractor beams?" asked Bo'tex. "That would've been a good idea."

"It *might* have been," Picard replied, "except for two things. First, the Abinarri were moving too quickly for us to get a lock on them. Second, our tractor capabilities had been disabled by that time."

The Caxtonian nodded judiciously. "I see."

Hompaq grunted disdainfully. "It's clear what he did. He deployed his escape pods and smashed them into the enemy's vessels. By the time he was done, the odds were more in his favor."

"Not a bad notion," Picard conceded. "That is, if we had still had any escape pods to deploy. When we took over the warbird and forced the Romulans to evacuate, they took anything and everything in the way of auxiliary vehicles. All they left us was a single shuttle, and it wasn't quick enough to catch up with an Abinarri assault ship."

Robinson looked around the table. "Any other guesses?"

No one seemed inclined to venture one—not even the gecko, apparently.

The Captain of the *Kalliope* smiled. "So . . . what *did* you do?"

Picard smiled, as well.

The Tale

As I said, a plan had begun to form in my mind. I turned to Abby and described it to her as briefly as I could.

She looked back at me, her pale blue eyes red with smoke. "Let's do it," she replied.

"Mr. Worf," I said, "establish control over the ship's transporters. Then contact the mercenary and tell our friends we'll be beaming over."

The Klingon had overheard our discussion. Under the circumstances, he could hardly question the wisdom of it.

"Aye, sir," he responded crisply.

I looked at Thadoc, apologizing in advance for what I was asking of him. "It'll be for only a minute," I said.

He glanced at me, knowing how long a minute could be in the heat of battle. "Take your time," he told me.

Turning the helm over to him, I got up and headed for the lift. Abby was a step ahead of me. We got in, punched out a destination code, and watched the doors close behind us.

As the compartment began to move, I drew a breath of untainted air through my burning, smoke-ravaged throat. Letting it out, I drew in another.

Abby had slumped against the wall and closed her eyes for a moment. Half her face was black-and-blue, and the shoulder of her tunic was ripped open, exposing a patch of burned skin.

"It won't be much longer now," I told her.

She opened her eyes to look at me. "Either way, eh?"

I grasped her firmly by her shoulders. "Listen to me," I said. "We're getting out of here. We can't allow ourselves to think any other way."

Abby smiled a sad and weary smile. "Whatever you say, Picard. But just in case we don't—"

The doors to the lift opened then, revealing the residential corridor where the Romulan commander had had his quarters. The place was almost shockingly pristine, untouched by the chaos that had scarred most of the warbird.

Abby and I exchanged glances. There was no time for her to finish what she'd begun to say. But then, she didn't have to.

Together, we raced down the winding corridor and slid to a stop in front of the commander's door. It opened for us without hesitation and we scrambled inside—only to find the place filled with smoke.

As it billowed out at us, encompassing us, I cursed and used my hands to clear a path for myself. Little by little, cough by throat-searing cough, I made it across the room to the spot where Abby had discovered the Klingon self-destruct device.

The mechanism was still lying on the floor where we left it, amid the selection of engineering implements Abby had gathered for me. Dropping to my knees, I picked the thing up and inspected it.

"Is it intact?" Abby asked, hunkering down beside me.

"It seems to be," I replied.

As I had told her on the bridge, it would be a lot easier to resurrect the thing than it had been to kill it. Still, it would take some time—and at the moment, time was in short supply.

The warbird shuddered terribly under the impact of another volley, forcing us to grab what we could to secure ourselves. A second or two later, the ship shuddered again.

"The Abinarri are closing in," Abby observed ruefully. "Thadoc can't elude them."

It came as no surprise to either of us. The fellow had the use of only one hand, after all, and I hadn't done much better with two of them.

Concentrating on the task before me, I began searching for my trusty charge inverter. The smoke made the job difficult, to say the least.

"Do you see it?" I asked.

Abby knew just what I meant. "No," she said after a moment. "Maybe it rolled away."

Eyes smarting, I groped about for it. Finally, I located the inverter near a leg of the commander's divan.

"Got it," I told her.

"Then get to work," she said.

My plan was a simple one, really. We would reactivate the self-destruct mechanism, set it, then beam off the Romulan vessel with the rest of the crew. Since the Abinarri had demonstrated an affinity for working at close quarters, we would allow them to do just that . . .

. . . until the moment the warbird's power source exploded in a frenzy of natural forces. Then if all went according to plan, the oppressor's ships would be caught in the blast.

As I said, a simple plan. But for it to work, I had to blow up the warbird before the Abinarri could.

Trying to see through the haze of smoke, I picked out one of the circuits that had fed the self-destruct device and began reactivating it. Unlike the last time, I worked in silence.

Abby and I could converse later, I thought. That is, if both of us managed to *survive.*

With some trouble owing to the stinging sensation in my eyes, I managed to restore the first connection. No sooner was I done than the warbird jerked again, sending me sprawling against the divan.

I bit my lip. Had the shock come a second earlier, I might have sent an unwanted charge through the circuit and blown up the ship prematurely. It was not a cheery thought, as you can imagine.

Abby helped me right myself. "Are you okay?" she asked.

"Right as rain," I assured her.

Spurred to a new sense of urgency, I went after the second connection. Again, we staggered under the force of the enemy's barrage—but this time I was prepared for it. Grinding my teeth together, I revived the energy flow and wiped sweat from my brow.

"Is it my imagination," I asked, "or is it getting hotter in here?"

"Hotter," Abby confirmed. "The damned Abinarri must have knocked out our life-supports."

I chuckled grimly to myself. The enemy seemed determined not to make this easy for us. Rude of them, I mused, as I turned my attention to the third and final connection.

It was trickier than the others. Apparently, I had done too good a job rendering it ineffective. The ship bucked and shook all around me, reminding me how little time I had to accomplish my task.

Sweat trickled into my eyes, making them smart even worse than before. The smoke was making me cough rather violently, which didn't help matters, and I was beginning to feel light-headed from a lack of oxygen.

Still, I plugged away with the Romulan charge inverter. And in time, I restored the deadly connection.

All that was left was to set the timer. I gave us three minutes to reach the transporter room and pulled Abby to her feet.

"Done?" she asked.

"Done," I said.

"Will it work?" she wondered, as I tugged her across the room in the direction of the exit.

"It had better," I replied. "Otherwise—"

I never finished my sentence. Indeed, my entire reality seemed to turn inside out in a single, blinding moment.

The next thing I knew, I was stretched out on the deck—ears ringing, pain awakening with spectacular results in the whole right side of my body. Abby was lying beside me, inches away, her face turned away from my own.

I tried to speak her name, to no avail. I tried to extend my hand, to reach for her, but I couldn't do that either. In fact, I could barely roll my head to assess our situation.

Yet when I tried it, something strange and miraculous and thoroughly horrifying greeted my eyes through a break in the smoke. I found myself staring at the spattering of distant suns outside the ship—and not through the protective medium of an observation port. The stars were standing there before me, big and fierce and naked in the void.

How was that possible? I asked myself. How could the stars have invaded the sanctity of our vessel?

Then I saw a flicker of blue-white current and, deep in the folds of myself where my mind still functioned, I understood. The hull had been breached, I realized—but the warbird's structural integrity field was still holding our atmosphere inside.

And us as well.

But that could change at any moment. Another well-aimed blast and the integrity field would shatter as well, allowing us to be sucked out into the vacuum. And I was too dazed, too battered to do anything about it.

Worse, we had less than three minutes before the warbird destroyed itself. Perhaps by then we had only two minutes, or one—or a matter of mere seconds. I had no way of knowing.

Abruptly, out of the corner of my eye, I saw movement. Not Abby, but something else. Some*one* else, I realized. A powerful-looking figure, making its way toward us through the roiling fumes.

He loomed closer and I recognized him. It was *Worf.*

Kneeling, he gathered me up and slung me over his shoulder. Then he slung Abby over the other. Finally, rising under the weight of his double burden, he turned and headed for the exit with some urgency.

I was upside down, bouncing helplessly with each step, but I had an inkling of where we were going. We entered a lift, exited again, then negotiated corridor after spark-filled corridor.

After what seemed like a long time, too long for the warbird to still have been in existence, we arrived in the ship's transporter room. Worf set Abby and I down on the transport grid, crossed the room to work the controls, then joined us a second later.

I must have blacked out at that point. When I came to, I was on the bridge of the Orion ship, lying in a corner where soft, purplish lighting bathed me in violet shadows. Worf was hunkered down next to me, watching the bridge officers apply themselves to their various tasks.

On the vessel's diamond-shaped viewscreen, I could see two Abinarri ships. As I looked on, one of them was stabbed by a bolt of disruptor fire. A moment later, the vessel shivered and exploded in a flare of pure, white light.

"Got him!" exclaimed the weapons officer, an awkward-looking fellow with four arms and jet black skin.

"We've still got one more!" roared the being in charge—a ponderous female with wrinkled, gray flesh and eyes like tiny, glittering diamonds. "Target and fire, Mastrokk!"

With an effort, I sat up. Every part of me felt bruised to the bone, but the ringing in my ears seemed to have stopped for the most part.

My lieutenant turned to me. "Captain . . .?"

Weakly, I held up a hand. "I'm all right," I assured him, though it came out little more than a whisper.

Then I remembered, and my throat constricted.

"Where's Abby?" I asked him.

Worf jerked his shaggy head.

Following the gesture, I saw her. Abby was lying in another corner of the bridge, surrounded by Thadoc, Dunwoody, and three of her other crewmen. Even in the eerie, purple lighting, she looked paler than the living had a right to be.

My god, I thought.

I remembered what Abby and I had said in the turbolift just a little while earlier. *"We're getting out of here,"* I had told her. *"We can't allow ourselves to think any other way."* And she had replied, *"Whatever you say, Picard. But just in case we don't . . ."*

I got up on shaky knees and started across the bridge. The Klingon grabbed my arm as gently as he could, hoping to restrain me—but I shrugged him off and kept going.

It can't be, I told myself. Not after we've come so far.

Thadoc and the others looked up at me as I approached. Their faces were grim, their eyesockets dark and hollow-looking—though not half as hollow-looking as Abby's.

Sinking to my knees in front of them, I reached out and touched her cheek with the back of my hand. It felt cold, waxy to the touch.

"Abby," I said.

Suddenly, her eyelids fluttered. A moment later, she opened them and took in the sight of me.

It took me a second or two to come to grips with my surprise. "You're not dead," I observed wonderingly.

Abby's mouth pulled up at the corners. "No," she agreed weakly. "But I think you may be." She shook her head. "You look awful, Picard."

I grinned, though my skin was so bruised, it hurt mightily to do so. "As matter of fact," I told her, "I *feel* awful."

Just then, someone yelled "Fire!" It turned out to be the female in charge of the vessel.

Before our eyes, the last of our attackers spasmed and blew herself to atoms in a moment of terrible splendor. Abby frowned.

"The last of them?" she asked. Apparently, she hadn't had her eyes closed the whole time.

I nodded. "The last of them."

Madigoor

"Then it worked?" asked the Captain of the *Kalliope*.

Hompaq grinned at the thought. "The warbird blew up and took your enemies with it?"

"So it would seem," said Picard.

The Klingon pounded the table with her fist. "Well done!" she rasped. "A feat worthy of a warrior!"

The captain nodded. "Thank you, Hompaq. Of course, I would rather have settled our differences with the Abinarri another way . . ." He shrugged. "But as I noted, they didn't leave us a great many options."

"But why did your lieutenant have to come and get you?" asked Flenarrh. He leaned forward in his chair. "What prevented him from simply beaming you out of the commander's quarters?"

"A good question," said Picard. "Apparently, by that time, site-to-site transports had been made impossible by the release of plasma gas all over the ship. Worf had no choice but to fetch us personally."

"It's a good thing it was the Klingon," Dravvin noted, "and not someone less powerful."

"Or less determined," Robinson added. "The warbird might have destroyed itself at any moment. Yet your man ignored that fact, risking his life to save your own."

Flenarrh grunted. "A brave man, that Worf."

"A warrior," Hompaq pointed out.

The Captain of the *Kalliope* chuckled. "Your first officer certainly knew what he was talking about."

Bo'tex looked at him. "His first officer?"

The Captain of the *Kalliope* nodded. "Early on in Picard's story, the man said Worf was worth several ordinary officers. The facts seemed to have proved him right."

"To be sure," Picard agreed.

"But surely," said Robinson, "you're not finished, Picard? What became of the fair Lady Abby? And her stalwarts?"

"And Brant?" the Captain of the *Kalliope* added. "What happened to him and his rebels?"

"And their Hoard?" Flenarrh wondered.

The gecko perked his head up. It seemed he had some questions of his own, if he could only voice them.

"You're right," Picard told them all. "There's more of my story to be told . . . if only a little."

The Tale

WE NEVER BEAMED BACK DOWN TO BRANT'S WORLD. RATHER, BRANT AND his fellow rebels beamed up to the mercenary vessel, along with all the equipment and supplies we had seen on the planet's surface.

And the Hoard as well.

Then we left the vicinity. Apparently, the rebels were well prepared, having decided in advance where they would rendezvous if they were ever attacked while their fleet was away.

Fortunately, the mercenary vessel had sustained little damage at the hands of the Abinarri. Cruising at warp eight, we would reach the rebellion's new headquarters world in a little less than two days.

In the meantime, we were treated for our injuries and given a chance to convalesce. Even Worf allowed his wounds to be dressed and subjected to a healing device of some kind. However, he refused to remain in the rebels' too bright, makeshift sickbay, preferring to prowl the purple-shadowed precincts of the ship.

I didn't have the strength to prowl with him, nor did I pretend to. I remained in sickbay, Abby's bed just a few feet from my own. I remember lying there as weariness and my medications conspired to overwhelm me, glad to see her color starting to come back a little.

After all, I had begun to care about her. To care *deeply.*

Finally, I succumbed to sleep—a wonderful sleep, peaceful and without dreams. When I woke, I was surprised to learn I had been out for eighteen hours straight—and that Abby was gone.

I searched for her throughout the ship. A few of the rebels said they had seen her, speaking here and there with the survivors of her crew. Then one of them directed me to the observation lounge.

That's where I found her. She was standing with her brother, gazing at the streaking stars through a large, diamond-shaped port. They were cast in a purple light, like almost everything else on that ship.

If our vessel had still been operated by its original owners, the Orions, the place would have boasted a wide variety of gambling paraphernalia. As it was, it contained just a few tables and chairs. I made my way through them to join the Brants.

Abby turned and smiled at the sight of me. She looked a lot better than when I had glimpsed her last. Her pallor was gone and her eyes were as bright as before.

"Picard," she said.

I nodded. "Or anyway, what's left of me." I turned to Brant. "I take it our journey has been without incident thus far."

"It has," he confirmed. "With any luck, it'll stay that way."

"We need to talk," Abby told me.

"I guess that's my cue," said Brant. "Glad to see you're up and about again, Picard." Then he made his way out of the lounge, leaving his sister and me alone.

Abby was silent for a moment, strangely pensive. Then she said, "I've spoken to my men."

"How are they?" I asked.

"They're fine," she replied. "I . . . told them I was sorry."

"For what?" I asked.

Abby shrugged. "For letting them think there was a pot of gold at the end of the rainbow. One they could keep, I mean."

"You didn't know there wasn't," I reminded her.

"But even if I had," she insisted, "I would still have led them on. I would have done whatever it took to put a crew together."

"Only because your brother's life was at stake. At least, that's what you thought at the time."

"Still," said Abby, "there's no way I could have carried off this gambit without them—no way I could've made it to Hel's Gate, much less gotten through to this universe and helped turn away the Abinarri."

She had a point. Had her crew been any less capable or courageous, Abby would never have survived her encounters with the Cardassians and the Romulans—not to mention the pirates we kept running into.

"So they risked their lives over and over," Abby said, "and for what? In the end, they had nothing to show for it—except my unending gratitude and affection, as if that were worth anything on the open market."

"What did they say?" I asked.

"What do you think? Thadoc told me there was no need for an apology. He was glad to have followed me anywhere, for any reason." She grinned. "Dunwoody told me I'd have to make it up to him—say, with another voyage. After all, he said, Dujonian's Hoard isn't the only treasure in the universe."

I smiled. "That sounds like him."

Abby's smile faded. "I thanked him for the sentiment, of course. But I said that it wouldn't be possible for us to make another voyage. He would have to find someone else with whom to seek out those treasures."

"And why is that?" I inquired.

She glanced at me meaningfully. "Because I have decided to stay here with the rebels."

Somewhere deep inside, I believe I had known she would say that. Still, it knocked the stuffing out of me. As I noted earlier, I had grown rather fond of Abby Brant.

"I see," I said.

Perceiving that I was less than ecstatic about her announcement, she took my hand. "Try to understand," she told me. "This is a second chance for me. A chance to do some good for people, to fight the good fight the way some of those privateers fought it—whether you believe that or not."

"Abby . . ." I said softly.

"And this time," she finished, "I don't intend to screw it up."

The observation lounge echoed with the force of her words. Blushing, she looked away from me, as if she had suddenly taken an interest in the stars outside our ship.

"Thadoc said one word," she went on. "It was 'no.' I asked him not to make my decision any harder than it had to be. 'Who's making it harder?' he asked. 'Your brother needs all the help he can get.' "

"Then Thadoc's staying, as well?" I asked.

Abby nodded, her eyes sparkling with reflected light. "Dunwoody, too. He said he could use a change of scenery—if I'd have him."

"And you told him you would, of course."

She chuckled. "In a minute."

Abby had asked the other survivors as well, all three of them—but they hadn't been quite so eager as Thadoc and Dunwoody. They wanted to go home to their own universe.

She turned back to me, her eyes seeking mine. "It'll feel good to have a couple of familiar faces around while I'm chipping at the Abinarri."

"No doubt," I said hollowly.

Abby's brow creased. "It'd be even better to have one more around. Say, for instance . . . *yours.*"

I didn't respond.

"You and I," she said, "we've been through a lot in the short time we've known each other. We've proven we make one hell of a team, haven't we? Why not make it . . . a permanent one?"

I searched Abby Brant's features—her wise, pale blue eyes, her fine, freckled nose, her full and inviting lips. There was a great deal to keep me there, I mused.

And if I left, I would likely never see her again. After all, Brant's rebels would have to establish one new base after another. Even if I managed to reach this reality a second time, I would have no way to find them.

No way to find *her.*

To be honest, I was tempted by Abby's offer. There were worse ways to live than to fight every day for a cause. The problem was, I already had one. It was called the Federation.

Telling myself that didn't make my decision any easier. But it made me see it was the only decision I could make.

"We do make a hell of a team," I told Abby, "and part of me wants very much to remain. But like you, I've made a commitment—to others and to myself—and I cannot help but see it through."

For a moment, she looked as if she would argue with me, try to talk me into staying. Then it seemed she thought better of it.

"I understand," Abby told me, her voice wavering only slightly.

"I knew you would," I replied.

And that was that.

We spent the next night on the surface of another barren planet, helping the rebels set up their camp—while a select few of them used the Orion's transporter to bury their Hoard. I met people from races I had never seen before and would probably never see again. And I spent a few precious hours with Abby Brant.

The next morning, Worf and I—along with the three other men who had decided not to join the rebels—gathered in the center of the camp. We said good-bye to the friends we had made. Then Richard Brant called the mercenary vessel and told her captain to beam us up.

I gazed for the last time at Abby, doing my best to memorize everything I could about her—her eyes, her manner, her bearing. Then I found myself on an Orion transporter pad, alongside Worf and the others.

The transporter technician was slight and angular, with black, staring eyes, a bluish white topknot, and skin the color of bronze. He looked up at us after a moment.

"You're sure you want to go back?" he asked.

I nodded. "Yes."

"Too bad," he said, making no effort to hide his disappointment. "The Gate gives me indigestion."

"I'm sorry to hear that," I told him, but my mind was elsewhere.

Exiting the transporter chamber, I made my way out into the corridor and located a diamond-shaped observation port with a view of the world below us. As I stood there, we began to break orbit.

"Captain?" said a deep voice.

I turned and saw Worf standing behind me.

"Do you mind if I join you?" he asked.

I found I was glad for the company. "No," I told the lieutenant. "I don't mind at all."

Together, we watched the rebels' new home dwindle beneath us, until it was the size of a ball and then a coin and then barely visible at all. At last, I lost sight of it.

And, regrettably, Abby with it.

Nonetheless, I found I was happy for her. Happy beyond words.

After all, she had found a treasure far more precious than anything she might have hoped for . . . an opportunity to start her life anew.

But if Abby Brant had found a treasure, Jean-Luc Picard had lost one. And no matter how far I traveled, no matter how many exotic star systems I explored, I knew I might never see its like again.

Madigoor

As the story ended, there was silence around the table. Picard's companions looked at one another. Then they nodded.

"A good story," Bo'tex decided.

"A *very* good story," Dravvin insisted.

"Just very good?" Robinson responded.

"Masterful," said the Captain of the *Kalliope.* "I won't even attempt to tell one of my own."

Hompaq grumbled in agreement. "Why waste it when the contest has already been won?"

Flenarrh smiled at Picard. "I'm glad Lafitte didn't run you through before you could tell it."

"As a matter of fact," the captain replied, "so am I."

Just then, the gecko roused itself and skittered to the edge of our table. With a last look around, it leaped off and lost itself in the crowd.

"Talk about your fair-weather friends," commented the Captain of the *Kalliope.* "Show's over and he's *gone.*"

Smiling in his beard, Robinson leaned closer to his fellow human. "Answer a question for me, Picard."

The captain of the *Enterprise* shrugged. "Ask away."

"If your story's true," Robinson inquired, "why have I never heard of Hel's Gate before? As long as I've frequented the Captain's Table, and that's long indeed, why has no one ever mentioned such a phenomenon?"

"I was wondering that myself," said Bo'tex.

"Though perhaps you were too embarrassed to admit it," Dravvin suggested. He drew disapproving looks from around the table. "Perhaps . . . almost as embarrassed as *I* was," he confessed grudgingly.

Flenarrh looked relieved. "Thank Trannis. I thought I was just *me.*"

Hompaq nodded ruefully. "You shamed us all into silence, Picard. I don't know whether to slap you on the back or spill your blood."

"Well?" said Robinson, his eyes narrowing mischievously as he regarded Picard. "Is it possible you've woven a yarn for us—and a wonderful yarn it was—with no basis in fact?"

Picard looked around the table—and smiled. "That," he said, "is something that must remain between myself and my conscience."

"That's all you'll tell us?" Hompaq rasped.

"That's all," the human confirmed.

"It's an outrage!" the Klingon bellowed, attracting the attention of other captains in the vicinity.

"No," Robinson told her. "It's an enhancement."

Again, those assembled at the table looked at one another, considering the proposition. And again, they nodded slowly in agreement.

"It makes the story that much more exciting," the Captain of the *Kalliope* observed. "Never to know if it's fact or fiction, spun from personal experience or the imagination."

"Never to know if Hel's Gate really exists," Dravvin added. "Or for that matter, the dimension beyond it."

"Or the lovely Red Abby," Robinson noted.

Hompaq grunted, the lone dissenter at the table. "And never to sleep again for wondering."

Flenarrh quirked a smile. "I salute you, Picard."

"And I as well," Bo'tex told him.

Robinson clapped Picard on the shoulder. "Well done, my friend."

"Jean Luc!" came a voice.

Turning in his seat, Picard saw Neil Gleason making his way toward them. And he had a female on his arm.

"Gleason," Picard declared, unable to conceal his exasperation. "Where the devil have you been?"

His fellow captain gestured to the female. "This is Captain Prrghh," he said. "An old friend. We've been . . . er, catching up on old times." He smiled at Prrghh. "Isn't that right, my love?"

Prrghh smiled back at him with her vaguely feline features. "Yes," she purred. "Catching up."

It didn't quite explain the suddenness of Gleason's disappearance. However, it did seem to explain why it had taken him so long to turn up again.

"Pleased to meet you," Picard told Prrghh.

"Likewise," the female responded. She nodded to the other captains at the table, then turned to Gleason. "I suppose you have to go now."

He sighed. "Duty calls. We've got an early-morning meeting we don't dare miss on pain of death."

Prrghh laughed. "Until next time, then." And she kissed Gleason softly on the cheek.

Gleason reddened. "Till next time," he echoed.

By then, Picard's tablemates had begun some new discussion, which had nothing to do with either Hel's Gate or Prrghh. Picard took advantage of the fact to stand and approach his friend.

"You abandoned me," he told Gleason.

His friend glanced at the table where Picard's companions still sat. "No one stays abandoned in this place for long," he said. He looked at Picard. "And can you say you didn't have a good time?"

Picard considered his surroundings and frowned. "Perhaps *abandoned* is too strong a word. Nonetheless, you could have warned me you were going to disappear. I was concerned that something might have happened to you."

Gleason chuckled. "Something *did.* But it was a most pleasant something, I assure you." He gestured. "Shall we?"

Following the gesture, Picard saw the door by which he'd entered the place.

He felt a tug on his sleeve. It was Robinson, reaching over from where he sat. "Don't tell me you're leaving us," the bearded man said.

"I'm afraid so," Picard told him. "Perhaps we'll meet again."

Robinson shrugged. "I'll be here."

Picard was about to say how unlikely it was he'd return to Madigoor IV. After all, if not for the conference, he might never have come here in the first place.

But that didn't mean he wouldn't return to the Captain's Table. In fact, he would make a *point* of returning.

Bo'tex waved good-bye. "Take care of yourself," he told Picard.

"Good voyaging," Dravvin chimed in.

"Fair ports," Flenarrh wished him.

Hompaq lifted her chin. "Qapla."

Picard smiled. "The same to you." He glanced at the Captain of the *Kalliope,* who smiled back at him. "To all of you." Then he nodded to Gleason, and they headed for the door.

Before they could quite reach it, however, someone shouted to them. Turning, Picard saw it was the fellow behind the bar.

"I'm sorry," he told the bartender. "I didn't hear you."

The man cupped his hands and called out again. "Give my regards to Guinan, won't you?"

It took Picard by surprise—not that the fellow knew Guinan, since she had been to any number of places in the course of her long life. But how had he known that *Picard* knew Guinan?

Then he remembered. He had identified himself to his tablemates as the captain of the *Enterprise.* Obviously, someone else had overheard and mentioned it to the bartender.

Yes, he thought, that was it. It *had* to be.

"Of course," he finally shouted back. "I'll be happy to."

The bartender waved his thanks and went back to his duties. And Picard, even more intrigued with the place than before, nonetheless resumed his progress toward the exit.

He took one last look at the Captain's Table—at the people, the place . . . the eerie, uncertain, and yet insistently familiar landscape. And then he followed his friend Gleason into the night and the fog.

For a while, they walked in silence. And when Picard looked back, he couldn't find the sign anymore that identified the Captain's Table. But somehow, he knew, if he searched long and hard enough, it would be right there before his eyes.

Reaching into the pocket of his jacket, he found and extracted the good-luck charm he had taken to carrying with him—a diamondlike jewel the size of a uniform pip.

"What's that?" asked his friend.

Picard shrugged. "A souvenir."

Of course, had Gleason been more of an archaeologist, he might have suspected the stone was a genuine glor'ya. But it was only a replica, given to Picard by one of the Federation scientists who had analyzed the real thing.

The captain had been tempted to show the gem to his comrades in the Captain's Table. However, as Robinson had noted, that would have detracted from the mystery surrounding his tale.

"Well?" asked Gleason. "Was the place everything I said it would be?"

Picard looked at him. "It was pleasant, all right."

"Just pleasant?" his friend probed.

The captain of the *Enterprise* took a deep draft of night air. "You mean, do I have as much on my mind as I did before?"

"Uh-huh. And do you?"

Picard shrugged. "Perhaps not. Or if I do, at least it isn't weighing quite as heavily." He smiled wistfully. "But then, a little fencing match always did put things into perspective for me."

The Mist

Benjamin Sisko

as recorded by

Dean Wesley Smith and

Kristine Kathryn Rusch

To Mark and Laura Nelson

One

On a vast front spread through the Alpha Quadrant, the battle between the Federation and Dominion waged on, ship by ship, sector by sector. Moving through an unusually empty section of space near the Klingon/Federation border, three Jem'Hadar ships raced to reinforce four other Dominion ships in a losing fight against the Federation starship *Defiant* and the Klingon battle cruiser *Hutlh*.

Without warning, and directly in front of the three Jem'Hadar reinforcements, a white line formed in the blackness of space, slowly filling into a large area of mist, as if it were a cloud building before a storm. It had no substance that registered on any instrument, and the three ships entered it, expecting their shields to protect them against the thin anomaly. They were within two minutes of the fight and they had no time to detour around a simple cloud of space debris.

But no ships reappeared on the other side of the thin area of mist.

A few moments later the mist faded and was gone, as quickly as it had come, leaving the space empty and black.

No Jem'Hadar reinforcements arrived at the battle, and the Federation starship *Defiant* and the Klingon battle cruiser *Hutlh* fought and destroyed the four Dominion ships, holding the line of the war for one more day.

The disappearance of the three Jem'Hadar reinforcement ships became an unexplained footnote in the records of a long and deadly war.

But sometimes wars are won in the footnotes.

• • •

The cool metal handle on the massive wooden door fit into Captain Benjamin Sisko's hand as if it were made for him. The feeling so startled him that he paused and glanced down, opening his hand without taking his fingers off the metal.

The handle's design was Bajoran, shaped almost like another hand reaching out, yet without the delineation of a hand or fingers. It was clearly very old and very well made. The surface was worn smooth, polished by use. Sisko couldn't see anything that attached the handle to the door, almost as if the handle grew from the dark wood.

Above Sisko's head was a carved wooden sign that read simply, THE CAPTAIN'S TABLE. The sign was an extension of the door frame and the letters on the sign were dried and cracked, obviously from the heat of the Bajoran summers. Yet the sign, along with the door and the griplike handle, seemed to reach out to Sisko and pull him in, welcoming him as if he were coming back to a childhood home.

A few weeks before, a captain of a Jibetian freighter had pulled Sisko aside on the Promenade and asked if he knew where a bar called the Captain's Table might be. Sisko had said he'd never heard of the place. Instead, he recommended Quark's.

The Jibetian had simply laughed and said, "If you ever get the chance, have a drink in the Captain's Table. There is no other bar."

Sisko had put the man's suggestion out of his mind until this morning. He was on Bajor because Dr. Bashir had threatened to have Sisko relieved of command if he did not rest. It was impossible to rest in the middle of a war, Sisko had argued, but Bashir was adamant. A Starfleet doctor did have the power to relieve someone of command, and rather than go through that fight, Sisko had agreed to two days on Bajor, two days without meetings, without Starfleet protocol, without decisions.

If he had stayed on the station, he wouldn't have been able to relax. Somehow the staff seemed to believe that Sisko had to decide which replicators remained on-line, which messages should be forwarded through the war zone, which ships would be allowed to dock. He had a competent crew; it was time, Bashir had said, to trust them with the details, and to sleep.

Bashir had wanted Sisko on Bajor for a week. Sisko wanted to stay overnight, and return in less than twenty-four hours. They had compromised on two days.

"Two *full* days," Bashir had said. "If I hear of you on this station before forty-eight hours are up, I will order you to the infirmary for the remainder of your holiday."

"I'll keep that in mind," Sisko had said, deciding that he'd rather remain on Bajor than subject himself to sickbay for even one hour. Bashir had smiled, knowing that he'd won.

Sisko spent his first day on Bajor in his rented cabin, sitting outside and wondering what the planet would be like when he retired there. If he got a chance to retire there.

By that afternoon, he was restless—despite Bashir's worry, Sisko had too much energy to relax. His concerns for the Federation, for the entire quadrant, would not allow him to rest. Not completely. And no matter how much he loved Bajor, it didn't take his mind off the problems he would face when he returned.

He wandered the streets of the nearby village, and had passed this very door more than once. On his third pass, the sign had caught his attention and the Jibetian captain's words had come back to him. Sisko had had his fingers wrapped around the handle before he'd even realized that he'd made a decision.

The door was so massive-looking that Sisko expected it to feel heavy as he pulled it open. Instead it moved easily, almost as if it had no weight at all.

Inside, the coolness and darkness gripped him, pulling him out of the heat of the Bajoran day. Instantly he could feel the sweat on his forehead, where moments before the dryness of the afternoon air had pulled it instantly away. He let the door swing shut slowly behind him, seeming to plunge him into complete darkness. His eyes struggled to adjust from the bright sunlight to the dim light. The coolness now wrapped completely around him like a welcome hand. In the cool air, he was suddenly more thirsty than normal.

Part of his thirst came from the smell. The interior had a soft scent, like the smell of fresh-baked bread long after it had been eaten. Or the scent of coffee just percolating in the morning. Familiar smells. Welcoming smells. Smells that made him think of comfort and of home.

He stood still, with his back to the door, and dim shapes appeared as his eyes adjusted.

Walls.

Pictures on the walls.

Soon he could tell that he was in a short hallway fashioned out of smooth wood and decorated with images of old water-sailing ships. Only a single indirect light above the ceiling illuminated the small passage. Deeper inside he could hear talking and an occasional laugh. He stepped forward and around a corner.

In front of him was a large yet comfortable-feeling room. The ceiling was low and a stone fireplace filled part of the wall to his left, a small fire doing nothing to take the comfortable coolness from the room. Most of the right wall of the room was filled with a long wooden bar fronted by a dozen or more stools. The surface of the bar looked worn and well used. A tall, thick man stood behind the bar, and at least a dozen patrons from different races sat around some of the tables in small groups.

Sisko stopped in the entrance, giving his eyes time to finish adjusting to the dim light. It was then that he noticed the grand-style piano in the corner to his left. It seemed old and very well used, its surface marred by what looked like hundreds of glass and bottle imprints.

Beside the piano a humanoid sat. He was from no race that Sisko recognized. The humanoid had slits for eyes, lizardlike skin, and four long talons on each hand. Sisko felt no fear or revulsion, but merely a sense of curiosity and a feeling of comfort coming from the creature.

"Welcome, Captain," the large man behind the bar said, smiling and motioning Sisko forward. With one more glance at the unmoving humanoid, Sisko turned and stepped toward the bar.

The bartender wore a white apron with an open-necked gray shirt under it. He had unruly white hair and a smile that seemed to take the dimness out of the air. Sisko liked the man instantly, not exactly knowing why, and not willing to explore why. Sisko was on vacation. It was time he relaxed. He usually knew better than to be lulled into a feeling of safety, and yet here he was. He was conscious of his back, conscious of the people around him, but he wasn't really wary. Not yet. And he wouldn't be unless something made him feel that way.

Sisko stepped between two of the bar stools. To his surprise, he had to look up to meet the gaze of the man behind the bar.

"They call me Cap," the bartender said in a deep, rich voice that seemed to have a touch of laughter floating through it. "Welcome to the Captain's Table. What's your drink of choice?" He wiped his hands on a bar rag, and then waited.

Sisko glanced down the long back bar filled with glasses of all shapes and sizes. Above the glasses were what seemed like hundreds of different bottles of liquor. He couldn't spot a replicator. He had a thousand choices, but at the moment he wanted something to take away the last of the Bajoran heat and dryness.

"Do you have Jibetian ale?"

Cap laughed and nodded. "You'll have to go a great deal more than that to stump this place. We have just about everything. Would you like your ale warm, cold, or lightly salted?"

Sisko had never liked the Jibetian habit of salting their ale. "Cold," he said. "No salt."

Betraying a lightness on his feet that didn't seem natural to a man his size, Cap spun and opened up a cooler under the back bar. A moment later he slid a cold, damp bottle of Jibetian ale into Sisko's hand.

"Thanks," Sisko said, tilting the bottle toward Cap in a small, appreciative salute.

Jibetian ale was the perfect drink for Sisko's mood. It was hard to come by, almost impossible since the start of the war with the Dominion. Quark claimed to have one bottle left in his stock, and the price he placed on it made it seem as if it were the last bottle anywhere in the universe. Sisko had thought he would have to forgo Jibetian ale until the Federation defeated the Dominion.

Almost as if he had read Sisko's mind, Cap said, "I think I got a few more where that came from."

"Excellent," Sisko said. "I wish I had time for more than one."

Cap just smiled as if what Sisko had said had amused him. Then the bartender turned back to cleaning glasses.

Sisko watched him for a moment, then took a drink. The rich, golden taste of the ale relaxed him, draining some of the problems he carried, almost as if they didn't exist. He downed half the bottle before finally forcing himself to stop for a breath. He very seldom drank, so going too fast wasn't the best idea, no matter how good it tasted. And this was real ale, not synthehol. Its effects would be real as well.

Cap was still washing glasses, so Sisko turned and studied the bar. He had half expected, in the middle of the afternoon, to be the only one inside. But that clearly wasn't the case. Five of the ten tables had groups at them, the sounds of their talking filling the low-ceilinged bar with a full background sound. If Sisko focused, he could hear individual conversations, but overall the noise level was not too loud.

The patrons of this bar were an odd mix. A number of humans, a young, almost childlike man from a race Sisko couldn't identify, and a half-dozen other races he had seen on the station. He would have thought this mix normal at Quark's, which had the entire quadrant to draw on. Here, in a small out-of-the-way bar on Bajor, the mix was odd indeed, especially since there were no Bajorans present.

A huge Caxtonian sat at the opposite end of the bar, nursing a drink. The Caxtonian looked as if he never left that stool, which struck Sisko. He had never heard of a Caxtonian ever visiting Bajor. There were a number of strange things about this place, and yet, he still didn't feel uncomfortable. Perhaps that was the strangest of all. He had been on alert ever since the threat to the Alpha Quadrant began; he'd thought he wouldn't relax until the situation was resolved.

Perhaps Bashir was right. Perhaps Sisko had needed this.

He had finished off another quarter of the bottle and was about to ask Cap about some of the customers when behind him a loud, grating voice boomed over the background talking.

"Sisko! You are a long way from your precious station."

As Sisko turned, the mostly empty ale bottle in his hand, he noticed that Cap wasn't smiling quite as much as he had been a moment before.

"I could say the same for you, Sotugh," Sisko said, turning to face the Klingon who stood near a table on the far side of the room. Sisko hadn't seen him a moment before, yet he knew that voice without even seeing its owner. And now he was even more surprised at the patrons of this bar.

Sotugh, head of the House of DachoH, commanded a large percentage of the Klingon fleet under Gowron. He was loyal to the Empire almost to a fault, and made clear his disgust at the current alliance between the Federation and the Klingon Empire against the Dominion. Yet he had fought many brilliant battles in the course of the war. The last time Sisko had heard, Sotugh and his ships were patrolling a sector of the Cardassian border.

"Bah," Sotugh said, waving his hand in disgust at Sisko's comment. He was a large man, even for a Klingon. His graying hair flowed over his clothing which, surprisingly, was not his uniform. Sisko wasn't sure if he'd ever seen Sotugh out of uniform before.

"Gentlemen," Cap said, his voice stopping Sotugh from continuing. "Instead of yelling across the bar, I suggest you sit down together and continue this conversation."

"Sit with Sisko," Sotugh said, laughing at the suggestion of the bartender. "I will fight with him against the Dominion, but nothing more."

Sisko leaned over his ale. "Still mad at me for the Mist incident, I see."

Sotugh's hand went to his knife. "The Mist would be members of the Empire if not for your action. Their weapons would help us fight the Cardassian and Dominion scum."

Sisko smiled. "As usual," he said deliberately, "your opinions blind you, Sotugh."

Sotugh stepped forward, his hand gripping his knife.

"Sotugh!" Cap said, his voice stopping the Klingon warrior in midstep. "Only a coward draws on an unarmed man. You are not known as a coward."

Sisko placed the bottle on the bar and opened both his hands to show Sotugh that they were empty. The bartender clearly knew how to handle Klingons. Around the bar a few other patrons laughed softly.

Sotugh only looked angry, but his hand left his knife.

"It seems," Cap said, "that since the Mist are considered nothing but legend, there is a story behind this. Am I right, Captain?"

Sisko picked up his bottle and finished the last of the ale. "There is a story," he said. He grinned at Sotugh, who only sneered in return. All the patrons in the bar now had their attention riveted on the two.

While the tension held the bar in silence, Cap opened another bottle of Jibetian ale and slid it down the bar, stopping it just beside Sisko's hand. Then he quickly poured what looked like a mug of blood wine. "Arthur, hand this to Sotugh."

The young-looking alien, the one who looked like a slender child, grabbed the mug from the bar. He moved easily across the floor, his robes flowing around him, and handed the mug to Sotugh as if the glowering Klingon were nothing more than a happy patron.

"I would be very interested in hearing a story about the Mist," Cap said. "Would anyone else?"

It seemed that from the yesses and applause, everyone agreed. Sisko only shook his head in amusement at Sotugh's expression of disgust. It had been a number of years since the meeting with Sotugh over the race called the Mist. There was nothing secret about the incident. But it hadn't become widely known, since shortly after it happened the Klingons invaded Cardassia. Now the story would only add to the legend of the Mist.

"Pull a couple of those tables together," Cap said, pointing at a few tables in the center of the room. "Does anyone need refills before the story starts?"

The young Arthur took Sotugh's blood wine before the Klingon had a chance to drink and set the mug on an empty table. To Sisko's surprise, Sotugh did not seem to mind. He went to the nearest chair, chased away a yellow-and-green gecko with a stumpy tail, grabbed his mug, and took a long drink, slopping some of the liquid down the side. Miraculously, Arthur managed to avoid getting drops on his robe.

Two patrons quickly pulled another table over to Sotugh's. Sisko nodded to Cap and moved over to the group table, sitting across from the Klingon. After a moment everyone in the bar, except for the Caxtonian at the bar and the strange lizard-man near the door, had gathered at the large table with drinks in their hands.

"Sotugh," Sisko said, smiling at his old adversary. "Would you like to start? Klingons are legendary for their ability to tell a story."

Sotugh simply waved his hand in disgust. "Klingons tell stories of honor. But this story has no honor for anyone. You tell it. I will correct your errors."

Sisko took a quick sip from the bottle of cold ale, then nodded at Cap, who stood near the bar.

"In my years in Starfleet, I have seen many strange things," Sisko said. "But little as strange as the Mist."

"Now that," Sotugh said, "is something I agree with."

Sisko smiled at Sotugh. He had known it would be impossible for the Klingon to keep silent during this story.

Cap laughed. "Sotugh, you have given the story over to Captain Sisko. Please let him tell it."

Sotugh sat back in disgust, the mug of blood wine clutched in his hands.

"Go ahead, Captain," Cap said.

"As you may have gathered, most of this story will be hard to believe. But I'm sure Sotugh will correct anything I may get wrong."

Sotugh only grunted.

"I first heard the legend of the Mist," Sisko said, "when I was a cadet in Starfleet Academy, but I didn't encounter them until many years later. By then I had almost forgotten who and what they were. . . ."

Two

My contact with the Mist occurred during the period of tension between the Klingon Empire and the Federation, just before this quadrant's problems with the Dominion began. For those of you who do not know, I command *Deep Space Nine,* a former Cardassian space station, one of the farthest outposts of the Federation. We are the guardians of the wormhole between the Alpha and Delta Quadrants.

We run a twenty-four-hour clock on *Deep Space Nine,* following the long-standing Federation tradition of maintaining an Earth Day in space. I am in my office—which used to be the Cardassian commander Gul Dukat's office—in Operations by 0800 hours, and my staff knows not to disturb me until I have finished my first and only glass of *raktajino.* It is not that I awaken slowly, or even in a bad mood. I simply prefer a few moments of silence at the beginning of my day, since I know that, if the day runs true to form, those will be the only moments of silence I will have.

So that morning, when my first officer, Major Kira, our liaison with Bajor, knocked and did not wait for my response to enter, I knew we had trouble.

She stood in the doorway, with a slightly apologetic look on her face. She held a padd in her left hand.

"What is it, Major?" I asked, my hand wrapped around my steaming—and so far untouched—glass of *raktajino.*

"I am sorry to interrupt you, Captain," she said. "But I think you need to look at this."

I should say here that Kira is one of the best officers I have on *Deep*

Space Nine. She breaks protocol only when necessity calls for it. An interruption from Kira is never frivolous, and always deserves my attention.

I took the padd.

Kira nodded once, then turned and left my office, the door hissing shut behind her. Through that door, I could see my morning staff at their usual positions, and I found comfort in that. Kira spoke briefly to Jadzia Dax, a joined Trill who sat at the science station, before going to the replicator to get her own morning glass of *raktajino.*

Before I turned my attention to the padd, I took what would be my only sip of *raktajino* that day. Then I read the report the major had prepared for me.

It seems that a few moments before my arrival, the station picked up a distress call. Sent in an ancient Earth code that had not been used since the early days of human interstellar travel.

But perhaps the most intriguing feature of the distress call was that it originated in an empty area of space near the Klingon border. The area did not have a planetary system, or large space debris, and our equipment could not pick up any sign of a ship or space station for light-years around.

A distress call was coming out of nothing.

"Your equipment. Bah!" Sotugh said. His outburst startled Sisko and others around the table. "I do not think the fault was with your equipment. Your people do not know how to run a proper scan."

Sisko slid his chair back slightly. "Your people had trouble as well."

"Let him tell the story," said a humanoid woman who had been sitting at the end of the bar. She stood. She was tall and slender, with catlike features and peach fur. She kicked a chair away from the table with a dark boot, and then twisted it, so that it faced the bar. She sat on it backward, placing her arms on top of the seat, and resting her chin on her arms. "I think it's fascinating."

"You would," Sotugh snapped.

"Leave your conflicts outside," Cap said. Then he nodded to Sisko. "Please continue, Captain."

Sisko nodded in return. "The report documented the anomalies I mentioned a moment ago," he said, with a glance at Sotugh, "but I felt they were strange enough to warrant another look. . . ."

I left my office and entered Ops.

The day crew is my most experienced and efficient. My chief engineer, Miles O'Brien, had once served on the *Starship Enterprise,* and falls into that legendary category of Starfleet engineers, the kind who can make a starship out of spitballs and twine. Lieutenant Commander Worf, a Klingon . . .

• • •

Sisko looked pointedly at Sotugh as he said that. Sotugh scowled into his blood wine and said nothing.

. . . who had also served on the *Enterprise*-D under the captaincy of Jean-Luc Picard. Worf has the finest sense of honor of any Klingon I have ever met. He also values perfection and brings a level of detail to his work that I find rare even in the ranks of Starfleet.

Jadzia Dax has been my friend through two different incarnations, and I find her wisdom and intelligence an essential part of our crew. I discovered later that she was the one, not Major Kira, who discovered the distress signal. But Dax has known me a long time, and she prefers to let someone else interrupt my morning routine. It goes back to the days when Dax was joined to Curzon, a rather surly old man who influenced me more than I care to say. But that is another story, for another time.

"Major," I said as I walked down the steps to the main section of Ops. "Are you still reading the signal?"

Kira balanced her glass of *raktajino* on her knee as she glanced at her console. "Yes," she said.

"There is still nothing in that section of space," Dax said. "I have run every scan I can think of."

"As well as some she shouldn't have," Chief O'Brien said.

Dax smiled at him. "It didn't put any strain on the equipment."

"This time," he said testily.

This sort of interaction was common among my morning crew, and it rose out of their sense of perfection.

"Notify Starfleet," I said. "I would like to investigate this further, but its proximity to the Klingon border could create problems that the Federation does not need."

"Captain," Kira said, before she carried out my order. "This might be a trap."

Out of the corner of my eye I could see Dax shaking her head as she stared at her board.

"It may be a trap," Worf said from his security station, "but it is not a Klingon trap."

"Worf knows his people," Sotugh said.

Sisko took the momentary break to sip from his Jibetian ale. He wasn't used to talking this much; his mouth was getting dry already.

"So then what happened?" asked a green-skinned woman in a blazing pink uniform. Sisko wondered how, with such colors, he had missed her when he first scanned the bar.

"We notified Starfleet," Sisko said, "and they approved of the mission.

I ordered the crew, along with our doctor, and several others, to be on our starship, the *Defiant,* within the hour. I left the station in Major Kira's capable hands."

"Very interesting," the catlike woman said. Perhaps it was better to describe her response as a purr. She leveled her bright green gaze on Sisko and smiled at him. "So *that* is what the Federation was doing. Yet you said this happened near the Klingon border. What were the Klingons doing?"

The dozen bar patrons sitting around the large double table shifted their attention from Sisko to Sotugh, waiting for him to answer. Cap leaned against the outside of the bar near the table, smiling. Sisko got the sense that, even though the catlike woman had directed the comment at him, she clearly had meant it as a jab at Sotugh.

But her question did seem to spark a lot of interest. A human couple, who had taken seats above the table at the bar to listen to the story, leaned forward. The woman watched closely while sipping from a cup of hot tea. The man, however, had abandoned his dark, carbonated beverage on the bar. "Yes," he said, with genuine interest, "did the Klingons hear the distress call?"

Sotugh nodded. "We did. And we understood its ancient language and message. But as Sisko said, there was nothing there. A waste of valuable time to investigate."

"Yet," the catlike woman said, still looking at Sisko, "you criticize the captain here for improperly using his equipment. What of yours?"

"We did not have time to chase ghosts in space," Sotugh said. "We trusted our readings and our equipment. Nothing was there to investigate."

"You didn't think that later," Sisko said, setting down his bottle of Jibetian ale.

"Things changed later," Sotugh said. "You are not telling everything, Sisko."

"I would, if you'd give me a chance," Sisko said evenly, making sure he was smiling.

In disgust, Sotugh downed the last of his blood wine. With a wide sweeping motion that almost caught the side of the Jibetian woman beside him, he handed his cup back to Cap, who without missing a beat slid it down the bar to Arthur, who was standing behind the bar. Obviously the young-looking Arthur was functioning as the assistant bartender.

"Please go on with your story, Captain," Cap said. "It seems clear that something was sending out that distress call after all."

Sisko raised his bottle of ale in a motion of agreement. "Oh, there was a ship sending out the distress call, all right. But our instruments, and Sotugh's, were correct. There was nothing there."

Sisko smiled at the puzzled expression on Cap's face before taking another long drink and going back to his story.

Three

The *Defiant* is the toughest starship in the Federation. It is sleek and streamlined, yet has more power than the Galaxy-class starships most people think of when they hear the word "Starfleet." The *Defiant* can run efficiently with a minimal crew. It is also the first Federation ship to be equipped with a cloaking device, a fact that we have relied on greatly in our current conflict with the Dominion.

I must be honest with you: As much as I like running the station, I love captaining the *Defiant.* When I sit on the command chair in the center of that bridge, I feel the way I always imagined I would feel when I was a boy dreaming of a career in the stars. Captaining the *Defiant,* even when we take her out on a routine maintenance spin to see if her parts are in working order, is like I imagine captaining an old seafaring vessel would have been. Sometimes I think, as the docking clamps release and the ship heads out into the blackness of space, *There be dragons here.*

I know that Dax shares my feelings, for whenever she and I stand on the bridge together, she gives me a look filled with mischief and awe. In her eyes, I see old Curzon and hear his lusty laugh as we are about to embark on yet another adventure.

There are adventures on *Deep Space Nine,* often more adventures than I would care for, but there the adventure seems to come to us.

On the *Defiant,* we head out into territories unknown, seeking the adventures ourselves.

That day, I thought of the old sailing maps and dragons as I sat on the command chair. I should have been thinking more along the line of pirates.

Dax had the helm. Behind me, Chief O'Brien was checking the systems. Commander Worf was checking our route, scanning as per my order, for anything that might seem like a trap. Should anything happen, he would be in charge of our weaponry. Cadet Nog, the first Ferengi to serve in Starfleet, monitored our communications.

Our station's chief medical officer, Julian Bashir, was powering up sickbay. I had a hunch—not an entirely pleasant one—that we would need his services before the adventure ended. I have found, in my years at *Deep Space Nine,* that leadership is one-third knowledge, one-third common sense, and one-third a deep-in-your-heart, unprovable moment of absolute certainty, based solely on pure gut instinct. The best leaders learn how to separate that instinct from wishful thinking. It is, I think, the hardest thing of all to do, even harder than preparing a beloved crew for war.

It was Cadet Nog who set the tone for the early part of this mission. I saw many of you frown when you heard me mention that a Ferengi had gone to Starfleet Academy, but he had done so at my recommendation. The very features that make Ferengi the true capitalists of the Alpha Quadrant are the features that will make Nog into one of Starfleet's best officers one day. Not their unmistakable avarice, but their attention to detail, their willingness to learn anything if it will benefit them, and their complete desire to be the best at anything they do.

Nog has never forgotten that it was my recommendation that opened the doors to Starfleet Academy, and he has been trying, in the most earnest manner I have ever seen, to repay me ever since.

For my part, I test him at every opportunity I get. At first, I did so because I did not want this recommendation to haunt me in future years, but later, the tests became my way of setting the bar as high as possible for the young cadet. I see in him officer material if he can shed a few of his Ferengi habits.

We had barely cleared the station when Nog said, "The distress signal continues, Captain." His voice was steady, considering he was only a cadet at the time, and it was his first time on the *Defiant.*

From my position, I could not see the cadet without turning my head. But I had a clear view of the side of Dax's face. She was grinning at Nog's obvious excitement. Like me, she felt responsible for the boy, and liked to encourage him. So she said, "There's still no sign of a ship, Benjamin. Or even debris."

"I do not like this," Worf said. "I recommend we go into the area with shields up."

"Noted," I said.

Worf had a point. With tensions running as high as they were at that time in the Alpha Quadrant, we could have been heading into something quite unpleasant. We had also had enough experiences this deep in space to show us that nothing was impossible.

Now, please understand another reason for my desire to explore this strange signal. I am rather fond of stories of lost ships. We had found one once, earlier in my tenure at *Deep Space Nine,* and I had been harboring a secret hope that we were about to find another.

"Old man," I said to Dax. "Are there any records of lost ships in this area from the time of that signal?"

Dax shook her head. "The signal dates from the early days of Earth's expansion out to the stars. They didn't keep the kinds of records we keep now. In those days more ships vanished than reported back."

I knew that, and I knew that the list of possible candidates would be endless. In addition to ships of exploration, many of those early Earth ships were colony ships, leaving Earth never intending to return. Only a few of them had found homes.

The distress signal continued as we approached its coordinates. As we reached the right area I asked Chief O'Brien if he had found the signal's source.

"No, sir," O'Brien said, not taking his eyes off his panel. He had calibrated one of the ship's sensors to search for any signs of a technology that might be hiding a ship or any unusual space anomalies. "In fact, I'm not finding anything at all. Frankly, sir, I don't like this."

Now, I have been on countless missions with the chief, and on many of them, he did not locate the source of the problem we were investigating on his first pass. His comment surprised and intrigued me.

"What exactly don't you like, Chief?" I asked.

He shook his head while continuing to stare at his panel. "Not only is there nothing in the area of that signal, but the entire area of space for almost a light-year in diameter is clear of all debris. Even the dust molecule content is way, way down."

"That cannot be," Worf said.

Now I understood what he was talking about. Even though space seems empty, it never is. There is always some form of matter in forms of asteroids or small dust clouds too thin for the naked eye to see.

"What would wipe an entire area of space clean?" Dax asked.

"I do not see how such a thing is even remotely possible," Worf said.

"I find it curious," I said, "that we would be getting a distress call from an area of space so empty that a dustball would seem conspicuous." I leaned forward. The display on the screen before me showed only darkness.

No one had a response for that, so I said, "Okay, old man, take us in slow and easy. Mr. Worf, go to alert status. Screens up."

"Aye, Captain."

The sound of the relief in Worf's voice made me smile slightly. Dax also smiled in fond amusement without taking her attention from her controls. Recently Dax and Worf married, but at the time of this mission, their relationship had not yet begun. I saw the relationship reflected in tiny gestures like Dax's. It did not interfere with their duties and seemed to make them even more efficient officers.

The chief's mention of discomfort seemed to travel through the crew. I was cautious, but not uncomfortable. I was fascinated by the puzzle, and ready to discover the secrets behind it.

I would discover those secrets sooner than I expected.

"We're almost on top of the signal," Dax said.

"We are less than one thousand meters away," Worf said.

"Chief?" I asked, without turning from the empty space showing on the viewscreen in front of me.

"I'm still not reading anything," he said.

"Have you checked the systems?"

"They're fine, sir. The problem isn't us." He turned and pointed at the blackness on the screen. "It's out there."

"That signal *has* to be coming from somewhere, people," I said, putting an edge in my voice. I wanted an answer before we got into a situation we could not predict. "It could be a cloaked ship, a time anomaly, anything. And I want to know what."

"We are five hundred meters away, Captain," Dax said, reverting from the familiar to my title, as she usually did in military situations.

"Take us to two hundred meters and hold that position," I said.

It took only a moment for Dax to report, "All stop. We are two hundred meters from the point of the distress call."

I still saw only emptiness on the viewscreen. "Magnify," I said.

"We're already at full magnification, sir," O'Brien said. "At this range, we would be able to see the pattern in the metal on the side of any ship."

I leaned forward, intrigued and mystified. There was a distress call coming from a point so close I could almost reach out and touch it, and yet nothing was there. Not even space dust.

"The message continues to repeat," O'Brien said, "coming from a point one hundred meters directly in front of us. Nothing is there that any of my instruments can see."

"How can that be?" I asked. I was ready for some answers. I was tired of my crew telling me that they found nothing. Something had to be sending that distress call, even if it was a carrier wave bouncing off something in space.

"It's impossible," the chief said, "but that's what's happening."

"Chief, *something* is causing that signal."

"No, sir," the chief said, sounding more rattled than usual. "Nothing is. I've explored every possibility, and I can't find anything."

"Then, you haven't explored every possibility," I said. "Cadet, what, exactly, is the source of that signal?"

"Ah, sir, I'm not reading a source." Nog sounded almost frightened of me. Which was good. I wanted to scare a bit of efficiency into my normally brilliant crew.

"There must be a source, Cadet."

"Benjamin," Dax said softly, almost protectively, "they're right. There is no source. Only coordinates."

"So," I said, "you're telling me that if we moved the *Defiant* directly over that point, the message would come from right here on the bridge?"

The chief stood near full attention. He knew I wasn't happy.

Dax sighed.

Worf continued to run scans.

I turned slightly, and saw the cadet look from one senior officer to another, hoping they knew the answer that he did not. In all my years of service with this crew, I had never seen them so completely baffled.

"I would not recommend such an action, sir," Worf said, after a short moment.

"Actually, Commander," I said, turning to look at Mr. Worf, forcing myself not to smile, "I wasn't considering it. I was merely asking."

"In that case, sir," Worf said, "it would seem that your analysis is correct."

I didn't like that answer at all, but no one else contradicted him. "Do you have a better idea on how to discover what's out there?" I asked.

Worf looked me right in the eye, straightened his back slightly, and said, "I do not, sir."

"Sir!" Nog shouted.

I spun around to face the now far-from-empty viewscreen.

Where a moment before had been nothing but very empty vacuum was now a long slit, as if the fabric of space had just been ripped open. The edges of the split were shimmering as it expanded and opened, sending a faint cloud of mist into the void.

"What is that?" I asked.

"It's as if space just ruptured," Dax said sharply. "We're too close."

"Get us out of here, old man," I said.

"I can't," she said. "Too late."

The tear in space moved over and around us, like a giant mouth of a fish swallowing us whole.

The ship remained completely silent. No rumble, no movement.

Nothing.

Everything remained normal as the cloud passed over us and disappeared, all in just a fraction of a second.

Again the screen in front of me only showed space, but where there had been nothing but emptiness for light-years, there were now suns and planetary systems.

Impossible suns and planetary systems.

Yet they were there. And we were just outside one of the systems.

But they were not the most startling change. That appeared directly in front of us. An alien craft now dominated our viewscreen.

Shiny black, it was shaped like two swept-back wings that met in the middle, with no body in between. It seemed to hover in space instead of float, bringing back memories of hawks diving at mice and eagles soaring. In all my years of seeing alien craft, I had never seen such a beautiful, and deadly-looking, craft.

It was my first sight of a ship of the Mist.

The fire to Sisko's back popped slightly, but otherwise there were no sounds in the entire bar. Everyone was listening to his story. He paused and took a long drink of ale, signaling that others should do the same. Sisko glanced around at his listeners. They did, but reluctantly, as if unwilling to break the story's spell.

Even Sotugh had been interested, although Sisko would not have known that if he had not spent a lot of time observing Worf. Klingons had a unique ability to look distracted when they were concentrating hard.

The Jibetian ale soothed the dryness in Sisko's throat. He took a second sip before satisfying a question of his own.

"So, Sotugh," Sisko asked. "Is this the point you got interested in the distress call?"

Sotugh laughed. "Of course, Captain," he said, leaning forward over his mug of blood wine. "We were monitoring your little rescue mission from the moment you left your station. When your ship disappeared, your mission became more than one of curiosity. Suddenly it became a threat to the Empire."

Sisko nodded, hoping Sotugh would continue.

Sotugh sat back, obviously—and surprisingly—not going to say another word.

Sisko studied him over the bottle of Jibetian ale. Sotugh was not going to make the telling of this story easy in any fashion.

"Your ship *disappeared?*" the catlike woman asked, glancing first at Sisko, then back at Sotugh.

"So, Captain," Cap said. "Don't hold us in suspense. What happened next?"

Sisko smiled, settled into a more comfortable position, and told them.

Four

I STOOD. I DID NOT LIKE THIS NEW SHIP, THIS POSITION, OR THESE NEW impossible stars and systems.

"Dax," I said, "where are we?"

"According to my sensors, we haven't moved, Captain."

"We are at the same coordinates," Worf said, confirming what Dax had said.

"The distress call is gone," Nog said.

Something was very, very wrong. We had been lured here. My feeling had been right. Here there were dragons; there was one before us, and I was not pleased.

I returned to my chair. "I want to know who that ship belongs to and what it wants with us," I said. I sat forward and studied it.

The ship was beautiful in a way that even now I cannot describe. Its design looked aerodynamic, as if the ship would function well in atmosphere, under water, or in space. Upon closer observation, the two wings, which had seemed attached to each other a moment before, had a small bulge between them, as unnoticeable as the body of a monarch butterfly or a Carnuiin round beetle. Both wings tapered back to fine points. No ports or weapons marred the perfect gleaming black surfaces.

"I'm not finding this ship anywhere in our database," Dax said. "The computer can't match it, and I've never seen anything like it."

That was quite a statement. In her many lives, Dax had seen a multitude of ships.

"I believe their shields are up," Worf said. "These readings are clear, but I do not trust them. They do not seem to be powering their weapons, but that does not mean they are not doing so."

"Let me know the moment the situation changes, Mr. Worf."

"Aye, sir."

I frowned at the ship. I blamed it for our transfer to this new place, even though I did not yet know exactly what, or where, this new place was. At that point, I was wondering how we had moved from one area of space to another without our instruments reflecting it.

"Captain," Chief O'Brien said. "That empty area of space I mentioned. It's no longer empty."

"I noticed, Chief."

"I mean, everything's back. The space dust. The debris. Everything that should be in an area of space."

"And five star systems," Dax added. "All inhabited."

"Most likely by the people who built that ship in front of us," I said.

"Those systems are stable," O'Brien said. "They weren't just moved there. It's as if they've *always* been right there. But they are on no modern star charts, and they weren't there a minute ago."

I was becoming more and more convinced that space hadn't changed, but that we had. "I want a double check of our equipment. I want to know if our coordinates have changed."

"My readings show they haven't," Dax said.

"I don't care about your readings," I said. "It seems to me that our systems might have been affected by that strange rupture we experienced. I want to know if we have found a wormhole, perhaps, or something else, something that moved us from one area of space to another."

"Nothing in our systems show that, Captain," Worf said. "I have already performed the necessary checks. If we have shifted positions, then our readings do not and will not show it."

"What about time?" I asked. If we remained in the same area of space, perhaps we had moved either forward or backward in time. That, too, had happened before, and it was unsettling to say the least. It would explain, however, why the distress signal had disappeared, and why the interplanetary systems had appeared.

"No, sir," Worf said. "We seem to be in the same place in time as we were when everything changed."

"I've scanned for chroniton particles, sir," O'Brien said. "They were the first things I scanned for, and I haven't found anything."

"Cadet, has that ship made any attempt to contact us?" I asked.

"Not yet, sir."

I glanced at him over my shoulder. "Do you expect them to?"

"If a ship mysteriously appeared in my path, sir, I would hail them. Sir."

"As would I," I said. "Dax, scan the surrounding area. See what else has changed."

While she worked, I stared at the ship facing us, and the impossible star systems behind it. Moving or hiding inhabited star systems just wasn't something that was done. At least not by any science known to the Alpha Quadrant. The bridge was silent except for the beep of consoles as my crew tried to determine exactly what had happened to us.

"Captain," Dax said, her fingers flying over the board in front of her. "*Deep Space Nine* is still in place and it seems to be functioning normally. We are still on the border of the Klingon Empire, and nothing about those systems seems different either."

Of all of the news I had just received, that was the part I did not like. If the star system had simply appeared, why hadn't *Deep Space Nine* disappeared?

I turned to the chief. "Are there differences between the readings we're taking of *Deep Space Nine,* and the readings we're getting of these new star systems?"

"Sir?" O'Brien asked, in that vaguely puzzled tone that he always used when he didn't understand one of my orders.

"I am thinking that perhaps the ship and the systems—"

"Were planted into our data systems," Dax said. "Of course." She bent over her console. So did the chief and Worf.

They all looked at me at the same time, and I knew before anyone spoke what their responses would be.

"I'm sorry, sir," O'Brien started. "But—"

"Captain," Worf said. "Three Klingon ships have just crossed the border. They are heading for our position."

Of course. The shift had attracted their attention. Not the first time I welcomed the arrival of the Klingons.

"That is," Sotugh said, "because you could not handle what you saw."

Every patron froze. The woman who was part of the middle-aged human couple at the bar said, a thread of irritation clear in her voice, "It seems to me that the captain was doing just fine."

"Fine," Sotugh said. "If he had been doing fine, he would not have needed help."

"Don't throw stones, Sotugh," Sisko said softly. "Your part in this tale is still ahead of us."

Sotugh stood abruptly and headed to the bar. He slammed his mug of blood wine on the wood, and the sound echoed. The strange alien at the piano brushed against the keys, seemingly accidentally, but the instrument mirrored the sound Sotugh had just made.

Sotugh ignored it. "More blood wine," he said. "And this time, make sure it is true blood wine."

"Our drinks are authentic," Cap said evenly. During Sisko's tale, he had moved from the front of the bar to the back. "Perhaps you would like some blood wine that dates from a different time period? The days of Kahless, perhaps?"

"Do not toy with me, bartender," Sotugh said. "Sisko's lies have put me in a disagreeable mood."

"How strange for a Klingon," the catlike woman said.

"I want to hear the rest," said a small, bristly alien with a large snout. He was standing on a chair toward the back, his chin barely crossing its top.

Sisko nodded to him. "As I said," Sisko continued, "three Klingon ships had just crossed the border. . . ."

"Dax," I said, "when will the Klingons arrive?"

"In sixteen minutes," Dax said.

I hoped we would have some answers by then.

"Bah!" Sotugh said from the bar.

"Sotugh," the catlike woman cautioned. "Let the man talk."

"Everything changed when that cloud surrounded us," I said. "Let's analyze that."

"I have been," O'Brien said. "I kept thinking that it was the cause of the change, but I can't see what it's done. It went over us, and everything changed, but I don't know if that's because it went over us, or if it appeared just as the ship did."

"They did not even scan us," Worf said.

"The ship or the cloudlike thing?" I asked.

"Neither," Worf said.

I stared at the ship floating in the center of the viewscreen, silently watching us. There didn't seem to be much choice. Since we had no idea what happened, and since it didn't look like we were going to figure it out soon, we had to gather more information.

"Hail the ship," I said.

"Aye, sir," Nog said. Then he bounced in his chair, unable to contain his excitement. "They're answering us, sir."

"Put them on the screen, Cadet."

I stood just as the screen flickered and changed. To my great surprise, the image of another human being faced me. Beside and slightly behind him was a thin, tall, almost wisplike humanoid of a species I had never seen before. The alien had a thin face with large, pupilless eyes and an even larger partially open mouth.

The human wore an unfamiliar gold uniform topped by a gold yachting cap. His hair and skin were dark, his eyes a vibrant blue. He had broad shoulders, a large smile, and was clearly in command. The alien also wore a form of the gold uniform, only without the yachting cap around his bald head. On the alien the uniform looked like a robe.

"Captain Sisko," the human said. "It's a pleasure meeting you. I'm Captain Victor and this is Councillor Näna of the High Council."

His use of my name made me instantly wary, but I did not show it. Instead, I said, "Was it your distress call that we answered?"

Captain Victor smiled and nodded. "Actually, it was a far distant ancestor's of mine. My family's name was Tucker. We left Earth hundreds of years ago in a ship called the *Dorren.* I just borrowed that distant relative's distress call to attract you."

"Obviously, it worked," I said, this time letting more of my displeasure show. "But you are clearly not in distress. Why didn't you contact us directly instead of using an ancient distress call to set a trap?"

"How can you judge on such a brief meeting, Captain, whether or not we are in distress?" he asked, but the question sounded lighthearted.

"We do not take distress calls lightly," I said.

"We know. That's why we used one to contact you."

"What do you want with us?" I asked.

Captain Victor laughed. "The answers to some of those questions will take a long time to explain. However, we used the ancient distress call to achieve the exact result we got. You came and the Klingons didn't."

"I'm afraid they're on their way now."

Captain Victor waved a hand as if brushing away a fly. "They can send as many ships as they want. It will make no difference to us."

"Captain!" Cadet Nog broke in. "I'm getting—"

"Not now, Cadet," I said without taking my gaze away from the screen.

"Captain, sir!" Nog said. "This is important."

I hoped Nog was right. He was still very new to Starfleet protocol. "Excuse me," I said to Captain Victor. Then I turned to Nog. "This had better be good, Cadet."

"Sir," Nog said, swallowing hard, "the station is hailing us on all emergency frequencies. And they have dispatched ships to search for us."

"To search for us?" I asked.

Again Cadet Nog swallowed hard, then looked up at me. "They seem to think we've vanished."

"You have," Captain Victor said, smiling. "At least as far as your station is concerned."

Behind him, Councillor Näna only nodded, his mouth opening and closing slowly.

• • •

"Your disappearance surprised us all," Sotugh said, returning to his chair, the blood wine sloshing out of his mug.

For the first time, Sotugh's interruption didn't seem to bother the other patrons. Only the catlike woman glared at him.

"How did the *Defiant*'s sudden vanishing act seem to other ships?" Cap asked Sotugh.

"There was no energy surge, no sudden movement," Sotugh said, shaking his head in disgust at the memory. "The ship simply vanished from our screens at the exact same moment the ancient distress call stopped. Ships do not vanish in open space."

"Unless they're cloaked," the bristly alien said.

"We know how to read the energy signature of a cloaked ship," Sotugh said with less annoyance than Sisko would have expected at such a comment.

"So you were coming to investigate," the middle-aged man at the bar said.

"Of course," Sotugh said, his words becoming almost a snarl. "We assumed the Federation was testing a new weapon to be turned against the Empire."

"If we were," Sisko said, "we wouldn't have done so that near the Klingon border."

"Your people can be sneaky, Sisko. It might have been a way of warning us."

"Logical," Cap said, nodding his head.

"And very Klingon," Sisko said.

"You would have done the same," Sotugh said.

Smiling, Sisko raised his ale bottle to Sotugh. "I would have."

Yellowish light flooded the entryway to the bar.

Sisko and a few of the others at the large table turned slightly to look. The door had opened, but then closed before he could see who had come inside.

"Arthur," Cap said. "Make sure everyone who needs a drink gets one. I'll greet our new guest."

Sisko held up his now almost empty bottle of ale for Arthur to see, then watched as Cap moved down the bar just as a Trill came around the corner from the front entry, his eyes blinking as he fought to adjust to the dim light. He was young, dressed in a thick jacket of unfamiliar design, and looked cold. Sisko found that odd, since the day outside was one of the hottest Sisko could remember in this area of Bajor.

The Trill had short hair, his neck markings clearly visible. He smiled at the group, but the smile was tired.

Sisko frowned at him. He had seen the Trill before; he was sure of it.

But not that sure. Sisko never forgot a face, and he knew—just as clearly as he knew that he'd seen the Trill—that he hadn't seen the Trill look quite like this.

Besides that, what was a Trill doing on Bajor, in a bar? Sisko made a mental note to ask the Trill if he got the chance.

"Welcome, Captain," Cap said to the Trill. "We have a warm fire and anything you care to drink."

Sisko watched as the Trill nodded, seemingly relieved to take off his coat and warm up. The silence in the bar was palpable and, of course, the Trill noticed.

"I'm sorry," he said. "I didn't mean to interrupt."

"Yes," Sotugh said. "Continue your story. There is much drinking to do."

"And, it seems," the catlike woman said, "much story left to tell."

"There is, at that," Sisko said. He took the new ale from Arthur, and then, with one more glance at the new arrival, went back to his story of the Mist.

Five

I WAS TRYING TO COMPREHEND ALL OF THE INFORMATION I HAD JUST RECEIVED. The station had sent out calls on all emergency frequencies searching for us; it had also sent ships. The Klingons were coming, in three ships as well. They had not answered the distress call, but they were coming now.

And this man on the screen in front of me, this Captain Victor, was telling me that we had vanished, that he and his friend, Councillor Näna, had lured us with the distress call as bait, and then reeled us in with the cloud of mist once we arrived.

I did not like being the fish.

I made a small motion to Cadet Nog, indicating that I wanted the sound momentarily severed between us and Captain Victor. I turned, as if I were surveying my crew, and said softly, in case Nog had misunderstood the order, "I want you all to check and see if there is anything different about our ship, whether they have cloaked us, or if there is something different on a molecular level. Do so quickly and with no communication."

Then I signaled Nog to continue the sound as if it had not been cut off. I finished my scan of the bridge and turned back to the screen.

"Satisfied, Captain?" Victor said to me. "Do you see now that the others believe you are gone?"

"What I see," I said calmly, even though I was not feeling calm, "is that somehow our signals and signatures are not reaching the others. I am not prepared to say that we have vanished."

Then I made a show of turning to Nog. "Answer the station, Cadet. Give them our location, and tell them that, for the moment, we are all right."

"Aye, sir," Nog said, looking at me rather strangely. It was Starfleet protocol to answer any emergency hail. I could tell from his expression that he had already done so and had received no response. I did not care. I wanted him to do so again, while Victor and Näna watched, so that we could observe any manipulation they might be causing. Perhaps our equipment would be able to locate what was causing the change in instruments.

For that was all I believed it to be, at the time. My mind did not accept that entire planetary systems could be invisible. I believed we were in the grip of a massive, and highly advanced, cloaking system. I knew that some planets had their own cloaking system, and we had, of course, the technology to cloak ships. It was a small stretch to believe that we could cloak entire areas of space as well.

A small stretch was all that I was willing to take.

"You know they can't hear you," Captain Victor said.

I felt my eyes narrow and my entire face become rigid. Whenever I got that look, my wife used to say, entire galaxies would crumble.

Captain Victor did not flinch. I decided to say nothing to him at the moment. Nothing would be more productive than the things I was thinking.

I turned to Nog, partly to prevent myself from saying anything to Victor. "Is there any response, Cadet?"

"No, sir," Nog said.

"Commander Worf, what about the Klingons?" I asked.

If I looked angry, Worf looked thunderous. "We are sending, sir, but there is no response. They, too, are acting as if we have disappeared."

"You have," Captain Victor said, his smile reaching his blue eyes almost as laughter.

I wanted to cut off all communication with that man. But I did not. I continued to ignore him, until I could put the situation back under my control.

"Check everything," I ordered my staff. "And keep trying to hail the station and the Klingons."

Then I turned back to face the screen. "All right, Captain," I said, with a slight sarcastic emphasis on the word *Captain.* "You seem to have all the answers. Share them."

"Gladly, Captain," Victor said. He glanced at his companion. Councillor Näna had still said nothing. His round mouth opened and closed occasionally, as if the movement were involuntary.

"A few moments ago," Victor said, "you couldn't see our ship or our homeworlds, could you?"

"No," I said. I knew what he was going to say, and I knew it would not be the answer I wanted. I wanted whys, not whats.

"Now," he said, "you and your fine ship have simply moved into our reality."

"The shimmering opening," O'Brien murmured.

Victor heard him. "It is a sort of doorway."

"It is not that simple," I said, this time letting the anger I felt punctuate each word. It was as if I put a space between each one.

"No, it's not," Victor said. "I would gladly explain everything to you, including our motives. But I think it might be better if you first moved your ship out of your current position."

"You want us out of your doorway," I said, not willing to move. I wanted to get out of there, and to do so now. I did not like how any of this was going.

Captain Victor laughed. "Of course not. That opening can be made anywhere with the right equipment. I'm just trying to save you some massive disorientation when the Klingon ships arrive."

At that moment, I did not understand what he meant. I would shortly.

"We've handled Klingons before," I said. "We will stay right here."

"Be my guest," Captain Victor said, shrugging as if he really didn't much care. "We'll move a short distance away and stand by. We've found it's just easier."

"Easier than what?" I asked.

"You'll see," Victor said, and then winked off the screen. In his place, his beautiful spaceship appeared, with the stars beyond it. The ship was moving slightly.

I sighed. "Once," I said, "just once, I would like to encounter a strange group who did not enjoy being mysterious."

No one laughed. No one was supposed to.

I sat down in my command chair, and surveyed the bridge. My crew was working as efficiently as always, but beneath that efficiency was a tension that I had seldom felt before.

"What are our new friends doing, Mr. Worf?" I asked.

"They appear to be changing position," he said.

"Just like Captain Victor said they would," Dax said.

I nodded.

"Captain," Worf said, "the Klingon ships are still heading this way."

"Have they responded to our hails yet?" I asked.

"No, sir, but they are heading directly for us."

"Is this some type of battlefield behavior that I'm not familiar with, Mr. Worf?"

"No, sir."

I frowned. "Let me know when they get here."

"Aye, sir," Worf said.

"Still no response from *Deep Space Nine,* sir," Nog said, anticipating my next question.

"The station is acting exactly by the book," Dax said, "following procedures that indicate there's an emergency on a ship. To the station we've gone missing."

I nodded as on the screen the alien ship turned like a bird on a gentle wind and moved off at slow impulse.

"Keep a very close eye on them, Mr. Worf," I said.

"I have been, Captain," Worf said. Then he bent his head slightly. "Captain, the Klingon ships will arrive in less than a minute. They are heading directly for our position."

"Hail them, Cadet. On all channels. Priority one."

"Yes, sir," Nog said.

I drummed my fingers on the arm of my chair. Victor wanted us to move out of the way of the Klingons. He knew that something was going to happen. Perhaps the Klingons couldn't see us. But they would be able to read our energy signature. Klingons knew how to search for cloaked ships.

"I'm getting no response, sir," Nog said.

"Captain," Worf said, "the Klingon ships are approaching uncloaked and fast. They have shields up, but have no weapons powered."

"Acting as if they don't see us," Dax said to herself.

"Hold this position. These are the last coordinates they had for us. They will search for us here," I said. "And continue hailing both the station and the approaching Klingon ships."

"Yes, sir," Nog said.

"Klingon ships dropping to impulse, slowing," Dax said.

That was what I had wanted to hear. I had expected it, but I was relieved nonetheless. The alien ship had settled into a position some distance from its original spot, but it was still close to us.

"Cadet, have you reached the Klingon ships?" I asked.

"No, sir. There's still no response." Nog's voice went up as it usually did when he panicked. But he was working hard, no matter how out of control he sounded.

"The lead Klingon ship is a Vor'Cha-class battle cruiser, the *Daqchov,*" Worf said. "HoD Sotugh in command. He is not usually like this. He is quite responsive—"

"Too fast!" Dax said. "Two thousand meters and closing too fast. They don't see us."

I had not expected this. I had thought they would come near these coordinates, not fly through them. "Get us out of their way!"

My order came too late.

As the *Defiant* moved, the *Daqchov* suddenly was on top of us, and then without the slightest hint of impact, we were inside the *Daqchov.*

Not just rammed through the side, but we actually passed through their hull. For a brief instant I got a glimpse of Sotugh sitting in his command chair, seemingly interested in his viewscreen, but clearly not braced for any impact.

Then a wave of nausea swept over me, as if the entire world had been turned inside out, along with the insides of my ear. I had no memory of ever being so dizzy before. The ship spun, and I had to cling to my command chair to keep my balance.

The rest of the crew was clinging too.

We were all superimposed on the inside of the *Daqchov.* It was as if the *Daqchov* had swallowed the *Defiant,* as if we all occupied the same space, like two holographic images, one on top of the other.

As we moved apart, Klingon hands went through me, Klingon equipment slid through my chair, and Klingon hull went through our bridge.

Then, as quickly as it had happened, the *Daqchov* was gone, back outside in space where it belonged.

"Damage reports?" I asked, my voice clear despite my dizziness.

"None, Captain." Dax sounded as shaky as I felt. Shaky and shocked.

My eyes had not lied to me. Part of the Klingon ship had passed right through the *Defiant* without any impact. That wasn't possible, yet my eyes and my twisted stomach told me it was.

Somehow, the *Defiant* had become a ghost ship.

And we were all the ghosts.

"Ghosts?" the catlike woman said. "But you weren't dead." She plucked on his sleeve to emphasize her point. "How could you be a ghost?"

Sisko smiled. The entire crowd in the bar was watching him. Most had empty glasses or mugs. He suspected Cap was not happy about that.

"Believe me, I wondered," Sisko said. "All that training from my Earth upbringing. All those superstitions rose in my head and were as quickly discarded. But they were there. I wondered if perhaps we had died and had not known it."

"Amazing," the woman at the bar said.

"Later," Sisko said, "Chief O'Brien said he had wondered the same thing. Worf seemed quite shocked as well. I know that the Klingons are superstitious people, but he has never spoken of that moment. Nog could not keep quiet about it when we returned to the station, and it was there I learned that the Ferengi view of the afterlife is, as we all suspected, different from ours. It has something to do with profit and latinum—and nothing to do with ghosts."

"So what had actually happened?" asked the middle-aged man at the bar.

"I'll get to that," Sisko said, "as soon as everyone has a moment to refill their drinks." He looked around the bar to see where he could get rid of some of his.

"Cap," he said as he stood. "Would it be possible to get something to snack on while I finish this?"

"This story will take forever the way he is telling it," Sotugh said. "You had better feed us."

Cap smiled.

Sisko got out of his chair. His body creaked slightly. He had been sitting awhile. Sotugh was right; it was taking him a while to tell this story. But then, it had taken time to happen. His audience seemed interested, and as long as he had them, he could tell the story the way he wanted to.

He scanned the bar for the rest room.

Cap noticed what he was doing and nodded toward the back of the bar.

Sisko walked past the serving station, past some stairs, and across from a storage room he found the bathroom. He wasn't the only one who needed to use it; it seemed his entire audience stood after he did, using his break as an excuse for one of their own.

When he returned, the drinks were replenished, and bowls of bright green Betazoid fruitnuts graced each table. Sotugh had clearly complained about the choice. Before him, Cap had placed some *bregit* lung, a Klingon dish I hadn't thought possible to get in a bar like this on Bajor.

Another bottle of Jibetian ale sat in front of Sisko's place. He had had more to drink since he'd come in here than he'd had in months, but he wasn't feeling any effects yet. He wondered if it would hit him all at once.

He decided that he didn't care. Bashir had ordered him to relax and that was what he was doing. If they needed him, they knew where to find him.

"Where was I?" he asked as he sat down.

"Ghosts," several people said at once.

He smiled again. "Ah, yes," he said, and continued.

Our ships had separated, but my crew and I were still feeling the effects of the strange collision. We were all dizzy. Chief O'Brien was a pale shade of green. Cadet Nog had his hands on his lobes, as if he were trying to balance himself by holding his ears in a level position. At that moment, if that had worked for humans, I would have done the same thing.

Dizziness for a human is bad. I imagine that for a Ferengi it is intolerable.

Worf was clutching both sides of his console, but staring straight ahead.

Dax had her head bent, her eyes closed.

We all seemed to breathe in at the same time, to exhale together, as we tried to readjust our systems. Mine came under control quickly. Cadet Nog did not seem so lucky.

I was about to say something when the door to the turbolift opened, and our ship's doctor, Julian Bashir, staggered onto the bridge. He looked almost as green as the chief.

"What in heaven's name was that?" he asked. He put a hand out, used one of the consoles to keep his balance, and then steadied himself. "One moment I was getting sickbay ready, the next thing I know, sickbay has been invaded by a Klingon ship, and then suddenly, the thing is gone. *What happened?"*

"I'll tell you as soon as we know, Doctor," I said. "Dax, where are the Klingons now?"

"Setting up positions two thousand meters from our present location."

"Keep an eye on them. I don't want a repeat of that."

"Neither do I," Dax said.

Nog was leaning against his console to keep his head from moving. "Captain," he said, his voice a shadow of its former self, "Captain Victor is hailing us."

"Put him on screen," I said.

This time, the screen filled with Victor's face. I could not see the rest of his bridge or Councillor Näna. Victor pretended to show concern, but his blue eyes were twinkling. I didn't like or trust this man.

"Mistrusting him seems appropriate to me," Sotugh muttered into his blood wine. "You should have shot him on sight."

Sisko grinned at Sotugh. "That seemed appropriate to me too. But Starfleet wouldn't have approved."

"Starfleet does not approve of many appropriate things," Sotugh said.

"What did Victor say?" Cap asked.

"Are you and your crew recovering?" Victor asked. "The experience is not harmful, but not pleasant, either."

"We seemed to have survived whatever just happened with only a few lingering side effects," I said.

Now Captain Victor actually let himself chuckle. "The side effects will pass. But now do you understand why we moved out of the way of the Klingon ships?"

I did not answer his question. "I think it's time for that explanation," I said.

Captain Victor's smile grew. "Since I assume you would still like to remain in this area, would you like to join me on my bridge, or may I join you?"

I wasn't about to go to their bridge. "You are welcome to come on board here," I said.

Victor nodded, as if he expected me to say that.

"Mr. Worf," I said, "lower the shields."

The screen went blank. Then, before Worf could voice the objection I was sure he was going to voice, Captain Victor shimmered into form, facing me.

He had beamed through our shields, an event I didn't like in the slightest.

I stood slowly to make sure that my balance had returned. It hadn't completely. The cabin spun, as if the ship were out of control. Only I knew all the spinning was going on inside my own head. "Welcome, Captain," I managed to say.

"Please sit," Victor said, smiling. "I know how you must feel after passing through the Klingon ship."

I did not sit down. It was my ship, and I would be the one who gave the commands. Although I did wish that I had not stood up.

Slowly, the spinning eased.

"You promised answers," I said.

He nodded and walked to the main screen. I noted that all the members of my crew, from the doctor to Dax, watched him closely. If Victor tried anything, I doubted anyone on my crew would hesitate. He would find himself on the floor, stunned by a phaser, in a matter of seconds.

Apparently my crew disliked being dizzy as much as I did. And they seemed to distrust this Captain Victor as much as I did.

He stopped and faced the main screen in such a manner that he could partially face me and partially face the screen.

"I'll make this as quick as I can," he said. "There isn't much time."

I waited.

"The five systems you see in front of you," he said, pointing at the screen, "are the homeworlds of the Mist."

"The Mist?" I asked.

This time it was Dax who nodded. She was still staring at Captain Victor. "Of course," she said. "That's what happened to them."

She spoke as if everything had become clear to her.

It was not yet clear to me. Not in the slightest.

Six

THE DIZZINESS HAD VANISHED, LEAVING ONLY A SLIGHT RINGING IN MY EARS. I barely noticed the change. I was watching Captain Victor. He was watching me, apparently to gauge my reaction.

"Dax," I said. "You know of this?"

"I know of the Mist," she said. "But I'd rather hear what Captain Victor has to say."

"As would I," Worf said. Somehow his curt, clipped tone made those three words sound like a threat. Victor caught the implication too.

"I only know the Mist as a legend," I said. "Like the ancient Greek gods from Earth, or the bottle creatures from the lost worlds of Ythi Four."

"Yeah," O'Brien said. "I rather feel like an Englishman in Ireland, being told the little people are real."

"The Mist are real enough," Victor said.

"So how do real beings become legend and not get discovered?" I asked.

Victor glanced at the screen, a half-smile playing on his face. Then, with a dramatic sweep of his arm, he pointed toward the five star systems behind the Mist ship. "At one time," he said, "those five systems were in normal space. This was over a thousand years before Cochrane invented the first human warp drive."

Victor turned to me to see if I was listening. He seemed to like dramatic pauses. As he spoke, he would gesture broadly. Young Nog said later that it seemed as if Victor expected to be paid in latinum for each listener he convinced.

"About the time our ancestors were fighting through the dark ages," he said, including me, the chief, and Dr. Bashir in that statement, "the Mist were feeling crowded by the expansion of other races around them into space. The Mist of that time were a very private people who had no desire to expand beyond their own systems."

His use of the past tense bothered me, but I let him continue.

"Through a series of circumstances I'm not familiar with," Captain Victor said, "the Mist invented a device that simply shifts the molecular structure of all material slightly out of phase with normal matter. The shift is so slight that it almost can't be measured. The effect was that the shifted matter didn't exist in the normal universe."

"Not at all?" Nog asked, and then looked at me, as if I were going to chastise him for speaking. I did not even look at him directly, which, I believe, made him even more uncomfortable.

"Not at all," Victor said.

"Yet it's there," O'Brien said. "Completely invisible to those around it.

"So why can we see the normal universe," Dax asked. "And the shifted worlds can't be seen?"

"I honestly don't know the reason," Captain Victor said, "but I am sure one of our scientists could explain."

"Invisible systems and ships," Worf said.

Captain Victor said, "Not only invisible to those in the normal universe, but nonexistent."

"Thus the Klingon ship could pass through this ship," O'Brien said.

"And the effect we felt?" I asked.

"Simply a side effect of the fact that two bodies of matter are occupying the same basic space," said Victor. "Nothing more. And the Klingons felt nothing."

"We felt something," Sotugh said, *bregit* lung dripping off his fingers. "We have always felt something in that region of space. It is why we try to avoid it as much as possible."

"I know of the area of which you speak," said the small bristly alien. Until it spoke up, its snout had been resting on the chair's back. It had to lift its head to talk. "There are spacefaring legends of that sector. My people had strange dreams as they flew through that area. The Betazoids avoid it altogether. It makes them ill. Perhaps humans feel nothing, but it is not true of every species."

Around the room, a handful of others nodded. The Trill leaned back in his chair, a half-smile playing on his face. His gaze met Sisko's, and Sisko got the sense that the Trill was noting what he was: that it was becoming a contest among the patrons to see whose species was sensitive enough to "feel" the Mist.

Cap seemed to notice it too. And, like Sisko, he knew which way it was going to go. Add enough intoxicants, and every species reverted to childhood. Pretty soon, the entire thing would degenerate into a "my species is better than your species" brawl.

"So," Cap said loudly, effectively silencing the growing debate. "We know that Victor believed the Klingons felt nothing—"

Sotugh started to speak, but Cap continued—"even though we know that they did feel something. Then what?"

Sisko heaved a small sigh of relief. He was wondering how he was going to return to DS9 battered from a bar brawl and still convince Dr. Bashir that he'd rested.

"Well," he said, "I glanced up at the Klingon ship *Daqchov* floating near the Mist ship. Wouldn't they be shocked to know they were so close to another alien ship?"

"Shocked?!?" Sotugh said. "Klingons are not shocked. We are never shocked. We—"

"Sotugh," several patrons said at once.

The cat-woman finished the thought. "Would you kindly shut up and let him talk? How would you like it if someone continually interrupted your stupid operas?"

"They are not stupid," Sotugh said.

"Could have fooled me," the cat-woman said.

"Prrghh, Sotugh, please," Cap said. "The others want to listen to the story, not your bickering."

"That's what I was trying to tell him," the catlike woman, Prrghh, said haughtily.

"Then take your own advice, woman." Sotugh leaned back in his chair. "Continue with your lies, Sisko."

Sisko did not take the bait. He took another swig of Jibetian ale, and went back to the story.

Chief O'Brien looked as if the entire discussion was a revelation to him. "So that's why this area of space is so clear," he said.

Captain Victor nodded. "It has to be kept clear to cut down on episodes of the dizziness and dislocation that you felt."

"But the energy to maintain such a shift," Chief O'Brien said, "must be enormous."

Captain Victor shook his head. "Once shifted, the matter remains in that constant state unless purposefully shifted back."

Dax had a slight frown on her face. "When the planets shifted, the Mist would have had to shift everything. Air, food, water. Everything that sustained life, including the suns. I find that hard to believe."

"It happened," Victor said. "And more. The Mist called this the Great Move. Their history makes it clear that the shift was a gigantic undertaking that took years."

While I found all of this fascinating, and just vague enough to be confusing scientifically, I had other concerns. Many parts of this story made no sense, at least not with the things I could see.

"How did you shift into Mist space?" I asked.

Captain Victor laughed. "My ancestors ran into some problems near this area of space with their ship. The Mist saved the ship, as they have done with many other ships over the centuries. Many of my ancestors decided to remain on the Mist worlds. Like many other races, we have been accepted in their culture. I am now a tenth-generation member of the Mist community."

I made a small, noncommittal sound in the back of my throat. Dr. Bashir looked at me. He knew that sound was my way of continuing a conversation, but of letting my skepticism out.

"So," I said, "you claim the Mist have been completely out of touch with any other race, except for those members of those races that it has 'rescued.' "

I put quite an emphasis on the word *rescued.* I wondered if we had been "rescued" as well.

"Why would we be in touch with any other race? We opted to leave this part of space, to live in our own universe, so to speak," Victor said. "The affairs, the wars, of the normal universe do not affect us."

"Well," I said softly, "something must have affected you, Captain. You knew enough about our universe to lure us here."

"True," he said.

"And I suspect you would not have done so if your problem was restricted to your own space."

He smiled at me, but there was no laughter in the smile. And with that look I distrusted him even more.

"The Mist have no desire to expand," he said, "but we do have need of room for growth beyond our five systems."

"Oh," I said, not liking where this was heading.

Victor held up his hand for me to wait. "Two hundred years ago," he said, "we found another three systems that were uninhabited, in an area just beyond the Bajoran system. Since they were uninhabited, and no race seemed to be claiming them, they wouldn't be missed."

"You shifted them," Dax said.

"Exactly," Victor said. "We shifted the systems and began colonization."

"And you have had trouble with the colonies," Worf said. He sounded as coolly skeptical as I felt. Luring us away from *Deep Space Nine,* shifting us into their space, and then not giving us proper warning about the effect of the Klingon ship hadn't warmed any of us to Captain Victor.

Captain Victor glanced at Worf as if his question were rude. Worf glowered back, as only a Klingon can.

"We do not glower," Sotugh said.

Several patrons shushed him. Sisko suppressed a smile.

"It is a moody word," Sotugh said. "Klingons are not moody."

They shushed him again.

"Well," Sotugh muttered into his blood wine. "We are not."

Sisko forced himself to continue before he laughed. "It seemed that Victor did not like what he saw in Worf's face."

"Better," Sotugh said. "No human should like what he sees in a Klingon face."

"So," Sisko said, "Victor . . ."

. . . looked directly at me. "There were no troubles," he said, and then he sighed. It seemed as if some of the energy left him. "Until this last generation of colonists. Over half of the colonies' populations were made up of the descendants of ships like my ancestors. There are humans, Cardassians, Jibetians, Bajorans, and a dozen other races on those three colony systems."

"All living under the Mist system," Dax said, "but growing tired of the Mist rules."

Captain Victor nodded. "It would seem that way. Under the leadership of a human named John David Phelps Jackson, the colonies have been demanding more and more."

I crossed my arms. "You brought us to help your side?"

Captain Victor shook his head. "Not really. We lured you here to get you, your fine crew, and your ship away from *Deep Space Nine.*"

I had not liked this conversation from the beginning, but now I hated it. I felt O'Brien stir behind me. Worf leaned forward on his console. Dax clenched her teeth, making her jaw seem quite firm.

Dr. Bashir took a step forward and asked the question we all were thinking. "And why would that be?"

"Because," Captain Victor said, "Jackson and the Mist colonists are about to shift *Deep Space Nine* into our reality and take it over."

"What?" I came up out of my chair. "They have no right to our station. *You* have no right to our station."

Victor stood calmly before the screen, as if he had expected my reaction.

"Of course we don't," he said.

I turned to Dax. "Is the station still there?"

"Yes," she said. "It's still in normal space, and still acting like we've gone missing. But . . ."

She bit her lower lip and looked up at Victor. The look she leveled at him should have caused him to quake in his boots.

"But?" Bashir asked. He, too, seemed unnaturally calm, something he had learned in his days on *Deep Space Nine.* He had learned to mask the strong emotions—his anger—behind a veneer of calm.

"But," she said, "now I count twenty Mist ships taking up positions surrounding it."

I turned back to face Captain Victor. "It would seem," I said, "that by luring us here, you are helping them."

"Oh," he said, shrugging, "your presence on the station would have done nothing to stop the takeover." He sounded as if this sort of thing were routine.

Worf growled behind me. If I hadn't seen Victor's nervous glance at the commander, I wouldn't have realized that Klingons made him uneasy. But he went on as if he were fine.

"Imagine having twenty ships suddenly appear out of nowhere around your station."

"The station would be able to defend against twenty ships," Worf said.

"Maybe," Victor said, "but not as well with hundreds of men with weapons beaming in beside every member of your crew, before they had time to even react."

"Just as you beamed in here with our shields still up?"

"Exactly," Captain Victor said.

"They beam through shields?" Prrghh asked. "I hadn't understood that before."

"You should have been listening more carefully," Sotugh said, and belched loudly. He got up without excusing himself, moved around the end of the bar, and disappeared through the doorway leading to the bathroom.

"The captain mentioned it," the middle-aged woman at the bar said, "when Victor beamed in."

"I know," Prrghh said. "It's just the juxtaposition of details . . ." Then she smiled and held up the tiny glass of blue liquid she had been sipping from. ". . . or perhaps it is the nectar of Honeybirds." And then she laughed, a warm throaty sound.

Sisko smiled at her. He didn't feel as if he'd had too much Jibetian ale, although he could do with more than fruitnuts. "Do you have a kitchen?" he asked Cap.

"We serve some things," Cap said. "What would you like?"

"Let's see your bar menu," Sisko said.

"What about the story?" the bristly creature asked, lifting his snout off his chair.

"He was waiting for me," Sotugh said, adjusting his clothing as he walked. He was not walking quite straight.

"I am hungry," Sisko said.

"But the story—"

"I'm still thinking about beaming through shields," Prrghh said. "Can you do that, Sotugh?"

"Do you think I'd tell you if I could?" he asked and sat down heavily.

"What about your station?" the Trill asked. The question sounded more like a prompt than a need to know. "Did they take it over?"

"That's what we were trying to find out," Sisko said.

My crew, except for Dr. Bashir, were huddled over their stations, trying to discover exactly what was happening on *Deep Space Nine.*

"Captain," Dax said, her voice showing the worry she felt, "two Mist ships are shoving a large asteroid directly at the station."

"An asteroid?" I asked. I had not expected that. "How long until impact?"

"Two minutes and ten seconds," Dax said.

"Cadet, send a warning on all channels. See if you can send something slightly out of phase, if you can send a message from our reality to theirs."

"Captain, communications aren't really my—"

"Do it, Cadet. Dax, help him." I knew it was a long shot, but I wanted to try everything. "Chief, see if you can shift us back. We need to warn them. I will not just sit here while someone tries to destroy my station."

"Don't worry, Captain," Victor said in a voice that was much too smarmy for my liking. "The asteroid has been shifted into this reality. Its only function is to pass through the station."

"To disorient everyone," Worf said.

"Exactly," Captain Victor said. "After the asteroid passes through the station, they will shift the station and then beam in and take it over."

"Continue sending messages, Cadet. Chief—"

"I am, sir."

"I know," O'Brien said, huddled over his console.

"So," I said to Victor, "as far as any of the ships guarding the station, and the wormhole, are concerned, the station will suddenly disappear."

Captain Victor nodded.

I faced the Mist captain. "And just what do they plan to do with my station?"

Captain Victor shifted his gaze for a moment back to the viewscreen, then looked me right in the eye and said, "They plan on using it to conquer the Mist homeworld."

Seven

"YOU HAVE NACHOS?" SISKO ASKED, INTERRUPTING HIMSELF AS HE STARED at Cap's bar menu. "Chicago-style pepperoni pizza? Jambalaya? And dirty rice?" The selection was simply amazing. He was shocked.

The patrons around him groaned. "Captain, please, continue," the bristly alien said.

"And you have heart of *targ,*" Sotugh said, leaning over Sisko's shoulder. The smell of blood wine mixed with *bregit* lung was nearly overpowering.

"This is an extensive menu," Sisko said.

"Captain, please," the bristly alien said, slapping its fingered paw on the chair.

"If you see something you'd like, I'd suggest ordering it quickly," Cap said. "You don't want to see a Quilli get mad. At least not in here."

The bristles on the little creature were standing on end. "You have abandoned the story at a good section," it said, climbing on the slats of the chair's back. The chair tottered precariously. "I demand that you continue."

"I will," Sisko said. Those bristles did look like quills, and if the Quilli could shoot them, like so many bristled creatures could, it would be bad. Very bad indeed.

"Now!" the Quilli growled.

"Are your nachos real?" Sisko asked Cap.

Patrons began moving away from the Quilli. Some ducked under tables. Others headed toward the door.

"Yes," Cap said, edging toward the bar, his gaze on the Quilli.

"Good," Sisko said. "I'd like a large."

"Captain, I demand to know what happened next!" The Quilli's bristles were trembling.

"What happened next?" Sisko said, looking at the small creature. Its chair was wobbling. The Trill got up and steadied it. The Quilli simply climbed higher.

"I put my entire staff on finding a way to get us phased into our own space."

"That's all?" The Quilli's little voice was rising.

"No," Sisko said. "That's not all."

"Keep broadcasting warnings," I ordered Dax and Nog. "Try anything. Chief, find a way to get a signal across."

My crew moved swiftly. I was furious. I took a step closer to Captain Victor. I wanted nothing more than to force him to return us to our home. But I knew his agenda was greater than that.

He looked amused. His blue eyes were twinkling, although he was not smiling. Not quite. "I'm afraid that you won't be able to get any signal between the two realities. Nothing crosses from this way to the normal universe. However, we can listen in on anything going on in the normal universe."

"Captain, I can't find the phase variance, let alone break it," O'Brien said. "Not in this amount of time."

"He's right, Benjamin," Dax said. "Miracles simply aren't possible at the moment."

I crossed the bridge. I stopped in front of Victor. He was my height, except for that silly yachting cap. I wanted to yank it off his head, but I didn't.

"Take us back," I said.

"Captain, really," Victor started.

"*Take us back,*" I said again.

He shrugged. "If that's what you want, but warning your crew will only cause undue bloodshed."

"Shift us back. *Now.*"

"Fine." He took off the cap himself and stuck it under his arm, like those old nineteenth-century paintings of Napoleon. I almost expected him to put one hand in his shirt. "But if you want to come back across, simply return to this point and my ship will bring you here."

"We will not want to come back," I said.

"Don't be so hasty in your predictions, Captain," he said, and chuckled. Then he tapped his foot, and disappeared.

"That was a quick transport," O'Brien said.

"Maybe he was never actually here," Dax said.

"Check the logs later, people," I said. "Right now we have to warn the station."

At that moment a line in space seemed to form in front of the *Defiant,* widening and growing with a thin, white mist. It swept over the ship from front to back almost instantly and then was gone.

The Mist ship had disappeared.

"The Klingon ships and the station are hailing us, sir," Nog said.

Home. I hadn't realized how much I missed it. And yet I hadn't been out of sight of it.

"How long until the asteroid hits the station?" I asked.

"At the speed the Mist ships were pushing it," Dax said, "we have less than one minute. But I can no longer see it, or any of the Mist ships."

"Put the station on screen," I said. "Make sure the channel is secure."

"It is," Nog said.

"Secure, Captain," Dax said, at the same time, obviously double-checking the cadet on such an important order.

"Captain," Major Kira said as her face appeared on screen. "Where were you? We were—"

"Major," I said, "you have exactly thirty seconds before an attack on the station. Go to red alert. The first sign of the attack will be dizziness; then a hundred or so armed troops will beam into the station even though the shields are up. If you can't hold Ops, disable anything you can, especially shields and weapons. Do you understand?"

"Aye, sir," Kira said. She had already started to turn away, to issue orders, as the screen went blank.

"Dax," I said. "Move us two hundred meters closer to the station and hold that position."

Silence filled the bridge of the *Defiant* as I sat and stared at the screen.

"Captain," Nog said, breaking the silence. "The Klingons are insistent, sir."

" 'The Klingons are insistent,' " Sotugh mocked. "Of course we were insistent. You appeared out of nowhere, in a position that we had just flown through."

"Shhh," the Quilli said.

Sotugh turned. Half the patrons ducked again. "Don't shush me, you pointed pipsqueak."

"You are interrupting the story," the Quilli said. Its bristles slowly rose.

Sisko wondered if he should duck. That small alien seemed to make most of the patrons nervous.

"I am part of the story," Sotugh said. "I want to make sure Sisko gets it right." He leaned over his chair and waved at Arthur, the kid behind the bar. "Where is my heart of *targ?"*

Arthur looked at Cap, who rose from the back bar, holding a blue bottle. "I don't recall you ordering any," Cap said.

"Of course I ordered some," Sotugh said. "When Sisko ordered his—neshos."

"Nachos," Sisko said quietly.

"The story!" the Quilli shouted.

"Did you know," the Trill said, crossing his arms and smiling, "that stories are the most important form of commerce on the Quilli homeworld?"

"Are you saying I'm trying to steal this one for a profit?" the Quilli snapped. Its bristles were shivering.

"Of course not," the Trill said. "I was merely explaining your insistence. Humans can be sloppy storytellers, especially when they're drinking. Sometimes they begin a story and never finish it. Sometimes they start in the middle and insist on an audience. Sometimes they tell a story that's too long for everyone to follow. With humans you never know what you might get."

"And sometimes they are filled with their own importance," Sotugh said.

"Are you saying," Sisko asked, slightly offended, "that I am a sloppy storyteller?"

"You do allow a lot of interruptions," the Trill said.

"If he were a better storyteller, there would be no interruptions," Sotugh said.

"You comprise the bulk of my interruptions," Sisko said.

"See? I am here to make certain of your accuracy," Sotugh said. "And obviously you are not accurate enough."

"He is a fine storyteller," the Quilli said. "In fact, he is an excellent storyteller and the story is entertaining me. I object to the interruptions. I want them to stop."

"I don't think that's possible," the Trill said, "given the mixture of customers here." He smiled as he glanced around the table. "But then you should know that. How many stories do you leave here with, anyway?"

The Quilli whirled so fast that Sisko almost didn't see the movement. One bristle stuck out double the length of the others.

"Any more insults, Trill," the Quilli said, "and you will lose an eye. Is that clear?"

The Trill held up his hands. He did not stop smiling. "No harm meant."

The bristle slipped back into place. "None taken," the Quilli said. It turned back to its position. "Captain, I believe you had just gotten a message from the Klingons."

Sisko cleared his throat. "Yes," he said. "Right." He smiled impishly at his audience. "I had Dax put the Klingons on screen. Captain Sotugh appeared. He looked—younger—then—"

"Didn't we all?" Sotugh mumbled.

"—and quite dashing in his uniform."

"Enough of the flattery, Sisko," Sotugh said. "Go on with the story before the warthog decides to blind us all."

Sisko's grin grew. "You'll let me tell this part?"

"I am waiting for my heart of *targ,*" Sotugh said.

"I take that for a yes," Sisko said. "Well, Captain Sotugh appeared on screen and said, without preamble . . ."

"Captain Sisko, we know you just sent a message to the station. What kind of trick is this? We demand to know what sort of cloaking device you are using."

"It is no trick," I said. "Train your sensors on *Deep Space Nine* and stand by."

"I cannot see why I—"

I told Nog to cut the communication, and he did. Now, remember, this is during that recent period of hostilities between the Federation and the Klingon Empire. I knew that I was taking a risk—

"Yeah, you know, I was wondering . . ." A chalk-colored alien rose from his spot against the wall. Sisko tried not to blink in surprise. He had thought the alien was a line of dirt until he moved. "If you had hostilities, how come you let one of their number on your ship?"

"Worf always was different," Cap said.

Everyone looked at him. Sisko wondered how he knew Worf.

"I don't care!" the Quilli said. "It's not relevant to the story. Will you please do something about these interruptions?"

"Actually, the question is slightly relevant," Sotugh said. "But of greater relevance is the risk that Sisko took in cutting me off. I followed his instruction—any good commander would, just to see what kind of trick he was playing—but I also raised my shields and gave an order to power my weapons. If we had not seen—"

"What did you see?" the little creature was shaking with fury.

Sisko met Sotugh's gaze. "I'll take it from here," Sisko said softly.

"I think that's best," Sotugh said.

"The station disappeared," Sisko said. "Oh, not right away. First, Dax said . . ."

"The asteroid should be passing through the station right about now."

We knew what they were going through. I don't know about the others, but my ears rang in sympathy, my inner ear spun slightly, and a hint of dizziness returned.

It happened too quickly, and Captain Victor knew he had sent us back too late. I could only clench my fists and hope that my first officer, Major Kira, who had fought in more tight situations than the rest of us had seen together—with, perhaps, the exception of Dax—would find a way out of this one too.

And that was when the station disappeared.

"It's gone, Benjamin," Dax said softly.

The silence on the bridge was intense.

I sat for one moment.

One long moment, feeling more fury than I had felt since my wife died. Captain Victor had played us like we were his favorite violin. He had taken each string, plucking and plucking, until we became the melody he wanted.

The melody, the chords, the over- and undertones. We had been played, and he had known what he was doing.

I could see his smile as he beamed off our ship. *Don't be so hasty in your predictions, Captain,* he had said, and then he had chuckled.

Chuckled!

Knowing that his people were about to steal my station.

"Captain," Nog said. "The starships around the station are going crazy. There are more hails here than I've ever seen. And the Klingons are demanding to speak to you, sir."

I stood. I would take care of this, and then I would take care of the Mist.

All of them.

"Cadet," I said, "open a channel to all the Federation ships in the area of the station, and send this message directly to Starfleet headquarters. And patch in the Klingons."

"Yes, sir," Nog said after a moment of looking very fearful. I saw Dax bend over her instruments, and move a hand, helping him. Finally, Nog said, "Channel open, sir."

I took a step toward our screen.

"This is Captain Sisko on the *Defiant. Deep Space Nine* has been taken by a rebel group of the legendary people called the Mist."

I paused for a moment to let that surprising statement sink in to all who were listening. "My information on this takeover is limited, but as soon as I know more, I will send it to you on this channel. Please stand by."

I had Nog cut the broadcast.

"Sir, we are being hailed by everyone," he said.

I ignored that. I knew my statement would provide more questions than answers.

"Old man," I said to Dax. "Move us back to the coordinates where we came out of Mist space."

Dax nodded.

"We are going back over?" Worf said.

"Do you have any other ideas, Commander?"

"No, sir," Worf said. He scowled at his panel, then said, "But it is a trap."

"People," I said, glancing around at my bridge crew, "that band of Mist have just declared war on the Federation, whether they intended to or not. And we need the other band of Mist to help us get our station back."

"I don't believe we can trust them, sir," O'Brien said. "They want us to go back."

"The chief is right, sir," Bashir said. "If they truly wanted to prevent the capture of the station, they would have approached us sooner."

"Captain Victor is not to be trusted," Dax said.

"This is not a debate," I said, and my crew fell silent. But right at that moment I agreed with everything they were saying. I knew it was some sort of trap, I knew Victor couldn't be trusted, yet at that moment I had no choice if we were ever going to see *Deep Space Nine* in real space again.

"We're in position," Dax said.

As she finished her statement, a rift in space opened up. For the second time in one day, the Mist swallowed us.

Eight

The five impossible planetary systems had returned, and with them, the beautiful but deadly-looking Mist ship, with its arching wings and small main section. The shift was as disorienting as coming out of hyperspace for the first time. The mind cannot accept the difference: it knows where it was, and believes it should still be there.

I stood as we crossed through, wondering why we did not feel any real physical effects. Apparently Dr. Bashir wondered the same thing, for he frowned and took an empty console, quickly going to work.

Dax was watching the screen and the helm. The chief was monitoring the shift so that he might repeat it, working to figure out exactly what was happening.

I spread my legs slightly, bracing myself. I was tired of the games the Mist were playing. For the second time we had crossed into their space, and for the second time, I felt as if we were lured, even though this time it was my decision to come. The first time had been a rescue signal. The second time was *Deep Space Nine.*

Bait.

They had my station and I had gone for the bait. Yet they did not know what they had done. By taking the station they had left ships abandoned in space. They left the wormhole vulnerable, Bajor vulnerable. An entire section of space normally policed by the Federation was now open to attack from any and all sides.

We had to resolve this quickly, or there would be great loss of life—losses of a type that I couldn't even predict except that they would happen.

I wondered about the station: what was going on inside her. Kira and Odo could handle themselves. But what of Quark's and the other businesses on the Promenade? What was happening in the Bajoran temple and Garak's tailor shop? Had the Mist placed its troops all over the station or just in Ops?

I longed to know. I wanted to be both there and here, in order to fight properly.

"Captain," Dax said. "The station is now visible to us."

"And the Klingons are screaming at us, sir," Nog said. He sounded breathless.

At the moment, I did not care about the Klingons.

"We cared about you," Sotugh said. "You had vanished again. We thought that perhaps you were planning some sort of military maneuver."

The Quilli growled.

Sotugh ignored it, and leaned back, shouting, "Where is my heart of *targ?*"

"Coming, sir," Arthur said.

Sisko proceeded as if the interruption hadn't happened.

I did not look at the cadet. I had a rudimentary plan, and its key was timing. "Hail Captain Victor," I said.

"Yes, sir," Nog said.

"Chief, what have you learned?" I asked while I waited for Victor to respond.

"There's a lot of information here," O'Brien said, "but I'm not sure it's what I need."

"Figure it out," I said.

"Yes, sir," he said.

Then Nog said, "I'm putting Captain Victor on screen, sir."

Captain Victor's face filled the screen. He was grinning, his teeth impossibly white against his skin. He still had his cap off, and his dark hair was sticking up in tufts. Behind him, I could barely make out Councillor Näna, his strange face staring unblinkingly at me through his huge eyes.

"All right," I said. "We are back. But we are here to retrieve *Deep Space Nine.* I expect your assistance, and I expect it now."

"Captain," Victor said, spreading his hands. "We have done nothing but assist you."

"You have done nothing but play games with us," I said. "And the games are over. Now. The loss of *Deep Space Nine* will cause a crisis of unparalleled proportions in the Alpha Quadrant. We must recover the station before word of this gets out."

• • •

"Too late," Sotugh said. "Word of it was already getting out. Within a minute of your second disappearance, I was picking up distress beacons from several ships."

Arthur swooped by with a platter heaping with nachos. The shredded beef smelled spicy. Jalapeños and black olives mixed with several cheeses and tomatoes on top. They were covered with homemade guacamole and real sour cream.

Sisko's mouth watered. He reached for a chip, then pulled back as the grease burned his fingertips. The nachos were too hot to eat.

"The story," the Quilli said, and tilted its chair toward Sisko.

"Oh, *relax,*" the Trill said, putting a foot on the chair's rung, and slamming it to the floor. The Quilli fell backward, its bristles sticking in the nearby tabletop, breaking its fall.

"On Quilla," it said, "you would die for that."

"On Quilla," the Trill said, "I would never do that."

Sisko sighed softly. He would have to wait a moment anyway to eat the nachos. He might as well continue.

"Where is my heart of *targ?*" Sotugh yelled.

"Coming," Arthur said, and scurried behind the bar.

"Captain Victor did not seem to care about the problems *Deep Space Nine*'s disappearance was causing in the Alpha Quadrant," Sisko said.

"I need to know what information you have about my station," I said to him, "and I need it now."

Victor's grin faded as I spoke to him. Apparently, in that instant, my return had ceased to be a joke to him.

He glanced at Näna, whose head moved up and down in time to his opening and closing mouth. That seemed like a nod to me, but I might have been anthropomorphizing.

"We've intercepted some colonist transmissions," Victor said, smiling. "It seems the colony forces met with more resistance than they had expected and some of the station's equipment has been damaged."

They were fighting then. Trust the major to respond to such a command with quick, sure strokes.

"What kind of equipment?" O'Brien said, in a voice that had an edge of fatherly panic.

I raised a hand to silence him.

"My first officer responded quickly to my message," I said. I wanted Victor to know that my people were competent, even on the station. I still did not feel as if I could trust him. I wanted to warn him in as many ways as I could about provoking me.

• • •

"It seems to me that he had done a good job so far, and you had done nothing," Sotugh said. He reached for the nachos, pulled out one, and ate it, then spit it out. "Bah. Tastes like plastic field rations. How could you order this, Sisko?"

Sisko took a chip. The cheese formed a string as he pulled and he had to break it with his fingers. He licked them off. These were excellent nachos. He had ordered them because he was picky about his jambalaya. Now that he knew the nachos were a success, he might share them, and then order jambalaya.

"These are the best nachos I have had since I left Earth," he said to Cap.

Cap nodded. "We have a captain who comes in here regularly who loves them."

"Aren't you going to answer the Klingon's point?" the middle-aged man at the bar asked. "I kind of agree with him. I don't think you responded well to the challenge at all."

Sisko smiled. "I'm not a Klingon. I do not respond aggressively to every attack. I like to gather information first."

"It makes you seem weak," Sotugh said, craning his head for Arthur. There was still no sign of the heart of *targ.* Sisko wondered how long it would take before Sotugh got really upset.

"It makes you seem overly cautious," said the alien who had recently detached himself from the wall.

"It prevents costly mistakes," Sisko said, speaking around another beef-and-cheese-covered chip. He had gotten some guacamole this time, too, and it was fresh and extremely well made.

"I suppose we will have to wait for you to finish eating now before you continue the story," the Quilli said. It had freed itself from the table during the last bit of the story. It was sitting a little farther away from the Trill now.

"It is considered rude among humans to talk with their mouths full," the Trill said.

The Quilli shot him a nasty look. "It is not considered rude among Quilli."

"Well, then," Sisko said, pulling a large chip from the center, "I shall talk and eat. Unless there are other objections?"

"Please continue," someone said.

"Who cares about human customs?" someone else asked.

"It is rude for Klingons *not* to talk and eat at the same time," Sotugh said.

Sisko smiled and reached for the pile of napkins that Cap had set on his table. "I continued to ask Captain Victor for information," Sisko said, as he tried to pry yet another chip out of the middle of the nacho pile. "It seemed to me that if he were telling the truth, he was in as much trouble as I was."

"How is that?" the woman drinking tea at the bar asked.

"The Mist colonists would be using *Deep Space Nine* against him and his faction," Sisko said. "Victor had been, in his own way, proposing that we become allies. I was willing to accept that in the information exchange, but I was also listening closely, keeping an eye on him, and trying to make certain that what he told me matched what I saw."

"Your first officer's actions might buy us some time," Captain Victor said to me.

I hoped for more than time. I hoped that Kira would be able to subdue the invaders, and then we would be able to take the station back to our own space.

"What is your defense plan?" I asked.

Victor glanced at Näna. The councillor had moved away, and all I could see of his face was one large unblinking eye, set in his gray lifeless skin. "Our ships are not set up for fighting," Victor said. "We outnumber the colonist ships, but we would stand no chance against that station of yours."

"If you are not set up to fight," Worf said, "then what does it matter if you outnumber the colonists' ships?"

I had been about to ask that question myself, but it sounded better coming from Worf. Victor seemed startled by the question.

"I—we—can fight. Sort of," he said.

I resisted the urge to shoot a triumphant glance at Worf. "Sort of," I repeated. "What are you leaving out, Captain?"

Victor glanced in Näna's direction, but the councillor had moved completely out of our visual range. I could see only Victor's half of their interaction. He seemed worried.

"Captain," I said, my voice deep and filled with warning.

He turned back to me, his skin darkened by a flush. "The Mist are not a fighting people," he said. "For centuries, they have avoided conflict by simply not taking part in what they observed going on in the normal space around them."

"They hid," I said, feeling contempt mixed with a deep anger. I had a hunch I knew where this was going.

"Actually, yes," Captain Victor said. "And now they're faced with a conflict of their own making and most Mist simply won't fight."

"But humans will," I said, "which explains why you captain a Mist ship."

He nodded. "Contacting you was my idea. I felt that if we were going to win, we needed the help of those who knew how to fight."

"The Federation does not usually get involved in internal disputes," I said. "And when we do, we do so as a mediator. We do not take sides."

Unless forced to when one of our space stations was captured. But I did not say that to him. Not yet.

Victor's flush deepened. "But most Mist on the homeworlds simply want to let the colonists take over," he said, his voice rising in a forceful tone.

"Then perhaps that is what should be done," I said.

"No," Victor said. "You don't understand."

"Apparently not," I said.

He ran a hand through his tufted hair. "The colonists," he said, "don't share the goal of keeping the Mist reality and the normal space reality separate."

"What does that mean, exactly?" Worf asked.

But I knew already. I was beginning to understand. And so was Dax.

"It means that they have no qualms about phasing into our space and stealing a space station," she said to Worf.

"Exactly," Victor said. "That act of aggression against your station is only the beginning. Imagine the advantage a warlike group with the ability to shift anything, at any time, into this form of space would have."

"We'd have to develop whole new weapons to fight them," O'Brien said.

"We'd never see them coming," Bashir said.

"They could control this sector before we even knew what hit us," Dax said.

Captain Victor only nodded.

I didn't like Captain Victor and liked the message he carried even less.

"This is where you made your mistake," Sotugh said, shaking a goo-covered finger at Sisko. The heart of *targ* had been served while Sisko was talking, and Sotugh had eaten it quickly, scooping it with his fingers like a human child who hadn't been taught how to eat properly.

"And how is that?" the man at the bar asked.

Sotugh didn't even look to the questioner, but only at Sisko. "If you had become allies with the other faction, we would have that technology now. Imagine using it against the Dominion. Imagine going into the Delta Quadrant, phasing the Jem'Hadar into one area of space, and the Founders into another. They would never be able to find one another, and we would be free of them forever."

"Or we would have destroyed each other by now," Sisko said. "No one could keep secrets, since no one would know if a shifted person was nearby. For all we know, a Mist might be listening to this conversation right now."

"It would have to be a Mist captain," the Trill said with a twinkle in his eye.

"Provided Cap knew he was here," Prrghh said, and everyone chuckled.

"I am serious," Sotugh said. "It was a missed opportunity."

"At the time," Sisko said. "I did not recognize that the opportunity was there. I was concerned with *Deep Space Nine.* And what it meant that it was missing from normal space."

"Captain," I said to Victor, "are the colonist ships as unarmed as yours?"

"More or less," he said. "Over the last few years they have managed to install some weapons, but it was only a short time ago that we learned of their entire intent."

I stroked my chin as I thought. It was clear that we were going to need help. There were at least twenty colonist ships near the station. And if Kira hadn't gotten the station completely disabled, then the *Defiant* wouldn't be a match. Either way, we needed help.

And I still did not have enough information to formulate a plan.

I moved my hand from my chin, and let it fall at my side. I was standing at attention and I didn't even realize it.

"Captain," I said, "let me get this straight. You used your ship to bring us here, right?"

"Yes," Victor said.

"Can all Mist ships do that?"

"If they have the right technology," Victor said.

I nodded. I didn't like how this was shaping up. In any fight between ships from our space and the Mist, the Mist would win. All they had to do was use their technology to send us back to our own space. End of fight.

"So," I said, thinking of the shift that had just occurred with *Deep Space Nine,* "all the colony ships have the same technology, then, too."

Victor seemed to understand where I was going. "No," he said.

"No? But they kidnapped *Deep Space Nine.* Some of the ships had to have the correct technology."

"Some," Victor said. "Actually two."

"How do you know that?" Worf asked.

Victor smiled. "The secret of the technology is very closely guarded by the High Council. Trust me. Only two colony ships have the ability to shift objects."

I didn't trust him, but I said nothing.

"But why couldn't the colonists take the equipment apart, learn how it works, and just make more?" O'Brien asked.

"Because," Captain Victor said, "simply tampering with the shift device on board a starship causes the device to destroy itself. As I said, the High Council has guarded the secret carefully, and successfully, for thousands of years."

So my vision of a fight in which the ships from our space lost was not a correct one after all. "Well then," I said, "it seems we can safely go for help."

"For help?" Dax said. She looked at me as if she did not understand.

"You are thinking of going to the Klingons?" Worf asked.

I smiled at him.

"The Klingons are a very warlike race," Captain Victor said. "I'm not sure that would be a good idea."

I shrugged. "You need all the help you can get, and there's only one Federation starship close enough to do us any good."

"But I do not want to trade one problem for a worse one."

"Oh, you won't," I said. "As long as you can shift the Klingons and us back to normal space when this is under control. Sometimes you have to fight fire with fire."

Captain Victor nodded. "But I would prefer to not get burned."

Sotugh hit the platter of nachos with one hand and sent it clattering off the table. It landed on the floor, scattering nachos in every direction, and shattering the platter.

"You!" he shouted. "You set this up? You dragged us into your problem? Do you know what you did?"

"Denied myself some nachos," Sisko said, looking at the ruined meal longingly.

"This is not a joke, Sisko," Sotugh said.

The other patrons had backed away. Sisko hadn't moved.

"But it is long over," Cap said. He put a hand on Sotugh's shoulder. Sotugh threw him off, but to Sisko's surprise, Cap did not fall back. "Let the man finish his story."

"He is without honor. He does not deserve to tell stories!" Sotugh said.

"Oh, shut up," Prrghh said. "Let him finish. You might learn something. You can kill him when he's done." She smiled at Sisko, revealing small pointed teeth. "Tomorrow might be a better day to die."

"You mock me, Prrghh," Sotugh said.

"It's just that you're getting so tiresome, Sotugh," she said. "Can't you—?"

Sotugh jerked forward and let out a large groan of pain. He turned and pulled a bristle out of his buttocks. He held it up and shook it at the Quilli.

"I warned you, warthog—"

"No," the Quilli said. "I warned you. I want to hear the rest of this story."

"No one will hear the rest of it, if things don't settle down right now," Cap said.

"Oh, what can you do to us?" Prrghh said.

"Close the bar," Cap said.

"Close the bar?" Prrghh asked. "You've never closed the bar."

"I will, rather than have a fight between a Klingon and a Quilli on the premises. Or a Klingon and a human." Cap looked meaningfully at Sisko and Sotugh.

Sisko leaned back in his chair. "I don't want you to close," he said. "Now that my nachos are gone, I'd like to try your jambalaya." Then he smiled. "And please put them on Sotugh's tab."

"You are pushing things, Sisko," Sotugh said.

"And you'd better clean that wound," the Trill said, "before the poison sets in."

"Poison?" Sotugh said, frowning at the Quilli. "Have you a med kit?" he asked Cap.

"In the bathroom," Cap said.

Sotugh shot a glance at the Quilli. "You and I will have business when we leave here."

"I'm willing to let it go if you allow Sisko to finish his story," the Quilli said.

"I'm not," Sotugh said, and stalked off to the rest room.

"Poison?" the middle-aged woman at the bar asked the Trill. "I'd never heard that Quilli bristles are poisonous."

The Trill grinned. "They're not. But that got him to shut up." He nodded to Sisko. "You can continue now."

The gecko climbed back up into Sotugh's temporarily vacant chair.

Nine

"ALL RIGHT," CAPTAIN VICTOR SAID. "WE SHALL BRING THE KLINGONS here." He turned to his crew.

I took a step closer to my screen. "Wait!" I said. I had a sudden image of the Klingons being brought into the Mist reality with no warning at all. They would have attacked first and asked questions later. "I need to warn them. You can't just bring them across."

"Captain, really," Victor said. "We brought you across with no warning, and you were fine."

He raised a hand.

"You said so yourself," I said quickly. "The Klingons are a warlike race. They won't respond as we did."

Victor's hand came down. He turned to me. "What do you suggest?"

"Send me back. Let me talk to them. I'll hail the Federation starship *Madison* as well."

Victor grimaced. "All right," he said. "But make it short. I do not know how long it will take for the colonists to take control of your station."

Probably longer than you expect, I thought. But I did not say so. "We will return to these coordinates after I have spoken to them," I said.

Victor nodded. He was ready, and so was I.

Sotugh was standing near the bar. He had returned from the rest room during Sisko's last part of the story. "You were right," he said. "We would have attacked first, and then you would have had no hope of getting your station back. This is the first smart thing you have said all day, Sisko."

Sisko didn't know if he should thank Sotugh or ignore him. So he ignored him.

The line of Mist swept over the *Defiant,* and Captain Victor's ship instantly disappeared, along with the Mist homeworlds. *Deep Space Nine* and the Mist colony ships around it also vanished off our sensors as we returned to the normal universe.

I did not like this form of shifting, and I could tell that my crew did not either. Dax shook her head slightly as she looked at the console. Worf gripped the edges of his, as if steadying himself. Dr. Bashir actually rubbed his eyes as if he could make the images change.

"Captain," Nog said, "we are being hailed by the *Starship Madison,* sir."

"They are within range," Worf said. "I will be able to get them on screen shortly."

"And Captain," Nog said. "The *Daqchov* is demanding that you talk to them."

"I will speak to both of them at once, Cadet," I said. "Open a secure channel, and put both captains on screen."

I clasped my hands behind my back and waited as Nog completed my orders. I was secretly pleased that the *Madison* was the nearest starship. Captain Paul Higginbotham was an old friend of mine, and I knew how he would respond in battle. Captain Higginbotham was a judicious man who weighed all his options carefully and always seemed to make the proper choice.

"And what is your opinion of Captain Sotugh?" Prrghh asked, leaning near Sisko. "Aren't you going to summarize him for us as well?"

Sotugh frowned.

Sisko leaned back, closer to Prrghh, and said, "I don't think I have to. You all know Captain Sotugh. He is in battle much as he is here, opinionated and aggressive. Those are good traits for a warrior."

Sotugh lifted his mug of blood wine. "Well said, Sisko."

"And diplomatically, too," Prrghh whispered in his ear.

Sisko smiled at her, and then continued.

Captain Higginbotham was a tall slender man who perched in his commander's chair like a judge, hands templed before him as he contemplated me through the screen. Nog had split the images so that next to Captain Higginbotham, Captain Sotugh looked as if he might slash right through the screen at me.

"Captains," I said, holding up my hand to stop both of them before they could even speak. "We're in a situation that threatens both the Federation and the Empire and we have very little time to act, so if you'd wait until I've explained what has happened before you ask questions, it would help."

"It's your game, Ben," Higginbotham said.

"Your analysis had better be correct," Sotugh said, looking even more disgusted.

It took me less than two minutes to explain the situation with the Mist, the Mist colonies, and the reason *Deep Space Nine* had disappeared. I finished by explaining that the Mist colonists wouldn't stop with just taking over their own homeworld. The entire sector was in danger.

"Understand," I said, "that the information I have is through Captain Victor, and to be honest, I don't trust him. But I see no other choice."

"Had it been any other Starfleet captain telling me such a pack of wild tales, I would not have believed them," Sotugh said.

"Nonsense," Prrghh said. "I've heard that you once worked with Picard."

"Picard." Sotugh waved a hand in disgust. "Picard never explains anything to me. He simply expects me to follow him."

"Have you?"

"Followed him? No! We worked together at my direction," Sotugh said.

"That sounds like a story for another time," Cap said.

"Perhaps when we finish this one," the Quilli said, rubbing its front paws together.

"I won't tell a story so that you can sell it," Sotugh said. He crossed his arms. "Unlike Sisko here."

Sisko grinned. "May I continue?" he asked.

"Certainly," Sotugh said. "Go on. You are being surprisingly accurate at this time."

"Would it be fair to say that you were staring at me as if I were a crazy man when I finished?" Sisko asked.

"More than fair," Sotugh said. "I thought you were insane for saying these things, and I thought *I* was insane for believing you. Higginbotham, however, seemed to believe everything you said, no questions asked."

"Paul and I have served on some interesting missions together," Sisko said. "He knew that I would not lie to him or exaggerate anything, no matter how improbable."

"If those colonists have the station up and working," Higginbotham said, after I had finished, "it's going to take a lot more than two starships and three Klingon warbirds to stop them."

I nodded. I knew that. I also knew that our time was limited. The longer we delayed, the more critical the situation got in both phases of space.

"My people on the station only had thirty seconds' warning before the attack," I said. "I have no idea how much time they bought us, but I do know they managed to cause some damage."

"If I had not seen your ship vanish and reappear so easily," Sotugh said, "and did not have the evidence of the space station disappearing, I would never believe such a wild story."

"Neither would I, Captain," I said. "But I have been to this phase of space twice now, and I need to go back. The threat is very real."

"I understand that," Sotugh said. "These 'Mist' may attack Klingon ships or the Klingon homeworld. So we must act swiftly. We must not allow this technology to be used in such a dishonorable manner."

I knew that he was speaking not only to me, but to his crew and the other two Klingon warbirds.

Sotugh grinned. "Perhaps you should not tell stories," he said. "You are usually such a quiet man and we Klingons think that much misses you. But it is becoming apparent that nothing does."

Sisko raised his eyebrows. "Thank you," he said. "I think."

Sotugh took his seat again quickly, almost crushing the gecko, who barely snuck out from under him in time.

"I will be at your location in less than ten minutes," Higginbotham said. "The *Idaho* is thirty minutes away. Six other Starfleet ships are within an hour. I will notify them of the situation. But I have to warn you, Ben. I'm afraid the situation is going to get worse before it gets better."

"Cardassians?" I asked.

"I'm afraid so," Higginbotham said. "They have a fleet coming across the border, heading for the former location of *Deep Space Nine.*"

"The Empire is also sending ships," Sotugh said.

"Wonderful," I said. "Let's just hope in thirty minutes they won't be needed."

Captain Higginbotham and Captain Sotugh said nothing.

"Stand by, Captain Sotugh," I said. "Captain Higginbotham, rendezvous with us halfway between this point and the former location of *Deep Space Nine.*"

"Will do, Ben," Higginbotham said, and cut the connection.

"We stand ready to fight," Sotugh said.

"Thank you, Captain," I said, and signaled for Nog to cut the channel.

"Okay, people," I said, glancing around at my bridge crew. "Let's go get our home back. Dax, move us into position so that Captain Victor will know that we are ready."

"Yes, sir," Dax said.

A moment later a white line of mist opened in space and a thin cloud swept over first the *Defiant,* then the *Daqchov* and the other two nearby Klingon warbirds.

Ten

"So, Sotugh," Prrghh said, leaning closer to Sisko and placing a tiny hand on his shoulder. "Is going through that barrier into Mist space like Sisko says?"

Sisko bent down to pick up a piece of glass from the broken plate that had lodged against the leg of the table. He then used that as an opportunity to move slightly away from Prrghh. He didn't know what her agenda was, but he suspected that if he allied himself with her in any way, he would make an enemy of Sotugh.

He and Sotugh had a bickering respect for one another. The last thing he wanted to do was lose that.

As he sat up, Sotugh's gaze met his. Arthur moved between them, picking up the empty heart of *targ* dish. He took the piece of glass from Sisko with a bit of a grimace. Arthur had worked hard during the last part of Sisko's tale to clean up the mess that Sotugh had made with the nachos.

"Well?" Prrghh purred.

"Sisko has described it accurately," Sotugh said.

"Suddenly," she said, "you seem quite reluctant to talk. Are you tiring of this, or do you think Sisko is being accurate?"

Sisko felt a flash of irritation, but he suppressed it as quickly as it flared. He asked Arthur to bring him some bottled water as well as another Jibetian ale when he brought the jambalaya.

Arthur nodded.

"Sotugh, you do not answer the lady," the wraith from the wall said.

"She is trying to make trouble," Sotugh said.

"But you have been making trouble all along," the wraith said.

"Not the kind Prrghh is making," Sotugh said. "She likes nothing more than disagreements among the people around her."

"So you do disagree with Sisko," the wraith said.

"I do not," Sotugh said. "I am listening to his part of the story. It gets tricky from this point on."

"That it does," Sisko said. He wiped his hands on a napkin, and leaned back. "Do you want to hear more?"

"Yes!" the patrons shouted in various tones and warbles.

To his surprise, Sotugh grinned at him. "It is a successful story so far, Sisko," he said. "Do not keep your public waiting any longer."

Sisko smiled. "As soon as I saw the five improbable planetary systems . . ."

. . . and the beautiful Mist ship, its wings arcing darkly against the blackness of space, I had Cadet Nog open a secure channel to Captain Victor.

Within seconds of our arrival, Captain Victor's face appeared on the main screen. He had replaced his ridiculous little yachting cap, covering the tufts of his hair. It made him look like a young man playing games like Victory in Space. Behind him, Councillor Näna was almost completely visible. I didn't like the look of the councillor. Each time I saw him, he seemed no different, his gray scaly skin ghostlike, his eyes unblinking, and the mouth constantly opening and closing without saying a word.

After a quick glance at Näna, I addressed all my comments to Victor. "Before we go any further," I said, "I want to make certain that you can send our ship and the Klingon ships back to normal space at any time."

"At any time?" Victor repeated.

"Yes." I didn't want to explain myself any more than that, but I did want to be certain that the Mist could save themselves from us, as well as from the colonists.

"At the moment, we can," he said. It was a hedge, but a small one. Dax glanced at me. There was a warning in her eyes that I didn't completely understand. But before I could say anything, Victor continued. "We will bring over the *Starship Madison* at the point you designated to meet it."

"Good." I glanced at Nog. He was monitoring everything. He seemed to have grown more mature, just in the space of this mission. "Hail the *Daqchov.* But keep this channel secured."

Nog worked for a moment; then the main screen split, showing both Captain Victor and Sotugh. Sotugh looked slightly disoriented.

• • •

"Ah," Sotugh growled. "This is where your perception is incorrect. You were disoriented upon your arrival in Mist space. I was merely gathering data."

Sisko suppressed a smile. "My mistake," he said. "Captain Sotugh looked as if he had been hastily gathering information."

"I don't care how he looked," the Quilli said. "What happened next?"

"I introduced Captain Sotugh to Captain Victor and Councillor Näna," Sisko said.

"And in this Sisko was not exaggerating," Sotugh said. "Näna was one of the most disgusting aliens I had ever seen. But I did not say so at the time. I was too intent on the mission at hand."

"In fact, he began the communication by insulting me," Sisko said, his smile widening.

"Sisko," Sotugh said, "I see you were not lying. But retaking your station with five ships is an idea of a fool."

The Klingons were never polite, not even when we were allies. But Victor seemed taken aback by Sotugh's words. I did not try to soothe him. Instead, I stood my ground, which was always the best course with Klingons.

"True enough," Sotugh muttered.

"I hope you have a plan," Sotugh said.

"Of course I do," I lied. I had the beginnings of a plan, but not a full-fledged one. Not yet. "While it is true that five ships aren't enough to take a space station, I am assuming that Captain Victor and his forces will help, since they have an interest as well."

"It still seems risky," Sotugh said.

"I thought Klingons liked risk," I said.

"We calculate risk just like you do, Captain," he said. "Only we act upon it differently."

"I figured you would help with this fight."

"And I will," Sotugh said. "We seem outnumbered."

"Perhaps," I said. "But Captain Victor has stated that the colony forces are limited."

Victor had been watching our exchange with increasing nervousness. He clearly feared the Klingons.

"A healthy and wise response," Sotugh muttered.

"Their forces are limited," Victor said. He tugged on the bill of his cap, securing it on his forehead. "But we must be careful. You must not destroy the two ships with the ability to shift objects from the main universe."

This was news to me, but it was Sotugh who asked the question, or rather, barked it.

"Why?"

Captain Victor glanced nervously at Councillor Näna. Näna's mouth opened and closed, he did not blink, and yet Victor seemed to have gotten something from the exchange. He said, "Only the same instrument that shifted the station into the Mist space can shift it back to normal space."

I froze. I did not like the way that Victor played these games. "Let me get this straight," I said. "You're saying that if your ship is destroyed, the *Daqchov,* the *Defiant,* and the other two Klingon ships will be stranded in this space."

"That is correct, Captain."

"And if we destroy the ship that shifted the space station it will remain shifted," Sotugh said. He sounded as if he were contemplating the idea.

"That also is correct," Captain Victor said.

I didn't like the look on Sotugh's face, but I did not challenge it at that time.

"Sisko," Sotugh said, "you are suggesting that I would intentionally destroy the colony ship that shifted the station."

Sotugh seemed unnaturally calm about this accusation. Sisko slid his chair slightly farther away from Prrghh's. The bar was quiet. The others seemed to think that Sotugh was upset.

Sisko smiled. "Of course I am," he said. "It would have been a brilliant move. If you destroyed the ship and stranded DS9, you would have, with one blow, made quite a difference in any conflict with the Federation. We would have lost—permanently—a very valuable and strategic asset."

"True," Sotugh said. His eyes twinkled. He *had* thought of it. Sisko kept his own expression neutral as Sotugh continued. "But at the time I felt the station would be more of a threat to the Empire in the hands of the Mist. I did not as yet know that would not be possible."

Sisko shrugged. "It's my story. And, at the time, I thought what I thought."

"It seems logical," the middle-aged man at the bar said.

Sisko nodded slightly in his direction. But Sotugh frowned. He did not seem to like the fact that someone else agreed with Sisko.

"What would you have done in my position if our roles had been reversed?" Sotugh asked.

Sisko raised his bottle of ale with a slight smile. "I would have considered destroying the colony ship that had shifted the station."

"We are more alike than you like to acknowledge," Sotugh said.

"I thought you were the one saying we were different."

"Only at the beginning of the battle, Sisko," Sotugh said. "Only at the beginning."

• • •

This new wrinkle had me very disturbed. Suddenly, we had no margin for error. "Captain Victor," I said, "how can we tell which two colony ships are the ones with the ability to shift?"

Again Victor glanced at the councillor. The councillor's mouth continued to open and close. One of his eyes shifted slightly as if it were looking at Victor, and then shifted back, all unblinking.

That seemed to mean something to Victor. He said, "There is no way to tell, but the ships with the shift modules won't have weapons. Most likely they will back away from any fight."

"That is not good enough," Sotugh said.

I agreed, but did not say so. I wanted as much information as I could gather. I did not want any more surprises.

"What kind of weapons are we facing with the colony ships?" I asked.

"Actually, Captain," Victor said, "our intelligence tells us that only two, maybe three of the colony ships have been outfitted with any sort of weapons. But neither of them would be a match for one of your ships. It was the firepower of the station the colonists were gambling on getting."

"Then let us hope Major Kira managed to disarm the station's weapons," I said. "Is there anything more you need, Sotugh?"

"We are ready to fight," Sotugh said.

I nodded. "We take Ops first. From there we can control the rest of the station."

"Understood," Sotugh said, and cut his communication.

I had Nog cut the communication, then I said, "Set course for *Deep Space Nine,* warp factor five."

"Yes, sir," Dax said. "We'll be there in exactly twelve minutes."

As we turned and jumped to warp, O'Brien said, "I don't like this."

"Neither do I," Nog said.

"What is there to like?" Worf asked.

I sat down. Sometimes I could learn a lot by listening to the digressions of my crew.

"There's just something odd going on with Captain Victor," O'Brien said. "Something he's not telling us."

"He hasn't told us a lot of things," Dax said. "And I would guess that much of what he has said is lies."

"And we will deal with that," Worf said. "But first we must recapture the station. That is our first priority."

Dr. Bashir had been quiet through all of this, studying the screen and the console before him. Finally he looked up. "Doesn't it strike anyone else odd that five systems full of people, plus another three systems full of colonists, have existed in this region for centuries and none of them have ever turned up outside of legend?"

"You have a good point, Julian," Dax said. "I have early memories of the legends about the planets of the Mist disappearing. But I don't remember hearing anything about someone meeting their race. Nothing but legends."

Bashir was tapping his console. "I don't like the way these things are adding up," he said. "I have a few facts from my console, and I know the chief does as well. Combine that with this lack of information, and I think there may be more to this shifting than we're initially seeing."

I didn't entirely follow Dr. Bashir's logic, but then he often left out crucial details when he was thinking aloud. It led, in the early days, to people underestimating him around the station. I had not underestimated him in years. His hypotheses usually had some basis in fact.

"Check it out," I said.

Bashir nodded and quickly left the bridge.

"There's going to be a crowd waiting for us," Dax said.

I could see what she meant. At least twenty Mist colonist ships surrounded the station. Among them were twenty or so vessels in normal space that had been docked to the station or in orbit around the station when it vanished.

On top of that, a half-dozen unaligned Cardassian ships, privateers not part of their regular fleet, were approaching and would arrive at the station just minutes before we did. Attacking the station was going to take running an obstacle course first.

"You could have warned us, Sisko," Sotugh said. "Obstacle course indeed. More like a gauntlet of pain and dizziness. Do you know what happens to Klingons when they get dizzy?"

"I bet it improves their disposition," Prrghh said sweetly.

"So you and the Klingons went through that obstacle course?" the Quilli asked, resting its paws on the top of its chair.

Sisko smiled at it. When it got its story, it was actually quite a charming creature. "We did," Sisko said. "But Sotugh has jumped a bit ahead of our story."

"Don't get that warthog mad at me again," Sotugh said. "I didn't do anything wrong this time." He rubbed his left buttock absently as he spoke.

"Ah, that's right," the Quilli said. "The *Madison* isn't there yet."

Sisko nodded. "But it was just a half second later that Dax reported . . ."

"The *Madison* has shifted and joined us." She bent over her console, fingers working rapidly. "We'll be at the station in five minutes."

"Sir!" Nog said. "Captain Higginbotham is hailing us."

"Put him on screen," I said.

Captain Higginbotham's serious face filled the screen. "What an amazing place you found here, Ben."

"It is startling, isn't it?" I said.

"What's your plan?"

"We're going in to take Ops first."

"It's going to get crowded in there," Higginbotham said. "Fighting in such close quarters is not going to be easy."

"Granted," I said. "Avoid passing through a ship in real space."

"You can do that?"

I nodded. "And it's not pleasant. Most of the colonists' ships are supposedly unarmed, but I don't trust that information. The biggest problem we have is we can't let any of the ships escape, and unless they fire on us, we can't destroy them, either."

"That's unusual," Higginbotham said. "What's the idea behind that?"

"It's complicated, Paul," I said. "But in abbreviated terms, we think we need the colonist ships with the transfer equipment to shift the station back, or it's stuck here, invisible, forever."

"Does that affect us as well?" he asked.

"Yes," I said, and told him about Victor's ship.

"Got it," Higginbotham said. "We'll back you up and keep as many of the Mist ships rounded up as we can."

"Thanks," I said, and had Nog cut the communication.

"Captain Victor's ship is dropping back," Dax said. "And being joined by half a dozen other Mist ships."

"I did not expect to see more Mist ships," Worf said.

"Me, either," Nog said.

"He mentioned them," O'Brien said uncertainly.

"Are they joining us?" I asked Dax.

Dax shook her head. "We're out here alone, Benjamin. It's just the three Klingon ships, the *Madison,* and us."

"I don't like this," O'Brien said to himself.

Right at that moment, I completely agreed. Something felt wrong. Very wrong.

Eleven

My heart was pounding as I leaned forward in my chair. It seemed as if I had already been in battle, judging by my body's reaction. I knew that I had to be prepared, and already I was on alert.

"Worf," I said, "I need to know the status of the station as soon as you can give it to me."

"Aye, sir," he said.

"We'll be in scanning range within one minute," Dax said. "The *Madison* and one Klingon ship are taking positions between the station and the colonists' home planets."

"Are the station's shields up?" I asked as we dropped out of warp.

"Shields are down, sir," Worf said. "Cardassian ships, led by Gul Dukat, have stationed themselves near the wormhole."

I expected as much. From Gul Dukat's point of view, the station was gone. That meant the wormhole was up for grabs. Dukat was going to be in for a large shock when the station suddenly reappeared.

"We'll worry about Dukat later," I said. "Right now, we concentrate on regaining the station."

"Captain," Worf said. "I am reading phaser fire in a dozen places around the station, including Ops."

Dax smiled. She knew, as I did, how difficult the station would be to take. Months later, it would take the Dominion and the Cardassians working together to capture *Deep Space Nine*—after a long and difficult struggle. The colonists did not have that kind of force.

• • •

"You don't have the station anymore?" Arthur asked from behind the bar. He was cleaning glasses. Sisko wondered what happened to his drink and jambalaya orders.

"Oh, I do," Sisko said. "The struggle with the Dominion and the Cardassians is another story, and believe me, I do not have time for that one even if I were to quit telling this one now."

"Don't quit," the Quilli said.

The Trill grinned, and cast a sidelong glance at the Quilli. "It might be dangerous for all of us."

The Quilli frowned at him, its bristles moving forward with the furrowing of its tiny brow. "I'm not always violent," it said. Then it climbed on the back of its chair. The chair tottered precariously. "I wouldn't mind hearing the Dominion story after this one, though."

"Greedy bastard," the middle-aged man at the bar said just loudly enough for everyone to hear.

Sisko held up a hand. "I'd love to tell it," he lied. "But I don't think my voice will hold out that long." He held up his empty ale bottle. "When's my refill coming?"

Arthur blushed. "I thought you wanted it with the jambalaya," he said.

"You're cooking the jambalaya from scratch, aren't you?" Sisko said. Somehow he had expected them to have it on the stove, waiting. "I think I'd better have the ale now. And the water."

"It won't be long for the food," Cap said.

"Still," Sisko said. His voice was rasping against his throat. He still had a lot of story to tell, and with this crowd, it wouldn't do to run out of voice before he ran out of story.

"Coming right up," Cap said.

Sisko nodded, and then cleared his throat. "As I was saying—"

"Dax had smiled," the Quilli said breathlessly. Sisko was shocked at its memory. It grinned—a shaggy, toothy smile—and put its paws under its chin, bracing itself. "She knew how difficult the station was to take—"

"And on and on," the Trill said.

The Quilli ignored him. "The colonists didn't have that kind of force. Over to you, Captain."

"Um," Sisko said, still slightly shocked. "Right. Um. Oh, yes . . ."

"Our people are still putting up a fight," O'Brien said, his voice excited.

I had done the right thing, leaving Kira in charge. She could defend the station with sticks and rubber bands if she had to. I was as pleased as my crew was at the news of the continued fighting.

"Now we must help them," I said. "Dax, you have the bridge. Help the

Madison keep those Mist colony ships in a tight group. Worf, Chief, you're with me."

Without another word I turned and headed for the transporter room. I wanted my people to beam into the station before the Klingons had a chance to get there.

"What did you think we would do, Sisko? Join forces with the Mist?" Sotugh wiped the blood wine off his mouth with the back of his hand as he spoke.

"No," Sisko said. "But I had a balancing act. I had to remember that in our space, you and I were on the verge of total war. It wouldn't do to have Starfleet troops running around the Empire at that time, would it?"

Sotugh scowled. "Point taken," he said.

We had just reached the transporter room when Dr. Bashir joined us. I had seen him in many states over the years—from a green doctor on a far station outpost to one of the most skilled, and calm battlefield surgeons—but never before had I seen him look like this. His angular face was white with shock. He looked both determined and angry.

"What is it, Julian?" I asked.

He scanned us. His gaze stopped for a moment on the transporter operator, a young Vulcan who was fresh out of the Academy. She nodded at him, her features impassive. He turned away.

"I found one of the items that Captain Victor failed to mention," he said.

I did not like the sound of this. It was something large enough to distress Dr. Bashir. "Make it quick, Doctor. We must get to the station."

" 'Quick' is the operative word, Captain," Bashir said. "If we stay in this altered space longer than two hours and six minutes, we won't ever go back to our own space."

"Not ever?" O'Brien asked.

The three security officers I had sent for while we were on the turbolift arrived. They looked at all of us as if our very expressions were alarming. I held up a hand to them, and they waited.

"Not ever," Bashir said.

"How can that be?" I asked.

"Matter alters in this space," Bashir said. "The shift changes the property of matter in such a fashion that it can never be shifted back. Us, the station, the Klingons. Everyone."

"Our molecular structure is changing?" Worf asked with a tone of complete disgust.

"That's right," Bashir said. "And according to my calculations, the change will be irreversible in a little over two hours."

"Two hours and six minutes from our last shift."

"Exactly," Bashir said. "And not one moment longer."

"So that's why no one sees the Mist," said the Caxtonian at the bar.

Sisko jumped. He had known the Caxtonian was there—Caxtonians were hard to miss, what with their incredible body odor and forceful opinions—but this one had been silent until now.

"Right?" he asked.

Sisko nodded. "That, in fact, was what clued Dr. Bashir into the problem in the first place."

"That's right," the Quilli said. "He mentioned something about it on the bridge."

"And then he started to investigate it," Sisko said, "and he came up with this."

"I hear that Bashir is abnormally intelligent," Sotugh said.

"More blood wine?" Arthur said, holding another mug. Sotugh looked up. Sisko was glad for the distraction. He didn't want to answer that question.

"Yes," Sotugh said, taking the mug.

"After hearing that news," Sisko said, starting into the story quickly so that Sotugh couldn't say anything more. "I realized we had a lot to do and very little time in which to do it. Because if we had two hours in which to act, the station, which had crossed over earlier, had even less time. And they didn't know it yet."

"Are you absolutely certain?" I asked him.

"I double- and triple-checked my figures," Bashir said. "I'm quite certain."

I got on the transporter pads and signaled the rest of my team to join me. Worf was already on his. O'Brien climbed to the platform, followed by the three security officers who were, I must say, looking quite confused.

"I wouldn't push the time limit if we can help it," Bashir said. "My figures are accurate, but I'm not certain how the gradual shift will affect us if we cross back to our space, say, two hours and four minutes from the point of shift."

"Are you saying that it could be painful?" O'Brien asked.

"He is saying that it might kill us," Worf said.

"Or it might make us wish we were dead," one of the security officers said.

"Actually," Bashir said. "It's more like trying to go through water that is slowly turning to ice. I doubt it will harm us, but one should be careful."

"I see your point, Doctor," I said. "We will hurry. How much time do we have?"

"If we're going to save the station," Bashir said, "we have one hour and ten minutes. The *Defiant* and the Klingons have about twenty minutes longer, thanks to that last visit back to normal space. The *Madison* a little longer."

"All right." I nodded at Bashir. "Excellent work, Doctor." Then I looked at the transporter operator. "Beam us into the middle of Ops."

"Aye, Captain," she said, and started the transport.

Sisko paused. The spicy scent of jambalaya made his stomach rumble. Arthur came out of the back, carrying a large bowl in one hand. The bowl was steaming. In the other hand, he held silverware. He set the bowl down in front of Sisko.

Sisko's mouth watered. There, mixed with the rice (which was properly browned before someone added the liquid), were pieces of ham, pork, and authentic Creole sausage. He picked up his fork and pushed the food apart, locating fresh shucked oysters. He had no idea how Cap had found those on Bajor, but he didn't care.

He forgot the story; he forgot everything else. It had been a long, long time since he'd had an authentic jambalaya. He scooped some rice and sausage onto his fork, and brought it to his mouth. He was about to taste it when Prrghh said,

"Well?"

He sighed and set the fork down. "Well, what?"

"Did you get to the station or will we be forever stuck in transport?"

He was tempted to say that they all died in transport, their molecules scattered to the seven seas—or some appropriate metaphor. Instead, he gazed longingly at his jambalaya and said,

"No. We arrived in the middle of a firefight."

Smoke filled the air. Dozens of small fires burned under and near panels. Ops had been clean and well lit and in prime condition when I last saw it. Now it was dark and filthy and littered with smashed equipment.

We had arrived in the very center of Ops. In case I didn't tell you, our Operations area is built in a sunken circular pattern, and we were in the middle of that sunken circle. Although I knew there were others in the room, I could not see them, except as shadows in the smoke. O'Brien, proprietary as always about his engineering work on the station, made a small sound of dismay at the mess, but that was the only reaction we were allowed.

A phaser shot cut between me and Worf, spinning one of the security officers around behind me. The chief and I ducked behind Kira's station as Worf rolled to a position under the security panel. The other two security-team members dragged the injured officer to a sheltered position near Dax's station.

"Good to see you, Captain," Major Kira's voice rang out over the craziness.

"Good to be seen, Major," I said.

More phaser fire cut into the panel near my head, scattering metal. One piece stuck into Worf's arm, but he didn't seem to notice as he returned fire, sending a colonist twisting up and backward in pain.

Through the smoke, I did my best to get a grasp on the situation. It seemed that Kira and three others were pinned down against the wall near the turbolift by a dozen Mist colonists near my office. But, from the looks of things, she had made sure that even if the colonists had captured the station, it wouldn't be working for a time.

I tapped my comm link. "Dax?"

"Go ahead, Captain."

"Lock on to the life signs nearest my office and beam them into the brig."

"Aye, sir."

For a moment the firing continued; then suddenly it stopped as the Mist colonists were beamed away. It took a moment before Kira and her group realized it was over.

"That's it?" Kira said, standing up. "That's it? Beam them away and it's all over?"

She sounded almost disappointed.

"No, Major," I said. "This stage is over. We still have a long way to go."

"Boy, do we," O'Brien said, brushing some dirt off himself, and staring at the mess.

Dax's voice came clearly over the now silent room. "Captain, we have six colonists in the brig. The Klingons have beamed onto the Promenade and are taking care of the remaining colonists there."

"Good," I said. "Beam Security Officer Thomason to sickbay. Stand by to beam me back to the *Defiant*'s bridge."

"Aye, sir," Dax said.

Thomason became a series of light-colored particles, and then vanished. Worf moved a piling aside. The other security officers began putting out the fires. O'Brien found the environmental controls and brought the lights back up.

That was a mistake. The edges of the smoke reflected the light, while the interior sucked the light inside. My eyes felt as if someone had rubbed them raw.

Then the exhaust fans started, gathering the smoke and sending it through long vents toward the vastness of space.

I felt an internal clock ticking away. We didn't have much time. I turned to Worf. "Secure this area and set up a guard. Be prepared for any beam-in attacks."

"Yes, sir," Worf said, quickly turning and directing the remainder of Kira's crew and the two security-team members to positions.

"Chief," I said, "you and Kira need to get this place back up and running as quickly as you can."

"That might not be so easy," Kira said. She pushed a strand of hair out of her face. She was covered in soot. Two long gashes had nearly severed the sleeve of her uniform.

"I understand," I said. "But do what you can. I plan to make this station reappear in the middle of all those Cardassian ships. In the very least, I would like to have shields. Ideally, I would like weapons to go with them."

"We'll see what we can do, sir," O'Brien said.

"At least we sabotaged them," Kira said. "We know how we broke them. We should know how to fix them."

"It's easier to break things than it is to repair them," O'Brien said.

They continued bickering—which was sometimes their best work method—as I beamed out of the station. In those few seconds between leaving the station and arriving on the *Defiant,* I felt hope. Hope that we could accomplish the goals we set out to accomplish. Hope that we would make it back.

But the moment I materialized on the *Defiant,* that hope vanished. It seems that there were a few more things about the colonists and this entire situation that Captain Victor hadn't told us. If Dr. Bashir was right, it looked as if the station was never to leave Mist space.

"And I," Sisko said with a grin, "am going to have a bite of this jambalaya if it kills me."

"It very well might, Captain," the wraith said.

"You can't stop there!" the Quilli said. "What did you see?"

"Let the man eat," the Trill said. "The last thing you want him to do is pass out from hunger."

"I could finish this," Sotugh said.

Sisko ignored them all. His taste buds were enjoying the perfect blend of rice, meat, butter, and vegetables. Cap had done the spices exactly right—just enough cayenne and chili powder, and the all important cloves.

He sighed in gastronomic ecstasy as all around him, the patrons of the bar began pounding their fists on the table and bar, demanding that he continue with his story about the Mist.

Twelve

"SILENCE!" SOTUGH SAID, STANDING UP. HE HELD HIS HANDS OUT, PALMS down, as if he were directing an orchestra to play its music softer.

The patrons stopped pounding, but their hands or paws or limbs rested on the edge of the tables, waiting.

Sisko took advantage of the moment. He hadn't realized how hungry he was, or how long it had been since he had had any jambalaya besides his own. This was wonderful. And it went very well with Jibetian ale.

"I will tell you about the fight for the Promenade," Sotugh said.

"No!" several voices yelled.

"We want to know what Sisko saw!"

"What happened next?" the Quilli was standing on the very back of its chair. The Trill had his booted foot resting casually on the chair's seat, so that it wouldn't tip over.

Cap crossed his arms and leaned against the bar. He was grinning. "You have them, Captain," he said.

"Suspense is good," Sisko said around a mouthful of food.

"But not always the best for my bar," Cap said. "I promise you, the jambalaya will remain warm."

Sisko sighed, swallowed, and pushed the bowl away. Around him, patrons applauded, and the little Quilli fanned its bristles in joy.

"What I saw," Sisko said, and stopped, his throat closing around the words. The very thought of the destruction angered him to this day.

"What I saw," he began again, softer, and to an audience that was leaning forward in anticipation, "seemed as strange to me as those impossible planets had when I first entered Mist space."

"Was everyone dead?" the middle-aged woman at the bar asked, breathlessly.

"On the ship, no," Sisko said. "But in space—" He shook his head. "In space, the destruction was indescribable."

The first words I heard were Dr. Bashir's. He was standing at his console, near the command chair, where Dax had beamed me aboard.

"I can't believe it," he said, and if anything, he looked even more shocked than he had when I had first left the *Defiant.* I couldn't believe that he wasn't already in sickbay. I had beamed the injured security officer to him not a few moments before.

I frowned at him, and was about to say something, when I realized that everyone on the bridge was staring at the screen.

I turned.

And felt all of the breath leave my body.

Let me try to explain this, for what I saw was a jumbled mess that at first made no sense to me at all. It took almost a half a minute for my brain to process the images.

Deep Space Nine remained in its normal place. That, as I have told you before, was how it looked from Mist space. Around it floated Cardassian ships, the handful of other ships that had been at the station when it disappeared, and, of course, the wormhole. All in normal space.

At first glance, this was what I saw, because this was what I expected to see. This was what I always saw when I was in the *Defiant* near *Deep Space Nine.*

"Minus the Cardassian dogs," Sotugh said.

Sisko nodded in his direction. "That's right," he said. "They would not normally be near the station unless there was trouble."

And believe me, I processed their presence that way: as trouble. To the Cardassians, of course, the station was gone, and they were guarding the wormhole. The approaching Klingon fleet would surely challenge that idea. A dozen other ships from different races were holding off toward Bajor, waiting.

That was what I expected to see, and what I did see.

It was in Mist space where everything had gone wrong.

Sisko cleared his throat. This was hard to say. He took a swig of Jibetian ale and that didn't help. Finally he downed half the bottle of water, wiped his mouth with the back of his hand as Sotugh had done, and looked at the other patrons. They watched his every move.

"Oh," he said when he regained his voice, "the *Madison* was still there, and the Klingon ships . . ."

. . . but the Mist ships had been destroyed.

Completely.

Imagine twenty of those lovely Mist ships, the wings arched over the small bodies, black against the darkness of space. Then imagine them shattered, those black pieces shrapnel, space debris, junk, floating and twisting in a grotesque imitation of dance. The pieces spun all over space, going through—at least to my eyes—the Cardassian ships, spinning out of control toward the wormhole.

I sank into the command chair.

All the hope that I had held, all the feelings that I had had, the beginnings to the end of this nightmare, were gone. *Deep Space Nine* would now be forever a part of Mist space. That was what I thought at that moment.

The implications were incredible: there would be a war for the wormhole. The Klingons and the Cardassians and the Federation, not to mention Bajor, and of course, the Dominion—although at that time I had no idea of the scope and power of the Dominion—would all battle for this small sector of space. Kira, Odo, and the others would have to remain here, in this strange reality, for the rest of their lives.

"But that didn't happen," the wraith said. "You've talked about the station since."

"Shhhh," said everyone around him.

I said nothing to the doctor. I knew that he had already thought of this implication. That is why he looked even more shocked than he had before.

What I first needed to know was who made this tragic error—and then I needed my best medical and engineering minds on finding a way to get my station back to its proper place in space, before that sector of space became a battleground.

"What happened?" I asked. My voice felt as if it had come out of a deep well.

"I've never seen anything like it," Dax said, and in her voice I could hear the same shock that I felt. "Two of the ships tried to make a run past the *Madison*."

"*Paul* did this?"

"I honestly don't know. I don't think so," Dax said. "But the way it happened . . ."

"Get a grip on yourself, old man, and then tell me what you saw."

Dax swallowed and nodded. Apparently she, too, was thinking of the loss of the station, and what it meant to the entire sector. What it meant to our friends.

She took a deep breath. "The *Madison* simply exploded a photon torpedo in front of them, to warn them to stop. It didn't explode anywhere near the ships, but at that moment, every Mist ship exploded."

Every Mist ship. I stared at the debris floating around and through the ships in my usual reality. *Every Mist ship.*

"Could this have something to do with the differing molecular structures that you were talking about?" I asked Dr. Bashir.

"I don't think so," he said, not taking his gaze off the screen. "You see how the two kinds of matter interact. It's as if one can flow through the other."

"But a weapon—"

"A weapon should work the same way," Bashir said. "Otherwise you'd accidentally blow up ships in Mist space when you used a photon torpedo in ours."

Of course. Of course. This was beginning to make some sort of sense to me, but in a subconscious way. Over the years, I have learned to trust that feeling, to allow it, and not my conscious brain, to sort through things I did not entirely understand.

"Explain what happened again, old man," I said to Dax. "How did those ships explode?"

"It was as if someone pushed a button and they all just exploded."

"All at the same time?"

She nodded.

"Was it a chain reaction?"

"Oh, no," she said. "It happened too fast."

I felt cold. My subconscious brain did not like that.

I leaned forward in my captain's chair. I could not see anything on that screen but the exploded Mist ships overlaid on the Cardassian, Klingon, and alien ships.

"What about Captain Victor and the other homeworld ships?" I was almost afraid of what her answer might be. If they were gone, we, too, were trapped in Mist space. Forever.

Her hands flew across her console. Apparently, in her concern and shock, Dax had not thought of our situation.

"They're fine," she said, and I felt a relief that I hadn't thought possible. "They're standing half a light-year off."

"I doubt it was the photon torpedo that caused this," I said. "Given what I understand of this, if it were the torpedo, the ships would have cascade-exploded in a chain reaction. They did not. So either there's a phenomenon we don't understand happening with our equipment or something else is going on."

And considering how difficult the situation had been with Captain Victor, how little he told us, and how often we found out the truth was slightly different, I would have wagered all of Quark's latinum that something else was going on. Perhaps the ships had had weapons, or, what I considered to be the more likely scenario, they had self-destructed when we took the first prisoners.

Prisoners. That brought me back to other matters.

"Doctor, we have wounded in sickbay," I said.

"I know," he said. "I was just heading there when this happened." He gazed at the screen. "I would like to use the science station to see what caused this. If I get a chance, I'll run some tests in sickbay."

"Good," I said, doubting he would get that chance in the time we needed it.

He headed toward the turbolift. As he did so, I scanned the bridge. Dax had brought up replacement officers for my away team. They seemed as stunned as we were. The Vulcan transporter operator was here. Her name was T'Lak, and she was a competent engineer. O'Brien had hopes for her.

"Ensign T'Lak," I said, "take over the science station. See what you can determine."

My words reached her. She moved with military precision from her position near the turbolift to the science station. The security officer who stood in Worf's usual place, a young Bajoran man named Orla, met my gaze. In his eyes, I saw all the concern I felt for our own region of space. He knew as well as I did that we had to resolve this or Bajor was lost forever.

"Help her, Lieutenant Orla," I said.

He nodded, then bent over his console.

I didn't expect them to find anything—I don't even know if they knew what they were looking for—but I had to keep them busy while I thought this through.

I ran my hand over my scalp as if I still had hair to smooth. Dax looked at me, her eyes wide.

"None of this makes sense, old man."

"I know, Benjamin," she said. "I've been trying to think it through—"

"It makes sense to me," Cadet Nog said.

Dax and I both turned to him. He shrugged and gave us both a sheepish grin. He said, "My people believe there is profit to be made from both sides of a war. Sometimes playing one side against the other brings higher profits."

He was right, of course. It was an option I hadn't thought of because it was something that went against every inch of my being. I would have come to it eventually, but it would take time. That sort of betrayal—the kind that cost lives—was anathema to me.

"Thank you, Cadet," I said as I stood. "Dax, you have the bridge. I have some prisoners to talk to."

"Bah," Sotugh said. "You take advice from a Ferengi, and a Starfleet cadet at that."

Sisko smiled at Sotugh. "I take good ideas where I find them. And you must admit, he was right."

"Don't! Don't!" the Quilli said. "You're spoiling the story. Don't let that Klingon get you ahead of yourself."

Sotugh gave the Quilli a horrid threatening look. The Quilli's bristles rose and seemed to grow longer.

"I will close the bar," Cap said.

"Ah, Cap, it's a good old-fashioned stare-down," the Trill said. "Let them be."

But Sotugh broke the look. He waved a hand again. "I do not waste my time with creatures one-tenth my size."

"And who have a hundred times your brainpower," the Quilli said.

Sotugh growled softly, but did not turn. Instead, he leveled his frown at Sisko.

"So tell them what you discovered from the prisoners," Sotugh said. "Just remember that while you were sitting, talking, I was fighting a pitched battle to save your station. Even though *they* do not want to hear of it."

"Does that matter?" Sisko asked. "You enjoyed every moment of that fight."

"True," Sotugh said, his frown suddenly changing to a laugh. "It *was* glorious."

The six prisoners filled the *Defiant*'s brig. They were an odd mix of humans, Bajorans, and Jibetians. They were all dirty and one seemed injured. She was lying on the cot, a hand over her face.

I stood facing the forcefield. "Who's in charge here?"

A human stood and moved to face me. He was squarely built. His dark eyes and rounded cheeks seemed more suited to laughter than to war.

"I am in charge," he said. "My name is John David Phelps Jackson."

I motioned for the guards to drop the forcefield for a moment, then indicated that Jackson should come with me. He glanced at his compatriots, as if in apology, then followed me to a small table where I sat and indicated that he do the same.

For a moment he looked as if he would remain standing, but I again indicated the chair. "Sit. We need to talk."

He did, making certain that his friends in the brig could still see his face.

"I'm afraid," I said, "that your ships have all been destroyed. What is left of your force on the station is in a very heated and, most likely, losing battle with Klingons."

"Destroyed?" Jackson said, his face going gray. "Why did you do that? They had no weapons."

"We did not," I said. "I can assure you of that. And neither did the Klingons. Your ships exploded all at the same moment. We have no explanation, yet."

Jackson leaned back in his chair and closed his eyes for a moment. When he sat back up there was a haunted look behind his eyes, as if he'd just seen a ghost and that ghost was going to kill him.

"What do you want from me, Captain Sisko?"

"I want to know what's going on. All I've been told is one side of this fight. Captain Victor and Councillor Näna's side. I would like to hear yours."

The frown of puzzlement that crossed Jackson's face made no sense to me at that moment. Then he leaned forward. "You have talked to Captain Victor?"

"Yes," I said.

"Then you know our side as well."

Now it was my turn to be confused. "He has told me of your intentions with the station, and of your desire to be free from the homeworld rule, but—"

"Free of their rule?" Jackson said. "What are you talking about?"

I glanced at the people behind the forcefield, then back at Jackson. I sighed. It seemed, once again, that Captain Victor had been less than honest with me.

I leaned toward him and said, "I think it is time that I hear your side of exactly what is going on here."

Thirteen

JACKSON LOOKED AT ME AS IF I WERE CRAZY. REMEMBER, WE HAD FOUGHT him and his compatriots, and then we had captured them, easily. Suddenly I was asking for his side. I must have seemed capricious and strange.

He glanced over his shoulder at his friends in the brig. Four of them were watching intently. The woman remained on her bunk.

"First," he said, "I need medical attention for Sasha. Then I'll talk to you."

I frowned at the two security officers. They did not meet my gaze. It was their duty to report any injuries among prisoners—injuries that were more serious, say, than a slight cut or bruise—and these officers hadn't done so. I knew that the anger at the capture of the station was running high, but it was not an excuse for dereliction of duty. Theirs would be noted in their files, and I would take care of the situation when this crisis was over.

I hit my comm badge. "Dr. Bashir," I said. "We have a patient needing treatment in the brig."

"I'm nearly finished here, sir," he said. "I'll send a member of my team down immediately."

"Good." Then I laid my hands flat on the table. "Your friend will be taken care of. Now, talk to me. We don't have much time."

Jackson studied me, eyes narrowing. "I don't see why I should tell you anything."

I had had enough. I was tired, I was worried, and I was under a very real deadline. "We both are facing a crisis," I said. "You have just lost all your ships. My station has been yanked into a part of space where it does not belong, causing a serious crisis in my space. We did not destroy your ships, and I have a hunch I know who did. Captain Victor told me you were his enemy, which leads me to believe you and I are both being used."

"I'm the *enemy?"* Jackson said, again sitting back and closing his eyes as he took in the information.

I decided the best course was to push. "Captain Victor said that you and the rest of the colonists were tired of Mist rule. He said that you had a plan to take the station and use it to control the Mist homeworld. He brought us and the Klingons into this space to stop you."

Jackson sat bolt upright, his eyes bright, his gaze focused on mine. "The rumors have been rampant for years that the Federation and Klingons intended to invade the Mist and use our technology. Captain Victor's plan was to take over your station and use it as a defense against your attack."

My left hand clenched into a fist. I was angry, not just at Captain Victor, but at myself. All through this crisis, my gut had said things were not as they appeared. And although I noted the reaction, I did not act upon it.

"Until Captain Victor lured us into your space," I said, "we did not even know the Mist existed outside of the legends."

"You never intended to attack us?"

"Of course not," I said. "We usually don't attack without reason, and we never intentionally attack something we don't know exists."

Jackson stared at me for a moment, holding my gaze. There was power in those dark eyes. The man was a natural leader. "So, if you weren't going to invade us, none of this makes sense."

"Oh, it's making sense to me," I said, thinking of Nog's comment about profit. "But the only truth I know at the moment is that someone blew up your ships, and it was not us."

Then we heard the whine of a pneumatic door. Two medical technicians entered, and hurried to the brig. The barrier winked out, and they stepped inside. It immediately winked up again.

Jackson turned to me, his gaze level. I was keeping my promise; we both knew that. And I was not acting like a man bent on conquering a section of space.

He swallowed hard. "Is every one of my ships gone?"

I nodded.

He slapped a hand on the table and stood. The guards made a move toward him, but I signaled them to stay back. Thirty ships were gone; he had to have lost a lot of people. A lot of friends.

"All the ships near the station are gone," I said as gently as I could. "I assume those were yours. Including the two special ships."

"Special ships?" He turned and grabbed the back of his chair, looking down at me.

In his confusion, I knew the last of it, the last of it all. Captain Victor had lied to me about *everything.* I still did not understand his purpose in doing so, nor his point in bringing the *Defiant* over *before* the capture of the station, but I suspected it was all part of an elaborate ploy, a ploy that was beginning to unravel.

"Captain Victor told me that only two of your ships had the capability of bringing the station from the normal universe," I said. "He also told me that the station could only be returned by the same device."

Jackson half laughed. It was a desperate, bitter sound. "All our ships have the ability to bring something over from normal space. And any of them can return it if it hasn't been here too long."

"We did discover that problem on our own," I said. "If our calculations are correct, we may stay here a little over two hours. Right now, we have used up much of that time."

Jackson didn't seem to hear me. He appeared to be lost in his own thoughts. Slowly he sank back into his chair. "With the people thinking you destroyed all our ships, the war fever will reach an unstoppable level," he said. "Hundreds of Mist systems will declare war on your Federation, and the Klingon Empire."

"Hundreds?" The extent of the lies that I had been told—and that I had not had the time to check—was astounding me. Captain Victor was really an accomplished manipulator. His mixture of truth and falsehood was creative and plausible.

And worthless, now.

We were on the brink of a devastating war. Not only would we have the problems within our own space that I've already outlined—the defense of the wormhole, the problems with the Cardassians and the Klingons and, ultimately, the Dominion—but we would have to fight the Mist because *they* believed they were victims of an unprovoked attack. With their technology, they would defeat us in a matter of hours.

"I thought there were five systems," I said, my voice flat. I already knew that I was wrong.

"No," Jackson said. "There are two hundred and eight Mist systems in this quadrant."

"Ah, phooey," the Quilli said, and sat down, hard, in its chair. The Trill had to move his foot quickly before bristles stuck in his boot.

"Phooey?" Cap said, eyebrows raised.

"Yeah," the Quilli said. "Phooey. I thought this was a great story until now."

"You have an opinion, warthog?" Sotugh asked, sounding as offended as if he had been telling the story.

"Yeah," the Quilli said, "I do. I believe that there could be five Mist systems, but not two hundred and eight. First of all, where'd they get all the space? And secondly, if what Sisko said is true, they had to steal their population from our universe. Wouldn't *someone* have noticed?"

Sisko took a forkful of jambalaya, knowing now that the Quilli wouldn't care. The food was still hot, just as Cap predicted, and just as delicious.

"Sisko," Sotugh said. "It is your story."

Sisko swallowed, held up his hand so that he could get a moment, and then had a few gulps of ale. "I talked to Jackson about this later," he said. "The Mist learned how to shift out of normal time over two thousand years ago. There were five systems full of Mist at that time. Eventually, they expanded."

"But one new system every twenty years?" the Caxtonian said. "Come on."

Sisko wiped his mouth with his napkin and looked pointedly at the Quilli. "It was easy for them to find a system with no intelligent life and to bring it over," he said. "They needed the new systems for minerals, food, and manufacturing to supply the ever-expanding culture."

"But they had to have life-forms on those systems," the Quilli said. "You can't make me believe they had that kind of population explosion."

"I do not expect you to believe anything," Sisko said. "I'm telling you what Jackson told me."

"And he could've been lying like Captain Victor was."

Sisko smiled, thinking of John David Phelps Jackson. The man probably could lie, but would not do so unless he had to do so to save lives.

"He could have been," Sisko said, "but Jackson was not that kind of man. Remember, the Mist were constantly bringing in other races. The growth was solid and expanding. They also had no natural enemies. I later learned that there were over a million human Mist spread across twenty planets."

"And very few Klingons," Sotugh said.

"Fewer than a thousand," Sisko said. He looked at Sotugh and grinned. "And you know, they all have different facial features than you do."

"Bah," Sotugh said. "They left the Empire centuries ago. They are Klingon only by birth."

"Convinced now?" the Trill asked the Quilli.

The Quilli frowned, and its bristles moved forward. The frown was one of those expressions that made dangerous tiny creatures appear harmless and cute. Sisko was not fooled. "It is the first thing that has broken me out of the story's magic—naturally broken me out, not interrupted it," it said, looking at the others. Then it stood again, and bowed slightly to Sisko. "But in each story, the teller is allowed one impossible thing. I will give you this one. Do not have any more."

Cap put a fist to his mouth and turned away, hiding a grin. Sotugh rolled his eyes.

Sisko nodded solemnly. "I'll do my best," he said.

"Obviously," I said to Jackson, "Captain Victor and Councillor Näna want to start a war between normal space and Mist space. We do not have time to discuss why. You and I need to call a truce between our forces. My people are running out of time."

Behind Jackson, the medical team helped the injured woman up. She was between them. They put their arms around her, and half carried her out of the brig. The remaining prisoners did not try to get away.

Jackson watched this, as I did, and then turned to me. "If you can return my belt," he said, "I can order a cease-fire."

I instructed the guard to do as Jackson asked, then release the others. I tapped my comm link. "Dax," I said. "Patch me through to Sotugh."

"Aye, Captain," she said.

One of the guards had left. The other still stood before the door. Jackson's people crowded near the barrier.

Then I heard Sotugh's voice over the comm link. "Go ahead, Sisko," he said.

"Cease hostilities," I said. "We have no fight with those on the station."

"Is this a trick, Sisko?" Sotugh said.

"If I had known you were doing this on the strength of one man's word," Sotugh said, "I would never have stopped the fighting."

Sisko had learned to take these interruptions as part of his story. He had taken, enjoyed, and swallowed a quick bite of jambalaya while Sotugh talked.

"Have you never taken a man on his honor before?" Sisko asked.

Sotugh scowled. "Human honor is a difficult concept, often debated among the Houses of the Empire."

"But it does exist," Sisko said.

"Sometimes," Sotugh conceded.

"This is not a trick," I said to Sotugh. "We have a much larger enemy and very little time to fight him. Meet me in Ops. We have a battle plan to discuss."

The guard had given Jackson his belt. He was using it to order a cease-fire.

There was a momentary pause, and then Sotugh said, "Bah, they have stopped fighting. There is no honor in killing men who do not fight. I will meet you."

I turned back to Jackson, who nodded to me. The worry lines on his face had eased slightly, and I realized he was a much younger man than I had initially thought. Young or not, he was clearly in control of his people.

"We need to figure out just what Captain Victor is up to," I said, "and then we need to stop him. But first, we are running out of time for my station. We must shift it back to real space. Do you know how we can do that?"

"With all of my ships destroyed," he said, "I don't think we can. Your station is going to be stuck in this space."

"Unacceptable," I said. "That is exactly what Captain Victor wants to happen, and we're not going to give it to him."

Fourteen

"Bravo!" the Quilli said, clapping its tiny paws together.

"The story's not over, warthog," Sotugh said.

"It doesn't matter. I like tales of heroism and derring-do."

The Trill raised an eyebrow. "I take it that you have forgotten your disapproval."

"We may quibble about details," the Quilli said, "but quite frankly if the story's good, the details can be changed."

"You are going to sell this!" the Trill said.

"I never said that," the Quilli said, looking at Sisko, paws out as if it were shrugging its tiny shoulders. "I'm merely trying to help the captain here with his tale."

The Trill shook his head. "Don't trust a Quilli. Make sure it pays you something before it leaves. Believe me, it'll make a profit off you otherwise."

Sotugh's scowl grew. "The warthog seems to be fairly unpredictable. We will wait until Sisko is done before we will discover if this story meets the warthog's ideas of 'derring-do.' "

"You don't think it will?" Sisko asked him.

Sotugh shook his head. "The warthog is a little tiny creature covered with poisoned darts. Who knows what will please it?"

"It would please it to continue with the story," the Quilli said.

Cap actually laughed.

Sisko only smiled, and complied.

• • •

Jackson and I beamed into Ops to discover that the smoke had cleared, the fires were out, and my crew was hard at work repairing the station. Chief O'Brien was on his back near some fried paneling, his hands covered with soot as he worked.

Major Kira had not bothered to clean the dirt off her face or fix the sleeve of her uniform; she was sitting at her station, seeing what parts of *Deep Space Nine* were still on-line. From one of the comm links, I heard Security Chief Odo's voice growling about looters, but I could not tell to whom he was talking.

It did not matter. At this moment, we had to take care of the station.

As Jackson and I stepped off the transporter pad, Kira saw us. She raised a phaser so quickly that I did not see her hand move.

"Captain!" she said. "Stand aside. That's one of the men we were fighting."

"I know, Major," I said. "You can put your weapon down. Jackson and I have discovered a common cause."

Kira put down her phaser, but she narrowed her eyes in her "this had better be good" look.

I ignored it. "Major, I need a status report."

She sighed, knowing that I would not answer her unasked question immediately. She glanced at O'Brien. Except for a brief moment to observe the verbal altercation, he did not look away from his work.

"We'll have shields up in five minutes," she said. "Weapons are going to take another ten."

"She did a good job sabotaging the place," O'Brien muttered. He did not sound pleased.

"As she was ordered to do," I said. "Just put it back together as soon as you can. But the weapons are now our first priority."

"Captain, the shields—"

"I understand, Major," I said. "But the situation has changed. We need those weapons and we need them now."

"Yes, sir," Kira said.

O'Brien rolled away from the panel he was working on. Without bothering to close it, he moved to another, pulled it open, and started to work there.

At that moment Captain Higginbotham beamed onto the transporter pad. Higginbotham is a tall man who looks no different than he did when we were at the Academy together—except for the silver threading his dark wiry curls.

He wrinkled his nose at the stench of fried circuitry. "Remind me when I need a good saboteur to hire Major Kira," he said as he stepped off the pad.

"The situation has changed, Paul," I said.

"I gathered that when I saw the ships," he said. He nodded at Jackson, who did not nod back.

Then the turbolift clanged into place. The unusual sound made O'Brien lift his head from his work. Sotugh, his uniform covered with two phaser burns, stepped off.

"Four," Sotugh said. "Four phaser burns, Sisko. We were having a glorious pitched battle on the Promenade until you cut it off."

"Excuse me," Sisko said, not willing to quibble over details, although he was convinced he had only seen two phaser burns, "*four* phaser burns. No matter how you looked, we can agree on what you said."

"I said, 'Your explanation had better be a good one,' " Sotugh said.

"And I did not answer you immediately."

"No, you did not."

"Instead I turned to Major Kira."

"Are the sensors working?" I asked.

"Yes, sir," she said. "I didn't see any point in sabotaging those."

I moved over to a nearby panel and keyed in the main screen showing the scene outside. The Cardassians were still holding their positions near the wormhole but now there were at least a dozen Galor-class warships.

"A Klingon fleet of six will be here in less than thirty minutes," I said. "Three Federation starships will also be here by that point."

"It will be a glorious battle," Sotugh said.

"Yes," I said. "But it will be a fight staged by Captain Victor and the Mist. And I, for one, don't like fighting other people's battles."

"Staged?" Sotugh said.

I switched the screen to show the fleet of Mist ships now surrounding Captain Victor's ship half a light-year away. There were at least thirty, maybe more.

"Grey Squadron," Jackson said, staring at the screen with a look of shock. "I've never seen or heard of more than two in one place before."

"Grey Squadron?" Higginbotham asked.

Jackson half swallowed, then nodded without taking his gaze from the main screen. His eyes were touched with a hint of fear. "The Grey Squadron is made up of the only fully armed Mist ships. They've functioned as a sort of police force for centuries, keeping the peace among the hundreds of systems."

"Hundreds of systems?" Higginbotham asked, glancing sharply at me.

"Armed with what?" Sotugh demanded.

Jackson only shrugged. "No one really knows."

"Oh," I said, "Captain Victor knows. And our problem is that we must capture one of those ships within thirty minutes or we're not returning to normal space."

"What?" Major Kira said.

"Explain yourself," Sotugh demanded.

"Yes," Higginbotham said. "It seems there is a lot we haven't heard."

"I was beginning to think that I was the one who had been tricked," Sotugh said. "By you."

Sisko nodded. "I can understand that. You certainly were not set up to trust the Federation at that point in our histories. It is to your credit that you helped us and did not abandon everything at that point."

"I still think you are too gullible," Sotugh said, obviously pleased at Sisko's compliment.

"I think events were transpiring too fast to proceed on anything other than gut instinct," Sisko said.

"If I had done that, Sisko," Sotugh said, "I would have taken over your station myself."

Sisko shrugged and sipped his Jibetian ale. "That only proves my point, Sotugh. Events were transpiring too fast for us to do much more than stay ahead of them."

It took me a few short minutes to brief Captains Sotugh and Higginbotham, Major Kira, and Chief O'Brien.

"It seems that our focus," Higginbotham said, after I finished, "is to get a device under our control to shift us back to normal space. We shift the station first to get it out of here, and to forestall any problems in our space. Then we shift our ships back momentarily to buy more time."

"A good idea," Sotugh said.

"I think it's critical," I said, "that we don't let the station fall into Captain Victor's hands."

"And from the looks of those Cardassian ships," Major Kira said, "the station needs to be in normal space to stop a war."

I glanced at the screen. There were now more than a dozen Cardassian privateer ships near the wormhole and the number seemed to be growing by the minute. I turned to Jackson. "Do you have any other ships close by with the ability to shift?"

"Every starship has the shift device hooked to its warp drive," Jackson said. "But the closest ship would take an hour to get here, if it could get through the Grey Squadron."

"That's too long," I said.

"What about the debris?" Chief O'Brien asked Jackson.

"I don't understand," Jackson said, staring at the chief before glancing at me.

"Your ships," O'Brien said. "Is there any chance that one of the shift devices might have survived whatever blew them apart?"

Jackson glanced at the main screen, but none of the debris was visible. His entire face sagged. I knew that he saw not just debris, but the bodies of his crewmates. "One of them might have," he said after a moment. "They are well protected."

"Jackson, work with the chief to see what you can find." I turned to Captain Higginbotham and Sotugh. "If we end up fighting the Mist ships, we need to remember that they can beam through our shields."

"And more than likely shoot through, also," Higginbotham said.

"Five against thirty," Sotugh said. "I would welcome such odds if we had shields. Without shields, there is only stupidity in such a death."

"So we need to find a way to shield against their weapons," I said.

"You know," Higginbotham said, stroking his chin and staring out the screen at the Grey Squadron, "if they have such an advantage, how come they aren't pouring in here to destroy us?"

"The way that Victor has set things up so far," I said, "has been to allow Jackson to do the fighting for him. I suspect he believes we are still fighting. It doesn't matter to him, as long as we remain here past our time limit. Then we will be trapped in the Mist's space."

"At which point they come in, call us invaders, and destroy us," Higginbotham said.

"I would imagine that is Captain Victor's plan."

"A coward's plan," Sotugh said.

"Captain," Chief O'Brien said. "We've found one shift device intact."

"Excellent, Chief. Beam over to the *Defiant* and get it hooked up."

"Captain," Jackson said, and three of us turned to him. He grinned for the first time since I met him, an infectious look. No wonder he was an effective leader.

"Captain Sisko," he corrected. "With our device hooked up, your ship will not be able to transfer your space. It will only be able to transfer other objects."

I glanced at Higginbotham and Sotugh.

"In fact," Jackson went on," anything that has been in Mist space too long will stop the shift."

Higginbotham gave me a concerned look. Sotugh shook his head, as if this obstacle was yet another personal affront.

• • •

"You must admit, the difficulties of this mission were increasing by the minute," Sotugh said. "I prefer quick, clean battles, with the sides carefully drawn."

"How Klingon of you," Prrghh said.

I did not like it either, but we had been lucky enough to find a device. We were going to use it.

"Chief," I said, "get busy. We need to get this station back where it belongs."

"Aye, sir," O'Brien said. He contacted Dax, and together they worked on a plan to get the device on board the *Defiant* while he beamed over.

"Gentlemen," I said to Captains Sotugh and Higginbotham, "I need your crews to work on a solution to the problem of the shields. Captain Victor beamed onto the *Defiant.* I'm sure we have information about the effect that beam-in had on our equipment. I'll have Dax transfer that to your ships. It will give your people a place to start."

"You still see a coming fight with Captain Victor, don't you?" Higginbotham asked.

I nodded. "Even if we retreat back into normal space, he's going to tell everyone that we destroyed the ships in an aborted invasion into Mist space."

"Why would he do that?" Higginbotham asked. "I have been trying to figure this out and it makes no sense."

"I have been wondering the same thing," I said. I glanced at Jackson. He was working with Kira and not monitoring our conversation. "Greed, perhaps? Control? Some kind of power transfer? I plan to ask Captain Victor the next time I see him."

"Right before you kill him, if I have not done so first," Sotugh said.

Higginbotham opened his mouth, probably to tell Sotugh that that is not the Federation way, when I caught his eye and shook my head. Higginbotham said nothing.

"Which was a good thing," Sotugh said. "The last thing I would have wanted to know was that I was fighting alongside men without honor."

"We have honor," Sisko said. "It's just different from yours."

Sotugh looked at the other patrons. "And now you see why we Klingons debate the nature of human honor. It is as slippery and changeable as a Belopian eel."

Sisko grinned. "I ignored the question of killing Captain Victor, and instead said . . ."

• • •

"If we don't get him stopped now, the Mist will declare war on the Federation and Empire and that will be the end of both our cultures."

Higginbotham nodded. The full impact of what we were facing was slowly dawning on him. "They can transfer one ship at a time into their space and destroy it."

"Or one person at a time," I said.

"There is no honor in fighting an unseen enemy," Sotugh said.

"Then we fight them now, while we can see them," I said. "We need shields, gentlemen. And we need them quickly. Get your crews working on the solution. Then we will come up with a battle plan."

"The sooner the better," Higginbotham said.

"If we do this right, the battle will be glorious," Sotugh said.

"Maybe," I said. "If that shift device works and we can modify the shields to stop Mist fire."

"Details," Sotugh said, waving his hand and looking more confident than he had since he arrived in Ops. "Those are nothing but petty details."

Fifteen

"PETTY DETAILS?" PRRGHH SAID, STANDING UP AND STRETCHING, ARCHING her back slightly and touching the tip of her small tongue to her upper lip. Her back was impossibly flexible. She straightened and looked at Sotugh. "Trust a Klingon to be overconfident."

"We were not overconfident," Sotugh said. "I knew it was going to be a glorious battle."

"Seems to me it either had to be glorious or you were all dead." The Trill got up and went to the bar. He ordered Canar, which made everyone look at him as if he were crazy.

Everyone except Cap, that is. He turned around, took a bottle of Canar off the shelf, and asked the Trill if he wanted a glass or the entire bottle.

"The entire bottle, of course," the Trill said. "If it's good Canar."

"You drink that Cardassian garbage?" Sotugh asked.

The Trill shrugged. "Just because you disagree with a race's political habits doesn't mean you should ignore the things they do well. I usually go for a good blood wine, but tonight, during this story, I prefer Canar."

Tonight? Sisko frowned. He wondered how long he had been in here. Sometimes it felt like days; sometimes it felt like minutes. He'd been here long enough to ruin a plate of nachos and to have Cap's cook make jambalaya from scratch. Several hours at least.

"I'm a little confused," the wraith said. It moved away from the wall, looking almost like an opaque shadow in motion. "Can I see if I have the facts straight?"

"Shoot," Sisko said, picking up his fork. He might be able to finish this jambalaya after all. He took a bite. Wonderfully, the jambalaya was *still* warm. What kind of bowl did Cap use? Did it have its own heating source?

"Okay." The wraith folded itself on top of a table, looking like a bit of wax that was bending itself into a vaguely human shape. "This is how I understand it. In normal space, you have a possible battle between a Cardassian fleet and a Klingon fleet over control of the wormhole. Correct?"

"And the Federation," Sisko said, around a mouthful of jambalaya. His words were nearly unintelligible.

Sotugh seemed to notice and added, "Three starships would arrive on the scene at the same time as the Klingons."

The wraith stretched a thumb. It extended and thinned like a piece of taffy. Only when the wraith let go of it, it snapped back into position with a loud *thwap!* "And the only thing that might stop the fight is the return of *Deep Space Nine* to normal space?"

"That is what we believed," Sisko said, being as cagey as he could. He didn't want to spoil the story, not after he had put this much time into it.

"We thought," Sotugh said, "that with the station and its firepower there, the Cardassians might not try to control the wormhole, or risk a war with the Federation."

"Seems unlikely to me," the Caxtonian said, his fetid breath filling the bar. Sisko's eyes watered, and he had to put his fork down. "But then I've always believed that the Cardassians let that station go too easily."

Sotugh shot him a withering glance. The Caxtonian didn't even seem to notice.

Neither did the wraith. It stretched a forefinger. "Then in Mist space," it said, letting the finger *thwap!* into place. Sisko suddenly realized this must be its equivalent of the human gesture of raising fingers to count. "The *Defiant,* Sotugh's three battle cruisers, and the *Starship Madison* are facing a fleet of Mist ships. And you don't have shields that are effective against them."

"Exactly," Sisko said.

The wraith took its middle finger. As it started to extend it, the Trill at the bar took a step over and grabbed the wraith's hand. The Trill looked a little green.

"You're putting me off my Canar," the Trill said softly.

"Oh!" The wraith glanced at him. "Sorry." It reached for its finger again, then—literally—balled up its hand and let it absorb into its waxlike body.

"If you were to keep the station," it said, "you would stand a chance against the Mist fleet, but you must send the station back to keep it from getting stuck in Mist space."

"And stop the fight between the Cardassians and Klingons," Prrghh said. "It's really not that complicated a story. You're making it harder than it is."

"I just want to be clear," the wraith said.

"Don't you find this to be another impossible situation?" the middle-aged woman at the bar asked the Quilli.

"No," it said. "I find it fascinating, and I would like to hear more. But I have decided to have patience. I believe that these interruptions must be a human way of storytelling."

"It's the way stories are told in bars," the middle-aged man said.

Cap grinned at him. "You sound like an authority."

The man shrugged, then put an arm around the middle-aged woman. The casualness of the gesture told Sisko that either these two had been together a long time, or they were married or both. "After seventeen years of bartending," the man said, "you get to be an expert on just about anything that happens in a bar."

"A Quilli telling a story in a bar would never allow this many interruptions," the Quilli said.

"A Quilli telling a story in *this* bar wouldn't have a choice," the Trill said. He took his bottle of Canar and returned to his table. "So, our finger-snapping buddy over here is pretty clear on the concept and since no one else is asking questions, I assume everyone else is. You could probably continue."

"Good," Arthur said from behind the bar. "Because I've been wondering what plan you and Captain Sotugh and Captain Higginbotham come up with to solve this and keep the Mist from attacking normal space."

"If you'd let him finish his story," the Caxtonian said, "we'd all know."

Sisko reluctantly pushed the jambalaya away. "Well," he said, settling back into the story. . . .

It took us less than five minutes to work out a plan of attack—

"Ah, geez, you aren't going to tell us the plan, are you?" Arthur said.

"Shh," the Quilli said. "It's a storytelling ploy, and a good one for building suspense. Go on, Captain."

Captains Sotugh and Higginbotham had beamed back to their ships. I went to help Major Kira while Odo, my chief of security, made certain that all of Jackson's personnel and equipment were on board the *Defiant.*

Despite what Kira had said earlier, she and Chief O'Brien had done a great deal of work on the weapons. It only took the two of us two and a half minutes to get the weapons on-line. It took another two and a half minutes to get them powered to eighty percent. It took us another two minutes to get the screens back on-line. That left exactly fourteen minutes to shift the station or have it forever trapped in Mist space.

I used the station's communications to contact the *Defiant.* "Chief," I said without preamble. "We're running out of time."

"This is one strange machine," O'Brien said. "I haven't had much time to study it, but I think we've got it working." He paused for a moment, then added. "Dax tells me she's found another intact shifter in the debris."

"Good," I said. "Tell her to get it on board. If she finds any more, have her beam them on as well. Let's take as many precautions as we can while remembering our time constraints."

"Will do," O'Brien said.

"After she beams that on, stand by," I said.

"Aye, sir."

I closed the communication with the *Defiant* and immediately contacted the *Madison.* Higginbotham appeared on our screens. He was doing hands-on work. I could tell from the smudge of grease along his left cheek.

"Well, Paul?" I asked. "How are the shield modifications coming?"

"To be honest, Ben," Higginbotham said, "I have no idea if what we've done will work. My engineer and my science officer have differing opinions. My engineer is uncertain, but Dr. Jones is adamant. She says it will work."

I'd met Jones. She was one of the sharper minds in Starfleet. "Let's hope that Dr. Jones is correct," I said, "because we are out of time and options. I'm going to shift the station, the *Madison,* and the Klingon ships back to real space in exactly four minutes."

"Got it," Higginbotham said. "Good luck."

His image disappeared from our screen.

I turned to Major Kira. "Get those shield modifications from the *Madison* in case I have to bring you back to Mist space. When we shift the station back over to normal space, it will be up to you to deal with the Cardassians."

She smiled. Her teeth were very white against her filthy, battle-worn skin. "Oh, that will be my pleasure," she said.

"Major," I said, both enjoying and worrying about her enthusiasm, "deal with them peacefully, if possible."

"You take all the fun out of it," she said, her grin widening. I knew that she would do her best, and that she would stay within the parameters set by Starfleet. I also knew that this situation could get out of hand, quickly.

"As soon as I reach the *Defiant,"* I said, heading to the transporter pad, "be prepared to shift to our home space. But remember, we may need your help here if things start going sour. So be ready."

"Understood," she said. "Good luck."

That was the second time someone had wished me good luck in the space of five minutes. Such a wish usually meant that the speaker had no faith in the procedure ahead. I knew that we were operating on a by-gosh and by-golly basis. Our chances for success depended on a series of happy coincidences and on the ability of our engineers—mine and Captain Higginbotham's—to analyze and compensate for unfamiliar equipment, and then make it work the first time.

I had faith in Chief O'Brien and I knew that Higginbotham's new engineer, Braun Ginn, was one of the best in the fleet. But sometimes we asked too much of these talented people.

Apparently Higginbotham and Kira both thought this was one of those times.

"You mean," said a man at the bar who hadn't spoken until now, "that you've gone through situations before where a plan like this would work?"

He sounded completely skeptical. Sisko had been watching him during the story. The man was large, with a full white head of hair and matching beard. He smoked a meerschaum pipe that made him look as if he belonged in the nineteenth century instead of the twenty-fourth. Even his clothing had that old-fashioned sense.

Sisko smiled. "The history of Starfleet is filled with engineers who have made things work on a whim and a prayer," he said. "Beginning with Zefram Cochrane."

"You could make the argument," said the middle-aged man at the bar, "that the history of human spaceflight is filled with engineers like that. Think of the Mir space station in the twentieth century. That thing was up there for at least a decade longer than it should have been and I swear by the time they retired it, it was held together by spit and glue."

"Humans have always been that way," the woman beside him said. "Think of the Wright brothers."

"Columbus," the Trill said.

"I've always thought of him as an incompetent," the white-bearded man said. "Imagine sailing one way and believing you were sailing another."

"Robinson," Cap said, "we'll have time for your opinions later."

"You let Bo'Tex express his," Robinson said.

"Yes," Cap said, "but I didn't warn him two days ago about antagonizing the other patrons, like I had to warn you."

"Nope," Robinson said. "You just reminded him to bathe!"

At that moment, Sisko realized they were talking about the Caxtonian. No wonder the place didn't smell completely like Caxtonian body odor. Cap kept his customers in line.

"Someday," Sisko said, "I will tell you stories about the great engineers of the post-warp era, starting with Cochrane, going through Ty'lep and Montgomery Scott, and ending with a few that I know personally, like Miles O'Brien."

"I'd like to hear it," Robinson said, obviously mollified.

"Maybe next," the Quilli said, clapping its tiny paws together.

"What, do you have a quota or something?" the Trill asked. "You've been asking for a lot of stories."

The Quilli shrugged. "Maybe I like stories better than I like"—it grimaced at the bottle of Canar—"liquor."

"Or maybe you see a way to make a small fortune off this place," the Trill said. "Hey, Cap. Is it legal for a Quilli to be here?"

"If it's a captain, it is," Cap said. "I don't ban patrons from this place just because they act according to their culture's precepts."

The Trill narrowed his gaze, and then grinned. "Touché," he said. "Hadn't thought of it that way. So this is a sort of 'storyteller beware' place."

"Every place is," Cap said. "Some just aren't as obvious as others."

"Does it bother you to have the Quilli listening?" the middle-aged woman asked Sisko.

Sisko smiled at the small creature. "It's a good audience," he said.

"Thank you," the Quilli said, making a small formal bow. "And I am finally getting used to these interruptions. Although I would like to know if you got the station back to its own space."

"Yes," the Trill said dryly. "I think we're all ready for a fight."

Sisko didn't know if the Trill meant inside the bar or inside the story, and he didn't really care. He pushed the nearly empty bowl of jambalaya aside and went back to the tale.

After the destruction I had been dealing with on the station, it felt good to be back on the *Defiant,* where things appeared to be running smoothly. Worf had returned to his security post. Dax was still at the helm. Cadet Nog looked like he belonged on communications.

Dax had the Grey Squadron on the screen. Individually, those ships had been beautiful. En masse, they looked like a fleet of ancient warships about to attack a defenseless village.

I dropped into the command chair and contacted Chief O'Brien in engineering. "Chief," I said. "Are you ready?"

"As ready as I'll ever be," the chief said. "This will work like a charm. I've got the shifter attached to the warp coil and the controls hooked up on the tractor beam. Jackson and two of his people are right here to help me."

That eased my worry a bit. Jackson, at least, should have known how this shifter worked.

• • •

"Your faith in an unknown human astounds me," Sotugh muttered.

"I've noticed that humans are an incredibly optimistic species," the Trill said.

"That's a charitable way of putting it," Prrghh said, as she crossed her arms and leaned back in the chair.

I asked the chief, "How about the shields?"

"I've made the shield modifications that the chief engineer of the *Madison* suggested," O'Brien said. I could almost hear him shrug. When he spoke like that, his attitude was that the idea might work, but he wasn't going to stake anything important on it. I never knew how to take that attitude. O'Brien usually didn't trust any engineer's work but his own—unless, of course, he had trained that engineer from the ground up.

"Good," I said to him. "Stand by."

"Standing," he said.

I grinned. We were always at our best at moments like this.

"Dax," I said. "Are all of Jackson's personnel aboard?"

"People and equipment," Dax said.

"Cadet, open a secure channel to both the *Madison* and the *Daqchov,*" I said.

"Yes, sir," Nog said.

A moment later the main screen split. Sotugh was on one, still looking battle-scarred with his four phaser burns—

"Finally got it right," Sotugh said.

—and Higginbotham was on the other, wearing just a bit more grease. After working to repair the station, I must have looked in the same sort of state.

"We're ready," I said. "We will shift the station first. Then we will shift your ships, Sotugh, and then the *Madison.*"

"Get us back quickly," Higginbotham said. "The Mist fleet is going to be on you in no time."

"Oh," I said, "I have no desire to fight them alone."

"Good," Sotugh said. "No point in taking all the glory."

I indicated that Nog should cut the communication.

"Chief," I said. "Ready?"

"Ready, sir," he said from engineering.

"Okay, old man," I said to Dax. "Put the station back where it belongs."

Sixteen

DAX BENT OVER HER CONSOLE. HER FINGERS MOVED WITH GREAT CONFIDENCE, but she was biting her lower lip again.

"I'm turning on the beam," she said, "and pointing it at the station."

I gripped my chair.

Worf raised his head to watch.

Nog sat down for the first time during this mission.

Dax continued to work.

On the main screen, a line of white mist seemed to form in space, expanding like a cloud and flowing over the station, making it look slightly hazy. It seemed as if we were at sea, and the station were being covered by a great fog. The normally clear outline of the station became indistinct; then it blurred.

And then, suddenly, clarity returned.

The white mist disappeared. From our vantage, it looked like the station had passed through a very thin cloud and emerged on the other side, completely unchanged.

I could see nothing different. The station hung in its normal place. The Cardassian ships hovered near the wormhole, and a half-dozen Klingon ships were dropping out of warp.

"It didn't materialize on anyone?" Prrghh asked with great disappointment. She had a bloodthirsty look in her eyes that Sisko had suspected was there but hadn't seen until now. "I've been waiting this entire story to see what would happen when the station reappeared in the spot where someone else was."

"I thought I had been clear about that," Sisko said. He took a sip of Jibetian ale. "I had said that the station looked the same, with the ships around it, even though it was phased into Mist space."

"Yeah?" Prrghh said. "So?"

"So no one had moved into the space that the station had previously occupied," Sisko said.

"No one?" Prrghh asked.

"No one," Sisko said.

Prrghh shook her head, and leaned her chair back on two legs. She looked over her shoulder at the Quilli. "There's another impossible thing for you," she said. "I'd say the story's worthless."

"Nonsense," the Quilli said. "You just don't pay attention."

"I do," Prrghh said. "But with all those ships, one of them would have moved into the station's space."

The Quilli patted down its bristles as if it were wearing a suit and searching its vest pockets for something. The habit appeared to be a nervous one.

"Forgive me for being so bold," the Quilli said.

"As if you were not bold before," Sotugh growled.

"But what Sisko said about the station makes perfect sense to me. In fact, it seems illogical for someone to move into the station's spot," the Quilli said.

"It doesn't seem illogical to me," Prrghh said.

"It would if you were there," the Quilli said. "Imagine going to a space station you always go to. Then it disappears. Vanishes, right before your eyes. Would you fly your ship in those coordinates? Especially right after the thing vanished?"

Everyone in the bar turned to Prrghh. It was a captaining question, a leadership question. Would you take your precious ship with its valuable cargo and its even more valuable crew, and risk it on an insignificant shortcut through a bit of space occupied by something as large as a Cardassian-built space station a moment before?

Prrghh seemed to struggle with the question, not, Sisko believed, because she would make such a grievous mistake, but because she didn't want to lose face. She set her chair back down on all four legs.

"Well," she said, "when you put it that way, no. I wouldn't."

"See?" the Quilli said. "Not impossible at all."

"Well," the Trill said. "One war's been averted. Let's see if Sisko averted another one."

Sisko smiled. "After the white mist vanished, Dax said . . ."

• • •

"Transfer complete."

I couldn't tell the difference. I squinted at the screen. "Are you certain?"

Dax checked her instruments. Behind me, I heard corresponding beeps as Worf checked his.

"I'm positive, Captain," she said.

"Then let's get Sotugh's ships transferred. Quickly." I hit my comm badge. "Jackson, I need you on the bridge at once."

"All right, Sisko," Jackson said. He was making a point of not calling me by my title. It was, I think, his way of regaining some personal power after being held prisoner.

"I'm turning on the beam," Dax said, "and aiming at the Klingon ships."

She rarely used so many words to describe a procedure, but we had no shorthand for this one. I turned to the screen just in time to see another white line of mist form, expand into a small cloud, and flow over the Klingon ships. They, too, became indistinct, almost ghostly forms of their selves, and then they became solid again.

The white mist disappeared.

I remember thinking, *What an odd device,* and also *This must be how people without transporters regard our technology.*

"Transfer complete," Dax said. She was shaking her head slightly as if she couldn't believe what she was seeing either.

Cadet Nog swiveled his chair toward me. "Major Kira is hailing the Cardassians," he said.

I had to take care of one problem at a time. "Dax, transfer the *Madison* to normal space."

"Beginning transfer," she said, finally developing a way of describing what she was doing.

The white mist formed, and engulfed the *Madison.* The starship seemed small and insignificant in the mist. I wondered if that was because the white mist mimicked a natural phenomenon on my home planet, Earth. No matter how far we go into the stars, the natural phenomena of our homes always seem more powerful than we are.

The *Madison*'s clean lines became blurry. Then the mist evaporated, and the *Madison* looked like herself again.

"Transfer complete," Dax said for a third time.

"Captain." Nog sounded panicked. "Captain Victor is demanding that he speak with you. Captain Sotugh is talking to the Klingon ships, and the *Madison* has contacted the other Starfleet vessels. Major Kira is still hailing the Cardassians."

"It sounds like the Tower of Babel out there, doesn't it, Cadet?" Dax asked with a grin.

"Huh?" Nog said, clearly not understanding the reference.

• • •

"I don't either," said the Quilli.

Several other alien voices chimed in as well.

"It's an Earth reference," the Trill said. "From one of their religious documents."

"How do Trills know about it?" the wraith asked.

The Trill smiled. "Trills make a point of knowing every good reference in the quadrant," he said.

Behind me, I heard the doors to the turbolift open. I spun my chair in time to see Jackson stride across the bridge. He seemed calm and self-assured. It was a nice contrast to the cadet's burgeoning panic.

"Everything has shifted back," I said to Jackson. "Are you ready?"

"I hope this works," he said, and I heard worry in his voice. Already he had mastered one of the main elements of command. No matter how concerned you are, always seem calm. If he lived through this, he would be a fine commander someday.

"That does not work with Klingons," Sotugh said, as he stood to get more blood wine.

"All we need is a little time," I said to Jackson. Then I stood and gave Jackson my command chair. He looked at it as if sitting in it would be a violation of some unwritten rule. Instead, he stood in front of it, much as I did when I spoke to others on screen.

"Dax," I said. "Make certain that the focus is on Jackson only. Everyone else remain quiet. Nog, I want this conversation to go out on a very wide band."

"Understood," Dax said.

"Yes, sir," Nog said.

"Connect him with Captain Victor," I said.

I moved over and stood near Nog, monitoring the young cadet. So far, he had acquitted himself well, but he did not dare make a mistake now. And as we all know, monitoring such wide and varied communications, while handling important ones of your own, can make for some interesting—and deadly—mistakes.

As it turned out, I needn't have worried. Nog handled the situation just fine. But at the time, I monitored everything.

Captain Victor appeared on screen. He was wearing his yachting cap low over his forehead, nearly obscuring his dark eyes. He did not look happy. Councillor Näna, beside him, seemed the same as ever. Näna's round mouth opened and closed for apparently no reason. His left eye wandered, and his right one was obscured by the screen.

Jackson put his hands on his hips and grinned. It was a powerful, cocky look, one that not many men could have carried off. Jackson made it look normal.

"Captain Victor," Jackson said. "Councillor."

"Jackson!" Victor sounded panicked. "What happened?"

"We captured this ship," Jackson said, "along with the station. However, it was clear that the Federation and Klingons had nothing to do with the destruction of our ships, and have no ability to shift into our space. They were brought over against their will, so we sent them back."

"You sent them *back?!"* Victor took a step closer to the screen as if he wanted to come through it and strangle Jackson himself. "You were not authorized to do that!"

Jackson let his grin slip. His expression hardened. It was clear just how dangerous this man could be. "I didn't realize I had to be authorized to take appropriate action."

"Jackson, your action was not appropriate," Victor said, obviously trying to get control of himself. "You don't understand what you have done!"

"Oh, I think I do," Jackson said. "Your information was incorrect about the Federation invasion. Up until you brought one of their ships over, and tricked my crews into bringing over their station, they didn't know we existed."

Captain Victor stiffened up like a statue. Beside him, Councillor Näna's mouth closed, and remained closed.

"How dare you accuse me of such things?" Victor said.

"I don't dare anything, Victor," Jackson said. His expression was now so hard that he looked nothing like the man who had grinned at Victor a moment before. "I have proof that you and your Grey Squadron blew up my ships. My planet's representative to the High Council will not be happy when he learns of your ploy. The entire High Council will not be happy."

For a moment Captain Victor seemed to hold his breath as his face reddened. Then slowly his eyes grew cold and his face seemed to change. "The High Council," he said, as if he were speaking of an annoying child. "The High Council is no longer important. We will simply destroy you, bring the station back over, and rule the Mist with it."

"An excellent plan," Jackson said, letting his arms drop. "In fact, an elegant plan, given its simplicity. It probably would work too, if the Grey Squadron were with you."

"They're with me, Jackson," Victor said. "They've always been with me." He moved closer to the screen. "And you have just guaranteed your death."

Then the screen went blank.

• • •

"Excellent," the wraith said. "You were broadcasting to the entire Mist. They saw Captain Victor for what he was, to stop them from thinking the Federation had attacked."

"That was my hope," Sisko said, nodding. Then he went on with the story.

"The Greys are moving," Dax said.

"Put it on screen," I said. "Let's keep a close eye on them, while we get the Federation and the Klingon ships back here."

"Aye, sir," Dax said. She bent over her console, performing the unfamiliar procedure.

"Transferring now," she said.

A white mistlike strip formed in space near the *Madison,* expanded to a cloud, and swept over it. Then the same thing repeated over the other two Federation starships. As I watched, the same cloud swept over the *Daqchov* and the other eight ships of the Klingon fleet.

I left communications in the cadet's capable hands, and walked over to Jackson. He grinned at me. "I think I could get used to commanding one of these."

"You'd have to go through Starfleet Academy first," I said, grinning back. "Although I must say, you might want to join the Mist version of the Royal Shakespeare Company. That was a hell of a performance."

"Very convincing," Nog said without looking up from the communications array.

"I think you bought enough time for the ships to adjust their shields," I said. "Good work."

"I hope so," Jackson said. "With that man ruling the Mist, nothing in this quadrant will be safe. In either space. That much has become very clear."

"Captain," Dax said. "In one minute, the Greys will be in range."

"Messages are coming in from the *Daqchov* and the *Madison,*" Nog said. "They're ready."

"Good," I said. "Open a hailing channel to Captain Victor. Again make sure this is broadcast as far as possible."

"Yes, sir," Nog said.

Both Jackson and I turned to face the screen as Captain Victor's face appeared. Until that day, I had never seen a human being's face turn purple with rage. But Captain Victor's did. He sputtered a moment before getting a word out.

"A Federation trick," Captain Victor said. "I thought so."

Councillor Näna had moved far away from him. Näna's mouth remained closed, and it appeared that his left eye had rolled inside his gray head.

"It was no trick," I said. "Jackson told the truth. And he's asked us and the Klingons to help him stop you from taking control. We have agreed."

"That is the truth," Jackson said. "You will not disband or destroy the council."

"I thought you didn't interfere in the internal affairs of others," Victor said to me.

I almost laughed. But I was conscious of our audience. "You brought us into this, Victor. You are responsible for our presence. You must live with the consequences."

"No," Victor said. "You must. You think a few weak Starfleet ships and some broken-down Klingon cruisers can stop the Grey Squadron?"

Jackson smiled. "Oh, I think so. And for the sake of the council and all the Mist worlds, I hope so."

"Be prepared to die," Victor said, and severed the communications. After a moment of darkness, the screen went back to showing the Grey Squadron. The ships looked even more menacing than they had before. They were well named.

"They'll be here in thirty seconds," Dax said.

"We have another problem, Captain," Worf said.

"I knew this resolution was too easy," the Quilli said, rubbing its paws together with glee.

"It's the Cardassians," Worf said. "They have taken up attack formation around the station."

I looked at the scene before me. Beyond the Grey Squadron, the station floated in its normal space. The Cardassians had formed an attack squadron around it. Suddenly we had a two-front battle, and to be honest, I wasn't sure we could win either of them.

Seventeen

"DID YOU FORGET ABOUT YOUR OWN SHIP?" THE WRAITH ASKED, PULLING on its fifth finger. The finger stretched and stretched, looking like a thin piece of gum.

The Trill was out of his seat, heading toward the wraith, as the wraith let go. The *thwap* echoed throughout the bar.

Several patrons—not just the Trill—shuddered.

Sisko found the whole finger thing kind of fascinating, but he was glad he was no longer eating.

The Trill grabbed the wraith's hand and squeezed it until it formed a doughlike impression of the Trill's fist. "Don't do that again," the Trill said. "It's disgusting."

"My people find it rather sexy," the wraith said.

The Trill made a face, and wiped his hands vigorously on his pants. Sisko got the sense that the wraith was grinning.

The wraith's hand re-formed into a normal, human-shaped hand. "Well?" he asked. "Did you forget?"

"No, I hadn't forgotten," Sisko said. "I simply hadn't had time to remind my crew of the problem. Besides, we could not do anything until the *Madison* or the *Daqchov* were back in Mist space. And when that happened, our hands were suddenly quite full."

"Oh, no," Prrghh said. "Don't tell me you lost your ship."

Several patrons groaned.

"Sisko strikes me as the sort of man who would go down with his ship," Robinson said. "I suspect the *Defiant* was fine."

"I think we're getting a little ahead of the story here," the Quilli said, sounding more like Sisko's first-year intergalactic literature instructor at the Academy than Sisko would like to think about.

"We have a two-front battle going on, and all you people can do is chatter. Have you no discipline?" Sotugh asked.

So the end of the story interested him, despite everything. Sisko suppressed a grin.

"We have discipline, just not when we're drinking," the middle-aged man said.

"I'm sorry," the wraith said. "It's just that I was curious—"

"It was a good question," Sisko said, "and one I needed to deal with because time was running out. However, I had the Grey Squadron and the Cardassians to worry about at that moment."

"Couldn't you have let the station take care of the Cardassians?" the Quilli asked, then clapped a paw over its mouth. The entire bar burst into laughter. The Quilli had learned some bad habits in the Captain's Table.

"If you do that on Quilla," the Trill said, "you lose your license to tell stories."

"I was just getting into the spirit of things," the Quilli said through its paw.

"To answer your question," Sisko said, "no, I could not. Even though I captained the *Defiant,* my true command was—and is—of *Deep Space Nine.* If I lost her to the Cardassians, the results would have been disastrous."

"I never did understand why the privateers attacked. Did they know of the Cardassian-Dominion alliance that soon?" Sotugh asked.

"No," Sisko said. "I have not understood it either, but my best guess is one that Dr. Bashir put forward after we recaptured the station."

"And the theory was?" Sotugh asked.

"They were acting like all pirates, looking for profit. They were planning to hold the wormhole for ransom."

"The Grey Squadron!" someone yelled from the back. Surprisingly, several patrons turned as if the fleet were coming through the door.

Sisko grinned. "Sorry," he said, and spun his empty Jibetian ale bottle with his fingers. Cap took it from him, and went back to the bar, probably to get him a new one.

"I told Dax," Sisko said, "to put us in the middle of the Federation and Klingon ships. That way, if it looked like any of them were getting into trouble—"

"You could shift them back to normal space, out of trouble!" the wraith said.

"Exactly," Sisko said.

• • •

Dax instantly implemented my order. Then I turned to the cadet.

"Nog," I said. "I want you to monitor the situation between the Cardassians and the station. If the Cardassians attack, I want to know at once."

"Yes, sir," Nog said.

"Second, Cadet," I said, "I want this battle broadcast on an open band. I want all the Mist worlds seeing what is happening here."

Nog nodded, and bent over his panel. After watching him work a few moments before, I had a great deal more confidence in his abilities. The cadet would be an excellent officer one day.

"Bah!" Sotugh said. "Such confidence in a Ferengi."

Then I turned to Commander Worf. He was glowering at the situation in front of him. "Mr. Worf," I said. "Put our shields up and have our weapons ready."

"Aye, sir," Worf said.

On the main screen the nine Klingon ships had spread out on the left, taking up an attack formation facing the approaching Mist fleet.

On the right, the *Starships Madison, Idaho,* and *Cochrane* were in position, forming a wedge. Dax had placed the *Defiant* in the middle, and slightly behind the rest, giving us a complete view of the coming battle.

The Grey Squadron of the Mist was a both intimidating and beautiful sight. Their swept-back wing configuration made them look more like a flock of birds fanning out through the blackness of space. They were no more than half the size of most of the ships they were facing. Even the *Defiant* was larger than the largest Mist ship. Yet they outnumbered us by almost two to one.

And I had no idea if our shields would hold against their weapons.

We were going to either give them a fight, or get torn from space. At that moment I had no idea which it was going to be.

"If I had any idea you were such a pessimist, Sisko, I would never have agreed to fight with you," Sotugh said. "I knew we would overcome the Mist."

Sisko smiled and took a new Jibetian ale from Cap. "My people believe overconfidence is dangerous," he said.

"My people believe that unrealistic pessimism is grounds for demotion," Sotugh said.

"Sounds like you were ready to face anything that was going to come at you," the Trill said. He was not being sarcastic.

"I like to think we were," Sotugh said. "Obviously Sisko did not."

"I had a lot to think about then," Sisko said. "At that moment, Dax told me the Grey Squadron had come into range."

The squadron formed a line in front of us, like thirty ravens, bent on destruction.

"Let them fire the first shot," I said, more to myself than to anyone else.

For a moment I honestly didn't think anyone was going to fire. Then Captain Victor's ship fired a bright blue beam, hitting the *Defiant* and rocking us slightly.

Our shields held.

I wanted to cheer, but didn't.

A second later, space was full of bright blue beams, cutting through the blackness like flashlights cutting the dark as all the Grey Squadron opened fire on us.

The Mist ships scattered and attacked randomly as they swept in on the Klingons and Federation ships.

The *Defiant* was caught with two blasts, rocking us so hard that Jackson was tossed to the floor and I was almost knocked from my chair.

"The shields are holding," Dax said, confirming what I already knew. She sounded surprised.

"They are holding on all of our ships," Worf added. He was clutching his console as the *Defiant* continued to rock.

"Return fire, Mr. Worf," I said.

Instantly I could feel the surge of the laser fire. The phaser cut a path ahead, catching a sweeping Mist ship like a bird in flight.

It exploded.

The Mist ship simply burst directly in front of us like a balloon stuck with a pin.

Our phaser had cut through it without any interference.

"What?" Prrghh said. "You've got to be kidding. Didn't they have a defense against your weapons?"

"They thought they did," Sisko said. "But they hadn't thought the situation through like we had."

"They hadn't modified their shields," the Caxtonian said.

"Exactly," Sisko said. "I'm not even sure they knew they had to."

"Okay," Prrghh said. "Explain this one."

"Sisko already has," Sotugh said.

"Explain it again," Prrghh said.

"I never realized that you were so slow," Sotugh said.

"And I never realized that you could be this rude," Prrghh said, sneering at the Klingon captain.

To forestall more fighting, Sisko said, "The difference between normal space and Mist space causes the shields to be slightly out of phase with the weapons. So they could have gone through our shields if we hadn't made the modification, and since they didn't modify their shields, our weapons went through theirs."

"And you wouldn't have known that if Captain Victor hadn't beamed through your screens when you first met," the Quilli said, obviously delighted at this turn of events.

"Exactly," Sisko said.

"So, I assume, you let Sotugh kill Captain Victor?" Prrghh asked.

"Sisko wouldn't do that," the wraith said. "Remember the argument about honor?"

"What did you do about Victor?" the middle-aged woman at the bar asked.

"And your ship?"

"And the Cardassians?"

"Well," Sisko said, feeling slightly overwhelmed by the questions, "you forget. The battle wasn't over yet."

A dozen other Mist ships exploded almost simultaneously, as the Klingon and Federation vessels returned fire. Debris flew everywhere. The scene was as devastating as the destruction of Jackson's ships. Jackson, by the way, pulled himself to his feet and watched, saying nothing. To this day, I do not know what he thought of that destruction.

Even though we were outnumbered two to one, the battle wasn't really a battle. They had no chance at all. Our weapons simply cut them apart while their weapons were useless against our modified shields.

It was an eerie battle as well. Imagine the Mist ships exploding in space, phasers and bright blue beams cutting through the darkness of space, and all around the devastation, other ships, Cardassian ships, hovered, as if nothing else was going on.

"To them nothing was," Sotugh said. "They were concentrating on *Deep Space Nine.* They could not even see us like we could see them."

"Exactly," Sisko said. "But we needed to pay attention to the coming fight, and with the mercifully short battle, we got our chance."

The fighting was over in a matter of seconds. Jackson looked stunned. The famed Grey Squadron of the Mist had been reduced to rubble in the time it took him to get to his feet.

"Nog," I said. "Open a channel to the starships and the Klingons."

"Aye, sir," he said. "Go ahead."

I stood. "Don't destroy Captain Victor's ship. Surround and hold it."

• • •

"I still think you should have let me kill him," Sotugh said.

"It would have made things easier," Sisko said. "But I didn't know that at the time."

"Even if you had known that," Sotugh said, "you would not have killed him."

"You're right," Sisko said. "That's not how Starfleet fights its battles."

And we fought this one by the book. The *Madison* and three Klingon ships, including the *Daqchov,* moved toward Victor's ship while the remaining Klingon ships chased the fleeing Mist ships, cutting them apart with ease.

All Captain Victor had to do was surrender. The battle was over. He had lost. It was clear to everyone, even Victor himself, I'm sure.

But the clarity made no difference. Captain Victor was not going to surrender. And even though it seemed at that moment that we could take him easily, Captain Victor had other plans.

He put them into effect immediately.

Eighteen

"WHAT OTHER PLANS COULD HE HAVE HAD?" PRRGHH ASKED. "HE CLEARLY had no options. He had no defense against your weapons; his fleet was being destroyed; Jackson had the sympathy of the Mist worlds—didn't he?"

Sisko smiled. "He did," Sisko said.

"Victor's plan was the plan of a fool," Sotugh said.

"A desperate fool," Sisko said.

"But sometimes," the Quilli said, climbing on the back of its chair, "desperate fools make dangerous enemies."

"True," the Trill said, placing one booted foot on the seat of the Quilli's chair. Sisko wondered if the Quilli even knew that the Trill kept saving it from falling over.

"Quite true," Sisko said, "and we were thinking like Captain Prrghh. Any rational man would know he had lost. Unfortunately, Victor was not rational."

He kept firing at us. The shots rocked the ship, but did no damage.

"What's he doing?" Jackson asked, as he held on to one of the consoles.

"I hoped you could tell me," I said. Victor's ship cut past the *Defiant,* shooting as it went. We rocked again.

"He's heading toward the station," Dax said.

"Screens holding at ninety percent," Worf said.

I stood. Perhaps Captain Victor had not understood what I had been saying to him. "Hail Captain Victor."

"I am hailing," Nog said, "but he's not responding."

"Open a channel anyway, Cadet, and broadcast this message to Victor on all frequencies. Ready?"

"Aye, sir," Nog said.

I nodded. "Captain Victor, cease-fire or be destroyed with the rest of your ships."

In response, Victor shot at the *Defiant.* The bright blue beam hit our shields directly, and bounced harmlessly off them.

"I don't think he's going to surrender," Dax said.

"He's a fool," I said.

"You said you were going to destroy him," Jackson said, "but there are some good people on those ships who are simply doing their jobs. They don't know what's going on."

I knew that. It was that way in any war. That's why wars were so devastating. I did not answer Jackson, not then.

"The captain does not believe in unnecessary bloodshed," Worf said.

"I think taking out Victor would have been necessary bloodshed," Sotugh said.

"You could have done so," Sisko said.

Sotugh shrugged. "I figured it was your fight, Sisko."

Sisko looked at him, not entirely believing that. "The *Daqchov* flanked Victor's ship on the right, and the *Madison* flanked him on the left. . . ."

They flew in and around the Cardassian ships as if they were flying around posts.

Victor's ship headed directly for the station. For a moment I thought Victor was attempting to use the station as some sort of shield, even though it was in normal space and he was in Mist space.

Then a white line of mistlike clouds appeared near the station and expanded, flowing over the station like a bad storm over the top of a mountain.

"He's bringing the station back over," Dax said.

"You're kidding," the Trill said. "What about the Cardassians?"

"To them," Sisko said, "the station had yet again disappeared."

"I wish I could have seen the expression on their faces," Sotugh said.

Sisko grinned. He hadn't thought of that before. "So do I," he said.

"Imagine planning an attack on an outpost that winked in and out like a strobe light," the wraith said, laughing.

"There have been stranger things in this world," Arthur said cryptically.

"Did he think he could take over the station?" the Quilli asked. "Jackson had failed. What was his plan?"

"The plan of a desperate man," Sotugh said. "He seemed to be inventing it as he went along."

"And our team was matching him move for move," Sisko said, "invention for invention."

As the white mist cleared, and Victor's ship moved under one of the docking pylons, I told the cadet to hail Major Kira.

A moment later Kira's dirt-smudged face appeared on the screen. "Since there is now a Mist vessel on my screen, I assume we've been pulled back into their space."

She did not sound happy.

"That's Captain Victor's ship," I said. "We're trying to catch him alive."

"Someday you will explain this obsession with letting your enemies live," Sotugh said.

"And someday you can explain to me why you think death is preferable to a long life spent contemplating crimes," Sisko said.

"Go on!" several patrons yelled.

Sisko smiled. "I said to Major Kira . . ."

"Have you engaged the modification in your shields?"

She glanced down at her panel. "It'll be engaged in fifteen seconds," she said. Then she sighed. "You know, I wondered why you insisted we get those specs. Did you know he'd do that?"

"You once said, Major, that the best commander is the prepared commander."

She grinned. "So I did."

"Stand by," I said. "We'll return you to normal space as quickly as possible."

Her image disappeared from the screen. In front of me now, I could see the station, surrounded by the Cardassians, with Victor's ship near the docking pylons, the Klingons and the *Madison* also nearby, and all the debris from the destroyed Mist ships.

"The Cardassians are moving again," Cadet Nog said.

He was right. On the screen it seemed as if every Cardassian ship in the fleet had suddenly started to move at once, in all directions. The effect of the station disappearing from the midst of their ships had been like kicking an ant pile. The ants were scattering.

"I don't think Dukat would like to hear you compare him to an ant," Cap said with a grin.

"Fortunately he's not here," Sisko said with an answering grin.

• • •

Dax noticed the problem first. "The *Daqchov!*" she said.

I could see exactly what she was talking about. As the *Daqchov* had come around to flank Victor's ship, a Cardassian battle cruiser had suddenly, and without warning, turned and accelerated. The *Daqchov* didn't stand a chance.

Sisko waited for Sotugh to add something. It was, Sisko knew, a slightly dirty trick. This was probably the part that Sotugh did not want to discuss.

Sotugh took a long drink from his blood wine. Then he wiped his mouth with the back of his hand. When he looked up, everyone in the bar was watching him.

He scowled at Sisko, then said, "Those filthy Cardassian dogs went right through us. I could see their bridge. Almost smell their stench."

Everyone waited.

Sotugh said nothing else.

"That's not all that happened," Sisko prompted, knowing that the Klingons had felt the extreme dizziness and nausea just as his crew had when the Klingon ship had gone through them earlier.

Sotugh's gaze met Sisko's. In Sotugh's eyes, Sisko could see the memory of that horrible experience, but Sotugh shrugged.

"We felt a little discomfort," Sotugh said. "It was nothing to a Klingon warrior."

"It was enough to remember," Sisko said, grinning.

"The entire battle was strange enough to remember," Sotugh said. "That does not make it important."

"It would have been important if we had lost," Sisko said.

"But we didn't," Sotugh said.

"No," Sisko said, "we didn't."

"I would imagine," Dax said, "that the *Daqchov* is out of commission for a few minutes."

"I think you're right, old man," I said. "Is there any movement from Captain Victor's ship?"

"No, sir," Worf said.

"Let's try this again, Cadet. Hail Victor's ship."

"I'm hailing them, sir," Nog said, "but they are still not responding."

"He won't respond," Jackson said. "Not now."

"What makes you say that, Jackson?" I asked.

"I know Victor. He can be incredibly stubborn."

"Obviously," Dax muttered.

I shook my head. I had no respect for leaders who jeopardized their people in pursuit of a cause already lost. "Cadet, broadcast this on all frequencies. Ready?"

"Aye, sir."

"Captain Victor," I said. "There is nowhere for you to run. Surrender your ship now."

"Sir," Nog said, swiveling his chair. He looked surprised. "We have a response now."

"Uh-oh," Jackson said softly.

I ignored him as Captain Victor appeared on screen. His yachting cap was long gone, his hair stood up in tufts, and his uniform, which had been crisp before, appeared rumpled. He had a wild look in his eyes and beads of sweat dripped from his forehead. Councillor Näna was still beside him, but was no longer facing the screen. All I could see was his left eye rolling slowly in its socket.

"Sisko," Victor said, "I will blow up this ship and take your station with it."

"Oh," Prrghh said. "I hadn't thought of that one."

"It would have been a good option if his weapons worked against Federation defenses," the wraith said.

"Did he modify his equipment?" the Quilli asked, breathlessly.

"He didn't have time," Sisko said.

"So what did you do?" the middle-aged man at the bar asked.

I laughed.

Then I said, "The station's screens are adjusted for your space and are much stronger than any ship's. All you'll manage to do, Victor, is kill yourself and murder your crew. You don't want to do that."

Now the wild look in his eyes became even more intense and he cut off communications without another word.

Prrghh shook her head. "You laughed at an insane man?"

Sisko smiled. "I did," he said.

"Which only drove him crazier, I'll bet," the Trill said.

"The plan to take over an essentially peaceful people was insane from the start," Sisko said. "Being laughed at was the last thing he wanted."

"Sisko," Sotugh said. "You surprise me."

"I know," Sisko said. "I surprised Victor too."

Less than ten seconds after I had laughed at Captain Victor, his ship turned and cut away, firing randomly at the ships blocking him. None of them fired back, but they kept on his tail, flanking him.

"Dax, shift the station back to normal space," I said as Victor cleared the area. "Then follow him close."

"Transferring," she said.

The white line formed in space near the station, then expanded to a cloud that passed over the station.

"Transfer complete," Dax said. "The station has returned to normal space."

"Let's hope it stays there," I said as the *Defiant* turned. We headed after Victor's ship and caught up to it moments later.

He shot at us again, rocking us slightly as the bright blue beam bounced off our shields. Dax positioned the *Defiant* directly behind the Mist ship.

"Shields holding," Worf said.

"*Madison* and *Daqchov* are pacing Victor's ship on either side," Dax said.

"Where does he think he's going?" Jackson asked. "He has no way of escaping."

"He is insane," Worf said as if he were explaining to a child that space is a vacuum. "Do not ask for logic."

"Cardassians are again taking up attack positions near the station," Dax said.

"Major Kira is again warning them off," Nog reported.

I had had enough of Captain Victor. "Let's end this," I said. "Cadet, open a channel to Captain Victor's ship."

"Open, sir," Nog said.

"Captain, cease-fire and come to a complete stop or be destroyed. This is not a bluff."

I motioned for Nog to cut the communications.

"So all this noble talk of allowing your enemy to live is just a lie," Sotugh said. "You simply wait until you tire of his antics and then you kill him."

"No," Sisko said. "I decided that Victor was a loose cannon. If we couldn't stop him, and quickly, he would cost other lives, especially with what was developing in normal space."

"That's certainly a reason to take someone out," the middle-aged woman at the bar said.

"It's called giving someone enough rope to hang himself," the middle-aged man added. "We humans do that a lot."

"It is more efficient to kill the offender early so that time is not wasted in senseless pursuit," Sotugh said.

Sisko grinned at him. "Or so that the pursuers don't have a Cardassian ship sharing their position in out-of-phase space."

"I did not say that," Sotugh said.

"But if Sisko had taken out Captain Victor earlier, you would have missed that wonderful experience," Prrghh said.

"Believe me," Sotugh said. "It was worth missing."

"So did you catch him?" the Quilli asked, climbing even higher on his chair. The Trill had to put his other foot on the seat to keep the chair from tipping over. "Or did you kill him?"

"Captain Victor?" Sisko said. "I had Worf target his ship."

"Fire on my mark," I said.

"Ready, sir," Worf said.

With one final shot at the *Madison* that bounced harmlessly off its shields, the Mist ship suddenly stopped firing, slowed, and stopped.

"Well, that's a surprise," Dax said.

"A trick, sir," Worf said.

"Hold position and we shall see," I said.

"They are hailing us, sir," Nog said.

"On screen."

Councillor Näna appeared, his gray features dominating the screen. His mouth was opening and closing as it did before. Behind him, two humans were holding a struggling Captain Victor on the ground near an instrument panel.

Councillor Näna's mouth opened. "We," it said. Then the mouth closed. A second later, it opened again. "Surrender." Its eyes rolled forward toward me, and I realized just how hard it was for the councillor to speak aloud.

"Excellent," I said.

I turned to Jackson. He was watching Näna with his mouth open. When he saw me look at him, Jackson's mouth closed. Apparently he had never heard Näna talk before either.

I grinned at Jackson. "Do you have enough healthy personnel to take over and control that ship?"

"I do," Jackson said.

"Then it's all yours," I said.

"Thank you, Captain," Jackson said. For a moment, his gaze met mine. The respect, it seemed, was finally mutual. Then he quickly spun and headed for the door.

I turned back to Councillor Näna. "Jackson and some of the others will be taking control of your ship. Do not fight him."

Councillor Näna nodded slowly. Before the screen cut off, one of the men sitting on Captain Victor slugged him, knocking him out. Clearly Captain Victor's days of leadership were over.

• • •

"I had hoped for a glorious battle," Sotugh said. "Instead, I chased a few weak ships, shot our weapons a few times, and did nothing. The battle was without honor. We fought an enemy that looked powerful, but in truth, had nothing but weakness at its core."

"That's some story, Sisko," the wraith said, pulling its entire left hand. The Trill yelled a caution from the other side of the room. The wraith immediately flattened its hand against its chest.

"Yes, it is quite a story, despite Sotugh's disappointment," Prrghh said. "It reminds me of the time—"

"The story is not over yet," the Quilli said, waving its tiny paws. "How did the *Defiant* get back to normal space? Did you meet your time limit?"

Sisko smiled. "I am amazed at all of you. You have forgotten an important detail."

"And that is?" the Trill asked.

"The Cardassians," he said, "are still about to attack the station."

Sotugh slammed down his empty mug of blood wine. "That's right!" he said. "We still had to deal with those filthy Cardassian dogs!"

Nineteen

"You don't seem to like the Cardassians much," the Trill said, with a slight smile playing on his face.

"They are a lying, duplicitous race, worthless in the extreme," Sotugh said. "They exist only to create trouble, and to spread their vileness throughout the quadrant."

"Sounds like Klingons to me," Prrghh said, moving just far away enough that Sotugh couldn't reach her.

"Actually," Arthur said, "Klingons have honor. They don't try to spread their vileness throughout the quadrant."

Sotugh nodded at him, in grateful acknowledgment.

"Could've fooled me," Prrghh said.

The Quilli was frowning again. "I thought you said that the Cardassians ran like—ents?—whatever those are. I thought you said they were gone."

"Ants," the Trill said, "an Earth insect, usually about the size of your nose bristles. They live in colonies—the ants, not your nose bristles—often called anthills. When one is kicked, the ants scatter."

"How come you seem to know all this stuff?" the Quilli said to him.

"Because I *understand* stories," the Trill said, "instead of collecting them."

"Is he right?" the Quilli said. "About the ants?"

"Yes," Sisko said.

"Then they scattered. Or you used the wrong metaphor."

Sisko smiled at the small, fierce creature. "No, I didn't. Ants scatter, but sometimes they return to the nest, especially if their queen is inside. Sometimes they even rebuild that nest—"

"Which is a perfect analogy for Terok Nor," Sotugh said, "which is the Cardassian name for the Cardassian-built station *Deep Space Nine.*"

"It was theirs?" the Quilli said.

"Initially," Sisko said. "How we came to be in possession of it is yet another story."

"You won it in a war?"

"Not exactly," Sisko said.

"Wow," the Quilli said. "Another story. If this one ends like I think it will, I'll want to hear the others."

"Another time," Sisko said. "I am not done with this one yet."

"So," the wraith asked, "what happened when the station shifted back to normal space? What did the Cardassians do?"

"They saw the station's double disappearance and return as an opportunity," Sisko said. "And a weakness, especially with all the Klingon and Starfleet ships gone."

"Like dogs on a dying animal," Sotugh said. "Cardassians are nothing better than scavengers. We should have wiped them out when we had the chance."

"You want to wipe everyone out," Prrghh said.

"Some more than others," Sotugh said, glaring at her.

"When the station reappeared for the second time," Sisko said, "Gul Dukat must have been going slightly crazy himself, attempting to discover what was happening."

"Yes," Sotugh said. "Another hint as to his future."

"So," Sisko said, "he decided to take over the station and ask questions later."

"Typical Cardassian stupidity," Sotugh said.

"Captain," Worf said. "The Cardassians are in attack positions around the station."

This was the last thing I needed. I was tired of Dukat trying to take advantage of every situation that came his way. The man had lost *Deep Space Nine* years ago, but he had never gotten over it. I wished he would stop trying to take it back.

"Is the station able to defend itself?" I asked.

"According to my readings, it is," Dax said. "They have recalibrated the shields for normal space."

"But they will not last long with a full-out attack," Worf said. "There are too many Cardassian warships."

"Major Kira is warning them to stand down again," Nog said. "She is being very clear about it."

Kira was yet again going head to head with Gul Dukat. I think, in some ways, he was her greatest nemesis, the one person she could not seem to get out of her life, no matter how hard she tried.

"The Cardassians are not responding."

How unlike Dukat. He usually crowed over his battle plans. He was probably uncertain as to what sort of trick the Federation was playing on him now. I wished he would respond as he normally did. Then I would have known what sort of battle loomed before my crew.

I studied the mess I saw on the screen in front of me. An entire fleet of Cardassian Galor-class warships surrounded *Deep Space Nine.* In Mist space, invisible to the Cardassians, were three Starfleet starships and nine Klingon battle cruisers. If the starships and Klingon fleet got back to normal space before the Cardassians attacked, the odds would be in our favor. Dukat would not fight such a force. We would win without firing a single shot.

"Cadet," I said, "open a channel to the *Madison,* and *Daqchov* and connect in the rest of the Klingon and Starfleet ships."

"Open, sir," Nog said as the image on the screen changed.

Captain Higginbotham was in his command chair, the grease wiped from his skin. His eyes were bright, and he appeared to be exhilarated from the earlier battle.

Captain Sotugh was on the other side of the screen. He was looking a bit queasy—

"Klingons do not get 'queasy,' " Sotugh said.

"Dizzy, then," Sisko said.

"Klingons do not get—"

"Come on, Sotugh," Sisko said. "I know you felt the effects of that ship going through yours. Do you want to describe it?"

"I was looking a bit—off-balance," Sotugh said.

"I don't think that's better," the Trill said, with a laugh.

"It doesn't matter how he looked," the Quilli said. "What did he do?"

"Actually, it's what I did," Sisko said. "I told them . . ."

"The Cardassians are about to attack the station," I said.

"I already noted that, Ben," Higginbotham said. "Shift us back over. They'll think twice about it then."

"I hope so," I said. "Make the necessary adjustments to your shields and gather in this area."

Sotugh looked disgusted. "Someday we will take care of Cardassia, once and for all."

• • •

"But you haven't yet, have you?" Prrghh said.

"Bah," Sotugh said, moving his hand in dismissal. "They will run from us, tails between their sorry little legs."

"One story at a time, please," the Quilli said, and leaned even harder on its chair back. The Trill had to bend his knees to accommodate the shift in weight.

"At that moment," Sisko said to the Quilli, "I didn't care about the future either."

"Today," I said, "let's just concentrate on *Deep Space Nine.*"

"My ship will remain here to help you," Sotugh said. "Send the other Klingon cruisers back."

I hesitated for a moment, then said to Sotugh, "Adjust your shields anyway. In case we both have to cross back over quickly. Sisko out."

"You had no intention of letting me stay, did you?" Sotugh asked, his mood shifting suddenly. "You lied to me. Are you without honor, Sisko?"

"Honor, shmonor," Prrghh said. "I think we all know that Sisko has honor. Come up with a new accusation, Sotugh."

"Of course I wasn't going to let you stay," Sisko said. "The destruction of the Mist Grey Squadron was over and I couldn't deprive you of a good fight with the Cardassians."

"That is not why you sent me back," Sotugh said.

"Helping me with the Mist was not why you intended to stay," Sisko said. "You wanted the Mist's device."

"Of course," Sotugh said. "They had already crossed into our space once. Who is to say they would not do so again?"

"No one," Sisko said. "But we didn't need that device."

"You are not one to make decisions for the Klingon Empire!"

Sisko smiled. "At that moment, I was. I was the only one who controlled whether or not you remained in Mist space."

"And you sent me back."

"I sent you back," Sisko said.

"The Cardassians are powering their weapons," Worf said.

"Dax," I said. "Are the three starships in position, close enough to shift?"

"Yes," Dax said.

"Cadet," I said. "Warn them they have thirty seconds until we shift them."

"Aye, sir," Nog said.

"How about the Klingons?"

"Taking formation now," Dax said.

• • •

"I was a fool to listen to you," Sotugh said. "If I had not taken that position—"

"Good," I said to Dax. "Shift the Klingons as close together as possible."

"All of them?" Dax asked, glancing back at me.

"All of them," I said.

"You had no right, Sisko!" Sotugh said.

"I had every right," Sisko said. "This was my fight, from the beginning."

"Sisko's right," the Trill said. "The Intergalactic Rules of War have been the same throughout all of my lifetimes."

"There were devices floating in that debris," the wraith said. "Sisko said as much. You had a chance. You blew it."

"We were searching for devices," Sotugh said. "We did not find any."

"The story! Please!" the Quilli said.

"You can't change the past," the Trill said. "You may as well accept it, Sotugh."

"I accept it," he said. "I simply do not like it."

"Well," the Quilli said, focusing its beady eyes on Sisko. "What next?"

"Before we could transfer the starships," he said, "the Cardassians attacked the station."

They engaged in a full frontal assault, concentrating on the station's weak areas. Dukat knew where those areas were. He had been the head of the station for years. He might have even known the station better than I did.

What he did not know was that Kira had already sabotaged many of those weak areas, when the Mist had attacked. I knew that. And I knew that, if we did not hurry, Dukat would take over the station in no time at all.

Laser fire lit up as it hit the station's shields. Just as I had expected, Dukat was targeting the weak points in the station's defense systems.

"The station's shields are holding," Worf said. "But I do not know for how long."

"Get them help," I said.

"I'm transferring the starships," Dax said.

On the screen the white line of mist formed, then expanded into a large cloud covering the three starships, blurring their outlines. Then, as quickly as it had formed, it was gone.

"Transfer complete," Dax said.

All three starships instantly went into motion, moving with phasers firing at the attacking Cardassian ships. Once again, I was glad that Higginbotham was on my side.

"Transferring the Klingon fleet," Dax said.

The white cloud expanded, covering every Klingon ship for a moment before vanishing.

"Transfer complete," Dax said.

Even though I knew that Sotugh was surprised to be transferred back to normal space, he was thoroughly professional. He sent his ships directly into the battle, each ship focusing on a different Cardassian vessel.

"You are being charitable, Sisko," Sotugh said.

"I'm telling it as I saw it, Sotugh," Sisko said.

It felt very strange to just sit and watch a battle rage around us. It also felt strange to see Klingon battle cruisers and Federation starships fight Cardassian battle cruisers. I did not know then that what I was seeing was merely a taste of the future, of the battles we would find ourselves in a few months hence.

When I think of the beginning of that war, though, I do not think of the Dominion attacks or the agreement it made with Cardassia. I think of this moment, of the fleets fighting, because in some ways, this was the beginning.

Two minutes after the Klingons arrived, the Cardassians were retreating. They did not have the strength to battle Starfleet and Klingons. Not then. But this battle helped the Cardassians with future battle plans. Of that, I am now certain.

A number of their ships were heavily damaged. Dukat's flagship was leading the retreat.

Sotugh kept his ships in hot pursuit all the way to the Cardassian border, where they broke off the fight.

"Nice of the Klingons to help out like that," Dax said, breaking the silence of the bridge.

"It certainly was," I said.

Twenty

"HOW NICE OF YOU TO ACKNOWLEDGE THAT," SOTUGH SAID, SARCASM SO great that Sisko half expected him to bow. "Here, at least."

"We acknowledged it there," Sisko said. "I'm telling you exactly what Dax said."

"I knew Dax as Curzon," Sotugh said. "He was rarely polite."

"You could say the same about Jadzia Dax," Sisko said. "She speaks her mind."

Sotugh inclined his head in Sisko's direction. It was, they both knew, Sotugh's way of letting bygones be bygones.

"So the story's over then," the wraith said.

"Weren't you paying attention?" the Quilli said. "The *Defiant* is still stuck in Mist space, perhaps permanently."

"It can't be permanent, or Sisko wouldn't be here," the middle-aged man said.

"You don't know that," the middle-aged woman said, jabbing him in the ribs. "For all we know, Sisko got his crew back to regular space and had to leave the *Defiant* behind."

"No captain would do that," Prrghh said.

"This place is a bit unusual," the wraith said, nodding toward Cap. "Perhaps Sisko came in from Mist space."

"I thought I was on Bajor," Sisko said.

"Blows that theory," the wraith said, shrugging. "So, how did you get the *Defiant* out? You had the only device on your ship."

"Not only that," Sisko said, "but we were nearly out of time. Even if we transferred the *Madison* back to Mist space, we would not have time to rig a device to her equipment."

The Klingons were after the Cardassians. There were other ships floating around *Deep Space Nine,* but none of them had the capabilities we needed. The debris from the destruction of Jackson's ships, and from the battle with the Grey Squadron, still drifted near us. The remaining Grey Squadron ships had not moved.

"Captain," Nog said. "Jackson is hailing us from Captain Victor's ship."

"Put him on screen," I said.

"Captain," Jackson said. "From the records on this ship, you were brought over to Mist space exactly one hour and fifty minutes ago."

"I know," I said. Getting us back to our own space was the next thing I had to do. "We're running out of time."

"You may already be out of time," Jackson said. "Nothing has ever remained in Mist space this long and been able to cross back to normal space."

"My doctor says we have two hours and six minutes," I said.

"Well," Jackson said, "what your doctor, able as he may be, says, and what our experience tells us, are two different things. I'm not even sure you should try this."

"Would you?" I asked.

Jackson flashed me that charismatic grin. "I tried to get out of here for two full months after I arrived."

"Well, then," I said, "we'll start beaming over the last of your people in anticipation of our departure. Are you ready to accept them?"

"We are," Jackson said. "And don't forget to remove the shift device and any other material that belongs in Mist space."

"He did not want you to have the technology," Sotugh said.

"It was a precaution," Sisko said, "and more than likely it allowed us to shift. Dr. Bashir told me later that if any Mist item or person had been left on board the *Defiant,* we would not have shifted."

"Fine," Sotugh said. "Believe what you want, but I do not."

Sisko only shrugged and went on.

"I'll remember," I said to Jackson, and had Nog cut the connection.

I stood and looked at the screen for a brief moment. Despite the debris, and the few Mist ships still floating around the station, it looked normal. The Cardassian fleet was out of visual range, and so were the Klingons.

Deep Space Nine, at least, had gone back to normal.

I hoped we could too.

I hit my comm badge, contacting the entire ship. "In exactly three minutes, Captain Jackson will shift us back to normal space. Every Mist resident and piece of equipment must be off this ship. This is priority one. Get to it, people."

"What exactly would happen if one of the Mist items remained?" the wraith asked.

"We weren't sure," Sisko said. "Beyond not being able to transfer. And just that was enough to worry me more than anything else."

"That must have been a scramble," Prrghh said. "Removing all that equipment and people."

Sisko smiled. "My crew is quite efficient," he said.

Dr. Bashir responded immediately. "Captain," he said. "You're going to have to beam most of these wounded directly out of sickbay. They're not yet able to go on their own."

"We'll beam them all," I said. "Make sure their clothes and every ounce of blood are either with them or in space away from the ship."

"Will do," Bashir said.

"Start getting Jackson's people out of here, old man," I said to Dax. "Put them on Jackson's bridge if you have to."

"Yes, sir," Dax said. "I have targeted their sickbay so that I'll be able to transfer the wounded directly."

"Do that first," I said. "I doubt you'll have time for any other precision maneuvers."

"You're probably right," she said, her fingers working her console as she spoke. Behind me, I could also hear Worf working. I knew that the other members of my crew were doing the same thing on different decks.

I hit my comm badge. "Chief, have you disconnected that shift device?"

"It'll take me at least ten minutes," he said. "If you want this ship working when it arrives home."

"I don't care if we're floating dead in space," I said. "You have two minutes. Do what you have to do."

"Yes, sir," O'Brien said.

I went to one of the consoles, and began beam-out work myself. I scanned the ship for foreign objects, using a parameter program that Dax had designed when she was looking for the shifting device in the debris. I found items scattered all over the *Defiant,* and I knew that other members of my crew were doing so as well.

I worked quickly—we all did—and because I was working quickly, I didn't have time to reflect. That was a good thing; I would have been worrying whether Dr. Bashir was right or whether John David Phelps Jackson was right. I was hoping that Bashir was right, that we had the full two hours, but common sense told me that Jackson had the edge.

It concerned me that no one had left Mist space after spending this much time in it. It would be hard to see our world and not be able to interact in it. In fact, I have always believed that would have been the hardest part of all.

Watching, but never being able to even say hello.

"Benjamin," Dax said, "we have less than a minute."

I left my console and went back to my command chair, hitting my comm badge on the way. "This is the last warning, people."

"Ready, sir," Bashir's voice said through the comm line.

"Chief?"

"Twenty more seconds," O'Brien said. He sounded frantic.

"Cadet," I said, "connect me to Jackson."

"Aye, sir," Nog said.

According to Dr. Bashir's original calculations, we had two minutes left.

Within seconds, Jackson's frowning face appeared on screen. Behind him, I could see members of his crew crowding the bridge. "I think it has been too long, Captain," he said.

"My people assure me we have two minutes to spare," I said. "Are you ready to send us home?"

"Ready when you are," Jackson said.

"Do it quickly," I said.

"Captain," he said, bowing his head slightly, "thank you."

"You're welcome," I said, not at all graciously. We could forgo the niceties as long as the *Defiant* went back to her own space. "Now get us back where we belong and we'll call it even."

He nodded and the screen went back to showing *Deep Space Nine.* The station looked so close, and yet so impossibly far away.

"Everything's off the ship, Captain," Dax said.

"Very good, old man," I said.

At that moment, a white line formed directly in front of the *Defiant,* then expanded and moved back over the ship, covering us. I felt a slight twisting of my stomach, and space itself seemed to shimmer. My hands looked indistinct, and the bridge seemed to fade slightly.

Or maybe I only imagined that change.

I never checked.

Jackson's ship was gone.

"Well?" I said, my mouth dry.

"We're in normal space," Dax said, turning and smiling.

"Excellent," Worf said.

"Yes," Cadet Nog said, holding up a fist. "For a moment, I thought I would never see my father again."

"Or my son," I said softly. I had managed to avoid that thought throughout this ordeal, but now that it was over, I felt incredible relief, and I knew that my greatest worry had been leaving Jake forever.

Then, at that moment, something happened that I never would have expected. A white line formed in front of us, expanding into a cloud and covering the *Defiant.*

Suddenly Jackson's ship was there. And no one needed to tell any of us that we were again in Mist space.

"What did he do?" the Quilli asked, shaking its tiny paws.

"Was he as tricky as Captain Victor?" the middle-aged man at the bar asked.

"They couldn't have developed another crisis that fast," the Trill said.

"I know," the wraith said. "You snapped back because you had been there too long."

"No," Prrghh said. "They had to have brought him back."

"But why?" Robinson asked.

Sisko smiled at their reactions. They were remarkably similar to the reactions on his bridge. Sisko held up his hand for silence. "I'll tell you," he said.

"I do not like this," Worf said.

"Captain," O'Brien's voice came over the comm. "Is everything all right?"

"I'll let you know, Chief," I said. I stood, arms crossed. I hadn't even had a chance to get used to being in my own space.

"Jackson is hailing us, sir," Cadet Nog said.

"Put him on screen," I said.

Later, Dax told me I did not speak the words. I just growled them.

The screen filled with Jackson, and his crowded bridge. He was grinning that infectious grin, and his dark eyes twinkled.

I did not know how to react to that. So I asked the question I had planned. "Did something go wrong?"

"You returned just fine to normal space," he said, his grin growing as he spoke. "Your bodies were reset by the process. You again have two hours in Mist space."

"Wonderful," Dax said softly.

"Then what do you need us for?" I asked. "Is there some unfinished business here?"

"Actually, Captain, there is," Jackson said. "Since you had to leave in such a hurry, there was a group that wanted to thank you. And the only way they could do that was for me to bring you back across one last time."

Even as annoyed as I was, I smiled at that.

"Please stand by," Jackson said.

A moment later the screen filled with the images of six robed figures. They were egg-shaped and their skin was a filmy white, as opaque as fog yet as see-through as mist burning off on a summer morning. They had standard features, but they were distorted, almost as if they couldn't hold their shape. These six figures obviously belonged to the original Mist race.

"I thought Näna was part of that race," Sotugh said.

"I did too until that moment," Sisko said. "He was a member of some other race that had transferred over, just like the humans and the strange-looking Klingons."

"You may allude to that all you want," Sotugh said, "but I will not tell you about those Klingons. It is not something we discuss with outsiders."

"Did they really want to say thank you?" the Quilli asked.

Sisko nodded.

The nearest figure floated toward the screen. That is the only way I can describe his movement. It was too smooth to be a walk.

"Captain Sisko," the figure said. It had an androgynous voice with a bit of a quaver, as if it were speaking through water. "I am Councillor Ell-Lee of the Mist High Council."

"Pleased" was all I could think to say.

"We asked Jackson," Councillor Ell-Lee said, "to bring you back to our space one last time for two reasons. First, we would like to thank you for stopping Captain Victor and Councillor Näna. In thousands of years of Mist history, this is the first time something like this has happened. We are profoundly embarrassed."

"No need to be," I said. "We are sorry that it happened too, but we are glad that everything could be resolved."

"Embarrassment is a good emotion," Ell-Lee said. "It tends to stop a repeat of the same action."

I laughed. "True enough."

Ell-Lee smiled. Or, at least I think it smiled.

"So, Captain, from all of the council and the hundreds of worlds of the Mist that we represent, we thank you."

"You are quite welcome," I said, bowing formally.

Dax looked at me, a slight smile on her face. Later, she would tease me for my formal reaction. But this did seem to be a formal occasion. It isn't often that we get thanked for doing our jobs.

Ell-Lee's smile faded. It raised its hands. "Our second reason is a simple one. We would like you to take a message to your government, and that of the Klingon High Council."

"Gladly," I said.

"Please convey to your governments that such actions that happened today will not take place again. We have no hostile intentions with the Federation or the Klingon Empire and simply wish to be left alone."

"I will gladly relay that message," I said.

Ell-Lee bowed its head slightly. "And now, I must be, in the eyes of your culture, rude. But we have discussed it and we see no choice."

I braced myself. This was the reason they had brought us back. Things never were as they seemed with the Mist.

"Please tell your governments," Ell-Lee said, "that any attempt to contact us, or transfer into Mist space, will be stopped at once. We have chosen isolation, and we prefer it. We will not be disturbed."

It was a clear warning. It was probably directed at me, and at my people, since we had gotten a hold of Mist technology and had a chance to study it before giving it back. The possibility existed that we could reproduce it.

"Do you think so?" Sotugh asked, suddenly interested.

Sisko did not answer him directly. But he looked at Sotugh as he said, "I told Ell-Lee that I would relay its warning. I did so at once to Gowron and now I have again."

Sotugh scowled and sat back.

"Good," Ell-Lee said, again smiling. "I am glad we are clear."

"Very clear," I said.

"Again, Captain," Ell-Lee said, "for all the Mist people, I apologize to you and your Federation. And to the Klingon Empire."

"We accept your apology," I said.

Ell-Lee lowered his hands and said, "Thank you."

And the screen returned to Jackson.

"I guess the council won't get caught like that again," he said with a sheepish grin.

"I hope not," I said, and then I smiled to take the sting out of my words. In truth, though, I did not want to come to Mist space again.

"Good luck, Captain," Jackson said. "And please accept a personal thank-you from me."

With that the screen cut back to showing the station.

A white line appeared in space and expanded, forming a cloud of mist that covered the *Defiant* for one last time.

A moment later we were again back in normal space.

Twenty-one

"EXCELLENT STORY," THE QUILLI SAID. IT CLAPPED ITS PAWS TOGETHER. "My congratulations."

"Uh-oh, here it comes," the Trill said.

"What?" the middle-aged woman at the bar asked. "It *was* a good story."

Sisko smiled. "I really do not think I have time for another story—"

"We'll discuss that in a moment," the Quilli said. It jumped off its chair, landing on all four feet, its bristles sticking straight up. Then it gripped the leg of the chair, and pulled itself upright. It waddled toward Sisko

Sotugh stood. "Warthog, you and I have unfinished business."

The Quilli stopped waddling, and looked up at the Klingon. It had to look up so high that the weight of its head almost tipped it over backward.

"You and I have settled our business," the Quilli said. "Your business is with that Trill. He lied to you. My bristles aren't poisonous."

"Is this true?" Sotugh bellowed.

Several patrons shrugged and looked away.

"Oh, dear," Prrghh said. "You've insulted the vaunted Klingon honor."

"Trill," Sotugh said. "You and I must settle this *now.*"

The Trill stood. "I'd love to," he said. "But we can't fight in here, and I doubt we can fight out there. I suspect we entered in completely different places."

Sisko frowned at that, not completely understanding it.

"Another time, then," Sotugh said. He grabbed his mug of blood wine, finished it, wiped the back of his mouth with his hand, and then shook the wet hand at the Quilli.

Blood wine draped its bristles. It narrowed its eyes; several bristles extended and then receded. "I suppose you owed me that," it said.

"That's enough," Cap said.

Sotugh ignored him.

"Sisko," Sotugh said, turning to him. "You are a fine storyteller, but if you ever trick me in battle again, we shall settle the matter in a purely Klingon manner."

"It would be my pleasure," Sisko said. He picked up his Jibetian ale, and then paused. "Sotugh?"

"Yes?" Sotugh said.

"The same goes if you ever trick me. Do we have an understanding?"

"I think so," Sotugh said. "Until the next battle."

"Until then," Sisko said.

Sotugh nodded toward Cap and headed out the door. The gecko he had displaced climbed back onto the now-empty chair. The Quilli waited until he was gone before proceeding.

When it reached Sisko's feet, it stopped. "As I said," the Quilli said, "a fine story."

It extended a paw. After looking at it for a moment to see if it had any bristles (it didn't), Sisko took it. It was too tiny to shake, but that didn't matter. Apparently the Quilli wasn't going for a handshake. It wanted leverage.

It pulled Sisko's hand as it climbed up his leg, over his lap, and onto the tabletop.

"There," it said, its soft breath hitting his face. The creature smelled like cinnamon. "I have a business proposition for you."

"You've got to be kidding," the Trill said.

The Quilli straightened. "I don't steal my material."

"Then you're the first Quilli I've met who doesn't," the Trill said.

"Theft is not allowed in the Captain's Table," Cap said. "It's grounds for permanent expulsion. Captain Zzthwthwp knows that."

"Indeed I do, as do all Quilli captains," the Quilli said. "And so," it said, looking at Sisko, "because I am an honorable Quilli, and because that is such a fine story, and because I know it will have a great audience among my people, I am prepared to pay you twenty thousand zwltys for your tale."

The Trill stood. "Quilli make a minimum of ten thousand zwltys for every performance they give of a good story. I think you're underpaying the captain."

The Quilli smiled. "You didn't let me finish. Twenty thousand zwltys up front, against a ten-percent cut of the total sum of all the fees paid on the story's performance."

"Paid biannually," the Trill said. "And you could probably give him more than ten percent."

"There are costs involved," the Quilli said. "Rental of performance space, advertising—"

"Paid biannually at least," the Trill said.

"You didn't let me finish," the Quilli said. "Ten percent paid biannually, the first installment to come in the month of Shedding."

"What's that?" Sisko asked Cap, trying to hide his amusement.

"I believe, in Earth terms, it would be called October."

"Do we have a deal?" the Quilli asked.

This time, Sisko did let himself grin. Then he shook his head.

"He doesn't know how much a zwlty is," the wraith said. "Can you do the conversion for him, Cap?"

Sisko held up a hand to stop Cap's answer. "Unfortunately," Sisko said, "I cannot accept any monetary payment for my story. My people frown on that sort of thing."

"But I will retell this story!" the Quilli said. "It's lodged in my brain!" It looked at Cap. "I thought I could pay for it."

"It looks like it would be theft," Cap said. "Guess you'll have to purge that one."

"It's too good to purge," the Quilli said.

"I do have a solution," Sisko said.

The Quilli frowned and sat down, rather like a spoiled child who wasn't getting its way.

"There is an orphanage on Bajor that I have sponsored. It is always in need of supplies and goods. If you would use my fee to provide for that—"

"I'm afraid that's not possible," the Trill said. "Captain Zzthwthwp has never been near Bajor, and probably will not be."

Sisko frowned. "But I—"

Cap held up his hand. "It's a long story, Captain. I will explain it to you later. But let's settle this first. If you and Zzthwthwp trust me, I will be the broker between you. I will make certain supplies and goods get to your orphanage in the correct time and place."

"That sounds fine to me," Sisko said.

"Me, too," the Quilli said. "So we have a deal?"

"How do you know he'll pay, though?" the wraith asked.

"That's where I come in," the Trill said. "Right, Zzthwthwp?"

The Quilli frowned. "You take all the fun out of everything."

"So you're a Quilli monitor?" the middle-aged man at the bar asked.

"Someone has to do it," the Trill said. "And I happen to like good stories well told. I'll keep track of the performances and make sure that this little Quilli translates your ten percent into the proper number of supplies for your orphans."

"What's your cut?" the middle-aged man at the bar asked.

"I'll take one additional percent of the Quilli's profits."

"Hey!" the Quilli said.

The Trill crossed his arms. "It's either that or you don't get your story."

The Quilli rested its chin on its paws. "I hate it when you do that."

Sisko's grin widened. "It's a deal, then," he said. "You're welcome to the story, my friend."

The Quilli brightened. "I'll tell it exactly as you did," he said.

"Interruptions and all," the Trill mumbled.

Sisko took a final sip of his Jibetian ale. He was tired—a good tired—and he knew he'd better leave before the Quilli asked for another story.

"You're going?" Prrghh asked.

Sisko nodded. "I am on a short leave. I have to get back to *Deep Space Nine* soon, and I seem to have lost all track of time."

"Not surprising," Cap said, smiling. "You're welcome to come again, Benjamin Sisko."

"Oh, I will," Sisko said. "You make the best jambalaya I've had outside of New Orleans on Earth—aside from my own, that is." He extended a hand. Cap took it, and they shook.

"I will tend to your orphans," he said softly.

Sisko nodded. He believed Cap. He wasn't sure why, but he did. "I appreciate it," Sisko said.

As he wound his way around the chairs, other patrons clapped his hand, or smiled at him. As he passed the lizardlike humanoid near the piano, the creature raised its head and blinked ever so slowly at him.

Sisko felt a surge of appreciation. Or that's what it seemed like. That seemed to be the creature's way of telling him that he liked the story.

Sisko turned past the piano toward the tiny entrance. As he did, a woman entered. She looked harried, her short hair mussed. She was shorter than he was, but moved with an air of command. She looked familiar—very familiar.

Clearly her eyes hadn't adjusted and she walked past him toward the bar without noticing him.

He was already in the short hallway, with his hand on the door, before a thought registered.

As quickly as it did, he shook it away. It couldn't be. She had vanished years ago in the Badlands. No one had heard from her since.

If she were on Bajor, he would know it.

Besides, as long as he had known her, she had worn her hair long.

They said that everyone had a double somewhere in the universe. He must have just seen hers.

He shook his head, and pushed the door open, stepping into the heat of Bajoran twilight. How many Jibetian ales had he had? He didn't know, and he really didn't care. For the first time in a long time, he had relaxed.

Bashir had been right. A few days of R&R were good. Now Sisko could return to his cabin and get a good night's sleep. He would tell Bashir when he returned—

Or maybe he wouldn't. No sense letting that doctor get too cocky. Bashir might try to pull something like this again sometime.

Sisko grinned and walked down the sidewalk, feeling better than he had in weeks.

Inside the Captain's Table, just moments after Sisko had walked toward the entrance, the Quilli jumped onto his chair. "You could have made him stay," the Quilli said to Cap. "I'll wager he had a dozen good stories in him."

"One was enough," Cap said. "In fact, you probably should refine it before you forget it. You have orphans to think of."

The Quilli frowned, jumped off the chair, and leaped onto the Klingon. The sound of their battle filled the bar, but most patrons simply ignored them, although some jumped in with glee.

A couple started down the stairs in the back. The woman was Klingon and the regulars recognized her as Hompaq. She had her arm entwined with that of a human male. He was shorter than she was, but seemed to measure up to her in presence. His dark brown eyes were made for laughter, and he had an infectious grin that made his charisma clear.

"You didn't tell me that story," she said as she led him down the stairs.

"There's not much to tell," he said.

"But to permanently capture Jem'Hadar," Hompaq said. "That's quite a risk."

"Not for us," the man said.

"I thought you weren't ever going to get involved over here in normal space again," she said.

His infectious grin widened. "We had a favor to repay," he said. "Besides, as we all know, sometimes wars are won in the details."

Fire Ship

Kathryn Janeway

as recorded by
Diane Carey

"Naow, about goin' back. Allowin' we could do it, which we can't,
you ain't in no fit state to go back to your home, an' *we've*
jest come on to the Banks, workin' fer our bread . . .
an' with good luck we'll be ashore again somewheres
abaout the first weeks o' September."

—Captain Disko Troop
Captains Courageous
by Rudyard Kipling

One

"AND JUST HOW DID YOU FIND YOUR WAY TO THE CAPTAIN'S TABLE?" A stout man in oilskins asked her.

"I smelled fire. And trouble."

"Both bad things at sea. Please go on."

Captain Kathryn Janeway sipped at her brandy, then did as she had been asked.

Maybe it was just cabbage stew. Trouble and cooked cabbage smelled a lot alike.

Dark planets always made me uneasy. Humans had sixth, seventh senses. I'd learned to listen.

"This way," I said with an unnecessary beckon.

"Why that way?"

"I don't know."

The narrow street was wet with recent rain, and there was a sense of steam around us. Dim figures came and went from doorways, cloaked and unspeaking. My mind made something of it, but perhaps the downcast eyes and drawn hoods were due only to the night chill. I hoped so, but . . .

"Captain?"

Back to work.

I turned, and tripped on a faulty brick in the street—doors, windows, banners, and signs spun, and so did I. All elbows, a knee—I tried to catch myself, failed—and Tom Paris caught me.

A clumsy captain. That's what every crewman wants to see—his elegant, surefooted, universally competent captain taking a spill on a grimy street.

"Shall we dance, madam?" Paris's college-boy face beamed at me, backlit by a gauzy streetlamp.

"Quit grinning, Lieutenant," I snapped. "Starship captains don't trip. And we *never* dance."

He smiled wider and arranged me on my feet, making me ponder courts-martial for a second or two. "I'm sorry, Captain, I just thought your injuries—"

"They're fine."

Another few steps padded away under our feet before I realized that my mood had completely changed. Caution had blended to intrigue. I could no more turn back than fly.

We were heading down an alley that made me think of Old London's back ways, heading toward a corner and another street. I wanted to get there, but caution boiled up a certain restraint. A few seconds wouldn't matter.

A passerby now looked up and nodded greeting. So other moods had changed too?

"This place feels *really* familiar," I mentioned.

"I thought I was imagining it," Paris said. "No place in the Delta Quadrant can possibly look familiar to us, unless we double back on our course—"

"—and we didn't do that," I abbreviated. "This place seems like an old movie to me . . . a Gothic mystery . . . one of those stories with the light in the castle tower and the woman in the diaphanous nightgown running across a moor, casting back a fearful glance—"

Paris bumped his head on a hanging sign. "Looks like a Western to me."

Casting him a glare, I said, "Lieutenant, let's get around that corner."

"Aye, aye, Captain."

An unexplained thrill ran down my arms as cobblestones kneaded our soles. Holmes, are you hiding there around the corner? Watson? Wet and foggy, yet cowled in city sounds and people's voices muffled behind shutters. There were no horses' hooves or wagon wheels—this culture was beyond that—but I found myself listening for a clop and clatter. The smoke-yellow streetlamps were electrical but inadequate. I had a feeling not of neglect but purpose. Just a feeling . . . nothing but a feeling . . .

Usually feelings didn't so completely guide me. Usually I depended upon rationality, upon keeping feelings reined hard, for they were inaccurate and undependable. Not how do I feel, but what do I think—that's what guided me, and so far had kept us all alive. Feelings were too susceptible to fears, and fear was a daily diet on this unending mission. And feelings were too sudden.

Even good feelings had been reined in a long time ago. I enjoyed a few things, but always kept control and never let myself enjoy too much. I never went over the top and forgot where we were and why. This kind of restraint, for a human being—a human woman—was unfortunate and even unnatural, but serviceable for me. If I kept my feelings in their place, good and bad, then I could handle the truly awful.

Like these last few days. Truly . . .

Just as I cast off my thoughts as beginning to be a little too Vulcan, I realized the voices we were hearing had gotten notably louder now that Paris and I had rounded the corner. Nothing raucous—just easier to hear, even delineate individuals. Somebody was having a pleasant time. Down the street, there was a rowdier place somewhere.

There were several doorways, each with some kind of hawker's sign swaying gently over it. When had a breeze come up?

I came to the first door on the left, snuggled into a leathery wooden archway by a good meter, and the heavy aged-oak door was propped open by what looked like an iron bootscraper. There was music, and a heady scent of fire and food. My memories stirred and pushed me toward the door.

"Tavern of some kind." I looked up at the dreary wooden sign and the carved letters.

"The Captain's Table . . ."

"Sounds nice," Paris commented.

I peered briefly at the faded paint in the shape of four stars in each corner of the sign. "Very nice, Tom. But why is it written in English?"

He eyed the sign again. "English . . ."

At a table to my right, voices muttered and drew my attention.

"—two months out of Shanghai when a gale mauled our rudder clean off. We hove to in high seas and sawed planks out of spare spars. For four days we fitted a jury rudder, then piloted with lines and tackles around the Cape."

"Eight thousand miles–a feat of seamanship wizardry for sure, Captain Moodie."

"A compliment, Charlie, from a man who ran the Bora in a steam launch."

"Oh, yeah, me and Rosie could move mountains, give or take them leeches."

As the two men paused, noticing me, I moved on into the pub, leaving them some privacy.

The wooden door wouldn't open without my shoulder involved. The wood was warm from inside, but dank on its surface from the fingers of fog slipping under the archway. I walked down a short corridor that guided me into a left turn, through a second archway with darkened timber and a whiff of sea rot. As I turned, the Captain's Table tavern opened before me.

A warm smoky cloak wrapped my shoulders and took me by the waist like an old friend's arm at a fireside, coddling me into the clublike environment of a country pub. To my left, there was a piano, but no one was playing. Its rectangled rosewood top sprawled like a morning airfield, reflecting incarnated gaslight from sconces on the paisley-papered wall. Before me was a raft of round tables, at the tables were people. Beings. Mostly men, a few women—most looked human but there were some aliens—who sat in wooden armchairs worn to a warm grousefeather brown.

Over there, to the right along the wall was a glossy cherry wood bar with moleskin stools. The age-darkened bar laughed with carved Canterbury Tales–type figures. Over a mirrored backsplash a shelf was crammed with whiskey jugs, ship's decanters, and every manner of bottle. Over the bar and bottles glowered a huge Canadian elk head with a full rack, which threw me for a moment because it was so undeniably of Earth. I looked down at my uniform, expecting to see an English shooting suit. If I looked out a window, would I see hedgerows and pheasants?

I might see England, except that the image would be rippled by the occupant of a majolica bowl on the piano . . . a lizard? At first I thought it was part of the ceramic design on the bowl, but no, it was a real live gecko, a mottled yellow-green chap with two-thirds of a tail, and he was enjoying feasting on the conch fritters in the bowl. I would've warned somebody that a creature had crawled in, except that several people from a table over there were watching the gecko and commenting on the length of its regrowing tail.

A British pub in the Delta Quadrant with conch fritters and a live-in lizard. Hmm . . .

Many of the people glanced up—some nodded, others raised their glasses to me, and still others glanced, then ignored me further. A young man in a cable-knit Irish sweater, with longish ivory hair and a voice like a Druid ghost's, softly greeted me, "Captain."

How did he know?

As I paused and returned his look, I noticed that there was glass crunching under my boot. As the company turned for their own look, a lull in the general movement of the place made me notice what they'd been doing—that several people were scooping up spilled food and righting toppled glasses and chairs. Here and there someone was nursing a bruised face or a bleeding lip. There'd been a fight.

Then a fellow wearing a maroon knit shirt, with a sailing ship and scrolled lettering embroidered on the left side of the chest, nodded and invited, "Welcome aboard, Captain. Relax. We'll have it all cleaned up in no time."

Beside him, a large creature, with a mirrored medallion on his chest and a set of antlers rivaling the elk's on his head, nodded elegantly as the lamplight played on the hollow bones of his face. He was demonic, yes, but still somehow welcoming. I didn't feel threatened at all. Even my instincts were voiceless.

The embroidery on the shirt didn't really surprise me—if a planet had water and wind, there was also some sort of sailing vessel. Common sense of function demanded certain designs, just as telling time and traffic control had a certain universal sense that could be counted upon just about everywhere. There were only so many ways to run an intersection.

But the two who had spoken were clearly human and shouldn't have been in the Delta Quadrant at all. My crew and myself were the only humans in the Delta Quadrant.

I rotated that a couple of times in my mind until I finally didn't believe it at all. *Most* of these people looked very human indeed, though quite a range of types—not unusual for a tavern in a spacelane, in a populated sector with civilized pockets.

"My crew was a mixture of types from all over," someone was saying—a young man's voice, but without the flippancy of youth. I looked at the nearest table and saw several people listening intently to a small-boned young man in a blue jacket with red facing running down the chest. His white neckerchief was loosened, and though he seemed relaxed, he also seemed troubled by his own story.

"The ship wasn't even ours. It was a converted merchantman on loan to us. Many of her timbers had rot in them, and though we possessed forty guns, several of those were inoperative. It was in the afternoon that the enemy closed on us, and the breeze was fading. We would soon be outmatched *and* crippled. On our last move, the enemy's sprit caught our mizzen shrouds—"

"Oh, my," someone uttered, and half the company shuddered with empathy.

The young man nodded somewhat cheerily at this. "Yes, but I lashed it there. Why not? I thought my ship would sink otherwise, and I wanted to fight! So I lashed up to something that would keep me afloat. My enemy's ship."

The table's company laughed in awed appreciation. I nudged a little nearer to keep listening.

"And I got it, by God, I got it," he said, shaking his head in reverie of a rugged moment. "Their shots passed straight through the timbers of our gun deck as if going through a straw mattress. They invited me to surrender before action became a slaughter. They had this odd conception that we didn't have it in us to establish ourselves as a power with which to reckon. But I'd hardly begun. I turned and simply told them such. My crew was so enthused that my riflemen in the tops dispatched the enemy's helmsmen one by one, and then a brisk fellow of mine vaulted the yards and dropped a grenade into the enemy's magazine. Such a roar! Their sails were lit afire!"

"And you were still made off to them?" the fellow in the maroon shirt asked.

I stopped moving forward because I was now listening to the dark-eyed young officer in the blue coat with red facings.

"Oh, yes," he answered. "If they sank, they would drag us down. I had only three guns left, but might as well keep shooting. But the other captain's ship was a goner and he soon struck. *Serapis*'s crewmen were well thankful to off-board their vessel, you might well understand. A sinking wreck is bad enough, but a sinking *and* burning wreck soon becomes legend. We unlashed, and off we limped. Our entire gun deck was gone."

An unfamiliar alien standing nearby asked, "So you won? Or you lost?"

The officer craned around for a glance at the question, saw that this creature might be someone who wouldn't or shouldn't already know the answer, and offered, "My opponent's ship was a brand-new warship. Mine was a half-rotted old merchant. My ship sank shortly after his, but his was the costlier loss and we denied the enemy domination of vital commerce and supply lanes."

The young captain took a sip from a horn-shaped mug that looked like pewter. He sank back a bit in his chair and stared at the tabletop, seeing something quite else. "I heard later that the other captain had been made a knight for that action. I told my men that if I ever met him again, by God, I'd make him a lord!"

Everyone laughed again—and so did I—and somebody, a woman, commented, "You're a brat, John."

The young man nodded. "Oh, thank you."

Someone else said, "That's a pretty fair story. Too short, though."

"It seemed rather lengthy at the time. I'll be longer winded from now on."

"Do that. Short stories are for musers, not doers."

For a moment the conversation died down and I heard other things. Faint music from somewhere, but not from the piano . . . Dueling pistols on a wall plaque, castle torchères, coach lamps, and railroad lanterns, a shelf with little unmatched stone gargoyles, a huge Black Forest cuckoo clock with a trumpeting elk carved on top of flared oak leaves and big pulls in the shapes of pine cones, devil-may-care patrons huddled around the tables like provocateurs in a novel, and a large silver samovar that needed polishing—this place boggled the mind with unexperienced memories. Was I hearing the groan of oak branches and waves against a seawall? The mutter of robber barons plotting in a back room? It was all seductively Victorian, and I felt right at home.

In a fireplace burned real wood, and somehow from it came the earthy aroma of autumn leaves like my grandfather had heaped up and burned outside the big farmhouse every October. He hadn't been a farmer, but he had a good time pretending.

Keeping my voice down, I turned my face just enough to speak over my shoulder to Paris. "This place looks like the *Orient Express* stopped at a Scottish pub in the Adirondacks. This isn't *like* Earth, Tom . . . this *is* Earth." He didn't respond, so I added, "I wonder if there's a back door to home. Somebody here has been to the Alpha Quadrant. Maybe they can show us their shortcut. Give me your tricorder."

I put my hand out, still looking around the pub, but Paris didn't give me his tricorder. Irritated that he could be so stupefied, I swung around to snap him out of it and found that he wasn't behind me anymore.

"Paris?" I called back toward the hooded entrance, but he didn't come out. I went to the archway and looked down the musky corridor to the street door, but he wasn't there.

I turned into the pub again and looked around, taking more care to check each person, each being. A pale-haired man, very thin and not tall, stood at the bar, dominating a group of others who were listening to him. His dark uniform coat, lathered with ribbons and medals, had a high collar and tails, and the right sleeve with its thick cuff was pinned up to the coat's chest—that arm was missing at the shoulder. He certainly wasn't Lieutenant Paris, and neither were any of those around him.

Down the bar a stool or two were some men in naval pilot coats and sea boots. I found myself surfing the walls for a portal back in time, and *way* off in space.

I looked up a set of worn wooden stairs with a spindled railing, but there was no sign of Paris.

Had he gone back to the street? Why would he?

I turned to go out, but someone caught my arm. I looked—a young man, human, five feet eleven, if I reckoned right . . . and if I was Kathryn Janeway, that was a United States Marine uniform. A captain. A flier. He smiled, and there was a very slight gap between his front teeth that gave a homey appearance to his narrow face, with its green eyes slightly downturned at the outside corners.

"Have a seat with us, Captain?" The Marine turned, not letting go of my arm, to a group of people at one of the larger tables, and he gestured to the nearest man. "Josiah, make room for the lady."

"Actually, I've lost track of my crewmate—"

"That's how it works at the Captain's Table," the woman said. "Don't fret over it. He'll be fine."

Annoyed, I peered at her briefly, pausing in the middle of a dozen thoughts and wondering if she were really a captain, as everyone here seemed to be. She wore a simple turtlenecked knit sweater, olive green, with three little crew pins on the collar, too small to read from here. She was unremarkable looking, average in most ways, yet self-satisfied, and had a bemused confidence behind her eyes that said she'd crewed a few voyages. Beside her was a pleasant-faced Vulcan, which pummeled the lingering theory that I was imagining the Alpha Quadrant elements. He had typically Vulcan dark hair, but swept to one side instead of straight across the forehead, and he wore a flare-shouldered velvet robe with a couple of rectangular brooches. Whether rank or ceremony, I couldn't tell. He motioned for me to take the chair they cleared, and the woman in the olive sweater nudged a little birch canoe full of walnuts toward me, showing a flesh-colored fingerless glove on her right hand. Looked like an old injury, but it didn't seem to bother her.

The man called Josiah, older and more grizzled than most others in the knot of patrons at this table, was now standing and offering me his chair. "Right here, madam."

Smoldering aroma of burning leaves . . . the musky scent of old wood . . . the comforting nods and touches of the people around me, the music, the elk head, the paisley wallpaper . . . I felt so much at home that I lowered into the chair in spite of having a crewman now missing.

". . . and that, my friends, is how I come to be sitting here with you, sipping this excellent brandy."

Standing over Janeway, the man called Josiah turned toward the bar and called, "Cap! Shake the reefs out, man! Let's have those mugs here while there's still a beard on the waves!"

She had no idea what that meant, but she liked the sound of it. Her hand didn't go through the table, at least. She lowered herself cautiously because she felt there was still the chance another part of her would go through the chair.

A tall man with white breeches and a double-breasted blue jacket left the clique around the one-armed man at the bar and approached our table. He had a deep voice, uncooperative dark hair, and he was irritatingly proper in his manner. "Captain, welcome to our little secret," he said. "Care for a game of whist?"

"Not right now . . . Captain," she said, daring the obvious while she tried to place his jacket in time and came up with about 1830. Maybe earlier. Noncommittally she added, "Just getting the feel of the place."

"It takes a moment for the logical mind," this tall man said, and pulled another chair up to the table for himself, tapping a set of playing cards on the table, then leaving the stack alone. Nobody else seemed to want to play cards right now, and he didn't seem willing to push.

"There's record of places like this," Janeway mused. "That planet in the Omicron Delta region . . . people see what they feel like seeing. Relive fond memories, great victories—"

"—or make new ones," the Vulcan said. Now the cloud of dimness rose a little more before her eyes, and she noticed that under the sleeveless velvet and satin panels of his ceremonial robe he was wearing a red pullover shirt with a black collar and gold slashes on the cuffs. It looked familiar . . .

In the flood of familiarity and comfort here, she dismissed the nagging hint.

The man who wanted to play cards sat rod-straight opposite her—how could he be sitting and still be standing?—and in the fingers of yellowish lamplight she could now see that his uniform was weathered, even frayed at the shoulders, and there was a little hole on one lapel. This didn't bother the others at the table or short him any of their respect as they turned to him while he spoke, and that told me something about him. So she listened too.

"This place has a mystical characteristic that newcomers find boggling," he said. "Certainly I did. I took the better part of the next voyage to dismiss the Captain's Table to a bad bottle."

"Magic comes hard to the organized mind," the Vulcan said.

Janeway looked at him, a little amazed. Vulcans didn't buy into mysticism any more than she did. Janeway saw in his expression that she was right—he was much more amused than serious. The woman in the olive sweater smiled and nudged the Vulcan as if he were being naughty. What an unlikely couple. They obviously knew each other very well, and she got the idea they always sat together.

"I don't believe in magic," Janeway told them. "There's obviously some bizarre science at work here. I've seen—"

The dark-haired officer's thick brows came down. "You call this science, Your Ladyship?"

She paused, waiting for a laugh at his calling her that, but nobody did laugh. Not even a chuckle. She sensed the lack of humor was something about him more than something about her.

"Once upon a time," she answered, "people thought fire was of the gods. We thought the stars were heaven. Then we made fire for ourselves and went to the stars. We learned there's no true alchemy, no 'magic' that can't be mastered eventually, but just science we haven't figured out yet." She glanced around again and sighed. "It's funny . . . I don't really want to figure this out. It looks like Earth, but . . . it's an Earth I'd make up myself. And that can't be real."

"Real enough, Captain," another voice interrupted. It was the elegant officer with the tailed coat and the medals and the missing arm. He now turned from the clique at the bar, most of whom followed him as he approached our table. "The competent commander takes events as they come and acts upon the dictates of duty."

"Duty often fails to proclaim its requisites before the crucial moment, Your Lordship," the Vulcan said.

The woman in the sweater grimaced and chided, "That's it—lip off to a historic luminary. Brilliant."

"It's 'an' historic," he dashed back fluidly. "Like 'an' horse."

"Or 'an horse's ass.' " The woman looked at me again. "Don't try to figure it out all at once. You'll just end up sitting in a corner making sock monkeys."

The Vulcan made one elegant nod. "I have seven myself."

Janeway squinted at him. Was this all a show by some benevolent traveling theater group?

"I think the captain should tell her first story right now," the woman went on, looking at me again. "No point wading through hot air we've already heard, right? Dive, dive, dive—"

"Perhaps," the Vulcan said to his cocky tablemate, "*you* would like to regale us with one of your tales of grand heroism. The time you sat on the barkentine's deck at dawn, cracking thirty dozen eggs for the crew's breakfast and feeding the drippings to the ship's cat. Or the time you fell off the trader's quarterdeck step while carrying a can of varnish—"

"They were defining moments," the woman nipped.

Janeway was about to politely decline the invitation to relive one of the many tense and disturbing incidents that had happened to her and her ship since the accident that had dropped them in the Delta Quadrant, when yet another blast of incongruity appeared at the entry arch.

Pushing to her feet, Janeway hissed, "That's a Cardassian!"

Her arms were clutched from both sides and she was pulled back into my chair.

"A Cardassian *captain,*" the Vulcan said. "All captains are given entry here."

Trying to get the pulse of this place, she buried what she really wanted to say and instead pointed out, "That can be its own kind of problem. It's one thing to club with other captains. It's something else to ask captains to club with those who have attacked our people and killed our shipmates."

They all fell silent at her words. They eyed the Cardassian just as Janeway did. Had each of them seen an enemy captain in this place? Had that been the cause of the bar fight they were now pushing out of the way?

The fact that they didn't argue with her was revealing. They were captains. Loyalties, emotions, and a sense of purpose tended to run deep among those who had held in their charge the lives of others, in such intimate conditions as a vessel. And more, many here must have defended innocents from various aggressors—Janeway saw that in their eyes right now and heard it in their silence. None of them wanted to tell her she was wrong.

Given entry, he had said. Not *were welcome.*

Suddenly Janeway thought this place a lot more interesting.

"Did you get another command, Captain Jones?" the Vulcan asked the man who had told the story.

"Yes," John said, and his gaze fell to his own hands cupped around his mug. "Yes . . . but one is most definitely not the same as another."

"That's hard on the heart, I know, John," the woman said to the man who had told the tale. "To move on to another ship after the one you love is destroyed."

Janeway added, "Somehow we find it in ourselves to move on if we have to."

"Have you 'had to,' Captain?" the Vulcan asked, his hazel eyes gleaming almost mischievously.

Janeway nodded.

"Go ahead," John invited, pushing a frothing mug toward her as several were delivered to the table. "Tell your tale."

Black spirits and white, red spirits and gray,
mingle, mingle, mingle, that you mingle may . . .
By the pricking of my thumbs,
something wicked this way comes.

Shakespeare, *Macbeth,*
Act IV, Scene i

Two

"Captain! My legs are on fire!"

And it *hurt*—

Confused by pain, distracted by the scratched crack of my own voice, I pounded my thighs with raw hands and called again for the captain in the smoke.

No answer, no answer . . . no one handing a fire extinguisher to me through the black cloud.

Pain was the immediate thing driving me crazy—I gasped a mindless wish to let go and float on.

Fight it or die . . . *fight it.*

"*Voyager,* this is Janeway! I know how to take down those ships! Do you copy!"

No answer. No response better than the crackle of static. Some kind of blanketing—

"Captain!" I called again over my shoulder, into the stifling heat of the tour craft.

Still no answer from the captain, no noise in fact other than the snap of destruction, the hiss of escaping atmosphere, and the slap of my hands on my own legs, and these were more like punctuations to the silence than noise in themselves. Yet I listened to them as if clinging to the last thread of a rope over a cliff.

No answer from the captain . . . was there anything worse on a ship?

Ship—only a touring craft, four meters by three, deployed from a larger vessel that now was only an exploded hulk to which we dared not return. A significant portion of its hull material was splattering through space at us, a hailstorm of hot knives, bits of metal impaling our craft's thin shell—*Pok! Pok!* And now as we lay on the butcher block, fire had broken out.

And on my ship, there was no answer from their captain either. Why wasn't I there? Why had I left? I had to get back. They couldn't do without me, they needed me—

There they were, locked in that damned spacedock!

I could just see my ship, shrouded by the massive girders of the low-slung spacedock, smothered in a gout of smoke and fire and destruction over the terraformed asteroid we had thought was such a great find. Have any of you ever experienced that kind of frustration? Usually we're on our ships when trouble comes, you know, at the first sign of it, we hurry right back to our bridges and alert our crews. Can you imagine what it was like for me? No warning, no hint of trouble coming, and I was off board when it came? All I could think of was my crew, scrambling to muster for action without their captain on board.

Yes, I can see that a couple of you know what that's like. Later, if you want, I could sure use a little commiseration. Would you tell me your stories of what happened to your ship when you couldn't get to it?

My ship hadn't been at red alert, or even yellow alert, and sure hadn't expected to be in the middle of an attack. Power was depleted, repairs were under way, half the ship was taken apart and being worked on. My ship . . . my crew . . . our whole world . . .

"*Voyager!* The enemy's power consumption curve is way off! It's got to be their shields! It's a bluff! Are you reading me!"

A puff of acidic breath from the little craft's helm panel choked off my cries. The electrical system—must be shattered. There was no light now except a single wide beam suffering through the forward viewport, gasping harder than I was. My scorched hands beat at embers on my legs. I crawled aft, my knees shuddering in weakness and pain. My fingers shivered to the left, the right—he had to be here somewhere. How could he be missing in four by three meters? Were my hands numb? Was I touching him and not even realizing it?

I pounded the commbadge on my chest, but would that work any better than the tough short-range comm on this tour vehicle? Down was down.

One more try, if I could just breathe—

"Their shields are limited to one band! That's why they seem so powerful! Find the frequency and shift your weapons phase! Are you reading me! Chakotay! Paris! Can you hear me! Recalibrate!"

Artificial gravity . . . slipping. I was now crawling along a wall. The deck was against my elbow suddenly, my left elbow. Was I still crawling aft? The burning carpet competed with me for the air that was left.

I waved frantically at the smoke and wiped off part of the side viewport, just enough to look out through my stinging eyes and witness hell unleashed on the innocent. Several ships were hovering over the populated areas, cutting away at the skin of the colony. The destruction of the settlement on the Iscoy Asteroid.

It boiled me in pure rage. The Iscoy had been hospitable to a fault. Unfortunately, this touring me around was the fault.

I'd allowed this to happen. I'd let myself fall into a state of relaxation. The ship was in much needed spacedock, being tended by her own crew and others we trusted, everyone was resting, well fed, happy, and I'd let myself suspend vigilance for a few hours. Now this.

The attack had come out of nowhere—no warning—I'd seen the same thing a dozen times, but not like this. The other times, we'd been out in open space, with room to maneuver, ready for action, not lulled and resting like this. The ship hadn't been in spacedock for some time. It had felt so good at first to settle her in there, with technicians other than ours, and the smiling faces of people willing to help. The Iscoy were country-inn hospitable. I liked the Iscoy. They liked us. They had a nice tidy spacedock and they'd welcomed us to it. They'd even invited us to stay with them if we wanted to abandon our struggle to get home. They'd thrown a thank-you luncheon in my honor, to thank me for letting them help us, no less, and now I was here, halfway to no place, screaming my head off into a vacuum.

The menacing ships were a gaggle of confiscated vessels from a bunch of cultures I didn't recognize. At least, it looked that way. No two were the same design. They'd come in, put up some damnable shields, and started cutting up everything in sight on and around the Iscoy Asteroid. A million Iscoy settlers, and my crew. Sitting ducks.

"Chakotay!" I hammered at the controls, now buried to my wrists in cottony smoke. "We can stop them with one wide burst! Chakotay, are you reading me!"

I pressed my nose to the viewport and looked from my cloudy cave out into clear space, and there I saw the spacedock, with my ship and my crew and the Iscoy technicians helping us out. I witnessed the largest menacing ship cut into the spacedock grid, saw the girders dissolve like sticks, saw the magnetic clamps shudder as they tried to let go of the ship's primary and secondary hulls.

Several more of the Menace crowded their ships against the insectlike girders and opened fire. My ship tried to fire back—a few feeble shots out of the dampening field that naturally surrounded a metal structure with power generating through it. The spacedock itself was becoming a trap.

Looking through a simple hole with just my bare eyes, I saw my ship tip up on her side. Then came a great cloud of evulsion behind her, beneath her. Her long cetacean hull was clamped tight to that spacedock and began to slide with it like a slab falling from a rock, the entire contraption, ship and dock, grinding toward the smoldering asteroid. If they couldn't compensate, natural gravity would take over.

Then, the nightmare parted, and hell came from its maw. As the ship slipped from the spacedock, a blinding ball of light erupted, forcing me to look away. When once again I could blink out the tiny port, I was met with the sight of white-hot metal shards spinning in every direction, like a flower opening without anything in the middle.

Without anything because the middle had just destroyed itself.

My lips parted to murmur my anguish, but nothing came out. I knew a warp reactor core detonation when I saw one.

My eyes should have been protected. I shouldn't have been looking. I shouldn't have had to see the death of everything I had been living for.

Relegated to mere spectator, I watched the demolition of my vessel and my crewmates. I'd seen something no member of any crew wants to watch. And I was too far away to help or to die with them.

The carpet beside me broke into flames. I tried to turn away with some grace but fell to one knee instead. My long hair caught the tip of a flame and ignited. *Sssszzzzzzt*—it lit like a fuse! Why did I wear it so damned long anyway?

I slapped at the ends of my hair madly, with only my hands to put out the fire. Human hair burned like flash paper, and if I didn't stop it, my scalp would be next. Halfway across my shoulder, I squeezed out the last burning bit. Now my hands were worse off as I tried to keep feeling along. I wanted to look outside again, but if I didn't get out of here soon, the smoke would kill me. I dropped to my hands and knees.

My left palm came down on a blade—I yanked back, suddenly dizzy with a whole new pain. Blood drained down my wrist into the stiff hot fabric of my sleeve, giving my blistered skin an odd kind of relief. I had cut myself on a piece of the Iscoy ship we'd come from. It had come to claim us the hard way. I couldn't remember its name.

Was there a life-pod in this thing? There had to be. Where, where . . . aft? Below?

I hunched my back and gagged my throat raw of the bitter electrical smoke, sucking enough oxygen out of the poisoned capsule to struggle another meter aft. There, I found the captain.

Crushed into a storage cubby, thrown there by the impact of his ship's explosion so nearby, he was stiff, coiled with spasms. I called to him again and again, pulled on his arms, his legs, the ridge of leaf-shaped spines down his back—what kind of stego-evolution is that? Air-conditioning?

No use for them now. His burned uniform virtually fell apart in my hands, just as mine was curling off my body, leaving scorched skin beneath. I grabbed one of his arms and a spinal fin and dragged him aft. When he came free of the cubby, I rolled him at the oddest of angles along the starboard wall.

Part of the light faded when our craft rolled away from the sun's meager comfort. We were moving, constantly moving, without power but pushed on our uncontrolled way by the explosion of the larger ship.

Where were the enemy ships? Would they come after a vessel this small? Did they know the captain was on board? Did they know I was here too?

Hot . . . hot . . . Sweat sheeted my face, wrecked my grip, got in my mouth, and made me spit. I pulled him, I dragged him, I dragged myself.

Then one thing went right. The aft part of the cabin was already waiting for us. The hatch to the escape pod was already open. Some kind of automatic safety feature. A little ventilator whirred madly, trying to keep the smoke mostly back in the main part of the craft. Like me, it was failing.

For a galling moment the captain's spine ridge caught on one of the impaling bits of metal poking through the craft's shuddering skin, and another convulsion stiffened his body in my cramping hands.

Casting one glance back toward the main viewport, I took my last glimpse of open space before committing myself to the pod, and there I saw a piece of gray hull streaking by, tumbling—a nacelle and part of the support strut, barely recognizable, covered with sparking damage and charred hull fabric.

I wanted to go forward again and look, try to find some figment of proof that I hadn't seen what I knew I had, but this touring craft was floating death if I didn't leave immediately. There was so little oxygen left, the escape pod would quickly exhaust itself trying to fill the poisoned cavity.

I was crawling into a coffin.

Shifting the captain's coiled body into the pod, I retrieved his feet from the entryway before feeling around for the controls. There had to be a button, a latch, something; it had to be simple, nobody would design anything complicated. Where was it?

I started pounding my fist on the sides of the pod, my eyes watering, blind, stinging. It had to be here.

As my lungs tightened to intolerance, I demanded rationality long enough to pound the curved wall in a pattern. I started at my own scorched legs and drove my fists in a straight line from my knees to behind me, then moved out six inches and repeated the pattern, mowing the lawn up to my side, over my head—

A sucking sound startled me. The hatch slid shut and the pod pressurized. Warning lights flashed through the murk on both sides of my head, hurting my eyes and making me feel insane.

Hostile sector. How could we have known?

I was *supposed* to know. I was supposed to have that special instinct. But intuition had failed. Usually I could forgive myself, but not this time. We were too tired from our own disaster. I'd let myself get tired. Experience had been dulled. I'd told myself the worst was over. I'd allowed myself a moment's peace.

Now this, now this.

Don't think about it, not yet, keep concentrating, survive, survive. One thing at a time. One small thing, then the next. Launch the pod.

I pounded again at the place that had shut the hatch. The release had to be in the same area. Nobody would design anything else. Anything different would be harder, and nobody in his right mind would design a safety feature to be complex. It was the same from culture to culture. Technological cultures found those things out early. Some things had to be the same, had to be common sense, or people would die all over the place.

I kept pounding. It *had* to be there! We were now a bug on the back of a run-over mole and we had to get off.

Something clicked. I heard it, but my hand was too numb to feel anything. A tremendous crack threw me against the bulkhead behind me. Just luck I was sitting in the right direction and ended up with a backache instead of a concussion.

Gravity changed. The pod had its own. I fell and landed on my side, half on top of the captain . . . Up wasn't where it had been a moment ago.

Silly visiting dignitary couldn't even find the floor.

We were loose! The artificial gravity bobbled momentarily and left me with a nauseated stomach as the pod tumbled through space, jolting in collision after collision with flotsam from the destroyed ships out there.

A faint little pink utility light came on, providing at least a sense of . . . no, it didn't provide much. At least I wasn't sitting in a black box. Now I was sitting in a hot murky haze. Even looking at my own tarnished body and alien captain's crumpled form was better than utter darkness.

How many enemy ships? Enough to bother coming after a two-man escape pod shooting past them?

I hugged my stinging legs, bit my lip against the pain, and waited to be blown to bits. Sometimes that's all there is—the last few seconds of waiting. Sometimes the ship disappears under you, and all you can do is take a deep breath. I'd heard that somewhere . . . some captain . . .

My hand drifted from my knee to the area in front of me. The alien captain shuddered once under my searching touch, then went suddenly and ominously still. The ventilator whirred madly, thinning the black haze to a gray veil. My eyes burned as I blinked and squeezed, trying to see the Iscoy captain's face.

His gentle face, his soft amber eyes with the double-slit pupils, his welcoming nod, and that snaky excuse for a smile had broken through the first twinge of alienness that came naturally to everyone, even the vaunted me. As my uniform smoldered against my skin, the fibers melting and sizzling, I drifted into a replay of the first greetings with the Iscoy, just four days ago. I wondered if my demeanor had been pleasant for him when I beamed onto his ship, declaring myself leader of a powerful troupe willing to trade. Had I seemed arrogant? Hard? Had I seemed a cold woman unable to mellow?

He hadn't seemed to take me that way.

Dredging up a flake of sense, I began peeling off my uniform. In my preoccupation with surviving, I hadn't realized my clothes were a garden of embers and I was still being scorched. Once the uniform lay on the curved deck of this purposeful bathtub, I stomped out the embers and tried to snuff the smoldering so it didn't eat any of the precious oxygen in here. Now I sat in only my underwear, a pathetic shell-colored chemise that brought little comfort. At least I wasn't so hot anymore.

The half-melted fabric of my uniform almost fell apart as I peeled the last of it off my legs, taking golfball-sized patches of skin with it. Curled, crispy fibers plucked at the melted skin and some stayed embedded in my legs. I needed treatment . . . I'd forgotten how much burns hurt.

I'd never been burned this badly before. Half my body was numb, the other half itching and sizzling. Was I in shock?

If it had been anyone but me, I'd have known what to do. For myself, I couldn't think. For long minutes I hugged my knees, blurring in and out of moaning consciousness, roused periodically by a loud thud on the hull as we crashed through the debris field from the attack outside. Were they still fighting? Or was it over now? Had the good guys won? I was blind, deaf, mute in here, grasping at the pitiful remains of my experience and imagination to figure out what was happening.

I knew what I'd seen. The boiling seltzer of warp core rupture. A ship blowing up.

A muffled whir inside the bulkhead stirred my mind after a while. Was this pod under power? Yes, there was a tiny engine of some sort keeping the pod stable, probably powering little thrusters. Made some sense . . . Power to get away from whatever calamity had caused the pathetic occupants to launch in the first place. It probably had a limit. After a while, the pod would be adrift.

Uniform . . . still smoldering somehow, eating oxygen. I shook myself into action and pushed at the clump of fabric with one boot. Where was the airlock? Oh, there—

I found the airlock release, opened the narrow hatch, shoved the uniform inside.

Oh—my commbadge!

Somewhere inside the hot fabric . . . there. I pulled off the small delta shield gold pin and clipped it to my chemise.

After a moment or two of guilty reflection, I rolled the Iscoy captain's body inside, also. Tears blurred my eyes as I felt the lingering warmth in his body, but I knew death when I saw it, when I could feel it. Awful, ugly responsibility, to consign the commander of another ship afloat without a proper burial, but I knew—we all knew—it might come to this. Dying was one of the clauses in the contract with deep space.

I didn't know whether or not his ship was still out there. He was gone. My ship was gone, and I was still here. Neither of us could go down with our ships. A terrible tragic thing.

"I'm sorry," I croaked to him. A miserable good-bye.

Don't look at me like that, Captain Cressy. You know about burial at sea. It's the same for us in space. All right, then, shall I go on?

Thanks.

A *clack,* a vacuum sucking noise, a second *clack* as the outer port closed again, and it was over for him. Now I had the whole dim bathtub to myself. Carefully I stretched out my legs, flinching at the crack of my own skin. I had to stretch out, or my muscles would contract permanently. Patches of skin on my thighs and calves cracked like cardboard as I extended my knees.

I closed my eyes and drifted through waves of agony. The tears for the captain drained down my hot face, drawing his memory upon my cheeks until I knew that I would never forget him. He had wanted so much to be back on his own ship when the attack came. How horrible it had been for both of us when we lost contact with our vessels.

Contact . . . I touched the commbadge on my chemise.

"Janeway to *Voyager* . . . do you copy?"

My head clunked back against the pod's inner skin. I waited for an answer.

Did this pod have a locator signal? If so, it must be automatic, because there was no control panel in here. Just the airlock, the hatch . . . What was this cubby hole? A survival kit! Of course! Food, liquid, maybe medical supplies?

Only the anticipation of some relief from the burns roused me from my sweaty fatigue. I fumbled for the commbadge again. Lucky I'd remembered it. In this state of smoke inhalation and pain I might've pushed it out the airlock with the uniform and my Iscoy friend.

"*Voyager,* this is Janeway . . . I'm in a survival pod. Location unknown . . .

The captain is dead. If you can read me, please try to respond . . . I've got severe burns . . ."

Were any of my people left out there to hear a call? Any friendly ears to listen?

In my experienced mind I knew better. I'd seen the magnetic clamps shudder, trying to let my ship go when the big strike came. They hadn't been abandoning the ship. They'd been rushing to battlestations and been destroyed trying. Pride encroached upon my misery.

Suddenly the whole pod shook around me. Had I been hit?

I crawled to my knees and looked at the overworked control panel and tried to remember what the Iscoy captain had told me about the readouts on these panels. Warp speed!

This escape pod was hyperlight! Some kind of mini–antimatter reactor core!

Not a bad idea, for an outpost so far away from the Iscoy homeworld, now that I thought about it. A non–warp pod wouldn't get anywhere. A warp pod might have a chance.

How fast was I going? Warp one? Two? That would be the max, in something this size. In fact, this pod might have only a warp surge reactor, with a time limit.

I had no way to know. It was saving my life but keeping me completely uninformed. At warp speed, even warp one, I might have a chance to be rescued by somebody other than the victorious menace out there.

If I had a chance to live, then I had to make myself survive. I started digging through the small cubbies and panels.

Food packets, dehydrated . . . a thermal foil blanket . . . hydrating capsules . . . medical kit. I wanted all of that, but mostly I wanted the med kit.

My hands shook as I lathered some kind of ointment over my arms and legs and my right hip, where the burns were worst. I didn't even know for sure if this stuff was for burns, because I couldn't read the alien writing on the tube, probably meant for fleas' chipped scales or something, but any ointment in a storm.

The little ventilation system worked frantically, and the pod was clearing now, allowing me to see in the flush of the pink utility light. As my eyes cleared, I flinched at a completely unexpected sight—an alien face looking at me through the haze.

I flinched like a schoolgirl and almost lashed out. Then it came to me that I was looking at some kind of video screen. It had no frame or hint of its existence until the screen actually came on. It was on now.

I was staring into the face of the enemy. They were communicating with me somehow, or perhaps only broadcasting a wide-range message to the conquered Iscoy, and this pod was picking it up. As I fought for rationality through my fury and fear, that became more likely. The square screen flinched and flickered—there was apparently damage to my box of survival—and there was no sound. The alien's mouth was moving. He was speaking. I heard nothing.

His face might have been beautiful in another circumstance, statuesque right down to its color, a glowing quartz violet. He was humanoid—not a surprise for advanced beings, since the basic form was so efficient and adaptable, and why was I thinking about this right now?—and his eyes were like a horse's eyes, big chestnuts set in soft round browbones. He had hair—a mass of pure white silky spools, like a decorated shower cap. Simple knit clothing, also white. He was like a mythological being, a lilac angel. He gazed and nodded and warned in silence from the pod's screen. And I hated him to his dirty murdering innards.

He and his kind were demons out of the night. They were slaughtering my crew and our new friends. I glared in pure despise at him as the screen fritzed and blinked, starving itself of power so I could survive. He became uglier and uglier as every moment of my utter helplessness came by.

I loathed him. I determined to loathe him forever. I wanted revenge. He was the Menace. He and all his kind.

Just as the hunger for revenge took a good grip on my warrior soul, the screen fizzled and winked out. Even my enemy's company had been company. Now I was completely alone.

Alone and wanting very much to fight. Life was cruel.

And now I was cold. The sweat was evaporating in the ventilation and I was covered with moist ointment. I hoped the ointment had a sterilizing compound in it. That might save me from infection, the real menace with burns.

Menace . . . violet skin, chestnut eyes, white hair, white clothes. I would never forget.

The chill of the pod's inner skin drew the heat out of my body—something I had wanted very much a few minutes ago.

I decided against swallowing anything in the med kit. Alien medication could just as easily make me grow feathers as do any good. What was this? Some kind of syringe. Antibiotics, maybe?

Or something else. Something more desperate, more final? If I were stocking a survival craft, would I offer a final solution?

No, I didn't think I would, but somebody else might. Space was cruel. Ways out were valuable.

I set the syringe in the med kit and promised myself to use it if the time came. How many weeks would I give myself?

Stay alive. Remember the Menace. Revenge and warning. Turn back the conqueror tide. Those were good reasons to stay alive. My teeth gritted with determination.

The copper-colored thermal foil blanket fit around me well enough but didn't stay in place unless I held it, and my hands hurt. I used a scalpel in the med kit to cut a slit in the middle of the brown foil, then pulled it over my head like a poncho and hoped the foil would keep me from going further into shock. I curled up inside my tiny tent and gave in to the pain, the drowsiness. The foil was crunchy and uncomforting, but it gave me something I very much needed right now.

A chance to rest, with a chance to wake up.

Wake up and fight.

Three

"OPEN IT."

"It's partially opened already. Jammed at the hinge—heavy damage on the outer skin. I don't recognize these marks."

"I don't know. Get the torches. Ruvan, are you reading life in there?"

"One heartbeat."

"Someone tell Quen."

"I'll go."

English . . . the words were like music.

No. No one speaks English in the Delta Quadrant except you and yours. It's the commbadge working.

I had no idea how long I'd huddled in the survival capsule. Hours had eventually blurred into days, and days became uncountable. I had no way to count, no way to measure time, except to watch my burned-off hair get longer. The days were a blend of boredom and pain, and many times I found myself gazing in mute challenge at the little syringe that might have life inside or death. It became a grim game. Would I win, or would it?

There was the other game too, the trick of extending my misery by rationing the dry food and the hydrating capsules. I rationed myself almost to starvation, and the challenge itself kept me going. Bones pushed outward against my thinning skin as I dotted ointment on my burns day after day.

When I went into the pod, part of my hair had been burned off above the shoulders. When I came out, it was an inch below the shoulder. How much time was that?

I thought I heard a bump. Then the airlock made its sucking noise, and hands were reaching for me.

Angels were reaching into the pod, drawing me out . . . beautiful people with glowing brown hair and light eyes, skin like hand lotion. I felt so dirty against them . . .

I wanted to walk. I tried, but had no idea where "down" was. My foil poncho crinkled and laughed as several strong hands lifted me. Dignity suffered greatly. What a sight I must be as they carried me away. I twisted my neck to look around at the sorry little pod that had saved my life. My scorched hand moved in a pathetic wave good-bye, thanks.

I saw figures over me, humanoid if not human, no outward spines or webs or bony formations. Just ordinary human forms with human faces, except for the coloring. Pale skin, hair in the dark greens and browns, and light eyes. And they weren't all the same, I began to notice. Some eyes were green, some amber, some pink. And their hair was different shades of forest green and umber. At least it was in the dim light here. By the time they laid me on the cot in their idea of sickbay, I'd collected lots of faces.

None of them seemed threatening, but I might be beyond that. A certain numbness sets in after a while, and it takes fear along with it. I just watched the goings-on. People dressed in dull clothing did things to my wounds, ran analytical tools over my body, then gave me injections with needle syringes similar to my little friend in the pod. These people didn't look like doctors or nurses. In fact, they didn't look any different from the crewmen who had pulled me out of the pod. I expected medical teamers to be dressed differently from everyone else.

And none appeared to be women. Was I imagining that? Were they just unfamiliar and I wasn't noticing the right things?

No women at all . . .

The lighting in this area was low, and the team had to work with handheld lights or lights attached to their uniforms, if these casual-looking clothes were indeed a uniform. The medical team didn't say much, except to agree from moment to moment on how to treat me, so I didn't say much either. Winced a lot, but didn't say much. Treatment of burns was almost as much fun as the burns themselves.

Once my wounds were dressed—these people had experience with fire—they fed me a thick warm liquid. What I wanted was a porterhouse steak, au gratin potatoes, and glazed baby carrots, but they were probably smart not to dare my weakened body with solid food.

And they didn't change my clothes or alter my appearance, except to sterilize my wounds for treatment. Why did they keep it so dim in here?

The doctor was a young man who reminded me of Tom Paris, except with lighter eyes and hair the color of the nocturnal sea; in certain light it was actually blue. He clicked off his utility light and raised my cot to a sitting position. Then he punched a signal button on panel and said, "She's ready."

"I'll be right there."

A simple comm system. Good. Something I could recognize. That was one. If I could get to a thousand, maybe things would work out.

I didn't bother to ask the doctor any questions. On my ship, I wouldn't have let the doctor answer anything in this situation, so I waited.

The door opened—not an automatic sliding panel, but a swinging hatch with a handle—and a wide-shouldered young man stepped into the sickbay. He had skin like butter and eyes almost the same color, but his wavy hair was the color of morning drizzle, not gray, but more into the silver blues. The pigmentation of these people was truly a fantasy, like a child had picked the colors for the painting—no rules. He wore a utility vest with several pockets, woolly trousers, and soft shoes.

"Do you understand me?" the young doctor asked.

"Yes, I do." My voice was raspy, smoke-rawed, and out of practice.

"I'm Ruvan, chief medic. This is Zell, our second in command." He turned to Zell and said, "She has burns over thirty percent of her body, but only four percent are deep damage. I have them treated and compressed. Her legs are the worst. She can walk, but slowly and with help. In fact, that would be a good thing. Another week in that pod, and her muscles would have retracted into atrophy. Would've been terrible, Zell, just terrible—"

"At least we found her in time." Zell gave the sensitive young medic a brotherly grip at the base of his neck, actually comforting him right there in front of a stranger. "Sit down and rest, Ruvan. You haven't been off your feet since yesterday. She's alive. We're all alive for now. It's good enough."

Through aching eyes I watched the two young men curiously. They acted more like family than crew. I suddenly felt very lucky, but there was something gray and fatalistic about their attitude.

The first officer turned to me and took a step closer. "Welcome aboard the *Zingara.* Our captain wants to see you."

"And I have things to tell him," I responded, letting them ease me to my feet—oh, my legs weren't happy at all with this. "There's something very powerful out there and I think it's coming this way—"

"You can tell the captain."

I clamped my mouth shut. No point wasting breath.

Zingara, Zingara. Pretty name for a ship . . .

The two men held me straight as I shuffled toward the doorlike hatchway. I didn't resist the help. There was no point in being prideful and ending up on my face, right?

At the door, I paused. "I should clean up before I meet your captain, shouldn't I?"

Zell shook his head. "He wants to look at you as you are, the way you came aboard. Afterward, you can clean and change your clothing."

"Makes sense."

"We have nothing new, but you can have ours. All we have is men's clothes, but—"

I offered him a thankful gaze. "I'll be honored to wear the clothing of those who rescued me."

He smiled but didn't say more. I wouldn't have said anything, either, if I'd been the first officer here.

They walked me through a narrow corridor and out a hatch in a transverse bulkhead, which turned out to be a portal to the large main deck. The wide underdeck of their ship had no corridors as I knew them, but instead was a broad open area. Crewmen were doing their jobs on an open platform that ran from beam end to beam end without partition. This deck seemed to be more or less in the middle, for I could see vertical hatchways with ladders that led up from here, and down from here. Most of the activity seemed to be down.

Curious eyes combed over me from every angle. They were a handsome but tattered lot, with the unpredictable coloring of Ruvan and Zell—hair in the muted greens, blues, grays, some lighter, and skin from gold to peach. Their hair was of various lengths, though mostly as if there were no barber on board and they trimmed their own or each other's, with a knife, with a machete. Handsome, shaggy, but in a child's drawing sort of way.

All were young, all male, all thin and . . . chilly. Most of them wore elbow-length shoulder capes, mismatched, no particular color, and many wore fingerless gloves. These weren't uniforms, because nothing was standardized. They just wanted to keep warm. I thought it had been just me, in this depleted condition, but this ship *was* cool.

And dim as a cloudy day. The crew worked by what I would've called utility lights, little bare bulbs of various colors that seemed piecemeal in their organization, and larger worklights set on the deck, powered by extension cords and umbilical cables skittered all over the place.

There was damage here, some of it heavy. Had they already encountered the Menace? Was my warning a needless one? Did they already know what was coming?

The crew paused in their work as I shuffled by. I looked at them and they at me, knowing we were completely odd-looking to each other. Some of them were working alone. Others were helping each other, holding tools, lifting mechanisms, sweating and struggling together. They had to assist each other because almost every one of them, I noticed, had some kind of injury. Some limbs were splinted, others bandaged, and some of the crew simply limped to show their troubles. They'd been through something, and been through it very recently. They were a mess.

Almost everywhere I looked, except for the deck we were walking on, the ship's inner skin was coated with little squares of colors ranging from ruby to orchid, mostly opaque or metallic, each slightly more than an inch across. These squares patched the innards of the ship above me and to the sides. Some of them were off, lying in neat boxes on the deck, and behind them were the guts of the ship, embedded right into the walls. There were little squares on the curved walls that obviously formed the shape of the ship, on the ceilings, in the archways—they were everywhere except where the crew had to walk to get to them. As Zell and Ruvan ushered me past one of the holes in the deck, I looked down the ladder to where more crew were working, and saw more sheets of squares. The whole ship seemed to be packed with them.

The rest of the technology looked about a hundred years behind mine. On the other hand, some of these mechanisms I didn't recognize at all. Possibly the technology wasn't just *behind* mine on a time scale, but sideways somehow as well. That happened now and then, even though most things had to be developed with a certain background supporting the inventions . . . Oh, well, my thoughts were drifting. Always the engineer, under what was left of my skin.

And another odd thing—as we passed working crewmen, both Ruvan and Zell paused here and there to check work or wounds, and during these little stops they touched hands with their comrades. Not the whole hand, like a handshake, but just a brief grip of fingers, or even just a brush of fingertips. I was reminded of the origins of the handshake on Earth: warriors approaching each other and gripping sword hands as an assurance that neither would go for the blade while they talked. This must be something like that, an old and culturally ingrained method of reassurance to each other. It struck me as kind of nice among these shaggy and obviously toil-hardened young men.

"Right here," Zell said, and eased me through a double-wide main hatchway in what my spacefarer's sense told me was the forward section of the ship. This was like an old-fashioned forecastle, crew quarters in the smallest area of the ship, with narrow quarters that had two bunks each, rather cluttered and lived-in. They looked average, just what anyone would've expected, except that most of the bunks had a blanket of some kind of fur. Might have been synthetic, but I doubted that. Looked like rabbit fur. In spite of an initial surge of disapproval, the warm comfort was too inviting to resist.

Zell led me to the farthest forward of these cabins. Before we went in, he turned to Ruvan. "I'll take her from here. You go and sit down in a quiet corner and eat something."

Ruvan smiled sadly. "I wish you would stop giving medical suggestions."

"It's not a suggestion," Zell told him. "It's an order."

"Mmm . . . all right." Ruvan reluctantly left us and headed back through the main deck. The last I saw of the worried young doctor was a glimpse of his hair in a work light as he knelt at someone's side to check a wound.

"This is Quen," Zell said, "our captain."

We stepped inside the cabin, which had only one bunk and a small desk. There, the captain sat hovering over his work.

The captain was another good-looking young man, with mushroom skin and soft shoulder-length hair the exact color of Scotch pine needles. What a storybook character he might've made, something out of a twentieth-century fantasy novel, except that through his good looks, he also seemed tired and overburdened. He didn't look up from a clutter of square metallic plates on his desk as I approached and forced myself not to lean on anything. Still feeling as if I'd been beaten with clubs, I also forced myself to wait a few seconds.

Finally he handed two of the metallic plates to Zell, and looked up at me. His expression changed to surprise—though we were basically similar, clearly I wasn't one of his species or any other that he recognized. I'd seen that look before.

Beyond that, what a sight I must have been. My legs were wrapped in Ruvan's compress dressings, my foil poncho was crinkled and cockeyed, and my hair—may the gods of cosmetics save us from this. Since part of it had been burned off, the right side was longer than the left side, as if I'd put a bad wig on crooked.

I gave him a moment to understand that the tattered mess he was looking at might not be the real me. Then I spoke up. A plaintive "It's dark in here" was the first thing out of my mouth. It should have been "thanks" but I wasn't in full control of my mouth.

"We conserve energy," he answered, without looking up. "Lights take energy. Zell, what did Ruvan say about her?"

"She's hurt, but she'll live. And if we don't get Ruvan some relief soon, I think his head's going to explode or he'll start bleeding from the eyes or his hair'll curl—"

"I know, I know . . . There isn't anybody to help him right now, Zell. The tiles have to be tended and the engine repairs are more important than medical. With the last find taken, that means more rationing until we can take another one. I don't have any spare hands. He'll just have to explode or curl up."

Zell smiled. These people had good smiles.

Now Quen leaned back and was abruptly stopped by a hard wince. His eyes snapped shut and he gripped his left arm near the shoulder. Zell stepped closer and firmly massaged what was obviously a recent injury to his captain's shoulder. Quen winced again but relaxed some. Neither of them seemed bothered to be showing either their familiarity or their weaknesses to a stranger.

After a moment Quen nodded to Zell and waved him off, then looked at me with clearer eyes. "So . . . who are you?"

Finally!

"My name is Kathryn Janeway."

"Do you want us to call you that?"

"Why not?"

"A little long for trouble, isn't it?"

I smiled. He had a point. "Well, you call me what you like. Spacefarers have to adjust, don't they?"

Something about that sentence bothered them.

"You're not . . . anything we recognize," Quen prodded. "You're not Berm, or Peliorine, Tauma, Omian—"

"We call ourselves Terrans. Humans, more generically. We call our species 'Homo sapiens.' What do your people call themselves, Captain?"

He glanced briefly at Zell again; what did those looks mean? "We're citizens of the Republic of Penza, on the planet Om. We call ourselves 'men' . . . 'people,' 'survivors,' 'Omian' . . ."

He seemed at a loss for what I was getting at.

I nodded. "Some things don't translate well. I've traveled many solar systems and the expanse of interstellar space and met many cultures. I understand."

He narrowed his eyes in obvious doubt. "Interstellar space . . . How are you understanding us if you're from so far away?"

Slipping my hand down the neck hole of my thermal sheet, I pulled off my commbadge and handed it to him.

He turned the small gold shield over and over in his fingers. "It translates?"

"Within a certain radius, yes."

"It's so small . . ." He peered closely at the commbadge and held it for Zell to see.

"If I hadn't pulled her out of the pod myself," Zell murmured, "I'd say she was a TCA agent, with something like this. If we could figure this out . . ."

"I know," Quen cut him off, but his tone was wishful and hungry.

Just as I began to fear for ever getting my precious little helper back, Quen simply handed it to me.

"It could help you?" I asked. "And you're just giving it back?"

Quen's brows drew together. "It's yours, not ours."

My recuperating fingers cramped slightly as I took the commbadge back and pinned it on the neck hole of my poncho.

"Your injuries have been treated?" he asked. "You're feeling all right?"

"Yes, and thank you for your doctor's help. I'm sure I was nearing the end of my rope when your rescue team found me."

"What were you doing in the pod?"

"Surviving," I said bluntly. "I was negotiating with the Iscoy when they were attacked by a mismatched fleet with a power curve that didn't make sense. But I recognized the pattern. It was an attacking fleet inflicting a total-destruction maneuver. It completely wiped out the Iscoy outpost."

"Iscoy?"

"You've never heard of them?"

"No."

"That's odd. If the pod was low-warp, the Iscoy Asteroid can't be all that far from here at cruising speed—"

"And there was an attack, you say?" Quen persisted.

"Not just an attack, Captain. A slaughter. I saw the weakness of their battle plan, but I saw it too late. I was off my ship. I tried to broadcast how to fight the Menace, but communications systems were being blanketed somehow. The Menace knew that if we talked to each other, we'd figure them out. They came in—" My hands begin to shake with deeply knotted emotion. "—and they put the entire Iscoy settlement to the torch. There was no warning, they took no prisoners, they refused to contact us with terms, they were completely heartless, soulless, they ignored cries for surrender or mercy—"

"You say you *saw* your ship destroyed? You're sure you saw this?"

His directness pulled me up short and made me realize where my tone of voice was going. I took a long breath and forced myself to calm down. "I saw the spacedock disintegrate. I saw a core explosion; I've seen them before. We were murdered, and we didn't even know why. Captain Quen, something is on its way . . . and we'd better be ready when it gets here."

"This thing that's coming . . . is it coming from the Berm and Kavapent routes?"

Uh-oh.

"I've never heard of those," I admitted.

"You were on the Kavapent route when we found you," Zell challenged. "You must've come in through the Berm Cloud. How did this ship of yours avoid the sands?"

What could I say? I had no answers. I'd come in blind.

"I'm new to this sector." Best I could do.

Quen watched me with an acute analytical gaze. "What ship were you traveling on?" he asked instead.

"It's a starship," I said, deliberately being a shade lofty. "The *U.S.S. Voyager.*"

"A what?" Zell asked.

"It's a fifteen-deck, seven-hundred-thousand-metric-ton light cruiser, registry number NCC 74656, Starfleet authorization, the defense and exploration agency of the United Federation of Planets. Currently exploring the Delta Quadrant. We were displaced by some kind of anomaly over which we had no control. We were trying to get home but were *very* far away—"

I paused because my legs were starting to hurt as Ruvan's anesthetic wore down, and also because both Quen and Zell were staring at me through the strangest doubts and worries. Had they picked up a lunatic?

Zell squinted and murmured, "Fifteen decks . . ."

Quen quieted him with a glance, then peered at me again. "You were a passenger? A traveler?"

My shoulders, slumped with cramped muscles, squared a little. "Neither. I'm the captain."

At this, Quen paused and passed his hand across his open lips. He held still briefly, deciding whether he had boarded a liar or a loon. He and Zell exchanged a suppressed glance that drove me crazy with frustration.

Quen pressed his lips flat, thinking. After a moment, he added, "No, uh . . . proof of this . . ."

Despite my injured legs, I managed to cock my hips and make a sorry motion to my foil poncho. "Well, not *on* me."

He shifted his injured arm. "If you're a captain, how long does it take at full speed to get from the largest sector star to the smallest?"

A legitimate question. Anyone in charge of a ship would have to know that, the simplest of area details, visible from multimillions of miles to anyone with the most basic of telescopic equipment.

Quickly I yanked up a shabby image of the star charts we'd made as we approached the Iscoy Asteroid and decided I just might know that one.

"At full hyperlight?" I asked.

"Yes."

"I'd estimate that would take my ship . . . about four days at maximum nonemergency warp speed."

The two young men looked at me as if I'd just grown green hair. Quen shifted his position to stretch a leg, but he was concentrating on what I'd just told him, adding it up. Finally he said, "It's a four-*month* journey with a light kick."

That's what comes from assuming. I shrugged. "Then your top speed is less than mine, that's all. Or your measure of time is different."

Zell heaved a doubtful breath and drawled, "No one's top light kick is better than Quen's."

Not getting anywhere on this tack, I decided to redirect the conversation.

"What's a light kick?"

"We use storage cells to funnel solar energy into our hyperligh t batteries and provide the kick of ignition up to light-speed."

My engineer's head started clicking. "Storage cells . . . you must mean some kind of capacitor."

Without committing himself, he continued, "Then the fusion engine takes over, and we can travel from star to star. One charge, one kick. If we get stalled in the interstellar void, we could suddenly be years away from home."

"I know the feeling."

"Power streams from the star to the skin of the ship, into the cell tiles, and we get the kick. Once we're kicked up to light-speed, the fusion engines can keep it up."

"But you can't initiate the warping process without solar collection?"

"Of course not," Zell said. "To build a fusion engine that could cold-start a light kick would take ten thousand times the mass of our engines. We can't go around towing a planet-sized fusion engine. It would take the resources of a million cities."

"You've never visited interstellar space, then?"

"Not willingly," Quen murmured. "And luckily, not us personally. We've heard of ships being stalled. The rescue process is almost a suicide mission itself. Some freelancers do it, but it takes just about half a lifetime."

"Besides," Zell added, "there's nothing in the void. Explorers have gone out and looked. They're gone half a lifetime, then they come back and tell us there's nothing there but dust. And they've been gone all that time just for dust. Nobody goes anymore. Not on purpose."

"Have you tried generational ships?" I shifted my legs, determined to stay upright long enough to plumb the culture that would be part of my life for . . . how long?

"There's no such thing as a perfect seal," Zell explained. "Everything leaks eventually. Even a cubic inch of loss a day means you're out of air eventually. If there's no air when you get where you're going, then you wake up dead."

With his slender hand again covering his mouth, Quen began shaking with amusement at his first officer's explanation. Laughing! In the middle of all this damage, with his own injuries still hurting, and after picking up a half-dead lunatic in a pod, he could still laugh!

I actually envied him.

With some halfhearted effort, he regained control of himself and straightened in his seat.

"Well," he asked, rather slowly, "what do you want?"

Here it came. A long steady breath . . . hold it a minute—

"I'm requesting you to take me back to my ship. If they're not destroyed, I've got to tell them how to defeat the Menace. I figured it out, but I was too late. I can make it worth your while in many ways."

"You said you saw your ship being destroyed," Quen reminded. He wanted clarity. Couldn't blame him for that.

I tilted my head and sounded like a scolding mother. "You must know nothing in a battle is that definite. I might be lying to myself. I *saw* the spacedock disintegrate and what looked like a warp core explosion . . . but I can't let that be my last try."

Zell picked up a small folding stool and moved it toward me. "Do you want to sit?"

"No!" I knocked the stool away. "Some of my crew might have survived! They might have salvaged sections of the ship. I can't just assume they're all gone. I have to see for myself and do an objective assessment. You *have* to take me there!"

Quen shared another glance with Zell—not one that cut me much slack for sanity—then came the hard question. "Where?"

"If you follow the stellar pattern directly across the red nebula at the narrowest point and broadcast a beacon I can encode for you, the Iscoy should be able to pick us up."

"Which spaceroad marker pattern?"

"I don't know anything about the markers around here."

"Did you notice any signals?"

"I was blind inside the pod."

"What about before you were in the pod?"

"No . . . I wasn't paying much attention. We had . . . an escort."

Not going well at all. Try again. "All you have to do is follow the stellar pattern in a direct line from the direction my pod came from. There wouldn't have been any deviation from a direct path—"

"We know which stars are in that direction," Quen told me. "The nearest one is a six-month journey."

"Six months . . ." I faltered momentarily, wondering if my translator were making his idea of a week into mine as it usually did, and if that meant I'd been drifting for at least that long. Was he talking about light-speed, and how high? What was his maximum light-speed with this kicking business?

Details, details. I was still having trouble thinking, adding up the trigonometry, the variants—

Going back to basics seemed like something they hadn't thought about in a long, long time. No surprise, there. This ship didn't strike me as a teaching vessel.

"What kind of power does your science use for hyperlight?" Quen asked. His calming tone brought me back to some self-control.

"Our hyperlight-speed," I began, "is fueled by matter/antimatter reaction, ignited by passing certain waves through dilithium crystals. We can generate an independent ignition any time we want to."

"Any time . . . Can you show us how to do it?"

I sighed at this, knew it was coming.

"Captain," I said, "I could be the best engineer in Star Fleet, and if I go back two hundred years in technology, I can't build a warp engine without the infrastructure that builds its million components. No matter what I tell you, you can't build warp drive without support. I can't say, 'Get me stone knives and bear skins, and I'll build you a warp drive.' But I can improve your systems to recover faster when you do fall out of warp. I might be able to help you eventually figure out a battery ignition system so you won't be slaves to solar energy. You won't have to live in a handful of forts with nothing but desert between. Our technology is generations beyond what I see out there on your deck, and so was the Iscoy's. My science skipped this jumping phase altogether. We know how to upgrade you to self-contained ignition. That would be worth your trouble, wouldn't it?"

I was careful to watch every word I said. I didn't want to make promises I couldn't keep. I was sworn not to violate the Prime Directive by providing unknown races with advanced technology. Even races with their own crude warp drive were covered until a decision was made by the Federation council. But if they could get me to *Voyager,* or any of her crew, then it was worth some prevarication. I'd find some way to reward them.

He watched me through weighted eyes but didn't offer any answer at all. Though my soliloquy had some elements of fascination to them, they looked at each other again—one of *those* glances.

"Well?" I prodded.

Seconds trucked by. My legs ached. My raw knuckles itched. The foil poncho had long ago lost its crinkle and now brushed pitifully against the edge of Quen's desk. Noise from the main deck outside interrupted us as somebody dropped something that went clattering abeam. None of us looked.

Finally, Quen sighed. His brows were drawn with an infuriating pity for me.

Zell shifted his weight in the most damnably clear universal body language I'd seen in a month.

"Nothing has fifteen decks," he uttered.

Damn, was I in trouble.

Their suspicion was both aggravating and understandable. Unable to avoid a tincture of desperation in my voice, I demanded, "What can I do to make you believe me?"

Quen seemed genuinely regretful, and in spite of my anger I couldn't help but empathize with him. "You don't know about the Berm and Kavapent," he said. "You don't know the marker patterns, signals, or spaceroads in this sector. You don't know about light kicks. Everyone who pilots any kind of ship knows those things. Every captain."

He didn't need to spell it for me. I felt my face harden and my glare turn fierce.

"You're not going to take me back?" I challenged. "You won't even try?"

"It would be against my pledge," he said with obvious conviction. "I have an obligation to my crew. If we make a light kick, and there's no star there—"

With one hand pressing on his desk, I leaned forward. "You won't need any solar power, Captain Quen, I told you. The Iscoy have the technology you need, and if any of my people survived, we have it, too. You'll get it. Your capacitors can be charged directly off a warp core. It's a ten-minute process! All you have to do is take me there!"

Only after it was too late did I realize my teeth were gritted and my fists clenched. From their point of view, I couldn't blame them. How did they know I hadn't been put off some other ship because I was nuts? Because my injuries were too extensive? Because I was some kind of danger? What was the past of this strange rubbish they'd scooped up? How long should I rave before they slapped me in their version of a padded cell and fed me applesauce? I realized my tune had better change quickly, or I would risk being put off the ship as some kind of spacesick Jonah.

And my plans would have to change, too. Quickly.

"All right, Captain," I began, gauging my tone like organ keys. "I don't want to be trouble or get in the way. I'll work my passage until we can come to an agreement. You can bunk me with one of the other women."

Seeming surprised at that last part, Quen looked at me quizzically. "There aren't any other women."

Oops—more trouble in River City.

"Your crew is all-male?"

He shrugged. "I've . . . never heard of anything else."

"Really? Then I'll bunk wherever you have room for me," I offered. "I'll do whatever work you have. Show me your engine room."

With both hands Quen brushed his shaggy emerald hair away from his drawn forehead, and frowned. "I don't like putting a woman to work. I'd rather send you—"

Before he finished that thought, I broke in. "I can assist your engineers significantly. My technical abilities can boost your power levels, your speed, and probably efficiency. I'll outwork anybody. I'll earn my place in your crew. Don't put me off until you give me a chance. I'm willing to trade improvements for a light kick as soon as you feel fully compensated."

Starfleet officer, sure. But I could haggle like Ferengi at a flea market.

Quen watched me as if waiting for me to break down and weep that it was all a pack of lies and I was playing some kind of game. That it was all a sorority prank. That I was really a princess pulling a fast one. I think I could've told him anything but the truth, and he'd have been relieved. After all, he already had the truth.

"If we try to contact a transport," Zell suggested, "we'll be giving up the salvage. Sasaquon or Oran is in the area. They'll move in on us."

"We couldn't go yet if we wanted to," Quen confirmed. "Don't worry. She'll just have to wait."

I had no idea what that really meant, but I got the idea that the situation they were in was buying me time. My mind raced briefly with plans, plots, ideas, and the long-range goal. The Menace was coming. I had to be ready. I had to make these people ready.

"Get clothes for her," Quen said. He started writing with some kind of stylus on one of the metal plates. I didn't know what those were, but this one had something to do with me. A log entry, maybe. Or recorded orders. "Assign her a bunk. Put her to work."

He handed the plate to Zell, who pocketed it in his vest.

"You," Zell told him then, "lie down for a while."

He plucked the stylus out of Quen's hand, then scooped up all the plates Quen had been working on.

"But I'm not finished," Quen protested. "Give me those back!"

"No."

"I want to get those out of the way before—"

"Bunk. You. Now."

Quen glowered at him. "Zell, I told you to quit giving me orders."

The first officer leaned over him and glared. "It's not an order. It's a threat."

He stuffed the metal plates into the hip pocket on his utility vest, as if to close the subject of Quen's doing any more work right now. He hoisted the fur blanket from Quen's bunk behind the desk and dumped it over his captain's head, leaving Quen sitting there, buried and chuckling.

Odd.

The crossroads before us was dim and disturbing as Zell ushered me out of the forecastle area and back to the main deck. He paused at a wall of lockers midships on the transverse bulkhead and opened one. From this he pulled a fur blanket, a small pillow, and two brown sheets, and from another cubby he pulled some clothes.

"If you'll show me to your engine room," I offered, "I can begin improvements right away. As soon as my hands and legs heal more, I'll be able to—"

"You're not going to the engines. You're going to work the tiles."

"But I can improve your—"

"We'll see later what you can do." His tone wasn't exactly patronizing, but it wasn't exactly encouraging either as he added, "Everybody starts at the tiles. Here are some clean clothes. We don't have any women's clothes—"

"That's all right."

I shook out the folded gear and discovered a simple pair of brown trousers that looked and felt like buckskin, an eggplant-colored knitted sweater with a thick cowl neck, and one of the shoulder capes that many of these men were also wearing. Apparently they put as little energy into heating as they could get away with and still function. It was chilly in here, but not enough to cause condensation. They seemed comfortable enough, probably because they'd grown accustomed to the chill. At least, I hoped so because that meant there was a chance in hell frozen over that I'd get used to it too. This was livably cool, as were the leaf-dropping crispy autumn days back home, but my shivering betrayed how spoiled I'd become to the warm and roomy accommodations on board my starship.

"Nobody here has feet as small as yours," Zell said, looking down at my boots. "I hope your mucks are good enough."

"They're just fine. I think my feet are the only part of me that didn't get cut, bruised, or burned."

"That's lucky."

Right there in front of the crew and the gods of luck and everybody, he helped me slip the trousers on over my bandaged legs. I'd gotten used to a captain's privileged privacy over the past few years, but there wasn't time for that. With a huff of relief I peeled off the crumpled foil poncho, and instantly every crewman on the long main deck turned away and suddenly got very interested in his work—not what I might've expected from the shipload of young men with no women on board.

"Your crew is very chivalrous," I mentioned, standing there in buckskin trousers and my silk chemise.

"What's that mean?" Zell asked, also conspicuously *not* looking at me.

"Polite."

Because my wrists were still stiff, he helped me pull the sweater on, then he fastened the clay-and-black checkered capelet over my shoulders. Felt like blanket fleece. Looked like Robin Hood. All I needed was a haircut.

"After you clean up and rest and Ruvan says you can work, you'll start over here."

Zell led me to the beam slightly forward of midships. He stooped and picked up a small tool with a scrubbing brush on one end and a pointed metal hook on the other. He handed this to me unceremoniously.

"The tool of your trade."

"It's a toothbrush," I said.

"It's a reamer," he corrected.

"What do I do with it?"

"Ream." He pointed at the bulkhead, which was encrusted from footboard to ceiling to the other side of the ship with those little metallic squares. "These are our cell tiles. They store energy, and when we need the energy they drain in an instant—"

"Capacitors. Giving you your power surge for the kick."

"And other things. Some of them are used for power flow on our fusion engines, our sensing probes—other things. It's complicated. Your job will be to ream out the crust that gets in between the tiles, keep the tiles absolutely clean and polished, and make sure they're fitted evenly and attached securely—"

I swung around to face him and almost twisted my leg off. "Are you telling me I'm a deck swab?"

He paused, then shrugged. "No . . . you're a tile reamer."

"But I'm a fully qualified and licensed chief engineer!"

"Not here you're not. Everybody starts at the tiles. I started there, Quen started there—"

Suddenly looking at months of working my way up to any real influence, I shook the little brush in his face and charged, "You don't have time for this! The Menace is coming!"

He gazed at me briefly with infuriating pity. "We'll keep a lookout."

"So did the Iscoy!"

"Zell!" one of the men at a side-mounted control stanchion called suddenly, and we both turned. "We've got approach!"

Zell took two steps toward the control stanchion, and was instantly thrown hard to his left by a jolt that rocked the whole ship. The *Zingara* heaved under us, actually leaving my feet by a couple of inches. I ended up on one knee, with the rest of the crew scrambling around me purposefully.

Frustration rocked through me as I realized I had no idea what to do or where to go, or even how to get out of the way and avoid making a nuisance of myself. Were we under attack? Had the Menace come sooner than even I expected?

Shoving to his feet and plunging to the control stanchion, Zell looked at the monitors and confirmed what was going on. He looked up and rasped out his order.

"Raid! Emergency posts!"

Four

QUEN APPEARED LIKE A PISTOL SHOT FROM THE FORECASTLE HATCHWAY, dragging his fur blanket caught on one boot. He came in so fast, in fact, that I barely saw the transition between when he wasn't here and when he was.

"Who is it?" he demanded.

Kind of an odd question—

"Sasaquon!" Zell answered. "Angle two-six over the prad."

All the crewmen had instantly jumped to their feet. On a Starfleet ship, when there was trouble, most people went to a post. There was no command chair or central arena on this deck, yet I got the idea that the general area with the helm was their version of a bridge. The helm was a standing console with one crewman manning it, which meant it was probably exclusively navigation and speed duty. Weapons, sensors, everything else must be somewhere other than that console. But where?

This empty, desperate feeling I had—it was nightmarish. I was a captain, but here I was nobody. A third wheel, a dunsel, with no idea what to do or how to help, or even what was going on. I should've been grateful for the crash course, but that was hard to appreciate while hanging here, completely impotent in the middle of trouble.

Standing near the helm officer, but not touching the helm itself, Quen ordered, "Hurry up, Vince, get us a corridor groove on standard trajectory. Othien, mark the racker and take weapons."

"The rod level is still down, Quen," Zell called, then he dropped into the lower deck through the big companionway right in the middle of the main deck.

I didn't understand their jargon, and obviously my commbadge didn't have a reference point from which to translate those words, so they just came through as the sounds Quen and Zell were making in their own language. Rod level, prad, corridor groove—I wanted to know what all that meant. I wanted to participate! I wasn't just a bird sitting in a cage, was I? I could help, but I didn't know how!

A few more lights popped on, all red ones, over control consoles where the crewmen now clustered around the perimeter of the deck. So their ocular physiology was like mine—red lights let us see what we were doing without forcing the pupils to contract. In the midst of my uselessness and confusion, it was good to find one thing I recognized.

Quen turned to one of his crewmen who was manning a panel of some kind aft of the helm. "Massus, let's have a full view."

"Full view." The crewman named Massus fed several metal plates like those I'd seen Quen working on into slots in his panel, paused, corrected something, then cranked a central lever all the way down.

The simple exchange showed me that repetition of orders had found its way into this culture too. Made sense. Clarity, control, understanding—

What in hell!

"Oh, my—" I choked, crouching in shock and looking around, overhead, to the sides.

It was as if the top half of *Zingara* had dissolved! We might as well be on an open-decked vessel in the middle of an ocean, with other vessels wheeling around us! Beautiful!

Beautiful, yes, but suddenly terrifying! We were virtually standing out in space! For a moment I actually held my breath, expecting all the oxygen to be gone. It took a firm shake of the senses to realize that this was some kind of artificial projection through the tiled inner skin that allowed Quen and his crew to see everything that was going on outside the ship, with the exception of directly below. What a great idea!

There's air . . . you're breathing . . . it's all right . . . you can breathe . . . out . . . out . . . out . . . let's go for an in . . .

I put my hand up, pressing it to the black sheet of space beside me; I could still feel the tiles, though I couldn't see them.

And, beyond my scraped fingers, this space was beautiful! I'd been used to looking through portals that had definite frames, or at the big bridge viewscreen aboard *Voyager.* Until now I hadn't realized how separate that view had been. This way, I was actually out in space, as if gazing at a mountain range from a canoe on a lake!

While feeling like I was about to exhale myself to death, I looked around and saw that a row of scanner readout screens had flickered to life below the disappear line. Most of them made no sense to me—no, that one did! Angle of vessel incline. One down. Forty or fifty to go. Oh—I got air!

Understand, Captains, those of you who work on an ocean, this was as if you jumped off your ships and ended up under water—or for us space captains, ended up outside our ships without a pressure suit—and suddenly realized you can still breathe. What a shock! What I was seeing just didn't link up to being able to inhale and function.

Convincing myself to behave as I might on a holodeck, that what I saw above me was a scanner illusion, a fabrication of the real thing, I pulled myself to my feet so I could see past the "rail," craned my neck, and peered out into open space,

Space here was indeed magnificent, crammed full of nebulae, bright sparkle clusters, a disturbingly close asteroid belt, and not much farther away an entire planet with a thick green atmosphere, a heavily watered surface, and frozen poles. To the other side was a fan of peacock-tail formations of chromatic gas-charged rings with dust plumes, as if someone had plucked the bird's feathers and laid them on a tabletop. For a moment the incomparable natural beauty caught my breath in my throat. I stared like an idiot. Until another shot rocked us—that woke me up.

To overcome the initial shock of what I was seeing, I retreated quickly to the logic of mathematics and engineering and clung to the anchor of figuring out this technology. It would never work unless these people had, like Starfleet, the ability to computer-magnify selected images. A ship passing close, say, fifty kilometers, would never be seen by the naked eye without help. We just hadn't evolved in space, so our senses were useless without machines adjusting things for our pathetic abilities. Good thing the machines needed us to design and build them, or they might get cocky.

The other ship, now wheeling past us from abaft to abeam on the port side, was relatively simple in configuration. It had a time-tried spaceborne design—functional and roughly cigar shaped with no appendages except weapons and broadcast arrays. The shape of the vessel presented the slimmest possible target at almost any angle except directly above and below. That explained why the intruder was staying on a level plane with *Zingara.* This added to the image of our moving about on an ocean's surface. Since Quen made no attempts to dodge under or over the other ship, I got the idea *Zingara* was a similar design.

And similarly banged up? That ship out there was patched and weathered as if it had been through a meteor shower and barely got out. Parts of the hull didn't match other parts, and sections were painted differently, as if made out of junk parts from other ships, and there were patches on top of other patches, creating a crazy quilt of a hull. Yet it looked strong—the repairs were tough and heavy, with thick welding strips visible even from here.

Beneath me the hull vibrated as powerful sublight engines revved to life. I winced—I knew a cold-start when I heard it. *Zingara* surged into a wheeling motion that countered the other ship's movements and forced them off their vector. The other ship corrected and started on a modified path downward from our plane, heeling to keep its slimmest profile to us.

"Sasaquon's moving to wing position, Quen," the crewman next to me informed.

"Don't let them get between us and the prize," Quen said. He wasn't responding, but passing an order to his helmsman, who immediately adjusted his controls, which included a joystick arrangement—probably thruster control.

"Absolutely quaint," I muttered, but after a moment of watching I recalled instead the retractable columns and yokes that once upon a time had been used to steer airplanes. As I watched *Zingara* being maneuvered, and the *Sasaquon* moving out there, my eyes scanned past a monitor that came on-line a few steps forward of me. I forced myself to watch it, to get used to it, to figure out what I was seeing. Three blue shapes in schematic, obviously vessels, flickering, changing position—

"I get it . . . ships in relation to each other . . ." The croak of my realization drew a look from the crewman manning that monitor.

He pointed at the shapes on the crackly screen. "This is *Sasaquon.* This is us. And this shape here is the prize we're defending. It's a derelict minesweeper. It's below the vid line right now."

"Thanks," I said, and scooted closer.

The third ship was below us, and clearly in pieces, like a wreck on the ocean floor, except that in space it was held together by some kind of tethers. At first it seemed the tethers might be inner cables that hadn't snapped. Then I changed my mind and concluded that someone had deliberately tied the pieces of the wreck together to keep them from drifting apart.

"I'm sorry you have to see this," he told me then.

"No—it's very interesting. I'm Kathryn Janeway."

"Lucas." He took a moment from his work to brush fingers with me. As he turned briefly, the blue form on his scanner reflected on his brown capelet and yellow hair, and I don't mean "blond."

"We have that name in my culture too," I mentioned. "Some people shorten it to Luke."

"That would work," he said. "Yours is long. You should shorten it for trouble. Duck down, please."

He pulled me to a crouch and looked over my head at the circling *Sasaquon,* then adjusted his scanner to compensate for speed.

"Did you shorten yours?" I asked.

"Everyone does. We have very long names."

"Then you'd better call me Janeway. There's not much of a way to shorten it. Jay . . . Jane . . ."

"What about the other one?" Lucas spoke as casually as if we weren't in a defensive maneuver, but carefully worked his equipment and kept his eye on *Sasaquon.*

"Well," I began, trying to be polite, "there are ways to shorten Kathryn. I've never done it. Kathy, Katie, Kate, Kay—"

"Kay is good. Short. Pardon me—" He reached past me and tapped some of the metallic squares near my elbow.

I noticed that he had no knobs, pressure panels, switches, or keys, but was running his fingers horizontally, vertically, or diagonally along some of these squares to adjust the picture on the scanner. The screen itself wasn't a screen at all, but dozens of these squares with each one broadcasting a fraction of the whole picture. A couple of them were "out," making little holes in the scene. This was a darn cute technology and I wanted in on it.

Later.

"What's your job here, Lucas?"

"Right now I'm keeping visual positions of everything in the challenge area. Usually, I map space."

"You're a stellar cartographer?"

"Usually. I also—"

As he started to say more, the sky above us blew to white—a hit on the hull directly above the midship section! Though only an illusion of what was going on outside, a shell had just exploded against the skin of the ship and we had seen it without any obstacles to our view, as if fireworks had exploded ten feet over our heads and sparkled over a glass ceiling. I flinched and ducked as the sparks rained and dissipated into a halo.

"It's all right," Lucas said. "We can take it for a while."

I made myself understand, with some effort, that what I was seeing was actually happening on the other side of an invisible ceiling.

Steeling myself in case we were hit again above the vid line, I asked, "Can you show me what *Zingara* looks like?"

Without answering, Lucas touched a square. Nothing happened. He corrected to another square, and the scanner screen changed. The three vessels suddenly took on a photographic realism. A miniature identical of *Sasaquon* veered past a clear image of *Zingara.* Quickly I added up the ships' similarities and differences. *Zingara* was somewhat more boat-shaped, possibly to accommodate her "vid" line, which for us created an illusion of a weather deck here, while the moving ship on the screen still had its decktops on. Mounted upon those tops were recognizable king posts with loading cranes, a rotating crane, and low-slung turret guns and cannons, but no living decks. All those, apparently, were down here on this level and below. Out forward was a barge bow with cushioned fenders for pushing, and aft was a stern transom that looked as if it might open and make a ramp. A fairly sensible working ship, able to defend itself. Like most ships, it wore its purpose on its sleeve.

The other ship was roughly the same basic shape, but its sheer line was broken with stacked housings amidships. It also had cranes, but all four of those were rotating cranes—no, there was one gantry crane mounted on the underbelly. The movements of the two ships looked like the *Monitor* and the *Merrimack* lumbering about in Hampton Roads.

From the CGI, with no frame of reference, I had no way of knowing the length of these vessels. Wait a minute—yes, I did. I had myself and these men standing around me. Turning, I eyeballed the distance from the forecastle transverse bulkhead to its correspondent aft and tried to remember walking it, even on bad legs. Maybe four hundred feet?

The steps might be wrong, but I thought the measurement was close. How far had I walked to get from that transverse bulkhead to Quen's cabin? Forty more feet?

Double that, add it up—*Zingara* bargained to be about five hundred feet overall, maybe five-fifty. A good, strong, serviceable tug size, not too big to turn tightly, not too small to have muscle. Made sense.

I compared my judgments with the CGI version of the ship, at the points where the hull started tapering toward the bow, and where it tapered toward its stern, and decided I was right—the two big transverse bulkheads were the markers for the midship section. That looked right, given my estimate of this deck with the other measurements. Well, I had to do something with my time while we were being fired on, didn't I?

"Why are they firing on us, Lucas?" I asked.

"They want to keep us from our claim."

"You mean that hulk out there?"

"Yes."

"Whose was it to begin with?"

"It was Shan. Derelict in the war."

Not much help.

"You just had a war and you're a salvage crew? How do you decide—"

My question was cut off by a hard hit forward of us from *Sasaquon.* The shots weren't like the long streaks of phaser bolts or the bloom of photon torpedoes. These shots were propellants of some sort, actual projectile weapons, not contained energy. As the *Sasaquon* fired and *Zingara* fired back, I could actually see solid projectiles spin across the space between us, and see the impact on the hulls, and over our heads on the vision of space, as if there were a glass ceiling over us. Impact and explosion. These weren't just solid iron like cannonballs. They were some kind of ballistic missile with a tracer stream. They wiggled toward us on a deadly trajectory, struck, and detonated.

Shots from *Zingara* did the same to *Sasaquon.* Both ships wobbled in the wash of enormous power and thrust as Quen's crew tried to work *Zingara* between the other ship and the wreck. How was the return fire handled? I didn't hear the captain giving orders to fire. That was how it was done on a starship—weapons officer taking specific orders to fire from the command officer, with the exception of "fire at will."

Had "fire at will" been given here?

I looked at Quen. He wasn't watching the big picture overhead. Instead he was huddled over a patch of squares with another crewman on the starboard side. Why wasn't he paying attention? Zell was belowdecks in the engine area, unable to handle command. Why wasn't Quen doing a captain's job?

Somebody was doing the shooting. Which of these men were the gunners? Or were the gunners not on this deck at all? Were they below? Or were they actually in the gun turrets?

Easy to solve.

"Lucas, who's handling the weapons?"

"Turretmasters," he answered.

"Aren't they waiting for orders?"

He looked at me, perplexed. "Orders? To shoot at Sasaquon? Nobody needs orders for that."

"Aren't you depleting your firepower with inefficient shots? The angles aren't coordinated with the ship's movements! Isn't somebody orchestrating the general activity?"

He squinted at me briefly, as if I'd asked him why his captain had green hair. "Everybody knows what to do," he said, perplexed and trying not to be rude to the dummy next to him.

Quen now straightened and watched as we slid downward and to the starboard, until we ran abeam of *Sasaquon.* He watched the other ship, but gave not a single maneuver order. Instead, he mildly spoke to a few of the crewmen here and there.

"Mark the rackers," he said. "Adjust the ergo stull and keep your corridor clear. Don't get fouled. Massus, cope the rod level."

"I'm watching it," Massus answered without turning. "It's not holding steady."

"Send the curry cards down to Zell so he can keep up the measure."

"All right."

No *yes, sir,* as I would have demanded. The lack of protocol and formality grated on me. Some things didn't translate, so I didn't even try to understand the technical jargon yet, but I knew inefficiency when I saw it.

Why wasn't anyone barking orders? Why weren't suggestions rushing across the crew?

In the middle of my criticisms, the enemy angled across our bow and got off a good shot directly at the left side of my forehead. Rationality hit the wind and I ducked. When I looked up, a quarter of the ceiling was blinking between here and not here. Quen and his crew watched it, wheeling underneath the jagged patch of reappearing upper bulkhead.

Zell appeared halfway up out of the companionway and craned at the reappeared section. Quen knelt by the companionway hole, spoke to Zell. Together they made some kind of decision, and Zell disappeared again. They left the ceiling as it was, partly there and partly gone. No one that I could see made any attempt to fix the damage so there would again be an unimpaired view of space.

"I can't see the *Sasaquon,*" I uttered, more or less thinking aloud. "Are they deliberately trying to impair our view? Is that why they're firing on the upper hull?"

Lucas was only half listening as he adjusted his screen, which was apparently the only mechanical visual reference to ships' positions. " 'The' *Sasaquon?"*

"Yes, that ship. The *Sasaquon.*"

"Oh. Sasaquon isn't the ship. Sasaquon is the captain over there. The ship is the *Aragore.*"

"You refer to your enemies by the captain's name?"

"Don't you?"

"Not really . . . that's a good detail not to get wrong. We put the names of our ships on the outside hull. What if you don't know the captain's name?"

"We know anyone who would attack us."

I shifted my aching legs and mumbled, "Like hell you do . . ."

Luckily, rather than add to a bad situation, my words were lost in a timely explosion on the lower decks. A ball of smoke piled out of the companionway. With it came a gout of choking crewmen, including Zell. Many of them staggered aside, and still more could barely walk. The rancorous smoke reached me just as I realized it was poisonous. I clapped a hand over my mouth and nose just in time to avoid a deep breath.

"Vents!" the second in command called, sending others running to select controls.

Quen helped Zell to his feet. "What happened?"

"Racker leaks," Zell gagged, waving at the smoke. It was clearing fast—and a good thing, that. "We had a choke catch, and then a . . . low-grade . . ."

He doubled over, clearing his lungs. Around them, a dozen crewmen were coiled on the deck, choking and seized up. Several had burned hands and scorched clothing.

Quen was damnably patient; I wouldn't have been. Low-grade what! What!

"Rod level drop," Zell finished.

"He's got us, then." Quen turned his tired eyes to the fracturing view of the enemy ship, just as the overhead bulkheads flickered back into existence.

"Quen, losing thruster control!" the helmsman called. "I can't hold against the pull."

"Steer right. Somebody get a window."

What pull? Gravitation from something? Were we too near a planet? He couldn't mean the wreck, could he?

I stood up and craned to see this area of space, to know what was going on, but as I looked upward, wide spans of damage in the panels flickered, reappeared, and shut out the vision of open space. We were once again in the shoebox. The overhead areas of the *Zingara* now showed patches of fracture, burns, and overloads. There must be a lot of mechanics packed up there, in order to provide a bulkhead-to-bulkhead computer-generated view of space beyond it, and also to carry ship's general systems. I was sure regular systems flowed through there; no fighting ship could afford such a big area to be devoted only to a viewscreen.

Steer right? Away from the wreck? Away from the one thing that could give us cover and a chance to win?

"Are you giving up?" I called.

To my left, Lucas flinched visibly and stared at me, but I was looking at Quen and Zell. They both blinked at me, and so did most of the crew—those who could still stand, anyway.

Then the most amazing thing happened. Zell turned his back. He faced Quen, and together they went to speak to Massus and two others over there in the aft corner, where the poison smoke was thinnest.

"Captain!" Angrily I pushed to my feet and stepped right over two recovering crewmen. "You can't actually be—"

Somebody hooked a hand in my elbow and whipped me around so fast that the words were snatched from my lips and I got a bad suck of that foul air.

Lucas and another crewman had me by both arms. I twisted against them and threw over my shoulder, "Captain, there's got to be more you can do!"

By now they'd hustled me to the far forward end of the shoebox, way down the deck from Quen and Zell.

Lucas pushed me into a corner and held me there while the other crewman stood back and watched, as if to let me know I couldn't get away from both of them.

"Don't bother Quen, Kay," Lucas warned. "We've lost the prize. Look at the crew—there's too much injury to keep on. Our vid is down, there's a rod level leak—"

"That doesn't mean you should give up," I said. "What kind of message is that to send to Sasaquon?"

"Sasaquon isn't like the others. He'll kill us."

Furious, I shook off his grip. "I don't understand the stakes here! What are you people doing? Is this a salvage operation, or are you invading somebody's claim, or what?!"

"We're not invading; it's a legitimate claim. Sasaquon's stealing what we need to surv—"

"Then why don't you defend what's yours?"

"We're too broken down now." He glanced at the other crewman who was guarding me, a lanky boy with scraggly brown hair and a gap between his front teeth.

"Use that wreck for cover!"

He and his friend stared at me, mouths agape, obviously with no answer for anger that seemed to make no sense to them.

"We can't move closer to the wreck," Lucas said, amazed that I would even suggest it.

But why was it amazing? Why!

"There are ways to fight, don't you know that?" I challenged. "Don't you people know anything about tactics? Don't you have tricks? Reserves?"

Lucas put his hands up to quiet me. "Do you want to be locked in a bunk?

For this he got a sock in the shoulder from a pointy fist. "I've just watched my ship get blown to pieces, and I'm not going to do it again. Both of you stand down!"

Though the punch didn't faze him, he was certainly stunned. He and Gap were actually afraid of me!

Intimidation worked in my favor as I shoved them both out of the way. Stalking back—all right, limping—toward the helm deck, I stocked up the half-dozen points I was going to make when Quen had no choice but to listen to me, which would be right now.

Coordinate maneuvers with firepower. Create a distraction. Bluff. Use the wreck for cover. After all, it's already a wreck!

What! A burly crewman with fuzzy rust hair done in a face-frame of braids had me by the wrist. I glared into his pale surly face as he said, "Don't bother Quen. We don't do that."

"Who are you?" I demanded.

"I'm Vince, the deck boss. Don't bother the captain."

"But I'm a captain too!"

"On board one day and you're a captain." He shoved me back. "Quen and Zell will handle the ship."

"You've got to trust me!"

He arched over me like a birch bending in a storm. "We don't *know* you!"

Lucas appeared at my side and squeezed between us, breaking Vince's grip on my arm. "Don't hit her, Vince!"

"I wasn't going to hit her!" the big deck boss snarled. "Get her out of the way!"

Nobody had to push me—the ship took care of that when it pitched up onto its starboard side and we all went crashing. I landed on top of the deck boss, and Lucas landed on top of me. There we were held as if by magnets through a surge of unseen power.

I dug my way out from under Vince's meaty leg and tried to see what was happening. Zell had disappeared completely under a wash of cables and equipment, and Quen was clawing his way up a deck that at this angle was virtually a wall.

At the aft transverse bulkhead, Massus held tightly on to a handgrip and shouted over the whine.

"We're caught in the Sands!"

Five

"SURGE THE COMPENSATORS!"

"They're oversurged already."

"Then bleed 'em!"

Orders fell like crackling leaves all around me. The weight of Vince and Lucas rose from me, and I was free to crawl along the tilted deck, maddened by the whine of straining engines and sizzling electronics, half of which were breaking and the other half crackling back to life as hasty repairs were made in every corner of the struggling *Zingara*.

I thought the ship must be finished, wallowing on such a tilt, groaning like an old scarecrow whose bones of wood and clothes of rags had begun to crack and shred in unkind wind. And there was nothing I could do about it, nothing I knew to do, no control that would recognize my touch, no way to know what had caught us or how to get out of its grip. The blind helplessness of the survival pod had been better than this poison helplessness and ignorance of what was happening and how to correct it.

The top half of the ship flickered, and part of the viewscreen came back on—which meant that jagged sections of the tile-encrusted bulkhead up there actually "disappeared," showing us a vision of what was happening out there. Now I saw what the problem was: Those peacock plumes of space matter and dust were now engulfing us in a sinister blue-green wash, sucking us deeper into the fans of energy. The Sands!

Instantly I realized I'd been wrong about the peacock plumes. They weren't just spewing dust left over from some ancient cataclysm. They were some kind of energy surge, with gravity sucking us in toward a collapsed or collapsing core. I'd completely misread what I'd seen. Quen's action to move away from the wreck was the right one, but even that had been too late to avoid the gravity wash. The ship was too weak to fight the pull into the Sands, so certainly it would now be too weak to claw its way out.

Did they have tractor beams? Could they latch on to something and take a purchase? At least hold themselves in place until repairs could be made? I hadn't heard anything like that. These ships didn't look as if they might be rigged for energy traction, not with all those cranes and booms and hauling hardware.

The ship around us screamed until I thought my brain would burst, engines relentlessly thrusting against the wavelike suction of the beautiful and deadly Sands. Like the giant eye in a peacock's feathers, the moon-sized center of this plume gorged itself on *Zingara,* washing against our hull with great arms of blue-green energy, as if we were being shoved again and again by ocean surf.

I'd never seen anything like this and didn't have any idea of how to fight it, though I struggled to come up with some wild plan to save the ship. As the crew scrambled around me, and the ship fought to put its own internal gravity back somewhere near upright so we could at least walk, the cold reality hit me that it wasn't my place to save the ship. I could have thirty ideas, but these people weren't interested in hearing them and would stand between me and Quen when I tried to tell him what I thought. No power, no influence, no one listening to me. No reputation, no rank, no confidence in me . . . I had nothing to offer that anyone here wanted. The weight of impotence almost crushed my chest.

"Look!"

It was Lucas, pointing furiously at an open part of the partial view above and to our sides.

I pulled myself to his side and looked out with my smoke-stung eyes. "Another ship!"

"It's Oran," Lucas gasped.

"Friend or foe?" I asked.

Through a glint of hope, he admitted, "That depends."

The new ship pulled out swiftly from behind a shimmering cloud and angled not toward us, but across our bow at an angle. At first I was irritated that the newcomers weren't rushing to our aid, then realized that they were steering clear of the surging Sands.

And those were some surges, if I was seeing right and measuring right. The peacock plumes were flowing and heaving back and forth against whatever gravitational power made them go, surging out and back by scores of kilometers, and they could easily strike out and capture a ship, which is probably what had happened to us. So the ship out there, Oran's ship, was smart to give way.

Why were they here? To help us or take advantage of our trouble?

Quen appeared between me and Lucas, gauged the distance of Oran's ship, its attitude, speed, and seemed also to be trying to guess its intent.

"Zell!" he called without turning.

"Down here." A voice, from somewhere below.

"Are the extenders up?"

"Yes, up."

"Go ahead and cast the harpoon cables. Hurry, hurry."

"Firing."

"Don't make him come to us."

"I won't, I'm casting. Vince! Get down here!"

Now Quen turned to the helmsman. "Keep the thrust up. Don't let us slip any more than we already have."

I pointed at another part of the jagged-edged view. "Here comes Sasaquon!"

Everyone around me looked where I was pointing, to Sasaquon's ship corkscrewing across our beam, firing salvos the whole way.

"Must be desperate," Quen muttered.

Though I didn't take it as a joke, several of the crew around me indulged in a gallows chuckle as they scrambled back to their posts and fought to compensate now not only for the suction of the Sands but the missiles hitting us.

Electrical damage sizzled through the systems around me and everything was suddenly hot with uninsulated energy. The view around us flickered, altered, some patches of tiles losing their ability to show us what was happening in space and others gaining it back, so that the view was inconstant and patchy.

What would Oran do? As the new ship wheeled in the distance, I still couldn't read intent in its motions.

Zingara jumped in place suddenly, and two cables fired outward from our lower hull, spooling into space between Sasaquon and Oran's ship as they came closer and closer to each other. Like a drowning swimmer being pulled under by a riptide, we had stuck a hand up to the surface and now hoped somebody would grab that hand.

Someone might just as easily slap it and push us under. Sasaquon was trying. Oran—an unknown factor.

I suddenly wanted my own viewscreen from *Voyager* in front of me. I wanted access to strong sensors and far-reaching communication, to order a view of Sasaquon himself so I could look in his eyes and know his face, memorize his expressions, and so he could see the determination in my eyes. I'd always cherished that face-to-face option with my opponents.

"Lucas!"

He was clinging to a handgrip with one hand and fingering tiles with the other, feeding information that scrolled across the scanner portion of tiles in front of him. I clasped another handgrip and squinted at the screen. A faulty image of our ship, Sasaquon's, and Oran's jockeyed with the giant fan of energy from the Sands, showing *Zingara* clawing against the generated wash of the plume, very artificial and somehow just as scary as the real thing visible in patches above and to the sides of us.

How strange!—it struck me again—to just look up and out as if the top half of the ship had opened up like the top of a box! Or the top of the coffin . . . The next few moments would tell. My teeth gritted so hard with frustration that I thought they'd crack.

"Lucas, can you show me what Sasaquon looks like?"

"What?" he called over the maddening whine of engines. "You want what?"

"I want to see Sasaquon!"

"Oh . . . now?"

"Yes!"

If I could've done it myself, I would have. The tile technology was a completely mystery, and I vowed to learn it as quickly as possible so I could get things for myself. He had to do two things at once to fulfill my request, but he did it and I was suddenly looking at a fuzzy picture of a strikingly handsome man, older than Quen, silver-haired with a good trim cut, with a ruddy complexion and dark eyes. Though his coloring was closer to human than any I'd seen yet, I could tell he was one of Quen's race. Something about the bone structure I was already getting used to. He wore the same kind of clothing as Quen's crew, except that the ragged shoulder capes were missing and Sasaquon wore instead a bright red vest. Though he seemed more like a businessman or an ambassador than a warrior, there was something effectively sinister in his appearance simply because I knew he was the one out there attacking us, trying to push us into the Sands.

The photo was some kind of communications record; though there was no sound, he was apparently just talking, not fighting, giving me the idea this had been recorded sometime in the recent past. Behind Sasaquon, crew members passed by wearing the same red vest and looking markedly healthier than Quen's crew. I resolved to ask about that later. Why were the enemy better dressed and better fed?

"What about Oran?"

"There's no time for this!" Lucas gasped. "We have to get out of the Sands! I have work to do!"

"All right, do it," I told him. There was really nothing I could do except stay out of the way.

As the ship shook and shuddered around me, I forced myself to concentrate on what Lucas did with the tiles and what the scanner screen made of them. A selection appeared on the screen with a bunch of little ships in profile, each on four tiles. So the four tiles were option files. He picked the ship that looked like Oran's, and the screen filled with the one ship. It made sense. I loved that it made sense. That meant I could learn all of this if I just had the time before we got crushed or smeared against a solid core somewhere at the hub of the Sands.

In the middle of near-disaster, I thought to myself, Great! Give me twenty minutes before I die, and I'll learn this stuff!

"He's almost got them!" Lucas called.

"I've almost got it!" Voices from the crew shouted back.

"Just a few more seconds!"

"Just another second . . ." Unable to affect what was going on in space, I fixated upon learning how to work the tile scanner and find out what Oran looked like. Now that Sasaquon's stylish and elegant appearance was burned into my memory, I wanted to know who and what else I might be up against. Know your friends, know your enemies, know yourself. Simple, simple—

Suddenly a jolt took the deck out from under me. I spun away from my scanner and missed the handgrip as I grabbed for it. The scanner flickered and changed to another menu, confused that I had left it without instruction, and I threw out one pathetic grasp toward the sorry tiles as I rolled away.

"What happened!" I shouted over the scrambling of the crew and the abrupt howl of the engines.

Nobody bothered to answer me, though several cast me surprised glances. Overhead, the view of space flashed and changed again as parts of the panorama changed back into bulkhead and other parts of the bulkhead flickered and changed to the outside view, which ironically was directly above my head as I ended up flat on my back, nestled under a coil of extension cord—and there, straight out in space, the two working cables that had gone out from our hull had been successfully captured by Oran's ship. They were going to pull us out of the Sands!

Friend or foe? Friend!

"And we need one!" I shoved the coil off my legs and clawed to my knees, crawling under two other crewmen who were stumbling around me. Heartened for the first time in weeks, I watched as Oran's ship fired on Sasaquon, and the turret guns of *Zingara* also fired in spite of our predicament. The combination of missiles from both ships drove Sasaquon to vector away and stop firing on us, at least for the moment.

Just before I was about to shout for action, demand we take advantage of the moment, Quen came out of an electrical cloud on the starboard side, dropped to one knee, and shouted down into the deck well, "Haul in!"

I heard Zell shout an answer, unintelligible under a squall of surging auxiliary power. This power was a different sound from the main engines, and I tried to identify it and what it was doing; soon enough I understood that this was some kind of donkey engine reeling in those tow cables. Oran's ship was providing us with anchorage, and we were hauling ourselves out of the Sands by reeling our own cables back in. *Zingara* was showcasing her nature as a working industrial ship.

"Haul . . . haul!" I encouraged, murmuring to the ship itself. I saturated my mind with the wonderful illusion of Oran's ship getting closer, though it was actually *Zingara* that was moving.

The color of hostile space filtered slowly from the surging aquamarine blue to the more comforting velvet black as we drew ourselves slowly out of the Sands. The pumping of the donkey engine took on a sensible regular pulse, though it was roaring almost as loudly as the ship's main engines and the power thrusters. There was at least a sense to the sound, a purposeful rhythm that said progress was being made.

In the distance, Sasaquon's ship wallowed, struggling, and flashed, with damage inflicted by the combined shots from us and Oran, but experience told me the respite wouldn't last if we didn't get out of here and fast. I was experienced enough with hostility in space to know that there were few buffers, few really good second chances that didn't somehow make things worse without a great deal of quick creativity, and I didn't know whether these people had that.

"It's working," Lucas uttered, his voice rough. His fear showed clearly now as I looked at his young face and his buttery hair flecked with dirt from the shattered panels above us.

His glint of hope caught me and I stopped looking for a picture of Oran, instead let myself be enthralled by the sight over the starboard rail. One ship, pendent against the blackness, helping another out of spaceborne quicksand—this was the best part of intelligent life, my favorite part, something I'd seen too seldom in the Delta Quadrant. I found myself hungering for the simple code of ethics employed so widely and freely in the Alpha Quadrant, established early on by the expansion of the Federation. Suddenly I wanted to go home more than ever.

Quen pulled himself along the slanted deck to peer over Lucas's shoulder at the proximity scanner. "How do we look?"

"Almost there," Lucas said, without committing himself with numbers.

Quen turned and called, "Resi, how's the helm feel?"

The young man at the helm, stiff-legged and breathing hard with tension, nodded, shrugged, and choked out, "I'm getting something back."

"Good," Quen gasped back. "I hadn't planned to die till the day after tomorrow."

He gazed out at the spectacle of Sasaquon's ship moving off, out of firing range, probably to duck away for repairs.

Possibly, if we had done enough damage, we'd have a buffer zone to repair our own ship before we came up against the efficient Sasaquon and his red-vested crew again. If only I understood why these people were fighting! Should I even be on the side of the people whose ship I was riding? I didn't have any idea whose team I should cheer for. Sasaquon had attacked us while we were down and damaged, of course, but some rules of war allowed for that perfectly honorably, and did I really dare judge before knowing the history of these people and what was going on?

I had to be on Quen's side for the moment, because that's where my life was and I had to fight for my own life. Whether that would hold, I'd have to see.

As he hovered near me, watching his ship slowly crawl out of the brilliant muck of space trouble, I watched the crease of his intelligent eyes and tried to see the hidden, ravaged youth under the fatigue and burdens he bore. His complexion was dusky, his eyes pouched. His hair, pine-colored, dirty, and dull, was the tired stuff of an overworked person who didn't take good-enough care of himself. There was great relief in his face, but his brow was still creased with worry. Did he think we might not make it?

At any other time I'd have blurted out the question. Not now, though, for I was learning that my voice, on this ship, wasn't so welcome as I was used to.

Was I spoiled by command? Could that be true? Had there been somebody belowdecks on *Voyager* whom I had stopped hearing?

If only I could go back and ask . . .

Abruptly the throbbing belligerence of the donkey engines fell off to a low rumble. Something had changed. The strain was gone. The Sands had released their hold on *Zingara.* Under us the deck heaved, then fell slightly, then came to an even keel. Compensators had found their center, and we could move again without hanging on or losing equilibrium. The difference was quite a physical surprise, like quickly getting up out of a rushing river.

"Quen." Zell appeared, just from the neck up, in the deck well. "We're clear."

"Keep the thrusters going. I want a buffer zone."

"Right."

"Send Vince back up here."

"Vince!"

Quen glanced at me as he turned back toward the view of Oran's ship. He said nothing to me, yet I knew he had in that instant registered my presence, my expression, my reaction, whether I looked afraid or not.

"Quen," Massus called from his place behind the helm, "Oran's releasing our cables. Should I reel in?"

"As quickly as you can," Quen confirmed. "Resi, steer us back toward the wreck, but go in an arch and follow the curve of the Sands so we don't get caught again. Protect the wreck, though."

"Protect it?" I blurted. "From what?"

He didn't answer me, and I almost shouted my question again, except that something about his manner silenced me. He gave me no more than the slightest glance as he concentrated hard on what was happening to his ship and the other two vessels. He was still worried. Why? We'd gotten out of the trouble, hadn't we? What was he still afraid of?

"Here he comes," Lucas said, riveted to his scanner just below where Quen and I were peering out into space.

Quen stepped back a few paces and to his right, away from me. There, he brushed some tiles with his fingertips and stood back again. A set of dark tiles glowed to life, and on came a vision of another ship's interior, another crew, and a helm similar to *Zingara*'s. That ship also was encrusted with tiles. So the general technology was the same, despite the fact that Oran's ship wasn't configured much like *Zingara* on the outside.

A young man who could easily have been in this crew, such were his looks and his clothing, appeared on the tiles. "You're going to have to move," he said bluntly, without the slightest protocol or formality.

"Get Oran, Jara," Quen responded, his voice suddenly brusk.

"Fine."

The man on the screen made a quick motion and stepped out of the screen. Another man appeared, taller, stronger, with coloring similar to Quen's, except that his hair was darker and almost into the navy blues, with glossy accents that were nearly black, and cut shorter.

"Are you out?" Oran asked. *"We can't see too well from here."*

Quen nodded. "Yes, and thank you."

"You're going to have to move out of our way now."

"We'll defend it."

"You don't have the power. We've been starving for a month. We'll take what we can. I'm sorry."

Quen simply nodded again. "Sorry too."

The tiles went dark. Briefly Quen gazed at the dark patch that a moment ago had shown the other captain's face. He rubbed his face, squeezed his tired eyes shut for a few seconds, then pressed both hands to his head as if to hold it on.

"Mmmm . . ." he complained inarticulately. With his eyes still closed, he stomped one foot on the deck. "Zell?"

From below: "What!"

"Get ready."

"Aw! Why can't two things in a row go right?"

"I don't know," Quen uttered. "Massus!"

"I know, I know," the other crewman said without turning.

I looked back there at Massus and, instinctively, all at once, got the idea that he corresponded with the on-bridge engineering office on Starfleet ships. Suddenly things made a little more sense.

Then the sense stopped. A bright white light appeared on the hull of our rescuer's vessel, then another and another. The lights bloomed wider, and at their centers were solid red dots—missiles!

Oran was firing on us!

Six

"I DON'T UNDERSTAND! THEY JUST SAVED US! THEY PULLED US OUT! THEY drove off Sasaquon! Why are they firing on us?"

"Later!"

A powerful voice sounded at my side, and two big hands shoved me physically to the side and down out of the way.

I twisted around to see who was manhandling me. Vince, the deck boss, whatever that meant, was back on the main deck, keeping me aside and barking orders to the others. His rusty hair was flecked with insulation and metal shavings—so there was damage below too.

Ducking lower than his grip, I squirmed away from him, and he instantly paid no more attention to me. Somehow I felt less insulted this time and cooperated by staying down and back. They had their hands full, and I didn't know how to help. Thrusting myself into the middle of the problem wouldn't do anything to solve it, and I should've known that from the start. I'd figure all this out, some way or other, I'd add up all that was around me, what I'd heard and seen, balance the inconsistencies, and pick at the technology until the curtains lifted. I'd do it myself, get my answers, and figure out what to do—later.

A flickering memory from my earliest days aboard Starfleet ships came sniggering back: what it was like to have people on board who didn't know what was going on but always tried to push themselves into the middle of things. I'd always hated that and taken solace in Starfleet crews with darned few civilian visitors crowding the bridge at critical moments.

Was that it? Was I spoiled? I'd come into Starfleet through all the right channels, always knowing the rules and understanding what was happening around me. Today I had been thrown into a situation I didn't understand, with a technology I didn't understand, and was being fired upon by people who had just saved my life.

Before I even finished that thought, the ship virtually dissolved around me. The vision of space overhead and to my sides disappeared and was replaced once again by the shoebox of tiled bulkheads, now draining cables and conduits and pieces of hardware, spitting sparks and spewing smoke. I ducked to keep my hair from catching fire again, and saw Quen slam to the deck, driven down by a double explosion directly over his head.

Dazed by the blast, he started to sluggishly roll over, waving at the sprinkle of ship guts spilling all over him, then threw one arm over his head. At first the motion confused me, but almost in the same instant I saw that he was protecting himself from a meter-wide piece of the ceiling material dangling from one fraying cable. He'd be killed if it fell!

I pushed away from the bulkhead where I was huddling and made a wild jump toward the hanging piece just as the cable parted. My left forearm and shoulder rammed the piece in midair and drove it only about two feet forward, but that was enough to miss Quen as the heavy material crashed to the deck and skidded against the forward side of the helm.

Surging forward on momentum and the fact that I was in a clumsy mood, I tripped on Quen's sprawled form and landed on one knee beside him. He reached out and caught my arm, keeping me from tumbling down the deck well, and together we struggled up.

"Are you hurt?" I asked, rasping through a cloud of insulation dust.

Leaning against the chunk of his ship that had almost crushed him, Quen pressed one hand to the back of his head, and another hand to his lower back. "I'll have to be hurt later. Thanks for the quick action; I'd have a hard time running the ship, cut in half."

His joke took me by surprise. "Well, yes . . ."

"Stand aside in case any more comes down."

Supporting himself from step to step, he moved away from me. More and more hits from Oran's ship, unremitting hits, hits without pause, missile after missile, until frustration soaked me as if I'd been dunked in a pond. This relentless attack was even more determined than Sasaquon's selective shots and maneuvers. Quen and his gasping crew fought back, less valiantly than I might've hoped, finally accepting their inability—or was it unwillingness—to fight hard enough to win or to die fighting.

Die? Did I want to die fighting for a hulk in space? There must be more to it, some value I didn't understand yet. They said they'd just had a war; was it really over, or were they lying to me? For the moment, I had to take the situation's word that the wreck out there was worth fighting for.

"Veer off!" Quen finally ordered to Vince, who had taken over the helm. "Give it to him. Lucas, signal that we're breaking battle."

"Hmm," I muttered. "Guess it's not worth a fight."

"After all this . . ." Lucas grimaced in misery, coughed, and turned to follow orders. "Now we starve . . ."

As soon as *Zingara*'s attitude changed, Oran's ship stopped firing on us. At least we had that. Sasaquon had kept firing even after we were caught in the Sands. The vessel around us struggled and crackled, with damage running through most of its systems. Injured crewmen gasped and struggled. Ruvan had appeared and picked his way from injury to injury. At last! Something I could do!

I pushed aside a jumbled coil of worklights and cords, and made my way to the nearest injured crewman. The man was barely breathing as I pulled him out of the way. I found a rag and pressed it to the wound on his neck. Rust-colored blood . . . about the color of Vince's hair. Different from humans, but not as different as Vulcans or Cardassians. Somehow the color was reassuring, silly as that was.

The deep-boned shuddering of *Zingara* gave way to a sick crackle as the old industrial vessel limped away from the wreck she had been defending. The doctor, Ruvan, stumbled to me and with a frightened and gratified glance took over stanching the dangerous wound of his shipmate. I managed a smile, trying to reassure him that things might start going better. That was my job as a commanding . . .

Pushing to my feet, I wiped bloody hands on my trousers, introducing stains of endangered life to the filth of a damaged ship, and made my way across the thirty or so feet to the helm.

"Vince," I began.

The big deck boss didn't even notice me, involved as he was in steering the ship, with a certain anger in his motions, handling two or three jobs at a time rather than just the helm as he should've been, and barking orders at crewmen through the smoke and sparks.

"Vince!"

"What do you want?"

"I'm going to help Ruvan triage the wounded."

"Do what to them?"

"Sort them for treatment. I know something about first aid and I can help."

"Fine. Go help."

"But if I do a good job," I said, "I want something from you when this is over."

"You *want* something from me? What do you want from me?"

Putting my hand on the helm console, I knitted myself to the ship and made a commitment that thirty minutes ago had been unthinkable.

"I want you to train me," I told him. "I'm going to learn how to run this ship."

The better part of a day went by before the *Zingara* settled down and the wounded were stabilized. Poor Ruvan nearly collapsed from exhaustion, trying to treat everybody on board, every injury, new and old. I did my best to help him, but my hands and legs were still bandaged, and there was a limit to my usefulness as a nurse.

I was just covering up a shocky young engineer when Vince appeared at my side and gruffly said, "Quen wants to talk to you."

"About time. Where is he?"

"In his quarters."

"You want to escort me or shall I just go on my own?"

The sarcasm was lost on him. Vince simply pointed forward and said, "You know where it is."

"I certainly do."

"When you come back," he said, "report to me."

Good. Now I could tell Quen I was sure I could help. All I needed was a few weeks of training to learn their engineering.

All this went through my head as I made my way across the half-wrecked deck to the forward bulkhead and to Quen's quarters. Mental lists of what I would say first, middle, and last scrolled through my mind. Wrapped up in my thoughts, I stepped right inside the captain's tiny quarters without even knocking.

Quen sat on the edge of his bunk, not at his desk, and he was speaking to Lucas, whose face flickered on one of the little tile screens. He noticed me but didn't break his communication.

"Go ahead, if you can put us through. I know he wants to talk to me," he said. "He's been trying all day. Can you make the connection?"

"I think I can do it now," Lucas said. *"They're being pretty cheap with the power down deck. I'll try to bleed off a little."*

The screen wobbled briefly, went dark, came light again, and struggled to focus on another face: dark navy hair, familiar bone structure—

Oran! I thought, stepping closer. Are you in communication with him? With the enemy?

"Quen?" our enemy on the screen began. *"I'm glad to see you. When we couldn't make contact, I got worried . . . You look exhausted."*

"I'm glad to see you too," Quen responded, his voice rough with fatigue. "I'm not exhausted. I'm just dusty. The tiles are dirty, too. You're not getting a good picture."

"Who's that with you?"

Quen glanced at me. "We picked up a rescue pod. This woman was in it."

"A woman? In space, here?"

"She's not from here," Quen said wearily. "Sorry we couldn't get your messages earlier. We're trashed over here."

On the flickering screen, Oran frowned. *"I heard you were hurt. Are you?"*

"No, no . . . just the same old aches."

"You're a bad liar," Oran told him. *"Listen to me now. I can trade the wreck in right away and arrange an air drop. You could pick it up on the other side of Lucarta Cluster, and no one will know."*

Quen moved his stiff shoulders. "Too big a risk for you. Sasaquon would find out. He's got eyes everywhere. And it's against your Pledge. I won't let you do that, Oran. We'll see to ourselves. I think we can make basic repairs in a month or so . . . but we've lost our rod level controls, and for that I need replacement parts. We're also down on fuel, and the forward top tiles are almost all fried."

Incredulous, I watched all this, but kept my mouth shut—and that took some doing. He was telling Oran details that could be useful to an enemy. Indignation gave a little way to curiosity. Somehow this all had to make sense eventually. The pieces of this dizzy puzzle would come together or I would simply force them into place. These two men, these enemies, spoke to each other with a strange warmth, even devotion. And only hours ago they had cut into each other's hulls!

"Have you got enough food?" Oran asked.

"Yes, plenty, no problem," Quen told him. "We made a good trade last month. Still living on it."

On the screen, Oran's expression was undisguised misery. He knew, and so did I, that Quen was lying.

Oran shifted his weight, forcing the screen to bobble to keep him in the middle. *"I don't like leaving you out here."*

"We'll have another chance. I have to go now."

"Take care, will you?"

"Don't worry."

Without any further words, Quen simply reached for the tiles and brushed them with his fingertips. The picture of Oran went dark, leaving only the dull brushed metallic tile squares now pretending to be a wall.

Quen pressed his hands to his face, rubbed his eyes, then drew a deep breath and turned to me. "I know," he said. "Oran's our enemy, and you don't know what's going on."

"No, I don't," I told him. "That was critical information you gave

Oran. You people have the strangest chivalry I've ever seen. Are these your enemies or not?"

"They're . . . our competitors."

"They tried to kill us."

"After they pulled us from the Sands," he clarified.

"And I don't understand that. Were they trying to give us a fair chance?"

Quen stretched one leg and winced, then rested back on his bunk, prompted on one elbow. "Oran had to fire on us until he could take the prize. He owes it to his crew, just as I owe mine."

"Why would you give him crucial information?"

"Why not? The battle's over. They won. They won't fight anymore."

"That's very naive of you, Captain," I said with a little shake of my head. "If it profits him to defeat you, eventually he *will* take advantage of any information he has."

"Not this."

"Why not? Why do you say that?"

"Because Oran's my brother."

Stunned, as he obviously expected, I sank back and leaned against a small ledge on the bulkhead. "Your brother. You don't mean that figuratively? You had the same parents?"

He nodded. "I used to steal his candy."

"And the relationship's amicable?" I pressed. "His attempts to help were genuine?"

"He'd still try to help us if I didn't stop him. So you don't have to worry about Oran. I'll do what I have to do for my ship and mates to survive. Oran's under the same obligation."

"What about Sasaquon?"

"He's . . . hard to understand sometimes. He'll kill us if he gets the chance."

"Then why didn't you accept Oran's offer of help?"

"Oran knows I can't accept. He's my brother and I don't want him compromised in the eyes of his crew. He's just torn between his Pledge and his brother." Quen flexed his shoulders again and sighed. "You're new here. There's a lot you don't know. Give yourself time to understand—"

"Yes, I'll understand everything eventually, but you have a very confusing operation going here. I know you think I've got some kind of space madness and you're treating me like a charity case. You just don't believe me, and I guess I can't blame you. After all, I can't suddenly develop transwarp for you. I could describe it, but you don't have the infrastructure to build it. I can make little improvements within your technological ability, but the question is . . . *should* I?"

"What do you mean, 'should' you?"

"My fleet swears to a directive that we won't interfere in developing cultures, but that starts to get vague once a culture discovers hyperlight travel. We can't explore *and* quarantine ourselves at the same time. We can't stand guard over a future that hasn't happened, or we'd never pull a drowning child out of a lake. I don't know what to do, really. Why should I care? You don't even believe me. Probably I wouldn't believe me, either."

My words trailed off as I realized I'd started to ramble, let my thoughts fall out of my head like seeds from a gourd.

Uneasily, Quen gazed at me, wondering just how crazy I really was. "Well, we don't know you . . ."

"No, you don't know me, but . . . damn it!" Frustration put a peak on my tone and I quickly fought for control.

"You don't know the roads," he said quietly, "you don't know the markers or lines, you talk about technology that can't possibly work, you want us to go somewhere without knowing how we'll get back . . . and you want us to treat you like a captain?"

I folded my arms and shook my head. "Sounds silly, I suppose."

"Well, far-fetched. This story about being 'thrown' so far from your home and trying to get back there . . . I've never heard of anything like that. And this civilization you say was attacked, we've never heard of them either."

"The Iscoy," I said, irritated. "They were decent people, incredibly helpful and welcoming. I didn't make them up, Captain. They lent us their spacedock, their materials, and even said that if we tired of our journey we could live with them. 'Stay with us,' they said, just like that. I'd be a liar if I said I wasn't tempted. A home for my crew, the warmth of a sun . . . but we're Starfleet officers and we belong in the Federation. We have a sworn duty to report what we know and take what we've learned back to the civilization that gave us our lives, our careers, and a ship to take us to the stars. We have as much obligation to them as to our families. The ship wasn't our personal plaything to possess and enjoy. It was an investment by the people of the Federation and we owe them. It's not just our desire to get home, it's our duty."

Yes, perhaps I was just venting, but it felt good to say all this to him. Maybe he would sense some trace of truth in my heartfelt words. So I let myself ramble. Often the truth spills from a toppled barrel.

His expression suggested a captain's empathy. He seemed to hear something in my tirade that the commander of a ship would understand. At least, if he didn't believe me entirely, he believed me a little bit.

Sensing it was time to throw him a bone of cooperation, I tried to appear more relaxed and cooperative by unfolding my arms and simply rubbing my aching fingers. "In light of that, I appreciate that you finally agreed to talk to me."

At this, Quen paused, got to his feet, and winced again at whatever was hurting him.

"Only to assure you," he began, "that hopefully within a month, two at the most, you'll be put off the ship."

Sharply I pushed away from the bulkhead. "Why! Why would you put me off?"

He gazed at me, both disturbed and confused by my reaction. "We have to find a place to trade for air. When we do, we'll make connections for you to go to a planet or an outpost where you can be comfortable and your injuries can—"

"But *why?*"

"Why . . ." Quen scratched his head, ruffled his hair out of his eyes, and frowned. "Women don't belong in space. We don't have women on our ships."

"Look, Captain," I began sharply, "I understand what your people believe, but I'm trained for space and I want to stay out here!"

"Already, some of our more suspicious men want you put off *Zingara* before anything happens to you, and I'm sorry to have brought you onto a ship that might be doomed. If we can't get air and supplies, we might be finished. If a woman died on my ship, I couldn't live with myself."

"Why didn't you accept Oran's help, then?" I asked again. "If things are that bad?"

"We can't join up. That would constitute a confederation. It's against the laws, and we always defend the laws. I just wanted to promise you that we would try to get you off as soon as possible. Until then, and we're sorry about this too, but you'll have to do some work."

My hands shook with bottled indignation and the cold realization that I could be in big trouble. The idea of being put off the ship terrified me. I'd come here hoping to be a hero, finally able to show how much I knew, tell them what they were doing wrong, show them how to fight. Instead, I was in the way, I was a woman, I was going to be put off. Stranded on some planet? Put off into a culture where I'd be the alien woman at the end of the block? Someday I'd graduate to being the weird old lady alien at the end of the block? No, thanks!

And I was very possibly the only person in the quadrant who knew how to defeat the Menace. What about that? I'd been in the wrong place at the wrong time, with the right knowledge to interpret what I was seeing, and I was being told there would be no chance for me to act upon it. When the Menace came, I'd be planet-locked.

My chin tucked as I tried to control my tone. "Captain, I already asked to be trained. Vince is going to train me."

"Train you?"

"Yes. I'm a Starfleet-licensed senior warp engineer. If Vince or somebody can familiarize me with your—"

"Vince already said you were getting in the way out there today."

That didn't do anything for my tone.

"In the way!" I erupted. "Was I 'in the way' when I saved your life?"

He shrugged and conceded with a nod. "No, that was very nice and quick of you."

"*Nice* and *quick* . . ."

"But you can't stay. We can't devote the resources to training you for the down decks because you won't be here to use what you learn. The crew would be very distracted by a woman on board all the time. They'd be looking out for you too much."

"I don't need looking after!"

"That wouldn't matter," he said quietly. The empathy in his face was absolutely enraging. "I'm sorry . . . I don't want *Zingara* to be the ship where a woman died. You're not staying. You've got a month. Maybe two. I hope just one."

Seven

MENIAL WORK. PETTY, MENIAL WORK. THE DULLEST, MOST REPETITIVE, most numbing task on this entire vessel fell to me. Me, the captain of a Federation starship, a qualified senior engineer, a top-scoring graduate of Starfleet Academy, with an enviable service record and socks older than most of these boys, and I was scraping tiles.

Things settled down quickly, out of necessity. The damage was being slowly repaired, and every day Ruvan scurried about like a mad hare, trying to treat the wounded. Nobody spoke much. Nobody complained at all. They joked some.

They wouldn't even let me repair the circuits behind the tiles. My job was to repair the tiles, clean the tiles, scrape the adhesive, ream the grout. The tiles were energy capacitors that stored solar power like batteries that emptied themselves in an instant, but there was more to them. They also served somehow as pixels in the huge virtual-space viewscreen and in smaller groups as scanner screens. As I worked on them, I became less and less sure that they were made of metal, though they looked metallic. They *felt* ceramic, but I came to doubt that too. They were made out of some kind of amalgam or composite. Some were beveled. Others had squared-off edges. My tools were the toothbrush, its reaming pick on the other end, a file, an adhesive neutralizer, a polishing gel, a shammy cloth, and creeping mental paralysis.

Hour by hour, day by day, I figured out that their idea of time was a little different from mine, but not unmanageable. Their idea of a day rounded out to my idea of thirty hours—comfortable with a little adjustment for sleeping. Their idea of a week was about the same as mine, and a month was a few days longer.

In actual function, I got *more* sleep than I was used to. The working day, though, was much longer. They ran two watches instead of three, and there was no real "off" time. We just worked all the time we weren't sleeping. There was certainly plenty to do.

Scrape, scrape, flake, flake, ream . . . sharpen, bevel . . . and the tiles weren't the same color, either. These in front of me were opalescent, pearly. Those over my shoulder were drab blue-gray. The only consistency was their size and the fact that they encrusted most of the interior of the *Zingara.* They had to be kept clean of crust, moisture, dust, and adhesive swell, or energy could bleed off—and polished, or they wouldn't show their pixel in focus.

I felt like I was doing somebody's fingernails. Ten thousand times.

Scrape, file, buff, buff, scrape, pick—

"Daughter of a Starfleet *admiral* . . . top of my *class* . . . Departmental Award in warp *physics* . . . used to have tidy *hair* . . . look at me *now* . . ."

One month, maybe two. I had one month to get out of this sector somehow. Or one month to show these people that I was worth having around. I fought to remember who put me in this position in the first place: the Menace. Mental calculations, guesses, bits of information, and mathematical voodoo kept nagging at me, telling me this: Given the kinds of methods I saw used by an aggressor civilization against the Iscoy, added up with the scarcity of large settlements in this sector, the Menace would eventually come here. Sooner or later, they would chew their way across the Quadrant, heading toward Quen's people because—what a target! They didn't have a clue how to fight!

A pair of boots appeared beside me—Zell, picking at the bulkhead beside me. As I scooted out of his way, I noticed that Quen was standing there too. Quen watched as his first officer twisted a couple of toggles and pulled open an access drum. Swallowing the pretty obvious annoyance that they thought I was now talking to myself and answering too, I listened to their conversation about the engineering. Making sense of their technical jargon through a translator had its limitations, so I was careful also to watch, to see which components they were pointing to and what they called them and what they said.

My stomach crawled as I listened—not because of anything they said or did, but because I realized I was learning a technology that might be in my future. I didn't want to admit that, to commit to this space, this life. Sitting here listening, etching into my memory a new technology, made me complicit in my own isolation.

I had a few suggestions but kept them to myself. Why should they listen to me? Why should they believe my stories? I didn't look like a captain, that was for sure. I didn't know anything about this space, the channels or markers, couldn't tell a warning from a nav beacon. I might be a spy or a Jonah. A lunatic. They were all uneasy around me, not used to having women around. Quen had put me to work because I was a mouth to feed and I should work my passage, and also, I knew, to help stave off suspicion.

Scrape . . . pick, pick . . . buff . . .

"Why don't you let your women and children into space?"

The question just popped out. Had to get this started somehow.

The two looked at each other with that "Is she crazy?" expression I was getting used to.

"We would never do that," Quen ultimately said. "It would be disrespectful."

His brows drew as he eyed me for reaction. He was disgusted that I'd even suggested it and was wondering what kind of people I came from. I was wondering the same about them, but also had to admit I'd misjudged their reasons for all-male crews.

"Life is hard and ugly in space," Quen continued when I didn't respond. "Women shouldn't have to see it."

Zell picked at a spool-shaped component in the thing they were working on and added, "I would never want my mother to see it."

"What if your mother wants to see it?" I asked.

"She wouldn't," he snapped back.

Quen finished, "I've never known a woman who wanted this kind of existence."

Whether they were deliberately giving me a dig, I couldn't really tell . . . No, I didn't think so. Though I watched carefully for indications that they were sending me a sideward insult, nothing surfaced but their contempt for the way they were forced to live. No point arguing the feminist case. After all, this wasn't my culture. Sooner or later I would find my way back to the Iscoy and chase the wild chance that anybody from my crew survived the Menace attack. Then we'd continue our voyage back to the Alpha Quadrant, back to home, where we fit in.

"If this life is so unsatisfying," I asked, "why stay yourselves?"

"We have to stay."

Continuing to scrape, pick, and buff, I decided to backtrack a little as long as they were held captive by the work they were doing, and press for a few answers.

"Because you lost your war?"

"Who told you that?" Zell blurted.

Quen motioned him silent. "Lost? We won."

I stopped working. "You certainly have a peculiar definition of victory.

What did you fight for? The right to squabble over salvage with Sasaquon and Oran? Are you telling me *they* lost?"

"No, they won too," Zell said. "We were all on the same side."

"Well, you're going to have to explain that one."

Dumbfounded by this ill-informed dolt they'd picked up, the two men eyed me, then each other again. I thought they were going to tell me to find out for myself, bother somebody else, don't disturb the command team, but Quen shrugged and told Zell, "If she's going to be here, she deserves to know. Make it short."

Insulted that he wasn't going to take the time to explain himself, I cast Quen my best disapproving glower as he pushed to his feet and climbed across a scatter of tools and cables, then disappeared into the lower deck well.

When I turned back, Zell was giving me a series of annoyed glances as he worked. He didn't want to talk to me. How infuriating! On my ship, I, the captain, would've taken the time to explain our situation to the lowliest of deckhands, and certainly to a rescued wayfarer. What kind of people were these?

"Well?" I prodded. "You have your orders, right?"

Unhappily, he huffed, "Keep working." Then he began: "The Assembly had to fight a war on the planet and in space with the Assosa Shan."

"Another planet?"

"No, it's the western continent on our planet. They wanted to absorb our nation into theirs again, using some ancient land claim as an excuse. We used to be part of them, but our forefathers fought for independence three centuries ago and established our own continental government."

"Sounds familiar. Sorry—go ahead."

"The Assembly had no fighting ships, so they hired all the private ships around and gave us the right to fight as official ships of war."

"Like privateers," I murmured.

He shrugged. "Whatever that means."

"It means a government issuing raiding rights to private ships during wartime."

"Well . . . that's it. What was that word again?"

"Privateers."

"That's a good word for it."

"What's your word for it."

"Our word for ourselves, you mean?"

"Yes."

"We're warranters."

"Warranters. That sounds almost the same as privateers. A warrant . . . letters of marque . . . a license to raid given by the current authority, right?"

Zell pondered all this, and I was struck by his apparent care and desire to get the story straight. Ultimately he decided, "Uh . . . I guess that's it."

"You won this war?" I pressed on.

"We won and their government collapsed. The Assembly absorbed them, and suddenly there were billions more people who had come from a destroyed nation, all scrambling to survive. I don't know how to explain this to you . . . We were being oppressed and we threw the oppressors off. Now we have to take care of their people too."

Zell paused now and stopped working, as if he couldn't do two things at once and explaining this to me in short form took all his concentration. I didn't say anything. Better he have the chance to organize his thoughts.

"After the war, the Assembly government was unstable," he said. "While we were trying to recover, the people we fought to get into power fell out of power, and a council of citizens came into power just long enough to stabilize everything. It's called the TCA. Temporary Civilian Authority."

"Uh-oh . . ." I stopped working and gave him a suspicious glare of understanding. "I don't like the sound of that. Just how long has this temporary authority been 'temporary'?"

Zell sniffed and wiped a greasy hand on his shirt. "Six years."

"Six years? You've been out here, like this, for *six years?* Six years is not temporary!"

He dived back into his work, and I could see that my words annoyed him.

I urged him to keep filling me in. "If you won the war, why don't you just go home?"

"After we won the war for them, the new Assembly didn't know what to do with us. They owe us payment for years of loyal service. They went into truce with the other hemisphere and mutually declared us on our own."

"Because they didn't want to pay you? Sounds like your 'new' government is corrupt."

"I don't know," he said morosely. "They aren't . . . living like we thought they would. They aren't using the principles we fought for."

"And you've been supporting yourselves by salvaging the wrecks from the war?"

"We're trying to survive until things change again. We scrupulously obey the laws because we don't want to turn into real pirates. If we start breaking laws, the Assembly can make their actions seem legitimate. Eventually things will change. Bad people will cycle out of power. It always happens . . . sooner or later . . ."

"Unfortunately it's usually later and after a lot of damage. 'Do your best and hope things change' doesn't usually work in the long run. Why can't you just go home?"

"Go home and live unfree? We face a prison sentence for not coming in, and after that's served, we'll be assigned to a farm or a factory, and be fed, and be given a cubicle to live in. That's not what we fought for. We won't go and be oppressed. If we can't live as free individuals, we won't go back. Everything we fought for will be given up."

"You mean they won't kill you, but you'll live as serfs?"

Zell twitched as if he'd suddenly developed a rash. Clearly he didn't like even reminding himself of these unfortunate facts. "The only way we can live as free individuals is in space. So this is our life now."

"Mmm," I uttered. " 'Live free or die.' "

He looked up. "What?"

"The state slogan of, uh . . . New Hampshire. 'Live free or die.' "

A mirthless chuckle huffed from him. "I like that."

"I've always liked it too," I told him, letting my solicitousness for their problem show through. "Sounds like your new leaders are setting the warranters up against each other."

His brow drew tight as my words galvanized thoughts that he didn't like hearing. "And passing laws that keep us from banding together."

"Like what?" I asked. "What kind of legal language could stipulate that?"

"Easy. If we join together in a common purpose, it constitutes a hostile confederation."

"Oh, yes—Quen mentioned that, but I didn't know what he meant. That does sound like the paranoid afterglow of a war."

"None of the captains would break the Pledge to his own crew. So we have to fight each other. We can barely keep our own crews and families alive. Especially now that Oran's got the salvage rights to that prize. That wreck would've fed us for half a year."

From across the deck, Massus interrupted, "Doesn't mean he can keep them."

And several of the men laughed as they relentlessly worked. Zell smiled and shared a glance with them.

"Can't you at least help each other in little ways?" I pestered. "Medical supplies, food?"

"Can't. If you do, you've broken the Pledge to your own crew."

"If you're so desperate," I asked carefully, "why did you rescue me, knowing you might end up with another mouth to feed?"

"Good question!" Vince's roar tumbled up from just inside the deck well.

Damn it! He was in a perfect position to eavesdrop down there!

Everybody laughed—except me. Then, after a moment and many relatively friendly glances from the crew, I did feel a smile creep over my dissatisfaction with all this.

"Most of us rescue survivors in good faith," Zell went on. "It's part of the Pledge."

"This Pledge . . . it bonds you to your ship and shipmates, but not to other ships?"

He paused, then agreed, "Basically. It bonds us to our ships and shipmates *first.* It also bonds us to the law we fought to defend."

"Laws like the one that says you're forming a hostile confederation if you help each other?"

He only nodded. Apparently he thought this was a raw deal.

I agreed. "That's why Quen and his brother are forced to compete and can't join forces?"

"They fought side by side for years. Now they have to fight each other, even kill each other, to keep their crews alive. We're all obliged to do anything we can to keep our ships and crews going. We're the last light of freedom . . ." His voice trailed off as he cranked on a tool and grimaced with the effort. "It's getting harder. But, if we band together, the TCA has authorized itself to confiscate our homes and arrest our women and children. As it is now, if we stay separate, they leave our wives and mothers alone."

"So you're forced into a situation where you have to compete to survive, like tribes in a desert. Or a pride of lions."

"Right. We have to compete."

"Why not go somewhere else? Take your families, make a light jump, find yourselves a comfortable planet somewhere, and settle it. Start over with—"

My words trailed out. The rest of the nearby crew had stopped working and were gazing at me with peculiar expressions of deep feeling. Their eyes, their silence, stopped me. Suddenly I felt bad about asking.

I held up a solicitous hand. "I'm sorry. Of all people, I should know . . . home is home. It's the civilization your fathers and mothers built, the one you want to fight for and keep on a good track . . . the one where you have a common heritage and a common future. There's something to that. I didn't mean to diminish it."

Contempt burned in Zell's eyes. "Enough talking. You'll learn what you need to know later. We have work to do."

Turning back to my tiles, I forced myself to accept that. While I was used to getting answers when I needed them, the message was seeping through my command skull that I wasn't the top of the totem pole anymore and couldn't just demand attention.

As Zell started down the deck well, I threw one more request over my shoulder. "I do have one more question."

Up to his shoulders in the well, he paused. "What's that?"

"Does anybody on this ship know how to give a haircut?"

• • •

Now I had the ducks lined up. There'd been a war on a planet with a spacefaring culture, so some of the war had lopped out into space. The salvagers were hired as privateers, "warranters," basically a makeshift navy, licensed to harass enemy shipping. But these were merchant guys, not soldiers. From what I'd seen, they'd developed a few basic tactics, but nothing like the training I'd received at Starfleet Academy or in my years in the service of starships. All the myriad tactics from hand-to-hand combat to space-battle strategic maneuvers were at my fingertips. For years I'd studied the history of warfare for two reasons, to avoid the mistakes and imitate the victories. These people had none of that training, nothing to call upon. They were merchant seamen trying to do what soldiers should do. They weren't soldiers. They didn't know how to *think* like soldiers.

And the corrupt new government was taking advantage of that. In my very few off-hours, I snuggled up with a tile screen and found my way through their basic recent history, and found some curious facts. These people had fought for certain principles of decency and rule of law, but after the war, during the time of upheaval that follows any total collapse, the leaders they'd fought for had been shoved out and nothing less than the old monarchy had wafted itself back into power. They had suspended the working government on the excuse of taking strong action to hold the Assembly together. I suspected from the news releases available that for six years the victory had been betrayed and the old monarchy was busy galvanizing itself while pretending to be temporary. The "Temporary Civilian Authority" was neither of those adjectives.

So here I was, trapped in a culture at least a hundred years behind my technology, where I recognized some things, but most were not up to my level, where warp two was the top speed, and scanners and sensors were weak by my standards. It was as if I'd been dropped on a Quaker farm with an idea of how an airplane might someday work but no way to build it. And I knew the big airplanes were out there and coming this way.

These thoughts I kept to myself. Neither Quen nor any of his crew really saw the scope of what could happen. There didn't seem to be anything like this in their history. They had no experience with government subversion except in theory. Certainly it was all over Earth's history, and I'd seen this kind of betrayal happen several times in the Alpha Quadrant at large—Klingons, Cardassians, Orions. If it hadn't happened in this sector, maybe they just didn't know what could occur. Maybe they really were naive.

I wasn't going for a degree in history, and truth be told, I didn't care that much. My immediate goal was to understand enough about the situation to get myself out of it. I was in trouble. I had a month to change things.

How could I possibly do that? I couldn't gain authority on this ship in a month . . . not past Zell and Vince, and certainly not past Quen.

So I scraped tiles and waited for my chance.

After a week or so, in fact, the strangest thing began happening to me—I got custodial about the damned tiles. I'd never really done deckhand work, and there was something therapeutic about this nonmental activity. I had used my hands for study, entertainment, art, interest, play, but rarely for ordinary everyday work. It started to matter to me that the tiles were clean, well reamed, properly filed, polished, and bonded back into place evenly. As I worked, I was slowly reducing myself from the artisan of overview I'd always been to the detail craftsman I'd never been. Before long, the most important thing became my tiles. Pride rested in the tile I'd just buffed. Challenge existed in the dirty one next to it. Satisfaction came in the nods and pats of approval from my shipmates . . . and then, the most ego-fluffing moment of all—two of the crew came over to me and asked me how I was getting the bevel so even, and how to do their tiles better! What a great feeling!

What a strange and unexpected gift, this peace of purpose . . . I'd never dropped down in my career. I'd only gone up. And started fairly high at that—fresh out of Starfleet Academy with credentials that put me above the noncoms on any ship. I was instantly part of any command team around me. I'd never vacuumed a corridor or worked the ship's laundry. For a long time I'd enjoyed the inflexibility of command, and now I was down in the decidedly elastic saddle of lower deck work. I had to be more buoyant than ever before. It had been a long time since I'd taken an order.

How strange it was to force myself not to care about duties that didn't involve me. Why were those two engineers hurrying? What was Quen talking to Vince about? Who was going to recalibrate that system over there? Why were we changing course? Suddenly I didn't have to listen to every conversation. The decisions weren't mine anymore. Here, sitting on the ignoble deck, scraping, reaming, picking, I was learning to be a crewman again.

Something else too . . . It was a relief, somehow. For the first time in years, I wasn't the one making the big decisions. I couldn't influence what was going on around me. So I concentrated on my tiles, and my mind began slowly to shut down and rest.

With the therapy of menial work, the quiet and peace of doing something with my hands instead of my brain, creeping comprehension stole in. The ship, my *Voyager,* was really gone. Destroyed, blown up, utterly out of reach. All the delusions that my former crew somehow might've gotten away finally came to land in the vacuum left by this new peace. Until now I had made myself believe, however fleetingly, that the *Voyager* escaped from the Menace attack and was on its way toward home.

Slowly, as I scraped and polished, reality crept in. The faces of Chakotay,

Paris, Seven, Tuvok, and all my crewmates began to swim past me as if waving good-bye. I knew what I'd seen. My goal was gone. Over. I was more than forty years old and wouldn't survive to see the Federation in my lifetime, not without a ship and crew who also wanted to go there, unique in our mutual dependence simply because we had no one else upon whom to depend.

Things were as bad as I could imagine. My ship was destroyed, my crew dead. I had failed to protect them, and failed again to go down with them. The adventure of our lifetimes had cost our lives.

Except for me . . . the captain who failed to go down with her ship. I didn't want to be alive anymore.

What I lacked was the courage to do away with myself. Instead, I scraped tiles and mourned. Probably I should be comforted that they died quickly, together, weren't left to watch each other suffer . . . I never knew it could be so shriveling to have nothing to live for.

I'd never given in to depression in my life. There had always been choices and chances, alternatives, tricks. Not this time. What did I have now to distract me? Not even dreams of the ship gone on its way without me. No images of my crew gone off on adventures to cheer and envy. All that remained to me was grim awareness that all my satisfactions to date had been fraudulent. Darkening in sorrow and nursing bitterness about *Voyager,* I became acutely aware of the curious glances from Quen's crew. Why did I feel their eyes like hidden creatures in a forest? Why did I hear their voices like crickets snapping silent the second I looked?

Damn everything! This was unmindful torture and I was doing it to myself! I was giving in to the sick awareness that I was probably the only human being left in the Delta Quadrant. Throw in a dash of guilt at having survived, spice with humility, and mix thoroughly. Bake on a deep dark deck until ripe and oozing.

Oh, I had to do better than this!

Instantly lightning flashed in my head and I knew what my problem was. Since I'd crawled into that rescue pod, I'd been trailing the events that happened around me. I had to get ahead of this game! I had to start *leading* events somehow. The key to that machine—shake off the quavering doubts of grief and ream, scrape, pick, and polish better than anybody ever had in the history of tile capacitors. That was the way to get ahead! Make yourself more valuable than the job you're doing. If you're going to swab a deck, make it the best-swabbed deck ever!

I went after the tiles as if they were my children, my salvation. I became the tile police. I buffed my assigned units, then took the initiative and went after places nobody else was tending. The interior of the ship actually started to glow a little, the tiles were so clean and even. There were no more dusty niches. Rewards came in the form of grudging respect and those nods of approval from my shipmates, and even from Vince—once.

There wasn't much time or energy for self-congratulation. We were heavily damaged. Food, power, water, everything was being rationed. After some days, when real hunger bit into my guts, I absorbed the true depth of Quen's struggle for survival. Losing the wreck to Oran deprived *Zingara* of a way to sustain itself in the immediate future. Medical supplies were very low too. Ruvan did not possess either the skills or resources of our medical program on *Voyager,* nor did he have the computer-calm objectivity of our Doctor. Ruvan was a bag of emotion and suffered greatly with each of his patients. When I looked at him, I saw a distraught kid, practically an intern, generally self-taught and trying to swim up a waterfall.

As I explored the ship and figured things out, I discovered that *Zingara* was about fifty feet longer that I'd first estimated, and below the main deck there was not just one engineering deck, but an engineering deck and a trying-out deck. On that lowest deck was a whole factory for processing salvage. A wreck could be pulled up to *Zingara*'s beam and very efficiently stripped, recycled down to its base metals, and stored as separate components, which could then be traded to anyone who needed those specific parts, metals, plastics, electronics, or anything else that could be salvaged.

We were saved from immediate extinction by discovery of a rather small free-roaming satellite left over from the war, no longer in any use, which we pounced on with relish, tried out, and sold to a passing broker of apparently dubious connections. This gave us enough supplies to struggle forward for a few more weeks, and it also gave me a chance to watch Quen's crew process a find.

The trying-out process was much quicker and less risky than towing a wreck some great distance to a place where it could be parted and brokered, and of course the wrecks were much more valuable already processed and parted out. I found myself wishing I could see it in full operation, with a big wreck.

No chance for that now; we'd lost our big wreck and apparently they were rare. Oran had possession and all the profits. If these people could find some way to band together, they could not only survive but flourish. They were holding scrupulously to a set of rules and laws, hoping to hold the upper hand someday, at which point they could also possess dignity and honor. If they lived that long.

Yes, the wrecks would be thinning out if this were the way of life for six years after a war. There could only be so many, after all. What would Quen and his crew, and the other warranters and their crews, do after all the wrecks were gone?

And what would an ill-starred expatriate do then? What would I do?

Eight

"HE'S BACK! HE FOUND US!"

"We've got an approach!"

"Where's Quen?"

"Othien, wake him up!"

"We're not ready . . . we're not ready . . ."

"Too bad Sasaquon didn't ask if we were ready. Get Quen!"

"Get this junk off the deck!"

"Are you at the scanners?"

"No, I've got to finish the jeklights!"

"Who's at the scanners?"

"Somebody come here with a hex shank and put this conduit back together!"

"They're firing!"

"Turn the ship! He's got us broadside if we don't turn!"

"What angle do you want?"

"Head-on!"

"Whose mucks are piled up on the compensator lid? Get these out of here!"

"The harpoon gunners aren't ready for head-on. We won't be able to aim."

"Secure the kick panel on the control stanchion, or somebody's going to get electrocuted."

"Vid's not up."

"Can somebody get over to these scanners, please? Because we're about to die. Morning, Quen."

"What's happening?"

"We're about to get killed."

"Before breakfast? Never mind the kick panel, Resi, just steer the ship. Don't step in that lube jelly. Angle nine over the prad and bleed the compensators while we have the chance. How close is he? What's his angle?"

Absolute chaos. I couldn't believe what I was seeing. They'd known all along that they were in a dangerous situation, depleted and damaged, yet they'd lulled themselves into a quiet recuperation and weren't prepared at all for what now knocked at our door. Sasaquon was coming back, probably before all his damage was repaired, just so he could get a jump on us while we were still weakened.

And here I crouched, holding my tile toothbrush and looking over a sea of cables and tools and tripping crewmen. The deck roiled under us as we took hits from Sasaquon's missile cannons. He'd gotten the jump on us and we were taking fast initial damage on the outer hull. Even as the off-duty crew tumbled out of their bunks and the watch team scrambled for their posts, emergency lights and warnings flashed all over the main deck tiles. Sparks flew everywhere, inflicting nasty little burns and breaking concentration all over the deck.

Near the aft transverse bulkhead, Quen pressed his hand against the helm stanchion to favor his injuries, not bothering to hide the strain and muscle tension of old-fashioned pain. He had too much on his mind and could hide only so much. Right now fear would have to be the hidden thing and pain would have to just show.

On the tile scanners that did manage to struggle to pictures, various images of Sasaquon's ship *Aragore* and our *Zingara* jockeyed for position, crowded into awkward maneuvers by the proximity of the crackling, rock-strewn Lucarta Cluster to our port side and something called Tauma, a lava flow of ancient but active gas eruptions, boiling below us.

They were either good cover or we were trapped—I couldn't tell which yet.

Thud.

"He's got a harpoon hook on us!"

Lucas's desperate cry rose above a bitter crashing sound that vibrated right up through my boots and into my bones. I stumbled to his side and looked at the tile scanner directly in front of him.

On the tiles was a computer generated representation of our ship, lumbering in space and turning on an invisible spit. A nasty-looking claw hook had embedded in *Zingara*'s side. Around us, as the thrusters heaved, the ship let out an *oof* at the piercing of her lung. Now a sinister string on the picture twisted through space, linking us to the powerful *Aragore.* On the ship-positional screen the cable was only a thread, but on the nearby analysis screen a cross-section of the cable showed a strong braided inner core, and a fully served outer sheath. Extrapolating the size of everything I saw, I guessed the cable was probably as big around as I was and, oh, a little tougher.

"What's he doing?" I demanded. "Why is he trying to take us under tow?"

Picking at the screens, trying to focus the tiles, Lucas panted through a grip of pure fear.

"If he gets a shock line on us, he can coat the ship with racker waves. Numb our nervous systems with it. You've never felt anything like it. I hate it! It's like your head is dying and your arms and legs are already dead. He'll be able to tow us over a zone limit and claim he caught us there. That violates the Assembly's edict about—"

"Never mind! I get the picture."

Now, don't forget I was still suffering in plenty of ways. My arms and legs hadn't entirely healed and were itching like bugs under the wrappings, half my mind lingered with the Menace, with the Iscoy victims whom I been forced to abandon, and I didn't know enough about this ship to jump in and do something drastic. Certainly the moment Sasaquon attacked I dropped the tile tools and at least started pulling the cords and parts aside so the crew could move around without ending up flat on their faces, netted by the trash of maintenance. It gave me something to do while I tried to think of something better.

Sure, I could've dropped through the deck well and started tampering with the engines, trying to boost power, redirect energy to the weapons and thrusters. Certainly I knew enough about physics and mechanics to help down there, but what good would it do to try? The engineers would gawk at me and shove me out of the way and demand what I was doing, and I didn't have time to explain or prove one damned thing.

I couldn't take them help; Othien had it now, though he seemed baffled by the maneuver Quen had ordered.

"Get insulated!" Quen called suddenly. "Don't touch anything! Othien, let go of the yoke!"

Did he see something I'd missed?

Pushing to my feet, I shouted, "Captain! What do you mean, don't touch anything! You're taking the crew away from their controls? Giving up the helm? Why!"

"Shut up!" Zell boomed as he crawled out of the well and vaulted over the railing. "You don't know what we're up against! Quit interrupting us!"

Stomping down the deck toward him, I put my nose right under his and glared up there. "I know you weren't prepared for what could happen and now you're in more trouble than you have to be, I sure know that! Why don't you shut down that processing station below and concentrate on your battle capabilities! It's a little late now, isn't it?"

"Woman!"

Oh, wonderful—Vince.

"Get back from the command deck! Leave Quen alone! Back in your place!"

I whirled to meet him as he thunked toward me. "My place? What am I, a parrot out of a cage? I can help you, if you'd just *let* me!"

Boom—another hit got us so squarely amidships on the upper hull that I felt like something had landed on my head. The deck-length vid system was down, so we couldn't see a damned thing through the overhead or abeam tiles. No more big window. Just the shoebox. We were really broken.

Quen pressed between us and shouted over the whine of the ship around us. "Insulate! Vince, you're standing in a puddle. Get one of your crew to buffer the starboard jeklights. Kay, this isn't the time."

Pure fury numbed my whole brain. I hated him for being calm and being right. My head started buzzing such as no anger had buzzed it before. My hands and feet tingled and my spine stiffened. What a time to have a dizzy flash.

Caught up in a rush of emotion that was obviously overcoming me, I stepped back to let Quen run his ship.

I *tried* to step back.

My feet wouldn't go.

Before me, Quen's face was turned upward toward the useless overview screen, which was showing him nothing. Why was he looking up there? There was nothing to—

His arms flared out at his sides, and a strangled gasp bolted from his throat. His silky grove green hair actually stood away from his face as his knees buckled and he dropped straight down before me, crashing into Zell as the first officer slammed sidelong to the deck.

Even with my muscles seized and my hands sizzling before me, I managed to turn enough to see fifty or more crewmen in the grip of this shipwide spasm. They were all falling . . . writhing . . . faces knotted in grimaces of pain and seizure. Some kind of neuralizer had them by the raw nerves.

What was that nerve thing Lucas had mentioned? Why wasn't I falling down?

Through the terrible freeze, I realized I still had some control. I was now the only person on the deck—probably on the ship—still standing. Why? If Sasaquon could zap the ship with some kind of energetic umbilical, why wasn't I down and out, too?

Human . . . I was human. For a moment I'd forgotten that I was an alien here. Of course their weapons would be organized to debilitate their own people, their own physiology. Oh, if only I could think. My nerve endings were in a grinder.

So I was the only person on *Zingara* left standing. Now what? Handle the ship and the engines and the weapons all alone? Run an offensive by myself?

The crew writhed at my feet and all around me in a pathetic carpet of twisting bodies. They weren't unconscious and my heart ached to see them in such torment. Pivoting weakly on one heel, I looked around and noticed that the interior of the ship was actually glowing with a graveyardish sulfur glow—the tiles!

My tiles! Whatever Sasaquon was hitting us with, the energy was coming right through our own capacitors! And I'd cleaned them and made sure they would work!

Damn it, I hated cooperating with the enemy.

This had to stop. We were under tow, the crew was down, the ship was in spasm, my feet were numb, and I was mad.

Though I couldn't feel my feet, I had some sensation in my knees. Cranking my neck downward, I managed to look at the deck, at my knees, and through massive concentration I made one leg move. Then the other. Through the foggy buzz in my head, I forced myself to concentrate on moving. Luckily, I was already facing the right direction.

Pressing both hands to my head, I held my brains in place and blocked some of the screaming electrical whine and shuffled toward the deck well. There it was . . . a lightly railed open hole in the deck, leading down through the engine room to the hold and the main service loading hatch.

There it was, a big hole . . . I shuffled toward it and forced down the stomach-wrenching caution that usually stops people from throwing themselves down a shaft. My feet scratched forward until there was no more deck, and the well opened before me. I plunged full-length into the well, barely missing getting my head smashed by the other edge, because I had no control to curl up but just fell forward like a bottle toppling over.

Where was I? Had I impaled myself on an engine mount? Would a pool of blood appear on the deck, inches from my face? My cheek was pressed to the deck. One arm was pinned beneath me.

I had to get up, get to my knees. Crawl . . .

The cluttered engine deck lay before me, an obstacle course for a person whose head was twisting off. Between me and the loading dock were two dozen more shuddering bodies of crewmen. As I picked my way past them, over them, my innards cranked with awareness of how many of them I'd come to know fairly well. When had that happened? We worked together, ate together; they accepted me in spite of their questioning glances, they had cared for me and tended my wounds, they hadn't locked me up. I wanted to help them . . . assure them, fix all this—

A flash of white metal caught my eye through the yellow glow from the tile-encrusted bulkheads. The pod! My survival pod! My little bathtub of salvation!

There it was, stowed safely inside the loading airlock, being saved for salvage or emergency use or whatever a thrifty culture might need. I had to get inside.

Wait, wait—first get the remote airlock control. I know I saw one last time I was down here. There it was, on its wall mount. At last! One thing in its place!

The cool white metal of the pod's hatch cuff was cool and vibrating slightly with Sasaquon's energy assault.

I tumbled inside the pod and landed curled up with my shoulder tucked under me and had to squeeze out of that and get my head in the right direction. Where were my hands?

Oh—here was one. I needed only one.

The controls were still working. The pod's airtight hatch rolled shut, giving me a brief but poignant memory of the Iscoy captain's body, burned and crumpled beside me. I ached as if remembering a severed limb and trying to use it.

A brief suction hurt my ears as the pod pressurized, but suddenly the ringing freeze of Sasaquon's neuralizer released me and my arms and legs started to come back. The pod was insulating me somehow—well, there were no tiles in here, were there? Nothing to conduct the debilitating energy surge. The tiny utility light clicked on, faintly illuminating the inside of the pod.

In icy fingers I cradled the airlock remote and picked at the squares of the control panel. Outside the pod, there was a distinct *chunk* as the airlock slid shut, protecting the engine room from the vacuum of space. All that remained was to key the outer hatchway and let the pod roll out, free of *Zingara.*

I put my hand on the launch control, a last cryptic sentence rattled out of my throat.

"*This* is the time."

"Come on . . . come on, grab me . . . come on, pull me in . . . here I am . . . grab me . . ."

What were they thinking on *Zingara?* Through the neuralizing zapper Sasaquon was using even now to fry the brains of those boys, were Quen and his crew thinking I had abandoned them? That I was a coward and getting away just because my physiology was different enough to let me move through the deep fryer?

I should've brought a weapon.

Come to think of it, I'd never seen a hand weapon of any kind on *Zingara.* Not a weapons locker, not even a stunner that could be used as a hand-to-hand defensive or offensive instrument. I should've brought a rigger's knife.

As I lay in the pod, waiting, I got an almost-comical mental picture of plunging over the rail of the *Aragore* with one of those pirate-story belaying pins in my teeth. At the moment, I'd have tried it.

What could I use? I wouldn't have the element of surprise on my side, even if this worked at all. There had to be something in here—a sharp edge of metal or even the heel of my boot? I could break a nose with that if I had to.

What indignity—I was winging through space in my steel ball, unable to control where I was going, counting on the actions of an enemy I did not know, being cursed as a coward by the people I did know. Charming.

All at once a sledgehammer hit me and I was over on my face, pressed to the curved side of the pod as if stapled there. A tractor beam! Or a cable, or something!

"I counted on that!" My rasping voice boomed inside the steel shell.

The pod was being winched in—toward the *Aragore!*

"I knew it! I knew you couldn't let me go! Sasaquon, I already know how you think! Here I come . . . keep bringing me in, just keep doing it . . . I'm almost ready . . ."

Talking to myself. There was progress.

Would they know I was here? Could they scan for life signs? Maybe, but I didn't know how soon or at what proximity. I'd have to assume they'd know I was here.

Where was that emergency medical kit? Where was the pressure adjustment?

There were a couple things in my favor. Primarily, I was a woman. They wouldn't expect much. Finally the chromosome quirk was proving useful.

Somehow I had to get that neuralizer turned off first, even if it were the only thing I accomplished.

But it couldn't be the only thing, because Sasaquon could always turn it back on. I had no way of knowing how long Quen and the crew could take that kind of torture. Sasaquon didn't care if they died, and who could know how long before their lungs shut down or they had internal damage?

From the medical kit I took a metal splint and jammed it into the hatch handle, so no one could open the door before I was ready. And I almost was.

Standard PSI arrangement, perfectly understandable, basically the same for your run-of-the-mill spacefaring technology. Very simple: adjust the interior pressure . . . more . . . more . . . turn the dial up . . . ouch . . . more, increasing the PSI inside. My eyes started to throb, my ears to ache and ring. Two atmospheres, three . . . my ears popped . . . three and a half . . . four . . . oh, boy . . .

A hard bump from outside declared that my little crucible had been successfully captured. I'd been reeled in and was being boated by Sasaquon. Ow . . .

No matter how much it hurts, don't jump the gun—let *them* open the pod.

Straps! Strap in—I had to get strapped to the pod's superstructure, or I'd be blown out the door when it finally opened. This pressure would pop the pod like a champagne bottle and I'd be the foam. Strap in . . . Where were the damned straps?

Ah, in a drawer. Good place for the safety straps. Inside something, completely out of sight, where they have to be searched for. Genius. Over the shoulders, buckle the chest belt, tie the free end of the belt to the . . . the thing keeping the hatch handle—splint, it was a splint. My head pounded so hard, I could hear it.

A metallic scraping noise. I was being hauled in. The last few seconds of docking were spent steeping myself in the idea of doing what I had to do, hardening myself to destroy what I had to destroy, even to kill whomever I had to kill to protect my ship and crew.

My ship . . . *my ship* . . .

God, my head hurt. My ears rang and rang. Quen and the other boys, caught in that neuralizer, suffering. They seemed like children to me, the Lost Boys trying to figure out how to fly.

Just as I had been the only one to survive the Menace attack, I was the only one who could maneuver through the neuralizer, and now this chance for action fell to me and I wouldn't give up my chance. Sometimes chances came by only once.

Somebody was rattling on the door! The hatch handle was shifting against the metal splint! Now, now!

I yanked on the belt that was tied to the splint. The splint jumped, danced, and popped out from the handle. The hatch blew open on its heavy hinges with a great sudden *crack!* My torso slammed forward against the safety straps. My arms and legs flew outward, my shaggy hair sprayed forward and recoiled against my face, and my neck got a good wrenching. The straps cut into my ribs with a sharp snap, and just as abruptly the whole deck equalized. A gush of warm air surged back into the pod and embraced me. I hadn't been warm in so long!

Just as I was yanked nearly out of my skin, all the loose gear in the pod, from the med kit to mini-scanners and tools Quen's crew were using to analyze the mechanics, went surging out the hatch and spattered one of Sasaquon's guards, whose faces I saw as only brief flashes in that first instant.

As I unstrapped myself, feeling bruises rise on my ribs and pelvis, I glared out into what looked like the lower decks of Sasaquon's ship, and at three burly guards sprawled on the deck, unconscious, maybe dead. The cannon of pressure had done its job exactly as I'd planned. Good for me because I really needed something to go my way.

The lady's luck wouldn't hold for long. The noise of the pressure release had probably been heard all over the ship. I had to move—both legs, kid—and crack out of here.

I staggered out of the pod into a well-lit airlock vestibule, my head still throbbing, most of my body sprained, and pawed at the collapsed guards' red utility vests. Nothing, nothing, ah! Was this palm-sized oblong box a weapon? It did have nice finger grooves molded into its housing, for a much bigger hand, which meant exactly nothing yet.

I took it anyway and veered down the nearest corridor. No bearings at all. A security team could just as easily come pounding toward me from the direction I was heading.

The first chance I got, I angled deeper into the ship, toward the throb of engines. The chances of a security team coming from the power center were less than from the crew decks. While stumbling along, trying to get my feet to work again, I also tried to figure out this box I'd taken off the dead guard. I hoped it was a weapon, but mostly it looked like some kind of musician's electronic metronome or a hand-held prospector. Then again, a Starfleet-issue hand phaser without the pistol grip didn't look like much either. Keep up the hope.

There weren't many shadows to hide in. This ship, unlike *Zingara,* had plenty of light. Which way was forward on this weapon thing? All I needed was to fire it and find myself minus an artery. Alien weapons—the ultimate crash course.

It was really warm here! How did Sasaquon's warranters have so much energy to spare? How could that be, when the others were running on threads and recycled parts?

Since the crew on board didn't know what they were looking for, they certainly weren't expecting a fairly lightweight woman who could duck into all the cubbies and hide in half the place needed to hide one of these lugs running past me. They hurried past me as I crunched into any possible nook, some of them involved in carrying equipment, and I got the idea that they weren't looking for me yet—at least, *these* crewmen weren't. Maybe somebody else was, but the word hadn't spread to the power decks. These men who rushed around were involved in the immediate business of crippling Quen's crew and taking *Zingara* in hostile tow.

And that was my immediate business too. I had to stop that neuralizer and bust the tow. Could this box in my hand do the job? Seemed awfully small for that kind of power, and I hadn't yet seen anything that packed the energy of a phaser into something this small. I could as well be rushing onto the engine deck to stick them up with a hand warmer, for all I knew.

I cut down through the processing deck, figuring that there wouldn't be many crewmen there during a battle situation, and found not only reduced production activity, but absolutely none at all. The whole deck was like a library. There was nobody here. Why was the processing deck quiet? Why was it clean? Where were the tried-out remains of the wrecks they were getting? The ship looked like hell from the outside, just like *Zingara* and Oran's ship, but inside, it was healthy, warm, well-provisioned.

The controls here were similar to Quen's ship, and I'd been learning about those. Certain things had to operate certain ways, and somebody like me, trained to Starfleet ships and general spacefaring technology, could translate what I already knew. Physics worked the same way here as in the Alpha Quadrant. Certain means had to be used to channel energy. Mechanics had to follow a certain logic. Propellants, fusion, atoms, controls had a few basic ways to work, and I knew the basics. Forward was forward, reverse was reverse, no matter how far we flew.

Thus, simple—find out where the energy was flowing and what it was flowing through, and disrupt it.

The neuralizer first, then the tow. If there was time for more, great.

Like *Zingara,* this ship had a coating of tile capacitors encrusting the inner decks. I ran my fingers along them, lightly brushing as I hurried down the very narrow corridor on what I thought was the power deck. Some of the tiles lit up, and I paused to look at what they were displaying. Not what I want . . . this wasn't either . . . nope . . . ah! A display of current heat flow through the ship!

Now, *this* I could use. The little schematic of the *Aragore* clearly showed where energy was flowing on this ship right now, and there was a convenient blinking blue dot that obviously was my current location. Smart. Somebody knew how to program a user-friendly system. *Zingara* had no such blue dot to show the crew where they were at any given time.

I was just aft of amidships, on the engine deck. Blue dot, yellow flashers . . . power emanations . . . computer banks . . . computer banks would do the job. There they were: my target.

And the tiles provided me with a map. As footsteps pounded toward me, I found the off-tile and ducked behind a laundry bin, just in time to avoid a thudding six-pack of Sasaquon's crewmen—and those sure weren't engineers. They all carried rifle-type weapons that looked, at the brief glance I got, clean and ready to fire. That was a security team, and they were looking for me.

After they raced unobservantly past me, which was the only reason they didn't notice my knee sticking out at the edge of the bin, I evil-eyed the little box I'd taken off the guard at the pod. If those rifles were their weapon of choice, what was this thing?

Hand warmer? I'll die comfortable.

It had fingertip pressure pads, color-coded, no dials, no numbers . . . This would be interesting. No instructions or hints about how to use it. Of course, a 1920s revolver didn't have instructions printed on the grip, either. Trial by error, and the error could take out the side of the ship if I was misjudging this baby box.

Once the six-pack had passed and the drum of their footsteps faded, I ducked back the way they'd come. Already minutes had been eaten up, long minutes of agony and damage for Quen and the boys. Move faster, Janeway, people are hurting.

The blue dot had showed me where I was, and the schematic had given me a goal. Aft, along another corridor farther to my right, possibly down this way—yes! Past the storage rooms and the bunking area . . . nobody asleep, of course, because they were in a battle situation. Nobody here to notice me, either.

Before long, I didn't have to rely on the dot map I'd bothered to quickly memorize. The pulsing sound of hot energy led me to what I hoped was the power center, or at least the center of something where great damage could be done. I wanted to do some damage. I could taste it.

My shoulders turned and I had to inhale to squeeze through two horizontal support stanchions. Crouching behind some crates, I surveyed the area quickly. Two crewmen tending that cylindrical thing over there with the clear housing through which the yellow energy flowed . . . Physically I couldn't take them both. Time to test the hand warmer.

There was a red button, and although ocular powers varied across the galaxy—and even between humans and dogs—I'd learned from Quen's ship that red was still red, a universal signal for heat among those who saw the same thing. This hand warmer had a red pad, several levels of gray, a gold one . . . no really good hints. If red meant what I thought it did, I'd better try out some grays first.

The lightest one. My thumb pressed the pad.

There was an actual *click.* Then, nothing.

Just when I was about to push another button, the box started to vibrate in my hand. Now it was humming—louder! I knew an overload when I saw one!

As if shedding a hot rock, I put it on top of the thing I was hiding behind and dived for cover, closed my eyes, plugged my ears, and made sure I wasn't leaning against anything.

The little box built up and built up, humming not really louder but certainly with more intensity—

Pop-*pieuw!*

My ears! The force of the pop knocked me over onto my side. If I hadn't been crouched already, I'd have been wrapped up in that batch of cables hanging over there. All that built-up power had been released at once!

It *was* a weapon! That or it was one heck of a welder.

Slowly I peeked out.

Before me, the whole cylindrical assembly, all its computer bank consoles, and half of the wall behind it were engaged in a complete meltdown! The whole bank was sinking into mush like a dessert mold being suddenly heated.

I felt no residual heat at all, but I sure saw the effect of something like it. "Please," I uttered, "let that have been the neuralizer . . ."

Stepping out onto the open deck area, I glanced around to make sure no one was coming immediately, and peered around the soggy mess I'd made of some very nice machinery. There on the deck, dead and partially *dissolved,* were the two crewmen who had been tending this area.

So I'd crossed that line. That ugly line. Now Quen, his ship, his crew, were embedded in my life for the rest of it. I'd killed for them.

Alarms started going off. If this had been a secret, if no one had been watching the monitors up there until now, the grace period was over. This machine had stopped working and would never be repaired.

I swung around, scooped up the hand warmer, and said, "Baby, you got moxie! Okay, Quen, I bought you time . . . think of something. Counterattack. There's got to be something you can do.

As I slipped back into the corridor, ran about twenty feet, and angled up a ladder hatch onto another level, I found a set of tiles and fingered them until they showed me the nearest intraship diagram. Wonderful! The yellow pulse of active energy had gone dark, and instead was flashing with red and purple emergency lights. The blue locator dot now showed me on the middle deck, aft, port side. It blinked dutifully, as if all else were well and I should be calmed.

Yet, there was a haunting whisper. Something I was missing.

Push, push on. The tow cable, before time ran out.

Nagging the tiles, I got them to show me where the controls were for the cable. Computers are the most wonderful pets, aren't they?

The activity on board was heating up. Footsteps and shouting voices rang all around me, but I had the advantage of knowing something about covert raiding. I knew how to lurk.

I crannied, nooked, niched, and cornered my way to the very lowest deck, the processing deck, figuring that since Sasaquon wasn't involved in salvage at this moment, preoccupied instead with a conquest, there wouldn't be very many crewmen down here. If I could avoid killing anyone else, I would, though not out of any misplaced humanity. These situations were hardly the kind where passivity played a part. I wanted restraint for one very clinical military reason: There was no way to predict what I'd need in my favor later on. Free-flung brutality might serve the immediate battle but might strangle deals later on. Nobody with a brain played the hands before they were dealt.

Therefore, when I get to the towing area, how could I clear it before using Moxie?

Sure was quiet down here . . . no machinery working or even warmed up. I paused and looked at the recyclers and processors. Not even lubricated. How could that be?

"Haven't been used in weeks," I muttered, touching one of the shredders.

And there were no crewmen down here at all. Nobody. Didn't they man this deck, even in trouble? I would've.

I didn't like abandoned decks, even when they did me a favor. While rushing almost the whole length of the ship down here, my suspicions grew and grew.

That blue locator dot was still blinking in my mind. Quen's ship didn't have anything like that. Oh, it had intraship diagrams, but no locator dots. Why would one ship need a blue dot for the crew, and another ship not need it? This wasn't exactly a vacation vessel that had lots of tourists on board who needed to find their way around with YOU ARE HERE signs. It had done me some good, but I was a saboteur. Pretty obvious they hadn't provided the blue dot for evil intruders like me.

I had a chance—a few seconds to myself—and I'd take them to figure out how Moxie worked. That meant pushing another color and firing it again. Working completely in ignorance of what these settings meant, I took a horrid chance and pushed the yellow pad.

Moxie vibrated to overload again, this time almost instantly, sizzling in my hand. I put it down and ducked for cover, but peeked out at it to see what the feisty box would do on yellow.

Charging up in just a second or two, this time Moxie gave no sudden plasma crack. Instead, a pinpoint beam speared from the box and drilled into the casing of a processor. In seconds, the processor was violated all the way through and the yellow beam, without diffusing at all, speared out the other side.

After ten seconds, the beam shut down, leaving a sizzling hole in the processor and a notable mark in a stanchion beyond.

I jumped up and reclaimed my new toy, blurting, "Oh, I've *got* to take this apart! Some kind of short-range plasma scalpel! Bet I could make you work on a large scale, baby."

If only I could find its stun setting. I'd have to remember that the plasma crack took several seconds to power up, but the scalpel almost no time at all. There'd be no way to test a stunner because I had no one to test it on. Sure couldn't stun a machine. I had a wide-range melter-killer and a pinpoint scalpel. Those would have to suffice.

Scalpel . . . Why was I bothering to look for a ladder or a conduit through to the tow cable tier?

I dropped to the deck, hit the yellow button, aimed, and let Moxie overload itself. The pinpoint beam spat onto the deck. The mini-torch spindle started boring through the deck. Top layer . . . structural beam . . . insulation . . . another beam . . . the ceiling of the deck below. As if peeling back layers of archaeology, I stripped my way through to the next deck, managing to keep any large pieces from falling through and giving away my position. Just to make sure nobody saw the beam, I scored only the last layer, then punched through and pried it back.

Slowly I poked my head down and looked around. I almost got a mouthful of some burly thug's blue hair as a team of crewmen dashed by. Armed. More guards. Why would a warranter ship need so much security?

They passed by, and an unlikely elf dropped from the ceiling. Moxie had done it again—I was minutes closer to the tow mechanism.

Break it, break it, break it. Concentrate.

As I made my way farther aft and down one more half-deck toward the cable tier, I did all the damage I could. I took Moxie's scalpel to every computer access point, every conduit, every bundle of wires, cords, cables, and circuits that I could expose quickly. I also threw every switch and reversed every control on every panel. Those would be easy to turn back on or off but might contribute to the general chaos I was conjuring. Quickness was the key. I had to break the tow and get the ships away from each other.

If only Quen were moving over there, doing something, crafting, conniving, cooperating with me. There must be some trick to use in their own defense. I hoped they were working on whatever that was. Ten bits of havoc popped into my mind right off, but so what? I was over here.

On the other hand, I could be all wet about everything. Maybe that yellow beam wasn't even the neuralizer. It could as easily have been the waste control plant. Maybe all I'd done was shut down the ship's heads.

Oh, well, keep a good hope. And keep moving, madam.

Footsteps! On this level! They resounded clearly as the corridor funneled the noise right to me. They were coming!

Of course they were! Where was my head! Was I slipping? What a fool! I'd been causing damage along my route, and that would be a dead giveaway about where I was heading. I should've restrained myself until the tow was broken!

I broke into a run—not what a clandestine saboteur would prefer—and raced dangerously around corners and through hatches without checking to see whether the coast was clear. Once I ran through a small area between two bulkheads where at least a crewman was working on something, facing away from me, and I don't think he even saw me at all.

The whole dash to the cable tier had a surreal craziness about it, and a swiftness that made me dizzy, but in seconds I was there, cracking out into a giant industrial garage the whole ship wide and several decks tall. Before me lay a flank of twenty-foot-tall winches and housings, and spools of extra cables. Here, across the deck from me, the next-to-last winch was squawking and working furiously. An automatic spray mechanism was dousing the whole drum and its cable in cold water every few seconds, keeping it from heating up as the winch furiously reeled and reeled. From the winch to a hawsehole in the aft bulkhead, a huge parceled and served cable ached its way back into the ship.

At the end of it, out there in space, was Quen's ship. This was it—the umbilical causing most of our troubles.

Behind me as I turned to glance was a huge computer bank, which I instantly recognized as primary drive controls. The engineering mainframe! What luck!

With footsteps drumming toward me, seconds eating away, I pushed the right pad on Moxie and placed my toy on the nearest winch brace, a housing that was taller than I was, and all it did was hold the winch. Moxie was now aimed at the winch that was working.

I dove for cover. Moxie vibrated, rattled, then hummed wildly as energy built up to overload. That was beginning to make sense to me: Somehow this culture had taken a turn that mine had skipped, concentrating on power storage, buildup, and sudden release. Moxie worked on the same principle as the capacitor tiles on these ships. Build up energy to a dangerous point, then suddenly—

Pop-*pieuw!*

The whole deck roared as the winch suddenly melted down. Around me the *Aragore* heaved up in spasm, and everything grated to a factory-level halt.

I ended up sprawled sidelong on the deck, my head ringing and my hair in my face. Scratching to my feet, I grabbed Moxie, fitted the grip-formed casing into my hand, ran to the far side of the deck, and swung around.

And I started to shout.

"Hold it! Hold it! Stop!"

Nine

MY SHOUT BROKE EVEN BEFORE ANY OF THE MEN CHASING ME TUMBLED into the cable tier. Five . . . six . . . eight of them, all in red vests. With Moxie aimed at them, they all ground to a halt and stared at me, aiming their rifle weapons but not firing. They knew better because in my hand Moxie wasn't aimed at them. It was aimed at their engineering mainframe. I could take out their whole bank even as they killed me, and they knew it.

Instantly one man plowed forward from the rear, and all the others let him come through.

And I recognized him.

Sasaquon.

And what a striking fellow he was, I must mention. He looked like the sort who might be an ambassador or a judge or one of the steam-pressed admirals back at Starfleet. His shoulders were straight, his complexion ruddy, his hair gunmetal gray with touches of white at the temples, and his eyes might have been friendly had I not known the underlying purposes and unforgivable methods of this attack dog.

He wasn't lean or pale like Quen's crew, nor were any of his men. This crew was well fed, well provisioned, healthy. Their clothing had no patches, their hands needed no gloves in the warmth of this vessel, and, strangely, they had no healing injuries. Oh, I saw a bruise or two, and one bandaged hand, but the bandage was clean and the bruises were all fresh.

It was as if these people hadn't been through a battle before today. Were they really that good?

He motioned to his men to restrain themselves, though no one raised his weapon. Neither did I.

"Who are you?" Sasaquon asked.

"Let Quen's ship go," I sternly warned. I aimed Moxie at the engineering computer bank. "Let it go right now. If you take any action, I'll melt this whole bank. It's not my first choice to leave anybody stranded in space, but I'll do it to you, be assured."

Sasaquon surveyed me cannily, trying to figure me out. I knew the look. I knew the pause. I'd used them myself.

After a moment of tense silence, he took a measured step toward me. "If she doesn't surrender in the next ten seconds, turn all the turrets onto Quen's ship and slice it to pieces."

Uh-oh . . . he'd figured out what I cared about. I'd given him a tool to use against me. My nearest chance for a win was to call his—no, he probably wasn't bluffing. Maybe I could call my own bluff somehow.

"I'm not putting the weapon down," I said. "This isn't a waltz, Captain. If you want to destroy that ship, then get to it. You're killing them in daily increments anyway. Make the commitment to murdering those men, or take a stand and tell them what you really want, but don't keep stringing them along this way."

"Stringing them? What's that mean?"

He actually had a nice voice. Rather mellow. He could read poetry.

"It means you're playing the part of just another warranter, but you're not playing it well enough for me. I've been deceived before and I know the signs. You're not in honest competition with these other men, are you? You wait for Quen or Oran or somebody to get a grip on a wreck, then you move in and take it from them. You're a barracuda, Mr. Sasaquon, you're raiding somebody else's catch before they get it out of the water. And where's the parceled salvage? This is your processing deck, isn't it?"

"What's any of this to you?" He moved toward me slowly, though not so close as to induce me to open fire because we both knew I'd do it. "Why do you come on board my ship and make all this destruction? Who are you? *What* are you?"

With far more satisfaction than I can describe or explain, I squared my shoulders and lowered my chin just enough to make an impression.

"I'm Kay Janeway, deckhand aboard the *Warranter Zingara.*"

Awww—that felt so good! The sheer humility of it was invigorating! Could I say it again?

Sasaquon squinted his doubts. "That's some kind of funny lie. Quen doesn't have any women over there. Why are you there? You're not Omian or anything we recognize. What are you?"

"That doesn't matter."

"Where did Quen get you?" he persisted.

"Doesn't matter."

"Did he hire you?"

"Doesn't matter. Where's your salvage?"

"Are you somebody's mother?"

"No. Why isn't your processing deck in operation?"

"Why would he bring a woman to space?"

"Doesn't matter."

He paced before me, then concluded, "I know why. He thinks I won't fire on a ship if I know there's a woman on board. Is that why he brought you?"

Stretching my arm to full length, I kept Moxie aimed at the center of that computer bank, letting him know that I wasn't about to ease the threat or hand him any answers.

"If you're not having any luck finding wrecks," I said instead, "or if somebody else is taking them away from you, then why aren't you starving? You got hit pretty hard at the Sands by two ships, Quen's and Oran's. How is it you're ready to attack again so soon? Why aren't these men bandaged? Why isn't anybody limping? I don't see any swellings. How did you get out of a battle with hardly any injuries? And just tell me this, Mr. Sasaquon, how is it you all have good haircuts?"

"Sasaquon."

A comm unit from somewhere spoke up with a mechanical buzz behind it.

"Go ahead," I told him. "Answer it, Captain. I want to hear the status report."

Sasaquon measured my demeanor carefully. He held his men back with a gesture, then pointed to the wall unit. One of the men clicked it for him.

"Go ahead," he responded.

"Clear to talk?"

"I said, go ahead and talk."

"Quen just severed the cable grapnel. He's moving off. Our cable's just flying out there. You want us to rig a retrieval or open fire?"

"Nothing yet. Is he getting away?"

"No, but he's drifting away. I don't think he's got control yet."

"Can we get repaired faster than he can?"

"Probably."

"Get working on it." He motioned for his crewman to click off the comm, then looked at the others. "You two go see what else she did and tell me how long to repair."

One of the men asked, "Me? Or—"

"No, Tor—Torma."

"Tirga," another man corrected.

"All right, Tirga and . . . you." He pointed at those he wanted to go.

They turned and ducked out the hatch. I probably should've opened fire on the bank. Still, I wanted to find out some things before I destroyed everything in sight.

Sasaquon turned to me again, narrowing his eyes. He took a few steps away from the bank.

"That won't do you any good, Captain." I kept my aim on the computers.

He stopped. "What won't?"

"Moving away and hoping my attention will follow you."

He gave up that tactic.

"Why didn't you know that man's name?" I asked.

Something about that stung him just right. Just wrong for me. Sasaquon grabbed one of his own crewmen, yanked the man off balance, and threw him across the deck toward me.

I had no choice but to fire. Moxie's scalpel beam cut across the deck and burned into the crewman's face, then down his neck and into his chest.

The poor man fell against me, knocking me backward. The diligent weapon in my hand went flying.

Sasaquon took that moment of distraction, balled one fist, slammed it into a two-switch panel on the stanchion he'd paused beside, and I heard the *snap* over my head. I tried to dodge—too late!

A crushing force slammed down on top of me, a smothering weight of fabric and lines, cargo netting and straps. How foolish not to have looked up just once! He'd hit a release!

Something cut into my lip. Another solid weight cracked the back of my head, and some kind of metal weight hit my right shoulder. A frazzle of pain left me numb for a few seconds, and then I started kicking.

At least two hundred pounds—probably more, because I could scarcely move. One leg hung in the open, and with it I lashed out and felt a connection with somebody who had plunged in to capture me.

The man tripped and with a hard grunt landed on the deck beside me.

The muffling weight lifted. I was hauled to my feet. One leg was still numb. Blood trickled down my chin from the side of my mouth. My shoulder burned, tingling all the way down to my fingers. My face burned too, but with pure indignation.

As Sasaquon picked Moxie up off the deck and squared off in his victory, I wrenched against the two men holding me so hard that one of them had to get a better grip on my arm. I watched the dying man on the deck, whose wounds now bubbled around the man's clawing fingers. As we watched, his body convulsed twice, rather horridly, and he reached out for Sasaquon to help him.

A moment passed, and the man's beseeching hand tumbled to the pile of straps and gear that had crushed me down.

I glared at Sasaquon.

"So tell me . . . why would a captain sacrifice a member of his own crew just to catch one scrawny woman?" I let the question ring and watched his men for a moment before looking at him again. "You could've hit that button without throwing him at me if you'd tried a little harder. Do your shipmates mean that little to you? Or is it that you just don't know them very well?"

My voice had an ominous rasp. As Sasaquon's men held me firmly before their captain, I licked my bleeding lip and stared at the man who had nearly killed Quen, the *Zingara* crew, and me.

"This isn't a pledged crew, is it?" I prosecuted. "You're getting fresh crew from somewhere."

"How can you guess something like that?" Sasaquon responded fiercely. "What do you know about our planet or our people? Who *are* you?"

"You're getting new clothing and stocks from someplace. Who are your suppliers? Why don't the other warranters have the same favors? You have a code of behavior, don't you? The Assembly has declared you outlaws, hasn't it? You're all on an even plane, aren't you? Aren't you, Mr. Sasaquon!"

His face flushed. His deeply exotic eyes speared me. I got the idea he wasn't quite as elegant and in control on the inside as the first impression he delivered.

"Did Quen send you here to do sabotage? He's never done that before. Why is he changing his tactics?"

"Maybe he's wising up, finally," I whipped back with unveiled sarcasm. "Why were you towing Quen's ship? You're taking us to a place where it's illegal for warranters to go, aren't you? Why would you do that except to prove to somebody the warranters are bad people? Who are you trying to impress? Are you under orders from somebody to turn public opinion against the warranters?"

Sasaquon's men shifted uneasily, their body language hardly needing a translator, so obvious that he scooped up a cargo strap and whipped it viciously at them, catching two of them across their faces. They instantly stopped giving things away, but it was really too late.

I smiled nastily at him. "I'll bet public opinion favors the warranters in the hemisphere, doesn't it? It's hard to hate Robin Hood, Captain."

Sasaquon scoured me with a disturbed glare. "Put her below with the other one."

• • •

We'd been passing a small star when Sasaquon jumped us. As cluttered as this area of space was, there were plenty of them. All I could hope was that Quen had been taking the time to maneuver closer to the star nearby and suck the solar energy into the capacitors. One light kick would put them far enough away from Sasaquon to have some time to put themselves back together, even if they went no farther than the next power pocket, any nebula or star where energy could be bled off.

Anywhere at all, just away from here.

Now Sasaquon's men were dragging me below to lock me up somewhere because Sasaquon was such a sweet guy that he didn't want to kill a woman. Quen's ship was now adrift out there. I'd apparently done enough damage to *Aragore* that Sasaquon couldn't reestablish his hold on Quen quite yet. The two ships were drifting within spitting distance of each other. A race of cleverness, resourcefulness, against time had begun.

How long Sasaquon's repairs would take, I had no way to know. Whether they could establish another tow with one of those other big winches, I also didn't know.

I hoped Quen and his crew were using this chance to get away if they could. Did they have motive power or was everything crippled?

Could they do anything at all, or were they helpless? Were they even conscious?

The questions, the doubts and dark unknowables ate at me as Sasaquon's men hauled me to a two-man lift, crammed in there with me, and delivered me to a lower deck.

This was some kind of bunking deck, with a dozen doors to small cabins. That made sense, their bringing me here. They probably didn't have anything like a brig.

All the doors had magnetic locks—I noticed that right away. They were going to cram me into one of these bunking quarters and bolt me in. I could be Houdini, and there was nothing I could do with a magnetic lock that had a central control.

Pretty regimental for a warrant ship, wasn't it? Lock and unlock all the crew cabins at the same time? Did they blow reveille too?

Another clue.

Halfway down this corridor of bunk doors, the men drew me to a stop. One of them punched a signal into a comm unit on the wall like the one Sasaquon had used back in the garage.

"Release the locks," this one said.

A few seconds passed before the order could be followed, but then the locks—all of them—up and down the corridor suddenly clacked and all the doors popped open like a row of cells.

With my last suspicious glance, the two men unceremoniously shoved me into the quarters and slammed the door behind me.

Momentum bumped me up against the opposite wall, where there were a sink and some drawers. On either side of me were four bunks with basic blankets and pillows dumped on them, unfolded and in heaps.

As I turned and looked around, one of the heaps moved. They did have somebody else prisoner! Why was Sasaquon taking prisoners? What authority could he possibly carry?

This wasn't the time to be polite. I pushed off the sink, grabbed the blanket that was moving, and yanked it clear of whoever was underneath.

Another woman! She lay with her back to me, and there was no mistaking the feminine form, unless I'd forgotten how to read the general formations of male and female humanoids in the galaxy. The shadow of the upper bunk muted what I was seeing, and the lights were indirect anyway, so I couldn't see much until she turned over.

"Come out of there," I ordered. "Who are you? Why are you being held here?"

Groggily, the woman turned over and moved her legs out of the bunk. Her head dipped under the top bunk, where a blanket hung halfway over, obscuring us from seeing each other.

She reached out to brush aside the hanging blanket, and the first thing I saw was her hand—a long-boned violet creation with a thumb and three fingers, not four. Instantly I knew she wasn't one of these Omian people, who all had five digits the same as I did.

She dipped her head to come out, and the second thing I saw was her hair . . . soft spools of vanilla silk lying flush against her scalp, thick skin the color of quartz.

She turned her face up now and looked at me. Large brown eyes, like chestnuts set in molded clay, blinking like a doe's eyes.

I dropped the blanket and stumbled back. Bumping my head against the opposite upper bunk, I pointed at her as a witch-hunter might point at a black cat.

My heart was ice. My voice was scarcely human.

"Menace!"

Ten

"MENACE!"

The alien woman flinched and stayed in her bunk, gazing at me in deep-riding suspicion and silence.

She was wearing a heavy and warm slipper-pink chemise, knotted at the shoulders, spreading out over her thick waist and hips, down past her knees. Her boots were simple brown mukluks. She wore no jewelry of any kind.

"Who are you!" I demanded.

She winced. "My name is . . . Totobet. Why are you shouting at me?"

"You killed my crew!"

Her quartz skin flushed almost purple at the intensity of my accusation. She paused, pondered what I had said, then tilted her head slightly.

"Were you . . . part of the big docked ship?"

I jabbed a finger at her. "It *was* you! You can't deny it!"

She blinked her chestnut eyes and seemed confused. "I haven't denied it."

"Then tell me why!"

"Because . . . it's what we do to survive."

"That's a lousy excuse."

We fell into bitter, doomful silence. I kept staring at her, no matter how she looked away from me or huddled or pulled blankets over herself. I looked at her hair spools. I looked at her skin. Her hands. I memorized everything about her for future despise.

These Menace people were humanoid, generally speaking, and had rather humanlike faces, except for the hair and the eyes, and of course the fingers were missing one. In my more lucid moments, when I could briefly banish the hatred eating at me, I tried to regain control of myself by analyzing what kind of evolution this was. Totobet had a slight bump of flesh and bone on each hand, in the place where I had a little finger. So the Menace had once been five-digited.

Like the human tailbone, the support for the little finger still existed even though the finger had evolved away. That might mean the Menace was farther along the evolutionary track than humans or Omians. Or Cardassians and Klingons. Perhaps maybe by as much as a million years. I thought of the comparisons with cats, dogs, even some reptiles and amphibians. All over the known galaxy, animals had five digits. There was something about that mechanism that nature liked. Some paleobiologists and anthropologists back home had explanations, but I'd never bothered to read them. Now I wished I had.

A million years' difference, but not technologically. The Menace was beatable—I knew that. It was a clear indication that technological and physical evolution didn't necessarily sail abeam.

As if I were some kind of scarecrow in a gutter, lost of mind and confused of spirit, I began to prick the air with ugly mutterings, scarcely even realized the simmerings were bubbling all the way out.

"Sitting there . . . looking so innocent . . . big brown eyes . . . Shirley Temple hair . . . trying to look so peaceable . . . You don't even know what you've done, do you?"

The Menace turned her head only enough to catch me in her considerable peripheral vision. She hugged her knees and tucked her chin.

I kept muttering.

"You and your kind . . . just fly in and start cutting into any civilization in your path . . . any ship in your way . . . don't know who's there or what they've been striving for. You don't pay attention. Don't even think about how much you're destroying beyond the lives and the buildings . . . how many aspirations and goals you've shot out of existence . . . I really *don't* like you."

Her narrow shoulders squeezed tight. She seemed afraid of me, and I liked it. I wanted her to feel in her bones the terror her people had caused and the misery in their wake. I narrowed my eyes and lowered my head as if I were a wolf on the hunt.

"Do you know what you destroyed that day? Do you really comprehend what you did?"

She turned to look at me now and quietly said, "Why are you treating me this way? Some things have to happen. Birth must come. Death must come. Why are you angry?"

A mirthless, vicious smile gnarled my lips. I spoke through the grating of my teeth.

"The *U.S.S. Voyager* was on its way back to the United Federation of Planets. We had a crew made up of Starfleet personnel, combined with Maquis rebels. You don't know what those are, but let's just say we didn't like each other at first. The Maquis captain became my first officer. His name is Chakotay and I miss him . . . I need him. Our first-watch helmsman was the son of an admiral and had a lot to overcome. Tom Paris, he was a brave young man who fought his own flaws and drove our ship through some of the worst conditions I've ever seen. Then there's Tuvok, who left a wife and five children behind. Even for a Vulcan, that's got to hurt in the middle of the night. Neelix, who tried so hard to make everybody happy . . . Harry and B'Elanna and our Doctor . . . He was so funny sometimes, even when he didn't mean to be . . ."

My chest was aching now, tight, muscles in spasm. Eyes hurt. Hands trembling. I didn't want her to see me cry. I wanted her to stay afraid of me.

I hadn't wept yet at all. Relentlessly I'd beaten off the grieving process, protected and distracted and tile-scrubbed myself past that. Now, suddenly, it wanted out.

No, no, not here! Not until everything I have to do is completely done.

In desperate defense I let the anger surge back over the misery, let hatred take over and raw contempt for Totobet and all her people be my guiding light.

Like a cobra I glared at her.

"We learned to work together," I said through gritted teeth. "We became a family. We absorbed expatriates from races we'd never met. We became a *bigger* family. We helped each other and supported each other. That's the kind of people you murdered. We even accepted a member of our most hated enemy into our ship, our lives . . . Her name was Seven. Yes, that's right, she was just a number to them. A lost child in a dangerous body. But to me and my crew she was becoming much more than that. She was just beginning to adjust. Then you came along. You didn't even give us warning. Didn't even give anybody a decent fighting chance. You just blew in and opened fire and burned all of those fine young people out of your way."

She did a good job of being pathetic. I wasn't buying it.

"Why do you do that?" I grilled. "Why do you fly in and start killing, just like that? Without even a word? Not even an explanation? Not even fair warning to get the children or the sick or old out of there? Why do you *do* that?"

"We have to," Totobet responded. Her voice was meek, but her words had no shame or regret. "We don't hate you . . . or your sevens or your toms . . . There is one survival device in the ocean, and I know you're going to fight me for it. When that time comes, we have to fight. I wouldn't hate you because of that. Why do you hate me because of it? Nobody's ever hated me. I don't understand you."

For the first time I hesitated. What was she talking about? Was that a metaphor for the Menace's murderous ways?

I offered only a nasty sarcastic huff. "You don't? Why not? Because the farmer's not supposed to hate the wolf for killing his sheep? Fine, but I can tell you this: I don't intend to *let* the wolf kill my sheep."

"No," she agreed quietly. "We understand when there's a fight. But we have to get room. There are too many of us all the time. We need more place. We have too many babies. There's never enough room."

"Wait a minute. Are you telling me . . . your slaughter of the Iscoy and my ship was part of some big overpopulation problem your people have?"

She blinked, paused, then shrugged. "Yes . . ."

My stomach twisted. I hoped this was a lie or a tall tale. "Are you out of your collective mind? That's one of the oldest problems of civilization and one of the easiest to solve! Why don't you use some kind of conception control?"

Totobet nodded in such a way as to tell me she'd heard all that before, and something about her manner made me believe her. "We have to conceive, or we die. Our men have to mate through their prime, or they die. Our women have to give birth and nurse, or we die. We have lots of babies. We need lots of place."

"Oh, swell," I droned. "A race of talking tribbles. Stay away from me. I'm busy."

Keeping as far from her as the cramped quarters afforded, I went back to the sink and pawed through the drawers. Nothing. Totally empty.

I turned to the bunks and investigated them. Just blankets, pillows, mattress—then, a bit of hope. On the underside of the top bunk were support slats for the mattress. Good enough.

A solid pull on a slat did nothing; they were riveted on. Casting a bitter glance at Totobet, who was watching my every move with a perplexed expression, I climbed onto the upper bunk, got my legs under me, braced my spine on the ceiling, and applied pressure.

"Why are you doing that?" Totobet asked.

"Shut up."

The bed started to squawk. The rivets were holding. I pounded with one foot, then the other. When that failed to work, I clawed the blankets away, then dumped the whole mattress overboard, until I was standing on the bare slats. Spreading my feet all the way to the sides, where the rivets were affixed, I slammed again and again, alternating feet.

This was dangerous. Any second now, one of the—

Snap. My left leg speared through the place where a moment ago there had been support. The rest of me followed, not very gracefully, except for my right elbow, which caught on another slat, and my chin, which hit the edge of the bunk. Dazed, I slithered through to the bottom bunk and fought off the blur of having socked myself in the jaw, but in one hand I had my prize. The metal bunk slat.

Well, part of it, anyway. A couple of good yanks demolished the second rivet and cut my palms pretty well too, but now I had a tool.

Totobet watched me. "Are you trying to build something?"

"None of your business." I stumbled off the bunk and went directly to the part of the wall where there must be some kind of internal circuitry. There were controls for temperature, lighting, air, and a comm unit. The comm had been deactivated, but maybe I could activate it again.

With the slat I pried off the wall panel and got to the bare circuitry. The circuits and mechanisms inside the cramped space behind the wall shivered and jumped in my fingers as I worked to find the live bits and connect them. Then the tiny speaker . . . there it was . . .

Behind me, a weak voice rose. "Are you trying to hear what they're saying?"

"Be quiet."

She was.

"ZZZZZZ . . . dzeeet . . . dssmuzzzbez . . ."

"Getting something!" I blurted. "Come on, come on . . ."

The sound was vibrating directly through the composites. If I could just hook it up to this speaker, I'd be able to eavesdrop on the ship's doings.

". . . levels frrraaapa . . ."

"Trajec—ards . . . erkk . . . ridor . . . before the prad on the rackers frrrasdisses . . ."

"Almost," I grumbled. "Almost!"

". . . grooves check on the curry cards bef—halo. Otherwise we'll have to make a strike before the fleet's ready."

"Got it! That's Sasaquon's voice! Fleet," I repeated. "Who's got a fleet?"

Must've looked weird, both hands pressed against the wall, talking into a hole. What if I'd made a mistake and also hooked up the send? They might be able to hear me!

I clammed up briefly and listened.

"—footway's blocked."

". . . cable befouled . . ."

So far so good—they hadn't heard me. I was effectively eavesdropping on a conversation between the command area and the engineering decks.

"What's that? What's he doing?"

". . . limping around, stern to—"

"They've launched something . . ."

". . . is it?"

"I don't recognize it."

Behind me, Totobet asked, "What are they talking about? Is there another ship out there?"

The blood boiled under my skin. "Yes, there's another ship. My ship."

"And they've launched a weapon?"

"Or something," I said. "Be quiet. I want to listen."

"It's got a clamp!"

Victoriously I slammed the heel of my hand into the wall. "Good boy, Quen! That's command thinking. Now, if only—"

"It's a drill clamp! Drill clamp!"

"Where'd they get that!"

"I think they built it."

"It's on! It's on the hull!"

"What's on the hull?" Totobet asked, a tremor in her voice.

She seemed to know nothing, but I could tell from that tremor that she was a spacefaring creature who at least lived aboard a ship, even if she didn't help run the ship. She knew we were in danger, knew that our lives depended exclusively upon the structure around us. As seafarers and spacefarers had for thousands of years before the two of us, we both knew the ship we were on meant our very lives. If it died, we died.

We were both aware of that, and of my lack of answer, when a fierce clacking noise hit the hull and rang through the metal bones of the ship. The clamping mechanism was above us somewhere, on *Aragore*'s upper external skin.

Even here in the lowest caves of the ship, we heard it reverberating, droning through the ship: *rowrowrowrowrowrowrow.*

And from the wall, the buzzing communication:

"What's it over?"

"The racker section! We've got no way to seal off that much area!"

"He knew that . . ."

"Who knew?" Totobet persisted. "Do they know something?"

At first I wasn't going to answer. Then I found myself talking, perhaps to sound out the logic for myself.

"My captain knew where to put a clamp on this ship, in a place where they can't seal off the chamber. If it drills through, this ship is hulled instantly."

The fear rose again in her voice. "Would he kill this ship? Knowing you're here on it?"

"I certainly hope so."

Fear widened Totobet's yellow eyes. "What would a hole do?"

"It'll punch through the skin of the ship and unequalize us. The whole ship is finished if it gets through."

"We'll be killed?"

"If we're still here."

Rowrowrowrowrowrowrowrow . . .

She turned away from me, curled up against a wall, and apparently decided there was no more to speak of since we were both dead.

"Are those your people in that other ship?" she asked. "But your ship was in the spacedock—"

"No, that's not the ship you're talking about. These are the people from here. They picked me up. I was in a survival pod. Just like Sasaquon picked you up."

"You escaped from the big ship?"

"I wasn't on board when you attacked."

"But how—"

"Shut up, I told you already."

Once she was silenced, I ignored her completely and listened carefully to the buzzing comm connection.

"That'll short out all the systems! We'll be down for days!"

"We'll be dead in ten minutes! Do it!"

The excitement vibrating through the comm drove Totobet to the enormity of touching me on the back of my arm and asked, "What does that mean?"

I cast her a smoldering glance and squelched the temptation to spit a suggestion that she live with the mystery. "They're probably going to send a surge of energy through the ship, trying to short out the mechanism on the—"

Suddenly I stopped, fitting together a dozen thoughts. Was it possible . . .

"Yes!" I bolted. Totobet flinched, but I didn't care. "That's it! Quen knew Sasaquon would have to flush the ship in order to turn off the drill! This door has a magnetic lock! He probably knows that too!"

She shook her head, confused. "What . . . what does . . ."

"Never mind," I snapped. "My captain's giving me a chance. I'm taking it."

I reached inside the wall until my fingers found the basic mechanism that powered this whole panel of lights, heat, and comm. With a single yank I pulled out the whole power coupling and wrenched it around to the hatch knob. Whatever went through this ship, I had to make sure it also went through that lock.

"Somebody's got a fleet," I muttered. "I think I know who that is. And it's ready to launch. Sasaquon's a traitor. Even worse, he's a cheater. I hate a cheater. I've got to warn Quen and the other warranters. They're up against something much bigger than they think."

"Why would you warn them?" Totobet asked. "They're not your people. They don't have your skin . . . they don't share your past—"

Fiercely I cut her off, yanking hard on the power cords as if these were the tendons of her throat. "They're my people if we believe the same things. I should've died in space anyway. Quen rescued me and gave me a few extra weeks. If they want to die out here, I'm ready to die with them. And I'm taking you with me."

"Me . . ."

"That's right. I'm going to keep my eye on you. You're not pulling any tricks while I'm around to stop you. No more."

I'd scarcely got the power cords secured on the hatch handle when the shout of a voice on the crackling comm got me by the instincts and I let go just in time. Well, almost in time—a surge of energy zapped my fingers in that last instant while my hands were still too close to the hatch. Conducted through the exostructure of the ship, the hull, the inner capacitor tiles, the bulkheads, and interior electrical system, Sasaquon's desperate attempt to shut down Quen's drill gave me a jolt that threw me backward.

My shoulder hit Totobet and knocked her into her bunk, and I fell against the sink, ramming my left hip hard on the edge. The sharp pain dazed me for an instant, and when I gained control I looked at the hatch.

A pencil line of smoke trailed up from the hatch handle, the only sign—other than my aching hip—that Sasaquon had tried his surge.

No . . . not the only sign! The *rowrowrow* sound had stopped! The drill clamp was out of commission!

My window was now closing.

Limping back to the door, I grabbed the handle, careless of whether or not the energy surge on the magnetic lock had caused a heat buildup. It hadn't. The handle turned in my grip. The hatch door clicked and opened as neatly as if I'd used a key.

Without pausing to enjoy my win, I reached back and grabbed Totobet unkindly and dragged her out of the bunk quarters, hauling her down the corridor at a quickstep.

"You do everything I say, or I'll kill you. Don't make any noise, or I'll also kill you. You understand killing, right? Sure you do. Get in my way, and it's all over. There are a lot of lives at stake. You're right on the top of the list right now."

I dragged her aft, running the diagrams of *Aragore* through my mind, trying to remember where I'd seen what I needed—a hangar area for several small craft. Probably the little workbees were meant for outside maintenance operations or salvage assistance. Didn't matter. Today they were going to be used to get me the hell out of here.

And with only a minor detour, why, here we were back in the winch garage, and right there was the sweet bank of computer systems I'd threatened before. Just how critical this bank was, I really couldn't guess, but I was here and so was a solid iron winch hammer.

In all the years of technology since the Middle Ages, my civilization had struggled to find some way to process metal to make it stronger, more pliant, less pliant, and always to make it lighter. For sheer weight—and even in deep space there were sometimes uses for the just plain heavy—there wasn't much of an improvement on good old iron. And these people had some, to be used, I guessed, to bludgeon a stuck winch into turning again or slam a twisted cable back into place.

"When in doubt," I uttered, heaving up the biggest iron I could lift, "use a sledgehammer."

Totobet hovered in the hatchway. "What are you doing?"

"Damage."

Wham!

One good swing of my hammer did the job. Luckily, I knew something about computer banks and was able to put that one swing where it counted—right where a blow resulted in a chain reaction that boiled through the whole bank. Totobet flinched and stared at what I had done, and for a brief moment I let myself watch the bank fry itself to a melted mass.

"I hope that's part of the main drive controls," I commented. "Let's go."

We were off again, before anybody could come down here and find us. There'd be no second chance. We had to get out right now and clear the *Aragore* while the chaos I hoped I'd caused still had a grip on Sasaquon's ship and crew.

The workbee craft, scarcely more than oblong bathtubs not much different from my rescue pod, were waiting for us, all lined up in a cute little row on the starboard side of the lowest deck, each sitting in its launch cradle, ready to go. Each had a little Plexi-viewport where the pilot could look out and see what was going on outside.

"Get inside!" I shoved Totobet to the nearest workbee and motioned for her to climb up to the open hatch. She had trouble, so I got under her and shoved. "You're heavier than you look. Come on, hoist. Get in there."

"What is this cubicle?"

"It's not a cubicle. It's some kind of free-flying maintenance scooter."

"It flies?"

"Yes! Inside. We're leaving."

With one leg inside the workbee, she tried to look back at me. "We're going out in space? In this little thing?"

"It'll be enough."

"Do you know how to fly it?"

"I do."

"Where are we going?"

"We're going back to *Zingara,* and I'm going to show you to Quen."

"Won't Sasaquon stop us?"

"He will if you keep stalling and they have enough time to get their cable system back up! *Move!*"

Eleven

I FELL OUT OF THE WORKBEE LIKE A FROG INTO A POND. A TERRIBLE screaming whistle on either side of my head—what was that awful noise?!

The airlock wasn't completely sealed! The hull must've taken so much damage that the cuff wasn't making a tight fit. The atmosphere from the *Zingara* spewed out with a ghastly shriek. I pushed to my knees, looking for some way to lock down the system, but before I could even stand up, several crewmen plunged in around me and went to work with the flanges and gaskets and valves.

"Don't jettison the workbee!" I called over the noise. "There's somebody in it! How soon can you make a light kick?"

It had been a rough ride. Sasaquon had fired on the workbee as I piloted away from his ship, and I was forced to go into a very uncomfortable series of evasive maneuvers that doubled the time it took to get back to *Zingara.*

The workbee was burning from Sasaquon's relentless open-fire, but I was heartened by the fact that Sasaquon hadn't managed to turn his ship to follow me. That meant I'd done some good sabotage.

Now Massus was standing over me and gave me a concerned glance, then snapped orders at the other crewmen, whose faces I couldn't see clearly through my watering eyes in the smoke. Within seconds—long seconds—the shriek diminished to a whine, then to a light hiss.

If that little remaining leak couldn't be securely patched, *Zingara* would be in trouble within days, but for now we could function.

"Kay!" Lucas exclaimed—at least one friendly voice. He appeared beside me out of a cloud of lingering electrical smoke, his bright hair so coated with dirt that it now looked gray. "I told them it was you over there! Zell thought you ran off!"

"No, I didn't run off. Where's Quen?"

As I crawled to my feet and looked up, Quen came limping toward me, with Zell helping him across the debris-strewn deck. The young captain looked ten years older, his pantleg torn at the knee, his left arm bandaged from the elbow to the fingertips with a stained rag, his hair crusted with lubricant and dirt. His limp was so pronounced as to indicate a possible hip or back injury, not just the leg.

"Did you do that, Kay?" he rasped. "Did you break us free from Sasaquon's tow?"

"Of course it was me!" After a pause to cough, I added, "You think they oversurged their own compensators and backflushed their own fusion?"

"It's a good thing," Zell admitted. "We were almost finished."

"How soon can you make a light kick and get out of here?"

"We're almost ready," Quen said, and that was a great relief to me.

At least we were thinking alike. I'd cut off the tow, he'd provided a distraction, forced Sasaquon to surge his own ship, and I'd taken advantage, done more damage, and gotten out of there. Now he was doing what I'd hoped, building up for an escape light kick. Not bad teamwork for one afternoon.

"We've almost bled enough solar energy into the tiles," Quen said. "Pretty soon, we'll kick."

"Sasaquon won't be able to follow you," I said with a gasp of relief, "if you move fast enough. We'll have time to make repairs and organize ourselves. Why didn't you fire on him when you had the chance?"

Quen blinked at the sudden accusation, but recovered quickly and said, "I couldn't fire on him as long as he had us in a tight tow. After you broke the tow, we were still drifting too close. The detonation would've done too much damage to *Zingara.*"

Begrudgingly, I muttered, "Well, that's a point, I guess." I turned to the workbee and called inside, "Come here."

Reaching in, I grabbed Totobet by one arm and yanked her forward, all the way out, and made her stand in front of Quen, Zell, Lucas, Massus, and everyone else who was looking.

Shocked by the appearance of Totobet, Lucas flinched in amazement—and bumped Massus, who also was staring.

Quen and Zell, the more experienced as command officers, managed to control their reaction, but I could see that they also were stunned that I'd shown up with this completely unexpected prize.

"Do you see this woman?" I demanded. "This is an alien woman. You haven't seen this race before, but I have. This is the race of people who attacked the Iscoy and slaughtered them mercilessly. This is what you're going to be fighting. Have you ever seen anyone like her before? Her eyes? Her skin? The little spooly hair things? Do you see her hands? Four fingers instead of five? That's alternative evolution! Look at her! Can you finally see what I'm warning your about? Can you see she's nothing like you?"

Quen and the others uneasily surveyed Totobet, her bleach-white hair, her silvery skin, her eyes, her hands. They seemed very uncomfortable, which I didn't know how to read, so I let the moments of silence speak.

Totobet held her breath and for a moment I almost felt sorry for her, though that didn't last long. I kept a firm grip on her arm, as if she were some kind of prize over which I had sole jurisdiction.

Drawing his own breath roughly in the acrid, dirty air, Quen shifted his weight from whatever hurt.

Carefully, he said, "You're . . . nothing like us either."

"I'm a lot more like you than this Menace!" Angry, I pulled Totobet a step closer to him. "But look at her and at least get it through your heads that I'm telling the truth about an alien race coming closer! These are the people who came out of nowhere and attacked the Iscoy and destroyed my ship! Here's living proof of the existence of the aliens I told you about! Here she is!"

"How did you get her?" Quen asked. "What's she doing here?"

Zell angrily pushed forward. "And what was she doing on Sasaquon's ship?"

"Sasaquon picked up another escape pod, just like you picked me up. She was in it. I found her in their brig."

"Their what?"

"Held prisoner on their processing deck. Which is another subject I have to discuss with you. But right now, do you at least see that there really are aliens you don't know about? Do you see that they're close enough that one of their escape pods got over here at roughly the same time mine did?"

I was kicking myself in the backside with this line of effort. From their faces I could tell they didn't know what to think or whatever to conclude. They saw was two little alien women in front of them, that's all, and Totobet certainly didn't look like much of a threat.

My next hand had better be well played.

"I'll go back to scraping tiles," I began carefully, "but first, I want to have my say."

They looked at each other like a panel of lawyers each waiting for the other to answer. Of course, the only one who could answer was Quen.

Eventually all eyes went where mine already lingered—Quen, our captain.

Soon it came down to him and me, gazing at each other on a much more level plane than ever before.

"You broke Sasaquon's grip," he began slowly. "You got him off us . . . risked your life and saved our ship. You deserve to have a say."

I nodded. "Good." I was about to turn my back on the one law every Starfleet official must uphold. That meant that for better or worse, I was in this for the long haul.

But at last, they were going to listen to me. After a moment to gather my wits, I decided where to start and took a header.

"I've been inside Sasaquon's ship. It's not like *Zingara* in there. It's warm, for one thing. They don't even have a working production facility. They're not processing the wrecks at all, Captain."

"But they fight for them," Massus said. "They tow them away—"

"I don't know what they're doing with the salvage," I responded instantly. "Mostly I suspect they're just keeping you from processing them. It's a good bet they've been driving down the worth of the wrecks you do manage to process."

"Why would Sasaquon do that? He has to live on the same deals we do—"

"No, he doesn't," I told him forcefully, with all the convictions of my belief and experience. "Sasaquon's being supported by the TCA."

"Do you have any kind of proof for this?" Quen justifiably asked.

"Not a shred. Just adding up what I saw over there. He's got food, good shoes, new tools, a full complement of supplies and fuel, and decent clothing that looks like it's on its way to being a uniform. Nobody living on the edge has all that. I can tell you with absolute assurance that the *Aragore* is not the ship of people who don't know what to do beyond survival."

More of the crew gathered behind Quen, Zell, Massus, and Lucas. They approached with both contempt and curiosity, taking the leads of their officers. None made a single sound as I went on. In fact, I raised my voice to make sure all could hear me. There might not be another chance.

"You warranters think you have a general mutual agreement going on, but Sasaquon's not living up to the code you've set for yourselves. His ship is all banged up on the outside, but inside it's warm and comfortable and his crew is well fed and well supplied. Sasaquon's sold his soul."

"What do you mean by that?" Zell challenged. "The TCA's only—"

"The Temporary Civilian Authority has no intention of being temporary," I said. "I've seen this kind of thing before. They don't intend to reestablish free elections or free speech. They're using the threat of the other hemisphere's rising again as a stall, so they have time to build power. They declare a crisis, then declare themselves the only solution. They're building a military for themselves, with captains like Sasaquon in collaboration. I'd bet they've promised Sasaquon a high position if he distracts the other warranters and keeps you from being healthy and strong and banding together. It won't be long before they're strong enough to just come out here and clean up. And the warranters will be too weak to resist."

To be honest, I couldn't tell from their expressions whether any of them had ever thought of this or not, or had tampered with it in the privacy of their own thoughts without ever admitting these possibilities to each other. They were troubled, obviously, by the ring of plausibility in my words. It seemed I was striking paydirt underneath their hopes that such ideas were just bad moods or loneliness.

Sympathy ran through me suddenly. Who would want to admit that their families might be at the mercy of tyrants? And admit to each other that they had no power to do anything about it?

"You *won,*" I offered, angling to keep some echo of their hopes alive. "What did you fight to protect? The TCA is having you compete with each other so they can debilitate you and solidify their power. Is that why you fought and won your war? For Napoleon's crown?"

They didn't know what that meant—I didn't expect them to—but I saw in Quen's face, in Zell's and those of the other crewmen, that they got the idea.

"All right, you fought a war," I went on. "Thought you won. You turned your back to lick your wounds, and while you weren't looking, the old tyrants slipped in and took over. The tyrants run the planet now and you can't bring yourself to rise against your own people. Are you harboring some delusion of someday being allowed to become merchant traders again? You're fooling yourselves. The TCA will always consider any free ship too dangerous. Your war isn't over, gentlemen. You just stopped fighting it."

Massus frowned and interrupted, "Are you suggesting we band together and attack our planet?"

"Will things be better tomorrow?" I asked. "Will you be weaker or stronger tomorrow? Maybe you've been too close to this situation. I'm a completely objective arrival here and I'm seeing things you're missing, boys. You've got to get over this idea that there's a bond between the warranters. There isn't! You're bound up by your Pledge and this weird code of chivalry between yourselves, but Sasaquon's not playing by the code. That means you're not bound to it either in dealing with him. He's turned this from a standoff into a siege, and you don't even realize it. Did you see that coming? If you can't expect him to play by the rules, why are you playing by them? One of the principles of conflict is that you must be willing to meet your enemy on his own level of behavior. Whether down or up, you've got to be willing to go there."

Around us the ship hummed and throbbed with its damage and efforts to live. The clank of repairs going on belowdecks rose through the metal and plastic of the bulkheads and put an eerie percussion on these new thoughts. The struggling, aching, tired old ship was putting in her two cents, saying she had almost reached her limits, that her time had come to make that last surge of effort or linger into ineffectiveness.

Somehow these thoughts were almost telepathic now.

"You'd better start reorganizing to fight again, before it's too late," I said. "Evolution sticks intelligent beings with a thing called stubbornness. Where's yours? There are principles here. You and the TCA want completely different futures. The governing system you fought for has been suspended and that's a bad thing. The TCA is suspending the laws you fought to live by, and you people just slog along from day to day, saying, 'This is how things are, it can't be stopped, and this is how we have to live.' You won your war, but you're still losing."

As I paused for a breath, I was heartened by the expressions on these young men's faces. They'd clearly never heard such things in their lives, never been spoken to this way by anyone, much less a women old enough to be their . . . aunt . . . their young aunt. As I had often found on board my own ship, being a little older than most of my crewmen could be a distinct advantage, if manipulated with the right panache and reserve.

Taking advantage of my sudden hitch upward in respect, or at least the shock factor, I paced a step to my left and put my hand against *Zingara*'s tired hull.

Beside me, still fast in my pointy little grip, Totobet looked at me and said, "You don't understand everything like you pretend to. You don't understand my people or what we're doing—"

"You be quiet! I don't trust you." I swung back to Quen. "You can't put me off the ship now, not now that she's here. You need me. There are things I know—"

Quen held up a volume-lowering hand. "I can't put you off anyway," he admitted. "Not until we find a fuel source. We don't have enough to get anywhere that I would want to leave you."

"Good, because I don't want to leave."

"That really doesn't matter. You're here and we have to let you stay—"

"Quen, she's still just a stranger!" Zell waved a hand at me fiercely. "We don't know her! How do we know she didn't sabotage *Zingara* so we couldn't fight? She was at the tiles everywhere on board. She could've done things. We don't really know her."

Quen turned to him, weary and troubled. "She's done good work for the ship. She went over there when we were all going to die and smashed Sasaquon. She could've gotten away, but she went over there instead. If we had even one turret working, we could destroy him. Then she got herself back here.

We're in better shape because of her, not worse." He motioned at Totobet, but looked at Zell. "She's been telling some version of the truth, Zell. I want to keep listening. I won't make any decisions right now, but I want to listen."

Without getting too full of myself, I understood that he was making absolutely no commitments to whatever I said. He was a better captain that I had first thought, and being more judicious than I expected, wise enough to at least listen to all the perceptions around him. I perfectly well understood that he might decide completely against me. Again, this might be my last chance to speak up. Take it, take it, take it.

"Thank you," I offered. "The first thing we should do is to stop thinking of Sasaquon as just another warranter. He's not competing with us—he's starving us out on purpose. I inflicted enough damage on Sasaquon's ship that he'll need weeks to repair. I also botched his communications so he can't call the TCA for help—at least not right away. That buys us time too. We should repair our own damage as fast as we can, forget about wasting time and energy on the processing deck, and concentrate on battle readiness. We should make a plan for action. Start organizing a plan of some kind. Start communicating with the other privateer captains. Start planning how to handle Sasaquon when he appears again. Start with your brother. Start!"

The crew who were gathered here stood as if under a kiln-hot pall. No one even twitched. They were absolutely stunned by the whole concept of aggression.

A distressed shudder, perhaps pure caution or an internal red alert, ran down my back. I had overloaded them, given them too much, too fast, just told them that their existence had a diabolical splinter, and now they were afraid.

Without turning, Quen eyed his crew sidelong as if to read these twitchy and taut undercurrents. There was great pressure on him now if even half of my words turned out to be true. Even a quarter. If only for the fact that Sasaquon was stronger and better supplied, there was danger and failure for the other warranters in the foreseeable future.

Quen sank back against whatever was behind him and leaned there, folded his arms, and consulted the deck. He closed his eyes for a brief moment as if fighting a headache, then pressed his lips tight and blinked with fatigue. Anxiety showed in his face.

Was I helping him or hurting him? Had I overstepped? Would I want anyone to do this to me? I'd been in his position so long, and after just a few weeks I'd forgotten what it was like to be in the hurricane's eye.

Caught up in my fresh adventure on Sasaquon's ship and what I'd discovered there, I had let myself get carried away and climbed a podium as if it were mine to pound.

Briefly suspending the press coverage of the crewmates standing nearby, watching and listening, I paused, genuinely regretted my grandstanding, and spoke intimately with Quen. "I'm sorry, Captain. I don't mean to outshine you."

He blinked at me, sighed, and made a limp gesture with his bandaged hand.

"Please," he uttered, smiling weakly, "outshine me."

With that simple gesture and those little words, my respect for him ratcheted up by half. Rare was the captain whose pride played so minimal a part in his command method.

Zell winced and wouldn't look at me. He turned away. Lucas seemed like a frightened child. His arms shook visibly. Massus touched Quen's arm in feeble reassurance, and Resi watched Zell for a cue of how to act.

Maybe there was a way I could've done this better, more diplomatically, less cruelly. I wished I'd paused to think, to realize how young they were, how desperate and tired they were, and how inexperienced.

I had to let them off the hook somehow, to cut through the sick fear just for a few hours, till they had time to think.

"We all have work to do," I began, searching, "and I'll do mine willingly, every tile. I'm asking only that you think about all this and . . . just let it settle until the captains can talk. Where's Vince? I should report to him now that I'm back on board."

A tremor of discomfort rolled visibly through the crew, as if I'd pinched them. Now they did twitch and shift, and looked to Quen suddenly.

"Vince, uh—" the captain said tightly. "He got a full dose of jeklight radiation. It was . . . over in seconds."

The announcement caught me by surprise. As close as I had been to death and dying the past few days, somehow the sudden death of such a strong, forceful crewman took me unawares.

I hesitated, perhaps too long, before saying, "I'm so sorry. He was an asset to the ship."

"He was." Quen's voice was rough, tired, and the touch of grief was unshielded. His words came with difficulty, as if he were forcing himself. To his credit, despite the struggle inside, he went on. "We don't judge by guesses and suspicions here. We judge by action. Merit means something to us here. You worked hard on the tiles, and when your chance came to flee a dangerous situation, you risked your life for the ship instead and it helped us. We have to keep you for a while, at least. It's my duty as captain to make the best use of any resource I have here."

He paused, limped a pace or two away under the cloying eyes of his own crew, then turned to me again, as if making the final commitment in a lingering decision.

"If you agree to take the Ship's Pledge," he said, "you'll be the new deck boss."

Twelve

"I, Kathryn Janeway, pledge my service and allegiance to this ship and this crew. I pledge to abide by the rules of engagement, to obey the order of any senior unless it violates the Ship's Pledge, and to put the ship and crew above my own life. I will not falsely accuse any crewmate. I will be honest in all pursuits. I accept the right of senior officers to punish me up to and including death if I violate the Ship's Pledge. If at any time I cannot keep to the Pledge, I will inform a senior officer and refrain from any activity until I can be put off the ship. I understand that all around me at this moment have also taken this Pledge, and to them I promise my devotion. From this moment forward I will use all my knowledge, experience, and talents to help and support my ship and my crewmates. I swear solemnly that this oath will . . . that this will supersede any previous oaths or obligations. On this day I, Kathryn Janeway, so pledge."

"Now turn, and face your ship and your shipmates."

Shivering like a midshipman, I turned. Before me, the main deck sprawled like a small stadium. Crowded before me was *Zingara*'s crew of one hundred nine, missing only the seven who were in the infirmary, still unconscious. They all looked at me, seeing weakness in my manner for the first time since I'd come on board, and I wondered if they held in full comprehension the reason for my little pauses.

My heart was splitting. That was the reason.

Beside me, having cleaned his hair to a soft pine shroud and changed into a fresh shoulder cape, Quen appeared more captainlike than I had seen him yet. He was quiet and circumspect, probably wondering whether or not he were making a mistake, pledging a woman, and someone whom they had met only a few short weeks ago.

We'd made our light kick. Now we passively drifted near a completely different star from the one we had used to power up the tiles. Hyperlight-speed had brought us to a place of relative safety, and we were slowly making repairs. Things were still very hard. There were almost no resources in this miserable solar system and scarcely any connections with which to get supplies. We were quite on our own, moving between distant settlements and deposits, trying to bribe, buy, trade, or collect what we needed to get along. And that was down to food and water, not just fancy composite for the ship's systems.

Somewhere on this ship, Totobet was locked in a bunk, just as she had been on Sasaquon's ship. Our nervous medic Ruvan was having a look at her, and I could only imagine his face at trying to figure out what she was. In the back of my mind, a thousand questions for her rose as logic set in over my raw disgust for her. I needed answers. Sooner or later, I'd get them from her. For now, there was only crushing emotion filling this rite of passage.

Sadness lay upon my chest. Tears pushed at the backs of my eyes. My own words, my new oath, galvanized the deep emotions that I could no longer banish. A profound weight had been lifted, and another came to rest on me. The universe had turned without me, and I was in a whole new place, never to see any other.

This was my life now. This was my place, my ship. I had a living duty, crewmates, and I had a captain to serve. There was nothing left between *Voyager* and me but misplaced fidelity. For me there was no more Prime Directive, for there was no more Federation, zero chance of ever returning, ever again fulfilling my oath as a Starfleet captain. Even the wind must someday accept that the storm has changed course.

Starfleet didn't expect us to sacrifice all that we knew and could offer to other life-forms; the Federation wasn't that stingy. If we were trapped, as I now was, in some distant place, they'd rather we live and survive, but not live like hermits. I'd want my crew to join a culture if they could, to assimilate and use what they knew to the betterment of any and all, wouldn't I? Even when *Voyager* was displaced, we were still all Starfleet officers. We always had that to cling to. But I couldn't cling all by myself.

Now, as I jumped up a step in rank on my new ship, I had obligations that no previous oath could smother. I needn't let go of my identity, hide my abilities, or forget my Earth heritage. The Federation had something to offer to this culture . . . and that something was me.

"I, Quen, pledged captain of the *Zingara,* promise to stand behind Kay Janeway, to consider her suggestions, to believe her words, and to act in her defense. Kay, your crew accepts your Pledge, and we pledge ourselves to you."

A miserable thank-you rattled in my throat, but my voice utterly failed. Not exactly graduation at the Academy, yet . . . a blessed moment in its way. A glance back, a step forward. Today, with my heart aching and my mind clear, I made a new oath, devoting myself to this ship, these young people, and this culture in upheaval. The real had to take precedence over the hypothetical. I was here now. I was *here* now.

That was all there was to it. Another major change in my life. No champagne reception, no shaking hands with admirals, no wondering whether my father would be proud of me. Deep sorrow for the crew engulfed me as they murmured their congratulations and shielded their doubts. This was all the ceremony these poor boys had. They didn't have much, but they were betting it all on me. This was much more poignant than momentous accolades and fanfare and pageant.

Those who were off duty wandered back to their bunks. Those assigned to other decks wandered to their posts. Those assigned here, on the main deck, assigned to me, stayed and waited and watched me, and watched Quen. There were about twenty of them. including Lucas, the helmsman Resi, and the strong and reserved engineer, Massus.

On quivering legs I turned to watch Quen make his way back toward his quarters. Had he promoted me out of some kind of strange chivalry that I didn't understand yet? Because I had freed the ship from Sasaquon? Or was there more to it—was he perhaps giving tacit approval to changes I might make? Had my words to him not fallen on barren ground, as I'd first suspected?

Until I knew, my plans would have to be careful and reserved. On the other hand, I was in charge of a deck watch now.

I was in the command line, one of very few officers on *Zingara*—the captain, the first mate, six deck engineers, and six deck bosses, of which I was now one. I would have to coordinate, somehow, with the two other deck bosses on my watch—a diplomatic tightrope to say the least. This was different from Starfleet, this sudden promotion business, and I didn't know how to handle it without churning up huge resentment among the crew.

Yes, there'd been a vote of confidence from the captain—or perhaps it was less than that, just a quick thank-you—but I could easily abuse that goodwill with the crew who had served him a long time already. In Starfleet, promotions came through many means, from time served to extraordinary action, but they didn't usually come suddenly and unexpected. Generally speaking, very few servicemen flew high and fast over the heads of those before them, rarely without great tragedy in that wake. For me to have launched myself over the heads of all these men wasn't necessarily a good thing.

On top of everything else, I was a woman and they were distressed with my presence.

On this ship there were four watches in a day, seven and a half hours each. The crew complement was immediately cut in half and shared the day, standing alternate watches into eternity, interrupted every other watch by the team that was now trying to get some sleep. That made for three deck bosses and three deck engineers awake and handling the ship, and either Zell or Quen in command. Zell had been in command when I came on board, which was why Quen had been in his cabin. In times of emergency, all hands came on deck, but the on-watch bosses and engineers called the shots. It was simple, redundant, workable, and generally familiar. I could live with it.

All this raced though my mind in those first few seconds as my watch crew looked at me and fretted over what the woman would do first. I had some authority, limited and tenuous, a captain to serve who felt obliged to give me some say, a first officer who doubted and suspected me, a crew who didn't know what to make of me but were now as pledged to me as I was to them.

A powder keg, if I wasn't very careful. The gloss of promotion came with a rusty edge.

As the crew dispersed, Quen faced me passively. He kept his voice quiet. "Do you feel all right?"

Blinking downward, I nodded, unable to keep a small hesitation out of it, speaking to myself as much as him. "I'm here now. I'm a member of *Zingara*'s crew. It'd be immoral to hold back my abilities. It's my obligation to be the best shipmate I can be . . . and give all my talents to you."

With the last phrase I raised my eyes to him. The pallor of his soft mushroom complexion had worsened with the stress of these past few days. His eyes were soft and deeply sympathetic. God, he looked so young to me.

"Choice is the blood of life," I finished. "No choice . . . no life."

Some things didn't need discussing.

He continued to gaze at me. If he did not somehow perceive what I had once possessed, he seemed to fully comprehend what I was giving up, and that even if it was a lunatic's wild fantasy, I at least very deeply believed it.

"When you're ready," he began, "we'll need a course of zero-nine-eight degrees. It'll take us to the Peliorine Belt, where we can pick up some ice chunks for water. We might starve, but at least we won't shrivel up."

"Zero-nine-eight degrees," I repeated. "Understood."

"Good luck." He caught my fingers in a light brush as he stepped away, just as he and his crewmen so often did to each other.

The cold creeps ran down my arms. He darned well knew he hadn't done me any favors.

Even colder was Zell's final glance as he disappeared down the deck well. Zell was the commanding officer for me now. Neither of us liked it much.

Lucas, Massus, Resi, and twenty-odd other young men on my watch lingered on the main deck before me, demoralized, curious, and waiting.

Would I turn their world upside down?

"I know you're all worried," I began. "This is a big change for me too. If we cooperate and take one thing at a time, we'll do very well together. I'm new to the ship. I'm a woman and that's unusual for you, but I have lots of experience in space. I'm asking you to trust me until you have reason not to. Is that fair?"

Lucas nodded right away. Massus and Resi glowered their doubt, but made no protest. The rest of the crew took their cue from Massus, who refused to make visible commitment. His wait-and-see attitude was nerve-wracking.

All right, I'd do without his approval.

I drew a deep breath, steadied myself, and tried to ignore the nagging facts about me that the crew was having such a hard time pretending weren't there.

"Okay, here are the immediate changes. I'm the deck boss. To me, that means if you have any problems or concerns, even about me, you'll come to me first. I'm bound to have lots of problems, and I want you to speak up and help me do better. The command structure under me will be Massus, then Levan, then Jedd. I know you've never done that before, but we're going to be prepared in case anything happens to me. We're going to one-hour watches on the wheel, sensors, power train, and ship check."

"What's a ship check?" Resi asked with a slight edge of challenge in his voice. "We checked. We know it's a ship."

I offered a smile, though he didn't return it. "It's a log of data we're going to check every hour. Rod levels, capacitor flow, compensators, thruster controls, rackers, pressure gauges, and the jeklight radiation charge."

"You want us to keep a log?" somebody asked. "Every hour?"

"That's right. That way we can monitor power usage and figure out how to be more efficient. Generally, it'll make us more familiar with our ship and how she works and how to help her work better. It sounds like extra work, and it is, but you'll get used to it."

They muttered and shifted, probably figuring I was crazy to watch things that didn't need watching. First step taken.

Next?

I held up a printout, written by the computer in the symbols of their language, and didn't bother to mention how many testy hours it had taken me to learn enough of their language to put this together. That was my problem.

"I've made up a station bill. It'll be posted right over there on the lateral support stanchion. It has all your names on it in rotation. It assigns helm watch, sensor watch, computer duty, spectroscopy and cartography, ship check, life support, tile duty, engineer's assistants, and standby, in those one-hour watches I told you about."

"Why an hour?" Resi asked. "Why can't we just get a post and stay there, like always?"

"Because, with the new rotation system, everybody gets a break and nobody numbs into a job for too long. And also, you get experience standing other posts, which is good in times of trouble. You'll learn to like it. You won't be as tired at the end of a watch. Oh, and if you're on standby, you've essentially got an hour off. Take it to rest or finish up something, change socks, or whatever you want, but stay available on the deck. Understood so far?"

They glanced at each other, wondering—oh, who knew what they were wondering—except for Massus and Resi, who were both glaring at me as if I'd grown pointed ears. They seemed to be two of the most experienced here, and the rest of the crew might take their leads. I'd have to win them over, or at least get them to keep any apprehension and skepticism to themselves for now.

"Mostly this work is for me over the next few days," I went on, "but I want you to know what I'm planning. I pledged to be honest with you, and to me that means letting you in on what I'm thinking about. I'll be making up an emergency station bill, and if you've got anything like this that I don't know about, please tell me and I'll try to keep close to whatever's familiar to you. Do you have a plan for abandon ship?"

They gawked at me, then Massus said, "Yes. Get out."

A nervous ripple of laughter ran through the crew, and in fact helped a little.

I smiled and shrugged.

"Good plan, but I'd like to refine it just a wee bit. Each of you will have an assignment for fire, rescue, abandon ship, and battlestations. Memorize your positions and get familiar with whatever equipment falls under your control in those positions. It sounds complicated, but it's not really. You have to memorize only three posts and get it into your head to go there. Each of the subbosses—Massus, Levan, and Jedd—will have an emergency leadership position. For instance, in the case of abandon ship, Massus will be in charge of one life craft. Those of you under his name on the bill will muster at that pod. As long as there are patients in the infirmary, some of you will have the assignment of getting the wounded to a pod—"

"What about the rest of the crew?" Levan interrupted. "We'll just leave them behind?"

Another roll of laughter, not quite so uneasy as before.

"That's right, we won't need them anyway," I said. "They'll just take up food."

Even Massus gave a grudging chuckle and tried to smother it behind a knuckle.

"I'll try to work something out with the other deck bosses," I assured. "They're sensible. They can be convinced to organize their crews too. We should all cooperate. We all have to abandon the same ship if it comes to that, right? Abandoning a ship means there's big trouble, so you've got to organize your thoughts and know where you're going long before that actually happens. A wild scramble is no good on a ship. Panic kills. No point letting it get a grip. Understand all that too, so far?"

A classroom nod bumbled across the deck. They didn't really understand all these unfamiliar and unexpected changes, but they were willing to give it a shot. I had to give them credit for not protesting right away. That was the sign of a good crew.

At first the station bills would be confusing, but then each man would get used to the fact that his name appeared only in select places, and he would memorize those places. For a while I'd float around every hour, making sure everybody was in place and knew what to do.

A few days from now, I'd start running emergency drills.

Oops—information overload. Better not mention drills just yet . . .

"What do you want us to do right now?" Resi asked, scratching his shoulder as if he were already tired.

"Oh . . ." I glanced around the cluttered deck. "Almost forgot about right now, didn't I? And I almost had you fooled that I knew what I was doing. Darn."

I cashed in on another ripple of smiles, which seemed to help everybody, including me.

"Well, let's start by squaring away."

"Squaring?" Jedd asked. "The tiles, you mean?"

"No. Everything. 'Squaring away' means to clear the deck. Coil the cords that aren't being used. Stow the work lights that we don't need right now. Sweep up the bits of junk all over and swab the spilled lubricant. Make this deck safe to walk around on. If we do have an crisis, there's no sense having a deck cluttered with shrapnel, is there?"

"Pick all this up?" Othien asked. "All the tools and everything?"

I looked at him. "Yes . . . Is there a problem?"

They glanced at each other, and then Levan said, "There's no place to stow all this. We usually just leave it out or push it aside. We always need things, so we don't put much below."

"Time to start. There's no organized storage for most of these tools and parts?"

They offered me only a collective shrug, but that wasn't because they didn't know the answer.

"Well," I said with a quick sigh, "we have to be ingenious, then. Take that skein of thin cord over there—yes, that's the one—and I'll teach you how to make gear nets. We'll hang them from these knees right at the edge of the decks and put the tools in one, the parts in another, electrical cords, maintenance gear, and so on. You'll get used to it. You might even like it. All right, let's consider ourselves on duty, shall we? When the watch is done, we'll gather amidships and go off watch together. Then we'll go belowdecks and eat together and discuss how it went. Levan, I believe you're up on the helm. If you'll take that position, please, and put us on a course of zero-nine-eight degrees, as Quen requested."

The crew began slowly to disperse, and I caught Levan's arm. "Repeat the order," I instructed.

Levan paused, and so did Massus, Lucas, and others who had heard. "What?"

"Repeat the order."

"You mean . . . tell you the order?"

"No, but acknowledge it by repeating what I tell you. Say, 'Zero-nine-eight.' "

He glanced uncomfortably at Massus, then frowned at me. "Zero-nine-eight . . ."

"Then say 'aye' so I know you heard me clearly and understood."

"Zero . . . nine-eight . . . 'aye'? Like that?"

"That's right."

"You want us to do that all the time?"

"All the time. You'll get used to it."

He sighed, shook his head, and picked his way toward the helm.

"Bet we won't," he muttered.

I watched them disperse, wondering whether I had given them too much to think about, attempted to change their ways too quickly. My self-doubts surged into my throat. It had been a long, long time since I'd run a deck.

When most of them were involved with coiling cords and swabbing lubricant, I moved across the deck, around the deck well, to Lucas, who was cleaning up the area around the lower port scanners amidships.

"Lucas," I began quietly, "you're assigned to the computer system right now, aren't you?"

He blinked at me, perfectly well knowing I'd assigned him here. "Yes . . ."

"I want you to do something for me but not discuss it with anyone else. Do you trust me?"

Offering a childlike shrug, he admitted, "I don't know. So far, I do."

"Thanks. I want you to start organizing lists of the other warranter captains and their ships. Help me get familiar with them. Type of ships, size, crew complement, power, communication codes, last known location. Can you do all that? Help me catch up with what everybody else already knows?"

He thought about what I was requesting, seemed to decide it was all innocent enough, or at least justified in my new position, and nodded. "I can do that."

"Thank you. Jedd, can I bother you a moment?"

What an odd thing . . . When I was a captain, all I had to do was stride into a room, catch a few eyes, and everybody was ready to tend my whims.

This was very different. I felt obliged to tend their needs, be more polite, make absolutely sure that any hint of arrogance remained muted. They had their jobs, and I shouldn't interrupt them, even if I assigned those jobs.

Jedd shoved his ratty blue hair out of his eyes and gave me a look I'd rather not see very often. "You're bothering me."

"Sorry. You know the weapons systems very well on this ship, don't you?"

"I built half of 'em."

"That's what everybody says. I need your help."

"What kind of help?"

"Would you teach me about the weapons? Show me the guts of the missiles, describe how the cables and clamps work, and make me understand the propellants?"

"Why? We know how they work."

Jedd was a rough sort of man, somewhat older than most of his shipmates, and I didn't know him except in passing, but I forced myself to stick to the promise of honesty until forced otherwise.

"Because you're not trained for this," I told him bluntly. "You fight to keep alive, but you don't know how to think ahead. Everything you've done so far has been weak and defensive. Only the most delusional minds think that a good quality of life can be had with weak defense. Now that I've got some authority, I'm going to help this ship grow antlers. For that, I need you."

His expression changed a little with the compliment and the confidence I showed in him—I'd have to remember that. For the first time, I saw a glint of anticipation in one of the crew.

"I'll show you everything," he said. "They're good systems. I like 'em. In no time, you'll know everything."

He stalked off.

I paused and took a deep breath before following.

"Bet I won't," I grumbled.

• • •

While the crew worked to adjust to the station bill and the new watch schedule, I worked also to familiarize myself with systems that any other deck boss would already know by heart. I'd always thought *Voyager* was a big ship, but I was finding out how little I really knew and that "big" was relative. *Zingara,* for an industrial tractor-processor, was a strong muscle in space that deserved much more respect from me than I had seen while gazing down my nose at her.

The other deck bosses, five of them, were variously indifferent or disdainful of my new methods, but how I ran my watch really didn't affect theirs, so any disdain soon wandered into curiosity. None suggested that it wasn't perfectly my business to run my crew in any way I saw fit, and even Zell, as commander on my watch, made no attempts to disparage the station bills. That was a relief, but I should've expected it. Running a ship had a certain intership, international, interstellar sense that just had to happen. Shipfaring from long ago had found its stride, and all over the galaxy we'd found similarities in management that just made common sense. For the commander to micromanage the crew was plain foolish and faulty to a point of danger. Zell had his job, I had mine, and the main deck crew was mine.

By the same token, I did not interfere in command, navigation, salvage decisions, or the running of the other decks, and I did not speak for the ship when we came up against other warranters or anybody else. The only other deck boss with whom I had interaction of necessity was a subdued fellow named Gashan who ran the other watch on the main deck. We had a few things to coordinate, such as which jobs still needed tending at the end of a given watch. I also arranged for both him and me to get our crews up and at theirs posts about five minutes earlier than the actual change of watch, then take over about two minutes early. This was something I'd learned on my very first ship. It didn't really change the duration of a watch, but just the illusion of getting off a couple minutes' early had a phenomenally encouraging effect on the crew. Everyone *thought* he was getting more rest and relief than he actually was, and the tiny attitude change worked miracles.

During the day's two meals, directly before and after each watch, we sat together on the processing deck—unless there was processing going on—and discussed problems and ways to improve things. Little things, not huge things. The huge things had been worked out long ago on ships like this. But incrementally, there was room for improvement. Gradually over the next few weeks, we improved.

The other deck bosses couldn't ignore the positive effects of my station posting tricks. My crew and Gashan's were better rested and in generally higher spirits than anyone else, and were more alert. Sworn, as I was, to do their best for the ship, the other deck bosses soon started trying similar methods. Some worked for them, others didn't, but they were experimenting with new ways, and from the general mutterings, that hadn't happened in a while.

After a time, with things running smoothly, I started using those quiet moments and off-watch times to get to know the technology. I discovered, for instance, that their energy storage methods weren't really different from what I was familiar with. I got the idea that the tile method, rather than being greatly divergent from the science of my culture, was just something my culture had skipped, and that this *Zingara* culture wasn't all that far from matter-antimatter propulsion. Already antimatter had been isolated and successfully maintained in a few of their facilities, so it was only a matter of time before they would figure it out.

As I figured out their technology, I started slowly to experiment with it. The tiles, my little square children, attracted me the most and I started to fiddle with their capabilities.

I kept my attempts to myself. What good would it do to stride around the ship prattling about microduotronics, reactant injectors, plasma distribution manifolds, and micron junction links? My job here wasn't to prance around showing off how superior I was. My job was to help these young men become superior too.

Besides, I wasn't superior. They knew a lot more about metallurgy and industrial recycling than I did. And much more about getting along day to day and surviving in a life-or-death situation than I did, right down to using real fur blankets because nature was sometimes hard to improve upon. Give or take the odd and rather limited adventure into stress I might've had while on board *Voyager,* no hardship had lasted as long as this for me, and certainly not as long as these men's working lives had been. I'd had a few hours, perhaps a few days at a time of trouble and strife. For this crew, trouble and strife were their whole existence. I came to laud less and less my own Starfleet-provided genius and appreciate much more the suffering-toughened resolve of *Zingara*'s crew. I even got used to the chill and dimness.

This had a bit of negative fallout. When I started fiddling, naturally I caught the eyes of the men on board. They wondered what I was doing and why. Loathe to sound pompous, I found myself explaining the general idea, but keeping the talk to a minimum. These fellows weren't stupid—they knew I was holding back. They started to wonder why. Funny little balancing act I found myself playing.

After a while, most of the crew left me alone to do my experiments unless they needed me, and I always made sure the watch was running smoothly before I got involved with anything of my own.

And those tiles kept attracting me. They seemed so simple, just capacitors, and yet they could do so many things—broadcast pictures, conduct communication, trigger mechanical response, and of course jump-start the fusion engines—and yet all this was simply through adjustments in the type, frequency, and modulation of their basic storage abilities. Fascinating little acorns on a very prolific tree.

While I was busy with my favorite tile experiment and getting some mind-boggling numbers, Quen happened to stroll by with a bowl of the oatmealy former livestock we too often called dinner. As he saw what I was doing, he ducked under the low-slung diagonal beam and peered at the single lonely tile I'd suspended on a coil wand. It stuck out of the bulkhead like a perverse flower on a stalk, glowing many times brighter than he was used to.

"Life from beyond the pyre?" he asked.

I looked up. "It's my grandmother, come for a visit."

"Is that . . . just one tile?"

"Just one sweet little slab. And it's holding two hundred twelve percent more energy than we're putting into any tile on board."

"Two hundred and twelve!" He put his bowl down on top of the jeklight meter and dipped under the beam, having to bend in order to join me under there.

He was prevented from crouching beside me by all the meters, sequencers, monitors, and transfer coils I had littered in a crude campfire circle around me, all working in combination to juice up that one tile and measure the changes. Quen couldn't even kneel with all this stuff on the deck, so he remained awkwardly bent and cupped a hand over the diagonal beam above his head to keep himself from falling forward.

The glow of my single tile emboldened his fine features and cast a Christmas sheen on his dark green hair.

"How did you do that?"

"I've been trying to figure out just how much energy could be packed into a tile if we didn't have to worry about burning up by getting too close to a sun. If it doesn't have to be radiant energy—well, watch this. The tile is completely isolated. There's no place for its energy to go, so it just has to keep absorbing, and I wanted to know how much cold power it could handle. Advance the coil valve . . . modify the rod level sequencers . . . Excuse me, but I can't see the network assembly—thanks. Direct feed off the fusion generator . . . Now watch the jeklight meter. Watch how much more one tile can hold."

On the end of its conduit wand, the tile began to whine with pumped-up energy and sizzled to a high green-white glow, so bright that Quen flinched, blinked, and put his free hand up to shield his eyes until they adjusted somewhat.

"Look at the rod levels," I told him.

"It's already red-lined."

"Keep watching it." As he adjusted his stance, almost hanging by his hand on the beam up there to twist and look at the indicator, I ticked off the numbers. "There's three hundred percent . . . four-eighty . . ."

The tile whined furiously, but did not vibrate, and shined with a glaring light.

"Five-twenty . . . six . . . eight . . . eight-ten . . . eight-fifteen . . . looks like it's topping out at . . . eight hundred seventeen percent."

The single tile was now brightly illuminating the whole lower deck, as if there weren't even any work lights on at all. Quen shielded his eyes from the glare and watched the meters in astonishment. "I had no idea a tile could do that!"

"I really didn't either," I said, "but there were enough similarities between this alloy and the properties of some things where I come from that it was worth a try. I just kept filling it and filling it. If you don't need a sun, you don't have to worry about the same limits."

Quen got a better grip on the beam overhead and leaned a little closer. "What can we do with it?"

"Ah," I accepted. "Those hard questions always serve to let us brilliant best-of-the-bests rise above the rabble and show what brainy wizards we are."

"Then what's the answer?"

"I don't have the foggiest idea."

He smiled. "There's got to be something . . ." He tilted a little to look at the conduit wand that so effectively isolated the single gleaming tile, and with his free hand reached around behind the tile.

I was watching the jeklight meter. I didn't see him reaching for the wand. Only as my peripheral alarms went off did I realize what he was about to do. I gasped an inadequate "Don't touch—!"

But my warning was swallowed by a lightning snap of power transfer. The force of sheer release drove me backward against the ship's rib, and from that low vantage I got a full view of the sheets of raw energy discharging from Quen's hand to his shoulder, through his body, arching upward through his other arm and into the beam over his head. His back arched convulsively as the tile purged all its stored power into him in a millisecond. His hair flew, his head shot back, and all I could see of his expression was his mouth gaping in shocky reaction and the triangle of his chin reflecting the sudden snap of light.

Using Quen's body as a conduit, the raw energy instantly bolted to the diagonal beam, popped a chorus of rivets, and cracked the wood to which the metal beam was bolted. The low overhead structure burst to shreds, shuddered as if suspended, then slammed on top of Quen as if driven down by the hands of titans.

Thirteen

THE BEAM AND ITS ATTENDANT STRUCTURE DROVE QUEN TO THE DECK and landed across his lower back and thighs. In seconds, there was nothing but the sizzle of burned wood and a faint wheeze from our captain's tortured lungs.

"Oh, no!" I crawled through hot wreckage, slamming aside my meters and monitors to get to Quen.

By the time I reached him, several men were piling down the ladder into the processor deck.

"Get Zell!" I called. "And Ruvan! Lift this beam off him!"

One of the men angled quickly back up the ladder, and three others came forward to lift the heavy metal beam off Quen's back.

Then Othien stooped in and started to grasp Quen's arm, a movement meant to turn the captain over. I quickly knocked him back.

"Don't move him . . . Get the top of that locker and bring it here. We'll use it as a backboard."

"Backboard?"

"We have to keep his spine immobile . . . My God, is he breathing?"

Sweat drained from my temples to my neck—the first time I'd perspired since crawling out of the pod into this chilly ship. A faint green glow made Quen look dead. He wasn't dead, was he?

Suddenly furious, I realized where the glow was coming from and lashed out to one side, cutting off the trail of power to the single tile, which was dutifully trying to recharge itself after the sudden discharge. Damn thing.

When I turned again to the terrible sight before me, Zell was there. He knelt at his captain's shoulder, his face a matte of misery and fear. He pressed his large hand to Quen's back with heart-wrenching tenderness. For a moment he just didn't seem to know what to do.

Nobody did. Nobody did . . .

Fourteen

"I WANT TO SEE HIM."

"He doesn't want to see you. Ruvan's still treating him."

"You mean *you* don't want him to see me. I'm one of the deck bosses. You can't just push me aside anymore, Zell."

"I'm your watch officer. You can report to me."

"Fine. I'm reporting that you know I have to be able to put my crew at ease in order for the ship to run smoothly. I can't do that if I don't know what's going on."

We were in dangerous territory. All around us, settlements teemed with contraband. Other warrant ships stole in and out over the past few hours. No matter how we tried to isolate ourselves, we had no choice but to barter for supplies. Word was spreading about Quen. That couldn't be good.

Unenthusiastic about much of anything, Zell shook his head and stepped into the pitifully inadequate infirmary. While I lingered back, he went straight to the treatment cot where Quen now lay. The first sound we heard was Quen's tight moan.

Quen's face was nearly white with pain, his eyes stricken. The dim light of *Zingara*'s thrifty interior did him no favors. Every breath was a knotted gasp. His hands clutched at the worn fur blanket draped over his hips and chest. Zell caught one of those hands, gazed at Quen's anguished face with the sincerest emotion I'd ever seen from him.

Ruvan flustered over a makeshift splint contraption holding Quen's pelvis and legs in place on the cot. Both legs were raised on a cushion and his feet were supported by another cushion. Didn't look very comfortable.

"Are his hips broken?" I asked quietly as Ruvan passed close to me coming around the end of the cot.

"Cracked pelvis," he said. "Lots of torn ligaments . . . possible spinal damage, three broken ribs. Almost every internal organ has been burned. There could be bleeding inside. Quen . . ."

The medic bent over our young captain and waited until Quen's eyes focused on him.

"I gave you something for the pain, but I can't treat all this. Not well enough. You've got to let us go back to Om and put you in a hospital. You need bone surgery. Maybe spinal surgery. There's no place to do that but on the planet."

Quen struggled to answer, managing a tight smile. "You do it . . . Zell's got a rigger's knife."

"Don't make jokes," Ruvan miserated. "Don't make jokes . . . please listen. We can't put you on another transport because I don't want to move you around. We have to take you back ourselves. It could be months for you waiting to heal without treatment."

"Ruvan's right," Zell intruded. "We can't load this all on him. It's not fair."

Sorrowfully Quen rolled his head on the small pillow to look at Zell. "We can't give in . . . we can't give in . . . Don't let anybody talk you into giving—"

A grueling spasm cut him in half. He twisted, valiantly fighting it. Zell held his hand, grimacing in anguish and empathy, and tried to keep Quen from harming himself further by shifting that damaged pelvis.

I found myself pressed back against the wall, arms folded so tightly that my ribs hurt. The two of them reminded me of Tom Paris and Harry Kim, just young men caught in a big ugly situation in which they were losing what little control they ever had.

Quen clamped his lips shut to bury the gasps, instead giving way to a series of compressed groans, one riding on each breath he drew. He pressed his left hand to his hip, crushed his eyes closed, and turned away from Zell. We could see the internal results of electrocution working on him, and could do nothing about it. For the first time in my life, I wished I'd gone to medical school.

Without trying to hide his inner torture, Zell looked at Ruvan. "Rig a traction. Do whatever you can for him. We're not going in."

Pain as deep-laden as Quen's cramped Ruvan's face. His shoulders hunched and he hung his head, envisioning months of ghastly discomfort for his patient.

Pressing a pale hand to his ribs, Quen opened his eyes wearily, reached out with the other hand, and caught Ruvan's wrist. When Ruvan looked at him, the injured leader of a ragtag crew heavily said, "I'm sorry I brought you here . . ."

The furtive glimpse into these boys' unspoken past gave me little information but somehow affected me deeply. In many ways they were lost, even more lost than *Voyager*'s crew had been, for we had at least known the way home.

"I'll need a couple of assistants to help with him," Ruvan rasped. "Someone'll have to build a slant-board. And I need nylon straps."

"Kay," Zell said instantly, "put two of your crew on infirmary duty."

"Right away," I responded. "I've got two men on standby."

"Straps and a slant board."

I nodded. "Less than twenty minutes."

He looked down at Quen and gripped his captain's hand reassuringly. "You . . . rest."

Quen offered him a minimal grin. "Between dances."

Zell, for a burly type who otherwise should've been guarding an end zone somewhere, was surprisingly gentle. He had trouble pulling himself away, but with a final glance at Ruvan that offered scant support, he forced himself out of the infirmary.

I caught him in the corridor, halfway to the main deck.

"Zell," I called. "Wait."

Turning to me, he visibly fought to regain control over his expression. "What?"

"We have to make a plan."

"Plan for what?"

"For battle. We're heading for one. We have to get the homeworld to understand there's an enemy coming. We can put the warranters in a stronger bargaining position if we all band together. Everyone has to unify in order to beat the Men—"

"We can't band together. I explained that."

"I know, hostile coalition. All I want is one face-to-face meeting with the other warranter captains and—"

"No!" He grimaced. "Aren't you tired of talking this way? You're making everybody scared for no reason."

"There's plenty of reason. We've got to be ready."

" 'Ready' how?"

"This sector doesn't stand a chance against Hell's Aliens if we don't organize. I can't teach you how to build a warp core—I can't even teach you how to build a pencil—but I can hike your fusion efficiency, enhance your long-range sensors, organize the warranter crews for battlestations. Your weapons can be made more efficient—"

"How?"

"Well, you've got turret guns supplemented by secondary guns on the casements. Instead of rotating the whole turret, why not mount the guns outside and just rotate the guns?"

"We tried that last year. The guns are unprotected and we have to go outside or retreat to make repairs."

"But we'd get better results. We should start targeting installations. We've got to start getting ready."

"Fine, get ready." Once again he tried to get back to the main deck and away from me.

With a hopeful lilt, I asked, "Is that a command?"

He stopped and glared at me. "What?"

"Is that permission to get the ship ready?"

Clapping a hand to his head, he rubbed his face harshly, then said, "What are you talking about?"

I held out a hand. "You're the captain now."

As he suddenly realized the scope of what I meant, he backed up so sharply that he bumped his head on a transverse beam. "I'm not the captain! Don't say that."

"Quen's incapacitated. He can't command from there—"

A big finger poked me in the shoulder. "Don't you say that to anybody on this ship or any other ship. Look, I have to deal with you, but I don't have to like it."

Though he tried to leave again, I plunged forward and caught him by the sleeve. "Zell, you have to take over!"

Yanking out of my grip, he snapped, "Stop saying that! I'm *not* the captain. Quen is *Zingara*'s captain. If things get worse . . . we'll have an election."

"Election?"

"I'm not captain until the crew makes me captain."

His big hand pressed against my shoulder and pushed me back, not roughly but very firmly. He fell silent for a few seconds, enough to put a buffer between us.

"Mind your own business, Kay," he warned. "Mind your crew and your business. Leave me alone."

Something in his voice made me give up. For a moment I'd forgotten that he was worn-out too, hungry, tired, probably frightened. He had spent his visible past in simple salvage operations and defending those salvages, a piratical but relatively simple and limited-range life. He had never before faced anything like what I was describing, and to his mind he had no reason to face it at all.

He filled up the hatchway as he stepped through to the main deck, leaving me blessedly behind. His respite was short-lived. Across the deck, now cleared of all the maintenance gear and safe to stride, came a wall of young men I didn't recognize. Warranters—and leading them was Oran!

Oran, Quen's brother—still, a competing warranter captain and a boarding party, on our ship!

If they'd been just boarders, I'd have known perfectly well what to do. Slam the hatch shut, lock it, and keep them from reaching our injured captain while I found a way to gas the main deck with sedative and knock everybody out.

The plan died aborning. Oran had more right to see Quen than I did. Brothers, right? What should I do?

Take Zell's cue—that was my second instinct.

Zell met the entourage halfway up the main deck. He and Oran squared off with something less than affection, but not animosity either. There was caution in the way they paused, looked at each other, exchanged a few words. Zell must be explaining what happened to Quen—yes, he was pointing at the wreckage that had crushed our captain to the deck. Then he put his hand on his own pelvis bone and his lower back and ribs, demonstrating some of the injuries.

Oran frowned in empathy with his brother, whom he hadn't even seen yet.

Quickly I dove for an equipment locker and pulled out several nylon harnesses and loading straps. Slipping back past the hatchway, I rushed toward the infirmary door, then controlled my motions so as to appear casual as I stepped inside.

Hovering over Quen, Ruvan looked up.

"Here are the straps," I said. "How much of a degree of incline do you want on the slant-board? Why don't you make me a little diagram of what you need."

That bought me enough time. When Oran and Zell appeared at the infirmary door, I was already inside.

Zell seemed plenty annoyed that I was still there, although Oran had attention only for his brother. Instantly Oran's captainlike distance and professionalism dissolved when he saw Quen lying there in a girdle of suffering.

"Oh, no," Oran moaned. "Oh, no . . ." His shoulders sank, and he thumped his hands on his thighs in frustration.

Quen gazed back at him. "You shouldn't be here," he whispered through the glaze of medication.

Ruvan's treatment had taken some effect. Quen's eyes were clearer and his motions less tormented as Oran came to him, and somehow they managed to get their arms around each other without causing any more damage. For a long time the brothers were nothing but a bundle of rugged clothing and forest-shadow hair. Ruvan and I stood aside, and Zell hovered near the hatch, letting them have this bonding moment. Apparently such times were rare in the lives of a warranter family.

Without really letting go, Oran raised his head enough that they could look at each other and talk.

"What is this?" he began roughly. "A pathetic excuse to get some sleep?"

Quen smiled, soon ruined as he tightened through a spasm. The sight of him cramped up like that drove the attempt at mirth away from all of us. Oran held his brother, and they endured the torment together until Quen managed to regain some control.

"You're going to have to accept help now," Oran said. "You know that, don't you?"

"We're . . . fine. We made two good . . . trades . . . and an ice catch . . . yesterday."

"Let me bring Murn over here. He knows something about internal injuries."

"No . . . no, Oran, don't."

"Ruvan can't handle this by himself. You're asking too much of him."

"He . . . likes it."

"Jokes," Ruvan mumbled disapprovingly.

Here were the captain, first mate, and chief medic of a working ship, yet they all seemed so very young to me as I watched them dealing with this tragic turn. I didn't want to be their mother, but maybe I had to be.

Keeping very careful control over my tone, I offered, "Quen, I agree with your brother. The warranters should start helping each other. This other way isn't working."

Had I lit a firecracker? You'd think so, the way they all looked at me. The whole idea of banding together was so foreign and dishonorable to them, given the promises they'd made to defend freedom on their planet and follow the rule of law, that even the mention of such a bond was some kind of transgression. They were all too decent for their own good. Now or never.

With my arms folded, trying not to appear overbearing, I took one measured step forward. "Captain Oran, may I speak to you about something very important?"

Suddenly enraged, Zell stepped in. "No, Kay!"

Oran looked at him, then back at me. "What's the matter? Who are you?"

"Nothing, nobody," Zell insisted. "Kay, get out."

I looked at Quen. "Captain . . . please?"

Still clinging to his brother, Quen studied my face for signs of honesty or insanity, trying to decide whether he knew me well enough to judge my character quite this deeply.

They were all watching me, though the only one I was interested in was Quen. I wouldn't speak again until he did.

Through a long gasping breath, he finally said, "Go ahead."

"Keep it short," Zell bruskly warned.

From the pocket of my trousers, I pulled a single curry card. "I planned on keeping it short. Here's an explanation of what I think is going on and why. I come from another ship, Captain Oran, a ship that was destroyed along with the outpost we were visiting and most of the people on it. There was a slaughter by an incoming force. It's all described there. I believe that force is a conquering body and it's on its way here. This whole sector will be obliterated if we don't organize ourselves. The warranters have to band together to fight the TCA fleet, or we all have to band together to fight the incoming Menace. And it's the second part that had better happen."

"TCA fleet?" Oran repeated. "The TCA doesn't have a fleet. *We* were the planetary fleet."

"I was on board Sasaquon's ship and overheard them talking about a fleet that'll be ready to launch soon. I believe the TCA has been using Sasaquon to keep the warranters from consolidating, long enough for the TCA to build up its own fleet to come here and wipe you out."

Zell snapped his fingers at me and said, "Get back on the deck where you belong."

But Oran looked at his brother. "You believe this, Quen?"

Quen's face took on the trouble of decision under the tightness of pain. "Some things she says . . . make sense . . . We believe she came from a . . . from a better science than ours . . . She knows some things . . . but there's no—"

A surge of new pain cut him off, and as Oran gripped him in helpless support, Zell stepped in to finish the sentence.

"No proof," the first mate charged. "No proof at all for this crazy talk."

"There's proof," I challenged. "We've got one of their women locked up in our forward section!"

"I want to see her," Oran said.

"You can see her," Zell agreed, "but she's not proof of anything. It's a big galaxy. Even if Kay's right, even if that woman's part of some force, this Menace she talks about could be headed in any hundred other directions. There are millions of stars. It could be centuries before they get to us."

"Or it could be tomorrow," I shoved in.

"Wait," Oran said, holding up a hand. "I saw things at Pelior Station and at Rymon Line. Things I didn't understand, but things that make sense if there's a fleet. That could explain why there's been so much activity at the Tuskan smelting facility."

"There's activity there?" Quen asked. "At this time of . . . year?"

"Lots of it."

For the first time there was a glimmer of suspicion in their eyes that didn't involve doubting me. Not Zell, of course, but the young captains. Like all captains, they were used to having to think more broadly than anyone else on any ship. They looked at each other, distilling almost psychically what they knew, and then both of them looked at me again.

This was hard—trying to convince other people of things that really mattered. On *Voyager* I had been the supreme authority, the person everybody else had to convince. All decisions were ultimately mine. I'd gotten spoiled. Now the shoe was on a whole other foot and I was scrambling for our lives without the voltage to make the action occur.

"Before we can fight the TCA fleet or the Menace," I went on, "first we have to be ready to fight, period. That's why I've been making new star charts, concentrating on coordinating depots, pockets of population, friendly bases, installations—"

"You are talking too much!" Zell shouted. "You're making it sound like we *have* to fight! If you build up to fight, it means you have to go out and look for a fight. If you put resources into getting strong and powerful, you have to go out and use that power! That's how people react to things!"

"Depends on the people," I said quietly. "We have to be so ready for a fight that everybody else knows we are. We have to make ourselves so scary that other people won't attack us. When the Menace shows up, I want to be out there already between them and our planets, with all the warranter ships and the TCA fleet, and I want to be too scary for anybody to attack us. That's how you *stop* a fight."

"This recording . . . it's just you talking?"

Oran looked at the curry card I'd provided him, and it seemed he was willing to pay attention, but only to a point.

"Not ships or aliens?" he asked. "It's not anything we can look at?"

"It's not proof," Zell clarified. "It's just her doing a lot of raving. She could be making it all up. She could be imagining all this Menace, slaughter, fleet."

"I don't think Kay's lying, Zell," Quen offered. At first I was heartened, but then to his brother he said, "It could be imagination. She was in very . . . bad . . ."

He winced hard. His eyes cramped shut, and he pressed against his brother's hands as pain dogged his crushed body.

Ruvan stepped to the cot, but there was nothing anyone could do except wait for the pain to pass. "That's enough," he said, and this doctorly order was the most authoritative thing I'd heard him say. Usually Ruvan was easy to push around, but clearly he'd had enough.

"Kay, you've had your moment," Zell ordered. "They've heard you, and it's time to get out and leave them alone. Let's go."

Neither of the captains countermanded his order. I was assigned to Zell's watch. He had command over me. My one chance, whatever it was worth, was over.

To his credit, Zell followed me out and motioned for Ruvan to come out too. He really did mean to let the brothers have a few moments of privacy.

What would the captains talk about to each other? How the woman was crazy? Or how there was some mysterious activity at the Tucker facility?

"Tuskan facility," I mumbled, correcting myself.

Zell and I stepped out onto the main deck and went our separate ways. He had his work to do, and I had mine. I had a crew to run.

There were tiles to be scrubbed. There was a slant-board to make. There was sabotage to plan. Time to get to work.

Fifteen

"LIGHT KICK! ZELL! ZELL!"

"What happened!"

"We're kicked!"

"Who made the buildup!"

"We don't know!"

"Why didn't anybody notice!"

"The readouts were shut down!"

"Can we stop it?"

"No, no! We're hyperlight!"

"How fast?"

"Full speed!"

"All right, don't stop it! Nobody touch anything! Kay! Where are you! Where is she?"

It had taken me nearly a week and a half to work out my plan. Finally, the button had been pushed and *Zingara*'s swelled-up capacitors released all their power at once, shoving the ship into light-speed, heading where I told it to go. It was an act of sabotage, even mutiny, and I'd done it with my own two little hands.

The way this technology worked, we were utterly committed. The capacitor tiles had skimmed off all they could of the nearest sun's energy as it streamed through the skin of the ship. Then, through some careful subterfuge and tricky crew assignments on my part, they'd built up to top-off without anyone's noticing. That could have gone on only for a matter of minutes. Soon the point of now-or-never had come, and I'd hit the switch.

The tiles had emptied of all their energy in an instant, funneling a massive surge into the fusion engines. *Zap*—we were at hyperlight speed. Now the fusion engines could keep up until we reached the destination I'd preprogrammed into the navigation system.

Most of the crew had been knocked to their knees by the sudden start. The rest had been dumped out of their bunks. With a little luck, Totobet would have landed on her head. I only hoped Quen was all right.

Yes, I felt awful about it. When *Voyager* needed me to be there and be a captain, I'd been somewhere else. I'd never make that mistake again.

When Zell and Massus appeared before me like a bulky wall, I wasn't surprised. When they grabbed my arms and hauled me across the deck, I didn't resist.

They dragged me past the astonished and confused faces of the current watch crew, a crew afraid to touch their own equipment. Their ship had come alive around them and gone off on its own. If anything changed, if they tampered, the light kick would shut down and they'd be stuck in the interstellar void with no way to power up for a return kick. They hovered around, monitoring things, afraid to do much. That was for the best. Now that I'd set things in motion, we had to go where we were headed.

Quen was still in the infirmary, tractioned up to a framework Ruvan had designed and my watch crew had built. His upper body was raised on the slant-board at about thirty degrees so he could breathe more easily with those broken ribs, and his legs were strapped to a pelvic splint that kept his knees slightly bent but prevented his shifting around.

Quen, Zell, Massus, Ruvan . . . a jury at a murder trial would've been more welcoming.

Their faces were gray and they looked old. And disaster-stricken. Quen was still in pain—that showed in his face—but the sharp spikes were under some control. He wasn't getting worse, and that was good luck. He could easily have had internal bleeding or some kind of damage that couldn't be handled with a slant board and splints. His broken ribs were bound, and obviously just breathing was still a trial for him.

Zell stepped in and yanked me after him. Massus came in, too, as the engineer on watch who had been completely taken by surprise. From Quen's expression, I could tell he already knew we were at hyperlight-speed.

"She initiated the light kick on her own," Zell bolted. "She didn't consult me or you or anybody."

Ruvan was here too, barely able to keep standing, he was so frightened.

They all fell silent for a few seconds and just stared at me with the most terrible expressions.

"This is unforgivable," Quen uttered. His voice had a slight wheeze from a stubborn lung infection that had damned Ruvan's efforts for a week and was finally starting to clear up.

With an agreeable nod, I said, "It sure is. I'm desperate. I know I'm blowing all the trust I've gained, but you have to understand what you're facing.

"You don't *know* any of this," Massus argued. Apparently he'd been talking to Zell, but I had absolutely no doubt that his thoughts were his own.

"We didn't log a jump with anyone," Zell ranted. "Even Oran doesn't know. If we get in trouble, nobody'll know what happened to us . . . We'll just be . . . we'll just . . ."

Looking like he was about to faint, he gripped a medicine shelf with both hands and shuddered fiercely.

In the void of brief silence, I said, "We're aimed for a star. We'll be able to get back."

"You can't possibly be that sure," Massus snapped. "We've never gone where you're sending us."

"I've navigated a lot of space. More than you."

Zell turned and found his voice. "How far did you come in your pod? Even you said you had no way to know!"

"I checked the pod. I calculated its top hyperlight, its fuel consumption and—"

"You can't be that sure," Massus said. "We never, *never* make a kick unless we're absolutely sure."

From his bed, Quen wiped his face with a shaking hand. "How can you know how far, Kay? Or if there's a solar source at all where we'll end up?"

"She doesn't understand!" Zell pounded the shelf he had just been leaning on. "If we end up even six months away from a solar source, we starve to death! We starve!"

Quen reached out and grasped Zell's elbow to quiet him, but though it silenced Zell, the comradely gesture did nothing to ease the moment's tension.

He watched me for a few long seconds, as if trying to read my eyes. "How could you do this to us?" he murmured. "You took the Ship's Pledge."

My chest constricted. The idea that they thought I'd broken their most cherished bond was hard to take. My stomach turned as their eyes worked on me.

"Oh, yes," I said, "and I meant every word. I promised to do what was best for the ship and crew, and this is it. If it takes proof to get action out of your people, I'll get proof. I need you to believe me."

They stared and doubted what they heard.

Getting nowhere plenty fast.

"Look, this won't hurt the ship, it won't hurt the crew, we're going to fly over to Iscoy space and have a look at the remains, and then we're going to power up the tiles and fly right back. We don't even have to stay. We just have to look."

"What if there's no solar source?" Massus insisted.

"There is. Prettiest little yellow lantern you ever saw, give or take my—"

"What if it's not where you think it is?" Zell challenged. "What if you've made mistakes? Our navigation isn't that precise. Our sensors are completely blind through the whole jump. What if your calculations are wrong and we end up in the void?"

"I've fine-tuned some of the sensors. When we get there, we should be able to analyze some things long-range. We won't even have to get close to the Menace ships to see them."

"*When* we get there—" Zell paced out some of his initial rage and now stalked the small infirmary in less anger and more genuine worry. "*If* we get there. *If* we're headed where you think we are, and *if* there's anything at the other end of this jump where we can power up—"

"How far are we going?" Massus asked. "Do you know even that?"

"It should be a nine-day jump, if all my calculations are correct."

"Nine days? We can't get anywhere in nine days," Zell said. "We'll be out in the middle of nothing!"

"No, listen," I said sternly. "I told you I'm an engineer. I've multiplied your warping effect by a significant factor. In nine days we'll be covering the same distance as you would normally cover in twenty-eight days."

"Twenty-eight!" Ruvan came to life suddenly. "Quen!"

Quen held up a steadying hand. "Shhh . . ."

Zell made a sharp gesture at me. "What if her calculations are no good? That's farther than we've ever gone before! We've never made a jump longer than fifteen days!"

Quen looked at Massus, the engineer, who tightly confirmed, "All this is guesswork. We could be headed in a completely wrong direction, not toward where she thinks she came from."

"I looked at your star charts," I told them. "And I remember mine. Mine were better—"

"Was your memory any better?" Zell demanded. "In that pod, in that condition?"

"It must be there." I tried to sound confident. "Unless I'm completely crazy, and it's a similar system over that way. I did computer simulations to see which stars are—"

"We've never gone this far," Quen said. "Nobody has. We've mapped a few key systems and routes to them, and that's where we go. We're not an explorer ship with stock on board to survive for months—"

A twitch in a muscle choked off his words. He clamped his hand to his ribs and gasped. Overcome, Zell stepped to the cot and lifted Quen up from the cushion a little until his captain's pain released him. The interfering cramp reminded us all just how very mortal we were.

Ruvan shivered and sank down to sit on his bunk. "We'll starve . . ."

Despite my conviction about what I'd done, I felt suddenly like a black banshee flying over their heads. No matter how the pie was cut, I was giving them the scare of their young lives.

And even worse, when it came down to bare porcelain, Zell had a point—I *wasn't* really sure. There *were* a lot of stars in the galaxy. The Menace could be headed in another direction entirely. Was I obsessed? Had I forgotten how to be a captain and see all the possibilities?

And poor Quen, lying here . . . I'd made a fool of him. He'd trusted me, put me above his own crewmates because he was trying to be the best kind of captain. How much more was he suffering because of me?

"She's insane," Zell mourned. Some of anger's heat had boiled out of him as he eased his captain back against the cushions. He pressed a hand to Quen's shoulder. "You take her out of power."

That wrenched me out of those thoughts.

"Now, wait a minute," I interrupted. "My watch methods have been helping. Trying to be the commanding officer on both watches hasn't done you any good, Zell. At least admit that things have been running well enough that you've been able to get some sleep while I'm on watch. If you tell the other deck bosses to organize their watches like mine, *Zingara* will be ready to defend against the Menace. This is bigger than just this ship or just the warranters. The TCA will have to be convinced too, so their fleet can—"

"You haven't seen this fleet," Quen pointed out.

"I don't need to see the wind blow either."

He shifted carefully, one hand pressed to his bound ribs, and looked at Zell. "What if her conclusions are right about the TCA? Zell, our own people . . ."

Rather than snapping a disagreement, Zell paused and contemplated. "We could go somewhere . . . get our families and go."

"If we do that," Quen said, "and the big attack comes that she's talking about, we'll have abandoned our own planet."

"What if she's just delusional?"

"Where did that other woman come from, then? With the—" Quen pointed at his hair and made a circular motion.

With a shrug, I told them again, "Either we're going to have a conflict with the Menace, or we're going to have a conflict with our planet, or we're going to have both."

Zell scowled at me. "*Our* planet?"

I shrugged and looked him right in the eye. "If it's yours, it's mine."

"But Zell's right, Kay," Quen said. "You don't know this Menace is coming. You don't know they'll attack if they do show up. You *think* they might."

"When they come, they'll attack. I know a strategy when I see one. I never got a chance to deal with them before, but I'm going to deal with them now. They destroyed my ship, they slaughtered citizens of a peaceful, progressive civilization, and when they get to our space, I'm going to be in a position to do something about them."

"Take her out of power, Quen," Zell repeated.

A small moan escaped Quen's lips. He sighed and said, "She hasn't been proven wrong yet. What if she's telling some version of the truth? What if we should be ready? Then we'll need her as deck boss."

"Either we get ready," Zell grumbled, "or we starve in the void. Until we know, I don't want to have to work with her. What if she does more trouble before the kick shuts down?"

Massus squeezed his hands into tense fists and muttered, "Nine days . . ."

Quen let his head fall back on the cushion and blanched visibly with the weight of his new decision, along with the discomfort of his traction and the throb of his injuries.

"We'll lock her in a berth until the kick is over. Then we'll see where we end up."

Quen gazed at me now, and the fear in his eyes nearly crushed us all.

"You've committed us, Kay," he said. "We have to go wherever you've sent us. If things aren't exactly as you say when we get there . . . I'm putting you off my ship."

Sixteen

NINE DAYS, CONFINED. NINE DAYS ALONE WITH MY THOUGHTS AND A FEW scanty meals. Nine days to fine-tune my plans to improve the warranter ships' abilities. Nine days of wondering what the crew was thinking of me, saying, and wondering.

What if Zell was right and I was wrong? What if my calculations were wrong and they wouldn't have any reason to believe me after all this? And then the Menace came anyway?

What if I was obsessed? Had a head injury in the pod?

No . . . obsessives didn't sit around wondering if they were obsessed.

Besides, on the starboard side, also locked in another berth, was that Menace woman. I sure hadn't obsessed her out of thin air.

The light kick was dangerous. If the fusion engine couldn't keep up, it would shut down and we'd be stranded in the interstellar void. If I'd miscalculated the engines' ability to keep up, we were all dead. They'd never gone this far in a single kick before. Most of their light kicks were a matter of hours. They were right—I couldn't be certain the ship could maintain thrust long enough.

We were committed to risk and danger—and if I was right, a terrible revelation—but none of that caused me the most worry. Strange, what really haunted me during these long hours was the attitude the crew might have about me now. In their minds, I'd let them down.

The heartache was insurmountable. That was what bothered me most.

Four . . . five . . .

I had to do something, get some answers. Parts of Totobet's story didn't add up. No civilization used up localities that fast. It would take centuries for a normal population to need that much room.

So I asked to speak to her. Nothing fancy, just put me in her room for a few minutes and stand outside and listen, and I promise not to pull her little spools out.

Zell didn't like the idea, but after a while he sent a couple of men to take me to Totobet. Apparently Quen wanted the facts known too, and had overridden Zell's big no.

She was resting in a bunk, wrapped in a fur blanket against the *Zingara*'s day-to-day chill.

"Get up," I ordered. "I want to talk to you."

As she came to the edge of the bunk, she quietly said, "You already talked to me. You told me to shut up."

"Well, I don't want to you shut up now. I want to know why your civilization needs so much area and needs it so quickly."

She nodded, seeming to understand the shortcut to answers. "We evolved reproducing," she attempted timidly. "We can't help it. If we don't find enough place, we have too many people to survive."

"So you think you can just come and steal the homes of others so you have a place to live?" I smoldered. "What if you don't find anybody? What happens when there's nobody to kill and no more room to grow? Have you ever thought about that?"

Her glossy chestnut eyes widened a little. "Of course. When that happens, we have to kill our children."

I stumbled backward as if she'd slapped me. I landed with my back against the locked door. Had I heard—

"What?"

She hunched her shoulders a bit. "We kill our children."

My arms were locked at my sides, my legs numb. Like lightning my mind processed what she had said, why she had said it, and distilled from her large brown eyes that this was no tall tale. I stared so hard, my face hurt. My soul hurt.

"We kill our children," she said.

Well, there was the missing element. There it was, right there. Right there.

My voice was shattered glass. "My God, I thought I'd heard it all . . ."

"You don't understand us," she attempted.

"Don't understand? I understand that a decent culture says, 'women and children first, and children more first'! You . . . your people, you say, 'Us first and children last'? Run out of space, so kill the kids? You're not helping yourself with me!"

Nauseated, I turned my back on her, but in just seconds I whirled to face her again.

"You can just say it out like that?" I charged. "They're 'killed'?"

Spreading her narrow hands, Totobet asked, "What should I say? That's what it is. Don't you have to stop things sometimes? What do your people say?"

A spike of rather hideous similarity went through my chest. "There are . . . euphemisms . . . 'aborted' . . . 'terminated'—"

"Are they killed?"

"Well . . . yes—"

"Then why don't you say 'killed'?"

She knew she had shocked me to the bone. At the same time her bluntness was strangely noble. They did this thing, but they owned up to it. How much had my own people done and called it something mild just to make it easy on ourselves?

Totobet's culture had apparently not bothered to make the intolerable into something you could mention in public without flinching. Why did she want me to know? Why had she said this? Why did I have to hear it?

"If we don't have a place to expand," she explained, "we have to resort to killing the babies. It's done decently, but it must be done. It's a terrible blow nature has dealt us. We have to survive by numbers. For most to live, many must die."

"You can be that heartless about it?" God, was that my voice? "Either you kill another race and take their planet, or you kill your own children? That's it?"

"When it comes to killing our own or killing others, we kill the others and have a place. If we can't find a place . . . we have a lottery."

"Lottery." I sank against the door until my pelvis got cold on the metal. "Damned whimsical . . . to kill your babies out of convenience."

"We have no choice."

"You haven't looked around enough," I spat back. "There's sure a lot here to dislike."

"We're not animals," Totobet protested quietly. "We're fully intelligent beings. In good times, we're really very pleasant. It's a terrible thing . . . Overpopulation is devastating. It ruins everyone. Rich, poor, young, old . . . The only way we can keep from revolution is if everyone's child has an equal chance. We can't lottery our adults because they're the ones who know things. The children can't build or grow food or make ships or fly them. Until we conquer another planet, most of the young are killed. If we have a place to expand, that's a big number of our children who can live. Some things have to happen . . . It's just survival."

A core-deep disgust forced bile into my throat, but not only because of what she had told me. It came because a part of me understood.

"This is a hard quadrant," I said.

• • •

For untold minutes I leaned against the door, shuddering, cold, absorbing the whole monumental concept of what I had been told, then rejecting it, then absorbing more. She was a liar. She was delusional. There was some other reason. It made no sense. It made perfect sense. Culture . . . habit . . . religion . . . biology . . . No answer served me today.

Savage, savage.

My lips pressed tight, I breathed in sharp sucks through my nose and turned back to the circuitry. I had to get out of here. I had to get out!

I had to change things in this sector. I had to have an effect or go crazy trying, or die maybe. Too often I'd accepted the role of onlooker in the Delta Quadrant, working hard at noninterference, even when involvement was forced by proximity or mandated by circumstance. Or by honor. And I had some.

More than she did. More than her people did.

Suddenly I wanted very much to change something. Even if it was only the condition of these goddamned circuits, why wouldn't they cut?

Population control taken to an extreme. Sickening. Couldn't use birth control because reproduction was a life-or-death deal with evolution. Us, them.

I felt as humbled and ineffectual as any human being, I think, had ever discovered himself or herself to be. Big things were happening around me, and there was such meager power in my scope that I could no longer affect them. That hadn't been the way for me all these many years in the captain's chair. I'd had many choices, some very hard, but the courses were mine to take or discard. Not for years had I been in a position of such diminished authority, such sweeping ignorance, and such utterly yeoman needs. Even as I struggled to hear what was going on in the sector at large, I was thinking about which of my tiles still needed grouting.

What was there to say? I pounded on the door until the crew let me out and took me back to my own bunk where I could curl up under my own fur blanket and sink into the hauntings that followed me there.

Six, seven . . . the ninth day.

The last hours were the longest. The last minutes almost strangled me. The ship was so quiet . . . only the soft murmur of the fusion engines and their supporting systems, and the whisper of life-support, artificial gravity, and all the things that gave us the illusion of security in space.

Children, children.

Thoughts of *Voyager* crept back in on me in the silent seclusion. Had we been fooling ourselves all along? Trying to travel tens of thousands of light-years—our lifetimes would've been eaten up by the trip. Our grandchildren, if we bothered to have any, would be the ones greeted by strangers in the Federation with whom they had no bonds. We had been the only human beings in the Delta Quadrant. There were only a hundred forty–some of us, not a big enough gene pool, but still the option had kept us going. If things got too bad, we could stop, join a culture like the Iscoy or, as I had, the Omians, and simply become part of another race, a new creed.

Yet, every time that chance came up, we rejected it. Our duty, our obligation, our Pledge was to keep paddling up that long river.

When the hatch to my small quarters cracked open, I jumped as if somebody had popped a balloon beside my ear. As I rolled off my bunk, my knees clicked furiously and I almost fell over.

Massus was at my door. So were Othien and Levan. They'd sent my own crew to bring me out.

"Are we there?" My voice, after nine days, was a croak. "Can you see anything?"

"Come on out," Massus said. He was tense and reserved.

"What's out there?"

"Go on."

He motioned for me to go in front of him out toward the main deck. Even before I got to the hatch I could see that almost the whole crew had crammed onto the main deck and were staring upward and out over the vid rail. The deck-wide video tiles above us had all been repaired and were working just fine. Just fine . . .

Standing in the middle of the deck, leaning on the rail that partly surrounded the deck well, Quen held himself in place with Ruvan's help. Beside him, Zell pivoted around, then around again, looking. Their faces, and those of the entire crew of the *Zingara,* were upturned toward the stunning full-wide view around us.

I had in my time seen plagues and I had seen battles. I'd seen the galaxy's ugliness and its breathtaking beauty. From life to death and back again I'd seen rather a lot. Until today, though, I had never seen an armada of so many ships that I couldn't count them, each bigger than my hometown.

That's what we were looking at through the great open window of the overhead vid tiles. From rail to rail, from transverse bulkhead to transverse bulkhead, there was nothing but a vast invasion fleet stretching off almost to infinity. The Menace.

Between us and the armada, only the slaggy haze of asteroids hid us from prying sensors. To our right was the pretty sun I'd remembered as being so welcoming and so much like Earth's sun when *Voyager* first accepted the Iscoy invitation to pull up and relax for a while. There was the largest asteroid, which the Iscoy had been using as a base, now peppered with new configurations of lights on its dark side, proving that the whole asteroid had been very quickly set up for full occupation.

And all around us, caught in the flow of the asteroid belt itself, were pieces of wrecked ships, torn violently to bits, along with the twisted and burned remains of the spacedock and several satellites.

The whole region, and its current occupants, spoke quite horridly for itself.

Good thing, because I couldn't speak at all.

Shuddering against the splints and bindings on his hips and legs, Quen shook like an old man. Staring out into the breadth of space, he scanned the massive armada, battleship after battleship, support vehicle after support vehicle, transport after transport.

I shuffled across the deck, looking around in such rapt attention that I tripped twice. Behind me, Massus and Levan bumped into each other as we stopped amidships, near where Zell was turning and turning.

Without really planning to, I ended up standing beside Quen. Together we gazed out at the two hundred battleships of the Menace armada.

Quen's breathing was labored. He did not look at me. "Did you expect this much?"

My head shook slowly, my lips moved, but there really wasn't much sound. "No . . ."

In spite of the minimal scratch of my words, the ship was so silent that I think everybody heard me. That old saying—one picture is worth a thousand words . . . I'd given them the thousand words, and none of them had the impact of these last five minutes. In virtual seconds I'd been proven at least partially right. The Menace existed, in invasion proportions. There had been a sudden and devastating battle here. If what Totobet said was true, and these people moved from place to place to have room to expand, then this little asteroid was nothing more than a temporary stop or a base of some kind. Maybe an outpost. There wasn't enough room on that asteroid for the occupants of even two or three of those ships to live.

"Whatever you do," I murmured, "stay hidden."

My voice was scarcely more than a whisper. We were hidden well enough, adrift with the flow of the Iscoy Asteroid Belt, and unless we drew attention to ourselves in some overt way, we could masquerade as part of the dusty mass of rocks, some of which were big enough to be moons.

Beside me, Quen rasped, "All this time, you were right . . ."

Though I'd expected to be happier, the win was cold as dead meat. "To tell you the truth . . . I was hoping I was crazy."

Through a haze of asteroid dust and the obscuration of larger asteroids rolling along with us in the flow of the belt, *Zingara* huddled with only docking thrusters to keep her from drifting into sight of the enemy.

I had the upper hand now. They trusted me again. Damned sour victory it was, too.

From behind me, Massus quietly suggested, "Maybe they're staying here . . ."

"No, they're not staying here," I said. "There's not enough living space for all the people on all those ships. It's got to be just a way station."

"On the way to us?" Othien wondered.

Offering him a supportive glance, I said, "That's what I suspect. A civilization like this doesn't stab in the dark. They must've sent advanced scouts around the sector. They know where the pockets of population are. They'll be heading toward us sooner or later."

A movement beside me made me step sideways, but then an unwelcome form caught my attention: Totobet. I slithered away from her, not wanting to be close.

She was moved past me by two crewmen and brought before Quen.

"Are these your people?" Quen asked her.

"Yes," she said. No reason to lie, apparently.

"Is Kay right about what your people do?"

Totobet gazed out at the ships of her civilization, and the remains of a battle from which she too had escaped. "About what we do, yes. Not why we do it."

"And are you on your way to our sector?"

She looked at him. "I have none of that information for you. I know only we go where people can live, and we take their place."

"All our troubles," Zell uttered suddenly, "the politics, the warranters . . . the TCA, Sasaquon, us . . . none of it matters anymore because we're about to be wiped out."

Quen started to say something else, but Massus burst forward in his torment and clawed at Totobet, stopped only by the rail around the deck well and two of his own shipmates, who drove him back a judicious step.

"No!" I shouted abruptly, stepping in front of Totobet. "It's not her fault. Not personally, anyway." With an extended hand, I held off the surge of angry crewmen for whom Massus's anger was contagious. "If what she told me is true, they can't even begin to make peace. They can't make friends or treaties with anyone. Within a couple generations, they're everywhere—eating resources, taking up room . . . Sooner or later there's got to be a fight. Nobody would even want them around."

"How do you know all this?" Zell asked.

"I've seen it before," I told them.

Zell rounded on Totobet, grasped her by the shoulder, and shouted, "Tell us how to stop you!"

"No, Zell!" Ruvan came to life beside Quen and pushed Zell back.

Ruvan actually getting physical? What was this?

"Don't hurt her," the medic said. "She's pregnant."

I shoved my way between them again. "She's what?"

"Pregnant."

"How pregnant!"

The medic gave me a very strange expression and said, "Extremely. She's going to have seven babies."

Oh, now, hadn't I heard enough for one lifetime? Didn't I have enough to deal with? Agony, agony. Seven?

Seven babies?

I grabbed Ruvan's arm. "*When* is she going to have them?"

"Oh, I don't know . . . months, yet. I've never seen anything like her before. But a few months, I think."

Stepping back, I looked at Totobet with this new information in mind and wondered where she was hiding this interesting turn of facts. True, she was thick at the waist and wide at the hips, and she wore that heavy smock-like tunic; if she had months to go, I guess it was possible.

"That won't save her," Massus growled. "If her people come after us and we can't do anything about it—"

Staying between him and Totobet, I put a hand on his shoulder and pushed him back a little. "Stop that," I said passively. "I think I know how to stop them. Quen, please—"

Quen motioned to the two crewmen who had brought Totobet to the main deck. "Take her back. Stand a guard. Ruvan . . . keep her comfortable."

"As soon as you're comfortable," Ruvan said, and refused to leave with the guards and Totobet. Instead he stayed, keeping a firm grip on Quen's arm.

"You were telling the truth this whole time," Quen said roughly, and it took a few seconds to realize he was speaking to me. "We're finished . . . I wish you hadn't told us."

"If I hadn't, they would still come." I flinched stupidly as an asteroid passed very close over our heads, forgetting for an instant that the view was only a tile screen vision and the body of the ship was still around us, protecting us from hits. "We *can* fight," I went on. "The trick is going to be convincing the TCA and their fleet and all the warranters to band together, fire up the boilers, and face the Menace when they show up."

Weakly he asked, "Lucas, is this recording?"

From somewhere in the crowd of crewmen, Lucas responded, "Yes . . . I've got it all."

"All—all these—" Quen started to speak, but then grasped the well rail and endured a harrowing wrack of pain.

Zell stepped to his side and made sure he didn't hurt himself further by falling, but there was no help for him or any of us. The crew watched him in undisguised empathy and worry—worry for him, worry for all of us and our future.

When he regained some control, our young captain looked up again with tired eyes and scanned the doomful armada.

"All these ships . . . they can go in the void without a kick?"

"Oh, yes," I confirmed. "They're fully flight-independent intragalactic interstellar vessels. See those elongated pods on the undersides and on top? Those are warp nacelles. They can go wherever they want, stop where they want, and start up again. No solar source required."

"Incredible," Massus murmured.

The rest of the crew was stunned absolutely silent by the concept. Silent and very obviously afraid.

There was something ominously endearing about that—despite the fact that they were all men, and all young, they didn't have a problem displaying that they were just plain scared. I liked that. It was honest. They'd still do their work, they'd fight if necessary and even die, but they wouldn't bother with any false bravado.

"We can't stay," Quen decided, which was a great relief to us all. "We have to go home and warn everyone. Massus, get ready to charge the tiles for another light kick."

"It'll take days," Massus complained. "If we can't get any closer than the belt, we'll have to make three or four passes."

"We don't dare leave the belt," Zell said. "We'll be seen by those . . . those people."

"Just charge up," Quen told them. "We can't just float here forever. Zell, anybody without a specific duty should sit down and stay calm. Don't attract any attention. No hull lights . . . no emissions. We've got work to do. We have to go home."

Without a word, Massus cast him a frightened glance, yet I could tell he was already working out the bleed-off in his engineer's mind. Soon, I hoped, his work would consume him and overcome that fear. I hoped that for the whole crew.

Yet we had days of charge-up and then another nine-day light kick ahead of us, during which all this would distill.

As the numb crew began slowly to disperse, another wave of agony swept over Quen. He faltered against Zell, unable to stand up anymore, even with the splints. Ruvan and Zell together managed to keep him from falling and harming himself further, but clearly his time on deck had run out.

"Othien," I spoke up, "bring that bench over here."

It was the first order I'd given in days, and it felt great. The fact that Othien did what I told him and nobody countermanded me, not even Zell, proved that I was once again the deck boss of my watch.

"If you lie him down on this," I suggested, turning to Zell, "we can carry him back to the infirmary. He won't have to strain himself."

From his expression, I could tell that Quen didn't like the idea, but also that pure anguish was working his resistance out of him. He made no protest as Ruvan supervised the process of laying his captain down properly on the plank.

By the time Quen lay upon the bench, ready to be carried back to his slant-board, he was worn out.

Zell gave an order to carry him away, but Quen caught Zell's arm and pulled him down to one knee beside him.

"One thing's certain," Quen weakly said, "we need a captain who's not bedridden."

The first officer shook his head. "No, Quen—a leader is his brain, not his body."

"I know that . . . I can run a small-cuff salvage, maybe, but I can't command battles, not like this." He gripped Zell's sleeve and gave it a gentle shake. "I'm on medication for pain, for infection, for respiration . . . other things I don't even know about. I'm awake, but I'm not sharp. I can feel it. Ruvan can't take me off the drugs or I'll die. Or the pain would be too much. I'm foggy, I'm tired, weak . . . and part of the Captain's Pledge is to admit it. We've got to have a vote."

"I don't want to have a vote." Misery rolled across Zell's face.

Dogged by the internal gnawing of his injuries, Quen rasped, "It always comes eventually, you know that. Nobody's captain forever." Resisting broken spirits, which would've been worse than fatal, Quen kept his composure in front of his crew and smiled tightly. "You set it up. When you're ready, we'll vote. It's just a formality, then you can take over."

I knew what that last part meant. There was no competition, no other candidate to consider but Zell. Of course not, he was first mate. On a Starfleet ship, there would be instant succession, without the "formality" of a vote. Things were different here. This ship was run like the old-time pirate ships on Earth, where the captains were elected or deposed by the crew. Suddenly a completely unexpected thought rammed through my skull and took root.

"Captain," I interrupted.

The sound of my voice actually surprised even me. I hadn't intended to speak up.

Everyone looked at me. Zell in particular glared harshly. My revelations had ruined his universe.

Keeping my voice down, I eased my body language too. Shoulders sagging a little, chin down, hands clasped unthreateningly in front of me.

"Zell deserves the job," I said, "if all we have to do is continue as warranters or even face the TCA fleet. But the goal is much more complicated. We have to do a lot of convincing over the next few weeks. We have to take recordings of all this and distribute them to everyone who will look. We have to unify a whole culture and reorganize battle readiness. With all respect—and I do respect you and I respect Zell very much—I'm best qualified to do those things. I'll do them either way, of course . . . I'll stand by *Zingara,* no matter who's in command. But you don't get anything in life you don't ask for, and that includes challenges. I have experience no one in the Omian sector has, not even Sasaquon. When the crew decides to have the vote for commanding officer . . . I'd like to be considered."

Seventeen

"APPROACH! ZELL, APPROACH! THEY SAW US! ZELL! THEY'RE COMING over here!"

So much for a moment's excuse for peace.

Quen was barely back in the infirmary when Lucas shouted the terrible warning that the Menace had spotted us, even in the shroud of the asteroid stream.

The ship coming up on us was huge beyond description, easily two hundred times the size of *Zingara,* and we weren't primarily a combat ship. It wasn't as if we were a stinger-fighter or a destroyer or a high-endurance attack vessel that could take on a more powerful ship even if it were something big and cumbersome. In fact, we didn't have anything going for us, battle-wise.

And the Menace was turning to attack. On several tile panels, screens popped on, reading firing solutions and showing increased energy production on the big ship. Didn't need to be an expert to know what that meant.

Lucas stood up from his screen and stared up at the monster on approach. "We're dead."

Clearly he saw in his mind what everyone saw: another wreck floating about in this space, cut to pieces relentlessly and with great experience.

Zell stared up, too. He didn't know what to do, either. I couldn't fault him for it. This ship was utterly outmatched, unable to fight, unable to run.

His voice was rough and shuddering. "Man the turret guns," he attempted, dry-mouthed. "Power up for maneuver . . . mark the rackers and . . . Levan, take the helm stanchion . . . thrusters on maximum . . . Somebody . . . somebody watch the rod levels."

He sounded less like a captain designing a red alert than a mortician designing an autopsy.

I couldn't let this happen. I'd promised to serve this ship, and that would be hard to do if there wasn't a ship here to serve, wouldn't it?

The Menace ship was almost on us. It was still miles, but the size of the vessel itself made that distance negligible.

Moving to the middle of the deck, I rather loudly claimed, "I got us into this. I can get us out."

Zell spun to face me, as fiercely as a man about to launch a barroom brawn. "Get us out how?"

"First we have to clear the asteroids," I said as the ship powered up around us, and the crew ran to their quaint version of battlestations.

"Leave the protection of the belt?"

"The belt'll be our grave if we don't get clear. We can't dodge asteroids *and* fire from that ship. We've got to power up for a jump—"

"We can't make a light jump," Massus challenged. "It would take hours to charge up the tiles! And we can't possibly outrun that thing!"

"We have to get out in order to charge up," I said, "and we have to be clear to shoot. We have to get out of the asteroid belt."

Shuddering with bitter resentment and who knows what else, Zell ground out his order. "She's right. We have to be able to shoot. Clear the belt."

As he and I stood in bald competition amidships, we were blanketed in the awful mutterings and desperate complaints of the crew . . .

"I knew I was going to die, but I at least thought I'd be home—"

"No one'll ever know what happened to us . . ."

"What good does this do us now?"

The Menace ship was getting closer. Zell turned and just stared at it. His attitude was one of misery as he gazed up there, like a man watching the guillotine being rolled out toward him.

"Are you giving up?" I asked.

He didn't look at me. "We're dead."

Clasping my hands behind my back as if I had all day, I stepped to him and looked up into his face. "If you've given yourselves up for dead anyway, then get out of my way. Am I going to make you deader?"

Lucas turned from his collection of screens again. "Zell, Quen wants to talk to you."

Zell stepped to Lucas's screens, one of which showed a schematic of ships' positions, and another which showed Quen's face against the cushion on his cot in the infirmary.

"They saw us?" Quen asked.

"We're in trouble," Zell gave by way of an answer. "No time to charge the tiles."

"Do whatever you have to," Quen told him. *"I'll stand behind any decision you make."*

That was clear. Quen was tersely communicating that he couldn't run a battle from a bed, just as he had said.

Tormented, Zell watched the Menace ship loom over us with its weapons ports glowing. "Kay—"

"Yes?"

"You know what to do?"

"I've got a couple of ideas."

"Take over."

"Thanks. Levan! Steer angle two-two-four under the prad! Wait, make it two-two-three."

Everyone in earshot turned and stared at me in horror, and at the helm poor Levan almost fainted. "That course doesn't make sense! It's a collision course!"

"What do you care? You're dead anyway. Steer the course."

Muttering something about his sisters and parents, Levan shook like a winter holly and steered the course I'd given him.

We surged out from the asteroids, took a stomach-wrenching dip, and came up under and behind the Menace ship and damned near rammed it. As one of the aft fins of the enormous ship sailed across our foreheads, Levan started to veer off.

"Hold that course!" I shouted. "Massus, plot a corridor groove and open the jeklights on the rod intakes. We can power up the cells for a light kick and get out of here."

"Are you crazy?" Massus shouted. "There's not enough sun way out here! We have to run or shoot or something!"

My hand sliced an abortive gesture between us. "No time to explain. You want to live? Do what I say!"

Enormous above us, like an elephant maneuvering beside a breadbox, the Menace ship was very clearly trying to come about, to keep us from getting a clear shot at their engine exhaust—a predictable battle maneuver, but *Zingara,* simply because we were smaller, was quicker. The Menace ship opened fire again, demolishing three of the king posts on our external salvage gear, and then we slipped behind them, out of the range of that particular weapons port—blessedly, because it was about to cut our whole bow off.

The *Zingara*'s automatic collision alarms went off, whooping at a fever pitch. Behind that noise, an overload bell from somewhere rang and rang, but that would have to be ignored.

Zell shouted, "Turret gunners, return fire!"

"I wouldn't bother," I muttered, but nobody heard me. Didn't matter. If they wanted to have the illusion of fighting back, no point stopping them.

Suddenly a bright sulfury wash blew over the whole vid screen, causing most of us to look away or shield our eyes.

"What is it?" Zell asked.

Massus fought with his controls. "We're in the wash from their main drive!"

"Massus!" I called. "Take the absorption safeties off!"

He looked at me, then at Zell, then back at me. "The tile safeties?"

"Yes! Take them completely off!"

"We'll be cooked!"

"No, we won't! We don't have to protect the ship because there isn't any sun. We can absorb energy almost instantly if there's a nonsolar source! I've been studying this! It's not all that different from the early-light technology where I come from. You've got the storage capacity, and the Menace has the source. Take the safeties off!"

Absolutely fuming, his fists balled and his legs locked, Zell glowered at me. "Take them off!"

A click, a surge, and suddenly all around us the interior tiles encrusting *Zingara* began to glow with anxious energy.

"What's happening!" Zell cried. "Why is this happening!"

Massus shouted his astonishment over the noise. "The tiles are swelling up with power directly off their drive wash! I've never seen the tiles swell so fast!"

"Don't overswell, whatever you do," Zell uttered, but he was watching the tiles for himself and didn't seem to think that was the big worry.

Ordinarily this powering process would take hours or even days, lurking as near a sun as was possible without being fried to a crisp, but here there was energy without the destructive solar violence. The tiles were sucking energy directly from the Menace's engines. What the hell—power was power.

"Levan," I called over the throb of power, "veer off and put us on a heading for home!"

"Veering off . . . heading locked in!"

"Next time listen to the old soldiers's stories," I said victoriously. "Never give up! Never give up until you're dead. Never give up and die. Don't go peacefully. Make them come and get you!"

Several men around me cheered in sudden awareness that we were instantly powered up for a light kick and we could get away. Even Zell grasped the well rail and pounded it in mute triumph.

I turned to Massus. "Are the fusion engines ready to take the start?"

"Ready!"

"Trigger the light kick! Let's go!"

The vid screen went dark, giving us a ceiling again, and almost immediately the tiles made their sudden drain, jump-starting the fusion engines to hyperlight speed.

From where we had been a moment ago, we were now gone.

As the tough old *Zingara* bolted to hyperlight speed and streaked away from an enemy against whom we could not possibly win, a crew who had thought themselves dead and decimated realized now that they could fight for their ship, for their lives.

"I want to talk to you."

In the dim confines of a bunk, starboard and forward on *Zingara,* away from the hum of the fusion engines that now carried us back toward our endangered sector.

Now that we were on the light kick, there was more to do, and the crew were using their hands to work out their shock. Part of that was shock that we'd lived through a confrontation with a Menace monstrosity. With everything running smoothly, if with a certain death-row resignation, I slipped forward to Totobet's bunk.

Without a word, the man guarding the door let me pass. Nobody stopped me from much of anything anymore.

Totobet raised herself on an elbow, saw me, then sat up on her bunk. "Thank you for defending me."

"I didn't defend you. I just kept my shipmates from turning into a mob. You're not worth that."

Sitting on the opposite bunk, I ticked away a few seconds, searching for a way to begin an impossible conversation.

"I just want to understand." I began finally. "Your people have a drastic overpopulation problem. Rather than try to control your number of conceptions, you go ahead and have the children, then expand to find room for them, and this is on a scale of hundreds of thousands. Right?"

She simply nodded.

"You've done this for a while, generations upon generations, using hyperlight ships. Has your technology advanced much since you started this interstellar assault?"

"Yes," she said. "We learn from those we must push aside, if we can. Sometimes there are ships left, buildings, businesses, laboratories . . . but we don't need much . . . We need only place."

"You need a scientific solution to conceiving so many babies. You haven't bothered looking for it, or you'd have found it already."

"We have looked."

"Not well enough. There are lots of ways for advanced beings to avoid conception."

"We can't avoid conception," she insisted mildly. Strange, I was arguing, but she wasn't. "That asteroid, the outpost there—"

"The Iscoy Asteroid," I snapped. "The people there were real living beings, not just targets with ground you needed. They were the Iscoy, and I liked them."

"The Iscoy Asteroid," she corrected willingly, "means a million of our young who don't have to die. My people will have that place now, and we make better use of area than anyone we've met."

"Anyone you've conquered."

"A million of us can live where two hundred thousand lived before. We're very thrifty. We can live a dozen where others live two."

"That's no justification. You're completely amoral and I despise you."

"I don't blame you."

"And I hate you for that too."

"I understand."

"Oh, shut up . . ." With a push to my feet, I started pacing, though there was scarcely room to take three whole steps.

Totobet watched me as I went back and forth, as if she knew I was trying to come up with some prosecution that she could not argue. Then I could declare her morally evil and somehow win.

"We've been driven back many times in our history," she said eventually. "When we're contained and can't expand, we are forced to revert—"

"—to devouring your own young," I blustered back at her. "The specter of your civilization gets uglier the longer I look at you."

She shifted her legs as if the stiffness of all these days were getting to her—no doubt it was—but she made no attempt to stand up because then she would be in my way.

"We're not stupid," she complained. "We know that someday we'll come up against a culture that can stop us. On that day, we'll probably all die. But until then, we expand."

Pausing to glare at her, I said, "I have trouble believing people like you will just go quietly into the night."

She shrugged one knobby shoulder under the soft tie of her tunic. "We won't like it . . . but this other culture who defeats us, they have to survive too. They can't just let us kill them. It's nature's way."

Something about her tone calmed me some. Her tone and her honesty about it all. Why couldn't she just be rapacious and without remorse? That would make things so much simpler.

"That makes rotten sense," I grumbled. "Your people aren't very creative. There's got to be some better way, some biological solution to this problem—"

"But we found a way to survive."

"You found a technological way. Have you kept up on your biological sciences? Have you kept trying to avoid conception?"

"We can't avoid conception. We must have mating. We must have birth. So I and my kind have to take place from others in order to have room. That's how things are."

I glowered fiercely at her, battling to keep from boiling over. " 'You and your kind'? 'Us and them'? That's how it is for you? Group mentality? Group rights? That justifies everything for you people?"

"It does for everyone, everywhere. It's natural to go with your own kind. Nature makes all life-forms at ease with others who look like them. Isn't that so where you come from?"

What could I do, argue with her? From alligators to elephants, she was right. From bacteria to skin color to religion, she was right. All life-forms of any level of development tended to cluster. It was natural, designed to be an aid to survival.

I hated that she was right.

"We have it," I allowed, "but we resist as much as we can."

"But you have it," she confirmed. She might be a mild individual, but she had no trouble facing me down on this. "You can scowl at me and hate me, but you have never faced this. Never faced starvation, anarchy, pestilence. Your culture has never contemplated mass-suicide. We considered it. That was when we made the lottery. We all accept it. You tell us we're wrong and immoral and we should find another way. What other way? This is the card nature dealt us. With the lottery, at least there is some chance that one or two of our children might survive out of each litter. This is how harsh nature has been on us . . . No other beings in the galaxy carry this burden."

A touch of indignation in her voice made me pause, and rightfully so. I'd failed in my moral duty to at least try to see things from their point of view. Perhaps it was a flaw of conflict—in order to be willing to fight, to kill, to win, it was normal to convince yourself that the other guy had no basis for his behavior.

"So you just give birth and drown the babies," I said. "Just get it over with, I suppose."

She gazed at me in a perplexed way, as if she didn't understand what I meant. Then she shook her head and I got the idea that I was the one who didn't understand, and she'd just figured that out.

"Oh, no," she said. "We can't kill them at birth. We have to keep them for many weeks. If a female doesn't give birth *and* nurse the babies for many weeks, she will die."

The berth fell to utter quiet. Only the soft hum of the fusion engines deep in the endless night. The cool room, the cool ship, seemed abruptly chillier.

I slowly lowered to sit on the bunk again. Empathy clawed at my heart.

"You mean . . . on top of this curse, you're required by physiology to get . . . attached to your babies? You have to take time to love them? Then you . . . That's . . . that's the cruelest thing I've ever heard."

"Very cruel. And hard," she agreed. "We've had to accept many hard things. To be completely evenhanded, and to keep parents from having to pick which of their children live and die, we invented the lottery."

"How long has this lottery been going on?"

"Four hundred of our years. Before that . . . we had a very ugly culture."

"I'll bet you did. You . . . your men . . . How do they handle all this?"

"The same as our women," she said with a little shrug. "We mate for life. Our men get as attached to the babies as our women. My husband was on one of the ships you saw."

"Are you a member of another ship's crew?"

"No, I just live there. We have to live in space, with each other, because we have to reproduce and nurse our children."

"One culture that has no choice for men and women but to ship out together, and another culture that never does. One that survives by never taking what's not theirs, and another that must take what's not theirs. The fabric of civilization is certainly tightly woven . . ."

Somehow at peace with all this, Totobet nodded sympathetically. How bizarre to sit here and see her sympathizing with me instead of the other way around, given the burden she and her people must bear.

We sat together in the oddest mutuality.

How had that happened? How had we gotten mutual?

Totobet watched me unthreateningly. After a while, she dug around in the heavy material of her sprawling dress and found what was apparently a big pocket hidden in the blanketlike fabric. She pulled a kind of thick notebook out, about five inches by three.

"You're the only person I know on this ship," she began again. "Although you hate me and I understand why, I think you're a good person. Would you help me with something?"

Now what?

She unsnapped the notebook's cover. Inside was an accordion-folded stream of laminated squares that fell out across her knees and went all the way to the deck. I tilted my head to see what was inside the laminate—

Pictures. Photographs. Little portraits. Big puppylike eyes set in lilac-moon faces.

"These are my litters," Totobet said, turning the stream of photos toward me. "My babies."

Oh, no. Somebody shoot me.

I slipped my hand under the trail of portraits. The faces of babies gazed back at me, so real I expected them to blink and make little noises.

"All these are . . ."

Totobet nodded. "Dead."

"But there are . . . ten, twenty, twenty-three children here. Are you telling me that . . ."

She nodded again, slowly, and gazed at the pictures. "I haven't been lucky in the lottery."

Why had I come to this stupid sector? Why had I accepted captaincy? Why had I signed up for Starfleet Academy? Why couldn't I just go home and, and . . . and—shoot myself?

Totobet ran her middle finger over some of the tiny mouths on the pictures, a distinctive mother's touch that only a brick wall could mistake for anything less. "Will you take these pictures and help me with remembering?"

I could barely speak. "Remembering?"

"It's the only way we have to honor their little lives. We give away pictures and help each other remember."

"Yes . . . yes, I'll help you remember them. Believe me, I'll never forget."

Anguished, hoping to get this over with, I started to hand the pictures back, but she pressed my arm away. "Don't give them back. We think that's a terrible insult. I know you don't realize."

With a stone in my stomach, I sat on the bunk, holding twenty-three babies. Most cultures with a pattern of abortion or infanticide did everything to forget that the children ever existed and that their lives were somehow less than precious.

"My babies that I'm carrying now," Totobet said, "if I die, will you take them back to my husband?"

I looked up sharply. "If you die? Why would you die?"

"Sometimes women die."

"Oh . . . yes, of course."

"I'd like to teach you their names, so you can remember. 'Tulu, Tessalit, Tamchaket, Totobet, Tishikot, Tippi, Tobarra."

Utterly wilted, I just stared at her. The babies weren't even born, but they were already named. My eyes hurt.

A nervous smile cracked my face. "Tippi?"

She blinked and smiled back at me. "It was my husband's mother's name. Now you say the names. Tulu . . ."

"Tulu . . ."

"Tessalit . . . Tamchaket . . ."

One by one we repeated the names of her unborn children. My voice was almost gone, my throat closed up so tightly that I could barely breathe.

Cursed with multiple births *and* a strong parental instinct, how could they keep from going insane? A culture that has to demolish its young would develop traditions like remembering if it didn't want to break down into anarchy. Or maybe it was even simpler than that. Maybe they just weren't the horrible race I'd thought they were. Stop the presses . . . maybe I was *wrong*.

As the names of her children rolled and rolled in my head, I forced up some very gravelly words. "I've misjudged your people."

"Do you have children?" she asked.

Uneasily, I glanced at her. "No . . . well . . . In a way, I guess I did . . ."

"What were their names? I can help you remember."

"Oh . . ." An unexpected smile trembled across my lips. "Well, all right . . . Chakotay . . . Paris . . ."

"Chakotay, Paris."

"Kim . . . Seven . . . Tuvok . . . Neelix . . . B'Elanna . . ."

She repeated the names, and before I knew it we were working our way down through crew members on *Voyager*—a dozen, another dozen—and then my voice trailed away. The weight of this ritual was too much for me.

"You have a big family," she told me, and she nodded in the strangest, most complete understanding I'd ever seen.

The most extraordinary thing occurred then. Totobet reached out for me, and I reached to respond. She gathered me into her arms and we met in the middle of the berth, sinking to the deck on our knees. Together we dissolved into a sobbing clutch.

Many long seconds trailed away as we crouched together, and the more we cried, the more we couldn't stop crying.

Into her ear I gulped, "Who are you? What do you call yourselves?"

So quietly that I could scarcely hear, Totobet squeaked, "Lumalit . . . Lumalit . . ."

The syllables spun from her lips like a strain of music from a harp. Such a beautiful, melodic word. They weren't the Kazon or the Klingons or the Cardassians, where the harshness of the word gave clues as to their ingrained disregard for others. They were a culture forced to kill their own beloved children in order to survive. They were the Lumalit . . . they loved their children. They understood their enemies. They were complex. They were sad. They were resigned.

My grip on Totobet tightened as sobs that should've come through me months ago came through me now. In my arms she shuddered and poured out her own misery. In her hand was one end of the laminate stream of photos of her babies, and in my hand was the other end. We held her children together and were utterly consumed with grief for her lost family, and for my lost family.

In the mild therapy of her desperate culture, Totobet began to murmur against my ear.

"Tulu . . . Tessalit . . . Tamchaket . . ."

Eighteen

"ZELL? YOU WANTED TO SEE ME?"

For two days we had bolted along on our light kick, heading back to an endangered sector, knowing that the Menace—the Lumalit—now knew we had seen them. The nature of a light kick caused us to head off in the very direction of our civilization. There had been no way to hide that. The fatal flaw was that, now that they'd seen us and we'd pointed the way home, even if they hadn't known we were there, they sure knew it now.

I didn't like that part. I didn't like aiding the enemy, even unwillingly, and I didn't like forcing the confrontation early, but that's what might have just happened.

Hell, at top warp, they could probably still beat us home.

All I could hope for was that the Lumalit weren't quite ready for another conquest yet. There was no way to know or even guess.

Totobet and I had had a good old-fashioned cry, and because of that I felt much stronger and much better directed. I had a very clear goal now—to stage a war, then trump the inevitable.

The commanding officer on my watch had summoned me, and here I was, meeting Zell in the quiet of the processing deck. The huge winches and cables around us were a strangely peaceful forest, even providing a trickling stream of spilled lubricant down the center of the deck.

Zell was sitting on a crank casement, his elbows on his knees, staring at the deck.

"It's not an easy job," he said, "being captain. You don't know much about salvaging. You don't even know the names of the other warranter ships or their captains . . . There are things about this ship you don't even know yet."

Without going into the overview of my past, I asked, "Are you trying to talk me out of running?"

He looked up. "Yes, of course I am. It's bad for the ship. You're not ready."

I'd have accused him of something else, of looking out for himself, but something about his expression stopped me.

"It's bad for the crew," he said. "You haven't been here very long. The rest of us, we've been together half our lives. We've been through everything together. We know each other better than our mothers know us. You've done good things around here, sometimes . . . Other things we don't like so well. Some people like you, and others think you're dangerous. But I'll tell you this . . ." He looked up now. "You don't have the votes. I know this crew. You can't win. By running for captain, you're dividing a crew that's never been divided on anything. Is there some way we can avoid this?"

Folding my arms, I paced away from him and back, then stood looking at the deck and playing with the lubricant puddle with my toe.

"I'd love to avoid it," I said. "But I took the Pledge. I promised to do what's best for the ship. This vote is not the worst thing for the ship. Not even close. Whatever you think, I'm not casually trying to depose you. I actually think you're a very good commanding officer. We haven't agreed on everything, but that's not required. But I know things you don't know. I have training you don't have. I even know things about your technology that you haven't figured out yet. A decision like this shouldn't be up to the crew, in my opinion, but if that's how this ship runs, I'll accept that. I don't think it's in the ship's best interest for me to withdraw, or I sure would. When the vote comes, we'll see what happens."

Zell rubbed a big hand over his face and sighed, then stood up. "We'll see now. Quen's called a crew meeting."

"Now?"

"Right now."

"Kay, you talk first."

Quen motioned weakly from the cot that had been moved out on the main deck for him. Apparently it was customary for all the crew to be present, excepting anyone who was unconscious or simply couldn't be moved. Quen almost fell into that latter category, but he insisted on being here, so here he was.

Here they all were, looking at me.

Over there, Zell stood between Massus and Lucas, leaning uneasily back on the transverse bulkhead with his arms folded and his ankles crossed. I got the feeling he'd have sat down if he'd thought it wouldn't look bad. It would.

Truly regretting what I thought was my duty, I stepped to a point amidships where most of the crew could see me. And I started talking.

"I've only been here a matter of months, I know that . . . I don't want to be your captain. When it comes down to time served, I don't deserve to be yet. Considering what we all saw two days ago, things are not normal. The fact is, you need me. This isn't salvage we're going into. It's either a confrontation with the TCA fleet for which the warranters haven't prepared, or it's a full-out war for your civilization's survival. Either way, I know how to do it and you don't."

Now I paused and raised my eyes, scanning the crew and trying to make contact with each of them in some small way.

"I'm a trained battle captain. I've been a commodore in two engagements. That means I've commanded more than just the ship I was on. I know how to coordinate several vessels. What we're facing is big, too big. I'm trained to face it and you're not. Believe me, right now I'd rather retreat to some quiet planet, put in earplugs, and start a garden. That's not . . . very good citizenship, though. The fact is, this is bigger than *Zingara* and bigger than everybody. The Mena—the Lumalit people have a huge problem, and the worst part is that they can't be allowed to slaughter other people's children so theirs can survive. It just can't be allowed. This is the nastiest situation I've ever faced."

Some of the crew shifted nervously. I gave them a moment to compose themselves and took the time to draw a long steadying breath.

Then I forced myself to go on, aware of how very unwillingly my soul tagged after.

"Please . . . understand this," I told them. "If you decide to elect Zell—and I think he deserves it very much—and you decide to march into the cannon's maw, I will march there with you. I took the Pledge and I'll absolutely stand by him. Whichever of us you elect, you must understand what's coming."

Deliberately, I didn't look at Zell. That would be uncalled for, cruel, competitive. It might even be taken as theatrical or calculated. I didn't want to take the slightest chance of anyone's misinterpreting my motives.

Changing my posture a little, I rubbed my chilly hands, gazed briefly at the deck, then looked up again.

"There are times in every civilization's history when there's no way to survive playing by the rules you're used to. You have to step outside. We have to suspend the normal way of doing things and take the only chance we have. We've got to adapt our technology to fight a very powerful force.

I've got a few ideas and they might work. Now, I'm not a politician making a speech and promising things I can't deliver. I don't know if we can win. This may be the death of the sector coming on. But if we play it right and don't squander the chance, we might not only survive but prevail. You might finally be free. This is a momentous time in history—a time when you, a handful of people, hold the fate of civilization in your grasp. You've taken incredible risks for so long . . . take one more."

Was there an echo in here? Why were my words rolling and rolling?

Some of the crew were staring at me, others refusing to look up. All were listening to my words again in their minds.

After a long pause, Quen gingerly turned his head to Zell.

"Your turn," he invited.

Zell scanned the crew, gave me a very brief glare, then gave a longer one to Quen that had some underlying communication in it. Quen offered a spontaneous grin without much cheer, but with a lot of support.

Slowly Zell pushed off the bulkhead but didn't unfold his arms. What would he say? And did it matter? These men had invested their whole lives in Quen and Zell, had trusted them for years and were still alive, still surviving, because of them. Whatever they had, it worked for them.

As the crew waited to hear what he had to say, Zell cleared his throat. Very resignedly, he let his arms fall to his sides. He never quite looked up.

"All of you who were going to vote for me," he said slowly, "vote for her."

Nineteen

"I, KATHRYN JANEWAY, ACCEPT THE POST OF COMMANDING SHIPMATE OF THE *Warranter Zingara.* I accept that this oath incorporates and assumes the Ship's Pledge. I accept the duty of judgment over any shipmate who violates the Pledge. I will administer justice according to the Pledge. I will remain captain until my crew releases me from my obligation. I swear that this obligation supersedes any previous oaths or obligations. I, Kathryn Janeway, so pledge."

With the exception of the pulselike murmur of the fusion engine carrying us in our light jump, the ship was eerily quiet.

I found Zell on the processing deck, sitting where he had been sitting the last time we talked, with his elbows on his knees again and his head in his hands. His eyes flicked a little when I came in, so he knew I was there, but he didn't change his position at all.

In a way that was nice—even he was comfortable enough around me not to put on any performances.

For a few moments we floated in comradely silence. Odd how much we seemed to understand each other now.

"I have a couple of ideas," I began finally. "We'll be back in two days. We should come out of the kick with a plan of action ready to implement. The first thing we should do is attract attention to ourselves as a signal to the TCA that things have changed."

"How?"

"Well, by creating a lot of sparkle and panic by bludgeoning automated outposts and maybe some TCA factories."

"Mock attacks?"

"Oh, hell no, real ones. Just very specifically targeted, with a bigger goal than just the destruction. It'll remind the TCA just who fought and won their war, and it'll focus public attention on the warranters. We'll need that."

"What do you want me to do?" he asked.

"We'll need a distribution network for our recordings of the Menace armada. As soon as we come out of the kick, we should fire off about a thousand copies of the recordings. You supervise making the distribution plan. Other warranter ships, media sources, TCA captains—"

"TCA captains?"

"Yes. Don't forget, there's a fleet."

"Oh . . ."

"You'll have to be ready to pin down the locations of any TCA ships in our range and broadcast that recording. I'll make a video introduction to what the problem is as I see it, a recording of Tobobet explaining very briefly the problem her culture faces and what they do about it, and then I'll narrate what we saw in Iscoy space, including a description of antimatter modes of power. Now, I need your advice . . . I think I'm overstepping propriety by narrating the recording myself. Do you think it'll be taken as grandstanding? I don't want to make the wrong impression. I'm not really out to make any impression of myself. I think Quen should do it."

Shifting his legs, he gazed at the deck.

"Quen should make the introduction," he suggested. "You should narrate the recording and explain the modes of power."

"All right, I can work with that. We have to be ready with something to give our armed forces, so they will be ready to fight the Lumalit."

He glanced up. "If this Lumalit Menace managed to destroy a force superior to ours, what can we do about them?"

My arms tightened around my ribs. "I think I've got that figured out. It's an old trick. Shields have to cover a huge band, a wide range of frequencies in order to protect against a range of destructive power. If you know your enemy's frequency, you could calculate its maximum, then concentrate all your shields to that, and make your shields seem almost invincible. It would give you a hell of a surprise advantage."

Looking like a shrunken doll, Zell nervously asked, "How do we beat that?"

"Well, if you're using energy weapons and you know ahead of time, you phase the frequency shift, and suddenly it's as if they have *no* shields. The Iscoy didn't have the technology to recognize that. You don't, either. They've been stomping whole civilizations because their shield trick hasn't been figured out. I've figured it out because my civilization came up against a group of beings called the Borg who could figure out what we were firing at them, and adapt so they couldn't be hurt. It's basically the same kind of trick. The Lumalit shields must have huge gaps. I know that because of their power consumption—well, never mind about that. In the Federation, nobody would get away with that trick for long because we all communicate. In this quadrant, though, with so many unaligned cultures, word doesn't get around . . ."

My words fell away and I stopped for a moment. There wasn't any point in scolding him about how his science hadn't caught up to mine yet. Really, that was never in my mind, but suddenly I was aware about how such things sounded. Zell didn't deserve this. Nobody here did.

I forced myself to change tack.

"They must be sending scouts ahead and analyzing weapons capabilities, then presetting their shields to those frequencies. You see, they weren't generating enough power to do what it looked like they were doing. If their shields were preset to be frequency-specific, then it made them seem a lot more powerful than they were. It gave teeth to their surprise attack. They've probably done the same thing to this area. They probably already know about our missiles and anything else we've got. But there's one thing they don't know—"

"That you're here," he handed out.

"Right. We need to use something they're not expecting at all, and hardshells won't do the trick. We need a wide-spectrum quantum discharge."

"What's that mean?"

"Mostly, it means spending the next forty hours or so finishing my experiments on the tiles."

Zell sat upright. "You mean, like what hurt Quen? Like *that?"*

"We have to be creative, Zell. We've got to have a computer program already on curry cards and ready to interface with any compatible system, any ship, any armed station on any planet. There won't be time for people to do what I have in mind. We have to let the computers do it all. I'll need one full watch crew for that, so we'll have to call all hands on deck. The on-watch crew will handle the ship, a second crew will work with me on the quantum discharge, and I want Lucas to head a team that will extend the capabilities of our long-range sensors. When the Lumalit come in, I want to know ahead of time."

"Lucas doesn't know how to do that."

"I've already told him how."

"Oh . . ." He leaned forward again and gazed at the deck, soaking up all this. "You'll need to know how the external gantries work and how to get them out of the way quickly. Jedd can show you that. And you should have

Levan or Othien explain the markers and signals we use on the grooves and corridors."

I tilted my head. "We're going into a battle situation. We won't need the usual signal and corridor rules."

He looked up briefly. "You'll need to know them so you'll know how to break them."

A trickle of embarrassment ran down my spine. "Mmmm . . . That's a pretty sad comment on how well you're getting to know me . . ."

"Didn't mean anything."

"I know you didn't."

Pacing off a few steps, half my brain working on all the things I suddenly had to learn in order to be captain of this ship, to deliver all the things I'd said were possible. Now that I had command, before me rose a mountain of surmountables.

I'd forgotten about that. Becoming captain didn't mean the height of knowledge or the pinnacle of accomplishment; it was in fact just the beginning of the learning process. Suddenly a restful sleep was a joke. There wasn't anywhere to shift any burden. Far from knowing everything, I now had to seek out those who knew and use their abilities to the best service of the ship and our purpose. Everybody here knew more than I did about *Zingara,* the warranters, and the culture I had adopted. This was not a time of lofty victory for me. It was a time of numbing humility.

Moving back to Zell, I paused, but not so close as to intimidate him in any way.

"I never wanted to be the captain," I told him honestly. "They'd have voted for you."

He scratched his head and sighed.

"They did what I told them," he muttered. "I got only two votes. Quen's . . . and yours." A mirthless chuckle jogged his shoulders. "Even I didn't vote for myself."

I offered a nominal smile. "What you did was uncommonly noble. You could've easily been captain."

Zell didn't look up. One shoulder moved in a small shrug.

"I took the Pledge," he said.

LIVE FREE OR DIE!

State slogan of New Hampshire

It was the forty-fathom slumber that clears the soul and eye and heart, and sends you to breakfast ravening.

— *Captains Courageous*

Twenty

"THE LUMALIT SHIELDS ARE FREQUENCY-SPECIFIC. THEY WON'T BE ABLE TO block more than five percent of a total wash. That's how we take them by surprise. They won't expect us to be able to blow through their shields. This discharge'll go right through."

"What are you going to use as a housing for this? Missiles?"

"Missiles are pretty fragile. But a ship isn't."

"Not . . ."

"No, not *Zingara,* don't worry. We'll tow a wreck in and use it. As long as it has the tile technology—"

"All the ships around us have tiles."

"Right, of course."

Massus, working at his engineering post before the aft transverse bulkhead, turned and called, "Kay, the engines are about to shut down from the light kick. We're almost back."

"Is the boarding party ready?"

"They're ready."

I turned to the crew and raised my voice. "Boys, this is it. Let's see how well we've learned our new tricks. Zell? Do your stuff."

With a dubious glance at me for last-second support, Zell cleared his throat, drew a tight breath, and tried his new trick.

"Orange alert!" he called.

With a quick laugh, I corrected, "Yellow!"

"*Yellow* alert! All hands to battlestations!"

• • •

"Engines are down. We're out of the kick!"

"Lucas, long-range sensors on."

"Long-range sensors . . . on."

"Massus, adjust engines for sublight."

"Adjusted."

"Say 'engines sublight, aye.' "

"Oh . . . engines sublight, aye."

Lucas suddenly turned. "Kay, there's a ship in our path!"

I leaned over his shoulder and looked at one of the tile screens that showed our ship approaching another. "Oh, well, there's a shock. The *Aragore.*"

"You want the overhead vid on?"

"No, too distracting. We'll just use the small screens. I don't want anybody craning his neck when he should be doing his job."

Zell appeared about twenty feet down deck from me. "You won't be able to see as much."

"We'll see enough. Everybody clear on what to do if he won't get out of the way?"

Around the deck, the fully mustered crew made anxious but purposeful shifts and nods, moving to their positions, keying on their tiles, testing their systems, making sure they were ready.

"Don't be nervous, anybody," I told them. "He's not scary enough."

Lucas turned his pale face to me. "You're not worried?"

"About Sasaquon?" I huffed. "He's the smallest potato around. Go ahead and hail him. Why wait?"

Tensely, he flattened his lips and touched the right tiles. A new screen appeared on a set of dark tiles. Sasaquon's communications man was standing there looking back at us.

"This is *Zingara,*" Lucas announced. "We want to talk to Sasaquon right now."

Without waiting for the formalities, Sasaquon shoved his comm guy aside and appeared on the screen. I moved next to Lucas to make sure Sasaquon could see me. Damn, that was a good-looking man. Why did he have to be a rat?

Not bothering with greetings, I asked, "How did you find us?"

"This is where you were last seen," he responded. *"You're all under arrest."*

"Arrest? Then you've decided to drop the act and stop pretending you're just another warranter?"

That one annoyed him. He scowled and demanded, *"Why are you talking for the ship? Where's Quen? I want to talk to him."*

"He's here. You'll have to talk to me."

"Is he dead?"

"No, he's not dead."

"Then where's Zell? Have you taken over that ship like you tried to do Aragore?"

Zell stepped up next to me so he was in the screen's capture range. "We've given her command, Sasaquon."

"Why would you? Is Quen dead?"

"We're making the best use of our crew's abilities. And Quen's not dead."

"You're moving in on us, Sasaquon," I said, making it clear that there'd be no sneaking up. "This is fair warning—don't get too close."

"I'm coming in to cable you. Your engines will be shut down and you'll be towed in under my authority."

"You a gambling man, Sassie?"

"What?"

"You'd better get out of my path. This civilization's way of doing business is all done."

"Why are we done?"

"Because I'm here now and I'm not letting this go on."

Even over the brushed surface of the tiles, with the grid of adhesive etching his face, Sasaquon's anger virtually glowed across space.

"Who are you to say?" he demanded.

How gratifying it was that I remained a mystery to him, that my presence in this sector and certainly my authority on this or any ship utterly confused him. The rules were changing and he didn't know what they were—what a grand advantage.

But that wasn't the answer. My answer was much better, far more satisfying to me.

"I'm the one that's here," I told him with firm and fiery conviction. "I'm the one who accepted command of a ship and said I'd use it to change things for the better. I'm the captain."

Around me the crew of *Zingara* bristled with underlying pride so crisp that I could feel it and was bolstered by their confidence.

"You're too late," Sasaquon said. *"Oran's gathered up all the warranters. They've formed an assault unit, and they're attacking our planet."*

With a single clap of my hands, I glanced around at my crew. "Hear that, everybody? The warranters are standing down the TCA's hired guns!"

A rallying cheer trumpeted through space over the comm lines.

Without waiting for the sound to fade, I said, "Sasaquon, you've got to move aside. We have critical information about an incoming armada. We've got to get to the planet. Whatever the political differences are, they've got to be stopped. If there are heavy casualties to the warranters or the TCA, there won't be enough—"

"It's called the CASF now. Civilian Authority Space Force."

"You can call yourselves the Starfleet Space Hockey Team, for all I care. What's important is that you get out of my way. Move and move now."

"There's no point in resisting," he countered. *"The battle at the planet is almost over. The warranters are negotiating a surrender. The Space Force has them surrounded. Since you and your crew fomented this revolt, you're under arrest. Accept defeat gracefully."*

"All right, that's it. Here's my idea of grace. Gentlemen, we have a little change of plans here. Red alert."

Zell's voice boomed across the long deck. "Red alert!"

"Turret gunners, fire! Massus, release *all* cables—proximity range!"

"Approaching home space, Kay."

"Understood. Maintain red alert. Have our engineering team ready to get off Sasaquon's ship if things go wrong. Is Sasaquon's crew locked down over there?"

"They're all tied hands and feet and locked in their bunks."

"Have somebody take an armed unit and go untie their feet, walk them through the airlock conduit, put them on our processing deck, and tie them up again."

"I'll do it myself."

"That's a good idea."

My conversation with Zell was far from private, and that was how I wanted it. Much better for the crew to hear my thought process and know what I had in mind. In order to fulfill my plan of attack, we needed a derelict ship. We'd been willing to go look for one, but since Sasaquon cooperated so nicely, we'd just use his ship.

The *Aragore* was under tow and we were making repairs from a remarkably quick assault. We'd made a good bet: Sasaquon had some authority, but he was a bad captain. He didn't have the loyalty of his crew. Sasaquon and his crew were soldiers pretending to be warranters. They hadn't expected to come up against warranters trained to fight, but that's what they got when they tried to stop us. Unlike any other warranters, we'd been ready for them and not on the defensive. We went instantly on the attack. The crew of *Zingara* were already at battlestations and ready to go on the offensive. Our turret gunners were already targeted, and Sasaquon was utterly overwhelmed by the quick unexpected firing off of not only guns, but cables. Twenty cables, all thicker around than I was, shooting at once and acting like a giant butterfly net.

Sasaquon tried shooting back, but by the time he figured out that he should be shooting at our cable releases instead of our turrets, the job was done. *Aragore* was netted and reeled in, instantly brought too close to continue firing without doing damage to themselves. While they tried to cut our cables, we plugged in an airlocked conduit and boarded an armed party, which they certainly hadn't expected.

None of that was the remarkable part . . . and I confess I hadn't counted on this. Sasaquon's crew, faced with armed guards who they knew were fighting for the freedom of their planet, had weak stomachs when it came to cold-blooded slaughter of warranters.

Of course! I hadn't expected that—the soldiers of the TCA perfectly well knew the warranters weren't dangerous. When it came right down to blood and bone, they wouldn't back up the corrupt government Sasaquon represented. Despite Sasaquon's posturing, *Aragore*'s crew surrendered.

Now they were on their way to the belly of *Zingara,* to await trial in a court of law if we could push this civilization to actually go back to a rule of law.

Time would tell—very soon. We were almost to the planet. Now we had only the TCA itself to deal with.

Even before the planet came into view around its nearest moon, we could see the flashes of battle casting a halo on the moon's perimeter. Ugly recognizable flashes of missile detonation spiderwebbed through open space, carrying sparkling debris and hot shrapnel.

"This is it," I said to my nervous crew. "That's the TCA fleet and the warranters. We avoided a big problem with Sasaquon. We might not be able to avoid one here. Massus, release the *Aragore.* We'll leave it orbiting the moon until we need it."

"Releasing the *Aragore,* aye."

"Lucas, get that broadcast ready. All right, boys, we're going to go in fighting! Everybody ready?"

They let me know with a rolling cheer that they were ready to back me up, and even though the decibel level on the cheer left something to be desired, I took whatever I could get. This was a crew that had been battle-trained to my strange methods for mere days, not years or even months. They didn't even know the history of the methods I was telling them to trust, but they were willing to give me all they possessed.

"One-half sublight speed," I ordered, and gripped the well rail while watching the largest of the tile screens on the starboard side. "Lucas, put the main action on the large screen like I showed you."

Lucas was juggling nearly a dozen screens, but we'd stationed two other screen guys there to help him. He had trouble delegating and was still trying to handle it all himself. I didn't interfere. After a few minutes, he had no choice but to concentrate and let the others help him.

The screens readjusted as he worked them, and right about amidships appeared a single wide-angle view of the action in space. Maybe I was just more comfortable with this arrangement because it looked more like Starfleet viewscreens than the huge overhead vid capabilities of the tiles. Right now I needed something familiar.

There were at least thirty ships visible on the large amidships screen, the gaggle of warranters, whose ships were all slightly different from each other, and a collection of brand-new ships, much more streamlined and obviously sliced by the same cookie cutter.

"Look!" I said. "There they are! Those are the TCA ships . . . there's Oran!"

"The warranters are almost surrounded!" Zell gasped. "Sasaquon was right!"

"They're not surrounded," I told him. "Look more closely—that's a wedge formation. They're still very much in the fight."

Blasts of missile fire and ensuing detonation rang across space, setting the hulls of the warranters ablaze.

"They're taking so many hits—" Lucas blurted, his hands shaking as he tended the screen, flinching with every new detonation.

"Yes," I said, "taking hits and fielding them. Those warrant ships are old and tough. Look at the damage on the TCA ships' hulls; they must be made of newer alloy, but they've been made on a budget, or too fast or something. They're being punctured."

"They must be double-hulled, though," Zell offered. "There's no atmosphere venting."

I squinted. "Oh, am I glad you noticed that! Good work! Jedd! Can you hear me?"

From down in the engineering well, Jedd called back, "I hear you!"

"Keep our strongest hull plates to the TCA."

"I can do that."

"Kay!" Lucas called. "They're turning on us!"

As we rushed through space toward the planet and the battle between here and there, a half-dozen TCA ships wheeled to meet us and opened fire.

Zingara rocked with missile impact but didn't crack.

"Hold your speed until we're closer," I called over the boom and rattle of detonation. "Turret gunners, target those missiles and detonate them in space."

"Don't you want them to fire on the ships?" Zell asked.

"Not yet." I gripped his arm. "Go below and supervise the gunners yourself. Don't waste ammunition!"

Without a response, he vaulted the deck rail and disappeared down the well.

"Lucas!" I came around the well. "Hail every ship in this area."

"H-hailing," he stammered.

To his left, a small screen popped out of nowhere on some dark tiles and showed a picture of me as the other ships would see me: head and shoulders, little cape, pale complexion, shaggy auburn mop, and notably more gaunt than I remembered myself.

"This is Kathryn Janeway, commanding the *Zingara.* I'm addressing all Space Force vessels. The warranters are not your enemy. Your true enemy is on its way from a distant solar system with an attacking armada of matter/antimatter–powered hyperlight vessels. It's absolutely critical—"

A direct hit slammed the ship sideways under me, and I hit the deck on my side. The ship vibrated horridly for ten seconds, then steadied down. Othian hauled me to my feet and I tried to remember what I was saying. Even as I talked, the firing continued. The TCA ships shot at us and at the warranters. Oran's ship moved in to help defend us, but I had another mission in mind.

"It's imperative that the Space Force and the warranters join forces immediately before any more damage is done," I continued, nearly shouting over the bang and ring of impact. "I recommend that the TCA step down and call elections. This sector has got to organize right away. Where I come from, there was once a state in a nation, and that state has a motto we would all do well to heed today. Those words are 'Live free or die.' I'm willing to do that. So are all the warranters. I challenge all of you today to look at what we are sending you now, and make a decision worthy of people who deserve to live free."

I paused briefly to let my words carry across space, and to watch the ships shooting at each other and at us.

"Lucas," I finally said, "broadcast the recording of what we saw in Iscoy space. Make sure they can pick it up on any frequency."

"What if they—"

"Doesn't matter. Broadcast."

Enduring a pounding that hearkened back to the most brutal I'd ever experienced, we steeled ourselves and took the hits as Lucas desperately sent and re-sent the message we'd so hastily created. Would the TCA think it was a hoax? Such things could easily be faked. Would they believe Quen on the recording? Would they believe me?

"Kay! Kay!"

Keeping a grip on the rail, I spun around. "What? Who is that?"

"It's me . . . it's—"

"Gashan, yes, what are you yelling about?"

"Look at this!"

Taking a step every second or so, between rockings of the ship around us, I pulled myself across the deck to where Gashan was crouched beside a tile screen we'd been generally ignoring. Luckily, despite the attraction of the battle being played out so near to us, he wasn't ignoring his station.

"Look at the readings . . ." He ran his finger along a sensory graph that made a strange series of dots on the tiles.

I didn't need Gashan to explain to me. Long-range sensors. I'd upgraded them myself.

"It's an incoming force," I murmured, suddenly hoarse. "Damn them . . . they're early."

My chest constricted as if some great flame had sucked the oxygen away. I pressed my lips tight and forced myself to breathe through my nose, just to keep from panting in front of my crewmates. The Menace was coming—the Lumalit, coming to inflict the terrible necessities of their culture on these people.

With my hands trembling in fingerless gloves and my pulse tenor-drumming in my ears, I struggled back across the vaulting deck to Lucas's side.

Zell climbed halfway out of the well and said, "Rod levels are two over the prad, and we've got a halo on the chokes."

I motioned him to come up here. Perplexed, he climbed up quickly and joined me. With a significant glance, I motioned back across the deck to Gashan's long-range scanner. Zell looked at it briefly as if he didn't understand . . . and then he did.

His face dropped its ruddy color, and for a moment I thought he'd stopped breathing, but then he collected himself and stood beside me as we looked at the TCA ships and warranters moving on the main viewer.

There, as many of the crew gathered around us to observe the ships moving on the screen, we watched the action and fought a private battle, each in his own head, to keep from going mad from the noise and the tension. If the pounding kept up much longer, we would have to launch serious retaliation or we would be cracked like a stone on an anvil.

We took the pounding and watched more of the TCA ships maneuvering to attack us. The warranters turned, also. Oran's ship veered in to fire at the nearest TCA ship. He was defending us. In deference to Quen and the honorable actions of his brother, I would soon open fire.

Soon . . . a few more seconds . . . long enough for that broadcast to reach every ship . . . soon there would be no choice.

Oran's ship took a hard hit from the nearby TCA ship. A stream of liquid, possibly fuel or lubricant, sprayed from the port-side aft section.

That was it. I'd have to start cutting hulls. There was no time left.

"Zell," I began, "go below and tell the gunners to target the TCA point-blank, full missile power. Don't hold back . . . kill them."

Shuddering, he put his hand on the well rail and maneuvered to climb down again. I heard his breath rattle in his chest.

"Kay?" Lucas's voice barely sounded over the thrum of missile detonations.

I turned back. "Yes?"

"Look . . . on the other side of the warranters . . . those TCA ships aren't shooting anymore. What does that mean?"

Now it was my turn to stop breathing.

Zell reappeared at my side.

The crew gathered tighter around us. The bleeps and hums of the working ship seemed to echo like the inside of a living body as we watched the TCA ships—first one, then another, and another across inner space—began to cease-fire.

Twenty-one

"IT'S AN OLD TRICK. IT'S CALLED THE 'FIRE SHIP MANEUVER.' IN THE oceanfaring navies on my planet in the past, they'd pack a ship with combustibles. Sometimes they'd even include incendiaries or explosives. Then they'd set the ship ablaze and send it sailing into a cluster of enemy ships. Everyone at sea is afraid of fire. In space, it's the same . . . everyone's afraid of energy."

"Are you sure it'll go through a vacuum? Shouldn't we put a timer on it?"

"If the potential is high enough, nothing'll buffer it. It'll discharge automatically when *Aragore* gets close enough to other ships. We've got to pack the fire ship with so much charge that it's unequal when it comes in proximity with another source, and the charge'll jump very much like lightning. It should even discharge through the vacuum of space."

"If the potential is high enough."

"If . . . it's high enough."

Beside me, Massus let out a doubtful sigh. "Well, the engines are adjusted to feed all their energy back into the tiles instead of thrust. I hope this works the way you say it will."

"I hope so too."

We weren't on board *Zingara.* We were on *Aragore.* Sasaquon and his crew were in custody back on the planet and were now somebody else's problem. Massus and I, with a team of five engineers from *Zingara,* were turning *Aragore* into a giant grenade when a call came from our ship.

"Kay!"

"Kay here, Zell."

"You better come back! They're almost to us!"

"All right, we'll come back."

"But we're not finished!" Massus protested.

"We're finished enough," I said. "He's the first officer. I should take his recommendation. He's right. If the battle starts and we get trapped over here, we're all dead. We'll try to finish by remote. Is the trigger in?"

"Yes."

"Let's go. Get the others."

Through the magnetic boarding cuff, into the airlock, and back onto *Zingara* we went, having left the *Aragore* rafted up to us and loaded with readjusted mechanics. We were on our way at top sublight to meet the incoming Menace armada. The farther away from the core of population, the better. That would give us room to confront them, and room to fall back if necessary.

Aragore was a virtually gutted ship. We'd scrambled to remove all the food supplies, water, blankets, mechanical portables, and anything else we might need if things went drastically wrong. No sense burning up stuff that could come in very handy in a survival situation, but of course all that took time and we had very little. We got what we could as the armada drew closer and closer.

The armada had reduced to sublight for their final approach, expected procedure for an assault that thought nobody was waiting for it.

"Are they changing formation at all?" I asked immediately as Massus and I joined Zell on the main deck of *Zingara.*

"No changes yet," Zell said.

"How many ships?"

"We've counted sixty-four."

"And we've got . . ."

"Nineteen Space Force ships and eleven warranters."

"Hmm . . . well, Nelson did it at Trafalgar."

"What?"

"I'll tell you later. Release all but the spring cable on *Aragore.* Massus, test the remote triggers. Make sure they'll start those engines. In fact, never mind testing them. Go ahead and start the engines. Charge it up."

Zell grasped my arm. "You want to start charging the tiles over there while *Aragore*'s still rafted to us? What if the charge jumps to us?"

"Then we'll be fried like fillets. Is the rest of the fleet ready?"

At his matte of screens, Lucas didn't turn to me. "Yes, they're in formation. We're in the lead . . . the warranters and Space Force ships are in formation behind us."

"Delta formation?"

"It looks like what you described."

"They should be able to handle that. It's almost the same as their wedge tactic. I hope so, anyway. Full overhead vid, please, Lucas."

"Oh . . . overhead, aye."

Lot of hoping going on here, I noticed, quite a nerve-wracking amount of it coming from me. My stomach quivered as the tile-encrusted ceiling and sides of the ship blurred and disappeared. Suddenly we were looking out into open space, able to see above and around us. I turned to check the formation of the Space Force and the warranters. To our right, Oran's ship flanked us just abaft our beam. It was good to see him there. I wished his brother could be here at his side, but Quen was under sedation as his broken bones and burned innards fought to recover. I felt deeply regretful about that; he deserved to be here. For a fleeting moment I thought of having Ruvan rouse him and station him here on his main deck for the big battle.

That would only be cruel, for I couldn't give back command. I was stuck with it.

"Zell," I began abruptly. When he looked at me I said, "Have Totobet brought to the main deck."

"That woman? Why?"

"I want her to see how we handle this. And I might have questions for her."

"She won't answer," he said. "I wouldn't."

"I wouldn't either, but bring her up anyway. I'd like her to watch this."

He stepped past me on his way to give that order, but quite unexpectedly he paused.

"You like this kind of thing, don't you?" he observed, keeping his voice low. "You seem . . . charged up."

I gazed back at him, a little embarrassed. What could I do? After all this, toe a pacifist line? Honesty was not only part of the Pledge, but generally a wise plan.

"Part of me likes it," I admitted. "I'd be lying to say otherwise. It's too easy to get away from."

"What's that mean?"

Pressing one hand on the well rail, I gave the old ship a warm rub of affection. "If you don't like heat and snakes, don't go to Tarkus II."

Zell was right. My whole body tingled with anticipation. My movements were darting, my orders inspired. I felt my eyes glow and my skin pulse with hot blood running just under the surface. Battle possessed undeniable intoxication for anyone trained to do it. Still, since I had met Totobet, spoken with her, understood her and the Lumalits' hideous natural burden, to have to fight them to the death became regrettable. The "us or them" rudiment of survival took on a rocky substance for me.

Of course, that wouldn't stop me either. I didn't hate the enemy. That wasn't required.

Totobet was here now, standing in the corner near the aft transverse bulkhead. She watched with her wide brown eyes as the armada of her people's advance flank streamed toward us out of the rhinestone-studded black fabric of space. She'd seen this before, of course, but not quite from this perspective.

"That's an advance team, isn't it?" I asked her. "There are only sixty-some ships there. We saw over two hundred in Iscoy space."

"All don't come at once," she said. Apparently she didn't see any reason to hide the obvious from me or try to tell me it wasn't true. "Others come later with the crew's families."

"Yes, transports," I responded. "That's how I'd do it. We can assume these ships are well armed, being the strike force, can't we?"

She watched the outflow of her people's armada. "Oh . . . yes."

I knew all this just from watching, but my crew needed to hear it. They needed to understand that they must do whatever the coming situation called upon them to do because there would be more of the enemy coming. And this enemy would not hesitate.

"Get ready to release the *Aragore.* Make sure we're at full sublight so she'll have the momentum we need."

Lucas craned to see me past the man crouching next to him. "Don't you want to hail them? Tell them who we are?"

"They know who we are," I said. "I've seen their tactics. They didn't give any warning to the Iscoy. I don't intend to give them any. Zell, hold back the *Aragore* until I give the order, no matter what happens. Is that understood?"

"It's clear . . . can't say I understand . . ."

"Kay, they're shooting! What is that!"

In the wide-open panorama around us, streaks of energy beams as white as the gleam off a knight's sword came bolting from the first flank of Lumalit ships. The first blasts sizzled across *Zingara*'s bow and the bows of Oran's ship and several others of our lines. They were directed hits, very effective, well targeted, and coordinated.

Very bright—we all shielded our eyes from the crackle of energy washing over our invisible hull.

And very noisy.

"Hold formation!" I called over the drumming hits.

Lucas would relay my choreography to the other ships. I hoped they would continue to take my suggestions, for certainly I hadn't been around enough for them to trust me as commodore and take actual orders from me.

"Oran wants to return fire!" Lucas called back.

"Not yet! Tell everybody to hold fire, batten down, and take the hits until we get closer!"

Massus stumbled to my side. "What kind of weapons are those white bolts?"

"Directed energy. Phased rectification using rapid nadions. It's got to do with high-speed reactions at the level of atomic nuclei. At least, that's what ours are. Theirs are some variation of that. The colors are different, sometimes the intensity, but the basic method . . . there are only so many ways to do it."

"Can you teach us?"

I glanced at him and raised an eyebrow. "If we ever get the time."

The Lumalit ships, once they had begun firing, continued to do so. Without shields in the sense I considered conventional, the warranters and the Space Force ships were cut horridly across the hulls, able to stand up to the pounding only because of their sheer toughness and overbuilt construction. They had nominal energy shields that were used only for protection from micrometeorites during the light kicks, and those managed to deflect enough of the Lumalit energy beams that the destructive power, by the time it reached the hull material itself, was depleted somewhat.

That might let us survive at this distance, but as we drew closer, as the angles on the beams became less glancing and more piercing, the slight advantage would disintegrate.

"Kay, they're getting close . . ." Zell paced back and forth behind me, his head swiveling as he watched the oncoming ships. "Are you sure we shouldn't fire back at them?"

"Not yet!" I snapped.

He didn't argue anymore. Everyone was tense, but to their credit they were not paralyzed. Crewmen stayed to their work, steadying the ship, plugging breaches, clearing damage, as *Zingara* rocked around us and we saw the other ships in our ragtag fleet also shimmy and suffer. Some fell from the formation, trailing great wedding trains of damage that painted space with lights.

"Keep forward motion, no matter what, Levan! Hold the course!"

"I'm holding it!"

"Massus, keep the speed up to one-half sublight."

"We're losing some speed—"

"Zell! Release the *Aragore!*"

"Releasing!"

"Levan, reduce speed and fall back. Lucas, tell everybody else to fall back, too. Massus, trigger the *Aragore*'s quantum buildup!"

"It's triggered! Hope it works—"

"How many ships have we lost?" I shouted. "Lucas! Can you hear me?"

"Yes . . . Oran's still with us, but thirteen ships are crippled!"

"Have the others close up formation!"

Part of the overhead screen went dark, and a second later that part of the hull exploded. Gutted mechanics, tiles, and structure crumbled on top of three men at the aft bulkhead, including Massus.

I pushed some of the hot junk aside and tried to see if they were alive. One wasn't. I couldn't be sure about Massus because I couldn't reach him.

Zell jumped to take over the controls. "Shouldn't we break up? Instead of making one big target?"

"Do you think so?" I asked.

"Seems it wouldn't let them concentrate their shots."

The rubble near me shifted—Massus! He crawled out from under the wreckage, shook his head, and let me help him to his feet.

I held his arm as he steadied himself, but I was still working on Zell's suggestion. "Or it might cause them to move apart and lessen our chances of taking out enough of them . . . All right, we'll try it your way. Lucas! Tell the other ships to break formation and draw fire. Othien, check the remotes on *Aragore.* Is there a buildup?"

Othian stumbled to Massus's screens and squinted at them. "I think . . ."

"Look!"

Zell stumbled to the middle of the main deck and pointed out, forward, at the *Aragore.*

As we fell back, still taking hits, *Aragore* surged forward like a good little robot, without a living soul on board, and the very body of the ship was beginning to gleam. All the tiles on board were mounting stocks of energy, building and building, without anywhere to release their stores. The skin of the warranter took on a brassy polish as energy built inside, sucking directly from the fusion engines that were turned inward upon themselves.

Predictably, the Lumalit ships began turning their attention to this single spearhead, assuming there were people on board and that *Aragore* was about to open fire on them.

How mystified they must be! *Aragore* took all their shots and returned none, sailing calmly into the mass of Lumalit ships as her hull was systematically seared by those energy bolts. The hull now glowed bright celery green against space, and a wide corona of radiant energy surrounded her as if she were painted with watercolors on a blotter.

"She's overloading!" Massus gasped.

"Not close enough," I muttered. "Closer . . . closer . . ."

Maybe I'd miscalculated. Maybe the Lumalit would destroy the *Aragore* before the ship could release its quantum discharge. Half the ship's tail section was flying like a kite behind her already. A few more shots—

A huge blue-white flash blinded us all. There was no sound, but inside my head was a single drum hit caused by the snap of bright light. When we looked again, there was another flash, and another!

Pure wide-spectrum energy branched again and again from *Aragore*'s overloaded tiles, conducting instantly through the vacuum of space, linking the former warrant ship with ten . . . fifteen . . . twenty-one Lumalit ships! Twenty-two!

Wave after wave of crackling blue lightning tied up the Lumalit ships near *Aragore,* setting them ablaze with raw deadly voltage. As we watched in a carnivalish combination of horror and delight, *Aragore* began to fall apart, chunk by chunk, destroying herself as energy blew from her tiles into the other ships.

Twenty-two enemy ships hit!

"Condition of those vessels, Lucas!" I called out. "What are you reading?"

"They're . . ." Lucas tapped his tiles and tried to keep a grasp on his panic. "They're . . . they're falling off! They're crippled!"

A cheer blasted from our crew in a single voice as nearly a dozen Lumalit ships rolled away from the center of the battle, obviously confused, damaged, and without the ability even to steer clear of other ships, which resulted in several collisions with the tight formation.

"Twenty-two ships crippled," I breathed. "Tell Oran and the others to move in while the Lumalit are confused. Open fire."

We all went in together, singling out a Lumalit ship and embarking on two dozen duels all happening at the same time. The Lumalit ships were faltering from radiant power that struck some of them when the fire ship released its quantum discharge, but they were slowly recovering and that worried me.

If the battle continued thus, this many ships against that many, we had a chance. Unfortunately, that wasn't how things were to go for us.

As we grappled in open space with our adversary, Lucas found me and tugged on the hem of my shoulder cape.

"Kay," he croaked. As I turned, he pointed across the deck at the long-range screen. "Uh . . . more . . ."

He didn't want anyone else to hear. In mere seconds, though, his gentlemanly forbearance wouldn't make a bit of difference.

On the screen were the jewel-clear blips that represented more ships coming in. Another wave of enemy vessels was about to fall out of hyperlight right on top of us.

Zell bent next to me to study the screen. "A second wave?"

"Looks like it," I grumbled.

"We can't beat them," he said. "We don't have any more fire ships to send in. They can take out our missiles too easily. Should we retreat?"

A brief silence crackled between us, and all around members of the crew listened to what we were saying. The silent moment had a damning voice: *What good would it do to retreat?*

"We're not retreating," I said. "We do have a ship to use against them. *Zingara* will be the next fire ship."

There were plenty of alternatives, but only one good alternative, only one that might give a message of example to the struggling fleet around us and show them all what we had to do, to what great lengths all people must go to live free.

I straightened up and paused for a second or two of deep consideration. When I spoke, my voice was strangely calm, almost melodic with purpose.

"Massus . . . adjust our engines to feed their energy back to the tiles. Levan, break off and set a course for the incoming armada."

Zell straightened and stared, but couldn't speak. His eyes worked furiously with all the emotions running past them. His fingers were splayed out pointlessly and trembling.

Massus stepped out from behind the helmsman. "You're sacrificing our lives? You get to decide? Just like that?"

I turned to face him. "That's right. Sometimes a decision just has to be made."

Stunned, he gawked at me. They all began to look at me. All over the deck young faces turned toward me, one after the other, as they realized I wasn't kidding. They had elected me as their captain, but that was where the concept of democracy ended. They knew me well enough by now to understand me. They'd have no choice but mutiny. Death or mutiny. Me or that danger out there. Which would they rather face? Two sailor's nightmares clashing up against each other. Orders or anarchy.

But there was more to it. Not just orders, not just death—the very depth of personal integrity was at stake. Everyone had to die eventually. A privileged few got to choose how and why they would die.

I had already chosen. I was willing to die for my adopted culture, and I hadn't even visited it in person yet. In the eyes of the crew, I was willing to die for *their* families, their nations, their planet.

Like the transfer of energy from the fire ship to our enemies, raw courage of conviction flowed from me to the crew. The change occurred before my eyes in utter silence, as skies clear from clouds to bright sunshine. Their shoulders straightened. Fear's pallor dropped from their faces. They crossed that line, to stand with me, to live free or die.

Without a further spoken word of our new bond, I gave them a sustaining nod.

"Zell," I said, "full sublight."

Our first officer slapped his hands on his thighs in that manner he had, then said, "Full speed, aye!"

He motioned to Othien and Levan, and we were on our way, heading into the nearest clutch of Menace ships to give up our lives and hope that others would follow. For this, sadly, would be the only way.

Twenty-two

"ZELL, HAVE RUVAN AND HIS ASSISTANTS BRING QUEN TO THE BRIDGE. HE should be here for this."

For our suicide mission, I avoided saying, he deserved to be here.

The interior tiles were beginning to glow with feedback, to pack themselves with potential energy.

"Everybody stay back from the tiles," Zell warned, then leaned down the well and repeated, "stay away from the tiles down there!"

When he straightened, I gave him a sustaining grin and said, "What difference does it make, really?"

He blushed, his hair taking on the cucumbery sheen of the glowing tiles, and his hands made a gesture of frustration and uselessness. Then he rubbed his face and couldn't help a miserable smile.

Out in space, the *Aragore* was still arching its last vestiges of blue snaggly energy to the nearest sources—whatever Lumalit ships hadn't been able to veer off in time.

"They're literally getting the shock of their lives," I muttered, then couldn't help a glance at Totobet, who was quietly watching the drama play out. Near her there was a movement, and my attention switched to Quen. He was being assisted through the hatch by Ruvan and Bren, one of the crew assigned to help in the infirmary. Quen was pale and groggy, but instantly looked up at the overhead vid to see what was happening, and as his expression changed I could see that he had figured it out already. He saw the tiles glowing with backfill around us, and he more than any here understood what that meant.

He was walking, though very stiffly, and there was still a canvas splinting device around his waist and hips. I could tell that most of his weight was being borne by Ruvan and Bren. Many of the crew reached for him and brushed his fingers in a sad and poignant gesture—they missed him. No level of experience offered by me could fill that void.

The bizarre part was that I missed him too. I wanted to have a captain again, to do hard hands-on work with the nuts and bolts of the ship and provide information to the command, then let somebody else broach the tricky decisions. Oh, I could *do* it . . . I'd just discovered something of great worth in myself that had been silent before this. A deckhand.

Like a long many-headed worm, the crew hovered in the middle of the deck now, unable to touch the tiles, and over our heads the vid screen tiles, even though we couldn't see most of them because they were busy projecting an illusion of open space, were washed in a sickly green haze.

The incoming armada still showed on the screen.

"They're close," I said aloud. "We'll see them in a minute."

These words were virtually our epitaph. As soon as we came within range of an unequal energy source, the power building up in our millions of capacitors would sizzle across space, frying us and everybody it could reach. The discharge, I hoped, would be abrupt and over quickly. With luck, we would not linger long to suffer the success of our mission.

Behind us, Oran's ship struggled to keep up, as did what was left of the warranters and Space Force vessels. They were regrouping, and I could only hope they had it within themselves to take our example if they had to, or the Menace children would live and multimillions of others would be killed. A ghastly balance—and if there were nightmares beyond the grave, this would be mine.

Watching his tiles from a less than safe distance, Lucas interrupted my thoughts. "Kay? Somebody's hailing us. I thought you said they wouldn't hail us."

I moved to where I could see his comm screen, but there was no way to touch a tile and respond to the hail. "They didn't hail anybody the last time. They just came in and started cutting."

"How can we answer?"

Cupping my hand on his shoulder, I said, "We can't. Just ignore it."

He didn't like that. His devotion to purpose was heartening as we stared down the barrel of suicide.

The first ship in the new wave came surging toward us on the screen, our energy-stuffed tiles still fighting to give us a craggy picture that was blurred and flickering. The first ship was of a different configuration than the rest, which seemed to be roughly cone-shaped.

I squinted against the glare of hot tiles. "Those don't look like Lumalit ships . . . at least nothing I've seen . . ."

"What's that big one in front?" Quen asked from a few steps away. "An assault vanguard?"

"I don't know," I said, "but let's hope it veers in to hit us. It'll get a hell of a shocking response."

It was the ship that would kill us, and that we would kill with our overpacked capacitors. Energy would crackle from *Zingara* to that ship and pulse its deadly poison across the vacuum of space, using that ship's own power against it, sucking back the wash of energy and recycling it into new charges. We'd be gone by then, fried by the first surge. Streaking across space, crackling now with furious stored energy in all our tiles, *Zingara* actually looked as if she were ablaze around us.

"They're not coming toward us!" Zell called over the whine of collected energy. "Why are they angling away?"

I shielded my eyes and tried to see the screen. We still couldn't see the incoming ships on the overhead—they were behind our visible bulkheads—but on the screen . . . Zell was right. The big advance guard and the triangular attackers behind it were splitting up and going wide around us. What kind of maneuver was that?

"They'll reach their own ships with that maneuver and miss us completely," I complained. "Why would anybody do that? Levan, prepare to come about if we have to. They're not getting by us!"

With all this stored up energy, I sure didn't want to just sit here in space and fry. If we had to die, we'd do a better job of it than that!

"Here they come!" Zell backed up and turned his face upward through the green snapping haze of energy that wanted so much to jump. He looked up and forward of us.

Quen turned also, as did the crew, and as did I. We stood shoulder to shoulder and watched the darkness of space while haze-shrouded forms took shape in the nearing distance as icebergs might appear on an ocean horizon. They were angling away from us in a reverse pie-wedge, making room for us to go down the middle corridor and completely miss them if we kept to our course. Did they smell a rat? Were they avoiding *Zingara* on purpose, assuming we were the best foot stepping forward and the ships behind us damaged, or more easily smashed? Not a bad assumption, unfortunately.

"Levan, one-quarter about!" I called.

"One-third," Quen suggested.

"Make that one-third!"

"One-third about," Levan shakily responded. He was handling the only control on the ship that wasn't encrusted with tiles: the helm.

The *Zingara,* rippling with green banshees, began slowly to swing about. This turned the forward bulkhead away from the incoming armada and let us see clearly the ships coming toward us, ships that exploded in my mind with all the force of warp core detonations.

Gasping, choking, shocked, I plunged to the helm and pushed Levan aside so hard that he nearly fell against the deadly glowing transverse bulkhead behind him.

"Out of the way!" My shout confused everybody. Even me.

The helm tingled in my hands, hot with radiant energy from the packed capacitors all over the ship, but I ordered myself to ignore that and force the ship to slow down, to stop turning.

"What are you doing!" Zell demanded. "We'll miss them if we slow down!"

"We have to miss them," I gagged, but the words cracked in my mouth.

The big advance ship soared overhead like an albatross on the hunt, so close that I was afraid the tiles would release their charge—and now I didn't want them to. The long cetacean lines were like a song played on a harp and vibrating against my heart. Now I understood why they had tried to hail us.

Zell rushed to me and put his hands over mine. "We've got to get them! We'll waste the charge!"

"No," I said, strangely quiet, buffeted by a sudden peace in my whole soul. "I don't want to destroy my ship."

He gawked at me. "What? You mean *Zingara?*"

My lips parted as we watched the big advance cruiser sail by us and open fire on the Lumalit ships that had survived our trick with the *Aragore.* I saw with great satisfaction that the bolts of energy from the attacking ship changed every few seconds; they'd figured out the Lumalit's shield adaptation and programmed the weapons to make random alterations in frequency. The cuts went right through the Lumalit shields and sliced into the skin of the ships, several at once, in a blaze of successful hits.

Quen hobbled toward me, and together we watched the monumental show.

"She doesn't mean *Zingara,*" he told Zell quietly. "Do you, Kay?"

Slowly, as tears drained down my face and were instantly warmed by the energy pulsing around us, I shook my head.

"No," I told him. "I mean *Voyager.*"

On the faces of my shipmates around me, I saw with great joy the sudden understanding. They knew what I meant, they understood what we were seeing.

There, before us, with a flank of Iscoy fighters following and now swooping in to blast the Lumalit ships away from the warranters and the Space Force ships, the *Starship Voyager* was for me, for us, the grandest sight in the universe. I was—we were—no longer alone.

Twenty-three

"CHAKOTAY! . . . TOM . . . TUVOK . . . HARRY!"

I fought back tears and rushed toward them as the airlock opened on *Zingara*'s loading deck.

They were alive, they were *alive!* I was alive! And all my closest associates were here to greet me. Chakotay, Tom Paris, Harry Kim, B'Elanna . . . they were alive, alive, alive.

Funny how this was so much harder to accept than getting used to the idea that they'd all died. In my chest bloomed the strange delight that they had done all right without me. The lesson in humility was as great as any parent could hope for while watching her children fledge. As indispensable as a captain would like to be, if the crew were well trained enough, then they could do fine without . . . me.

What a bittersweet thing that was. What a moment of pride and intimidation, sadness and satisfaction.

Behind me, Quen, Zell, Lucas, and many more of *Zingara*'s crew watched the unlikely reunion, and I couldn't hazard a guess about what they were feeling. Shock, I supposed, and a little touch of contrition that they had doubted me, but who could blame them for that? I'd landed on their ship and declared myself superior. They'd done the smartest thing: They'd handed me a broom and said, "Sweep."

"Kathryn" was all Chakotay could manage to say, and he said it at least three times until I finally started laughing and crying at the same time.

Somehow holding hands with all of them at once, I choked out, "You got the random frequency thing figured out!"

Chakotay said, "Their energy usage wasn't deep enough for the shields to be that strong."

"B'Elanna figured it out," Tom Paris managed.

B'Elanna Torres cast her Klingon reserves overboard and absolutely shook with affection. I saw a thousand questions race across her mind, but the one that finally popped out was "What happened to your *hair?*"

Oh, what I must look like to them! Here I stood, my hair chopped and shaggy, my hands still scarred from the burns in the pod, my clothing more like a medieval forester than a modern spacefarer, and standing here as I was, with my shipmates behind me in very much the same clothing, with the same shag and the same gauntness and the same hopes, I felt prouder than I ever had before.

Summoning a whole new courage, I mustered up the operative point. "I saw *Voyager* blow up . . . I saw a warp reactor detonation . . ."

Chakotay nodded. "You did see that. But it was the spacedock's auxiliary test engine blowing up. It had an antimatter reactor."

I openly stared at him. The stupid spacedock. An auxiliary reactor core. The blinding flash of antimatter detonation.

Like an idiot I kept staring at him, ready to declare him a liar and insist that the ship had blown up and they were really all dead and so was I because *Zingara* had discharged her energy and this was all the dream of the last second of consciousness before I got electrocuted into vapor.

Then Chakotay reached out and gripped my arm as if he knew what I was thinking, touching me with such plain human warmth and reassurance that I shuddered with emotion.

"The spacedock clamps failed to release us," Tuvok explained, buttering the moment with his Vulcan evenhandedness. "We had to let it disintegrate before we could break away. Mr. Chakotay was ready for it—"

"We hit emergency warp." Chakotay took over before he was forced to collect too much praise. "It knocked us all on our ears, but we were shielded by the blast of the auxiliary engine and ducked into the sun's corona. It's an old Maquis trick . . . from my 'better' days. You pretend you've been destroyed, and you get time to tend your damage. Once we'd made our major repairs, we met with the Iscoy survivors and just decided that these people weren't going to do this to anyone else if we could stop it. So when they warped out, we followed them."

Overwhelmed, I beat back a wave of new tears. "You deserve a commendation. If you ever do this to me again, I'll strangle you. Doctor . . ."

I reached out to him as he stepped through the airlock from the shuttlecraft linked up to *Zingara.*

"Captain," he said warmly, and with such emotion that I really believed for a moment that a computer-generated hologram could cry. I thought he was holding my hand, but then I realized he was examining my hand. "Look at these burns. You'll need skin grafts. Good thing I'm here."

"Yes, I'm very glad you're here," I told him. "We have one of the Lumalit people on board here. We need you to apply your medical analysis to her and try to figure out their reproductive systems. They've got a big problem—"

"Kay," Zell called from amidships, just below the deck well, "Lucas says the Lumalit flagship is hailing us. They want to talk to you."

"What's their condition?" I asked.

"All their ships are heavily damaged. Only two have motive power right now. They're all badly crippled . . . I think they want our terms for surrender."

His voice had a cautious lick of hope in it.

"Come on," I called, and waved everybody to follow me.

We dashed up the deck well onto the main deck, where Lucas had several of the now-calm tiles arranged in screens that showed many Lumalit faces, presumably those in command of various ships. They were harried and wounded. Defeated.

On the wide overhead video display, off to our starboard side, there hovered the enormous and beautiful *Voyager,* scarred from battle, many of her silvery hull plates scorched, lying in birdlike repose, having survived the unsurvivable.

How wonderful she was to my eyes. For the first time in my life, I loved two ships.

Nearby, Totobet stood in mute reflection as she watched me and both my crews come to the middle deck. I communed silently with her for a moment, then turned to the faces of anticipation.

"The jig is up," I told them boldly, without any greetings or formalities. "We know how to beat you. You're finished in this quadrant."

The Lumalit faces ran a gamut of reactions from misery to acceptance. Then one man about three screens away from me spoke up.

"We understand what you mean," he said. "What are your intentions? Will you destroy our transports? . . . How many of us will you allow to survive? . . . May we choose who dies? That is how we survive. Please allow it."

Again I glanced at Totobet. She returned my glance and quietly mentioned, "Please let me rejoin my people for this . . ."

"Don't be silly," I clipped. Stepping closer to the spokesman's screen, I pointed out, "You've got to be talking about millions of lives."

The Lumalit spokesman nodded. "Yes. If that is the best we can do, we will do it. It is the curse of our genetics."

Amazing.

Even after all this, the whole idea was still amazing to me. One more time I looked at Totobet, and in her eyes I saw the terrible burden of her people. She watched the scorched faces of those who piloted their attack fleet, and I knew she had seen such things before. These were people who had won many times, but also who had lost many times and been forced to enact their awful lottery. She looked upward and saw the ships crackling and breaking, and knew she was one of the vanquished.

In the pocket of my shirt under the shoulder cape, the small folded book of photographs ached against my chest. In my victory, I saw the inevitable civilian victims. That was Totobet. She was standing there looking at her smashed fleet, and realizing once again that the children she was carrying would be the ones to die.

As I watched her, I came down out of the saddle of my victory and stood beside the price of it.

Turning away from her, I moved to Quen's side.

"Doctor," I began. "This is Quen. He was the captain of *Zingara* before his injuries, and he rescued me from the pod, brought me on board, and offered me a new life. If you don't mind, please admit him to *Voyager*'s sickbay and treat his injuries." Quen looked at me, seeming a little hesitant to hand himself over to strangers on a strange ship, but I gripped his hand and assured, "You'll be much better very soon. You'll be surprised."

Chakotay and Paris, more than the others, had caught something in my words and now stepped forward together, and Paris blurted, "Wait a minute—"

At the same time, Chakotay said, "What do you mean, 'If we don't mind,' take him to sickbay?"

"You're coming with us," Paris finished.

This was the moment I had dreaded from the first instant when my mind believed what it was seeing—that the *Voyager* had survived and my spaceborne family was alive.

Standing between Quen and Zell, with Lucas nearby and Massus behind me, I squared my shoulders beneath the little cape and looked at *Voyager*'s boarding party. Despite what I expected, my voice didn't crack, my hands didn't tremble.

"I've sworn a Pledge to this ship," I said. "I can't be citizen of two countries or captain of two ships. I'm not going back with you. I'm staying here."

Twenty-four

Voyager . . . THE SICKBAY. SUCH A BRIGHT AND BEAUTIFUL PLACE, A LOCALE of so much knowledge, the medical lexicons of a hundred cultures, a place of modern miracles wrought by the brains of the living. The brightness was shocking. The warmth alien and unfamiliar, seeming suddenly unnecessary, even wasteful.

Here in the light of these rooms, I stood beside the diagnostic cot, making sure not to crowd Oran as he stood at Quen's shoulder. Quen lay on the cot, and *Voyager*'s doctor was finishing some of those modern miracles that suddenly dazzled me as if I'd never seen them before.

On the other side of the cot, behind the doctor, Zell also waited to see what would happen. On another cot a few steps away, Totobet sat and waited patiently with her crossed legs hanging over the side, not sure what her fate would be. I knew she hoped I'd return her to her people. I would, but I hadn't told her that yet.

"Pelvic bones fused . . . internal burns, well, almost healed. And that spleen is rather improved now, I should say." The doctor ran his diagnostics over his patient's body and somehow ignored Quen's winces and groans as medical science very quickly knitted tissues that otherwise would take months to heal. I'd been through some of that myself in the past—a rather stinging process at times.

"I'd like to avoid surgery," the doctor went on, narrating his activities as he usually did. "So you'll have some internal discomfort for a week or so. Otherwise, you can return to normal duty, provided you avoid heavy lifting."

"He's going to avoid everything," Oran said, raising his brother to a sitting position on the edge of the cot. "I'm going to tie him down and feed him some good food."

"We'll all have good food now," I told them. "We just got word that the TCA has collapsed. Their own military wouldn't back them up. When the Space Force figured out that the warranters would rather die than go on without freedom, they stood up to their own government. No more forcing the warranters to keep from banding together. Everyone can go home and work on setting up a decent government of, for, and by the people. Not bad for three days' work, wouldn't you say?"

"I can't believe it," Quen murmured, but he smiled. He clasped Oran's hand, then Zell's. "We can go home."

"That's right, and it's about time." I looked around, beaming at my shipmates, and found myself looking also at Chakotay, Tuvok, and Tom Paris, who had invaded the sickbay when they found out I was on board.

Pretty obvious why they were here. I hadn't changed my clothes. I hadn't gotten my hair fixed up. The burns on the backs of my hands were treated with freshly grown skin, but that was the only change. I saw the disappointment in their eyes as they came in. They wanted me to stay.

As Quen sat on the bed, with Oran and Zell at his sides, and tested his mended body limb by limb, I strode to Totobet and invited, "Doctor? Do you have anything to say to this young lady and her people?"

Voyager's vaunty physician stepped forward to my side. "Yes, after examining her for these few days, and the male prisoners we took, I do have a few things to say. Madam, your problem is hormonal. In my medical laboratories I have synthesized the various hormones. With a tightly controlled series of treatments, we can make the male body believe it has already sired. We're still working on the female physiology, but I think we're close to solving that problem as well."

"What about the multiplicity?" I asked. "The multiple births?"

"Hormonal as well," he said flatly. "A mere subsection of the other solution."

Chakotay smiled. "Some of our prisoners confirmed that they'd never run into anyone with advanced medical capabilities. At least, not as advanced as ours."

Playing up the moment, I pressed, "Oh, really? Can you explain that, Doctor?"

Accommodatingly the doctor said, "Certainly. They didn't have *me*."

"No, they didn't." I turned to Totobet and put an arm around her—what an unexpected gesture. "You and your people threw all your technology into survival and conquest. You gave up on curbing reproduction because your people died trying. We understand that, but as your technology advanced, you forgot to try again and again until a solution was found. This physician and the Federation *Starship Voyager* are significantly more advanced in medical sciences than anything you're familiar with, and I'll bet Captain Chakotay will be willing to look into your problem. You've always been on a footing geared to survival rather than betterment. Here's a dose of betterment."

She tried to speak, but nothing came out. I think she was stunned. A solution to all this that didn't involve further struggle and slaughter? A biological solution? Her children would no longer have to die?

That was right, but only because *Voyager* had survived the attack of her desperate people. Without this ship and its crew, neither the Lumalit, nor the Om, nor the Iscoy had such a depth of medical indices to conjure up an answer. We would've had to keep fighting until one side or the other was utterly destroyed.

Sudden sympathy rose in me for the civilizations of the past who had been forced to fight over monumental things whose answers today seemed so available. I didn't prefer to understand, but all at once I did.

Before temptation took over and things turned sour, I moved back to the other cot and took Quen's arm. "Let's get back to the *Zingara.*"

"Captain," Chakotay began.

I stopped him with a look. "Please, don't."

He actually held his breath. Behind him, Tuvok's scowl was dark as space and Paris looked like a gutted jack-o'-lantern.

"Thank you all," I said. "It's been my privilege to serve with you. But now I serve another ship, and I'm going back to her."

After three days of postbattle cleanup and rushed summits of regions' leaders all over the home planet, and all the admirals or whatever they called themselves getting together and deciding things, not to mention the good scare they'd gotten from the Lumalit, the people of this sector were remarkably resilient and ready to make changes.

I'd been standing back in rather a lot of awe, watching how fast things happened, considering that they'd been stalled in this political limbo for . . . how many years was it?

But now the tide had turned and there was no pulling it back. The warranters wanted to see their families and live normal lives, the former TCA leaders were in exile somewhere and being hunted down for trial, local dartboards had Sasaquon's face for a target, and in between the chaotic events were soaring moments of real hope and reason.

Shipments of food, fuel, water, and fresh clothing were coming in by the hour for the warranters, who were finally getting the appreciation they deserved for their eight-year standoff on behalf of freedom. With some regret I turned over my tattered shoulder cape for one that had been freshly made by a little girl on a planet I'd never even visited. How wonderful to be appreciated by those for whom you had put down your very life. I'd forgotten that part. It was as if my heart had been polished and given a lube job.

On board *Zingara,* members of the crew were involved in a cocktail of damage control and giddy partying. Have a drink and pass me that wrench. When I returned with Quen, Zell, and Oran, and the crew could see for themselves that Quen and I were both much improved from our injuries, their young faces gleamed with mystification and delight. There really *was* hope!

Communiqués were coming in from all over, ranging from questions to interviews to congratulations, and most of them were fielded by Lucas or Zell, but ultimately one came in for me, and nobody else could answer the strange and heady request.

"This is Kay," I responded when the portrait of a rather small-boned elderly man appeared on one of the smaller tile screens.

"I am Samda, newly appointed chief justice of the Om Planetary Court, Captain Kay. This communication is being wide-broadcast to all localities and ships. We no longer wish to work in secret. No more closed doors. May I thank you personally and publicly for your valiant participation in the past weeks' events."

"You're most welcome, Judge," I said. "It was my pleasure to serve. I'm glad I could be here when I was needed, but I can't take all the credit. The warranters endured years of isolation and struggle before I ever came here. They are your sons and the true valiant among us."

"And we shall reward them for a lifetime," the old man promised. *"For now, though, for the immediate future . . . we have an unorthodox request. We all have taken a vote here, and on the colonies. We all know about you and your Federation, and where you came from. You are the only person who isn't a representative of some faction or other, some hemisphere, some loyalty, or some bias. You're the only person that everyone here trusts. Captain Kay, will you come to the planet and become the imperial leader and show us how to set up a government that will not collapse under the weight of corruption? Will you come here? Will you lead us?"*

What had he said?

I leaned toward Quen and out of the corner of my mouth I muttered, "Is he offering me a planet?"

Quen smiled. "Sounds that way. Why don't you take it? You could get that haircut."

"Do I have to take the Planet's Pledge?"

He laughed. I guess he knew I wasn't going to go be a dictator, no matter how many planets I was offered.

"Judge Samda," I began after a moment, "I don't want to run your planet. But on the *Voyager,* if you'll let me contact Captain Chakotay on your behalf, there is a library of documents that would serve you very well during this time. No one can do this for you. You have to decide your own direction. You've been running your planet the way you should run a ship, and your ships the way you should run a planet. The planet should be a democracy. The ships shouldn't be. You don't have the wrong rulers, you have the wrong rules. Just read what I send you . . . and make your world. Thank you again and best luck."

With a brief nod of salute, I motioned to Lucas to cut off the communication. No more of that.

"Lucas, contact the *Voyager* and tell them I have a list of publications they should duplicate and give to the planet's media and bodies of authority."

"Why don't you contact them yourself, Kay?" Quen asked.

My lips pressed tight for a moment and I shook my head. "Lucas can do it."

I hadn't noticed, but now did, that most of the crew had gathered around me on the main deck. What was this, another celebration of my wonderfulness? Couldn't we be done with that?

"You can tell them yourself," Zell said.

"Why?" I looked at him, then at Quen. "I don't want to go back there."

"Well, you'd better. We took another vote. You've been deposed."

Suddenly trembling, I swiveled around and looked at the beaming faces of *Zingara*'s crew. "You're releasing me from my Pledge? But I didn't ask—"

"We're not releasing you from it," Zell protested.

"Not at all," Quen said. "We're just reassigning you. We've just elected you captain of the *Voyager.*"

Twenty-five

"So I said, 'Go ahead and make your world.' And they did, gentlemen, they did."

"And tell us, Captain . . . which documents did you send to the new government of that planet?"

"Oh, I imagine you could guess many of them yourself, Captain Troop. And the other captains here could guess the rest. The Magna Carta, the Bill of Rights, the United States Constitution, the United Federation of Planets Articles of Confederation, the Fundamental Declarations of the Martian Colonies, the Vulcan Treatises on Logic and the Living Condition, *The Death of Andor* . . . and many others. They just needed a little guidance. The Berlin Wall always falls . . . it's just harder to find inside a free society."

"This episode seems to have changed you as much as those around you who were affected by your presence."

Across the table, the man with one arm chased his sentence with an aristocratic blue glare. He'd been making comments like that all the way through my tale, probing not for what happened, but for which changes came of the happenings. Even in this odd environment, he was trying to learn from what he heard.

Around me like a smoky cloak, the Captain's Table murmured its comforting noises. Tales being told at other tables, the *clop* of footsteps up and down the stairs, someone picking out a one-fingered tune on the piano, glasses clinking, laughter, sighs.

"Yes, Your Lordship," I agreed. "I had always doubted . . . wondered if

I was captain because I had connections, or because of my father, or because I was lucky. What I found out was that you could burn my hair and clothes off, wrap me in foil, drop me on a ship, injured, alien, and raving, and I could still cope."

"That's right. You were captain again," the woman in the sweater said. "Whatever your pluses and minuses are, you could put that one away."

"Oh, but I was a captain greatly changed," I told her after a sip of my drink. "Silly as it seems, I kept wanting to go back to buffing the tiles. I found a deckhand in myself, and I like her. As a matter of fact . . . she'd better get back to her ship."

The table of interesting people raised their glasses to me but made no attempt to stop me from leaving.

"Fair weather," the woman said.

Her Vulcan companion echoed, "And best destiny, Captain."

The others, captains all, murmured their farewells. As I stepped away from the table and headed toward the arched entrance, another story had already begun. Something about a shipment of rice and the hold of a prize ship . . .

I was tempted to stay, but something else called to me. Somehow I knew this was time for me to leave, just as I had known before that it would be all right to stay awhile.

The warmth of the pub slipped down my back as if a cloak were being taken from my shoulders. I stepped out into the cobbled street, still moist from rain, and looked around.

"Captain!"

I swung about, and Tom Paris almost knocked me over.

"There you are!" he blustered. "Are you all right?"

"Yes, I'm really actually very well right now," I told him. "Where did you go?"

"I thought I was following you into that door, but I must've taken a wrong turn," he said. "I've been walking around corners looking for you."

"How long?"

He paused and frowned. "Well, I don't really know . . ."

Putting my hand on his arm before he went any farther, I said, "Just a minute. I want to check something." I tapped my commbadge. "Janeway to *Voyager.*"

"Chakotay here, Captain. Is anything wrong?"

"What's wrong with the comm network? I tried to raise you about an hour ago, but I couldn't get through."

"An hour ago? Captain, you just beamed down."

"How long ago did we beam down?"

"It's been . . . eight minutes, thirty seconds."

"Mmm," I uttered. "You've been in command of a Maquis ship, haven't you, Chakotay? You've been a captain."

There was a pause. *"Of course. You know that . . ."*

"Yes. Put Tuvok in command and beam down, would you? I'd like to check out a theory. I'm going to shove you through a big oak doorway and see what happens."

"Uh . . . understood. I'll be right there."

"Janeway out." I turned to Paris again. "He doesn't understand."

Paris shrugged and gazed at the foggy street.

"That's all right," I said. "Some things are better with a little mystery clinging to them. Some romances, some tales, some adventures . . . but listen, Tom, do me a favor, will you? Some time in the future, when things look bad and I really need a boost . . ."

"Yes?"

"Call me 'Kay.' "

Once Burned

Mackenzie Calhoun

as recorded by
Peter David

First Encounter

You never forget the first man you kill.

Man.

Well . . . that may be an exaggeration.

I was fourteen seasons at the time, a youth on my homeworld of Xenex. My father had died several seasons before that, beaten to death in the public square by our Danteri oppressors as a signal to all my people that we should know our place. It is my everlasting shame that I did not immediately retaliate. Instead I stood there, paralyzed. I can still remember my older brother digging his fingers into my shoulder, keeping me from attacking. That was what I wanted to do at the time. I wanted to charge from the crowd, leap upon the man who was inflicting such punishment upon my father, and sink my teeth into his throat. I wanted to feel his blood fountaining between my teeth.

Unfortunately, I was a child. My brother was probably concerned—not without reason—that I would be cut down before I got within twenty feet of my father's tormentor. So I stayed where I was, and watched, and wished the entire time that I could tear my eyes from my sockets, block out the cries from my father's throat.

Such a proud man, he was. So proud. What they did to him . . .

It fueled me several years later when I began my campaign against the Danteri.

There was a tax collector, a rather hated Danteri individual named Stener. A short, squat individual, he was, with a voice like a rockslide and a viciousness in attitude and deportment that made you cringe as soon as you look at him. He rode about on this mount, a large and hairy creature called a Pok that had been specially bred by the Danteri to be a sort of all-purpose steed. He always had several guards with him. On this particular day, he had three. They were massively broad, although it was difficult to get a precise idea of their build beneath their armor. They were not wearing helmets, however, possibly because it was hot and the helmets were sweaty. Instead their helmets were tucked under their arms. That would prove to be a costly mistake.

It was a very hot day, I remember. Very hot, the last day of a very hot week. Tempers were becoming ragged as it was, and whispers of my rabble-rousing were already beginning to reach the ears of the Danteri. At that particular time, though, they dismissed me as nothing they need concern themselves about. I was, after all, merely a loudmouthed teenager insofar as they knew. Perhaps more erudite than many, but nothing much more than that. Still, they saw the growing anger in the eyes of my people. The downward casting of glances, the automatic subservience . . . that seemed to be present less and less, and it very likely concerned the Danteri.

I was determined to give them more than cause for concern. I wanted to send them an unmistakable message. To let them know that my people would not tolerate their presence on my world any longer. To let them know that their torture of my father—rather than serving as a warning—had instead awakened the slumbering giant of Xenexian pride. And I wanted my hand to be the one that struck the first blow, that hammered the gong which would chime out the call to freedom.

Stener had collected the taxes in my home city of Calhoun, but he had very likely tired of the epithets, the curses, the increasingly aggressive sneers that greeted him. Nothing actionable or worth starting a fight over, but it very likely grated on him. He didn't know that I was following him, stalking him. He can be forgiven for his obliviousness. There were any number of scruffy, disheveled Xenexian youths around, so there was no intrinsic reason for him to focus on me any more than on anyone else. I stuck to the shadows, skulked around buildings, and whenever any of his men happened to glance in my direction, I managed to melt into the background, to disappear.

To a certain extent . . . it was a game. I was in the throes of youth, pleased with my skill and alacrity. As I paced them, keeping to myself but never letting them from my view, I felt an increasing sense of empowerment. Even—dare I say it—invincibility. That is naturally a very dangerous state of mind. Under such circumstances, one can become exceedingly sloppy. One should never underestimate an opponent, and I do not for a moment recommend it for anyone.

They reached the outskirts of Calhoun and still had not spotted me. Had they then decided to return to their vessel and depart, they might very well all have survived. But they didn't. That was their greed, their own arrogance and sense of invincibility . . . as dangerous to them as to me. Stupidity is remarkably evenhanded.

Since they were certain that my people were too subservient to pose a serious threat, they decided to make their way to the neighboring, smaller village of Moute. Everything was happening spur-of-the-moment. Had I given the matter any thought at all, I would have gone into it with something approaching a plan. But I was flying on instinct alone, which was a habit that I would thankfully not continue to indulge in for my future dealings.

There was only one road between Calhoun and Moute, and I knew they were going to have to take it. Stener's Pok was moving at a fairly slow pace, and his three guards had to walk slowly to match it. As a result I had more than enough opportunity to get ahead of them. I moved with an almost bizarre recklessness, searching out and finding higher ground along the rocky ridges that lined the road. Ideally there would have been something with sufficient altitude that I could have sent an avalanche cascading down on their damned heads. Unfortunately the territory was fairly low, the ridges rising no more than maybe ten feet, so that wasn't an option. So I had to resort to other means to accomplish my task. I examined the stones beneath my feet and around me as I kept in careful pursuit, selecting those stones that best suited my purposes. The best were smooth and round, capable of hurtling at high speeds if thrown with enough strength. Believe me, the way I was feeling at that moment, my strength was more than sufficient. Such was the confidence I had in myself that I only selected three stones. It never even occurred to me that more might possibly be required.

I moved with speed and stealth, getting farther ahead until I was satisfied with the distance I'd put between myself and my targets. Crouching behind one of the upright outcroppings, I held one stone in either hand, and popped the third into my mouth for easy access. I listened carefully to determine if there was any useful information I could derive from whatever chitchat I might overhear, but there was no crosstalk at all. They rode in an almost eerie silence, as if they existed only to be my victims and otherwise had no lives up until that point.

The sun was beginning to descend upon the horizon, but it would still be quite some time until night. I had no interest in waiting until darkness. I wanted to see their faces clearly. I wanted them to know that even in broad daylight, there was still nowhere safe that they could hide. Besides, they'd be easier targets in the daylight. However, everything was going to depend upon my speed.

My back against the outcropping, I took a deep breath to steady my racing heart. I knew that the main thing I had going for me was the element of surprise. The moment that was lost, only pure speed could help me. I sprang from my hiding place and hurled the first rock, flipped the second rock to my throwing hand as I spit the third out. The first rock struck the closest guard squarely in the forehead. It knocked him cold. The second guard whirled around to see what had happened to his associate, but the second rock was already in flight and this one struck as accurately as the first. The third guard didn't even have a chance to turn; my last missile hit him bang-on in the back of his head. He went down without a sound.

It had all happened so quickly that Stener hadn't fully had the opportunity to comprehend what was going on. His Pok was turning in place in alarm. It was everything that Stener could do to keep his grip on the beast. "What's happening? Who's there?!" he called out.

I admit, at the time I had something of a flair for the dramatic.

I leaped down from the rocks, landing in a feral crouch. My sword was still strapped to my back. Perhaps it was because of that that Stener didn't yet realize he was in any danger. The fact that three of his men had just been dropped in rapid succession didn't jibe with the unkempt teenager who was approaching him. He likely considered me some sort of prankster. "You, boy! Are you responsible for this?"

I took a mocking bow. "The very same," I said.

"These are my men! This is official business! How dare you—?"

"How dare you," I snarled back, quickly losing patience with the oaf. "How dare you and your people think that you can abuse my people indefinitely. Today begins the day we strike back. Today is the day we begin the long march toward freedom."

I unsheathed my sword, drawing it slowly from the scabbard on my back for maximum effect. It was that threatening sound, and probably the look in my eye, that made Stener truly comprehend that his life was being threatened. "Now, wait just a minute, young man," he said, but even as he spoke he tried to angle his Pok around, in obvious preparation for trying to make a break for it.

He need not have wasted his time. We were in a fairly narrow pass, after all, and it was no great trick to angle myself around and block his only real escape route. I brandished my sword in a reasonably threatening manner. Stener began to stammer a bit, his bluster become tangled with his concern for self-preservation. "Now . . . now wait just a minute. . . ."

"I have waited long enough already," I replied. "All my people have. We wait no longer. Today we strike back."

That was when a sword seemed to flash from nowhere.

My block was purely on instinct as I brought my sword up to deflect the blow. One of the guards I had struck—the one from behind—apparently had a harder head than I had credited him for. Perhaps it was a lesson I was being taught for attacking from the rear—a less than heroic tactic, I fully admit.

Our swords locked at the hilt. He was bigger than I was, and very likely stronger. But he was still slightly dazed from the blow to the back of his head. Even were I not the superior fighter, the fact that he was fighting at less than his best would have been more than enough to tilt the battle in my favor.

He tried to push me off my feet, but I disengaged my sword and faced him. He had put his helmet on, and it obscured his face, although his eyes seemed to glitter with cold contempt. He appeared to take the measure of me for a moment and then he swung his blade. Our swords clanged together, the impact echoing in the soundlessness of the place.

Stener was reining in his panicking Pok and attempting to send it back in the direction from which they had just come. I wasn't concerned; I was certain that I could dispatch my opponent and still catch up with Stener in time to kill him as well. Such confidence I had. Such confidence considering that I had never taken another life. The other two guards were unconscious only, as this one was supposed to be. Stener was intended to be my first blood, but my feeling at that moment was that the guard would do just as nicely.

He fought well, I'll give him that. For a moment or two, I actually found myself in trouble as his sword flashed before my face, shaving a lock of my hair off. I didn't even realize it until I found strands on the ground later. There were no words between us. Really, what could we have said? An exchange of names? Pointless. A mutual request for surrender? Beyond pointless. We both knew what was at stake, both knew that there would be no backing down. This was no coward I was facing; he was willing to die to do his job. Likewise, he must have known that I would never have staged the assault if I had not intended to see it through.

A parry, another parry, and I fell back. He smiled. He probably thought he had me, since I was retreating. He didn't understand that I was simply watching him expend all his "tricks" as I studied his method of attack, his offensive skills. They were, I quickly discerned, limited. I knew I could take him. I waited for the best moment, and eventually it presented itself. I appeared to leave myself open and he went for the opportunity. I blocked the thrust and my blade slid up the length of his sword, off, and then my blade whipped around and I struck him in the helmet with such force that I actually shattered the head covering. Understand, my sword was not some delicate, polite saber. This was a large blade, four feet long, heavy as hell. In later years, I'd be capable of knocking an opponent's head from his shoulders with one sweep. But I was still a young man, and hadn't quite "grown in" to my weapon yet. Nonetheless, the impact caved in the side of his skull.

Just that quickly, his body was transformed from something of use into a sack of bones with meat surrounding it. He went down with as sickening a thud as I'd ever heard. The abruptness, the violence of the moment, brought me up short. It just . . . caught me off-guard. I wasn't prepared somehow for the finality of it.

I heard the pounding of the Pok's feet as it put greater distance between us. I should have been concerned. I should have been immediately in pursuit. Poks are not renowned for their speed; even on foot, I could have overtaken it. But Stener was already forgotten. Instead my attention was focused on the guard. The other two were lying unconscious nearby, but they could well have been on one of Xenex's moons for all that it mattered at that moment.

I crept toward him. In retrospect, it's amazing how tentative I was. It wasn't as if he could be any threat to me. I had, effectively, killed him. But on some level that hadn't really registered on me. So I approached him as if he still might somehow strike at me. I drew closer, closer, until I was standing right over him. He was staring straight up, and he looked . . . confused. He didn't appear aware of where he was or how he had gotten there, and certainly he was unclear as to what had happened.

It was the first time that I actually had a chance to study him close-up. The pieces of his broken helmet had fallen away from his face, and I was able to see him clearly. I was stunned by his youth. He only looked several years older than I was. There was no belligerence in his face. He did not look . . .

. . . evil. That was it. I was expecting him to look evil. He was, after all, an agent of the enemy, a supporter of the evil oppressors. So his demeanor should have reflected that.

Except that I didn't know what evil was "supposed" to look like. The face of the enemy was not a great, monolithic thing, but rather millions upon millions of individuals, each with his own hopes and dreams and aspirations. And this face, this nameless face that was staring at the sky with a profoundly confused expression, had just had all his dreams shattered along with his helmet and his head.

I didn't know what to do. The Pok was long forgotten, Stener's getaway assured, and yet I didn't care. There were emotions tumbling through me, emotions that I had no clue how to deal with. Odd, isn't it. With all those emotions present, you would think that "triumph" would have been one of them. But I didn't feel that at all. In fact, it might well have been that I felt everything but that.

And then he said something that utterly confused me. He said . . ."Hand."

I was clueless as to what he was talking about. The word, bereft of context, meant nothing.

Then I saw that his fingers were spasming slightly. It took me a moment more to grasp fully what he wanted.

Slowly—even, I hate to admit, a bit fearfully—I reached out. Understand this: In the heat of battle, I was capable of slicing a man open, ripping his still-beating heart from his chest and holding it up into his face, and I say that with no sense of hyperbole. I actually did that, on several occasions throughout the years. I was not what anyone would call squeamish, and certainly had no trepidation over touching a dead or dying man.

But in this instance I did. My hand was actually trembling. I realized it and became angry with what I saw as my weakness. Taking a deep breath, I seized his hand firmly, still in a quandary as to why he appeared to want the gesture.

His fingers wrapped around mine and he looked into my eyes with infinite gratitude. I don't think he knew who I was. He didn't realize that I was the one who had struck the fatal blow. His mind was a million miles away. All he knew was that I was another being, another living, breathing soul. He knew that . . . and he knew, I have to believe, that he was dying.

In a voice that was barely above a hoarse whisper, he said, "Thank . . . you. . . ."

I knew that he was beyond help, and furthermore, that more of the Danteri would be back before too long. Not only that, but the unconscious soldiers would come around sooner or later. I tried to get up, to get away, to extricate my hand from his, but he gasped out, "No." He didn't seem afraid of dying. He simply didn't want to be alone.

I lifted him, then. I was surprised by how light he was. The entire business had taken a most bizarre turn, but I didn't dwell on any of that. I was operating purely on instinct, answering some moral code that I couldn't truly articulate quite yet. I ran with him, ran to an area of caves and crevices that I knew about not too far away. It was a labyrinthine area which I had known about for quite some time, and explored extensively in my youth. I knew I could hide there indefinitely, and there were underground passages as well so it wasn't as if anyone could reasonably lay siege to it.

I brought the young guard there, my mind racing with confusion. I was unable to determine any reasonable answers as to why I was doing what I was doing. I brought him to a secluded place within the caverns, and there I sat with him.

This was the enemy. I kept reminding myself of that, over and over again. He was the enemy, his people had enslaved my people. I had no reason whatsoever to feel the slightest bit of empathy for this individual. But I did. Here I had had my first taste of destruction, had taken down my first opponent . . . and I have never felt weaker. I wanted to get up, to flee the caves, to leave his rotting corpse for whatever scavenger creatures might take a fancy to it.

Instead I stayed. Perhaps I felt that leaving him behind would have been cowardice. Perhaps I needed to prove to myself that I was capable of taking it. Perhaps I was simply morbidly curious. It may have been all of those or none of those. In the final analysis . . . I just couldn't. I sat there with him, and his grip did not lessen on my hand. Every so often he would tremble, shuddering, his body convulsing slightly. He faded in and out, and never once that entire time did he comprehend that the man who had killed him was next to him.

I was looking into his eyes when he died. He had lain there, in the cool of the cavern, staring into space as if searching for some sort of answer. He said nothing. And then his head rolled slowly in my direction, his gaze fixing on me—truly fixing on me—for the first time. "You . . ." he managed to say.

I waited for the rest, or at least whatever it was he was able to manage. You destroyed me. You bastard, you took my life. You are the one who is responsible. You did this to me. Anything, everything, I was ready for it.

"Thank . . . you . . ." he told me. Then his head lolled to one side and I heard a sound that I would come to know all too well: a death rattle, his spirit leaving the meaty shell in which it had spent its mortal existence.

I stared at him for a very long time, and then I saw a large spot of wetness appear on his face. It took me a moment to fully comprehend what it was. It was a tear. It was not, however, from him. It was from me. Large, fat tears were rolling down my face, and I was so numb that I was unaware of it at first. Then they came faster and harder. My body started to tremble, great racking sobs seizing me. I couldn't believe it. I fancied myself already as a hardened warrior, determined and ready to lead his people to freedom. What sort of warrior and leader allows himself to fall apart in the face of killing an enemy? But the more I tried to pull myself together, the more the tears flowed.

I tried to stand up, tried to run, but there was no strength in my limbs. I collapsed and continued to cry, and I have no idea for how long it continued. It was probably minutes, but it felt like days.

Eventually it subsided, the sobbing tapering off. Still I lay there for some time, feeling the coolness of the stone against my face. Then I pulled myself together and dusted myself off. I picked up the body of the first man I had ever killed. He was significantly larger than I, and his body was even heavier dead than it had been alive. But my strength was rather formidable and I had no trouble hauling him out to the mouth of the cave. Prudence would have dictated that I simply leave him . . . it . . . there. After all, I was putting myself at risk weighing myself down, and if there had been any Danteri hunting parties passing by at that particular moment, I would have been at a disadvantage. The sun was already quite low in the sky, the shadows stretching like darkling fingers across the plains, as I left the corpse behind me and set off into the darkness.

I've often looked back on that day and wondered what possessed me. After all, I had known that slaying others would be necessary if I were to accomplish my goal and lead an insurrection that would result in Xenex's freedom. Why, then, did it affect me in such a way?

Perhaps I was mourning my lost innocence, or at least what passed for innocence. Never again would I be anything other than a slayer.

Perhaps the tears, in some way, were an expression of fear. In having irretrievably made that first strike, I had determined a course not only for myself, but for my planet. The Danteri would demand Xenexian blood by the ton in exchange for the assault upon their collector and the death of one of the guards. My people would not stand for it—that I would see to personally. Perhaps I was shedding tears in advance for those of my people who were destined to die in the insurrection. With a stroke of my sword, I had doomed them. They would die fighting for a greater cause, but they would die just the same, and so those deaths would be on my head.

Or perhaps it was simply because I never knew my victim's name, or anything about him. Did he have a wife back on Danter whom I had just transformed into a widow? A son who would never see his father again? He himself had parents, that was likely. How would they react upon learning that their son was dead? Would his mother still hear the cries he uttered as an infant, like a haunting, mournful song in her head, and cry until her heart broke over the loss of that child? Or perhaps he was an orphan, with no parents, and had not yet had time to marry or sire children. In that case, he would leave no one behind to mourn him or those accomplishments that he might have achieved had his life not been cut short. Here I was, planning to lead a rebellion that—if it succeeded—would definitely give me a permanent place in the annals of Xenex, and the first casualty in that course might be a young man who was so without attachment to the world that he might as well not even have lived in it.

There was no way for me to know, no way for me to ever know, and perhaps that was what caused me to cry my heart out. But once it had been cried out, I then carefully and meticulously began to build a great wall of brick around it. The slaying of the young man was the first brick, and more bricks would follow while their thickening blood provided the cement between them.

In the final analysis, it might have been all of those plus one more: the evil irony of a young man dying while thanking the one who had killed him since his delirium had prevented him from understanding who I was.

I returned home, told my older brother, D'ndai, what I had done. He blanched considerably, and then his jaw set in grim determination. At the time he had no great love for the Danteri, and was as susceptible to my exhortations as was any other man. Although I would be designated warlord within a very short time, at that time I was given the appointment of a rank we called *"r'ksha"* . . . or what you would term "captain." D'ndai had several private fliers, all of which were pressed into work as our preparation for battle against the Danteri loomed. The largest one was given to me, out of deference to the fact that my determination was setting the entire situation into motion. I also had my first crew, and ten truer and braver men never walked the surface of Xenex. "Men." What a word. More like young boys, they were. We all were, although we felt much older, of course.

Sadly . . . I was the only one who grew to become older. The rest of them died within the first year of combat.

The last of my crew was wiped out in a devastating raid on a Danteri outpost which went horribly wrong. I had had several early successes, you see, and became emboldened as a result. Consequently, I became sloppy. I trusted a tip from a source who proved to be not as reliable as I had previously thought. What I had intended as a surprise attack on a strategic outpost turned out to be a crafty trap by the Danteri. I have a "sixth sense" for danger, I always have. Just before their trap sprang shut, I sensed that we were heading into an ambush and tried to get us out of there before it was too late. In one respect, I accomplished that goal. Had I not realized when I did, we would have been slaughtered within seconds. As it was, we narrowly avoided capture, but the firefight that resulted from the nearly perfect ambush was catastrophic. My vessel limped back to the city, with my urging every last bit of speed out of its failing engines. I was hoping, praying that I would be able to save at least a few lives of the handful of men—boys—who were left to me. But by the time I made it back to the city, it was too late. The last of my crew died in my arms. Unlike the time with the first man I killed, though, this time I felt nothing. Absolutely nothing. The wall that I had built around my heart was a strong one by that point, and not easily pierced. No more tears would I, could I, shed over the deaths of others, be it at my hand or not.

That was the theory, at least. Nonetheless, the guilt weighed heavily upon me, despite D'ndai's assurances that it was not my fault, that I had no way of knowing. That was no excuse. I should have known. It was my first major setback, my first major loss to the Danteri, and part of me was angry that I had survived while the men who had been counting on me had lost their lives. My resolve was not shattered . . . but for the first time, I began to doubt myself. I had never wavered in my belief that I would triumph over the Danteri . . . until that moment.

I wandered the streets of Calhoun aimlessly that night. I had a slight limp from an injured leg, and I had not washed off the smoke and soot from battle or the crash of my vessel. My hair was wildly askew. In short, I wasn't especially pretty to look at, I can tell you. I passed the fortifications that had been erected around the city of Calhoun. The perimeter guards saluted me, nodding in approval as I passed, gave me gestures of assurance. All of it felt hollow, empty. They still had confidence in me, but I did not have it in myself.

Understand, I knew every foot, every square inch of the city. Nonetheless, after walking aimlessly for a time, I found myself in an area of town that was oddly unfamiliar to me. Furthermore, I was drawn to one particular door that had an odd sign hanging on it. In Xenexian, it read, "R'Ksha Foldes." Or, to translate into English: "the Captain's Table." I had no idea what it was referring to. I had never heard of the establishment, if such it was, and that alone was very odd since I had thought I knew every place of business in all of Calhoun.

I placed an ear against the door and heard what amounted to a faint murmur from within, but nothing I could distinguish. It sounded like voices, but I couldn't make out anything that anyone was saying. For a moment I thought of turning away, but something within me rebelled at the notion. It smacked too much of cowardice, and therefore was an intolerable option.

Taking a deep breath, I pushed open the door.

It was a very odd sight.

In many ways, it seemed no different than a standard Xenexian tavern. Weapons hung upon the wall as a convenience for drunken customers, as was always the case in Xenexian taverns. The reason, you see, is that customers who allow themselves to get too drunk to fight, but try and do so anyway, are too stupid to live and therefore duels with such individuals should be facilitated. That way they won't continue to cause mischief.

But there was something about the place that I couldn't immediately identify. A scent, perhaps, like sea air, and a breeze wafting through which was of mysterious origin considering that outside on that night there had been no breeze at all. Furthermore—and this, I assure you, was the oddest part—I couldn't help but feel that the floor was rocking ever so gently. Not a quake, most definitely, but just a very delicate swaying motion, as if I were standing on the deck of a ship of some sort.

What was most peculiar of all, however, was the astounding mixture of alien races who populated the place. At sturdy wooden tables were representatives of all manner of species, including any number that I could not identify. It's not as if Xenex has a large number of visitors. Despite the fact that Calhoun was one of the larger cities, Xenex was—and is—largely the province of Xenexians. Nevertheless, there were individuals with blue skin, green skin, red skin . . . every permutation of the spectrum, it seemed. Some with antennae, others with multiple eyes or no eyes, one with tentacles, another with a spotted shell and a perpetual scowl.

There was one man off to the side at a table by himself. Of the species I now know as "humans," he was dressed in blue, with a trim white beard. He was simply shaking his head as if in perpetual annoyance and confusion, and there was the sadness of the grave in his eyes. He kept muttering the same words over and over again: "Damned iceberg. Goddamned iceberg." I had no idea what he was talking about. I started to approach him, and then felt a hand on my shoulder.

I whirled because, of course, I had no idea who was behind me. I was conditioned to anticipate attacks at all times.

"Just leave him be, son. You'd be wasting your time anyway. Poor devil's off in his own world."

The man who had spoken, who had stopped me from going near the bearded man in blue, had somewhat unkempt white hair himself. He wore an apron, and had a ready smile that I found comforting somehow. He was not Xenexian, but in an odd and fleeting way, he reminded me of my father. "They call me Cap," he said.

"Are you the owner of this place?" I asked.

"Yes and no. In a way, we're all owners of this place. You, me," and he gestured to encompass the rest of the bar, "them. This is your first time here, but eventually you'll understand." He smiled. "Congratulations, by the way."

"For what?" For a moment I bristled. I was still angry, bitter over what happened to my men, and some part of me thought he was sarcastically alluding to that tragedy.

"For being the youngest captain ever to visit the Captain's Table. Previously the youngest we had was Alexander. He was only here once, and then on a technicality, since in truth he was a king. But he fancied himself a captain of great armies, and that was sufficient to gain him entrance in a sort of probationary status. It was just the one time, though. He tried to take over the bar." He shook his head resignedly. "Should have expected that."

"Should I . . . know this person you're speaking of?"

Cap tilted his head back and declaimed as if in the theater, " 'And Alexander wept, for he had no new worlds to conquer.' " The mention of the name drew glances from several of the other patrons, and there were what appeared to be grim smiles of acknowledgment and recollection.

I decided not to pursue it. As if sensing my thoughts, he guided me to a small table to one side. "I think it best, what with this being your first time and considering your age, that you simply observe rather than try to interact extensively. We do not, after all, want to have any problems."

"I . . . suppose not," I said. I was having difficulty understanding where I was or what was happening. Without really paying attention, I sat down at a table.

"No, not that one," Cap said quickly, and he pointed off to my left. "The one over here."

I was beginning to become annoyed. The eccentricity of the place, the odd atmosphere that was a bizarre blend of strange-yet-familiar, and my own state of mind thanks to my recent setbacks, were serving to put me on edge a bit. "This one seems fine," I told him. "I think I will stay right—"

A huge dagger slammed down into the tabletop with such force that it threatened to split the wood in half. The hilt quivered slightly.

"Captain Gloriosus," Cap said with clear warning in his voice. "You know the rules."

Slowly I glanced up, and up, at the man whose powerful hand had wielded the dagger. He was dressed in glittering chestplate armor and a metal skirt that ended at about midthigh. His legs were powerful, his arms no less so. He had a long, bristling beard so thick that it looked like wire, and a fierce scowl that showed from beneath a plumed helmet. The scabbard for his dagger was on the inside of his right calf, and from his left hip hung a massive sword.

"This pup is at my table," the one called Gloriosus said.

I did not appreciate the tone of his voice, and told him so. This seemed to amuse the one called Gloriosus, and he laughed in a booming tone that was unbearably condescending. "Cap," he bellowed, 'are we letting any upstart who wishes it to sit at the Captain's Table? Have we no standards anymore?"

"The standard is that patrons have to be captains of one sort or another," Cap told him as if addressing a small child. "He fits the criteria, Miles, as do you. As does everyone here."

The others were making no pretense of looking away anymore. About forty or so pairs of eyes took in the entire confrontation. They sat back and observed as if watching a vid or an adventure in a holosuite.

"That means," continued Cap as if unaware that this situation were anything other than the most intimate of disagreements, "that he is under the protection of the bar . . . as are you, Miles."

"A captain of the Roman legions needs no protection from a whelp," the one called Miles Gloriosus said.

I didn't like this tone, or his arrogance. More, I felt as if he had made it a point to try and shame me in front of the others who were scattered around the bar. I had no idea why the opinions of these strangers mattered, but something within me simply refused to allow myself to be treated as a laughingstock.

Captain Miles Gloriosus was continuing to boast about his own general fabulousness. I didn't bother to listen. Instead with my right hand I yanked the dagger from the table, and with the left I reached up and grabbed a fistful of his copious beard. Before he was aware of what I was doing, I yanked down as hard as I could. His head hit the table and I brought the dagger around and down, driving it squarely through the beard and into the tabletop with a resounding thud. Gloriosus was pinned, momentarily immobilized as his beard was entangled with the blade. Given time, of course, he would have managed to pull it loose, but time was not something I was inclined to afford him.

I was on my feet then. I could have used my sword, which was strapped onto my back, but instead I yanked out the Roman captain's own sword from his scabbard. He yelped in frustration and grabbed at the knife to extricate it from his beard . . . and suddenly he became very quiet, probably because he felt the edge of his own blade against the back of his neck. One movement downward and I could have severed his head.

The tavern, which had been bustling with energy only moments before, suddenly became very quiet. Every single individual was watching with stony, impassive silence. It was impossible to tell whether they approved or disapproved of my actions. Cap said nothing, but merely stood there with his arms folded, inscrutable.

I had his sword in a firm double-handed grip, and the blade did not waver so much as a centimeter. I had one of the cutting edges of the blade tucked just under the bottom of his helmet. Very quietly, very deliberately, I said, "It would appear you need some protection from the whelp after all. Wouldn't you say that's true?"

He muttered something that sounded like a curse, and I repeated, "Wouldn't you say that's true?" To underscore my point, and the delicacy of his situation, I pressed the blade down ever so slightly. A thin line of blood welled up. I couldn't see his eyes from the angle I was standing, but from the sudden tensing of his body I was quite sure he felt it.

"M'k'n'zy," Cap said warningly.

And then Miles Gloriosus growled, "Yes."

"Yes what?" I wasn't going to let him get off quite that easily.

"Yes . . . on reflection, I would say it's true . . . that I could have used . . ." He hesitated, and I applied just a hair more pressure. "Protection against the whelp!" he practically spat out as quickly as he could.

I stepped back then and he spun with a good deal of speed, forcibly tearing himself away from the table with such violence that a generous chunk of his beard was torn right from his chin. He didn't seem to notice. He was too busy focusing the fullness of his ire upon me. For a moment, just for a moment, I envisioned what it would be like to face him on a true battlefield. I had a sense of him, a feeling of the environment from which he came. I realized that the truth was that I had been rather fortunate. Had he not been so swaggeringly confident, I never would have been able to manhandle him so easily.

He extended a hand and I thought he wanted to shake mine. Then I realized that he wanted his sword back. I handed it over to him hilt first. This was a tactical gamble—some would say error—on my part. I was holding the blade as I offered the sword to him. Had he wished to do so, he could have grabbed the hilt, swung the sword around and tried to gut me like a freshly caught fish. Whether he would have succeeded or not is debatable, but he certainly could have had a good shot at killing me. Instead, however, he took his sword from me without comment and slid it into his scabbard. I was impressed by the soundlessness of it, since both the steel and scabbard were so well oiled. There was no hiss of the metal against the leather; instead it went in noiselessly, and presumably was pulled in much the same manner.

"You," he growled, "were lucky."

I couldn't disagree. I felt the same way.

"You would be well advised to stay out of my way," continued Gloriosus, "lest things not turn out quite so well for you the next time." Pulling together what was left of his pride, Gloriosus swaggered away.

My gaze swept the other captains who were in the bar. Many of them didn't seem interested in meeting my glance, but were instead suddenly very preoccupied with looking in other directions entirely. I felt very unwelcome and unwanted, and had no idea what the hell I was doing there. I started to rise from my seat, intending to head for the door, but Cap put a hand on my forearm and quietly said, "Stay. You have as much right to be here as anyone else."

"I doubt that," I said, but I sat anyway.

Cap placed a mug in front of me. I have no idea from where he pulled it, but there it was. "First drink for a first-time customer is always on the house," he said, gesturing to it. I reached for it tentatively.

My general paranoia and uncertainty made me hesitate, but then I sniffed at it and looked up curiously. "What is this called?" I asked.

"Beer."

"Bihr." I rolled the unfamiliar word around in my mouth, then took a sip of it. It was more pungent than I'd expected, but had a certain degree of kick to it. I must have been quite a sight: the scruffy barbarian, surrounded by men and women who were, for the most part, far more cultured and civilized than I could ever hope to be. Everyone was watching me, even those who were pretending to look in another direction. They probably wondered what I was doing there. So did I.

I swallowed half the beer and found the sensation somewhat relaxing. I looked at Cap, a gentle warmth beginning to develop in my gut, and I realized, "You called me by name before. How did you know my name?"

"How did I know you?" He feigned surprise that such a question could even be posed. "Why, everyone knows the name of the great M'k'n'zy. Weren't you aware of that?"

"I was not aware of any greatness," I said bitterly. "My men were depending on me, and I let them down. It was my fault."

"Yes. It was," Cap said, matter-of-factly.

I looked up at him. His comment was a stark contrast to D'ndai's words of consolation. "What should I have done, then? How could I have avoided it?"

"Oh, you couldn't have," said Cap. He had seated himself opposite me, and was holding an empty glass, which he was wiping clean with a white cloth. "There was nothing you could have done differently. You made all the correct decisions based upon the information you had available to you. Any other person here, in your position, would have done the same thing."

"But . . . you're still saying it's my fault. . . ."

"Of course it is. You're the captain. You're the leader. That makes it your responsibility. All these people," and he nodded his head in their direction, "oversee vessels or armies or crews, some of them numbering in the thousands. And whatever happens, these people here are the final authorities. Theirs is the final responsibility. Even when it's not their fault . . . it's their fault. Tell me, M'k'n'zy . . ." He leaned forward in a conspiratorial fashion. "Do you feel something filtering through the air? A sort of sensation, a distant heaviness that seems to settle around your upper torso?"

"I . . . suppose. Yes . . . yes, I think I do at that." I flexed my shoulders. "What . . . is that?"

"It's the weight of the world," Cap said with a ragged smile. "Everyone here carries it on them, and it just kind of leaks around and filters through the atmosphere of the Captain's Table. The nice thing about this place is that we all share each other's weight, and that makes it all the more bearable."

I stared at him skeptically, unsure whether he literally meant it or not. I found my gaze resting on the man in blue once more, the one with the beard who was off by himself. "What's his problem?" I asked.

"He lost his vessel," Cap told me. "Over a thousand souls perished, claimed by icy waters. As his vessel was sinking, he discovered a door on his deck that he had never noticed before. He stepped through it . . . and found himself here. He's been here ever since. Nothing for him to go back to, really."

"How long has he been here?" I asked.

"A few minutes. A few centuries." Cap pulled thoughtfully at his chin. "It's all subjective, really. Never an easy answer to that one. Somewhat like being a commander, really. The easy answers don't always present themselves readily."

A slow, eerie feeling began to creep over me. "Cap . . ." I said slowly.

"Yes?"

"Am I . . . are we . . . dead?"

He laughed loudly and boisterously at that. "No, young M'k'n'zy. We, and you, are not dead. Oh, in a sense, we're dead to the world, I suppose, in a small way. It's really the only way this bar can function, because there is so much responsibility borne by its patrons that they'd be pulled out of here by those demands if those requests could reach them. But in the standard sense, we are very much alive. The land of the living awaits just beyond the exit."

I looked in the direction he was pointing, and then I asked suspiciously, "How do I know that, if I pass through that door, I won't wind up splashing about in the icy waters that took his vessel?" I indicated the white-bearded captain.

"So many things you desire to know, young M'k'n'zy," Cap said, and if a man less charming had said it, it might have sounded patronizing. "I'm afraid that there will be some matters which you will have to take on faith. Besides, you have a destiny to fulfill, and that destiny certainly doesn't include sinking beneath the surface of the Atlantic Ocean."

"Of the what?"

"Of an ocean," Cap amended.

"And what would this destiny be?" I asked.

"How would I know that? I'm simply a bartender, M'k'n'zy. I'm not God."

"Are you certain of that?"

He didn't seem to answer at first, but merely smiled, and then I realized that the smile itself was indeed the answer. "If you need a refill," he said, "just hold up a hand and someone will attend to you directly. And M'k'n'zy . . . be aware of something. . . ."

"Yes?"

"Every single person here has had failures, setbacks, and frustrations. Every one has blamed himself, sometimes rightly and sometimes wrongly. The important thing is to keep to the hope of all the things you can do to benefit others. You can do great good, M'k'n'zy. Never forget that your men are depending upon you . . . but also never forget that you are not a god. You are not infallible. You are simply . . . a captain. Just worry about being the best captain that you can be, and let the rest sort itself out as it will."

"That's too easy, too facile an answer," I told him, but he wasn't there anymore. He'd moved away from the table, and a quick glance around the room did not reveal him.

I sat there for a time longer. A waitress would bring over another beer whenever I wanted it, although interestingly I never actually had to ask her for it. It was simply there. And when I had enough, the table space in front of me remained vacant.

I realized that Cap was right. What made me realize it was that I kept going over and over it in my mind, and I wasn't feeling any better over what had happened, but on the other hand I wasn't coming up with anything I would have, or could have, done that would have made it any better.

Eventually, I knew it was time to leave. To this day, I don't know whether the impulse came from within or without. But I was already in motion before my mind had fully adjusted to my imminent departure. I had left a random amount of Xenexian currency behind as a tip, having no clue as to how much would be appropriate. But Cap, who was behind the bar, tossed off a salute. I had never seen one before, since Xenexians tend to bow in deference to commanding officers. But I returned the gesture and from his approving smile I surmised that I had done so correctly. "M'k'n'zy," he called to me. I turned and waited expectantly. "Next time," he said, "a story."

I looked at him oddly. "A story? You'll tell a story?"

"No," he told me. "You will."

"About what?"

He shrugged. "Whatever." Then, effectively ending the conversation, he picked up another glass and whistled as he wiped it down. I was going to continue to ask him what he was talking about, but decided that it would be best simply to be on my way.

I walked out of the tavern back onto the Xenexian street. The evening had grown colder. I had no idea how much time had passed while I was in there. Drawing my cloak more tightly around myself, I started down the street . . . and then hesitated. His words about a story were still with me, and I felt myself overwhelmed with curiosity. I turned and retraced my steps so that I could ask Cap for clarification.

I couldn't find the place.

I was certain that I passed the tavern's location several times. It wasn't as if there was now a vacant area where once the tavern had been. The shops and eateries had simply closed ranks, as if they were hiding one of their own from prying eyes. On the off chance that I had headed down the wrong street, I went to the nearest intersection and circumnavigated the block. Nothing. Gone. Completely gone. It wasn't at all possible . . . but it had happened. The Captain's Table had somehow managed to make itself scarce.

I thought of ghost stories that I had heard, strange tales of visions and such that I had always half-kiddingly traded with my friends. I was convinced, though, that this night I had had an experience very much along those lines. Perhaps I had been given a preview of an afterlife set aside for warriors . . . such as your Earth's Norsemen, I would learn in later years, described their Valhalla. Or perhaps I had wandered into what could best be termed a haunted house. Perhaps some bizarre interdimensional anomaly had situated itself smack on a side street of the city of Calhoun and had allowed me into it.

Or perhaps I just wasn't getting enough sleep.

Resolving to do something about the last circumstance, at least, I went into the night without a backward glance. This was deliberate: Part of me was afraid to admit that I would not see the place again when it had so clearly been there, and the other part was concerned that the Captain's Table had somehow sprung into existence again. If the latter occurred, I would not be able to resist entering once more . . . and it might be that, given a second opportunity, I might never leave at all.

That was my first time at the Captain's Table.

This . . .

This is the second. . . .

Second Encounter

I WAS GOING OUT OF MY MIND WITH BOREDOM.

I read over, for what seemed the hundredth time, the dispatches from Starfleet regarding the Dominion War. When the chime sounded at the door of my ready room, I didn't even hear it the first time. That's how absorbed I was in the recounting of the various battles and skirmishes. In fact, it took the voice of my first officer, Elizabeth Paula Shelby—"Eppy," I called her, when I felt like being either affectionate or annoying—calling, "Captain!" through the door to get my attention.

I glanced up impatiently, wondered why she wasn't standing in front of me, and realized that she was still on the other side of the door waiting for permission to enter. "Come," I called.

The door slid open and Elizabeth entered.

Now there is something you should understand about Elizabeth: I love her. Deeply. Madly. Completely. Even when we broke off our engagement, I never stopped loving her. Even when looking at her was a knife to the heart, I never stopped loving her. She is my soul mate, my better half, my significant other . . . any nickname you choose to give it, that is what she is to me. However I can never tell her that. I know myself, you see. I need to be in control of situations, and to admit to her how I feel would be to surrender a part of myself that I am not willing to give up. In order for me to love Elizabeth as truly as I wish to, I must bring myself to a state of mind where I cannot live without her. In my time, however, I have seen too much death, too much slaughter. I have lost too many loved ones, time and again. I cannot remember a time where death was not a reality rather than an abstract concept. My very first memory, in fact, is someone dying. I don't remember the details; I could not have been more than two seasons old. But I remember the blood, and the death rattle, and staring into lifeless eyes before the strong hand of my father yanked me away.

If I ever reach a point where I cannot live without Elizabeth, then I will feel as if I have attached a beacon to her back that is serving to summon the Grim Reaper. I cannot leave myself as vulnerable as that. It would be wrong. Wrong for me, wrong for the crew . . . just . . . wrong.

So I keep my silence, wrap my feelings for her within a cloak of toughness mixed with irreverence. When I argue with her, what I truly want to do is hold her tight. Every time I say her name, I imagine myself brushing my lips across hers. She doesn't know any of this, or at least I pray she does not. Otherwise she might think the less of me. For in some ways, that mind-set makes me a coward, and it would pain me if she regarded me in that manner.

"Commander," I greeted her formally with a slight nod.

"Are you all right, Captain?" she asked without preamble.

"Fine. Why do you ask?"

"Well, you got those recent war updates, and you've been stewing in here ever since."

"Stewing?" I raised an eyebrow in mild offense. "I wouldn't say 'stewing.' "

"Then how would you term it . . . sir?" she asked.

I didn't reply immediately, because to be honest, "stewing" wasn't all that far off the mark. Finally I let out an annoyed sigh. " 'Smoldering,' perhaps. I have a good deal of anger, Eppy, and no clear idea of what to do with it."

"Anger? Why?" She sat opposite me. I could tell she was concerned about my state of mind, because she allowed my use of her hated nickname to pass without comment.

"We should be there," I said, tapping my computer. On the screen there was a display of Federation space with key points in the ongoing war marked for easy reference. "The *Excalibur* is as good a starship as any of them, Eppy, and this is a damned fine crew. A little odd in places, I admit, but I'd gladly lead any of them into battle and be confident that they'd give as good a fight as any opponent is likely to get. Instead we're out here, in Thallonian space. We're . . ."

"We're pursuing our mission, as per our orders, Mac," Elizabeth reminded me.

"Our orders, our orders. To hell with our orders. *Grozit,* Commander . . . Captain Picard ignored his orders when the Borg assaulted Earth. Starfleet had him rooting around the Neutral Zone. He followed his conscience and if it weren't for him, Earth would be the sole province of the Borg by now." I pointed in the general, vague direction of Federation space. "There are men and women I trained with in the midst of one of the most formidable wars since the Romulans first swarmed their borders, and I'm reduced to hearing about it secondhand."

"It was a different situation with Picard, Mac," Shelby replied. "He'd been assimilated into the collective at one point, and that made him suspect as far as the Fleet was concerned. But as he proved, it also made him uniquely suited to attack and defeat the Borg. That was a one-in-a-million set of circumstances."

"Our place is with the Fleet," I said firmly.

"Our place is where we're told to be," she shot back, but she didn't do so in an angry manner. I could tell that she was as torn up about the conflict as I was. For all I knew, she'd love to sit there and voice the same complaints. But it's part of Shelby's value to me that she will readily take an opposing viewpoint, if for no other reason than to make me think more carefully about whatever it is I'm saying. The fact is, she challenges me and I learn a lot from her. Not that I would admit that, of course.

"I smell Jellico behind this," I told her. At that point I rose from behind my desk and pulled my sword off the wall. It was the sword that I had taken off an enemy, back when the bastard had sliced open the right side of my face and left me with a permanent scar . . . or, at least, a scar that I had chosen to leave permanently. "He doesn't trust me any more than the rest of the Fleet trusted Picard. Perhaps I should respond the same way that Picard did." I swung the sword through the air. It made satisfying, sharp hissing sounds as it cut. Elizabeth flinched slightly; perhaps she was worried it was going to come flying out of my hand and decapitate her.

"It's more complicated than that, Mac. There's not one big battle going on where we can ride to the rescue. Besides," she continued in a less strident tone, "has it occurred to you that this might not simply be Admiral Jellico?"

"Believe me, Eppy, if anyone is capable of doing something to annoy me, it's Jellico."

"Perhaps," she admitted, "but Mac, the bottom line is: We don't know truly how the war is going. We know what Starfleet is admitting to, but it might be worse than they're letting on, and what we're hearing already isn't that great to begin with."

"Starfleet, less than candid?" I feigned horror at the very notion. "Careful, Eppy. You might cause the entirety of my world to come crashing down around me."

She didn't seem the least bit impressed by my dazzling repartee. I couldn't entirely blame her. The subject matter didn't lend itself to it; it felt clumsy and forced. Considering what she said next, I can somewhat understand why the conversation seemed labored.

"Have you considered the possibility that the Federation . . . could fall?"

It was not an easy question for her to pose. It was more than just a case of her tossing out a scenario and asking whether I had thought about it. In a way, she was voicing her own greatest nightmare.

I stared at her. The fact was, it hadn't even occurred to me. "Of course I've considered it," I lied smoothly.

"No, you haven't," she said, reminding me of the typical futility in trying to put something past her. "You're so convinced of the intrinsic 'rightness' of your 'side' that you haven't thought for a moment that the Federation might end up on the short end of the stick. If that happens, Mac, if things go badly," she said patiently, "they're going to need ships that they've held in reserve. Not only that, but those ships will need to be captained by the men with the most experience at operating on their own, without any guidance from home."

I knew precisely what she was referring to. All captains, particularly starship captains, function with a good deal of autonomy. But there are some captains . . . more than I care to think about, really . . . who are referred to as "homebodies." They check with Starfleet constantly about every move they make, wanting an official stamp on everything they do in order to avoid second-guessing or potential charges.

I was definitely not one of those types. Eppy knew that all too well. If anything, I tended to operate from the philosophy that rules were not only made for other people, but for other galaxies. If Starfleet disappeared tomorrow, I wouldn't give a single glance back.

"You're more comfortable on your own, Mac. Happier. Not only that," and she leaned forward on her elbows, "but how many captains out there actually have experience in rallying troops against oppressors. You led an entire planet in revolt before you were twenty. If you were brought in now, you'd simply be part of the fleet. You'd probably feel that the situation was cramping your style. Ahhh, but if it goes badly with the Federation, and we discover ourselves in a sort of frontier situation, who better than you to try and rebuild the society we've all come to know."

"I . . ." I let the thought trail off for a moment, and then shrugged. "I suppose you're right."

"Of course I am."

Her flat tone certainly sounded like the old Eppy. I smiled gamely at her. "Your confidence is most appreciated."

"One of us has to be confident." But then she reached across the table and took my hand. Her voice softened and she said, "Mac . . . I know you've spent your whole life refusing to settle. You look at the world around you and you say, 'How can I change it? How can I make it better?

How can I improve upon it so that it better suits the needs and desires of one Mackenzie Calhoun?' "

"You make me sound like the most self-centered bastard that ever walked the galaxy."

"No," said Elizabeth ruefully. "That title belongs to the guy I dated right after I broke off with you. I was never so angry, before or since, with a man. We won't discuss him."

"I owe him a great debt, then. How many men make me look good in comparison?"

"The point is, Mac . . . that mind-set of yours has made history. You looked upon the people of Xenex, saw where the problems were, saw what had to be done, did it . . . and an entire people breathes free because of you. That's one hell of an accomplishment, and no one can ever take that away from you. But sometimes, you just have to settle for the way things are. You have to allow things to happen in their own time and way. I can give you an example, from centuries ago . . ."

"I don't need to hear this."

"Yes, you do." She settled into her chair. "It used to be that when children's feet turned sharply inward, causing them to walk oddly, orthopedists would provide all sorts of elaborate braces and heavy-duty tools. And eventually the child would walk normally. And the doctors were all quite pleased with themselves until they did a study and noticed that all the children left untreated . . . eventually, they walked normally, too. There was no cause and effect; if left alone, the problem righted itself as time passed. All they had to do was let matters develop naturally. You see what I'm saying?"

"Yes. You're saying that if I trust in the natural order of things, then sooner or later my efforts will prove pointless and I'll be out of a job."

She sighed once more. "You're hopeless. And will you please put the sword away? I know it satisfies your notions of male posturing, but I'm always afraid it's going to fly out of your hand and give me another navel."

"That'd be a waste, considering you already have three." I replaced the sword on the wall. "I'm sorry, Commander. The fact is, I know I'm hopeless. My ex-fiancée has informed me of that, any number of times."

"Mac . . ." She regarded me with open curiosity, more so than I could recall in the past. "Speaking of ex-fiancées and such . . . do you ever wonder what would have happened if we . . . uhm . . . if we . . ."

"No," I said quickly.

"Neither do I," she was just as speedy to reply.

And we left it at that.

I wasn't able to sleep.

Despite my lengthy conversation with Elizabeth, despite the fundamental belief that we were doing what we were supposed to do, where we were supposed to do it . . . I still felt a sort of gnawing frustration. I was supposed to be doing my duty as a Starfleet officer, continuing on my mission of mercy in the former Thallonian space, Sector 221-G. And besides, Elizabeth was likely correct. The *Excalibur* was very possibly being held in reserve, minding our own business in Thallonian space while at the same time ready at a moment's notice to fight on behalf of the Federation. Perhaps it was my famous ego talking, but I was convinced that somehow, in some way, we could wind up making a difference.

But it was becoming quite clear that we weren't going to be given the opportunity. At best, we were being held in reserve. At worst—to speak in the spirit of the Borg—we were irrelevant, depending upon what angle you wished to view the matter from.

I was in my quarters, bursting with energy and having no outlet for it. I did some brisk exercises, trying to burn off some of the frustration. I imagined I had a sword in my hand, practiced stabbing and thrusting, my old instincts coming to the fore. I had removed my shirt and was moving so quickly I would have been a blur to any observers. At least, I like to think so. One does have one's mental images of how one looks.

After an interminable time, I stopped. There was a thin coat of sweat on my chest. Knowing that I wasn't going to be getting any sleep, I dried myself off with a towel, got dressed, and exited my quarters.

As I walked the hallways of the *Excalibur,* I tried to look as if I were heading somewhere definitive, or had deep thoughts on my mind. Anything except appearing simply as a restless commanding officer who didn't know what to do with himself. I nodded briskly and greeted assorted crew members, but didn't bother to engage in small talk. I wasn't feeling especially chatty.

For reasons that I didn't even fully comprehend at first, I stopped in front of the main holodeck. The controls on it indicated that it was not in use. The timing was fortuitous. Obviously I was meant to try and use the holodeck to let off some steam.

"Rigel Nine. Main marketplace, Tamaran City." I said. I was literally picking it at random. I'd been to Rigel IX once, many many years ago. Briefly stopped in at Tamaran City, had a look around, got rather drunk and consequently had little memory of the place. But I was reasonably sure that it was in the memory of the holodeck computers, since it was frequented by any number of Starfleet personnel.

Moments later the doors had opened and I was standing in a perfect replica of Tamaran City. As soon as I was in, the doors hissed shut behind me and blended seamlessly with the rest of the environment. I should have been used to it, I suppose; that was the whole purpose of the holodeck, to foster the illusion of reality if one was willing enough to accept it.

And what an illusion it was. The rather pungent smell of Tamaran City's marketplace filled my nostrils as I began to stroll along the main boulevard. Frying meats, and assorted potatoes on open grills, and every block that I walked more merchants would be running out into the streets with their wares. None of them were real, and yet they performed with such eagerness that one would have thought their very livelihood hinged on their making a sale. I politely nodded off each one of them. I didn't want anyone—even fake beings—to perceive me as an easily targeted sucker. Odd, when one thinks about it, how pervasive pride can be.

I wandered the streets, moving into the back sections, making my way through the alleys. I wasn't heading anywhere in particular; I was simply seized with an urge to amble aimlessly about. I still wasn't getting tired; not the slightest bit of fatigue was pulling at me. From the corner of my eye, I noticed a man sneaking valuables from the pocket of another—a holy man, of all things, a Tellarite. I stepped in and snagged the thief in the act. He pulled away from me and bolted into the crowd, and I was about to take off after him when I realized that it seemed rather absurd to be chasing a criminal hologram. That might be taking the compulsion for crime and punishment just a bit too far. So I allowed him to escape and started to turn away when the Tellarite's hand was on my shoulder. I turned toward him slowly. Most Tellarites were aggressive and warlike, but there was a small white-clad religious sect that was not only harmless, but generally considered wise, pious, and peaceful. Even among their own, they didn't really fit in.

"Are you troubled, my son?" asked the Tellarite.

"I'm fine. Really," I said, turning away.

"Do you know what you need?"

"I said that I would be fi—"

"You need a drink."

It was startling words to hear coming from a holodeck replication. I turned back and looked thoughtfully into his face. There seemed to be no artifice, no sense of guile. For someone who was fake, he seemed one of the most "real" individuals I had ever met.

"A drink, holy man?" I replied cautiously.

"Yes. A drink. I think that may be where you want to go," and he pointed toward the end of the street. "I have heard good things about it."

I looked where he was pointing, and couldn't even begin to believe what I was seeing. A sign hung outside. The logo was in Rigelian, but the meaning was abundantly clear:

The Captain's Table.

By that point I was nothing short of stunned, for even though my encounter with the Captain's Table had occurred decades ago, the memory of the place was as vivid as if it had happened the previous day. Was it staggering coincidence? Two places in two different star systems, both with the same name?

And what was most bizarre about the situation was that I had walked those actual streets in the past. Not holos of them, but the real items. If the holodeck was supposed to be an accurate representation of the area, why would it have manufactured a doorway to a tavern that wasn't there?

I turned back to the holy man, but there was no sign of him. He had disappeared back into the crowd. I looked to the door and rubbed my eyes, as if doing so would somehow expunge the contradictory sight. But no, it was still right there. I felt as if it were mocking me.

"All right. Enough's enough," I said. I walked up to the door of the Captain's Table and pushed it open.

The weight of the world was still there. It hit me the moment I entered. Somehow, though, it didn't seem quite as heavy as before. Perhaps I had built up strength in my upper torso from years of carrying it myself.

There was also that faint aroma, the smell of sea air. As opposed to the first time, when it had puzzled me, this time I felt invigorated. I inhaled deeply, and my lungs fairly tingled from the sensation.

Then my rational mind took over and informed me that this simply couldn't be. It was flat-out impossible for the Captain's Table, for the real Captain's Table bar, to somehow have materialized within the holodeck. Perhaps it was some sort of elaborate prank. Perhaps it was just wishful thinking. No matter what the case, there was no way that I was going to allow it to continue. The memories of that place were too deep, too personal to me. I couldn't permit a shadow of it to exist. Since I was in the holodeck, of course, there was a simple way to put a stop to it.

"End program," I said.

Nothing happened. The patrons of the bar continued in their conversations, although one or two of them might have afforded me a curious glance. It wasn't like the last time, when the presence of the incredibly scruffy and disheveled barbarian youngster immediately captured the attention of all the patrons. I was older, more "normal"-looking. Still, in many ways I was just as confused as I was the first time I'd walked into the place. I was simply a bit more polished in my presentation.

"Computer, end program," I repeated. Still nothing happened. That was a flat-out impossibility. "Computer, end program!" When I received no response, I tapped my communicator. "Calhoun to bridge." No response.

I started to head for the door, and then a very familiar voice stopped me. "Leaving so soon, M'k'n'zy? Oh, that's right. You go by 'Mac' these days. At least, 'Mac' to your friends."

I turned, knowing ahead of time what I would see. Sure enough, there was Cap. The fact that he was exactly as I had remembered him from more than twenty years earlier was almost proof positive that I was in a holodeck re-creation. "I'd like to think," continued Cap, "that I can still count myself among your friends. That is the case, isn't it?"

"How . . . is this possible?" I asked.

He looked at me strangely as if he found it puzzling that I could even question it. "Why shouldn't it be possible? It's the most natural thing in the world. You saw a door for the Captain's Table, you walked through it, and lo and behold, you're in the Captain's Table. It's not as if you entered a door with our sign on it and found yourself in the middle of a baseball field."

"It would make equally as much sense," I said.

"Mac," and he shook his head disappointedly, "are you going to spend all your time here complaining and questioning? Or are you going to . . ." He stopped and stared. "What's wrong?"

I had totally lost focus on what Cap was saying, because I had spotted . . . *him* . . . across the bar.

He was just as I remembered him. The only difference was that he seemed a bit younger than he appeared to me when I'd first seen him. Maybe it was because I felt so much older, or maybe it was . . .

. . . maybe it was something else.

His hair was that same odd combination of gray with white at the temples. The same heavy eyebrows, the same jowly face and eyes that seemed to twinkle with merriment which gave him, in some ways, an almost elfin appearance. His Starfleet uniform was as crisp and clean as I remembered it. And his comm badge was right in place, with no drop of blood on it. He was engaged in an active discussion with several other captains of assorted races, and he didn't even glance my way. I might as well have been invisible to him.

"Kenyon," I whispered. "Captain Kenyon."

He didn't hear me, of course. I was on the opposite side of the tavern. But I was going to change that very quickly.

"Mac," Cap said. I knew that tone of voice; it was the same warning tone that he had used when I had confronted the Roman captain. In this case, it sounded even more firm and strident than it had the previous time. But I didn't care; it wasn't going to slow me down for a moment.

I started to make my way across the pub, toward Kenyon. That was when things started to happen.

It was subtle, at first, and then it became more pronounced. A waitress getting in my way, turning me around. Then a crowd of revelers moved between Kenyon and myself. When they passed, I had lost sight of Kenyon . . . and then spotted him, apparently as he had been before except it seemed as if the table had relocated somehow. I angled in that direction . . . and encountered more bar patrons, another waitress. A busboy dropped a stack of dishes, and I reflexively glanced in the way of the crash. When I looked back, Kenyon was somewhere else again, except there was no indication that he'd moved.

"What the hell?" I muttered.

Cap was at my elbow. "Sit down, Mac," he said firmly.

"Cap, I . . ."

"Sit . . . down."

Had someone else taken that tone of voice with me, I would have bristled, barked back, had any of a hundred reactions, all of them aggressive. But something in Cap's look and tone prompted me to sit down as meekly as a first-year cadet. More meekly, actually, come to think of it, considering that in my first year at the Academy I dislocated the jaw of a third-year student when he made some condescending remarks.

There was sympathy in his eyes, but also firmness, as he sat opposite me. "There are certain rules of the Captain's Table, Mac," he said not unkindly. "And one of the big rules is that no one here can do anything to change the timeline or fate of anyone else. That falls under the category of duty, and at the Captain's Table, one is expected to leave one's duties at the door."

"But I can't just let him sit there and not know . . . not when I can tell him . . ."

"That, Mac, is precisely what you not only can do, but have to do. No man should know his own destiny. No man can know; otherwise he just becomes a pawn of fate and no longer a man."

"That's a nice philosophy, Cap. And I'm supposed to just stand by and—"

"Yes, Mac," and this time his tone was flat and uncompromising. "Rules of the house. I'm afraid that that is exactly what you're supposed to do."

I stared forlornly across the tavern at him. Never had the cliché, "So near and yet so far" had quite as much meaning to me. "Why am I here, then?" I asked in annoyance. "I mean . . . I would have thought that the reason one comes here is to relax."

"It is."

"How can I relax? How am I supposed to do that when I see Kenyon there, right there. It's within my ability to help him, to warn him . . ."

"It wouldn't help, Mac. In fact, it would very likely hurt, in ways that you can't even begin to imagine. You can't say anything. More to the point, you won't say anything."

My temper began to flare ever so slightly. "And if I simply choose to walk out the door rather than stay here under your rules?"

"All of us have free will, Mac. You can go as you please."

"But not necessarily come back?"

He smiled thinly. "We've always been a bit of a catch-as-catch-can operation, Mac. If you're looking for a guarantee that you'd be back, well . . . no promises. But if you did continue to try and flaunt the rules of the house, well . . ." He shrugged noncommittally.

I looked down. "I've never been much for rules."

"Yes, I know that," he said. "Sometimes that has served you quite well. After all, if you stuck to the rules, your homeworld would still be under the thumb of the Danteri. And you would not be as good a captain as you are."

"You think I'm a good captain?" I asked.

"Yes. But why does it matter what I think?"

"I don't . . ." I considered the question, and then said, "I don't . . . know. But it does. Maybe it's you. Maybe it's this place."

"Maybe it's a little of both," said Cap. "We bartenders, we're surrogates. Surrogate parents, father confessors, what have you. We try not to judge."

"That a house rule, too?"

"No. Just a bit of common courtesy." Suddenly he turned and snapped his fingers briskly once. I was confused for a moment, but then a waitress came over as if by magic and, without a word, deposited a beer in front of me.

"I take it your tastes haven't changed, even though your appearance has somewhat," he said. "The scar, in particular. Very decorative."

"Thank you," I said ruefully. "Sometimes I consider allowing someone else to lay open the other side of my face so that I'll have balance."

"Not a bad idea," Cap replied, and I couldn't entirely tell whether he was being sarcastic or not.

The glass was frosted, and the beer felt good going down. I lowered the mug and tapped it. "I take it I'm old enough that my drinks are no longer free."

"You take it correctly. There is a price attached. A story."

"A story. You mentioned that last time. You want me to tell you a story? It sounds rather juvenile."

"Not me," Cap said in amusement, as if the mere suggesting of such a thing was an absurdity. "No, I'm just the bartender."

"There's something about you, Cap, that makes me think you're not 'just' anything."

He let the remark pass. "No, the tales told here are for the customers, Mac. For your fellow captains, who love tales of adventure and derring-do."

"I don't think my do is particularly derring. Besides, I . . . don't particularly like stories. Especially stories about myself."

"I'm surprised you would feel that way, Mac. I would have thought that someone like you, a planetary hero, would be accustomed to hearing stories of his adventures bandied about."

"I am. That's part of the point." I took another sip of beer. "When I worked to liberate Xenex, I heard tales of my adventures and endeavors, spreading from town to town. Sometimes a storyteller would speak to an audience spellbound by the manner in which he wove tales of my exploits. And I would sit at the outer fringes of such gatherings and gather no notice at all, for the M'k'n'zy of Calhoun who featured in those tales was seven and a half feet tall, with eyes of blazing fire, muscles the size of mighty boulders. His preferred weapon was a sword so massive that it took either one M'k'n'zy or three normal men to wield it, and when he walked the ground trembled beneath his mighty stride and beautiful women threw themselves upon him and begged him to sire their children."

"And none of that was true?" Cap asked.

"Well . . . maybe the part about the women," I allowed.

We both laughed softly for a moment, and then I grew serious. "But I knew that these fables were just that, Cap . . . fables. They bore no resemblance to the real world. In those stories, I single-handedly slaughtered hundreds—no, thousands—of Danteri troops. My troops supposedly stood in awe of my prowess and fell to their knees in worship of me. It was all nonsense. Stories are not real life. In real life, good does not always triumph, and decent people suffer for no purpose and receive no final redemption. Stories are the antithesis of life, in that stories must have a point. I live in the real world, Cap. Sweet fictions have no relevance to me."

"Don't sell such fables short, Mac. You do them, and you, a disservice. Consider the effect such stories had on your own people. When they heard tales of the great M'k'n'zy, they drew hope from that. It sustained them, nourished their souls in their time of need. So what if there were exaggerations? Who cares if the reality did not match the fancy? What was important was that it took them out of themselves, gave them something to think about besides the difficulties of their lives. Dreams are very powerful tools, Mac. By hearing the stories of your great deeds, the Xenexians dreamed of a better life. From the dreaming came the doing. Life imitates art which imitates life in turn, and stories of your adventures are just part of that cycle."

"I suppose. . . ."

"No supposing. Take my word for it. And now, Mac, this is what you're going to do: You're going to find another captain or captains here, and you will sit him, her, or them down, and you will tell a story of your exploits. If you feel constrained to adhere to reality . . . if you must tell a story where good does not triumph, or decent people suffer . . . if that is what's required for you to maintain the moral purity of your soul, who am I to gainsay you?"

"Who are you indeed?" I asked. "That's actually something I've been wondering about. Who are you when you're not being you, Cap?"

"I am," Cap smiled, "who I am." He patted me on the shoulder as he rose. "Find a willing audience, Mac. Find it and share something of yourself. You owe it to them, to yourself . . ." He touched the mug of beer. ". . . and to your tab."

I watched him head back to his bar. I noticed for the first time that he walked with a very slight limp. I had no idea why, nor could I find it within me to ask. I had the feeling that I'd just get another roundabout, vague answer.

For a moment I considered getting up and heading out the door. But part of me was concerned that I really wouldn't be able to find the place again, no matter how hard I looked. I still wasn't entirely sure what I was doing there in the first place, or how I'd gotten to it. But it had become apparent that, when it came to questions about the Captain's Table, less was generally preferable to more.

"I still think it's a waste of time," I called after him.

He slowed long enough to say over his shoulder, "There are some things in this galaxy that are for us to think about. And there are other things that are for us to do. This is one of the latter. Understand?"

I didn't, but I said that I did.

I suppose the real truth of it is that I simply don't like to share things. I don't like to say what's going on in my mind. Call it my military upbringing, if you will. I tend to dole out information on a need-to-know basis. Otherwise I tend to keep things to myself.

But I like Cap, and I like this place. I would hate to think that I should never find my way back to it again, be it by happenstance, cosmic direction, destiny, or plain dumb luck. So for once even the mighty, rule-flaunting Mackenzie Calhoun will play by the rules. You seem like a worthy individual to tell my story to; indeed, you may be the best qualified here.

My previous post to the captaincy of the *Excalibur* was as first officer aboard the *Starship Grissom.*

Perhaps the name should have cautioned me. It was named after an Earth astronaut, Virgil "Gus" Grissom. His career in space started off impressively enough. Grissom was the second American in space, flying a suborbital vessel called the *Liberty Bell,* which was part of the Mercury program. He flew in the Gemini program after that. He was well liked and respected, and his career was on the fast track for greatness . . . just like mine seemed to be.

And then he died. He did so horribly, asphyxiating aboard a flight simulator which erupted in flames. A man like that, if he were to die in action, deserved to die in space. That's where his heart was, where his destiny was.

Instead his career was cut short thanks to a terrible accident. It should not have happened that way.

That reminds me of me as well.

But I knew none of that when the assignment aboard the *Grissom* was presented to me. I simply saw it as an opportunity, a chance to advance in the career that I was quite certain was to be mine by divine right.

I was to learn otherwise. And it all ended . . . rather badly.

Here's what happened.

The Interview

CAPTAIN NORMAN KENYON WAS THE EPITOME OF THE WORD "AVUNCULAR." (That means "uncle-like," in case you do not wish to scramble to a dictionary.)

Kenyon had been something of a lady's man in his younger days, and the ladies ostensibly loved it. In fact it was rumored—although never proven, at least to my knowledge—that there was a secret society which called itself "the Norman Conquests," and that it was something of a badge of honor to join the club. I have no idea whether meetings were held, secret handshakes were established. For all I know, the entire matter was apocryphal. I never quite mustered the nerve to ask the captain himself about it. Since Kenyon was always one of the more gentlemanly of men, I suspect that if I had, the question would likely have elicited nothing more than an enigmatic smile. And that, I daresay, is how it should be.

However, even the most rakish of men tends to settle down at one point or another. The good captain eventually married (and again, perhaps apocryphally, the Norman Conquests had a symbolic wake) and produced a daughter who was, by all accounts, quite impressive, a lively and intelligent daughter named Stephanie. I shall tell you more of her a bit later.

The marriage was quite happy, and Kenyon and his wife served together as a research team, while rising up the ranks together, and Kenyon eventually achieved the rank of captain. His wife—Marsha was her name, as I recall—served as his science officer aboard Kenyon's new command, the *U.S.S. Harriman.* However, two months into their tour of duty, the *Harriman* was caught in a crossfire between a Klingon and Romulan vessel. Casualties were light . . . but unfortunately, Marsha Kenyon was among the few. Light, I suppose, is cold comfort when it's your lover who is lying cold in the cargo bay awaiting transport back to Earth.

Norman Kenyon was devastated by the loss, of course. Starfleet offered him a leave of absence. He didn't take it. Stephanie was grown and following her own career, and to Kenyon, Earth was simply another alien world for all the meaning it had to him. Starfleet had a hearing over it, because they were concerned about his state of mind. Those who were witnesses said that Kenyon spoke on his own behalf in quiet, controlled tones that nonetheless were so moving that even hardened admirals were having trouble choking back tears. "I have lost my love," he told them. "Do not take my life from me as well."

They gave him command of the *Grissom.* From what I understand, the crew wasn't sure how to act around him at first. Obviously a captain is to be treated with respect, but the mood that can best be ascribed to the crew at that point was "tentative." They knew that he was mourning his loss, and consequently acted in a cautious manner. They needn't have done so. Kenyon was all business at first, and after a bit of time passed, became downright pleasant. As a captain, he was absolutely unflappable. Calm, patient, easygoing . . . and yet he never came across as a pushover. He had no trouble making the tough decisions, but never did so in anything other than an unhurried manner. In no time at all he knew the name, first and last, of every single person on the ship, and greeted them by name rather than rank. If he encountered a crewman who had some sort of problem, no matter how much the crewman tried to cover it, Kenyon always knew. Some people believed he was part Betazoid, even though he was born in Kansas from two very human parents. And Kenyon would take the crewman aside, even take him to Ten-Forward, and talk the difficulty out. Sometimes he came up with some angle that the crewman hadn't considered, sometimes not, but talking to him always managed to at least make the man in question feel better.

And no matter what situation he faced with other races that he encountered, not only did he always appear in control of matters, but he met every crisis with coolness and more than a modicum of charm. He had a ready smile, and even opposing captains tended to find him rather likable. It was easy to see how he would have been capable of amassing so many female admirers that he would have acquired his own followers, but once he became captain of the *Grissom,* and a widower, he had no known involvement with any women on board ship, or even on shore leave. He was urbane, even flirtatious on rare occasions, but that was as far as it went. Even though his wife was gone, he was still loyal to her. It was sweet in a way. Bittersweet, really.

There are command officers who are respected, there are those who are admired, there are those who are simply obeyed. Kenyon was all that and more: He was beloved. By the time I came on the scene, there wasn't a man or woman on the ship who wouldn't have been willing to walk barefoot on broken glass for him. He'd been serving as captain for two and a half years by that point. Kenyon's first officer, Paullina Simons, had just gotten her own command aboard the *U.S.S. Houston.* So Kenyon was interviewing for a new first officer.

Enter one Mackenzie Calhoun.

I already had something of a reputation as a hell-raiser. However, I also had a major supporter within Starfleet. His name was Admiral Edward Jellico, and considering how matters eventually turned out between us, it was really rather ironic that it was his recommendation which jumped my name to the top of the pile.

I cooled my heels at Starbase 27 for a couple of days, waiting to rendezvous with the *Grissom.* Mostly I kept to myself. It wasn't all that difficult; the savage known as M'k'n'zy Calhoun was much nearer to the surface in those days than now. I had managed to cloak him with respectability, paint him over with a thin veneer of civilization. But I would still reflexively appraise anyone who came near me, sizing them up, dissecting them with a glance. Looking to see if they had weapons, whether they were spies, whether they appeared to be a threat. It wasn't as if I was some spring-loaded, demented nut who was prepared to leap to attack at any time. I had that much reined in, at least. It was simply reflex, looking for danger at every turn. It was instincts that had served me well and saved my life any number of times, particularly back on Xenex when the Danteri started sending in spies to infiltrate us. One of them got so close to me that I barely had time to disembowel him before he took a shot at me. Got blood on my boots. It was quite a mess.

I'm getting off track here.

The point is that what had served me so well on Xenex was somewhat off-putting to the more civilized tastes of Starfleet and associated races. People rarely said anything about it directly to me because, really, what was there to say? I never said anything threatening, never attacked, never did something untoward. Were they supposed to go to their COs and say, "That guy over there with the scar and the purple eyes is looking at me funny!"

I was an object of curiosity, but not much more than that.

So I sat around and thought for two days. My life at that point was split into two times: Before I joined Starfleet, and after. It was a very curious circumstance for me, the first Xenexian to join up. I suppose that, deep down—or perhaps not so deep down—I felt a bit of a fraud. To me, everyone else who was in Starfleet seemed born to it. They had every business being there, and I didn't. No one else had that deep, abiding violence in their heart that I did. I was a wolf in Starfleet clothing.

I also missed Elizabeth.

There was something in her that had calmed me. I was able to bury myself in her, leave behind that part of me that in some ways I would almost have preferred to forget. Ultimately that may be what caused the relationship to be doomed. I wasn't ready for it, wasn't grown-up enough. I used her to satisfy my own needs and never really knew or understood what her own needs were. Not that I would have admitted to it, of course. Xenexian pride and all that.

At the time, though, sitting there in the starbase, I didn't have the emotional distance or maturity to understand that. All I knew was that I was angry, and lonely, and sullen, and resenting the hell out of Elizabeth. I also resented myself and my limitations, but I wasn't entirely able to admit that to myself. I wanted company, female company, but by the same token I didn't want to let anyone else near me. I had left myself vulnerable with Elizabeth Shelby, and when it hadn't worked out I was determined to be nothing but alone. Not the most reasonable of goals, but—as always—the instinctive one.

So when the *Grissom* arrived, I was not in the greatest of moods. Just where one wants to be when facing an interview that could make or break one's career.

I beamed aboard the *Grissom,* and I have no doubt that there were more than a few sighs of relief on the starbase once I was gone. She was a much larger ship than any I'd served on, with easily twice the number of crewmen. More than any other vessel I'd been on, she seemed like a floating city in space. To me, it was dazzling. But I tried not to let any of that awed attitude show through, since I felt that it would be viewed as unprofessional.

I was extremely surprised by the woman who greeted me in the transporter room of the *Grissom.*

She was a tall woman, with broad shoulders and an air of infinite superiority about her. Even though she was fully clothed in uniform, of course, I could tell that her body was lean and hard. She stood with her jaw slightly outthrust, her dark blond hair tied in a severe knot. Her eyes were cobalt blue and instantly captivating.

But her most prominent feature was something totally unexpected. She had a scar. Not exactly like mine, but not totally dissimilar. It was on the left side of her face, as opposed to mine on the right. It was thinner as well. My guess was that it had been made with some sort of a sword, as mine had been, but a thinner one: a rapier, perhaps. It had long since healed over, but it was still quite visible. Like me, she could of course have had the scar removed or repaired. With modern cosmetic repair techniques, it would have been the work of minutes at most. But she had chosen to keep hers, just as I had mine. I was curious about the reasons. Indeed, I was curious about her altogether.

The moment she saw me, I could have sworn that a fleeting look of amusement played over her features, but then she immediately covered it rather deftly.

"Commander," she said crisply. Her voice had the faint hint of a German accent. "I'm Katerina Mueller, ship's XO." She stuck out a hand and I took it in a firm grip as I stepped down from the transporter pad. She was about an inch taller than I was.

"I'm surprised to see you awake, XO."

She tilted her head slightly like a curious dog. "Sir?"

"The executive officer generally runs the night shift. Unless I've completely lost track of time, we're solidly in the middle of the day shift."

"That's correct. However, with Commander . . . I'm sorry, *Captain* . . . Simons having already departed for her command, I'm performing double duty until she's been replaced."

"Sounds rather grueling."

"We learn to adapt, sir." She gestured toward the door, and I preceded her out into the hallway.

I tried not to look around too much. It would have made me feel like a tourist. But I couldn't help but steal glances here and there, and I could only hope that I wasn't coming across as an idiot to XO Mueller. "How long have you been serving with the *Grissom,* Mueller?" I asked.

"Two years, one month, twenty-three days," she replied.

I smiled slightly. "Sounds to me like you might have some Vulcan blood in you, Mueller, with answers like that."

"Merely trying to be accurate, Commander."

"Not interested in the second-in-command slot yourself?"

"I don't feel I'm quite temperamentally suited to it. I prefer the nightside, and the duties of XO. The second chair is a stepping-stone to captaincy, and at this point in my career, I'm not angling for that."

"You seem to know yourself quite well, XO."

"If I don't, sir, who will?" She paused a moment and then said, "I know it's been a rather short period of acquaintance, Commander, but do you mind if I ask you a personal question?"

"Let me guess: My scar."

"Very perceptive, Commander."

"Got it in a fight. Someone came at me and I was a hair slow in dodging."

"I would say you were a hair fast. If you hadn't been, your opponent would have split your skull, by the look of it."

"That's about accurate, yes."

"You killed him, I take it?"

I looked at her with what must have been a puzzled expression. "You sound rather sanguine about it."

"It's just common sense. If someone endeavors to bisect your cranium, seeking to open negotiations doesn't quite seem to be a proportionate response. Clearly it was kill or be killed."

I nodded approvingly. "Quite right, XO." Oddly, I found myself warming to her quickly.

"May I ask how you attended to the wound at the time? It looks rather comprehensive. Why are there no stitches?"

"I fused it together myself using a laser welder."

She stopped dead in her tracks and stared at me. "Pardon?"

"I said I fused it with a laser welder."

She nodded, pondering this, and then picked up the pace once more. "Is that a procedure you would readily recommend?"

"Only for an enemy. Hurts like hell."

"I would imagine."

We stepped into a turbolift. "Bridge," said Mueller, and the lift immediately headed us toward the nerve center of the ship. Why in God's name the bridge, arguably the most important strategic point of the vessel, is an easy target at the top of the saucer section is something I never completely understood. Why not just paint a big target on your ship and write, "Aim here for best shot at the captain"? Unfortunately, no one in Starfleet had ever consulted me on techniques of vessel design.

"So how did you get—?" I tapped the side of my face, clearly referring to her own facial laceration.

"This?" She traced the length of her wound with her index finger and seemed to smile at the memory. "Heidelberg fencing scar."

"Heidelberg? That's a school, isn't it?"

She nodded. "University in Germany. Renowned, among other things, for its fencing. It was discontinued for a time, but a push for returning to traditional values brought it back about a hundred years ago. I picked up this memento during a fencing exercise."

"Shouldn't you have been wearing a protective face mask?"

She regarded me with open curiosity. "Why?"

"So you would have been protected."

"This is a badge of honor, Commander," she told me archly. "I wear it proudly . . . as, I suspect, do you."

"What about your opponent? How did he, or she, turn out?"

Without a word, she drew her finger across her throat in a swift cutting gesture. I laughed uncertainly. She showed no signs of indicating that she was kidding, and I decided that it might be best if I didn't try to press the point.

The turbolift opened onto the bridge. A man was seated in the captain's chair with his back to us, but his hair was blond and even from the back I could see that he was much too young to be captain. The man half-turned in the seat and saw XO Mueller. Immediately he rose to make way for Mueller, and seemed only mildly curious as to my presence there. Perhaps he'd had advance notice of my arrival.

He was the first blond Asian I'd ever seen. It didn't appear to be any sort of cosmetic change, but rather his natural hair color. His hair was fairly round. He had remarkably young features; indeed, if I didn't know better, I'd have thought he hadn't even started shaving yet. But with the rank of lieutenant, obviously he had a few years on him.

Mueller waved him off. "Take back the conn, Lieutenant, I'll be a few minutes still. Commander Calhoun, this is Lieutenant Romeo Takahashi, science and ops."

When he spoke, it was with a voice that was at odds with his face (which was already fighting with his hair). He spoke slowly and in an intonation that could best be characterized as a deep Southern drawl. "Call me Hash," said the lieutenant, shaking my hand firmly. "Ev'body does."

"No, we don't," Mueller said with what appeared as faint disapproval. But it was difficult for me to tell whether she was really annoyed by him, or whether she found him amusing.

"*You* don't, XO." He looked at me with what appeared to be a search for sympathy. "You'll find our XO, she tends to be on the formal side," Hash said.

Hash reached out and shook my hand, and I was astounded by the strength in his grip. He wasn't a particularly tall man, but he shook my hand so firmly that I thought he was going to break my fingers. "Why do they . . . or at least some people . . . call you 'Hash'?" I asked.

"Because," he replied, "aside from the obvious shortening of Takahashi, I also make the best corned-beef hash that anyone on this li'l starship has ever tasted. It's become so fundamental to so many people's diets around these parts, they're thinking of adding it to the periodic table as an element."

"Is that a fact?"

"No, it's not, Commander. This way," said Mueller, looking as if she felt enough time had been wasted on him.

"XO," Hash remonstrated her gently, "we have simply got to get you a sense of humor."

She stared at him as if he were a microbe. "Lieutenant, if it's not issued at the Academy, I live without it. Besides, the fact is that your own wit is just so devastating that, had I an actual sense of humor, I'd be too busy being convulsed with laughter and therefore unable to fulfill my duties."

"Then I suppose it's all worked out for the best," he said.

"Yes, I guess so," she agreed, and led me quickly to the captain's ready room. I caught Hash out of the corner of my eye grinning in amusement and shaking his head even as he settled back, however temporarily, into the command chair.

"Come," I heard a deep voice issue from behind the doors of the ready room. Mueller gestured that I should enter, but stood to one side. It was clear from her posture that she had no intention of going in herself.

My first impression of Kenyon was an air of unfailing pleasantness . . . but with an undercurrent of firm command. I sensed immediately that there were many layers to him, all hidden securely below the surface. I almost envied him that. Me, I was not tremendously skilled at keeping my "layers" out of sight. There was the Calhoun who was struggling to fit into Starfleet, wearing his façade of respectability like a too-tight second skin. And there was the Calhoun who was barely civilized enough to know how to fold a napkin . . . or even use it properly. He bubbled and percolated just below the surface. That pretty much summed up the extent of Mackenzie Calhoun.

"Captain Kenyon," I said, standing several feet away from him, "Commander Calhoun reporting for interview as instructed, sir." I wasn't entirely sure whether I was supposed to shake his hand or simply stand at attention and await his preference for how to conduct the interview.

I didn't have long to wait. As the doors started to hiss closed, with Mueller on the outside, Kenyon looked me up and down: my perfect posture, my eyes staring resolutely straight ahead as if I'd found something in midair incredibly fascinating. He said, "I'd invite you to sit down, Commander, presuming that you *can* bend at the waist with all that starch in your shorts."

I noticed that Mueller was smirking slightly, shaking her head, as the doors closed, blocking her from sight. I was rather glad. No . . . make that rather relieved.

I sat, feeling rather annoyed. "I can't say I particularly appreciate that assessment, Captain."

"It wasn't for you to appreciate, Commander. Just react to." He was studying what appeared to be my service record on the computer screen. "You come highly recommended by Edward Jellico. That's very rare. Jellico's a hard nut to crack."

"Yes, sir."

"And what's impressive is that you do not have exactly sterling recommendations from your commanding officers. That's also very rare. Generally everyone in Starfleet pulls together for mutual gain when it comes to climbing the ranks, which means you must have put a few noses out of joint along the way." He paused. "Not speaking up in your own defense?"

"I wasn't aware you were waiting for a reply, sir. Seemed like a fairly self-contained statement."

"Mm-hmm. So." He leaned forward, his hands folded. "You want to tell me why it is that Jellico sang your praises?"

"I . . . did him some small service. Him and his son."

"I see. Care to go into detail?"

"I don't see that it's necessary, sir."

"Just being modest?"

I shrugged. "Maybe."

"You don't seem particularly comfortable here, Calhoun."

"I'm not, sir. It's the starch in my shorts."

He guffawed at that and then quickly reined it in. "For what it's worth, you don't have to. Jellico told me all about it. Couldn't stop talking about it, actually."

"He probably exaggerated it, sir. You know these things . . . they always become bigger in the retelling."

"Something about how he'd been temporarily assigned to your previous ship for the purpose of him and his son going into a first-contact situation. The first contact went sour. The natives were not only restless, they tried to capture and/or kill both Jellico and his son. Mackenzie Calhoun, the ship's third officer and tactical officer, happened to be there, along with a security escort. In the melee, the entire security escort died in defending Jellico. It came down to Mackenzie Calhoun versus about twenty men who were trying to get to the admiral. And Calhoun, with a phaser that was tapped out, took them down barehanded despite suffering multiple abrasions, contusions, two broken ribs, and a skull fracture. Now, was any of that exaggerated?"

"Yes, sir," I said immediately.

"Which part?"

"It wasn't twenty men . . . it was fifteen. The phaser wasn't completely depleted, good for at least two more shots. And I wasn't barehanded. I managed to break apart a chair and use the legs for clubs."

"Oh, well, that's a completely different story." He rose from behind his desk and circled the room, his hands draped behind his back. "So anything that Admiral Jellico says about you should be attributed to the stress of the moment. Words like, 'heroic, bravery above and beyond, determination, stamina . . .' "

"Those could all be used to describe a long-distance runner, sir, but I don't know that I'd put one in charge of a ship," I pointed out.

"Don't you want to get ahead, Calhoun?"

"I hadn't given it much thought, sir."

"Oh, nonsense. What sort of career officer doesn't give much thought as to whether he wants to get ahead or not?"

He was behind me, but I didn't turn to face him. Instead I continued to look straight ahead. "The kind who doesn't want to worry about second-guessing himself. The kind who wants and needs to trust his instincts, without being concerned as to how it's going to look on his record or who it's going to upset so that he can't get good recommendations in the future. That kind."

I thought he nodded, although since he was behind me, I couldn't say for sure. "Previous commanders or superior officers describe you as headstrong. As insubordinate. As a maverick. As someone who thinks that the rules do not apply to him. Do you feel that the rules apply to you, Calhoun?"

"All but the stupid ones, sir."

"Indeed. And to whom do those apply?"

"Those who are too stupid to realize the stupidity of them."

"And who makes those judgments? You? Don't you have any respect for authority?"

Now I turned to face him. "I acknowledge authority. I acknowledge that those in authority have power over me. But that is not a condition that I take either lightly or for granted, no matter how much they endeavor to drill the chain of command into me. When those in authority are acting stupidly, I do not feel constrained to join them. That doesn't make for good officers. Just more stupidity. Rules and regulations are not handed down on high from the gods. They're made by people, mortal people, no more, no less. People who can't be expected to anticipate every eventuality. What some individuals perceive as immutable laws that restrict our actions, I see as guidelines that indicate what a particular body of opinion-makers believes to be the best way of completing a mission and coming home safely. But just because they believe it to be the best doesn't automatically make it so, and under no circumstance is it the only one. And if there are consequences for deviating from the limits that others have made, then I will accept those consequences. But no one, sir, with all due respect, is going to tell me how to live my life or force me to do that which I know, in my heart, to be wrong. I will be free, in thought and action."

"Have you considered the possibility, Calhoun, that you might be in the wrong field of endeavor."

"Every day since I entered the Academy, sir."

"And yet you stayed. Why?"

I laughed. It wasn't a particularly pleasant sound. More rueful than anything else. "Because, sir . . . I had nothing better to do."

"Well well," Kenyon said after a time. "I can see how you've managed to endear yourself to your superiors. You don't just take on responsibility for yourself. You don't just take the word of others. You feel it necessary to take on the entirety of The Way Things Are every time out, and let the consequences fall on you. You remake the galaxy in your image."

"I think that's overstating it, sir."

"Really? I don't."

I shrugged, seeing no reason to press the point.

"And what would you do if you were my first officer and I stepped out of line, eh? If I did something that you felt to be stupid. Or do you feel it wouldn't be your place to make that kind of judgment?"

"It would not only be my place, Captain, but my responsibility. If a j.g. down in the sickbay does something stupid, that doesn't necessarily have broad-ranging impact. If you do it, it could have dire consequences for everyone on ship."

"So you'd be second-guessing me."

"Every time, sir."

"And you wouldn't be afraid to tell me so."

"No, sir."

"In front of the entire bridge crew, if necessary?"

I didn't reply right away. The silence seemed to surprise him. "You hesitate," he said.

"Not in front of the bridge crew, no, sir."

"Really. You would curtail your right to voice objections?"

"There are limits, sir," and I smiled thinly, "even to me. It is possible to exercise one's right to judge others, and act on that judgment, without curtailing another's right to command. If I had a dispute with the way that a captain was handling matters, I would make certain that that dispute was handled in private. To openly argue with the CO could have a negative impact on the CO's ability to lead, and that would be . . . it would be inappropriate. Besides, think of the unnecessary damage to morale if I challenged the captain in front of the crew and it turned out that my concerns were groundless."

"Are you saying, Commander," and he feigned shock, "that you allow for the possibility that you might be . . . wrong?"

"It has been known to happen, sir," I allowed. "On one or two occasions."

"And if I were risking myself, and my personal safety, in a circumstance where the crew was not directly involved? Where it was just me and my conscience? If you thought I was misguided in my endeavors, would you allow me to risk myself?"

"Of course," I said promptly.

"You would?"

"You're a grown man, Captain. You have free will, you're a free man. If you felt strongly that you must risk yourself, it would be insulting of me to try and curtail that instinct. Insulting and condescending."

"So you would allow me to risk death."

"Yes, without hesitation."

He seemed most puzzled, as if he couldn't believe I was saying it. As if I'd admitted some horrible secret. "You would stand by and let me . . ."

"Stand by?" I made no effort to hide the surprise I felt. "Of course I wouldn't stand by. If you felt that facing danger was unavoidable, I would do nothing to stop you. But I would naturally feel constrained to share that danger. I could do no less."

"Why?"

"Because in making the decision to not oppose your intentions, I am taking on the responsibility to make certain that you get back to the ship in one piece. So I would have to be at your side to make sure that happened."

"Aren't you concerned that you might fail in that endeavor?"

"No."

"Some small measure of dou—"

"No," I repeated.

He shook his head in disbelief. "How can you be so positive?"

"Ask Admiral Jellico," I replied.

He laughed curtly at that. "Good point. Tell me, Calhoun: What do you feel is the single greatest responsibility that you, as a Starfleet officer, have?"

"To do the right thing," I said without hesitation.

"What about exploration? What about adherence to the Prime Directive? What about—"

"Captain," I cut him off, "I suspect you have a great many things to do. If you're going to ask me a question, get a straight answer, and then doubt and challenge my answers repeatedly, this is going to take a much longer time than I truly think you need to spend."

He sat on the edge of his desk, a foot away from me, and leaned forward. "Who decides," he said, "what is right?"

"The gods. I just do my best to interpret."

"And do you truly believe in gods, Mackenzie Calhoun? Do you?"

I smiled. "I believe in myself. That's generally been good enough."

To my surprise, he slapped his knee as if I'd just told him a fabulous joke. "You are an original, Calhoun, I'll give you that." Then, surprisingly fast, a change came over him. Very soberly, he said, "Do you know what my biggest problem is, Calhoun?"

"No, sir."

"I," he said with what seemed like great sadness, "am beloved."

"Most men would not consider that a problem, sir."

"My crew," he said, "has my best interests at heart. They are concerned about me. They watch out for me. No one ever disagrees with me, or challenges me, because I'm just so damned beloved, it could make you sick."

"I have a strong constitution, sir."

"I don't doubt it. I have to tell you, Calhoun, I never met someone who freed their entire world from planetary conquerors before they were twenty years old. Must have been somewhat difficult to find anything that challenging. You think being my first officer would begin to approach that?"

"Probably not, sir. But it'll do until something better comes along."

He stared at me . . . and then he laughed. This time it was a large, open, boisterous laugh that, to my surprise, I actually found was infectious. I started to laugh, too, which I hadn't been expecting at all. . . .

"The job's yours if you want it, son," he said. I would later find out that he tended to call people "son" a lot. Oddly, he never addressed any of the women by a similar endearment. Perhaps it was because he had a daughter, and didn't want to imply—even to himself—that anyone could possibly be a replacement for her.

"Yes, sir. Yes, I think I do."

"Good." He extended a hand and I shook it firmly. "Welcome aboard the *Grissom.* By the way . . . how'd you get the scar?"

"This? Bar fight. Three big guys, with knives. There was an argument over a woman, things got out of hand . . ." I shrugged. "It happens."

"Seems to me you got off lucky. Why didn't you have the scar removed?"

"Well," and I touched it gingerly, "I keep it around to remind me that no woman is really worth the aggravation."

"Oh, I would disagree with that, Commander. There are some women who are worth all that and more. Didn't you ever have a woman who stole your heart?"

I thought about Shelby, about her smiling at me. About the very first time that I'd seen her even before I knew her name . . . as an image of my future, smiling at me, naked and alluring, across the years.

"No, sir. Never. I keep my heart carefully hidden just to avoid any such situations."

The Battle

As it turned out, I was right. XO Katerina Mueller had a remarkable body.

There are some who will tell you that shipboard romances are a remarkably bad idea. This is nonsensical, of course. After all, it's not as if we can all work our shifts, then leave the ship at the end of the day and go home to someone else. The people we work with are the same people that we see in our off hours, and at any other given time of the day. So it's fairly inevitable that something will develop.

I wasn't expecting it with Mueller, though. Indeed, she would have been the last person I would have expected. Then again, calling it romance probably would have been an exaggeration. It was . . . recreational, I suppose. Letting off steam. Having a good time with each other, secure in the knowledge that neither of us needed or wanted more.

It came about in a rather unexpected fashion.

I had been serving aboard the *Grissom* for several months. Up to that point, everything had been surprisingly routine. I suspect that, to some degree, the crew didn't quite know what to make of me. My manner could be brusque, and I was not terribly skilled at suffering fools gladly. I suppose it could be rather daunting trying to deal with me, particularly at that point in my life. Certain of everything, confident in my opinions, not hesitating to tell other people that they didn't know what they were talking about . . .

Hmm.

Come to think of it, I guess I'm not all that different now. It's just that now I do it with a good deal more charm, I suppose. At least, I like to think so.

In any event, the crew seemed to be treating me with respect, and that was ultimately all that I needed or required. I was seen as something of a loner, and that was fine with me. I wasn't looking for attachments or to strike up friendships. If I sat in Ten-Forward, I did so alone. No one approached me. Really, I don't suppose I would have been upset if they had. It might have been . . .

. . . it might have been nice.

No matter. They didn't, and that was fine, too.

One day I had just gotten off shift, and I was passing by the holodeck on my way to my quarters. Normally you can't really detect any noise from within the holodeck, but my ears are fairly sharp and, besides, there was a noise coming from within that I couldn't possibly miss. It was the sound of steel on steel in quick succession. Swords. Someone was having a duel, with more than one opponent.

It was considered something of a breach of protocol to interrupt someone during a holodeck run, but as anyone who knows me can attest, I'm perfectly capable of tossing aside the rules when and where it suits my purposes. And the sound of swordplay was an irresistible lure to a barely contained savage such as myself. The door was sealed, but I tapped in the override code and it slid open obediently. I stepped in . . .

. . . and found myself on a battlefield red with blood. It was a wide field, the grass tinted with frost and crunching under my feet as I walked. I stepped over bodies and moved to the side of the dried blood that was everywhere. Ahead of me was a small, rather confined area where battle still seemed to be raging.

These were not small blades being bandied about. There were warriors with large, double-handed swords, the kind that were capable of gutting a victim from crotch to sternum with just one blow. They were dressed in furs, their faces painted blue, and they were emitting loud war cries as they battled others dressed in similar garb.

And in the midst of it all was Mueller.

She was attired similarly to the others, and she was whipping her own sword through the air with such speed that it seemed to buzz. She was quick and adept. I saw someone coming in behind her, but somehow she managed to catch the movement out of the corner of her eye and intercepted it. She had a look of burning fury in her eyes, and her clothes and face were splattered with blood . . . in all likelihood, the blood of her opponents.

Two men were coming at her from either side. She spun in place, her blade like a scythe, and her attackers went down. Her head snapped around and she saw me. She froze in place, clearly surprised to see me there. Her breath floated from her mouth in a lazy mist.

Then, from over a rise, there was another war cry. It drew both our attention and we saw a squad of attackers heading toward her. She had several allies still alive and remaining with her, and they lined up beside her, ready to battle. But her gaze had not left me.

"Well," she said finally. "Are you just going to stand there, or are you going to grab a sword and make yourself useful?"

The enemies were charging forward, their howling filling the air. Unhurried, I picked up swords off of fallen soldiers, hefting one in either hand. I tested the weight, chose the one that was in my left hand and dropped the other to the ground. Gripping it firmly, I whipped it through the air a few times.

You have to understand, my relationship with Mueller up until that time had been perfectly formal. She had struck me as coolly efficient, slightly disdainful, and not particularly interested in doing anything except her job. Hash had been correct in that humor did not seem to be her forte. We didn't have all that much interaction, what with being on different shifts. But what we had didn't begin to hint that she was capable of such brutal, bloody means of entertaining herself.

To be honest, I found it somewhat stimulating.

The first of the attackers were getting closer, closer. Something within me couldn't wait. I shouted *"Rakaaaash!"* and, my legs pumping, charged forward and met them while they were still about twenty feet from Mueller. I only had a second to wonder whether or not Mueller had overridden the holodeck safeties and whether I was in real danger. Then I promptly stopped caring as I gutted the first of my attackers. Without slowing in my turn, I cleaved open the second one and eviscerated the third, all in a matter of seconds.

A fourth man was coming at me, and I was prepared to block him when suddenly Mueller was there, stopping the downward thrust with her own weapon. She muscled him back and thrust forward with her own blade. The opponent's blood spurted onto my boots.

"Sorry," she said, noticing the stain.

"It'll come out," I replied. And that was all the exchange we had time for as the battle was truly joined. It was a symphony of clanging blades, of grunts and cuts and a cold fury that burned in the pit of your stomach and drove you onward, ever onward. In cases like that you tend to lose track of everything except survival. You draw a mental circle around yourself, and you concentrate on only those individuals who are attempting to enter that circle. Outside it you ignore them, inside it and your blade takes their life. It's as simple as that. You lose track of time, you lose track of yourself, and you only stop when they stop coming.

And eventually . . . they stopped.

As is always the case in such instances, I didn't realize it at first. My breath was slamming hard in my chest. I had not stinted in either my defense or offense simply because my opponents were holographic. A battle was a battle, a challenge still a challenge. My uniform shirt was torn in several places from slices by opponents that had gotten a little too close. Blood streaked my face, my hair was disheveled. My heart was pounding, and I realized I wanted more. More to conquer, more physical exertion. I felt more alive than I had in ages. I had never used the holodeck for much of anything, really. I had found the entire concept to be somewhat ridiculous and pointless: shadow dances that had no meaning. I certainly wasn't feeling that way anymore. To me, it seemed like I could actually feel my blood flowing through my veins.

I looked to see if there were any more opponents, any more challenges. There was only one other individual standing nearby, and that was Mueller. The rest of her allies had been struck down, but she had survived. Standing there clutching her sword, fire in her eyes, a wolflike grin on her face, she looked like a Valkyrie, like a warrior from a bygone age. Just us two, there on the blood-soaked plain.

I could tell from the look of her that she was undergoing the same roiling of feelings that I was. It might have been that mine was more intense; after all, I was the one who had been raised in a relatively barbaric society, had engaged in battles not too dissimilar from this one where my life was genuinely at stake, had known what it was like to fight for my life, for honor. The first man that I had killed, I had cried for . . . cried as much for myself as for him. I was long past those days. Now I felt nothing but triumph, and a euphoric exaltation.

She saw it in my eyes, and it attracted her, inflamed her, I was sure of it. She took a step toward me, another. And then she swung her sword around, the blade whistling straight at me. I intercepted the swing and the swords crashed together. Her blade slid down the length of mine, bringing us hilt to hilt, body to body, my chest pressed against her. Our breath was racing, our hearts beating together.

I said the only thing that seemed appropriate:

"My quarters, your quarters, or right here?"

"Right here," she said without a second's worth of thought.

The swords dropped down onto the ice-layered ground, and a moment later, so did we.

We never said a word.

And thus began one of the somewhat odder relationships I ever had, because we never did say a word. Whenever we encountered each other after that in uniform, we were all business. No one could have told that we were anything other than coworkers.

But every so often, as if we had a bond on some level, we would just . . .

know. I would show up at her quarters, unsummoned and unbidden, or she would turn up at my door. And we would . . . well . . . we would.

Without a word. Never was a word exchanged. As if to say anything would serve to break the spell.

Absolutely no one knew. Well . . .

. . . one.

There was one evening where we lay in my bed, basking in the afterglow. The perspiration on both our bodies was slowly drying. We'd had a particularly successful outing, and we were enjoying the time after . . . although, once more, in silence.

I felt as if I should say something, but I had no idea what. I couldn't say whether she felt the same way, but the moment simply seemed to require some sort of intercourse of the social kind. Just as I started to open my mouth, though, a chime came from the door.

"Yes?" I called.

"Commander?" came a familiar drawl. "Got something for you."

"Not now, Hash," I replied. "Could you come back later?"

"Got to strike on these things while the iron's hot, y'know, sir. It's just a li'l ol' thing. But I'd surely like to give it to you in person."

Kat Mueller looked at me with a certain degree of controlled franticness. The last thing we needed was Takahashi waltzing in with the two of us curled in bed together. "Really, Hash, later would be a better time. That's something of an order."

"There's no time like the present, sir."

"Is there any cliché he doesn't know?" Kat hissed in my ear. It was the first time that any words had been exchanged between us while we were unclothed. It certainly wouldn't have been the first words I would have wanted to hear.

"Hash, I'm going to be a while. . . ."

"S'okay, sir. I'll just wait out here. Got nothin' better to do, really."

I could have argued it, could have gotten forceful. He was a subordinate, after all. But the bottom line was, he was basically a nice guy, I liked him, and obviously he was trying to do something thoughtful, although heaven only knew what. I could continue to debate it, or I could endeavor to resolve it. "All right, hold on a moment," I said. Kat's eyes opened wider, and I whispered to her, "Do you think it's preferable that he stand outside for who knows how long and keeps calling through the door? Very subtle, that."

"Then what—?"

I pointed to the bathroom. "Wait in the head until he's gone."

She stared at me with unconcealed annoyance and then rolled off the bed. She gathered up her clothing as quickly as she could and made for the bathroom. As the door slid shut I thought she might have tossed me an obscene gesture, but I couldn't be sure. In retrospect, it was probably better that way.

I had gotten out of bed and pulled on a robe. I belted it tightly around my waist, went to the door, and said, "Okay, come."

Hash was standing there in the doorway. He was holding a large bowl with the aid of a couple of thick mitts. "Hot off the stove," he said proudly.

"Let me guess: hash," I said.

He nodded eagerly. "I keep promising to make you some of my specialty, but you never seem to have yourself around when it's being made. Thought you might wanna help your taste buds sing." He paused. "Y'all have taste buds on Xenex, right?"

"Last I checked. So . . . why don't you come back later and I can—"

"Eat it while it's hot. Got a fork right there in the top. Dig in." He walked in and placed it on a table, then stepped back and stood there with folded arms.

"You mean . . . right now?"

"It's your first time, Commander. Got to see how you react to your first time."

I was trying to be polite, to hold my temper, but it wasn't easy. "If I do, will you go away?"

He laughed as if I'd been joking.

Realizing that there was only one way to end it—well, two ways, but only one of them wouldn't get me court-martialed—I took a forkful of the proffered hash and ate it. Then I blinked in surprise. "This is good."

He grinned.

"I mean it . . . this is really good. No, this is great." I wasn't exaggerating. It was corned-beef hash and it was absolutely delicious.

Romeo backed away, bobbing his bizarrely blond head, and he said, "Enjoy it, sir."

"Do you want to stay to—?"

The moment the words were out of my mouth, I couldn't believe I'd said them. I'd completely forgotten that Kat was stranded in the bathroom. A prolonged stay wasn't going to endear me to her.

Fortunately enough, Romeo said suavely, "Oh nooo . . . no, I don't think that'd be wise. You enjoy the rest all by your lonesome . . . you and your lady friend."

Suddenly it seemed as if the temperature in the room had dropped twenty degrees. "Lady . . . friend?" I managed to get out.

"Well, yeah. The one you got hiding in the bathroom."

"How do . . . I mean, what makes you think that . . . ?" I asked in what had to be one of the clumsiest attempts at a save ever made.

He inclined his chin in the direction of the bed. "That yours?"

I glanced in the direction he was indicating. A bra was entangled in the sheets.

"Yes," I said tonelessly. "Yes. It is."

"Mm-hmm. Commander . . . I want to assure you that I am, despite all appearances to the contrary, a genuine Southern gentleman. Discretion is my middle name."

I thought, *And here I thought your middle name was "Lousy Timing,"* but I didn't say it.

He grinned once more and headed toward the door. He paused in the doorway and called over his shoulder, "Sayonara, y'all," and then exited whistling.

The door to the bathroom opened and a rather steamed Kat Mueller stood there. She was wearing her uniform. Her breasts did not appear to be sagging. "You know . . . I was never wild about Takahashi before. He's entirely too cheerful for my taste. But I never actively disliked him before."

I held up the bra. "Here," I said, not having anything else particularly clever to say.

"Thanks. I hear it's yours."

I tossed it to her.

"Mac . . . this is absurd." It was the first time she had ever addressed me as "Mac." When we were on duty she used my rank, and when we were intimate no words were exchanged. She turned her back to me, removed her uniform top and finished getting dressed. "We can't continue this way."

"We can't?"

"No. We can't. I'm afraid it's over."

I stared at her levelly as she turned around. "All right."

"We'll just be coworkers."

"That would probably be best."

"Probably, yes."

And that was that. She left.

She was back three days later, you understand . . . but it seemed like a very long three days.

The Assignment

CAPTAIN KENYON STRODE ONTO THE BRIDGE AND LOOKED IN A PARTICULARLY good mood. "Mr. Gold," he called to the man at conn. "Set course for Starbase Nine, warp factor four."

"Aye, sir. On our way." Mick Gold, Lieutenant j.g., was a conn officer with what could delicately be called a sense of self-aggrandizement. Since he piloted the ship, he had a rather impressive ego, and oftentimes wasn't afraid to display it. The thing was, he was extremely skilled at what he did, and also had an amazing instinct—possibly better than any targeting computers—when it came to a firefight. So to a certain extent, Gold's self-importance was merited. Still, Gold never waited for the captain to actually order the ship to embark on her new heading. He would simply announce, "On our way."

When this was pointed out to him by a somewhat irked Commander Paullina Simons, Gold calmly pointed out that standing on ceremony was silly. If the captain didn't want them to go to a particular place at a particular speed, then why in the world would he issue the order in the first place? Simons reported the exchange to Kenyon, who shrugged it off and said, "Well, when you get right down to it, he's right. If I know where we want to go, what's wrong with just going there?" Which left Gold to continue as he had been with the captain's tacit endorsement.

"Mr. Calhoun," said Kenyon, "conference lounge in ten minutes. You, Mr. Takahashi, Dr. Villers, and Mr. Cray." He turned and headed back out, still carrying himself in a very cheerful manner.

Dr. Villers was a Starfleet veteran. She was heavyset with gray hair, and had the bedside manner of a Romulan interrogator. She was also the most physically imposing woman I'd ever met. She wasn't tall, but she was wide: "Built like a Tenarian *vass.*" She worked out in the gymnasium every day, lifting weights and wiping the floor with karate partners. Part of me was almost perverse enough to mentally match her against Kat and wonder who would come out on top. I had the feeling it might be Doc Villers.

Cray was something else again.

Cray was an Andorian, the head of security. When he spoke, which was not often, it was just above a whisper so that you had to strain to hear him. I had witnessed him in combat situations—we had stumbled upon some Orion raiders while on a mineral survey—and he was easily one of the most vicious fighters I'd ever seen in action. He carried a phaser, but I'd never actually seen him use it. He seemed to prefer hand-to-hand, and he was frighteningly good at it. And he did not like me, not one bit. I make no bones about it, I may not have been the most popular first officer who ever sat in the second chair. There were those who simply didn't like my style. Who felt that I walked with too much swagger, or felt that I didn't act with sufficient deference to the captain (an opinion, I cannot emphasize enough, that the captain did not share). And there were crewmen who, as I told you earlier, felt disconcerted by what they saw in my eyes and felt constrained to look away. As always, Starfleet and I did not remain the smoothest of fits, and that caused occasional bumping of heads.

With Cray, though, it was different. Cray had no desire to remain in the security track. To be specific, he'd had his eye on the second chair. He was technically next in line after the first officer; the day I'd arrived, Hash had been at the conn because Cray was temporarily off the bridge attending to other duties. Cray had felt that the promotion was virtually guaranteed once Commander Simons had gotten her captaincy and Mueller had made no effort to step in for consideration. He had not expected Kenyon to seek a new first officer from outside of the personnel on the *Grissom,* and was convinced that the only reason I was there was because I'd had Jellico pushing for me. He might well have been right.

Much of Cray's state of mind I was able to garner from a few conversations with various crewmen. Cray, you see, hadn't been particularly reticent when it came to his feelings about me, especially once he'd gotten a few slugs of synthehol into him. Once I became aware of his feelings of annoyance, I tried to sit down with him in Ten-Forward to work things out.

I've told you how others didn't like what they saw in my eyes. I can assure you that, when I looked into Cray's eyes, I wasn't ecstatic with what I saw there, either. Our talk did not go particularly well, nor did I endeavor to pursue it in the future.

Not that he presented a danger to me, you understand. There was no reason to think that he would perform his duty in any way other than to the best of his abilities as a Starfleet officer. Nor did I think that he would expose me to danger, or that he wouldn't watch my back if we found ourselves in a sticky situation. On the other hand, I was reasonably certain that he would be among the first to laugh loudly if I made a muddle of things. It can be very disconcerting if you're aware that someone is waiting for you to screw things up. It can make you tense, make you second-guess yourself.

Not me, of course. Cray's attitude was his and he was welcome to it. I shut out my concerns with relative facility.

As per the captain's orders, we had assembled in the conference lounge at the appointed time. The captain's exceptionally good mood persisted, and within minutes he explained to us why.

We had been assigned to escort a diplomatic team to oversee peace talks between two races on two worlds in the Anzibar system. The world of Anzibar II, populated by a race called the Carvargna, was a temperate, even tropical world. The Carvargna were—perhaps not coincidentally—a relatively benign people who far preferred peace to bloodshed.

For millennia, the Carvargna was the only sentient race in the Anzibar system. Then an ark ship arrived in their system, carrying an entire race of people known as the Dufaux, themselves refugees from a system whose sun had aged out and rendered their world uninhabitable. The Carvargna extended their hospitality to the Dufaux, their reasoning being that on their world there was room for all. The Dufaux settled there, and turned out to be an extremely prolific race. They didn't breed quite as quickly as tribbles, but they were certainly not lacking in their birthing capabilities. Over the decades, not only did their populace increase exponentially, but so did their desire for land. They were also far more warlike and savage than the Carvargna, and when the Carvargna resources began to reach the stress point, the Dufaux simply resolved to obliterate the Carvargna. Obviously, the Carvargna—peace-loving as they were—nonetheless did not go quietly into that good night. The warfare became intense and bloody, and the Dufaux wound up being driven off the world of Anzibar II. Anzibar III was uninhabitable, so they wound up on Anzibar IV. It was not, however, remotely as hospitable a world as the one they'd left. Years had passed, but resentments had not cooled. The two worlds continued to snipe at each other, every so often launching missile attacks or sending in raiding parties. It was not a good situation.

The Carvargna had tired of the assaults and battles over the years. They had approached the Federation and asked that it take a hand in the matter. The Federation had long desired to bring in Anzibar II and the Carvargna, and this seemed like the ideal opportunity. Consequently, it had assigned a diplomatic team to go to the Anzibar system and endeavor to heal the wounds between the neighboring worlds.

It was the identity of the diplomatic team that apparently had Kenyon in such a good mood: Byron Kenyon, the captain's brother . . . and his attaché, Stephanie . . . Captain Kenyon's daughter.

"Wait until you have the pleasure of meeting her," Kenyon said to us. "Some of you who might remember her beloved mother, or might have met Stephie when she was a little . . . I guarantee you, you're in for a treat." He beamed at the memory. "She is the image of her mother, let me tell you. She has her mother's spunk, her vivaciousness. She's quite a young woman, my Stephie."

"I remember her very well, Norm," said Villers. Of everyone on board, Doc Villers was the only one who addressed the captain by his first name, no matter what the situation. "Although she couldn't have been more than ten last time I saw her. It was great seeing her with you. She seemed to idolize you. I always thought that she'd follow you into the Fleet."

"Yes. Yes, that's what I thought, too." For just a moment, there seemed to be extreme sadness in his face, and then with effort he forced it off. "So." He rose and clapped his hands briskly, which was his general signal for the end of the meeting. "Once we pick them up from the starbase, we bring them to the Anzibar system and stay on station for as long as they need us. Any questions?"

"Security," Cray said in that whispery tone of his. It was a word, a statement, and a question all rolled into one.

"Of course we'll want them to have a full security escort," Kenyon replied. "I'll want you to head up the squad, Cray."

"Honored."

"Permission to go planetside with them, sir, particularly if it's Anzibar Four which is potentially the more hostile," I said.

"Actually, I was planning to go down myself, Calhoun," said the captain.

"That, sir, is not an appropriate course of action," I replied.

"Oh? And why would that be?"

"Because," I told him evenly, "you would be going into a situation where you could not be counted upon to act in a dispassionate or reasonable manner. The fact that both your brother and daughter are involved may cloud or dull your judgment. It would be inappropriate of you to accompany them. You need someone with emotional distance."

"Are you saying," Kenyon asked, "that I am incapable of acting in a professional manner where my daughter or brother are concerned?"

"I have nothing upon which to make that judgment," I said. "However, sir, if it's all the same to you, I'd prefer not to find out. I think none of us would."

There were nods of agreement from all around the table, which I found surprisingly heartening. At first Kenyon seemed inclined to protest, but then he saw the prevailing sentiment and simply shrugged. "If that's how you all feel . . . then I must certainly acknowledge your concerns and act accordingly. Very well, Calhoun. You will accompany my daughter and brother planetside. And bring them back to me in one piece."

"We will," Cray said before I could get a word out. And he looked at me out the side of his eyes in a manner that indicated I would be wise to leave the particulars of this mission to him. It was rapidly beginning to develop into a situation that was making me exceedingly uncomfortable.

The Daughter

SHE WAS A STUNNER.

I had to admit that the captain had not exaggerated his daughter's attributes in any way. The moment she materialized on the transporter pad, where Captain Kenyon and I awaited the arrival of her and her uncle, I was captivated by her. If she indeed resembled her mother, then Kenyon had been one of the luckiest bastards in the galaxy.

She was slim and small-waisted, but she had an open face that seemed to appreciate the world it was looking at. Her hair was brown and straight and amazingly long, hanging to just below her hips, and braided down either side. When she smiled, which seemed her natural state of expression, she had dimples in either slightly chubby cheek. Her eyes were green, like a cat's, and she had a long slender neck around which she wore a simple choker. She was dressed in a pale blue dress that clung in the right places but opened out into a large, flowing skirt. When she moved, it almost seemed as if she were floating along the floor rather than treading upon it.

With her was Kenyon's brother, Byron, and if I had not known that they were brothers, I still would have figured it out immediately. Byron, even though he was the younger of the two, was nevertheless the larger of them. He had to be at least fifty pounds heavier, his hair was thinning at the top, and he had a thick mustache. Nonetheless, his general look and deportment made the familial link exceptionally clear. He and the captain embraced as Byron stepped down from the pad.

Stephanie was staring at me.

She seemed immediately captivated by me, and to be honest, she herself wasn't exactly difficult on these old purple eyes of mine. "Stephie," her father said, several times, before he managed to pull her attention away from me. It seemed to me that he was definitely aware of the interest she had displayed in me, but he chose not to comment on it. Instead he hugged her so tightly I thought he would break her in half, and then he gestured toward me and said, "May I present my first officer, Mackenzie Calhoun."

"You're Xenexian, aren't you," she asked.

I made no attempt to hide my surprise. "Why . . . yes. . . ."

She nodded as if she had needed to confirm this for herself. "Yes, the general coloring of the skin and cranial shape implied that. The purple eyes, of course, were a strong indicator. They're of a shade that one virtually never sees on Earth, but they are not uncommon in Xenex—relatively speaking—occurring in about thirty-eight percent of the populace."

"That much?" I let out a low whistle.

"Which would mean your name isn't really 'Mackenzie Calhoun.' "

Rather than shake her hand, I bowed slightly in a manner that encompassed both her and her uncle. "I am M'k'n'zy, of the city of Calhoun. I changed it, or at least unofficially modified it, once I got to the Academy. I got a little tired of hearing the properly accented way of pronouncing it mangled all the time."

"You mean they had trouble saying 'M'k'n'zy'?"

I made no effort to hide my surprise. Her accent had been damned near perfect, her pronunciation of the guttural and hesitant syllables unassailable. I'd never heard any lips other than Xenexian capable of saying it so accurately. If everyone on Earth had said it that perfectly, I'd never have changed it. Hell, she said it better than Elizabeth, and we were almost married, for pity's sake.

"It's hard to believe, I know," I allowed. "But call me 'Mac,' please."

"All right, Mac." If it was possible, her dimples seemed to sink in even more deeply.

Kenyon tapped his combadge. "Kenyon to conn. Gold . . . they're aboard. Set course for the Anzibar system."

"On our way," came back Gold's voice, not waiting as usual for the captain's go-ahead. Sometimes I wondered if Kenyon had an official rule book somewhere of just how far, and no farther, he could be pushed.

"It's good to see you, Byron," the captain said, an arm draped around his sibling. He slapped his brother's stomach. "You've put on weight."

"Not at all," replied Byron. "It's just that somewhere, someone else has lost it, and it came through space and leaped onto me. Fat, like matter, cannot be destroyed, but merely transferred to another host body. I'm doing you a favor, Norm. If I lose it," and he slapped his belly, "it'll probably all wind up leaping onto you."

"The sacrifices you make for me," said the captain.

I felt almost envious, seeing the two of them together that way. My own brother and I had never had that sort of easy, give-and-take relationship. There had always been an undercurrent of tension between us, even when we were allies against the Danteri. And in later years, my brother had made himself over into little more than a Danteri stooge, accommodating them wherever he could and selling out the greater concerns of our people in return for personal profit. Seeing Norman and Byron Kenyon interacting in that way—the teasing, the joy at seeing each other, the obvious affection they held for one another—it got to me a bit.

Naturally, though, I kept my true feelings buried. It was no problem, really; I'd had a lot of practice on that score.

We showed them to their respective quarters. I was certain that it was my imagination, but Stephanie appeared unable to take her eyes off me. I bowed slightly, formally, when the captain and I brought her to her quarters, and then as I turned to leave, she said, "Dad? Do you think I might get a tour of the ship?"

"Of course, honey." He gestured that she should precede him, thereby indicating that he himself would conduct the tour.

"Oh, Daddy, I wouldn't think of taking up your time," she told him. "If you'd want to assign . . . someone else?" She looked straight at me.

Credit the captain: Nothing slips past him. Of course, it's not as if Stephanie was being exactly subtle. "Commander." Kenyon turned to me, looking very formal. "Would you be so kind as to escort my daughter around the ship? Show her the points of interest?"

"I would be honored, sir."

"And, of course, I can trust you to be a perfect gentleman?" he added gravely.

"Of course, sir."

And that was when I heard Stephanie mutter, "Damn," under her breath.

Well, Stephanie turned out to be quite a woman, let me tell you. And no, before you start getting ahead of me and conjuring up scenarios in your own mind, I will tell you in advance: No. Nothing happened.

Not that it was for lack of trying.

Stephanie was easily one of the most charming, intelligent, sophisticated, and downright fun women that I have ever encountered. From the first tour that I gave her of the *Grissom,* to the time we spent dining together, to the late hours we spent debating everything from Federation politics to obscure strategies of ancient generals, Stephanie Kenyon proved to be nothing short of amazing.

"I feel guilty," I said to her at one point. "I think I'm monopolizing your time. You should be spending it with your father."

It was the first time that I actually saw her hesitate to say what was on her mind. "That . . . might not be wise," she said finally.

"Why not?" We were alone in one of the forward observation lounges. "Don't tell me you two don't get along with each other. I can't believe that."

"I just . . ." She paused. "I'd rather not discuss it."

"All right," I said readily. I was perfectly comfortable not discussing it. I genuinely liked Captain Kenyon, and felt a bit voyeuristic. I realized that I didn't want some sort of inside glimpse into his personal life. I was perfectly happy to keep that aspect of his life at a distance.

Naturally Stephanie took my being perfectly comfortable with not hearing her discuss it as an invitation to discuss it.

Women. Xenexian, Terran . . . they're all the same. Well . . . maybe not Vulcans, but otherwise, all the same.

"I just think that . . . well . . . my father is disappointed in me."

"Disappointed? How can you think that?" I was genuinely astounded. "He thinks the world of you. He talks about how proud he is of you. . . ."

"He also talks about how he wishes I'd gone into Starfleet, doesn't he. He's disappointed that I didn't."

I thought of the obvious sadness in his eyes when his daughter's career path had been casually brought up in the conference lounge. He had obviously endeavored to push it away, but it was there just the same. "No," I said quickly. "I didn't get that impression at all."

She smiled sadly. "Mac, you're a terrible liar."

"Actually," I protested, "I'm generally pretty good at it. I'm just not especially good at it with you."

She stared out at the stars that hurtled past us, and she seemed very sad. "My dad's had so much hurt in his life . . . I hate the thought of adding to it. I hate not being what he wanted me to be. But I couldn't . . . it was ego, that's all."

"Ego?"

"I didn't want to spend my life being Norman Kenyon's daughter. If I'd gone into Starfleet, that's exactly what I would have been. I would have had my life, my career, defined by my relationship to him. It's not that I don't love him; I do. It's not that I'm not proud of him; I am. But I wanted to do, and be, something that was separate from him."

"So you chose the diplomatic corps."

"It seemed a worthwhile direction in which to go. Besides," and she laughed, "I couldn't help but have the burned-in desire to meet and experience other races. That much, my father managed to make such a part of me that to deprive myself of those opportunities would have been like cutting off an arm. Living your own life is one thing, but one shouldn't have to be mutilated . . . oh. Oh God. I'm sorry."

"What?" I didn't try to cover the fact that I was puzzled. "Sorry about what?"

"Oh God, now I'm making an even bigger idiot of myself. I'm sorry, it's just . . . well, I was talking about mutilation, and you with that . . ." She touched the side of her face.

"Oh! The scar." I waved off her concern. "Don't worry about it."

"May I ask, uhm . . . how did you . . . ?"

"Jealous husband," I told her. "My fault. I didn't know she was married. Shouldn't have taken her word for it. One moment we're rolling around in the sheets, the next thing I know, I'm hearing bellowing from this man the size of a small asteroid heading toward me, waving an axe with a blade twice the size of my head. All things considered, I was damned lucky. *Grozit,* he could have taken my head off."

"Good lord."

Inwardly, I smiled. At least I wasn't a hopeless liar when it came to the daughter of Captain Norman Kenyon.

That was when she kissed me.

It was long and sensuous, and she gave freely of herself. And when our lips parted, she looked up at me with . . . I don't know what. Longing. Interest. Perhaps just a touch of boredom that she was trying to kill.

"I'll . . . walk you back to your quarters," I told her.

"Would you stay awhile?"

"I have duties to perform."

"Can they wait?"

"Probably. But they won't."

There was surprise on her face. I turned her to face me, taking her shoulders in my hands. "Stephanie . . . I think you're terrific. But . . . your father is my captain. I wouldn't feel comfortable."

"I'm a grown woman," she said. "Dad knows that. Do you think he doesn't know I find you very attractive? He respects my freedom."

"Good. But, you see . . . I respect *him.* I would not feel . . . right. Even if any involvement would be with his approval, even if he sent flowers and a balloon assortment. I would feel . . . not . . . right. And to be honest . . . I think you should be spending more time with him than with me. All right?"

She laughed softly, low in her throat. "I won't say I'm not disappointed."

"I won't say it either. But it's how I feel. And I know I can count on you to respect that."

"True enough. But I'm telling you, Calhoun," and she smiled in a very saucy manner, "sooner or later, you're going to regret it. Regrets are terrible things to have, because you know what? Life's just too damned short."

That was the last I saw of her that day, except for the very end of my shift. As I was about to go off duty, Stephanie showed up on the bridge, kissed her father on the top of the head, and together the two of them left the bridge to go to dinner. She cast a very quick glance in my direction, winking just before the turbolift doors closed.

When I returned to my quarters, Kat was there. She was fully dressed, sitting on the edge of my bed. "I hear you're quite the couple," she said without preamble.

"Oh, we're going to talk," I said with feigned surprise.

"Well? Are you?"

"If you're referring to Stephanie Kenyon and myself . . . I think she's terrific. A wonderful woman. Then again, considering her pedigree, it's not surprising."

"We're not discussing a dog, Calhoun."

"What happened to 'Mac'? I thought you were calling me 'Mac.' "

She stood. Although she was only an inch taller, at that point she seemed about two heads higher than me. "Are you involved with her?"

"What does it matter to you?"

Her expression hardened. I had the oddest feeling that there was about to be a lightning storm in my quarters. "It matters."

"Why?" I started to raise my voice, feeling a bit exasperated. "Why does it matter? Do we have a relationship, you and I? What the hell *do* we have? We have a . . . a mutual outlet for pent-up emotion, that's what we have. Are we supposed to build on that?"

"I'm not concerned about building. I'm concerned about the kind of man you are."

"I'm not following you."

"I'm curious to know," and she took a step closer, seeming to loom over me, "whether you're the type of man who would endeavor to solidify his position using whatever means necessary. Because that would drastically reshape my opinion of you."

It took a moment for it to sink in . . . and then I started to laugh. "Are you . . ." I was laughing so hard that I had to clutch my stomach because it hurt. "Are you . . . are you implying that I'm trying to . . . to sleep my way to the top?"

"Stop laughing."

I leaned against the bulkhead and waited until I was able to compose myself. "If you must know . . . if you really must . . . if Stephanie Kenyon were anyone else, I would most definitely be involved with her. But because she is who she is, I have made clear to her that friends are what we are, and friends are what we will remain. So it's the opposite of what you're suggesting. All right?"

Mueller seemed mollified at that. "You're being honest with me?"

"If you have to ask me that, then we really have nothing else to talk about."

"All right. Well . . . good. All right."

"So this was all because you were concerned with my integrity. Not because of any personal involvement that you and I might have, or feelings you might have for me."

"I don't have feelings for you, Mac," said Mueller. "We have what we have, and that's all. I don't want or need anything beyond that. I thought you didn't either."

I eyed her curiously. "Then why do you care about what sort of man I am? If it's purely about physical needs, then why should any aspect of my personality factor into it? Endurance, breath control . . . that should be all you're concerned about."

"I will be concerned about what I choose to be concerned about."

"Really. And what about me?" We circled each other in my quarters. "Should I be concerned about the fact that I'm involved with a woman who wants nothing beyond physical gratification? Why is that? Why is that all you care about?"

"It's not all I care about. But it's all I want."

"Why? Why are you this way?"

For a moment, there was a flicker of sadness in her eyes. "We are what we are, Mac. We are what circumstances make us."

There was a long silence between us . . . and, I had a feeling, something else between us as well. "Kat . . ."

"I have to go," she said.

She walked toward the door, and stopped short of it. She stood ramrod straight, her back to me. She didn't move from the spot.

"Kat . . . ?"

Her straight, squared-off shoulders were shaking ever so slightly. "I have to go . . . and I don't want to."

I took her by the arm, turned her around to face me. Her face was absolutely dry. All of her crying was on the inside.

I held her close to me, and one thing led to another . . .

. . . and once again, we didn't speak. But this time, it wasn't because we had nothing to say. It was because we didn't need to.

The Dufaux

ANOTHER MEETING HAD BEEN CALLED IN THE CONFERENCE LOUNGE, WITH the Anzibar system only hours away. The mood on the part of Stephanie Kenyon seemed fairly grim, as it did for the captain as well. It was immediately made clear to Doc Villers, Cray, Hash, and me just what the problem was. Byron wasn't there, which had me somewhat apprehensive. But Stephanie didn't seem inclined to wait.

"There's been a development," said Stephanie. She glanced at her father, but the captain simply nodded as if to indicate that she should continue. "We've been in touch with the Dufaux. Understand that it was the Carvargna who requested, and pushed for, the intervention of the Federation. The Dufaux were resistant to it . . . very much so. However, they finally agreed to it . . . albeit somewhat reluctantly. A recent missile barrage by the Carvargna helped to change their minds, I think."

"So what's the problem?" asked Hash.

"The problem is," the captain now stepped in, "that there's been an overthrow in the leadership of the Dufaux. Apparently, to some extremists, the fact that they were willing to talk at all was seen as a sign of weakness. There are new leaders in place, and they seem disinclined to meet with any UFP representatives."

"So we meet with the Carvargna only," said Hash.

"Pointless," whispered Cray.

Stephanie nodded. "I must agree with Mr. Cray. We're trying to put together a negotiation here. There has to be a meeting of minds, and that can't be one-sided."

"Where's Byron?" I asked.

"He's engaged in private communication with the Dufaux," the captain said. He didn't seem especially enthused about it. "I was there for the first few minutes of it. I can tell you, people, that I am not speaking with simple fraternal pride when I say that my brother is one of the best negotiators in the business. He's pulled off some miracles in his career. I'd say he's saved more lives through words and dogged pursuit of the peace process than everyone in this room combined, with all our starships, our weapons, and our strength. But these Dufaux . . . they sounded completely resistant. He said he'd be coming in here to give us an update, but I think you're going to see a very frustrated diplomat coming through that door."

"The captain's right," said Stephanie, being politic and avoiding a possibly cloying sentence such as, "Dad's right." "I've watched Byron in action. I know what he's capable of achieving, and this one seems to be a roadblock . . ."

The doors hissed open and Byron Kenyon practically marched into the room. His arms were swinging in leisurely fashion, and he was beaming. "So! What did I miss!" he said cheerfully.

"You missed the vote on your attitude for when you come in here," Villers told him. "I'm afraid you'll have to go out and come back in in a much worse mood."

"Byron, what happened?" asked a clearly surprised Kenyon.

Byron draped himself over one of the chairs. "I managed to make them see the light."

"You mean," said Stephanie, leaning forward, her elbows on the table, "that you got them to agree to meet with the Carvargna?"

"We must walk before we can run and, in this case, crawl before we can walk, Stephanie," Byron counseled her, sounding at his most sage. "I managed to convince the Dufaux leadership—headed up by an individual named Kradius—that they are presenting no risk to their current status by agreeing to meet with us. That no one ever died simply from talking about something."

"I can think of any number of martyrs who would disagree with you," I said. Now . . . I've always had a knack for sensing danger. Call it battle experience, call it reading signs, call it a psionic ability if you must, but I've had it before and I was having it at that moment. "This doesn't smell right."

"It'll be fine, Commander," Byron said calmly. "Oh, I know, they were resistant at first. But I've managed to work them past that. I have done this before, you know."

"Yes, and I've seen people die before who thought they were dealing with those who could be trusted," I said.

"Commander," and Byron was starting to sound just a bit angry, "I know that you are merely trying to express your concern, but to be blunt, you are coming across as rather condescending."

"That was not my intention, sir. But I would be doing you a disservice if I didn't speak up. If the Dufaux are genuinely interested in the peace process, let's hold the discussion up here on the *Grissom.* We bring up some of their people . . . this 'Kradius' you spoke of . . ."

"I suggested that," Byron said. "Unfortunately, Kradius wouldn't go for that. Remember, these are a suspicious and warlike people. They are convinced that whoever they send up might be used for hostages."

"Oh, that's absurd," Captain Kenyon spoke up. "The Federation doesn't operate that way."

"Captain," Byron told him, "we are outsiders to them, and they couldn't give a damn how we do and do not operate. They are judging us by their standards, not ours. Now I have . . . we," and he glanced at Stephanie, "have a job to do, and I regret that it will not be able to be done here. The Dufaux have requested a private audience, with Stephanie and me, on Anzibar Four. It took me hours to bring them to that point. I'm not about to turn around and risk tossing all that aside due to paranoia."

"Very well," Kenyon said with a sigh. Clearly he wasn't happy about it, but he had his orders as well and he knew it. He turned to Cray and said, "Prepare a security team, standard armament, to accompany—"

"Just us," said Byron. "Just Stephanie and myself."

There was dead silence for a long moment.

For Cray, one-word sentences were his more common oral stylings. When he got up above two, you knew that something serious was in the offing. "You're joking, of course," said Cray, this time speaking just above a whisper.

"No, I'm not joking."

"I won't permit it," Captain Kenyon immediately said.

"I beg your pardon?" Byron was staring at his brother. "Captain . . . this is not within your province."

"You're on my ship," Kenyon shot back. "My concern is for your safety and welfare."

"We are not part of your crew, Captain," replied Byron. "You are not responsible for baby-sitting us, holding our hands, or changing our diapers. I am perfectly capable of assessing a situation and dealing with it accordingly. And if you think that you are in a position to do so, then I strongly advise you to think again."

"This is madness," said Kenyon. "I won't allow—"

"Captain," Byron said with what appeared to be infinite patience. "Your powers aboard this ship are vast; I understand that. But they are not infinite, and I think that if you review regulations, you'll find that when it comes to a diplomatic mission, I have the right to refuse any action on the part of the captain which I think could be injurious to the successful completion of the mission."

The captain started to reply, but I immediately jumped in. "To hell with regulations," I said. "I've done some reading on the Dufaux. My people would be classified by some experts as savages, and I'm telling you right now, even we would be appalled by some of their activities. Brutalities, capricious cruelties . . ."

"Commander," began Byron.

But I wasn't letting him get a word in. "My people kill to defend themselves and to achieve freedom. These people kill to display their strength . . . or for fun."

"I'm familiar with the reports and surveys you've read, Commander, and I'm telling you they are outdated. The Dufaux, as they stand now, are not eager to continue the conflict."

"So say the people who killed their predecessors because they sought to achieve peace."

"Once someone is in power, Commander," Byron replied, "they tend to view things a bit differently. I believe that to be the case here."

"And you're willing to stake your life on that?" the captain asked. "Yours . . . and hers?"

And Stephanie suddenly spoke up, and she sounded far angrier than I would have imagined. "Don't you do it, Captain. Don't you dare. Don't you dare act in any way other than with the concept that I am a professional diplomatic aide, out to do my job. Our relationship doesn't enter into it, and if you act like it does, I will never forgive you for that."

It was as if a thunderclap had erupted in the room. No one quite knew what to say; the outburst had seemed to come from nowhere. Except I knew exactly where it came from: from deep in the heart of a young woman who was determined to make her own way in the galaxy, and would not do anything that required her, in any way, to live in her father's shadow.

It was Byron who broke the silence. "I have a job to do, Captain," he said. "I must be allowed to do it to the best of my ability, as must my aide. Not only do the regs back me on this, but you yourself know it to be true. You cannot allow your personal feelings to—"

For the first time, I actually heard the unflappable, the always patient, the perpetually cheerful Captain Norman Kenyon sound genuinely angry. "Do not," he said with a voice that could cut castrodinium, "presume to tell me my mind, sir. You overstep yourself. Is that clear?"

"Captain—" began Byron.

"Is that clear!"

Byron opened his mouth, clearly intending to say something else, but then closed it again and simply nodded.

Kenyon weighed the situation for a time, and then he turned to Doc Villers. "I want you to implant subcutaneous transponders on them, on the back of their forearms."

"Oh, for God's sake," said an annoyed Byron.

"What?" Stephanie looked momentarily puzzled. I was surprised; I had started to think that there wasn't anything she didn't know. "What are—"

"They're wafer-thin tracking devices," Villers explained. "They're inserted just under the surface of the skin. Not as sophisticated as a comm badge or communicator because you can't talk on them. "

"However," Hash said, "not only can we lock on to them, but you can send a simple pulse as a way of letting us know you're all right. Since the captain wants them implanted here," and he indicated the back of his arm, just under his uniform shirt sleeve, "all you have to do is press on them. It'll feel like you're pressing on bone. It'll send a brief signal burst to the ship on our tracking frequency."

"You'll do it every hour, on the hour," Kenyon told them. "That way, we know everything is all right. If you signal at any other time, or don't signal at all, we beam you up immediately on the assumption that there's trouble."

"You're already operating on an assumption, Captain," said Byron. "You're assuming that we'll be unable to fend for ourselves."

"Absolutely," Kenyon said readily. "If I go down to a planet on an away-team expedition, I bring security people, weapons, and comm badges. I don't go down in my underwear and socks and figure that I'll be able to fend for myself. I don't see why I should treat you any differently."

"Captain, I can handle the situation, and your condescension is—"

"Entirely my prerogative," said Kenyon. "Perhaps I can't stop you from going down. But there's nothing in the regs that says I can't unobtrusively keep track of you, and so help me, Byron, if you give me grief on this, then you are acting in blatant disregard to my authority. That is a violation of regs, and you can spend the next two weeks cooling your heels in lockup for it. Are we clear on this?"

Byron growled something unintelligible, and then he just shrugged. "Yes . . . sir," he added, almost as an afterthought.

"Good. You will accompany Dr. Villers to sickbay. Hash, coordinate with the doc to make sure of the transponder frequency and run a couple of tests on them. Cray . . . assemble a security squad and keep them on alert, just in case."

The captain hadn't given me any specific orders, and then I saw by the look in his eyes that he wanted me to stay put. I did so as the others left, and moments later it was just the two of us in the room. "You think I'm making a mistake, don't you," he said.

"I don't know, sir."

"You said it yourself. To hell with regulations."

"I have that luxury," I said. "I'm only the second-in-command. I only have to answer to you if I go outside the regs, and I'm reasonably sure that I'd get a fair hearing and—at worst—a slap on the wrist from you, as long as the outcome of my actions was one you approved of. You have other considerations."

"Yes. I do. Do you know what the hell of it is, Calhoun?"

"I can think of several, but I'd be interested in yours."

"That to a degree, Stephanie was right. If it weren't my daughter and brother involved, I wouldn't have hesitated to let them deal with the situation as they saw fit. As it was, I second-guessed them."

"You say that now, sir. You don't know that for sure. If you're asking my opinion, my guess is that you'd have reacted in the exact same manner no matter who was involved. You care too much about people to just let them recklessly risk their lives."

"And if you were in charge, Calhoun? What would you have done?"

"Probably the same thing you're doing."

In years to come, I would think about that meeting between Kenyon and me, the conversation we had as to what I would do and not do. Years down the line, I would face a similar situation shortly after I became a captain. A group of refugees whom the *Excalibur* had saved would accept the offer of asylum from a world about which I had suspicions. My instinct would be to keep them aboard the ship. Shelby, my first officer, would stridently inform me that I could not act against the wishes of the refugees. And I would end up yielding to her insistence. Against my better judgment, I would allow the people to go planetside. Almost immediately upon doing so, they would become pawns in a game with the planetary government as the government would endeavor to blackmail me into providing it with Starfleet weaponry and technology. A few people would die in that encounter, and I would end up counting myself lucky since it could have been a lot more people than just a few.

If I were writing the Starfleet regulations, they would boil down to exactly two: Rule 1—The captain is always right. Rule 2—When in doubt, see Rule 1.

Kenyon leaned back in his chair and stared up at the ceiling. "I hope I'm doing the right thing, Calhoun. I hope I am."

"You're doing the only thing you can do, sir," I said in what was meant to be a consoling tone.

He smiled at me. "Thank you, Calhoun. I needed to hear that."

And with those words . . . with what I had said to him, and his reply, which I had allowed to pass . . . I damned myself.

Because that wasn't what I wanted to say at all. But, damn me, for a moment I allowed weakness within myself. He had already made his decision, and I didn't want to make him feel worse. So I kept my silence.

They say that silence is golden.

They don't know what the hell they're talking about.

The Message

PLANETS ALWAYS LOOK SO PEACEFUL.

We sat in orbit around Anzibar IV, having beamed down Byron and Stephanie Kenyon. It continues to be amazing to me: I've been to planets where the various populations are waging wars with the intention being complete genocide. Where border skirmishes reign, where hatred and terror hold sway . . . and the planets continue in their path, unknowing, unheeding, and uncaring. Sometimes I wish I could take every warring race and haul them high above their world. I would make them look down at the sphere beneath us and say, "See? See what you have beneath your feet? What are you fighting over? Why are you bothering?"

On the other hand, if someone had endeavored to yank young M'k'n'zy off his homeworld of Xenex and given him a stern talking to about the joys of peace, M'k'n'zy would very likely have handed his head to him.

From the moment that the Kenyons had been beamed to the planet's surface, the bridge had settled into an extraordinarily quiet routine. Usually there was some chatter, some spirited back-and-forth, even casual conversation. Not this time. Captain Kenyon remained in his command chair as if bolted into it. His posture didn't change for ages. Crewmen approached him from time to time for exceedingly routine matters, such as fuel-consumption reports. He dealt with each and every call for his attention with brisk efficiency, but nothing more than that. His attention never wavered from the planet that turned on the screen.

At one point, though, in a very low voice, he said, "Commander . . ."

I turned to face him.

"They're going to be all right, aren't they."

I wasn't sure if it was a question or not. Trying to sound reasonable, I said, "I think so, sir. It's not as if your brother is a novice at this sort of thing. If his judgment was that he could handle the situation, I would be inclined—much as you were—to permit him to do so."

He nodded, but said nothing.

The first transmission from the planet's surface had gone without incident. Precisely on the hour, both Stephanie and Byron had quietly been able to push in on the top of their respective forearms. Takahashi got a beep on his ops board and, moments later, a second one. "Both accounted for, sir," he said and smiled in that broad, odd way he had. "Don't you worry about a thing."

Again Kenyon nodded but said nothing.

In one way, this drove home for me just how lonely a captain's life could be. It was the captain's job to make assignments, to treat everyone equally, to deal with crewpeople as crewpeople first and individuals second. If a captain formed truly strong attachments to anyone—and heaven forbid any of them should be romantic attachments—it made it exceedingly difficult for him to do his job. What if a particular member of the crew was the best suited to deal with some hazardous situation, but the captain was reluctant to send him or her because of personal feelings? Sending a less-qualified individual could endanger an entire mission. The captain owed it both to himself and to his crew to remain as neutral and uninvolved as possible.

And yes, yes, I know, before you say anything . . . when I became captain of the *Excalibur,* I appointed my former fiancée as my first officer. People search for purity of character, for perfection of consistency. Life doesn't happen that way. We set an ideal and just because we don't always manage to stick to it doesn't mean that the ideal is any less devoutly to be sought. I had a teacher back at the Academy, specializing in strategies, who would put forward one theory of warfare and then mention another that would seem to fly in the face of what he had taught earlier. What he was trying to put across to us was that rules of war are not immutable, and one has to be able to adapt quickly or one will run into trouble. On those occasions when he would give us conflicting information, he would always quote an Earthman called Walt Whitman, who apparently said: "Do I contradict myself? Very well then I contradict myself, (I am large, I contain multitudes.)" To be honest, I was never entirely sure what that meant.

The second hour went by, and the third and fourth, and each time there was a comforting signal that let us know the two of them were safe. I found myself falling into a rather exhausting rhythm: As we would come up on the appointed time, I would feel my pulse racing, my body getting tense.

We would come upon the hour, and occasionally a minute or two or three after the appointed time, at which point I would feel a cold sweat beginning to bead on my forehead. I would see Stephanie's laughing face in my mind's eye, the dimples, the long hair. I would hear the coy teasing of her voice, and the tempting way in which she had spoken.

I was regretting it already. I knew that I had done the right thing by not getting involved with her. But, damn, it would have been fun. Not wise, but fun. Still, even though I wasn't sure exactly where we stood with each other or what we meant to each other, there was still Katerina Mueller to consider. . . .

"Am I early?"

I looked up in surprise and realized that—for I don't know how long—I had completely lost track of the time. As if she had sensed my thoughts and materialized in response, Mueller was standing at the turbolift door. She was looking around in surprise to see that the day shift was still in place, with nobody apparently making any preparations to leave.

Slowly Captain Kenyon became aware that no one was moving. As if trying to reorient himself to the moment, he looked around and saw that Mueller was standing there with a mildly puzzled expression on her face. "Nightside already, XO?" he asked.

"This is generally when it's done, sir." She cocked her head in concern. "Anything I should know about?"

"If it's all the same to you, XO . . . I think I'll stay here a bit longer."

"She's your boat, sir. Stay as long as you like." She glanced around at the rest of the crew. No one said anything, but it became clear that no one else was budging. She looked to me and said, "One big happy family, is that it?"

"Seems that way."

She tapped her comm badge. "XO Mueller to night-shift bridge crew: All bridge crew hands, at ease until further notice. It would appear that the sun isn't setting quite yet. XO out." She turned to Takahashi. "Ops . . ."

"Yes, sir." For once, even Romeo's somewhat loose attitude was firmed up, as if he considered anything other than full attention at that point to be in somewhat bad taste.

"I've got the nightside squared away. Would you be so kind as to adjust the auto wake-up calls for everyone on the graveyard shift as well. Let them sleep in until we know what time we'll need them."

"Aye, sir." Hash set about doing as he was instructed . . . but then he stopped. He turned in his chair to face the captain. "Sir."

"It's running late, isn't it," Kenyon said. He spoke with absolutely amazing control. If I were in that situation, I doubt I could have maintained such equanimity. "The signal."

"Yes, sir, it is."

"How late?"

"Four minutes, sir. Going on five."

"Could be in the middle of a fairly heated debate, sir," I pointed out. But I was already starting to get an extraordinary sinking feeling.

Kenyon was up out of his chair. "Mr. Cray, would you be so kind as to raise—what was their leader's name? Kradius. Get me Kradius immediately."

The moments that passed as Cray endeavored to do so seemed endless.

"Five minutes," Hash said.

"Nothing," Cray said.

"Nothing?" His voice sounded hard although his face remained impassive. "They're ignoring us?"

"Yes."

"Five minutes, twenty seconds overdue."

"Bridge to transporter room," Kenyon said without another moment's hesitation. "Lock on to transponder signal and beam them the hell out of there, now! *Now!* Bridge to sickbay. Villers, get down to the transporter room. Bring two emergency setups, just in case. Bridge out. Mr. Calhoun, you have the conn."

"Captain, with all due respect, I suggest you stay here. I'll go."

He spun and looked at me with astonishment. "Why?"

He didn't have to ask, and I didn't really have to reply. We both knew why. We both knew that, just in case something really, truly horrific had happened, the captain would not be in a position of coming unraveled in front of any of his crew.

The unspoken exchange hung there, and then he turned to Mueller and said, "XO, the conn is yours. Calhoun, with me." He headed into the turbolift and I quickly followed.

The moment the door shut behind us, he rounded on me with as much anger as I'd ever heard. "Don't you ever do that again."

"Sir?"

"Condescend to me. Imply that there's something I can't handle."

"I never said there was something you couldn't handle, sir," I told him. "But there are some things you shouldn't *have* to handle."

Before he could respond, his comm badge beeped. "Transporter room to captain."

He tapped it in acknowledgment. "Kenyon here. Go ahead."

"Sir, we've locked on to the transponders. Beaming them up now."

"Is Villers there?" asked Kenyon. Now that he was speaking to someone other than me, his voice was its calm, unflappable, normal tone.

"She's right here. She's . . ."

The transporter chief stopped talking . . . but the comm line remained open.

"Transporter room, go ahead. What's happening?" said Kenyon with growing urgency.

"Oh my God," came the startled gasp from the other end.

"Transporter room, report! Have you got them?"

But the transporter room made no reply. Instead there were shouts, alarmed voices, and above them all the sound of Doc Villers shouting orders. The words "Get them to sickbay!" came loud and clear over the comm channel.

Kenyon took no time to demand further updates. Instead he cut the link and snapped at the turbolift controls, "Destination override. Sickbay." The lift immediately reversed course and sent us to the sickbay. During the trip, no words were exchanged. We both stood there in apprehensive silence. Both of us alone with our concerns and prayers, and both of us having the sinking feeling that we knew what we were going to find when we got there.

The turbolift doors opened and we charged down the corridor. I was in the lead, practically shoving crewmen out of the way if they didn't scatter fast enough. Kenyon was right behind me, and actually doing a fair job of keeping up. We darted into sickbay, and Villers was waiting for us . . . waiting for us just inside the door, and blocking the way.

"Captain . . ." she started to say.

"Where is she? And he. Where are they? Are they all right?" There was no panic in his voice, no sound of desperation. His tone of voice was that of a superior officer demanding information of a subordinate. How he managed to keep himself together considering what was going through his head, I haven't the faintest idea.

And then, Doc Villers—her face a dispassionate mask—said the two words one never wants to hear in that kind of situation.

"I'm sorry."

Kenyon froze where he was. I put a hand on his shoulder, but it was numb. I doubt he felt it at all. Instead he said quietly, "I want to see them."

"No. You don't," said Villers.

"Show me."

"Captain, nothing will be served by—"

Kenyon didn't hesitate. "Doctor, you're relieved of duty. Dr. Ross, show me my daughter and brother, if you please."

Doc Villers looked as if she'd been slapped across the face. But then the chunky woman simply stepped aside and turned to Dr. Ross, a tall, narrow-faced, and somewhat stunned-looking assistant. She nodded to him and Ross said, "Uhm . . . this way, Captain."

Kenyon seemed to have forgotten that I was there altogether. Consequently, I followed him without a word as Ross led him to the back section of sickbay. There, on two med tables, were the bodies of Stephanie Kenyon and Byron Kenyon.

At least, what was left of them was there.

In my time on Xenex I had seen brutality in all its forms. This was not the worst I had ever seen, but it definitely ranked high up there. I didn't have any medical training, but there were electronic representations of their bodies up on the monitors, giving a fuller picture of their internal structure, and even I could see what had been done to them.

Quite simply, they had been beaten to death. They had died brutally and horribly, their skulls crushed in, their bones shattered. There were rope burns on their wrists. They'd probably been stunned by blows to the head, and when they came to, their wrists being bound made it impossible to activate their transponders. There was blood everywhere, my God, it was everywhere. Their faces didn't look like faces, but rather like crimson masks. Stephanie's long hair was thick and matted with blood. Her mouth was hanging open and most of her teeth had been knocked out, as had Byron's. Their clothes were shredded, huge gashes laid open their thighs, the . . .

. . . I'm sorry. I need a drink. Excuse me.

You know . . . you'd think with everything I've seen, everything I've done . . . describing that wouldn't get to me. You'd think that, wouldn't you. You'd think enough time would have passed, that I could be more dispassionate. That I . . .

I think, for everyone, there comes a moment where they come face-to-face with their belief system. Something happens that is so ghastly, so calamitous, that you look not only deep into your soul, but to the being or beings who put that soul there in the first place. And you wonder if they're there, or if they're listening, or if they care about anyone and anything at all.

I think . . . I think that's when I lost my faith. Right then, right there. Oh, I have moments, I admit . . . moments now when I still pray out of habit. When I toss out a random request for help in a pinch. But in my day-to-day existence, in my endeavors to cope with each passing day, I have lost the conviction that there is some greater being watching over us. People don't usually have instant epiphanies, not really. What you usually have is a very small revelation, a tiny peek behind the fabric of our reality to see the gnawing, monstrous evil that hides behind it all. The darkness from which forlorn voices cry out in hopelessness and misery. It leers at you and knows with grim satisfaction that it can bide its time because, sooner or later, it gets you in the end. So it can afford not to worry.

Kenyon stood there, looking at the remains of his daughter and brother for a time. I kept waiting for him to scream, to rant, to moan, to cry . . . anything. To display some sort of reaction. But there was nothing, nothing at all. Instead he simply walked over to his daughter, took the blanket that was at the far end of the med table, and pulled it up and over her head to cover her. Then he went to his brother and did the same for him. As he did that, everyone in sickbay had lined up behind him, just watching. No one knew what to say. What could anyone say? "I'm sorry, Captain"? Something like that? How could any expression of sympathy even begin to approach the depth of agony that he had to be feeling at that moment?

His comm badge beeped and he tapped it. "Bridge to captain." It was Mueller's voice.

"This is the captain." I couldn't believe it. His voice sounded almost chatty.

"Sir . . . we received a reply, finally, to our hail to the Dufaux. It's from Kradius."

"Really. And what does he have to say?" He might have been discussing the technical aspects of tracing a warp signature for all the emotion that he was displaying.

"All it says is: Let that be a lesson to you."

"I see. Mr. Takahashi . . ."

Hash's voice cut in. "Aye, sir?"

"Hash . . . kindly arrange for the storage of two corpses. We'll need to make a convenient rendezvous for a cargo ship heading back toward earth. XO, if you wouldn't mind contacting the Kenyon family burial site. Inform them that we'll be having two new clients for them. Thank you."

"What? Capt—"

"That will be all. Kenyon out."

It was obvious to all of us that he was in shock. In comparison to what he was giving off, Vulcans were screaming mental cases. He rested one hand on the sheets which now covered his daughter and brother. "Go in peace" was all he said.

Then he turned and walked away from them with that same, confident gait he always employed. "Captain . . ." I said.

He blinked in apparent surprise. He *had* forgotten. He'd forgotten I was there. "Yes, Calhoun?"

"You . . ." Everyone was waiting for me to say something, and I didn't have a clue where to start. Then I noticed something as I looked down. "Sir . . . you have blood on your hand."

I indicated his right hand with a small nod. He held up the hand and looked at the crimson-tinged fingers in surprise. "I'll be. Must've happened when I pulled the blankets up over them."

"And on your comm badge too, sir," I said. "Must have happened when you replied to the hail, sir."

"Really." He looked down at the comm badge with only the vaguest interest. Then he removed it from his uniform jacket and flipped it to me. I caught it reflexively. "You can have it."

"Sir, it's yours . . ."

He wasn't listening. Instead he walked out of the sickbay without another word, walking at a slow saunter and appearing for all the world like a man who was simply ambling down a peaceful street of a small town, perhaps heading down to the local eatery to chat it up with the other townsfolk. He gave no indication at all of a man who had completely cracked.

That, of course, is what made him so dangerous.

The Blame

I WALKED STRAIGHT INTO KENYON'S QUARTERS AND TOLD HIM THAT HE should relieve me of my position.

He was sitting in a chair in the middle of his quarters, just sitting there as if it were a command chair. He didn't move from his spot, but instead simply fixed a gaze on me like an owl in a Starfleet uniform. "Why would I want to do that?" he asked. Again, he didn't sound surprised or stunned or anything. He sounded crushingly, frighteningly normal.

"Because I fell into the trap that I should not have fallen into, sir," I told him flatly. "You needed me to be honest with you. You needed me to tell you everything that was going through my mind. The fact of the matter is that I wanted to tell you not to allow them to go down. I wanted to fight you on it every step of the way. You needed to hear me say that, and I . . . I let you down. I was reluctant to contradict you because of . . ." I hesitated.

"Because of her," he finished. "You didn't want to risk embarrassing me in front of my daughter."

"More or less, sir. You . . . you gave me the opportunity to tell you what I really thought. You did so repeatedly. I should have ignored the dynamics of the interpersonal relations I was witnessing and gone with my instincts . . ."

"And your instincts said that the regs should have been ignored."

"Yes, sir. That's right sir."

"Don't worry about it, Calhoun." His voice sounded faint and distant.

"Don't worry about it?" I was pacing the room. "Captain . . . I was supposed to watch out for your best interests. And I fell into the same trap that everyone else here does. I went too easy on you. I didn't present

enough of a challenge. I let you down, and her and him down, and now they're dead because of it."

"What are you looking for, Calhoun? Absolution?" He gestured in the air several times as if he were tossing holy water on me. "I give you absolution, my son. Go. Go and sin no more."

"Captain, I . . ."

"Calhoun, it's not your fault." His tone had changed, become more confident, even conversational. "The captain is the final decision maker on the ship. If I'd been of a mind to violate regs, or second-guess my brother and daughter, I would have done so without your endorsement. By the same token, if—and this happened to be the case—I hadn't been convinced that ignoring both the regs and their wishes was the proper way to proceed, not a hundred Mackenzie Calhouns could have convinced me otherwise. Calhoun, it's . . . Calhoun, look at me."

I was mortified. I felt an actual stinging in my eyes. I hadn't cried in years, not since the death of my first victim, and I was not about to start bawling at that point. I managed to pull myself together and turned to face my captain.

"Calhoun . . . what these people did, these Dufaux . . . they did this. Their leader, Kradius, did this. We, you and I, did not do these . . . these terrible things. We can chastise ourselves all we want for not foreseeing it, or not managing to get Byron and Stephanie to foresee it. But the bottom line is that, as much as we care to blame ourselves for not preventing it . . . that doesn't automatically mean that we caused it. Let us keep the blame placed where it properly should be: with Kradius and his people. And if the blame is to be placed anywhere besides there, then it should be upon me. Mine was the decision, mine was the responsibility, and yours was simply one voice in the crowd. Whether you feel you should have been tougher with me or not is truly beside the point. The same thing would likely have happened."

I stared at him for a long time. His face remained impassive, except for the hints of a small smile at the edges of his mouth. "How can you be so calm?" I asked. "With all respect, sir, how can you seem so . . . so unaffected."

"My reactions aren't really for public consumption, Calhoun," he said easily. "Whatever's going through my head, I prefer to keep it in there. Do I feel grief? Of course. But beating my breast in the presence of my officers is hardly going to be of any use to anyone, is it. We still have a job to do. We still have a peace to negotiate."

"A peace?" I couldn't quite believe it. "A peace? Between the Carvargna and the Dufaux?"

"That was our assignment, I do believe."

"Captain . . . you can't be serious. The Dufaux are—"

"Oh, I have no intention of meeting with the Dufaux," he said. "I'll be meeting directly with the Carvargna myself."

I began to get that same feeling of danger that I had earlier. "Yourself, sir?"

"I am the ranking officer, last I checked," he said in that same eerily calm tone. "Why? Don't you trust me, Calhoun?"

I had the sense that I was treading in an extremely dangerous area. Choosing my words as delicately as I could, I said, "It's . . . not a matter of trust, sir. You've had a terrible shock, a traumatic loss. Perhaps . . . this isn't the time to pursue a matter that could just as easily wait."

"Wait?" He raised a curious eyebrow.

"They were at war before we got here, and they'll be at war after we leave."

"You were talking to me about responsibility, Calhoun. Taking responsibility for lost lives. If people die because we delayed trying to rectify the situation, then aren't those lives on our heads? At least to some degree?"

"Captain . . ."

"Mac," he said gently, "I'm fine. Truly. I'm fine. Perhaps . . . well, perhaps I'm still in shock in many respects."

"That thought had occurred to me, sir."

"Well, you may be right. And that's fine. The human psyche lets us deal with things in our own way and in its own time. I'm willing to let that develop naturally. In the meantime, I have a job to do, and I'll be damned if I let this setback stop me from doing it."

The word rocked me. *Setback?* Saying that he was simply in shock was turning into something of an understatement. I didn't think he was dealing with any aspect of it.

"The best thing that I can do," he continued, unaware of what was going through my mind, "is complete Byron and Stephanie's work. They always—both of them—they always were concerned first and foremost with the grand scheme of things. I can . . ." He smiled. "You'll say I'm foolish . . . but I can hear their voices in my head."

"Haunting you, sir?" It was not a concept that I lightly dismissed. On Xenex not only did we believe in visions, but connections with those who were lost to us were not uncommon.

"Nothing quite that exotic," he said. "I hear them as one would hear the advice of someone who is dear to you. And they are telling me that the last thing they'd want me to do is allow this, their last mission, to go unfulfilled. Now, I know what you're thinking, Calhoun, and you needn't worry. I will be consulting directly with Starfleet on this matter. This is a situation of some delicacy, and I wouldn't want to do anything that could make matters worse. Any actions I take, no matter what, will be done with the full approval and backing of Starfleet command."

"Any 'actions,' sir? Actions . . . such as what?"

He smiled once more. "Trust me," he said.

That should have been the moment. Right there. Even as I tell it to you now, I see it with such blinding clarity that I cannot believe, in retrospect, that I didn't do something right then and there. But what could I have done? Tried to relieve him of command? Simply because he was saying he was going to get the job done? How insane would that have been?

Besides, my overall imperative at that point was to protect him, to be the best first officer possible and support him in whatever decisions he was to make.

Within me, though, my blood was boiling, and it wasn't simply out of concern for completing a peace initiative. I was appalled to the core over what had been done to them. And more . . . even during our brief time together, I had felt a connection with Stephanie that perhaps even went beyond what Elizabeth and I had had. I fully admit, I may be adding to it at this point with the intervention of years. I may be looking back at what was the most brief of encounters, which might have led to absolutely nothing, and imbuing it with a richness and texture that wasn't really there. But, as are all mortals, I am limited to telling stories by how I remember them. It's difficult, impossible even, to separate hindsight and wishful thinking from whatever the reality of the situation was. To the best of my recollection . . . the loss of Stephanie, in particular, and the brutal way in which she died, inflamed a desire for revenge in me such as I had not felt in years. But I could not let that flame touch the captain. He had greater duties to which he had to attend. He had to stand for something more. He had to be shielded from the hurt and pain and anger. I had to help him . . . but had no idea how to go about it.

And he seemed

So

Calm.

It was frightening in a way. Even before anything happened, before any of the subsequent events occurred, I felt cold, burning fear in the pit of my stomach. Not for myself, but on the captain's behalf. It was a fear that I spoke of to Mueller. It was one of those rare instances where we were together, relatively alone, and fully dressed. We were in Ten-Forward, huddled close in at a table. The *Grissom* was on its way to Anzibar II—not a terribly long voyage at that point, mere hours at most—with the captain busily arranging for a meeting with that world's leaders. Indeed, the only thing that was delaying us was the captain, who was, good as his word, taking the time to consult with Starfleet before taking any actions. He was also handling all contact with the Carvargna himself. Said it was his preference.

No one was paying any particular attention to Kat and me. Everyone on the ship was shaken up by the turn of events, and the captain's welfare was on everyone's mind. I spoke in a low tone, saying to Kat, "Something's going to go wrong. I can feel it."

"You're not implying that the captain can't handle the situation, are you?"

"I'm not implying anything. I'm just stating concerns, that's all. You've served with him far longer than I have . . ."

"Yes. I have. And let me tell you this, Commander," and she leaned forward so that our faces were only inches away from each other, "I trust the man implicitly. He is the most thorough professional I have ever known. If he says he can handle the situation . . . if he says he's on top of things . . . then I say he can handle it. I say you shouldn't worry."

Kat Mueller's words were exactly what I wanted to hear.

Unfortunately, that worried me even more.

As it turned out, later on we would both be changing our tunes.

The Meeting

Captain Kenyon had his first meeting with the Carvargna leadership . . . and I did not attend. No one did, except the captain himself, and Lieutenant Cray, who went along as security backup. And even Cray told me that, at the actual meeting, he wasn't present. Kenyon had kept the meeting behind closed doors with the Carvargna. I felt all of the worry, all of the concern, flaring once more. Unfortunately, there was little I could do about it.

Actually, there was one thing.

I sought out Dr. Villers while the captain was on the planet's surface. I found her sitting quietly in her office, off duty, but with half a bottle of synthehol situated on her desk. One did not have to be a master detective to figure out where the rest of the bottle's contents had gone.

"Doctor? Doc?"

She looked up at me, bleary-eyed. "Yeah?" Her voice was slurred.

"I need to talk to you about something kind of important."

Immediately she sat up, the intoxicating effects of synthehol falling away from her. That was, of course, one of the joys of synthehol. It was also, to my mind, one of the drawbacks.

"What can I do for you, Commander?"

Taking a seat, I said, "I need your input about . . . competency."

"Don't be concerned, Commander," she said calmly. "I admit, your socialization skills are somewhat lacking, but I hardly think you'd qualify as incompetent."

"I wasn't referring to me. I was referring to . . . to the captain."

She stared at me for a moment and then growled, "That isn't funny, Commander."

"I wasn't joking, Doctor. I am becoming . . . concerned about the captain."

"And I am becoming concerned about you, Commander, as of this moment. Captain Kenyon is a great man . . ."

"And he's had a great loss," I pointed out. "I just wanted your medical opinion—"

"Medical opinion." She picked up the bottle and tossed back another deep swallow. I was reluctantly impressed by her imbibing skills. "In order to form a medical opinion, I would have to give him a medical examination. On what grounds do you suggest I do so?"

"You don't need grounds. You're the CMO, and all crewmen must submit to exams upon your request. That includes the captain."

"That is a very broad-ranging power I have, Commander. Since power tends to corrupt, it is not one I exercise lightly. And when the captain is involved, I do not exercise at all unless I feel it's unavoidable. Just because the captain isn't mourning on a fast enough schedule for you doesn't mean that it's going to make me the least bit concerned."

"It doesn't have anything to do with me, Doctor. . . ."

"Are you sure about that?"

I eyed her suspiciously. "May I ask what that is supposed to mean?"

"It means no more and no less than what you take it to mean."

I felt myself starting to get angry, and I pushed it as far down as I could. "That's a bit too vague an answer to satisfy me, I'm afraid. You're implying something, and I'd like to know what that is."

"All right," said Villers. She pushed the bottle aside and sized me up. "I've worked with Captain Kenyon for a damned long time. He's the best officer, and the best man I've ever known with the possible exception of my third husband, and even that's iffy. The fact is, I already had a long talk with him earlier today. He feels the loss, he mourns it in his own way. But he is preparing to carry on in the professional manner to which I have become accustomed. You, on the other hand . . ."

"Yes? Don't hesitate, pray continue."

"You, Commander, are what I would term a 'loose cannon.' Your service record is impressive in its accomplishments, and you have your curious supporters. There are some who even compare you to James Kirk in terms of your command style. But these days are not those, Commander. I dislike cowboys. Cowboys get people injured or killed. That means more work for me. Not that I'm lazy, you understand, but a day where no one comes through my door is a day that I consider a good one. Your record is shot through with foolish chances that need not have been taken, and wouldn't have been if you'd attended to the regs. The fact that things 'turned out' for you is irrelevant to me. They might not have. I don't like your command technique, and to be blunt—"

"Oh, you've been tactful until now?"

"—to be blunt, I don't like you. And I don't like what you're doing now: trying to take advantage of the captain's loss to clear the way for yourself."

I felt my throat constricting in fury. The scar on my face burned, which indicated to me that it was turning darker red. That's what usually happened when I got angry. "Is that your interpretation?"

"It's *an* interpretation. It's certainly the one I'm drawing. If that is not the case . . ."

"It is not."

"Then you may want to reconsider your actions so that you don't suggest to others that you're simply an opportunist who will do anything to get ahead."

"If that were the case, *Doctor,* then hasn't it occurred to you that—rather than being a 'cowboy' and a 'loose cannon'—I'd be doing everything I could to toe the line of regulations so that I could get ahead? I wouldn't act upon my conscience, or depend upon 'curious supporters.' I'd be trying to build as wide a base of support as possible instead of taking the actions that I felt necessary."

"Well," and she smiled in a very unpleasant way, "perhaps you're simply an inept opportunist."

"And perhaps you," I replied, "are so blinded by loyalty that you're refusing to see a bad situation developing right in front of your eyes."

"At least," she said, "some of us *have* loyalty."

There are certain comments that could best be referred to as "conversation enders." That was definitely one of them.

I'm sorry. That went a bit further afield than I was expecting it to. What was I talking about?

Ah yes. The meeting.

The captain, immediately upon his return, called for a meeting to be held in the conference lounge. I was, as it turned out, the last one to arrive. Already present were the captain himself, of course, Romeo Takahashi, Cray, Doc Villers, Katerina Mueller, and Rachel McLauren. McLauren was the chief engineer. She was easily the most diminutive engineer I'd ever seen. Word around the engine room was that that was one of her special skills. She was so narrow that she could worm her way into virtually anywhere with no problem at all. Some folks kiddingly referred to her as the "pocket-sized engineer." I couldn't say whether they ever mentioned that nickname around her, and I can only guess as to what her reaction would have been if she'd heard it. She had a shaved head and thick red eyebrows. When she was studying a situation, her deep blue eyes seemed capable of plunging to the depths of any problem and discerning not only the difficulty, but the solution, in a matter of seconds.

"Thank you all for coming," Kenyon said briskly, and he nodded toward Kat. "Particularly you, XO."

"Not a problem, sir," said Mueller. With no hint of irony, she endeavored to cover a yawn with the back of her hand. "No problem at all."

"I know this is off-duty hours for you, Mueller. Ordinarily I would just have the computer deliver a précise when you come on duty, but the extraordinary nature of the situation requires, I think, extraordinary measures."

No one really salutes in Starfleet. This didn't stop Katerina from tossing off a tongue-in-cheek semi-salute. It came across more like a waggling of fingers in greeting than a stiff salute. Kenyon didn't seem to notice, or if he did notice, he didn't mind

"However," Kenyon continued, "I wanted all key officers on this at the same time."

"On what, sir?" asked Hash. "Did the meeting with the Carvargna go well?"

"Better than well. Better than great." He folded his hands neatly and said, "The leaders of the Carvargna want to cooperate with us in whatever way possible. I've spent a good deal of time with them. They're considerate, they're thoughtful. Their emphasis is on love and poetry. How can anyone find fault with that?"

"I don't think anyone is out to find fault, sir," said Mueller. "I think, though, we'd all like to see what the point of this is."

"The point is, they fight only because they have to," said Kenyon. "They are worthy individuals and deserve to have their population safe from the ravages of the Dufaux. We are, after all, familiar with the sorts of atrocities that they're capable of perpetrating."

"The plan?" Cray asked softly, cutting as always to the heart of the situation.

"Ah yes, the plan. After lengthy discussions with all concerned . . . it has been decided that we are going to assist the Carvargna with improving and updating the weaponry of their vessels."

Rachel McLauren blinked as if in surprise. "I'm sorry. What?" There was a brief exchange of glances around the table as if everyone wanted to make sure that everyone else was understanding the matter in the same way.

"The Dufaux have more advanced weaponry than do the Carvargna." The captain seemed happy to elaborate. "The supposition is that they stole it from other races. Ultimately, the hows and whys aren't all that important. We are going to help the Carvargna win this war and stabilize the entire area of space."

Now understand—then as now—Starfleet regulations have no greater challenger than me. I'll complain about them when I feel like it, ignore them when I have to. But even I was caught flat-footed by the bald-faced assertion of the comment.

"Sir, with all respect . . ." I looked around the table and saw mostly puzzled expressions. "Sir, can we *do* that?"

"We most certainly can . . . and with the UFP's blessing, I might add. Look, people, considering the circumstances, I know it's going to sound odd when I say: It's nothing personal here."

"Odd" was something of an understatement. I was spiraling way beyond baffled at that point.

"What I'm saying," continued Kenyon, "is that whether the victims had been . . . who they were . . . or total strangers, that wouldn't change the outcome of the response to the Dufaux's actions." His voice became hard, an undercurrent of anger audible. "They took two legitimate, authorized representatives of the Federation and they slaughtered them. Animals butchered for food die in more humane fashion than those two people did. They went down at the invitation of the Dufaux, and their lifeless bodies were sent back as a clear warning. A clear warning necessitates a clear response. The Dufaux have spit in the face of the Federation, and they will be brought to task for it. Now . . . do any of you have a problem with that?"

"No, sir," said Cray. Naturally he was the first to respond, but Villers promptly voiced her support as well.

McLauren was already working up the logistics. "I'll just have to be careful not to give them too much too fast," she mused. "Last thing we need to do is jack up their weaponry to the point where they blow themselves up."

Kenyon turned to Hash expectantly. "Takahashi?"

"I'll prepare ship's services to provide any help it can," he said evenly.

"XO?"

"I'll coordinate with night and graveyard, Captain," she told him. "If you feel that round-the-clock is mandated, we'll be able to provide it."

"Good." There was a silence then. For me it seemed that it was a fairly long one.

Kenyon was waiting for my response. Waiting for me to chime in, either with a protest or a show of support.

I thought of how I had said to him that I would never contradict him in front of others. That support for the position of captain, and his long-term authority, was mandatory. I also thought of how my silence, my tacit agreement in his allowing Stephanie and Byron to go to the planet's surface, had set all of this into motion and cost two people their lives. If I spoke up now, lodged a protest, tried to block him . . . either way, in some aspect or another, I was risking doing the wrong thing. My choices were between one bad decision and another.

But I didn't know for sure that silence, that support, was automatically bad. After all, he had Starfleet backing on this.

I thought about Kirk.

Having been compared to him, I had felt it wise to study up on him, even beyond the required reading. There had been a time when Kirk faced a situation that was not dissimilar from what I was encountering now. A planet where two factions were at war with one another . . . and Kirk had discovered that the Klingons—our enemies at the time—were supplying one side with advanced weaponry. Well . . . relatively advanced. Flintlocks and such. So Kirk supplied the other side for the purpose of evening the score. Matters escalated and eventually Kirk, soured by the experience and feeling like a warmonger, pulled out. After he left, the tribe that he'd been backing was wiped out by the Klingon-supplied side. Ironically, with no one to fight . . . but with the advanced weaponry in their hands . . . the "victors" wound up turning upon each other, embarking in a power struggle that wound up wiping out every last one of them. Every so often, I still think about the Klingons walking among the corpses that resulted from their handiwork. Were they pleased? I wonder. Were they saddened? Did they care one way or the other? I would have liked to ask them.

But this situation . . . this one was entirely different. Kirk at least rationalized that he was simply giving a proportionate response to outsiders who had already interfered with the planet's development and business. Thus he was able to justify his actions. Here, in Anzibar space . . . we were the outsiders. We were the ones who were interfering. We were the Klingons . . . the enemy.

If we mixed in . . .

Then I saw Stephanie's bloodied corpse in my mind's eye. I saw Captain Kenyon, looking at me expectantly. I saw Byron that last time I'd seen him alive, insisting that a peace initiative was worth the risk. People always speak boldly of risks when, in their hearts, they believe that they're going to come out of a situation hale and hardy. I've faced death far too many times to have a limited sense of my own mortality, but there are many others who do have such a lack of perspective. Byron was one of them. And the Dufaux made sure that it cost him and Stephanie the ultimate price.

Even before my mind had fully wrapped itself around the problem and come to a reasonable conclusion, I heard my mouth say, "Whatever help I can provide, Captain . . . it's yours."

From the corner of my eye, I saw Doc Villers nodding with a small smile on her face. Perhaps she thought that I was just a cowardly little weasel who didn't mind going around behind the captain's back, but when put to the test face-to-face, I promptly sided with my commander. Perhaps she thought I had simply come around and she had "talked sense" into me. To be honest, I didn't care overmuch what she thought.

Instead my instincts led me to glance at Cray. I wasn't sure why yet . . . but I had the feeling that he might present the biggest problem.

Cray wasn't looking at me at all. That, in and of itself, was strange. After all, the captain had just addressed me directly, and I had spoken in reply. The instinct for anyone at the table would have been to be looking my way. But Cray was staring straight ahead, almost as if he were making a point of ignoring me. That, to my mind, did not bode well at all.

"What you can provide, Mr. Calhoun," said the captain, leaning forward eagerly, "is your expertise. I've been treading the spaceways a good few decades now. Lord knows I've been involved in my share of skirmishes. But I've never coordinated a war before. You have. For those of you who might be unaware," he said (and I might have been crazy, but it sounded to me as if he were speaking with a modicum of personal pride, as if he were a proud father), "the commander here, while still in his tender teen years, led an entire world to freedom as warlord of the Xenexians."

That was when Cray spoke. Always in that quiet, almost sibilant voice, he asked with what sounded like gentle mocking, "Should we bow?"

Kenyon didn't respond directly. Instead he continued speaking to me. "The Carvargna, as I've noted, tend to be a more peaceful race. They could use work on strategy, on coordinating attacks with limited resources. It's not as if we're going to be heading in there, leading an attack with the *Grissom*'s phasers blasting. . . ."

"We're not?" I tried not to sound surprised.

"No, Mr. Calhoun, we're not," he assured me. "We're simply here to help, not storm. Teach them. Guide them. Fill them in about basic strategy, about coordinated attacks, about air versus ground assault. You're certainly suited for it."

"As am I," said Cray. At that point, Cray was indeed looking at me. Somehow the unblinking stare I was getting from him was hardly mollifying.

"No slight intended, Mr. Cray," said the captain. "But I feel it would be best if Mr. Calhoun handled this. If he's up for it, that is. Are you . . . Calhoun?"

The challenge was unmistakable. This wasn't simply an assignment. He wanted to make damned sure that I was on his side. That I wasn't going to countermand him, or doubt him. He needed to know that he had my support going in. I'm not entirely sure why it was so important to him. Perhaps it was a normal, human instinct for him to have. All of us want approval in some form or another, even if it's from those we would consider to be our subordinates.

"Absolutely, sir," I said firmly. "Just tell me where and when, and I'll be there."

"Good!" He slapped the table and it shuddered slightly. "I knew I could count on you. On all of you. And together," and he spoke more loudly, more boldly than I'd ever heard him, "we're going to show the Dufaux that there are some fundamentals of decency that are not tampered with, some lines that are not crossed. We're going to show them what the Federation stands for . . . and that to spit in the face of that is to pay a terrible price."

As for me, I couldn't help but wonder what sort of price we were all going to pay.

It's just that . . .

There's something you have to understand.

There are aspects of myself that I don't like. Aspects that I've tried to grow beyond.

As much as I draw upon the strength of my "barbaric" upbringing, part of me is almost . . . almost ashamed of it. That's always been a conflict that I've carried around within me. Wanting to move beyond what I've been . . . but finding it impossible to leave behind because I need it, depend on it.

I've seen the face of anger, the face of hatred, the face of revenge. I've seen it reflected in the eyes of men I was about to kill as they looked in fear upon me. I saw it reflected in the water of a stream, when I went to dry my face after sobbing over my father's execution. I've seen it mirrored in the faces of men who fought by my side, seeking to avenge themselves against their oppressors.

I didn't want to see it in Norman Kenyon. I liked and respected him too much for that. He deserved better than to be . . .

. . . to be me.

Then again, I've noticed that life tends not to cooperate with those things that are the most important to us. And ultimately . . . we cannot save those who do not want to be saved.

But if we are to go down, the least we can do is go down in flames. We all owe ourselves that, at least.

I'm sorry. I'm getting off topic and I was . . . distracted . . . a bit . . .

The Questions

Mick Gold, the officer at conn, was the first one to come to me.

Gold fancied himself a bit more of a maverick than he actually was. He tended to walk with such a pronounced swagger that Villers had taken one look at him and prescribed an ointment for his upper thighs on the assumption that he was having a serious chafing problem.

It had been several days since the captain had instituted what he had come to refer to as "the Initiative." We'd been working with the Carvargna to the best of both our and their ability. I had been somewhat underwhelmed by their military "leaders." They had been given the rank and the responsibility, but there was very little that they actually understood about the strategies and techniques of warfare. I walked them through some of the basics, gave them what I considered some required reading—everything ranging from the annals of Garth of Izar to Julius Caesar's *De Bello Gallico.* I will credit them that what they lacked in firsthand knowledge they more than made up for in pure enthusiasm. They wanted to learn. And it wasn't simply for the sake of trying to save their own skins (skins which were, I should add, a rather startling shade of green) but also, it seemed to me, out of interest in knowledge for its own sake.

Other than me, McLauren had the heaviest burden. The ship's weaponry that the Carvargna possessed was on par with simple disruptors. It was not even in the same league as the phase-generated pulsers the Dufaux possessed. The pulsers, in turn, were no match for our phasers, but the captain's instruction was not to arm the Carvargna with firepower beyond that which the Dufaux had at their disposal. "We want to insure that the Carvargna will be safe and capable," Kenyon had told us. "We don't need to arm them so heavily that they're tempted to abuse the armament and go elsewhere to display their new strength." In short, we didn't want to risk turning them into that which we were trying to combat.

I was stepping into a turbolift, on the way to my quarters, when Lieutenant Gold ran up calling, "Hold the lift!" I did so and he stepped in beside me. As the lift started to move, he turned to me and said, "Have you seen them?"

"Them?" I wasn't quite sure what he was talking about, and it was evident from the confusion on my face. "Them . . . who?"

" 'Them' the orders from Starfleet."

For a moment I was still clueless, and then I understood. "You mean the orders that instruct us to aid the Carvargna."

He nodded. "Yup. Them."

"No, I haven't. Nor do I need to. The captain has said they exist and it's my duty to carry them out."

"It's your duty not to let something be pulled on you, sir." I have to admit, that's one of the things I liked about Gold. He never mucked around with such disclaimer phrases as "with all due respect."

"Do you have reason to believe that the captain is falsifying orders? Because, Mr. Gold, that is a very serious charge."

He looked at me for a long moment, and then said quietly—uncharacteristically quietly, in fact—"No. No, I have no reason."

"I see."

"I'm just the suspicious type."

"I see," I said again. "That being the case, you might want to consider rethinking your current career path and seek instead a career in security. That is certainly the environment for someone who is of a suspicious nature."

"Security is the environment for someone who obeys blindly and follows the captain right or wrong."

" 'Right or wrong'?"

"Look . . ." Gold shifted uncomfortably from one foot to the other. "I love a fight as much as the next guy. But I generally like to know what I'm fighting for. I feel badly about what happened to the captain's kid and his brother. Everybody does. And I don't even object to the idea of kicking in the teeth of the bastards what did it. But I just want to make sure that everything's on the up and up, that a proper course is being steered. It's just my nature, y'know?"

I couldn't blame him for being concerned. After all, I'd had a not dissimilar discussion with Doc Villers . . . and had been roundly shot down for my troubles. Now I found myself in the odd position of defending the captain from the very sentiments that I had been voicing not all that long ago. But there was no way that I was going to convey any doubts that I had—particularly when, as of this point, they were still unfounded—to a subordinate. It just wasn't right.

"I will take your concern under advisement."

"So you're not going to check."

"For the first officer to contact Starfleet directly," I said, "would be a circumvention of procedure." Something within me recoiled, horrified, at the rote sound to my words. I was actually falling back on regs to excuse behavior. What the hell was I coming to? Nonetheless, I continued, "Verifying orders, as if the captain's word were being doubted, would set off bells all through Starfleet. They'd want to know why anyone was questioning the captain's orders, what there was about the captain's conduct that warranted that type of concern. And if I don't have any easy answers for those questions, then I would not only be wasting the time of all concerned, but I would be unfairly undermining the captain with Starfleet."

"So you're not going to check," said Gold as if I had not spoken at all.

"Under. Advisement," I said.

The lift doors opened not a moment too soon. Gold stepped through them, turned, and tossed off a mock salute. The doors hissed shut, closing me back in and leaving me to wonder just who and what it was that I had become. Was I being concerned over how Kenyon would be seen? Or, as the prospect of my own command began to loom before me, was I suddenly turning into a conservative, line-toe drone who valued the Proper Order of Things above all else?

It was not a situation that I wanted to dwell upon.

Nor was there anyone with whom I could discuss the matter. After all, the core of the problem involved support for the actions of the captain. If I chose to try and converse with someone about the situation, I was then, by definition, undermining Kenyon . . . which is what I was trying to avoid doing.

Mueller also floated a question to me in a much more cautious fashion. I had just returned from one of my sessions with the Carvargna. Kat and I had just had some . . . recreation . . . and she turned over, her head lying on my shoulder, and she fingered my chest hair. "Are you sure about this?" she asked. Her voice was a low whisper, as if she was concerned that someone might overhear us.

"This? Yes . . . I'm, uh . . . I'm sure this is chest hair, if that's what you mean."

"I mean are you sure about the captain. About what we're doing."

I wanted to lie to her, tell her that the captain had my full confidence. That not for a moment did I doubt the rightness of our actions. Instead I replied honestly: "No."

She made a thoughtful noise in the bottom of her throat and then, without moving away from me, she said, "I'm not sure, either."

Considering the unswerving support she'd voiced earlier, perhaps that's why she would not go into detail, even though I gently coaxed her.

I should have coaxed her less gently.

The Time Between

Now, for storytelling purposes, it would probably be ideal if nothing else happened at this point in my narrative. However, life has an odd habit of not working out in ways that best suit the needs of storytellers.

"Communiqué from Starfleet, sir," Lieutenant Cray reported after we had spent nearly two weeks instructing and teaching the Carvargna the fine art of war, and working to equip them in such a way that they would be more easily able to deal with their opponents.

I watched the captain's expression carefully to see how he would react to this news. He didn't bat an eye, but instead said simply, "I'll take it in my ready room, Lieutenant." He disappeared into there for some minutes.

I was waiting for him to come out and announce that our instructions were to blow up the Dufaux. Had that happened, well . . . it would have been easy, then. It would have been so easy. But you know, the funny thing about the road to ruin is that you rarely stride down it. It's taken in small, delicate steps, and you don't realize how completely doomed you are until you're much too far along.

Kenyon emerged from the ready room. I tensed, as if I were preparing to take a shot to the head. Without saying a word, he settled into his command chair. "Cray," he said. He spoke more loudly than usual, as if he were calling across a large room rather than addressing someone who was positioned directly behind him.

"Yes, sir."

"Please get Barhba on screen for me."

Barhba was the Carvargna head counsel who had been mainly responsible for coordinating the *Grissom*'s efforts. In less than a minute after Kenyon had made the request, Barhba appeared on the screen. In some ways, he reminded me of Kenyon himself. Green skin, a head of hair that was similarly green, but lighter in color. Hash had said at one point that the Carvargna had reminded him of a broccoli stalk, only a bit more personable. Fortunately he had not said it within the earshot of Barhba, although for all I know, the Carvargna might have agreed.

"Honored Kenyon," Barhba said. "News?"

"Unfortunate, I'm afraid, my friend," Kenyon replied. "We have other assignments to which we must attend."

"Not unexpected." Barhba smiled with his green teeth, which was, quite frankly, a bit unsightly. Natural, but unsightly. "There are others who would benefit from your help. It is a large galaxy, after all. We appreciate the aid that you have given us thus far."

"I only regret," Kenyon said, "that our efforts were not able to lead to the peace that you so richly deserve."

"Perhaps not. But you have prepared us for the alternative, as undesirable as that may be. At the very least, the Dufaux would be wise if they did not attack us anytime soon. They know of the help you have given us, and would be most foolish to challenge us again."

"If they do . . . don't let them get away with anything."

"We will not. And my warmest regards to you, Honored Calhoun, as well."

I rose and bowed slightly, as was the custom of theirs that I had observed. "You have learned well the ways of war," I said. "Let us hope that you do not have to use any of them."

"That is always to be desired," said Barhba diplomatically.

And that, as far as I knew, was that.

The *Grissom* promptly set course for the Neutral Zone. According to Starfleet, there had been talk of a Romulan buildup at one of the outlying borders, and we had been asked to investigate it.

And we did. It turned out to be not the Romulans, but instead an Orion pirate fortification that was the beginnings of a possible alliance with the Romulans. The Orion pirate ring was smashed by our efforts, and of course the Romulans denied any knowledge of the Orions' becoming their allies.

We then headed for rendezvous with the transport that would be picking up the bodies of Stephanie and Byron. At the point where the transfer was made, a memorial service was to be held. Most of the crew attended. Only a handful of them had actually met either of the decea—

Had met Stephanie or Byron. Most of them attended out of respect for the captain and his grief. For a brief time, the captain contemplated taking a leave of absence to return to Earth and see their bodies back there, but decided against it.

I know I should say "home" instead of "Earth," since most people refer to it that way. Then again, I'm not from Earth. Oddly . . . I've discovered that I've stopped referring to Xenex as home. In many ways I . . . don't feel as if I have one.

I should feel sad about that, I suppose.

Hmm.

Ah well.

At the memorial service, Kenyon was the picture of calm. That alone was enough to ring a few warning bells in my head, but I said nothing. He was unfailingly polite and supportive, accepted all condolences with unfailing equanimity. Once during all of that, he glanced my way and—for some odd reason—winked at me. It was as if he was saying, Don't worry about me, I'm going to be fine. There's no problems on this end.

Understand, I wanted nothing more than for that to be the case. You see, well . . .

Hell, how do I put this.

In many ways . . . Kenyon reminded me of my father.

I know, I didn't say this earlier. I was afraid . . .

. . . well, I was afraid it would sound trite to you. Or you might feel sorry for me. "Poor Calhoun, spending his entire life looking for a father substitute." That's not it at all. It's just there was some physical resemblance, although not tremendous, but some. And in the way he carried himself, in his infinite patience, in . . . well, in any number of ways.

You'll think it's foolish.

Well . . . the hell with you. It's my story. And I'm telling you, that's how I felt. If that's not profound enough or deep enough for you, then that's your problem, not mine.

What I'm simply trying to convey to you is that . . . I've seen people change.

I saw my father as the oppression of the Danteri wore down on him. I saw him become angry, more bitter, more defiant. I saw those attitudes drive him, consume him, until the final confrontation that saw him beaten to death in the public square.

So I was alert to it, looking for signs of it in the captain as well.

The thing is, when you look for something, more often than not you find it.

After the memorial service, we embarked on assignment after assignment. Much of it was routine, a couple of them had an element of danger. As for the captain . . . he was . . .

. . . he was different.

It was in small ways, at first, subtle ways. Nothing that anyone would really notice or pay attention to if they weren't looking for it. I was. He seemed shorter-tempered to me than before. Angrier. He stopped greeting people by name as he made his way down corridors. Previously one of the more sociable of men, he tended to keep more to himself.

I sensed problems.

I'm not a telepath, or a Betazoid. I spoke to the ship's counselor at one point, a decent enough fellow named Nugent who had several degrees in counseling and was, by all reports, a very good listener. Like Dr. Villers, Nugent had also taken time to speak with the captain, and he likewise came away from the meetings positive that—although Kenyon was understandably grieving over the loss of his daughter and brother—he was coping with it.

I wanted to believe it. I wanted to believe it more than I can possibly express. I wanted it so much that in large measure I forced myself to believe it. Certainly the captain seemed testier, more easily angered, but so what? The professionals believed that everything was going to be okay.

And who was I to judge? I am the first to admit that I don't always have the healthiest outlook upon the world. There is a layer of anger that boils within me just below the surface that is always there. It colors everything that I do, everything that I perceive. We all come into any given situation carrying our own experiences, which help to shape our viewpoints, and my experiences were certainly more traumatic than most.

The savage M'k'n'zy of Calhoun, the one who never doubted himself, the one who was confident in his convictions, was coming squarely up against Mackenzie Calhoun, trained by Starfleet to accept the rules, obey his superior officers, shut up and do the job. It was easily one of the most uncertain times of my life. I was completely torn inside . . . and the problem is that it's only now, with the distance and cool assessment that only the passage of time can provide, that I fully understand what my problem was. At the time, all I knew was that my instincts, upon which I had always depended, were in turmoil.

I let things progress.

My curious nonrelationship with Kat Mueller continued, neither advancing nor regressing. It just . . . was. In some ways, there was as much passion in our time together as there would have been in running a few brisk miles. In sex between two genuine lovers, the lovers complete a need within each other. We were fulfilling a need within ourselves. Not the same thing at all . . . but it was satisfactory, it was good exercise, no one was being hurt by it, and neither of us wanted or needed more. At least, that's what we told ourselves, although every so often the image of Stephanie Kenyon would float to me unbidden. Once I even accidentally cried out her name, but Kat didn't hear me. At least, I like to think she didn't.

I tried to approach the captain on a social basis. Not that I suggested we date or something like that. But I spoke of going for drinks in Ten-Forward, or engaging in some sort of absurd holoadventure in the holodeck. Each time, though, I was politely but firmly rebuffed. "I have work," he would say, or "I have other things on my mind right now, Calhoun," or even more simply, "Another time, perhaps."

And so time passed.

Then it all fell apart.

The Return to Anzibar

"INCOMING MESSAGE FROM STARFLEET, SIR."

"In the ready room, Mr. Cray," said Kenyon.

It was no different than any other time . . . and yet, for some reason, it felt different to me. I found myself looking around at the others on the bridge to see whether, for whatever reason, they were reacting to it in the same manner. It was as if I had seen a ghost and was trying to determine, without making too big a fuss over the matter, whether others had seen it as well. But there was no reaction. No one seemed to think anything of it, and I began to wonder why I was reacting to it the way that I had. It was as if I was looking for trouble.

This time, when Kenyon emerged from the ready room, he seemed different, more energized than I had seen him in ages. He cast a quick glance at Cray, and then said, "Calhoun, conference lounge, five minutes. Mr. Cray, Mr. Takahashi, Mr. Gold, you too." He walked out without another word.

That Cray and Hash were being summoned to a meeting was more or less standard operating procedure. But Gold did nothing to hide the momentary surprise. What, he clearly wondered, could require the presence of the conn operator?

I looked to Cray. "Any idea what that was about, Lieutenant?" I asked.

He simply shook his head. No reason he should know. Most communiqués from Starfleet were strictly between the captain and headquarters.

Five minutes later, we had assembled in the conference lounge. Also present were Kat and Villers, Kat—as usually was the case in these circumstances—rubbing the sleep out of her eyes. Fortunately enough, Mueller had become accustomed to being roused from sleep at odd hours. She had developed the ability not only to come to full wakefulness at a moment's notice, but also to nod off just as quickly. I'd seen her do it. She'd tilt her head back, close her eyes, and be asleep just like that. Most impressive, really.

"Mr. Gold," said the captain, "you are to set us a course for the Anzibar system."

Gold looked as if he thought he hadn't quite heard the captain properly. "Anzibar, sir? Weren't we . . . weren't we just there?"

"Yes. And Starfleet has ordered that we return."

"Why, sir?" asked Mueller. She looked puzzled.

Kenyon, in a surprisingly sharp tone, said, "Are you questioning orders, XO?"

It took a bit more than a jarring attitude from the captain to throw Katerina Mueller off stride. "No, sir," she replied, utterly composed. "Merely curious as to the circumstances that engendered them."

"Yes. Of course. We . . . have been asked to check back with the Carvargna. The Dufaux have apparently been making serious noises about a new, even more concentrated strike against the Carvargna. Starfleet simply wants us to make our presence known. To let the Dufaux know that we're . . ."

"That we're what, sir?" I asked when no immediate completion to the sentence seemed forthcoming.

He looked at me as if his mind had been light-years away, and he forcibly pulled himself back to the conversation at hand. "That we're there. That we're watching. That we're aware of the types of people that they are, and that we're not prepared simply to abandon more innocent lives to them."

"Captain . . . what are you saying?" Mueller asked slowly. "Are you saying that we're going to . . . attack . . . ?"

"Attack? No! No, of course not!" Kenyon laughed. It was a jarring laugh in that it was eerily evocative of the genuine, full-bodied laugh he'd once possessed . . . except there was something missing from it. Mirth, perhaps, or a genuine sense of joy. "We do what we're ordered to, XO, and nothing beyond that. Come now . . . I'd think you'd know better than that."

"Yes, sir. I do," said Kat. The message was clear . . . at least to me. She knew better. She was wondering whether he did.

"Mr. Gold," Kenyon said as if the matter were settled, "I'll want you to stay on full alert once we're in Anzibar space. You too, Mr. Cray."

"Yellow alert, sir?"

"I don't think it's necessary to put the entire ship on yellow alert, Lieutenant. I just want you and Mr. Gold to keep a particularly close eye on sensors, and on lookout for anything that is the least bit unusual. The Dufaux are a crafty and deceitful race, and we should not take anything for granted. I don't think they'd hesitate to attack us in any way they could, if we give them half a chance to do so. Half a chance is twice as much as I want to provide them. Understood?"

Cray and Gold both nodded, although Gold looked more than a little puzzled. I wasn't entirely surprised. It wasn't as if Gold wasn't always keeping a weather eye out for any possible threat. Same with Cray, although he was far too stoic to allow any of his thought process to make itself evident. Cray maintained his usual careful deadpan.

We returned to our respective stations and Kenyon said, "Mr. Gold, set course for the Anzibar system. Warp factor five.

"Aye, sir." After a moment's work, he said, "Course laid in, sir. Warp on line."

And then . . . silence.

Kenyon sat there for a time, and then he realized that we weren't on our way toward Anzibar. It took him a moment to grasp why that would be. "Why, Mr. Gold," he said in exaggerated surprise. "Why don't you have us under way already?"

"I . . . thought you would want to order it yourself, sir."

Gold's voice was carefully neutral. It was impossible to read what was going through his mind. Kenyon's eyebrows knit for a moment as he tried to see if Gold was somehow being difficult or insubordinate, or for that matter simply a smartass. But Gold's face was impassive, and besides, what could Kenyon possibly accuse him of? Daring to follow protocol?

"Very well. Punch it, Mr. Gold."

"On our way, sir."

The *Grissom,* in response, leaped into warp space and headed out for her last mission under the command of Captain Norman Kenyon.

The Attack Fleet

"OH . . . MY GOD . . ."

It was Hash who whispered it in amazement, and since the reserved Southerner was usually somewhat unflappable (the most drastic response he ever made was usually a prolonged "Wellllll"), it had to be a fairly impressive sight to get that kind of reaction out of him.

It was indeed.

All around the world of Anzibar II, there were ships. This was not simply a scattered assortment. This was a fleet. For a moment I was pleased to see that, as I had taught them, they were flying in protective formations. But that pride was short-lived as the enormity of what I was seeing hit me. They were clearly prepared to go to war. And something about the timing of the whole thing was hitting me very badly.

I looked to Kenyon to see his reaction. He seemed as startled as any of us. "Mr. Cray," he said, "raise—"

"Head counsel Barhba calling," Cray interrupted.

"Great minds," murmured Kenyon. "On screen."

Barhba appeared moments later on the screen. He looked slightly different than he had last time I'd seen him. Before, he'd been dressing in muted colors. Now he was wearing something bolder, brighter. He seemed—although I might have been imagining it—more challenging.

"Honored Kenyon," he said. "It is good to see you once more."

"We need to talk, Barhba. We need to do so now."

"For you, Honored Kenyon? Anything. I would be happy to bring you and any associates over to my flagship."

Flagship. Yes, yes I could see from his surroundings: He wasn't on the planet's surface anymore. He was in one of the ships. I had the oddest feeling it was the biggest one.

"Captain," I said quickly, "perhaps it would be best if I—"

"We will be right over there to talk, Honored Barhba," Kenyon said. He was already on his feet. "Takahashi, get the coordinates for beaming over. Cray, with me. Calhoun, you have the conn."

I spoke with more urgency than before. "Captain, if I could have a moment before you—"

He faced me and anger practically radiated off him. "Calhoun, we may not *have* a moment. I'm going to go over there and find out what's going on. I need a battle-experienced veteran at the conn, because for all we know, the Dufaux are going to attack at any moment. Now do you have any problems with that?"

"No, sir," I said tightly.

Without another word, Kenyon and Cray walked off the bridge.

There was a long silence then, and I realized that every eye on the bridge was upon me.

I had said I would support the captain. I had promised him.

To hell with the Dufaux. They'd killed Stephanie. There was no reason, I figured, that I should give them a moment's more thought.

"Attend to your stations, people," I said. I moved over and stood next to the command chair, but didn't sit. "Stay frosty. We have no clear idea what's happening yet . . . which means anything can happen." After a moment's more thought, I added, "Hash . . . take us to yellow alert."

"Yellow alert, aye."

Ensign Barbosa had stepped in at tactical. "Go to weapons hot, sir?"

I considered it. "No. I want people on station, but let's not run the full gamut yet. Not until the captain returns . . . and hopefully tells us what's happening."

We stayed that way for half an hour. The time seemed to crawl past. The yellow-alert klaxon had been sounding, but after about five minutes of that unbelievably irritating noise, I ordered status maintained but the alarm shut down. I'm not entirely certain what sort of signal I would install on a ship to indicate a yellow alert, but it would definitely be something other than the headache-inducing wailing we presently have.

After what seemed an interminable wait, Captain Kenyon and Lieutenant Cray returned. Once again we all met in the conference lounge . . . and this time, I was stunned by what Kenyon told us.

"They're launching an attack on Anzibar Four," Kenyon informed us.

"They are? And Starfleet picks now to send us here?" noted Mueller. "How's that for a stroke of luck."

"Yes, I know," agreed Kenyon. He was speaking in such a carefully neutral tone that it was impossible to get any sort of impression as to how he felt about the development. Before any of us could react to that tidbit of information, though, he then added the bombshell follow-up: "And we are going to be part of the attack fleet."

Mueller was first on her feet. *"What?!"*

"Sit down, XO."

"Captain, you can't be serious!"

"Mueller," I spoke up. She looked to me and with a flicker of my eyes I indicated that she should take her seat.

"We're not actually going to participate in the attack . . ." continued Kenyon.

"Captain, come on!" It was now Gold who was speaking. "If we're converging on the Dufaux and the shooting starts, are we supposed to just let stray shots ricochet off our shields? It's ridicu—"

Kenyon slammed a fist down on the table with such explosive force that we all jumped. None of us had ever seen him display that level of anger. *"I am not accustomed to being interrupted repeatedly during a briefing, is that clear!"*

No one said anything. There were nods of several heads, and I felt—rightly or wrongly—that everyone was looking to me. "Clear, sir," I said, speaking on behalf of all of us.

"Good." Kenyon didn't seem especially mollified. "The Dufaux have made repeated attempts at warfare during the time that we've been gone. The Carvargna have resisted their repeated incursions, mostly thanks to the aid that we gave them. But the leadership has come to the realization, as difficult a conclusion as it may be to reach, that the Dufaux are never going to stop coming. That they will continue to attack and attack, to wear down the armaments and energy of the Carvargna.

"And so the Carvargna have assembled a fighting force. A force composed not only of their own vessels, but other ships from nearby systems. They've formed alliances as a means of mutual protection, for they are certain that—should the Dufaux eventually triumph and obliterate the Carvargna—nothing will stop them from spreading their campaign of war to other worlds. They have chosen to end it here and now. It is, frankly, a decision that I can respect and support." He paused and surveyed us around the table. It was almost as if he was daring us to say something, to try and find some flaw in what he was saying. We were all mute. It seemed the wisest course.

"I have emphasized to High Counsel Barhba that we cannot actually join in the battle. We will not violate the Prime Directive. But I'll . . ." He hesitated. There seemed to be just the slightest crack in the veneer of toughness that he had created for himself. "I'll tell you something, people, and this is the brutally honest truth: I want to be there. I want the Dufaux to see this vessel, a symbol of everything that they turned away from, coming right down their throat surrounded by an army of vessels arrayed against them. An army composed of people who have said, 'No more. Enough. Enough mindless warfare. Enough callous disregard for life. We have decided to put an end to you and your kind.' This . . ." He waved a hand in the general direction of the fleet outside. "This is one of the most glorious days in the history of the Carvargna. Until now they have been largely victims. But they have refused to allow that to continue. Instead they have risen up with the confidence, weaponry, and guidance that we gave them and they are going to rid themselves of a pernicious threat once and for all. And people, I intend to be there for every minute of it. Every glorious minute. Is it petty of me? Perhaps. Vindictive? If you say so. But these people, these Dufaux . . . they are evil. Evil in its purest form, violence at its essence. I want . . ." His voice choked slightly. It was the first time he'd shown any vulnerability since the death of those whom he had loved so dearly. "I want to see them brought down. We're being offered a front-row seat for it, and I, for one, intend to occupy it. Now . . . do any of you have any problems with that?"

There was a long moment of silence.

"Permission to speak freely, sir?" said Mueller.

"Absolutely."

"I think it's sick."

Kenyon blanched. Villers's mouth thinned to the point of invisibility. Gold and Hash looked as if they'd been gut-punched, although it was difficult for me to tell whose side they were on. Cray was his usual deadpan.

Mueller was up and moving. "We're supposed to stand for something, Captain. This crew, this ship . . . we're supposed to stand for something bigger than death and carnage. War is, at best, a necessary evil, but evil nevertheless. If we are to be any different than the Dufaux, then we should not be rejoicing in their downfall. We should be mourning for lives and wasted opportunities. Not in a 'front-row seat,' rejoicing over the fall of a foe like stargoing ghouls. We should not—must not—do this thing. Faced with possible annihilation, the Dufaux might be willing to talk . . ."

"No more talk." It was Cray who had spoken.

"The time for talk is long past," agreed Villers. "If it could have been settled by now, it would have been. I'm with the captain on this. You, XO, weren't the one who had to pick up the pieces of Stephanie and Byron Kenyon—sorry, Captain."

"It's all right," said Kenyon.

"I, uhm . . ." Hash said slowly, his drawl becoming even more pronounced, "I . . . well, the XO, what she's sayin' and all . . ."

"Spit it out, Romeo," Kenyon said impatiently.

"Look . . . me and the XO, we never seen eye to eye all that much, but I gotta say, she's making a piece of sense here. Captain, if you and the Carvargna, perhaps y'all could . . ."

"Could what? With the Dufaux seeing a sizable opposition coming their way, they'd have nothing to gain by fighting. They'll want to negotiate a peace, which they'll toss aside the moment that the alliance has been disbanded. In fact, the next time they attack, they'll come at the Carvargna harder than ever because they won't want to take a chance that another attack force might be mounted. Certainly you must see that."

"We're going to be pulled into a fight," Gold spoke up, shaking his head. "We can talk about not violating the PD all we want, but let's not kid each other. We're going to be smack in the middle of it."

"Not up to the challenge?" asked Kenyon.

"It's not a matter of that, sir," Gold said, bristling. "It's not a question of whether we *can,* but whether we *should!"*

"My God." Kenyon looked around the table, making no attempt to hide his disbelief. "An innocent man and woman died because the Dufaux cannot be trusted! The peace-loving residents of the Anzibar system have allied themselves to say, 'Never again.' We have to bear witness to that achievement! Anything else would be an insult to all they've achieved! We owe it to them! And to . . . to *them!"* None of us had to ask for clarification as to who the second "them" was. Suddenly he turned to me. "Calhoun . . . your thoughts on the matter?"

All eyes turned to me.

I never felt more alone in my entire life. It wasn't as if a vote were being taken: ultimately the captain would do as he saw fit. But my opinion was going to carry weight. If there was anyone who might be able to dissuade the captain from this course of action, it would be me.

And, of course, there was the other, more dreaded aspect. Namely, if there was anyone who was in a position to challenge the captain's authority in this matter, it was also me. It was the first officer's responsibility to take action if the captain was not making competent decisions.

My instinct . . .

My instinct was to go with what Mueller and the others had said. Everything about this smelled wrong. I had a feeling that we were heading into nothing but disaster, and it was within my ability to put a stop to it, quickly and cleanly. At least . . . I thought it was.

But I looked at the captain, and I realized for the first time that his eyes were very much like Stephanie's. I could almost sense her looking out at me from within him.

I've told you that, to Xenexians, ghosts and shades of the past are very real considerations. That remained the case with me, particularly at that moment. I felt as if the ghost of Stephanie had moved into the room and was just watching me, judging me.

They were murderers, the Dufaux were. Murderers and oppressors. Any number of arguments could be made for why they weren't worth shedding a tear over. . . .

But should the *Grissom* be there? Should it be on the scene? Kenyon had more or less said it himself. This was no longer about a mission of peace. This was a mission of war . . . more, it was a mission of vengeance. Blood lust and an urge to see a hated race suffer close-up were the motivators that were driving Kenyon now. It wasn't worthy of him, it wasn't worthy of the *Grissom.*

When I led Xenex to victory over the Danteri, I had always felt . . . outside of myself to some degree. As if I were being impelled by the dictates of a history already written: I was merely a player in the grand scheme of things, my presence preordained, my victory assured. I felt as if I were part of something that was greater than myself, greater than any individual. One of the main reasons that I had joined Starfleet was to be in an environment where that state of mind would be perpetuated. Starfleet, the UFP, these were bigger than any one person. To pilot the *Grissom* into a war zone purely as a means of witnessing personal revenge . . . it was . . . it was petty. It was the desires of one person overwhelming what Starfleet was all about.

But who was I to make those judgments? I was not the one who had lost his family . . . well, not recently at any rate. It had never been more clear than now that the loss had been eating away at Kenyon. He needed this, needed to see it, to be a part of it. Otherwise he would never have closure. It needed to be finished for him so that he could move on with his anger, move on with his life.

And ultimately . . . what was the harm? Really, when it came down to it . . . what was the harm? Starfleet had ordered us out here. There was no intrinsic reason that we shouldn't be witnessing firsthand the end of the hostilities in the Anzibar system. Stephanie would see it through the eyes of her father, I was positive of that. See it and smile in relief that it was over, and that those who had killed her and her uncle had paid the price.

All of this went through my mind within a second or two. There was a barely perceptible hesitation before I said, "I'm with you, Captain."

Kat looked at me as if she'd been slapped. "What? You can't be serious. . . ."

"I just don't see the conflict here," I lied. I saw the conflict perfectly well, but was choosing to try and finesse my way around it. "The Prime Directive is not at issue. We aren't instigating this battle; the Dufaux have started it, and the Carvargna have finished it. We will simply observe. It's no different than if we were watching a star die."

"You're right," Kat Mueller said. Her chin was raised high and she seemed very cold, very distant. I had the sneaking suspicion that sex wasn't in our future anytime soon. "It isn't different. Because a dying star can become a black hole . . . and we're being sucked deep into something dark and unpleasant, and there's not going to be any way out of it. You mark my words."

Looking back on it, I still don't know which to be more impressed by: that Katerina was the first person I'd ever met who used the phrase "mark my words" in normal speech . . . or that Katerina was absolutely, one hundred percent right.

The meeting broke up shortly thereafter, the growing tide of resentment and protest by the junior officers having been unexpectedly quelled by me. "Thank you, Calhoun," the captain said, clearly grateful. "I thought it was going to start getting ugly in there."

"Do me a favor, Captain: Don't let it get ugly out here."

He patted me on the shoulder. "Just leave everything to me," he said confidently.

I felt the hair on the back of my neck stand on end. My hair was brighter than I was.

I ran into Mueller on the turbolift. Katerina wouldn't even look at me. "Kat . . ." I started to say.

"I think," she said thoughtfully and with just an edge of disgust in her voice, "it would be preferable for the moment if you simply addressed me as 'Mueller' or 'XO.' "

"Kat, it's going to be fine. Don't you think that, if I didn't believe that, I would have stood up to the captain?"

She was only supposed to be an inch taller than me, but it felt as if she was looming over me. Impressive how she did that. "So you admit you backed down from him."

"No . . . well . . . I suppose, but . . . no, I didn't. You're twisting it, Kat."

"What's twisted is this situation, Commander, and I'm frankly shocked and disappointed that you can't see that."

"I'm not refusing to see anything. I just don't happen to agree with your sentiment in this matter. This is important to the captain. Didn't you ever have anything important to you?"

"Yes. I did. And it died several years ago," she said. "Under rather ugly circumstances, too. But I didn't risk an entire Starfleet vessel to make up for it."

"You're exaggerating."

She looked up and said, "Turbolift, override. Halt." Immediately the lift car came to a halt.

"Am I? Where am I exaggerating? He's risking the saucer section, but not the warp drive? He's risking the lives of the crewmen, but only the boring ones? Where and how have I exaggerated?"

"Don't lecture me, *Kat.* It wasn't all that long ago you told me you trusted him completely."

She sighed. "Don't remind me." She looked me in the eyes. "Deep down, you know what to do. But you're being kindhearted. In others, that would be a laudable ambition. But it doesn't fit you well, Mac. Do you know why?"

"Why." I didn't really want to know, but I had a feeling she wasn't going to let the question go.

"Because you're not a nice guy, Calhoun. That's why. You're not a nice guy, and every time you try to be a nice guy, it gets you into trouble. Well, the captain doesn't need a nice guy riding herd on him. He needs a son of a bitch. He needs a bastard to sit him down and say, This isn't our fight. We're a starship, a Federation starship, and we do not hover over a field of battle like filthy vultures, displaying our appreciation for the rapidly growing stack of bodies. That's what you should have said, that's what he needed to hear from you. From his first officer. The warrior that I encountered in the holodeck wouldn't have been afraid to hurl himself against his commanding officer for the good of the ship and the Fleet." She paused and, to my surprise, regarded me with curiosity. "That reminds me . . . I never got around to asking you. In the holodeck, you shouted something. '*Rakash,*' I think it was. What was that?"

I was almost relieved that the subject had switched away, however momentarily, from my shortcomings as a first officer. "A Xenexian war cry. It means, 'To the hilt.' When faced with an opponent, the concept is that you won't back down until your knife blade is buried in the body of your enemy up to the hilt."

"Charming." She nodded a moment, and then we simply stood there for a time.

"Are you . . . planning to send us on our way anytime soon?" I asked.

"Oh! Uhm . . . turbolift. Resume." The lift promptly started up again.

"So are . . . we okay?" I asked. "You and I?"

"Us. No . . . no, Mac. I think we're light-years away from okay. Because the bottom line is that I know you agree with me. You know that vengeance diminishes us all. . . ."

And for a moment, my temper flared. I stepped in close to her and suddenly she didn't seem taller than me anymore. In a low snarl I said, "I never managed to find the man who beat my father to death, or the man who ordered it done. If I were captain of a vessel, and the opportunity presented itself, I would cross the galaxy from one side to the other just to have a shot at crushing their windpipes with my bare hands and feeling the slowing and stopping of their pulse against my palm. You speak of necessary evil? One of those necessities is that if innocents must suffer, the guilty must suffer more. And the warrior that you so respect can empathize completely with what the captain is going through."

The door hissed open behind us. Without taking her eyes from me, Kat said evenly, "Then I guess the captain and you are well matched at that. A far better match than you or I could ever be."

The door closed and I was so angry that it took me a few moments to realize I'd gotten off on the wrong deck. I was on the deck where my quarters were situated. I'd meant to go up to the bridge.

I stood there, stewing. And as occasionally happens at such times, my mind started wandering in different directions. I thought about what Mueller had said, even though I didn't want to . . . and then, more to the point, I thought of something very specific she had said. But it wasn't during our turbolift ride. It was something earlier, almost a passing remark back in the conference lounge. . . .

The Lie

AND STARFLEET PICKS NOW *TO SEND US HERE? HOW'S THAT FOR A STROKE OF LUCK.*

Kat's offhand comment had thrust itself into my consciousness. It was beginning to bother me greatly the more I thought about it.

Here was an entire battle fleet ready to strike at Anzibar IV, and we showed up just in time to be there for the kill. It seemed . . . too coincidental. Too convenient. Of course, it was possible that somehow Starfleet had been aware of the buildup, had known the timing of it when they sent us in. If that was the case, then Kenyon simply hadn't been completely forthcoming, or perhaps he didn't even know. Perhaps it was just damned good timing, luck of the draw.

But perhaps it wasn't. Perhaps it was something else, something even more sinister.

I went to my quarters, convinced that I was being paranoid. As I entered, my combadge beeped at me. It was the captain, demanding to know where the hell I was. "A . . . momentary illness, sir," I told him. "I'm just taking some quick medication for it. I'll be there in a few minutes."

"See that you are, Commander." The captain sounded slightly mollified, but not overjoyed.

"Computer," I said as soon as I got to my quarters.

"Working," came the crisp reply.

"Access communications log, reference Starfleet communiqués."

"Starfleet communiqués communications log is confidential under security seal," the computer informed me.

"Security seal override, by authority of Calhoun, Mackenzie, first officer, security clearance zero-zero-one-zero-one."

"Processing." There was a pause of only a second and then the computer said, "Override accepted."

I couldn't get into specifics of messages addressed to the captain. Those were under direct seal of the captain himself and inaccessible to anyone with the exception of a board of inquiry composed of the top three officers below the captain. But I didn't need to get into what the message said . . . at least, not yet. One potential crisis at a time. "Read out of time for all Starfleet communiqués received within the last forty-eight hours."

"Working." And again, after the briefest of pauses, the computer informed me, "No Starfleet communiqués received within last forty-eight hours."

The sentences, damning, hung there for a moment. "None at all?" I said.

"Affirmative."

"Check again."

I have no idea why I said it, but I did. Naturally, it made no difference to the computer. It simply repeated, "No Starfleet communiqués received within last forty-eight hours."

Cray had been the one who claimed that a communication had come in.

He'd lied.

There was going to be hell to pay, and I had every intention of collecting that debt. But first the captain had to be notified . . . and then, *grozit* . . . this would be straightened out once and for all.

The Confrontation

I WALKED ONTO THE BRIDGE AND LOOKED STRAIGHT AT CRAY. HE DIDN'T even bother to glance at me. I didn't think he was aware that I knew what he had done; I was reasonably sure that his own security board would not have informed him that I had been researching his comm log. I glanced at the screen and saw, as I suspected, that we were already under way. The attack fleet surrounded us as we made our way toward Anzibar IV. Obviously it was not going to take us a long time to get there. That meant I had to speak to the captain quickly, because if Cray had faked the message from Starfleet, then who knew what else he had lied about. Perhaps he was a spy, I thought. At the very least, he was a traitor. It was a good thing that Andorians weren't telepathic, or I would certainly have been giving him a mental earful right about then.

Kenyon looked at me with clear concern. "Are you quite all right, Calhoun?"

"We need to speak privately, sir. Now."

"Calhoun, it will have to wai—"

"It can't wait, sir."

"What the hell is wrong with you?"

"Sir. Privately. Now."

There was something in my voice that got through to him, that let him know that this wasn't simply some casual conversation we were about to have. "Mr. Cray, you have the conn," he said. This was obviously not a choice that thrilled me overmuch, but I didn't want to say anything just yet.

It would be okay; the situation could stay as it was another few minutes and it wouldn't be especially problematic. At least, that's what I was hoping.

Kenyon didn't look any too pleased as he walked into his ready room with me trailing directly behind him. He didn't even bother to go around his desk. Instead he turned to face me as soon as the doors were closed. "This had better be good, Calhoun."

"Good? By no stretch of the imagination, sir." I took a deep breath and launched into it. "Lieutenant Cray has been giving you false information."

He raised an eyebrow. "Really?" His voice didn't go up at the end of the word. It wasn't a question so much as an interested statement.

"We have received no communications from Starfleet command within the last forty-eight hours. So any claims to the contrary—including the orders that we received to come here—are false. Mr. Cray lied about any transmissions from HQ."

"And you know this how?"

"Ran a check from my own computer station, sir."

"Used the security block override protocol, did you."

"Yes, sir." I nodded.

He didn't seem particularly upset. Indeed, he seemed almost amused by it. He leaned back and stroked his chin thoughtfully. "And what do you recommend we do. About it, I mean. About Mr. Cray."

"I'll inform a security squad that they should come up here and place Mr. Cray under arrest. I also recommend that we tender our regrets to high counsel Barhba and depart this system immediately. We don't know for certain what Cray might have cooked up, but for all we know this is some sort of ambush. I simply need your authorization to have him taken into custody."

Kenyon pursed his lips and said nothing.

And something began to dawn on me.

It came to me very slowly. Indeed, it's rather embarrassing to admit to it now. To look back on it after all this time, it seems fairly self-evident. But at that point I was far more "in the moment," carried away by the current of events. But in Kenyon's attitude, in his demeanor, something began to click for me. I couldn't quite believe it. I certainly didn't want to. But there were particular conclusions which were slowly starting to seem inevitable to me, whether I wanted to arrive at them or not.

Taking a chance that maybe, just maybe, I was fortunate enough to be completely off the mark, I said, "Sir . . . I see you're preoccupied. That is very understandable. I'll attend to Mr. Cray's arrest myself, then."

"I . . ."

I waited for the rest of the sentence.

"I . . . wouldn't," he finished ruefully.

I nodded. All was becoming clear to me. "Cray . . . didn't fool you about anything, did he."

He shook his head. Amazingly, he almost looked proud of me that I had figured it out.

"He wasn't betraying you," I continued. "He was providing you with an alibi. You needed witnesses to see that the message had come in from the Fleet."

"That's right."

"Because you wanted to come back here. You knew this was going to be happening ahead of time."

He nodded. "Barhba and I worked out a timetable."

"Grozit . . . and the previous message? The one that said we were supposed to help them?"

"We received a message from Starfleet, yes." He shrugged, clearly seeing no reason to hide the truth anymore. "It indicated that we were to stay on station here for a short time more, yes. But for the purpose of trying to reestablish peace talks. Can you imagine?" He shook his head in clear amazement. "Peace talks . . . with those animals . . ."

"So you took it upon yourself to arm and educate their enemies instead."

"They're animals," he said again. I might as well not have been in the room.

"You took it," I said again, underscoring the severity of the situation, "upon yourself . . . to arm and educate—"

"THEY'RE ANIMALS!"

It was fortunate that the ready room was soundproof so that they couldn't hear that one outside, because people would have come running in with phasers drawn in consternation.

The anger, the misery that previously had only been hinted at in the earlier meeting was nothing compared to what I saw in Kenyon's face now. Blind, savage fury had completely taken hold of him. His body was quaking, and there were tears pouring down his face, his mouth contracting in a rictus of a scream that wouldn't come out.

"They killed my brother . . . they killed my baby . . . those animals, they'll pay," and he kicked over a chair, *"they'll pay, those bastards, I'm going to make them pay!"*

It would have been the exact perfect time for me to keep my cool. The angrier he got, the more reserved I should have become.

When you punch someone, it's never a good idea to make a fist and hit them on the chin. Bone on bone. Always a bad tactic. Good way to hurt yourself.

Meeting anger with anger is nearly as bad. Unfortunately, that's exactly what I did.

"You lied to me!" I shot back. "I supported you, I trusted you, and you lied to me! You and Cray! You brought Cray in as an ally to cover for you, and all of it so that you could pursue your witch-hunt against the Dufaux! How dare you!"

"How dare *I?* This is no witch-hunt, Calhoun! This isn't a search for evil where none exists, where innocent people are hurt because of superstitious nonsense! These monstrous animals don't deserve to live! And I'm going to see them wiped out!"

"To the last man, woman, and child? Every innocent will die. . . ."

"There are no innocents! The men are slaughterers, the women aid in producing more of the men, and the children will grow up to be butchers in their turn!" His voice was rising to a fever pitch and I knew then, beyond any dispute, that if he wasn't already clinically insane, then he was hurtling there fast with no brake in sight. "It's a mercy killing, Calhoun! I'm showing mercy for the entire sector!"

"You're crazy," I told him. "You've completely snapped . . . your loss, everything that's happened since . . ."

His face was purpling with rage, the veins distending on his forehead, and he was trembling with uncontained fury. "They killed my little girl. They do not deserve to live, *and I will not suffer them to live, and even if I have to tear out their living hearts with my bare hands, I will see to it that they don't!"*

"You lied to me!" I said again. "You used me, you set me up to support you out of concern and kindness and wanting to see justice done, and then I find out that it was all a lie! You scheming son of a bitch!"

"How *dare* you!" he thundered. *"How dare y—"*

He hit the desk again, and the entire ship shook.

For one insane moment I actually thought that he himself had caused it, even as I tumbled to the floor. Kenyon had been leaning against his desk and stumbled against a bulkhead, but as a result he wasn't thrown to his feet. He lurched out of the ready room, me following him in a rather undignified fashion, hauling myself forward on my hands and knees and staggering upright as I went.

The red-alert klaxon was screaming as Kenyon shouted, "Status report!"

"Dufaux battle fleet attacking, sir!" Gold called.

The screen was alive with ships. Whereas the Carvargna and their allies were in relatively large, not-terribly-maneuverable vessels with lots of firepower, the Dufaux were in smaller, faster-moving vessels. Like hornets they descended upon the fleet, buzzing about and firing with their pulsers.

In previous circumstances, the Carvargna fleet would have been more hard-pressed to stave them off. But the shield improvements had made them nearly invulnerable as far as the Dufaux ships were concerned, and the armament they were carrying was targeting and picking off the Dufaux ships. However, many were slipping through and still causing damage. Credit the Dufaux: They certainly knew how to fly.

"They're firing on us," Gold called. "Apparently they're unaware that we're just the cheering section." If there was one thing that Gold wasn't particularly skilled at, it was subtlety.

"Get us out of here!" I called. "Retreat to a safe distance. . . ."

"Belay that!" Kenyon shouted over me as two more Dufaux vessels took potshots at us. Our shields were rattled but they held.

"Incoming message from the flagship, sir," Lieutenant Cray called. He was addressing Kenyon, but he was looking straight at me. He had to know. He had to. "They've taken several heavy hits. Hit to the engine room. Pulsers off line. Barhba is asking for our assistance."

Kenyon didn't even hesitate. "We're not about to stand by and watch good people die at the hands of barbarians. Target the Dufaux vessels near the flagship, Mr. Cray. Fire on my order."

"Belay that."

It was I who had spoken, and what was impressive was just how quiet a bridge can become even when there's a red-alert klaxon blaring.

Kenyon stared at me as if from another universe. There were no hints of the tears that had been streaming down his face. Amazingly, he looked more composed than I'd ever seen him.

"Mr. Gold, plot us a course to a safe distance," I continued. "Captain Kenyon, I regret that I must relieve you of command. If you stand down now . . ."

"If I stand down now . . . you'll what?" he asked quietly. "Not have me arrested? You seem to forget, Commander, who's in charge here. Mr. Cray . . ."

"No . . ." I said.

"Fire at will."

"No!"

The *Grissom*'s phasers lashed out in the direction of the flagship. Our weaponry, more powerful than the Dufaux's, more powerful even than what we had given to the Carvargna, made short work of the Dufaux vessels that they struck. Two were sliced completely in half, another was blasted into space dust.

"Again," Kenyon said.

"No!" I lunged toward Cray, in order to shove him back and away from the tactical station.

It was exactly what the Andorian was waiting for. I never even saw his hands move, he was that fast. All I knew was that suddenly what felt like a ten-pound weight slammed against the side of my head. It was his fist. It whipped my head around and I felt a muscle pull in my neck even as light exploded behind my eyes. Then his other hand smashed my upper lip, and I tasted my own blood between my teeth. I stumbled back, hit the floor and lay there for a moment, the world spinning around me even as I heard the ship's phasers blast out again. More Dufaux died at our hands.

The rest of the bridge crew was stunned, unable to believe what they were seeing. At the time part of me was angry that they weren't springing to my defense. In retrospect, I can see the problem. They didn't know what I knew. They didn't know that Kenyon had lost it. They didn't know that he was pursuing a vendetta, as justified as that need for revenge might seem. They didn't realize that, after decades of service, he was throwing it all away because the voices in his head had cried for vengeance so loudly that they had drowned out everything else, including reason and sanity.

Gold was trying to watch the front screen, his instruments and me. Hash's mouth was moving but I couldn't hear his voice, which meant either I'd gone deaf or he was whispering. Considering the ringing in my head, which was aggravated by the red-alert klaxon, it might have been a little bit of both.

"Security team to the bridge," Cray was saying.

I'm not entirely sure where I drew the strength from at that moment. But suddenly I was on my feet, and I gripped the railing, swung my legs up, and vaulted over the railing with the intention of slamming my feet into Cray's face. Cray was too quick. He ducked under the sweep of my legs, came up before I'd completely cleared him, and threw me into the wall behind him with such force that I was positive that he'd just broken my face. Certainly it was numb down the entire left side.

From below, Kenyon called, "I regret you've forced me to take these actions, Mr. Calhoun. You were a good officer. I'm sorry it's come to this."

I propped myself up on one elbow and looked at him through an eye that was already swelling shut. And the weird thing was . . . I could see it in his face. He *was* genuinely sorry that it had come to this. Although his face was set and determined, in his eyes was more misery than I had ever seen in any sentient being in my life. It was as if a decent and moral man was trapped inside of the individual who inhabited the name and body of Norman Kenyon. Trapped and unable to find a means of communicating *Help me . . . I'm still here . . . I still exist . . . I'm still alive . . . help me, please . . .*

Had I not been spitting up my own blood at that point, I might actually have felt really sorry for him.

No one ever accused me of knowing when to quit. I started to pull myself to standing once more. This time Cray didn't even have to exert himself (although truthfully, I don't know if he'd been working up much of a sweat up to that point). The Andorian reached out with one foot and brought it down on the back of my head.

Fight him! It was the savage within me, shouting in my mind. *Fight him! Get him! Kill him! Rip him to shreds, the blue-skinned antennaed bastard! Don't let him do this to you!*

But I had no room to maneuver, no weapon in my hand, and he had been far too efficient in his physical dismantling of me. At that point my entire goal was simply to try and get away, to regroup.

I heard the turbolift hiss open. Several security men entered.

"Commander Calhoun has attempted mutiny," Kenyon said. "Take him and toss him in the brig."

I tried to say something—anything—but I couldn't even stand up. Hands were beginning to reach toward me . . .

. . . and then I disappeared.

The Reprieve

THERE MAY HAVE BEEN TIMES IN MY LIFE WHERE I WAS MORE CONFUSED than I was at that moment, but none leap readily to mind.

One moment I was on the carpeted floor of the bridge . . . and the next thing I knew, I was on the platform of the transporter room. My senses were so confused that the floor itself wasn't my first tip-off of my location. Rather, it was the fading hum of the transporter beams.

I raised my head slowly in confusion and looked up. My head was throbbing and I couldn't see beyond my immediate field of vision . . . that is, I could see straight ahead, but everything to the side was just a fuzzy gray area. "What's . . . ?"

The face of Katerina Mueller filled my entire vision. "Mac . . ." she called to me. Her normally stern face was filled with such worry that for a moment I was concerned that I was dying. I didn't think anything else could get that sort of reaction from her. "Mac . . . can you hear me? Say something. . . ."

"You look . . . really lovely from this angle . . ." I told her. "Did they build a tunnel in here?"

"Don't stand up until you feel you're ready to." Then, to my surprise, she pulled off my combadge, tossed it on the floor, and slammed her heel down on it. I heard the badge shatter under her foot. She turned back to me and saw the obvious surprise on my face. "You know why I did that, of course."

"Well . . . if I'm remembering the custom correctly . . . according to Jewish law, we're now married."

"Very funny."

"I wasn't trying to be funny," I said.

"You succeeded beyond your wildest hopes." As I lay there tending to the wound left by the thrust of her rapier wit, she turned to the woman, Lieutenant Melissa Shemin, at the transporter. "Now . . . you didn't see this, Melly," she said flatly. "We weren't here. In fact . . . now would be a good time for you to go on your break."

Lieutenant Shemin shook her head and smiled in an amused way. When she spoke, it was with a faint British accent. "You realize, Katerina, if this were anyone but you . . ."

"I know, I know."

Shemin looked at me and then winked, much to my surprise, before heading out the door. By that point the world was beginning to lose some of the haze that had pervaded it. "What was that all about?"

"She would have flunked out of the Academy if I hadn't helped her out."

"All right," I said once the ship had stopped spinning. "Tell me what happened."

I was seated on the floor, rubbing the throbbing that remained in my temples. Katerina slid down the wall until she was seated next to me. "You can thank Hash," she told me.

"I thought you never called him that."

"I do from now on. Through the ops board, he told me what was happening. I got to the transporter room while you were having the crap kicked out of you and beamed you here."

"Maybe they'll think I was beamed out of the ship completely."

She gave me a pitying look. "Perhaps you were hit in the head harder than I thought. We're on red alert, remember? Battle situation? Combat? People shooting at us?"

I thudded the back of my head lightly against the wall. "Of course. Our shields are up. No one could possibly beam me out. Which means that they'll know I'm somewhere in the ship and . . ."

We stared at each other. Her unflappable demeanor, her somewhat superior attitude, slipped for a moment as she realized the immediate problem.

"Shit!" we said at the same time.

We were on our feet in an instant. She pointed at the wall. "That grating . . . pull it out. Fast."

"That's just a storage bin! It doesn't go anywhere!"

"I know that." Her hands were flying over the controls. The transporter beams were humming into existence. I didn't understand what she was doing, but I obediently yanked open the storage bin. There would be enough room for the two of us if we squeezed in tightly enough. The transporter beams faded out. Mueller barely waited for them to disappear and then she crammed her way into the storage bin. She clambered over an array of boots and other equipment. "Hurry!" she said. "I hear them coming!"

I heard them as well. We had perhaps a few seconds at best. I pulled the bin covering closed and prayed that it was tight enough.

We could hear, but not see, the noise from within the transporter room. From my rough guess, there were at least four security men stomping around in there. "Check activity," came a voice that I recognized immediately as security man Meyer. "Once we finish here, we check the other transporter rooms."

"Should we be searching the rooms themselves, sir?"

"As if Calhoun and whoever bailed him out would be stupid enough to stay around chatting in the transporter room," Meyer said.

I had a feeling that Katerina was rather pleased at that moment that it was dark in the storage bay. That way she didn't have to look at my pitying expression.

"What the hell is going on in here?" It was Shemin's voice. She'd come back in.

"Where were you, Lieutenant?" Meyer did not sound particularly in a forgiving mood.

"Checking the section 28-A flow regulators. They sounded a bit off. It happens even to the best of us."

"We're on red alert. You abandoned your post during a red alert."

"Great idea, Meyer. I should stay at my post and let the flow regulators break down, on the off chance that someone shatters the laws of starship physics and beams something through our shielding. I took three minutes that may have saved our lives. You don't like it, go tell Starfleet to build the ship differently."

"Transporter activity less than a minute ago, sir," one of the security men said.

"What? That's impossible." Shemin came across as utterly shocked. She might have missed her calling; she was a damned fine actress.

"See what happens during your absences, Lieutenant?" Meyer scolded her. "Destination?"

"Utility shaft, deck thirteen, section four."

"Beam them back, Shemin."

"Beam who back?"

"Commander Calhoun!"

I heard her operating the transporter controls for a moment, and then she said, "I'm trying to get a transporter fix on his comm link. I'm not getting anything. Perhaps it . . . wait! Look there, on the floor. Someone crushed a combadge. Bet it was him. Without his combadge, I'll never be able to sort his pattern out from everyone around him . . . particularly if he makes his way down to engineering from there. With all the neutrino fluctuations from the engines, I can't possibly get a lock on him. This equipment wasn't really designed for—"

"Okay, okay! We get the message. Let's go. Shemin . . . you're on report."

"I'm devastated."

We heard the receding footsteps of the security team as they ran out the door, with Meyer already informing Cray, via comm, of our presumed whereabouts. We waited until they were safely gone, and then kicked open the storage bay. Shemin jumped at the noise, then she gaped at us. "What are you doing here?"

"Don't mind us," I said. "We were stupid enough to stay around chatting in the transporter room."

"Give me a break, will you?" demanded Mueller. "I'm nightside, okay? I just woke up. I haven't had any coffee yet. You're damned lucky I even remember your name."

"Well I just got kicked in the head!"

"Shhhh!!!" hissed Shemin. "Excuse me! But I don't need to be found out as an accessory to attempted mutiny! I don't know about you, but I can think of better things to do than spend the next ten years in the Starfleet lockup! So will the two of you please shut up! Or hasn't it occurred to you they might have left someone nearby to guard against your return, and if you raise your voices too loud, he's going to come in here with phaser blasting?"

It hadn't occurred to us, actually.

"All right. Tell me what happened," Mueller said.

I told her, in as quick and concise statements as I could manage. She listened carefully, never interrupting, and finally shook her head in slow amazement. "Incredible. We have to get word to Starfleet. This situation cannot continue."

"The problem is—"

At that moment, we heard the captain's voice throughout the ship. "All hands . . . remain at battle stations, but you are to keep an eye out for Commander Mackenzie Calhoun. Mr. Calhoun, acting in defiance of Starfleet orders, has attempted to take over this vessel by force. His attempt has been beaten back, but he is at large and apparently has allies in his cause. It is possible that he is under Dufaux influence."

"Oh, terrific," I muttered. "Why not say I'm a disguised Romulan while I'm at it."

"All personnel are to maintain sidearms at all times. If Commander Calhoun is seen, do not hesitate to fire. Phasers on stun unless deadly force is absolutely mandatory."

"This is just getting better and better," Mueller said.

Shemin was studying her board and frowning. "What did you beam to the utility shaft? You couldn't have just activated the beams; it wouldn't have read into the log as a transmission. You'd never have fooled them."

"Air," said Mueller. "Air has mass, weight. I simply sent a chunk of air to the shaft." She turned to me. "Thoughts?"

"All right," I said slowly. "None of the command staff, with the exception of Hash, knows that you're involved, and he can't tell anyone without tipping himself off. So he's in. I think you should proceed as normal at this point."

"As normal? There's nothing normal about the present situation, Mac."

"I know. I need you to, very quietly, get a feel for what's going on out there. We can't let the captain continue in this manner."

"What 'continue'? From what I hear, we're helping to destroy the Dufaux. It won't go on for much longer."

"Trust me . . . it will. Once the desire for vengeance fully gets going, there's no stopping it. Believe me, I know. Find out who, if anyone, is backing up the captain . . . particularly on the command crew. Check with your people especially. Night shift might not have the same attachment to the captain as the day shift does; they work with him so much less. As for graveyard, hell, they might not even know the captain's name."

"What about you? They might come back here once they find you're not where they think you are. They're going to tear apart every square inch inside this ship."

I thought about that a moment . . . and then looked at the storage bin, looked at the equipment that was in there.

"You're probably right," I said. "Which leaves one logical alternative."

As it turned out, Mueller was right once again. Within ten minutes another security team was back at the transporter room. Shemin, however, was one of the more ingenious transporter operators we had, and she'd been able to rig the transporter log so that its most recent beaming transmission had disappeared from the records.

Which left yours truly, Commander Mackenzie Calhoun, in an EVA suit, clinging to the rear of the saucer section of the *Grissom,* watching the demolition of the Dufaux fleet.

The Slaughter

IF CAPTAIN KENYON THOUGHT HE HAD A GOOD SEAT FOR THE DISMANTLING of the Dufaux fleet, he should have seen mine.

From my position outside the saucer section, I was able to see everything.

What was eerie was the silence of it all. I mean, explosions naturally don't make any noise in space. But when you're on a bridge and you're witnessing a battle, there is at least all the noises one comes to expect from within the starship itself. The talking, the sounds of the instrumentation, even that annoying red-alert alarm. But I was on the ship's exterior, in a Low Pressure Environment Garment, and the only noise I heard was the sound of my own breathing. Oddly, that can be one of the loneliest sounds in the galaxy.

I had magnetic boots on the LPEG, of course, to aid me in adhering to the hull. Moreover, there were magnetic grasping plates in the palms of the gloves. Normally one did not want to spend excessive time outside in the LPEG. The advantage of the suit was that it was lighter in weight and more easy to maneuver in than the more high-powered Standard Extravehicular Work Garment, or SWEG. The problem with the LPEG was that it provided far less protection than the SWEG, since its simple multilayer construction gave it almost no protection against such hazards of space as micrometeoroids and radiation. But at least at the moment, as long as the shielding remained in place, that would provide me all the protection I needed. Besides, the LPEG was what had been in the storage bin of the transporter room. It wasn't as if I'd had a lot of choice.

High above me the shielding glowed in place around the ship. Naturally nothing could beam beyond that point . . . but there was nothing that prevented the transporter being able to move someone from inside the ship just to the other side of the hull. All in all, it was actually a fairly devious place to hide. It wasn't the type of place that anyone would generally think to look. Moreover, a starship is pretty damned big. Noticing one person against the ship's exterior would be quite a challenge, even if you were looking for them.

So there I clung to the ship and watched the slaughter.

The *Grissom* was still firing on Dufaux ships. I had to admit that Kenyon and Cray made a fairly formidable team. With Cray marshaling the security forces, and Kenyon finding ways to justify his actions, they were virtually unassailable.

The Carvargna forces assumed the bulk of the work and responsibility. They assaulted the Dufaux from all sides, making certain not to let themselves be drawn out of formation. They divided the Dufaux vessels from one another, cutting them off and assailing them individually or as small, easily controllable units.

But helping to herd them all together was the *Grissom.* Sometimes the starship fired warning shots that drove them toward the Carvargna squadrons. Other times they simply opened fire directly on the ships themselves. Space was alive with bursts, like fireflies battling one another in coordinated fury. Every time I saw the *Grissom* responsible for another Dufaux vessel erupting in quickly-snuffed-out flames, my heart would die a bit more.

There were so many ways I wanted to explain what had happened to Captain Kenyon. He had been . . . I don't know . . . possessed. Possessed by an evil free-floating creature. Or perhaps he'd been replaced by an evil twin. A shapeshifter had come aboard the ship, that was it. A shapeshifter who was impersonating the real Kenyon. Even better . . . not only was this not really Captain Kenyon, but evil shapeshifters had impersonated the corpses of Stephanie and Byron as well in order to make the entire charade seem more credible. They weren't really dead, but instead being held captive by the Dufaux, who themselves were part of an insidious plot . . .

And so on, and so on.

How nice that would have been. How gloriously involved, and wonderfully dismissive of the realities of life.

Would that it were that way, or had been that way.

Because that way, you see, I wouldn't have had to deal with the truth of it. And the truth of it is that sometimes good people go somewhat crazy.

We all have the darkness in us. No matter how good, how decent we are, there is the beast residing within us, waiting to get out. I know, because he lurks within me, never far below the surface. The violent, brutal being I tapped into for the purpose of freeing my people. I made extensive use of him for a very long time, and then, when I tried to bottle him away, he did not go quietly or willingly. To this day he rumbles around in my head, spoiling for a fight. I try not to indulge him.

It's not as if he's my personal demon. He's in you. He's in all of us.

James Kirk wrote an autobiography, you know. Much of it was dismissed by critics as a collection of tall tales. Some believed that Kirk had a penchant for exaggerating. Outrageous stories of planets of sorcery, or confrontations with Greek gods or Abraham Lincoln, or the removal of his first officer's brain (which some more waggish commentators claimed was not so extraordinary, considering that there were ostensibly any number of Starfleet officers for whom such a loss would not make any noticeable difference). Many felt that the reason Kirk's legend was so phenomenal was that he himself took great pains to build it. Some referred to him as the Baron Münchausen of space, and the fact that his friends and officers backed him up was written off as simple personal loyalty.

I never believed that. Never believed it for a minute. Because space is vast and unknowable, and it's the height of presumption to consider any aspect of it and toss it aside as unbelievable. Once upon a time, to the people of Earth, the idea of beings from another planet was preposterous. Yet here I am. To some, the very notion of this place, the Captain's Table, would likewise be considered absurd. Yet here we are, telling stories.

Stories.

I'm getting off track. I'm sorry. Why did I start talking about Kirk . . . ?

Oh. Yes.

There was one particular thing that Kirk wrote that stuck with me, that truly hit home for me. He was writing of officers he had met who, as he put it, had "lost the vision." They had forgotten what they were supposed to be, what they were intended to represent. He encountered several of them in his career: Captain Tracey of the *Exeter,* who—not unlike Kenyon—used advanced weaponry to interfere in a planet's local politics. Or Captain Merrick of the *Beagle,* who brought his crew, one by one, down to a planet's surface to fight in an atmosphere reminiscent of Roman gladiatorial bouts. Another man, a historian rather than an officer, named John Gill, who reshaped an entire world into Nazi Germany. One of his own men, Lieutenant Kevin Riley, who attempted to kill a man he suspected to be a war criminal. A commodore—although he didn't name him for some reason, but just described him in general terms—who completely lost his reason and started taking reckless chances when his entire crew was killed in a confrontation with an alien artifact. A few others, I think.

The thing is, Kirk said that whenever he encountered someone like that, he saw something in their eyes . . . that seemed to stare back at him. He would think of all the vast power that was at his command, and the number of times he himself played reckless games with the principle of noninterference in order to suit his own ends. That things turned out well for him oftentimes seemed as much a matter of luck as anything else. I remember exactly what Kirk wrote on the subject:

"I'd look into their eyes and see the choices they made . . . and not only would I be able to understand how and why they made them, but I could also—on some level—see myself doing the same thing. I'd like to tell myself it could never happen. It might have, though. We like to think that we would behave in a consistently moral and worthy manner, and it's only the others, the failed others, who fall by the wayside. I think that's too simplistic, though, and too denying of human nature. Every time I look at one of those fallen from the vision of Starfleet, I cannot help but say to myself: There, but for the grace of God, go I."

I doubt that there is a God, or gods. But if there is, then He exists as a divine spark in each of us. That spark had been lost in Captain Kenyon. He had turned away from it, turned away from himself.

Like Kirk, I knew the feeling. I knew what was going through his mind, knew the tragedy that he was experiencing. There was no alien invasion of his soul, no fiendish doppelgänger. He had instead succumbed to the darkness within us all. His loss . . . was a diminishment to all of us. Darkness and loss, grief pervasive and everlasting. To be so low in one's soul that the light which guides us is forever extinguished, or at least so it seems.

There, but for the grace of . . . whatever . . . went I.

And I was determined to bring him back from that. To pull him out of the abyss. Perhaps because, in a way, to help him would be to help myself.

Cray, on the other hand, I wanted to beat the crap out of. Nobility of motive only goes so far, after all.

I had a lot of time to think on such matters as I clung to the outside of the ship.

One by one the Dufaux fell. In my imagination I could almost hear Captain Kenyon laughing in joy over the disaster that had befallen the slayers of his daughter and brother. I could only hope that the Dufaux leaders—particularly the one called Kradius, who had sent the defiant message to the *Grissom*—had already died in the assault. If they still lived, and the opportunity for further revenge came into Kenyon's possession, it would be a terrible, terrible thing.

The *Grissom* advanced, meter by meter, along with the rest of the fleet. In short order, we were within range of Anzibar IV. That was when the true horror began.

The fleet started firing upon the surface of Anzibar IV. Whereas before

I had fancied that I heard Kenyon's laughter, now I was hearing the screams of those countless millions below. The fleet surrounded the planet, firing from all sides. I lay there helplessly, watching it all. The *Grissom* was not one of those raining destruction down upon the world itself. My suspicion is that even Kenyon knew he couldn't push matters that far. The entire bridge crew would likely rise up in protest if he attempted that. But even though he wasn't attacking the planet directly, his was still the responsibility. He had made it all possible, had galvanized and focused the Carvargna. And so had I, at his instruction. My hands were as red with blood as his own. Unfortunately I was the only one who could see that.

All over Anzibar IV, there was flare after flare as more strikes hit. They had some ground defenses that they were able to launch against the invaders. I can only be grateful that none of them struck the *Grissom,* because that might have given him the excuse he needed to open fire on Anzibar itself.

The bombardment continued forever, it seemed. I lost all track of time, minute stretching into hour, and into what seemed like days. Miles away on the planet below, it seemed like some parts of it were . . . moving. No, not moving. Burning. Entire continents were on fire, shimmering as if black snakes were undulating across them. Madness.

Madness.

Anzibar IV was burning.

I wondered if the Carvargna were taking any joy in it. These had ostensibly been a peaceful people. Yet I knew that, when I had been teaching them about military tactics, they had taken to it with almost gleeful abandon. Perhaps they weren't peaceful so much as they were repressed bullies, cheerfully happy to annihilate an opponent once they had big enough weapons and ships backing them up.

I closed my eyes against the sight, but that didn't stop me from hearing their voices in my head. I could hear them calling. . . .

"Mac . . ."

The suddenness of the voice startled me and it took me a moment to realize that it was inside my helmet rather than in my imagination. It was Mueller's voice. She was remarkably in control, but I could hear the edginess in her tone. "Are you seeing it?"

"Yes."

"My God, Mac . . . what have we done."

"The question isn't whether you're asking that, Kat. The question is whether the rest of the crew is. Where are you? Do they suspect . . . ?"

"No. No, not at all. At least, I hope not. There's all sorts of rumors flying throughout the crew about what happened. The captain made that announcement about you—"

"And people know that it's not true?"

"Well . . . no. There's discussion about it."

"You mean they're not rejecting it out of hand?"

"Some do. A lot . . ." Her voice trailed off.

I shouldn't have been surprised, I suppose. I'd made no effort to really get close to the crew. I liked keeping my distance, wanted to maintain my loner status. Consequently, it had cost me. When it came down to the word of a beloved captain versus the actions of a suspicious newcomer and outsider, one should easily have been able to expect that reaction.

Nonetheless, it hurt. It hurt far more than I ever would have expected.

"Mac . . . are you still there?"

"Yes." I shook it off. "Yes . . . I'm here. . . ."

"Your air supply . . . how's that holding up?"

I checked my on-line systems and realized that I'd been paying no attention to it at all. That was probably not the brightest move on my part. "It's running low. Eighteen minutes before I'm breathing my own carbon dioxide in here. Are you planning to beam me in?"

"That . . . could be a problem."

I suddenly started to feel icy, as if the vacuum of space was seeping through my suit. "A problem . . . how?"

"Lieutenant Cray doesn't want a repeat of your vanishing act. So he has security guards at all the transporter stations until further notice."

"Oh . . . perfect. How am I supposed to get back in? Crawl up a photon torpedo tube?"

There was dead silence.

And she said, "Well . . . actually . . ."

The Tube

IT'S AMAZING HOW SLOWLY YOU CAN MOVE WHEN YOU WANT TO GO very, very quickly.

Keeping an eye on the time that it took to maneuver in the weightlessness, even as I was being anchored by the magnetized boots, I felt as if it was taking an achingly long time to get from point A to point B. With my air supply ticking down as I went, it wasn't as if I had a good deal of time to waste.

I was closer to the aft torpedo tube than I was the forward, so that was obviously where I wanted to be. The air was already becoming stale in my helmet, my breathing more and more labored as I exerted myself. I knew that the torpedo tube would be wide enough for me to climb through, although it would be a fairly tight fit, particularly with the LPEG suit. On the other hand, I could remove the LPEG suit as soon as I was inside the tube. There was air in the tube, after all . . . naturally, because the far end of the tube opened up directly into the Torpedo Bay Control. It's not as if everyone at the TBC was in danger of being sucked out into space or losing all their air every time we launched one of the damned things.

The fact that the tube opened into the TBC was one of my major problems. There were always two people on station there, particularly during time of red alert. The tube itself was thirty feet long, with the first twenty-five or so sufficiently obscured by shadows and such that they'd never see me coming. But the last five feet were going to be the trickiest, because they'd see me emerging from the tube and have enough time to alert security as to my whereabouts.

First thing was first, though. Before I could worry myself about what I would do upon emerging from the torpedo, I had to get to the tube first.

Five minutes' worth of fresh air left, and the tubes still seemed miles away. Four, and I was becoming more light-headed. It was requiring greater and greater effort to maintain my focus. Three minutes, and my magnetized feet felt as if iron weights had been attached to them. I heard a buzzing in my helmet, a distant voice, and it sounded like Kat Mueller, but I couldn't be sure. I couldn't be sure of anything except that I felt like lying down and taking a nap. Certainly the rest of the distance could wait for a few minutes. Just a few minutes more so that I could shut my eyes and take it easy . . .

"Mac!" came her urgent voice again, snapping me momentarily out of my fog. I was tired, my lungs felt so damned heavy. Kat's words were racing over me in a torrent, something about a ship, but I wasn't paying attention. I shut off the communications beacon to my helmet because her voice had become so irritating to me. Everything bothered me at that moment. I just wanted the entire galaxy to go away and let me get some sleep.

I could smell the burning.

It wasn't possible, of course. There was no way that I could possibly smell the conflagration that had consumed the world of Anzibar IV. It was my imagination, my imagination spurring me on. It was enough to prod me forward, to keep me going and think about what had been done and what had yet to be done. And suddenly, just like that, the photon-torpedo tube was just ahead of me.

I looked at my instrumentation and saw that I was out of clean air. The tube was still ten feet away. It felt like ten yards. I came to the realization that I'd stopped moving. I had no idea how long I'd been like that. I shoved myself forward, going to my hands as well as my knees, pulling myself forward foot by foot. The tube drew closer, closer, and then I was right at it. My head was swimming as I pushed my way through the annular forcefield that covered the business end of the torpedo tube. It was the same type of forcefield that was employed in the shuttlebay, the kind that permitted solid objects to pass through it. Objects such as shuttlecrafts, or photon torpedoes, and even the occasional renegade officer were able to move through an annular forcefield with impunity, but air remained within the confined area.

I hauled myself completely into the torpedo tube. The moment I was through, my breathing inside the helmet sounded completely different to me. I disengaged the clamps of the helmet, twisted it, and removed it. I sucked air greedily into my lungs and waited for the light-headedness to disappear. I also tried to keep it as quiet as possible, concerned that any loud noises might echo up the tube and alert crewmen at the other end.

I sat curled up in the tube for a few moments, composing myself and letting my thudding heart slow to a more normal speed. It was tight inside there; I'd certainly known more comfortable fits in my life. I also knew that I was going to have to move quickly once I got out of the tube. The simple fact was that I was going to have to knock out whatever crewmen were at the other end before they summoned security. I wasn't looking forward to it, but it had to be done. However, if I was clomping around in an LPEG suit when I was trying to do it, I'd never be able to move quickly enough. The LPEG was more formfitting than other, bulkier suits, but it still wasn't going to allow me the full mobility I was going to need.

The rest of the LPEG suit was one piece, gloves and boots all attached. Of course, it was generally designed to be removed in some place that was slightly more spacious than the inside of a photon-torpedo tube. But I didn't see that I had much of a choice. I unlatched the back restraints, slid my torso out, and then shimmied the rest of my body out of it. I took one more deep breath and then twisted around to see the far end of the tube. The way seemed pretty clear. The trick was going to be making the approach with sufficient stealth.

Leaving the suit behind, I hauled myself forward on my elbows. Slowly I made my way forward, the tube running at a slight incline just to make my life that much more exciting. I listened carefully, straining to hear if there was any discussion going on. I wanted to know how many people were going to be waiting for me. I desperately needed more information than I had. Because the less I knew, the more chance there was of something going wrong.

I covered ten feet with no incident. Up the darkened tube I went, fifteen feet, halfway there. I kept my elbows tight, moving forward, ever forward, and I heard the toe of my boot squeak against the interior of the darkened tube. I froze, hoping that the noise hadn't tipped anyone off. I thought I heard someone ahead, at the far end. At least two voices, talking with one another, and I drew myself closer. I'd covered twenty feet. Another five or so, and then we were going to get to the hardest part, because I'd be visible to anyone at the other end. I called upon all my strength, all my speed, hoping and praying that I would be up to the task.

Suddenly the inside of the tube lit up.

There are moments in your life where you should really understand instantly what's happening. But the situation becomes one that is so horrendous, so problematic, that your brain spends a few moments in ignorance or denial or both. In this case, it was definitely denial.

Ten feet ahead of me, a photon torpedo was shoved into place, blocking my intended exit. "Lock and load!" I heard.

"Aw, *grozit,*" I snarled, no longer being quite as concerned whether I was heard or not.

I started scrambling frantically backward. There was no time or space to turn myself around, so I just kept shoving as fast as I could.

The photon torpedo started to roll forward, caught up in the inevitable process that would send it hurtling into space. It wasn't armed yet. If it was employing the standard cycle, it wouldn't go active until just under two seconds after it cleared the ship. But it would still have more than enough power to blast me into space. Granted the shields were up and that would prevent me from spiraling away into the void, but I'd still be sufficiently far enough away from the ship—with no means of propulsion—that I'd never be able to get back before I asphyxiated.

I pushed myself back, faster and faster. As if it were caught up in the spirit of a race, the photon torpedo casing began to build up speed as well. It was gaining on me. I completely lost track of where I was in the tube, or how far I had to go before I was clear at the end. All I knew was that the torpedo was catching up. I was practically nose to nose with the damned thing. I shoved back faster, driven by building panic, and then my feet became entangled in something. It was my LPEG suit. The photon torpedo was practically on top of me, and I grabbed my helmet and shoved it under the torpedo. The obstruction momentarily jammed it. I heard the buildup of energy as the torpedo pushed against the helmet that had been wedged into the clearance area. I grabbed up the rest of the suit but there was no time as the torpedo, driven by the explosive forces of the building energy that was to propel it at near-warp speeds, slammed forward. It ran over the helmet, crushing it, and then the torpedo was coming right at me.

At the last second I suddenly sensed the void directly behind me. My instinct was to take a deep breath, but that would have been exactly the wrong move. The pressure of the vacuum would have tried to equalize the pressure and I would likely have had my rib cage crushed in no time. Instead I blew all the air out of my lungs and hurled myself backward into space, clutching onto the suit for dear life.

I'd seen old vids and such from centuries ago, featuring fanciful depictions of people exploding in a vacuum, their eyes bulging out of their heads, their major organs exploding into a rather impressive rain of red liquid.

Very decorative. Not correct, but very decorative. You don't explode. You don't combust. You simply either freeze to death or you suffocate, and it happens fairly quickly. I'm not entirely certain whether that's any improvement, but it certainly requires far less clean-up.

The cold was beyond anything imaginable. A million knives stabbing into all my pores and twisting couldn't begin to approximate the cold of space. I tried to twist myself around to get back to the ship, my body already slowing down as the frigidity of the vacuum worked its way into my joints, my muscles, and that was the instant that the torpedo blasted out of its tube. The light from the release of the energy was blinding and I closed my eyes against it.

The torpedo just barely grazed me as it passed, but even the slightest impact was enough to send me spiraling. By what easily qualified as the one bit of luck that I was having at the moment, the angle of the sideswipe actually sent me tumbling back toward the *Grissom.* But I was stunned, freezing to death, no air in my lungs . . .

From the corner of my eye, I saw a ship in the distance. It was a small one, a Dufaux fighter. It must have been a straggler, a survivor of the massacre. It was firing upon the *Grissom.* Obviously, rather than be satisfied with simply surviving, the ship's pilot had chosen to attack, as futile a gesture as that might have been. The pilot's blasts bounced off the shields harmlessly, and then the photon torpedo struck home. The ship disappeared in a flash of distant light.

Would that I had been in a position to admire the marksmanship.

I hit the hull about two feet away from the torpedo tube and then bounced off and away. There was nothing to stop me from tumbling off to my death.

Nothing except the suit that I was still clutching in my numb fingers.

My brain sent commands to my arms, trying to get them to function. I couldn't feel any part of my body. I couldn't get anything to move. *Not like this,* I thought furiously, *not like this! I will not die like this!*

I think I shocked my arms into movement with the vehemence of my anger. I was still clutching the sleeve of the suit. I didn't have a choice; my fingers were frozen in a paralyzed rictus around it. I swung the suit around in an arc, like a lifeline, and the magnets of the boots slammed into the hull . . . and held.

I floated in space, clutching the suit, adhering to the side of the ship through only the slimmest of margins. The nearness of a possible salvation galvanized me. I refused to attend to the fact that my body wasn't responding, and instead forced it to do so through sheer ire. My lungs were beyond airless, and in the deathly silence of space, I heard my heart pounding. It was the single loudest noise I'd ever heard.

Hand over hand, I pulled myself toward the ship. The entire time I was terrified that the magnets would come loose, or that the cloth of the suit would slip through my numbed fingers. I drew closer, closer, and just at the very end I was convinced that I wasn't going to make it. I was positive that I was going to die right there, right then, inches away from my destination.

Then my conscious brain completely shut down. That's the only explanation I can really provide for it. I was functioning entirely on autopilot. I must have been, because I don't even remember hauling myself back into the photon-torpedo tube. It took a minute or two for me to realize that I was safe, jolted back to consciousness by the sting of air in my lungs. My lower legs were still freezing and I realized I hadn't completely pulled myself into the tube. With a low grunt of pain I hauled myself completely in and then lay there for an eternity, just making sure that I was in one piece.

To some extent, all I wanted to do was rest. But I didn't dare take the chance. For all I knew, another ship might show up behind us and the captain would consider it a good idea to blow it to bits with an aft torpedo as well. I might not have any time at all.

Working completely on adrenaline, I clambered back up the torpedo tube as fast as my body would readily let me. I covered the distance faster than I would have thought possible. On the way I grabbed up the scattered pieces of the helmet, since I'd suddenly come up with a quick use for them. When I reached the point where I'd found myself staring down the barrel of a torpedo, I flinched inwardly. But there was no repeat performance. I drew to within the critical five feet where I would be visible and paused a moment.

There were two crewmen, going about their business. They weren't staring straight at me, but from the angle that I was coming and from where they were standing, they would unquestionably see me before I was ready to be seen.

I gathered the crushed pieces of the helmet tightly in my right hand. The edges were sharp and a couple cut my hand. I couldn't even feel it. Lucky me.

I cocked my arm, took a breath (an action for which I had never been quite as grateful before), and threw. The pieces sailed over the heads of the crewmen and bounced off the far wall. The noise immediately distracted them as they moved toward the origin of it to investigate. With only a couple of seconds to act, I hauled myself up and clear of the tube. I rolled off the loading section and the instant my feet hit the ground, they turned with questions on their faces.

Clear astonishment registered in their expressions. Actually, for all I knew, they were sympathetic to my situation. But I couldn't take the chance. Making the element of surprise work for me for all it was worth, I charged, grabbed each of their heads in either hand, and slammed their heads together with all my strength. They sagged to the floor, unconscious. I sagged with them.

To no one in particular, I muttered, "I'm not getting paid enough for this."

The Developments

I TENSED AS THE DOORS TO THE TORPEDO STATION OPENED. I SUDDENLY realized that I was too tired to move, momentarily having given everything that I had to give. If this was a security team, or even a very irate tribble, I was not going to be able to do anything to fight back.

Katerina Mueller walked into the room.

When she entered, she did so looking extremely businesslike . . . and yet she was also determinedly casual. I realized immediately that she was attempting to appear as if she were simply making a routine check on whatever activity was presently going on in there. She knew that's where I was going to wind up . . . if I was damned lucky. But the instant that she saw me, as well as the two unconscious crewmen, she immediately relaxed . . . only to tense up again as she got a good look at me. "My God, Mac, what happened?" she asked. She went to me and touched my hair. "There's frost on it. It's all stiff. Your lips are blue . . . what—?"

I told her, in as quick and unvarnished a way as I could. I tried not to make it sound worse than it was. Unfortunately the facts alone were enough to cause the once-unflappable German XO to turn several shades of pale.

"Are you all right?" she asked when I finished. "I mean, now."

"Do I look all right?"

"Well . . . your lips are starting to turn a lighter shade of blue. How are your extremities?"

I flexed my hand and, inside of my boots, squeezed my toes. "Still numb . . . but they're moving, at least."

"Hold on. Let's check."

And she leaned over and kissed me, slowly and longingly on the lips. It was the single best kiss we'd ever shared. We separated and she nodded in approval. "Recovering nicely, I think. I think that warmed it up a bit."

"My lap feels chilly."

"Don't push it, Calhoun." She moved over to the fallen crewmen and checked them. "They're breathing steadily. Strong pulse. They'll be okay, I think."

"They'll have serious headaches, though."

"You've got your own headaches. So do I. There's been some developments."

Walking out into the corridor would not have been the best idea in the world. Instead we scrambled up a service ladder and, moments later, were crawling through the ship's utility shafts. Once we'd put sufficient distance between ourselves and the torpedo room, Mueller found a fairly secure area for us to hole up.

"Okay . . . here's the situation," she said, getting down to business. "The Carvargna battle fleet has been, to put it mildly, a success."

"That's no surprise."

"The Dufaux have surrendered unconditionally. That's also no surprise," she continued before I could say anything. "They were outnumbered, outgunned . . . there was nothing else they could do. The Carvargna are hailing Captain Kenyon as a galactic hero."

"A hero." I shook my head in disbelief. "He's a tortured man."

"Don't tell me you feel sorry for him. After everything he's put you through . . ."

"I helped bring it about, Kat. If I'd taken a stronger hand when I should have, I might have prevented all of this. Instead I let it happen. I did that."

"Mac, you can't blame yourself for everything."

"I have to stop him. I have to stop him before it goes any further."

She stared at me in disbelief. "Further? Mac, Anzibar Four is in smoking ruins. The Dufaux are, for the most part, crushed, begging for an end to it. They've been defeated. . . ."

"It may not be over," I warned her. "The leaders. The Dufaux leaders . . . Kradius, and whoever his associates might be . . . do you know if they're dead? If so, then maybe . . ."

"Actually, Kradius is alive. The Carvargna have him in custody on the planet's surface right now. That was part of the terms of the surrender as dictated by . . ."

"By Captain Kenyon."

"We don't know that for sure," she told me.

I shook my head. "Perhaps not. But I wouldn't bet against it. In fact . . . I bet I can tell you how the rest of it is going to go."

"Dazzle me with your knowledge, Calhoun." Despite the seriousness of the situation, the delicacy of our position . . . she actually managed to sound remarkably casual about the entire thing. She was quite a woman, our Katerina was.

"They're putting Kradius on trial," I said. "The trial will be overseen by the Carvargna rulers and the heads of the alliance they've formed. And they've invited Captain Kenyon to take a position at the trial, a position that he's accepted. In fact, he's probably already down there. No reason to delay matters . . . particularly since the longer he delays, the more chance there is that somehow Starfleet will manage to shut this all down and stop him from exacting the full measure of his vengeance."

Despite her faintly sarcastic air from moments before, she actually looked at me with genuine amazement. "I'm impressed," she said. "How did you know all that?"

"Because, Kat, things don't happen in a vacuum . . . well, most things," I added ruefully, touching my lips, which were only at that point starting to have some degree of sensation in them. "I've seen scenarios like this play out, time and again. Some in Earth history, some on other worlds. These things tend to turn out depressingly the same. The wrinkle in this instance is that Captain Kenyon is a part of it."

"Right now I'm less concerned about the captain than I am about you," Kat told me. "We've got a serious problem here. I'd hate to see them put you on trial for court-martial. It'll be your word against the captain's and Lieutenant Cray . . ."

"It's not going to come to that," I said.

"Mac, this isn't the time for false confidence."

"That's not it. Cray isn't going to want to take any chances."

She stared at me as if she couldn't believe what I was suggesting. "You're not saying that he's . . . you think . . . ?"

"He'll try to kill me."

"No." She shook her head vehemently. "No, I don't believe it. . . ."

"Mueller, there's too many ways to get at the truth. Computer readouts, telepathic scans . . . the works. The last thing that Cray is going to want to risk is my living to tell exactly what happened."

"He's a Starfleet officer, dammit!"

"He's an Andorian, first and foremost," I told her. "There are certain traits that are part and parcel of being an Andorian."

"Don't be a bigot, Calhoun."

"It's not bigotry, it's simply observed. Andorians speak quietly on the whole, but when it comes to an opponent they can be absolutely ruthless."

"So can you," she reminded me.

I smiled grimly. "That's true. That's how I know just what it is he's going to do. That's one of the reasons I've been trying to stay out of lockup. Not for a minute do I believe that I would live to get to a starbase for trial if I were in Cray's hands."

"I don't know that I believe it. But for sake of argument, we'll say you're right. In that case, then we've only one choice," Mueller said reasonably. "We have to get to the captain directly. We have to . . ." Her confidence faltered a bit. "We have to . . . what?"

"I don't know," I admitted. "I have to get through to him. To make him realize that what he's done is horribly, horribly wrong. There may be no way that he can make amends. But we can stop him from making it worse."

"You said that before. How could it possibly be worse?"

"That's easy," I said. "He could kill Kradius."

"Kill? You mean . . . murder? He'd . . . he'd never do that. . . ."

"Oh, yes he would. Where his state of mind is at the moment . . . he absolutely would. It's one thing to rationalize firing on the Dufaux vessels that fired upon the *Grissom.* We were acting to protect ourselves. Likewise he could explain away to himself the defense of the Carvargna flagship. But to cold-bloodedly stand there and execute a helpless opponent . . . doing something like that changes you forever. I wouldn't wish that on anyone, least of all the captain."

It seemed to me that she was dissecting me with her eyes. "You did it once . . . didn't you?"

"No."

"No?"

"No. More than once. Many . . . more times than once. Don't you see, Kat? No one . . . should have to be like me. No one."

She said nothing for a long moment. And then, to my surprise, she reached over and hugged me. "Why did you do that?" I asked.

"My own reasons. And they'll remain my own." She considered the situation a moment, stroking her chin thoughtfully. Then she tapped her combadge. "Mueller to Takahashi," she said in a very soft voice.

"This is Hash. Go ahead." His voice was also soft. Clearly they had coordinated earlier.

"I'll need the coordinates for where the captain beamed to on Anzibar Four."

"Hold on." Obviously he was double-checking them off his ops board. After a moment he told Kat, and she repeated them carefully to make sure she had it right.

"That's it."

"Much obliged. Mueller out."

"Okay, we know where he went. Now what?"

"Now we get down there," she said as if it were the most reasonable thing in the world.

"How? We jump?"

"No. We're going to have to get to one of the transporter rooms. It'll probably necessitate overpowering the security guard. If you don't think you're up for that . . ."

I raised an eyebrow. "Is that to be considered a challenge, XO?"

"Whatever you want to call it."

"Kat . . ." I hesitated. "There's . . . there's really no way I can thank you for all this. I—"

"You're right," she said immediately. "So it's probably better that you don't even try."

She moved off down the utility shaft, and I immediately followed her. I had to admit it: It was tough to argue with logic like that. It probably *was* better that I didn't try. We made our way through the utility shaft, approaching the main transporter room. The plan was going fairly well. By sticking to the utility shafts, we were able to stay out of sight. If we were able to get close enough to the transporter room, then we might face minimal opposition once we got there.

In fact, according to Mueller, we might face even less than I had previously thought.

"There's a lot of people who aren't thrilled with the way all of this has turned out," she told me. "Not the majority of the crew, certainly. But enough. Enough to make people wonder whether all of this has gone down properly. It might not just be your word against the captain and Cray. . . ."

"Whether people believe or don't believe is up to them," I said as we climbed down one of the ladders. I took each step slowly and carefully. The last thing I needed to do was slip and break my ankle or something similarly intelligent. "I'll be perceived as the instigator. What we have to do is—"

I didn't get a chance to finish the sentence, because suddenly the utility shaft was filled with a terribly familiar noise. It was the whine of transporter beams, and before we could do anything at all we were caught in their grip. The utility tubes dissolved around us and suddenly we found that we were in the main transporter room.

Lieutenant Cray was standing there with his phaser aimed levelly at us.

The Andorian

There was no one else around. Just Cray. Cray, Mueller, and me. Kat looked dumbfounded, staring at Cray as if she couldn't comprehend what she and I could possibly be doing there.

As if he'd read her mind, Cray spoke in that same eerie whisper of his, "You and he. Obvious."

"He figured you were the one who helped me, Katerina," I said. I didn't bother to raise my hands. "He's head of security, after all, and he's very thorough. I strongly suspect that he knows just about everyone's business aboard this ship."

He inclined his head slightly in acknowledgment.

"So he locked on to my combadge," she said in slow understanding, "and beamed me and whoever was with me here, on the assumption that it would be you."

He nodded again. His blue lips thinned in a self-satisfied smile.

For a moment, no words were spoken. Then I said, "Cray . . . it's pointless to discuss this further. We're two of a kind, you and I. We both know what needs to be done here. The only question will be whether you do it as a coward . . . or as an Andorian. Oh . . . I forgot. That's pretty much the same thing, isn't it."

The amusement vanished from his face.

"What are you doing?" Mueller said softly out of the corner of her mouth.

I ignored her. "Tell you what, Cray. I'll make it easy for you. This is what your kind prefers, after all." I turned my back to him. "Here. That's your method of operation, isn't it."

"This won't work," he said softly.

I faced him once more. "Cray . . . don't waste my time or yours. We both know you're going to fire the phaser from a nice, safe distance. No stomach for hand-to-hand, to show who's the better man. Finish us off, nice and quick. No witnesses. That's the way you want it, isn't it. You've probably already made adjustments to your log to fake receiving entries from Starfleet, so no one else can find out your deceit as I did. But just out of curiosity . . . how long do you think that's going to last? Once the real investigation starts . . . whatever entries you've cooked up will never stand up to scrutiny. You've totally miscalculated the game, Cray. You thought by cooperating with the captain, doing whatever he wanted, that would be how you'd get ahead. Plus there was certainly no love for me lost on your part. If my career, and I, had to be destroyed, well . . . you weren't going to shed any tears about that. Correct?"

He said nothing. The phaser hadn't wavered. This wasn't a good sign. Cray wasn't going for the taunting, wasn't allowing his advantage to slip away. There was only one thing that could possibly make the situation worse.

Katerina Mueller drew herself to her full height. "Cray . . . put it down. Now. That's an order."

That was it.

Cray turned and fired at Katerina.

I saw it coming about a half second before he fired. I shoved her to the right as I lunged to the left. But Katerina didn't move fast enough as the phaser blast clipped her right shoulder. Kat let out a howl of pain and crumbled to the ground. Cray wasn't screwing around. The phaser was set on kill. If he'd struck a vital area, such as her heart, she would have been dead before she hit the floor.

"Don't move," he said. The order wasn't addressed to Kat, but to me. He had the phaser aimed at her head and the threat was clear. If I didn't make myself a nice easy target, she was dead.

But she was dead anyway. We both were.

I spit at him.

It was the purest means by which I could express contempt, and certainly the most pointed. The wad of spittle sailed across the room and struck Cray on the right side of the face. His eyes went wide with fury as, in silence, he felt the spittle trickling down.

And then, very slowly and very deliberately, he placed the phaser down on the control console.

"You will never . . ." It was as if every section of his sentence was an effort. ". . . insult Andorians . . . again. . . ."

I struck a defensive pose. He matched it. Slowly we circled the cramped quarters of the transporter room. There wouldn't be a lot of room for maneuvering. Despite the fact that he was an enemy, I couldn't help but admire the fluid way in which he moved.

"You will receive . . . what you desired," he said, his hands tracing elaborate patterns in the air. Slowly I paralleled his steps, keeping the console between us. I moved slightly to the left and he already moved in anticipation of it. His eyes glittered with fury. "No weapons, save our hands. We will see . . . who is the coward. We will see . . . who is the better man. We will see . . . who is the . . ."

Calmly, I reached over the console and picked up the phaser that he'd put down and I aimed it at him.

His face twisted in contempt. "Coward!"

"Idiot," I replied, and fired. I hit him squarely in the chest. The impact of the phaser blast lifted Cray up off his feet and sent him slamming back into the far wall of the transporter room. He hit it with a most satisfying thud and slid to the ground, his head slumped to one side, his eyes closed.

I knelt down next to Kat, took her arm gently, and tried to bend it at the elbow. "Does this hurt?" I asked.

"A little. I can handle it." She started to sit up, her teeth gritted against the pain that she was obviously feeling. She glanced at Cray. "Is he dead?"

"I doubt it. Andorians are fairly tough, actually."

And suddenly Cray was sitting up.

There was red-hot fury in his eyes and, without slowing down, he lunged at me. The hole where I had nailed him was still smoking from the blast.

"*Fairly* . . . tough?" he snarled, as if the modifier was the worst insult I could have hurled. His hands were around my throat.

I tried to bring the phaser around but he released one of his hands briefly enough to knock the phaser away, sending it clattering into a far corner of the room. He straddled me, choking me, and Kat tried to throw herself against him to knock him off me. Without even looking away from me, Cray swung his right fist around and caught Mueller squarely on the point of her chin. Her eyes rolling up, Katerina sank to the ground and Mueller returned to the important business of crushing my larynx.

My hands were gripping his wrists, pulling as hard as I could. It didn't seem nearly to be enough. His powerful fingers, like iron bars, dug deeper and deeper.

I rammed the heel of my hand into his nose.

I felt a satisfying crack beneath my fingers and knew that I had just busted his nose. He was momentarily dazed as I shoved him to one side and got to my feet, facing him.

He didn't look happy.

I wanted to finish it quickly and swung a roundhouse. No chance. He blocked it as if I were moving in slow motion and drove a fist into my gut. I gasped, doubled over, and he spun and slammed a foot into my head. I went down, tried to stand and he was moving so fast that I never even saw the backspin that sent me crashing to the floor when it connected. I tried to roll back out of the way, but he was up and kicking me in the torso, causing me to tuck my legs up as if I were assuming the fetal position. He grabbed me by the scruff of the neck, hauled me to my feet, spun me around and slammed me face first into the wall. The impact expelled air from me, winded me. He released me for a moment, much to my surprise, and I stood there and wavered as I tried to mount a defense. No chance again. Leaping high, he spun in midair for the purpose of crushing the front of my face with his feet. Fortunately enough I managed to block it partly, but that wasn't enough to save me from the full impact. Someone dropped an anvil on my skull as I collapsed again under the superior hand-and-footwork of Cray. I was getting knocked about so badly that my thoughts were completely tattered. *We should hire this guy, he's good,* I mused. That's how bad a shape I was in.

Cray reached down, snagged my shirtfront in his huge hands, and hauled me to my feet with the very likely purpose of finishing me off. I had been right. Right straight down the line. Why, dammit, why did I have to be right all the time?

"Die," he growled.

I grabbed one of his antennae atop his head, got a firm grip, and pulled as hard as I could. Cray hadn't realized what I was doing until I actually did it. There was a nauseating ripping sound and antennae suddenly tore free of his head and came up, truncated and bloody, in my hand.

Cray was beyond agony. He screamed as loudly as I've ever heard a sentient being scream. He dropped to one knee, clutching at his head, blood pouring out and staining his head of white hair. I leaned against a wall, gasping, observing Cray's discomfort.

"You . . . bastard!" he managed to get out.

"You're still an idiot," I replied, and I hit him as hard as I could.

I knew instantly that something had broken, although whether it was his jaw or my fist was a bit hard to tell. He went down, his eyes rolling up and back, and then he keeled over and thudded to the floor.

I immediately went over to Katerina and shook her gently. Her head lolled a bit, but slowly her eyes opened. "Are you okay?" I asked.

"Oh . . . fine," she managed to get out.

"I need you to beam me down to the planet. Do you remember the coordinates that Hash gave you?"

She grinned lopsidedly and tweaked my cheek. "You're cute," she informed me.

"That's a relief to hear. Get up, Katerina. Can you get up?"

"Why? Is it time for school?"

I realized that the process of bringing her out of it was going to take slightly longer than I had anticipated.

The Sentence

Perhaps matters might have been a bit more difficult for Captain Kenyon if Kradius had at least looked repentant. Or, for that matter, had even looked remotely like someone sympathetic.

It didn't help that Kradius had horns.

In point of fact, he looked almost demonic. Kradius was huge, over six feet, and about as wide as a shuttlecraft. He had a huge head of hair that bore a resemblance to the mane of a lion, an impossibly huge brow, and small horns situated just above the hairline. His eyes were dark red, and there was a thin covering of what appeared to be fur on him.

He was surveying his captors with open contempt.

The Carvargna board of inquiry and trial sat in a row of chairs, regarding Kradius with what appeared to be equal amounts of boredom and disdain. To say that they were in a room might be to overstate it. They were in the burned-out remains of what once had been the central government site of the Dufaux. Now it was smoking ruins, the ceiling gone and the night sky glittering. There was a faint chill wind cutting through, but nobody seemed to be paying much attention.

There were no other Dufaux there aside from Kradius. All of the government officials had either died in the assault or were in a holding facility awaiting their own "trial" . . . much too generous a word, really. Kradius's accusers were arrayed before him, and most prominent among them was Captain Kenyon.

He sat in the middle of the line of judges. He stared at Kradius, his eyes half-lidded, hiding whatever thoughts were going through his mind. Hatred seeped from him like a toxic waste. Barhba was next to him. And Barhba . . .

Barhba seemed tired of it all. It was as if the immensity of their activities, the full weight of the slaughter that they had perpetrated, was starting to weigh upon him. The novelty, such as it was, had worn off. The Dufaux were no threat anymore, and the sooner that this business was ended, the sooner Barhba would be able to return home and put all of this behind him.

Except it was unlikely that he would. Far more likely was that he would lie awake at night, imagining the screams of terror of the Dufaux people as death hammered down on them from on high. He would probably think about his finger on the trigger, his involvement in the eradication of the Dufaux. He would begin to wonder if, indeed, there hadn't been some other way possible. A chorus of imaginary shrieks of despair and death rattles would be the serenade that would sing him to sleep at night and the alarm that roused him in the morning. No, Barhba did not have an enviable life ahead of him.

Kenyon, on the other hand, did not look tired at all. He was completely focused on Kradius. Kradius did not appear to notice him. Either that or he held him in such contempt that he simply didn't bother to acknowledge his presence.

Doc Villers was standing directly behind Kenyon, and there were two security men, Meyer and Boyajian, directly behind her. The guards were armed, and even Kenyon had a phaser on his belt.

Kenyon had no greater supporter aboard the ship than the irascible Doc Villers, but even she seemed a bit daunted by the proceedings. She kept looking at Kenyon as if she were trying to urge him, mentally, to give up his seat on the tribunal and return to the stars. For in truth, he had no business here. Not really.

Yet here he was.

"Kradius," Barhba said, sounding fatigued, "this board has found you guilty of crimes against sentient beings of this sector. You have remained silent during your trial, offering no defense. Would you speak now?"

His gaze swiveled toward Barhba and he appeared to be aware of the Carvargna, as well as the Carvargna's allies, for the first time. When he spoke his voice was surprisingly low. "Why?"

"Why?" The question seemed to puzzle Barhba. "In order . . . to have your side heard. To explain yourself."

"To you?" Kradius dripped contempt. "I do not acknowledge that you have power over me."

"Whether you acknowledge it or not, your life is in the hands of this board."

He snorted derisively. "My life is in the hands of our god. He does with it as he sees fit. You are simply the instruments of his will."

This pronouncement appeared to intrigue Kenyon. He leaned forward, his fingers interlaced. "You have a god?" he asked in clear amazement. "You believe in something greater than yourselves?"

"Greater than ourselves. Greater than you," Kradius replied. "We are his chosen. You . . . are nothing."

"Oh. We are nothing. I see." Kenyon rose from his seat at that point and slowly started to approach Kradius. The huge Dufaux posed no threat, his hands bound in front of him. "Is that how you see it, then? Is that how you justify your actions?"

"We do not need to justify anything," said Kradius. "We do what we will. If you do not like it, that is your problem."

"Ohhhh no," Kenyon said, shaking his head. "It's your problem. It is entirely your problem now, sir."

"Captain." It was Villers who had spoken. She was looking increasingly uncomfortable with everything that was happening. "Captain, please . . . perhaps it would be best to . . ."

"Quiet, Doctor," Kenyon said, cutting her off. There was a demented gleam in his eye, as if he were running a fever. "I want to hear about this bastard's religion. I want to hear what he has to say for himself. To hear him spout about his superiority while he is standing here in chains awaiting his punishment."

Kradius was looking Kenyon up and down, and then comprehension appeared to dawn on his face. "I thought you looked familiar to me," he said at last. "The Federation ambassador . . . he was related to you in some way, wasn't he."

"He was my brother." Kenyon fairly shook with anger. "And the girl was my daughter. They were the last of my family, and you killed them. You did that. I'm now alone in the galaxy. You did that, too."

"Norman . . ." Villers started again.

"Shut up, Doctor."

This was the second time Kenyon had rebuked the doctor. Meyer and Boyajian glanced at each other, looking a bit nervous. The relationship between Kenyon and Villers was well known as one of total respect and genuine admiration. For Kenyon to have cut Villers off at the knees in that way . . . it indicated that something was truly very, very wrong.

But Barhba spoke up at that point. "This is accomplishing nothing, honored Kenyon. We see no reason to continue with it. Kradius, it is the decision of this board that you be executed. Said execution, in the interests of mercy, will be performed in as timely and painless a manner as can readily be devised."

"You are alone in the galaxy?" Kradius was addressing Kenyon as if the others hadn't spoken. "You? I had three mates, human. Three. Nineteen children. They are all dead now. Dead, thanks to the barrage from you and your associates. Do not speak of being alone to me, human. You cannot even begin to grasp the definition."

"You brought it on yourself. You killed . . ."

"I killed trespassers."

"You killed representatives of the Federation that you yourselves gave permission to come to your world!"

He shook his head violently. "I refused permission. It was subsequently granted by a lieutenant of mine who had no respect for my wishes in the matter. Who felt that the attitudes of my government were too extreme. He desired that I speak at length with those whose opinions were different from mine. The moment I discovered his schemes, I had him executed. I gave the Federation representatives the opportunity to leave unmolested. They insisted on trying to speak with me." He had been speaking in an almost conversational voice, but now his tone became louder. "I refused them. They insisted and insisted. Imagine the disrespect, to ignore my wishes in that matter. I am Kradius. *I am Kradius,"* and he sounded indignant over the mere thought of how he had been "treated" at the hands of those he had killed. "They were overconfident. They were certain that I would desire to listen to them. Warning after warning I gave them, and still they would not leave. They desired to talk when I had no interest in doing so. I had no choice in the matter. To treat me with disrespect, before my advisers, before all of the Dufaux, by not honoring my wishes. They had to die for that offense."

"You butcher," Kenyon snarled. "You goddamn butcher."

"They had their opportunities to survive. They had their chances and chose not to take them," Kradius replied. "Those were offered to them by me. What chances did you offer my mate and children, eh?" He looked at all of them then, not just Kenyon. "What chance did you offer? My understanding—from what I hear your soldiers tell—is that I put up a considerable fight when they came for me. The truth is that when your soldiers arrived, I was sitting in the ruins of my house cradling the body of my newborn son. I said nothing to them, did not lift a hand against them. That is the tale of the mighty Kradius at bay . . . but it's not remotely as interesting, is it. So it has to be built up, exaggerated."

"Your crimes are no exaggeration. Your brutality is documented," Kenyon told him.

"I do not care for your opinion of me, human. Perhaps you'd be well advised to save it for those who do."

"Honored Kenyon," Barhba addressed him. He rose from his chair and took a couple of steps in Kenyon's direction. "The anger you bear this man is quite clear. We," and he indicated himself and the council, "feel it right and just that you handle his execution. He has committed crimes against us, of course, but yours are the most personal and therefore it is the most appropriate that the requirement of blood be settled by you and only by you. His life . . . will be in your hands."

"Thank you," said Kenyon, bowing slightly. He turned to Meyer and Boyajian. "Gentlemen."

"Yes, sir?" said Meyer.

"Line up, please."

They did as they were told, still clearly a bit puzzled. But Villers was ahead of them and Kenyon. "Norm," she said urgently, "don't do this. This is crossing a line."

He ignored her. Instead he stepped in close to Kradius and grabbed him by the elbow. With a force that was surprising in the older man, he shoved Kradius back against a wall, or at least what remained of a wall. Carvargna and other allies who were observing made sure to clear away. Kenyon stepped back, leaving Kradius standing there by himself. His huge fists were clenched.

"Norm!" She was becoming more insistent.

"Not now, Doctor. Security team . . . weapons up."

The reality of what they were being faced with slowly began to dawn on Meyer and Boyajian. Acting automatically, they removed their weapons from their belts and gripped them firmly, but there was nothing but uncertainty and even confusion on their faces, as if they were in the middle of a truly demented nightmare.

"Ready . . ." began Kenyon. "Aim . . ."

They didn't aim. They just stood there, holding their weapons but down and at the side. Meyer, who had been all for attending to the captain's wishes back in the transporter room, seemed racked with indecision. "Captain . . . this is . . ."

"Problem, Mr. Meyer?" Kenyon asked icily.

"Captain . . . we're security guards," Boyajian now spoke up. "We're not . . . we're not executioners. We're not acting on behalf of the Federation here. We don't even have a death penalty in the UFP. . . ."

"Yes, but we're not on one of the United Federation of Planets members now, are we," Kenyon said with forced calm. "We're on a world where brutal deaths are apparently part of the standard policy. The death that has been ordered for this . . . person . . . is far more merciful than what he dealt out to the two UFP representatives who were here weeks ago. Now do as you're ordered. Weapons up."

They looked at each other, as if trying to decide what to do.

"My God," Villers said in low astonishment, "Calhoun was right. How could I not have . . ."

"This is not a noninterference question, gentlemen. This thing has been condemned to die!"

"They said it was in your hands, Norman," Villers spoke up. She turned to Barhba. "Does that mean that . . . that if he doesn't . . ."

"If the honored Kenyon shows mercy, I do not see how we could do less," Barhba said. He looked to the others, who nodded in agreement.

"There will be no showing of any such thing. Now I'm not going to order you again!" Kenyon said, his ire mounting. He walked right up to Meyer and Boyajian. Kradius observed the entire scene with cool amusement.

"That . . . is fortunate, sir," Meyer said. "Because I've never disobeyed a direct order before. And I . . ."

"Typical," Kradius said.

"You shut up," Kenyon said sharply.

For someone whose death was being debated, Kradius seemed remarkably detached from the whole thing. "So typical. Your own soldiers cannot carry out a simple execution."

"I'm warning you . . ."

"Would you like to know the real reason that we were not interested in becoming involved with your Federation?" Kradius asked. "It's because we sensed your weakness. Your whining brother came across as an effete, petulant snob rather than someone who should be attended to. His death was inevitable the moment he set foot on our world. He didn't have the strength of character to survive."

Kenyon started to turn a distinct shade of purple. "You . . . heartless bastard," he snarled. "Not enough that you killed him . . . killed my child . . . now you say these things . . ."

"You Starfleet men are seekers of truth, are you not?" said Kradius. "Here is the truth for you, then. I handled his execution myself. I did. He seemed so weak, so insufferable, that I wanted to see how much he could take. To see how much pain he could endure before he cried like a child, begged for his life. It took almost no time at all. Then I continued to beat him so that I could see how long it would take him to realize that begging would do no good. That took a much longer time. Actually . . . he never stopped begging. Right until the end. He died with whimpering and pleading on his lips, or what was left of his lips."

"I'll . . . kill you . . ." whispered Kenyon.

"Yes, by all means, do so," sneered Kradius. "For all your posturing, prove to me at the last that you're no different. Would you like to hear of your daughter's death as well? She had more bravery, I will grant her that. She only begged at the end . . . and I believe she called for you repeatedly, although you of course didn't come. . . ."

Kenyon snapped. His own phaser forgotten, he grabbed instead the first weapon that he saw, which was Meyer's phaser. He snatched it right out of the hands of the startled security officer, took several steps forward, and brought it to bear on Kradius, ready to shoot him down on the spot.

And that was when I stepped forward.

I had been able to secret myself easily enough in the crowd of onlookers. It wasn't as if Kenyon was particularly looking for me at that point. Mueller had recovered enough to beam me down, and I had stayed out of sight during the entire confrontation, hoping and praying that Kenyon would do the right thing on his own. But that, it was becoming clear, was not going to be the case.

I was holding the phaser that I had taken off Cray, and now it was leveled directly at Captain Kenyon. There I was, first officer of the *Grissom,* with my commanding officer at gunpoint. As I said to you before . . . if one is going to go down, best to go down in flames.

Amazingly, Kenyon didn't seem surprised to see me. "Hello, Calhoun," he said as if I'd happened to wander in during a family picnic.

This didn't seem the time for niceties. "Put the phaser down, Captain."

"You first."

"I can't do that."

"Well, then we have a problem, don't we."

His phaser didn't waver from being pointed at Kradius.

"Meyer, Boyajian . . . back away from him. Doctor, you too. This is between the captain and me."

I was pleased to see that they didn't dispute or debate me. They did precisely as I was ordered. It was entirely possible that it was the last order I was ever going to wind up giving. At least it had been obeyed.

What I found most significant about the moment was that Kenyon hadn't fired yet. In point of fact, there was nothing stopping him. I wasn't in the way, and even if I fired upon him after he squeezed the trigger, there was nothing I could do about his killing Kradius. I couldn't knock Kradius out of the way, and I certainly couldn't move faster than the beam of light that was the primary discharge of a phaser. But if Kenyon hadn't fired yet . . . then it was entirely possible that something deep within him was stopping him. Perhaps he wanted me to talk him out of it somehow.

"Between you and me?" Kenyon asked with faint amusement, echoing my words. "Calhoun . . . there's nothing between you and me. It's all me," and he gestured with the phaser, "and him. That . . . thing who killed my—"

"I know what he did, Captain. And believe it or not—and I know it's not going to feel like much consolation at the moment—but I know what you're feeling. But I cannot let you do this thing. There has to be a point at which this ends."

"Yes. That point is his death," and he indicated Kradius.

"No, sir. Enough has already happened. Enough is enough. Don't you see? If you turn away from this now . . . turn away from the vengeance that's presenting itself to you . . . there's still a chance for you. Still a chance to—"

"A chance? You mean like the chance he gave my baby . . . my Stephie . . ."

"Captain . . ."

"This tribunal has condemned him to death. I'm simply carrying out their will. . . ."

"This tribunal wouldn't be here if it weren't for you, Captain! You set this entire thing into motion! You made it possible! All of it, possible!" I kept my phaser leveled on him. "My God, Captain, think of all the people who have died thus far! Died because of the guiding hand provided by the *Grissom!* It has to end, sir!"

"It does. It ends with him."

"If that's the will of these people, then let them attend to it. But not you. You're not one of them. You're separate from them, you're . . ."

When Kenyon spoke, it was as if from very far away. "You can't stop me, Mac," he said. "Whether you approve or not . . . whether it costs me my command or not . . . I am going to do this thing. I . . . I can hear them. . . ."

And before my eyes, before the eyes of everyone, Kenyon came completely unraveled. It was the man whom I had seen losing control of himself in the ready room, but this was worse, far worse. He lost it completely, tears pouring down his face. Kradius sneered in contempt at the sight, and I could only be grateful that Kenyon was so much in a world of his own at that point. For if he had seen Kradius's expression at that moment, nothing in the universe would have been able to prevent him from blowing off the Dufaux's head.

"I can hear my brother . . . my . . . my little girl . . . begging me for help, I can hear them in my head . . . begging me, cursing me because I let them down . . . I can't live with that, Mac. . . ." His voice was going in and out, louder and softer, a bizarre mixture of laughing and crying.

"Captain," I said desperately, "I'm trying to save a fine officer . . . a fine and distinguished career. . . ."

I knew I was losing him then. Because I saw his finger starting to tighten on the firing control. "If you want to stop me . . . you're going to have to kill me. . . ."

All the options raced through my mind at that moment.

I could try to shoot to stun or wound. But that might not stop Kenyon in the state of mind that he was in. He might still manage to get a shot off and kill Kradius.

The problem was that I was a practical man. Always had been. And I knew at that point that there was really only one possibility open.

Kradius had to die.

Kenyon was too far gone. Weeks of imagining his daughter's and brother's awful deaths had completely unhinged him. The voices were in his head, voices crying for vengeance that I knew only too well. I had lived with them all my life, and would continue to do so. But Kenyon, he was too new at this, too good a soul to have to tolerate it.

The harsh but inescapable reality of the situation was that, as long as Kradius was alive, Kenyon could never heal. Never be the man that he was. It was possible that it was too late for that anyway. . . .

Possible . . . but not impossible.

I had pledged to watch out for the captain. To support him. He was going to have enough difficulties defending his actions up until that point. Cold-blooded murder would be damned near impossible. It was possibly the difference between being asked to retire after a distinguished career and being brought up on charges, being forced out in disgrace.

There was already so much blood on my hands, so much blackening of my soul . . . what was one more death, really, laid at my doorstep? And if they tried and convicted me, court-martialed me and stuck me in a prison camp somewhere, well . . . so what? Small loss in the grand scheme of things. Just another commander with only a semi-promising future at best. That couldn't even begin to compare to what Kenyon would be giving up.

The answer was obvious, really.

Understand . . . I didn't really give a damn about Kradius. I had killed far less worse than him, with far less provocation. It was what he represented in terms of Kenyon's own life and career that concerned me.

If Kradius's life ended . . . then Kenyon's at least had a prayer of continuing in something vaguely resembling its previous form. If Kenyon were the one who killed him, that was pretty much it for Kenyon. It was going to be bad enough as it was; Starfleet would roast him alive if he took that final step. Plus, I was convinced that Kenyon was in the throes of a temporary insanity, driven there by the trauma of losing those who were so beloved to him. If and when that madness passed, everything that he had done would come crashing down on him. I desperately wanted to avoid homicide being added to the list.

If Kradius lived, however, then the drive for vengeance would continue to eat away at Kenyon. I knew from personal experience what that was like.

That left only one option.

I didn't know what to do. I was completely torn, and the savage within whispered, *Just do it. Get it done.*

Before I had given it rational thought, before I was completely resolved, I had already swung my phaser in the direction of Kradius. All it would take was a quick squeeze and the problems would be over.

And as fiercely as the savage had called to me, the would-be civilized officer within me begged me not to.

I hesitated for a split instant . . .

. . . and then I aimed at Kradius and blew his head off.

Because at the last second, the moment of indecision before I knew absolutely what I was going to do, that was when I had seen the phaser in Kradius's hand. Even though Kradius's hands were shackled, somehow he was holding a phaser in them. As his headless body started to tumble forward, I glanced at the only source I could think of and saw that I was right. The phaser was gone from the captain's belt. When Kenyon had pushed him up against the wall, he had been so irate that he hadn't noticed Kradius palming his phaser.

And Kradius had chosen now, this very moment, when Kenyon and I seemed totally distracted by, and wrapped up in, each other, to try and take a shot directly at Kenyon. His arms were already half raised in Kenyon's general direction when my phaser blast had drilled right through his face and splattered his brains on the back wall. The phaser slipped from his nerveless hands and Kradius, or what was left of him, pitched forward and hit the ground with such impact that the floor shook beneath our feet.

"My . . . God . . ." Villers said in amazement. She looked at me with something that I had never thought I would see in her face: admiration. "You're the fastest shot I've ever seen. You're lightning! I didn't even see the phaser until just now. You saved the captain's life."

I couldn't believe it. I absolutely couldn't believe it. They had thought that I was acting to prevent Kradius from shooting Kenyon, when in point of fact I had been totally unaware that Kradius posed any sort of threat until the very last instant. I was "lightning" only because I was already in motion before I knew Kradius posed a threat.

I said the only thing I could, given the circumstances:

"Thanks."

Kenyon hadn't moved from his position. He still had the phaser leveled at Kradius, or at least where Kradius had been. His eyes were wide, his brow still covered with sweat.

"Captain . . . it's over," I said gently. I took a step toward him. "Kradius is dead. It's done. So just lower the phaser now . . . and we can all go home. . . ."

And Kenyon turned to look at me with a more haunted expression than I had ever seen in any man . . . including myself.

"You didn't understand me, Mac. I said I couldn't live with their voices in my head. Killing Kradius would balance the scales . . . but it wouldn't stop the voices . . . only one thing can do that. . . ."

I saw it coming an instant before it happened.

Kenyon reversed the phaser, aimed it at himself, and fired.

The Hearing

I STOOD BEFORE THE STARFLEET TRIBUNAL ON EARTH AND OFFERED NO defense whatsoever. I refused to have defense counsel. I refused to utter a word as to why I had done anything that I had done, because I felt that my actions should speak for themselves. The main reason that I did so was that I felt like a total and complete failure.

I was exonerated anyway.

Officer after officer came before the tribunal and testified as to my bravery, to my diligence. Mueller called me the greatest officer she had ever known. Villers blamed herself for not flagging the problem earlier, blinded by loyalty. Takahashi admitted his culpability in the *Grissom* mutiny and wound up getting a commendation, as did Mueller. Cray was tossed into a Starfleet prison camp for a sentence of five years for attempted murder and falsifying Starfleet orders.

And I was hailed as a hero.

When the verdict came down, I sat before the tribunal, disbelieving. Dead center, beaming, looking proud as anything, was Admiral Jellico. Jellico, whose life I had once saved and who was one of my biggest boosters as a result. There in the council room, with the crewmen who had testified on my behalf present, Jellico read the unanimous decision of the tribunal. I had acted in a manner in accordance with Starfleet regulations, and was not to be blamed for any aspect of the unfortunate behavior which had resulted in the mutiny and Kenyon's unfortunate demise. They even held up my shooting Kradius as an example of exemplary behavior.

I sat there, stunned. I simply couldn't believe it. I had failed, failed in every way possible. My sworn duty was to protect Kenyon. I had failed. I might have averted the entire thing if only I'd been firmer, if I'd stepped in when there was still the opportunity. I had refused to do so. And I had been *that* close to shooting a man dead in cold blood . . . probably would have, given another second . . . but it hadn't looked that way to anyone who had been present.

They thought me a hero.

I was a fraud.

I heard them speaking of captaincy, of advancement. Of being a shining example of everything that Starfleet stood for. All I wanted to do was vomit.

I rose from behind the table where I was seated and approached the tribunal. They were smiling, clearly figuring that I would be pleased over their decision. Without a word, I removed my combadge and placed it on the table in front of them.

"I quit," I told them.

"What?" Jellico actually laughed, as if he thought I was joking.

"I quit. I resign my commission. I'm out," I said. I turned away and started to leave.

Jellico was around the table inside of a second, and he grabbed me by the arm, sputtering. "Commander . . . we know this has been a great stress on you. If you give it some time, however, we're sure you'll see . . ."

"You know this has been a great stress? Admiral, believe me when I tell you: You know nothing. Nothing." Inside I was furious, furious with myself, and I took it all out on Jellico. "What you don't know could fill volumes. I resign. I quit. I'm out. You are no longer a superior officer; you're just a man holding my arm. Let go."

Anger started to darken Jellico's face. "Don't talk to me that way, Calhoun. I went to bat for you. You owe me. Now sit down and we'll discuss this in a—"

"Let go of me," I told him, "or I will knock you down."

"Calhoun . . ." he started to say, and he pulled on my arm again.

I never heard the rest of what he was going to say. I'm sure it would have been very interesting. It might even have made a major difference in my life.

My fist swung around and caught him squarely in the side of the head. Jellico went down, landing hard on his rump and staring up at me in open astonishment. The other two admirals were on their feet. If I had suddenly ripped off my head to reveal I was a Regulan blood worm in a man suit, they couldn't have looked more surprised.

"I warned you," I said.

I didn't even look back over my shoulder as I heard Jellico raging,

"You're finished, Calhoun! You hear? You're finished in Starfleet! Finished!"

Considering that I had just resigned, that wasn't a threat I was particularly concerned about.

I went back to my apartment to clear out my stuff. What I could carry I simply shoved into a suitcase that would be easy to travel with. What I couldn't carry . . . furniture and such . . . I was going to leave behind.

There was a chime at my door. "Go away," I called.

"Mac," came a familiar voice.

I sighed, knowing that standing there and arguing wasn't going to do any good where she was concerned. "Come," I said.

Katerina Mueller entered. And stood there.

"So?" I said.

I was curious as to how well she truly knew me. Whether she would bother to try and argue. Whether she would give me grief, or tell me how I was throwing away my career, or besiege me with any number of unasked-for and unwanted reasons why I was being an idiot.

For a long moment, no words were spoken.

And then she said simply, "One for the road?"

I smiled and accommodated her. It seemed only polite.

The End

I LEFT EARTH SHORTLY THEREAFTER AND BEGAN TO WANDER. AFTER ABOUT a year, I was found by one Admiral Alynna Nechayev, who had her own plans and interests for me. I cooperated with her for a time, doing things that were of interest to me and of service to her because it seemed an equitable arrangement. And one thing led to another, and I eventually found myself as a captain once more in Starfleet. Becoming involved in Starfleet, serving on a starship . . . I wasn't particularly anxious to embrace the concept. I'd done it before, and as the old saying goes, once burned, twice shy. Then again, it wasn't such a terrible thing, I suppose, going back. If nothing else, it allowed me to be here at the Captain's Table.

When I took command of the *Excalibur,* I wound up bringing some associates with me. Lieutenants Hash and Gold work the nightside on the *Excalibur.* Katerina Mueller is likewise along, serving as ship's XO as she did so capably for the *Grissom.* It's an odd situation, really, since my first officer and former fiancée, Elizabeth Shelby, doesn't know about how closely Mueller and I served together before. She probably wouldn't care if she did . . . but then again, on the other hand, it's probably better that she not know.

And then there's Captain Kenyon.

Right there. Seated right there, on the other side of the Captain's Table, obviously having wandered in from an earlier time in his life. He has no idea what's to come, and thanks to the rules of this place . . . I can't warn him. Can't let him know what's to come.

I still have his combadge, tinted with blood. It's right here, in fact. I keep it with me to remind me . . .

. . . to remind me of . . .

. . . to hell with it.

Here.

Here, you take it. Let me pin it on you . . . there. There. It actually looks rather good on you.

I've never spoken of this to anyone. Not in all the detail. No one truly knows all the aspects of it, not even Mueller. I suppose that I was holding on to the badge . . . until I found someone that I could trust with the story. So I've trusted you now. You have the combadge, you have the story. I've opened myself up to someone, as I promised Cap I would. I chose you. Do with the story, and the badge, as you will.

As for me . . . I was just trying to meet my obligations as best as I was able to. Which, in the final analysis . . . is all any of us can do.

Nice talking to you.

Captain Mackenzie Calhoun stood up, ignoring the Gecko that scurried quickly from under his chair, and looked once more in a forlorn manner across the bar. Then he turned away from Captain Kenyon and started to head for the door.

Cap, the bartender, intercepted him halfway out. He looked at Calhoun with a slightly scolding air. "You cheated, Mac," he said.

"Cheated? You said I owed a story. I did exactly as you said. I sat down at a table and told my story to another captain."

"The purpose is for you to share aspects of yourself, Mac. To open up, to air things out. You, of all people—the most tightly wrapped, the one who is mostly likely to internalize everything and keep it to yourself—you, most of all, could have used that release. Instead you dodged it."

"I told the story. And I figured if anyone could appreciate a story about a disaster, *he* could."

"Yes, but you know damned well he didn't hear a word you said."

Calhoun shrugged.

Cap tried to look gravely at him and ream him out some more, but ultimately he wasn't able to. Instead he laughed. "You know . . . you remind me of an arrogant, disheveled kid who came in here thinking he was smarter and better than everyone else."

"Yeah. Whatever happened to him?"

"He was in here just yesterday."

"Really?" Calhoun smiled. "Seems like ages."

He clapped Cap on the back and headed toward the door.

And behind him, at the table he had just left, a man continued to sit there. A man with a white beard and an old-style naval uniform, circa early 1900s. A man who just sat there as he had for so long, and would continue to do, shaking his head and murmuring over and over, "Damned iceberg. Goddamned iceberg."

And on his chest, hidden among various medals and service ribbons he'd received, a blood-tinged Starfleet communication badge sat unobtrusively and glinted faintly in the subdued lighting of the Captain's Table.

—THE CAPTAIN'S TABLE—

Where Sea Meets Sky

Christopher Pike

as recorded by
Jerry Oltion

For my brother, Ray,
who introduced me to Star Trek
and helped tune it in
by leaning out the basement window
to turn the beam antenna
while I fiddled with the knobs
on the black-and-white TV.
We did this even when it was 20 degrees below zero.
That's dedication.

Acknowledgments

The idea for the titans came from a convention panel a long time ago in Billings, Montana. We were trying to come up with plausible creatures that might live in space, and we designed something pretty close to what I describe here, but for whatever reason I never could find the right story to feature them in until now. They somehow seemed perfect for Captain Pike to discover, buried deep in a file cabinet in my study.

So for everyone in the audience that afternoon at Treasurecon III, and for Phil Foglio, who drew sketches during the panel (I still have those!)—a great big *Thank You!* Our crazy space whales have finally found their ocean.

One

Evening painted the sky orange, and a chill wind off the Bay made Christopher Pike shiver as he walked along San Francisco's waterfront. Red and yellow leaves swirled in the air and danced around the other pedestrians on the street. Coming toward him, a young couple struggled to keep control of both their hovercart full of baggage and their exuberant four- or five-year-old son, who called out happily as he passed, "We're going to Affa Centauri!"

"That's nice," said Pike, who had often traveled to Alpha Centauri and beyond. During his ten years as captain of the *Enterprise* he had gone many places indeed, most of them far more distant—and far more exotic—than Sol's nearest neighbor.

History moves in cycles, he thought as the family swept past. The street on which he walked had once been named the Embarcadero because it ran along the wharves, and it was from the wharves that people embarked on sailing ships in their travels around the world. When the age of ships had given way to the age of the airplane, the street had become a commercial center, full of warehouses at one end and tourist shops at the other, but nobody had set out on long journeys from there. Then had come space travel and the need for a good place to launch and land passenger ships. The airport was already too busy, and acreage elsewhere was at a premium for living space, so the fledgling industry had turned to the last open space near the sprawling city: the Bay. Now, four centuries after the Embarcadero's genesis, the same street was once again busy with travelers. They were boarding shuttles to take them into orbit rather than wooden ships that plied the ocean, but the spectacle of families struggling with overpacked bags looked the same no matter where they were headed.

Pike wished them all well, but he was glad to be on solid ground again. He'd done his time in space, and now he was putting that experience to use as fleet captain, assigned to Starfleet Headquarters right here on good old Mother Earth. He had the best of both worlds: an adventurous past and a position of responsibility on his own home planet.

So why did he feel so unfulfilled?

He'd been telling himself for the last year or so that he was just growing restless. It had been five years since he'd brought the *Enterprise* back home for refitting and renovation. He'd originally thought he would resume the conn when the ship was ready to fly again, but it had taken two years to replace all the worn and outdated machinery on board and to increase the crew compliment from 203 to 430, and by then Starfleet had already promoted him out of the job and given it to James Kirk. Pike didn't begrudge him the post; Kirk was a good officer, if a bit impulsive. He would do well if he didn't get himself killed in some defiant act of bravado. And Pike had come to enjoy his new position, but he had to admit he sometimes missed the thrill of facing the unknown.

Not very often, though. That thrill usually came hand in hand with mortal danger, and even when Pike survived it, other members of his crew often didn't. He had lost more friends than he cared to count during his decade on the *Enterprise,* and he had no desire to experience that again. Maybe some captains could go on after a crew fatality without blaming themselves, but he had never been able to. Every time it happened he went through days of anguish and self-recrimination. And every time he took the ship into danger again he worried that his actions would lead to more deaths.

No, he didn't envy Kirk the job.

Another gust of wind bit through his light topcoat. He had underdressed for the weather. Mark Twain had often said that the coldest winter he ever spent was a summer in San Francisco—well, he should have tried it in autumn. The western horizon was clear enough to allow a sunset, but the sky directly overhead threatened rain and the air was humid enough that it felt like mist already. Pike looked at the buildings along the waterfront, seeking a store he could duck into to warm up for a moment, and his eyes came upon a sign he hadn't seen before.

It was an old-style wooden sign, with letters carved deep into planks held together with black iron bands. It projected out over a windowless doorway and swung gently in the wind, its iron chain squeaking softly. The orange light of sunset made the words THE CAPTAIN'S TABLE stand out in bold relief on its rough surface.

Something about the place seemed inviting, yet Pike hesitated before the door. He couldn't very well just duck into a bar for a minute. He would have to order something, and it was a bit early in the evening to start drinking. That wasn't what he had come down here for anyway. He had merely wanted to get some exercise and some fresh air.

On the other hand, he didn't have any place special he had to be.

The first few drops of rain on his face decided him. He was willing to put up with cold, but cold and wet wasn't part of the plan. He reached for the wrought-iron handle on the solid door and tugged it open, noting a faint tingling sensation as he touched it. A security field of some sort? Or . . . a transporter? He turned and looked behind him. The Embarcadero was still there. Not a transport beam, then. It sure had felt like it, though.

"Close the door!" someone shouted from inside.

Pike nearly let it swing back into place without entering, but the rain was picking up so he ducked in and pulled the massive wooden slab closed behind him.

He couldn't tell who had spoken. Everyone in the bar was looking at him. There were a dozen or so people, mostly human, seated in twos and threes at tables between him and the bar itself, where a Klingon woman held down a stool and a tall, heavyset man stood on the other side, polishing a beer glass. The glasses were either very small, Pike thought, or the bartender had huge hands to go with the rest of his bulky frame.

Fortunately he also wore a smile to match. "Don't pay no mind to Jolley, there," he said. "That's just his way of saying 'Hello.' "

Pike nodded. He wouldn't. All his attention was on the Klingon woman. Not because of the unusual bony ridges on her forehead, nor her exotic face with wide, full lips and an enigmatic grin, nor even the ample cleavage revealed by her traditional open-chested battle garb, though Pike found the latter alluring enough for a second look. What drew his attention was the fact that she was there at all. The Klingon Empire and the Federation had been in conflict for nearly fifty years. All-out war seemed imminent, yet here sat a Klingon in a bar on the waterfront not a kilometer from Starfleet Headquarters.

She had to be a member of a peace delegation. She had probably snuck away from their hotel to check out Earth without a chaperone breathing down her neck. Maybe she thought she could seduce someone here in the bar and learn military secrets from them.

She had undoubtedly recognized Pike the moment he walked in. A fleet captain would be well known to the enemy. Well, Pike would keep his eye on her, too. One of the other patrons was no doubt a Secret Service agent assigned to tail her, but it wouldn't hurt to back him up.

He looked for a good place to sit. There was a piano to his immediate left, and a single small table wedged in next to the piano. A lizardlike alien with slits for eyes and talon-sharp fingers was sitting at the table, sipping at a glass full of something red. Pike didn't look too closely; he just nodded and stepped past, unbuttoning his jacket.

Most of the tables were to his left, clustered in a semicircle around a large stone fireplace that popped and flared as if it were burning real wood. The ones nearest the fire were obviously the popular places to sit. Pike didn't see any vacant tables there as he approached the bar.

"What'll you have, Captain?" the bartender asked.

Pike wasn't wearing a uniform, but he assumed the bartender called everyone "captain," after the name of the place. He looked to the mirrored shelves on the back wall to see what kind of stock they kept here, and was surprised to see several bottles of rare and expensive alien liqueurs in among the more common bourbons and gins. He was tempted to ask for Maraltian Seev-ale just to see if they had it, but he wasn't in the mood for the green stuff tonight. "Saurian brandy," he said instead. He had picked up the taste for that on the *Enterprise,* and it was still his favorite drink.

The bartender poured a snifter full from a curved, amber-colored bottle. Pike took a sip and smiled as the volatile spirits warmed their way down, then turned away to look for a quiet table. He didn't want to sit at the bar; he would either have to sit right next to the Klingon woman or close to a scruffy-looking fisherman who had taken a stool halfway between her and the wall.

There was a stairway to the right of the bar and two tables in an alcove between that stair and the front door. Neither table was occupied. Pike went over to the smaller of the two and sat facing the rear of the bar at an angle, neither turning his back on the others nor staring at them. He sipped his brandy and examined the decor while conversations started up again at the other tables.

There was plenty to look at. Artifacts from dozens of worlds hung on the walls. Pike saw drinking mugs with handles for nonhuman hands, wooden carvings of unrecognizable creatures, and metallic hardware that might have been anything from engine parts to alien sex toys. A Klingon *bat'leth* stuck out just overhead, its curved blade buried so deeply into the wood that Pike doubted anyone could remove it without a pry bar. A thick layer of dust on it provided evidence that few people even tried. A Vulcan harp hanging from a peg next to it apparently came down more often; there was no dust on it, and the strings were discolored near the fingerboard from use.

That was a good sign. Pike liked music better than fighting, too.

The fisherman belched loudly, then said to the bartender, "Another tankard o' grog." He looked over at Pike while the bartender refilled his stoneware mug. Pike looked away—the guy had a drunk and despondent air about him—but when the fisherman got his drink he stood up and walked over to Pike's table anyway.

"You look like a man who's got a lot on his mind," he said as he pulled out a chair and sat down uninvited. Pike could smell the salt and fish and seaweed on him.

"I suppose I might have," Pike admitted, "but I didn't really come here to talk."

The fisherman didn't take the hint. He leaned back in his chair—the wooden frame and leather seat squeaking under his weight even though he was lightly built—and said, "What then? To drink yourself into oblivion? I've tried that. It doesn't work."

Pike laughed softly. "I came in because it was cold outside and starting to rain."

"An admirable reason for a drink," said the fisherman. He took a gulp of his grog—Pike could smell the rum from across the table—and belched again.

How could he make this guy go away? "Get lost" would probably do it, but for all Pike knew this was the bar's owner. Or the Secret Service agent. "I'd really rather not—" he began, but the fisherman waved a hand in dismissal.

"Now me, I drink because my wife and son were killed on a prison colony."

His statement hung in the air between them like a ghost. The short, brutal intensity of those few words and the deep sadness with which they were spoken left Pike gasping for breath even as he tried to think of a response to them.

"I—I'm sorry to hear that" was all he could manage.

"Tortured to death," the man went on. "Right in front of me. A place called Rura Penthe."

What had Pike gotten himself into now? He looked up toward the bar, saw the Klingon woman flinch as she heard the name of the place, but he had no idea why. It meant nothing to him.

"They damned near killed me, too," his unwelcome companion went on. "Forced me to work in the mines, digging nitrates and phosphates for gunpowder while I held the secret that would make their puny chemicals obsolete overnight! I held it, too. Never told a soul. Saved the world, I did."

"I'm sure you must have," Pike said. "But perhaps you shouldn't be talking about it now, if it's such a dangerous secret."

The man laughed, a single, quick exhalation. "Ha! What do I care now? It's apparently old news. Nuclear power! Splitting the atom! The most elemental force of the universe—only two hours ago in this very bar someone told me it was nothing compared to antimatter annihilation. And that's apparently nothing compared to zero-point energy, whatever that is." He looked at Pike with eyes red as cooked shrimp. "I held my tongue for *nothing*."

Who *was* this guy? Talking as if the secret of nuclear fission was something new. Pike looked at him more closely. His clothing was rough, coarse cotton and wool dyed in drab brown and blue, and he wore a red bandanna around his neck. He had a high forehead and wide-set eyes, and he sported a two- or three-week beard that hadn't been trimmed since he'd started it, but his features underneath it were fair. And young. His general appearance had made him look older, but his hair was still coal black and his skin smooth. He couldn't be much over thirty-five, if that.

"Who are you?" Pike asked him.

"A fool, apparently," he replied. "One who's seen and suffered more than should be required of any man." He slurped noisily at his grog, then said softly, "At first I tried to serve humanity, then when I realized what I had discovered I tried to protect it, but now I find that I despise humanity and all it stands for." He looked Pike directly in the eyes and said, "And a man who despises humanity must needs despise himself as well. Many's the day I've wondered if I should put an end to it all."

Pike heard the sincerity in the man's voice, and his experience as a ship's captain raised the hackles on the back of his neck. Just his luck. He'd come out this evening to dwell on his own problems, and now it looked like he might have to talk someone out of suicide.

"Come now," he said. "Whatever your past, you're safe now. You're a free man, warm and dry with a drink in your hand and a roof over your head. Your future can be whatever you make of it." *Especially with a little psychiatric help,* he thought, but he left that unsaid.

"Oh, aye, I'm aware of that," said his unwelcome visitor. "I'm clever enough to make a go of it if I choose. I *have* made a go of it, come to that."

"Oh?" asked Pike. That sounded promising.

The fisherman took the bait. "Well, sir, not to brag, but I masterminded an escape from the prison island. I and twenty men stowed away in empty powder casks and let the stevedores load us on board a warship. It was cramped, but no worse than what we suffered in our barracks at night. And there was no worry of being mistreated in a powder cask!" He grinned, then took a drink. "We waited until the ship was at sea, then rose up in the night and took her. The men pronounced me 'captain,' and we became pirates of a sort, preying on our former captors until they brought in too many ships for us to match. We eventually took damage too heavy to repair ourselves, so we withdrew and set sail here for refitting." The glint faded from his eyes and he shook his head sadly. "It may not be worth the effort. Even if we return to Rura Penthe, no amount of battle has yet managed to vanquish the memory of what I have suffered."

The man told his story with the air of someone who believed every word. Yet how could any of it be true? A prison colony, in the twenty-third century? Mining nitrates for gunpowder? And transporting it by sailing ship? This guy was about four hundred years out of phase with the rest of the world.

Yet he was so convincing that Captain Pike actually looked around the bar again for confirmation that *he* wasn't somehow in the wrong time. He found it in abundance: the Klingon woman on her stool, the Vulcan harp overhead, the Saurian brandy in his glass. He took a sip of it and savored the tart, smoky explosion of flavor.

His gaze fell on the alien by the door. He had seen a few lizardlike humanoids in his travels, but never one like that. It was from an entirely new species. And its kind had to be fairly common for one to be here on Earth, unescorted, in a hole-in-the-wall bar in San Francisco. Pike wondered how he had missed hearing about them before this.

The fisherman—if that's what he was—noticed where Pike was looking. He shook himself out of his reverie and said, "Yes, strange things are about. But I've seen stranger."

"Have you now?" Pike asked, interested despite himself.

"Aye, that I have. Under the sea. Even a single fathom below the surface, everything is different."

"So I've heard," Pike said. He had grown up in Mojave, and even after he'd moved away he'd never felt comfortable in the water.

"So I've *seen,*" the seaman said. "Manta rays bigger than sails, fish with lanterns dangling before their noses so they can see in the black depths, pods of whales all the way to the horizon, making the sea boil as they breached and dove."

Now Pike knew the man was having him on. There hadn't been a whale on Earth for two centuries.

Well, if he was just telling tales then Pike had a few of his own to share. And maybe he could get this guy's mind off his troubles for a while. "I saw some whales once," he said. "But these weren't in the ocean."

His companion considered that a moment. "I've heard there are lakes in China where—"

"Not a lake, either. These were in space."

The man snorted, but when he spoke there was an air of sophistication that hadn't been there before. "Sir, you force me to express doubt."

Pike laughed out loud. "I didn't believe them myself when I first saw them, but they were real enough." He took a sip of brandy and settled back in his chair. "It was back when I was captain of the *Enterprise.* We were out in the Carrollia sector, mapping subspace anomalies and looking for new sources of dilithium, when we received a distress call from a planet called Aronnia. They had a problem with their interstellar fleet. Seems all their starships had run away. . . ."

Two

I WAS ON THE BRIDGE (SAID PIKE) WHEN THE CALL CAME IN. I HAD Communications Officer Dabisch put it on the main screen. A floor-to-ceiling image of Commander Brady, from Starbase 7, looked out of the screen at me and said, "Hello, Captain. How far are you from the Aronnia system?"

I looked over at my first officer, Lieutenant Commander Lefler, whom I generally called "Number One." She had been running the navigation console during our mapping sweep; she would know the figure or be able to retrieve it in seconds.

But Spock, my science officer, beat her to it. Without even consulting the computer he said, "Fourteen point two seven light-years."

Number One gave him a look that said plainly, "Thanks for nothing," but Spock's Vulcan upbringing practically guaranteed he wouldn't understand.

Brady merely smiled at what he no doubt thought was a simple case of one-upmanship among my bridge crew and said, "Close enough. We've just gotten an urgent request for assistance from the Aronnians. They were admitted to the Federation a few years ago under peculiar circumstances; their spaceflight capability is entirely biological. Now they've got some kind of problem with it, and they can't cross interstellar distances. They've asked for the loan of a starship until they can get things straightened out."

"Loan them a starship?" I asked, hardly believing my ears. "Not the *Enterprise?"* We were the pinnacle of Starfleet, a veritable city on the move. They wouldn't just loan us out as a taxi service, would they?

Commander Brady saw the concern on my face. "I want you to find out what their problem is and see if you can help them solve it. Failing that you can request a cargo transport or whatever's appropriate for them to use while they work on it themselves."

"Understood," I said.

"Very good. Brady out." His face blinked out, and the viewscreen switched back to the starfield we had been mapping.

Number One said, "Biotech? Sounds like a job for Dr. Boyce."

I laughed at the thought of our ship's chief medical officer waving his diagnostic scanners over a spaceship, but I wondered how far off that image would turn out to be. None of us had much experience with biotech. We would soon have quite a bit more, I imagined.

"Set course for Aronnia," I said. "Time warp, factor seven."

"Aye, sir," said Number One. She worked at her controls for a moment, then said, "Course locked in."

"Engage," I said. She fed power to the engines and we leaped away.

At warp seven we would get there in eight days. I hoped that would be soon enough, but I wasn't willing to overload the engines unless I knew for certain we needed to get there sooner, and this situation didn't seem that desperate.

Spock turned to his computer console and busied himself studying what we knew of Aronnia. I gave him a few minutes, listening to the busy bleeps and pings of the ship's instruments while I waited, then asked, "So, what's this place like, Mr. Spock?"

"Aronnia is a class-M planet," he replied. "Surface gravity point nine three standard gees, atmosphere twenty percent oxygen, seventy-eight percent nitrogen, and the rest trace gases. Three major landmasses, mostly desert in their interiors. There are twenty-three cities with populations greater than one million, seven hundred and—"

"How about the biotech?" I asked. Spock could get a bit didactic if you let him. "How do these spaceships of theirs work?"

Spock frowned. "The record is incomplete. The Aronnians were able to demonstrate interstellar flight capability to the scout team who discovered them, and they were invited to join the Federation on the basis of that ability, but apparently they consider the actual workings of their technology to be classified information. Later investigators were not allowed to board the ships, nor witness their construction."

"Do we have any visuals of them?" I asked.

"We do."

"Put it onscreen."

Spock did so, and I found myself looking at an oblong blob with fins sticking out the sides. It looked like an old-fashioned rocket ship, except it had a blunt nose with an enormous mouth, and the fins ended in tentacles. The fins were big, like the wind vanes on a blimp. In fact, that's what the whole starship looked like: a living blimp. There were eyes about a third of the way back; from the two on the side I could see I guessed there were four of them spaced ninety degrees apart around its circumference. The body tapered down to a narrow tail with two side-by-side bulges. From the bell-shaped nozzle one was clearly a rocket engine, but the other had no openings.

This wasn't just biotech, using self-replicating and self-healing organisms for various ship functions; this was one complete organism. "Their spaceships are living creatures!" I whispered.

"That is correct," Spock replied unnecessarily.

Its skin was gray-black, hard to spot against the darkness of space. A tiny silver bubble looked completely out of place on its back, like a single barnacle marring the smooth line of a ship's hull. Just at the limit of discernibility, I thought I could see faint markings on the silver dome.

"What's the scale on this?" I asked.

Spock turned to his computer console and said, "Here is the *Enterprise* for comparison."

The familiar saucer and warp nacelles of a Constitution-class starship appeared above the Aronnian "ship." We were larger, but only by a quarter of our length. That meant the "space whale," as I was already beginning to think of it, was at least two hundred meters long. I had never seen anything like it.

"Expand the silver dome on top," I said. Spock did so, and we could tell now that the markings I had seen were windows and an airlock. The Aronnians had tied a sealed habitat module to the creature's back. If their doors were of average size for most humanoid races, then the entire living space was only ten meters high and twenty across at the base.

"This is what they call a spaceship?" I asked incredulously.

"They do have more conventional craft for interplanetary travel," Spock replied, putting on the screen an image of a winged metal spaceplane. It looked boxy and primitive, with stubby wings for atmospheric flight and oversize reaction control rockets for spaceflight, but it looked like it should work well enough. It had no warp nacelles, though, and without them it would never leave its own solar system.

"But the space whale can travel from star to star?" I asked, just to be sure I was interpreting things correctly.

"That is what the record states," Spock replied. "I theorize that one of the two bulges at the tail of the creature—the one without a rocket nozzle—must be a warp engine."

Number One laughed. "How could a living creature develop a warp engine? Or a regular rocket for that matter? It's ridiculous."

"Yet it exists," said Spock.

There was no denying that.

"It must be the result of genetic engineering," said Dabisch. He scratched his left ear just under his transparent cranium. To someone who hadn't seen how many humanoid species filled the galaxy he would no doubt look like a genetics experiment himself, but the Galamites had evolved on their own, just like humans had.

"We don't know that," I told him. The clunky look of their interplanetary ships made me doubt that the Aronnians were capable of something that sophisticated. And if they were, why didn't they just breed smaller versions of the creatures for in-system use? It didn't add up, and we didn't have the information we needed to understand it. "Let's not jump to conclusions," I said. "If we do that we'll arrive with preconceived notions that we'll probably just have to unlearn. We're better off simply asking the Aronnians how it works when we get there."

"They were not forthcoming with information before this," Spock reminded me.

"They weren't asking for help before, either," I reminded him right back. But he had a point. They weren't likely to tell us any more than they had to, even if we were there to help.

When we arrived, I immediately had Spock scan for signs of the immense biological spaceships, but he reported none within sensor range. That meant none in the entire planetary system, since the *Enterprise*'s sensors would certainly have been able to pick up a life-form that large if one had been there.

There weren't many of the boxy in-system ships, either. Nor were there any satellites. Normally there are at least a few defense satellites around any inhabited planet, but Number One brought the *Enterprise* into a surprisingly empty orbit around Aronnia, and from all appearances nobody there even knew we had arrived until Communications Officer Dabisch hailed them.

His hail was answered immediately by a slender humanoid with large green eyes, silvery hair, and smooth brown skin with dark stripes on the forehead and cheeks. Its wide smile revealed even, white teeth, and its voice was softly melodious.

"I am Consil Perri, director of spaceflight," said the Aronnian. "Thank you for coming to our assistance."

"I'm Christopher Pike, captain of the *Enterprise,*" I said, wondering if I was talking to a male or a female. It probably shouldn't have mattered, but it always made me more comfortable to know, especially when I was talking with someone as close to the human phenotype as this. It made for fewer misunderstandings. Trouble was, you couldn't just ask an alien—no matter how humanoid it looked—what its gender was. Some societies would consider it too personal for discussion with an outsider, and others might consider it an insult. A Klingon would probably try to kill someone who asked that question. I had no idea what an Aronnian would do, so I merely kept my eyes and ears open for clues while I said, "We're told you have a problem with your starships."

"That's right," said Perri. "They haven't returned from their annual migration."

"Migration?" I asked. I glanced over at Spock, whose poker face revealed none of the intense interest I was sure he felt. Biotech was different enough, but we did at least have some experience with that on a limited scale. Starships that migrated were something entirely new.

The Aronnian hesitated, evidently unwilling to divulge more than was necessary about their technology, but after a moment's consideration said, "Every year the titans leave for a neighboring star system called Devernia, where they mate and raise their young. They return here to feed in the atmospheres of our gas-giants planets. For the last few years their numbers have been dwindling, but this year the migration stopped completely. We sent messages to the Devernians asking if they knew what had happened, but we got no response, so we sent the few tame titans we had kept with us to go see for ourselves, but they never returned. We are now out of starships, so we are asking you to help us investigate."

"I see," I said, feeling the hair on the back of my neck start to tingle. I hated going into situations where other ships were known to have disappeared, even if those others appeared much less capable than we were of defending themselves from attack. *Something* had happened to them, and we would no doubt have to face that something as well. It had apparently silenced the Devernians, too. If it was anything like what we had seen already, it would be completely different from anything we had faced before.

Headlong into the unknown, with danger waiting when we got there. I knew what I was getting into when I signed up with Starfleet, but at times like these I wondered if it had been a mistake. Nevertheless, that was what we were here for, so I said to Perri, "Very well, let us beam you aboard and we'll go have a look."

Three

Captain Pike paused in his story. The fisherman, or escaped prisoner or sea captain or whoever he was, had a puzzled expression on his face. "Something wrong?" asked Pike.

The seaman shrugged slightly. "Have you ever experienced the feeling that someone is using English but they're nonetheless speaking a foreign tongue?"

"Ah," said Pike. "Sorry. I sometimes forget that not everybody has been in space."

The seaman drained his near-empty mug. "I am still struggling with the idea that *anybody* has. But you tell a convincing tale, Captain. I am willing to believe in your *Enterprise,* and in these 'titans' you speak of as well. I want to hear what you discovered at Devernia, but I fear I must replenish my beverage before we continue. May I get one for you?"

This would be the opportunity to say, "My, look at the time; sorry, but I have to be somewhere at seven." Pike considered it, but he had been enjoying his reminiscence despite the somewhat unusual company. And besides, the Klingon woman was still at the bar. She had stopped talking with the bartender and was listening to Pike now, drinking from a pewter tankard of Warnog as she eavesdropped. When she saw him hesitate, she smiled at him, her pointed teeth making it both an invitation and a challenge. Typical Klingon. Pike glanced at her openly displayed cleavage again before he looked away; if that was typical as well, Klingon men were happier at home than they seemed in public.

Pike felt a bit surprised to realize that he enjoyed her attention. He even enjoyed the seaman's attention. What had started out as a gloomy walk on a rainy day had turned into an interesting, if unusual, evening, one that he was in no hurry to end.

"Yes, thank you," he said to his drinking companion. "I'm having Saurian brandy." Pike drained his snifter and handed it over.

"Very good. I shall return." The seaman stood and walked to the bar, narrowly missing someone who had just come down the stairway. He did a theatrical double take when he saw that he had nearly run down a peach-colored felinoid woman, but when she smiled and said, "Hi there, sailor," in an exaggerated drawl, he merely shook his head and continued on his way.

Pike watched her cross the bar and sit at a table with two young human men. Her graceful body was covered in short fur, but in deference to human custom—or maybe just to enhance her natural charms—she also wore a tight bodysuit of iridescent material that flashed between white and pale violet when she moved. She laughed at something one of the men said, and Pike smiled at the sound of her voice. He had always been a cat person.

When he looked over to the bar again he saw that the Klingon woman was scowling. That, too, was typical. Klingons hated anything soft or delicate or beautiful. No, that wasn't fair. It wasn't hate they felt, but disdain. Klingons valued strength and honor above all else, and had little respect for anyone who didn't feel likewise.

Pike glanced at the cat-woman again, then back at the Klingon, glad he could appreciate both kinds of beauty. But he wondered what had happened to the Klingon's forehead. Some kind of accident? If so, it looked pretty serious. That looked like ridges of bone just under the surface.

Beside the Klingon at the bar, the seaman reached into a pocket and withdrew a metal coin, which he held out to the bartender. It shone bright gold in the light. The bartender held out his hands and shook his head, smiling as he did so, and the seaman shrugged and pocketed the coin. Pike wondered once again just who this person was, but his first attempt to ask had been turned aside, and as with the Aronnian director of spaceflight, he didn't want to risk trouble by pushing too hard for an answer. He would learn it in time.

The seaman returned with Pike's brandy and a second snifter of it for himself instead of the grog he was drinking earlier. "I decided to broaden my horizons," he said as he handed one to Pike. "It smells intriguing."

"It is that," Pike replied. "Potent, too. Go easy on it." He held up his glass. "Cheers."

"Cheers," the seaman replied. They drank, and his eyes widened. "Whoo!" he said when he could breathe again. "Whoever the Saurians are, they know a thing or two about brandy."

"True enough," Pike said.

"I did, too, at one time." The seaman's expression faltered, but he settled into his chair and said, "So then, where were we? You were about to face certain death at Devernia, I believe. . . ."

Four

So I feared, anyway (said Pike). The Aronnian seemed a bit nervous as well, especially after beaming aboard, but I couldn't tell if that was from being reduced to elementary particles and rebuilt in our ship's transporter, or from the prospect of what faced us at our destination. Or perhaps it was the ship itself. I had gone down to the transporter room to welcome our new passenger and offer him a guided tour of the *Enterprise,* but we had just boarded the turbolift for the bridge when I noticed that his normally wide eyes were even wider than usual and he was clutching the handgrip for dear life.

After seeing him in person, I had decided that Perri was male. I still couldn't see any obvious secondary sexual characteristics, but that very lack argued for masculinity. Plus there was something in the way he carried himself, an indefinable combination of attitude and bearing that spoke to me even across the species barrier.

His apprehension in the turbolift didn't change that. I didn't ask what was the matter; that, too, could be a mortal offense in some cultures. I merely said to the computer, "Cancel bridge. Take us to deck six." To Perri I said, "Let me show you to your quarters first. There'll be plenty of time to tour the ship when you've settled in."

Perri laughed softly. "You are most kind, Captain, but I will be fine. It merely struck me how large your vessel must be, in order to need a transportation system just to move about within it."

"It's pretty big," I admitted. "But these beasts you ride—'titans,' you call them?—are nearly the same size. I would think you'd be used to spaceships of this scale."

"Our ships may be large overall, but the passenger space is small. Titans do not like to carry large structures." Perri looked at the marker lights flashing past just beyond the turbolift's translucent window. "As for me personally, this is my first time in space, though I must admit it hardly seems like I've gone anywhere."

"Oh, we're definitely in space," I said. "Your stateroom has a nice view directly out the starboard side. We're still in orbit; you'll probably be able to see Aronnia from there."

"I will?" He really *hadn't* been in space before. You can always tell a dirtsider by the twinkle in their eyes at the idea of seeing their planet from above.

The turbolift stopped at deck six and the doors slid open on the circular corridor that ran around the perimeter of the *Enterprise*'s saucer section. "Here we are," I said, stepping off and gesturing for Perri to follow. As we walked along toward the guest quarters, Perri staring at everything and peeking into every nook and cranny we passed, I said, "I would have thought the director of spaceflight would get into orbit quite regularly. Maybe even live there."

He laughed again. "Oh no, Captain. It's much too dangerous for that. Space is for the adventurous."

"That's true enough," I agreed, remembering all the dangers I had encountered during my years in Starfleet. And I had seen what the Aronnians used for ships, both interplanetary and interstellar. I wouldn't want to trust my life to them either. But I didn't really know that much about them, did I? I had been too busy trying to decide whether my passenger was male or female to learn more about the ships.

That, at least, I could simply ask about. I might not get much response, but it was worth a try. "So tell me more about these titans," I said. "Who does ride them? And how do you control them?"

Perri said nothing. I turned to see if I had given offense, but I couldn't detect any difference in his expression. "It's . . . complicated," the Aronnian said at last. "You see—"

Just then Yeoman Colt came around the bend in the corridor, holding a datapad in one hand while she tugged her strawberry blond hair into a ponytail and tried to tie it in place. She abandoned the effort when she saw me, letting her hair fall down around her oval face to her shoulders as she said, "Captain, I was just heading to the bridge to see you. I have those inventory figures you wanted."

I had been concerned about perishable supplies, since it had been some time since we had put in at a starbase. "Thank you, Yeoman," I said, taking the datapad from her. Nodding to each of them in turn, I said, "Yeoman Colt, Director of Spaceflight Perri of Aronnia."

If I had any remaining doubt over Perri's gender, the looks they gave one another erased it completely. Their eyes might as well have been sending out tractor beams by the way they locked together. Colt's pale skin turned light pink. The dark stripes on Perri's forehead and cheeks grew darker still.

"Um, pleasure to meet you," Colt said, offering her hand.

"Yes," he replied. "It is." He grasped her hand, held it in his for a moment—clearly unsure what our customs were—then let go and said to me, "My delight with your ship grows with each passing moment, Captain."

Colt blushed even more. I felt myself grow slightly annoyed by the attention he was paying her. She was my yeoman, after all, and he was on a mission that could have serious consequences for his home planet. He had best keep his mind on business if he wanted to accomplish anything.

I didn't say so, of course. I merely said, "I was just showing Mr. Perri to his quarters."

Colt nodded. "Yes sir. I made sure guest suite number one was prepared. If you need anything else," she said to Perri, "just ask."

"I will," he replied, and I knew he would.

"Thank you, Yeoman," I said again, and I led the Aronnian away to his quarters.

He forgot all about Yeoman Colt the moment the door slid aside. "Oh," he said, stopping in the doorway and looking out at the starfield beyond the windows. The guest suite has three large windows in each of its two rooms. They lean outward, following the curve of the ship's hull, so a person can actually lie down against them and get the sensation of flying through space. The ship's artificial gravity gets a bit odd that close to the edge of the field, pulling to all sides rather than down, but that merely adds to the impression of free flight. Perri didn't try that right away; it was all he could do to step inside and let the door slide closed behind us.

He stood rooted to the spot for maybe half a minute. I didn't rush him. When a person encounters the vastness of the universe for the first time, he generally needs a while to soak it all in. Perri finally started moving again on his own, taking slow steps closer and closer to the windows until he stood right in front of one, holding on to the edge of the deep-set frame for support.

"Oh," he said again. I came up beside him and looked out. Aronnia carved out a white, blue, and brown arc below us. I noticed that the continents stood out in sharp detail under sparse cloud cover—Spock hadn't been making up that bit about "mostly desert." The atmosphere blurred the boundary between planet and space ever so slightly, softening the impression a little, but the planet looked harsh and uninviting to me.

Not so to Perri. He took a deep breath and said, "Many have died for a chance to see this. I have often wondered if we were right in pursuing such a risky dream, but now I know. This alone makes it worthwhile."

"The director of spaceflight, a skeptic?" I asked. "You surprise me again and again."

He turned away from the window to look at me. "Even the most vocal advocate can harbor doubts. When you control as risky a venture as I do, your doubts practically define your life. I worry about every mission as though my own children were at risk."

I remembered stories from the dawn of human spaceflight, when hundreds of controllers would fidget during a manned mission, entire rooms full of people smoking addictive tobacco to calm their nerves while they waited for disaster to strike the astronauts and cosmonauts in orbit. We had come a long way since then, but I imagined that some fleet captains back home still bit their nails to the quick for every starship they sent into the void.

For that matter, I worried enough about my own crew to understand how Perri felt. The *Enterprise* was far stronger than any of the Aronnians' ships, but we were still a fragile bubble of humanity compared to some of the forces waiting for us in deep space.

One of which might be waiting for us later today. Devernia was only a few hours away.

The sooner we got there, the sooner we would find out what we faced. I said, "It's time we were going. Would you like to accompany me to the bridge, or would you rather watch the trip from here?"

"Oh, the bridge by all means," Perri said, turning nonetheless reluctantly away from the window. I suspected he would pull the bed over so the stars were right over his head when he slept here that night.

He seemed completely at ease in the turbolift this time, and when we arrived at the bridge he broke into a big smile. "It's round," he said. "And domed overhead. It looks just like the control pod on a titan." Then he took in all the science and navigation instruments and said, "Considerably more advanced, of course."

I introduced him to the bridge crew. He looked at Spock for a long moment, no doubt wondering about the Vulcan's pointed ears and green hue, but when he looked over to Dabisch his mouth fell open. The Galamite's transparent cranium, glowing fuschia eyes, and scaly purple skin must have seemed like a hallucination.

"Pleased to meet you," said Dabisch, who was used to it by now even though he'd only been on board for a few months.

His voice has a distinctive timbre to it, a hum like a low-frequency carrier wave that his vocal cords modulated for sound. "We spoke earlier," Perri replied when he heard it.

"Yes," replied Dabisch. "I did not use video when I set up the call. I have found that it leads to confusion when the rest of the crew turns out to be human."

"I can see how that could be a problem," said Perri. He turned back to me. "You do have an . . . um . . . interesting ship."

"Thank you," I said. Our regular navigator, Lieutenant Tyler, was back at the controls. "Mr. Tyler, set course for Devernia, warp factor seven. Let's go see what happened to the titan migration."

"Aye, sir," he said, calculating the coordinates and sending the information to Number One at the helm controls beside him.

I nodded toward the main viewscreen, on which the image from straight ahead was displayed. Aronnia curved away to left and right, and stars glinted steadily above. When Number One engaged the warp engines, however, all that changed in an instant. Aronnia whirled crazily around, first to the left, then overhead as the *Enterprise* came around to the right coordinates. Then it vanished like a punctured balloon and the stars leaped toward us in long white streaks.

Perri gripped the handrail that encircled the command and helm stations, but internal gravity had kept us from feeling a thing. He let go with visible reluctance, and said, "I don't believe it's this smooth riding a titan."

"I suspect not," I admitted.

Devernia was less than two light-years away, but we still had a few hours to kill before we got there even at warp seven. I let Spock and Dabisch show our guest around the bridge while I went over the supply report that Yeoman Colt had given me; then, when I was satisfied that we wouldn't starve before we reached our next starbase, we went back downship for lunch. Dr. Boyce joined us in the cafeteria, first scanning our guest with his medical tricorder to make sure none of our foods would poison him.

"Stay away from onions and garlic, but otherwise it looks like we're fairly compatible," Boyce told him when he was done.

I smiled when he said that, since I had just been thinking how his white hair was nearly the same color as Perri's. There was a certain similarity about their faces, too, though one was marked with stripes and the other with worry lines. Their size was their biggest difference. Boyce was taller and heavier, big even for a human. He may have been older than the average starship crewman, but he was all muscle. Perri was thin and wiry, but at first glance he and Boyce could have been father and son.

Boyce questioned him like a father grills a son who comes home late from his first date, that much was sure. "What kind of metabolism do these titans of yours have?" he asked before he'd taken his first forkful of vegetables. "How do you control them?" "How intelligent are they?" And so on.

Perri answered some of his questions, but diverted others. Titans were fairly intelligent, he said, but only in certain ways. They were very territorial, for instance, and would band together to protect their feeding grounds—which presented quite a problem for anyone who wanted to approach one of the Aronnian system's gas-giant planets. The titans scooped raw materials directly out of their atmospheres, dropping out of orbit to make a blazing, meteoric run through the upper regions with their immense mouths unfolded to ten times their body width.

"That must be quite a sight," Boyce said. "What are they going for in the atmospheres? Hydrogen? Or do they filter out life-forms for food?"

"Both," said Perri. "They use the hydrogen for fuel and reaction mass, and the tiny airborne creatures for nourishment."

"Pretty slick system. Must save you a bundle on fuel and construction costs. How'd you develop something like that, anyway?"

Perri was picking at his green beans, but I suspected it wasn't the food he was concerned with. "Um, yes, it certainly does provide cost-effective spaceflight," he said. "You must understand, however, that I cannot discuss the details of their production. That would compromise Aronnian trade secrets."

"Hmmph." Boyce was a scientist; he wasn't the kind to let trade secrets get in the way of understanding. But Perri was obstinate; he would tell us only that the creatures were a relatively new development, and that the population was self-sustaining once established. "We also use . . . um . . . by-products of the technology for manufacturing. It's an important part of our economy. We have considered exporting titans to other star systems," he said, "but naturally we want to make sure we retain control of the technology if we do. From what we've seen of the Federation we're a relatively young race, and that's the only real trade item we have to offer."

Boyce shrugged. "You never know what's useful and what isn't, except of course for booze. That outsells practically everything else. You got any good alcoholic beverages to export?"

"We're introducing a distilled liqueur through an independent distributor named Harcourt Fenton Mudd. He promised us a large return on our investment, but so far sales have been disappointing."

I didn't know this Mudd fellow from Adam, but I said, "Be careful of independent contractors. Most of them are reputable, but there are some shady characters out there. You're better off dealing directly with planetary governments."

"We are beginning to understand that," admitted Perri. "That is why we are proceeding more slowly with the titans."

"How come they migrate?" Boyce asked. "That seems to be a big weakness, especially considering your current situation."

Perri ate the last of his dinner roll and washed it down with coffee, though I could tell from his expression that he didn't particularly care for Centauri roast. "We do seem to have made a miscalculation, haven't we?" he asked. "I can only hope it isn't as serious as it seems." He turned to me. "Captain, it was late evening my time when you picked me up, and I find that this meal has made me somewhat drowsy. Is there time for me to take a short nap before we arrive in the Devernia system?"

"Yes, certainly," I told him. "I'll wake you before we get there."

"Thank you." He rose from the table, and Dr. Boyce and I got up as well, but he motioned us back down. "You need not interrupt your own meals. I think I can find my way. If not, there seem to be plenty of people to ask directions."

That was true enough. "Very well," I said. "Pleasant dreams."

When he left the cafeteria, Dr. Boyce said, "He's hiding something."

"He admits he's hiding something," I reminded him.

"I think he's hiding something else."

"Maybe. I'll be taking us out of warp with shields up, that's for sure."

"Good idea," Boyce said. "And I'm going to count our spoons while he's on board. I wish you hadn't given him free run of the ship."

I laughed. "Critical systems are always under guard when guests are on board, you know that. Besides, where can he go? Unless he's got a pocket full of titan seeds—and the whole cargo deck to grow one in—I think we've got him pretty well under wraps."

"I hope so," said Boyce. "But something about him doesn't feel right."

I'd learned to take his opinions seriously. He was one of the *Enterprise*'s first crew members, after all. He'd served under Captain April before me, and he'd examined more aliens more closely than I ever would.

"Okay," I said. "I'll keep my eye on him too. But I'm expecting more trouble from whatever's ahead of us than from him."

My hunch proved correct. When we dropped out of warp, Perri was rested and standing beside me on the bridge. The computer had reported him in his quarters the entire time. Whatever he might be hiding, he had caused no trouble so far, and he was as horrified as I was by the scene we encountered near Devernia.

There was an all-out battle going on. We had approached from a distance, far beyond synchronous orbit around the system's one habitable planet, but that wasn't far enough. The viewscreen was full of titans, their dark bodies eclipsing the stars and their rocket exhaust drawing bright lines through the darkness. Smaller spacecraft darted in and out among them, and the flash of deep-space explosions were visible even under low magnification. The collision alarm sounded almost immediately. "Incoming missile," Spock reported.

"Evasive action," I ordered, but Number One said, "It's too close. It's going to hit us."

"Red alert!" I said. "Brace for impact." I gripped the arms of my chair as the claxon began to wail. Perri, beside me, grasped the handrail. As I had promised Dr. Boyce, we had dropped out of warp with the shields up. They would absorb an explosion, but the inertial damping fields couldn't compensate instantaneously for the shock.

The viewscreen lit up with the flash, then went dark as the outside sensors were momentarily overloaded. The ship lurched, lights blinked, and sparks flew from the navigation controls. Lieutenant Tyler cursed and jumped up from his chair, but a second later he was back at his post, ascertaining the damage. Number One, beside him at the helm controls, had hardly flinched.

The ship steadied out, and the starfield slowly returned to view. In it we could see the ion trails of many small spacecraft under power, and hundreds of titans sweeping gracefully around them. Devernia was a bright crescent against the stellar backdrop, peppered with the black silhouettes of the swirling combatants.

"Damage report?" I asked.

"Navigation is down," Tyler reported.

"Helm's not responding," Number One said. "Switching to backup control systems."

"Shields at ninety percent and falling," said Spock. "Radiation damage to starboard warp nacelle. Warp engines off-line." The lights blinked again, and his screen filled with more information. "Impulse engines also off-line. Main power off-line."

We wouldn't last long under auxiliary power. I jabbed the intercom switch on the arm of my command chair, years of experience guiding my fingers almost instinctively to the right button, and said, "Engineering, get that power back on!"

A moment later I got my response. Unfortunately it wasn't the resurgence of power I wanted, but just a worried-sounding technician who said, "We're working on it."

The air stank of burned electronics. I turned to look at Spock, unsure I had heard him properly. "Radiation damage? What kind of radiation?"

"The missile carried a fission warhead. Relatively low yield—I estimate less than twenty kilotons—but the nuclear reaction produced a neutron and gamma ray flash that was nearly as deadly as the explosion itself."

I could hardly believe my ears. Bombs. The Devernians were throwing nuclear bombs at each other.

Five

THE SEAMAN SLAMMED HIS BRANDY SNIFTER TO THE TABLE, BREAKING THE pedestal right off the stem. He hardly noticed in his agitation.

"That's exactly what I was afraid of!" he said. "The same reaction that could drive a ship around the world on an ounce of fuel could also wipe out a city in the blink of an eye." He noticed his broken glass, drained the brandy in a single swallow, then set the glass upside down next to its pedestal and said, "But your *Enterprise* was evidently made of sterner stuff. Why wasn't it vaporized in the blast?"

Captain Pike shrugged. "We would have been if we weren't shielded. Even so, we took damage. The shields are mostly good against phasers and photon torpedoes. We weren't ready for the radiation or the electromagnetic pulse. *That* was the real problem. Warp engines are essentially big coils of wire, you know—"

"No, I didn't," the seaman said.

Pike didn't let the interruption derail his train of thought. "They are. And the pulse induced an enormous current in them. It surged straight down the main power bus into the matter-antimatter reaction chamber, where it diverted the antimatter stream for a moment, which tripped all the alarms and shut down the engines. And that in turn put us on battery power in the middle of a battle. Plus another pulse traveled to the bridge on the navigation control lines and fried our helm."

Out of the corner of his eye he saw the Klingon woman at the bar and he suddenly realized she was listening intently to his every word. Of course she would be; details of how to cripple a Federation starship would be worth a fortune on her homeworld. "Of course we've upgraded our shield technology to prevent that from happening again," he said loudly.

She grinned at him with her pointed teeth. "Of course," she said. She held his gaze for a moment longer, then turned to the bartender and whispered something to him.

The seaman had contained his agitation. "I apologize, Captain," he said softly. "It was a great shock to learn that my fears as well as my triumph had already come to pass, but I see that they are apparently old news as well." He shook his head sadly. "I must have been on the prison island longer than I imagined."

Pike didn't know how to respond to that, so he decided to change the subject. "I don't know your name," he said. "Mine's Pike. Christopher Pike."

The seaman nodded. "I gathered that from your tale." He hesitated, frowned, then said, "Considering my current profession, I fear you will have to call me no one."

"That's not much to call a man you're drinking with," Pike said.

"It is if you spell it N-O-W-A-N," said the seaman. "Nowan is a family name of long-standing nobility."

"It just doesn't happen to be yours," Pike said, not bothering to hide his disappointment.

"Ah, but it is," said the seaman. "It describes me, and I answer to it. The rest of my family is dead, so I leave nobody orphaned by my choice. I am Nowan."

Pike couldn't decide whether to point out the psychological implications of what "Nowan" had just said, or simply let it go. The Klingon woman decided the issue for him when she walked over from the bar with two more snifters of Saurian brandy and set them down on the table. "I noticed you were out," she said, gathering up Pike's empty glass and the pieces of the seaman's broken one.

"Thank you," both men said automatically. She didn't reply; merely turned away and walked back to the bar.

Pike took one of the glasses and sniffed it. No detectable poisons. Of course that left a couple of thousand undetectable ones she might have dropped in it, but he didn't think the odds of that were very high. She wouldn't risk an interplanetary incident just to kill a fleet captain. She was probably hoping to get him drunk and learn more about the *Enterprise*'s weaknesses.

Fat chance of that. Pike hadn't been born yesterday. He raised his glass slightly in her direction, nodded to her, and took a sip. The rush of evaporating spirits on his tongue felt the same as usual.

He wasn't going to get much more out of this Nowan, he could tell. And in truth, that was as good a name as any. So he leaned back in his chair and picked up his story. "As I was saying, we're better equipped to handle fission bombs now, but at the time we were dead in space, with more missiles coming right down our throats. . . ."

Six

We had a few seconds before the next impact. We couldn't maneuver, but we did have weapons of our own. "Target phasers on those missiles," I ordered. "Fire."

Number One and Tyler both reached to their weapons controls. Red beams of energy shot outward, spearing the two approaching missiles and exploding them at a safe distance.

As the billowing clouds of superheated gas expanded into nothing, Number One consulted her instruments and said, "Sir, neither of those missiles were aimed at us. Nor the first one either, apparently."

"Who are they shooting at, then?" I asked.

"It looks like the titans. We were just unlucky enough to get in the way. Look." She pointed to the upper right corner of the screen, where the bright spark of another missile reached out for one of the magnificent beasts.

I could hardly hear her over the wail of the red-alert klaxon. "Cancel red alert," I said, "and expand that view." The image grew to fill the screen. The titan was firing its fusion engine, turning to get away from the approaching missile. But it was running the wrong way!

"Go *across* the flight path, not with it!" I whispered, feeling the agony of anyone who has ever watched a cartoon hero try to outrun a rolling boulder. But the titan was smarter than I had given it credit for; it wasn't just running. It was using its fusion exhaust as a weapon, spraying the million-degree plasma into the path of the oncoming missile.

It would have worked if the missile hadn't been so small. The titan's superheated plume of exhaust swept across it once, but the missile dodged and kept coming, and before the titan could correct its aim, it struck.

For a moment it appeared as if the warhead was a dud, but then I realized it had merely been fused to go off *after* impact, so it would concentrate its force inside its target. That was an effective strategy; the entire rear half of the titan's body erupted in a white-hot fireball, throwing a spherical cloud of ejecta outward into space. The front half tumbled end over end, spewing blue-green blood and entrails and charred flesh in a vast pinwheel.

Perri, standing beside me, moaned at the sight. Number One frowned and looked away. I felt the contents of my stomach shift, but I forced myself to watch. I might learn something about Devernian battle tactics.

The ship that had fired the missile let the corpse drift without further assault. It was a small, primitive craft like the ones the Aronnians used for in-system flight, but it was light and agile. It darted around among the titans like a bee among flowers, never keeping to a straight path for more than a few seconds. The titans, being so much more massive, couldn't follow it—and for some reason they weren't using their warp drives to get away either.

Agility was about the only thing to recommend the Devernian ship. Its missiles were mounted in racks outside the hull, vulnerable to attack. They used simple reaction drives; I could see black streaks along the fuselage from their rocket exhaust. The ship had no shields, no warp engines, and from the way it maneuvered on tongues of bright yellow flame I suspected it used chemical propellant. I would have laughed at their rudimentary technology if the *Enterprise* weren't drifting crippled in space because of it.

"The titans," Perri said, his voice full of anguish. "We have to protect the titans."

"We'll do what we can," I said, "but we can't stop that many fighters. Mr. Dabisch, open a channel to one of those ships."

"Yes sir." I heard bleeps and whistles as the ship's computer tried to establish a connection, but after a moment Dabisch replied, "No one answers our hail."

"Are they talking with one another? Break into their communications channels."

"There is no regular message traffic. Occasional burst transmissions only. It appears each craft is operating autonomously." Dabisch turned back to his board, saying, "There is also considerable microwave emission coming from the titans themselves. I detect no meaningful patterns there, either. It appears to be a radar locating system."

"Is that how they navigate?" I asked Perri.

He nodded. "Yes. They also use the questing beam to locate food. And, one would hope, Devernian attackers."

"Doesn't look like it's doing them much good." I tried the intercom again. "Engineering, what's your status?"

The same junior tech who'd replied the first time said, "Uh . . . we've got a lot of fried circuitry down here, Captain, but we'll have main power back in a moment. Impulse power should be restored along with it. Warp power will take a bit longer."

"Keep on it," I said. "We may need those engines soon."

"Understood."

"There goes another one!" Perri exclaimed, pointing at the viewscreen where a tiny ship had fired a missile at another titan. "Captain, you must stop this carnage."

I didn't really want our first act in the Devernian system to be hostile, but neither did I want to stand by and watch more of this slaughter. And we *had* tried to communicate.

"Target that missile," I said. "And this time fire a warning shot across the bow of the ship that launched it, too. Don't hurt them, but I want to get their attention."

"Yes sir," said Number One.

The ship's phasers lanced out twice. The missile vanished in a puff of vapor; the second shot came close enough to fry the paint on the ship's forward hull.

"That was probably a bit tight," I said.

"Sorry," said Number One. "I forgot these ships aren't shielded."

The Devernian craft swiveled around with tiny bursts from its chemical thrusters until it was pointed at the *Enterprise;* then its main engine sprayed flame and it accelerated toward us. "Well, we certainly got their attention, anyway," I said. "Get ready for incoming missiles. Don't let them even get *close* to us."

"Yes, sir."

We waited nervously while the Devernian ship drew closer. I glanced over at Perri, who gripped the handrail next to my command chair. He was breathing hard and studying the viewscreen intently, but I thought I could see a faint hint of a smile on his face. Who'd have thought he would turn out to be the type who enjoyed battle? Or maybe he didn't understand how precarious our position was. Two other ships broke away from the titans they were chasing and came toward us as well. "This doesn't look good," I said.

"I detect low-power laser emissions from all three craft," Dabisch said. "Not a communication signal. Possibly guidance for their missiles."

"Jam it," I told him.

The first ship fired a missile. Number One didn't wait to see if it could lock on to us; she fired the phasers at it as soon as she had a clear shot.

Both of the other ships fired as well. They were farther away, though, so I said, "Hold up a second. Let's see what happens."

Number One waited with her finger poised over the fire button. The missiles raced toward us—but the first one veered ever so slightly to the left and the second one angled overhead. Our jamming signal was apparently doing something, at least.

"Let them go," I said. "Save power." The phasers drew energy directly from the main power banks; we didn't have much reserve without the matter-antimatter generators on line.

We watched the two incoming missiles search in vain for a target, but then the closest ship fired another one. It was near enough that I didn't want to take a chance. "Shoot that one down," I ordered.

She did so. The two other missiles swerved toward the explosion, then lost their focus as it dissipated. One must have struck a piece of shrapnel; it flared into a yellow ball of flame as its fuel tanks ruptured, but its nuclear warhead didn't explode.

The other one, however, suddenly locked on target and accelerated again—not at us or at the remains of the other rocket, but straight at the closest of the three Devernian ships.

"Stop that missile," I ordered.

Number One moved to comply, but just then the lights flickered again and her targeting computer lost its fix. The phaser shot went too high, and by the time Number One could fire again more accurately, the missile had nearly reached its target.

The explosion sent the tiny ship fluttering like a leaf. A white fog of escaping air billowed out around it. The hull had been breached.

I hit the intercom switch again, this time a couple of buttons down from engineering. "Transporter room, lock on to the disabled ship off our port bow. Transport any survivors out of there immediately."

"Scanning for life-forms," came the reply. "I've found one. Transporting. . . . He doesn't look good. Sickbay, Dr. Boyce to transporter room one on the double."

The transporters and sickbay were both on the same deck for just that reason. The few seconds it took to get a patient from the receiving platform into the turbolift and out again could mean the difference between life or death.

Dr. Boyce would save the injured Devernian if anyone could. And just in case he wasn't as badly hurt as it sounded, I sent a security team to meet them and make sure we didn't let a hostile alien loose on board the ship.

In the meantime, we were still under attack from outside.

"That flicker had better have been main power going on line," I said.

"Affirmative," said Spock. "Shields are now at full strength. Impulse engines are operational again."

"Then take us out of here," I ordered.

Number One complied immediately. The safest place in a battle is usually behind your enemy; the viewscreen image swirled around with dizzying speed, then we shot right past one of the approaching ships before it could fire another missile at us. Number One didn't bring us around for a counterattack, however, but continued on into deep space.

"Where to now?" she asked.

"Back into the fray, of course," said Perri. "We must protect the titans!"

"There are thousands of them," Number One said. "And hundreds of Devernian ships. We can't stop them all."

Perri slapped the handrail. "We must! What they are doing here is insane. If we let them continue, they will exterminate the titans, and our livelihood with it."

He had a better opinion of our chances than I did, but I wasn't exactly happy with what I saw, either. I looked at the viewscreen for a moment, trying to get a handle on the situation. Activity seemed centered around the Devernian home planet. The titans had drawn into a dozen or so tight groups for protection from their attackers, a strategy that might have worked fine against an enemy similar to themselves, but against nuclear weapons it was the worst strategy possible. The Devernians only needed to shoot into the herd, and they were practically guaranteed to hit something every time.

Space was littered with the corpses of dead titans. At first I hadn't noticed, since their skin was so dark, but the more I looked the more I saw. Thousands—perhaps millions—of slaughtered beasts drifted through space for as far as I could see. I looked to the planet and saw long streaks of light in the atmosphere where some of them blazed in a meteoric funeral pyre.

Perri was right; we couldn't just stand by and let this continue. "Take us into the nearest group of titans," I said, and while Tyler and Number One worked on the course I asked Perri, "What do you call a bunch of them together? A pod? A herd?"

"A fleet, of course," he said, forcing a smile despite the carnage outside. "They are spacecraft, after all."

"Of course." I watched as we drew closer. "Get between them and the Devernians. Number One, you fly; Tyler, you shoot down the incoming missiles. Nuclear bombs aren't cheap; maybe after they lose a few dozen they'll decide to talk."

The Devernians knew we were coming. They veered toward us, but Number One easily outflanked them at full impulse power. Tyler didn't even have to fire at their missiles; their chemical rockets couldn't approach our top speed.

The titans saw us coming, too. I suppose I was expecting gratitude, but I realized my mistake the moment we came to a halt amid them. These weren't just strange-looking starships with humanoid crews. There were no control domes on these beasts, no Aronnians inside pulling the reins or whatever they did to direct them. These were wild animals. *Panicked* wild animals big enough to smash us to pieces, which was just what they tried to do.

Half a dozen of them came at us from all sides. The screen filled with the enormous mouth of the one in front, offering us a view down a gullet big enough to fly a dozen shuttlecraft through in formation. The inside was lined with scaly plates of material hard enough to withstand the intense heat of passage through a gas giant's atmosphere. Those plates were hinged to turn forward as well; it came at us with them projecting ahead like pointed battering rams. Under full thrust it could only produce half a gravity or so of acceleration, but once moving its mass gave it the momentum of a small asteroid.

Shields were no good against something like this. "Evasive action!" I ordered. Number One reached out to comply, but before we had moved an inch the *Enterprise* shuddered under a blow from behind, then another from the starboard side.

We began to turn aside just as the one in front slammed into us. We lurched backward and heard its jaws squeal against the hull; then Tyler fired the phaser straight into its mouth. He used low power at first, no doubt hoping to drive it away without hurting it, but it hardly felt the blast through all that armor. It lunged at us again, biting down on the edge of the saucer-shaped hull, so he increased power and fired again.

It felt that, but it still didn't back off. The ship rang with its fury as it thrashed and bit; then two more titans struck us from above and below.

"To hell with this," I said, hanging on for dear life. "Ahead half impulse power. We'll knock them loose."

That was easier said than done. The one in front hung on like a bulldog, jerking back and forth in an effort to tear us apart, while more and more of them piled into us from the sides and the rear.

"Full impulse!" I ordered.

The *Enterprise* leaped forward under heavy acceleration. The battering from the sides and behind stopped as the titans there fell away, though one of them must have clung to the starboard warp nacelle for a moment. Unbalanced by its mass, we spun halfway around under full thrust before it dropped off. That motion finally wrenched loose the one in front as well; a deep groan echoed through the hull as it slid free, taking a generous swath of antennas and sensor arrays with it.

Even then we weren't out of the woods. The titans pursued us at top speed, darting ahead on warp drive and rushing us, only to be driven back by Tyler's phaser fire. And the rest of the "fleet," as Perri had called it, joined in the chase.

Seven

"Oh yes," said the seaman, Nowan. "I've seen many a ship battered to pieces by a pod o' whales. They get to playing with you and it's all over."

"These weren't playing," Pike told him. "They were trying to kill us."

"Ah, but that's often play to a man, now isn't it? Who's to say it's not the same to other creatures as well?"

"Point taken," Pike said. "Whatever their motive, these titans had it in for us. We'd already sustained enough damage to cripple the ship and still they came on; I imagined them cracking us open like a crab shell and sucking out the entire crew."

"A nasty image, that." Nowan leaned forward, his elbows on the table. "So what did you do, turn and fight again?"

Pike shook his head. "It wouldn't have done any good. We were hopelessly outnumbered. We had all the advantage of superior technology, but it was useless against the sheer bulk and determination of all those angry titans." He took a sip of brandy and said, "Oh, we probably could have launched a few photon torpedoes at them and scattered bloody pieces halfway across the Devernia system, but we were there to help save them, not kill them wholesale. I wanted a better option."

"Did you have one?"

"Barely."

Pike looked up. Every face in the bar was turned his way. Even the felinoid woman seemed interested. He felt heat rush into his cheeks at the realization that he was now the center of attention.

Nowan didn't care. "So what was it?" he demanded. "Out with it! Did your Mr. Tyler save the day with his fancy harpooning? Did Dabisch suddenly learn to speak Titan? What?"

Pike laughed. "Nothing so prosaic, I'm afraid. I merely remembered what I had seen the Devernian ships do—darting around like bees—and I realized they had already discovered the titans' weakness. They were bulky, and thus slow to maneuver. The *Enterprise* wasn't exactly a stunt fighter, but we could outfly a titan. So I order a full stop, a ninety-degree rotation out of the plane of the ecliptic, and a return to full impulse power. That shook off the pursuit—at least for a few seconds. . . ."

Eight

When we were once again under way and the titans were still trying to catch up, I hit the intercom switch and said, "Engineering, now would be a very good time to get those warp engines back on line."

This time the chief engineer replied. He was a New Yorker named Michael Burnstein, but I just called him "Burnie." "We're working on it," he said, "but that starboard field generator is in bad shape. We can maybe give you warp two, but the two engines won't be putting out the same thrust. The unbalanced field would tear the ship apart if we tried any more than that."

"Warp two is better than nothing," I said. "Number One, you heard the man; get us out of here."

"Aye, sir," she said. I heard the doubt in her voice, but she didn't question my order. She just entered the command into the helm console, then said, "Brace yourselves, this is liable to be rough."

The *Enterprise* had already taken a beating unlike anything she'd been designed for. Now we torqued the frame with unequal thrust on top of all her other damage. A deep bass rumble shook us to the core, and we heard the squeal of metal sliding on metal somewhere within the walls, but Burnie knew our limits. The ship held together—and the titans dropped farther behind. Either their biological engines couldn't keep up or they just lost interest in the chase when we made it more difficult, and I didn't care which it was. We plowed on alone for another full minute before I finally said, "That's far enough. Bring us out of warp."

We came to a halt about fifteen light-minutes away from Devernia.

Everyone on the bridge held their breath as Spock scanned the space around us, and when he said, "I find four thousand six hundred and twelve titans in the spherical volume of space one light-minute across." I heard a collective groan, but then he added, "But none seem to be concerned with our presence here," and everyone sighed with relief.

Into the silence I said, "That seems to me like an awful lot of titans."

Perri, apparently deciding that he wouldn't be shaken to the floor again soon, released his death grip on the handrail and said, "During their migration they sometimes seem to fill the entire planetary system, but that is largely an illusion. There are seldom more than a few million of them altogether."

"A few *million?*" I asked, incredulous. The entire Federation didn't have a million starships. The ones we had were more useful than these, to be sure, but still, there was something to be said for sheer numbers. The Aronnians and Devernians were apparently sitting on a gold mine.

Spock turned back to his science station for a moment, then reported, "Sensors indicate seven million, eight hundred and twelve thousand, six hundred and eleven spaceborne life-forms of size comparable to the titans in the Devernian planetary system. There are three million, two hundred and six thousand, four hundred and seventy-six smaller life-forms of one-quarter scale or less. Would these perhaps be their young?"

Perri said, "Three million of them? Impossible. That many have never hatched in one year before."

"Hatched?" I asked, surprised. "I naturally assumed they gave birth to live young. But they lay eggs?"

His brows furrowed, and I realized he hadn't intended to reveal that fact to us. I couldn't see how it mattered, but it was plain that it did to him. It was too late to hide it now, though, so he said somewhat reluctantly, "Yes, they do."

"Where?" I asked.

He looked from me to Spock to Number One, then back at me. "On, um, small, rocky worlds. Ones with liquid water."

"In other words, habitable planets," Spock said.

"Yes."

Spock narrowed his eyebrows. "How do the titans land? Their bodies do not seem designed for planetary surfaces."

"They aren't," Perri said. "They drop their eggs from orbit."

"How large are the eggs?" I asked.

Perri didn't like answering questions, but he had no good excuse not to. "About two or three times as long as you or I am tall, and maybe half that wide. They're oblong, with fins on the back and a heat shield in front for atmospheric entry."

"Fascinating," said Spock. "I surmise that this is how you domesticate them, then? By bonding with them when they are young?"

"That's right."

"How do you—"

Just then the intercom whistled for attention, and Dr. Boyce said, "Captain, I've got a very agitated patient here who demands to see you. You want me to put him out until you've got time, or what?"

"Just a moment," I said. I hit the engineering button and said, "How are those repairs coming?"

Burnie replied, "We're just getting started on the warp engine. It'll be three or four hours at least before it's up and running."

Some engineers pad their estimates so they look like heroes when they beat the deadline. Burnie wasn't that type. If he said it would take three or four hours, that's how long it would take.

"All right," I said. "We'll try not to need it before that. Sickbay, looks like we're not going anywhere for a while. I'll be right down." I stood up and said to Perri, "Come on, let's go see what he has to say."

Boyce was right about the "agitated" bit. When we got to sickbay we found the patient strapped to an examining table with wrist, ankle, and chest restraints, and he was still struggling. "You have no authority to hold me!" he shouted. "This is an act of war! I demand to speak to your commanding officer."

"Whoa, whoa," I said, stepping up to his side. "Calm down a minute. Maybe you didn't see what happened out there, but we rescued you from one of your own people's missiles. *You* were shooting at *us*."

"Who are you?" he demanded.

I took a good look at him before I replied. He had the same general build as an Aronnian, the same facial stripes and wide eyes. They were definitely from the same genetic stock. I couldn't tell from a sample of two if their populations still interbred, but it was obvious they at least had common ancestors not long ago.

"I'm Christopher Pike, captain of the *Enterprise,*" I said. "Who are you?"

"Name's Lanned, independent pilot on loan to the thirteenth Devernian attack group. You entered our space without invitation. What is your purpose here?"

I nodded toward Perri and said, "We came to find out what had happened to the titans. It looks like we've found that out, but we still don't know why."

"Why what?"

"Why are you slaughtering them?"

"Because they're slaughtering *us!"* He glared at Perri. "You—you *Aronnian!* You didn't tell them that, did you?"

Perri swallowed hard. "Of course I didn't, because it's not true. You Devernians have blown the situation completely out of proportion."

"Tell that to the orphans whose parents were eaten by titans," snarled Lanned. "Tell that to the parents whose *children* were eaten. Tell that to the homeless whose cities were burned."

Perri stepped closer. "The threat is not as great as you make it out to be. If you exercised even the simplest precautions, you wouldn't—"

"You murderous idiot!" Lanned lunged for Perri, nearly jerking the exam table off its mount. His head had the most mobility; his teeth met with a snap only centimeters from Perri's hand.

Perri flinched backward. Lanned said, "You and your precious Federation. 'Got to have star travel to be a member,' you say. 'Got to breed titans to sell on the interstellar market.' Well, every one you harvest comes with a price *we* have to pay, and we're not going to put up with your greed any longer." He spit a piece of tooth at the Aronnian.

Perri clenched and unclenched his fists as if he might try throttling the Devernian. He actually reached forward until I held out my hands—careful to keep them out of Lanned's range—and said, "Gentlemen, gentlemen, let's lower our voices and discuss this rationally. There's obviously a great deal of misunderstanding here."

"Discuss it rationally?" asked Lanned. "While I'm tied to a table?" There was a black gap between two of his front teeth. The broken one must have hurt terribly, but he betrayed none of the pain.

I looked at Dr. Boyce, then back to him. "We'll let you up when you convince us it's safe to do so. But Mr. Perri is our guest, and if you threaten him you will have to stay under restraint."

He scowled. "Unlike the Aronnians, we Devernians don't want to kill anyone. But we will wipe out every titan in our star system, and neither of you had better try to stop us."

Perri sighed. "He's an extremist. They're all extremists. They refuse to listen to reason."

Maybe so, but I wasn't exactly happy with Perri, either. He'd known what we would find here. This sounded like an ongoing argument, and he'd apparently expected us to sweep in with our superior technology and rout the opposition merely because the Aronnians were members of the Federation.

"I don't like being used," I told him. I drew my hand laser, then nodded to Dr. Boyce. "Let him up."

He looked at me askance, but didn't say anything as he unbuckled Lanned's feet, then his chest, then his hands. Lanned let him do so without hindrance, then slid his legs off the exam table and stood before us, rubbing his wrists.

"Thank you, Captain," he said. "And thank you, Doctor, for repairing my wounds."

Boyce bent down and picked up the fragment of tooth off the floor. "Here," he said, "let me fix this, too. Nobody walks out of my sickbay with a toothache."

Lanned drew a breath to protest, but we all saw him wince as air hit the nerve. "I wouldn't want to compromise your reputation," he said, sitting back down on the edge of the table.

A few minutes later, his smile restored, I led Lanned and Perri and two security officers to a conference room. Spock met us there, and we got down to business.

"First off," I said, standing at the head of the table with the star-filled windows behind me while the others sat, "I want to know what happened to the Aronnians who came here before us. Assuming you actually sent the ships you told us you did," I said to Perri.

"We did." The pained expression he had been wearing for the last few minutes intensified. "Captain, you really have the wrong impression of us."

"I think you have the wrong impression of us, too," I told him. "The Federation doesn't intervene in disputes between neighbors. We will assist in negotiating a treaty, but we won't fight your wars for you. Is that clear?"

"Very. That's all we ask," Perri said.

"Yet you deliberately let us come here under the impression that we were investigating a natural phenomenon, knowing what we would actually find."

"We had no idea what we would find!" Perri said. "That was the whole point of coming here! The Devernians didn't answer our signals. None of the titan riders we sent to investigate returned. I told you that."

"But you knew you had a dispute with the Devernians, didn't you?"

Perri nodded slowly. "Y-yes."

"And if your investigators didn't come back, you knew they had probably been killed in battle."

"Not so," he said. "You, with your glorious *Enterprise,* don't understand how dangerous it is to ride a titan from star to star. We sent eight riders. We expected four to make it here. Of those, we expected two to return with news."

Spock cleared his throat. "You lose *half* your interstellar missions?"

"We do," Perri said defiantly, daring him to comment. But Spock merely nodded and entered something into his datapad.

I felt the hair on the back of my neck stand up. Half their astronauts were lost in space! Yet people went out anyway, knowing the odds. I didn't know whether to admire them or pity them.

I said to Lanned, "So four of them presumably made it through. What happened to them when they got here?"

"What do you think happened?" he asked.

"I think you killed them. Did you?"

He shifted uncomfortably. "Not me personally, no, but we all have orders to shoot anyone who interferes with the eradication effort. If the Aronnians tried to stop us, they would have been fired upon."

" 'Would have been,' " I said mockingly. "Were they or weren't they?"

"They were," he admitted.

"Which could only be considered an act of war," I pointed out.

"It was an act of desperation," he protested. "We have no other choice. It's either the titans or us, and anyone who tries to prevent us from doing what we must will be stopped. That includes you, Captain."

Perri snorted. "You have all kinds of choice. People have coexisted peacefully with titans for centuries; there's no reason why we can't continue to do so indefinitely."

Lanned didn't even reply to him. He kept his eyes on me as he said, "Did he tell you how they breed?"

"They lay eggs on your home planet," I replied.

"Has he told you what happens next?"

"No."

"Let me describe it for you. The eggs fall with the force of a small bomb." He slapped his hand on the table. "They don't usually kill anyone when they hit. Planets are big, and our population is small, which means we generally don't even see where they come down. Most often the first sign we have that one has landed is when the young hatch out.

"You've seen the adults. You've seen the tentacles on the ends of their guidance fins. Well the young ones are all tentacles. That means they're mobile, and as strong as they are they can move fast as lightning. And they're carnivorous. They have to build up a great deal of body mass before they return to space, so they eat practically anything in sight—including *us.*"

Spock had opened his mouth, no doubt to correct Lanned for saying "carnivorous" instead of "omnivorous," but he stopped with his mouth open when the Devernian's final words registered.

"It used to be something we'd hear about maybe once a year," said Lanned. "It was always in some other city and everyone would say 'What a shame' and that would be the end of it. But as our population expanded and so did that of the titans, it became more common. Plus, as the titans who fed upon us matured and went into space, it seemed that they deliberately began dropping their eggs near cities. We had to kill them the moment they landed, or the hatchlings would pillage entire towns. They're nearly impossible to stop after they hatch. And if by chance anything survives their depredations, it goes up in flames the moment they launch themselves into space with their fusion engines."

Perri said, "They're not dangerous if you feed them. You could domesticate them if you wanted to. That's what we do with the ones that hatch on Aronnia."

"Oh, yes," said Lanned. "All three of them. We get thousands, and they each eat tons of food every day for weeks while they grow. Where is that supposed to come from?"

Perri shrugged. "We feed them fish. You have far more ocean than we do; that shouldn't present a problem."

"The oceans are barren! The titans ate everything in them before they started dropping their eggs on land."

"Nonsense," said Perri. "If you have trouble with your oceans, it's because of industrial pollution. If you had been more careful the titans would have stayed offshore and you wouldn't have a problem."

"What do you know about oceans?" Lanned asked. "Aronnia is a desert. That's the only thing that has saved you; you don't have enough water to support a breeding population."

"We could breed them if we wanted to. Until you messed things up so badly there was no need."

Perri and Lanned looked as if they might leap up from the table and come to blows, and I wasn't sure if I would bother to stop them if they did. I was rapidly losing sympathy for either side of their argument.

The two security guards by the door lowered their hands to their lasers, but Spock interrupted before the situation could escalate any further. Tapping his datapad's screen for emphasis, he said, "When the Aronnians applied for membership in the Federation, you implied that the titans were the result of bioengineering. However, it is becoming increasingly clear that you had no hand in the creation of these creatures, nor even in their husbandry. I suspect that you discovered them already as they are, and merely took advantage of a natural resource. Is that not correct?"

Perri didn't answer. Lanned said mockingly, "Why don't you tell him?" He said to Spock, "The titans came to Devernia about five hundred years ago. To *us,* not to them. There *weren't* any Aronnians until a few Devernians foolish enough to domesticate the titans strapped airtight tanks to their backs and rode them from our star to theirs. We colonized Aronnia. And now they claim the titans as their own handiwork." He laughed. "And as for 'taking advantage of a natural resource,' do you want to know what they use them for? I mean besides riding around on them like the fools who started it all?"

"I would be happy to learn anything you wish to tell me," Spock said.

"They scoop up their dung."

"Their dung?" I asked to be sure I'd heard him properly.

"That's right. Adult titans feed in the atmospheres of gas-giant planets, and they filter dust and small particles out of the rings of any planet that has them. Devernia only has one gas giant, but Aronnia has three, so the titans migrate there to fatten up before they come back here to breed. But they don't need everything they eat. Their excrement is rich in rare elements, which the Aronnians gather for raw materials."

The stripes on Perri's forehead and cheeks darkened. I wondered if he was blushing, to have us learn this apparently humbling fact about his race.

"You use it too," he said to Lanned.

"Of course we do. We'd be foolish not to. But we don't base our whole economy on it."

"Nor do we." Perri took a deep breath, then said, "Captain Pike. Regardless of our differences of opinion, you can plainly see that the Devernians have embarked upon a campaign of indiscriminate slaughter that will adversely affect both our planets. As members of the Federation, we have asked for your help in stopping this carnage. You've seen what they're doing here; you can't approve of it."

I looked out the windows. Even from here, I could see the distant flash of nuclear explosions. Devernia was a bright crescent in the far distance. "You're right," I said, "I don't approve of it. But my approval isn't required. All that's required before I act on anyone's behalf is that I understand what's going on, but the simple truth here is that I don't trust either one of you two as far as I can throw you." They both began to protest, but I cut them off. "Save your breath. You've both talked enough. I want to examine the situation firsthand."

Perri looked puzzled. He said, "You have. You are here. What more is there to see?"

I nodded toward the bright planet in the distance. "Devernia itself. When you're looking for a solution, go to the source of the problem."

Lanned said, "You haven't been invited."

I replied, "Then invite us. You need our help just as badly as the Aronnians do. You can't really think hunting them down will work, can you? Spock says there's millions of them out there. Do you have any idea what exploding a million nuclear bombs will do to your environment? Radioactive debris will rain down on you for generations."

"What else do you propose?" he asked. "We won't stand by and let the titans destroy our cities any longer."

"I don't have a proposal yet," I told him. "That's why I want to go have a look for myself. Maybe my crew and I can figure out something more agreeable for everyone involved—including the titans."

Lanned snorted at my presumption, but he said, "Very well, Captain. I will show you Devernia, on one condition."

"What's that?"

He looked at Perri and grinned. "That this arrogant dung-sifter come with us and see for himself what it's like."

Nine

In the Captain's Table, Nowan chuckled softly. "I'll wager he nearly wet his pants at that, eh?"

Captain Pike smiled, but shook his head. "If he did, he hid it pretty well. He spluttered around a bit, of course, said it was a complete waste of time, but in the end he didn't have much choice. Lanned had shamed him into it."

"He no doubt enjoyed that. He strikes me as a rather crude fellow. From your description of him, I fancy he enjoyed laying waste to so many great beasts. No doubt it gave him a sense of power."

"I don't know if he enjoyed it or not," Pike said, "but he thought he had good reason for doing it."

"Oh, aye," said Nowan. "Every man who's ever thrown a harpoon has found some way to justify taking the life of a leviathan, but so many have done it that you will forgive me if I suspect their motives. It sounds to me as if the entire Devernian society had gone a bit mad, if they truly thought they could solve their problem through such massive slaughter."

Pike rocked his brandy snifter around in a circle on the wooden tabletop. "Like Lanned said, they were desperate. They didn't go out hunting titans just because they wanted to. But yes, I suspect the solution they picked answered an emotional need as well as a practical one."

"That is an easy trap to fall into," the seaman said. "After our escape from the prison island, my own crew wanted to avenge ourselves on every ship that entered the bay, be it civilian or not. I found it difficult to deny them, in part because I felt their desire myself. But a true man will rise above his bloodlust and not let passion rule his actions."

"Spoken like a Vulcan," Pike said.

"How so?"

Pike felt a moment's confusion. How could anybody miss that reference? "They're all logic," he explained. "They don't give in to emotion at all."

"An admirable trait," said Nowan.

From her stool at the bar, the Klingon woman said, "A cowardly trait, you mean."

Both Pike and Nowan looked over to see her leaning forward with her lips pulled back in a snarl.

"To overcome one's passion is in no way cowardly," said the seaman. "It often requires great courage."

"Passion is part of life," the Klingon replied. "Deny it, and you deny the very core of your being."

"Then you think the Devernians were right to slaughter the titans, merely because they felt the need to strike back at them?"

Her lips pulled back even farther. "The Devernians sound like cowards, too. There is no honor in fighting dumb animals with nuclear weapons. A Klingon would pit himself against them on more equal terms as a test of his honor."

Nowan's eyes narrowed. "Men who need to kill things to prove themselves have no honor," he declared.

The Klingon woman snarled at him, a sound like a lion about to pounce. "What do you know of honor, prisoner? A Klingon would never allow himself to be captured alive."

They stared at one another for a moment, fire smoldering behind their eyes. Everyone else in the bar had frozen in place, Pike noticed, except for the felinoid woman, who laughed musically and scratched at her left arm beneath its iridescent covering. The Klingon looked over at her with open disdain, but her expression turned to surprise when she saw the tiny hand phaser the felinoid had drawn from its hiding place and now held with the business end pointed straight at her head.

"Zap," said the felinoid. "You're my prisoner."

"Hey!" shouted the bartender. "No drawing weapons in here, you know that," but the Klingon didn't wait to see if the cat-woman would put it away. With a scream that chilled the blood of everyone in the bar, she leaped from her stool, picked up a chair from the empty table in front of her, and swung it around in an arc that knocked the phaser from the other woman's grip.

The weapon flew through the air toward the piano, but disarming her opponent wasn't enough. She brought the chair back around for another blow, this one aimed at the cat-woman's head, but the moment she had leaped from her stool Captain Pike had also reacted with instinctive speed. He had his phaser out of his boot before the cat-woman's even hit the floor, and he leaped to his feet and shouted "Drop it!" while the Klingon was still raising the chair over her head.

The Klingon didn't even hesitate. The chair came down in a swift arc toward the surprised felinoid's head, but it never connected. Pike fired as soon as he realized she wasn't going to stop, and the chair vanished in a puff of dissociated atoms.

It was a split-second decision. He could have stunned her instead, but if she was part of a peace delegation that could have terrible consequences. Even disarming her might cost more than humanity was willing to pay, but he couldn't let her hurt someone when he could prevent it.

She whirled around to face him, her face full of rage, but he held his phaser on her and said calmly, "Emotion or logic? Your move."

Just then the fire popped, and one of the men at the table with the cat-woman flinched so hard his chair scooted back with a screech.

Pike felt his finger twitch on the phaser's fire button, too, but he held steady. The Klingon woman held her eyes on him a moment longer, and Pike was just beginning to think he might have to stun her after all when she threw back her head and laughed. Her voice rattled the bottles on their shelves behind the bar and her long black hair swung from side to side as she shook her head.

"Well done, Captain," she said, stepping away from the felinoid's table. "I would welcome the chance to spar with you hand to hand."

"Perhaps another time," Pike said.

"I look forward to it." She walked over to the piano and Pike was afraid she was going to go for the cat-woman's phaser, but instead of picking it up she merely crushed it beneath her heavy black boots. *Then* she picked it up, and carried the pieces back to the cat-woman. "Here's your phaser, dear," she said sweetly. She walked back over to the bar, took a long drink from her tankard of Warnog, then sat down again—but not in her original place. She deliberately scooted down to the end of the bar closest to Pike, which still left her well beyond arm's reach, but not far enough to suit him.

"Dammit, Hompaq," said the bartender, "if you do that again I'll kick you out of here so fast they'll hear the sonic boom halfway around Qo'noS."

Hompaq, Pike thought. Typical Klingon name to go with her typical Klingon bravado.

"I was provoked," she said.

"You were insulting and threatening my customers, and I won't have it. Behave yourself or find another bar."

She shrugged and looked away. Conversation slowly started up again. Pike sat back down and tucked his phaser back in the loop at the top of his right boot.

Nowan watched him in open-eyed astonishment. "I have no idea what I just witnessed," he said, "but I will tell you this: I am no longer inebriated."

Pike smiled. "Nothing like a little adrenaline to burn out the alcohol." He looked around the bar and shook his head. "This place is just full of surprises, isn't it?"

"That it is," said his companion. "That it is. But I fear this particular surprise has diverted you from your story. You had me hooked, sir; I am ready to be reeled in. What did you discover on Devernia?"

Pike had to think a minute to recall where he'd been. Devernia, Devernia. Ah, yes.

Ten

We couldn't go down immediately, of course. The warp engines weren't repaired yet, and I wasn't about to try running the gauntlet of titans around the planet on impulse power alone. So I took the time to fill in the landing party on what we had learned. To accompany me I chose Spock, one of the two security officers who had already overheard much of our discussion, and Yeoman Colt.

Perri was delighted to see her again, and Lanned seemed equally smitten, but they both expressed surprise that I would choose a petite young woman for the mission. I confess that when I had first seen her I had shared their skepticism, but she had long since proven herself to me, and I told them so. She blushed prettily at my words of praise, which only made her seem even more fragile and beautiful, but when I began issuing our equipment she took on a somewhat different appearance. A phaser rifle held at parade rest puts a certain edge on anyone's character.

I wondered if rifles would be enough. After seeing how little effect the ship's phasers had on an adult titan, I knew a hand laser wouldn't be worth much against a juvenile, but I wasn't sure if a phaser rifle would be much better. Unfortunately it was the best I could do without hauling around a full-fledged phaser cannon, and I didn't think the Devernians would appreciate that. The rifles were going to be problematic enough.

I asked Lanned if he needed to contact his commanding officer, but he only laughed and said, "You presume a great deal more order than actually exists, Captain. I haven't had a commanding officer for weeks."

"You haven't?" I asked. "Who coordinates the battles? Who arranges for supplies? You must have some kind of leader."

He shrugged. "I'm sure someone back home fancies himself a leader. There might even be some who follow him. But anyone left who's worth following is out on the front lines in a ship of his own, battling the menace from space."

"Your chain of command has collapsed?" I asked, stunned at the prospect of a leaderless planet in a time of crisis—and at how cavalier he was about it.

"We all know what needs to be done," he said.

"So you think," said Perri. He was looking at our phaser rifles enviously, but I had declined to issue one to him or Lanned. I didn't want to have to protect myself from them as well as from titan hatchlings.

I did outfit everyone with survival equipment: medical kits, a day's rations, warm clothing. With all the activity in space around the planet, I didn't know if the *Enterprise* would be able to stay on station continuously. If there was no central authority to grant us permission to approach, there might be times when Number One would have to take her out of orbit to avoid hostilities.

I wondered what kind of reception we would receive on the ground, but Lanned said we would be welcome so long as we didn't try to interfere with their efforts to eradicate the titans. I didn't know whether or not to believe him, but I had little choice but to beam down and see.

At last, after the promised three and a half hours, Burnie pronounced the warp engines ready for flight. I led my landing party to the transporter room, then called the bridge on the intercom and said, "Take us in, Number One."

Lanned had given us coordinates for his home city, a seaport called Malodya on the south end of a large island. I waited nervously while Number One brought us into position directly overhead, darting in at warp three to slip past the titans and the Devernian warships without detection. The moment we re-entered normal space over the planet, however, she said, "Whoops! Here they come. Titans incoming at warp one point six, and Devernians following at full impulse power. We've got about thirty seconds before things get exciting."

"We're on our way," I told her. "Take the *Enterprise* out of range as soon as we're gone and wait for our pickup signal."

"Aye, Captain. Be careful down there."

"You be careful up here." I stepped up onto the transporter platform, where the others were already waiting. "Energize," I said to the technician at the controls, and a moment later the *Enterprise* faded away—

—to be replaced by a muddy street with gray stone buildings on either side of it. A line of scraggly yellow trees grew between the most traveled part of the street and the face of the buildings, but there was no sidewalk, no demarcation between vehicular and foot traffic. The street had apparently been covered with stones at one time—either that or it had never been cleared of them—but now so much mud had worked up around them that they presented more of an impediment than an aid to travel.

There were fifteen or twenty Devernians on the street, either walking or riding in ungainly wheeled vehicles that looked like they had all been assembled out of spare parts. No two cars looked alike. Some were improbably tall and narrow and looked like they would tip over at any moment, while others were wider and lower to the ground. They were all angles, apparently made out of stamped sheet metal and riveted or bolted together. The sound of them clanking and rattling down the uneven street assaulted us like an earthquake in a restaurant kitchen, and the air was thick with the aroma of partially burned hydrocarbons.

At least half of the vehicles had no paint that I could see beneath their thick coating of brown mud. The sea air—I could smell the salt from where we stood—was busy rusting them out. Besides the rust, their only common features were wide, large-diameter wheels that presumably helped them churn through the muck. I looked out at the oozing brown surface, then up at the gray sky that threatened to drop more rain on it at any moment, but I held my tongue. I had learned as a cadet that one doesn't criticize alien societies on first impressions. Maybe they had a good reason not to pave their roads.

We had materialized in a parking lot. Only one Devernian had witnessed our arrival—an old woman who had been tying down a pile of wooden crates on the back of a flatbed truck. She looked at us curiously, still tugging on the rope; then she narrowed her eyes and peered intently at Lanned. "Ortezi, is that you?" she asked.

Lanned shook his head. "No. I'm Lanned, Ortezi's brother. Ortezi was killed three years ago by a titan."

"Ah," she said, nodding sadly. "I thought so, but the way you all popped up from nowhere, I . . ." She trailed off and finished tying her knot, asking as she worked at it, "How did you do that?"

Lanned held his hand out toward me and my four crew members. "These people are from the Federation. That's how they get from place to place. They came here to stop us from killing the titans."

"Did they now?" Her expression grew cold.

"We're here to help you solve your problem," I said quickly. That wasn't strictly true, of course. The Prime Directive prohibited interfering in a society's development, either for good or for bad. If Aronnia hadn't been a member of the Federation we couldn't do anything at all, but they were and they had asked for help, and Devernia was arguably part of their society, so I felt comfortable at least investigating the situation. Whether or not we acted on it, however, depended on what we learned.

The old woman didn't warm up any, but she said, "Hah. If you could make 'em all vanish the way you appeared just now, you'd be welcome enough. Can you do that?"

"No," I replied. "I'm afraid that's beyond our ability."

"Pity," she said. She looked back to Lanned. "Your brother was a good boy. I used to hire him to help me skin trinis at harvest time." She rapped a wrinkled knuckle on one of the crates, and whatever was inside hissed loudly through the vent hole in the side.

Lanned smiled at her. "He showed me the scars. How is the farm doing now?"

She spat on the ground, which was spongy but hadn't given over to mud there in the parking lot. "Can't complain. People still have to eat, even when the sky's falling around 'em. I could do with a bit less rain, though." She looked again at the four of us from the *Enterprise* and said, "I don't suppose you can do anything about that, can you?"

"No, sorry," I said.

"Not much good to us then, are you?" she asked pointedly.

I saw Yeoman Colt trying to stifle a grin and I gave her a warning look, but that only made it harder for her to contain.

I looked away lest I start laughing too, and our surroundings quickly robbed any mirth from the situation. I said to the old woman, "We'll do what we can."

"See that you do," she said. She checked her knot, then climbed into the cab of her vehicle. The engine started with a belch of black smoke and a whine that rose in pitch until it howled painfully just near the threshold of hearing; then, with a clashing of metal against metal and a momentary spinning of wheels, the woman put it in gear and drove away.

Spock wiped a bit of mud from his pants leg, but considering our surroundings it seemed a futile gesture.

Perri didn't even try to hide his disgust. "What a trini pen!" he said, wrinkling his nose. "How can you people live this way?"

Lanned gave him a withering look. "What's the matter, desert dweller? Can't take a little moisture?"

"It's not the water, it's the—the *miasma* that's so disagreeable. Have you people no pride?"

"We don't have time for pride," Lanned said. "Unlike you—"

"And we don't have time to stand here insulting each other, either," I said before they could take off on another riff. "Come on, let's have the tour."

Lanned seemed happy to drop it. Perri's comment had apparently stung. I wondered if life here had always been like this, or if we were seeing evidence of the decline Lanned had spoken of. He didn't elaborate; he just said, "Very well," and walked toward the street, leaving the rest of us to follow or not as we wished.

It's hard to be unobtrusive when you're carrying phaser rifles. Some of the Devernians carried weapons, but they were usually handguns, and the few rifles we saw were definitely projectile weapons rather than directed energy beamers. At least our dark jackets covered our blue and yellow and red shirts, but people still gawked at us as we marched along the street, stepping carefully to avoid sinking to our ankles in mud. The locals wore mostly subdued browns and grays themselves, probably because they were going to *get* brown and gray within a block no matter what color they started out. Every horizontal surface was covered with mud, and every vertical one with dark soot. When I caught glimpses of the skyline between buildings I could see plumes of smoke rising into the clouds, smudging the already-dark sky. Even the rain was probably dirty, I imagined.

I tried not to be judgmental. Earth had gone through a period like this. Two of them, actually. We'd climbed out of it once, then bombed ourselves back into it again before Zefram Cochrane invented the warp drive and lifted us out of the squalor once and for all.

I wondered if the titans might do the same for the Devernians, but if Lanned was to be believed then the titans were responsible for the situation in the first place.

Or maybe they were responsible for more than that.

I stopped dead in my tracks. Yeoman Colt, who had been speaking quietly with Perri, bumped into me from behind and jumped back.

"Oh! Sorry, sir."

"My fault," I told her. "Lanned, how old is this city?"

"Malodya?" he asked. "Seventy or a hundred years, maybe. Why do you ask?"

"How old is the oldest city on Devernia?"

He shrugged. "I don't know. Old. Maybe four hundred years?"

Four hundred years was *old?*

"And how long ago was Aronnia colonized?"

Perri answered that. "Two hundred and seventeen Aronnian years ago. That would be about one hundred and eighty-something Devernian years."

Colt said what I was thinking. "You're so young! How could anybody go from the birth of cities to spaceflight in two hundred years?"

Lanned laughed softly. "The spaceships were free. We only had to develop the sealed containers to ride in. And the titans provided the raw materials for that, too. Their bones are mostly metal, and their eggshells make excellent refractory crucibles for smelting it."

That's what I had thought. I could easily imagine tribes of hunter-gatherers or early agrarian farmers watching the creatures come and go on their fusion flames, wondering how they did it and making their own experiments with fire. Two hundred years was fast, but it would be long enough for them to learn to work metals and build the machinery of civilization—even their own spaceships—if they had an example to strive for.

Any problem I had with the Prime Directive paled in comparison to the interference that had already happened here. Now I wondered which would be worse, helping them eliminate the titan influence or leaving them alone.

Spock had been taking tricorder readings since we had arrived. Now he spoke up and said, "Ion dating of the building materials supports Lanned's figures. This section of the city is forty-seven years old."

"You want to see the oldest part?" Lanned asked.

"It might help us understand your culture," Spock replied. I didn't really know what we were looking for, but I supposed looking at the city's history might give us a direction to expand our investigation so I said, "Yes, let's have a look."

Lanned led us down the block to the intersection with another muddy street, turned right, and headed toward a cluster of ten- to fifteen-story buildings that I assumed was the center of town.

I looked at the smaller structures we passed on the way, and I noticed a peculiarity in their design. There were no windows at all on the ground floor, and the doors were heavy sheets of steel, banded for strength. "Are those doors designed to keep hatchling titans out?" I asked.

Lanned shook his head. "Nothing will keep them out if they decide there's food inside. The doors are only designed to delay them long enough for someone on the opposite building to get a shot at them." He pointed to the roof of the building across the street from us, where I saw a notch in the waist-high wall and in the notch the round end of what looked like a medieval cannon pointing at us. It must have had a bore the size of my fist.

I turned to my security officer, Lieutenant Garrett, who nodded grimly. He saw it too. And now that we were looking, we could see them atop every building all the way down the street.

I didn't see anyone up there with the cannons, so I assumed that they were left unmanned until someone sounded the alert. "How often do you need to fire one of those?" I asked.

"We test them every week," Lanned replied. "So far we haven't actually had to shoot a titan this far into town, but there's always a first time. We're ready."

That they were. I shivered at the thought of needing a cannon on every rooftop, but it probably made the city's inhabitants feel safer.

We continued walking toward the downtown area, but we turned aside before we got there. After crossing several muddy cross-streets, we came to a wide, tree-filled park, and the moment he saw it Lanned suddenly smiled and said, "Oh, the *big* gun! Of course you must see that." He led the way under the canopy of yellow leaves toward a circular pond in the middle of the park.

When we reached the edge of it, Lanned said nothing; he merely turned to look at us, a peculiar smile on his face. I looked at the black surface of the pond, maybe five meters across and ringed in rusting metal about knee high; then I turned once around and examined the park. Wide-leafed trees, bushes here and there, a low ground cover that looked more like tiny fern fronds than grass—but no gun.

Was the pond the remains of its turret, perhaps? Maybe there had been some kind of artillery emplacement here and this was all that was left. It was circular enough to be a turret, and the rim of metal around it could be a track . . .

Or a barrel.

I looked into the black water again, trying to spot the bottom. If there was one, I couldn't see it.

"How deep is that, Mr. Spock?" I asked.

He was already examining it with his tricorder. "I read two hundred and seventy-four point three meters," he said.

I felt my insides tighten up as if I'd just been transported to the top of a cliff. I backed away from the edge and looked to the side to keep my balance. What kind of people would leave a hole that deep in the middle of town without a fence around it? Even if it was full of water. I said to Lanned, "You can't mean to tell me this is a gun barrel."

"Oh, but it is," he said, grinning wide now. He glanced momentarily at Yeoman Colt, then looked back at me. "I'm glad to see that something we did can impress you Federation people."

"You've certainly managed . . . two hundred and some *meters?* What in the world did you *shoot* with it? And what did you shoot *out of* it?"

"Titans," Lanned said. "Titans to both questions. Their eggs make excellent projectiles going up as well as coming down. We just sent them back upward with considerably more velocity than what they arrived with."

"But straight up? You'd have to be incredibly lucky to hit anything with it."

Lanned said, "Not so lucky as you might think. The eggs shatter under the stress of the explosion, so it's really a cloud of fragments rather than a single egg. That means less impact when it hits something, of course, but when your target is moving at orbital velocity all you really have to do is put the projectile in front of it."

Spock's tricorder made whistling sounds as he continued to take readings. "That would be an effective weapon. An egg fragment weighing only a kilogram would strike with 28,543,209.88 joules of energy."

"How much is that in kilotons?" Colt asked.

"A lot," I told her before Spock could make an equally precise conversion. "Did it work?"

Lanned nodded. "Oh yes. We shot down twenty-six titans with it before the barrel cracked."

"Fascinating," said Spock.

"Of course, that was before we developed our own spaceships. After that we just carried rocks into retrograde orbit and pitched them out. That meant they hit with *twice* the power. Much more effective."

"But you gave that up, too, in favor of nuclear bombs," I said. "Why?"

Lanned lost his grin. "We kept hitting too many of our own rocks. Projectiles from the gun fell back into the sea if they didn't hit anything, but orbital debris stays up there for months. Besides, by the time the titans get into orbit, they're already close enough to release their eggs. We had to take the fight farther out."

"You realize, of course," said Spock, "that by attempting to drive them from Devernia you have disrupted their migration pattern and caused them to remain here year-round instead."

"We know that now. We didn't expect it to work that way when we started killing them, but we're trying to take advantage of it and eliminate them while we've got the chance."

I edged closer to the enormous gun barrel and looked down into the water again. My reflection stared back out, just as awed as I. These people weren't afraid to think big, that much was certain.

Just then I saw a flash of light in the sky reflected in the water, and a moment later we heard a whistling sound overhead, followed by a concussion we could feel in the soles of our boots. I blinked and saw another flash—no doubt the afterimage in my retinas. Concentric rings rippled outward into the middle of the flooded gun barrel.

"What was that?" I asked, knowing the answer already.

Lanned confirmed it. "Eggfall!" he said, and the tone of his voice carried both fear and satisfaction.

Eleven

CAPTAIN PIKE PAUSED TO TAKE A DRINK, AND FOUND THAT HIS BRANDY snifter was empty again. So was his drinking companion's. They eyed one another for a moment, then Pike looked over at the bar where the Klingon woman, Hompaq, sat. The other bar patrons had gone back to their own conversations and their own concerns, but she had hardly moved for the last quarter hour. She didn't even look as if she was paying attention to Pike anymore, but he doubted that she had forgotten their confrontation. She was probably just waiting for the chance to stick a knife in his ribs.

Nowan knew exactly what he was thinking. "Arm-wrestle you for it," he said.

Pike laughed softly. "No, it's my turn. Be right back." He picked up both glasses and stood up.

"I'm right behind you if there's trouble."

"If there's trouble, I'm probably going to be on my back," Pike said, not really sure he was joking. He squared his shoulders and walked over to the bar anyway, setting the glasses down on the polished wood with a soft click. Hompaq bared her teeth at him, and he felt his skin crawl as she reached down to scratch her bare midriff, but she brought her hand back up empty.

The bartender had been restocking the cooler midway down the bar. He turned his head at the sound, and Pike said, "Two more."

He nodded, but finished transferring dark green bottles of ale before he stood up.

"Relax, tiger," the Klingon said. "If I was mad at you, I'd have let you know it before this."

He looked sideways at her. "How? By swinging a chair at my head?"

"I never use the same tactic twice. It's bad form. No, if I were angry at you, I'd probably do something disgustingly personal and very painful." She grinned again, showing all of her pointed teeth. "Of course to a Klingon, that's practically indistinguishable from making love."

"How charming," he said. Was she coming *on* to him? Impossible. Wasn't it?

The bartender took down the curved brown bottle of Saurian brandy from the shelf, got two fresh glasses from beneath the bar, and poured.

"Maybe we should just take the bottle," said Pike.

Hompaq chuckled softly. It was all she needed to say; Pike felt warmth in his cheeks.

The bartender shook the bottle gently, said, "Actually, there's not much left in this one," and poured the rest into the glasses, leaving them each a centimeter shy of the top. "Want a fresh one?" he asked.

Good grief, thought Pike. Had he actually drank half a bottle of Saurian brandy already? On an empty stomach? No wonder he had phasered the chair out of Hompaq's hands. And no telling what he would do after a whole bottle. "No thanks," he said. "That's probably more than we need."

"Try some Warnog," said Hompaq, raising her tankard. "It'll grow hair on your chest."

Pike couldn't resist. He looked back at her, let his gaze slide deliberately down from her face to the rounded targets her half-exposed breasts made, and said, "Hasn't worked on you yet."

She looked down in surprise, then burst out laughing. "Ha! Very good, human. I think I like you." She slapped him on the back hard enough to make his teeth rattle.

Pike thought of half a dozen replies to that as well, but he prudently let them all slide. Picking up the brandy snifters, he raised one slightly toward her, said, "Cheers," and went back to his table.

"Well done," Nowan said when he sat down.

Pike shrugged. He'd gotten past her without violence, but he wasn't particularly proud of the accomplishment. There'd been a time when he would have welcomed the chance to wipe the bar with her. That wasn't necessarily better, but he felt somehow let down by the thought that he was mellowing out, and he suspected that Hompaq felt the same disappointment. Nothing would please her more than a good brawl.

She was still watching him. He winked at her. Let her wonder what it meant.

"So now, where was I?" he asked Nowan. "Had Colt fallen into the gun barrel yet?"

"No!" Nowan exclaimed. "Did she?"

"Nope." Pike grinned at him. "Just checking to see if you were listening. You sure you want to hear all this?"

Nowan drew himself upright in his chair. "Sir, if you leave me stranded at this point I will join the scantily clad woman in rending you limb from limb. Proceed at once. The egg had fallen. What did you do?"

"I'll tell you what we *should* have done," Pike said. "We should have run away while we had the chance. . . ."

Twelve

BUT OF COURSE WE RAN TOWARD IT. IT WAS HARD TO TELL WHERE IT HAD come down, what with all the buildings in the way, but Spock kept scanning for life-forms with his tricorder and he kept us pointed in the right direction. We couldn't follow the locals; Devernians were running every which way. I eventually realized there was a pattern to their movement—parents and their children going one way and people with guns going the other—but that wasn't apparent at first. All I saw was a city that looked like a kicked anthill, an anthill full of angular ground vehicles with bad brakes.

We were nearly run over half a dozen times as we sprinted toward the fallen titan egg. Once we came upon an intersection that was clogged with crumpled cars, and I realized with horror that they had no structural integrity fields, no artificial gravity, not even crash harnesses to restrain their passengers. Only the poor condition of the streets prevented a worse disaster; nobody could drive fast enough through the rutted mud for a collision to be fatal.

At last we rounded a corner and found the impact site. The egg had struck a building at a low angle and smashed right through a second-story wall, crashed through the floor inside, and come to rest in a ground-floor room on the other side of the building. The cannons from the buildings around it were useless in this situation, but a couple dozen Devernians had climbed to the roof of the one that had been hit and were busy removing the gun from its mount so they could carry it inside to fire point-blank at the egg.

"Make way!" Lanned shouted as we neared the crowd of onlookers on the ground. "Coming through!"

There were hundreds of people milling around with their hand weapons drawn, but so far nobody had fired one at anything. Those nearest to us turned to see who had shouted, and when they saw us following Lanned, armed with our phaser rifles, they backed away. They had probably never seen a phaser before, but the rifles were deliberately designed to look deadly, and that apparently was just what they wanted to see. "Inside!" some of them shouted. "Blow it up! Kill it! Kill it!"

"How long—" I asked, gasping for breath after running so far. "How long before it hatches?"

"Who knows?" Lanned answered. "It used to take about nine days, but now that we're keeping the mothers at bay they're developing further before they drop. Sometimes it's just hours. Others hatch on the way down."

We pushed our way into the building just as a loud *boom* shook it. We heard shouts from within, and I thought the egg must have hatched, but when we reached the room where it had fallen we saw that it was still intact, an oblong spheroid big enough to hold a full-grown elephant. It was scorched black by its fall through the atmosphere, it surface crinkly and stinking of hot metal and complex organic compounds. Its nose was buried in the floor and its tail stuck up through the ceiling, the fins on the back making it look for all the world like a cartoon bomb.

The noise we'd heard had come from a more realistic bomb that someone had placed beneath the egg and touched off, but that had had no effect other than temporarily deafening everyone in the building and scattering shredded paper like confetti all around the room. It had apparently been an office a few moments ago. I noticed a few other people with clumsy-looking grenades as well as slug-throwing handguns dangling from their belts, but it was clear that those kinds of weapons were no match for what we faced here.

"Out!" Lanned shouted, waving everyone away. "Get out of here! We'll take care of it."

Of course nobody left, but nobody tossed another grenade, and the ones closest to the egg backed off to make room for us. Spock stepped forward and ran his tricorder along the surface of the egg. "What's he doing?" someone asked.

"Ascertaining the danger," Spock replied. He stepped around the egg, sidling along the wall where it was a tight fit, his tricorder whirring the entire time. The novelty of it held the Devernians at bay until he had made a complete circuit.

"Well, Spock?" I asked when he didn't speak right away.

"A moment, Captain." We were standing under one of the fins; he frowned at his tricorder's display and moved around to the side of the egg again. It was warm, I noticed, but not as hot as I would have expected from its fiery passage through the atmosphere. Its shell must have functioned as an ablative heat shield, the outer layers vaporizing and carrying away the energy before it could cook the layers below.

"I read intense metabolic activity," Spock said finally, "but I do not detect any motion. I believe the embryo is still developing."

"Good," someone said. "That'll give us time to blast it apart."

Lanned was looking at Spock and the tricorder. "You can see through the shell with that thing?" he asked.

"Only on Q-band," Spock said. "It is opaque to all other frequencies, but Q-band is designed for high-penetration and long-distance scans, so it does allow me to take at least some readings."

"How about the other way around? Can you put energy *into* it?"

Spock considered his request. "That would theoretically be possible, but not with this unit. I assume you wish to irradiate and sterilize the embryo?"

"That's right."

"Given its biomass and its resistance to heat, I suspect it would take more energy than even a phaser battery contains to assure its destruction through irradiation alone. Molecular disruption remains a much more cost-effective option."

Perri had been catching his breath at the back of the room, but now he spoke up. "What are you talking about killing it for? If it's not due to hatch right away, then this is the perfect opportunity to domesticate it. Get some food handy so it will have something to eat when it crawls out of the egg, and it'll bond with the first person it sees."

"Are you volunteering to be that person?" asked Lanned.

Perri swallowed, and I was sure he would find some way to weasel out of it, but he surprised me. "Yes, of course," he said. "If no one else wants a starship of their own, I certainly won't turn it down."

Lanned was just as surprised as me. "I—well—" he stammered, looking from Perri to the others and back, "I—we don't have the food even if we wanted to let you," he said.

If Perri was relieved by that news, he didn't show it. "You're letting a priceless resource go to waste," he said.

The other Devernians looked at him as if he'd just sprouted horns, and one of them raised his handgun threateningly, but Lanned waved him back and said, "Maybe in a different time they were a resource. Now they're only a menace. Captain Pike, can your phaser rifles kill this egg before it hatches?"

"I don't know," I said. "Spock?"

He consulted his tricorder, frowning at the results. "The shell is composed of an unknown organic molecule with a hyperconnected bond structure. It is a superconductor of heat and electricity, and is opaque to most frequencies of electromagnetic radiation. Our phasers will not penetrate deeply, but they may be able to burn through under sustained fire." He looked up at me. "However, since there is no immediate danger, doing so prematurely will only destroy a valuable opportunity to study the development of a titan embryo."

"What good will that do?" one of the Devernians asked. "We already know how to kill 'em. Cannons don't do it on the first shot either, but if you hit 'em enough times in the same spot, you eventually punch through."

Spock raised a single eyebrow. "I am sure you do," he said. "However, additional knowledge can only improve your ability to deal with the titans, either to exterminate them more effectively or perhaps to discover a more benign way of handling the situation. In either case, knowledge is more useful than indiscriminate action." He reached out to touch the blackened surface of the egg just ahead of one of its fins. "For instance, were you aware that this egg has a defect right here which reduces its strength by twenty-six percent?"

"It does?"

"It does. It also has a tracery of microfissures emanating from this point here"—he stretched to tap a spot high around the curved surface—"which I presume is the pressure point that allows the egg to be opened from within." He took another tricorder reading, and nodded. "The position of the embryo lends support to that hypothesis. All its tentacles are clustered beneath this region, presumably to assist in pushing it outward."

"Hmm," said the Devernian. "What else do you see in there?"

Spock never got the chance to answer, because the team of men who had dismounted the cannon from the roof arrived with it just then. "Stand back!" they shouted. "Gun coming through!"

That cleared the path. Six Devernians, carrying the cannon between them like a coffin, struggled through the doorway with it and set it on its tripod a few steps from the surface of the egg. Now that I had a closer look I could see that it was a little more sophisticated than my first impression of it; it had a hinged breech for loading, and the gunners carried cartridges the size of their forearms tipped with armor-piercing slugs.

Even so, it was the wrong tool for the job. "You can't actually be thinking of shooting that thing in here," I said. "The ricochets would be more deadly than the titan."

"You've got a better idea?" one of them asked, mopping sweat from his forehead.

"Yes, as a matter of fact I do," I told him, raising my phaser rifle, but careful to point it toward the ceiling. "We'll take care of the egg when the time is right, but in the meantime Spock is studying it for weaknesses."

"He's already found a soft spot," the man who had been arguing with him before said.

"Then let's shoot it in the soft spot and be done with it!" the cannoneer said. "Where is it?"

"Right here," the other man said, slapping the weak area ahead of the fin.

"Yeah!" someone else shouted, and other people took up the cry as well. "Kill it! Kill it now, before it hatches!"

"Wait!" I shouted, but my voice was lost in the din.

The cannoneers aimed their gun at the side of the egg, and one of them pulled back a cocking lever. "Take cover!" he yelled.

"Wait!" I shouted again, but it was plain that they weren't about to.

So I did the only thing I could do. I shot the cannon. It wasn't made of a hyperconnected organic molecule; it was simple iron, and its atoms dissociated instantly under the blast of a phaser rifle.

There was a shocked silence, into which I said, "We've got the situation under control."

We didn't, of course. The Devernians weren't big on authority, and they weren't happy at all about losing a cannon to some upstart alien. I heard angry muttering and knew that in a moment it would become an angry roar. And most of these people were armed.

Yeoman Colt and Lieutenant Garrett held their phaser rifles ready, but it was all for show. We couldn't shoot these people, not until they shot one of us, and by then we'd probably all be dead.

I could only think of one thing that might appease them. "Sorry, Spock," I said, raising my phaser rifle and firing at the egg's weak spot. They were going to kill it in a few minutes anyway, I told myself, right after they finished with us.

An area about the size of my outstretched hand began to glow. Red at first, then orange, intensifying through yellow and green and blue to white. Sparks, then whole tongues of flame shot out from the target site, but it didn't burn through.

"Add your phasers to mine!" I ordered, and two more energy beams converged on the spot as Colt and Garrett fired. Spock continued recording, since a fourth rifle shouldn't have been necessary. There was enough energy pouring into that one spot to punch through a small asteroid, but the egg still resisted. I felt my phaser grow warm in my hands, but I kept firing.

Sparks and flames continued to gush from the incandescent spot; then at last, just as I was beginning to wonder if our power would hold out, we cut through to softer tissue. In one last gout of flame our beams lanced into the creature within, which convulsed in a frantic attempt to break free. The spot that Spock had identified as the fracture point bulged outward; then a piece the size of a dinner plate blew free with explosive force, barely missing his head. It clanged off the ceiling and fell at Lanned's feet, and a mass of writhing tentacles reached a couple of meters out through the hole. One of them caught the arm of a Devernian who stood too close and wrapped around it with incredible speed, then yanked the man off his feet and smashed him into the side of the egg.

I shifted my aim to the tentacles and held my finger down on the trigger. Even they were amazingly resistant to our energy beams, but they weren't as tough as the shell. Within a second or two they began to crisp, and the creature dropped the Devernian and yanked them back inside. All four of us continued to fire while the egg rocked back and forth and the baby titan screeched in agony, but at last it subsided and after a few more seconds for good measure we let off. Smoke rose from both holes in the egg, and the air reeked of cooked flesh. The titan was dead, but even with that much continuous fire we hadn't managed to vaporize it. I checked my phaser charge: I was down to twenty percent.

The Devernians' anger at us had given over to awe at the pyrotechnic spectacle. "Where can I get me one of those things?" one man asked.

"I think your cannon would probably have done a better job," I said, disgusted with our poor showing.

That was apparently the right thing to say. The man who had asked the question laughed, then someone else joined him, and pretty soon the whole room full of people were laughing and slapping one another on the backs. The man who had been grabbed by the arm got up and dusted himself off, wincing when he moved but laughing nonetheless. Colt and I and Garrett even exchanged wide grins. No matter who had done the actual job, the titan menace had been stopped, and that was cause for celebration.

Except for Spock, of course, who was still taking readings of the corpse with his tricorder. And frowning. He turned away from the egg and stepped through the office debris to the wall farthest from it, his tricorder still whirring softly as he waved it from side to side.

"Problems, Spock?" I asked.

"I am still detecting metabolic activity consistent with a titan embryo," he replied. "Not, however, from this egg."

"You mean there's another one nearby?"

"That is affirmative."

I felt a chill run up my spine. I had seen a second flash in the sky, but I had thought it was just an afterimage. Apparently it had been another egg. If I had sounded a warning, the Devernians could have taken care of that one as well.

Maybe they had anyway. We couldn't tell what was going on even a block away from where we were. But I knew we had better have a look.

"Let's go!" I said. "Spock, how far is it?"

"That is difficult to ascertain, Captain. Perhaps three or four hundred meters. As we draw closer I will be able to pinpoint it more accurately."

"Lead on," I said, sounding a great deal more confident than I felt. Now that I'd seen what we were up against, I had a lot more respect for the danger. Those tentacles coming out of the egg would haunt me for weeks. Plus we were about out of phaser energy, and we couldn't just run back to the *Enterprise* to recharge.

It took a moment to get out of the building. The Devernians farther away from us had no idea what was going on; they thought the action was still inside. We managed to push our way out, and once they saw a group of their own people following a tall, pointy-eared alien with a humming instrument in his hand, they joined in and we became a good-sized mob advancing up the street. We were a fairly slow mob, since Spock set the pace and he couldn't watch his tricorder and his footing at the same time; plus it was hard to run in the muck.

Lanned was right beside me as we slogged along after Spock. I asked him, "Isn't it a bit coincidental that two eggs dropped on the same city at the same time?"

"There's no coincidence about it, Captain," he replied. "They followed your ship in. Since we began shooting at titans in space and driving them away, whenever one nears the planet they drop as many eggs as they can."

I groaned. "Oh, wonderful. You're saying we actually *brought* them here."

He nodded. "Don't be too hard on yourself. I suspected it might happen. You wanted to see what the titan threat was like on the ground; I thought this would be as good a way as any to show it to you."

"You could have warned us," I said.

He gave me a calculating look. "And why should I? You have to agree that the surprise is part of the experience."

I supposed it was that, but I could definitely have done without it. Of course that was Lanned's whole point. All of Devernia could do without it, and that's why they were doing what they were doing.

Yeoman Colt had overheard our exchange. Now she said to Lanned, "It sounds to me like you just need to run a blockade rather than hunting titans with bombs. If you can keep them from coming near enough to lay their eggs, then you don't have to actually kill them. You could even let a few titans through the blockade over uninhabited places if you wanted."

"Whatever for?" asked Lanned.

"To keep the population going," she answered. Lanned snorted derisively, but she pressed on. "You and the Aronnians both need them for raw materials. If you kill them all, both your economies will suffer. What's wrong with a blockade, if it will keep them from dropping eggs on your cities?"

Lanned held his arms out wide. "You of all people should be able to understand the sheer magnitude of an entire planet. It's costing us everything we have to keep them at bay even now that we have reduced the population by half. If we don't kill them all this year, we won't have the resources to keep up the effort next year. How could we maintain a perpetual blockade?"

He had a good point, at least from the Devernian point of view. But Colt said, "How about a network of phaser satellites? I know phasers aren't much good against eggs, but they did seem to sting what was inside it. Automated satellites could fire on any titans that came close, except over whatever breeding ground you set aside for them. Pretty soon they'd get the idea."

Lanned considered it. "Aside from the fact that we don't have your less-than-wonderful phaser technology, how many satellites do you suppose that would require?"

"I don't know," Colt said, "but I'll bet it would be a lot fewer than the number of missiles it takes to blow them all up."

Spock hadn't appeared to be listening, but now he lowered his tricorder and said, "Aside from the obvious Prime Directive violation, the number of satellites is not trivial. A typical phaser cannon of the magnitude that could be installed in a satellite has an effective range of perhaps a thousand kilometers. To guard the surface of a spherical volume of space within synchronous orbit around a planet of this size, even with minimal overlap, would require seven thousand and fifty-six satellites."

"Oh," she said.

Spock turned back to his tricorder, the issue settled as far he was concerned. "I believe the second egg is somewhere in the next block," he said. "Twenty degrees to the right of the street's path and seventy meters distant."

I estimated the range. There was a three-story building about that far away; twenty degrees to the right of the street would put the egg just behind it. As we jogged toward it we heard shouts and a sharp *pop, pop, pop* that I assumed was the report from Devernian handguns.

"Sounds like someone else discovered it already," I said.

Just then a screech like a wounded tyrannosaur split the air.

Lanned turned white. Even the dark stripes on his face faded to practically nothing. He reached instinctively to his side for a weapon that wasn't there—he hadn't been wearing one when we beamed him aboard the *Enterprise,* and he hadn't picked up one since—then turned to me and said, "It has hatched already."

"I kind of gathered that," I told him, checking to make sure my phaser rifle was still set on maximum output.

Colt and Spock and Lieutenant Garrett did the same, and we advanced toward the source of the noise. Most of the Devernians who had followed us did so too, but I noticed a few backing away. Even some of the ones with weapons. Not a good sign.

Thirteen

"WHAT'S A TYRANNOSAUR?" THE KLINGON WOMAN ASKED.

Pike looked over at her. So she was still listening, eh? Of course she was. And of course she wouldn't know what a tyrannosaur was.

"It's a big lizard," he told her. "About fifty meters tall, carnivorous, with a mouth big enough to park a shuttlecraft in."

"Where are they found?" she asked eagerly. "They sound like they would make interesting pets."

"They're found underground, these days. Fossilized. They lived on Earth a hundred million years ago, but they died out after an asteroid impact."

"Oh. Pity."

Pike laughed. "I'm not sure about that. Especially after what I saw on Devernia. Big monsters and people don't mix."

"What happened?" Nowan asked. "Who got killed?"

"Who didn't?" Pike asked, sobering somewhat. "I mean, think about it. The Devernians had a pretty decent planet, from what I saw of it. Their ancestors were minding their own business, making their own discoveries and working toward their own particular style of civilization, when all of a sudden these huge, ravenous beasts started dropping out of the sky. You can imagine what happened to the first guy who grew curious about an egg. And the first settlement near a landing site. Devernian history is full of death and destruction, all of it because of the titans."

Hompaq nodded approvingly. "Which no doubt strengthened them beyond measure. If you humans had lived when these tyrannosaurs did, you would have a more adventurous spirit."

"You think so?" asked Pike. "That's not what I found on Devernia. What I saw there was a society in collapse. They'd risen a long way, certainly, but they were on their way back down when we got there."

"Then they did not have a warrior's heart," Hompaq said, as though that were a moral failing worth damning an entire race for.

"You're right about that," Pike told her. "The only good thing I can say about the situation is that the Devernians had never discovered war. Oh, they knew about it. They understood the concept. They might even have gotten around to having one or two, if they could just take care of those pesky titans first. But their common enemy united them like nothing else could."

Nowan pursed his lips, considering that statement for a moment, before he said, "Perhaps that was not such a bad trade-off, if the outside threat truly eliminated warfare. Think of all the suffering humanity would have been spared if only we had fought against nature rather than one another."

Pike shrugged. "Eaten by dinosaurs or blown up by bombs; dead is dead."

"But the moral price to society is far less acute."

"True enough." Considering where this guy said he'd come from, Pike wasn't surprised he felt that way. "I agree with you," he said, "at least in principle. But when I remember what it felt like staring into the mouth of a wounded titan, I'm not so sure I would have appreciated the distinction at the time."

"So it did attack you?" asked Nowan.

"Oh yes. And everyone else within reach, too. We had quite a time with it."

" 'Quite a time'? A monster from the gates of Hell attacks and you had 'quite a time'? Sir, I'm afraid I must accuse you of understatement, if not false modesty as well."

Pike cocked his head sideways, and an impish grin slowly crept across his face. "Okay, then, we had a hell of a time. Bodies everywhere. Blood and guts and bullets and phaser beams flying back and forth, and the titan snarling and coming on like a runaway hovercar and the wounded screaming to be put out of their misery and heroic action on all sides and—"

"Enough, enough! I preferred 'quite a time.' "

Pike laughed. "I thought so. But it really was that."

"So divulge your secrets forthwith. Who went down the beast's gullet? This is your tale, so we know who played the hero, but who helped you bring it to its knees?"

Hompaq said, "It didn't have knees."

"I was speaking metaphorically," Nowan replied. Of Pike, he asked, "What did it look like, then? Like an octopus, perhaps?"

"A little," Pike replied. "Or a spider. Of course it was moving so fast what it mostly looked like at any given moment was a muddy ball of snakes. With big, triangular teeth . . ."

Fourteen

We couldn't go through the building; the people inside had slammed the heavy steel doors and weren't willing to open them for anyone. So we had to run down a narrow alley between that building and the next one. I expected the titan to rush toward us at any moment and catch us in the cramped space, but we made it to the alley in back without incident.

What we found there, however, was just as chilling as what I'd feared. The egg had come down in a courtyard garden, splashing up a wall of muddy soil which the hatchling now hid behind while it gulped down the body of a luckless Devernian. The mud had blocked off a corner of the courtyard, so the titan had two walls for protection behind it, and the mud in front. Fragments of eggshell sticking up from the mud also helped shield it from attack. All I could see of it was its mouth, round and lined with concentric rings of triangular teeth which all pointed inward to prevent their prey from escaping. The Devernian was beyond trying; only his legs stuck out now, and they betrayed no sign of life.

The others were firing a nearly continuous barrage from their projectile guns, but the beast kept too low for them to hit anything vital. The muddy bank spattered with ricocheting bullets, and I heard a few of them whiz past over our heads as well. I looked upward to see why the cannoneers on the rooftops hadn't fired yet, and I realized that the ones on the building right beside the creature couldn't shoot straight down on it. The building across the alley was only a single story tall, which gave the cannon there little better vantage than what we had from the ground. They were no doubt holding their fire for a clear shot.

The baby titan finished swallowing; then snarled again and stuck its head up over the edge. The cannon roared and the titan jerked backward, but I couldn't even see a wound where the projectile had struck. I saw where it bounced to, though; from the titan's nose it smashed into the stone steps by the building's back door, which acted like a perfect right-angle reflector and lofted it right back at the gun that had fired it. Fortunately gravity and air resistance had taken their toll, and it merely struck the building below their feet and fell to the ground, hissing as it cooled on the mud.

"Spock," I said, leaning close so he could hear me over the barrage of gunfire. "Can you find the weak spots here, too?"

"Affirmative, Captain," he replied, looking up from his tricorder. "Its body appears to be a compressed version of the adult form—an aerodynamic oblong with a large ramscoop mouth at the front and four small fins at the back which end in three tentacles per fin. Its skin is made of overlapping scales of the same material from which the eggshell is made, but it has four eyes set at equidistant points around the base of its mouth. The eyelids are also shielded, of course, but much less so than the rest of the body. If we could burn through the lids, the sockets beneath offer access directly to the brain."

"Great! How big are those eyes?"

"Approximately ten centimeters across."

"Oh." Maybe it wasn't so great after all. Ten centimeters across was hardly bigger than the palm of my hand. I was a fair shot with a phaser, but to hit a spot that size on a moving target, and hold the beam there until it burned through to the vital organs beneath, wasn't going to be easy.

We had to try it, though. I turned to Colt and Garrett and shouted, "Next time it shows itself, aim for the eyes!"

I considered moving closer, but that would put me in the path of the Devernians, and they didn't seem to be very cautious in their aim. What I really needed was high ground, but there were no trees in the courtyard and the building was smooth-sided and windowless. So we just shouldered our rifles and waited for the titan to rise above its shelter.

We didn't have to wait long. One Devernian was apparently not enough to assuage its hunger, or maybe it was smart enough to realize it couldn't stay hidden forever, but whatever the reason, it leaped out from behind the mud bank and raced toward us, its mouth open wide and its tentacles churning like multiple jointed legs to propel it along.

All I could see was mouth. I fired a quick burst at that, hoping to turn the creature aside, but its overlapping teeth were made of the same stuff as the eggshell and it hardly felt a thing. The Devernians fired dozens of shots directly into its gullet as well, with no more effect.

Colt and Garrett split apart to try and flank it. Even Spock clipped his tricorder back on his belt and raised his phaser rifle, but he held his fire until he could see an eye.

The rooftop cannon roared again, but the shot fell behind the creature. It was moving fast, covering the fifteen or twenty paces between its hiding spot and its attackers in a couple of seconds. They didn't stick around for it, however; the crowd split apart in two separate waves racing in either direction down the alley.

The titan turned to the right, toward us instead of broadside to us, which meant we still didn't have a good shot at it. And now it was coming straight at Lieutenant Garrett.

He fired his phaser down its throat. I aimed for the tentacles, the only other part of it I could see. Colt, off to our left, fired at its flank.

The triple combination definitely got its attention. And that probably saved Garrett's life, because the titan couldn't see what it was charging with its enormous ramscoop mouth opened wide. It slammed the mouth closed and turned its head sideways to get a better view of what had stung it, and all four of us immediately fired on the exposed eye.

The titan whipped around again, opening its mouth and roaring in pain. Our shots hadn't penetrated deeply, but we had definitely blinded that eye. And now that it had turned toward Spock and me, Garrett had a clear shot at the eye on the other side. His red energy beam lanced out, and the titan screeched and whirled around toward him, which let us have another shot at the eye we had already hit.

It had stopped advancing, but now it held its eyelids closed over its two damaged eyes, and the way it shook its head from side to side we couldn't hold our fire long enough to burn through to the brain.

The rooftop cannon fired once more, and this time the shot had an effect. The gunners were also aiming for the creature's eyes, and even though they missed the top one the massive slug struck with enough force to drive the titan's head momentarily to the ground. The armor-piercing core had ripped a ragged hole in its scaly hide, from which thick bluish green blood began to well up.

We took the opportunity to fire once more on the eye we could see, burning away the eyelid before the titan whirled around and fled for cover again.

"One more shot and we'll have it!" I shouted to the others.

That was easier said than done. The titan had hunkered down between the mudbank and the stone building and didn't present so much as a tendril for us to shoot at.

Perri and Lanned had both stayed with us during its charge. I felt flattered at their confidence in our ability, but considering how hard these things were to kill I also thought that confidence was a bit misplaced. My phaser was down to seven percent now. I had about two more good shots before I might as well start using it as a club.

Lanned didn't know that, of course. He said, "Come on, let's get closer. It's half blind now; we should be able to get within easy range."

"Getting within range is only part of the battle," I reminded him. "Surviving to do any good once we're there is just as important."

The look he gave me said "Chicken!" just as clearly as words. I believe he would have walked right up to the wounded titan and fired at it point-blank if I had given him my phaser, but I didn't.

Yeoman Colt had come back toward us again, and was looking toward its hiding place with a thoughtful expression on her face. "Captain?" she said.

"Yes?"

"What about those fragments of eggshell?"

They were still sticking up out of the ground on our side of the mud bank that the entire egg had splashed up when it struck. And some of them were big enough for a person to hide behind.

"The titan could flatten those in an instant," I said.

"Not that curved piece."

There was a hemispherical section of shell resting on its side near the top of the mud slope. A person could crouch down beside it, and if the titan rushed him the shell would fall over and cover him like a bomb shelter. Maybe. If the titan didn't rip it away and eat him instead.

"There's got to be a better way than that," I said, looking around at the courtyard to see what it might be, but the building was no more scalable than it had been before, and no trees had grown in the few minutes since we had arrived.

A few Devernians trickled back down the alley toward us, but the courtyard had grown quiet as we all—even the titan—waited for something to happen. Every moment we waited, though, gave it time to regain its strength, maybe even to heal the wounds we had given it. I had no idea how fast it could do that, but I didn't want to learn the hard way.

I picked up a fist-sized rock near my feet and flung it over the embankment. It hit the titan with a loud crack, but the creature didn't raise a tendril. Could we have killed it? We couldn't be that lucky. No, it was just too smart to leave cover again without good reason.

"Trade me rifles, Mr. Spock," I said, holding out my phaser to him. He didn't protest; he simply exchanged his nearly charged phaser for my nearly depleted one, then said, "The upper and lower eyes are still functional. Be careful."

"Right. The rest of you get close together so you can all aim for the same eye we hit before. Fire the moment it comes into view." I took a couple of steps toward the eggshell.

"Wait, Captain." I turned around. It was Colt. "You can't . . . I mean . . . it was my idea."

"And it's a good one," I said. "If it works, you'll receive a commendation."

"That's not what I meant, sir," she said stiffly.

"I know it isn't." I smiled. "When you're captain, then it'll be your turn to have all the fun."

I turned back and walked toward the egg, stepping lightly so the titan couldn't hear my approach. For once the soft ground helped out; I couldn't have made noise if I'd wanted to.

The eggshell stank. I didn't care; I didn't plan to stay there long. I approached it cautiously, made sure I knew where to jump if I had to, then peered around it to see if I could spot the titan.

It was looking right at me. The eyes on either side of its head were black and bubbling, but it held its head up so it could use the lower one. For a split second we stared at one another, then the titan roared a challenge and leaped up. I fired at its good eye, held the beam as long as I dared, then jumped for cover. As I flew through the air I saw three more phaser beams converge on a spot right over my head, and I had just enough time to curse my stupidity for taking the most fully charged phaser with me before the eggshell slammed down around me and the world went dark.

Devernia tasted terrible. I spit out a mouthful of salty mud, then pulled my arms and legs in close to my body. I didn't have room to get to my knees; I had to lie on my left side and hold the phaser rifle next to my chest. The eggshell muffled sound, but it couldn't block it completely, and I could hear the titan screeching right overhead. I expected it to crush the eggshell and flatten me into the mud at any second, but the noise went on and on and I felt only a few thumps against the shell. I heard a distant boom and knew that the cannon had fired again, then more screeching and the ground shook like jelly.

The eggshell slammed downward, pressing me deeper into the mud. I tried to move my feet, tried to raise my head, but I was pinned. I could move my hands just enough to feel that I had less than an arm's reach of space in any direction, which meant I had enough air for maybe five minutes at most.

The way it stank, running out might be a blessing.

I still held the phaser rifle. Its emitter was right near my head, and I didn't have room to turn it around. I didn't want to fire it in the enclosed space anyway; I had seen how long it took to burn through the eggshell material, and I didn't want to breathe the fumes it would generate while it did.

No more noise came from outside. They must have killed the titan, then. Much good would that do me; I suspected its body was lying directly on top of me.

I tried scratching at the ground to see if I could dig my way out, but the eggshell had been driven deep into the muddy soil and I could only dig a little ways before the hole began to fill again.

Suddenly I heard three soft thumps on the shell. Someone was out there! I thumped back with my fist, but it was like hitting a boulder. I could barely hear it even on my side. I grasped the phaser rifle and swung its butt against the shell near my knees and that did the trick. I pounded out three sharp raps in reply.

There were a couple more thumps from outside, then silence. I listened for a voice, but if anyone was calling to me, the shell blocked the sound.

"Hello!" I shouted, just in case they could hear *me.* "I'm okay, but I'm running out of air!"

Nothing. I thought I saw light, but then I realized it was phantom tracers in my own eyes. I didn't have much time left.

I tried to think of something I'd missed, but it was getting hard to keep my mind on the problem. I was getting sleepy, and I could hear a great rushing sound in my ears as I started to black out.

Well, I thought, *at least they're not going to find my body next to a full phaser rifle.*

I held the emitter up to the surface of the shell as far from my head as I could, and pulled the trigger. Bright light nearly blinded me as layer after layer of the tough polymer vaporized under its blast, but there was more shell than I had strength for. The phaser wavered, cutting a wide groove, before I braced my arms and held it on the original spot again. The tracers in my eyes grew worse, and my lungs felt as if they were on fire, but I held my finger on the trigger until the phaser beam sputtered and flared out.

The light didn't die. I saw a tiny circle of white, decided it had to be an afterimage in my eyes from staring at such an intense glare, but then just as I was about to lose consciousness the thought struck me: Afterimages of bright spots were dark, not light.

I awoke to a wet, sucking sound that I thought at first must be the noise a body makes as it slides down a monster's throat, but after a moment I realized I was still under the eggshell. Light was pouring in through a ragged hole in its side—light and sweet, wonderful air.

The sucking sound came again. Somebody was lifting the shell off me! Air rushed in through the hole to fill the partial vacuum created as it rose, and I stuck my face into the stream and breathed greedily. Who cared what it smelled like; it held oxygen!

Then I had a bad thought: What if it was the *titan* prying up the eggshell? I had just used up the last of my phaser charge.

I didn't have more than a few seconds to worry about it before the shell slid free of the mud and flew up over my head. I uncurled and sat up, ready to shove the rifle down the creature's throat ahead of me, at least, but instead of its ravenous mouth I saw dozens of people encircling me.

"Captain!" shouted Colt and Garrett. A cheer went up from the Devernians. I rose shakily to my feet and said, "Thank you!" but nobody could hear me.

There was so much shouting and backslapping that I was afraid the Devernians would finish the job that the titan had started, but they stopped just short of breaking bones. Colt offered her arm to steady me as I staggered under the assault, and I managed to stay on my feet.

On top of the embankment lay the body of the titan. Smoke rose from the side of its head where its right eye used to be. Its tentacles lay limp now, dangling from undeveloped stabilizing fins that would never guide it through an atmosphere. I supposed I should have felt bad about its death, but at the moment I couldn't. I looked over at Perri, but the Aronnian looked more stunned than dismayed.

He also looked completely disheveled. So did everyone else, now that I thought about it. I looked down at my own clothing, which was covered in mud all along the left side. I had mud in my hair as well. I must have looked even worse than the others, but at the moment I didn't care. The titan was dead and I was alive.

When things died down a bit I noticed Spock—who barely had a hair out of place—scanning the body with his tricorder again. His expression was that of a scientist making a major discovery.

"What is it, Spock?" I asked him.

"Fascinating," he replied. "In addition to its digestive organs and nervous system, this immature titan already has a partially developed warp engine, a fully operational fusion engine, and a microtubule hydrogen storage tank of surprising capacity. The tank is empty now, but next to it is an osmotic filtration system capable of filtering enough deuterium from seawater to completely fuel it within two weeks' time."

Its fusion engine was already developed? "We're lucky it wasn't fueled when it hatched," I said, "or it could have fried us all in a heartbeat."

"That is true," he replied, "but luck may have played less of a role than simple evolutionary pressure."

"Evolution?" I asked. "How so?"

Spock continued scanning with his tricorder as he answered. "Deuterium is a precious resource in space, but it is relatively abundant on planets. Since the hatchling would not normally need flight capability until it was ready to leave for space again, there would be no reason for the mother to deplete her own supply of deuterium by providing any to the developing egg."

"I guess that makes a certain amount of sense," I replied. "Although I find it hard to believe that anything could evolve a fusion engine in the first place."

"Nevertheless," Spock said, "I find considerable evidence that the osmotic fueling system, at least, is a relatively new addition to their genetic code. I have a theory, based on my study of the unhatched egg and this more developed specimen. Are you familiar with the concept of neoteny?"

I realized I was standing there in the middle of a devastated courtyard, tired and wet and covered with mud, while my science officer was about to expound on the origin of the creature that had nearly killed me. "No, Spock," I said. "I'm not familiar with it, but I don't think this is the time to go into it. I want a hot shower first, and a good meal."

He nodded stiffly, obviously disappointed that he couldn't share his theory with everyone, and went back to gathering more information.

I took my communicator from my belt and flipped it open, but it didn't respond. Not surprising; it was full of mud.

I sighed. "Yeoman, could you please call the *Enterprise* and request beam-out?"

"Yes sir," she replied. She took out her communicator and opened it with both hands. "Colt to *Enterprise.* Come in, *Enterprise.*"

"*Enterprise* here," Dabisch replied.

"Six to beam up."

"We're on our way, but it'll take a few minutes. These titans have been chasing us halfway around the system."

"Understood." She paused a moment, then said, "Captain, if they come in over the city again, the titans who follow them will just drop more eggs."

She was right. "Tell them to stay over the ocean and beam us out from there," I said.

She relayed the order, then closed her communicator.

Lanned said, "I'm not sure I want to go back to your ship. I've got a planet to help defend here."

I couldn't argue with him. Not after what I'd seen. Even Perri didn't seem inclined to protest.

Spock, however, said, "If my theory about their origin is correct, we may have need of someone who understands their habits."

"So what's your theory?" Lanned asked.

"The short version," I said. "We've only got a few minutes."

"Understood. I think it is quite obvious that the titans are not indigenous to the Devernian nor the Aronnian planetary systems. Their metabolic processes share nothing with the local biology, and we have Lanned's own testimony that they appeared only five hundred years ago. They must therefore come from a neighboring system. From the stages of development that I have studied, I find evidence that they are evolving at a rapid rate. This indicates to me that they are adapting to a new ecological niche, which in turn indicates that they had a considerably different living arrangement wherever they came from."

"So?" asked Lanned. "It's what they're doing here that concerns us."

"Just so," said Spock. "What they are doing here, essentially, is breeding without check. Yet they cannot breed like this everywhere they go, or they would have overrun the galaxy already. Therefore, if you wish to stop them from doing so here, I suggest finding out what keeps them in check elsewhere. If we can do that, we can perhaps stabilize their population at a less dangerous—and ultimately more useful—level."

"I'm not sure I want to find something big enough to eat a titan," Perri said nervously.

"And I'm not sure I'd want it in my solar system if we found it," Lanned said. "It could easily cause more trouble than even the titans do."

"Predators do not have to be larger than their prey, nor even more fearsome," said Spock. "On my home planet, Vulcan, the sehlat is our most efficient predator, yet it is no larger than me and gentle enough to be kept as a pet. On Earth, where Captain Pike comes from, wolves are a similar predator. There are also parasites and disease to consider, either of which can limit the population of creatures far larger than themselves."

Lanned thought it over for a moment. I heard a murmur run through the crowd around us as Spock's idea passed along from person to person. I was thinking about it, too, but from a different angle than they were. I was trying to decide if we had a Prime Directive problem on our hands.

The Prime Directive stated that Starfleet personnel were prohibited from interfering with the normal development of a society. Generally that meant no interference whatsoever, but the key phrase in the rule was "normal development." Devernia hadn't enjoyed anything like "normal development" since the titans had arrived. How bad was an outside influence to correct another outside influence?

I could have radioed Starfleet Headquarters for advice. They would mull it over for a year or three, kick it up to higher authority for review, and eventually come to a decision about the time the last Devernian was eaten. And if that happened it would be my fault, because *I* was supposed to be the higher authority. It was my job to be Starfleet's representative on the scene. I knew the rules as well as anyone, I knew the exceptions that had been allowed before, and I knew the disasters that had happened when they were ignored. I also—at least theoretically—knew the situation at hand better than anyone else.

So it was my call. If I made the right decision, I could become a hero. If I made the wrong one, I could face a court-martial, though I might still be a hero to the people my decision saved.

When I thought about it that way, the choice didn't seem that difficult to make.

Lanned must have been thinking along the same lines. Besides which, I could see the same gleam in his eyes that I had seen in Perri's when he had first arrived on board the *Enterprise.* Lanned had been in space before, but he had never ridden a titan. The prospect of an interstellar flight definitely appealed to him. And if he returned home a hero, well, so much the better.

"Very well," he said. "I will accompany you on your search for the home of the titans."

Fifteen

In the Captain's Table, the seaman who sat across from Captain Pike had the same gleam in his eyes. He shook his head slowly, in the manner of a man who doesn't know whether or not to believe what he's just heard. "Sailing from star to star," he said. "What man wouldn't jump at the chance?"

"Oh, lots of them," Pike replied. "Even nowadays there are millions of people who won't leave the planet."

"Millions? That implies that millions have the choice, does it not?"

"Well, sure, but even when spaceflight was limited to just a few trained astronauts, there were millions of people who didn't want *them* to go either. Humanity has always had its share of stay-at-homes." He looked over to Hompaq and said, before she could make the obvious snide comment, "And so do the Klingons, or your homeworld would be a ghost planet."

She had indeed been about to say something, but she stopped with her mouth open, then laughed softly and said, "That's not necessarily true. We could all come and go."

"You could. But you don't, do you?"

"No."

Nowan looked at the two of them for a moment, biting his lower lip while he worked up his nerve to say something. Pike noticed his hesitation and asked, "What?"

He breathed deeply, exhaled, then said, "I mean no offense, but when you first began your tale I felt confident that you were merely a skilled fabulist. The very things you described lent credence to that theory, for I knew they could never actually happen. Yet you speak so convincingly of them, and pile detail upon detail, until I can no longer maintain my disbelief. You *do* voyage among the stars, do you not?"

"I did," Pike admitted. "Nowadays I've got a desk job just up the street."

"And this disturbs you. You have lost something valuable, a part of your life that you are afraid you may never recover."

"Guilty," Pike said, surprised at how obvious his melancholy must be.

"That merely caps the edifice of credibility you have been constructing all evening. Somehow, in some way I cannot yet fathom, you travel the stars. She also travels the stars. And this . . . being over here—" he nodded toward the reptilian humanoid near the door, who blinked one eye and dipped a long, orange tongue into his bloodred drink "—could only come from another star himself. For you, this apparently isn't even unusual."

Pike laughed softly. "Oh, it's unusual enough. I've never seen our friend by the door's species before, nor the curvaceous cat-woman's, either. Klingons I've seen aplenty, but finding one in a bar half a kilometer from Starfleet Headquarters is a bit out of my experience as well." He looked around the bar as he spoke, slowly building up his own nerve to ask the question that had now become foremost in his mind. He felt a bit silly actually voicing it, but he could no longer ignore the evidence. "I imagine my confusion is slight compared to yours. Tell me, what was the stardate when you entered this bar?"

"Stardate? If you refer to the Julian method of calculation, that has been out of vogue for more than a century. In the Gregorian reckoning, today is August twelfth, 1861."

The only surprise Pike felt came when he realized how little Nowan's words surprised him. He had already suspected something like this. He had no idea how it could be possible, but he knew this guy was the genuine article.

Nowan, too, was ready to believe. "And what was the date when you entered?" he asked. "No, wait, let me guess. Your *Enterprise* is the size of a small city. It is the pride of your star fleet, but it is not the only one of its kind. Millions of people have traveled in ships like it, or had the opportunity. For this to happen, I would guess fully two hundred years must have passed between my time and yours."

"Good guess," Pike told him. "But you didn't figure on two world wars before spaceflight even got started, and a whole generation of people who thought it was more expensive than it was worth, plus the Eugenics Wars and another world war after that. When I woke up this morning it was stardate 1626.8. In the Gregorian system that would be, let's see . . . times eight, carry the six . . . October third, 2266. Or is it the seventh? I can never remember the conversion factors."

It didn't matter to Nowan. "Good God! Over four hundred years. I am dust and bones to you."

"Maybe, maybe not," Pike said. "You're here now." He turned to Hompaq. "How about you?" he asked. "What's your era?"

She bared her teeth. "I could dance on your grave, Captain Pike, if I could reach it."

"Do tell," he said casually, but inside he felt as if he'd just grasped a live plasma conduit. She could be playing games with him, but he didn't think so. There were too many discrepancies in this bar for him to be in the right time either. And it was all fine and good to think of the poor seaman as a castaway on the shoals of time, but when he suddenly found himself the anachronism, things became a great deal more personal.

He couldn't let it go, though. "Where am I buried?" he asked.

"Do you really want to know?"

Did he? Probably not, but he'd always hated those hokey tri-vids where the characters backed away from information that later turned out to be vital. The location of his grave was probably the most vital information he was likely to get, so he said, "Sure. Where am I buried?"

"Remember Talos IV?" she asked.

"How could I forget?" For Nowan's benefit he said, "Yeoman Colt and Number One and I were captured by aliens there once. They had the power to completely cloud our minds, to make us see anything they wanted us to. We barely got away." To Hompaq he said, "Talos IV has been interdicted. It's a capital offense even to communicate with the Talosians. Why would anyone take my body there?"

"Maybe you're not dead when you go," she said.

Again he felt that shock of dissonance. How easily she spoke of his demise! Killed by Talosians after all. What a rotten way to go. And the worst part of it was, he would probably not even know he was there. They would make him think he was back on the *Enterprise,* or horseback riding in Mojave, while he was really strapped to a dissecting table in their filthy underground warrens.

"Why would I ever go back?" he asked. "Can they lure me there over this kind of distance? If so, then nobody is safe."

The bartender had been listening quietly, but now he spoke up. "Calm yourself, Captain," he said. "Talos is no threat to anyone. But you could be, if you followed that line of thought."

Pike didn't even have to ask what he meant by that. An entire career of interstellar duty had driven home the Prime Directive and all that it implied. Partial knowledge could be more dangerous than ignorance. If Pike thought the Talosians were mounting an attack on the Federation, he could set into motion a preemptive strike that would drain Federation resources at a time when they were already facing threats on too many fronts. Not to mention starting a battle with someone who might not deserve it—though Pike had no love for the Talosians.

Nor Klingons, when it came to that, yet he found himself strangely attracted to Hompaq. He looked more closely at her. That heavily convoluted forehead wasn't normal for Klingons. At least not Klingons of his era. Nor, he suspected, was it the result of an accident. Hompaq must have been from far enough in the future that her race had actually evolved into this form. Or maybe this was a cosmetic thing, a personal choice she had encoded into her own genes for amusement.

Or for battle. He would hate to butt heads with her in a dark alley.

"So tell me, are we at war with one another?" he asked her.

"In whose time?"

"In—" He stopped, realizing how utterly meaningless his question was. They weren't at war yet in his time, and Hompaq could be from anywhen. He looked back to the bartender. "What date is it *here,* right *now?"*

The bartender shook his head. "I can't answer that."

"Why? Prime Directive?" Pike asked him.

"More like meaningless question."

"Okay, then, *where* are we?"

"Equally meaningless."

"Then how did I get here?"

"You walked through the door. And if you ever want to find this place again after you leave, that's about all the more you want to ask about it."

"Why?" Pike asked. The bartender rolled his eyes, and Pike realized he was being a pest. And maybe he was jeopardizing something truly special. He had heard of places like this before, in legends of fairy rings and disappearing magic shops. Always the newcomer was warned not to inquire too closely into the secret. He was the newcomer here, and he had just received the same warning, but he had never been satisfied with the legends and he wasn't satisfied now. "What does it matter if I know where this place is, or when it is?" he asked.

The bartender sighed. "When did you say you were from? 2266?"

"Yeah."

"Then you are familiar with the Heisenberg Uncertainty Principle."

"It's impossible to know both the position and the velocity of a particle at any given time. So?"

"So that's three variables. The velocity of the envelope of space-time that encompasses this bar is negligible. That means you can either know its position or the time, but not both. Take your pick, but hold on to your hat if you decide on the time."

"That's—we have Heisenberg compensators on our transporters to get around that very problem."

"We don't," said the bartender. He looked at Pike with a steady gaze, waiting for him to decide.

"So I'm just supposed to relax and accept it?" Pike asked at last.

"That's the general idea." The bartender smiled, then turned away and began to polish his glassware.

Pike looked at Hompaq, who also smiled in her pointy-toothed way, then he looked at the other bar patrons, who all wore amused expressions as well. Even the seaman at his own table was grinning.

"Why do I feel like the ghost at the banquet?" Pike asked him.

"It appears we're all ghosts at this particular banquet," Nowan replied. "And while I have never heard of this Heisenberg mystery you refer to, I suspect our esteemed host has the right of it. My inquiry, and yours following it, have proved to be a herring in the path of our Devernian fox. We turn aside at our peril, and disappoint all who follow the hunt."

Pike saw that everyone else in the bar had once again stopped what they were doing to follow what he and Nowan were saying. He felt a bit put on the spot. Didn't these people know that it wasn't polite to eavesdrop on someone else's conversation?

At least it wasn't polite in Pike's time. But customs varied from time to time and place to place, and as he had been gently informed just now, he wasn't in Kansas anymore. Nor San Francisco, most likely. Nor, for that matter, in 2266.

But if any custom was likely to be universal, he imagined it was the one that said it was impolite to stop telling a story in the middle.

There would be time enough later to unravel the mystery of the Captain's Table, if he decided to pursue it.

He took a cautious sip of his Saurian brandy—he had drunk quite enough of that for a while, but he did need to lubricate his throat a bit—then said, "Very well, the Devernians. Let's see . . . Spock had decided that the titans had opened the wrong door and wound up someplace they didn't belong, so we were about to head off in search of their rightful home. Fortunately we didn't worry about the Heisenberg Uncertainty Principle, or we might never have tried. . . ."

Sixteen

I STAYED IN THE SHOWER FOR A GOOD HALF HOUR, LETTING BOTH WATER and ultrasonics scour away the memory of Devernia. I suspect the rest of my landing party did the same; none of them surfaced again for at least an hour after our return. Except for Spock, of course. He was already on the bridge when I got there, poring over star charts for the local region of space. I settled into my command chair and said to Number One, "Status?"

"All systems operational, sir," she reported. "Engineering is still repairing minor subsystems all through the ship, but the engines and helm controls are back up to specs. Shields are functioning at one hundred percent, and energy reserves are at full capacity. We're ready for space."

"Good. Mr. Spock, have you figured out where we should go yet?"

"I have identified seven stars as likely candidates for the origin of the titans," he said. "Unfortunately my selection criteria must remain rather crude until I receive further data, so these seven are merely the ones that are closer to Devernia than Aronnia and which also possess gas-giant planets."

"I would think that would include half the galaxy," I said. "How did you narrow it down to seven?"

"By factoring in the calculated speed and maximum range of the titans. Their energy source is deuterium fusion, not matter-antimatter annihilation, so they have a much more limited range than we do. By calculating the size of their fuel tanks and estimating the efficiency of their warp engines, I came up with a figure of fifteen light-years as their maximum range without refueling."

"Very clever," I said. "So which one of our targets is the closest of the seven?"

Spock put a star map up on the main screen, and used the computer's pointer to indicate one of the myriad stars on it. "This one here, which is actually a G2-F6 double, designated merely by a survey record number of L2334.45."

"A double star, that's good," I said. "Two chances of finding something in one place."

"It also has the advantage of being on the edge of an unexplored sector," said Spock. "I assume that we would have records of titans from other survey teams if anyone had encountered them; therefore it seems likely that what we seek is in unexplored space."

"Very likely indeed," I said. "Mr. Tyler, you have the coordinates. Number One, take us there, warp factor seven."

"Yes sir." As soon as Tyler keyed in the course she engaged the warp engines and the *Enterprise* leaped away from Devernia. I wasn't sorry to see it fall away behind us when we switched the viewscreen back to the exterior view.

I busied myself with the detailed ship's status report that Dabisch had prepared for me, noting that a work crew had gone out in a shuttlecraft to check the damage we had received to the outer hull when the titans had physically attacked us. The video of that was pretty sobering: dents in the duranium from direct impacts, long gashes from the titans' armor-plated ramscoop mouths, sensors torn entirely free . . . it would take months to repair it all. The video tour zoomed in on one window with a star-shaped crack in it and I wondered if anyone had been inside the room when it happened. Possibly; the damage report indicated that the window was in observation room J-12, which might have held off-duty crew members interested in watching our approach to Devernia. Somehow what they would have seen seemed even scarier than what I had faced on the planet, though I couldn't explain even to myself why the prospect of being sucked into space by explosive decompression and then eaten was any worse than simply being eaten.

The repair crew had not yet repaired the window; until they could get to it they had merely covered it with an external sealant and closed the room to use. It wouldn't have done anyone much good to go in there now anyway, I noticed, since the sealant was black.

When I finished the status report and still hadn't heard from either of our guests, I asked the computer to locate them for me.

"Both Perri and Lanned are in the cafeteria," it replied in its synthesized female voice, which I had always thought sounded just like Number One's. I sometimes kidded her about it, telling her that it must mean she had the theoretically perfect pitch and intonation for easy understanding, but this time the computer's words robbed all thought of teasing from my mind.

"Uh-oh," I said. The two of them together unsupervised sounded like a good way to start a food fight.

"Number One, you have the conn," I told her as I headed downship to stop it.

When I got there, however, I found them both at the same table, chatting happily with Yeoman Colt. All three of them glowed from recent showers, and Colt glowed even more from all the attention she was receiving. I felt a momentary pang of annoyance, but I quashed it immediately. It was part of her job to help entertain guests; if she happened to enjoy it, so much the better.

I almost turned away to leave them to their conversation, but Perri looked up and saw me at the door before I could go. "Ah, Captain," he said. "I see we are under way already." He nodded out the windows to where the white starlike streaks that formed the subspace representation of interstellar space were sweeping past.

"No sense wasting time," I replied. "There's a lot of places to search, and not much time if we want to save both Devernia and the titans."

He nodded. "After seeing conditions there I must say I'm not sure how both can be saved, but I agree we must try."

Lanned made a rude noise with his lips. "Such a selfless position, for someone who stands to benefit greatly if we succeed."

"As will you," said Perri. "You seem determined to declare yourself at cross-purposes with me, but the truth of the matter is that we are both now interested in the same thing."

"Indeed," said Lanned, and he turned his attention back to Colt.

She laughed. "You had better keep your minds on the titans."

"What's the hurry? It will be a day at least before we arrive at the first star system. A great deal can happen in a day."

"Can it really?" she asked innocently, but she kept smiling.

"Well," I said, "it looks like you've got the situation here under control. I'll leave you three to it." I turned away, then remembered where we were and turned back to Lanned. "I don't know if Dr. Boyce mentioned this to you yet, but you can't have onions or garlic. You either, Mr. Perri. Don't forget."

Lanned said, "Yes, I received the unfortunate news. And now of course my tongue yearns for this exotic flavor that's forever denied me." He said to Colt, "You will have to describe it to me in full sensual detail."

"Onions?" she asked. "Sensual?" Then she got a mischievous look on her face and said, "Well, maybe so. Under the right circumstances."

"See?" cried Lanned. "I knew it. Ah, cruel fate!"

"Be glad that's the only thing you're denied," I told him, then I took my leave.

He seemed a bit taken aback at my tone of voice, but I didn't even try to explain. Maybe Colt could explain it to him, but I really didn't know.

As I walked back to the turbolift I thought about the strange quirks of fate that put some people in position to enjoy a thing that someone else could not. It could certainly be frustrating. I imagined it seemed quite unfair to anyone caught on the receiving end of a Prime Directive problem, for instance. Or the not-receiving end, as it were. It would be tough enough to discover someone who had solved a problem that still loomed large in your own society, but how much harder it must be to watch them leave without telling you how they'd done it.

I wondered if that was what we would find somewhere ahead of us. Spock said he'd found evidence that the titans were evolving, but I had a hard time imagining what they could have evolved *from.* The way I figured it, they had to be genetically engineered, and that implied a society somewhere ahead of us that could do it. Ahead both spatially and technologically.

The *Enterprise* had already met a few superior races, and without exception those encounters had been unpleasant. We'd been captured, toyed with, dismissed, and demoralized more than once, and I didn't want it to happen again. Yet it could happen at any moment out here in uncharted space. No Federation ship had ever been to this star we approached now; we could find just about anything there.

Lanned had been right: at warp seven it would be a day before we arrived. I knew I should try to get some sleep before then, but I was too keyed up. If I tried in this condition, I would just toss and turn and feel worse than if I didn't bother.

Fortunately I had learned a good trick for putting myself to sleep when I needed to. The gym was on the same deck as the cafeteria; I walked around the curved corridor until I reached it, then went inside to tire myself out lifting weights.

We approached the G2 component of the double star system first. Not because we suspected any more likelihood of finding anything there, but simply because it was a tenth of a light-year closer to Devernia than the F6 star at this point in their orbit.

We dropped out of warp with our shields down. It was always a gamble to do that, but the energy attenuation fields cut the effectiveness of our sensors, and I preferred being able to see what was out there rather than hunkering down and waiting for it to come knock on our shell. At Devernia I had chosen the opposite tactic and it had paid off, but a captain learns to play his hunches, and I had a hunch we wouldn't find a war in progress here.

Spock was ready at the science station. The moment we emerged into normal space, he said, "Scanning for energy signatures. . . . No spaceborne sources within sensor range. Scanning planetary surfaces. . . . No artificial sources there either. Scanning for life-forms. . . ."

It took a little longer to do that, but the result was the same. "No life-forms registered in the entire planetary system."

"What do we have here for planets?" I asked.

"Two class K, marginally habitable, one gas giant, class T, and asteroid fields of astonishing density in each of the interorbital spaces between planets." He frowned and adjusted a sensor. "The asteroids are unusually uniform in size. They are, in fact, the same size as adult titans."

"But no sign of life?" I asked.

"None, sir."

"Take us closer," I said to Number One.

We swept into the system under impulse power, and as we approached the first asteroid belt, I said, "On screen, high magnification."

The view expanded, stars rushing off the screen to be replaced by tiny, dim points of light. As the *Enterprise* drew closer, they grew from points to tiny oblongs, and from tiny oblongs to bigger oblongs.

Perri and Lanned stood on either side of my command chair, having finally allowed Yeoman Colt to escape their attentions. I didn't allow myself to wonder if either of them had succeeded in winning her affection. I said to them, "Look familiar to you?"

"They are titans," Perri said softly. "Millions of them. All dead."

"What happened to them?" asked Lanned.

"Spock?" I asked.

Information flowed onto his monitors faster than a human could follow, but he seemed to have no problem interpreting it. "I see signs of violence. Fins torn away, some bodies partially eaten. Others seem intact, but thinner than desiccation alone would account for."

"How long ago did all this happen?" I asked.

He consulted his instruments. "Exact dating is difficult, but from the amount of heavy ions deposited by the solar wind, I calculate no more than a thousand years. Perhaps as little as two hundred."

"So these could have been the ones that seeded the Devernia system."

"That seems likely."

"And then they all died out."

Perri grew agitated. "Could this happen to our titans as well? Spontaneous death of the whole species?"

Spock said, "Death is seldom spontaneous. I believe we can safely assume that this many creatures died of some external cause."

"What is it, then?"

"I do not know—yet." Spock turned back to his monitors.

"Take us to within ten kilometers," I said to Number One. "Get ready to raise shields."

"Yes, sir."

If something external had killed them, I didn't want to find out what it was the hard way. But as we drew closer, it became more and more apparent that most of the titans were still intact. They looked thin, though. I could see their skeletons through their scaly hide: hexagonal and pentagonal matrices like geodesic domes, narrowing down to their bulging engines at the tail.

"They look emaciated," I said. "Did they starve to death?"

"That appears to be the case." Spock consulted more instruments, switching to different sensors and frowning when he realized the ones he wanted were gone. "Though I cannot rule out poisoning or pathogens."

"What about the ones that are damaged?"

"The wounds are consistent with the bite patterns we suffered when titans attacked our ship. It looks as if they tried to eat each other."

Starving creatures often did that. It sometimes even worked, if there was a possibility of rescue or if the survivors could last until the famine ended. But nobody had come to rescue these poor beasts, and apparently their food supply had dried up for good.

Then I remembered what they ate. "How could they run out of *hydrogen?*" I asked. "We're talking about the atmosphere of a *gas giant* for a food source here."

Spock said, "The titans need more than just hydrogen. Spectroscopic analysis of their bodies reveals carbon, sulfur, potassium, and seventeen other trace elements."

"All of which are found in gas-giant atmospheres, aren't they?"

"Normally that is so," Spock said. "However, this system's gas giant is atypical. It is class T, which means it is mostly helium and heavier gases surrounding a rocky core. That core, however, displays many of the internal characteristics of a class-U planet, which has a significantly higher ratio of hydrogen, methane, and ammonia in its atmosphere. I theorize that this once *was* a class-U planet, until its hydrogen and hydrocarbons were consumed by titans."

I couldn't believe it. They skimmed off an entire planet's atmosphere? Then I looked out at the drifting carcasses, millions of them—probably billions of them—filling the solar system. There were so many they actually formed rings around the star. They reminded me of Saturn's rings, with their gaps where shepherd moons orbited and kept the particles from drifting away. Except each of these "particles" was two-thirds the size of the

Enterprise. Suddenly it didn't seem so unlikely that they could have consumed an entire gas giant's hydrogen supply.

"I wonder what they did to the terrestrial planets?" I asked.

Spock put an image of one on the screen. The planet was mostly brown, with small ice caps on the poles. There didn't seem to be much cloud cover, but then there didn't seem to be a lot of water to create clouds with. I didn't see any evidence of oceans. I couldn't see much other detail; on that scale it was hard to see anything smaller than a few square miles.

"Take us in for a closer look," I told Number One. The planet was a third of the way across the system, so she had to fly us up out of the plane of the ecliptic to get past the ring of titans. While we traversed the seemingly infinite plain of dead bodies, I said to Perri and Lanned, "Looks like there's a lifetime supply of free fusion drives and warp engines out there if someone could figure out how to harvest them and adapt them to a conventional spaceship."

"We have tried," said Perri. "Without the circulatory system to provide them with nutrients, they break down."

"Break down? As in 'malfunction' or 'decompose'?"

"Decompose," he replied. "There appears to be an enzyme in their cellular structure that triggers the process after they die." He considered his words a moment, then said, "However, studying them is how we learned to build our own fusion engines."

"But not warp engines," I said. "For those you still use live titans. Why?"

"Well, um . . ."

"Because we can't figure them out," said Lanned.

"That's not true!" Perri protested. "We just don't—"

"It is so," Lanned said. "You managed to fool that Federation first-contact group into thinking you built the titans, but the fact is you don't know the first thing about them."

"That's no surprise to me," I told him. "Nor is it any concern of mine, other than simple curiosity. You possess interstellar flight capability; that's one of the criteria for membership in the Federation. Unless you stole it, which doesn't seem to be the case, how you got it is not an issue."

Perri looked surprised, and I laughed. "You've been trying to hide your ignorance from us all along, but it really doesn't matter. The Federation is as inclusive as we can be without interfering in a society's development. We're not going to kick you out because you get your spaceships for free."

"I would hardly call it 'for free,' " Lanned said.

"Good point."

We were approaching the planet by then. Its gravity had cleared a wide space in the ring of titan bodies, so Tyler set up a standard polar mapping orbit four hundred kilometers above the surface and Number One brought us in. Spock locked the telescope onto a spot below and increased the magnification until we were looking straight down on a dry streambed that cut through a rocky desert. I didn't see anything growing, nor any evidence that anything had ever grown there—except for titans. Bodies of young ones as well as old littered the ground, the old ones crumpled up in the middle of craters that attested to their inability to land once they achieved adulthood. They must have been so desperate they tried it anyway, or else they knew they were committing suicide.

As we swept around the planet in our orbit, the telescope lost its lock and began to show us a moving image of the surface directly below. We saw more and more titans, some of them piled up in drifts, for thousands of kilometers.

A steep cliff swept past; then the character of the ground changed from the heavily eroded badlands we had been looking at to a smoother surface. Wind blew dust into swirling tornadoes a kilometer high. Then I saw a few flat-topped mesas with little mountains on the tops of them and I realized what this had to be.

"Those are islands!" I said. "Spock, freeze that image."

He did so, and I pointed to the fried-egg features on the landscape. "See the reefs around the edges, and the long, gentle slope that used to be beach? This dusty ground used to be seafloor, and that cliff we saw a minute ago had to be the continental slope at the edge of what used to be land."

Spock said, "I believe you are correct. Deep-penetration radar shows a much thinner rock crust in this area, which is consistent with a seafloor. We must assume that the oceans have dried up."

"Been swallowed up, more likely," I said. "By baby titans filtering deuterium from seawater."

Lanned said softly, "This is what Devernia will look like in time."

"Not if we can help it," I said. "This is just more proof that the rest of their ecosystem didn't come with them. It's obvious they can't live without an outside influence to keep their numbers in balance. We'll find out what it is, don't worry."

"Don't worry?" he said. "Captain, this sight will haunt me to my dying day, whether we find a solution to the problem or not. Just knowing this *could* happen to us will always make me worry."

I shrugged. "Maybe that's smart. You're less likely to be surprised by the next thing fate drops in your lap. Mr. Spock, unless you need to take more readings, I suggest we continue our search."

"I believe my sensor log has recorded sufficient detail here," he said.

"Good. Tyler, set course for the other half of this binary system. I suspect we'll find the same thing there, but we're so close we might as well look and see."

"Yes sir." He supplied Number One with the coordinates and she brought us out of orbit, then engaged the warp engines, and we left the devastated planet and the rings of dead titans behind.

Seventeen

NOWAN SHOOK HIS HEAD SADLY. "THAT MUST HAVE BEEN A SIGHT. I'VE seen an entire bay filled with whales slaughtered for their oil, but I've never seen anything of the magnitude you describe."

"Neither had I," Pike told him. "It was a pretty sobering sight. Rings clear around a *star,* all made up of dead bodies. It gave me the creeps."

" 'The creeps.' An interesting phrase. Evocative. I may steal it."

"Feel free," said Pike. "It's not original with me."

Nowan laughed. "It no doubt comes from a century or two before your time. That would make me only two or three centuries ahead of mine when I use it." He shook his head. "I will no doubt take away more than just that from our discussion here today. But there is one thing I am afraid I must leave behind."

"And what is that?" Pike asked him.

"The brandy!" Nowan laughed at his own joke, then scooted his chair away from the table and stood up. "If you will excuse me for a moment, I must find the necessarium."

"Of course," Pike said.

Nowan turned once around, looking for the proper door. When he looked toward the corner beyond Hompaq, she tilted her bony forehead toward the back of the bar instead. "Behind there."

"Ah, thank you." He hurried away.

Pike got up and carried their empty glasses over to the bar. "Two more, please," he asked the bartender, who was mixing something green and fuming for one of the men at the cat-woman's table.

"Coming up."

He felt less nervous standing next to the Klingon woman now, though he really didn't know any more about her than he had before. Less, actually. She could be anyone, from anywhere. If this bar was like the places of legend, then she might have stepped into it from the Klingon homeworld, or from halfway across the galaxy.

He looked at the other patrons' reflections in the mirror. Even the humans could be from anywhere, or anywhen. He wondered how many of them recognized him. How many of them knew his fate.

Hompaq apparently did, though he had a hard time believing he would wind up on Talos IV again. The fact that she even knew about the place argued that she knew something about him, though. He wondered what else she knew.

"So tell me," he said, "has anyone made it safely through the Galactic Barrier yet?" Just last year Captain Kirk had discovered an energy field around the outer edge of the galaxy, an enormous barrier that prevented ships from crossing either in or out without serious damage to ship and crew. If it turned out to be a serious threat, the galaxy could become a pretty crowded place in a few millennia.

Hompaq shrugged. "It's been done a few times, but always at high cost. Not many people think it's worth trying. There's a lot of nothing on the other side."

"There's the entire *universe* on the other side," Pike said.

"And it's over a thousand years to Andromeda even at warp nine."

"So we haven't found anything better than warp drive, then."

She swiveled around on her stool to face him more directly. "Define 'we.' There's evidence that somebody has done it. One of your Starfleet ships will even find itself in the Delta Quadrant by accident."

"What? Which ship? In the *Delta* Quadrant?" It would take them a century to get home from there at conventional warp speed. Pike had to prevent that from happening! After all, looking after the welfare of the fleet was his *job.*

She shook her head. "I don't remember the name." But there was just the trace of a grin on her lips.

"You do too," Pike said.

"And so what if I do? Cap's right." She nodded toward the bartender, who had finished the fuming green drink and was now pouring Pike's brandy. "We could turn this place into a great big traveling trans-chrono anomalizer, or we can stop fishing for information and enjoy our time here."

"Yes, but—"

"No 'but.' "

"Innocent people will be hurt."

"Innocent people are always hurt. You stop this one and something else will happen to somebody else. Maybe this ship in the Delta Quadrant will discover something you need to know."

"Like what?"

She shrugged. "Like how to kill Borg, maybe."

"Borg?"

"See? It's an infinite regression. Galactic Barrier, warp drive, Delta Quadrant, Borg, Q, Trelane, *tribbles*"—she scowled in distaste at that word—"and so on indefinitely, but you probably don't recognize half the references. Each one will lead you to another fistful of concepts you don't understand, and so on for as long as you'd like to go. Or"—she picked up his brandy snifter and took a sip, then scowled almost as badly as she had over the word *tribble*—"we can ignore all that and enjoy one another's company without giving ourselves indigestion. Want some Warnog?" She held her mug up under his nose where he could smell its oily, almost petrochemical odor.

"Uh, no thanks."

"Smart man. Want to arm-wrestle?" She thumped her right elbow on the bar, forearm held high.

Pike laughed. He and Dr. Boyce had sometimes arm-wrestled in the forward lounge after hours. Boyce was a big man, but Pike lifted weights almost daily; he usually won. That was a long time ago, though. He hadn't lifted anything heavier than a reference book since he'd taken the desk job. Still, he hadn't gone completely to seed yet.

"Sure," he said, carefully scooting the brandy snifters down to the end of the bar where they wouldn't get knocked over. There was a cup full of pens there. Clear plastic ballpoints with octagonal barrels, by the looks of them. Pike had never seen one of those outside of a museum.

Hompaq didn't give him time to investigate. "You're not as smart as I thought," she said with a sneer as she leaned forward eagerly and wiggled her fingers to loosen them up. Pike did the same, then sat down on the stool next to her and took her hand in his. Her skin was warmer than he'd expected, and softer. Apparently being a Klingon warrior didn't mean you had to mistreat yourself.

They adjusted their grip, then gave a tentative push to make sure they were ready. "Okay," Pike said. "On the count of three. One . . . two . . . *three.*"

Hompaq lunged so quickly his knuckles nearly rapped the bar, but he recovered just in time and struggled to bring his hand back up. He felt himself slipping off his stool, wrapped his left leg around its post, and held on.

Hompaq growled and pushed harder, but Pike leaned into it and slowly brought their hands back up to vertical, then beyond. She leaned forward as well and stopped him from going any farther, but neither of them could gain any ground after that. They strained for fifteen or twenty seconds, both of them starting to shake with the effort.

Then Pike noticed what else was shaking. He'd been concentrating on the contest so hard he hadn't realized where he'd been staring until the jiggling motion became impossible to ignore. Hompaq must have realized it just about the same time, because she laughed and shook her body even harder. A moment later his hand smacked painfully against the bar and it was all he could do to keep from falling backward off his stool.

"Treachery," he said, letting go and rubbing his forearm with his left hand.

"A warrior should learn to keep his mind on the battle," she told him, grinning wide with her pointed teeth.

Just then Nowan came back around the corner from behind the bar. He saw Pike next to Hompaq, and came over to stand beside them, a bemused expression on his face. "I expected considerable advances in plumbing," he said, "but I must confess I still expected *plumbing.*"

Both Pike and Hompaq laughed, and Nowan added, "I must have spent five minutes trying to decide what went where. I hope I did it right."

"You're still here," Hompaq told him. "If you'd gotten it wrong, you'd probably have been sucked into an alternate dimension."

"That sets my mind at ease."

Pike shook his fingers to get the circulation going in them again, then picked up his brandy snifter. Nowan took his from the end of the bar and went back to their table.

"You could, uh, come sit with us, if you'd like," Pike said to Hompaq.

"I could, could I?"

"If you'd like."

"How do I know you won't shoot my chair out from under me?"

He shrugged. "I never use the same tactic twice. It's bad form."

"So it is." She rapped her mug on the bar. "Hey, Cap. Top this off for me, will you?"

The bartender did so, filling the mug from a tap rather than a bottle. Klingons must come here fairly often, Pike thought. Either that or Hompaq drank too much.

They went back over to the table by the stairs. Pike took a quick peek up the dim stairwell before he sat down, but he saw only a landing and the beginning of a hallway leading off to the left.

"Interested in what's up there?" Hompaq asked playfully. She had taken the chair with its back to the room, but she had turned it so she sat sideways to the table.

"I don't know what's up there to be interested in it," Pike said.

"You want to find out?"

He settled into his chair. "I thought I wasn't supposed to poke too deeply into the mysteries of this place."

"Hah! True enough. Besides, you weren't finished with your story. You'd found the great titan graveyard, and were about to investigate the companion star. What did you find there?"

"You sure you're supposed to know this?" Pike asked her. "It could lead to an infinite regression. Titans, Bork, K, Tremaine—what if we found tribbles? Whatever they are."

"You didn't."

"You know that for certain, don't you? Maybe I should let you tell the rest of the story."

She scowled. "Maybe you shouldn't. I don't know everything about you, Captain."

"That's encouraging."

"Good. So tell your tale."

He took a sip of brandy, then shrugged. "All right. Let's see, we were headed for the F6 star. It was just a few minutes away at warp seven . . ."

Eighteen

. . . So we didn't have much time to wonder what we'd find. Of course we had trouble even before we got there. Titan bodies kept looming up in the sensors, and Number One kept having to dodge them at warp speed all the way across from star to star. They must have eaten every source of raw materials in both systems—every moon, every asteroid, every meteor—and then they had spread out to eat the comets. And those weren't in a nice flat plane, so we couldn't even rise up over them the way we had deeper in-system.

We slowed to warp six, then to warp five, and on down the scale as the titan density increased. Spock scanned ahead with long-range sensors and found the gaps where planets had swept their orbits clean, and we aimed for the first of those, dropping back into normal space just a few light-minutes from the outermost planet.

At first glance it looked like a terrestrial world, not much larger than Earth. It was too far from its sun—even a brighter F6 like this one—to ever support humanoid life, but it showed definite signs of titan influence. Their bodies littered the surface here, too, though we found no young ones this time. There were a great many unhatched eggs, all split open from impact. The cause was readily apparent: there was no atmosphere left at all to slow their fall.

I couldn't see any evidence that this planet had ever had continents or oceans. It looked more like Mars than Earth, only much darker and without the heavy cratering that Mars endured. I wondered why it hadn't been bombarded by asteroids early in its life, but Spock soon gave me the answer.

"Fascinating," he said, finally looking up from his monitors. "This planet used to be a gas giant."

"What?" I asked. "How could that be? It's bare rock now."

"This is the core of a class-S planet, much like your Saturn. It did at one time have a metallic hydrogen envelope surrounding it and a gaseous hydrogen and helium atmosphere, but that appears to have been entirely removed by the titans, as have the atmospheres of all the planets inward from here. When I calculate the mass removed and compare it to the estimated mass of the titans in both star systems, I find that the two figures agree within three percent."

"My god," said Number One. "They completely stripped the planets."

"Take us inward," I told her. "Let's see what else they've done."

Now that we were within the planetary disk, where gravitational perturbation would keep loose bodies in the plane of the ecliptic, we could rise above the rings of titan bodies and move steadily inward, scanning the planets as we went. The next two were just like the first, rocky cores of what had once been huge gasballs, but the fourth one had the familiar characteristics of a class-M planet. It still held its atmosphere, probably because nitrogen and oxygen weren't useful to the titans in quantity, but it had suffered the same fate as the class-K planet we had examined in the other star system. Titans had filtered every bit of water out of the oceans, and they had blasted the surface to rubble.

"Any life-forms at all?" I asked Spock as we dropped into mapping orbit.

"None," he said. "However, I do show a power signature of some sort."

"What kind of power?"

"Electrical. Nearly a megawatt. It just cleared the horizon."

"On screen."

At first I saw just a jumble of rock and dead titans, but then I realized there was a pattern to the rubble. Straight lines ran outward in six directions from the center, meeting with other lines to form a hexagonal array.

"A *city?*" I asked.

"It would appear so. The power signature is coming from a geothermal generator six hundred meters below the surface. I suspect it provided electricity to the buildings, when they were standing."

"Any sign of the inhabitants?"

"The titans are the only biological form in evidence larger than microbes."

"Figures," I said. "Any indication that the inhabitants might have gotten away before this happened?"

"Unlikely, Captain. The level of technology displayed in the power turbine is lower even than the Devernians' or Aronnians'. No offense intended," he added to our guests.

"None taken," said Lanned. "I know where we stand in the overall scheme of things."

"Are there any other cities?" asked Number One.

Spock consulted his sensor displays. "Now that I know what to look for, I find several. None have operating power sources, and none show any surviving aboveground structures at all."

"Anything interesting underground?" I asked.

"A few open spaces that might have been parking facilities for ground vehicles," Spock said. "Subway tunnels. Storage space."

I had been considering a landing party, but that didn't sound promising. I said, "Whoever lived there obviously didn't have the answer to the titan problem. I don't see what good it would do to investigate firsthand. Let's mark this on the charts for an archaeological mission and go on to the next candidate star. Mr. Spock, which one would you recommend next?"

He put the map on the screen. "There are three stars within seven light-years of here—half a titan's maximum range. We could go straight ahead, farther from Devernia, turn twenty degrees to galactic south, or turn seventy degrees to galactic north."

It didn't take long for me to decide. We'd found titans on our first stop; that meant they came from somewhere in this direction. I didn't see any reason to turn aside. "Straight ahead," I said. "Let's see if we get lucky twice in a row."

"You call this luck?" asked Perri.

"We came out here to find titans," I told him. "We did that."

He shivered. "Yes, we did, didn't we?"

It took us another day to cross the immense distance between stars. Our guests spent the time competing for Yeoman Colt's attention—and doing it so blatantly that I took her aside on the pretext of going over the damage reports with her and asked her straight out, "Are those two bothering you?"

We were the only people in the conference room, me seated at the table and her standing beside it. I assumed she could give me a straight answer without embarrassment, but she blushed when I asked the question and I realized I must have overstepped my bounds.

"If they aren't, it's none of my business," I said hurriedly, "but if they are I'll put a stop to it. You shouldn't have to put up with unwanted advances from anyone."

She played with a loose strand of her reddish blonde hair, winding it around her finger and letting it slip free. She didn't look at me, but instead addressed the window behind me. "It—it's all right. I can't say I'm not flattered. If I thought it was going to go on for long I'd probably feel different, but we'll only be doing this for what, another week or two? To be perfectly honest, that will be just about right." She glanced at me, then back out the window. "I actually find them attractive in a strange way. The lure of the exotic, I suppose. Neither one of them is really my type, but they're both interesting."

She tucked the loose hair into her ponytail and lowered her hand. "I appreciate your concern, sir."

"Just doing my job. I think."

"You are."

I sighed. "Thanks for saying so."

She looked at me quizzically.

I fumbled for an explanation. "I . . . what I mean to say is . . ."

"Sir?"

I laughed. "Maybe you should sit here and I'll stand over there and it'll be easier to say."

"How about if we both sit?" she asked. She pulled out a chair and spun it around so she could lean forward against its back.

"That's the same way Yeoman Leon used to treat a chair," I said, smiling at the memory.

"Oh. I'm sorry." She moved to get up.

"No, that's fine," I said quickly. "That's what I wanted to say, actually. It's fine. You are. I mean, you're doing a fine job." I plunged ahead with reckless abandon, knowing I'd better elaborate or look even more foolish than I already did. "I know I said some pretty harsh things when you first came on board. Leon was a good friend as well as my yeoman, and losing him was hard. I didn't want someone to take his place, and when Starfleet assigned a young woman to the job I thought they were crazy, but I can see now that they knew what they were doing. And so do you, as it turns out. I just want to make sure you know I realize that. You're doing great, and I'm sorry I ever doubted you."

She tilted her head a little, embarrassed again. "Thank you."

"And don't worry about being compared to Leon all the time. I haven't done that since your first few days on board. You've got your own way of doing things, your own personality, and I appreciate that."

"That's . . . a relief."

"I thought it might be." I realized I was tapping my fingers nervously on the table and forced them to stop. "That's all I had to say, besides making sure you weren't being bothered by our guests."

She nodded, but she didn't move to go. I didn't want to chase her out, either, so I waited for her to say what was on her mind. When she did, it wasn't what I'd expected.

"Why did you join Starfleet?" she asked.

That was a tough question. I was still trying to decide if I wanted to answer it when she elaborated.

"I have this theory that there are two kind of people who join. There's the duty and honor and glory guys who want to be part of something great, and there's the strange new worlds people who want to see what's out there. I'm guessing you're the strange new worlds type, but if I'm going to work closely with you it occurs to me that I should know for sure why you're here. It might make a difference sometime when we have to understand each other in a hurry."

"It might," I admitted. I had been about ready to jump on her for getting too personal, but she had a point. Leon and I had known each other that well. In fact, he could probably have answered her question easier than I could, since I had to get past all the internal clutter that hid my true motives even from myself. She had made a pretty good guess, though. "I think you're right," I answered. "I came out here for the adventure. I inherited the duty and honor bit when I became an officer."

"Thought so."

"That's not to say duty and honor isn't worthwhile," I pointed out. "If we all came out here for the adventure we'd probably get the whole shipload of us killed the first planet we came to."

"Maybe."

She started toying with another strand of hair. I watched for a few seconds, hypnotized; then I broke away and said, "How about you? Adventure, right?"

"Right."

"Which is why Perri and Lanned don't bother you."

She grinned sheepishly. "Guilty."

"Have an adventure, then," I told her. "But be careful you don't get hurt."

"I will." She straightened up on her chair, then stood and flipped it back around under the table. "Thank you, sir," she said again. "Will, um, will that be all?"

"Yes," I told her. "Carry on."

She giggled. It was the first time I had ever heard her do that. "So to speak," she said.

I shook my head. "So to speak."

She turned to go, and I watched her walk to the door, wondering if I had overstepped my bounds as far as it felt like I had. I had no idea. A captain and his yeoman should be able to talk about anything, at any time. As she had said, it might make a difference sometime when we had to understand each other in a hurry. So why did I feel like I'd just navigated my way without sensors through an asteroid belt?

Our next star proved disappointing. It was an A-type, big and bright and hot, and the rocky planets close-in were just that: rocks. All the water had been boiled off epochs ago, leaving nothing for titans or anything else to use. The outer planets held more volatiles, but they were all giants, which left no breeding ground.

"I suppose they could have come through here on their way to that last system," I said when Spock delivered the bad news. "Adults could refuel in those atmospheres, couldn't they?"

"They probably could," he replied.

"So we still don't know whether to go on, or to try galactic north or south."

"No, sir. Except the stars to the north are more densely packed, which means we could search more of them in a shorter time if we go that direction."

"Sounds good to me," I said. "North it is."

Our luck changed at the very next star. It was a K-type, dimmer than Sol, and with a wider range of planets. When we dropped out of warp, Spock almost immediately said, "I read titan fusion drives throughout the system."

"Proximity?" I asked.

"None within one hundred thousand kilometers."

Good. I didn't want a repeat of what had happened to us when we'd arrived at Devernia. "What does their population density look like?"

"Not as high as what we found around L2334.45, but significantly higher than that around Devernia."

"Other life-forms?"

"None register at this distance; however, simple spectrographic analysis indicates life other than titans on at least two of the inner planets."

Life. I thought of what Colt and I had talked about earlier, how we were both in Starfleet to see what we would find in the depths of space. Thousands of people had discovered life on alien planets, starting with the first expedition to Mars even before Zephram Cochrane invented the warp drive, but it still gave me a little thrill to do it again. I looked over at Colt, standing behind Number One. She was smiling too. "What kind of life?" I asked.

"Impossible to determine from here," Spock replied calmly, his Vulcan heritage momentarily winning out over his human half and preventing him from betraying any emotion he might have felt. "All I read is a molecular signature similar to chlorophyll."

Most likely plants, then, but I understood Spock's reluctance to say for sure. We could find a planet covered with green animals just as easily as anything else.

"Take us closer," I said to Number One. "But be ready to get us out of here in a hurry if there's trouble. Mr. Spock, is there any indication of power generation?"

"None yet, but the titans' energy signatures may be masking anything more subtle."

"Any communication signals, Dabisch?"

"Only the microwave bursts coming from the titans themselves, the same as those we found around Devernia."

That would be their primitive radar beams. "Still no information content?" I asked, just to be sure.

"None," he confirmed.

We accelerated toward the inner planets on impulse power, watching carefully for any sign of aggression from the titans or anyone else, but we came within a half-million kilometers before they even noticed us.

When they did, the reaction was immediate. There had been thousands of them orbiting the planet; a hundred or more whose orbital motion was aimed near our position suddenly lit their fusion engines and accelerated toward us.

"Interesting," Spock said, examining the monitors. "I detect a significant disturbance in the stellar magnetic field. I believe they are using that as well as their rockets for motive power."

"They're coming fast," said Number One.

"Shields up," I said. That hadn't made any difference the last time, but it wouldn't cost us anything but sensor range to power them up, and we already knew the titans were coming. I didn't like waiting for them without some kind of defense, however ineffective it might be. And in the back of my mind was the thought: If they could manipulate the stellar magnetic field, what else could they do that we hadn't seen yet?

"Mr. Perri," I said, "do you know anything about this magnetic propulsion?"

He said, "The only magnetic effects we have observed are the containment fields for the fusion reaction chamber and the subspace effects of the warp coils."

"Lanned?"

"He's right as far as I know."

"Spock, did you notice anything like this in your sensor scans around Devernia?"

"Negative, Captain."

"One hundred thousand kilometers and closing," said Tyler at the navigation console. "Seventy-five. Fifty."

As tightly as a fighter squadron flying formation, the titans spun end-for-end and decelerated toward us on their fusion engines. The plasma stream from their exhaust struck our shields, the flash momentarily blinding us until our sensors shifted to a wavelength they could see in. I was glad I'd raised our shields; the hull could take fusion exhaust without harm from this distance, but the radiation wouldn't do the crew any good.

"Magnetic activity increasing," Spock said, watching his monitors carefully. "Plasma stream is being affected. It is drawing tighter. Curious. That would reduce the efficiency of—"

Suddenly the viewscreen lit up with a red flash so bright that some of the individual pixels blew out before the automatic gain control could compensate. I blinked and saw afterimages, and when I looked back to the screen there were dark spots where the elements had failed.

"Hull temperature rising," Spock said. "Shields unable to compensate."

"Get us out of here," I said. "Warp eight." I had no idea what had just hit us, but I didn't want to find out the hard way.

Number One complied instantly. The warp fields wrapped around the ship and hurled us a couple of light-minutes across the planetary system within seconds.

"Any sign of pursuit?" I asked.

"None, sir," Spock said.

"Full stop," I ordered. When the stars settled down and we ascertained that no more titans were in the vicinity, I said, "All right, what hit us back there?" I looked around the bridge: Spock busy correlating all the information available to him on his science station, Number One checking fire control and helm response, Tyler scanning nearby space. Colt and Perri and Lanned were gripping the handrail and looking at the forward viewscreen, which showed a serene starscape that betrayed none of the violence we had just endured.

Dabisch looked up from his communications board and said, "I picked up an incredibly strong signal at the low end of the visible-light spectrum. All carrier wave, though; there was no information in it."

"It was not a communications beam," Spock said. "It was a simple laser."

"A *laser?*" I asked. "Was there someone riding those titans?"

"Negative."

"Then where did it come from? That was one almighty powerful laser to punch through our shields like it did."

"It came from the titans themselves," Spock replied. "Or more precisely, from their fusion drive exhaust stream. Observe." He switched the main viewer to the aft sensor array and increased the magnification until I saw a gleaming white starship on one side of the screen and a fleet of a hundred or so titans approaching it from the other. It was the *Enterprise* and the titans that had attacked it; the light from the event only now catching up with us.

The titans flipped over and sprayed rocket exhaust at us. "Most of the plasma comes from atomic hydrogen," said Spock, "mixed with a small amount of helium from the fusion reaction. It is harmless, except when compressed magnetically to a uniform density, as you see here." Sure enough, the jet of gas grew narrower, becoming a bright red pencil-line drawn between titans and starship.

"At this point, with energy still pouring into it from the fusion engines, the gas conduit lased at a wavelength of 670 nanometers."

I stared open-mouthed at the screen as the red line suddenly increased in brilliance a thousandfold, bathing the *Enterprise* in scintillating fire. Our shields flared like a nuclear blast, radiating most of the energy outward, but unable to reflect every erg of it. I knew from the design specs that the leakage was less than one percent, but with a laser that size, even one percent had nearly cooked us.

The ship on the screen winked out of existence. That was when we'd engaged the warp engines. The titans released their magnetic hold on the exhaust stream and braked to a halt where we had been, milling around like hunting dogs looking for a downed bird in tall grass.

"My god," Number One said, "that's more firepower than *we* have."

"It is an impressive capability," Spock said.

Lanned made a soft humming sound deep in his throat. "I've never seen them do that before."

"You're lucky," I said. "A laser that size could fry one of your ships in a second."

"How could it be that these titans have lasers and the ones around Devernia don't?" asked Colt.

"I don't know," I said. "Spock, any ideas?"

"None at this point, Captain. I would need further data on which to base a theory."

"I was afraid you'd say that. Where do you want to look first?"

"The nearest planet would be most logical," he replied. "We will want to investigate them all if possible."

"If we survive that long," said Tyler, but he keyed in the coordinates.

Nineteen

"You actually went back?" asked Hompaq. "I'm impressed."

Pike gave a little shrug. "It wasn't as dangerous as it seemed. We could always outrun them."

"Until they burned out something vital."

"True. We tried hard not to get hit a second time."

"I'll bet you did. Too bad you didn't have a cloaking device."

"A what?"

"Invisibility, Captain. It blocks visual, electromagnetic, even subspace emissions. Very useful in sneaking up on something."

"I bet it would be!" Pike said. "How long are we going to have to wait before that becomes available?"

She looked nonchalantly up at the ceiling. "A while."

Nowan cleared his throat, then said, "For him, or for me? 'A while' for him is forever for me. Assuming I go back where I came from when I leave this drinking establishment."

"You do," said Hompaq.

"Invariably?" he asked. "What if I leave with one of you?"

She shook her head. "You still go back to your home time and place. You think Cap's gateway can't handle two people at once?"

"Cap, that's the bartender?" asked Pike. He looked over to see the man watching them with a thoughtful expression on his face.

"It's his place," said Hompaq. "It's the Captain's Table, so we all just call him 'Cap.' "

Pike looked back to her. "How often do you come here, anyway?"

"Often enough."

"Why?"

"Not to answer your questions," she said pointedly.

He took a deep breath, let it out slowly. "All right, I'll stop prying. But this place has got me damned curious."

"Good," she said. "You're supposed to be curious, but the mystery is yours, not mine or anyone else's. You wound up here because of something inside *you,* not me. If you have to figure out anything about this place, figure out why you're here first."

Pike chuckled. "Like I told this fellow here, I came in because it was raining and I was cold."

"Sure you did. And you went back into that mess of titans because you told Perri and Lanned you'd help them solve their problem. But that's not the real reason."

"What was the real reason?"

"You just told us not ten minutes ago."

He tried to remember what he'd said. "Did I? If so, I must have forgotten it."

She snorted loudly. "Your yeoman knows."

Comprehension dawned on his face. "Ah. Adventure. Yes, perhaps you're right. It's a good thing Spock and Number One were there for duty and honor, or I probably would have gotten us all killed, just like I told Colt."

"Why?" asked Nowan. "What did they do?"

"Called it quits when the going got too tough," said Pike.

"What?" demanded Hompaq. "This is heroism?"

"No," said Pike. "It was realism. And logic."

"Logic," she spat. "Vulcans value it far too much."

Pike took a sip of brandy. "Well, it proved valuable to us, or I wouldn't be here to tell you about it."

She sighed heavily. "Very well, tell me how this Vulcan's *logic* saved the day. But you had better figure in heroically again or I will make you regret wasting my time with this prattle."

"No pressure, eh?" asked Pike. He stretched, rubbed his neck, then said, "All right, here's heroism for you: I went in with our shields down, knowing we'd have a few seconds to bring them up again before we were attacked, and knowing that Spock could get better sensor readings in those few seconds. How's that?"

"That's bravery. Heroism is bravery when you expect to fail."

"Oh," said Pike. "Then that came a bit later. In fact, the first time through was a piece of cake."

Twenty

We went back into the system at warp six. It was too hard to stop exactly where you wanted to at warp seven or eight, and the way we intended to do things, precision counted more than speed. The Devernian titans' top speed had seemed to be about warp two, so unless these differed from them in that regard as well we probably could have gone in even slower than that, but we didn't know if they could detect us in motion so I decided to catch them completely by surprise if I could.

Spock had already gotten sensor readings of the outermost planet before the titans had chased us away, so we went to the next one in from there. Tyler calculated a course that let us drop out of warp only a thousand kilometers above its surface—a banded, churning, Jupiter-like surface—where we got about ten seconds of scanning time before the local titans noticed us and closed in. When the first hint of fusion exhaust licked out toward us, I told Number One, "Next planet," and she took us away before they could start their laser.

We did the same thing there. There was no time to do more than monitor our scanners; we would be hours going over the recorded data once we were clear of the titans. At the third planet, however, where Spock had found evidence of life, he kept his eyes on the life-form readouts as they scrolled past.

"Time to go," I said when the titans rushed toward us, but he said, "One moment, Captain."

I gave him his moment, then said, "Go," and Number One took us to the next planet, but Spock said, "We must go back. There was evidence of land-dwelling animals."

"Other than titans, you mean?" I watched the screens warily while our sensors automatically scanned planet number four.

"That is unclear, which is why we must return for closer examination." He spoke without looking at me, still watching his monitors. "And now I find similar life-forms here."

"You've got about fifteen seconds to do something about it," I told him, watching the titans gather. "Ten. Five. *Go.*"

We went.

The inner planets contained no surprises. When we had scanned them all, I had Number One take us out of the ecliptic, over the south pole of the star, while we decided what to do.

"How much more time do you need?" I asked Spock.

"At least thirty seconds," he replied. "A minute would be preferable. Our rapid scan indicated life-forms on both inhabited worlds, neither of which fit the immature titan profile. I must locate and do a full scan on at least three of each type in order to determine their genetic makeup."

"Why three?" asked Colt.

"Because any single specimen could be a mutant. Only by comparing multiple samples can the true genotype be mapped with any degree of confidence."

"We're not going to *get* a minute," I told him. "And by the way they're behaving, I doubt we'll get even thirty seconds. Look." I pointed to the main viewscreen, on which Dabisch had put a magnified image of the inner solar system. The space surrounding each of the planets was abuzz with milling dust motes, from which tiny lines of red light speared out.

"It looks like they're fighting among themselves now," Lanned said.

"Or just rattling their swords," said Number One. "Are they actually hitting anything?"

Dabisch expanded the view of one of the planets Spock wanted to return to. Now we could see individual titans and their odd magnetically induced laser beams, but as Number One had suspected, they weren't shooting at each other.

"We certainly got them worked up," I said. "But I think we can still manage to catch them by surprise. Mr. Tyler, set a leapfrog course for those two planets, and try to pick a region where the titans are least active to jump into. We may have to run through each system a few times, but we'll get our data even if it's a piece at a time."

"Course laid in, sir," he said.

"Spock, are you ready?"

"Ready."

"All right, then, engage."

We streaked toward the first planet under warp power, then stopped only a hundred kilometers above its surface. Spock started his scan while we watched out for titans.

They saw us instantly. Unfortunately one happened to be pointing almost directly away from us, and it wasted no time in firing its fusion jet at us. Magnetic fields constricted the jet a few seconds later. There was only the one titan this time, so we might have been able to withstand its lone weapon, but I didn't want to guess wrong. "Go," I said, just as the plasma lased and the beam shot out at us. The viewscreen flashed again and hull temperature sensors sounded the warning, but Number One already had her finger on the button and we streaked away to the other planet before we took any serious damage.

We had only a few more seconds there before the titans spotted us. This time three of them fired from three different angles, and we took another hit before we jumped free.

"Spock? Did you get anything?"

"One life-form detected and scanned at each planet," he replied. "Three samples of each type of life-form are required for unambiguous speciation. We will need two more passes to ensure good data."

"Great," I said. "Mr. Tyler, again, please. Pick a new spot near each planet. Maybe they'll all be looking for us where we were last time."

"Yes, sir." He calculated the coordinates, fed them to Number One's control board, and she took us back in.

Space was filled with titans. We had to dodge half a dozen of them before we even broke out of warp, and by slowing down to do so we evidently gave ourselves away. They were waiting for us when we arrived, their fusion flames crisscrossing the space in front of us. The moment we stopped they all went into laser mode, blasting us from at least three sides.

"Abort!" I shouted over the howl of alarms. Number One slapped her control panel and we jumped into warp again, skipping the other planet and rushing back out into interplanetary space. Some of the titans followed us until we increased speed to warp five and left them behind.

"I'm beginning to take this personally," I said when the alarms shut off. "Tyler, try a polar approach. Maybe they won't be looking up."

"Aye, sir," he said. He sounded dubious, but he set the coordinates.

"Ready, Spock?"

"Ready. However, I believe that shields will not impair our sensor efficiency enough to make their use counterproductive."

I wasn't going to argue with that. "Shields up, then. Take us in, Number One."

We streaked inward again, arching up out of the ecliptic and down over the planet's north pole, but the titans were on the alert all around the globe. They gave us no more time than on our last pass before their lasers struck again and I ordered us away.

"I'm tempted to paint a shuttlecraft silver and go in with that," I said. "Let them shoot at a mirror for a change."

"Even silver paint would not reflect one hundred percent of all impinging light," Spock pointed out. "It would burn through within seconds, and the shuttlecraft's hull would take little longer."

"How are they *finding* us so fast?" I asked. "Can that microwave radar of theirs possibly be that efficient?" Starfleet hadn't used radar since the invention of subspace field distortion sensors, but I supposed it could still be useful in normal space.

Spock checked his long-range scanners. "Microwave field intensity has increased among the titans who are most alarmed," he said.

"Can we jam it?"

"Possibly," Spock said. He played with the science station's controls for a few seconds, frowned, and said, "They use two frequencies, one at the natural resonant frequency of deuterium oxide molecules, the other at a much shorter wavelength. The first one will be relatively easy to block with an anti-phase return wave, but the second one will be much more difficult."

"Why is that?" I asked.

"Its frequency is high enough that it is nearly in the infrared light spectrum. As we have seen with the laser beams, we cannot mask ourselves completely from light, nor can we send a return beam of sufficient complexity to cancel our reflection. At best we can attenuate it by a factor of two."

"Let's try it anyway," I said. "Maybe it'll give us the few extra seconds we need to get a good scan of those planets."

"Very well," he said. He worked at the controls for a few minutes, during which time Number One said, "Is this really worth it?"

"The data I have already received seems to suggest that something with the same metabolic processes as titans is living on the surface of these planets," said Spock while he worked. "Since we came here to learn about titan ecology, it would be useful to know more about them."

"It would be useful to know why they attack us on sight, that's for sure," Colt said. "Do we look like some ancestral enemy, or do they just hate spaceships?"

"A good question," said Spock. "Unfortunately that will be difficult to answer with just one ship to experiment with."

"Yours attacked us too," I said to Lanned, "but I had assumed until you started shooting at them they left your ships alone. Was I wrong?"

"No, you're right," he said. "They tolerated our ships at first. Of course when we started killing them they swarmed the planet and attacked anything that rose above the atmosphere, but we didn't mind. That way we didn't have to waste fuel tracking them down."

"I wonder if your size made you appear less of a threat, until you proved yourselves otherwise."

"Maybe. We'd never seen how they react to bigger ships until you showed up, and by then they were mad at everybody."

"Perri?" I asked. "How did the titans around your planet react to the first Federation survey ship?"

He rubbed his forehead as he tried to remember. "I believe all but the tame ones had migrated to Devernia at that time."

Lanned laughed. "Incidentally making it easier for you to claim the few remaining ones as our own creation."

Perri nodded. "It was a misconception which we did not attempt to correct. I have admitted that, and Captain Pike has said it made no difference anyway."

"Not to him."

Before Lanned and Perri could get into another argument over it, Spock said, "I am ready with the jamming signal."

"All right, let's do it. Mr. Tyler, let's try the other planet first. They've had more chance to calm down over there."

"Aye, sir," he said, and he entered the course.

"Number One, engage."

She did, and we raced back in-system one more time. When we popped out into normal space above the planet, I held my breath while we waited to see if we would be spotted. There were hundreds of titans within easy striking distance, but they didn't seem concerned. I counted ten seconds, fifteen, twenty—then one of them suddenly turned toward us.

Dabisch said, "They have shifted frequency!"

"Spock, can you compensate?"

"Not in time."

"Number One, get ready to take us out of here."

The news of our arrival spread like a ripple on a pond. Titans turned first toward us, sending their radar beams out ahead as they accelerated on magnetic fields and fusion power, then they flipped over and fired their plasma streams at us.

"Time to go," I said.

We left, but not before their lasers clipped us. Our shields flared, and another few pixels of the main viewscreen blew out. Then the hull-breach alarm wailed for attention.

I slapped the control to silence it. "Damage report?" I asked when we dropped back into normal space at the edge of the star system.

Dabisch listened to the in-ship communications link for a moment, then said, "Pressure loss in observation room J-twelve. No injuries."

J-12. That was the same room that the Devernian titans had damaged. The repair crew had sprayed black sealant on the window, which, since it now absorbed any light that struck it, had undoubtedly grown hot under each laser blast we had received. It would have cooled down while we prepared for another approach, only to be heated again by the next laser, expanding and contracting each time until the already-cracked window shattered under the stress.

"It's all right," I said. "Isolated incident. I assume the pressure doors are holding?"

"They are. A repair team has been dispatched."

"Tell them to paint the patch silver this time," I said. "It may not work for long, but it's better than starting out black." I turned to Spock. "How much more data do you need?"

"How much more can we *afford?*" asked Number One.

Spock looked at his displays, on which I could see several genetic maps scrolling past side by side. "Actually," he said, "I believe I have gained sufficient information. The land creatures we discovered are degenerate forms of titans, rather than a distinctly different species."

"What do you mean by 'degenerate forms'?" I asked.

"They have evolved into their present shape so recently that they share their entire genetic code with the spaceborne form. Only the expression of certain features has changed, such as the atrophy of the fusion and warp engines in favor of greater tentacle strength and a body more balanced for running."

So they had given up spaceflight and adapted to life on land. At least some of them had. The others, apparently, had evolved laser weapons. "What about those lasers?" I asked. "Why didn't the ones around Devernia have that capability?"

Spock recalled the data from there and compared it with what he had just recorded. "I did not detect any magnetic field manipulation in those specimens, other than in the fusion engine. My study of the embryonic and neonatal forms on Devernia indicated that the magnetic containment field coils developed first, followed by the fusion engine. The adult titans we observed here have much less efficient fusion engines, but they make up for that by using their ability to manipulate magnetic fields as a propulsion system."

"And to create that laser effect in their exhaust plumes."

"Correct. Evolutionarily, it would be a fair trade."

I shook my head. "I have a heck of a time believing that anything, even if it had somehow evolved a fusion engine in the first place, could evolve a *laser.*"

"Actually, I was thinking in the other direction," said Spock. "Losing the laser effect is a fair trade if it results in a more efficient engine, so long as the solar system in which they live contains no natural enemies."

"Like Devernians?" asked Perri. "From the titans' point of view they must certainly look like enemies."

Spock nodded. "They are indeed, but that is a new threat. The titans have not had time for evolutionary pressure to alter their genome to meet it, but I suspect it will eventually shift back to providing them with lasers now that the threat has become evident."

Lanned's eyes grew even wider than usual. "How long before it happens?" he asked.

"That is impossible to predict. Evolution typically takes generations, but the titans seem to evolve quickly, on the order of years rather than millennia, and the genetic code they need is already there to be expressed. It could happen with the very next hatchling."

Lanned's knees buckled, but he caught himself on the railing and pulled himself back to his feet. He turned to me, his striped face as pale as my own, and whispered, "We have to go back!"

"And do what?" I asked.

"Warn them!"

"What would you do differently? Stop killing the titans? They would overpopulate and destroy Devernia as surely as they did the double star we investigated two days ago."

"Then you must go back and help us exterminate them quickly, before they mutate into these—these fire-breathing monsters."

I looked at the viewscreen again, once more showing the star system with its myriad dust motes winking with ruby threads of light. "We don't have that kind of firepower. Your nuclear bombs are probably more effective than our phasers, when it comes to killing titans. Photon torpedoes would probably do the job, but we don't have enough of them to even put a dent in their population."

"But we must do something!" Lanned said. "The threat is even worse than we realized."

"We're doing it," I said. "We're learning more about them every day. Somewhere out here is the answer to your problem. Out here, not back at Devernia."

"You hope," he said.

"I'm sure of it," I replied confidently. Not that I believed it, of course, but it's a captain's duty to keep his crew inspired. Before Lanned could say anything more, I turned to Spock and said, "What's our next target star?"

Twenty-one

Pike paused in his story to take another sip of brandy. Then, scooting back his chair, he said, "If you don't mind my pausing for a few minutes, I think it's my turn to visit the head."

"We should make you stay here until you're done," Hompaq said, grinning evilly.

"Oh," said Pike. "All right, then. Let's see, at the next planet we found a transdimensional entity with godlike powers who agreed to go back to Devernia with us and turn all the titans into giant space butterflies instead. Fragile as cobwebs, of course, but beautiful. Now Devernia is a popular tourist attraction for people who want to see the famous veiled sunsets."

Hompaq growled deep in her throat. "If that's the end of your story, I will throw you headfirst into the fireplace."

"And I will help," said Nowan.

"Hmm," said Pike. "Perhaps I can come up with something a bit more exciting. Let me go think on it for a moment." He stood up before either of them could protest any further and stepped through the door marked Humanoid Male at the back of the bar.

Nowan had been right; there was no plumbing, not even in the sink. Instead of a washbasin, there was just a flat metal plate on the countertop. Pike waved his right hand over it and heard the unmistakable hum of a transporter. His hand tingled momentarily, but nothing prevented it from continuing through its arc. On a hunch he dug into his pocket for a pen, drew an "X" on the palm of his left hand, and waved it above the plate. The transporter hummed again, and when he looked at his hand the "X" was gone.

"Amazing," he said aloud. Yes indeed, they did some interesting things with transporters these days. Whenever "these days" were.

He heard a bang from out in the bar, then Klingon laughter. Had she thrown another chair at someone? He opened the door a crack and peered out, saw her still sitting at the table, and opened the door the rest of the way.

Nowan was rubbing his arm and saying, "You have an unconventional way of wrestling, madam."

She nodded toward Pike. "Like I told the storyteller here, a warrior should keep his mind—and his eyes—on the battle."

Pike settled into his chair again and said, "Yes, let's. We were just about to head for yet another star system. . . ."

Twenty-two

WE INVESTIGATED FIVE MORE IN THE NEXT FIVE DAYS. FINDING TITANS was never the problem. Avoiding them long enough to collect any meaningful data was the difficult part. In every star system where we encountered them, they were without exception hostile.

They all had laser capability, which led Spock to believe that that was the standard from which the Devernian titans had evolved. Other characteristics, however, seemed completely variable. Some populations had bigger ramscoop mouths than others, and that seemed to vary with the density of the atmospheres they scooped nutrients from. Some, like the Devernian titans, had teeth within the ramscoops, which appeared to arise when there were planetary rings or asteroids to feed on. The tentacles had atrophied on one species which lived in a system with no rocky planets to breed on. There the adults laid their eggs on comets instead, and the young fed on the ice until they were ready to launch themselves into space.

"This is a classic example of evolution in action," said Spock on the afternoon of our fifth day. "Like the finches on Earth's own Galápagos Islands that convinced Charles Darwin of the theory, I find each star system filled with a population perfectly adapted to local conditions." He had just discovered a correlation between the strength of the titans' radar signals and the availability of deuterium in the water of their hatching grounds. "Here, for instance, they use the low-frequency radar signal to locate deuterium sources for their young, and then drop their eggs in areas of highest concentration. Yet in planetary systems where there is no concentrated deuterium source, they lose that ability and instead adopt a cometary birth strategy."

Number One and I were looking over his shoulders at the data. Perri and Lanned had tired of the study and had gone off to explore the ship some more, and Colt had gone along to keep them out of trouble. Number One said, "The problem with your evolution idea is that none of these populations are stable. They're all headed toward overcrowding and eventual starvation."

"That does seem to be the case," said Spock. "I can only assume that we are seeing the same problem repeated here as we saw on Devernia: none of the ancillary life-forms that evolved with these creatures has managed to cross the interstellar gulf with them. Even with the rapid rate of evolution we have witnessed here, one species in isolation cannot evolve fast enough to provide the necessary diversity to keep the ecosystem in balance."

"You're making one big assumption," she said.

"And what is that?"

"The assumption that they *did* evolve. What if they were made?"

Spock thought it over. "My argument still holds. Even an artificially produced organism cannot exist in isolation. If the titans were genetically engineered, other organisms were also created to feed them, and to feed *on* them."

"They seem to find plenty to eat on their own," I pointed out. "It's just the latter part that's missing."

"No," said Spock. "Dr. Boyce has helped me identify developmental abnormalities among all the races I have studied. They are missing key nutrients, which has led to weakened internal organs and shorter life spans than they might otherwise have."

I wasn't sure if a longer-lived, stronger titan was a good idea, but I imagined that Spock and Boyce probably knew what they were talking about. "That still doesn't give us any idea where the rest of this ecosystem of theirs *is,* does it?" I asked.

"Perhaps it does," Spock said. "One thing that seems universal among them is the low-frequency radar with which they seek out deuterium sources. That is a very specific signal, and while it would be quite weak at interstellar distances, it would still be detectable."

"So we can scan this entire sector of space and we'll know which stars have titans," said Number One. "We could have done that all along."

"We could have, but since we found titans at all but one star so far, we have not wasted our effort. What I propose now, however, should cut our search down even further."

"Good," I said. "What's your plan?"

"I am assuming that what works for titans would work for other creatures as well. In space it would be very useful to search out nutrients with radar before expending significant amounts of energy to go harvest them.

However, other creatures would presumably need other nutrients than titans do, and therefore their radar frequencies would be different from the titans'. If we search for a planetary system from which multiple frequencies emanate, there would be a high likelihood of finding multiple species there."

"I don't know," I said. "The titans a few planets back already used two different frequencies themselves, and they shifted to a third when we riled them up."

"That has so far been an isolated case. All the other titans we have studied have used only one frequency."

"Well, I guess it wouldn't hurt to try it," I said. "Scanning is a lot quicker than actually going to look at every star in the sector." I turned to Dabisch at his communications board, ready to give him the order, and saw that he was already working on it.

He put his results on the viewscreen as they came in. The blown-out pixels had been replaced, so the picture didn't have gaps in it anymore. I saw a scattered starfield, on which one star after another turned red as Dabisch found the "standard" frequency of radar emanating from it. I had expected to see a spherical distribution, but it looked more like a cancer with long arms reaching out from various barely connected nodes. I saw that Devernia was at the tip of one such arm, down which we had traveled maybe a third of the distance.

"I'll bet what we're looking for is in one of those joining points," I said, just as the one farthest from us lit up in red, then green, then yellow. "Multiple frequencies there," Dabisch announced.

"That's twenty light-years away," I said, looking at the scale on the bottom of the screen. "Over a week of travel time. Keep scanning."

Dabisch did so, but it soon became apparent that Spock had been right: the homeworld—if that's what we were seeing—was unique in all the sector.

It was so deep in unexplored territory that it didn't even have a catalog number. I sighed. "Mr. Tyler, set course for that star. Looks like we're going for a bit longer trip than we'd hoped."

We spent the week making repairs to the ship. We couldn't go outside while under way, but we could reach all the critical sensors through the Jefferies tubes and access hatches, so by the time we arrived at our destination we were back in fairly good condition. Not full battle specs, but after what we had endured I felt glad to have as much working as we did.

Of course that lasted about an hour. It would have been even less, but I brought us back into normal space well out of our target system so we could scan for life-forms before we proceeded inward. The monitors lit up like Christmas trees, color-coded dots showing different types of creatures scattered all through the system. I could see free-flying dots at random between planets—those I assumed were titans—but there were heavy concentrations of life-forms in the gas-giant atmospheres, in their ring systems, and in the three separate asteroid belts between planetary orbits. The terrestrial planets didn't seem to have many life-forms on them, but the gas giants and the asteroids more than made up for that lack.

"How many species?" I asked when the map finally stabilized.

Spock said, "At least six. Perhaps as many as ten. It is difficult to ascertain true species differences with long-range sensors."

He sounded happy—at least as happy as Spock ever sounded. But I was disappointed. "That few?" I asked. "I had thought we would find hundreds, if this is where they originated."

"This is far more than we discovered anywhere else," he pointed out. "And the population densities seem consistent with a stable ecosystem."

"How so?"

"The smaller creatures exist in the greatest numbers, with population density decreasing in inverse proportion to the mass. This would seem to indicate that the smaller species provide nourishment for the larger ones, all the way up the food chain to the titans."

"It's a pretty small food chain with only six links in it." I leaned back in my command chair and looked at the screen. With all that color-coding it looked complicated as hell, but I had never heard of an ecosystem with so few species. "Dabisch, is there any sign of civilization here?" I asked.

"No communication signals. If there is power generation, it is masked by the titans' own power signatures."

"I guess we'd better go in for a closer look," I said. "Are the titans using just the one frequency of radar here?"

"Affirmative," said Dabisch.

"Then maybe we'll have a better chance of slipping in undetected. Get ready to start our jamming signal. Number One, kill our exterior beacons. We're going in dark this time." I pressed the shipwide intercom button. "All hands, this is the captain. We are going to stealth mode two. Extinguish all lights visible from the exterior of the ship, and opaque all windows."

I didn't really think that would matter much—the hull was painted white, after all—but every little bit might help. Especially if we could stay out of the light.

"Do you have a preferred starting point, Mr. Spock?"

"This gas giant." He used the pointer to indicate the third one in toward the star. "It has the greatest biodiversity of any one planet, with separate species in its ring system and on each of its moons as well as in the atmosphere. It seems to be a microcosm of the entire system."

"All right. Mr. Tyler, Number One, are you ready?"

"Ready."

"Ready."

"Approach at warp five. Bring us to a stop in the shadow of one of the smallest moons. Be prepared to raise shields, but leave them down until we're attacked. And don't wait for my command if you see a threat."

"Yes, sir," they said in unison.

I looked to either side of my command chair. Lanned, Perri, Colt, and Dr. Boyce had all come to watch. Boyce was helping Spock collect data at the control panel beside his science station; the other three were gripping the handrail already. Good. I hoped they wouldn't need the support, but it was better to be prepared.

I leaned forward and grasped the armrests of my chair. "Take us in."

We slid into the moon's shadow as quietly as a cat stalking a mouse. The planet's immense ring system spread out in front of us, sparkling with gold and silver highlights in the sunlight. Spock immediately started scanning for life-forms and mapping their genetic code, while Boyce busied himself with determining each organism's role in the food chain. The rest of us held our breath, waiting for the first sign of discovery. Every ping and bleep from the ship's instruments seemed magnified, spooky, though we all knew sound was the one thing that couldn't betray us in vacuum.

"The rings are full of little photosynthesizers," Boyce said. "Looks like plankton or something similar. Hydroplankton? They use solar energy to collect deuterium and compress it in little bubble tanks about a millimeter across. I see titans scooping them up by the millions. There's bigger butterfly-like things, too, that look like they concentrate carbon into their wings. It looks like titans eat those as well."

"Do you see anything eating *titans?*" I asked. "That's what we want to find. Something that'll limit their population."

"I'm looking for parasites or signs of disease," he replied. "No luck so far. This really is a simple ecosystem."

"Something's got to be keeping them under control," I said.

"Something obviously is," Boyce said, "but I haven't found it yet. Give me time; we just got here."

Our radar jamming seemed to be working. There were seven or eight titans feeding in the rings less than a thousand kilometers from us, but they didn't seem to notice us at all. And in the shadow of the tiny moon, even our white hull reflected only the soft glow of the rings and the banded orange planet beyond.

I should have known we wouldn't be the only ones to think of that trick. I was just beginning to relax when Tyler said, "That's strange. This moon has a moon of its own."

I looked over his shoulder at the navigation display, where he had zoomed in on a bumpy asteroid only a few dozen kilometers away. It was about three hundred meters across, and its surface was heavily cratered and zigzagged with cracks. It looked like it must have once been hit hard enough to nearly shatter it. Not surprising this close to a planetary ring system, especially one with life in it; there must have been tons of debris flying around just waiting to smack into something.

"Anything living on it?" I asked.

"Let me check," said Boyce. He retrained his sensors on the asteroid, said, "Several small life-forms on the surface. Something else underneath . . . let me see." He frowned. "Hmm. That can't be right. Spock, let me borrow the deep-penetration array for a second."

"Certainly," Spock replied. "What have you found?"

"It reads like one big life-form inside, but that can't be. There's no opening for it to come and go."

"How big?" I asked, the hair standing up on my neck.

"Bigger than a titan," he said, "but it's got to be a false reading. Just a second."

We never got that second. We didn't need to; the answer became obvious when the asteroid split apart into dozens of thin shards of rock and a creature straight out of a nightmare came flying toward us.

It looked a lot like a juvenile titan, only scaled up. Its dozen tentacles were each as thick as the support columns for our warp engines. Its mouth was the size of a hangar bay. It wasn't designed for filtering hydroplankton, either. It was all fangs, multiple rows of them for ripping big chunks out of its prey. It didn't have a fusion drive; it came at us like a magnet to steel, accelerating fast.

Twenty-three

"PIZZA!" PIKE SAID SUDDENLY. HOMPAQ JERKED BACKWARD IN SURPRISE, then growled.

"Pizza?" she asked. "What is pizza?"

"He meant to say 'phaser,' " said Nowan. "Didn't you? Only your incredible phasers could save you from such a beast."

"No, no," Pike said, laughing. "I meant pizza. It's food. Bread with meat and cheese and stuff on it. Great for filling an empty stomach—and for sharing with friends. I just realized I've missed dinner, and so have you, I'd bet. How about we share a pizza? That is, if this place serves food."

"Cap has a replicator," Hompaq said.

Pike had never heard of a replicator, but he took that as affirmative. The name was suggestive enough.

Nowan shrugged. "I know not what this 'pizza' is like, but I eat bread and meat and cheese. 'Stuff,' on the other hand, sounds ominous. What sort of 'stuff' do you propose?"

"Oh, you can put all kinds of things on pizza. Olives, green peppers, mushrooms, anchovies, haggis . . ."

"Anchovies?" Nowan made a face. "Not the little fish?"

"Yeah, that's right. Cured in salt."

"I would prefer not. I have eaten my fill of salted fish for quite some time."

Pike nodded. "I suppose you probably have."

Hompaq said, "I have heard of mushrooms. They are a fungus, are they not?" She also had a disgusted look on her face.

"Well, yeah," said Pike. "But they're not slimy or anything."

"Klingons do not eat fungus."

"All right, then, what do you eat?"

"With bread and cheese? Gagh would be good."

Now it was Pike's turn to make a face. "Gag? I already don't like it. What is it?"

"Serpent worms. Best when served live, but they can also be stewed, for those with *delicate* stomachs." She sneered at Pike as she said that.

"Hey, don't delicate me," he said. "I can eat mushrooms. But I'll pass on the gag, thank you."

"Haggis sounds equally unpleasant," said Nowan.

"What is it?" Hompaq asked. "The name, at least, is close to gagh."

"It's ground-up heart and liver and lungs mixed with oatmeal and boiled in a sheep's stomach."

"That sounds acceptable," she said.

Nowan paled and shook his head. "No, not for me. Sorry."

Pike sighed. "You know, pizza has been around for at least three hundred years, and it's always this way when more than one person tries to order one. Let's try it by process of elimination: Who doesn't like sausage?"

Neither Hompaq or Nowan spoke.

"North American Protectorate bacon?"

"What is that?" Hompaq asked.

"Sliced pig."

"Ah. Pigs are much like our targs. Acceptable."

"Good. Olives?"

"Cap keeps them for martinis. Salty but acceptable."

"Green pepper?"

"I prefer my peppers hot. Humans have no peppers worthy of the name, but jalapeños are adequate."

"Uh, let's skip the peppers. Pineapple?"

Neither of them complained.

Pike nodded. "Let's not press our luck. That ought to be enough. Just a minute." He stood up and walked over to the bar. On the way he realized he hadn't asked about tomato sauce, but he decided not to go down that path. Pizza without tomato sauce was no better than a sandwich.

Cap was waiting at the end of the bar. Before Pike could tell him what he wanted, Cap said, "New York, Chicago, or Italian style?"

"Uh . . . New York," said Pike.

"Just a sec." Cap walked halfway down the length of the bar to a silvery alcove in the back wall, said, "Pizza, New York style, large, with sausage, NAP bacon, green olive, pineapple, standard cheeses." He waited a moment, just long enough to scratch his head, then reached in and lifted out a steaming pizza on a round wooden board. "Here you go." He set it in front of Pike, laid a handful of bar napkins beside it, and said, "Paramecium cheese?"

"Uh . . . no thanks," said Pike. He looked down at the pizza, then over at the slot in the wall. "Replicator" was a good name for it.

He wondered where the template had come from. The pizza certainly smelled fresh. Had chefs competed for the chance to create the perfect one from which all further replicas were made? Then at just the right moment, when all the flavors were blended and the dough cooked just so, it would be scanned into a transporter buffer and stored as an information pattern. Signal degradation from the data compression necessary to store the pattern would be too great to re-create actual living cells, but the proteins would be okay.

"Amazing," he said out loud. Starfleet could do this now, with existing technology.

"No, pizza," said Cap.

Pike nodded and picked it up, along with the napkins, and carried it back to his table.

"Dig in," he said. He sat down and pulled off a slice, stringy with melted cheese. He blew on it to cool it, then took a bite. *Mmmm.* Good as the real thing.

Hompaq tried a slice, her expression dubious for an entirely different reason, but after the first bite she nodded and said, *"Mot bah!"*

Nowan wrapped his slice in a napkin so he wouldn't get his hands oily, and when he bit he was careful not to let cheese dangle from his mouth. Victorian manners, Pike assumed. Nowan waited until he had swallowed before he said, "Yes, quite good. And quite welcome. It has been a long time since my last meal."

"Eat up, then," Pike said. "I get the impression there's a lot more where this came from."

He devoured his slice, then another, before leaning back and wiping his mouth with his napkin. "All right, that's better. Now, where was I?"

"About to face the same fate as this pizza," Hompaq said.

"Oh, yes. The kraken. It was coming fast . . ."

Twenty-four

"Shields!" I ordered, and a moment later, "Evasive action!" but we didn't have time for either strategy to do any good. We had demonstrated around Devernia that our shields wouldn't prevent a head-on collision with something that big, and a ship the size of the *Enterprise* can't move instantly. The impulse engines had just powered up when the creature struck.

The hull shuddered under the blow, made doubly hard by our forward acceleration. Everyone on the bridge hung on until the inertial dampers could compensate for it, but the monster didn't sit still. It swarmed over the ship like a giant squid, hanging on with its tentacles and biting at anything that looked vulnerable. Its extra mass threw us off balance, making us spin around in a dizzying spiral until I ordered Number One to try full reverse.

Again we lurched nearly out of our chairs—those of us who had them. Everyone else went tumbling. The dampers were calibrated for a mass of 190,000 tons, not twice that, so they actually yanked the crew backward faster than the ship with its passenger could move. The creature, of course, hung on with all twelve tentacles, hardly budging until I ordered, "Full stop!"

Colt and our passengers picked themselves up off the floor. We could hear the creature slide across the hull, scraping ominously just overhead, but we couldn't see it. All our sensors pointed away from the ship, not toward it. The best we could do was infer its position by the sensors that showed scaly gray hide or total darkness, but that seemed to be the entire top half of the saucer section.

"Dabisch, launch a signal buoy," I said. Buoys exited the ship from near the middle of the saucer, and they were designed to penetrate an asteroid's surface so they could cling tight and serve as a navigation warning. One of those ought to give the monster a bellyache.

It definitely got its attention. We heard the thump of launch, then the screech of tentacles and heavy banging as the creature thrashed in pain. Then the overhead sensors cleared.

"Where did it go?" I asked. "Are we free?"

"Negative," said Spock. "It has moved to the starboard warp nacelle."

That we could see. "Give me visual," I said, and a moment later the viewscreen lit up with the view aft from the top of the saucer. The hull curved away like a gentle hillside, but the warp engines peered up over it like two enormous eyes—one of which wore a patch. A *big,* writhing, multilegged patch that seemed bent on ripping the entire engine loose from its mount. If the structural integrity fields hadn't been operating it probably could have, but it wasn't dealing with simple metallic strength. The integrity fields kept the engines from ripping loose during the extreme accelerations of warp drive, but they weren't designed for random motion any more than the inertial dampers were. If we let that thing tug at the engine long enough, it would break the support pylon. And if it did that we were as good as dead, because there was no way we would survive long enough in this system to reattach it and get away.

The phasers were purposefully designed so they couldn't fire on our own ship. The only way we could hit the creature now would be to go out with phaser rifles and shoot at it by hand, but I had already seen how effective they were against titans and I had no reason to expect them to be any more useful against this.

The ship continued to shake as the creature yanked at the engine. "Can we go into warp with it clinging to the nacelle like that?" asked Colt. Half of her hair had fallen out of its ponytail and she hung on with both hands to the railing to keep from being thrown to the floor again.

"Negative," Spock replied. "The stress would rip the ship apart."

"How about if we just let the engine build up a subspace field?" I asked. "Don't actually engage the flight controls. Maybe the magnetic effect will damage it somehow."

Spock didn't immediately object, so I said, "Try it, Number One."

She worked the controls and I watched the swirling lines of the subspace field intensity monitor above Spock's station shift to their familiar cruising pattern. But the viewscreen showed the creature stubbornly clinging on, apparently none the worse for the energy pouring through its body.

A piece of the asteroid it had used for camouflage drifted past, tumbling end over end. It was thin and sharp-edged from where it had been broken off the main mass. If only we could put an impulse engine on *that,* I thought, and steer it into the monster on our ship.

"Wait a minute," I said. The asteroid fragment didn't need an impulse engine; *we* had that. And we had a bigger target to work with, too. "Forward view," I said. The screen flickered, then showed us the moon in whose shadow we were hiding, and off to the side, the remains of the asteroid. As I had thought, the greatest part of its mass was still concentrated in one chunk. The titan-eater sheared off thin pieces to cover itself with, keeping the main mass to use over and over again. Well, we could use it too.

"Mr. Tyler," I said, "set a course for that asteroid. Offset its radius, plus forty-five meters to port, twenty meters down from ship's centerline." That was how far out the warp engine stood. Any captain who's ever taken his ship into space dock knows those figures by heart. And so does his pilot. "Number One, follow that course exactly. To the *centimeter.* And don't forget to compensate for the extra mass."

She gulped. "Aye, sir."

"Course set," Tyler said.

"Ahead half impulse power."

The ship lurched and the asteroid veered downward in the viewscreen, but Number One brought us back onto Tyler's trajectory and we watched the rocky surface approach. "Shields down," I ordered, suddenly realizing they were still up. I didn't want anything to slow the asteroid's impact by even a single erg.

It grew larger and larger, nearly filling the viewscreen with its deeply scarred surface. We could see tooth marks and fracture lines from where the creature had ripped pieces loose. It seemed as if it would smash straight into us, and I thought for sure that Tyler or Number One had miscalculated.

"Brace for impact!" I yelled.

Someone behind me shouted "Aaah!" and we all winced, but just as it seemed we would crash headlong into the stony surface, it started to slide upward. That was actually us gliding past it, just far enough away to miss it but close enough to scrape off paint. And close enough, I hoped, to scrape off unwanted passengers.

We were moving at a couple of hundred kilometers per second by then; the impact jarred us worse than anything we had yet felt. I wound up draped over the helm controls between Tyler and Number One. When I struggled back to my chair I saw Colt and Perri and Lanned folded over the railing, struggling to get their feet under them again. Spock, unperturbable as ever, picked himself up off the floor and dusted himself off before sitting back down on his stool. Dabisch had turned his long-backed chair around and ridden it out in comfort. Now he flipped the viewscreen to the aft view again and we saw the monster struggling with the asteroid, which seemed to have crushed a couple of tentacles when it struck.

"Let's go!" I said. "Warp speed, anywhere but here."

Number One engaged the engines, but a harsh alarm sounded and she instantly slapped the Abort button. "Field asymmetry is beyond safe limits," she said. "It must have damaged the engine."

"It's coming back!" Perri shouted.

"Full impulse power," I ordered. "Keep some distance."

Number One flew us toward the moon, trying to stay in its shadow, but the beast flung itself loose from the asteroid and pursued us.

"Ready phasers," I said. "Full power. Number One, bring us about." We whirled around, the effect entirely visual now that the inertial dampers had only our normal mass to work with, and Tyler fired a full spread from the phaser banks. The beams converged on the monster and its scaly hide sparkled with energy discharge, but they had no effect other than that.

I considered using a photon torpedo, but then we would probably have to fight a dozen titans that were alerted to the battle as well. "Forward again," I said. "Spock, can we get any more power out of those phasers?"

"Power is not the problem," he replied. "Penetration is. Like the titans, this creature's armor is opaque to all but Q-band radiation."

"Can we modulate the phasers to emit Q-band?" I asked.

"I believe so."

"Then do it. And fast. We don't have much time."

While he worked I pressed the intercom switch. "Engineering, see what you can do about that warp field asymmetry."

Burnie didn't sound happy. "We're trying, Captain, but it's a real mess out there. The Jefferies tubes have lost their seal at the junction so I've had to send a crew out in pressure suits. We don't even know what's wrong yet, much less how to fix it."

"You've got to do something," I said. "We can't stick around here much longer."

"Phasers are ready," Spock said.

"Number One, bring us around. Mr. Tyler, fire at will."

The creature was considerably closer now; he hit it with full power and this time the effect was instantaneous. Two of its immense tentacles blew free, whirling around like bolas. Tyler fired again and another arm twitched and jerked away like a separate beast.

One last shot and the creature's body erupted in a shower of debris, accompanied by a bright flash of light. We had apparently hit its magnetic field generator.

"Captain," Colt said. "The titans have seen us."

I hit the intercom again. "Burnie, do something *now*."

"The best I can do is lower the efficiency of the port engine," he said. "That'll balance the subspace field, but we won't be able to do better than warp one point five."

"Warp one and a half is better than eaten alive," I said. "Do it." I looked up at Number One. "You heard the man. Get us out of here as soon as Burnie adjusts the port engine."

It took him nearly a minute, during which we watched the titans draw closer. I thanked fate that our radar jammer still worked. As it was they were only investigating a bright flash, not a foreign spaceship in their midst. One of them came close enough to spot us visually, though, and Tyler had to fire on it as well. The explosion was just as spectacular—and just as bloody—as the Devernian nuclear bombs.

That only brought more of them in. Space was starting to get pretty thick with large bodies.

"Burnie," I said, hitting the intercom button. "Do your stuff."

"It's ready," he replied, just as another titan saw us and accelerated on its magnetic fields straight for us. It flipped over and fired its plasma jet, but before it could initiate its laser Number One engaged the engines and we leaped into warp.

Of course we weren't out of the woods yet. The titans could do warp one point five, too, and they were definitely unhappy with us. Flashes of light were a curiosity; ships traveling at warp speed were evidently the enemy.

"What have they got against starships?" I asked.

"Maybe they're guard dogs," Colt replied. Number One turned away from her control board long enough to give her one of her patented withering looks, but Colt shrugged it off and said, "Well, that's how they act. Sniffing around peaceful as can be until they see an intruder, and then *bam!*"

"Yes," Spock said, "there are similarities in their behavior. If the analogy holds true, then as soon as we are out of their territory they should lose interest in us."

"And if it doesn't?" Number One asked.

"Then we will either have to stand and fight, or continue running until they exhaust their fuel supply."

"Fifteen light-years?" I asked. "That's a lot of running at warp two."

Spock said, "That was a theoretical calculation. I may have been in error by as much as seven percent."

That was comforting. Maybe we would only have to run fourteen light-years instead.

Or maybe Colt was right and we just needed to make it out of the solar system. We crossed the heliopause, the invisible boundary where solar wind stops pushing away interstellar dust, and plunged on into deep space. Most of the titans kept following us, but a couple of the stragglers turned back. I held my breath, waiting to see if any more would, and eventually a couple more turned away, then more and more after that until there was only one titan on our tail.

"There's always one showoff, isn't there?" I asked. "Number One, take us out of warp and bring us about on my mark. Mr. Tyler, phasers at quarter power. Shoot to injure if possible, but if it gets too close, go to full power."

"Yes, sir."

I waited a moment longer, hoping the titan would tire of the chase on its own, but when it was only a few seconds away I sighed and said, "Mark."

Number One brought us back into normal space and whirled us around so fast the viewscreen actually showed a brief image of the ship rushing toward us. Right behind it came the titan. Tyler fired and struck it head-on with the phaser banks and it lurched to the side, but it kept coming so he hit it again and this time it curved away. He gave it a third shot broadside just to make sure, and that sent it completely around the way it had come, its tentacles tucked tightly up against its body.

"Guard dogs," I said. "What do you know. Good guess, Yeoman."

"Thank you, sir."

Number One didn't look up from her helm controls.

"Any other life-forms nearby?" I asked.

"Negative," said Spock.

"Did you check for mysterious hollow asteroids, too?"

"I did."

I nodded. "All right, then, let's rest up here until Burnie gets the engines up to specs again. In the meantime, let's take stock of what we've just seen. Are these big things what keeps the titan population in check, or is it more complicated than that? And what do we do about it either way?"

Lanned said, "If they're the answer to our problem, I think I prefer the problem."

"I agree," said Perri. "I don't want them anywhere close to Aronnia, either."

"I think it's a moot point," I told him. "There's no way we could take something that size back with us. And even if we could somehow manage it, it would take dozens of them to even make a dent in the titan population."

The bridge grew quiet for a moment as we all pondered the situation. We could hear the electronic bleeps and pings of instrumentation and the hum of life-support machinery keeping us comfortable inside our metal cocoon, but we were all thinking about what lived on the other side of the walls. If this was what we had come here to find, then we were on a fool's errand.

"What do we call them?" Yeoman Colt asked. "Gargantuans?"

That pretty well summed up what we were all thinking. The problem we faced, the voyage we had undertaken, the creatures we had encountered along the way—all seemed overwhelming. Especially now that it was clear the titans weren't the largest nor the fiercest monsters we were liable to face.

"How about krakens?" suggested Dr. Boyce. "It's an old name for a mythological sea monster."

"I wish these *were* mythological," I told him. "With surprises like this waiting for us it's going to be damned difficult to learn anything useful."

Spock said, "On the contrary, Captain. We have already learned a great deal of useful information. It is true that none of it offers an immediate answer to the Devernians' problem, but we *are* learning how the ecosystem functions."

"By nearly becoming part of the food chain," I said. "I don't think we can take much more of that." I leaned back in my chair and said, "No, we need to figure out a better way of gathering information. We need to find out what eats krakens, and what eats whatever eats krakens, without attracting any more attention to ourselves."

"Maybe that's our problem," Colt said.

"Maybe what is?" I asked.

"Maybe we're too conspicuous. If it's really true that the titans see us as a threat, maybe the trick isn't to hide from them so much as it is to look like less of a threat."

"And how do you propose to do that? Paint the ship to look like a titan?"

She swallowed. "No, sir. I was remembering what Lanned said, that the titans didn't attack the Devernian spaceships until they started shooting at them. Maybe it was because the ships were too small to trigger their defense mechanism. I was thinking maybe we need to be smaller."

Dr. Boyce snorted. "Smaller? How do you plan to do that? Separate the saucer and go in without the warp drive? That would be suicide."

"No," she said. "Even the saucer would probably be too big. If the titans are guard dogs, we need to be mice. I was thinking of going back in a shuttlecraft."

"A shuttlecraft?" Boyce said. "That's insane. You'd be eaten alive."

I agreed with him at first, but after I had a moment to think about it I started to change my mind. "Maybe not," I said. "The Devernian ships—the non-living ones—aren't much bigger than a shuttle, and they held their own even under attack. They could outmaneuver the titans, for one thing. That's been our biggest liability in the *Enterprise;* we can't dodge fast enough when they come after us."

Boyce stood up from his science station and came over to the handrail around my command chair. "You're seriously considering this?" he asked. "The shuttles have no warp drive to get you out of trouble. Their phasers have maybe a tenth the power of our main batteries. Even if we tech them around to emit Q-band, that'll probably just be enough to annoy a titan. And as for a kraken, well, that'd probably just get his attention."

"We won't even try to get their attention," I told him. "That's the whole point."

"The easiest way to not get their attention is to stay the hell out of their way."

"But that won't accomplish what we came here for. We've got to go back somehow, and this is the best idea I've heard yet." I looked at the people on the bridge, wondering who I should take with me on the mission. Spock, certainly. Dr. Boyce as well, despite his objections. Perri and Lanned, to acknowledge their involvement in all this if nothing else. And Colt? It was her idea, but was that enough reason to let her endanger her life?

She looked at me with undisguised eagerness, and I remembered our discussion in the conference room a few days ago. This was the sort of thing she'd come into space for. That wasn't a good enough reason by itself, either, but she was observant and quick-thinking, both useful qualities on a mission into hostile territory.

I glanced over at Number One. Equally capable, much more calm and reasoning, with more experience and better understanding of the ship's systems. Which made her absolutely invaluable on board the *Enterprise* while I was gone. Only a fool would take all his senior officers on a dangerous mission and leave nobody experienced to mind the ship.

I briefly considered sending her to command the mission and staying here myself. That would be the most prudent course of action, the sort of thing Starfleet Command would recommend. From their point of view, the *Enterprise* and I were indispensable; I was not to risk either of us unnecessarily. But I had a pretty low opinion of the kind of captain who would send someone into a danger he wouldn't face himself, and despite their policy I suspected Command did, too. No, if anyone was going, I would lead them.

I pressed the intercom switch on the arm of my chair. "Engineering," I said. "Have someone prepare a shuttlecraft for in-system reconnaisance. Load it with full-spectrum scanning equipment, and recalibrate the phasers for peak output in Q-band." I let up on the button and said to the bridge crew, "All right, we'll try this once more, this time the sleek and silent way."

Twenty-five

In the bar, Nowan shook his head and said, "I can't fault you for courage, but there's a fine line between courage and foolhardiness. Taking a dinghy into a pod of whales is a good way to get yourself smashed to smithereens."

"I thought whales didn't mind small boats," Pike replied. "Unless they're carrying harpooners, of course."

"Oh, aye, they don't mind 'em, not in either sense of the word. If you have the bad luck to be in their way, they'll never even know you're there."

"Ah." Pike picked at the remains of the pizza. "We had a little more room to maneuver. And we didn't go straight for the biggest concentration of titans. We wanted a broader overview of the ecosystem. And we had collected quite a bit of data already. I let Spock and Boyce go over it while we prepared the shuttle, and they figured out where the gaps in their knowledge were so we were able to target our mission a little more accurately than we had the first time. We didn't just waltz in there and hope for the best."

Hompaq was toying with a napkin, tearing it into little pieces and smiling in a distracted sort of way. Pike thought she hadn't been paying attention, but now she said, "You were—what is the human term? You were sweet on her, weren't you?"

"Who?" Pike asked.

"Don't 'who' me. Your yeoman. You took her with you everywhere you went."

"That's what a yeoman is for," Pike said. "Besides their clerical duties, they're the captain's personal assistant in practically everything, and she was highly qualified for her job."

She grinned. "I'll bet she was. It must have really rankled to see her and those two aliens consorting with one another."

Pike shook his head. "It wasn't like that."

"It should have been," said Hompaq. "On a Klingon ship, sleeping with the captain is an honor. If you truly cared for her you would have let the rest of the crew know she was your chosen mate."

Pike blushed. "That's not the way we do things in Starfleet."

"Your loss. So where is she now?"

"Science officer on board the *Bozeman.*"

She laughed. "You knew that pretty quickly."

"I approved her transfer," he replied. "I'm fleet captain now, in case you don't remember that from your history books."

"Oh, I remember," she said. "Science officer? That's quite a jump in responsibility in such a short time. One would almost suspect she pulled a few strings to get there. A few heartstrings, maybe?"

Pike leaned toward her and said softly, "Don't insult either of us by that insinuation. She got where she is today by hard work and intelligence. And ambition. When the *Enterprise* went into spacedock for refitting she didn't want to stick around for two years waiting for it to fly again, so she transferred out. And up. I was happy to give her a recommendation, but that's the extent of my influence."

"Of course." Hompaq tore a few more pieces off her napkin, adding them to the loose pile in front of her. Without looking up, she said, "You want a little piece of friendly advice?"

He considered it for a moment, ready to turn her down, but at last he shrugged and said, "Sure. What?"

"Transfer her back."

He felt a little shiver run up his spine. "Why? Does something happen to the *Bozeman?*"

"Not that I know of," she said. "Nor to her, either. But that's not what I'm talking about. I'm talking about *you.* For your sake, bring her back."

Pike rolled his eyes. "I'm hardly a pining schoolboy," he told her. "Even if I *did* harbor some personal affection for her—which I'm not admitting I do—I'm not about to cut short her career just to bring her close to me again. It wouldn't work anyway. Can you imagine how she'd feel about that?"

"Can you imagine how you're going to feel when—"

"Hompaq." The voice wasn't all that loud, but it cut through the conversation in the bar like a sonic stunner. Everyone turned to look at the bartender, who stood at the near end of the bar, a glass in one hand and a towel in the other. "Don't go there," he said.

"But he's—"

"Come here."

Her aura of bravado drained away, and she stood up without protest and walked over to the bar. They whispered back and forth for a minute, during which Pike could only catch the phrases "delta radiation" and "out of the picture anyway."

Nowan cleared his throat and said, "I suspect you must feel a little like the condemned man awaiting clemency. She clearly knows something about you."

"She certainly seems to," said Pike. "I've got to wonder, though, if she's just yanking my chain again."

"The bartender seems concerned enough to reprimand her."

"Yeah." Pike listened nervously for more clues, but Cap and Hompaq had reduced their volume. "It makes me kind of twitchy knowing they know my future," he said.

"Likewise," said Nowan.

Pike laughed. "Nobody knows *your* future. Unless you'd care to give me more of a name than 'Nowan.' "

The seaman smiled enigmatically and shook his head. "No, Captain. 'Nowan' is sufficient. As our bartender is almost certainly telling Hompaq, we are not here to upset history. The less you know about me, the better, I believe."

Pike nodded, chastened. "You're right, of course."

Hompaq and the bartender finished their argument—a rather one-sided argument, it looked like—and she came back to their table. "Just in case you were wondering, you live happily ever after," she said as she sat down again.

"That's a comfort."

"It wasn't intended to be."

Across the bar, the cat-woman stood up and led one of the human men at her table toward the stairs at the back. They were giggling as they passed Pike's table, but when Hompaq growled deep in her throat the cat-woman hissed at her and bared her fangs. Pike tensed, waiting for Hompaq to leap up and start a hand-to-hand fight, but she stayed in her chair. Too many run-ins with the bartender already tonight; she evidently didn't want to get kicked out just yet.

"There's certainly no love lost between you two, is there?" Pike asked when the cat-woman and her companion had gone up the stairs.

Hompaq snorted. "Long story. And you were still in the midst of yours."

"So I was," Pike said, just as eager as she was to leave the last few minutes behind. "Let's see, we were getting ready to head back into the titans' home system in a shuttlecraft. . . ."

Twenty-six

We took the *Kepler,* our newest shuttle. It was already set up for planetary reconnaissance, so it required less refitting than the other shuttles, which mostly served as landing craft when the transporters couldn't handle a planet's ionosphere or when the target area was shielded. The *Kepler* had room for six, but not much more than that. I sat in the pilot's chair while Spock took the copilot's position, but he concentrated on the sensors while I flew. Colt and Boyce sat in the back, monitoring the additional scanning equipment that the engineering crew had added to the hull. Perri and Lanned sat in the middle where they could look over Spock's and my shoulders or at Colt's and Boyce's monitors, whichever seemed most interesting at the time.

It would have taken us hours to fly back into the system under impulse power, so we waited until Burnie had gotten the *Enterprise*'s warp engines back up to specs, then let it ferry us into position using the same trick we had used the first time. We went back to the same planet, but we picked a different moon to hide behind, and the moment the ship dropped out of warp we launched the shuttle, flying out of the moon's shadow toward a lone titan feeding in the rings. If they weren't going to tolerate our presence, we wanted to know it while the *Enterprise* could still pick us up and get us out of there.

We waited nervously for the titan to notice us, but if it did it gave no sign. I piloted the shuttle right up to its starboard flank while Spock, Dr. Boyce, and Colt directed scanners at everything around us. Perri and Lanned and I watched through the windshield for trouble, peering down into the jumble of dust particles, ice flakes, rocks, and occasional boulders that stretched away toward infinity before us, but long minutes ticked past without any sign of aggression.

"Any evidence of krakens?" I asked.

"One," Spock replied, "but it is four point three thousand kilometers distant."

"How about hidden ones? Would you be able to spot one covered in rock?"

"Now that we know what to look for, I believe so. But I find only the one I mentioned within sensor range."

"How about other predators?"

"None in evidence," he said.

Boyce added, "Boy, you were right about how basic this ecosystem is. I get two different types of hydroplankton, the butterfly things, one species of salmon-sized filter feeder, and then the titans and krakens. Nothing in between."

"That doesn't explain what keeps the population in check," Lanned said. "There must be something else."

"If there is, it doesn't live in the rings," Boyce said. "Not this part of 'em anyway."

"Should we go elsewhere?" I asked.

"Why don't we do an overflight?" he said. "One complete circuit around the rings. That would tell us a lot."

It was easier said than done. The rings and everything in them were already in orbit around the gas giant, so for us to move relative to them meant that we had to *leave* orbit and hold our position under power while the rings moved beneath us. Fortunately the planet's gravity wasn't so strong that we needed full thrust to do it, but I would have to keep my attention on piloting.

"Pike to *Enterprise,*" I said, keying the in-dash communicator. "We're commencing a sweep of the ring system. Take the ship to safety and wait for our pickup signal."

"Yes, sir," said Number One. "Request permission to try scanning the inner planets while we wait. The titan population dwindles closer to the sun, and that would actually put us closer to you than if we left the system completely."

She was right. "Good thinking, Number One," I said. "Permission granted. Pike out."

The shuttle seemed to grow even smaller then. We were alone now, with just one thin metal wall between us and the unknown quantities outside. Yet our tiny refuge hummed with reassuring efficiency. The air recirculator hissed softly, pulling the excess moisture and carbon dioxide out of our exhalations, and the monitors bleeped and chimed musically as they relayed their information to us. The control panel added its own sounds as the navigation array warned us of debris within our path. Clothing rustled as people shifted position, and Perri cleared his throat a few times.

"Commencing sweep," I said, taking the shuttle straight out from the rings. I wanted to get up above the ring plane a few hundred kilometers before we started moving alongside it. That would give us a better vantage from which to scan for life-forms, and it would also reduce our chances of hitting something. Most planetary rings were only a kilometer or two thick, but I didn't want to take chances here. With all these titans knocking things around, there could be debris ten times as far away as usual.

A gas giant's ring system is a big place. We drifted along above it for hours, a tiny dust mote above an immense river. Occasionally Spock would say, "I read a denser concentration of hydroplankton," or Boyce would say, "There's a subspecies of filter-fish here," and when we passed near a kraken or a moon they would grow busy for a few minutes scanning that, but as time passed it became clear there was little new to discover.

At one point we saw a kraken eating a titan, ripping it apart and devouring its internal organs. The titan was freshly killed; the ends of its tentacles were still twitching.

"I guess that settles that," I said. "Krakens eat titans."

"Obviously," said Spock.

My behind had started to grow tired from sitting on it for too long. "So what we've got here," I said, "is little plankton gizmos and butterfly things that concentrate nutrients for the filter-fish, and the titans who eat both, and the krakens who eat filter-fish and titans. That seems awfully basic. What are we missing?"

"Nothing, as far as I can tell," said Spock. "However, by definition, if we were missing something I would not be aware of it."

"What I'm wondering," said Colt, "is why the filter-fish? The titans and krakens would do fine without them, wouldn't they?"

"Not necessarily," said Boyce. "Ecosystems with only one path through the food chain are dynamically unstable. A minor fluctuation in any part of the chain sends ripples all through it."

"How so?" asked Perri.

Boyce leaned back from his monitors and rubbed his eyes. "Imagine what would happen if there was only one kind of plankton, or just the titans to eat it. If the plankton died back for some reason, so would the titans. And then the krakens. Without the titans feeding on it the plankton would probably bloom again, and the titan population would boom pretty soon after, which would lower the plankton population just about the time the kraken population was rising in response to the increased number of titans, so the titans would starve *and* be hunted down to nothing, and the cycle would keep repeating itself under positive feedback until something died out completely. But with two types of plankton and with butterflies and filter-fish in the mix, there's a second food source for everything, which serves to buffer the system and prevent feedback loops from developing."

"Is that what we're missing at home then? These little filter-fish?"

"Maybe," said Boyce. "But you're missing the plankton, too, for that matter. Your titans feed directly on gas-giant atmospheres, even when there's no plankton there. That's probably the adaptation that let them colonize other star systems, but it plays hell with their natural control mechanisms."

"What if we introduced the plankton *and* the filter-fish?" asked Lanned. "It seems counterintuitive to feed them when we want to reduce their population, but if that is what it takes . . ."

"You'd probably have to introduce krakens too," said Boyce. "And that would still leave them laying their eggs on Devernia."

I dodged a meter-wide rock that the navigation array tagged as being on a collision course, then said, "So where do the titans in this system lay their eggs?"

Spock said, "Our early scans of the inner planets showed little activity there. However, I have spotted sixty-two immature titans in the rings. They must have come from nearby. It is possible that these titans lay their eggs on the moons."

"What do the hatchlings eat, then?" I asked.

"There are hydroplankton subspecies in the moons' atmospheres and in the surface ices," he replied. "There are also land-dwelling variants of filter-fish. Plus the moons contain direct deposits of deuterium-oxide ice, which the parents can seek out with their radar when they are ready to lay their eggs. When the young have absorbed enough nutrients there to lift off into the rings, they could eat spaceborne butterflies and filter-fish until they were large enough to scoop up hydroplankton directly."

"That's *it?*" I asked. "That's the complete ecosystem?"

"Substantially," said Boyce. "We could still find a few surprises, but what we've seen here is theoretically enough."

"So what does that mean for Devernia?" Lanned asked. "Suppose we seed our gas-giant atmospheres and their rings and their moons with this hydroplankton, and release butterflies and filter-fish to feed on that. Suppose we even import krakens to feed on the titans. Even so, how do we train the titans to breed on the moons instead of Devernia?"

"Good question," said Boyce. "They've got five hundred years of experience breeding on planets. More than that, actually, since they've probably bred on them halfway from here to there. That's a lot of conditioning to overcome."

We drifted along over the rings, each lost in our own thoughts for a while. How could we retrain an entire population of titans to breed somewhere else? Providing them with the alternative site wouldn't be enough; they would just use both. We would somehow have to make Devernia not worth the effort, but if killing them with nuclear bombs hadn't discouraged them I didn't see what would.

Back on Devernia, after we had witnessed the first eggfall, Yeoman Colt had suggested fencing the titans out with phaser satellites. Spock had pointed out how impossible that was, but I couldn't help thinking we had missed something else that would make it feasible. We knew how to make the phasers more efficient now; that would help, but it hadn't been the efficiency Spock had objected to. It was the sheer number of satellites it would take to provide complete coverage.

What we needed was a way to make the titans not want to go near Devernia in the first place.

"What about jamming?" I asked.

"Jamming?" asked Spock.

"Yeah. I was thinking of Colt's fence idea. That won't work, but what if we put up a few jamming satellites? Keep the titans from getting a radar signature from Devernia."

Boyce laughed. "You can't mask a *planet.* Titans have eyes as well as radar."

"But it's the radar that tells them there's deuterium on the surface," I said. "We could jam *that,* couldn't we? Without the deuterium signature, would they still lay their eggs there?"

"I don't know," said Boyce. "Spock?"

"I do not know either." Spock turned to the copilot's control board. "But there is an easy way to test the theory."

"How?" I asked.

"Mask the deuterium signature around one of the small moons that they lay eggs on here, then watch and see what happens."

That wasn't the answer I was looking for. "It could take weeks to prove that the titans are avoiding it."

"It could. On the other hand, if we find an obvious hatching ground it could take a day or less."

"And how are we going to find an obvious hatching ground?"

"By searching for immature titans. If we find a concentration of them near a moon, that would be strong evidence that the moon is where they originated. We can then scan any adult titans in the area for mature eggs in their oviducts and observe their behavior."

That sounded reasonable enough. If they moved away and laid their eggs on another moon, that would be pretty good evidence. "How many satellites will we need?" I asked.

"Two should be sufficient for the test. One in high orbit on either side will provide coverage of the entire moon."

"And we just happen to have two jamming devices on board," I pointed out. One was hooked up to our main deflector to help hide the shuttle from curious titans if that became necessary, and we had a spare in case the first one was damaged. "Good enough. Let's try it."

It didn't take long to find a suitable moon. There were over a dozen to choose from, starting with the hundred-kilometer snowball nearest the rings. When I flew us close to it we discovered its icy surface crawling with the planetbound versions of filter-fish, and we could see circular craters dotting the ice like dimples on a golf ball. The resemblance was uncanny, for the craters were all the same size. That couldn't happen from impacts; meteor craters would be completely random.

"Blast craters?" I asked when I saw them.

"Affirmative," said Spock. "I presume they are made when the young titans fire their fusion engines to leave the surface."

I looked from the cratered landscape to Lanned, who peered over my shoulder. "Oh yes," he said, seeing the expression on my face. "Our planet is bigger than this moon, and it takes a great deal of thrust to break free of its gravity. Imagine what a city looks like after one has lifted off from within it."

I could easily envision the destruction a fusion flame strong enough to carry a titan would wreak on a city, even one made of stone buildings. "If any of this pays off," I told him, "they'll be taking off from one of your system's moons from now on. Spock, any evidence of krakens?"

"One, Captain," Spock said. "It is hidden in an asteroid much like the first one we encountered, drifting well below us in a twenty-kilometer orbit."

"Keep an eye on it," I told him. "The moment it breaks cover, we're out of here. In the meantime, let's set up our jamming signal and see what happens."

While I piloted the shuttle up to the synchronous-orbit level above the moon's surface, Spock got up from his seat and worked his way back through the shuttle's other passengers to the cargo lockers in the rear, where he removed the backup jamming device. It was a squat rectangular box about the size of a suitcase with a detector/emitter dish on top. The programmable electronics inside had been set to return an antiphase signal to nullify any signal it received, effectively canceling out meaningful reflections. It was old technology; people had been using similar devices for centuries to block everything from police radar to orbital surveillance satellites. I had no doubt it would work against the titans' simple deuterium-location system, but whether that would discourage them was the big question.

Spock set the jammer for automatic operation, then put it in the airlock and closed the inner door. He pressed the button that opened the outer door, and with a thump of breathing air it tumbled free of the shuttle. It stabilized itself with internal forcefields and began echoing signals.

"So much for this half of the moon," I said. "Taking us around to the other." I piloted us over the pole and down to synchronous orbit on the far side, where we parked the shuttle and I activated the jammer mounted on the outer hull.

Then we settled back to wait.

Six people in a shuttlecraft is about two too many even when they're all occupied. Six people just sitting there waiting for something to happen could be the legal definition of a crowd. Spock and Boyce continued to scan the moon below us and surrounding space for life-forms, but the rest of us had little to do besides sit in our chairs and talk about what we had seen so far. When that grew old we broke out our rations and ate a meal; then Perri and Lanned, whose bodies had not yet adapted to twenty-four-hour days, took a nap.

Colt and I played a game of three-dimensional chess on the fold-up board from the emergency survival kit, while Spock eyed our progress and tried his best not to kibitz when we made dumb moves. Neither of us was exactly a master at the game, but we were at least evenly matched, except that I kept getting distracted by the faint but unmistakable smell of garlic on her breath. I didn't even want to know what that signified, but I couldn't help wondering. She was either using it as an excuse to keep Perri and Lanned at a safe distance or she was using it as an alien aphrodisiac, and the more I thought about it the more preoccupied I became.

We traded half a dozen pieces before Colt eventually trapped my king on one of the upper platforms and began systematically wiping out my defenses, keeping one move ahead of me until I finally conceded defeat.

"Good game, Yeoman," I told her, helping fold up the board again. "Any progress yet?" I asked Spock.

"Sixteen titans have approached the moon, sent questing signals out, and turned away when they received no deuterium signature," he replied. "Of those sixteen, six carried eggs. Those six have since moved on, and two at the extreme limit of our sensor range have lain their eggs on other moons."

"So it seems to be working," I said.

He shook his head slightly. "Two eggs deposited elsewhere is hardly a significant trend. However, we have experienced no laying behavior here since we activated the jammers, so our theory has yet to be disproved, either."

"Yes, quite," I said, thinking, *Ask a Vulcan a question . . .*

Dr. Boyce spoke up. "The kraken's asteroid has come around to our side again." Its close orbit had taken it twice around already.

"Is it still in hiding?" I asked.

"I'm checking. Looks like it—no, wait a minute." He increased the sensitivity of his scanner. "I'm getting life-form readings, but it's not the kraken. Looks like . . . eggs?"

Spock looked at his monitor. "I concur. The kraken has deposited a clutch of nine eggs."

"Why'd it leave them?" I asked. "And where'd it go?"

"Unknown," said Spock. "It does not register on our sensors. It is either on the far side of the moon, or it has left for cislunar space while it was shielded from view."

"Leaving its eggs behind," Boyce said. "It snuck them in under our radar net."

"It was already inside our orbit," Spock pointed out. "And leaving eggs behind seems to be the nature of all life here. Even the filter-fish follow the same pattern."

I looked out at the tiny asteroid with its cargo of eggs, and a crazy notion blossomed in my mind. "How long before the eggs hatch?" I asked.

"Difficult to determine," said Spock. "They are shielded from our sensors by thirty meters of rock. However, comparing what metabolic readings I can get with those taken of titan eggs, I estimate at least a week. Perhaps two."

Maybe two weeks. Not a whole lot of time, but maybe enough. "I think it's time we summed up our observations, gentlemen," I said. "Do we or do we not have enough evidence to support our theory about setting up a stable ecosystem?"

Boyce looked at me with a puzzled expression. "Spock just told you it's too soon to tell for sure."

"I don't want for sure. I want probability. Does it look like it will work? And more importantly, how much of the ecosystem do we need to take back with us to *make* it work?"

"Why are you in such an all-fired hurry all of a sudden?" He grinned. "There's a bathroom in back, you know."

I laughed. "That's not it. I'm just thinking that if we're going to transport krakens back to the Devernian system, there's an opportunity right below us we're not likely to find again."

I swear Boyce's hair turned even whiter when I said that.

"You can't be serious," he said. "You want to steal eggs from a kraken's nest?"

"If krakens are important to the ecosystem, I do."

"They are undoubtedly important," said Spock. "We have witnessed nothing else that preys on titans."

"Then put on your pressure suits, boys and girls," I said. "We're going to raid the henhouse."

Twenty-seven

"You didn't," said Nowan.

"We did," Pike replied, grinning proudly.

"Without even knowing where the parent had gone?"

"We made a quick orbit around the moon first and made sure it wasn't lurking close by. We didn't find any sign of it, so we figured it must have gone away. So we parked the shuttle near the asteroid and went in with jet packs." He laughed. "Of course, six of us suiting up in that cramped little shuttle was a comedy in a closet, but we managed it. It went considerably easier after I turned off the gravity."

"You took your entire crew?" Hompaq asked, just as Nowan said in the same astonished tone of voice, "You turned off the gravity?"

"No," Pike said. "I left Dr. Boyce with the shuttle, but I wanted him suited up in case we needed him in a hurry. And yes, I turned off the gravity. It gave us a lot more room to maneuver in. Five of us would duck down and the sixth would float lengthwise in the cabin while we dressed them for space. Of course Perri didn't like that much, since he'd never experienced free fall before, but he took to it pretty quickly. And Colt turned out to be a regular gymnast. She didn't need any help getting her suit on, although Perri and Lanned both helped her anyway."

Hompaq snorted. "While you stood by and gallantly held her helmet."

"Hey, who's telling this story, anyway?"

"If I was telling it, you'd have killed the gravity hours earlier and enjoyed yourselves."

Pike rolled his eyes. "You're incorrigible."

"Damned near insatiable, too," Hompaq admitted, leering at him.

Nowan laughed nervously, then scooted his chair back. "Time to refill our beverages," he said, picking up the two brandy snifters and the Warnog mug and carrying them to the bar. While the bartender refilled them, he came back for the pizza board and the napkins and set them on the end of the bar. Pike watched him take a pen from the mug full of them and look at the nib, then draw on a napkin with it. The nineteenth-century man couldn't hide his astonishment at seeing a ballpoint; he drew a few more lines with it, then pocketed the pen and the unused napkins.

Hompaq had been watching Pike instead. "Really, Captain," she said, "you should get out more. Beat your chest and battle some enemies. Or make savage love with exotic strangers."

"I should, should I?" he asked, eyeing her dubiously from under narrowed eyebrows. "And what makes you say that, Miss Alien Psychiatrist?"

She scratched an itch in an area that most women would have considered private, then said, "The way you tell your tale, and the way you looked when you came in here. When you walked through that door you looked like someone whose whole life had dried up and blown away, but you've shed ten years in the last hour."

He had managed to forget why he'd gone on his walk this evening, but at her words the full load of frustration and self-doubt returned like a stifling cloud of oxygen-poor air. His days as a space explorer were long past, and despite the temporary rush he felt in reliving them, no amount of barstory nostalgia could bring them back.

"That was interesting," Hompaq said.

"What?"

"You can switch it on and off like a light."

"Can I." It wasn't a question.

Nowan came back with their drinks, carefully set them in front of their respective owners, and sat down.

"Is it just me," he asked, "or has a chill blown through here in the last few moments?"

"We were discussing whether Captain Pike here should get out more," Hompaq said. "I think we both voted yes."

"Ah," said Nowan. He, too, lost a little of the gleam in his eye, and Pike remembered how he had looked at first. And acted. A Victorian gentleman who had renounced everything, including his manners. He had gotten them back, but Pike had just witnessed how temporary these bar changes could be.

Temporary or not, he wasn't ready to give it up just yet. Nor was Nowan. The seaman held up his glass and said, "To getting out more." They drank, then he added, "I believe you were about to get out of your shuttle to go raid a kraken's nest. How, pray tell, did that expedition fare?"

"Well enough, at first," Pike replied, glad for the respite. "Once we got out of the shuttle." He took another sip of brandy, reluctant now to go on, but both Hompaq and Nowan were waiting. He took a moment to gather his thoughts, trying to recapture the moment, then set his glass down. "As I said, I left Dr. Boyce there to guard our transportation and to warn us if the kraken returned, and the rest of us jumped to the surface of the asteroid. It was so small there was hardly any gravity to draw us down, so we had to move carefully." Pike smiled, remembering. "It was Perri's first time in a spacesuit, so he was pretty clumsy. And I think he was probably terrified, too, but he never let on. Except we could hear him panting so hard over the radio that Colt reached over to his chest controls and turned down the oxygen level in his air so he wouldn't hyperventilate."

"Why didn't you just leave him behind?" Hompaq asked. "He sounds like a liability."

"I wanted the manpower," Pike replied. "Those eggs were big, and we needed at least two of them. And I wanted the extra phaser in case there were any surprises on the asteroid. The eggs were down inside it, in a cavern the kraken had hollowed out a couple dozen meters below the surface. Our sensors couldn't detect anything in there besides eggs, but I'd been surprised before."

As Pike talked, Nowan took out the pen he had gotten from the bar and began to doodle on the napkins. He was a good artist, and quick. With a few bold strokes of the pen he had rendered a titan with its streamlined body, immense mouth in front, and betentacled fins at the rear. And the kraken, shorter but bigger around, with much larger tentacles. Both rushing toward a tiny box with stick figures floating haphazardly around it.

"You're getting ahead of me," Pike told him.

"What? Oh." Nowan blushed. "Just trying out this pen. It's amazing." He traced the wrinkles in his hand with it, then added a few extra curves and circles for eyes and it suddenly became the face of a wizened old man.

"You're not half bad with that," Pike said.

"Thank you. But I interrupt your story. Please continue." He set the pen down and leaned back in his chair to listen.

Pike shrugged. "No problem. So anyway, the five of us in spacesuits pushed off for the mouth of the cave where the eggs were. . . ."

Twenty-eight

I'd issued everyone a phaser rifle this time. Perri and Lanned had long since put aside their differences, and even though the phasers had been modified for peak output in Q-band I wanted as much firepower as I could get in case of trouble. I showed both men how to shoot and warned them not to unless it was absolutely necessary; then we used our jet packs to move off across the asteroid's scarred surface toward the kraken's nest.

We looked like a procession of snowmen. Our suits were white and bulky, and even with constant-volume joints they resisted movement, so we tended to move our whole bodies when we turned or bent down to look at something. I heard plastic creak as I moved, and the gentle hiss of air through the recirculator reminded me that there was hard vacuum about an inch away from my nose. The helmet had a generous faceplate so I could see to either side without turning my head, but its opaque back still made me feel like something was following me.

There was no dust on the surface, just bare rock. It was dark gray, almost black except when we shone our headlamps directly at it and it sparkled with pinpoints of reflected light. We couldn't walk on it—there wasn't enough gravity to hold our feet down—but we drifted along with our legs pointed that way out of habit. Except for Lanned, who moved headfirst like a torpedo, pulling himself along with his hands. He probably had the most experience with zero-g of any of us, I realized, since his primitive fighter craft had no provision for gravity.

Spock had his tricorder out and was scanning the surface for life-forms. The horizon was only a few dozen meters away and a tricorder couldn't go through very much rock, so I wasn't sure how much good it would do, but it was better than nothing.

"See anything?" I asked him.

"I detect no significant life-forms."

"Here's the opening," Lanned said, bringing himself to a stop at the lip of the cavern. He stuck his legs upward for the rest of us to stop ourselves with, but Perri missed and drifted out over the cave mouth.

"Ahh!" he cried out, swinging his arms wildly for balance, but Lanned snagged his left boot and pulled him back.

I thought about linking everyone together with our safety lines, but that would cut down on our mobility. Perri would be okay in the cave, I figured. There wouldn't be that much room for him to drift before he bumped into a wall.

We peered down into it, our headlights making little circles of brightness on the rock. It was a rough-hewn tube about three meters wide, but instead of running straight down to the egg chamber it curved, so we could only see a few meters into it. It looked empty.

"We're going in," I said for Boyce's benefit.

"I see you," he replied from his vantage a hundred yards overhead. "Be careful."

I pulled myself over the lip and fired my jet pack downward, going in feet first. The rest of us followed one at a time, Lanned bringing up the rear and helping Perri. The rock walls closed in on us, and after we'd negotiated the first turn and couldn't see the stars behind us anymore I felt a twinge of claustrophobia, but I fought it off and continued on. We wouldn't be in here long.

"Anything, Spock?" I asked.

"I can detect the eggs," he replied. "Anything smaller would be beyond the sensitivity of a handheld tricorder through this much rock."

"Smaller I'm not worried about," I said. "I just don't want to surprise a kraken sitting on the nest."

My own shadow preceded me, cast by the others' headlamps as I led the way deeper into the asteroid. I shifted my phaser from hand to hand so I could push off from whichever side of the tunnel I was close to, and I peered around each bend as cautiously as I could, but anything in there had to know we were coming.

It flashed toward us without warning. Spock barely had time to say "Captain, I read—" when two silvery forms burst out of the darkness and came straight for us.

I shouted and got off a quick shot at one of them, but I was way too slow. Nobody else even tried, for which I was thankful. The radio filled with our shouts of alarm as the two creatures bore down on us, then zoomed past without slowing. I never even got a good look at them; all I could see were two bodies about the size of house cats streaking outward, never touching the walls of the cave. Evidently they had the same magnetic propulsion capability that the titans and the kraken did.

Boyce's signal cut in and out, but I heard him say, "What the . . . that? Are . . . right in there?"

"We're fine," I said when I got control of my voice again. "Filter-fish?" I asked Spock.

"Affirmative," he replied.

"I'm glad there's plumbing in these suits," Perri said.

Lanned laughed, and Colt said, "Me too."

"Cut the chatter," I told them. "Let's go."

I led them deeper into the cavern, and after two more turns we found the egg chamber. It was spherical, maybe five meters across. The eggs were coffin-sized and stacked against the back wall, their gray and scaly surfaces almost indistinguishable from the rock. With nine of them and five of us the place felt crowded. I wondered how a kraken could fit in here, and decided it couldn't. Not with its wide body and thick, scaly hide. It must push the eggs down here with its tentacles.

"How close to hatching are they?" I asked Spock, who was waving his tricorder over them.

"Fascinating," he replied.

"That's not a number," I told him. "Will they make it back to Devernia without hatching?"

"I believe so," he said. "The embryos have barely begun to differentiate yet. But what development I do see shows clear evidence of genetic engineering."

"What kind of evidence?" I asked.

He continued to scan as he talked. "The nervous system is essentially a trinary computer, not yet running but already programmed. Even in its simple form I cannot decipher the program without help from the ship's computer, but I can identify sections that clearly represent pattern-recognition subroutines. They are almost certainly a catalog of images. I suspect these will turn out to be a list of objects to either attack or defend in adult life."

Its brain was a *computer?* "Do the titans have this same kind of system?" I asked.

"Undoubtedly. I did not recognize it as such because I was unable to observe such early embryonic stages in their development, and therefore did not detect the simple underlying program that directed their actions, but from what I did see of the later forms, they are built in substantially the same fashion."

Guard dogs indeed, I thought. Ones that came pre-trained. "Could the program be modified?" I asked.

"It probably could," he replied. "In this pristine form it would be relatively easy to alter the code. Once it was running it would be more difficult. I suspect the creatures were designed this way to give their creators an opportunity to modify their programming before releasing them into the wild."

"You're right," I said, "it's fascinating. And maybe even useful if we can figure out how to tap into their programs to make them less aggressive toward starships. But for now we're in the middle of a nest made by one that hasn't been reprogrammed, and every minute we stay here we're pushing our luck that much further. Come on, let's grab a couple of eggs and go."

"We will need three," Spock said.

"Three? There's three sexes?"

Spock shook his head, a gesture that was barely visible outside his pressure suit. "They do not reproduce sexually, at least not as we understand it, but there are three distinct types. We should have a specimen of each."

"Okay, then, three. Which ones?"

He ran the tricorder over the eggs. "The top three will do," he said after a moment.

I let go of my phaser rifle and tugged the first one free. It pulled slowly loose from the others, and I pushed it over to Colt and Perri. I shoved the next one toward Lanned, and I took the last one myself.

A burst of static washed over the radio and I heard Boyce trying to say something, but the signal couldn't penetrate that much rock. "We're coming out," I said, just in case the shuttle radio could pick up our signal better than we could his.

We had just made it to the first bend when Colt shouted "Look out!" and shoved Perri back toward the rest of us. Reaction sent her forward straight into the tentacle that snaked down the tunnel toward us.

It was as big around as a tree trunk, but flexible enough to wrap around her waist the moment it touched her. The only thing that saved her was the egg she was pushing; it bumped into the tentacle and the creature paused to loop itself around that, too. By then all four of us had opened fire on it, aiming for the spot just ahead of where it held her. The tentacle twitched and Colt screamed in pain, but a moment later our phasers blew the end of it free and it loosened its grip on her.

The ragged ends oozed blue-green blood which spattered on our white spacesuits and smeared our visors, but we kept firing at the end that was still attached to the kraken until it vanished back up the tunnel.

I pushed myself over to Colt, who was bent over and clutching her left side. "Are you all right?" I asked, knowing already that she wasn't. I could hear her breathing hard over the radio, and there was an ominous bubbling sound to it.

"I think it—broke some ribs," she said.

There was nothing we could do for that here. We'd have to get her out of her suit and let Dr. Boyce go over her with a protoplaser . . . provided *he* was okay.

Her spacesuit had taken a beating, too. It had deep gouges on the chest and arms where the kraken's scaly hide had slid around it. I checked the pressure gauge. The external readout on her chest control unit read 1.02 atmospheres. That meant the suit wasn't leaking, but I wondered why the pressure was high. I watched it for a moment, and it clicked to 1.03. The internal sensor had been damaged.

We were only thirty or forty meters from safety, provided the kraken had left the shuttle alone. Colt would make it that far without overpressurizing.

"Let's get out of here while we can," I said. "Come on." I pushed the kraken egg into the tunnel ahead of me, then gently helped Colt along behind it. We all advanced with our phaser rifles ready, but the kraken didn't poke its tentacles down the hole again.

We saw why when we got to the surface. Dr. Boyce had taken the shuttle out of harm's way and tried to warn us by radio when the kraken approached, but when we didn't respond and he saw it going for the cave he had returned to shoot at it with the phasers and scare it away. Trouble was, it wasn't scaring. It moved like a ghost, bobbing and weaving through space on its magnetic drive while it lashed out at the shuttle with its tentacles. We had removed the last couple meters of one, and Boyce had blown another one off at the base, but that still left it ten good ones to fight with.

Boyce was doing a good job of piloting. The shuttle darted around the kraken on its impulse engines, and whenever he got a second to reach the phaser controls he would fire at the creature's head, but he had his hands full just staying out of its way.

"Open fire!" I said, and all five of us—even Colt—raised our phaser rifles and shot at the kraken.

"Hey, the cavalry's here!" Boyce said. "Boy am I glad to see you. I was afraid you'd been smashed to pulp down there."

"It almost got Colt," I told him. "She's got—look out!"

The kraken had whirled around to face the new sting in its side, and when it saw us at the edge of the cave with three of its eggs floating into space in front of us, it rushed toward us. We scattered like ejecta from an explosion, firing our jet packs at maximum thrust in six different directions. I spun myself around and kept firing at it with my phaser, hoping to draw it away from the others, but they all had the same idea.

The kraken had its own ideas as well. Boyce had followed it in, firing steadily at its backside, but the kraken hit the asteroid, flexed its tentacles, and sprang back at him with surprising speed.

"Reverse thrust!" I yelled at him, but it was way too late. The kraken struck the shuttle a direct body blow, then it wrapped its tentacles around it and started to squeeze.

Boyce fired the phasers again point-blank. There was a big explosion and two tentacles flew away, but the blast must have taken out the phaser emitter as well because he didn't fire again.

We shot at it from below, still aiming for the thing's head, but it was hard to reach anything vital through the writhing tentacles.

The kraken squeezed hard and the shuttle's windshield blew out in a howl of breathing air. "Boyce, get out of there!" I shouted.

"Just a minute," he said. The shuttle lurched forward under full thrust, slamming hard into the kraken, but the tentacles didn't release their hold on it. Our phasers were having no better effect. The kraken tightened its tentacles again, and we could see the body of the shuttle constrict like an hourglass.

"Jump, dammit!" I shouted.

"Yeah, that looks like a very good idea," he said. He didn't bother with the airlock; he just leaped out through the hole where the windshield had been. He brushed one of the tentacles on his way out and it curled around to snare him, but he fired his jet pack and shot upward, then curved back behind the shuttle and out of the tentacles' reach.

"Hold your fire," I said. "We're not hurting that thing a bit from here. We're just wasting energy."

Our phaser beams winked out, and we watched the kraken crush the shuttle. It was still facing away from it, but we watched it twist around, pulling its head in through the knot of tentacles and rotating them around until it could get its mouth into position.

It took the entire shuttle in one gulp. I watched its massive jaws come together and grind sideways, eerily silent in the vacuum of space, but I knew what it was doing to the shuttle inside that armored maw. Then, suddenly, I realized what was about to happen.

"Take cover!" I shouted. We were too far apart for anyone to help anyone else; I just jetted for the cave entrance and hoped the others could make it as well. Perri and Lanned joined me there, but Colt and Spock and the doctor took off around the curve of the asteroid, putting its entire bulk between them and the kraken.

I hit the first curve in the tunnel feet first and actually ran around the corner, the centripetal force holding my feet to the floor. I used my hands and my boots to bring myself to a stop, and I helped Perri and Lanned do the same. We waited for a few seconds, breathing hard, while I wondered if I had misjudged the situation, but just as I was about to go peek around the corner there was a bright flash and a chunk of blue-gray flesh smacked wetly into the exposed face of the tunnel.

"Fuel tanks?" Lanned asked.

"Fuel or air," I said. "Either one was under a lot of pressure."

We crawled back out of the tunnel. There was no sign of the shuttle, and of the kraken I could only see tentacles whipping around in pinwheels as they receded into space.

Boyce and Spock and Colt came back over the horizon. I noticed that Boyce was helping Colt, who held her arms close to her chest. "Now what?" asked Boyce.

"Did you manage to get out a distress call?" I asked.

He snorted. "Things were a little busy there."

"I imagine they were. Well, let's try it now." I switched from the suit intercom frequency to the general hail frequency. "Pike to *Enterprise.* Come in, *Enterprise.*"

No response. Of course there wouldn't be; we were on the dark side of the asteroid, and Number One had taken the ship into the inner system.

I kicked off from the surface and dodged kraken debris until I made it into the sunlight. We were quite a ways from the star, but it was still bright enough to cast shadows. I called on the general hail frequency again, "Pike to *Enterprise.* Come in *Enterprise.*"

Still no reply. I switched back to the intercom frequency. "Let's all try it," I said. "Maybe our combined signal will reach."

So we all jumped free and radioed for help, but that had no better effect.

"They'll come investigate pretty soon when they don't hear from us, won't they?" asked Perri.

"I'm sure they will," I said, "but Colt's got broken ribs and a busted pressure sensor in her suit. We don't have long."

"Add a punctured lung to that," Boyce said. "She needs help as quick as we can get it."

Spock was holding his tricorder up to his faceplate and pointing it out toward the gas giant. "The explosion seems to have attracted the attention of the titans," he said.

Of course it had, I thought. Things hadn't been bad enough yet. "How many?" I asked.

"Fifteen."

"The *Enterprise* couldn't pick us up even if they knew we were in trouble," I said. "Not with them just waiting for the ship to pop out of warp."

I looked down at the cavern mouth. If we hadn't had an injured crew member we could have hidden in there until the titans went away and the *Enterprise* could come get us. We didn't have that kind of time, though. We had to get completely away from here, and we had to do it *now.*

Out in the rings, which we saw edge-on from our vantage point, fifteen tiny points of light grew brighter. The titans were coming fast.

"Wait a second," I said. "Perri, how do you actually control a titan once you've saddled it up?"

"Saddled?" he asked.

"Harnessed. Put your pressure dome on it. How do you make it go where you want it to?"

"We run electrical current through its skin at sensitive spots along the tail fins and nose. Um . . . why do you ask?" His tone of voice made it clear he was hoping for a different answer than what he thought it would be.

I had to disappoint him. "Because I think we've got just one chance to get Colt to safety in time."

"By riding a *titan?*" asked Boyce. "That's suicide."

"Are you willing to let her die while we hide out and wait for rescue?"

Colt said, "Captain, I'm not hurt that—" but she coughed and we could all hear the gurgling of blood in her lungs. It took her quite a while to stop coughing, during which the rest of us floated helplessly, unable to do anything for her.

I didn't wait for her to protest any more. "Come on," I said. "The krakens have already shown us how to sneak up on a titan. Let's use those eggs for cover and set ourselves adrift before they get here."

We used our jet packs to chase down the eggs, which were tumbling end over end from the explosion. Spock and Lanned and I brought them together and all six of us crowded into as tight a ball as we could, using our safety lines to tie ourselves to the eggs and holding them like a shield between us and the advancing titans. We jetted away from the explosion site, then waited to see what the titans would do when they got there.

The first ones shot through the debris field with their mouths closed, letting the hunks of kraken meat bounce off them as they looked for danger, but when they found nothing threatening they moved back through and began feeding. The later ones caught up with them and they began pushing one another around, fighting for the choicest pieces. Some of them bit into pieces of the shuttle and spit them back out, only to have others try the same thing. They looked a little like fish in an aquarium right after you've dropped the food in, but I kept reminding myself that these fish were nearly as large as the *Enterprise.*

One of the titans kept getting pushed aside, and I noticed that it was drifting farther out of the group—the *fleet,* as Lanned called it. It ate a few tiny bits of shredded kraken when it came upon them, but mostly it just drifted motionless with its nose pointed toward the others, looking for all the world like somebody's younger brother who's been left out of all the fun.

"That's our baby," I said, pointing at it. "Let's see if we can sneak up on it from behind."

"We . . . really don't . . . have to . . ." Colt said.

"Save your breath, Yeoman," I told her. "Let's go."

We fired our jet packs and moved closer, keeping the rocky surface of the eggs between us and the titan. Just as we had almost reached its broad tail fins it saw something it wanted and surged away, but a moment later it was knocked back by a more aggressive companion. One of its fins sailed past just a few meters beneath our bellies; then the rough hide slid by, growing closer and closer as we worked our way up the thickening body.

I pulled out a long loop of line from my safety tether's belt reel, and just as the eggs bumped into the creature's skin I reached out and ran it around one of the dinner-plate-sized scales. The skin twitched, nearly throwing us off, but I tugged us back down and the others each looped a line around a scale.

I peeked out from under our cover. We were on the top of a gently curving hillside. The huge fin behind us stuck up like a ten-story building, its three tentacles reaching forward to scratch an itch they couldn't quite reach. I shivered, thinking how lucky we had been not to hit the fin.

I saw the bulge of an eye socket up ahead, watched it swivel around, but it couldn't move far enough to let the creature see us, either. Another ripple ran along its hide, but we rode it out easily. If that was the best it could do then we were set.

"So, Mr. Perri, where do we zap it to make it go?" I asked.

Twenty-nine

"AHAB," SAID NOWAN.

"Gesundheit," Pike said automatically.

"No, no, *Ahab.* Melville's character. Though I suppose it's a stretch to hope a book that was already ten years old and obscure in my time would still be read in yours."

Pike laughed. "You mean *Moby Dick?* Sure we still read it. It's assigned in school alongside *Fear of Flying* and *The Shining.* It's been a long time since I studied it, but didn't Ahab come to a bad end?"

"You might say. Dragged to his death in the sea by the whale he'd chased half his life."

"Yeah, that's right. I hope you don't think I'm going to end my story that way."

Nowan shook his head. "I rather doubt that, since you're here to tell it. I was just caught by the similarity to Ahab in his moment of desperation, entangled with his nemesis even after it destroyed his ship."

Hompaq yawned and stretched, a motion that drew the attention of both men at the table. "I do not know this Ahab," she said, "but I know that human books contain much silliness and soul-searching when action would better suit them."

"Act first, think later?" Pike asked her.

"Act first, then act again while your opponent lies unconscious," she replied.

"Uh-huh." Pike edged away theatrically.

She laughed, then reached out and slapped him on the back. "Relax, Captain. You would enjoy my way of rendering *you* unconscious."

Klingons certainly weren't subtle, that much was certain. Pike wasn't sure exactly what she had in mind, but he got the general drift of it, and while he was flattered that she thought him heroic enough to consort with, he wasn't sure if he was willing to risk broken bones in order to prove anything more to her.

But oh, how tempting it was.

Nowan was squirming in his chair like a five-year-old at a museum. Victorian ladies apparently didn't talk about such things in public. Or even in private, if the history books were to be believed. Pike took pity on him and said, "Anyway, the titan dragged us through plenty of space, but it didn't drag us to our deaths. We found death aplenty on board it, though."

"What?" he asked. "I was sure you had gotten away unscathed. Save for your yeoman's injury, of course."

"We thought so too," said Pike. "And for the first million kilometers or so we did, but we had a couple hundred times that far to go, and an asteroid belt full of more titans and krakens to get through."

"Not again!" cried Nowan.

"That's what we said, too, when the first one came after us." Pike leaned forward in his chair. "Especially when we realized we'd picked a slow titan."

Thirty

IT TURNED OUT THE WAY TO GOOSE A TITAN WAS TO HIT IT ON THE TRAILing edge of its tail fins. There was no way I would let my crew get close to the tentacles that reached forward from there, so we had to make do with shooting from high on the flanks with our phasers set on "stun." And then we had to hang on for dear life, because a titan's first response to being hit in the privates is to twitch a whole lot harder than it had when we tied ourselves down to it.

I heard Colt cry out the first time it happened, but the titan hadn't gone anywhere so I ordered everyone to fire again. It was just Spock and Perri and Lanned and myself with phaser rifles; Dr. Boyce stayed with Colt to do what he could for her, which at the moment meant holding her hand and occasionally venting her suit when its air pressure built up to the danger level.

Our second volley got it moving, but slowly, so we fired again and this time it really took off. It wasn't pointed toward the inner reaches of the solar system, though, so I had Perri fire at the outermost fin and that turned it inward. It took some fine-tuning, but we eventually had it aimed straight at the star and then we poured on the fire until it was booming along at thousands of kilometers per second. There was no way to tell by eye how fast we were going, of course, but Spock could triangulate on the planets with his tricorder and calculate it out.

"At this rate we will reach the primary in four hours, thirteen and a half minutes," he said.

"Boyce?" I asked. "Will that do?"

"Maybe," he said. "If she doesn't run out of air first. I'm having to blow off a couple liters a minute just to keep her suit from overfilling."

"Let me see," I said. I tugged myself down to the mottled gray titan hide by my safety line and pulled myself over to Colt, who had curled into a loose fetal position beside the kraken eggs, which Boyce had tied down as well. I bent down to look at her suit's chest controls, trying to see if I could override the internal pressure sensor somehow, but those things were designed to be idiotproof. The linkage was completely internal, and short of opening her suit to vacuum and adjusting the sensor by hand there was nothing I could do.

Her air supply was down to sixty percent. It had only been fifteen or twenty minutes since her injury. She wouldn't make it at this rate.

I looked at her face, pasty white and sweaty. She had always looked like a little girl to me; now she looked even younger. I felt like five times a fool for bringing her out here. Adventure, pah! What kind of adventure was it to drown in your own blood while tied to the back of an alien monster a hundred light-years from home? And I was the man who had led her there.

Her eyes fluttered open and she looked up at me. It was all I could do to keep from turning away.

"Don't try to talk," I said. "You're going to be all right. We're on our way to the *Enterprise* now."

She nodded slightly. She knew I was lying to her, knew she was going to die.

Her pressure gauge read 1.3 atmospheres. Boyce let off more air, but stopped at 1.2. "The suit's safe at that," he said. "I've upped the oxygen content, too. With all the blood she's losing and that lung filling up, she needs all she can get."

"Good," I said. "Keep her going. We'll share our air supply if necessary."

"How?" he asked. "We've got no hoses, no couplings, nothing. I don't even have my damned emergency kit."

"We'll think of something," I told him. "You let me worry about that; you just keep her alive."

"Yes, *sir!*" he said sarcastically. From anybody else I'd have reprimanded him on the spot for insubordination, but I felt like I deserved worse.

I stood up and pushed off toward Perri. "How do you get them to go into warp?" I asked.

"You don't want to try that," he replied.

"I do. How do we do it?"

"Captain," he said. "One-half of all attempts end in failure. This is with *trained* pilots, and tame titans."

"That's for interstellar flights," I replied. "I'm just talking about going for five minutes or so until we're in radio range."

He turned around and looked at the star, a hard, bright dot not much bigger than Venus or Jupiter seen from Earth.

"We haven't got a choice," I said.

He sighed. "Very well. We must stimulate the warp engine directly."

The warp engine was in one of the two bulges right at the very tip of the tail. Down around the curve of the creature's tapering flank. "We can't reach it from here," I said.

"No, we can't," he replied. "One of us will have to go down among the fins and shoot at it from there."

"How do you stop it once it's going?" I asked.

"You stop shocking it—or in this case stop shooting it—and then you pray," he replied.

"Great," I muttered. "All right, you guys make damn sure it stays aimed for the inner system. If it veers off course at warp speed, we're all in deep trouble." I turned away and pulled myself down toward one of the fins, looping my safety line around half a dozen scales as I went along.

"Captain, no!" Colt said. She could hear everything we said over the suit intercoms.

"I'll be fine," I told her. "Don't worry. Spock, you calculate how far we've gone, and tell me when we need to stop."

"Very well, Captain," he said. I could tell he didn't think much of the idea, either, but he was officer enough not to question my order.

I looked down toward the tentacles, all reaching for me. The titan couldn't see me back here, but it could feel the tug on its scales. That's what I was counting on. I kicked off toward the back, then tucked my feet up so I wouldn't touch anything and unreeled safety line as I drifted toward the creature's tail. My line kept a steady pull on the scales up ahead.

It was a long glide. At one point I got disoriented and felt like I was falling down an infinite cliff, but I kept myself from grabbing the line and halting my progress. I passed between two fins, just below the questing tentacles, and on toward the back.

I didn't stop until I was well out of reach behind the titan. From that vantage it was easy to see which bump was the fusion engine and which one was the warp drive. I pulled myself forward a ways until I was out of the blast cone if it lit the engine, eyeing the tentacles to make sure I wasn't in their reach either, then said, "Everybody brace yourselves. Here we go," and fired my phaser at the warp engine.

The tentacles all whipped around toward the back. One of them grazed my tether and snapped me forward, but I stopped myself with my jet pack and fired again at the warp engine.

The *Enterprise*'s engines are set way in back of the living quarters for a reason. The intense subspace distortion right next to the field generators can turn a person inside out if they're too close. It can scramble your brain and short out every nerve in your body. The titan's engine wasn't nearly as powerful, and I was probably twenty meters away from it so I didn't get the full effect, but I saw plenty of crazy images when the titan finally decided to engage it. The stars seemed to bulge in front of us and narrow down behind us, and bright streaks of intense white light rushed toward me. I knew then how Zefram Cochrane must have felt in his unshielded ship when he made humanity's first warp-drive trip across the solar system.

I let out a little more line, continuing to fire the phaser one-handed while I put some distance between me and the engine. I didn't want to get *too* far away—if I fell out of the warp field entirely I would be left behind in interplanetary space—but I figured another dozen meters or so would be safe enough.

Then the titan, in full panic, fired its fusion drive as well, and a moment later the magnetic squeeze effect turned it into a laser. A two-meter-wide, bloodred death ray, beside which I bobbed on the end of my tether, my boots maybe one foot's width from the edge of the beam.

My heart froze, then lurched back into action.

I quit firing my phaser and scrambled hand-over-hand up the line again. The titan continued on under warp drive for a few more seconds, then dropped back into normal space. I looked outward and saw hundreds of scintillating points of light in all directions.

"Asteroid belt?" I asked.

"Affirmative, Captain," Spock replied.

"Let's see if we're close enough to reach the *Enterprise* now," I said. "Hold on." I switched over to the hailing frequency and called, "Pike to *Enterprise,* come in *Enterprise.*"

After a few seconds I heard Dabisch's voice, buried in static. *"ssss . . .* that you? Say again . . . *ssss."*

"Dabisch, this is Pike! We're in the asteroid belt. Come get us!"

*"ssss*teroid belt? How'd you *sssss?"*

"Long story. We need pickup *now.* Do you copy?"

"Give us *sssss.* We'll *ssssss."*

"Drop whatever you're doing and come *now.* Immediate pickup. Do you copy?"

There was a moment with no carrier at all, then, *"ssss* on the ground. *sssss* abandon *sssss?"*

Dammit. Number One had sent someone down to the surface of one of the planets. "Negative, negative," I said. I wasn't going to endanger one group to rescue another. "Do not leave anyone behind. Pick up your ground party first, but hurry!"

"Under*ssss.* We'll be there as *ssss* possible."

"Good. Pike out." I switched back to intercom mode, leaving the receiver set to pick up anything on either channel. "I got through," I reported. "They've got to recall a team on the ground first, but they'll be coming as soon as they do that."

"Good," said Boyce. "Her condition's deteriorating."

I pulled myself up the line to where he and Colt had tied themselves to the titan's scaly hide. We were in free fall again, so it was relatively easy to reel in line as I went. "Hang in there, Yeoman," I said. "Help's on the way."

"G-glad to . . . hear that," she whispered.

"Unfortunately, more titans are also on the way," Spock said.

I looked out at the asteroid field. Sure enough, the specks of light were now distinct bodies, approaching fast. "Let's hope they just want to check out the newcomer," I said.

That seemed to be the case at first. When the other titans arrived they drifted up alongside ours, their immense bodies sliding past slowly like starships in spacedock, but suddenly one of them turned away and sprayed hot exhaust plasma at us. The brunt of it hit farther up, toward the creature's head, but there was enough scatter to set off my suit alarm.

I whirled around and fired at the fins to prod our ride into action, but there was no need. Our titan didn't like the welcome any more than we did. It surged away, but the others chased it, one of them roaring past and firing its fusion engine again. This time the exhaust plume lased, and the fiery beam streaked along the creature's flank only a dozen meters from us, throwing out gouts of vaporized flesh. It raked across one of the fins and sliced it off as cleanly as a knife before winking out.

The titan shuddered and the radio filled with voices as everyone shouted at once. I prepared to leap for the back and zap the warp engine, but there was no need for that, either. The titan did the job itself. Space folded up on us again and we streaked away from our attackers.

It didn't last long. I felt a nauseating sensation in the pit of my stomach, like intense gravity waves passing through me, then we dropped back into normal space.

"The titan's subspace field generator has burned out," Spock said.

We were still in the asteroid field, but the titans who had chased us were long gone. Apparently whatever had set them off wasn't worth going into hyperspace for.

"Let's hope the *Enterprise* gets here before we're discovered again," I said.

The titan was shuddering like a ground car on a bumpy road. Dark blood bubbled into space from the severed fin. I didn't think it was going to survive its wounds.

"I wonder what set them off?" Lanned asked. "I've never seen titans attack one another before."

"I thought it was us they were shooting at," I replied.

Perri said, "I don't think that was it. The ones back home don't seem to even notice the life-support modules we put on them."

"They did seem to be targeting the titan itself," Spock replied.

Boyce straightened up and jetted over to Spock. "Let me see that tricorder for a minute."

Spock handed it over and Boyce crouched down to the titan's skin with it, then moved down to the gaping wound and scanned that for a moment. "Well I'll be damned," he said. "This thing's sick. There's some kind of disease organism all through its tissues."

Sick? I hadn't imagined that something this huge could get sick, but I supposed it had to be possible. I said, "The others must have sensed it somehow, and were trying to drive it off before it infected them."

"That'd be my guess," Boyce said. "Spock, have you got a sample vial?"

"I do." Spock jetted down to where the doctor was and helped him collect a sample of the sticky, bubbling blood.

Our brief jump into warp had taken us to a less densely populated area of the asteroid belt, but I could still see specks of light moving around out there. It wouldn't take long before the local titans discovered us and came to finish the job.

I switched to the hailing frequency again. "Pike to *Enterprise.* What is your status?"

Static, then, "Landing party *ssss* on board. Proceeding to *ssss.*"

"Pour on the coals," I said. "The natives are hostile."

"Say again?" Dabisch replied.

"Just get out here!" I ordered.

"We're coming."

Over the intercom I said, "Get ready for pickup." We all crowded together near Colt, holding on to one another in a rough hexagon. Boyce let her stay on her side so she would be lying down when gravity returned.

I looked out toward the other titans and saw them coming. "Any time now," I said, then switched frequencies.

"Enterprise?" I called. "Are you in range yet?"

"We're entering the asteroid belt, but we can't locate the shuttle," Dabisch said. His voice came through loud and clear now.

"We lost that," I told him. "We're on the back of a titan. Home in on my signal."

"On the back of—affirmative." I heard him relaying our situation to Number One, and a moment later he said, "We've spotted you."

I saw at least six blimp-shaped bodies drawing nearer. "So have the titans," I said. "Hurry."

A moment later the *Enterprise* hove into view. It stood at about a seventy-degree angle off our port side, its underside glistening bright white in the sunlight. I just had time to say "There she—" before the transporter locked on to us and I finished my sentence on the receiving platform.

"—is. Get Colt to sickbay immediately. Bridge, stay on station." While Perri, Lanned, Boyce, and Spock all lifted Colt as gently as they could and rushed her across the hall, I twisted off my helmet and said to the transporter chief, "We left three kraken eggs on that titan; beam them aboard too." I wasn't about to leave empty-handed, not after all we'd been through.

"Kraken eggs?" he asked, but he was already scanning for them. "Ah, found them. Transporting."

The eggs materialized on the platform, standing erect like people until the containment field released them and they fell over with three loud bangs.

"All right," I said into my helmet, which Dabisch was presumably still listening to. "They're on board. Get us out of here."

The ship lurched sideways as a titan struck us, but a second blow never came. I went to the intercom panel on the wall and hit the bridge button. "Damage report?"

"Minor hull damage to deck five, starboard side," Dabisch reported. "We are now fleeing at warp six."

"Good. Bring us to a stop once we've reached safety. We're not quite done here yet."

I switched the intercom over to security and ordered a team to take the kraken eggs and put them in a cargo hold under a tight force field; then I peeled out of my spacesuit, leaving it piled on the floor, and crossed over to sickbay. Colt lay on her back on an exam table, unconscious, her suit in shreds beneath her where Boyce had cut it away. He stood beside her, still suited except for his helmet, and ran some whirring gadget back and forth above her chest.

Perri and Lanned stood by the side of her bed, also still in their suits, not quite getting in the way while Boyce worked. Spock had apparently headed for the bridge already.

"Is she all right?" I asked.

"As all right as you can be with a punctured lung," Boyce replied, "but she'll be okay in a day or two."

Perri was looking down at her face. It's always hard to read aliens' expressions, but I thought the simple lust I'd seen in him before had become a bit more complicated now. He looked up and saw me watching him. "She saved my life," he said softly.

"Yes, she probably did," I told him. "She probably saved us all."

There was little else anyone could say. I left them in the sickbay and took the turbolift to the bridge, where I found Spock and Number One already comparing notes.

"Welcome back, Captain," said Number One.

"It's good to be back," I told her, settling down in my familiar command chair again. "It sounds like you found something on one of the inner planets that was worth a closer look. What was it?"

She sat down at the helm controls. "We discovered ruins on the second planet that date back over a million years. There's not much left, but what we found looked like a bunch of tombs."

"Tombs? As in dead bodies?"

"That's what it looked like. They were full of big buglike exoskeletons. It's like the whole population just filed into these things and lay down in a heap. But the kicker was what we found on the *out*side."

"What?"

She pushed a stray wisp of hair into place. "More guard dogs. Long dead from some disease, but their skeletons were all over the place. About twice the size of a person and shaped almost exactly like an immature titan. I found enough organic residue for a gene scan and the code is pretty close. Definitely the same basic plan. But it's not anything like the bugs' code."

I rubbed my stubble-encrusted chin. We knew the krakens were genetically engineered, and by implication the titans as well. And probably these things outside the tombs, too. Dead bugs, guard dogs on the ground, and guard whales in orbit. "Somebody really didn't want people disturbing their graves," I said.

"That's the way I read it," she said. "Whatever happened, though, it was a long, *long* time ago."

"We'll leave it for the archaeologists to puzzle out," I said, then I laughed. "If they want to try. I've had my fill of this place. Mr. Spock, I assume we need to gather a few filter-fish and some hydroplankton before we go?"

"We do," he replied. "Fortunately, that can be done with the transporters from a safe distance."

"See to it," I said. I turned to Number One. "The moment we get the specimens, take us back to Devernia, warp eight."

"Warp eight, sir?" she asked. "We can't sustain that for the entire trip."

"Run at that speed for as long as we can," I told her. "We've got eggs in the cargo hold I'd just as soon didn't hatch there."

She nodded. "Understood."

I went back downship to clean up, but I had just gotten to my quarters when the intercom whistled and Dr. Boyce said, "Captain, have you got a minute?"

"I—sure. Be right there."

I hurried down to deck seven, afraid something unforseen had happened to Colt, but she was sleeping peacefully on a diagnostic bed, the overhead monitors all reading normal. Perri and Lanned and Dr. Boyce were in the lab across the hall from the intensive-care room. "Take a look at this," Boyce said when I stepped inside. He pointed at a desktop monitor on which a microscopic organism of some sort crawled along with tiny cilia.

"This is one of the species of hydroplankton," he said. "Now look at this." He pressed a switch and the image blinked over to a similar picture.

I couldn't tell much difference, and said so.

"This," he said, "is the bug I got from that sick titan's blood. It's a mutated plankton. Mutated to eat *titans*. It's really slow, but I did a comparative scan of the genetic code and found where the changes are. It would be child's play to tweak it a little further and make it work faster."

I looked at the tiny bug on the screen. It was little more than a mouth and a collection of little bubbles for storing and metabolizing food. "You could create a titan plague?" I asked.

"I think so."

I looked over at Perri and Lanned. Lanned's eyes were bright, and he was smiling wide. Perri looked considerably less pleased.

"We don't need to do that," he said. "We have already figured out how to control them naturally."

"This is natural," Lanned said. "As natural as the titans, at any rate. And it would certainly control them."

"Exterminate them, you mean! This is no better than your previous policy of reckless slaughter."

I looked from one to the other, then back to the monitor. What were we trying to protect, anyway? All these creatures were apparently the result of some paranoid alien race's dying wish for isolation. Maybe it would be simplest to wipe them out. We could spread the disease among the various populations of titans all the way back to Devernia and prevent them from causing any more damage.

I heard Yeoman Colt's soft breathing from the intensive care room, thought about what had happened to her and what had happened to so many Devernians over the centuries. What would they say?

I knew what I had to say. "Make the enhanced organism," I told Boyce. Perri started to protest, but I cut him off. "I don't know yet whether we'll use it or not, but I want that option. *You* want that option, believe me. After what we've seen on the way out here, I think everyone would sleep better at night knowing there's a fast way to control these monsters."

Perri had no response to that, but Lanned nodded and said, "I agree, Captain. I, at least, will sleep better. Let the doctor make this disease, and let us go home and decide then whether or not to use it."

"I've already given the order," I told him. "We're headed back as soon as Spock finishes collecting specimens."

I saw the satisfaction those words brought to both him and Perri. After all they had been through, they were going home again, each bringing their own brand of solution to the problem that had sent us out here.

Thirty-one

"You couldn't!" exclaimed Nowan. He slapped his hand on the table for emphasis. "The entire species, wiped out in a heartbeat? Tell me you didn't do it!"

Pike held out his hands, palms up. "I don't know," he said. "It was pretty tempting. They were artificial, after all, and they had already gotten loose and destroyed dozens of solar systems. They could still destroy Devernia if our plan to import their natural ecosystem didn't work. And releasing krakens into inhabited space didn't seem like as good an idea as I'd originally thought. Not after fighting one hand-to-hand."

"It seems like a fine idea to me," Hompaq said. "Klingons would give much to know the location of these creatures. If they still exist, that is."

"Oh, they exist," Pike said. "Nowan's right. We couldn't just sow the plague among them and watch them die off. They might have had artificial origins, but they had been around for a million years already. Longer than the human race. I couldn't kill that off with a wave of my hand." He shook his head, remembering. "We tested the enhanced disease organism on a couple of titans to make sure it would work, then we dropped their bodies into the sun and took the disease back to Starfleet Headquarters for safekeeping. Lanned wasn't happy with me, but I didn't care. Beggars can't be choosers, after all."

"Hah," said Hompaq. "You talk a fine rationale, but I know why you saved them. Admit it: You did it for the adventure. You're a better man than you think, Captain Pike."

"For the adventure? That's ridicu—" He stopped, his eyes narrowed. "Well, okay, maybe that was part of it, but—"

"A sufficient part. No Klingon could survive what you did and then slay the beasts in such an ignoble fashion. And neither could you. You left them alive for others to pit themselves against." Hompaq took a drink of her Warnog.

"I—no, really that wasn't . . . I mean, maybe a little, but—"

Nowan said, "I think she has the right of it, Captain. Remember why you and your yeoman, at least, were there in the first place."

Pike scowled. "If she'd died, I'd have spread the plague through every star system in the sector."

Hompaq nearly sprayed Warnog on him. She managed to swallow it instead, then said, "Hah! You don't care for her, no, not at all."

"Look, she was a crew member," Pike said impatiently. "I cared about her the same as I cared about anyone else."

"As you wish," said Hompaq. "So what did you do when you got back to Devernia? Distribute the krakens and plankton and so forth?"

"Yes," said Pike. "I was afraid the kraken population would boom because of all the food available to them, but Spock spent his time on the trip back studying the embryos and he discovered that they were already programmed to limit themselves to a fraction of the number of titans. A hundredth of a percent or so, which meant when the titan population stabilized there would only be a hundred or so krakens in the entire planetary system. Lanned decided he could live with that. And Perri figured the Aronnians would probably want to import the entire ecosystem to their own gas-giant planets so they wouldn't have to depend on the migration from Devernia anymore."

"Did it work?" Nowan asked.

"Last I heard it was starting to. It'll take a while to know for sure. There's still a sample of the mutated hydroplankton in the Starfleet gene lab just in case it doesn't, but we haven't gotten a distress call from either planet yet."

"And the Aronnians are still riding their magnificent beasts from star to star?" asked Hompaq.

"As far as I know. It's been a few years." As Pike said that, he felt a blanket of melancholy descend on him again, and at that moment he made a decision. To hell with his groundside job; he was going back into space. It had been so long since he'd flown anything that he had lost his proficiency rating, so he would have to requalify for pilot's status, much less a captain's chair, but even a trainer would be more fun than flying a desk. He could pull a few strings, get himself assigned to one of the class-J ships Starfleet used to train cadets. From there it would be relatively easy to get his own ship again.

Nowan seemed a bit lost in reverie, too. He had been drawing something else on a napkin while Pike finished his story; now he was looking at it and rubbing his chin, but he raised his head when he realized Pike and Hompaq were looking at him.

"Sorry. I was just thinking what it must be like for you. Exploring strange new worlds. Going where no man has gone before." He looked toward the door. "Eighteen sixty-one awaits me out there, doesn't it?"

"If that's when you came from," said Hompaq.

"Is there no way to leave with one of you instead?"

" 'Fraid not. But the Captain's Table will always be here whenever you need it."

He nodded. "That is some comfort, I suppose."

Pike was looking at the napkin. He reached out and turned it around so the drawing was right side up for him. He had thought at first that it was another drawing of a titan, but now he saw that it was more like a fish. The nose came to a sharp point, and the top of its head had some kind of bony ridge sticking out of it—rather like Hompaq, Pike realized. The fish's midsection had a round oval like her cleavage-baring outfit, as well. It had a more aquatic-looking dorsal fin and tail, however, except that the tail was cut out and a tiny figure eight stood in the gap.

Then the entire picture seemed to morph in his mind as he realized that the figure eight was a propeller. The open waist was a large porthole, and if the tiny dots above and below it were normal-sized ones then the entire vessel was large indeed. The dorsal fin was actually a conning tower, and the bony forehead was a massive spur, jagged-edged for ripping the bottoms out of boats.

"Not as grand as your *Enterprise,*" said Nowan, "but it's a start. If I must stay in my own era, there is at least one domain left to explore." His expression grew darker. "And a few warships left to avenge myself against."

Pike looked at it with his mouth agape. "It's . . . it's the *Nautilus.*"

"It's nothing but a gleam in a bitter man's eye, at this point," said Nowan. "But that's not a bad name." He retrieved his napkin, drained his brandy, and pushed back his chair. "On another night I would tell you a tale of my own to match yours, but my mind is filled to bursting with strange notions and strong drink, and I feel the need for solitude. Besides, if Hompaq is to be believed—and she undoubtedly is," he added hastily when she bared her teeth at him, "then we will have other opportunities." He stood up and extended his hand.

Pike shook it, still somewhat stunned. "You—I—" he stammered, but Nowan had already turned to Hompaq. She held out her hand to clasp arms in the Klingon fashion, but he lifted her fingers to his lips and kissed them instead. "I do, milady," he said, then Pike realized he was speaking French.

He turned toward the door, but before he left he stopped at the piano and pressed a few keys down at the low end. Pike recognized the first few notes of Bach's *Toccata and Fugue in D Minor.*

"Fitting music to exit by," he said.

"It sounds better on a pipe organ," said Nowan. He nodded to Pike and went to the door. When he opened it, the clop-clop of horses' hooves could be heard for a moment before it closed again behind him.

The other patrons in the bar had watched him leave, then turned back to their own concerns. Pike looked over at Hompaq. "Do you know who that was?" he asked.

She shrugged. "He called himself Nowan. Beyond that, I have no idea."

Pike looked over at the door again. Could it be? He took a deep breath, trying to clear his mind. He'd drunk a lot of Saurian brandy tonight. But *that* much?

"Whoever he is," he said at last, "I bet in a few years he'll have tales to tell that'll make mine seem tame."

He heard a squeal of high-pitched laughter and a thump from upstairs as a door opened momentarily, then slammed. Had that been the catwoman? It had sounded more like a wild animal.

"What's up there?" he asked.

Hompaq laughed softly. "You want to find out?"

She was looking at him with the frankly appraising eyes of a predator sizing up its prey. "I, uh, well," he stammered, feeling himself growing warm. He had a pretty good idea what would be up there for the two of them.

"Come on," she said. "Where's your sense of adventure?"

She held out her hand. Pike took it, and when she stood up he found himself following her.

"You sure know which buttons to push, don't you?" he said.

She grinned at him as they took their first step upward. "Not yet, I don't, but you'll be amazed how fast I learn."

The gecko awoke when a dollop of beer landed on his nose.

Waking—sleeping. He recognized little difference between the two states. One involved snuggling his belly tight against whatever heat source was available and soaking up as much warmth as possible for as long as possible; the other involved doing the same thing with his eyes open.

So he opened his eyes.

The fireplace stones still hummed with residual heat, even though the flames responsible for that warmth had died to ash hours ago. Feet in more styles than his olfactory-oriented brain had ever conceived of clumped back and forth on the wood planks beyond the hearth, and the unpleasantly tepid splash of beer dripping off his wedge-shaped nose raised him up on his front legs in a defiant bob of protest. It was the last casual indignity from these huge and raucous mammals. His sensitive belly receptors had already begun to complain that the stones beneath him were cooling, and he'd found only one careless spider to eat during his last perambulation along the baseboards. Even the beautiful, fierce princesses who'd whispered sweet promises and tickled his throat had long since lost interest and wandered away. It was time to shake the kinks out of his newly regrown tail and head home.

Little five-toed feet stepped delicately onto wood planking so old and well trod it had taken on the color and softness of amber. What mammals felt as a warmness in wood was really little more than a lack of cold; his sensitive belly recognized room temperature for what it was, and identified no delineation between the air above him and the floor below. He padded methodical S-curves into the chaos of shoes and bare feet, feeling like he was flying through his own single-temperature world.

It took a few steps to get his rhythm—the regrown tail followed behind without the sinuous undulations of his long-lost original. That had been a beautiful tail, fat and long and supple all the way down to its brown-banded tip. He'd regrown—and relost—its replacement so many times by now, he could no longer remember when or how it first happened. All he retained now was a patch of lizard memory, like skin that never shed, which sometimes reminded his dreams how it had been to shake his tail for a harem of pretty admirers.

He knew the path to the door by rote, where to speed up, when to swerve. Toes larger than his head brushed past close enough to bite, but he'd long ago given up hissing at them. They never heard, or didn't notice, and his splinter-sized brain didn't come with the luxury of paying attention to more than one thing at a time. He kept his tiny bright eyes fixed on his goal, waiting for the moment light cracked around its edges, then kicked his little legs until they slipped on the floorboards in his hurry to dash out before the door swung closed.

The advantage of a regrown tail was that it didn't hurt when it was bitten, or stepped on, or slammed in a closing door. He realized he'd been caught only because his feet skidded back and forth in place on the metal deck outside without taking him anywhere. By then, it was too late. Whatever primitive mechanism in his primitive biology identified a pinned tail as life-threatening had already cinched closed the blood vessels running past the base of his spine. With a little hop, he detached himself from the bulb of trapped flesh and scampered off with new lightness. Tails came and tails went. There was no room for regret in a lizard mind. He'd almost forgotten the weighty burden by the time he made the first corridor junction and turned by instinct in the direction of his home.

He recognized the smell of home by the metallic cleanness of its air, recognized the light's burnt-cayenne tint when he skittered past windows and transparent aluminum doors. The dusty musk of his native sand made his toes tingle with excitement. A rise in temperature, slow and pervasive, hurried him along, and the feel of warm, moist earth beneath his toes welcomed him back to his quiet little kingdom.

A long walk for little legs. An eternity of travel to a little lizard mind. He found his favorite rock, the tallest and roundest of the slate mountains erratically cluttering his home. Well placed at the foot of a long, unobstructed length of window, it drank in the warmth of the sun all day, then offered it back into the nighttime with such sweet jealousy that it could make a lizard happy until sunrise. He liked the view from here, well above the sandy ground and even most of the low-lying plants. He especially loved the diamond scatter of stars that filled the window like spots on a female's long back. If a lizard could conceive of gazing into forever, he might have understood. If a lizard could appreciate the awe of standing so close to the edge of the infinite, he might have named the swirl of pleasure that curled through him at the sight. Instead, he let instinct take him as high up on the rock as he could climb, not realizing when he passed from warm rock to warm trouser leg until a gentle voice greeted softly, "Well, hello there, little guy. What happened to your poor tail?"

The hands which lifted him were even warmer than his accustomed rock, and he felt no fear when he looked up into the friendly golden face smiling down at him. Snuggling his belly into the human's palm, he dropped his eyes to half-mast and enjoyed the mammalian heat as he tipped his chin up toward the stars.

The human chuckled. "Looks like I'm not the only one who likes this view." He lifted the somnolent lizard even with his red-jacketed shoulder and rotated his hand to offer a better vantage. "That's my ship there, the *Excelsior.*" He pointed to one of the shining motes outside the window, and smiled again. "I'd offer to give you the captain's tour, but you're probably not the adventurous type."

The lizard blinked placidly up at the timeless sea of stars, but didn't reply.

Transparent aluminum spun a delicate membrane between the spindly green of transplanted Martian foliage and the blue-black Martian sky. As he watched one of the shipyard's many crew transports crawl patiently starward along a sparkling length of duranium filament, it occurred to James Kirk that man-made atmospheres were always the most fragile. Mars's chilly surface, although no longer the frigid wasteland of just a few centuries before, still clung to the planet only through the heroic efforts of her tenants. Outside the tame habitat of interlinked domes and tunnels, carefully tended flora lifted from Earth's highest mountains and harshest tundras braved Mars's seasonal extremes, while the excess carbon dioxide from captured comets and a few million adventurous humans preserved just enough liquid water on the surface to reward the plants with the occasional rainshower. The end result was a certain defiant beauty—spidery junipers and upright bracken reaching toward the teal spark of a homeworld their ancestors had left generations ago.

Not unlike humanity. Granted, humans pampered themselves with heaters, oxygen co-generators, and pressurized suits and homes. But they still survived where nothing larger than a dust mote had survived before them, and Kirk liked the view they'd created.

Utopia Planitia's shipyards stretched from the skirt of the colony's main dome to beyond the horizon, arcing magically upward in the guise of shuttle-bees and crew elevators. The twinkling strings of force and fiber bound the orbiting ships only temporarily. Some nearly finished, others bare skeletons of the great leviathans they would become, they'd all turn outward soon enough. Darkened engine rooms would thunder with the pulse of great dilithium hearts, and the blood and muscle organs in the chests of her eager crew would leap up in answer, until what finally ignited her sleeping warp core was that combined symphony of animal and mineral, creature and machine. It was a song that kept an officer's heart beating long after no other passion could. *Old captains never die . . .*

Kirk stepped off the moving walkway in the northmost Agridome, the one dedicated to the sparse rock gardens and dark succulents of a Terran gulf environment whose name Kirk no longer remembered. It wasn't crowded the way so many of the lux-enhanced Agridomes always were. Everyone wanted to watch the crews ship out while surrounded by bright Colombian parrots or Hawaiian orchids, as though they'd never really dared to leave Earth at all. But here the lack of tall plant life offered an unobstructed view through the sides and top of the dome, and the foliage reflected the reddish moonslight in silver washes, as though leaves and stems were spun from raw pewter. Kirk remembered coming here as a freshly minted ensign the night before he rode a crowded elevator up to his first assignment on board the *U.S.S. Farragut.* He'd stayed here until dawn, trying to count the multitude of stars he could see in the single patch of sky surrounding the ship that was to be his home, his life, his family for the next five years. That was more than forty years ago, but it felt like only yesterday. He could still hear the reverent hush of the leaves against his trousers as he picked a path through the foliage, and he still remembered the cool surface of the rock that served as his perch at the foot of the dome's widest panel. Best seat in the house.

He found the man he was looking for seated in exactly the same spot, shoulders square, head high, hands folded neatly in his lap. Beyond him and a thousand miles above, the brilliant glow of a refurbished starship dwarfed the dimmer signatures drifting around her.

Kirk smiled, and paused what he hoped was a respectful distance away. "Quite a view, isn't it?"

The younger captain rose, turning with an alert smoothness born of courtesy rather than surprise. That was something Kirk would always associate with Hikaru Sulu—the politeness which came to him apparently as naturally as breathing, with no taint of impatience or condescension. That, and an endless capacity for brilliance.

Sulu mirrored Kirk's smile, looking only a little embarrassed as he stole one last look at the magnificent ship hanging over his shoulder. "All the way into forever." He kept one hand cradled close to his waist, and extended the other as he stepped away from his now vacated stone seat. "Admiral."

His grip was firm and even, as befitted a man of his position. Kirk returned the warm handshake in kind. "Captain."

"I didn't realize you were in-system," Sulu told him. "If I'd known, I would have stopped by to give my regards." It might have just been politeness, but Kirk could tell from his former helmsman's voice that the sentiment was sincere.

"Just passing through on my way to finalize the Khitomer negotiations," Kirk assured him. "I heard at the commodore's office that you were laid over to take on your new executive officer." A movement from the vicinity of Sulu's cupped hand caught Kirk's attention, and he found himself suddenly eye-to-eye with the small, spotted lizard who had clambered up onto Sulu's thumb for a better view. "He's shorter than I remember."

Sulu glanced fondly down at his stubby-tailed companion, tickling it under the curve of its bemused little smile until it blinked. "Actually, we're not scheduled to rendezvous for another two hours. This is just one of the friendly locals." Or as local as any living thing on Mars. Its anteriorly bilateral eyes and five-toed little feet hinted at a Terran origin, but it was the nearly identical gold-and-brown speckled relatives Kirk could now see lounging among the thick-leafed shrubs that gave its ancestry away. The Martian Parks Service didn't like mixing one planet's flora with another planet's fauna. Therefore, Terran landscaping equaled Terran lizards.

Each chubby little eublepharid had staked out its own rock or branch or hummock, blunt little noses lifted skyward, hind feet splayed out behind them as though they were laconically bodysurfing on their own bliss. Kirk envied their abandon.

"Anything on your agenda for those next two hours?" he asked Sulu.

The younger captain shrugged one shoulder, startling his small passenger into an aborted scrabble partway up his wrist. It paused there, as though forgetting where it meant to go, and Kirk noticed that unlike its lounging neighbors, this lizard's tail looked recently broken and rehealed. Its curiosity and boldness must have gotten it in trouble recently. "I've got nothing in particular to do," Sulu admitted. "Just some long-overdue relaxation while I have the chance." Kirk wondered if he'd been watching the meditating lizards instead of his own starship after all. "Did you have something in mind?"

"Some*place*." Kirk caught the politely questioning cock of Sulu's head, and smiled. "The perfect spot for overdue relaxation, as a matter of fact."

"Sounds good." Sulu glanced down as the lizard squirmed determinedly under the cuff of his uniform jacket. Before he could stop it, all that was left was a sausage-shaped bulge and an exposed nubbin where its brown-banded tail should have been. "Are they friendly toward nonhumanoids?"

"I've never known that to be a problem before," Kirk assured him. "And I'm sure that in the lizard world, that little guy was the captain of its very own rock somewhere. He'll be welcome in the Captain's Table."

He led a willing Sulu back out of the Agridomes and down the stately, curving avenues that led eventually to the spaceport and the feet of those rising elevators. The door to the bar was where Kirk remembered it, looking as always like the entrance to a supply cabinet rather than to the cozy tavern he knew lay within. Plain, nearly flush with the Martian stone of this ill-lit subterranean passageway, it was set apart from the other more ostentatious establishments on either side by nothing except a neatly painted sign just to the right of a hand-operated doorknob: THE CAPTAIN'S TABLE.

Sulu cocked his head with a thoughtful wrinkling of his brow, and Kirk knew he was trying to remember why he'd never noticed the little entrance before. "This must be new," the younger captain decided at last. He still held his arm balanced across his midsection in deference to the small passenger up his sleeve.

Kirk hid his smile by stepping forward to take hold of the door. "I found it the first year I commanded the *Enterprise,* but some other captains I know claim it's been here for dozens of years before that."

Sulu gave a little grunt of surprise, then moved back to let the door swing wide. "Sounds like the Federation's best-kept secret."

A gentle swell of warmth, and sound, and scent rolled over them like a familiar blanket. "More like the galaxy's most exclusive club." And, just as a dozen times before, Kirk found himself inside without specifically remembering stepping through the doorway.

The Captain's Table had never been a large establishment, and that didn't appear to have changed over the years. A brief, narrow entry hall spilled them abruptly into the bar's jumble of tables and chairs, and Kirk found himself veering sideways to avoid tripping over the tall alien seated directly in his path. Slitted eyes shifted almost imperceptibly within an almost featureless skull; one long, taloned finger dipped into a fluted glass half-full of viscous red liquid. It was a dance they'd performed the first time Kirk came into the Captain's Table thirty years ago, not to mention every other time he'd stumbled onto the place on Argelius, Rukbat, or Vega. He stopped himself from laughing, not sure the lizardine patron would appreciate his humor, and instead nodded a terse apology before turning to join Sulu in search of their own table.

"Jimmee!"

It seemed everyone was here tonight.

Kirk spun around just in time to catch Prrghh at the height of her leap. It wasn't one of her more spectacular jumps—Kirk would never forget watching her pounce from the second-floor banister to land on her feet amid a particularly rousing discussion—but she still contacted him almost chest-high and entwined legs and arms around his torso in lithe, feline abandon. Kirk felt himself blush with pleasure more than embarrassment when she stroked her own sleekly furred cheek against his. Acutely aware of all the other eyes in the bar, he resisted an impulse to wind his hands in her long primrose mane.

"James!" The bartender's roar collided with the low ceiling and ricocheted all over the room. "How in hell are you? Long time gone, boy-o!"

At least seven years, Kirk admitted to himself. But not a damned thing about the place had changed. Not so much as a dust mote.

"Don' bee *fex,* Cap!" Prrghh squirmed around in Kirk's arms to look back over her shoulder, a position that would certainly have dislocated the spine of any anthropoid species. "Jimmee allas heerr!"

"Everyone is always here," a gruff voice behind them snarled. "Especially tonight." The female Klingon pushed past Kirk as though she had somewhere to go, then stopped abruptly and crouched to thrust her nose into Prrghh's pretty face. "If you're staying, sit down. If not, get out of the way and take your *mris* with you."

Prrghh's hiss was dry but rich with hatred. Kirk turned them away from the Klingon, already knowing where things could lead once Prrghh's ruff had gotten up. "Why don't we find a seat, then?" he suggested smoothly. The Klingon grunted, but made no move to follow.

Kirk swung Prrghh to the floor as though he were twenty years younger or she twenty kilograms lighter. He let her fold her hand inside his, though, basketing his fingers with lightly extended claws. Her palm felt soft and familiar despite the years that had passed since it had last been fitted into his. Beside him, he noticed Sulu's failed efforts to hide a knowing grin by pretending to check on the lizard now peering curiously from beneath his cuff. Kirk wondered briefly what sorts of tales the younger captain might tell out of school, considering his former commander's reputation. This time the heat in Kirk's cheeks had a little bit more to do with embarrassment.

It might have been a Saturday night, the place was so packed with bodies and voices and laughing. But, then, Kirk's memory said that it *always* looked like Saturday night, no matter what the day or time. Never too crowded to find a seat, thank God, but always just threatening to burst at the seams and overflow into the rest of the world. Kirk snagged Sulu by the hem of his jacket when the captain started toward the bar along the long end of the crowded room.

"A seat," Sulu said by way of explanation, lifting his lizard-filled hands to indicate his objective. Kirk glanced where the captain pointed and shook his head. The empty seat in question—several of them, in fact—surrounded a grossly fat Caxtonian freighter pilot who appeared to have congealed around a tankard of milky brown fluid.

"He's Caxtonian," Kirk said. "By this time of night—"

Prrggh wrinkled her delicate nose. "—hee stinkk feersly!" Her long, supple tail snaked up between the men to twitch their attention toward the foot of the stairs. "Thees othur qhuman dances for you."

The captain Prrghh pointed out looked human enough, at least. Salt-and-pepper beard, with hair a matching color that hung just a little longer than the current civilian standard. Kirk liked the well-worn look of his leather jacket, with its rainbow shoulder patch and anomalously fleece-trimmed collar. He was lean and wiry, with an earnest smile and tired but friendly eyes. Two other seats at his table were already filled by a rapier-thin dandy with his black hair pulled back into a neat queue, and a broad bear of a man with a wild white beard and a curl of pipe smoke covering most of his head. When their leather-jacketed comrade waved again, Kirk acknowledged his gesture by slipping between a knot of standing patrons to blaze a path to the table.

"Gentlemen. Welcome to the Captain's Table." The salt-and-pepper human took Kirk's hand in a firm, somewhat eager shake. "Humans?" he asked, with just the slightest bit of hopefulness in his tone.

Kirk glanced at the freighter designation stenciled beneath the ship name on the leather jacket's patch, and recognized the wearer for a fellow captain. Of course. "The genuine article." He stole a chair from the table next door and offered it to Prrghh as Sulu conscientiously offered the freighter captain his left hand for shaking to avoid disturbing the reptilian passenger sprawled happily across his right palm.

The freighter captain pumped Sulu's hand without seeming to notice either the deviation from convention or the little passenger. "I'm sure pleased to see you," he grinned. "We were feeling a bit outnumbered tonight." He tipped a cordial nod to Prrghh as she slipped into her seat. "No offense, Captain. I just sometimes get real tired of aliens."

Her ears came up and green eyes narrowed on the other captain's lean face. Kirk recognized the expression—she liked a challenge. "Purrhaps you haf not met the ryght ailyens."

The freighter captain lifted an eyebrow, and Kirk suspected he enjoyed his share of challenges, too. "Perhaps not," he admitted with a smile. "Maybe you can educate me."

". . . a surprisingly trusting lot, all points considered." The black-haired dandy tipped the tankard in his hand and squinted down its throat to verify it was empty. He hadn't interrupted his story for Kirk and Sulu's arrival, and didn't interrupt it now as he waved the tankard over his head to catch a server's attention. "They brought us neatly upside, lashed our hulls together, and came aboard with every thought of liberating our hold of its treasures. Alas, our only cargo was a crew of well-armed men and the good old Union Jack. By the time we'd taken our due, that was one Jolly Roger which never flew again."

"A clever story." The white-haired captain bit down on his meerschaum pipe and nodded wisely. "You're a cunning man, Captain, using that pirate crew's own expectations against them."

"The best judge of a pirate is one of his own," the Englishman admitted. His tankard still waggled above one shoulder. "My duties may seal me now to the queen, but I'm loath to believe that any man who never ran with pirates can ever be their match."

Kirk straightened in his seat, stung by the remark. "Oh, I don't know about that."

The table's patrons turned to him almost as a unit, and he found himself momentarily startled by the frank challenge in their stares.

"Do you mean to disavow my own experience?" There was steel in the dark-haired Englishman's voice despite his friendly countenance.

The white-haired bear lifted one big hand in an obvious gesture of placation. "Easy, my friend. He sounds like a man with experience of his own."

"Some." Kirk settled back as a wiry serving boy scampered up to their table with a tray full of drinks. He gave the others first pick from the offerings since he knew whatever he wanted would be still left when they were done. "Pirates were never my primary business, but I've run across my share." He wrapped his hands around the mug of warm rum the boy placed in front of him, well familiar with the price every captain had to pay for the first round of drinks after his arrival. "Let me tell you about a time when I rescued the victims of some pirates, only to find out they weren't exactly what I'd expected. . . ."

• • •

I told myself it wasn't resentment. I didn't have the right to resent him. He hadn't killed my helmsman; he'd never placed my ship and crew in danger; he hadn't forced my chief medical officer to retire. He hadn't even murdered my best friend. He had never been anything but responsible, conscientious, and reliable. In these last few weeks, he'd stepped into a position made vacant by my own actions—not because he wanted it, or because he hoped to prove anything to anybody, just because it was necessary. He was that kind of officer; service without complaint. Duty called, and he answered.

Still, I hadn't quite figured out how to separate him from everything that had come before. So while he stood there in the gym doorway, waiting for my answer with his damned, impenetrable patience, my first instinct was to tell him to go to hell. Instead, I asked in the mildest tone I could muster, "Mr. Spock, can't this wait until later?"

I must not have sounded as patient as I'd hoped. He lifted one eyebrow a few micrometers, and peered at me with the same keen interest he probably applied to alien mathematics problems. Subtle emotions often had that effect on him, I'd noticed. As though he couldn't decide what informational value to assign such a random variable, and it annoyed him to settle for an imperfect interpretation.

Except, of course, annoyance was a human emotion.

"Regulations stipulate that a starship's captain and executive officer shall meet once every seven days to coordinate duties and exchange pertinent crew and mission information." He didn't fidget. He just folded his hands around the datapad at his waist and settled in as though there was no place else he needed to be. "Our last such meeting was eleven days ago."

I turned back to my interrupted workout, leaving him to recognize the implied dismissal. "Then a few more hours won't make any difference." I aimed a high sweep-kick at the sparring drone, and earned a flash of approving lights for smashing into the upper right quadrant target.

Spock was silent for what seemed a long time, watching me with his usual cool fascination, no doubt, as I did my best to sweat out my personal demons at the expense of a supposedly indestructible robot.

In the end, they both managed to outlast me. I stopped before I started to stumble, but not before I was forced to suck in air by the lungful, or before I raised dark welts on the edges of both hands. I still secretly believed that if I could push myself just a little further, a little longer, I'd finally beat out the last of my uncertainty and guilt. But I'd entertained this secret belief for at least three weeks now, and hadn't yet found the magic distance. I refused to fall down in front of my new executive officer while I still struggled to find it.

He gave me what was probably a carefully calculated amount of time to catch my breath, then said to my still-turned back, "May I remind the captain that when he is not eating, sleeping, or engaging in some necessary physical activity, he is on duty. As senior science officer, my duty shift is concurrent with the captain's. As acting executive officer, my second duty shift coincides with when the captain is off-duty. Logic therefore suggests that rather than disrupt the necessary human sleep function, the most efficient time period during which to conduct our required conferencing would be during the one hour fifteen minute interval between the termination of my secondary duty shift and the beginning of your regular tour." He paused as though giving my slower human mind a moment to process his argument, then added blandly, "Which is now."

I swiped a hand over my eyes to flick away the worst of the sweat, and heaved an extra-deep breath to even out my panting. "Is this your way of telling me you're working a few too many hours, Mr. Spock?"

Both eyebrows were nearly to his hairline; I could almost feel the lightning flicker of his thoughts behind those dark Vulcan eyes. "No, Captain." As deadly serious as if I'd asked him to contemplate the course of Klingon politics over the next hundred years. "My current schedule allows ample time for research, personal hygiene, and the intake of food. Since Vulcans are not limited by the same stringent sleep requirements as humans, I find the hours between my shifts more than sufficient for meditation and physical renewal."

I tried not to sigh out loud. My entire Starfleet career would be a success if I could teach even one Vulcan to have a sense of humor. "What would you like to discuss, Mr. Spock?" I asked wearily.

Where anyone else—anyone human—would have promptly flipped up the padd to consult its readout, Spock announced, apparently from memory, "According to the first officer's log, there are currently eight hundred fifty-four individual crew evaluations which are late or incomplete."

I paused in scooping up my towel to frown at him. "There are only four hundred and thirty crew on board the *Enterprise.*"

Spock acknowledged my point with a microscopic tilt of his head. "Four hundred twenty-four evaluations are still outstanding from the quarter ending stardate 1013.4. The other four hundred thirty were due at the end of the most recent quarter, which ended on stardate 1298.9."

And Gary—perpetually behind when it came to such mundane administrative duties—died before he had the chance to turn in even one from the most recent batch. I tried to disguise a fresh swell of frustration by scrubbing at my face and scalp with the towel. "Since last quarter, Lieutenant Lee Kelso was killed in the line of duty. Dr. Elizabeth Dehner—killed in the line of duty. Lieutenant Commander Gary Mitchell—" I hid a bitter scowl by turning and banning the sparring drone back to its storage locker.

"—killed." The word still tasted like cold gunmetal in my mouth. "I've ordered the lateral transfer of Lieutenant Hikaru Sulu and Ensign David Bailey from astrosciences to cover the vacant bridge positions, and have accepted Lieutenant Commander Spock's application for temporary assignment as ship's first officer." Snatching up my tunic and boots with a brusqueness that surprised even me, I came to a stop just shy of touching Spock, knowing full well what a discomforting situation that tended to make for Vulcans. "On a brighter note, Chief Medical Officer Mark Piper has retired to a safe, well-paying civilian position at Johns Hopkins University on Earth, and his replacement, Leonard McCoy, seems to be adapting nicely." That last was half a lie, since I hadn't actually spoken to my old friend since the day McCoy first came aboard. I hadn't managed to say much even then, thanks to the doctor's colorful tirade against the ship's transporter. I hadn't remembered him being quite so technophobic, and found myself wondering if this was going to be a problem. "Why don't you put all that in Gary's files and call them done?"

Spock said nothing as I pushed past him on my way to the shower room, merely stepping neatly to one side to avoid any unseemly physical contact. These were the kinds of little skills he must practice daily, I realized. Memorized patterns of behavior, movement, and response based on the thousands—perhaps millions—of social interactions he'd endured with a species whose conduct must seem positively arcane to him. I doubted he even understood much of the social data he mentally collected about his crewmates—he simply made note of what interactions produced what results, and adjusted his model accordingly. If there was a difference between that and how a soulless machine would make use of the same information, at that particular moment I couldn't see what it was.

He followed me into the shower room at what was no doubt a carefully calculated distance. Why did his patient silences always make me feel so guilty about whatever random bitterness popped into my head? Probably just another side effect of his conversational style. I made a note to read up on Vulcan social customs, naively believing that I might find some understanding in their workings.

"The completion of Commander Mitchell's reports should pose no undo difficulty. I calculate that, by committing only forty-two point three percent of my on-duty time, I can deliver the reports to you within sixty-eight hours."

I hoped he didn't expect me to vet them quite so quickly. Eating and sleeping aside, I still had too much shoring up to do with the ship's new crew assignments to catch up on nearly nine hundred reports over the next three days.

"I must confess, however . . ."

Reluctance? I paused with the water crashing over my head to stare at him.

He all but rushed on before I could say a word. "I find the guidelines as laid out by Starfleet . . . baffling."

That admission of near-weakness surprised me more than almost anything else he could have said. I turned off the water and leaned out to study him. "How so?"

If he were human, I almost think he might have blushed. Not in embarrassment, but in the stone-faced frustration young children sometimes display when confronted with an impenetrable question they secretly suspect is a joke at their expense. I wondered if Vulcan children ever teased each other, or if the Vulcan Science Academy practiced hazing.

"The precise goal of such record keeping in the format specified is unclear," he said, quite formally, yet somehow without actually meeting my eyes. "There are no statistical data to be compiled, no discreet procedures to be followed. The desired end result is entirely inadequately conveyed."

I felt a strange warmth when I realized what he was saying. Sympathy, almost. "The desired end result is insight." He looked at me, and I smiled gently, explaining, "It's the first officer's job to be liaison to the crew. As captain, I depend on your observations—your instincts and feelings about the crew's state of mind."

Any emotion I might have imagined in his features evaporated with the infinitesimal straightening of his shoulders. "I am Vulcan. I have no instincts or feelings, only logic."

But the crew is human, I wanted to tell him, *just bubbling over with emotion.* Who in God's name had ever thought a Vulcan could serve as a human crew's XO?

The chirrup of my communicator saved us from pursuing a discussion neither of us was sure how to follow. I ducked out of the shower, careless of the water I dripped as I scooped up the communicator and flipped back the grid. "Kirk here. Go ahead."

The communications officer's honey-rich voice seemed strangely out of place in the conflicting Vulcan-human landscape of our interrupted conversation. "Sir, sensors have detected a disabled ship two point two million kilometers to our starboard. There's some shipboard functions, but they don't respond to our hails."

A real problem. Not overdue reports, Vulcan emotional illiteracy, or misplaced captain's angst. A way to avoid feelings of helplessness by directing all my energy toward something I could change. "Plot a course to intercept, and scan the ship for survivors. I'm on my way to the bridge." I was already shaking my tunic free from the rest of my clothing by the time I snapped the communicator shut and tossed it to the bench. "I'm afraid you're on your own with those reports, Mr. Spock." I flashed him a grin over the collar of my shirt, one that was probably as reassuring as it was strictly sincere. "Just do the best you can."

The bridge felt alien and strangely too quite when the turbolift deposited us on its margins. I missed Gary's laughter. It had been omnipresent—sometimes irritatingly so—and I found myself missing the sudden guilty hush that meant Gary had been sharing some particularly bawdy story with the rest of the crew before my arrival. I missed his liar's smile, and his all-too-innocent "Captain on the bridge" to announce my arrival.

Instead, the smoothly deep voice of my new helmsman made the call, and nobody abruptly ceased what they were doing or ducked their heads to hide a sudden onset of blushing. Decorum reigned, and I felt like I'd stumbled onto some other captain's vessel.

Still, I made that first step beyond the turbolift's doors without any outward sign of hesitation, briskly taking the steps down to my chair as Spock rounded behind me to head for his own station at the science console. "Mr. Sulu, report."

The helmsman—*my* helmsman, I reminded myself firmly—half turned in his seat, one hand still hovering possessively over his controls. "Sensors detect life on the vessel, but still no response to our hails. Their power exchange is in bad shape—the distress call might be on automatic."

Meaning the crew either couldn't use ship's systems to respond, or were too badly injured to make the attempt. I drummed my fingers on the arm of my command chair, thinking. On the viewscreen, the flat, elongated vessel drifted lazily clockwise, passing into a long silhouette, presenting us her nose, wafting lengthwise again. Her engines had been burned down to nubs, and the characteristic shatter of disruptor fire carved jagged stripes down her sides. It looked like at least half the ship was in vacuum, and the other half looked too dark to be getting anywhere near normal power. If there was anything or anyone still alive on board, they wouldn't stay that way forever.

"Spock, do we have any idea what kind of ship that is?"

He was silent for a moment. I gave him that—I'd figured out early on that he didn't like giving answers until he'd looked at all the data.

"Sixty-three percent of the identifiable ship's components strongly resemble an Orion Suga-class transport," Spock said at last, still scanning the computer's library screens. "Eleven point six percent are from an Orion-manufactured slaving facility. Four point two percent still bear the registration codes for a Klingon unmanned science probe. The remaining twenty-two point two percent resemble nothing currently on record."

I rubbed thoughtfully at my chin. "Could they be Orions?" I asked after adding up those bits and pieces. "Or maybe Orion allies?"

"Starfleet has reported no recent Orion pirating activity in this sector." While it wasn't exactly an answer to my question, it still led me a few steps closer to something that was. Spock swiveled in his own chair to lift an eyebrow at the screen. "To my knowledge, the Orions have no allies."

Which told you everything you needed to know about the Orions. Still . . . "Just because we don't know about any allies doesn't mean there are none." I resisted an urge to toss Spock a puckish grin he wouldn't appreciate. "After all, even the Devil had friends."

He tipped his head in grave acknowledgment of my point, and I felt for one startled moment as though he were teasing me. *He's a Vulcan, not Gary Mitchell. Vulcans don't tease.* I turned forward again to hide my chagrin, and tapped my chair intercom with the side of my hand. "Bridge to transporter room."

"Transporter room. Scott here."

It worried me sometimes that my chief engineer spent so much time with the transporter. I tried to reassure myself that it was a fascinating piece of equipment, with all manner of systems to explore. But sometimes I just couldn't shake the suspicion that there was more to Scott's constant tending than mere affection. Probably not something I should mention around Dr. McCoy. "Scotty, can you get a fix on the life-forms inside that alien vessel?"

"Fifteen to twenty of them," he reported, managing to sound pleased with himself and a little frustrated all at the same time. "Maybe as much as twenty-four—the numbers are hopping all over the place."

"See if you can isolate them with a wide-angle beam." I muted the channel and glanced aside at Spock. "What sort of environment does that ship hold?"

He opened his mouth, took a small breath as though to say something, then seemed to change his mind at the last minute. Without having to reconsult his equipment, he informed me, "Slightly higher in oxygen and nitrogen than Earth normal, and at a slightly greater atmospheric pressure. Fluctuations in their gravitational equipment average at just a little less than one Earth gravity." Then he continued on without pausing, saying what I suspected had been the first thing to cross his mind. "May I infer from your questions that you intend to bring any survivors on board?"

"Indeed you may." I sent an automated request to security for a small reception committee, and a similar request to sickbay for an emergency medical team. "I've never ignored another ship's distress signal, and I don't intend to start now."

Spock stood smoothly as I jumped up from my chair, his own quiet way of announcing that he was following me down to the transporter room. "And if the captain who initiated this distress call is an Orion ally, as you speculate?"

I looked up at the viewscreen, quickly refreshing my image of its crumpled superstructure and ruptured sides. "Then they still need rescuing." We certainly couldn't tow them anywhere—I doubted their ship would stand up to the grasp of the tractor beam, much less to having its tumble forcibly stilled and its whole mass accelerated along a single vector. Besides, towing wouldn't take care of their wounded. I wouldn't put any captain in the position of being helplessly dragged along while his crew died around him. Not if I could help it.

"Don't worry, Mr. Spock," I continued as I circled my command chair and took the stairs to the second level in a single step. "We can isolate our guests in rec hall three until arrangements are made to drop them off with whatever allies they're willing to claim." The turbolift doors whisked aside for me, and I slipped inside with one hand on the sensor to hold them open as Spock caught up. "No one's going to get free run of the ship just because we're giving them a ride."

He stepped in neatly beside me, pivoting to face the front of the lift with a precision that seemed to be just a part of his movement, not something he planned. "Worry is a human emotion," he stated, as though correcting me on some particularly salient fact.

I stepped back from the doors and let them flash closed on us, taking up my own place on the opposite side of the turbolift. "Of course it is," I said, rather flatly. I kept my eyes trained on the deck indicator to avoid having to look at him. "How could I have forgotten?"

Never the end . . .

Biographies

Christopher Pike

by Michael Jan Friedman

Christopher Pike grew up in the Mojave region on Earth, a part of North America that had been uninhabitable desert only two hundred years earlier. However, by the time of Pike's birth in the early part of the twenty-third century, the Mojave had been converted into a paradise of glittering cities and wide belts of lush, green parkland.

It was here that the young Pike learned to ride horses—particularly his beloved Tango—and to enjoy the wide-open spaces, passions which remained with him throughout his life. It was here as well that Pike first glimpsed the stars in the crisp night sky and knew he wanted to devote his life to their exploration.

Even before he took command of the *U.S.S. Enterprise*, in 2250, Pike was known throughout Starfleet as a bright, dedicated, and compassionate individual—prime command material. Never one to crack a joke, he took his duties and responsibilities as captain quite seriously.

According to his critics, he may have taken his responsibilities too seriously on occasion. For instance, when the *Enterprise* was involved in a violent conflict on Rigel VII and three crew members were killed, Pike blamed the incident on his own carelessness in not anticipating hostilities on the part of the Rigelians—even though his colleagues on the ship assured him there was nothing else he could have done.

In 2254, Pike and the *Enterprise* were en route to the Vega colony when they received a distress call from the *S.S. Columbia*—a spacegoing vessel that had disappeared near the Talos star group some eighteen years earlier. His investigation led to the discovery of the *Columbia's* crash site on planet Talos IV and, subsequently, contact with the planet's indigenous inhabitants—a race of technically advanced humanoids.

The Talosians captured Pike and attempted to detain him with their ability to create realistic illusions. Their aim was to mate him with a human female in their possession in order to breed a line of captive humans. However, Pike managed to outwit the Talosians and win his freedom. His behavior convinced them that humans are unsuitable for captivity.

Nonetheless, the human female whom Pike encountered—Vina, the lone survivor of the *S.S. Columbia* crash—opted to remain with the Talosians. Apparently, she had been badly disfigured in the crash and had come to prefer illusion to reality.

Pike left Vina there, though he felt a strong emotional attachment to her. Soon after, Starfleet Command imposed General Order 7 on Talos IV, prohibiting Federation contact with that planet on pain of death.

Pike went on to conduct two complete five-year missions of exploration, the second ending in 2261. He relinquished command of the *Enterprise* to James Kirk in 2263, at which time Pike was promoted to fleet captain.

For three years, Pike proved a capable and creative administrator. Then, in 2266, he suffered severe radiation injuries in an attempt to save lives during an accident aboard a class-J training ship.

Wheelchair-bound as a result of delta-ray exposure, Pike found life difficult, to say the least. Always a very active individual, his disability drove him to the edge of despondence.

Finally, with the help of the Vulcan Spock, who had served on the *Enterprise* under Pike, the fleet captain managed to return to Talos IV despite General Order 7. Once there, he took the Talosians up on an offer they had made to him twelve years earlier—an offer to use their power of illusion to give him a life unfettered by his physical reality.

Though little is known of Pike's life after that, Starfleet chroniclers have speculated that he lived out his natural life in Vina's company, as happy and fulfilled as any human could be.

Though Pike himself left Starfleet, his accomplishments went on to inspire a great many of the fleet's finest officers. One of them was the aforementioned Spock of Vulcan, who later served under James Kirk, Pike's successor as captain of the *Enterprise.*

Pike City, a town on the Federation planet Cestus III, was named for the sometimes grim, always unpretentious, and yet stirringly adventuresome Captain Christopher Pike.

James T. Kirk

by
Michael Jan Friedman

His Early Life

JAMES TIBERIUS KIRK WAS BORN IN 2233 IN THE REGION CALLED IOWA, ON planet Earth. He and his older brother, George Samuel Kirk, grew up on their father's farm, where they learned hard work and an appreciation for the facts of life and death.

In 2246, at the tender age of thirteen, James Kirk was one of the surviving eyewitnesses to the massacre of some 4,000 colonists on Tarsus IV by Kodos the Executioner. Later on, as a Starfleet captain, Kirk would identify and apprehend Kodos, thereby bringing a sense of closure to the surviving members of the colony.

Kirk was admitted to Starfleet Academy in 2250. One of his most influential instructors was a man named John Gill, who would later violate the Federation's Prime Directive by inadvertently creating a tyrannical regime on the planet Ekos.

Early on at the Academy, Kirk was tormented by an upperclassman named Finnegan, who frequently chose Kirk as a target for his practical jokes. Kirk found a measure of satisfaction years later, in 2267, when he had a chance to wallop a replica of Finnegan created on an "amusement park" planet in the Omicron Delta region.

One of Kirk's heroes at the Academy was the legendary Captain Garth of Izar, whose exploits were required reading. Years later, Kirk helped save his hero when Garth became criminally insane and was being treated at the

Elba II penal colony. Another of Kirk's personal heroes was Abraham Lincoln, sixteenth president of the United States of America on Earth.

As an exemplary student, Kirk was asked to serve as an instructor at the Academy. One of his students was Gary Mitchell, a fellow human who would become Kirk's best friend. Years later, on the planet Dimorus, Mitchell would risk his life by taking a poisonous dart meant for his friend Jim. Mitchell also arranged for Kirk to date an unidentified "little blonde lab technician," whom Kirk almost married.

Another of Kirk's friends from his Academy days was Benjamin Finney, who named his daughter, Jamie, after Kirk. A rift developed between Finney and Kirk in 2250 when the two were serving together on the *U.S.S. Republic.* Kirk recorded a mistake that Finney had made in the duty log, and Finney blamed Kirk for his subsequent failure to earn command of a starship.

Shortly thereafter, Kirk and the *Republic* visited the planet Axanar on a peace mission. The operation was a major achievement for Captain Garth, who spearheaded the mission, while Starfleet awarded Kirk the Palm Leaf of Axanar for his smaller role in the effort.

Kirk continued to serve aboard the *Republic* until his graduation from the Academy in 2254. Before leaving, he distinguished himself as the only cadet ever to have beaten the "no-win" *Kobayashi Maru* computer-simulation problem. Kirk accomplished this by secretly reprogramming the simulation computer to make it possible for him to win, earning a commendation for original thinking in the process.

After graduation, Kirk's first posting was as a lieutenant on the *U.S.S. Farragut,* under the command of Captain Garrovick. While serving aboard the *Farragut* in 2257, Lieutenant Kirk encountered a dikironium cloud creature at planet Tycho IV. The creature ended up killing some 200 members of the *Farragut*'s crew, including Captain Garrovick.

At the time, Kirk felt guilty for the deaths, believing that he could have averted tragedy if he had fired on the creature more quickly. However, he learned years later that nothing could have prevented the deaths of his captain and his comrades.

Sometime in his youth, Kirk was exposed to and almost died from Vegan choriomengitis, a rare and deadly disease which remained dormant in his bloodstream. In 2268, the disease was used by the people of the planet Gideon to infect volunteers willing to die to solve their planet's overpopulation crisis.

In 2263, Kirk was promoted to the rank of captain. A year later, he assumed command of the *U.S.S. Enterprise,* taking over for Captain Pike, and embarked on a five-year mission from 2264 through 2269 that made him a legend in the annals of space exploration.

It was during this five-year mission that Kirk's friendships with

Commander Spock and Chief Medical Officer Leonard McCoy developed. These were friendships that would last the three men the rest of their lives.

The Legendary Five-Year Mission

In 2265, Kirk and the *Enterprise* discovered a strange energy barrier. Exposure to the energies in the barrier initiated a transformation in Kirk's friend and colleague, Lt. Gary Mitchell, changing him into a being with tremendous psychokinetic powers. An attempt to quarantine Mitchell at the Delta Vega mining facility was unsuccessful and Kirk was tragically forced to kill his friend to save the *Enterprise.*

Kirk demonstrated his ability to "tap dance"—in other words, to create innovatative solutions to urgent problems—when he encountered a giant spacecraft which identified itself as the *Fesarius.* When the commander of the *Fesarius* threatened to destroy the *Enterprise* if it didn't move off, Kirk told his alien counterpart that Starfleet vessels are equipped with a "corbomite" system which would destroy any attacker. The *Fesarius* refrained from initiating hostilities and Kirk eventually established friendly relations with its lone occupant.

Kirk lost his older brother, George Samuel Kirk (whom only James called Sam), and sister-in-law, Aurelan Kirk, on the planet Deneva when it was invaded by neural parasites in 2267. Kirk's nephew, Peter, survived the invasion. Sam Kirk also had two other sons who were not on Deneva at the time of the tragedy.

James Kirk became the first starship captain ever to stand trial when he was accused of causing the death of Benjamin Finney. However, Kirk's court-martial, held at Starbase 11, exposed a plot by the embittered Finney and proved the captain innocent of any wrongdoing.

Early in his five-year mission, Kirk recorded a tape of last orders to be played by officers Spock and McCoy upon his death. Some time later, while trapped in a spatial interphase near Tholian space, Kirk vanished with the *U.S.S. Defiant* and was declared dead. Spock and McCoy honored their captain's last wishes by working together against the Tholian threat, despite their differences—at least until they realized he wasn't dead after all.

In 2267, Captain Kirk and a handful of his officers were thrust into a mirror universe after trying to beam down to a planet during an ion storm. They found it to be a savage place, governed by a brutally oppressive regime. In this frame of reference, Starfleet officers climbed the ranks through assassination and mutiny.

One of Kirk's earliest nemeses was Harry F. Mudd, a slippery interplanetary swindler. In the captain's first meeting with Mudd, the con man was trying to sell off his "cargo" of three women—the beneficiaries of a Venus drug that kept them young and beautiful.

In another encounter, Kirk's ship was taken over and brought to a planet full of androids—among whom Mudd resided. Mudd had made plans to rule the androids as they expanded throughout the galaxy, but the androids—recognizing Mudd as a flawed example of humanity—decided to strand him with the crew of the *Enterprise* when they left the planet. With Mudd's help, Kirk took back his ship. But when the *Enterprise* departed, Mudd was left behind.

Of course, not all of Kirk's adversaries were completely human. In 2266, Kirk took aboard young Charles Evans, the lone survivor of a spaceship on the planet Thasus 14 years earlier. When Charlie demonstrated remarkable telekinetic powers, causing crewmen to disappear and taking over the *Enterprise,* Kirk was presented with the difficult problem of dealing with this enfant terrible.

Shortly thereafter, Kirk's *Enterprise* tracked down a Romulan vessel that had attacked Starfleet outposts along the Romulan Neutral Zone. Engaging the ship, Kirk guessed that its actions were a test of Federation resolve. Despite the fact that the Romulans enjoyed a cloaking device and superior weaponry, Kirk outmaneuvered the commander of the Romulan vessel and forced him to self-destruct as an alternative to surrender.

On another occasion, Kirk was split into two distinct personalities by a transporter malfunction. With the help of his chief engineer, Montgomery Scott, Kirk arranged for his two halves to be rejoined.

In 2267, Kirk found himself at odds with his first officer when Spock hijacked the *Enterprise* and took it to Talos IV against the express dictates of Starfleet's General Order 7. It was only when the *Enterprise* arrived at its destination that Spock's plan was revealed—the transport of former *Enterprise* Captain Christopher Pike, crippled in a recent accident, to an environment where he could live out his life in happiness.

Kirk encountered Trelane, an illogical but extremely powerful alien, in the middle of the *Enterprise*'s original five-year mission. Although Trelane appeared to be an adult humanoid fascinated with Earth's history, Kirk recognized that there was more to the being than met the eye. His suspicions were confirmed when Trelane's parents intervened—and Trelane himself was exposed as an alien child.

On the planet Cestus III, the super-advanced Metrons pitted Kirk against a representative of the merciless, lizardlike species known as the Gorn in a one-on-one competition for survival—in which the loser's crew would be destroyed. Using his wits against the Gorn's brawn, the captain defeated his opponent, but refused to kill him. Impressed, the Metrons allowed both crews to live.

The captain also encountered a being who called himself Apollo, a member of a band of space travelers who lived on Mount Olympus, on old Earth. Though Apollo declared the *Enterprise* crew to be his children, Kirk and his officers refused to stay and worship him—and destroyed Apollo's temple, the source of his amazing powers.

Kirk made one of his greatest enemies when the *Enterprise* discovered a sleeper vessel from the late twentieth century. Its crew turned out to be a group of eugenically created and cryogenically preserved supermen. Their leader, a magnetic but ultimately contemptuous individual named Kahn, tried to take over the ship. However, Kirk defeated Kahn and dropped him off on a virgin world, where he could put his superhuman abilities to the test.

Then again, not all of Kirk's challenges were quite so adversarial. Some of them were a good deal more complex.

At one point, the gravitational forces of a black star hurled the *Enterprise* back in time to the twentieth century, where it was sighted by a pilot named John Christopher. So as to leave the time line intact, Kirk beamed Christopher aboard the *Enterprise.* However, when Spock pointed out that Christopher's son would become an important space explorer, Kirk returned the pilot to Earth.

In 2267, Kirk came upon two worlds engaged in a war in which randomly selected casualties, who willingly sacrificed their lives in antimatter chambers to prevent the resumption of a real conflict. Kirk destroyed the computers on one of the combatant-worlds, thereby forcing the two worlds to engage in a bloody fight or seek peace.

When Spock entered the ponn farr, the Vulcan mating cycle, Kirk was forced to return his first officer to his native planet. However, through a series of machinations, Kirk wound up not as a visitor to a marriage ceremony, but as a participant in a deadly combat—pitted against the inhumanly strong Spock. Only an injection by Dr. McCoy allowed Kirk to escape his dilemma by appearing dead and thereby ending the combat.

By 2267, Kirk had earned an impressive list of commendations from Starfleet, including not only the Palm Leaf of Axanar, but the Grankite Order of Tactics (Class of Excellence) and the Preantares Ribbon of Commendation (Classes First and Second). Kirk's awards for valor included the Medal of Honor, the Silver Palm with Cluster, the Starfleet Citation for Conspicuous Gallantry, and the Kragite Order of Heroism.

In 2268, Kirk and two of his officers were abducted by a group of advanced beings called the Providers and forced to fight as gladiators for the Providers' amusement. To save his people and his ship, Kirk wagered their freedom on his ability to defeat three of the Providers' best thralls—a feat he then carried off.

Soon after, Kirk took the *Enterprise* into Romulan space and feigned a nervous breakdown due to overwork. Spock denounced his captain and gave the appearance that he had killed Kirk, thereby attaining his way into the trust of a female Romulan commander.

However, it was all part of a scheme to gain possession of the Romulans' cloaking device, the efficacy of which Kirk had experienced firsthand a couple of years earlier. In disguise, the captain beamed aboard the Romulan flagship, stole the device, and escaped.

Kirk was known to violate Starfleet directives when he saw no viable alternative. In 2268, for instance, the Klingons armed one component of a planet's population—the Hill People—with firearms, thereby endangering another component of the population. In violation of the Prime Directive, the captain reluctantly restored the balance of power by arming the endangered tribespeople as well.

His Romances

Kirk was notably unsuccessful in maintaining long-term liaisons with the opposite sex. Although he was romantically involved with a great many women during his life, his intense passion for his career always seemed to interfere with his relationships.

In 2252, Kirk dated a woman named Ruth. Not much is known about her, though she seemed to occupy Kirk's thoughts for years afterward. Later on, while still attending the Academy, Kirk spent a year or so with a woman named Janice Lester. Some fifteen years later, Lester would attempt to switch bodies with her old flame in a bizarre attempt to realize her dream of becoming a starship captain.

A few years prior to his command of the *Enterprise,* Kirk became involved with a scientist, Dr. Carol Marcus. The two had a child, David Marcus, but Kirk and Carol did not remain together because their careers took them in different directions.

Other significant romances in Kirk's life included Janet Wallace, an endocrinologist who later saved his life from an aging virus; Areel Shaw, who, ironically, prosecuted Kirk years later in the case of Ben Finney's apparent death; and Miramanee, a beautiful primitive woman Kirk married in 2268 after he was struck with amnesia on a landing party mission. Miramanee became pregnant with Kirk's child, but both she and her unborn baby were killed in a local power struggle.

Kirk fell in love with a woman named Antonia after his first retirement from Starfleet, and for the rest of his life regretted not having proposed to her. However, Kirk's most tragic romantic involvement was with American social worker Edith Keeler, whom he met when he traveled into the 1930s through the Guardian of Forever. As it turned out, Keeler's existence was a focal point in time, and Kirk was forced to watch her die to prevent a terrible change in the established time line.

Kirk was not involved with the upbringing of his son, David Marcus, at the request of the boy's mother, Carol Marcus. In fact, Kirk had no contact with his son until 2285, when Carol and David were both working on Project Genesis and Kirk helped rescue the two from Kahn's vengeance. Later, Kirk and his son were able to become friends. Tragically, David was murdered shortly thereafter on the Genesis Planet by a Klingon officer named Kruge, who sought to steal the secret of Genesis.

His Later Career

Following the return of the *Enterprise* from its five-year mission in 2269, Kirk accepted a promotion to admiral and became chief of Starfleet operations, while the *Enterprise* underwent an extensive refit. At the time, Kirk recommended Will Decker to replace him as *Enterprise* captain.

However, when V'ger—a highly destructive mechanical life-form—approached Earth in 2271, Kirk accepted a grade reduction back to captain in order to reassume command of the *Enterprise* and deal with the threat. In the end, he defused the problem, thanks to the willingness of Decker and a Deltan female named Ilia to merge themselves with the V'ger entity.

Kirk's first retirement from Starfleet took place some time thereafter. Nonetheless, unable to ignore the siren call of duty, he returned to Starfleet in 2284 and became a staff instructor with the rank of admiral at Starfleet Academy.

Before long, however, Kirk found himself dissatisfied with ground assignment. He returned to active duty in 2285 when Khan Noonien Singh hijacked the starship *Reliant* and stole the Genesis Device, a revolutionary terraforming tool. Commander Spock, Kirk's close friend, was killed in the effort to retrieve the device.

Upon learning that Spock's katra—or personal essence—had survived the incident, Kirk hijacked the *Enterprise* to the Genesis Planet to recover Spock's body and take it to Vulcan. There, on the planet of his birth, Spock was brought back to life, his body and katra reunited.

In the course of retrieving Spock, Kirk was forced to destroy the *Enterprise,* to prevent the ship's capture by Klingons. Later, in 2285, he was charged with nine violations of Starfleet regulations in connection with the hijacking of the *Enterprise.*

All but one charge was dropped. Kirk was found guilty of that one remaining charge—disobeying a superior officer.

However, the Federation Council was so grateful that Kirk had saved

Earth from the devastating effects of an alien probe, it commuted his sentence and granted him the captaincy of a second starship named *Enterprise,* known colloquially as the *Enterprise-A.*

Kirk was an intensely motivated individual who loved the outdoors. His greatest accomplishment in that regard was free-climbing the sheer El Capitan mountain face in Yosemite National Park on Earth.

The captain was an accomplished equestrian as well. He kept a horse at a mountain cabin that he owned during his first retirement. Another companion at his mountain cabin was Butler, his Great Dane. He sold the cabin some time after his return to Starfleet.

Kirk's bitterness over his son's murder by Kruge colored his feelings about the Klingons for years after. He therefore opposed the peace initiative of Klingon chancellor Gorkon in 2293. Nonetheless, Starfleet appointed him the Federation's "olive branch" and assigned him the duty of escorting Gorkon to Earth.

During that mission, Kirk—along with his friend and fellow officer, Dr. McCoy—was arrested and wrongfully convicted of the murder of Gorkon. It later turned out that Gorkon had been killed by Federation and Klingon forces conspiring to block his initiatives. Escaping from Rura Penthe, a cold and deadly Klingon prison-planet, Kirk played a pivotal role in saving the historic Khitomer peace conference from further attacks. He retired from Starfleet a second time about three months after the Khitomer conference.

Shortly after his second retirement, Kirk was an honored guest at the launch of the Excelsior-class starship *Enterprise-B* in 2293. When the vessel ran into trouble on its maiden voyage, Kirk was believed dead.

However, it was later learned that he had actually disappeared into a unique temporal anomaly called the nexus. Kirk remained in the anomaly until 2371, when he was contacted and roused from his "paradise" by twenty-fourth-century *Enterprise-D* captain, Jean-Luc Picard.

Working alongside Picard, Kirk emerged from the nexus to help save the inhabitants of the Veridian system from the machinations of a deranged El-Aurian scientist, Tolian Soran. However, Kirk's heroic effort cost him nothing less than his life. Throughout his illustrious career, he had cheated death at every turn, until, at last, he could cheat her no more.

James T. Kirk is buried on a mountaintop on the planet called Veridian III. Fueled by a burning curiosity to see "what's out there" and armed with an unparalleled resourcefulness, Kirk will long be remembered for going boldly where no one had gone before.

Hikaru Sulu

by
Michael and Denise Okuda

SULU BEGAN HIS CAREER IN STARFLEET UNDER THE COMMAND OF CAPTAIN James T. Kirk on the original *Starship Enterprise.* Sulu, born in San Francisco on Earth was initially assigned as a physicist in 2265 but later transferred to the helm.

Sulu assumed command of the *Starship Excelsior* in 2290, and subsequently conducted a three-year scientific mission of cataloging gaseous planetary anomalies in the Beta Quadrant. Sulu and the Excelsior played a pivotal role in the historic Khitomer peace conference of 2293 by helping to protect the conference against Federation and Klingon forces seeking to disrupt the peace process.

Sulu demonstrated his loyalty and courage when he risked his ship and his career by violating Starfleet orders and attempting a rescue of his former shipmates James T. Kirk and Leonard McCoy. During the attempted rescue, Sulu narrowly escaped a Klingon patrol commanded by Captain Kang in the Azure Nebula. Sulu never entered the incident into his official log.

Sulu had a wide range of hobbies, including botany and fencing. The latter interest surfaced when Sulu suffered the effects of the Psi 2000 virus in 2266, and Sulu threatened everyone in sight with a foil. Old style handguns were another of his hobbies.

Hikaru Sulu had a daughter, Demora Sulu, born in 2271.

—Adapted from *The Star Trek Encyclopedia*
by Michael and Denise Okuda

Jean-Luc Picard

by
Michael Jan Friedman

His Early Life

JEAN-LUC PICARD WAS BORN ON EARTH IN 2305 TO MAURICE AND Yvette Gessard Picard, and raised on a family farm in LaBarre, France, along with his older brother, Robert. Maurice Picard was a tradition-bound French vintner who didn't approve of advanced technology and encouraged both his sons to follow in his footsteps.

However, from a very young age, Jean-Luc had his eyes on the stars. As a boy, he enjoyed building ships in bottles, the pride of his collection being a legendary Promellian battle cruiser—a vessel he would one day discover in his voyages aboard the *Enterprise-D*.

These toy ships served as a springboard for the future captain's imagination. In his daydreams, he was in command of the vessels after which the toys had been modeled, a true heir to the legendary starship commanders who had gone before him.

Against his father's wishes, Picard applied for entrance into Starfleet Academy in 2322, at the age of seventeen. Unfortunately, he fell short in this effort. Undaunted, the young Frenchman tried again and was admitted to the Academy a year later.

As a first-year cadet, in 2323, he ran the grueling Starfleet Academy marathon on Danula II. By passing four upperclassmen on the last hill of the forty-kilometer run, he became the only freshman ever to win the event. Picard won top academic honors at the Academy as well, scoring high enough to be named class valedictorian.

Still, his record at the Academy was not flawless. He committed a serious offense that was never made public. Years later, Picard credited Academy groundskeeper Boothby with helping him to rectify his error, thereby making it possible for him to remain a cadet in good standing.

Shortly after graduation with the class of 2327, Picard was on leave with several classmates at Starbase Earhart, where he picked a fight with three Nausicaans at the Bonestell Recreation Facility. One of the Nausicaans stabbed Picard through the heart, necessitating a cardiac replacement procedure and leaving Picard with an artificial heart.

Years later, as a young lieutenant, Picard met the legendary Sarek of Vulcan at the wedding of the ambassador's son. Picard was awed by Sarek, whose negotiations had helped to shape the Federation. On another occasion, Picard distinguished himself by leading an away team to Milika III to save an endangered Federation ambassador.

In 2333, Picard was a staff officer on the *U.S.S. Stargazer* when the ship's captain was killed. The twenty-eight-year-old Picard took charge of the bridge and for his coolheadedness in the emergency was offered command of the *Stargazer*—thereby becoming one of the youngest Starfleet officers ever to captain a starship.

Sometime later, Picard became fast friends with Jack Crusher, one of the officers reporting to him on the *Stargazer.* In 2344, Crusher introduced Picard to his fiancée, a medical student named Beverly Howard, to whom Picard was strongly attracted. However, as Crusher was a close friend, Picard never mentioned the attraction, either to Crusher or to Beverly.

Jack Crusher married Beverly Howard in 2348. The couple had a child, Wesley, a year later. When Jack was killed in the line of duty in 2354, it was Picard's sad task to inform Beverly Crusher of her husband's death. Picard still declined to reveal his love for Beverly at the time, because he felt to do so would be to betray his friend.

Picard commanded the *Stargazer* until 2355, when the ship was nearly destroyed by an unprovoked sneak attack near the Maxia Zeta star system. The assailant in the incident was unknown at the time but was later found to be a Ferengi spacecraft.

The captain would later recall that an unidentified vessel suddenly appeared and fired twice at point-blank range, disabling the *Stargazer*'s shields. Picard saved the lives of his crew by employing a tactic to be known as the "Picard maneuver."

However, the *Stargazer* was too badly damaged to repair. Picard abandoned the vessel, albeit reluctantly. The surviving crew, including the captain himself, drifted for several long weeks in lifeboats and shuttlecraft before being rescued.

Following the loss of the *Stargazer,* Picard was court-martialed, as required by standard Starfleet procedure. In the end, he was exonerated. The prosecutor in the case was Phillipa Louvois, with whom Picard had had a love affair.

Picard would see the *Stargazer* again, some years later, in an encounter with a revenge-seeking Ferengi. However, the vessel would be destroyed before the captain could salvage it.

While captain of the *Stargazer,* Picard had also been romantically involved with a woman named Jenice. Although Picard and Jenice were strongly attracted to one another, the captain feared commitment and eventually broke off the relationship. It was a move he would come to regret.

Picard and Jenice would be reunited in 2364. At that time, the crew of the *Enterprise-D* would save the life of Jenice's husband, Dr. Paul Manheim, following a serious laboratory accident on planet Vandor IX.

The *Enterprise-D*

Picard was appointed captain of the *Enterprise-D,* the fifth starship to bear the name *Enterprise,* in 2363, shortly after the vessel was commissioned. It was in this capacity that he carried out his greatest accomplishments and achieved his greatest glory.

Still, Picard had served on the *Enterprise* for less than a year when he was offered a promotion to the admiralty by Admiral Gregory Quinn, who was attempting to consolidate his power base against a supposed alien conspiracy within Starfleet Command. Picard declined the offer, citing his belief that he could better serve the Federation as a starship commander.

Later on, however, the captain found that the conspiracy was real. A number of Starfleet officials had been taken over by a species of intelligent parasites, whose presence was marked only by a quill-like protrusion from the host's neck. With the help of his officers, Picard foiled the parasites' plans to take control of the fleet.

Picard's most frequent nemesis was the seemingly omnipotent, extradimensional being known as Q. Actually, Q was a single component of an entire continuum that called itself by the same name. Despite his amazing powers and long life, Q displayed a childlike petulance and sense of playfulness.

The captain's first encounter with Q took place during his first mission on the *Enterprise-D,* in 2364. Q detained the ship and made Picard the defendant in a twenty-first-century courtroom drama, in which Q accused captain and crew of being "grievously savage."

On his second visit to the *Enterprise-D,* Q offered First Officer William Riker a gift of Q-like supernatural powers. On his third visit, Q transported the *Enterprise-D* some seven thousand light-years beyond Federation space to System J-25, where Picard and his crew first encountered the powerful and dangerous race known as the Borg.

In 2367, Q cast Picard and his officers into an elaborate romantic fantasy based on the old Earth legends of Robin Hood. Two years later, Q presented Picard with what he claimed was the afterlife, allowing the captain to see what his life would have been like had he not made some of the rash choices of his youth. However, Picard discovered that it was partly the brashness of his youth that had made him the man he was.

In 2370, the Q Continuum decided to test Picard again, devising a paradox whereby he would be responsible for the destruction of mankind by creating an antitime phenomenon. Q himself added the wrinkle of having Picard shift among three time periods, with awareness of what was happening in each.

After Picard succeeded in solving the paradox, Q informed him that the experience had been a test. The Q Continuum had wanted to see if Picard could expand his mind and explore the unknown possibilities of existence—abilities he had demonstrated to the Continuum's satisfaction.

One of Picard's senior officers on the *Enterprise-D* was Beverly Crusher. As the vessel was designed to accommodate family life, Crusher was accompanied by her young son, Wesley. Another of his officers was Data, an android created by the legendary cyberneticist, Noonien Soong.

In 2365, an energy vortex near the Endicor system created a duplicate of Picard that had originated at a point in the time line six hours in the future. Although the "future" Picard was identical to the "present" Picard, the captain had difficulty accepting the existence of his twin—largely because he believed his duplicate might have been responsible for the destruction of his ship. To Picard, this was a deeply repugnant idea.

Picard's artificial heart required routine replacement. This happened most recently in 2365, when complications in the cardiac replacement procedure performed at Starbase 515 necessitated emergency assistance by Dr. Katherine Pulaski. Pulaski had joined the crew of the *Enterprise* just a few months earlier, temporarily replacing Beverly Crusher.

In 2366, in an inadvertent violation of the Prime Directive, Picard was mistaken for a god by the Vulcanoid natives of Mintaka III. While he couldn't erase their knowledge of him, he was able to convince them to nonetheless follow a "rational" path in their development.

The captain met Sarek of Vulcan again in 2366, when the Vulcan ambassador's final mission was jeopardized by Bendii Syndrome. The disease caused Sarek to lose control of his emotions, a source of great embarrassment to a Vulcan. Picard mind-melded with Sarek to lend the ambassador the emotional stability he needed to conclude a historic treaty with the Legarans.

In 2368, Picard visited Sarek's deathbed to investigate rumors that Sarek's son, Spock, had defected to the Romulan Empire. Sarek told the captain that Spock perhaps was only attempting to reunite the Vulcan and Romulan peoples. Disguising themselves as Romulans, Picard and Data ventured to Romulus to discover the truth—and aided Spock when he was double-crossed by his Romulan allies.

The captain of the *Enterprise-D* enjoyed a great many friendships. One of his warmest and most unique associations was with a being called Guinan, who came to serve on the *Enterprise* as the bartender in its Ten-Forward lounge in 2365.

Guinan was a member of the El-Aurian race, which was nearly wiped out by the Borg in the late twenty-third century. While fleeing from the Borg 2293, she was briefly swept into an alternate reality known as the nexus—along with James T. Kirk and a number of other El-Aurians.

Like all her people, Guinan was long-lived. Born sometime in the nineteenth century, she was about five hundred years old when she served aboard the *Enterprise-D.* Guinan and Q were acquaintances, having met each other in the twenty-second century, but their relationship was a hostile one.

Guinan possessed an unusual sense that extended beyond linear space-time. She alone was intuitively aware of the damage to the "normal" flow of time when the *Enterprise-C* was swept some twenty-two years into its future, creating an alternate time line. Guinan warned Picard that history had been altered, persuading him to return the *Enterprise-C* to 2344 to repair the time line.

Picard also maintained a close rapport with Data. In 2365, the captain served as the android's attorney when a hearing tested Data's status as an enfranchised being. With Phillipa Louvois hearing the case, Picard argued successfully that all beings are created but not owned by their creator. Louvois's decision made it clear that Data was no one's property.

Picard formed a brief friendship with a Tamarian captain named Dathon in 2368. Dathon perished saving Picard's life, but managed to facilitate peaceful contact between the Tamarians and the Federation in the process.

Later that year, Picard accepted Ensign Ro Laren, a Bajoran with a checkered past, as a member of his crew. Two years later, Ro disappointed him by aligning herself with the rebel Maquis and exposing a Starfleet ambush Picard had set for them. Reportedly, her greatest regret was betraying her captain, who had placed so much faith in her.

One of Picard's greatest sorrows as captain of the *Enterprise* was that he could not save the life of Tasha Yar, his first chief of security on the ship. Yar was destroyed by a creature called Armus in an attempt to rescue *Enterprise* personnel trapped on Armus's world.

In 2366, on the pleasure planet Risa, Picard met and fell for a beautiful and roguish woman named Vash. A year later, he played Robin Hood to her maid Marian in a fantasy environment created by Q.

The Borg

Picard was abducted by the Borg in late 2366 as part of a Borg assault on the Federation. Helpless in the hands of the invaders, Picard was surgically mutilated and transformed into a Borg entity called Locutus. As Locutus, Picard was forced to cooperate in the devastating battle of Wolf 359, in which he helped destroy thirty-nine Federation starships and the majority of their crews.

The captain was finally rescued by an *Enterprise-D* away team, then surgically restored to his human form by Dr. Crusher. However, he carried the emotional scars of his experience for quite some time.

Following his return from Borg captivity, Picard spent several weeks recovering from the terrible physical and psychological trauma. While the *Enterprise-D* was undergoing repairs at Earth Station McKinley in 2367, Picard took the opportunity to visit his hometown of LaBarre for the first time in almost twenty years.

In LaBarre, he stayed with his brother, Robert—and met Robert's wife, Marie, and his son, Rene, for the first time. Fiercely old-fashioned, Picard's brother had remained on the family vineyard to continue his father's work after Jean-Luc left to join Starfleet.

Robert was resentful of his brother's stellar achievements, though Robert's son seemed inclined to follow his uncle Jean-Luc to the stars. Once Robert's resentment was out in the open, the Picard brothers came somewhat to terms with one another. Jean-Luc even briefly toyed with the idea of leaving Starfleet to accept directorship of the Atlantis Project, but he eventually realized his place was still on the *Enterprise-D*.

In 2368, Picard encountered the Borg again, when the *Enterprise* recovered a lone Borg survivor of a spaceship crash. Scarred by his experience as Locutus, the captain fought his impulse to allow the Borg to die.

Cut off from his race's collective consciousness, the Borg became an individual referred to as "Hugh," not a threat as Picard had expected. When he was returned to the collective, Hugh's individualism figured to act as a virus, disabling a portion of the Borg collective as no weapon could have.

On two occasions, Picard had to save his ship single-handed. In 2369, he was forced to outwit a pack of thieves who had snuck aboard while the *Enterprise-D* was shut down for maintenance work. In 2370, when a bizarre virus transformed the crew into their various evolutionary forebears, the captain had to work his way through the ship to stun a devolved Worf and facilitate a cure devised by Commander Data.

Picard also had to fight the *Enterprise-D* itself when it developed a network of nodes reminiscent of a neural web and began acting of its own volition. Eventually, the captain realized that the ship was indeed fostering its own embryonic intelligence. When that intelligence departed in the form of a fully mature entity, the *Enterprise-D* returned to normal.

Picard assumed an unprecedented role in Klingon politics when he served as Arbiter of Succession following the death of Klingon leader K'mpec in 2367. K'mpec took the highly unusual step of appointing an outsider as arbiter so as to ensure that the choice of K'mpec's successor would not plunge the Empire into civil war. Under Picard's arbitration, council member Gowron emerged as the sole challenger for leadership of the High Council.

A Man of Parts

The captain of the *Enterprise-D* was known as something of a Renaissance man, whose areas of interest ranged from drama to astrophysics. In particular, he was an accomplished fencer and wine connoisseur. His favorite beverage was "tea . . . Earl Grey . . . hot."

Picard was also an avid amateur archaeologist who was intrigued by the legendary ancient Iconians while still at Starfleet Academy. He occasionally published scientific papers on archaeology, and even addressed the Federation Archaeology Council in 2367.

Early in his career, at the urging of his teacher, noted archaeologist Richard Galen, Picard had seriously considered pursuing archaeology on a professional level. Picard's path later crossed Galen's again just before Galen's death in 2369, when Picard helped complete Galen's greatest discovery—the reconstruction of an ancient message from a humanoid species that had lived some four billion years earlier.

The captain actually had the opportunity to visit the mythical planet Iconia in 2365. However, an Iconian computer virus endangered the *Enterprise* and prevented him from exploring the place.

In 2370, Picard's expertise as an archaeologist stood him in good stead. Captured by pirates bent on finding a psionic superweapon developed by the ancient Vulcans, the captain was able to survive by posing as a renegade archaeologist.

Picard was also an accomplished equestrian. One of his favorite holodeck programs was a woodland setting in which he enjoyed riding a computer-simulated Arabian mare.

The captain played the piano when he was young, at the urging of his mother, but his deep love of music may have stemmed from an incident in 2268 when his mind received a lifetime of memories from the now-dead planet Kataan. At that time, he experienced the life of a man named Kamin, who had died a thousand years earlier. Kamin had played a Ressikan flute; Picard treasured the instrument because he shared Kamin's memories.

Picard's affinity for music led him to become romantically involved with Neela Daren, an *Enterprise-D* crew member, in 2369. When Daren was nearly killed on an away assignment, she and Picard realized they couldn't remain lovers while working as commander and subordinate, and she requested a transfer off the ship.

In 2369, Picard—like several members of his crew—was turned into a twelve-year-old child after passing through an energy field. With the help of Dr. Crusher and *Enterprise-D* engineer Miles O'Brien, they were restored to their original ages.

Picard suffered profound emotional abuse that same year when he was captured by Gul Madred, a high-ranking Cardassian officer. Madred tortured Picard for Starfleet tactical information. Picard resisted, but later confessed that the experience so brutalized him that he would have told Madred anything had he not been rescued.

The same occasion marked the only time a non–crew member was ever in command of the *Enterprise-D* during Picard's stint as captain. That individual was Edward Jellico, who took the captain's seat while Picard was in the custody of the Cardassians.

In 2354, Picard had been romantically involved with a woman named Miranda Vigo during shore leave on Earth. Although Picard and Vigo attempted to keep in touch, he never saw her again.

In 2370, a Ferengi named Bok found Jason Vigo, the son of Miranda Vigo, and resequenced the boy's DNA to make it seem as if he were Picard's son. Bok, who had plotted against Picard before, planned to kill Jason in retaliation for the captain's supposed murder of Bok's son in 2355. Fortunately, the plot was exposed and Jason Vigo's life was preserved.

Beverly Crusher finally learned of Picard's feelings for her in 2370, when she and the captain were implanted with psi-wave devices so she could read his thoughts. To his surprise, Picard learned that his feelings were reciprocated, though the two opted not to act on those feelings for a while.

Picard enjoyed taking part in a series of hard-boiled holonovels featuring fictional twentieth-century detective Dixon Hill. On one occasion, a computer malfunction disabled the fail-safe mechanism that protects holodeck users, allowing a crew member to perish in the holonovel environment.

On another occasion, in 2365, a Sherlock Holmes holonovel gave rise to Moriarty, a villainous holoconstruct who tried to take over the ship. It took all Picard's powers of persuasion to convince the Moriarty construct to release his hold on the *Enterprise.*

The Moriarty construct appeared again in 2369. This time, Picard and Commander Data created a separate holoreality and outwitted the resourceful Moriarty into inhabiting it, forever unaware that he had not escaped the holodeck after all.

Tragedy and Triumph

Jean-Luc Picard was proud of his illustrious family history. One of his ancestors fought at the battle of Trafalgar, another won a Nobel prize for chemistry, and a handful of Picards were among those who settled the first Martian Colonies.

On the other hand, Picard felt guilt over the role of another ancestor, Javier Maribona-Picard, who helped crush the Pueblo Indian Revolt on Earth in 1692. This became evident in the captain's dealings with a colony of Native Americans on Dorvan V.

For a long time, Picard wasn't confortable with children around him. In fact, almost from the moment he took command of the *Enterprise-D,* he foisted his child-related duties as captain onto his first officer, Commander William Riker. However, after being trapped in a turbolift with three young winners of a shipboard science contest, Picard came to appreciate children for their courage and optimism.

Still, he had no urge to start a family of his own. That is, until the tragic death in a fire of his brother, Robert, and his nephew, Rene—his only blood relatives, in 2371. At that point, the captain realized that he was "the last Picard," and regretted his earlier decision not to have children.

Picard's command of the *Enterprise-D* came to a premature end in 2371, when the ship was destroyed at Veridian III in an attempt to prevent Dr. Tolian Soran from destroying the Veridian system. Picard's partner in his effort to thwart Soran was James T. Kirk, captain of the original *Enterprise.* Kirk, who had been missing for some seventy-eight years following the launch of the *Enterprise-B,* was killed in the battle against Soran.

As captain of the *Enterprise-E,* Picard uncovered a Borg plot to go back in time and prevent Earth's initial contact with the Vulcans, thereby nullifying the formation of the Federation—and making the Borg's conquest of the sector in the twenty-fourth century a much easier task.

Picard took his vessel back in time as well and thwarted the Borg scheme. However, he had to face his own inner demons in the process, coming to grips with the fear and anger that still plagued him as a result of his assimilation into the Borg collective.

As the captain of the fifth and sixth starships called *Enterprise,* Jean-Luc Picard will always be known as one of the great space explorers, scientists, and interstellar diplomats of the twenty-fourth century, a man whose considerable accomplishments were forged in the fires of wisdom, compassion, and conscience.

Benjamin Sisko

by
Michael Jan Friedman

His Early Life and Career

BENJAMIN SISKO WAS A DEVOTED FAMILY MAN WHO GREW UP IN NEW Orleans on Earth. His father, Joseph Sisko, was a gourmet chef of Creole descent who ran a small bistro in New Orleans.

The elder Sisko insisted the family dine together, so that his "taste testers"—his wife and two children—could sample his new recipes. This love of cooking, particularly with regard to his native Creole dishes, manifested itself in young Ben as well, allowing him to become an accomplished chef in his own right later in life.

While Sisko's sister moved to Portland, Oregon, the future captain himself attended Starfleet Academy in San Francisco. He distinguished himself there as a promising command officer.

Sisko met Jennifer, his future wife, at Gilgo Beach on Earth in 2353, just after Sisko's graduation from the Academy. After a short courtship, during which Jennifer expressed reservations about marrying a Starfleet cadet, she and Sisko married. The couple had a son, Jake, in 2355.

Early in his Starfleet career, Ensign Sisko was mentored by Curzon Dax, a Trill whom he met at Palios Station. The two later served on board the *U.S.S. Livingston* together and remained friends for nearly two decades. Curzon Dax was in the habit of assigning Sisko the duty of escorting VIP guests so the Trill wouldn't have to deal with them.

Sisko also was friends with Calvin Hudson, a fellow Starfleet officer with whom he had attended the Academy. Sisko was sorely disappointed when Hudson later turned out to be a member of the infamous Maquis rebellion.

One of Sisko's earliest Starfleet experiences was a stint in the war between the Federation and the Tzenkethi. He served aboard the *U.S.S. Saratoga* as executive officer with the rank of lieutenant commander until early 2367, when the ship was destroyed by the Borg in the battle of Wolf 359.

Though Commander Sisko and his son survived the destruction of the *Saratoga,* his wife, Jennifer, tragically did not. Sisko was devastated by the loss, which caused him to withdraw into himself for a time and shun the idea of serving again on a starship.

Out of respect for his personal tragedy, he was assigned to the Utopia Planitia Fleet Yards on Mars, where he spent three years overseeing starship construction. One of Sisko's projects at Utopia Planitia included design work on the experimental warship *Defiant,* which he would later command.

However, Starfleet had no intention of letting such a valuable officer languish for long at Utopia Planitia. Sisko was eventually promoted to full commander and assigned to station *Deep Space Nine*—a former Cardassian facility near the planet Bajor, which had been occupied and exploited by the Cardassians for several decades.

On *Deep Space Nine*

Commander Sisko was not at all pleased with his posting to *Deep Space Nine,* as it didn't seem like the ideal place to raise a young boy. In fact, he was seriously considering civilian life as an alternative.

He also was not pleased with the officer who turned over the "keys" to the place—Captain Jean-Luc Picard, of the *Enterprise.* After all, the last time Sisko had seen the man was at Wolf 359—where Picard, as the Borg named Locutus, coordinated the Borg attack that resulted in the death of Jennifer Sisko.

However, after the Bajoran wormhole was discovered, the commander came to understand the strategic importance of *Deep Space Nine* and the challenge of bringing Bajor into the Federation—and rose to the challenge. He even overcame his negative feelings toward Picard in order to continue his role as Starfleet's presence on the station.

Among Sisko's staff at *Deep Space Nine* was science officer Jadzia Dax, a Trill who carried the memories and experiences of Curzon Dax. Sisko initially found it difficult to relate to his old friend in the body of a beautiful young woman, but the two eventually came to renew their friendship.

Shortly after his posting to *Deep Space Nine,* Sisko made contact with the mysterious life-forms identified as Bajor's legendary Prophets. These beings existed in the Celestial Temple—also known as the Bajoran wormhole—which was located in the Denorios Belt. Their nonlinear perspective on existence helped Sisko come to grips with the loss of his wife.

As a result of his contact with the Prophets, Bajoran religious leader Kai Opaka indicated that Sisko was the Emissary described in ancient prophecies as the one who would save the Bajoran people. Sisko was uncomfortable with his role as Emissary for some time, but felt obligated to respect Bajoran religious beliefs.

From the time of his wife's death, Sisko was reluctant to form another romantic relationship. It wasn't until 2370 that he took an interest in a mysterious woman called Fenna, who bore a strange resemblance to the wife of a scientist visiting *Deep Space Nine.* Much to Sisko's dismay and disappointment, Fenna turned out to be a mere psychoprojection created by the scientist's wife under stressful circumstances.

Sisko's next relationship had its share of rough spots as well. In 2371, he began dating an attractive freighter captain named Kasidy Yates, who shared his love of baseball. Their relationship blossomed rapidly into a serious love affair.

Thus, Sisko felt betrayed when Yates was exposed as a Maquis sympathizer, who was helping to smuggle supplies into the Badlands. He confronted Yates with his knowledge of her activities, after which she gave herself up and served time in a Federation penal colony. As he had promised, Sisko was there for Yates when her sentence was over.

It was also in 2371—specifically, stardate 48959.1—that Sisko was promoted to the rank of captain, in recognition of his accomplishments on *Deep Space Nine.* Though rank had never been particularly important to Sisko, his subordinates thought the promotion was long overdue.

Commanding *Deep Space Nine* brought Sisko his share of difficult decisions. In 2370, for instance, a proto-universe threatened the safety of his station, but he refused to arbitrarily destroy the proto-universe. He felt that to do so would have been to act with the same indifference to life that the Borg had shown to the Federation.

In 2371, Sisko was abducted by a man who appeared to be Miles O'Brien, *Deep Space Nine*'s chief of operations. This man turned out to be the Miles O'Brien of the mirror universe originally discovered by Captain Kirk. The mirror O'Brien wanted Sisko to help a Terran rebellion, to fight an interplanetary group of oppressors known as the Alliance.

Sisko was disconcerted to learn that the counterpart of his late wife, Jennifer, was still alive in the mirror universe. It was Sisko's difficult job to convince the mirror Jennifer to abandon her work for the Alliance, and to persuade her to instead join the Terran rebellion. Fortunately for the rebellion, he succeeded.

The captain entered the mirror universe again a year later, following his son after Jake was lured there by the living counterpart of his late mother. By then, the Terran rebellion had built its own *Starship Defiant,* but was having trouble making the warship operational—and needed Sisko's help to fend off an oncoming Alliance fleet.

Helping to get the *Defiant* shipshape, Sisko subsequently volunteered to lead its rebel crew into battle. His leadership enabled the rebels to emerge victorious—but not before the mirror Jennifer was killed, leaving Sisko and his son to deal with Jennifer's loss a second time.

In 2371, an automated Cardassian self-destruct program was accidentally activated on *Deep Space Nine.* Sisko, trapped in an ore-processing bay with his son and Miles O'Brien, risked his life to reach a control junction and successfully redirect the destructive force into space.

The Dominion and Other Foes

Sisko's greatest challenge as commander of *Deep Space Nine* was the threat posed by the Dominion, a powerful and hostile alliance of planetary groups in the Gamma Quadrant. The Dominion had been established by the mysterious and reclusive Founders, who were almost never seen, though a species of brutal soldier called the Jem'Hadar savagely ensured compliance with the Founders' rule.

Sisko first encountered the Dominion during a father-son bonding trip to the Gamma Quadrant, during which he ran into a group of Jem'Hadar. Some time later, hoping to avert a Dominion invasion by demonstrating the Federation's peaceful intent, Sisko took the newly commissioned *Defiant* and his officers into the Gamma Quadrant to find the Founders.

It turned out the Founders were shapeshifters, like Sisko's *Deep Space Nine* security chief, Odo—and that they were unlikely to accept the idea of a peaceful coexistence with the Federation. Sisko and his people returned to the Alpha Quadrant, sobered by the knowledge that war with the Dominion might be inevitable.

A year later, evidence that the Founders were targeting Earth for invasion sent Sisko back to his home planet, where he and Odo had to prevent—or prepare for—war with the Dominion. However, the more immediate threat was a Starfleet plot to wrest control of the Federation to better defend it against the Dominion. Sisko exposed the conspiracy and restored order on Earth, refusing to let fear conquer his homeworld for the Dominion.

In 2373, Sisko, Odo, and O'Brien disguised themselves as Klingons and joined Commander Worf, formerly of the *Enterprise*-D, on a suicide mission into Klingon territory. Their purpose was to expose Gowron, the Klingon leader, whom they suspected of being a changeling. However, it was General Martok, Gowron's right-hand man, who turned out to be the changeling in question.

Later on, Sisko and some of his officers came across a crashed Jem'Hadar warship while exploring a world in the Gamma Quadrant. When another Jem'Hadar ship showed up, Sisko and his enemies contended for the vessel—but neither side got what it wanted from it.

After learning that Cardassia had joined the Dominion, Sisko was forced to deal with what appeared to be a devastating assault force made up of cloaked Jem'Hadar and Cardassian warships. However, the attack turned out to be a ruse to conceal a more insidious plot—to transform Bajor's sun into a supernova, destroying Bajor and *Deep Space Nine* in the process.

Sisko was sometimes forced to join forces with his enemies. In 2372, he succeeded in stopping a group of Jem'Hadar renegades from gaining immense power by working alongside a sanctioned group of Jem'Hadar. Though the captain saved the life of the Jem'Hadar leader with whom he was aligned, the Jem'Hadar threatened to kill Sisko next time they met.

The captain also found it necessary to ally himself with the Cardassians on occasion. In one such instance, Thomas Riker—a duplicate of the *Enterprise*-D's Will Riker—stole the *Defiant* on behalf of the Maquis. Concerned that the Cardassians would believe the Federation had made an alliance with the Maquis, Sisko was forced to help his Cardassian nemesis, Gul Dukat, find and destroy the *Defiant*. In the end, Sisko was able to negotiate a deal to retrieve his ship and preserve Thomas Riker's life.

On another occasion, when the Klingons invaded Cardassia, Sisko deemed it necessary to warn the Cardassians and even do battle with the Klingons. Eventually, the captain was able to convince Gowron, the leader of the Klingon High Council, that a split among the Federation, the Klingons, and the Cardassians was just what the Dominion wanted to see.

Officer and Emissary

Though skeptical of his role as the Bajoran Emissary, the captain gradually came to embrace it, seeing the potential for doing good it brought him. A key point in this process was an incident in 2371, in which Sisko ignored an ancient Bajoran prophecy of doom to undertake a joint scientific venture with the Cardassians. When the prophecy came true, albeit in a symbolic way, Sisko developed a new respect for Bajoran mysticism—and for his own prophesied part in Bajor's fate.

A year later, Akorem Laan, a legendary Bajoran poet who had vanished into the wormhole two hundred years earlier, claimed that *he* was the Emissary. Sisko stepped aside without argument to let Akorem assume the position—until he saw the misery caused by Akorem's reverence for Bajor's ancient caste system. In the end, the wormhole aliens known as the Prophets confirmed that Sisko was the true Emissary.

In 2373, Sisko was plagued by life-threatening visions that enabled him to find B'hala, Bajor's legendary lost city, which seemed to hold the key to Bajor's future. When his life was saved by the station's physician, Dr. Julian Bashir, the visions went away—and the captain felt the loss deeply.

That same year, Sisko and some of his officers traveled back in time to a pivotal moment in the history of the original *Starship Enterprise.* Arne Darvin, a surgically altered Klingon, had used a Bajoran orb to send the *Defiant* back into the past, aiming to kill Captain James Kirk and alter history in his favor. Rubbing elbows with Kirk and his legendary crew, Sisko and his people managed to foil Darvin's plot and preserve the time line.

One of Sisko's favorite recreational activities was a holosuite program of the pastime known as "baseball," in which he was able to pit his skills against the sport's greatest players—including Buck Bokai, Tris Speaker, and Ted Williams. Using this program, Sisko was able to teach his son, Jake, how to play the game. The program also allowed him to cheer his hero, Buck Bokai, in the sparsely attended 2042 World Series that heralded the end of professional baseball.

Sisko was an aficionado of other aspects of twenty-first-century Earth history as well. This interest stood him in good stead when he and Dr. Bashir were transported to the San Francisco of 2024—the time and place of the infamous Bell riots.

The captain enjoyed collecting ancient African artifacts. In fact, he tried to bring one back with him every time he visited Earth.

One of Sisko's most remarkable recreational activities was his construction of a Bajoran solar-sail vessel of ancient design, which he completed in 2371. Along with his son, Jake, Sisko piloted the vessel to Cardassia, dramatically demonstrating how ancient Bajorans might have accomplished the same feat some eight centuries earlier.

Sisko had a "problem" with losing, as evidenced by his preoccupation with the Maquis leader Michael Eddington. Eddington had served aboard *Deep Space Nine* for eighteen months as Starfleet security officer before showing his true colors as a rebel. Taking the deception personally, Sisko finally apprehended Eddington by casting himself as the villain of the piece and appealing to the rebel's penchant for self-sacrifice.

Despite his soft-spoken and often charming demeanor, no Starfleet officer has ever been as strong-willed, as tough, or as downright courageous as the estimable Benjamin Sisko.

Kathryn Janeway

by

Michael Jan Friedman

Her Early Life and Career

KATHRYN JANEWAY WAS RAISED IN A TWENTY-FOURTH-CENTURY AGRICULTURAL park in the region known as Indiana, on Earth. Her father, Edward Janeway, was a career Starfleet officer who rose to the rank of vice-admiral before his untimely death.

During the latter stages of Kathryn's childhood, the elder Janeway spent increasing amounts of time away from home, dealing with the burgeoning Cardassian threat to the Federation—a threat that would ultimately erupt into armed conflict. Young Kathryn responded to these absences by trying to excel at the activities her father had laid out for her, becoming an outstanding mathematician, scientist, tennis player, and ballet artist in an attempt to impress and please him.

Once, after losing a tennis match, Kathryn Janeway set out to trek twenty miles through rainy woods rather than take a ride back to her home. It would not be until later in life that she learned to deal well with failure, though she remained driven to succeed in every aspect of her life.

Janeway accompanied her father to Mars at the tender age of nine and developed an affinity for the terraformed world that would bring her back on several other occasions. As a young woman, after completing her senior honors thesis on vertebrate anatomy, Janeway discovered what appeared to be a chordate skeleton while cave-diving on Mars—suggesting that there had been vertebrate life on Mars at one time. The discovery brought her a certain amount of fame in scientific circles at an early age.

Originally, Janeway aspired to become the science officer on a deep-space exploration expedition, and even completed a doctoral degree in quantum cosmology toward that end. However, the young woman changed her mind about her career direction while serving as an ensign under Admiral Owen Paris on the starship *Icarus*.

Janeway's assignment to the *Icarus* was her first in space. In the course of it, both she and Admiral Paris were briefly taken prisoner by the Cardassians, whose actions the *Icarus* was investigating. After Janeway aided in the admiral's escape, he suggested that Starfleet would better benefit from her services as a command officer.

Janeway went on to serve under Paris as science officer on the *Al-Bataani,* but later took his advice and switched to the command track. It was at about the same time that Janeway's father and fiancé were killed in the crash of a shuttlecraft on Tau Ceti Prime.

Janeway, who had been piloting the vessel, was only injured in the crash. Still, she carried its emotional scars for some time afterward, even sinking into a clinical depression.

Her mother, Gretchen, and her younger sister, Phoebe, are credited with having brought Janeway out of that depression. Janeway also benefited from the company of Petunia, a dog she rescued from a snowstorm near her family home, and the support of Mark Johnson, a childhood friend and a member of Earth's Questor philosophical symposium.

Janeway went on to become romantically involved with Johnson, though she had never before seen him in a romantic light. Nonetheless, their relationship didn't keep Janeway from pursuing her aspirations to explore deep space as a Starfleet officer.

Her first mission as captain was a six-month venture into the Beta Quadrant. Afterward, a Vulcan ensign named Tuvok was asked to assess her efforts as the commanding officer of a starship. He found her lacking in respect for military exercises. Though Janeway was nonetheless commended for her tour of duty, Tuvok was assigned to accompany her on her next command—to make sure she conducted the necessary tactical drills.

Janeway and Tuvok went on to become fast friends and staunch comrades. The captain came to rely on the Vulcan's clear, logical vision and technical expertise. When she was placed in command of the cutting-edge starship *U.S.S. Voyager,* Janeway named Tuvok her tactical officer.

The *Voyager* Adventures

Starfleet Command "borrowed" Tuvok from Janeway and had him infiltrate the revolutionary group known as the Maquis. However, in 2371, the

Maquis ship to which the Vulcan was assigned fell victim to an anomaly in the region of space known as the Badlands.

Janeway took *Voyager* into the Badlands in an attempt to locate Tuvok, but fell victim to the same anomaly. Both she and her ship were swept into the distant Delta Quadrant of the galaxy, some 70,000 light-years from the nearest Federation border.

After the destruction of the Maquis vessel, which had also been drawn into the Delta Quadrant, Janeway recovered Tuvok and accepted the Maquis crew aboard her ship. Furthermore, she invited its commander, Chakotay, to become her first officer on *Voyager.*

Janeway's courage and leadership were instrumental in the survival of her ship and its occupants as they made a long and difficult journey back to the Alpha Quadrant. One of her earliest challenges in this area was to meld the Starfleet and Maquis components of her crew.

To accelerate the process, Janeway named other Maquis besides Chakotay to staff officer positions. Prominent among these appointments was that of B'Elanna Torres, a half-Klingon, half-human female who was placed in charge of the engineering section.

Tom Paris, the son of Admiral Owen Paris, served as helmsman on *Voyager* during those difficult days. Though the younger Paris had been discredited for lying and ousted from Starfleet, Janeway valued his skills as a pilot and had him removed from a penal colony to take her into the Badlands. Though he couldn't keep *Voyager* and her crew from being thrown into the Delta Quadrant, Paris proved his mettle as a pilot and an officer, and justified Janeway's faith in him on numerous other occasions.

Captain Janeway encountered a number of intriguing and dangerous species in her journey across the Delta Quadrant. Prominent among them was the Kazon, a savage and acquisitive people divided into individual sects, each one hostile to Janeway and her crew. At one point, the captain tried unsuccessfully to forge a defensive alliance with a number of Kazon sects.

The captain also encountered the Vidiians, a species ravaged by a virus called the Phage, which gradually destroyed the organs of their bodies. To fill their increasing need for new organs, the Vidiians captured individuals of other species and used them as involuntary donors.

In 2371, Janeway and Tom Paris were investigating a world laid waste by a polaric energy explosion, when they were thrown back in time through a subspace fracture. Arriving at a point just prior to the explosion, they managed to prevent it—and thereby save an entire planetary population from extinction.

That same year, Janeway sought Chakotay's help in experiencing a vision quest in search of her personal animal spirit guide. Her quest indeed yielded her a guide—a lizard.

Soon after, Janeway got the opportunity to meet one of her heroes—the twentieth-century female pilot Amelia Earhart. Apparently, Earhart had been abducted from Earth in 1937 by an alien species and brought to the Delta Quadrant, where she was preserved in suspended animation.

The captain's feelings for her father were reawakened when she allied herself with a local eccentric on an alien planet, in an attempt to recover Tuvok and B'Elanna Torres from a prison cell. When the man took a fatal wound helping her, Janeway recognized his courage by going along with his illusion that she was his long lost daughter.

In 2372, Janeway ran into the entity known as Q for the first time, when she encountered another Q with a death wish. A year later, Q returned to *Voyager* to ask the captain to have his baby, over the objections of a jealous female Q.

On another occasion, Janeway took *Voyager* through a void in space and discovered an identical ship and crew existing in a parallel universe. With the help of her counterpart, the captain saved *Voyager* and her crew—though, in the process, her own Ensign Harry Kim was replaced with the Kim of the other universe.

Janeway was extremely protective of her subordinates. At one point, she found it necessary to enter a computer program and pit herself against the embodiment of a race's fear. Some time later, the captain risked her life to save Kes, a member of her crew, from a coma—the result of Kes's encounter with the Nechani homeworld's "spirit" realm.

Late in 2372, Janeway and her crew were boarded by the Kazon and beamed off *Voyager* onto the surface of a savage planet. Using their most basic skills, the captain and her people survived the rigors of that world and went on to recover their vessel.

In 2373, Janeway had to fight for her life and that of her crew once again. This time, she was pitted against a spreading macrovirus threatening to take over *Voyager.*

Also in 2373, Janeway and her crew got their wish and were transported back to Earth—but in the wrong century. In returning to their own time, they also were forced to return to the Delta Quadrant.

Janeway experienced her first brush with the Borg when *Voyager* encountered a disabled Borg ship in the Delta Quadrant—as well as the ship's besieged planetbound survivors. Fortunately, the survivors turned out to be friendly to Janeway and her people. They created a Borg-like neural network and destroyed the cubeshaped vessel before it could come back to life.

A lifelong dog lover, Janeway grew up with a wire-haired mutt named Bramble. At the time of *Voyager*'s disappearance, Janeway's Irish setter, Molly, was about to give birth under Mark Johnson's watchful eye.

During her off-duty hours on *Voyager,* Janeway enjoyed participating in a Gothic romance holonovel set in old England on Earth. In the program, which was referred to as Janeway Lambda-1, Janeway played the governess of two children whose mother had died.

Janeway was also an accomplished pool player. She got a chance to demonstrate this in another holo-setting, a recreation of a French pool hall called Chez Sandrine, favored by Tom Paris during his Academy days.

Janeway considered coffee to be her only vice. Even though replicator privileges on *Voyager* were strictly rationed, she always had at least two cups of coffee a day.

Kathryn Janeway will be remembered as an individual who always rose to a challenge, inspired others with her unflagging optimism and ability, and never took no for an answer.

Mackenzie Calhoun

by
David Mack

Captain Mackenzie Calhoun was well known as the leader of the planetary revolution that freed the planet Xenex from Danteri control before he entered Starfleet Academy.

During Calhoun's tenure in the Academy, he earned a reputation for being high-energy and quick with his fists, and for never backing down from any confrontation.

Calhoun is never afraid to say precisely what's on his mind; nor does he suffer fools gladly. Although he understands and appreciates the chain of command, respect and loyalty are not commoditi es he gives to superior officers simply because they are of higher rank. He feels those privileges must be earned.

Captain Calhoun's given name on his homeworld of Xenex was M'k'n'zy. When he joined Starfleet he changed it to Mackenzie, the closest Terran equivalent, and adopted the name of his home city, Calhoun, as his surname.

Calhoun has an older brother, D'ndai, who conspired with Thallonian Chancellor Yoz to overthrow the Thallonian royal family.

—from the Star Trek: New Frontier Minipedia